PENGUIN CLASSICS  DELUXE EDITION

# KRISTIN LAVRANSDATTER

SIGRID UNDSET was born in Denmark in 1882, the eldest daughter of a Norwegian father and a Danish mother, and moved with her family to Oslo two years later. She published her first novel, *Fru Marta Oulie* (*Mrs. Marta Oulie*) in 1907 and her second book, *Den lykkelige alder* (*The Happy Age*), in 1908. The following year she published her first work set in the Middle Ages, *Fortællingen om Viga-Ljot og Vigdis* (later translated into English under the title *Gunnar's Daughter* and now available in Penguin Classics). More novels and stories followed, including *Jenny* (1911, first translated 1920), *Fattige skjæbner* (*Fates of the Poor*, 1912), *Vaaren* (*Spring*, 1914), *Splinten av troldspeilet* (translated in part as *Images in a Mirror*, 1917), and *De kloge jomfruer* (*The Wise Virgins*, 1918). In 1920 Undset published the first volume of *Kristin Lavransdatter*, the medieval trilogy that would become her most famous work. *Kransen* (*The Wreath*) was followed by *Husfrue* (*The Wife*) in 1921 and *Korset* (*The Cross*) in 1922. Beginning in 1925 she published the four-volume *Olav Audunssøn i Hestviken* (translated into English under the title *The Master of Hestviken*), also set in the Middle Ages. In 1928 Sigrid Undset won the Nobel Prize in Literature. During the 1930s she published several more novels, notably the autobiographical *Elleve aar* (translated as *The Longest Years*, 1934). She was also a prolific essayist on subjects ranging from Scandinavian history and literature to the Catholic Church (to which she became a convert in 1924) and politics. During the Nazi occupation of Norway, Undset lived as a refugee in New York City. She returned home in 1945 and lived in Lillehammer until her death in 1949.

TIINA NUNNALLY has translated all three volumes of *Kristin Lavransdatter* for Penguin Classics. She won the PEN/Book-of-the-Month Club Translation Prize for the third volume, *The Cross*. Her translations of the first and second volumes, *The Wreath* and *The Wife*, were finalists for the PEN Center USA West Translation Award, and *The Wife* was also a finalist for the PEN/Book-of-the-Month Club Translation Prize. Her other translations include Hans Christian Andersen's *Fairy Tales*; Undset's *Jenny*; Per Olov Enquist's *The Royal Physician's Visit* (Independent Foreign Fiction Prize); Peter Høeg's *Smilla's Sense of Snow* (Lewis Galantière Prize given by the American Translators Association); Jens Peter Jacobsen's *Niels Lyhne* (PEN Center USA West Translation Award); and Tove Ditlevsen's *Early Spring* (American-Scandinavian Foundation Translation Prize). Also the author of three novels, *Maija*, *Runemaker*, and *Fate of Ravens*, Nunnally holds an M.A. in Scandinavian Studies from the University of Wisconsin-Madison. She lives in Albuquerque, New Mexico.

BRAD LEITHAUSER is the author of several novels, including *Darlington's Fall*, *A Few Corrections*, *The Friends of Freeland*, and *Equal Distance*, as well as poetry and essays. His work appears regularly in *The New York Review of Books*, his awards include a MacArthur Fellowship, and he is Emily Dickinson Lecturer in the Humanities at Mount Holyoke College, where he teaches courses in writing and literature.

SIGRID UNDSET

# Kristin Lavransdatter

I: THE WREATH

II: THE WIFE

III: THE CROSS

*Translated with Notes by* TIINA NUNNALLY

*Introduction by* BRAD LEITHAUSER

PENGUIN BOOKS

PENGUIN BOOKS
Published by the Penguin Group
Penguin Group (USA) Inc., 375 Hudson Street, New York, New York 10014, USA
Penguin Group (Canada), 90 Eglinton Avenue East, Suite 700, Toronto,
Ontario M4P 2Y3, Canada (a division of Pearson Penguin Canada Inc.)
Penguin Books Ltd, 80 Strand, London WC2R 0RL, England
Penguin Ireland, 25 St Stephen's Green, Dublin 2, Ireland (a division of Penguin Books Ltd)
Penguin Group (Australia), 707 Collins Street, Melbourne, Victoria 3008, Australia
(a division of Pearson Australia Group Pty Ltd)
Penguin Books India Pvt Ltd, 11 Community Centre, Panchsheel Park, New Delhi – 110 017, India
Penguin Group (NZ), 67 Apollo Drive, Rosedale, Auckland 0632, New Zealand
(a division of Pearson New Zealand Ltd)
Penguin Books (South Africa), Rosebank Office Park, 181 Jan Smuts Avenue, Parktown North 2193, South Africa
Penguin China, B7 Jiaming Center, 27 East Third Ring Road North,
Chaoyang District, Beijing 100020, China

Penguin Books Ltd, Registered Offices:
80 Strand, London WC2R 0RL, England

This edition first published in Penguin Books 2005

19 20 18



*The Wreath*, *The Wife*, and *The Cross* are published in individual volumes by Penguin Books.

These works were originally published in Norwegian by H. Aschehoug & Company, Oslo: *The Wreath* under the title *Kransen* in 1920; *The Wife* as *Husfrue* in 1921; and *The Cross* as *Korset* in 1922.

Mr. Leithauser's introduction first appeared in *The New York Review of Books.*

LIBRARY OF CONGRESS CATALOGING IN PUBLICATION DATA
Undset, Sigrid, 1882–1949.
[Kristin Lavransdatter. English]
Kristin Lavransdatter / Sigrid Undset ; translated with notes by Tiina Nunnally ;
introduction by Brad Leithauser.
p. cm.
Originally published as 3 separate works: New York : Penguin Books, 1997–2000.
Contents: 1. The wreath—2. The wife—3. The cross.
ISBN 978-0-14-303916-7
I. Nunnally, Tiina, 1952– II. Title.
PT8950.U5K713 2005
839.82'372—dc 2005048941

Printed in the United States of America
Maps by Virginia Norey

CONTENTS

# INTRODUCTION

## LADY WITH A PAST

My first foray into the world of *Kristin Lavransdatter*, the Nobel laureate Sigrid Undset's celebrated trilogy of novels set in fourteenth-century Norway, turned out to be a reading experience like no other. I'm thinking here less of the books themselves (though these were an unexpected delight, a convincing twentieth-century evocation of medieval Norway) than of the personal encounters the books fostered.

The trilogy runs over one thousand pages in the old three-in-one Knopf hardcover I'd picked up secondhand, and I chose to read it slowly, for weeks on end, lugging the hefty, handsome volume everywhere I went. One of its themes is the stubborn power of magic—the bewitching allure of pagan practices in a society that had officially but not wholeheartedly embraced Christianity—and the trilogy did seem to work magical effects: it drew elderly women to me.

Memory tells me that this must have happened seven or eight times, but probably it was more like four. In any event, the encounters were much of a piece. An older woman sitting by me on the subway, or waiting beside me in a line at the Department of Motor Vehicles, or having lunch at a nearby table, would cross the boundary separating strangers in order to volunteer that she, too, had once read *Kristin Lavransdatter*—a remark accompanied by that special glow which comes at the recollection of a distant but enduring pleasure.

### 1.

Early in the trilogy arrives a moment emblematic of Undset's overarching ambitions and designs. For the first time in her life our heroine, Kristin Lavransdatter, age seven, leaves the valley that has heretofore circumscribed her existence. A new sort of panorama beckons and beguiles:

> There were forest-clad mountain slopes below her in all directions; her valley was no more than a hollow between the enormous mountains, and the neighboring valleys were even smaller hollows . . . Kristin had thought that if she came up over the crest of her home mountains, she would be able to look down on another village like their own, with farms and houses, and she had such a strange feeling when she saw what a great distance there was between places where people lived.

The revelation is geographical for Kristin but temporal for the reader, who also is to be granted a breathtaking new vista, as a world many centuries old emerges with crystalline clarity. Indeed, the book's deepest pleasures may be retrocessive. The trilogy advances with a relentless forward motion, following Kristin methodically from the age of seven until her death, at about fifty, from the Black Death, but the reader's greatest thrill is the rearward one of feeling tugged back into a half-pagan world where local spirits still inhabit the streams and cairns and shadowy forests. The trilogy sets us in an earlier age that looks back, uneasily, on a still earlier age.

*Kristin Lavransdatter* was a publishing phenomenon. My own edition was the seventeenth printing—an elaborate clothbound hardcover published in 1973, a half century after the trilogy first appeared in English. The trilogy was a main selection of the Book-of-the-Month Club, where its striking success elicited an unprecedented testimonial: "We consider it the best book our judges have ever selected and it has been better received by our subscribers than any other book."

Continuously in print for three-quarters of a century, *Kristin Lavransdatter* is today that rarity of foreign twentieth-century novels: one with competing translations available. Still, it plainly hasn't captivated later generations as it once did. Though Undset may well be, even now, the best-known modern Scandinavian novelist in the United States, she has been little embraced by academia (which has overlooked Scandinavia generally, apart from its playwrights), and the trilogy is perhaps gradually moving, in the language of the blurb, from "beloved masterpiece" to "cult classic." When, in 2001, Steerforth Press brought out *The Unknown Sigrid Undset*, a collection that presented both Undset's wonderful early book *Jenny*—a novel set in modern Rome—and a sampling of her letters, its title raised the question whether there is a "known" Undset in this country.

*Kristin Lavransdatter*'s dense, decade-spanning plot might be summarized as the story of a daddy's girl who refuses daddy's choice of a husband and marries for love, with often harrowing long-range consequences. Kristin's father wishes her to marry Simon Andressøn, an honorable, thoughtful, devoted, and woefuly unglamorous man. Kristin falls instead for Erlend Nikulaussøn, a proud, impulsive, fearless young knight who seems constitutionally unable to steer clear of scandal. After having pledged her love to him, she finds out that Erlend has already fathered children through an adulterous liaison, and when he and Kristin are wed—for the headstrong girl squelches all paternal objections and marries the man of her choice—she is already secretly pregnant. For Kristin, the wedding turns out to be a literally nauseating dissimulation, an unshakable bout of morning sickness as her father gives her away with all the pomp appropriate to a virgin bride. No matter how many children she has under the sanction of holy wedlock—she and Erlend wind up with seven sons—she still feels like a transgressor.

Like the earlier *Jenny*, whose heroine is a modern Norwegian art student in Rome who disdains a suitor for the suitor's father, *Kristin Lavransdatter* is the tale of a scandalous woman. That the trilogy's readers are meant to regard Kristin sympathetically is but one sign of Undset's bold and nuanced treatment of sexuality. Although the trilogy's sex is hardly graphic (almost the only reference to genitalia arises when, in a skirmish, Erlend receives a spear wound to, significantly, his groin), Undset repeatedly lets us know that her heroine is a slave to carnal desires, as when, not long before his death, Erlend discomfits his wife with a casual, jesting reference to those days when her nails dug so deeply into his skin as to leave him bleeding.

In the annals of literary "fallen women," Kristin Lavransdatter, that twentieth-century/fourteenth-century literary figure, occupies a curious and fascinating place. After they fell, a number of Kristin's nineteenth-century counterparts were whisked offstage, often to meet a premature end. In the latter part of the twentieth century, many of Kristin's successors were sexual adventuresses whose exploits were pure and liberated triumphs. Writing in the first quarter of the twentieth century, Undset chose a middle path for her heroine. Kristin never doubts that she has covertly sinned, and the pain of her deceptions remains a lifelong affliction. Even so, her unshakable guilt in no way paralyzes her and she carries on with her life. Throughout the trilogy, Kristin is an indomitable presence in every role she undertakes—mother, mistress of an estate, and even, in her final days, sometime religious pilgrim who chooses to close her life in a nunnery.

Kristin's painful wedding is both a commencement and a culmination: her life progresses as though her squalid seduction, set in a brothel room obtained by Erlend as a means of protecting their privacy, must forever discolor connubial relations. "The Devil cannot have so much power over a man that I would ever cause you sorrow or harm," Erlend naively vows after seducing her, yet he has already planted the seeds of distress that eventually will all but destroy his beloved. Actually, their doomed marriage—they eventually part physically, although psychologically they can never sever the tortured bonds between them—is but one of the trilogy's numerous portraits of domestic discord and blight. At the very close of the first volume, we learn that the marriage of Kristin's parents is also rooted in deception. Undset's characters are near-contemporaries of Chaucer's pilgrims, and they might likewise "speke of wo that is in mariage."

Undset's greatest literary strength reveals itself bit by bit, in the way the passions of Kristin, Erlend, and Simon Andressøn play out in all their intricate and lingering aftereffects. Simon's transformation is particularly affecting. He begins as a promising and enthusiastic suitor of a beautiful young girl, Kristin Lavransdatter; comes to harbor doubts about her devotion; discovers her affair with Erlend and, brandishing a sword, seeks to "rescue" her; in time enters a kind of collusion with the lovers, who convince him not to disclose the affair to Kristin's father; and eventually marries a homely but wealthy widow, leaving unspoken much of the hurt and regret he clearly feels. The trilogy achieves an exceptional sense of accumulating dailiness, of momentous actions concatenating in all sorts of minute and unexpected evolutions.

The burning lust between Kristin and Erlend feels doubly real, not merely plausible but also proximate. But no less real is that variable, volatile mixture of remorse, shame, loyalty, and fondness which their youthful passion retrospectively stirs. It's one of the reasons the two of them can never fully part—the memories of a passion so urgent that all other considerations, moral and practical, were subsumed by it. When you enter *Kristin Lavransdatter*, you enter a marriage, a contract expansively unfolding through time. Disturbingly, fascinatingly, it's a union of two people who share a proud, combative stubbornness that ultimately undoes them.

## 2.

As a writer renowned for her medieval epics, Undset came by her calling honestly. Born in Denmark in 1882, she grew up in Norway, within a household permeated by vanished societies. Her Norwegian father and well-educated Danish mother collaborated professionally, he as an archeologist and she as his secretary and illustrator. Sigrid was reared among archeological relics and manuscripts. Her naturally derived feeling of being at home in earlier centuries protected her from the great occupational hazard of the historical novelist: the urge to display just how much scholarship has gone into the past's disinterment. *Kristin Lavransdatter* reflects deep reading, as well as a close-at-hand tactile familiarity with the everyday objects of fourteenth-century Norway, but Undset's research is mainly concealed. You never sense the burden of heavy labor in her prose. Yet she seems intimately acquainted with the clothes and the diet, the customs and the politics, the architecture and the thinking of the people she writes about. The farm where Kristin grows up feels like a working farm.

When Sigrid's beloved father died, in 1893, the family found itself in sharply reduced circumstances. She abandoned her formal education while still in her mid-teens and took a secretarial job in an electrical company. She worked there for ten years. She wrote in her spare hours, embarking unsuccessfully on a pair of novels set in medieval times. An influential editor advised her to abandon such projects: "Don't attempt any more historical novels. You have no talent for it. But you might try writing something modern. You never know."

The pursuit of "something modern" led to *Fru Marta Oulie*, a contemporary tale of infidelity, published in 1907 and not yet published in English, and a collection of stories, presumably drawn from life—a number are about Norwegian office workers—followed a year later. The books were respectfully received and sold well. Nonetheless, Undset's passion for an older world was unquenchable, and in 1909 she published a short novel set in the Middle Ages. (Under the title *Gunnar's Daughter*, it first appeared in English in the thirties, and resurfaced as a Penguin Twentieth-Century Classic in 1998.)

The first volume of *Kristin Lavransdatter* was published in Norway in 1920, with the second and third volumes appearing in succeeding years. The trilogy was quickly translated and just as quickly embraced across the globe. A medieval tetralogy, *The Master of Hestviken*, which also has at its heart a pair of passionate but troubled and guilt-stricken young lovers, followed in the mid-twenties. In 1928, at the age of forty-six, Undset received the Nobel Prize, chiefly for her medieval epics. She had surmounted every obstacle. In sales, number of translations, significant honors and reader loyalty, Sigrid Undset in 1928 was probably the most successful woman writer in the world.

Perhaps it's unsurprising that things proceeded less smoothly in her personal life. In 1909, while traveling in Italy, she fell in love with Anders Castus Svarstad, a Norwegian painter thirteen years her senior. He was married, with three children. After an eventual divorce, Svarstad wed Undset, once more fathering three children, one of them severely retarded. In time, their marriage foundered and in 1924, after Undset converted from Lutheranism to Catholicism—a seemingly inevitable move for someone whose imagination was rooted in a pre-Reformation Europe—the marriage was annulled.

During the decade of her marriage, Undset published a book of feminist essays. As her translator Tiina Nunnally wryly points out in a helpful introduction to the trilogy's first volume: "Her written positions were often in direct contradiction to her own life choices." (Svarstad turned out to be a highly demanding partner, and it was only after she separated from him, in 1919, that her work took off.) For all the upheaval in her personal life, she remained steadily industrious and generous. She donated all her Nobel Prize money to charity and, a decade later, when the Soviets invaded Finland, she sold her Nobel medallion to support a relief fund for Finnish children. When the Nazis invaded Norway, Undset fled to the United States, settling in Brooklyn for a five-year exile, during which she traveled on many speaking tours on behalf of her homeland. She returned to Norway after the war to find her house seriously vandalized. Her health was broken, and she died in 1949, at the age of sixty-seven.

For an English-language reader, much about Undset's life remains inaccessible, locked away in bibliographies that point toward Norwegian books and articles. This situation was somewhat amended by *The Unknown Sigrid Undset*, also translated by Nunnally, which includes *Jenny*, a pair of stories, and—especially welcome—a selection of Undset's letters that throws welcome light on those apprentice years when the lowly office worker dreamed of a higher life. All of these letters were addressed to Andrea Hedberg, a friend who shared Undset's literary interests and ambitions. The correspondence, which lasted more than forty years, originated through a Swedish pen-pal club. For any reader who has succumbed to the spell of *Kristin Lavransdatter* or *The Master of Hestviken*, there's a privileged thrill in having these letters available, in hearing an elusive authorial voice, previously filtered through the Middle Ages, speaking immediately of its own concerns, whether in youth ("I'm only happy when I'm alone in the woods") or in full adulthood ("On the morning of the 24th I gave birth to a son—a big strong boy—5 kilos").

It's a voice, one should add, that offers few surprises—insofar as the earnest, fervent, ambitious, far-seeing young electric company secretary is so recognizably, while yet in embryo, the author of the mature novels: Undset was high-minded from start to finish. She spoke freely and unselfconsciously to Hedberg about her coalescing artistic aims. Here is Undset at age seventeen:

> Sometimes I want so much to write a book . . . I've started a few times, but nothing comes of it, and I burn it at once. But

> it's supposed to take place in 1340 . . . and there isn't a single romantic scene in it. It's about two young people—of course—Svend Trøst and Maiden Agnete, whose unhappy story . . . an unhappy marriage that I won't bother you with right now.

And here she is two years later:

> But it's an *artist* that I want to be, a *woman* artist, and not a pen-wielding lady. . . . Furthermore, marriage makes most women stupid, or they dilute their demands on life, on their husband, and on themselves so much that they can scarcely be counted as human, or they become uncomprehending, vulgar, coarse, or unhappy.
>
> Yes, my dear Dea, I certainly hope you will take great joy and comfort from this edifying epistle. I'm keeping one consolation for my own use: I *will!*
>
> I will hold my head high, I will not buckle under.
>
> I will not commit suicide—will not waste my talents. If I have any, I will also find them and use them. I will be whatever I can be.

While *Kristin Lavransdatter* is firmly rooted in a specific place and era—southern and central Norway in the first half of the fourteenth century—I suspect for most American readers the story has always been set in some misted Long Ago and Far Away. The medieval historian may find in it a careful account of political maneuvering and uncertainty, but the shifting intrigues following, say, the death of King Haakon (who reigned from 1299 to 1319) are likely to feel impossibly remote to the general reader. The trilogy's earlier translation, by Charles Archer, may also have worked to deracinate the plot from its historical grounding. Archer's many archaisms ("Yet did he look in his coarse homely clothing more high-born than many a knight," "he had wrought scathe to the maidenhood of her spirit") encourage us to transplant the plot into a realm detached from time, some enchanted Arthurian landscape of gallant knights and comely maidens.

Nunnally's translation redirects our attention. The florid constructions and whimsical quaintnesses have dropped away, and

Undset emerges as a writer of spare vigor. Nunnally unquestionably brings us closer to the heart of the book than Archer did. While I have a lingering fondness for the Archer translation—he was the museum guide who first led me to the tapestry—on the grounds of lucidity and authenticity the nod must go to Nunnally, who has surely done as much as anyone in recent years to bring Nordic literature to this country. (She has translated, with fluency and grace, Knut Hamsun, Jens Peter Jacobsen, and Peter Høeg's *Smilla's Sense of Snow.*)

If Archer's translation scanted the trilogy's treatment of medieval history, it may thereby have encouraged comparisons to figures less remote in time. Readers may have found in the trilogy's headstrong and often self-destructive heroine a distant cousin to *Vanity Fair*'s Becky Sharpe and *Gone with the Wind*'s Scarlett O'Hara. In Erlend and Kristin's ill-starred but unstoppable love affair, they may have detected a kinship with *Wuthering Heights*'s Heathcliff and Cathy. But *Kristin Lavransdatter* has a dimension these other books rarely aspired to: an encompassing religiosity. Only in the third volume does it grow apparent that the trilogy registers a gradual but inevitable repudiation of the flesh. The appetites of the young girl who lost her virginity in a brothel grow distant and Kristin finally winds up in a nunnery, ministering to others with extraordinary courage and selflessness during a sort of hallucinatory apocalypse—the arrival of the Black Death, which some historians estimate may have wiped out at least half the country's population.

The growing call of religion renders richly ambiguous the culminating events of Kristin's life. One might view the trilogy as an accelerating accretion of tragedies, as Kristin's poor abandoned suitor, Simon, whose love for her is hopeless and perpetual, goes to his deathbed with his faithfulness largely unnoticed or misunderstood by Kristin; as her marriage founders and she loses Erlend to a spear; as illness and blindness and plague pluck her children from her, one by one. The story might also be viewed as the record of a long, hard-won, noble victory, as the passionate teenager who brooks no curbs on her desires, recklessly sowing pain and destruction in the process, decades later renounces the decaying kingdom of the flesh for the indestructible domain of the spirit.

Undset owed an incalculable debt to the anonymous Icelandic

sagas of the thirteenth century, as she was the first to acknowledge. When she was ten, she fell under the spell of the longest and perhaps greatest of them, *Njal's Saga*, whose elaborate chronicling of violent and implacable feuds overwhelmed her young imagination; she later declared this the "most important turning point in my life." *Kristin Lavransdatter* reflects many of the signature traits of the sagas: a matter-of-fact abruptness when unexpected catastrophe supervenes; a tendency to view characters externally, with only occasional ventures into the inner workings of their minds; a wry stoicism in the face of life's merciless cruelty (Undset notes about Kristin's mother, who lost her three sons in infancy: "People thought she took the deaths of her children unreasonably hard"); a fondness for characters prone to lengthy brooding silences finally punctuated by shattering admissions, as when Kristin's mother stuns her husband by announcing, "I'm talking about the fact that I wasn't a maiden when I became your wife," or when she declares, "I've always known, Kristin, that you've never been very fond of me."

A particular poignancy attends the reading of very long novels, especially those which, for all their undeniable charms, you're unlikely to read again. Weeks, even months of your internal life are given over to some new cast of characters, who vaporize when the book is closed.

A few such novels may escape this tinge of melancholy. I felt little of it while reading for the first time *Don Quixote* or *David Copperfield* or *Vanity Fair* or *In Search of Lost Time*, since I never doubted I'd one day return to them. But it's the fate of most long books never to be revisited. I don't suppose I'll ever get around to rereading John Hersey's *The Call*, though it's the only novel I've ever read that convincingly situated me in China, or Shimazaki Toson's *Before the Dawn*, even if it deposited me deep in rural Japan during the Meiji restoration, or Austin Tappan Wright's *Islandia*, although parting from its imaginary Thoreauvian country was a little like leaving the land of the lotos-eaters.

Doubtless many of those readers who adored *Kristin Lavransdatter* in its original translation never got around to rereading it, and the story faded into a distant glimmering. If the trilogy's plot embodies an ultimate stripping away of worldly concerns, as

Kristin moves slowly but steadily from bodily to spiritual priorities, in readers' memories a counterpart sort of paring may take place. Again, for most readers, the book's political machinations—King Haakon and all the rest—probably fled the memory in rapid order, as did any strong feelings about Undset as a prose stylist. What lingered was a feeling of having been transported; what lingered was enchantment. Each time a woman approached me to say, "I once read that book," she was responding to a literary gratitude so durable it insisted on being expressed to a stranger.

What was *another world* has now found its way into another world: Nunnally's new translation, with its cleaner motivations and phrasing, its nuanced balancing of the blunt and the taciturn. Throughout all the tribulations of her life, Kristin winds up being not merely a survivor but an explorer: her hardy soul is on a pilgrimage. It's heartening to think of a new generation of readers following Kristin's explorations, and in the process amassing memories so rich they might induce a stranger to approach a stranger and say, "I once read that book."

# A NOTE ON THE TRANSLATION

THIS TRANSLATION from the Norwegian is based on the first edition of Sigrid Undset's epic trilogy, *Kransen*, *Husfrue*, and *Korset*, which appeared in 1920, 1921, and 1922, respectively. All of the novels were originally published in Oslo by H. Aschehoug & Company, which continues to publish Undset's works in Norway today.

The three volumes of *Kristin Lavransdatter* were translated into English in the 1920s, but the translators chose to impose an artificially archaic style on the text, which completely misrepresented Undset's beautifully clear prose. They filled her novels with stilted dialogue (using words such as *'tis, 'twas, I trow, thee, thou, hath,* and *doth*), and they insisted on a convoluted syntax.

Nowadays the role of the translator is different. Accuracy and faithfulness to the original tone and style are both expected and required. In Norwegian Undset writes in a straightforward, almost plain style, yet she can be quite lyrical, especially in her descriptions of nature. The beauty of the mountainous Norwegian landscape is lovingly revealed in Undset's lucid prose. In her research for *Kristin Lavransdatter,* she immersed herself in the customs and traditions of medieval Norway. She was meticulous about using the proper terms for clothing, housewares, and architectural features, but she did not force archaic speech patterns on her characters. To readers of the twenty-first century, the dialogue may sound slightly formal, but it is never incomprehensible.

Misunderstandings and omissions also marred the English translation from the 1920s. One crucial passage in *The Wreath* was even censored, perhaps thought to be too sexually explicit for readers at the time. Most serious of all, certain sections of *The Wife*, scattered throughout the novel and totaling approximately eighteen pages, were deleted. Many are key passages, such as

Kristin's lengthy dialogue with Saint Olav in Christ Church, Gunnulf's meditation on the mixture of jealousy and love he has always felt toward Erlend, and Ragnfrid's anguished memory of her betrothal to Lavrans. I have restored all of these passages, which offer the reader essential insight into the underlying spiritual and psychological turmoil of the story. The Penguin Classics edition is thus the first unabridged English translation of Undset's trilogy. Part of this translation has been published with the support of a grant from NORLA (Norwegian Literature Abroad).

Throughout the text I have retained the original spelling of Norwegian names. The occasional use of the letter ö instead of ø in proper names is intentional—the former is used in Swedish names, the latter in Norwegian. The original Norwegian text contains thousands of dashes, which tend to impede rather than enhance the reading. In most cases I have chosen to replace the dashes with commas or semicolons, or, occasionally, to create separate sentences. I have also decided to keep the Norwegian masculine title "Herr" and the feminine title "Fru" rather than to translate them into the somewhat misleading English titles of "Sir" and "Lady." Only those men who are clearly identified in the story as knights are given "Sir" as their title. Readers should note that Norwegian surnames were derived from the father's given name, followed by either "-datter" or "-søn," depending on the gender of the child. For example, Kristin's mother is named Ragnfrid Ivarsdatter, while her mother's brother is named Trond Ivarsøn. They are also referred to as Gjeslings, since they are descendants of the Gjesling lineage.

It is a testament to the power of Sigrid Undset's story that, in spite of a severely flawed early translation, *Kristin Lavransdatter* has been so beloved by generations of readers. I hope that with this new translation many more readers will now discover Undset's magnificent story of a headstrong young woman who defies her family and faith to follow the passions of her heart.

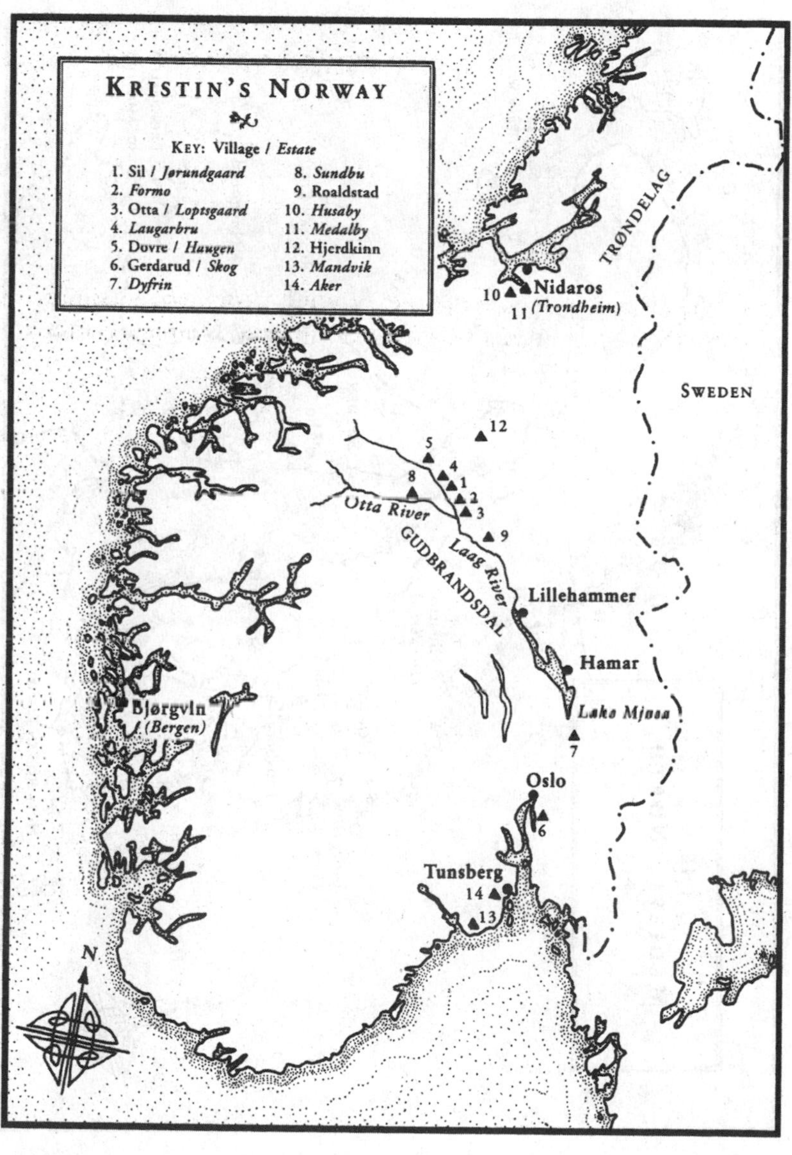

Kristin's Norway
Key: Village / Estate
1. Sil / Jørundgaard
2. Formo
3. Otta / Loptsgaard
4. Laugarbru
5. Dovre / Haugen
6. Gerdarud / Skog
7. Dyfrin
8. Sundbu
9. Roaldstad
10. Husaby
11. Medalby
12. Hjerdkinn
13. Mandvik
14. Aker
Trøndelag
Nidaros
(Trondheim)
Sweden
Otta River
Laag River
Gudbrandsdal
Lillehammer
Hamar
Lake Mjøsa
Bjørgvin
(Bergen)
Oslo
Tunsberg
N

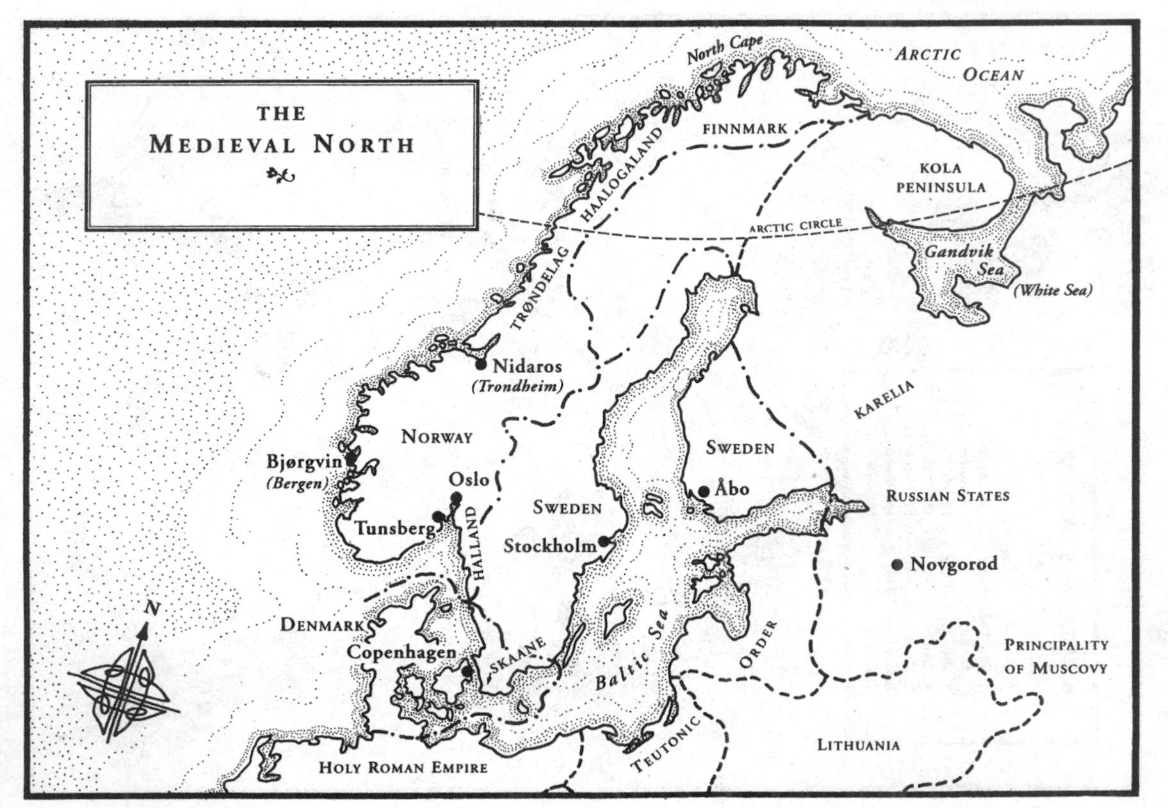
THE
MEDIEVAL NORTH
North Cape
ARCTIC
OCEAN
FINNMARK
HAALOGALAND
KOLA
PENINSULA
ARCTIC CIRCLE
Gandvik
Sea
(White Sea)
TRØNDELAG
Nidaros
(Trondheim)
KARELIA
NORWAY
SWEDEN
Bjørgvin
(Bergen)
Oslo
Åbo
SWEDEN
RUSSIAN STATES
Tunsberg
HALLAND
Stockholm
Novgorod
N
DENMARK
Copenhagen
SKAANE
Baltic Sea
ORDER
PRINCIPALITY
OF MUSCOVY
TEUTONIC
LITHUANIA
HOLY ROMAN EMPIRE

# I: THE WREATH

PART I

# JØRUNDGAARD

## CHAPTER 1

WHEN THE EARTHLY GOODS of Ivar Gjesling the Younger of Sundbu were divided up in the year 1306, his property at Sil was given to his daughter Ragnfrid and her husband Lavrans Bjørgulfsøn. Before that time they had lived at Skog, Lavrans's manor in Follo near Oslo, but now they moved to Jørundgaard, high on the open slope at Sil.

Lavrans belonged to a lineage that here in Norway was known as the sons of Lagmand. It originated in Sweden with a certain Laurentius Östgötelagman, who abducted the Earl of Bjelbo's sister, the maiden Bengta, from Vreta cloister and fled to Norway with her. Herr Laurentius served King Haakon the Old, and was much favored by him; the king bestowed on him the manor Skog. But after he had been in this country for eight years, he died of a lingering disease, and his widow, a daughter of the house of the Folkungs whom the people of Norway called a king's daughter, returned home to be reconciled with her kinsmen. She later married a rich man in another country. She and Herr Laurentius had had no children, and so Laurentius's brother Ketil inherited Skog. He was the grandfather of Lavrans Bjørgulfsøn.

Lavrans was married at a young age; he was only twenty-eight at the time he arrived at Sil, and three years younger than his wife. As a youth he had been one of the king's retainers and had benefited from a good upbringing; but after his marriage he lived quietly on his own estate, for Ragnfrid was rather moody and melancholy and did not thrive among people in the south. After she had had the misfortune to lose three small sons in the cradle, she became quite reclusive. Lavrans moved to Gudbrandsdal largely so that his wife might be closer to her kinsmen and friends. They had one child still living when they arrived there, a little maiden named Kristin.

But after they had settled in at Jørundgaard, they lived for the most part just as quietly and kept much to themselves; Ragnfrid did not seem overly fond of her kinsmen, since she only saw them as often as she had to for the sake of propriety. This was partially due to the fact that Lavrans and Ragnfrid were particularly pious and God-fearing people, who faithfully went to church and were glad to house God's servants and people traveling on church business or pilgrims journeying up the valley to Nidaros.[1] And they showed the greatest respect to their parish priest, who was their closest neighbor and lived at Romundgaard. But the other people in the valley felt that God's kingdom had cost them dearly enough in tithes, goods, and money already, so they thought it unnecessary to attend to fasts and prayers so strictly or to take in priests and monks unless there was a need for them.

Otherwise the people of Jørundgaard were greatly respected and also well liked, especially Lavrans, because he was known as a strong and courageous man, but a peaceful soul, honest and calm, humble in conduct but courtly in bearing, a remarkably capable farmer, and a great hunter. He hunted wolves and bears with particular ferocity, and all types of vermin. In only a few years he had acquired a good deal of land, but he was a kind and helpful master to his tenants.

Ragnfrid was seen so seldom that people soon stopped talking about her altogether. When she first returned home to Gudbrandsdal, many were surprised, since they remembered her from the time when she lived at Sundbu. She had never been beautiful, but in those days she seemed gracious and happy; now she had lost her looks so utterly that one might think she was ten years older than her husband instead of three. People thought she took the deaths of her children unreasonably hard, because in other ways she was far better off than most women—she had great wealth and position and she got on well with her husband, as far as anyone could tell. Lavrans did not take up with other women, he always asked for her advice in all matters, and he never said an unkind word to her, whether he was sober or drunk. And she was not so old that she couldn't have many more children, if God would grant her that.

They had some difficulty finding young people to serve at Jørundgaard because the mistress was of such a mournful spirit and because they observed all of the fasts so strictly. But the servants lived well on the manor, and angry or chastising words were seldom heard. Both Lavrans and Ragnfrid took the lead in all work. The master also had a lively spirit in his own way, and he might join in a dance or start up singing when the young people frolicked on the church green on sleepless vigil nights.[2] But it was mostly older people who took employment at Jørundgaard; they found it to their liking and stayed for a long time.

One day when the child Kristin was seven years old, she was going to accompany her father up to their mountain pastures.

It was a beautiful morning in early summer. Kristin was standing in the loft where they slept in the summertime. She saw the sun shining outside, and she heard her father and his men talking down in the courtyard.[3] She was so excited that she couldn't stand still while her mother dressed her; she jumped and leaped after she was helped into every garment. She had never before been up to the mountains, only across the gorge to Vaage, when she was allowed to go along to visit her mother's kinsmen at Sundbu, and into the nearby woods with her mother and the servants when they went out to pick berries, which Ragnfrid put in her weak ale. She also made a sour mash out of cowberries and cranberries, which she ate on bread instead of butter during Lent.

Ragnfrid coiled up Kristin's long golden hair and fastened it under her old blue cap. Then she kissed her daughter on the cheek, and Kristin ran down to her father. Lavrans was already sitting in the saddle; he lifted her up behind him, where he had folded his cape like a pillow on the horse's loin. There Kristin was allowed to sit astride and hold on to his belt. Then they called farewell to her mother, but she had come running down from the gallery with Kristin's hooded cloak; she handed it to Lavrans and told him to take good care of the child.

The sun was shining but it had rained hard during the night so the streams were splashing and singing everywhere on the hillsides, and wisps of fog drifted below the mountain slopes. But above the crests, white fair-weather clouds climbed into the blue sky, and Lavrans and his men said it was going to be a hot day later on. Lavrans had four men with him, and they were all well armed because at that time there were all kinds of strange people in the mountains—although it seemed unlikely they would encounter any such people because there were so many in their group, and they were only going a short way into the mountains. Kristin liked all of the servants. Three of them were somewhat older men, but the fourth, Arne Gyrdsøn of Finsbrekken, was a half-grown boy and Kristin's best friend. He rode right behind Lavrans because he was supposed to tell her about everything they saw along the way as they passed.

They rode between the buildings of Romundgaard and exchanged greetings with Eirik the priest. He was standing outside scolding his daughter[4]—she ran the house for him—about a skein of newly dyed yarn that she had left hanging outdoors the day before; now it had been ruined by the rain.

On the hill across from the parsonage stood the church; it was not large but graceful, beautiful, well kept, and freshly tarred. Near the cross outside the cemetery gate, Lavrans and his men removed their hats and bowed their heads. Then Kristin's father turned around in his saddle, and he and Kristin waved to her mother. They could see her out on the green in front of the farm buildings back home; she waved to them with a corner of her linen veil.

Kristin was used to playing almost every day up here on the church hill and in the cemetery; but today she was going to travel so far that the child thought the familiar sight of her home and village[5] looked completely new and strange. The clusters of buildings at Jørundgaard, in both the inner and outer courtyards, seemed to have grown smaller and grayer down there on the lowlands. The glittering river wound its way past into the distance, and the valley spread out before her, with wide green pastures and marshes at the bottom and farms with fields and meadows up along the hillsides beneath the precipitous gray mountains.

Kristin knew that Loptsgaard lay far below the place where the mountains joined and closed off the valley. That was where Sigurd and Jon lived, two old men with white beards; they always teased her and played with her whenever they came to Jørundgaard. She liked Jon because he carved the prettiest animals out of wood for her, and he had once given her a gold ring. But the last time he visited them, on Whitsunday, he had brought her a knight that was so beautifully carved and so exquisitely painted that Kristin thought she had never received a more marvelous gift. She insisted on taking the knight to bed with her every single night, but in the morning when she woke up he would be standing on the step in front of the bed where she slept with her parents. Her father told her that the knight got up at the first crow of the cock, but Kristin knew that her mother took him away after she fell asleep. She had heard her mother say that he would be so hard and uncomfortable if they rolled on top of him during the night.

Kristin was afraid of Sigurd of Loptsgaard, and she didn't like it when he took her on his knee, because he was in the habit of saying that when she grew up, he would sleep in her arms. He had outlived two wives and said he would no doubt outlive the third as well; so Kristin could be the fourth. But when she started to cry, Lavrans would laugh and say that he didn't think Margit was about to give up the ghost anytime soon, but if things did go badly and Sigurd came courting, he would be refused—Kristin needn't worry about that.

A large boulder lay near the road, about the distance of an arrow shot north of the church, and around it there was a dense grove of birch and aspen. That's where they played church, and Tomas, the youngest grandson of Eirik the priest, would stand up and say mass like his grandfather, sprinkling holy water and performing baptisms when there was rainwater in the hollows of the rock. But one day the previous fall, things had gone awry. First Tomas had married Kristin and Arne—Arne was still so young that he sometimes stayed behind with the children and played with them when he could. Then Arne caught a piglet that was wandering about and they carried it off to be baptized. Tomas anointed it with mud, dipped it into a hole filled with water and, mimicking his grandfather, said the mass in Latin and scolded them for their scanty offerings. That made the children laugh because they had heard the grown-ups talking about Eirik's excessive greed. And the more they laughed, the more inventive Tomas became. Then he said that this child had been conceived during Lent, and they would have to atone before the priest and the church for their sin. The older boys laughed so hard that they howled, but Kristin was so filled with shame that she was almost in tears as she stood there with the piglet in her arms. And while this was going on, they were unlucky enough that Eirik himself came riding past, on his way home after visiting a sick parishioner. When he saw what the children were up to, he leaped from his horse and handed the holy vessel abruptly to Bentein, his oldest grandson, who was with him. Bentein almost dropped the silver dove containing the Holy Host on the ground. The priest rushed in among the children and thrashed as many as he could grab. Kristin dropped the piglet, and it ran down the road squealing as it dragged the christening gown behind, making the priest's horses rear up in terror. The priest also slapped Kristin, who fell, and then he kicked her so hard that her hip hurt for days afterward. When Lavrans heard of this, he felt that Eirik had been too harsh toward Kristin, since she was so young. He said that he would speak to the priest about it, but Ragnfrid begged him not to do so, because the child had received no more than she deserved by taking part in such a blasphemous game. So Lavrans said nothing more about the matter, but he gave Arne the worst beating he had ever received.

That's why, as they rode past the boulder, Arne plucked at Kristin's sleeve. He didn't dare say anything because of Lavrans, so he grimaced, smiled, and slapped his backside. But Kristin bowed her head in shame.

The road headed into dense forest. They rode in the shadow of Hammer Ridge; the valley grew narrow and dark, and the roar of the Laag River was stronger and rougher. When they caught a glimpse of the river, it was flowing icy-green with white froth between steep walls of stone. The mountain was black with forest on both sides of the valley; it was dark and close and rank in the gorge, and the cold wind came in gusts. They rode over the footbridge across Rost Creek, and soon they saw the bridge over the river down in the valley. In a pool just below the bridge there lived a river sprite.[6] Arne wanted to tell Kristin about it, but Lavrans sternly forbade the boy to speak of such things out there in the forest. And when they reached the bridge, he jumped down from his horse and led it across by the bridle as he held his other arm around the child's waist.

On the other side of the river a bridle path led straight up into the heights, so the men got down from their horses and walked, but Lavrans lifted Kristin forward into his saddle so she could hold on to the saddlebow, and then she was allowed to ride Guldsvein alone.

More gray crests and distant blue peaks striped with snow rose up beyond the mountainsides as they climbed higher, and now

Kristin could glimpse through the trees the village north of the gorge. Arne pointed and told her the names of the farms that they could see.

High up on the grassy slope they came to a small hut. They stopped near the split-rail fence. Lavrans shouted and his voice echoed again and again among the cliffs. Two men came running down from the small patch of pasture. They were the sons of the house. They were skillful tar-burners,[7] and Lavrans wanted to hire them to do some tar distilling for him. Their mother followed with a large basin of cold cellar milk, for it was a hot day, as the men had expected it would be.

"I see you have your daughter with you," she said after she had greeted them. "I thought I'd have a look at her. You must take off her cap. They say she has such fair hair."

Lavrans did as the woman asked, and Kristin's hair fell over her shoulders all the way to the saddle. It was thick and golden, like ripe wheat.

Isrid, the woman, touched her hair and said, "Now I see that the rumors did not exaggerate about your little maiden. She's a lily, and she looks like the child of a knight. Gentle eyes she has as well—she takes after you and not the Gjeslings. May God grant you joy from her, Lavrans Bjørgulfsøn! And look how you ride Guldsvein, sitting as straight as a king's courtier," she teased, holding the basin as Kristin drank.

The child blushed with pleasure, for she knew that her father was considered the most handsome of men far and wide, and he looked like a knight as he stood there among his servants, even though he was dressed more like a peasant, as was his custom at home. He was wearing a short tunic, quite wide, made of green-dyed homespun and open at the neck so his shirt was visible. He had on hose and shoes of undyed leather, and on his head he wore an old-fashioned wide-brimmed woolen hat. His only jewelry was a polished silver buckle on his belt and a little filigree brooch at the neck of his shirt. Part of a gold chain was also visible around his neck. Lavrans always wore this chain, and from it hung a gold cross, set with large rock crystals. The cross could be opened, and inside was a scrap of shroud and hair from the Holy Fru Elin of Skøvde, for the sons of Lagmand traced their lineage from one of the daughters of that blessed woman. Whenever Lavrans was in the forest or at work, he would put the cross inside his shirt against his bare chest, so as not to lose it.

And yet in his rough homespun clothing he looked more high-born than many a knight or king's retainer dressed in banquet attire. He was a handsome figure, tall, broad-shouldered, and narrow-hipped. His head was small and set attractively on his neck, and he had pleasing, somewhat narrow facial features—suitably full cheeks, a nicely rounded chin, and a well-shaped mouth. His coloring was fair, with a fresh complexion, gray eyes, and thick, straight, silky-gold hair.

He stood there talking to Isrid about her affairs, and he also asked about Tordis, Isrid's kinswoman who was looking after Jørundgaard's mountain pastures that summer. Tordis had recently given birth, and Isrid was waiting for the chance to find safe passage through the forest so she could carry Tordis's little boy down from the mountains to have him baptized. Lavrans said that she could come along with them; he was going to return the next evening, and it would be safer and more reassuring for her to have so many men to accompany her and the heathen child.

Isrid thanked him. "If the truth be told, this is exactly what I've been waiting for. We all know, we poor folks who live up here in the hills, that you will do us a favor if you can whenever you come this way." She ran off to gather up her bundle and a cloak.

The fact of the matter was that Lavrans enjoyed being among these humble people who lived in clearings and on leaseholdings high up at the edge of the village. With them he was always happy and full of banter. He talked to them about the movements of the forest animals, about the reindeer on the high plateaus, and about all the uncanny goings-on that occur in such places. He assisted them in word and deed and offered a helping hand; he saw to their sick cattle, helped them at the forge and with their carpentry work. On occasion he even applied his own powerful strength when they had to break up the worst rocks or roots. That's why these people always joyfully welcomed Lavrans Bjørgulfsøn and Guldsvein, the huge red stallion he rode. The horse was a beautiful animal with a glossy coat, white mane and tail, and shining eyes—known in the villages for his strength and fierceness. But toward Lavrans he was as gentle as a lamb. And Lavrans often said that he was as fond of the horse as of a younger brother.

The first thing Lavrans wanted to attend to was the beacon at Heimhaugen. During those difficult times of unrest a hundred years earlier or more, the landowners along the valleys had erected beacons in certain places on the mountainsides, much like the wood stacked in warning bonfires at the ports for warships along the coast. But these beacons in the valleys were not under military authority; the farmer guilds kept them in good repair, and the members took turns taking care of them.

When they came to the first mountain pasture, Lavrans released all the horses except the pack horse into the fenced meadow, and then they set off on a steep pathway upward. Before long there was a great distance between trees. Huge pines stood dead and white, like bones, next to marshy patches of land—and now Kristin saw bare gray mountain domes appearing in the sky all around. They climbed over long stretches of scree, and in places a creek ran across the path so that her father had to carry her. The wind was brisk and fresh up there, and the heath was black with berries, but Lavrans said that they had no time to stop and pick them. Arne leaped here and there, plucking off berries for her, and telling her which pastures they could see below in the forest—for there was forest over all of Høvringsvang at that time.

Now they were just below the last bare, rounded crest, and they could see the enormous heap of wood towering against the sky and the caretaker's hut in the shelter of a sheer cliff.

As they came over the ridge, the wind rushed toward them and whipped through their clothes—it seemed to Kristin that something alive which dwelled up there had come forward to greet them. The wind gusted and blew as she and Arne walked across the expanse of moss. The children sat down on the very end of a ledge, and Kristin stared with big eyes—never had she imagined that the world was so huge or so vast.

There were forest-clad mountain slopes below her in all directions; her valley was no more than a hollow between the enormous mountains, and the neighboring valleys were even smaller hollows; there were many of them, and yet there were fewer valleys than there were mountains. On all sides gray domes, golden-flamed with lichen, loomed above the carpet of forest; and far off in the distance, toward the horizon, stood blue peaks with white glints of snow, seeming to merge with the grayish-blue and dazzling white summer clouds. But to the northeast, close by—just beyond the pasture woods—stood a cluster of magnificent stone-blue mountains with streaks of new snow on their slopes. Kristin guessed that they belonged to the Raanekamp, the Boar Range, which she had heard about, for they truly did look like a group of mighty boars walking away with their backs turned to the village. And yet Arne said that it was half a day's ride to reach them.

Kristin had thought that if she came up over the crest of her home mountains, she would be able to look down on another village like their own, with farms and houses, and she had such a strange feeling when she saw what a great distance there was between places where people lived. She saw the little yellow and green flecks on the floor of the valley and the tiny glades with dots of houses in the mountain forests; she started to count them, but by the time she had reached three dozen, she could no longer keep track. And yet the marks of settlement were like nothing in that wilderness.

She knew that wolves and bears reigned in the forest, and under every rock lived trolls and goblins and elves, and she was suddenly afraid, for no one knew how many there were, but there were certainly many more of them than of Christian people. Then she called loudly for her father, but he didn't hear her because of the wind—he and his men were rolling great boulders down the rock face to use as supports for the timbers of the beacon.

But Isrid came over to the children and showed Kristin where the mountain Vaage Vestfjeld lay. And Arne pointed out Graafjeld, where the people of the villages captured reindeer in trenches and where the king's hawk hunters[8] lived in stone huts. That was the sort of work that Arne wanted to do himself someday—but he also wanted to learn to train birds for the hunt—and he lifted his arms overhead, as if he were flinging a hawk into the air.

Isrid shook her head.

"It's a loathsome life, Arne Gyrdsøn. It would be a great sorrow for your mother if you became a hawk hunter, my boy. No man can make a living doing that unless he keeps company with the worst kind of people, and with those who are even worse."

Lavrans had come over to them and caught the last remark.

"Yes," he said, "there's probably more than one household out there that pays neither taxes nor tithes."

"I imagine you've seen one thing and another, haven't you, Lavrans?" Isrid hinted. "You who have journeyed so deep into the mountains."

"Ah, well," Lavrans said reluctantly, "that could be—but I don't think I should speak of such things. We must not begrudge those who have exhausted their peace in the village whatever peace they may find on the mountain, that's what I think. And yet I've seen yellow pastures and beautiful hay meadows in places where few people know that any valleys exist. And I've seen herds of cattle and flocks of sheep, but I don't know whether they belonged to people or to the others."

"That's right," said Isrid. "Bears and wolves are blamed for the loss of cattle up here in the mountain pastures, but there are much worse robbers on the slopes."

"You call them worse?" said Lavrans thoughtfully, stroking his daughter's cap. "In the mountains south of the Raanekamp I once saw three little boys, the oldest about Kristin's age, and they had blond hair and tunics made of hides. They bared their teeth at me like young wolves before they ran away and hid. It's not so surprising that the poor man they belonged to should be tempted to take a cow or two for himself."

"Well, wolves and bears all have young ones too," said Isrid peevishly. "And you don't choose to spare them, Lavrans. Neither the full-grown ones nor their young. And yet they have never been taught laws or Christianity, as have these evil-doers that you wish so well."

"Do you think I wish them well because I wish for them something slightly better than the worst?" said Lavrans with a faint smile. "But come along now, let's see what kind of food packets Ragnfrid has given us for today." He took Kristin's hand and led her away. He bent down to her and said softly, "I was thinking of your three baby brothers, little Kristin."

They peeked into the caretaker's hut, but it was stuffy and smelled of mold. Kristin took a quick look around, but there were only earthen benches along the walls, a hearthstone in the middle of the floor, barrels of tar, and bundles of resinous pine sticks and birchbark. Lavrans thought they should eat outdoors, and a little farther down a birch-covered slope they found a lovely green plateau.

They unloaded the pack horse and stretched out on the grass. And there was plenty of good food in Ragnfrid's bag—soft bread and thin *lefse*,[9] butter and cheese, pork and wind-dried reindeer meat, lard, boiled beef brisket, two large kegs of German ale, and a small jug of mead. They wasted no time in cutting up the meat and passing it around, while Halvdan, the oldest of the men, made a fire; it was more comforting to have heat than to be without it in the forest.

Isrid and Arne pulled up heather and gathered birch twigs and tossed them into the flames; the fire crackled as it tore the fresh foliage from the branches so that little white charred specks flew high up into the red mane of the blaze. Thick dark smoke swirled up toward the clear sky. Kristin sat and watched; the fire seemed happy to be outside and free to play. It was different; not like when it was confined to the hearth back home and had to slave to cook the food and light up the room for them.

She sat there leaning against her father, with one arm over his knee. He gave her as much as she wanted to eat from all the best portions and offered her all the ale she could drink, along with frequent sips of the mead.

"She'll be so tipsy she won't be able to walk down to the pasture," said Halvdan with a laugh, but Lavrans stroked her plump cheeks.

"There are enough of us here to carry her. It will do her good. Drink up, Arne. God's gifts will do you good, not harm, all you who are still growing. The ale will give you sweet red blood and make you sleep well. It won't arouse rage or foolishness."

And the men drank long and hard too. Isrid did not stint herself either, and soon their voices and the roar and hiss of the fire became a distant sound in Kristin's ears; she felt her head grow heavy. She also noticed that they tried to entice Lavrans to tell them about the strange things he had witnessed on his hunting expeditions. But he would say very little, and she thought this so comforting and reassuring. And she had eaten so much.

Her father was holding a chunk of soft barley bread. He shaped little pieces with his fingers so they looked like horses, and he broke off tiny scraps of meat and set them astride the bread horses. Then he made them ride down his thigh and into Kristin's mouth. Before long she was so tired that she could neither yawn nor chew—and then she toppled over onto the ground and fell asleep.

When she woke up, she was lying in the warmth and darkness of her father's arms—he had wrapped his cape around both of them. Kristin sat up, wiped the sweat from her face, and untied her cap so the air could dry her damp hair.

It must have been late in the day, for the sunshine was a gleaming yellow and the shadows had lengthened and now fell toward the southeast. There was no longer even a breath of wind, and mosquitoes and flies were buzzing and humming around the sleeping group of people. Kristin sat quite still, scratching the mosquito bites on her hands, and looked around. The mountain dome above them shone white with moss and gold from the lichen in the sunshine, and the beacon of weather-beaten timbers towered against the sky like the skeleton of some weird beast.

She started to feel uneasy—it was so odd to see all of them asleep in the bright, bare light of day. Whenever she woke up at home in the night, she would be lying snugly in the dark with her mother on one side and the tapestry that hung over the timbered wall on the other. Then she would know that the door and smoke vent of the room had been closed against the night and the weather outside; and she could hear the small noises of the sleeping people who lay safe and sound among the furs and pillows. But all of these bodies lying twisted and turned on the slope around the small mound of white and black ashes might just as well have been dead; some of them lay on their stomachs and some on their backs with their knees pulled up, and the sounds they uttered frightened Kristin. Her father was snoring heavily, but when Halvdan drew in a breath, a squeak and a whistle came from his nose. And Arne was lying on his side with his face hidden in his arm and his glossy light-brown hair spread out on the heath. He lay so still that Kristin was afraid he might be dead. She had to bend over and touch him; then he stirred a bit in his sleep.

Suddenly it occurred to Kristin that they might have slept a whole night and that it was now the next day. Then she grew so alarmed that she shook her father, but he merely grunted and kept on sleeping. Kristin felt heavy-headed herself, but she didn't dare lie down to sleep. So she crept over to the fire and poked at it with a stick—there were still some embers glowing. She added some heather and small twigs, which she found close at hand, but she didn't want to venture outside the circle of sleepers to find bigger branches.

Suddenly there was a thundering and crashing from the field nearby; Kristin's heart sank and she grew cold with fear. Then she saw a red body through the trees, and Guldsvein emerged from the alpine birches and stood there, looking at her with his clear, bright eyes. She was so relieved that she jumped up and ran toward the stallion. The brown horse that Arne had ridden was there too, along with the pack horse. Then Kristin felt quite safe; she went over and patted all three of them on the flank, but Guldsvein bowed his head so she could reach up to stroke his cheeks and tug on his golden-white forelock. He snuffled his soft muzzle in her hands.

The horses ambled down the birch-covered slope, grazing, and Kristin walked along with them, for she didn't think there was any danger if she kept close to Guldsvein—he had chased off bears before, after all. The blueberries grew so thick there, and the child was thirsty and had a bad taste in her mouth. She had no desire for any ale just then, but the sweet, juicy berries were as good as wine. Over in the scree she saw raspberries too; then she took Guldsvein by the mane and asked him nicely to come with her, and the stallion obediently followed the little girl. As she moved farther and farther down the slope, he would come to her whenever she called him, and the other horses followed Guldsvein.

Kristin heard a stream trickling and gurgling somewhere nearby. She walked toward the sound until she found it, and then she lay down on a slab of rock and washed her sweaty, mosquito-bitten face and hands. Beneath the rock slab the water stood motionless in a deep black pool; on the other side a sheer rock face rose up behind several slender birch trees and willow thickets. It made the finest mirror, and Kristin leaned over and looked at herself in the water. She wanted to see if what Isrid had said was true, that she resembled her father.

She smiled and nodded and bent forward until her hair met the blond hair framing the round young face with the big eyes that she saw in the water.

All around grew such a profusion of the finest pink tufts of flowers called valerian; they were much redder and more beautiful here next to the mountain stream than back home near the river. Then Kristin picked some blossoms and carefully bound them together with blades of grass until she had the loveliest, pinkest, and most tightly woven wreath. The child pressed it down on her hair and ran over to the pool to see how she looked, now that she was adorned like a grown-up maiden about to go off to a dance.

She bent over the water and saw her own dark image rise up from the depths and become clearer as it came closer. Then she saw in the mirror of the stream that someone was standing among the birches on the other side and leaning toward her. Abruptly she straightened up into a kneeling position and looked across the water. At first she thought she saw only the rock face and the trees clustered at its base. But suddenly she discerned a face among the leaves—there was a woman over there, with a pale face and flowing, flaxen hair. Her big light-gray eyes and her flaring, pale pink nostrils reminded Kristin of Guldsvein's. She was wearing something shiny and leaf-green, and branches and twigs hid her figure up to her full breasts, which were covered with brooches and gleaming necklaces.

Kristin stared at the vision. Then the woman raised her hand and showed her a wreath of golden flowers and beckoned to her with it.

Behind her, Kristin heard Guldsvein whinny loudly with fear. She turned her head. The stallion reared up, gave a resounding shriek, and then whirled around and set off up the hillside, making the ground thunder. The other horses followed. They rushed straight up the scree, so that rocks plummeted down with a crash, and branches and roots snapped and cracked.

Then Kristin screamed as loud as she could. "Father!" she shrieked. "Father!" She sprang to her feet and ran up the slope after the horses, not daring to look back over her shoulder. She clambered up the scree, tripped on the hem of her dress, and slid down, then climbed up again, scrabbling onward with bleeding hands, crawling on scraped and bruised knees, calling to Guldsvein in between her shouts to her father—while the sweat poured out of her whole body, running like water into her eyes, and her heart pounded as if it would hammer a hole through her chest; sobs of terror rose in her throat.

"Oh, Father, Father!"

Then she heard his voice somewhere above her. She saw him coming in great leaps down the slope of the scree—the bright, sun-white scree. Alpine birches and aspens stood motionless along the slope, their leaves glittering with little glints of silver. The mountain meadow was so quiet and so bright, but her father came bounding toward her, calling her name, and Kristin sank down, realizing that now she was saved.

"Sancta Maria!" Lavrans knelt down next to his daughter and pulled her to him. He was pale and there was a strange look to his mouth that frightened Kristin even more; not until she saw his face did she realize the extent of her peril.

"Child, child . . ." He lifted up her bloody hands, looked at them, noticed the wreath on her bare head, and touched it. "What's this? How did you get here, little Kristin?"

"I followed Guldsvein," she sobbed against his chest. "I was so afraid because you were all asleep, but then Guldsvein came. And then there was someone who waved to me from down by the stream. . . ."

"Who waved? Was it a man?"

"No, it was a woman. She beckoned to me with a wreath of gold—I think it was a dwarf maiden, Father."

"Jesus Christus," said Lavrans softly, making the sign of the cross over the child and himself.

He helped her up the slope until they came to the grassy hillside; then he lifted her up and carried her. She clung to his neck and sobbed; she couldn't stop, no matter how much he hushed her.

Soon they reached the men and Isrid, who clasped her hands together when she heard what had happened.

"Oh, that must have been the elf maiden—I tell you, she must have wanted to lure this pretty child into the mountain."

"Be quiet," said Lavrans harshly. "We shouldn't have talked about such things the way we did here in the forest. You never know who's under the stones, listening to every word."

He pulled out the golden chain with the reliquary cross from inside his shirt and hung it around Kristin's neck, placing it against her bare skin.

"All of you must guard your tongues well," he told them. "For Ragnfrid must never hear that the child was exposed to such danger."

Then they caught the horses that had run into the woods and walked briskly down to the pasture enclosure where the other horses had been left. Everyone mounted their horses, and they rode over to the Jørundgaard pasture; it was not far off.

The sun was about to go down when they arrived. The cattle were in the pen, and Tordis and the herdsmen were doing the milking. Inside the hut, porridge had been prepared for them, for the pasture folk had seen them up at the beacon earlier in the day and they were expected.

Not until then did Kristin stop her weeping. She sat on her father's lap and ate porridge and thick cream from his spoon.

The next day Lavrans was to ride out to a lake farther up the mountain; that's where some of his herdsmen had taken the oxen. Kristin was supposed to have gone with him, but now he told her to stay at the hut. "And you, Tordis and Isrid, must see to it that the door is kept locked and the smoke vent closed until we come back, both for Kristin's sake and for the sake of the little unbaptized child in the cradle."

Tordis was so frightened that she didn't dare stay up there any longer with the baby; she had not yet been to church herself since giving birth. She wanted to leave at once and stay down in the village. Lavrans said he thought this reasonable; she could travel with them down the mountain the next evening. He thought he could get an older widow who was a servant at Jørundgaard to come up here in her place.

Tordis had spread sweet, fresh meadow grass under the hides on the bench; it smelled so strong and good, and Kristin was almost asleep as her father said the Lord's Prayer and *Ave Maria* over her.

"It's going to be a long time before I take you with me to the mountains again," said Lavrans, patting her cheek.

Kristin woke up with a start.

"Father, won't you let me go with you to the south in the fall, as you promised?"

"We'll have to see about that," said Lavrans, and then Kristin fell at once into a sweet sleep between the sheepskins.

## CHAPTER 2

EVERY SUMMER Lavrans Bjørgulfsøn would ride off to the south to see to his estate at Follo. These journeys of her father were like yearly mileposts in Kristin's life: those long weeks of his absence and then the great joy when he returned home with wonderful gifts—cloth from abroad for her bridal chest, figs, raisins, and gingerbread from Oslo—and many strange things to tell her.

But this year Kristin noticed that there was something out of the ordinary about her father's trip. It was postponed again and again. The old men from Loptsgaard came riding over unexpectedly and sat at the table with her father and mother, talking about inheritances and allodial property,[1] repurchasing rights, and the difficulties of running a manor from a distance; and about the episcopal seat and the king's castle in Oslo, which took so many of the workers away from the farms in the neighboring areas. The old men had no time to play with Kristin, and she was sent out to the cookhouse to the maids. Her uncle, Trond Ivarsøn of Sundbu, also came to visit them more often than usual—but he had never been in the habit of teasing or playing with Kristin.

Gradually she began to understand what it was all about. Ever since he had come to Sil, her father had sought to acquire land there in the village, and now Sir Andres Gudmundsøn had offered to exchange Formo, which was his mother's ancestral estate, for Skog, which lay closer to him, since he was one of the king's retainers and seldom came to the valley. Lavrans was loath to part with Skog, which was his ancestral farm; it had come into his family as a gift from the king. And yet the exchange would be advantageous to him in many ways. But Lavrans's brother, Aasmund Bjørgulfsøn, was also interested in acquiring Skog—he was now living in Hadeland, where he had a manor that he had obtained through marriage—and it was uncertain whether Aasmund would relinquish his ancestral property rights.

But one day Lavrans told Ragnfrid that this year he wanted to take Kristin along with him to Skog. She should at least see the estate where she had been born and the home of his forefathers if it was going to pass out of their possession. Ragnfrid thought this a reasonable request, even though she was a little uneasy about sending so young a child on such a long journey when she was not going along herself.

During the first days after Kristin had seen the elf maiden, she was so fearful that she kept close to her mother; she was even frightened by the mere sight of any of the servants who had been up on the mountain that day and who knew what had happened to her. She was glad that her father had forbidden anyone to mention it.

But after some time had passed, she thought that she would have liked to talk about it. In her own mind she told someone about it—she wasn't sure who—and the strange thing was that the more time that passed, the better she seemed to remember it, and the clearer her memory was of the fair woman.

But the strangest thing of all was that every time she thought about the elf maiden, she would feel such a yearning to travel to Skog, and she grew more and more afraid that her father would refuse to take her.

Finally one morning she woke up in the loft above the storeroom and saw that Old Gunhild and her mother were sitting on the doorstep looking through Lavrans's bundle of squirrel skins. Gunhild was a widow who went from farm to farm, sewing furs into capes and other garments. Kristin gathered from their conversation that now she was the one who was to have a new cloak, lined with squirrel skins and trimmed with marten. Then she realized that she was going to accompany her father, and she jumped out of bed with a cry of joy.

Her mother came over to her and caressed her cheek.

"Are you so happy then, my daughter, to be going so far away from me?"

Ragnfrid said the same thing on the morning of their departure from Jørundgaard. They were up before dawn; it was dark outside, and a thick mist was drifting between the buildings when Kristin peeked out the door at the weather. It billowed like gray smoke around the lanterns and in front of the open doorways. Servants ran back and forth from the stables to the storehouses, and the women came from the cookhouse with steaming pots of porridge and trenchers of boiled meat and pork. They would have a good meal of hearty food before they set off in the cold of the morning.

Indoors the leather bags with their traveling goods were opened up again, and forgotten items were placed inside. Ragnfrid reminded her husband of all the things he was supposed to tend to for her, and she talked about kinsmen and acquaintances who lived along the way—he must give a certain person her greetings, and he must not forget to ask after someone else she mentioned.

Kristin ran in and out, saying goodbye many times to everyone in the house, unable to sit still anywhere.

"Are you so happy then, Kristin, to be going so far away from me, and for such a long time?" asked her mother. Kristin felt both sad and crestfallen, and she wished that her mother had not said such a thing. But she replied as best she could.

"No, dear Mother, but I'm happy to be going with my father."

"Yes, I suppose you are," said Ragnfrid with a sigh. Then she kissed the child and fussed with the maiden's clothes a bit.

At last they sat in the saddles, everyone who was to accompany them on the journey. Kristin was riding Morvin, the horse that had once been her father's. He was old, wise, and steady. Ragnfrid handed the silver goblet with one last fortifying drink to her husband, placed a hand on her daughter's knee, and told her to remember everything that she had impressed upon her.

Then they rode out of the courtyard into the gray dawn. The fog hovered as white as milk over the village. But in a while it began to disperse and then the sun seeped through. Dripping with dew and green with the second crop of hay, the pastures shimmered in the white haze, along with pale stubble-fields and yellow trees and mountain ash with glittering red berries. The blue of the mountainsides was dimly visible, rising up out of the mist and steam. Then the fog broke and drifted in wisps among the grassy slopes, and they rode down through the valley in the most glorious sunshine—Kristin foremost in the group, at her father's side.

* * *

They arrived in Hamar on a dark and rainy evening. Kristin was sitting in front on her father's saddle, for she was so tired that everything swam before her eyes—the lake gleaming palely off to the right, the dark trees dripping moisture on them as they rode underneath, and the somber black clusters of buildings in the colorless, wet fields along the road.

She had stopped counting the days. It seemed to her that she had been on this long journey forever. They had visited family and friends who lived along the valley. She had gotten to know children on the large manors, she had played in unfamiliar houses and barns and courtyards, and she had worn her red dress with the silk sleeves many times. They had rested along the side of the road in the daytime when it was good weather. Arne had gathered nuts for her, and after their meals she had been allowed to sleep on top of the leather bags containing their clothes. At one estate they had been given silk-covered pillows in their beds. On another night they had slept in a roadside hostel, and whenever Kristin woke up she could hear a woman weeping softly and full of despair in one of the other beds. But every night she had slept snugly against her father's broad, warm back.

Kristin woke up with a start. She didn't know where she was, but the odd ringing and droning sound she had heard in her dreams continued. She was lying alone in a bed, and in the room where it stood, a fire was burning in the hearth.

She called to her father, and he rose from the hearth where he was sitting and came over to her, accompanied by a heavyset woman.

"Where are we?" she asked.

Lavrans laughed and said, "We're in Hamar now, and this is Margret, Shoemaker Fartein's wife. You must greet her nicely, for you were asleep when we arrived. But now Margret will help you get dressed."

"Is it morning?" asked Kristin. "I thought you would be coming to bed now. Can't you help me instead?" she begged, but Lavrans replied rather sternly that she should thank Margret for her willingness to help.

"And look at the present she has for you!"

It was a pair of red shoes with silk straps. The woman smiled at Kristin's joyful face and then helped her put on her shift and stockings in bed so that she wouldn't have to step barefoot onto the dirt floor.

"What's making that sound?" asked Kristin. "Like a church bell, but so many of them."

"Those are our bells," laughed Margret. "Haven't you heard about the great cathedral here in town? That's where you're going now. That's where the big bell is ringing. And bells are ringing at the cloister and the Church of the Cross too."

Margret spread a thick layer of butter on Kristin's bread and put honey in her milk so that the food would be more filling—she had so little time to eat.

Outside it was still dark and frost had set in. The mist was so cold that it bit into her skin. The footpaths made by people and cattle and horses were as hard as cast iron, so that Kristin's feet hurt in her thin new shoes. In one place, she stepped through the ice into a rut in the middle of the narrow street, which made her legs wet and cold. Then Lavrans lifted her up on his back and carried her.

She peered into the darkness, but there was little she could see of the town—she glimpsed the black gables of houses and trees outlined against the gray sky. Then they reached a small meadow that glittered with rime, and on the other side of the meadow she could make out a pale gray building as huge as a mountain. There were large stone buildings surrounding it, and here and there light shone through peepholes in the wall. The bells, which had been silent for a while, started ringing again, and now the sound was so powerful that it made icy shivers run down her spine.

It was like entering the mountain, thought Kristin as they stepped inside the vestibule of the church; they were met by darkness and cold. They went through a doorway, and there they encountered the chill smell of old incense and candles. Kristin was in a dark and vast room with a high ceiling. Her eyes couldn't penetrate the darkness, neither overhead nor to the sides, but a light was burning on an altar far in front of them. A priest was standing there, and the echo of his voice crept oddly around the room, like puffs of air and whispers. Lavrans crossed himself and his child with holy water, and then walked forward. Even though he stepped cautiously, his spurs rang loudly against the stone floor. They passed giant pillars, and looking between the pillars was like peering into coal-black holes.

Up front near the altar Lavrans knelt down, and Kristin knelt at his side. Her eyes began adjusting to the dark. Gold and silver gleamed from altars between the pillars, but on the altar before them, candles were glowing in gilded candlesticks, and the holy vessels shone, as did the great, magnificent paintings behind. Kristin again thought of the mountain—this is the way she had imagined it must be inside, so much splendor, but perhaps even more light. And the dwarf maiden's face appeared before her. But then she raised her eyes and saw above the painting the figure of Christ himself, huge and stern, lifted high up on the cross. She was frightened. He didn't look gentle and sad, as he did back home in their own warm, brown-timbered church, where he hung heavily from his arms, his feet and hands pierced through, and his blood-spattered head bowed beneath the crown of thorns. Here he stood on a step, his arms rigidly outstretched and his head erect; his hair was gleaming gold and adorned with a golden crown; his face was lifted upward, with a harsh expression.

Then Kristin tried to follow the priest's words as he prayed and sang, but his speech was so rapid and indistinct. At home she was able to distinguish each word, for Sira Eirik had the clearest voice, and he had taught her what the holy words meant in Norwegian so that she could better keep her thoughts on God when she was in church.

But she couldn't do that here, for she was constantly noticing things in the dark. There were windows high up on the wall, and they began to grow lighter with the day. And near the place where they were kneeling, a strange gallowslike structure of wood had been raised; beyond it lay light-colored blocks of stone, and troughs and tools lay there too. Then she could hear that people had arrived and were padding around in there. Her eyes fell once more on the stern Lord Jesus on the wall, and she tried to keep her thoughts on the service. The icy cold of the stone floor made her legs stiff all the way up to her hips, and her knees ached. Finally everything began to swirl around her, because she was so tired.

Then her father stood up. The service was over. The priest came forward to greet her father. While they talked, Kristin sat down on a step because she saw the altar boy do the same. He yawned, and that made her yawn too. When he noticed that she was looking at him, he stuck his tongue in his cheek and crossed his eyes at her. Then he pulled out a pouch from under his clothing and dumped out the contents onto the stone floor: fish hooks, lumps of lead, leather straps, and a pair of dice; and the whole time he made faces at Kristin. She was quite astonished.

Then the priest and Lavrans looked at the children. The priest laughed and told the boy that he should go off to school, but Lavrans frowned and took Kristin by the hand.

It was starting to get lighter inside the church. Sleepily, Kristin clung to Lavrans's hand while he and the priest walked under the wooden scaffold, talking about Bishop Ingjald's construction work.

They wandered through the entire church, and at last they came out into the vestibule. From there a stone stairway led up into the west tower. Kristin trudged wearily up the stairs. The priest opened a door to a beautiful side chapel, but then Lavrans told Kristin to sit down outside on the steps and wait while he went in to make his confession. Afterward she could come in to kiss the shrine of Saint Thomas.

At that moment an old monk wearing an ash-brown cowl came out of the chapel. He paused for a minute, smiled at the child, and pulled out some sacking and homespun rags that had been stuffed into a hole in the wall. He spread them out on the landing.

"Sit down here; then you won't be so cold," he said, and continued on down the stairs in his bare feet.

Kristin was asleep when Father Martein, as the priest was called, came out to get her. From the church rose the loveliest song, and inside the chapel, candles burned on the altar. The priest gestured for Kristin to kneel beside her father, and then he took down a little golden reliquary that stood above the altar. He whispered to her that inside was a fragment of Saint Thomas of Canterbury's bloody clothing, and he pointed to the holy image, so that Kristin could press her lips to the feet.

Lovely tones were still streaming from the church as they went downstairs. Father Martein told them that the organist was practicing while the schoolboys sang. But they had no time to listen, for Lavrans was hungry; he had fasted before confession. Now they would go over to the guest quarters at the canons' house[2] to eat.

Outside, the morning sun gleamed gold on the steep shores of distant Lake Mjøsa, so that all of the faded leafy groves looked like golden dust in the dark blue forests. The lake was rippled with little white specks of dancing foam. The wind blew cold and fresh, making the multicolored leaves float down onto the frost-covered hill.

A group of horsemen appeared between the bishop's citadel and the house belonging to the Brothers of the Holy Cross. Lavrans stepped aside and bowed with his hand to his breast as he nearly swept the ground with his hat; then Kristin realized that the horseman in the fur cape had to be the bishop himself, and she sank in a curtsey almost to the ground.

The bishop reined in his horse and greeted them in return, beckoning Lavrans to approach, and he spoke with him for a moment.

Then Lavrans came back to the priest and the child and said, "I have been invited to dine at the bishop's citadel. Do you think, Father Martein, that one of the canons' servants could accompany this little maiden home to Shoemaker Fartein's house and tell my men that Halvdan should meet me here with Guldsvein at the hour of midafternoon prayers?"

The priest replied that this could easily be arranged. Then the barefoot monk who had spoken to Kristin in the tower stairway stepped forward and greeted them.

"There's a man over in our guest house who has business with the shoemaker anyway; he can take your message, Lavrans Bjørgulfsøn. And then your daughter can either go with him or stay at the cloister until you return. I'll see to it that she's given food over there."

Lavrans thanked him and said, "It's a shame that you should be troubled with this child, Brother Edvin."

"Brother Edvin gathers up all the children he can," said Father Martein with a laugh. "Then he has someone to preach to."

"Yes, I don't dare offer you learned gentlemen here in Hamar my sermons," said the monk, smiling, and without taking offense. "I'm only good at talking to children and farmers, but that's no reason to tie a muzzle on the ox that threshes."

Kristin gave her father an imploring look; she thought there was nothing she would like better than to go with Brother Edvin. So Lavrans thanked him, and as her father and the priest followed the bishop's entourage, Kristin put her hand in the monk's and they walked down toward the monastery, which was a cluster of wooden houses and a light-colored stone church all the way down near the water.

Brother Edvin gave her hand a little squeeze, and when they glanced at each other, they both had to laugh. The monk was tall and gaunt but quite stoop-shouldered. The child thought he looked like an old crane because his head was small, with a narrow, shiny, smooth pate above a bushy white fringe of hair, and perched on a long, thin, wrinkled neck. His nose was also as big and sharp as a beak. But there was something about him that made Kristin feel at ease and happy just by looking up into his long, furrowed face. His old watery-blue eyes were red-rimmed, and his eyelids were like thin brown membranes with thousands of wrinkles radiating from them. His hollow cheeks, with their reddish web of veins, were crisscrossed with wrinkles that ran down to his small, thin-lipped mouth. But it looked as if Brother Edvin had become so wrinkled simply from smiling at people. Kristin thought she had never seen anyone who looked so cheerful or so kind. He seemed to carry within him a luminous and secret joy, and she was able to share it whenever he spoke.

They walked along the fence of an apple orchard where a few yellow and red fruits still hung on the trees. Two friars wearing black-and-white robes were raking withered beanstalks in the garden.

The monastery was not much different from any other farm, and the guest house into which the monk escorted Kristin closely resembled a humble farmhouse, although there were many beds. In one of the beds lay an old man, and at the hearth sat a woman wrapping an infant in swaddling clothes; two older children, a boy and a girl, stood near her.

They complained, both the man and the woman, because they had not yet received their lunch. "But they don't want to bring food to us twice, so here we sit and starve while you run around in town, Brother Edvin."

"Don't be so angry, Steinulv," said the monk. "Come over here, Kristin, and say hello. Look at this pretty maiden who is going to stay here today and eat with us."

He told Kristin that Steinulv had fallen ill on his way home from a meeting, and he had been allowed to stay in the cloister's guest house instead of the hospice because a kinswoman who was living at the hospice was so mean that he couldn't stand to be there.

"But I can tell they're getting tired of having me here," said the old man. "When you leave, Brother Edvin, no one will have time to take care of me, and then they'll probably make me go back to the hospice."

"Oh, you'll be well long before I'm done with my work at the church," said Brother Edvin. "Then your son will come to get you." He took a kettle of hot water from the hearth and let Kristin hold it as he attended to Steinulv. Then the old man grew more tractable, and a moment later a monk came in, bringing food and drink for them.

Brother Edvin said a prayer over the food and then sat down next to Steinulv on the edge of the bed so he could help the old man eat. Kristin sat down near the woman and fed the little boy, who was so small that he couldn't reach the porridge bowl, and who spilled whenever he tried to dip into the bowl of ale. The woman was from Hadeland and had come with her husband and children to visit her brother who was a monk at the cloister. But he was out wandering among the villages, and she complained bitterly about having to sit there wasting time.

Brother Edvin spoke gently to the woman. She must not say that she was throwing her time away when she was here in the bishop's Hamar. Here were all the splendid churches, and all day long the monks and canons celebrated mass and chanted the offices of the day. And the town was so beautiful, even lovelier than Oslo itself, although it was somewhat smaller. But here, nearly every farm had a garden. "You should have seen it when I arrived in the springtime," the monk said. "The whole town was white with flowers. And since then the sweetbriar roses have bloomed . . ."

"Well, what good does that do me?" said the woman peevishly. "And it seems to me that there are more holy places here than holiness."

The monk chuckled and shook his head. Then he rummaged around in his straw pallet and pulled out a big pile of apples and pears, which he shared among the children. Kristin had never tasted such luscious fruit. The juice ran out of her mouth with every bite she took.

Then Brother Edvin had to go off to church, and he said that Kristin could come along. They cut across the cloister courtyard, and through a little side door they entered the church's choir.

Construction was still going on at this church too, and scaffolding had been set up at the juncture of the nave and the transept. Brother Edvin told Kristin that Bishop Ingjald was having the choir renovated and decorated. The bishop was immensely wealthy, and he used all of his riches to adorn the churches of the town. He was an excellent bishop and a good man. The friars of Olav's cloister were also good men: celibate, learned, and humble. It was a poor monastery, but they had received Brother Edvin kindly. His home was at the Minorite[3] cloister in Oslo, but he had been given permission to beg for alms here in the Hamar diocese.

"Come over here," he said, leading Kristin to the foot of the scaffolding. He climbed up a ladder and rearranged several planks high above. Then he went back down and helped the child to ascend.

On the gray stone wall above her, Kristin saw strange, flickering specks of light, red as blood and yellow as ale, blue and brown and green. She wanted to look behind her, but the monk whispered, "Don't turn around." When they stood together high up on the planks, he gently turned her around, and Kristin saw a sight so glorious that it almost took her breath away.

Directly opposite her, on the south wall of the nave, stood a picture that glowed as if it had been made from nothing but glittering gemstones. The multicolored specks of light on the wall came from rays emanating from the picture itself; she and the monk were standing in the midst of its radiance. Her hands were red, as if she had dipped them in wine; the monk's face seemed to be completely gilded, and from his dark cowl the colors of the picture were dimly reflected. She gave him a questioning glance, but he merely nodded and smiled.

It was like standing at a great distance and looking into heaven. Behind a lattice of black lines she began to distinguish, little by little, the Lord Jesus himself, wearing the costliest red cloak; the Virgin Mary in robes as blue as the sky; and the holy men and maidens in gleaming yellow and green and violet attire. They stood beneath the arches and pillars of illuminated houses surrounded by intertwining branches and twigs with extraordinary, bright leaves.

The monk pulled her a little farther out toward the edge of the scaffold.

"Stand here," he whispered. "Then the light will fall on you from Christ's own cloak."

From the church below the faint smell of incense and the odor of cold stone drifted up toward them. It was gloomy down below, but rays of sunlight were entering diagonally through a series of windows on the south wall of the nave. Kristin began to see that the heavenly picture must be some sort of windowpane,[4] for it filled that type of opening in the wall. The others were empty or closed off with panes of horn in wooden frames. A bird appeared, perched on the windowsill, chirped briefly, and then flew away. Outside the wall of the choir the sound of metal on stone could be heard. Otherwise everything was quiet; only the wind came in small gusts, sighed a little between the church walls, and then died away.

"Well, well," said Brother Edvin with a sigh. "No one can make things like this in Norway. They may paint with glass in Nidaros, but not like this. But in the lands to the south, Kristin, in the great cathedrals, there they have picture panes as big as the portals of this church."

Kristin thought about the pictures in the church back home. The altars of Saint Olav and Saint Thomas of Canterbury had paintings on the front panels and the tabernacles behind. But those pictures seemed dull to her and without radiance as she thought about them now.

They climbed down the ladder and went up into the choir. There stood the altar, naked and bare, and on its stone top were stacked up small boxes and cups made of metal and wood and ceramic; odd little knives, pieces of iron, and pens and brushes lay next to them. Then Brother Edvin told Kristin that these were his tools. He was skilled in the craft of painting pictures and carving tabernacles, and he had made the exquisite paintings that stood nearby on the choir chairs. They were intended for the front panels of the altars here in the friars' church.

Kristin was allowed to watch as he mixed colored powders and stirred them in little ceramic cups, and she helped him carry the things over to a bench next to the wall. As the monk went from one painting to the next, sketching fine red lines in the fair hair of the holy men and women so curls and waves were made visible, Kristin followed close on his heels, watching him and asking questions. And the monk explained what he had painted.

In one of the paintings Christ sat on a golden chair, and Saint Nikulaus and Saint Clement stood near him under a canopy. On either side was depicted the life of Saint Nikulaus. In one place he was an infant sitting on his mother's knee; he had turned away from the breast she offered him, for he was so holy, even in his cradle, that he refused to nurse more than once on Fridays. Next to this was a picture of him placing the money bags at the door of the house where three maidens lived who were so poor that they couldn't find husbands. Kristin saw how he cured the child of the Roman knight, and she saw the knight sail off in a boat with the false golden chalice in his hands. The knight had promised the holy bishop a golden chalice, which had been in his family for a thousand years, as payment for returning the child to good health. But then he tried to betray Saint Nikulaus by giving him a false golden chalice instead. That's why the boy fell into the sea with the real golden chalice in his hand. But Saint Nikulaus carried the child unharmed beneath the water, and he emerged onto shore as his father stood in Saint Nikulaus's church, offering the false goblet. All of this was shown in the picture, painted with gold and the most beautiful of colors.

In another painting the Virgin Mary sat with the Christ child on her knee. He had put one hand up under his mother's chin, and he was holding an apple in the other. With them stood Saint Sunniva and Saint Kristina. They were leaning gracefully from the hips, their faces a lovely pink and white, and they had golden hair and wore golden crowns.

Brother Edvin gripped his right wrist with his left hand as he painted leaves and roses in their crowns.

"It seems to me that the dragon is awfully small," said Kristin, looking at the image of the saint who was her namesake. "It doesn't look as if it could swallow up the maiden."

"And it couldn't, either," said Brother Edvin. "It was no bigger than that. Dragons and all other creatures that serve the Devil only seem big as long as we harbor fear within ourselves. But if a person seeks God with such earnestness and desire that he enters into His power, then the power of the Devil at once suffers such a great defeat that his instruments become small and impotent. Dragons and evil spirits shrink until they are no bigger than goblins and cats and crows. As you can see, the whole mountain that Saint Sunniva was trapped inside is so small that it will fit on the skirt of her cloak."

"But weren't they inside the caves?" asked Kristin. "Saint Sunniva and the Selje men?[5] Isn't that true?"

The monk squinted at her and smiled again.

"It's both true and not true. It seemed to be true for the people who found the holy bodies. And it seemed true to Sunniva and the Selje men, because they were humble and believed that the world is stronger than all sinful people. They did not imagine that they might be stronger than the world because they did not love it. But if they had only known, they could have taken all the mountains and flung them out into the sea like tiny pebbles. No one and nothing can harm us, child, except what we fear and love."

"But what if a person doesn't fear and love God?" asked Kristin in horror.

The monk put his hand on her golden hair, gently tilted her head back, and looked into her face. His eyes were blue and open wide.

"There is no one, Kristin, who does not love and fear God. But it's because our hearts are divided between love for God and fear of the Devil, and love for this world and this flesh, that we are miserable in life and death. For if a man knew no yearning for God and God's being, then he would thrive in Hell, and we alone would not understand that he had found his heart's desire. Then the fire would not burn him if he did not long for coolness, and he would not feel the pain of the serpent's bite if he did not long for peace."

Kristin looked up into his face; she understood nothing of what he said.

Brother Edvin continued, "It was because of God's mercy toward us that He saw how our hearts were split, and He came down to live among us, in order to taste, in fleshly form, the temptations of the Devil when he entices us with power and glory, and the menace of the world when it offers us blows and contempt and the wounds of sharp nails in our hands and feet. In this manner He showed us the way and allowed us to see His love."

The monk looked down into the child's strained and somber

face. Then he laughed a little and said in an entirely different tone of voice, "Do you know who was the first one to realize that Our Lord had allowed Himself to be born? It was the rooster. He saw the star and then he said—and all the animals could speak Latin back then—he cried, *'Christus natus est!'*"

Brother Edvin crowed out the last words, sounding so much like a rooster that Kristin ended up howling with laughter. And it felt so good to laugh, because all the strange things that he had just been talking about had settled upon her like a burden of solemnity.

The monk laughed too.

"It's true. Then when the ox heard about it, he began to bellow, *'Ubi, ubi, ubi?'*

"But the goat bleated and said, *'Betlem, Betlem, Betlem.'*

"And the sheep was so filled with longing to see Our Lady and her Son that he baa'd at once, *'Eamus, eamus!'*

"And the newborn calf lying in the straw got up and stood on his own legs. *'Volo, volo, volo!'* he said.

"Haven't you heard this before? No, I should have known. I realize that he's a clever priest, that Sira Eirik who lives up there with you, and well educated, but he probably doesn't know about this because it's not something you learn unless you journey to Paris. . . ."

"Have you been to Paris then?" asked the child.

"God bless you, little Kristin, I've been to Paris and traveled elsewhere in the world as well, and yet you mustn't think me any better for it, because I fear the Devil and love and desire this world like a fool. But I hold on to the cross with all my strength—one must cling to it like a kitten hanging on to a plank when it falls into the sea.

"And what about you, Kristin? How would you like to offer up those lovely curls of yours and serve Our Lady like these brides that I've painted here?"

"There are no other children at home besides me," replied Kristin. "So I will probably marry, I would think. Mother has already filled chests and trunks with my dowry."

"Yes, I see," said Brother Edvin, stroking her forehead. "That's the way folk dispatch their children these days. To God they give the daughters that are lame and blind and ugly and infirm; or if they think He has given them too many children, they let Him take some of them back. And yet they wonder why the men and maidens who live in the cloisters are not all holy people. . . ."

Brother Edvin took Kristin into the sacristy and showed her the monastery's books, which were displayed on stands. They contained the most beautiful pictures. But when one of the monks came in, Brother Edvin said he was merely looking for a donkey's head to copy.

Afterward he shook his head at himself. "There you see my fear, Kristin. But they're so nervous about their books here in this house. If I had the proper faith and love, I wouldn't stand here and lie to Brother Aasulv. But then I could just as well take these old leather gloves and hang them up on that ray of sunshine over there."

Kristin went with the monk over to the guest house and had something to eat, but otherwise she sat in the church all day long, watching him work and talking to him. And not until Lavrans came back to get Kristin did either she or the monk remember the message that should have been sent to the shoemaker.

Kristin remembered those days she spent in Hamar better than anything else she experienced on that long journey. Oslo was no doubt larger than Hamar, but since she had already seen a town, it did not seem so extraordinary to her. Nor did she think Skog was as beautiful as Jørundgaard, even though the buildings were finer. She was glad she wasn't going to live there. The manor was set on a hill, and below lay Botn Fjord, gray and melancholy with black forests, while on the opposite shore and beyond the buildings the sky reached all the way down to the tops of the trees. There were no towering or steep mountainsides like those back home to lift the sky high overhead or to soften and frame the view so that the world was neither too big nor too small.

The journey home was cold; it was almost Advent, and when they had traveled a short distance into the valley, they came upon snow. They had to borrow sleighs and ride for most of the way.

The exchange of estates was handled in such a manner that Lavrans turned over Skog to his brother Aasmund but retained the right of repurchase for himself and his descendants.

## CHAPTER 3

IN THE SPRING after Kristin's long journey, Ragnfrid gave birth to a daughter. Both parents had no doubt wished that the child would be a boy, but this did not trouble them for long, and they developed the deepest love for little Ulvhild. She was an exceedingly pretty child, healthy, good-natured, happy, and serene. Ragnfrid loved this new child so much that she continued to nurse her even after she turned two. For that reason Ragnfrid followed Sira Eirik's advice and refrained from participating in her usual strict fasts and devout rituals for as long as she had the child at her breast. Because of this and because of her joy for Ulvhild, Ragnfrid blossomed; and Lavrans thought he had never seen his wife look so happy and beautiful and approachable in all the years of their marriage.

Kristin also felt it was a great joy that they had been given her little infant sister. She had never thought about the fact that her mother's somber disposition had made life at home so subdued. She thought things were as they should be: her mother disciplined or admonished her, while her father teased and played with her. Now her mother was gentler toward her and gave her more freedom; she caressed her more often too, so Kristin didn't notice that her mother also had less time to spend with her. She loved Ulvhild, as everyone did, and was pleased when she was allowed to carry her sister or rock her cradle. And later on the little one was even more fun; as she began to crawl and walk and talk, Kristin could play with her.

In this manner the people of Jørundgaard enjoyed three good years. Good fortune was also with them in many ways, and Lavrans did a great deal of construction and made improvements on the estate. The buildings and stables had been old and small when he came to Jørundgaard, since the Gjeslings had leased out the farm for several generations.

Then came Whitsuntide of the third year. At that time Ragnfrid's brother Trond Ivarsøn of Sundbu and his wife Gudrid and their three small sons were visiting. One morning the grown-ups were sitting up on the loft gallery talking, while the children played in the courtyard. There Lavrans had started building a new house, and the children were climbing up onto the timbers that had been brought by wagon. One of the Gjesling boys had hit Ulvhild and made her cry, so Trond went down and scolded his son as he picked Ulvhild up in his arms. She was the prettiest and most amenable child that one could imagine, and her uncle had great affection for her, although he was not usually very fond of children.

At that moment a man came walking across the courtyard from the barnyard leading a huge black ox, but the ox was mean and intractable, and it tore away from the man. Trond leaped up on top of the pile of timbers, chasing the older children ahead of him, but he was carrying Ulvhild in one arm and he had his youngest son by the hand. A log suddenly rolled beneath his feet, and Ulvhild fell from his grasp and down the hill. The log slid after her and then rolled until it came to rest on the child's back.

Lavrans dashed down from the gallery at once. He came racing over and tried to lift the log. Suddenly the ox charged toward him. He grabbed for its horns but he was knocked off his feet; then he managed to seize hold of its nostrils, pulled himself halfway up, and held on to the ox until Trond recovered from his confusion, and the men who came running from the house threw harnesses over the animal.

Ragnfrid was on her knees, trying to raise the log. Lavrans lifted it enough so that she could pull the child out and place her on her lap. The little girl whimpered terribly when they touched her, but Ragnfrid sobbed loudly, "She's alive, thank God, she's alive."

It was a great miracle that Ulvhild had not been crushed; the log had fallen in such a way that it had come to rest with one end lying on top of a rock in the grass. When Lavrans straightened up, blood ran from his mouth, and his clothes had been ripped to shreds across his chest from the ox's horns.

Tordis came running with a sheet made from hides; carefully she and Ragnfrid lifted the child onto it, but she sounded as if she was suffering intolerable pain at even the slightest touch. Ragnfrid and Tordis carried her into the winter house.

Kristin stood pale and rigid on the pile of timbers; the little boys clung to her, crying. All the servants of the farm had now gathered in the courtyard, the women weeping and wailing. Lavrans ordered them to saddle Guldsvein and one more horse. But when Arne brought the horses, Lavrans fell to the ground when he tried to mount. Then he ordered Arne to ride over to the priest while Halvdan would travel south to bring back a wise woman who lived near the place where the rivers converged.

Kristin saw that her father's face was grayish white; he had bled so much that his light-blue clothing was completely covered with reddish-brown spots. Suddenly he straightened up, tore an axe out of the hands of one of the men, and strode over to where several servants were still holding on to the ox. He struck the beast between the horns with the blade of the axe so that the ox sank to its knees, but Lavrans kept on hammering away until blood and brains were spattered everywhere. Then he was seized by a coughing fit and fell backward onto the ground. Trond and one of the men had to carry him inside.

Kristin thought her father was dead; she screamed loudly and ran after him as she called to him with all her heart.

Inside the winter house Ulvhild had been placed on her parents' bed. All of the pillows had been thrown to the floor so that the child could lie flat. It looked as if she had already been laid out on the straw of her deathbed. But she was moaning loudly and incessantly, and her mother was leaning over her, stroking and patting her, wild with grief because there was nothing she could do.

Lavrans was lying on the other bed. He got up and staggered across the floor to console his wife.

Then she sprang up and screamed, "Don't touch me! Don't touch me! Jesus, Jesus, I am so worthless that you should strike me dead—will there never be an end to the misfortune I bring upon you?"

"You haven't . . . my dear wife, this is not something you have brought upon us," said Lavrans, placing a hand on her shoulder. She shuddered at his touch and her pale gray eyes glistened in her gaunt, sallow face.

"No doubt she means that *I* am the one who caused this," said Trond Ivarsøn harshly.

His sister shot him a look of hatred and replied, "Trond knows what I mean."

Kristin ran to her parents but they both pushed her aside. And Tordis, who came over with a kettle of hot water, took her gently by the shoulders and said, "Go over to our house, Kristin. You're in the way here."

Tordis wanted to attend to Lavrans, who was sitting on the step of the bed, but he told her that he was not gravely wounded.

"But can't you ease Ulvhild's pain a little? God help us, her moans could arouse pity from the stone inside the mountain."

"We don't dare touch her until the priest arrives, or Ingegjerd, the wise woman," said Tordis.

Arne came in just then and reported that Sira Eirik was not at home.

Ragnfrid stood there for a moment, wringing her hands. Then she said, "Send word to Fru Aashild at Haugen. Nothing else matters, if only Ulvhild can be saved."

No one paid any attention to Kristin. She crept up onto the bench behind the headboard of the bed, tucked up her legs, and rested her head on her knees.

Now she felt as if her heart were being crushed between hard fists. Fru Aashild was going to be summoned! Her mother had never wanted them to send for Fru Aashild, not even when she herself was near death when she gave birth to Ulvhild, nor when Kristin was so ill with fever. People said she was a witch; the bishop of Oslo and the canons of the cathedral had sat in judgment on her. She would have been executed or burned at the stake if she hadn't been of such high birth that she was like a sister to Queen Ingebjørg. But people said that she had poisoned her first husband, and that she had won her present husband, Herr Bjørn, through witchcraft. He was young enough to be her son. She did have children, but they never came to visit their mother. So those two high-born people, Bjørn and Aashild, sat on their small farm in Dovre, having lost all their riches. None of the gentry in the valley would have anything to do with them, but secretly people sought out Fru Aashild's advice. Poor folk even went to her openly with their troubles and ills; they said she was kind, but they were also afraid of her.

Kristin thought that her mother, who was otherwise constantly praying, should have called on God and the Virgin Mary instead. She tried to pray herself—especially to Saint Olav,[1] for she knew that he was kind and he had helped so many who suffered from illness and wounds and broken bones. But she couldn't collect her thoughts.

Her parents were now alone in the room. Lavrans was lying on the bed again and Ragnfrid sat leaning over the injured child, occasionally wiping Ulvhild's forehead and hands with a damp cloth and moistening her lips with wine.

A long time passed. Tordis looked in on them now and then; she wanted so desperately to help, but each time Ragnfrid sent her away. Kristin wept soundlessly and prayed in silence, but every once in a while she would think about the witch, and she waited tensely to see her enter the room.

Suddenly Ragnfrid broke the silence. "Are you asleep, Lavrans?"

"No," replied her husband. "I'm listening to Ulvhild. God will help His innocent lamb, my wife—we mustn't doubt that. But it's hard to lie here and wait."

"God hates me for my sins," said Ragnfrid in despair. "My children are in peace where they are—I don't dare doubt that. And now Ulvhild's time has come too. But He has cast me out, for my heart is a viper's nest of sin and sorrow."

Just then the door opened. Sira Eirik stepped inside, straightening up his enormous body as he stood in the doorway, and pronounced in his deep, clear voice, "God help those in this house!"

The priest placed the box containing his medical things[2] on the step of the bed, went over to the hearth, and poured warm water over his hands. Then he pulled out his cross, raised it to all four corners of the room, and murmured something in Latin. After that he opened the smoke vent so that light could stream into the room. Then he went over and looked at Ulvhild.

Kristin was afraid that he would discover her and chase her away—usually very little escaped Sira Eirik's eye. But he didn't look around. The priest took a vial out of his box, poured something onto a tuft of finely carded wool, and placed it over Ulvhild's nose and mouth.

"Soon her suffering will lessen," said the priest. He went over to Lavrans and attended to him as he asked them to tell him how the accident had occurred. Lavrans had two broken ribs and he had received a wound to his lungs, but the priest didn't think he was in danger.

"What about Ulvhild?" asked her father sorrowfully.

"I'll tell you after I have examined her," replied the priest. "But you must go up to the loft and rest; we need quiet here and more room for those who will take care of her." He put Lavrans's arm around his shoulder, lifted up the man, and helped him out. Kristin would have preferred to go with her father, but she didn't dare show herself.

When Sira Eirik returned, he didn't speak to Ragnfrid but cut the clothes off Ulvhild, who was now whimpering less and seemed to be half asleep. Cautiously he ran his hands over the child's body and limbs.

"Are things so bad for my child, Eirik, that you don't know what to do? Is that why you have nothing to say?" asked Ragnfrid in a subdued voice.

The priest replied softly, "It looks as if her back is badly injured, Ragnfrid. I don't know anything else to do except to let God and Saint Olav prevail. There's not much I can do here."

The mother said vehemently, "Then we must pray. You know that Lavrans and I will give everything you ask for, sparing nothing, if you can convince God to allow Ulvhild to live."

"I think it would be a miracle," said the priest, "if she were to live and regain her health."

"But aren't you always talking about miracles both day and night? Don't you think a miracle could happen for my child?" she said in the same tone of voice.

"It's true that miracles do occur," said the priest, "but God does not grant everyone's prayers—we do not know His mysterious ways. And don't you think it would be worse for this pretty little maiden to grow up crippled and lame?"

Ragnfrid shook her head and cried softly, "I have lost so many, priest, I cannot lose her too."

"I'll do everything I can," replied the priest, "and pray with all my might. But you must try, Ragnfrid, to bear whatever fate God visits upon you."

The mother murmured softly, "Never have I loved any of my

children as I have loved this one. If she too is taken from me, I think my heart will break."

"God help you, Ragnfrid Ivarsdatter," said Sira Eirik, shaking his head. "You want nothing more from all your prayers and fasting than to force your will on God. Does it surprise you, then, that it has accomplished so little good?"

Ragnfrid gave the priest a stubborn look and said, "I have sent for Fru Aashild."

"Well, you may know her, but I do not," said the priest.

"I will not live without Ulvhild," said Ragnfrid in the same voice as before. "If God won't help her, then I will seek the aid of Fru Aashild, or offer myself up to the Devil if he will help!"

The priest looked as if he wanted to make a sharp retort, but he restrained himself. He leaned down and touched the injured girl's limbs again.

"Her hands and feet are cold," he said. "We must put some kegs of hot water next to her—and then you must not touch her again until Fru Aashild arrives."

Kristin soundlessly slipped down onto the bench and pretended to sleep. Her heart was pounding with fear. She had not understood much of the conversation between Sira Eirik and her mother, but it had frightened her greatly, and she knew it wasn't meant for her ears.

Her mother stood up to get the kegs; then she broke down, sobbing. "Pray for us, nevertheless, Sira Eirik!"

A little while later her mother came back with Tordis. The priest and the women bustled around Ulvhild, and then Kristin was discovered and sent away.

The light dazzled Kristin as she stood in the courtyard. She thought that most of the day had passed while she sat in the dark winter house, but the buildings were light gray and the grass was shimmering, as glossy as silk in the white midday sun. Beyond the golden lattice of the alder thicket, with its tiny new leaves, the river glinted. It filled the air with its cheerful, monotonous roar, for it flowed strongly down a flat, rocky riverbed near Jørundgaard. The mountainsides rose up in a clear blue haze, and the streams leaped down the slopes through melting snow. The sweet, strong spring outside made Kristin weep with sorrow at the helplessness she felt all around her.

No one was in the courtyard, but she heard people talking in the servants' room. Fresh earth had been spread over the spot where her father had killed the ox. She didn't know what to do with herself; then she crept behind the wall of the new building, which had been raised to a height of a couple of logs. Inside were Ulvhild's and her playthings; she gathered them up and put them into a hole between the lowest log and the foundation. Lately Ulvhild had wanted all of Kristin's toys, and that had made her unhappy at times. She thought now that if her sister got well, she would give her everything she owned. And that thought comforted her a little.

Kristin thought about the monk at Hamar—he at least was convinced that miracles could happen for everyone. But Sira Eirik was not as sure of it, nor were her parents, and they were the ones she was most accustomed to listening to. It fell like a terrible burden upon her when she realized for the first time that people could have such different opinions about so many things. And not just evil, godless people disagreeing with good people, but also good people such as Brother Edvin and Sira Eirik—or her mother and father. She suddenly realized that they too thought differently about many things.

Tordis found Kristin asleep there in the corner late in the day, and she took her indoors. The child hadn't eaten a thing since morning. Tordis kept vigil with Ragnfrid over Ulvhild that night, and Kristin lay in her bed with Jon, Tordis's husband, and Eivind and Orm, her little boys. The smell of their bodies, the man's snoring, and the even breathing of the two children made Kristin quietly weep. Only the night before she had lain in bed, as she had every night of her life, with her own father and mother and little Ulvhild. It was like thinking about a nest that had been torn apart and scattered, and she herself had been flung from the shelter and wings that had always warmed her. At last she cried herself to sleep, alone and miserable among all those strangers.

On the following morning when Kristin got up, she learned that her uncle and his entire entourage had left Jørundgaard—in anger.

Trond had called his sister a crazy, demented woman and her husband a spineless fool who had never learned to rein in his wife. Kristin grew flushed with rage, but she was also ashamed. She realized that a grave impropriety had taken place when her mother had driven her closest kinsmen from the manor. And for the first time it occurred to Kristin that there was something about her mother that was not as it should be—that she was different from other women.

As she stood and pondered this, a maidservant came up to her and asked her to go up to the loft to her father.

But when she stepped into the loft room Kristin forgot all about tending to him, for across from the open doorway, with the light shining directly in her face, sat a small woman, whom she realized must be the witch—although Kristin had not expected her to look like that.

She seemed as small as a child, and delicate, for she was sitting in the big high-backed chair that had been brought up to the room. A table had also been placed in front of her, covered with Ragnfrid's finest embroidered linen cloth. Pork and fowl were set forth on silver platters, there was wine in a bowl of curly birchwood, and she had Lavrans's own silver goblet to drink from. She had finished eating and was wiping her small, slender hands on one of Ragnfrid's best towels. Ragnfrid herself stood in front of her, holding a brass basin of water.

Fru Aashild let the towel drop into her lap, smiled at the child, and said in a lovely, clear voice, "Come over here to me!" And to Kristin's mother she said, "You have beautiful children, Ragnfrid."

Her face was full of wrinkles but pure white and pink like a child's, and her skin looked as if it were just as soft and fine to the touch. Her lips were as red and fresh as a young woman's, and her big hazel eyes gleamed. An elegant white linen wimple framed her face and was fastened tightly under her chin with a gold brooch; over it she wore a veil of soft, dark-blue wool, which fell loosely over her shoulders and onto her dark, well-fitting clothes. She sat as erect as a candle, and Kristin sensed rather than thought that she had never seen such a beautiful or noble woman as this old witch whom the gentry of the village refused to have anything to do with.

Fru Aashild held Kristin's hand in her own soft old hands; she spoke to her kindly and with humor, but Kristin could not find a word to reply.

Fru Aashild said to Ragnfrid with a little laugh, "Do you think she's afraid of me?"

"No, no," Kristin almost shouted.

Fru Aashild laughed even more and said, "She has wise eyes, this daughter of yours, and good strong hands. And she's not accustomed to slothfulness either, I can see. You're going to need someone who can help you care for Ulvhild when I'm not here. So you can let Kristin assist me while I'm at the manor. She's old enough for that, isn't she? Eleven years old?"

Then Fru Aashild left, and Kristin was about to follow her. But Lavrans called to her from his bed. He was lying flat on his back with pillows stuffed under his knees; Fru Aashild had ordered him to lie in this manner so that the injury to his chest would heal faster.

"You're going to get well soon, aren't you, Father?" asked Kristin, using the formal means of address. Lavrans looked up at her. Never before had she addressed him in that manner.

Then he said somberly, "I'm not in danger, but it's much more serious for your sister."

"I know," said Kristin with a sigh.

Then she stood next to his bed for a while. Her father did not speak again, and Kristin could find nothing more to say. And when Lavrans told her some time later to go downstairs to her mother and Fru Aashild, Kristin hurried out and rushed across the courtyard to the winter house.

## CHAPTER 4

Fru Aashild stayed at Jørundgaard for most of the summer, which meant that people came there to seek her advice. Kristin heard Sira Eirik speak jeeringly of this, and it dawned on her that her parents did not much care for it either. But she pushed aside all thoughts of these things, nor did she pay any heed to what her own opinion of Fru Aashild might be; she was her constant companion and never tired of listening to and watching the woman.

Ulvhild still lay stretched out flat on her back in the big bed. Her small face was white to the very edge of her lips, and she had dark circles under her eyes. Her lovely blond hair smelled sharply of sweat because it hadn't been washed in such a long time; it had turned dark and had lost its sheen and curl so that it looked like old, windblown hay. She looked tired and tormented and patient, and she would smile, feeble and wan, whenever Kristin sat by her on the bed to talk and to show her all the lovely presents she had received from her parents and their friends and kinsmen far and wide. There were dolls, toy birds and cattle, a little board game, jewelry, velvet caps, and colorful ribbons. Kristin had put it all in a box for her. Ulvhild would look at everything with her somber eyes, sigh, and then let the treasures fall from her weary hands.

But whenever Fru Aashild came over to her, Ulvhild's face would light up with joy. Eagerly she drank the refreshing and sleep-inducing brews that Fru Aashild prepared for her. She never complained when the woman tended to her, and she would lie still, listening happily, whenever Fru Aashild played Lavrans's harp and sang—she knew so many ballads that were unfamiliar to the people there in the valley.

Often she would sing for Kristin when Ulvhild had fallen asleep. And sometimes she spoke of her youth, when she lived in the south of the country and frequented the courts of King Magnus and King Eirik and their queens.

Once, as they were sitting there and Fru Aashild was telling stories, Kristin blurted out what she had thought about so often.

"It seems strange to me that you're always so happy, when you've been used to—" she broke off, blushing.

Fru Aashild looked down at the child, smiling.

"You mean because now I'm separated from all those things?" She laughed quietly and then she said, "I've had my glory days, Kristin, but I'm not foolish enough to complain because I have to be content with sour, watered-down milk now that I've drunk up all my wine and ale. Good days can last a long time if one tends to things with care and caution; all sensible people know that. That's why I think that sensible people have to be satisfied with the good days—for the grandest of days are costly indeed. They call a man a fool who fritters away his father's inheritance in order to enjoy himself in his youth. Everyone is entitled to his own opinion about that. But I call him a true idiot and fool only if he regrets his actions afterward, and he is twice the fool and the greatest buffoon of all if he expects to see his drinking companions again once the inheritance is gone.

"Is something wrong with Ulvhild?" Fru Aashild asked gently, turning to Ragnfrid, who had given a start from her place near the child's bed.

"No, she's sleeping quietly," said the mother as she came over to Fru Aashild and Kristin, who were sitting near the hearth. With her hand on the smoke vent pole, Ragnfrid stood and looked down into the woman's face.

"Kristin doesn't understand all this," she said.

"No," replied Fru Aashild. "But she also learned her prayers before she understood them. At those times when one needs either prayers or advice, one usually has no mind to learn or to understand."

Ragnfrid raised her black eyebrows thoughtfully. When she did that, her light, deep-set eyes looked like lakes beneath a black forest meadow. That's what Kristin used to think when she was small, or perhaps she had heard someone say that. Fru Aashild looked at her with that little half smile of hers. Ragnfrid sat down at the edge of the hearth, picked up a twig, and poked at the embers.

"But the person who has wasted his inheritance on the most wretched of goods—and then later sees a treasure he would give his life to own—don't you think that he would deplore his own stupidity?"

"No bargain is without some loss, Ragnfrid," said Fru Aashild. "And whoever wishes to give his life must take the risk and see what he can win."

Ragnfrid jerked the burning twig from the fire, blew out the flame, and curled her hand around the glowing end so that a blood-red light shone between her fingers.

"Oh, it's all nothing but words, words, words, Fru Aashild."

"There is very little worth paying for so dearly, Ragnfrid," said the other woman, "as with one's own life."

"Yes, there is," said Kristin's mother fervently. "My husband," she whispered almost inaudibly.

"Ragnfrid," said Fru Aashild quietly, "many a maiden has had the same thought when she was tempted to bind a man to her and gave up her maidenhood to do so. But haven't you read about men and maidens who gave God all they owned, and entered cloisters or stood naked in the wilderness and then regretted it afterward? They're called fools in the holy books. And it would certainly be a sin to think that God was the one who had deceived them in their bargain."

Ragnfrid sat quite still for a moment. Then Fru Aashild said, "Come along with me, Kristin. It's time to go out and collect the dew that we'll use to wash Ulvhild in the morning."

Outside, the courtyard was white and black in the moonlight. Ragnfrid accompanied them through the farmyard down to the gate near the cabbage garden. Kristin saw the thin silhouette of her mother leaning against the fence nearby. The child shook dew from the large, ice-cold cabbage leaves and from the folds of the lady's-mantle into her father's silver goblet.

Fru Aashild walked silently at Kristin's side. She was there only to protect her, for it was not wise to let a child go out alone on such a night. But the dew would have more power if it was collected by an innocent maiden.

When they came back to the gate, Ragnfrid was gone. Kristin was shaking with cold as she put the icy silver goblet into Fru

Aashild's hands. In her wet shoes she ran over to the loft where she slept with her father. She had her foot on the first step when Ragnfrid emerged from the shadows beneath the gallery of the loft. In her hands she held a bowl of steaming liquid.

"I've warmed up some ale for you, daughter," said Ragnfrid.

Kristin thanked her gratefully and put her lips to the rim. Then her mother asked, "Kristin, those prayers and other things that Fru Aashild is teaching you—is there anything sinful or ungodly about them?"

"I can't believe that," replied the child. "They all mention Jesus and the Virgin Mary and the names of the saints."

"What has she been teaching you?" asked her mother again.

"Oh, about herbs, and how to ward off bleeding and warts and strained eyes—and moths in clothing and mice in the storehouse. And which herbs to pick in sunlight and which ones have power in the rain. But I mustn't tell the prayers to anyone else, or they will lose their power," she said quickly.

Her mother took the empty bowl and set it on the steps. Suddenly she threw her arms around her daughter, pulled her close, and kissed her. Kristin noticed that her mother's cheeks were hot and wet.

"May God and Our Lady guard and protect you against all evil—we have only you now, your father and I; you're the only one that misfortune has not touched. My dear, my dear—never forget that you are your father's dearest joy."

Ragnfrid went back to the winter house, undressed, and crawled into bed with Ulvhild. She put her arm around the child and pressed her face close to the little one's so that she could feel the warmth of Ulvhild's body and smell the sharp odor of sweat from the child's damp hair. Ulvhild slept soundly and securely as always after Fru Aashild's evening potion. There was a soothing scent from the Virgin Mary grass spread under the sheet. And yet Ragnfrid lay there for a long time, unable to sleep, and stared up at the little scrap of light in the roof where the moon shone on the horn pane of the smoke vent.

Fru Aashild lay in the other bed, but Ragnfrid never knew whether she was asleep or awake. Fru Aashild never mentioned that they had known each other in the past, and that frightened Ragnfrid quite badly. She thought she had never felt so bitterly sad or in such an agony of fear as she did now, even though she knew that Lavrans would regain his full health—and that Ulvhild would survive.

Fru Aashild seemed to enjoy talking to Kristin, and for each day that passed, the maiden became better friends with her.

One day when they had gone out to pick herbs, they sat down next to the river in a little grassy clearing at the foot of a scree. They could look down at the courtyard of Formo and see Arne Gyrdsøn's red shirt. He had ridden over with them and was going to look after their horses while they were up in the mountain meadow gathering herbs.

As they sat there, Kristin told Fru Aashild about her encounter with the dwarf maiden. She hadn't thought about the incident for many years, but now it suddenly came back to her. And as she spoke, the strange thought occurred to her that there was some resemblance between Fru Aashild and the dwarf woman—even though she realized full well that they did not look at all alike.

But when she had finished telling the story, Fru Aashild sat in silence for a moment and gazed out across the valley.

Finally she said, "It was wise of you to flee, since you were only a child back then. But haven't you ever heard of people who took the gold the dwarf offered them, and then trapped the troll in a rock afterward?"

"I've heard of such stories," said Kristin, "but I would never dare do that myself. And I don't think it's the right thing to do."

"It's good when you don't dare do something that doesn't seem right," said Fru Aashild with a little laugh. "But it's not so good if you think something isn't right because you don't dare do it." Then she added abruptly, "You've grown up a great deal this summer. I wonder if you realize how lovely you've become."

"Yes, I know," said Kristin. "They say I look like my father."

Fru Aashild laughed softly.

"Yes, it would be best if you took after Lavrans, both in temperament and appearance. And yet it would be a shame if they married you to someone up here in the valley. Farming customs and the ways of smallholders should not be disdained, but these gentry up here all think they're so grand that their equals are not to be found in all of Norway. I'm sure they wonder how I can manage to live and prosper even though they've closed their doors to me. But they're lazy and arrogant and refuse to learn new ways—and then they blame everything on the old enmity with the monarchy in the time of King Sverre.[1] It's all a lie—your ancestor reconciled with King Sverre and accepted gifts from him. But if your mother's brother wanted to serve the king and join his retinue, then he would have to cleanse himself, both inside and out, which is not something Trond is willing to do. But you, Kristin, you ought to marry a man who is both chivalrous and courtly. . . ."

Kristin sat staring down at the Formo courtyard, at Arne's red back. She hadn't been aware of it herself, but whenever Fru Aashild talked about the world she had frequented in the past, Kristin always pictured the knights and counts in Arne's image. Before, when she was a child, she had always envisioned them in her father's image.

"My nephew, Erlend Nikulaussøn of Husaby—now he would have been a suitable bridegroom for you. He has grown up to be so handsome, that boy. My sister Magnhild came to visit me last year when she was on her way through the valley, and she brought her son along with her. Well, you won't be able to marry him, of course, but I would have gladly spread the blanket over the two of you in the wedding bed. His hair is as dark as yours is fair, and he has beautiful eyes. But if I know my brother-in-law, he has already set his sights on a better match for Erlend than you would be."

"Does that mean I'm not a good match, then?" asked Kristin with surprise. She was never offended by anything Fru Aashild said, but she felt embarrassed and chagrined that Fru Aashild might be somehow better than her own family.

"Yes, of course you're a good match," said Fru Aashild. "And yet you couldn't expect to become part of my lineage. Your ancestor here in Norway was an outlaw and a foreigner, and the Gjeslings have sat moldering away on their estates for such a long time that almost no one remembers them outside of this valley. But my sister and I married the nephews of Queen Margret Skulesdatter."

Kristin didn't even think to object that it was not her ancestor but his brother who had come to Norway as an outlaw. She sat and gazed out over the dark mountain slopes across the valley, and she remembered that day, many years ago, when she went up onto the ridge and saw how many mountains there were between her own village and the rest of the world. Then Fru Aashild said they ought to head home, and she asked Kristin to call for Arne. Kristin put her hands up to her mouth and shouted and then waved her kerchief until she saw the red speck down in the courtyard turn and wave back.

Some time later Fru Aashild returned home, but during the fall and the first part of winter she often came to Jørundgaard to spend a few days with Ulvhild. The child was now taken out of bed in the daytime, and they tried to get her to stand on her own, but her legs crumpled beneath her whenever she tried it. She was fretful, pale, and tired, and the laced garment that Fru Aashild had made for her from horsehide and slender willow branches plagued her terribly; all she wanted to do was lie in her mother's lap. Ragnfrid was constantly holding her injured daughter, so Tordis was now in charge of all the housekeeping. At her mother's request, Kristin accompanied Tordis, to help and to learn.

Kristin sometimes longed for Fru Aashild, who occasionally would talk to her a great deal, but at other times Kristin would wait in vain for a word beyond the casual greeting as Fru Aashild came and went.

Instead, Fru Aashild would sit with the grown-ups and talk. That was always what happened when she brought her husband along with her, for now Bjørn Gunnarsøn also came to Jørundgaard. One day in the fall, Lavrans had ridden over to Haugen to take Fru Aashild payment for her doctoring: the best silver pitcher and matching platter they owned. He had stayed the night and afterward had high praise for their farm. He said it was beautiful and well tended, and not as small as people claimed. Inside the buildings everything looked prosperous, and the customs of the house were as courtly as those of the gentry in the south of the country. What Lavrans thought of Bjørn he didn't say, but he always received the man courteously when Bjørn accompanied his wife to Jørundgaard. On the other hand, Lavrans was exceedingly fond of Fru Aashild, and he believed that most of what people said about her was a lie. He also said that twenty years earlier she would hardly have required witchcraft to bind a man to her—she was sixty now but still looked young, and she had a most appealing and charming manner.

Kristin noticed that her mother was not happy about all this. It's true that Ragnfrid never said much about Fru Aashild, but one time she compared Bjørn to the flattened yellow grass that can be found under large rocks, and Kristin thought this an apt description. Bjørn had an oddly faded appearance—he was quite fat, pale, and sluggish, and slightly bald—even though he was not much older than Lavrans. And yet it was still apparent that he had once been an extremely handsome man. Kristin never exchanged a single word with him. He said little, preferring to stay in one spot, wherever he happened to be seated, from the moment he stepped in the door until it was time for bed. He drank an enormous amount but it seemed to have little effect on him. He ate almost nothing, and occasionally he would stare at someone in the room, stony-faced and pensive, with his strange, pale eyes.

They had not seen their kinsmen from Sundbu since the accident occurred, but Lavrans had been over to Vaage several times. Sira Eirik, on the other hand, came to Jørundgaard as often as before, and there he frequently met Fru Aashild. They had become good friends. People thought this a generous attitude on the part of the priest, since he himself was a very capable doctor. This was also probably one of the reasons why people on the large estates had not sought Fru Aashild's advice, at least not openly, because they considered the priest to be competent enough. It was not easy for them to know how to act toward two people who in some ways had been cast out of their own circles. Sira Eirik himself said that they caused no one any harm, and as for Fru Aashild's witchcraft, he was not her parish priest. It could be that the woman knew more than was good for the health of her soul—and yet one should not forget that ignorant people often spoke of witchcraft as soon as a woman showed herself to be wiser than the councilmen. For her part, Fru Aashild spoke highly of the priest and diligently went to church if she happened to be at Jørundgaard on a holy day.

Christmas was a sad time that year. Ulvhild was still unable to stand on her own. And they neither saw nor heard from their kinsmen at Sundbu. Kristin noticed that people in the village were talking about the rift and that her father took it to heart. But her mother didn't care, and Kristin thought this was callous of her.

One evening toward the end of the holidays, Sira Sigurd, Trond Gjesling's house priest, arrived in a big sleigh, and his primary mission was to invite them all to visit Sundbu.

Sira Sigurd was not well liked in the surrounding villages, for he was the one who actually managed Trond's properties for him—or at least he was the one who was blamed whenever Trond acted harshly or unjustly, and Trond tended to plague his tenants somewhat. The priest was exceedingly clever at writing and figuring; he knew the law and was a skilled doctor, although not as skilled as he thought. But judging by his behavior, no one would think him a clever man; he often said foolish things. Ragnfrid and Lavrans had never liked him, but the Sundbu people, as was reasonable, set great store by their priest, and both they and he were greatly disappointed that he had not been called on to tend to Ulvhild.

On the day that Sira Sigurd came to Jørundgaard—unfortunately for him—Fru Aashild and Herr Bjørn were already there, as were Sira Eirik, Arne's parents Gyrd and Inga of Finsbrekken, Old Jon from Loptsgaard, and a friar from Hamar, Brother Aasgaut.

While Ragnfrid had the tables set once more with food for the guests and Lavrans pored over the boxes of sealed letters that the priest had brought, Sira Sigurd asked to see Ulvhild. She had already been put to bed for the night and was sleeping, but Sira Sigurd woke her up, examined her back and limbs, and asked her questions—at first kindly enough, but with increasing impatience as Ulvhild grew frightened. Sigurd was a small man, practically a dwarf, but he had a big, flame-red face. When he tried to lift her onto the floor to test her legs, Ulvhild began to scream. Then Fru Aashild stood up, went over to the bed, and covered her with the blanket, saying that the child was sleepy—she wouldn't have been able to stand up even if her legs were healthy.

The priest began to protest vehemently; he was also considered a capable doctor. But Fru Aashild took his hand, led him over to the high seat[2] at the table, and started talking about what she had done for Ulvhild as she asked his opinion on everything. Then he grew more amenable, and he ate and drank of Ragnfrid's good repast.

But when the ale and wine began to go to his head, Sira Sigurd was once again in a foul mood, quarrelsome and bad tempered. He was quite aware that no one in the room liked him. First he turned to Gyrd, who was the envoy of the Bishop of Hamar at Vaage and Sil. There had been numerous disputes between the bishopric and Trond Ivarsøn. Gyrd didn't say much, but Inga was a hot-tempered woman, and then Brother Aasgaut joined in the discussion.

He said, "You shouldn't forget, Sira Sigurd, that our worthy Father Ingjald is your prelate too; we know all about you in Hamar. You revel in all that is good at Sundbu, and give little thought to the fact that you are dedicated to other work than acting as Trond's eye-servant, helping him do everything that is unjust so that he endangers his own soul and diminishes the power of the Church. Haven't you ever heard about what happens to those disobedient and unfaithful priests who contravene their own spiritual fathers and superiors? Don't you know about the time when the angels led Saint Thomas of Canterbury to the gates of Hell and let him peek inside? He was greatly surprised not to see any of those who had opposed him as you oppose your bishop. He was just about to praise God's mercy, for the holy man wished all sinners to be saved, when the angel asked the Devil to lift his tail. With a tremendous roar and a horrid stench of sulfur, out spewed all the priests and learned men who had betrayed the interests of the Church. And then he saw where all of them had ended up."

"You're lying, monk," said the priest. "I've heard that story too, but it was friars, not priests, who were spewed out of the Devil's behind like wasps from a wasp's nest."

Old Jon laughed louder than all the servants and cried, "No doubt it was both, I'll bet it was. . . ."

"Then the Devil must have a very wide tail," said Bjørn Gunnarsøn.

And Fru Aashild smiled and said, "Yes, haven't you heard it said that everything bad has a long rump dragging behind?"

"You be quiet, Fru Aashild," shouted Sira Sigurd. "You shouldn't talk about the long rump that bad people drag behind them. Here you sit as if you were the mistress of the house instead of Ragnfrid. But it's odd that you haven't been able to cure her child—don't you have any more of that powerful water you used to use? The water that could make a dismembered sheep whole again in the soup pot and turn a woman into a maiden in the bridal bed? I know all about that wedding here in the village when you prepared the bath for the despoiled bride. . . ."

Sira Eirik jumped up, grabbed the other priest by the shoulder and flank, and threw him right across the table so that pitchers and cups toppled and food and drink spilled onto the tablecloths and floor. Sira Sigurd landed flat on his back, his clothing torn.

Eirik leaped over the table and was about to strike him again, bellowing over the din, "Shut your filthy trap, you damned priest!"

Lavrans tried to separate them, but Ragnfrid stood at the table, as white as a corpse, wringing her hands. Then Fru Aashild ran over and helped Sira Sigurd to his feet and wiped the blood from his face.

She handed him a goblet of mead as she said, "You shouldn't be so stern, Sira Eirik, that you can't stand to hear a joke late in the evening after so many drinks. Now sit down, and I'll tell you about that wedding. It wasn't here in this valley at all, and it's my misfortune that I was not the one who knew about that water. If I had been able to brew it, we wouldn't be sitting up there on that little farm. Then I'd be a rich woman with property out in the big villages somewhere—near the town and cloisters and bishops and canons," she said, smiling at the three clergymen.

"But someone must have known the art in the old days, because this was in the time of King Inge, as far as I know, and the bridegroom was Peter Lodinsøn of Bratteland. But I won't say which of his three wives was the bride, since there are living descendants from all three. Well, this bride probably had good reason to wish for that water, and she managed to get it too. She prepared a bath for herself out in the shed, but before she managed to bathe, in came the woman who was to be her mother-in-law. She was muddy and dirty from the ride to the wedding manor, so she took off her clothes and stepped into the tub. She was an old woman, and she had had nine children by Lodin. But on that night both Lodin and Peter had a different kind of pleasure than they had counted on."

Everyone in the room laughed heartily, and both Gyrd and Jon called to Fru Aashild to tell more such ribald tales.

But she refused. "Here sit two priests and Brother Aasgaut and young boys and maidservants. We should stop now before the talk grows indecent and vulgar; remember that these are the holy days."

The men protested, but the women agreed with Fru Aashild. No one noticed that Ragnfrid had left the room. A little later Kristin, who had been sitting at the far end of the women's bench among the maidservants, stood up to go to bed. She was sleeping in Tordis's house because there were so many guests at the farm.

It was biting cold, and the northern lights were flaring and flickering above the domed mountains to the north. The snow creaked under Kristin's feet as she ran across the courtyard, shivering, with her arms crossed over her breast.

Then she noticed that in the shadows beneath the old loft someone was pacing vigorously back and forth in the snow, throwing out her arms, wringing her hands, and moaning loudly. Kristin recognized her mother. Frightened, she ran over to her and asked her if she was ill.

"No, no," said Ragnfrid fiercely. "I just had to get out. Go to bed now, child."

Kristin turned around when her mother softly called her name.

"Go into the house and lie down in bed with your father and Ulvhild—hold her in your arms so that he doesn't crush her by mistake. He sleeps so heavily when he's drunk. I'll go up and sleep here in the old loft tonight."

"Jesus, Mother," said Kristin. "You'll freeze to death if you sleep there—and all alone. What will Father say if you don't come to bed tonight?"

"He won't notice," replied her mother. "He was almost asleep when I left, and tomorrow he'll get up late. Go and do as I say."

"You'll be so cold," whimpered Kristin, but her mother pushed her away, somewhat more gently, and then shut herself inside the loft.

It was just as cold inside as out, and pitch dark. Ragnfrid fumbled her way over to the bed, tore the shawl from her head, took off her shoes, and crawled under the furs. They chilled her to the bone; it was like sinking into a snow drift. She pulled the covers over her head, tucked up her legs, and put her hands into the bodice of her clothing. And she lay there in that way, weeping—alternately crying quite softly, with streaming tears, and then screaming and gnashing her teeth in between her sobs. Finally she had warmed up the bed enough that she began to feel drowsy, and then she cried herself to sleep.

## CHAPTER 5

IN THE SPRINGTIME of Kristin's fifteenth year, Lavrans Bjørgulfsøn and Sir Andres Gudmundsøn of Dyfrin agreed to meet at Holledis *ting*.[1] There they decided that Andres's second son, Simon, should be betrothed to Kristin Lavransdatter and that he would be given Formo, the property which Andres had inherited from his mother. The men sealed the agreement with a handshake, but no document was drawn up about it because Andres first had to arrange for the inheritance of his other children. And no betrothal ale was drunk either, but Sir Andres and Simon accompanied Lavrans back to Jørundgaard to see the bride, and Lavrans gave a great banquet.

Lavrans had finished building the new house—two stories tall, with brick fireplaces in both the main room and the loft. It was richly and beautifully decorated with wood carvings and fine furniture. He had also renovated the old loft and expanded the other buildings, so that he could now live in a manner befitting a squire. By this time, he possessed great wealth, for he had been fortunate in his undertakings, and he was a wise and thoughtful master. He was especially known for breeding the finest horses and the best cattle of all types. And now that he had arranged things so that his daughter would acquire Formo through marriage with a man of the Dyfrin lineage, people said that he had successfully achieved his goal of becoming the foremost landowner in the village. Lavrans and Ragnfrid were also very pleased, as were Sir Andres and Simon.

Kristin was a little disappointed when she first saw Simon Andressøn, for she had heard such high praise of his handsome appearance and noble manner that there was no limit to what she had expected of her bridegroom.

Simon was indeed handsome, but he was rather heavyset for a man of only twenty; he had a short neck, and his face was as round and shiny as the moon. His hair was quite beautiful, brown and curly, and his eyes were gray and clear, but they seemed slightly pinched because his eyelids were puffy. His nose was too small and his mouth was also small and pouting, but not ugly. And in spite of his stoutness he was light-footed and quick and agile in all his movements, and he was an able sportsman. He was rather impetuous and rash in his speech, but Lavrans felt that he nevertheless showed both good sense and wisdom when he spoke to older men.

Ragnfrid soon came to like him, and Ulvhild developed at once the greatest affection for him; he was also particularly kind and loving toward the little maiden who was ill. And after Kristin had grown accustomed to his round face and his way of speaking, she was entirely satisfied with her betrothed and pleased that her father had arranged the marriage for her.

Fru Aashild was invited to the banquet. Ever since the people of Jørundgaard had taken up with her, the gentry of the nearest villages had once again begun to remember her high birth, and they paid less attention to her strange reputation; so now Fru Aashild was often in the company of others.

After she had seen Simon, she said, "He's a good match, Kristin. This Simon will do well in the world—you'll be spared many types of sorrow, and he'll be a kind man to live with. But he seems to me rather too fat and cheerful. If things were the same in Norway today as they were in the past and as they are in other countries, where people are no sterner toward sinners than God is Himself, then I would suggest you find yourself a friend who is thin and melancholy—someone you could sit and talk to. Then I would say that you could fare no better than with Simon."

Kristin blushed even though she didn't fully understand what Fru Aashild meant. But as time passed and her dowry chests were filled and she listened to the constant talk of her marriage and what she would take to her new home, she began to yearn for the matter to be bound with a formal betrothal and for Simon to come north. After a while she began to think about him a great deal, and she looked forward to seeing him again.

Kristin was now grown-up, and she was exceedingly beautiful. She most resembled her father. She was tall and small-waisted, with slender, elegant limbs, but she was also buxom and shapely. Her face was rather short and round; her forehead low and broad and as white as milk; her eyes large, gray, and gentle under finely etched brows. Her mouth was a little too big, but her full lips were a fresh red, and her chin was round like an apple and nicely shaped. She had lovely thick, long hair, but it was rather dark now, more brown than gold, and quite straight. Lavrans liked nothing better than to hear Sira Eirik boast about Kristin. The priest had watched the maiden grow up, had taught her reading and writing, and was very fond of her. But Lavrans was not particularly pleased to hear the priest occasionally compare his daughter to a flawless and glossy-coated young mare.

Yet everyone said that if the accident had not befallen Ulvhild, she would have been many times more beautiful than her sister. She had the prettiest and sweetest face, white and pink like roses and lilies, with white-gold, silky-soft hair that flowed and curled around her slender neck and thin shoulders. Her eyes resembled those of the Gjesling family: they were deep-set beneath straight black brows, and they were as clear as water and grayish blue, but her gaze was gentle, not sharp. The child's voice was also so clear and lovely that it was a joy to listen to her whether she spoke or sang. She had an agile talent for book learning and for playing all types of stringed instruments and board games, but she took little interest in needlework because her back would quickly tire.

It seemed unlikely that this pretty child would ever regain the full health of her body, although she improved somewhat after her parents took her to Nidaros to the shrine of Saint Olav. Lavrans and Ragnfrid went there on foot, without a single servant or maid to accompany them, and they carried the child on a litter between them for the entire journey. After that, Ulvhild was so much better that she could walk with a crutch. But it was not likely that she would ever be well enough to marry, and so, when the time came, she would probably be sent to a convent with all the possessions that she would inherit.

They never talked about it, and Ulvhild was not aware that she was any different from other children. She was very fond of finery and beautiful clothes, and her parents didn't have the heart to refuse her anything; Ragnfrid stitched and sewed for her and adorned her like a royal child. Once some peddlers came through the village and stayed the night at Laugarbru, where Ulvhild was allowed to examine their wares. They had some amber-yellow silk, and she was set on having a shift made from it. Lavrans normally never traded with the kind of people who traveled through the villages, illegally selling goods from the town, but this time he bought the entire bolt at once. He also gave Kristin cloth for her bridal shift, which she worked on during the summer. Before that she had never owned shifts made of anything but wool, except for a linen shift for her finest gown. But Ulvhild was given a shift made of silk to wear to banquets and a Sunday shift of linen with a bodice of silk.

Lavrans Bjørgulfsøn now owned Laugarbru as well, which was tended by Tordis and Jon. Lavrans and Ragnfrid's youngest daughter Ramborg lived with them there; Tordis had been her wetnurse. Ragnfrid would hardly even look at the child during the first days after her birth because she said that she brought her children bad luck. And yet she loved the little maiden dearly and was constantly sending gifts to her and to Tordis. Later on she would often go over to Laugarbru to visit Ramborg, but she preferred to arrive after the child was asleep, and then she would sit with her. Lavrans and the two older daughters often went to Laugarbru to play with the little one; she was a strong and healthy child, though not as pretty as her sisters.

That summer was the last one that Arne Gyrdsøn spent at Jørundgaard. The bishop had promised Gyrd to help the boy make his way in the world, and in the fall Arne was to leave for Hamar.

Kristin had undoubtedly noticed that Arne was fond of her, but in many ways her feelings were quite childish, so she didn't give it much thought and behaved toward him as she always had, ever since they were children. She sought out his company as often as she could and always took his hand when they danced at home or on the church hill. The fact that her mother didn't approve of this, she found rather amusing. But she never spoke to Arne about Simon or about her betrothal, for she noticed that he grew dispirited whenever it was mentioned.

Arne was good with his hands and he wanted to make Kristin a sewing chest to remember him by. He had carved an elegant and beautiful box and frame, and now he was working in the smithy to make iron bands and a lock for it. On a fine evening with fair weather late in the summer, Kristin went over to talk to him. She took along one of her father's shirts to mend, sat down on the stone doorstep, and began to sew as she chatted with the young man inside the smithy. Ulvhild was with her too, hopping around on her crutch and eating raspberries that were growing among the stones piled up on the ground.

After a while Arne came over to the smithy door to cool off. He wanted to sit down next to Kristin, but she moved away a bit and asked him to take care not to get soot on the sewing that she was holding on her lap.

"So that's how things have become between us?" said Arne. "You don't dare let me sit with you because you're afraid that the farm boy will get you dirty?"

Kristin looked at him in surprise and then said, "You know quite well what I meant. But take off your apron, wash the coal from your hands, and sit down here with me and rest a while." And she made room for him.

But Arne lay down in the grass in front of her.

Then Kristin continued, "Now don't be angry, dear Arne. Do you think I would be so ungrateful for the lovely present that you're making for me, or that I would ever forget that you've always been my best friend here at home?"

"Have I been?" he asked.

"You know you have," said Kristin. "And I'll never forget you. But you, who are about to go out into the world—maybe you'll acquire wealth and honor before you know it. You'll probably forget me long before I forget you."

"You'll never forget me," said Arne and smiled. "But I'll forget you before you forget me—you're such a child, Kristin."

"You're not very old yourself," she replied.

"I'm just as old as Simon Darre," he said. "And we can bear helmets and shields just as well as the Dyfrin people, but my parents have not had fortune on their side."

He had wiped off his hands on some tufts of grass. Now he took hold of Kristin's ankle and pressed his cheek against her foot, which was sticking out from the hem of her dress. She tried to pull her foot away, but Arne said, "Your mother is at Laugarbru, and Lavrans rode off from the farm—and from the buildings no one can see us sitting here. Just this once you must let me talk about what's on my mind."

Kristin replied, "We've always known, both you and I, that it would be futile for us to fall in love with each other."

"Can I put my head in your lap?" asked Arne, and when she didn't reply, he did it anyway, wrapping his arm around her waist. With the other hand he tugged on her braids.

"How will you like it," he asked after a moment, "when Simon lies in your lap like this and plays with your hair?"

Kristin didn't answer. She felt as if a weight suddenly fell upon her—Arne's words and Arne's head on her knees—it seemed to her as if a door were opening into a room with many dark corridors leading into more darkness. Unhappy and heartsick, she hesitated, refusing to look inside.

"Married people don't do things like this," she said abruptly and briskly, as if with relief. She tried to imagine Simon's plump, round face looking up at her with the same gaze in his eyes as Arne now had; she heard his voice—and she couldn't help laughing.

"I don't think Simon would ever lie down on the ground to play with my shoes!"

"No, because he can play with you in his own bed," said Arne. His voice made Kristin feel suddenly sick and helpless.

She tried to push his head off her lap, but he pressed it harder against her knees and said gently, "But I would play with your shoes and your hair and your fingers and follow you in and out all day long, Kristin, if you would be my wife and sleep in my arms every night."

He pulled himself halfway up, put his hands on her shoulders, and looked into her eyes.

"It's not proper for you to talk to me this way," said Kristin quietly and shyly.

"No, it's not," said Arne. He got to his feet and stood in front of her. "But tell me one thing—wouldn't you rather it had been me?"

"Oh, I would rather . . ." She sat in silence for a moment. "I would rather not have any man at all—not even . . ."

Arne didn't move. He said, "Would you rather go into a convent then, as they've planned for Ulvhild, and be a maiden all your days?"

Kristin wrung her hands in her lap. She felt a strange, sweet trembling inside her—and with a sudden shudder she realized how sad it was for her little sister. And her eyes filled with tears of sorrow for Ulvhild's sake.

"Kristin," said Arne gently.

At that moment Ulvhild screamed loudly. Her crutch had lodged between some stones and she had fallen. Arne and Kristin ran over to her, and Arne lifted her into her sister's arms. She had cut her mouth and was bleeding badly.

Kristin sat down with her in the doorway to the smithy, and Arne brought water in a wooden bowl. Together they began to wash Ulvhild's face. She had also scraped the skin on her knees. Kristin bent tenderly over the small, thin legs.

Ulvhild's wailing soon stopped and she whimpered softly, the way children do who are used to suffering pain. Kristin pressed Ulvhild's head against her breast and rocked her gently.

Then the bell up in Olav's church began ringing for vespers.

Arne spoke to Kristin, but she sat there as if she neither heard nor sensed what he said as she bent over her sister. Then he grew frightened and asked her whether she thought the injuries were serious. Kristin shook her head but refused to look at him.

A little later she stood up and started walking toward the farm, carrying Ulvhild in her arms. Arne followed, silent and confused. Kristin looked so preoccupied that her face was completely rigid. As she walked, the bell continued to toll across the meadows and valley; it was still ringing as she went into the house.

She placed Ulvhild on the bed which the sisters had shared ever since Kristin had grown too old to sleep with her parents. Then she took off her own shoes and lay down next to the little one. She lay there and listened for the bell long after it had stopped ringing and the child was asleep.

It had occurred to her, as the bell began to peal, while she sat with Ulvhild's little bloodied face in her hands, that perhaps this was an omen for her. If she would take her sister's place—if she would promise herself to the service of God and the Virgin Mary—then maybe God would grant the child renewed vigor and good health.

Kristin remembered Brother Edvin saying that these days parents offered to God only the crippled and lame children or those for whom they could not arrange good marriages. She knew her parents were pious people, and yet she had never heard them say anything except that she would marry. But when they realized that Ulvhild would be ill all her days, they at once proposed that she should enter a convent.

But Kristin didn't want to do it; she resisted the idea that God would perform a miracle for Ulvhild if she became a nun. She clung to Sira Eirik's words that so few miracles occurred nowadays. And yet she had the feeling this evening that it was as Brother Edvin had said—that if someone had enough faith, then he could indeed work miracles. But she did not want that kind of faith; she did not love God and His Mother and the saints in that way. She would never love them in that way. She loved the world and longed for the world.

Kristin pressed her lips to Ulvhild's soft, silky hair. The child slept soundly, but the elder sister sat up, restless, and then lay down again. Her heart was bleeding with sorrow and shame, but she knew that she could not believe in miracles because she was unwilling to give up her inheritance of health and beauty and love.

Then she tried to console herself with the thought that her parents would never give her permission to do such a thing. Nor would they ever believe that it would do any good. She was already betrothed, after all, and they would undoubtedly be loath to lose Simon, whom they liked so much. She felt betrayed because they seemed to find this son-in-law so splendid. She suddenly thought with displeasure of Simon's round, red face and his small, laughing eyes, of his leaping gait—it occurred to her all of a sudden that he bounced like a ball—and of his teasing manner of speaking, which made her feel awkward and stupid. And it was not such a splendid thing, either, to be given to him and then move only as far as Formo. And yet she would rather have him than be sent to a convent. But what about the world beyond the mountains? The king's castle, and the counts and the knights that Fru Aashild had talked about, a handsome man with melancholy eyes who would follow her in and out and never grow tired. . . . She remembered Arne on that summer day long ago when he lay on his side and slept with his shiny brown hair spread out on the heath—she had loved him as if he were her own brother back then. It wasn't proper for him to speak to her the way he had today, when he knew they could never have each other.

* * *

Word was sent from Laugarbru that her mother would stay there overnight. Kristin got up to undress and get ready for bed. She began to unlace her dress, but then she put her shoes back on, wrapped her cloak around her, and went out.

The night sky, bright and green, stretched above the mountain crests. It was almost time for the moon to rise, and at the spot where it waited below the ridge, small clouds drifted past, gleaming like silver underneath; the sky grew lighter and lighter, like metal gathering dew.

Kristin ran between the fences, across the road, and up the hill toward the church. It was asleep, black and locked, but she went over to the cross that stood nearby—a memorial to the time when Saint Olav once rested there as he was fleeing from his enemies.

Kristin knelt down on the stone and placed her folded hands on the base. "Holy Cross, the strongest of masts, the fairest of trees, the bridge for those who are ill to the fair shores of health . . ."

As she spoke the words of the prayer, she felt her yearning gradually spread like rings on water. The various thoughts that were making her uneasy were smoothed out, her mind grew calmer, more tender, and a gentle sorrow, empty of all thought, replaced her troubles.

She stayed there on her knees, aware of all the sounds of the night. The wind was sighing so oddly, the river was roaring beyond the groves on the other side of the church, and the stream was flowing nearby, right across the road—and everywhere, both close at hand and far away in the dark, her eyes and her ears caught hints of tiny rivulets of running and dripping water. The river flashed white down in the village. The moon glided up over a small gap in the mountains; stones and leaves wet with dew shimmered faintly, and the newly tarred timbers of the bell tower near the cemetery gate shone dull and dark. Then the moon vanished again where the ridge of the mountain rose higher. Many more gleaming white clouds appeared in the sky.

She heard a horse approaching at a slow pace higher up the road, and the sound of men's voices, speaking evenly and softly. Kristin was not afraid of people so close to home where she knew everyone; she felt quite safe.

Her father's dogs came rushing toward her, turned around and bounded back to the grove, then turned again and raced back to her; then her father called a greeting as he emerged from among the birches. He was leading Guldsvein by the bridle; a bunch of birds dangled in front of the saddle, and Lavrans was carrying a hooded hawk on his left hand. He was in the company of a tall, hunchbacked man in monk's clothing, and before Kristin had even seen his face, she knew it was Brother Edvin. She went to greet them, and she couldn't have been more surprised than if she had dreamed it. She merely smiled when Lavrans asked her whether she recognized their guest.

Lavrans had met the monk up by Rost Bridge. Then he had persuaded him to come home with him and stay the night at the farm. But Brother Edvin insisted on being allowed to sleep in the cowshed: "For I've picked up so many lice that you can't have me lying in your good beds."

And no matter how much Lavrans begged and implored, the monk was adamant; at first he even wanted them to bring his food out into the courtyard. But finally they coaxed him inside the house, and Kristin put wood in the fireplace in the corner and set candles on the table, while a maid brought in food and drink.

The monk sat down on the beggar's bench near the door, but he would only take cold porridge and water for his evening meal. And he refused to accept Lavrans's offer to prepare a bath for him and to have his clothes washed.

Brother Edvin scratched and rubbed himself and his gaunt old face beamed with glee.

"No, no," he said. "The lice bite better at my proud hide than any scourges or the guardian's words. I spent this summer under an overhang up on the mountain. They had given me permission to go into the wilderness to fast and pray, and there I sat, thinking that I was as pure as a holy hermit, and the poor people over in Setna valley brought food up to me and thought they beheld a pious monk, living a pure life. 'Brother Edvin,' they said, 'if there were more monks like you, then we would soon mend our ways, but when we see priests and bishops and monks shoving and fighting like piglets at the trough . . .' Well, I told them that was not a Christian way to talk—but I liked hearing it all the same, and I sang and prayed so my voice resounded in the mountains. Now it will be to my benefit to feel how the lice are biting and fighting on my skin and to hear the good housewives, who want to keep their houses clean and neat, shouting that the filthy monkhide can just as well sleep in the barn during the summer. I'm heading north to Nidaros now, to celebrate Saint Olav's Day, and it will do me good to see that people aren't so keen to come near me."

Ulvhild woke up. Then Lavrans went over and lifted her up in his cape.

"Here is the child I told you about, dear Father. Place your hands on her and pray to God for her, the way you prayed for the boy up north in Meldal—we heard he regained his health."

The monk gently put his hand under Ulvhild's chin and looked into her eyes. Then he lifted one of her hands and kissed it.

"You should pray instead, you and your wife, Lavrans Bjørgulfsøn, that you will not be tempted to bend God's will with this child. Our Lord Jesus himself has set these small feet on a path so that she can walk safely toward the house of peace—I can see in your eyes, blessed Ulvhild, that you have your intercessors in that other house."

"I heard that the boy in Meldal got well," said Lavrans quietly.

"He was the only child of a poor widow, and there was no one to feed or clothe him when the mother passed away, except the village. And yet the woman only asked that God give her a fearless heart so that she might have faith that He would let happen whatever was best for the boy. I did nothing more than pray alongside her."

"It's not easy for Ragnfrid and me to be content with that," said Lavrans gloomily. "Especially since she's so pretty and so good."

"Have you seen the child they have over in Lidstad, in the south of the valley?" asked the monk. "Would you rather your daughter were like that?"

Lavrans shuddered and pressed the child close.

"Don't you think," Brother Edvin went on, "that in God's eyes we are all like children for whom He has reason to grieve, crippled as we are by sin? And yet we don't think that things are the worst in the world for us."

He walked over to the painting of the Virgin Mary on the wall, and everyone knelt down as he said the evening prayer. They felt that Brother Edvin had offered them great comfort.

But after he had left the house to find his sleeping place, Astrid, who was in charge of all the maids, vigorously swept the floor everywhere the monk had stood and hastily threw the sweepings into the fire.

The next morning Kristin got up early, put some milk porridge and wheat cakes into a lovely red-flecked bowl made from birch roots—for she knew that the monk never touched meat—and took the food out to him. No one else in the house was awake yet.

Brother Edvin was standing on the ramp to the cowshed, ready to leave, with his staff and bag in hand. With a smile he thanked Kristin for her trouble and sat down in the grass and ate, while Kristin sat at his feet.

Her little white dog came running over to them, making the tiny bells on his collar ring. Kristin pulled the dog onto her lap, and Brother Edvin snapped his fingers, tossing little bits of wheat cake into the dog's mouth, as he praised the animal.

"It's the same breed that Queen Eufemia brought over to Norway," he said. "Everything is so splendid here at Jørundgaard now."

Kristin blushed with pleasure. She knew the dog was particularly fine, and she was proud to own him. No one else in the village had a pet dog. But she hadn't known that he was of the same type as the queen's pet dogs.

"Simon Andressøn sent him to me," she said, hugging the dog as he licked her face. "His name is Kortelin."

She had planned to speak to the monk about her uneasiness and ask for his advice. But now she had no wish to spend any more time on her thoughts of the night before. Brother Edvin believed that God would do what was best for Ulvhild. And it was generous of Simon to send her such a gift even before their betrothal had been formally acknowledged. She refused to think about Arne—he had behaved badly toward her, she thought.

Brother Edvin picked up his staff and bag and asked Kristin to give his greetings to the others; he wouldn't wait for everyone to wake up, but would set off while the day was cool. She walked with him up past the church and a short way into the grove.

When they parted, he offered her God's peace and blessed her.

"Give me a few words, as you did for Ulvhild, dear Father," begged Kristin as she stood with her hand in his.

The monk poked his bare foot, knotty with rheumatism, in the wet grass.

"Then I would impress upon your heart, my daughter, that you should pay close attention to the way God tends to the welfare of the people here in the valley. Little rain falls, but He has given you water from the mountains, and the dew refreshes the meadows and fields each night. Thank God for the good gifts He has given you, and don't complain if you think you are lacking something else that you think would be beneficial. You have beautiful golden hair, so do not fret because it isn't curly. Haven't you heard about the woman who sat and wept because she had only a little scrap of pork to give to her seven hungry children for Christmas dinner? Saint Olav came riding past at that very moment. Then he stretched out his hand over the meat and prayed to God to feed the poor urchins. But when the woman saw that a slaughtered pig lay on the table, she began to cry because she didn't have enough bowls and pots."

Kristin ran off toward home, and Kortelin danced around at her feet as he nipped at her clothing and barked, making all his tiny silver bells ring.

## CHAPTER 6

ARNE WAS HOME at Finsbrekken for the last time before he left for Hamar. His mother and sisters were outfitting him with clothes.

The day before he was supposed to ride south he went to Jørundgaard to say farewell. There he asked Kristin in a whisper whether she would meet him on the road south of Laugarbru on the following evening.

"I would like us to be alone, just the two of us, the last time we meet," he said. "Do you think that's too much to ask? We who have grown up together as brother and sister?" he added when Kristin hesitated a moment before replying.

Then she promised to come if she could slip away from home.

The next morning it snowed, but later in the day it began to rain and soon the roads and fields were nothing but gray mud. Wisps of fog hovered and drifted along the mountain ridges, occasionally dropping down and twining into white mist at the foot of the mountains, but then the weather closed in again.

Sira Eirik came over to help Lavrans put together several boxes of letters. They went into the hearth house because it was more comfortable there in that kind of weather than in the larger house where the fireplace filled the room with smoke. Ragnfrid was at Laugarbru, where Ramborg was recuperating from an illness and fever she had suffered earlier that fall.

So it was not difficult for Kristin to slip away from the farm unnoticed; she didn't dare take a horse, so she went on foot. The road was a morass of slushy snow and withered leaves; the air smelled mournfully raw and dead and moldy, and now and then a gust of wind would blow the rain right into her face. Kristin pulled her hood up over her head and held her cloak closed with both hands as she walked briskly onward. She was a little apprehensive—the clamor of the river sounded so muffled in the oppressive air, and the clouds were black and ragged, drifting above the mountain crests. Occasionally she would stop and listen behind her, thinking that she might hear Arne.

After a while she became aware of a horse's hooves on the sodden road, and then she stopped, for she had reached a rather desolate spot and thought it would be a suitable place for them to say goodbye to each other undisturbed. A moment later she saw the rider appear behind her, and Arne jumped down from his horse, leading it forward as he walked toward her.

"It was good of you to come," he said, "in this awful weather."

"It's worse for you, who will have to ride such a long way. But why are you leaving so late in the evening?"

"Jon has invited me to stay at Loptsgaard tonight," said Arne. "And I thought it would be easier for you to come here at this time of day."

They stood in silence for a moment. Kristin thought she had never before realized how handsome Arne was. He wore a shiny steel helmet, and under it a brown woolen hood that framed his face and spread out over his shoulders; underneath, his thin face looked so bright and fair. His leather breastplate was old, flecked with rust, and scratched from the coat of mail that had been worn over it—Arne's father had given it to him—but it fit snugly on his slender, lithe, and strong body. He wore a sword at his side and carried a spear in his hand; his other weapons hung from his saddle. He was a full-grown man and looked imposing.

Kristin put her hand on his shoulder and said, "Do you remember, Arne, that you once asked me whether I thought you were as splendid a fellow as Simon Andressøn? I want to tell you something now, before we part. You seem to me as much his superior in fair appearance and bearing as he is held above you in birth and wealth by people who value such things most."

"Why are you telling me this?" asked Arne breathlessly.

"Because Brother Edvin impressed on my heart that we should thank God for His good gifts and not be like the woman who wept because she had no bowls when Saint Olav multiplied the meat for her. So you shouldn't fret over the fact that He hasn't given you as much wealth as He has physical gifts. . . ."

"Is that what you meant?" said Arne. And when Kristin didn't reply he went on, "I was wondering whether you meant that you would rather have been married to me than to that other man."

"I probably would, at that," she said quietly. "For I know you much better."

Arne threw his arms around her so tight that he lifted her feet off the ground. He kissed her face many times, but then he set her down.

"God help us, Kristin. You're such a child!"

She stood there with her head bowed, but she kept her hands on his shoulders. He gripped her wrists and held them tight.

"I see now that you don't realize, my sweet, how my heart aches because I am going to lose you. Kristin, we've grown up together like two apples on a branch. I loved you before I began to realize that one day someone else would come and tear you away from me. As certain as God had to die for us all, I don't know how I can ever be happy again in this world after today."

Kristin wept bitterly and lifted her face so that he could kiss her.

"Don't talk like that, my Arne," she begged, patting his arm.

"Kristin," said Arne in a muted voice, taking her in his arms again. "Couldn't you consider asking your father . . . Lavrans is such a good man, he would never force you against your will. Couldn't you ask him to wait a few years? No one knows how my fortune may change—we're both so young."

"I must do what those at home want me to do," she sobbed.

Then tears overcame Arne too.

"You have no idea, Kristin, how much I love you." He hid his face on her shoulder. "If you did, and if you loved me too, then you would go to Lavrans and beg him sweetly—"

"I can't do that," sobbed the maiden. "I don't think I could ever love a man so dearly that I would go against my parents' will for his sake." She slipped her hands under Arne's hood and heavy steel helmet to find his face. "You mustn't cry like that, Arne, my dearest friend."

"I want you to have this," he said after a moment, giving her a small brooch. "And think of me now and then, for I will never forget you, or my sorrow."

It was almost completely dark by the time Kristin and Arne had said their last farewells. She stood and gazed after him when he finally rode away. A yellow light shone through the clouds, and the light was reflected in their footsteps, where they had walked and stood in the slush of the road; it looked so cold and bleak, she thought. She pulled out the linen cloth covering her bodice and wiped her tear-streaked face; then she turned around and set off for home.

She was wet and cold and she walked fast. After a while she heard someone approaching on the road behind her. She was a little frightened; it was possible that strangers might be traveling on this main road, even on an evening like this, and she had a lonely stretch ahead of her. Steep black scree rose up on one side, but on the other there was a sharp drop-off, covered with pine woods all the way down to the pale, leaden river at the bottom of the valley. So she was relieved when the person behind her called her name; she stopped and waited.

The person who approached was a tall, thin man wearing a dark surcoat with lighter colored sleeves. When he came closer, Kristin saw that he was dressed as a priest and carried an empty knapsack on his back. She now recognized Bentein Prestesøn, as they called him—Sira Eirik's grandson. She noticed at once that he was quite drunk.

"Well, one departs and the other arrives," he said and laughed after they had greeted each other. "I met Arne from Brekken just now—and I see that you're walking along and crying. So how about giving me a little smile because I've come back home? The two of us have also been friends since childhood, haven't we?"

"It's a poor bargain to have you come back to the valley in his stead," said Kristin crossly. She had never liked Bentein. "Quite a few people will say the same, I'm afraid. And your grandfather was so happy that you were getting on so well down south in Oslo."

"Oh, yes," said Bentein with a snicker and a sneer. "So you think I was getting on well, do you? Like a pig in a wheat field, that's how it was for me, Kristin—and the end result was the same. I was chased off with a shout and a long stick. Well, well. He doesn't have much joy from his offspring, my grandfather. Why are you walking so fast?"

"I'm freezing," said Kristin curtly.

"No more than I am," said the priest. "The only clothing I have to wear is what you see. I had to sell my cape for food and ale in Lillehammer. But you must still have warmth in your body from saying farewell to Arne. I think you should let me come under your furs with you." And he seized hold of her cloak, threw it around his shoulders, and wrapped his wet arm around her waist.

Kristin was so startled by his boldness that it took a moment for her to regain her senses—then she tried to tear herself away, but he was holding on to her cloak and it was fastened with a sturdy silver clasp. Bentein put his arms around her again and tried to kiss her, shoving his mouth close to her chin. She tried to strike him, but he was gripping her upper arms.

"I think you've lost your mind," she seethed as she struggled against him. "How dare you manhandle me as if I were a . . . You're going to regret this bitterly tomorrow, you miserable wretch."

"Oh, tomorrow you won't be so stupid," said Bentein, tripping her with his leg so that she fell to her knees in the mud of the road. Then he pressed his hand over her mouth.

And yet Kristin still did not think to scream. Now she finally realized what he intended to do to her, but rage overcame her with such fury and violence that she hardly felt any fear. She snarled like an animal in battle and fought against this man who was holding her down so that the ice-cold snow water soaked through her clothing and reached her burning hot flesh.

"Tomorrow you'll know enough to keep quiet," said Bentein. "And if it can't be concealed, you can always blame Arne; people will sooner believe that. . . ."

He had put a finger in her mouth, so she bit him with all her might, and Bentein screamed and loosened his grip. As quick as lightning Kristin pulled one hand free and shoved it into his face, pressing her thumb as hard as she could into his eye. He bellowed and got up on one knee. She wriggled free like a cat, pushed the priest so that he fell onto his back, and then ran off down the road as the mud spurted up behind her with every step.

She ran and ran without looking back. She heard Bentein coming after her, and she raced off with her heart pounding in her throat, as she moaned softly and peered ahead—would she never reach Laugarbru? At last Kristin came to the part of the road where it passed through the fields. She saw buildings clustered on the hillside, and suddenly realized that she didn't dare go to her mother—not the way she looked, covered with mud and withered leaves from head to toe, her clothing torn.

She could feel Bentein coming closer. She bent down and picked up two big rocks, and when he was near enough she threw them; one of them struck him so hard that it knocked him down. Then she started running again and didn't stop until she stood on the bridge.

Trembling, she stood there holding on to the railing; everything went black and she was afraid that she would sink into unconsciousness—but then she thought about Bentein. What if he came and found her like that? Shaking with shame and bitterness, she kept on going, but her legs could hardly bear her, and now she felt how her face stung from the scratches of his fingernails, and she had hurt both her back and her arms. Tears came, hot as fire.

She wished Bentein would be dead from the rock she had thrown; she wished she had gone back and put an end to him, that she had taken out her knife, but she noticed that she must have lost it.

Then she realized again that she dared not be seen like this at home; it occurred to her that she could go to Romundgaard. She would complain to Sira Eirik.

But the priest had not yet returned from Jørundgaard. In the cookhouse she found Gunhild, Bentein's mother. The woman was alone, and then Kristin told her how her son had behaved toward her. But she didn't mention that she had gone out to meet Arne. When she realized that Gunhild thought she had been at Laugarbru, she didn't dissuade her.

Gunhild said very little but cried a great deal as she washed Kristin's clothing and mended the worst rips. And the young girl was so distressed that she didn't notice the glances Gunhild cast at her in secret.

As Kristin was leaving, Gunhild put on her own cloak and followed her out the door, but then headed toward the stable. Kristin asked her where she was going.

"Surely I should be allowed to ride over and tend to my son," said the woman, "to see if you've killed him with that rock or what's happened to him."

Kristin had nothing to say in reply, so she simply told Gunhild to make sure that Bentein left the village as soon as possible; she never wanted to lay eyes on him again. "Or I'll speak of this to Lavrans, and then you can well imagine what will happen."

Bentein headed south hardly more than a week later; he carried letters to the Bishop of Hamar from Sira Eirik, asking the bishop if he could find some occupation for Bentein or give him some assistance.

## CHAPTER 7

ONE DAY during the Christmas season, Simon Andressøn arrived at Jørundgaard on horseback, quite unexpected. He apologized for coming in this manner, uninvited and alone, without kinsmen, but Sir Andres was in Sweden on business for the king. He himself had been at home at Dyfrin for some time, but there he had only the company of his younger sisters and his mother, who was ill in bed, and the days had grown so dreary for him; he suddenly felt such an urge to come and see them.

Ragnfrid and Lavrans thanked him warmly for making the long journey at the height of winter. The more they saw of Simon, the more they liked him. He was well acquainted with everything that had been agreed upon between Andres and Lavrans, and it was now decided that the betrothal ale for the young couple would be celebrated before the beginning of Lent, if Sir Andres returned home before then—otherwise, at Easter.

Kristin was quiet and shy when she was with her betrothed; she found little to talk about with him. One evening when everyone had been sitting and drinking, Simon asked her to go outside with him to get some fresh air. As they stood on the gallery in front of the loft room, he put his arm around her waist and kissed her. After that, he did it often whenever they were alone. She wasn't pleased by this, but she allowed him to do it because she knew there was no escape from the betrothal. Now she thought of her marriage as something she had to do, but not something that she looked forward to. And yet she liked Simon well enough, especially when he was talking to the others and did not touch her or speak to her.

She had been so unhappy the entire autumn. It did no good to tell herself that Bentein had done her no harm; she felt herself defiled just the same.

Nothing could be as it had been before, now that a man had dared to do such a thing to her. She lay awake at night, burning with shame, and she couldn't stop thinking about it. She remembered Bentein's body against hers when she fought with him, and his hot ale-breath. She was forced to think about what might have happened, and she was reminded, as a shudder rippled through her flesh, of what he had said: that if it could not be concealed, then Arne would be blamed. Images raced through her head of everything that would have followed if she had ended up in such misfortune and then people had found out about her meeting with Arne. And what if her mother and father had believed such a thing of Arne? And Arne himself . . . She saw him as he had looked on that last evening, and she felt as if she were sinking down before him in shame simply because she *might* have dragged him down along with her into sorrow and disgrace. And her dreams were so vile. She had heard about the desires and temptations of the flesh in church and in the Holy Scriptures, but it had meant nothing to her. Now it had become clear that she herself and everyone else had a sinful, fleshly body encompassing the soul, biting into it with harsh bands.

Then she imagined how she might have killed Bentein or blinded him. That was the only consolation she could find—to indulge in dreams of revenge against that hideous dark figure who was always haunting her thoughts. But it never helped for long; she would lie next to Ulvhild at night and weep about everything that had been visited upon her by violence. In her mind, Bentein had managed to breach her maidenhood all the same.

On the first workday after the Christmas season, all the women of Jørundgaard were busy in the cookhouse. Ragnfrid and Kristin had also spent most of the day there. Late in the evening, while some of the women were cleaning up after the baking and others were preparing the evening meal, the milkmaid came rushing in, screaming as she threw up her hands.

"Jesus, Jesus—has anyone ever heard more dreadful news! They're carrying Arne Gyrdsøn home in a sleigh—God help Gyrd and Inga in their misery."

In came a man who lived in a house a short way down the road, and with him was Halvdan. They were the ones who had met the funeral procession.

The women crowded around them. On the very outskirts of the circle stood Kristin, pale and trembling. Halvdan, Lavrans's own servant who had known Arne since he was a boy, sobbed loudly as he spoke.

It was Bentein Prestesøn who had killed Arne. On New Year's Eve the bishop's men were sitting in the men's house drinking, when Bentein came in. He had become a scribe for a priest, a Corpus Christi prebendary.[1] At first the men didn't want to let Bentein in, but he reminded Arne that they were from the same village. So Arne allowed him to sit with him, and they both began to drink. But then they came to blows, and Arne fought so fiercely that Bentein seized a knife from the table and stabbed Arne in the throat and then several times in the chest. Arne died almost at once.

The bishop took this misfortune greatly to heart; he personally saw to it that the body was properly tended to, and he had his own men accompany it on the long journey home. He had Bentein thrown in irons and excommunicated from the Church, and if he had not already been hanged, then he soon would be.

Halvdan had to tell the story several times as more people crowded into the room. Lavrans and Simon also came over to the cookhouse when they noticed all the noise and commotion in the courtyard. Lavrans was much distressed; he ordered his horse to be saddled, for he wanted to ride over to Brekken at once. As he was about to leave, his eyes fell on Kristin's white face.

"Perhaps you would like to go with me?" he asked. Kristin hesitated for a moment, shuddering, but then she nodded, for she didn't dare utter a word.

"Isn't it too cold for her?" said Ragnfrid. "Tomorrow they will hold the wake, and then we'll all go."

Lavrans looked at his wife; he also glanced at Simon's face, and then he went over and put his arm around Kristin's shoulder.

"You must remember that she's his foster sister," he said. "Perhaps she would like to help Inga attend to the body."

And even though Kristin's heart was gripped with fear and despair, she felt a warm surge of gratitude toward her father for his words.

Then Ragnfrid wanted them to eat the evening porridge before they left, if Kristin would be going along. She also wanted to send gifts to Inga—a new linen sheet, candles, and freshly baked bread.

She asked them to tell Inga that she would come to help them prepare for the burial.

Little was eaten but much was said in the room while the food stood on the table. One person reminded the other about the trials that God had visited upon Gyrd and Inga. Their farm had been destroyed by a rock slide and flood, and many of their older children had died, so all of Arne's siblings were still quite young. But fortune had been with them for several years now, ever since the bishop had appointed Gyrd of Finsbrekken as his envoy, and the children they had been blessed to keep were good-looking and full of promise. But Inga had loved Arne more dearly than all the rest.

People felt sorry for Sira Eirik too. The priest was loved and respected, and the people in the village were proud of him; he was well educated and capable, and in all his years with the Church he had not missed a single holy day or mass or service that he was obliged to observe. In his youth he had been a soldier under Count Alv of Tornberg, but he had brought trouble on himself by killing a man of exceedingly high birth, and so he had turned to the Bishop of Oslo. When the bishop realized how quick Eirik was to acquire book learning, he had accepted him into the priesthood. And if not for the fact that he still had enemies because of that killing in the past, Sira Eirik would probably never have stayed at that little church. It's true that he was quite avaricious, both for his own purse and for his church. But the church was, after all, quite attractively furnished with vessels and draperies and books, and he did have those children—but he had never had anything but trouble and sorrow from his family. In the countryside people thought it unreasonable to expect priests to live like monks, since they had to have women servants on their farms and might well be in need of a woman to look after things for them when they had to make such long and arduous journeys through the parish in all kinds of weather. People also remembered that it was not so long ago that priests in Norway had been married men. So no one blamed Sira Eirik for having three children by the housekeeper who was with him when he was young. On this evening, however, they said that it looked as if God wanted to punish Eirik for taking a mistress, since his children and grandchildren had caused him so much grief. And some people said that there was good reason for priests not to have wives or children—for enmity and indignation were bound to arise between the priest and the people of Finsbrekken. Until now they had been the best of friends.

Simon Andressøn was quite familiar with Bentein's conduct in Oslo, and he told the others about it. Bentein had become a scribe for the provost of the Maria Church and was considered a clever fellow. And there were plenty of women who were quite fond of him; he had those eyes and a quick tongue. Some thought him a handsome man—mostly women who felt they had been cheated by their husbands, or young maidens who enjoyed having men act freely toward them. Simon laughed; they knew what he meant, didn't they? Well, Bentein was so shrewd that he didn't get too close to those kinds of women; with them he exchanged only words, and he won a reputation for leading a pure life.

It so happened that King Haakon, who was a pious and decent man himself, wanted his men to maintain disciplined and proper behavior—at least the younger men. The others he had little control over. But the king's priest always heard about whatever pranks the young men managed to sneak out and take part in—drunken feasts, gambling, ale-drinking, and the like. And then the rascals had to confess and repent, and they received harsh punishment; yes, two or three of the wildest boys were even sent away. But at last it came to light that it was that fox, Bentein *secretarius*, who had been secretly frequenting all of the ale houses and establishments that were even worse; he had actually listened to the confessions of whores and had given them absolution.

Kristin was sitting next to her mother. She tried to eat so that no one would notice how things stood with her, but her hand shook so badly that she spilled some of the porridge with every spoonful, and her tongue felt so thick and dry in her mouth that she could hardly swallow the bread. But when Simon began to talk about Bentein she had to give up all pretense of eating. She gripped the edge of the bench with her hands; terror and loathing took such a hold on her that she felt dizzy and filled with nausea. He was the one who had tried to . . . Bentein and Arne, Bentein and Arne . . . Sick with impatience she waited for the others to finish. She longed to see Arne, Arne's handsome face, to fall to her knees and grieve, forgetting everything else.

When Ragnfrid helped Kristin into her outer garments, she

kissed her daughter on the cheek. Kristin was unaccustomed to receiving any kind of caress from her mother, and it felt so good. She rested her head on Ragnfrid's shoulder for a moment, but she could not cry.

When she came out to the courtyard, she saw that there were more people coming with them—Halvdan, Jon of Laugarbru, and Simon and his servant. She felt unreasonably anguished that the two strangers would be going along.

It was a biting cold night; the snow creaked underfoot, and the stars glittered, as dense as frost, in the black sky. After they had gone a short distance, they heard howls and shouts and furious hoofbeats south of the meadows. A little farther along the road the whole pack of riders came storming up behind them and then raced on past. The sound of ringing metal and vapor from the steaming, frost-covered bodies of the horses rose up before Lavrans and his party as they moved out of the way into the snow. Halvdan shouted at the wild throng—it was the youths from the farms south of the village. They were still celebrating Christmas and were out trying their horses. Those who were too drunk to take notice raced on ahead, thundering and bellowing as they hammered on their shields. But a few of them understood the news that Halvdan had yelled after them; they dropped away from the group, fell silent, and joined Lavrans's party as they whispered to the men in the back of the procession.

They continued on until they could see Finsbrekken on the slope alongside the Sil River. There was a light between the buildings; in the middle of the courtyard the servants had set pine torches in a mound of snow, and the firelight gleamed red across the white hillock, but the dark houses looked as if they were streaked with clotted blood. One of Arne's little sisters was standing outside, stamping her feet, with her arms crossed under her cloak. Kristin kissed the tear-stained face of the freezing child. Her heart was as heavy as stone, and she felt as if there was lead in her limbs as she climbed the stairs to the loft where they had laid him out.

The sound of hymns and the radiance of many lighted candles filled the doorway. In the center of the loft stood the coffin Arne had been brought home in, covered with a sheet. Boards had been placed over trestles and the coffin had been lifted on top. At its head stood a young priest with a book in his hands, singing. All around him people were kneeling with their faces hidden in their thick capes.

Lavrans lit his candle from one of the candles in the room, set it firmly on the board of the bier, and knelt down. Kristin was about to do the same, but she couldn't get her candle to stand; then Simon stepped over to help her. As long as the priest prayed, everyone remained on their knees, repeating his words in a whisper, so that the steam hovered around their mouths. It was ice-cold in the loft.

When the priest closed his book, the people rose; many had already gathered in the death chamber. Lavrans went over to Inga. She was staring at Kristin and seemed not to hear Lavrans's words; she stood there with the gifts he had given her, holding them as if unaware that she had anything in her hands.

"So you have come too, Kristin," she said in an odd, strained tone of voice. "Perhaps you would like to see my son, the way he has come back to me?"

She moved a few candles aside, grabbed Kristin's arm with a trembling hand, and with the other she tore the cloth from the dead man's face.

It was grayish-yellow like mud, and his lips were the color of lead; they were slightly parted so that the even, narrow, bone-white teeth seemed to offer a mocking smile. Beneath the long eyelashes could be seen a glimpse of his glazed eyes, and there were several bluish-black spots high on his cheeks that were either bruises from the fight or the marks of a corpse.

"Perhaps you would like to kiss him?" asked Inga in the same tone of voice, and Kristin obediently leaned forward and pressed her lips to the dead man's cheek. It was clammy, as if from dew, and she thought she could faintly smell the stench of the corpse; he had no doubt begun to thaw out in the heat from all the candles.

Kristin remained leaning there, with her hands on the bier, for she did not have the strength to stand up. Inga pulled aside more of the shroud so the gash from the knife wound across his collarbone was visible.

Then she turned to the people and said in a quavering voice, "I see that it's a lie, what people say, that a dead man's wounds will bleed if he's touched by the one who caused his death. He's colder now, my boy, and not as handsome as when you last met him down on the road. You don't care to kiss him now, I see—but I've heard that you didn't refuse his lips back then."

"Inga," said Lavrans, stepping forward, "have you lost your senses? What are you saying?"

"Oh, you're all so grand over there at Jørundgaard—you were much too rich a man, Lavrans Bjørgulfsøn, for my son to dare court your daughter with honor. And no doubt Kristin thought she was too good for him too. But she wasn't too good to run after him on the road at night and dally with him in the thickets on the evening he left. Ask her yourself and we'll see if she dares to deny it, as Arne lies here dead—she who has brought this upon us with her loose ways. . . ."

Lavrans did not ask the question; instead he turned to Gyrd.

"You must rein in your wife—she has taken leave of her senses."

But Kristin raised her pale face and looked around in despair.

"I did go out to meet Arne on that last evening, because he asked me to do so. But nothing happened between us that was not proper." And as she seemed to pull herself together and fully realize what was implied, she shouted loudly, "I don't know what you mean, Inga. Are you defaming Arne as he lies here? Never did he try to entice or seduce me."

But Inga laughed loudly.

"Arne? No, not Arne. But Bentein didn't let you play with him that way. Ask Gunhild, Lavrans, who washed the filth off your daughter's back, and ask any man who was in the men's quarters at the bishop's citadel on New Year's Eve when Bentein ridiculed Arne for having let her go and then was made her fool. She let Bentein come under her fur as she walked home, and she tried to play the same game with him—"

Lavrans gripped Inga by the shoulder and pressed his hand against her mouth.

"Get her out of here, Gyrd. It's shameful that you should talk this way before the body of this good boy. But even if all of your children lay here dead, I would not stand and listen to your lies about mine. And you, Gyrd, will have to answer for what this demented woman is saying."

Gyrd took hold of his wife to lead her away, but he said to

Lavrans, "It's true that Arne and Bentein were talking about Kristin when my son lost his life. It's understandable that you may not have heard it, but there has been talk here in the village this fall. . . ."

Simon slammed his sword into the nearest clothes chest.

"No, good folks, now you will have to find something other than my betrothed to talk about in this death chamber. Priest, can't you harness these people so that everything proceeds according to custom?"

The priest—Kristin now saw that he was the youngest son from Ulvsvold who had been home for Christmas—opened his book and took up his position next to the bier. But Lavrans shouted that those who had spoken of his daughter, whoever they might be, would have to eat their words.

And then Inga screamed, "Go ahead and take my life, Lavrans, just as she has taken all my solace and joy—and celebrate her marriage to this son of a knight, and yet everyone will know that she was married to Bentein on the road. Here—" And she threw the sheet that Lavrans had given her across the bier to Kristin. "I don't need Ragnfrid's linen to wrap around Arne for burial. Make yourself a kerchief out of it, or keep it to swaddle your wayside bastard—and go over to help Gunhild mourn for the hanged man."

Lavrans, Gyrd, and the priest all seized hold of Inga. Simon tried to lift up Kristin, who was lying across the bier. But she vehemently shook off his hand, and then, still on her knees, she straightened up and shouted loudly, "May God my Savior help me, that is a lie!"

She put out her hand and held it over the nearest candle on the bier.

It looked as if the flame wavered and moved aside. Kristin felt everyone's eyes upon her—for a very long time, it seemed. Then she suddenly noticed a searing pain in her palm, and with a piercing shriek she collapsed onto the floor.

She thought she had fainted, but she could feel Simon and the priest lifting her up. Inga screamed something. She saw her father's horrified face and heard the priest shout that no one should consider it a true trial—this was not the way to ask God to bear witness—and then Simon carried Kristin out of the loft and down the stairs. Simon's servant ran to the stable and a moment later Kristin, still only half conscious, was sitting on the front of Simon's saddle, wrapped in his cape, as he rode down toward the village as fast as his horse could carry them.

They had almost reached Jørundgaard when Lavrans overtook them. The rest of their entourage came thundering along the road far behind.

"Say nothing to your mother," said Simon as he set Kristin down next to the door. "We've heard far too much senseless talk tonight; it's no wonder that you fainted in the end."

Ragnfrid was lying awake when they came in and she asked how things had gone at the vigil. Simon spoke for all of them. Yes, there were many candles and many people. Yes, a priest was there—Tormod of Ulvsvold. Of Sira Eirik, he heard that he had ridden south to Hamar that very evening, so they would avoid any difficulty at the burial.

"We must have a mass said for the boy," said Ragnfrid. "May God give Inga strength. She has been sorely tried, that good, capable woman."

Lavrans fell in with the tone that Simon had set, and in a little while Simon said that now they must all go to bed—"For Kristin is both tired and sad."

Some time later, when Ragnfrid had fallen asleep, Lavrans threw on some clothes and went over to sit on the edge of the bed where his daughters were sleeping. In the dark he found Kristin's hand, and then he said gently, "Now you must tell me, child, what is true and what is a lie in all this talk that Inga is spouting."

Sobbing, Kristin told him of everything that had happened on the evening that Arne left for Hamar. Lavrans said little. Then Kristin crawled forward on the bed and threw her arms around his neck, whimpering softly.

"I am to blame for Arne's death—it's true what Inga said. . . ."

"Arne himself asked you to come and meet him," said Lavrans, pulling the covers up around his daughter's bare shoulders. "It was thoughtless of me to allow the two of you to spend so much time together, but I thought the boy had better sense. I won't blame the two of you; I can see that these things are heavy for you to bear. And yet I never imagined that any of my daughters would fall into ill repute here in our village. It will be painful for your mother when she hears this news. But you went to Gunhild instead of coming to me—that was so unwise that I can't understand how you could act so foolishly."

"I don't want to stay here in the village any longer," wept Kristin. "I don't dare look a single person in the eye. And all the sorrow I have caused those at Romundgaard and at Finsbrekken . . ."

"Yes," said Lavrans, "they will have to make sure, both Gyrd and Sira Eirik, that these lies about you are put in the ground along with Arne. Otherwise it is Simon Andressøn who can best defend you in this matter." And he patted her in the dark. "Don't you think he handled things well and with good sense?"

"Father," Kristin begged, fearful and fervent, as she clung to him, "send me to the cloister, Father. Yes, listen to me—I've thought about this for a long time. Maybe Ulvhild will get well if I go in her place. Do you remember the shoes that I sewed for her this autumn, the ones with pearls on them? I pricked my fingers so badly, I bled from the sharp gold thread. I sat and sewed those shoes because I thought it was wrong that I didn't love my sister enough to become a nun and help her. Arne asked me about that once. If I had said yes back then, none of this would have happened."

Lavrans shook his head.

"Lie down now," he told her. "You don't know what you're saying, my poor child. Now you must try to sleep."

But Kristin lay there, feeling the pain in her burned hand; bitterness and despair over her fate raged in her heart. Things could not have gone worse for her if she had been the most sinful of women; everyone would believe . . . No, she couldn't, she couldn't stand to stay here in the village. Horror after horror appeared before her. When her mother found out about this . . . And now there was blood between them and their parish priest, hostility among all those around her who had been friends her whole life. But the most extreme and oppressive fears seized her whenever she thought of Simon—the way he had picked her up and carried her off and spoken for her at home and acted as if she were his property. Her father and mother had yielded to him as if she already belonged more to him than to them.

Then she remembered Arne's face, cold and hideous. She remembered that she had seen an open grave waiting for a body the last time she came out of church. The chopped-up lumps of earth lay on the snow, hard and cold and gray as iron—that was where she had brought Arne.

Suddenly she thought about a summer night many years before. She was standing on the loft gallery at Finsbrekken, the same loft where she had been struck down this evening. Arne was playing ball with some boys down in the courtyard, and the ball came sailing up to her on the gallery. She held it behind her back and refused to give it up when Arne came to retrieve it. Then he tried to take it from her by force, and they had fought over it on the gallery, then inside the loft among the chests. The leather sacks full of clothes that were hanging there knocked them on the head when they ran into them during the chase. They had fought and tumbled over that ball.

And now she finally seemed to realize that he was dead and gone, and that she would never see his brave, handsome face or feel his warm hands again. She had been so childish and heartless that it had never occurred to her how he would feel about losing her. She wept in despair and thought she deserved her own unhappiness. But then she started thinking again about everything that still awaited her, and she wept because she thought the punishment that would befall her was too severe.

Simon was the one who told Ragnfrid about what had happened at the vigil at Brekken the night before. He made no more of the matter than was necessary. But Kristin was so dazed from grief and a sleepless night that she felt a purely unreasonable bitterness toward him, because he could speak of it as if it were not so terrible after all. She also felt a great displeasure at the way her parents let Simon act as if he were the master of the house.

"So you don't think anything of it, Simon?" asked Ragnfrid anxiously.

"No," replied Simon. "And I don't think anyone else will either; they know you and her and they know this Bentein. But there's not much to talk about in this remote village; it's perfectly reasonable for people to help themselves to this juicy tidbit. Now we'll have to teach them that Kristin's reputation is too rich a diet for the peasants around here. But it's too bad that she was so frightened by his coarseness that she didn't come to you at once, or go to Sira Eirik himself. I think that whorehouse priest would have gladly testified that he had meant no more than some innocent teasing if you had spoken to him, Lavrans."

Both parents agreed that Simon was right. But Kristin gave a shriek and stamped her foot.

"But he knocked me to the ground. I hardly know what he did to me. I was out of my senses; I no longer remember a thing. For all I know, it might be as Inga says. I haven't been well or happy for a single day since. . . ."

Ragnfrid gave a cry and pressed her hands together; Lavrans leaped to his feet. Even Simon's face changed expression; he gave Kristin a sharp look, went over to her, and put his hand under her chin. Then he laughed.

"God bless you, Kristin. You would have remembered it if he had done you any harm. It's no wonder she's been feeling melancholy and unwell since that unlucky evening when she was given such a fright—she who has never met with anything but kindness and goodwill before," he said to the others. "Anyone can see from her eyes, which bear no ill intent and would rather believe in good than evil, that she is a maiden and not a woman."

Kristin looked up into the small, steady eyes of her betrothed. She raised her arms halfway up; she wanted to place them around his neck.

Then Simon went on. "You mustn't think, Kristin, that you won't forget all about this. I don't intend for us to settle at Formo right away and never allow you to leave this valley. 'No one has the same color of hair or temperament in the rain as in the sun,' said old King Sverre when they accused his 'Birch-Leg' followers[2] of growing arrogant with success."

Lavrans and Ragnfrid smiled. It amused them to hear the young man speak as if he were a wise old bishop.

Simon continued. "It would not be proper for me to admonish you, the man who is to be my father-in-law, but perhaps I might say this much: we were dealt with more strictly, my siblings and I. We were not allowed to move so freely among the servants as I see it is Kristin's custom. My mother used to say that if you play with the cottager's children, in the long run you'll end up with lice in your hair; and there is some truth to that."

Lavrans and Ragnfrid said nothing to this. But Kristin turned away, and the desire she had felt for a moment to put her arms around Simon Darre's neck had vanished completely.

Around midday Lavrans and Simon put on their skis and went off to tend to several traps up on the ridge. Outdoors it was now beautiful weather, sunny and not nearly as bitter cold. Both men were relieved to slip away from all the sorrow and tears at home, so they skied a great distance, all the way up to the bare rock.

They lay in the sun under a steep cliff and drank and ate. Then Lavrans talked a little about Arne; he had been very fond of the boy. Simon joined in, praising the dead man, and said that he didn't find it strange that Kristin should grieve for her foster brother. Then Lavrans mentioned that perhaps they should not pressure her so much, but give her a little more time to regain her composure before they celebrated the betrothal ale. She had said that she would like to go to a cloister for a while.

Simon sat up suddenly and gave a long whistle.

"You don't care for the idea?" asked Lavrans.

"Oh, yes, yes," replied the other man hastily. "This seems to be the best counsel, dear father-in-law. Send her to the sisters in Oslo for a year; then she'll learn how people talk about each other out in the world. I happen to know a little about several of the maidens who are there," he said and laughed. "They wouldn't lie down and die of grief over two mad boys tearing each other apart for their sake. Not that I would want such a maiden for my wife, but I don't think it would do Kristin any harm to meet some new people."

Lavrans put the rest of the food in the knapsack and said, without looking at the young man, "You are fond of Kristin, I think."

Simon laughed a little but did not look at Lavrans.

"You must know that I have great affection for her—and for you, as well," Simon said brusquely, and then he stood up and put on his skis. "I have never met any maiden I would rather marry."

* * *

Right before Easter, while it was still possible to drive a sleigh down the valley and across Lake Mjøsa, Kristin made her second journey to the south. Simon came to escort her to the cloister. So this time she traveled with her father and her betrothed, sitting in the sleigh, wrapped in furs. And accompanying them were servants and sleighs full of her chests of clothing and gifts of food and furs for the abbess and the sisters of Nonneseter.

PART II

# THE WREATH

# CHAPTER 1

EARLY ONE SUNDAY morning at the end of April, Aasmund Bjørgulfsøn's church boat glided past the point on the island of Hovedø as the bells rang in the cloister church, and bells from the town chimed their reply out across the bay, sounding louder, then fainter as the wind carried the notes.

The sky was clear and pale blue, with light fluted clouds drifting across it, and the sun was glinting restlessly on the rippling water. It seemed quite springlike along the shore; the fields were almost bare of snow, and there were bluish shadows and a yellowish sheen on the leafy thickets. But snow was visible in the spruce forest atop the ridges framing the settlements of Aker, and to the west, on the distant blue mountains beyond the fjord, many streaks of white still gleamed.

Kristin was standing in the bow of the boat with her father and Gyrid, Aasmund's wife. She turned her gaze toward the town, with all of its light-colored churches and stone buildings rising up above the multitudes of grayish-brown wooden houses and the bare crowns of the trees. The wind ruffled the edges of her cloak and tousled her hair beneath her hood.

They had let the livestock out to pasture at Skog the day before, and Kristin had suddenly felt such a homesickness for Jørundgaard. It would be a long time before they could let out the cattle back home. She felt a tender and sympathetic longing for the winter-gaunt cattle in the dark stalls; they would have to wait and endure for many days yet. She missed everyone so—her mother, Ulvhild, who had slept in her arms every night for all these years, little Ramborg. She longed for all the people back home and for the horses and dogs; for Kortelin, whom Ulvhild would take care of while she was gone; and for her father's hawks, sitting on their perches with hoods over their heads. Next to them hung the gloves made of horsehide, which had to be worn when handling them, and the ivory sticks used to scratch them.

All the terrible events of the winter now seemed so far away, and she only remembered her home as it had been before. They had also told her that no one in the village thought ill of her. Nor did Sira Eirik; he was angry and aggrieved by what Bentein had done. Bentein had escaped from Hamar, and it was said that he had run off to Sweden. So things had not been as unpleasant between her family and the people of the neighboring farm as Kristin had feared.

On their way south they had stayed at Simon's home, and she had met his mother and siblings; Sir Andres was still in Sweden. She had not felt at ease there, and her dislike of the family at Dyfrin was all the greater because she knew of no reasonable explanation for it. During the entire journey she had told herself that they had no reason to be haughty or to consider themselves better than her ancestors—no one had ever heard of Reidar Darre, the Birch-Leg, until King Sverre found the widow of the baron at Dyfrin for him to wed.

But they turned out not to be haughty at all, and Simon even spoke of his ancestor one evening. "I have now found out for certain that he was supposed to have been a comb maker—so you will truly be joining a royal lineage, Kristin," he said.

"Guard your tongue, my boy," said his mother, but they all laughed.

Kristin felt so oddly distressed when she thought of her father. He laughed a great deal whenever Simon gave him the least reason to do so. The thought occurred to her that perhaps her father would have liked to laugh more often in his life. But she didn't like it that he was so fond of Simon.

During Easter they were all at Skog. Kristin noticed that her Uncle Aasmund was a stern master toward his tenants and servants. She met a few people who asked after her mother and who spoke affectionately of Lavrans; they had enjoyed better days when he was living there. Aasmund's mother, who was Lavrans's stepmother, lived on the farm in her own house. She was not particularly old, but she was sickly and feeble. Lavrans seldom spoke of her at home. Once when Kristin asked her father whether he had had a quarrelsome stepmother, he had replied, "She has never done much for me, good or bad."

Kristin reached for her father's hand, and he squeezed hers in return.

"I know you'll be happy with the worthy sisters, my daughter. There you'll have other things to think about than yearning for us back home."

They sailed so close to the town that the smell of tar and salt fish drifted out to them from the docks. Gyrid pointed out the churches and farms and roads that stretched upward from the water's edge. Kristin recognized nothing from the last time she had been there except for the ponderous towers of Halvard's Cathedral. They sailed west, around the entire town, and then put in at the nuns' dock.

Kristin walked between her father and her uncle past a cluster of warehouses and then reached the road, which led uphill past the fields. Gyrid followed after them, escorted by Simon. The servants stayed behind to help several men from the cloister load the trunks onto a cart.

The convent Nonneseter and all of Leiran lay inside the town's boundaries, but there were only a few houses clustered here and there along the road. The larks were chirping overhead in the pale blue sky, and tiny yellow Michaelmas daisies teemed on the sallow dirt hills, but along the fences the roots of the grass were green.

As they went through the gate and entered the colonnade, all the nuns came walking toward them in a procession from church, with music and song streaming after them from the open doorway.

Kristin stared uneasily at the many black-clad women with white wimples framing their faces. She sank into a curtsey, and the men bowed with their hats pressed to their chests. Following the nuns came a group of young maidens—some of them were children—wearing dresses of undyed homespun, with black-and-white belts made of twisted cord around their waists. Their hair was pulled back from their faces and braided tightly with the same kind of black-and-white cord. Kristin unconsciously put on a haughty expression for the young maidens because she felt shy, and she was afraid that they would think she looked unrefined and foolish.

The convent was so magnificent that she was completely overwhelmed. All the buildings surrounding the inner courtyard were made of gray stone. On the north side the long wall of the church loomed above the other buildings; it had a two-tiered roof and a tower at the west end. The surface of the courtyard was paved with flagstones, and the entire area was enclosed by a covered arcade supported by stately pillars. In the center of the square stood a stone statue of *Mater Misericordiae*, spreading her cloak over a group of kneeling people.

A lay sister came forward and asked them to follow her to the parlatory, the abbess's reception room. Abbess Groa Guttormsdatter was a tall, stout old woman. She would have been good-looking if she hadn't had so many stubbly hairs around her mouth. Her voice was deep and made her sound like a man. But she had a pleasant manner, and she reminded Lavrans that she had known his parents, and then asked after his wife and their other children. At last she turned kindly to Kristin.

"I have heard good things of you, and you seem to be clever and well brought up, so I do not think you will give us any reason for displeasure. I have heard that you are promised to that noble and good man, Simon Andressøn, whom I see before me. We think it wise of your father and your betrothed to send you here to the Virgin Mary's house for a time, so that you can learn to obey and to serve before you are charged with giving orders and commands. I want to impress on you now that you should learn to find joy in prayer and the divine services so that in all your actions you will be in the habit of remembering your Creator, the Lord's gentle Mother, and all the saints who have given us the best examples of strength, rectitude, fidelity, and all the virtues that you ought to demonstrate if you are to manage property and servants and raise children. You will also learn in this house that one must pay close attention to time, because here each hour has a specific purpose and chore. Many young maidens and wives are much too fond of lying in bed late in the morning, and of lingering at the table in the evening, carrying on useless conversation. But you do not look as if you were that kind. Yet you can learn a great deal from this year that will benefit you both here and in that other home."

Kristin curtseyed and kissed her hand. Then Fru Groa told Kristin to follow an execeptionally fat old nun, whom she called Sister Potentia, over to the nuns' refectory. She invited the men and Fru Gyrid to dine with her in a different room.

The refectory was a beautiful hall. It had a stone floor and arched windows with glass panes. A doorway led into another room, and Kristin could see that this room too must have glass windowpanes, because the sun was shining inside.

The sisters had already sat down and were waiting for the food. The older nuns were sitting on a stone bench covered with cushions along the wall under the windows. The younger sisters and the bareheaded maidens wearing light homespun dresses sat on a wooden bench in front of the table. Tables had also been set in the adjoining room, which was intended for the most distinguished of the corrodians[1] and the lay servants; there were several old men among them. These people did not wear cloister garb, but they did wear dark and dignified attire.

Sister Potentia showed Kristin to a place on the outer bench while she herself went over to a seat near the abbess's place of honor at the head of the table, which would remain empty today.

Everyone rose, both in the main hall and in the adjoining room, as the sisters said the blessing. Then a young, pretty nun came forward and stepped up to a lectern which had been placed in the doorway between the rooms. And while two of the lay sisters in the main hall and two of the youngest nuns in the other room brought in the food and drink, the nun read in a loud and lovely voice—without pausing or hesitating at a single word—the story of Saint Theodora and Saint Didymus.

From the very first moment, Kristin thought most about showing good table manners, for she noticed that all the sisters and young maidens had such elegant comportment and ate so properly, as if they were at the most magnificent banquet. There was an abundance of the best food and drink, but everyone took only modest portions, using only the tips of their fingers to help themselves from the platters. No one spilled any soup on the tablecloth or on their clothes, and everyone cut up the meat into such tiny pieces that they hardly sullied their lips; they ate so carefully that not a sound could be heard.

Kristin was sweating with fear that she wouldn't be able to act as refined as the others. She also felt uncomfortable in her brightly colored attire among all the women dressed in black and white. She imagined that they were all staring at her. Then, as she was about to eat a piece of fatty mutton breast and was holding it with two fingers pressed against the bone while in her right hand she held the knife, trying to cut easily and neatly, the whole thing slipped away from her. The bread and the meat leaped onto the tablecloth as the knife fell with a clatter to the floor.

The sound was deafening in that quiet room. Kristin blushed red as blood and was about to bend down to pick up the knife, but a lay sister wearing sandals came over, soundlessly, and gathered up the things. But Kristin could eat nothing more. She also noticed that she had cut her finger, and she was afraid of bleeding on the tablecloth, so she sat there with her hand wrapped up in a fold of her dress, thinking that now she was making spots on the lovely light-blue gown that she had been given for her journey to Oslo. And she didn't dare raise her eyes from her lap.

After a while she started to listen more closely to what the nun was reading. When the chieftain could not sway the maiden Theodora's steadfast will—she would neither make sacrifices to false gods nor let herself be married—he ordered her to be taken to a brothel. Furthermore, he exhorted her along the way to think of her freeborn ancestors and her honorable parents, upon whom an everlasting shame would now fall, and he promised that she would be allowed to live in peace and remain a maiden if she would agree to serve a pagan goddess, whom they called Diana.

Theodora replied, unafraid, "Chastity is like a lamp, but love for God is the flame. If I were to serve the devil-woman whom you call Diana, then my chastity would be worth no more than a rusty lamp without fire or oil. You call me freeborn, but we are all born thralls, since our first parents sold us to the Devil. Christ has redeemed me, and I am obliged to serve him, so I cannot marry his enemies. He will protect his dove, but if he would cause you to break my body, which is the temple of his Holy Spirit, then it shall not be reckoned to my shame, as long as I do not consent to betray his property in enemy hands."

Kristin's heart began to pound, because this reminded her in a certain way of her encounter with Bentein. It struck her that perhaps this was her sin, that she had not for a moment thought of God or prayed for His help. Then Sister Cecilia read about Saint Didymus. He was a Christian knight, but he had kept his Christianity secret from all except a few friends. He went to the house where the maiden was confined. He gave money to the woman who owned the house, and then he was allowed to go to Theodora. She fled to a corner like a frightened rabbit, but Didymus greeted her as a sister and the bride of his Lord and said that he had come to save her. Then he talked to her for a while, saying: "Shouldn't a brother risk his own life for his sister's honor?" And finally she did as he asked; she exchanged clothes with him and allowed herself to be strapped into his coat of mail. He pulled the helmet down over her eyes and drew the cape closed under her chin, and then he told her to go out with her face hidden, like a youth who was ashamed to be in such a place.

Kristin thought about Arne and had the greatest difficulty in holding back her sobs. She stared straight ahead, with tear-filled eyes, as the nun read the end of the story—how Didymus was led off to the gallows and Theodora came rushing down from the mountains, threw herself at the executioner's feet, and begged to be allowed to die in his place. Then those two pious people argued about who would be the first to win the crown, and they were both beheaded on the same day. It was the twenty-eighth day of April in the year A.D. 304, in Antioch, as Saint Ambrosius has written of it.

When they rose from the table, Sister Potentia came over and patted Kristin kindly on the cheek. "Yes, I can imagine that you are longing for your mother." Then Kristin's tears began to fall. But the nun pretended not to notice, and she led Kristin to the dormitory where she was going to live.

It was in one of the stone buildings along the colonnade, a beautiful room with glass windowpanes and an enormous fireplace at the far end. Along one wall stood six beds and along the other were all of the maidens' chests.

Kristin wished she would be allowed to sleep with one of the little girls, but Sister Potentia called to a plump, fair-haired, fully grown maiden.

"This is Ingebjørg Filippusdatter, who will be your bedmate. The two of you should get acquainted." And then she left.

Ingebjørg took Kristin's hand at once and began to talk. She was not very tall and much too fat, especially in her face; her eyes were tiny because her cheeks were so fat. But her complexion was pure, pink and white, and her hair was yellow like gold and so curly that her thick braids twisted and turned like ropes, and little locks were constantly slipping out from under her headband.

She immediately began asking Kristin about all sorts of things but never waited for an answer. Instead, she talked about herself and reeled off all her ancestors in all the branches; they were grand and enormously wealthy people. Ingebjørg was also betrothed, to a rich and powerful man, Einar Einarssøn of Agan;aes—but he was much too old and had twice been widowed. It was her greatest sorrow, she said. But Kristin couldn't see that she was taking it particularly hard. Then Ingebjørg talked a little about Simon Darre—it was strange how carefully she had studied him during that brief moment when they passed each other in the arcade. Then Ingebjørg wanted to look in Kristin's chest, but first she opened her own and showed Kristin all of her gowns. As they were rummaging in the chests, Sister Cecilia came in. She reproached them and told them that was not a proper activity on a Sunday. And then Kristin felt downhearted again. She had never been reprimanded by anyone except her own mother, and it felt odd to be scolded by strangers.

Ingebjørg was completely unperturbed.

That night, after they had gone to bed, Ingebjørg lay there talking, right up until Kristin fell asleep. Two elderly lay sisters slept in a corner of the room. They were supposed to see to it that the maidens did not remove their shifts at night—for it was against the rules for the girls to undress completely—and that they got up in time for matins at the church. But otherwise they didn't concern themselves with keeping order in the dormitory, and they pretended not to notice when the maidens lay in bed talking or eating treats they had hidden in their chests.

When Kristin awoke the next morning, Ingebjørg was already in the middle of a long story, and Kristin wondered whether she had been talking all night.

## CHAPTER 2

THE FOREIGN MERCHANTS who spent the summer trading in Oslo arrived in the city in the spring, around Holy Cross Day, which was ten days before the Vigil of Saint Halvard. For that celebration, people came in throngs from all the villages from Lake Mjøsa to the Swedish border, so the town was teeming with people during the first weeks of May. It was best to buy goods from the foreigners during that time, before they had sold too many of their wares.

Sister Potentia was in charge of the shopping at Nonneseter, and on the day before the Vigil of Saint Halvard she had promised Ingebjørg and Kristin that they could go along with her into town. But around noon some of Sister Potentia's kinsmen came to the convent to visit her; she would not be able to go out that day. Then Ingebjørg managed to beg permission for them to go alone, although this was against the rules. As an escort, an old farmer who received a corrody from the cloister was sent along with them. His name was Haakon.

By this time, Kristin had been at Nonneseter for three weeks, and in all that time she had not once set foot outside the convent's courtyards and gardens. She was astonished to see how springlike it had become outside. The small groves of leafy trees out in the fields were shiny green, and the wood anemones were growing as thick as a carpet beneath the lustrous tree trunks. Bright fair-weather clouds came sailing above the islands in the fjord, and the water looked fresh and blue, rippled by small gusts of spring wind.

Ingebjørg skipped along, snapping off clusters of leaves from the trees and smelling them, turning to stare at the people they passed, but Haakon reproached her. Was that the proper way for a noble maiden to act, and one who was wearing convent attire, at that? The maidens had to take each other by the hand and walk along behind him, quietly and decorously; but Ingebjørg let her eyes wander and her mouth chatter all the same, since Haakon was slightly deaf. Kristin now wore the garb of a young sister: an undyed, pale-gray homespun dress, a woolen belt and headband, and a simple dark-blue cloak with the hood pulled forward so that her braided hair was completely hidden. Haakon strode along in front of them with a big brass-knobbed stick in his hand. He was dressed in a long black coat, with an *Agnus Dei* made of lead hanging on his chest and a picture of Saint Christopher on his hat. His white hair and beard were so well-brushed that they glinted like silver in the sun.

The upper part of the town, from the nuns' creek and down toward the bishop's citadel, was a quiet neighborhood. There were no market stalls or hostelries, only farms belonging mostly to gentry from the outlying villages. The buildings faced the street with dark and windowless timbered gables. But on this day, the lane was already crowded up there, and servants were hanging over the farm fences, talking to the people walking past.

As they came out near the bishop's citadel, they joined a great throng at the marketplace in front of Halvard's Cathedral and Olav's cloister. Booths had been set up on the grassy slope and there were strolling players who were making trained dogs jump through barrel hoops. But Haakon wouldn't let the maidens stop to watch, nor would he allow Kristin to enter the church; he said it would be more fun for her to see it on the great festival day itself.

On the road in front of Clement's Church, Haakon took them both by the hand, for here the crowd was even bigger, with people coming in from the wharves or from the lanes between the townyards.[1] The girls were going to Miklegaard, where the shoemakers worked. Ingebjørg thought the dresses that Kristin had brought from home were pretty and nice, but she said that the footwear Kristin had with her from the village could not be worn on fine occasions. And when Kristin saw the foreign-made shoes, of which Ingebjørg had many pairs, she thought she could not rest until she had bought some for herself.

Miklegaard was one of the largest townyards in Oslo. It extended all the way from the wharves up toward Shoemaker Lane, with more than forty buildings surrounding two big courtyards. Now booths with homespun canopies had also been set up in the courtyards, and above the tents towered a statue of Saint Crispin.

There was a great crush of people shopping. Women were running back and forth to the cookhouses with pots and buckets, children were getting tangled up in people's feet, horses were being led in and out of the stables, and servants were carrying loads in and out of the storage sheds. Up on the galleries of the lofts where the finest wares were sold, the shoemakers and hawkers in the booths called to the maidens below, dangling toward them small, colorful, gold-stitched shoes.

But Ingebjørg headed for the loft where Shoemaker Didrek had his workshop; he was German but had a Norwegian wife and owned a building in Miklegaard.

The old man was conducting business with a gentleman wearing a traveling cape and a sword at his belt, but Ingebjørg stepped forward boldly, bowed, and said, "Good sir, won't you allow us to speak with Didrek first? We must be back home at our convent before vespers, and you perhaps have more time?"

The gentleman greeted her and stepped aside. Didrek gave Ingebjørg a poke with his elbow and asked her with a laugh whether they were dancing so much at the cloister that she had already worn out all the shoes she had bought the year before. Ingebjørg gave him a poke back and said that they were hardly used at all, good heavens, but here was another maiden—and she pulled Kristin over to him. Then Didrek and his apprentice brought a chest out to the gallery, and he started taking out the shoes, each pair more beautiful than the last. Kristin sat down on a box and he tried the shoes on her feet. There were white shoes, and brown and red and green and blue shoes; shoes with painted heels made of wood, and shoes with no heels at all; shoes with buckles, shoes with silken ties, and shoes made from two or three different colored leathers. Kristin almost thought she liked them all. But they were so expensive that she was shocked—not a single pair cost less than a cow back home. Her father had given her a purse with one mark of silver counted out in coins when he left; this was to be her spending money, and Kristin had thought it a great sum. But she could see that Ingebjørg didn't think she could buy much with it at all.

Ingebjørg also had to try on shoes, just for fun. It didn't cost anything, said Didrek with a laugh. She bought a pair of leaf-green shoes with red heels, but she had to take them on credit; Didrek knew her, after all, as well as her family.

But Kristin could see that Didrek did not much care for this, and he was also dismayed because the tall gentleman in the traveling cape had left the loft; they had spent a long time trying on shoes. So Kristin chose a pair of shoes without heels made of thin, blue-violet leather; they were stitched with silver and rose-colored stones. But she didn't like the green silk straps. Then Didrek said that he could change them, and he took them along to a room at the back of the loft. There he had boxes of silk ribbons and small silver buckles—things which shoemakers were actually not allowed to sell, and many of the ribbons were too wide and the buckles too big for shoes anyway.

Both Kristin and Ingebjørg had to buy a few of these odds and ends, and by the time they had drunk a little sweet wine with Didrek and he had wrapped up their purchases in a homespun cloth, it had grown quite late, and Kristin's purse had grown much lighter.

When they came out onto East Lane again, the sun was quite gold, and the dust from all the traffic in the town hung like a faint haze over the street. It was so warm and lovely, and people were arriving from Eikaberg with great armfuls of new foliage to decorate their houses for the holiday. Then Ingebjørg decided that they should walk out toward Gjeita Bridge. On market days there was always so much entertainment going on in the paddocks along the river, with jugglers and fiddlers. Ingebjørg had even heard that a whole ship full of foreign animals had arrived, and they were being displayed in cages down on the shore.

Haakon had had some German beer at Miklegaard and was now quite amenable and in good spirits, so when the maidens took him by the arm and begged so nicely, he relented, and the three of them walked over toward Eikaberg.

On the other side of the river there were only a few small farms scattered across the green slopes between the river and the steep incline. They went past the Minorites' cloister, and Kristin's heart shrank with shame, for she suddenly remembered that she had wanted to offer most of her silver for Arne's soul. But she had not wanted to speak of this to the priest at Nonneseter; she was afraid of being questioned. She had thought that perhaps she could go out to visit the barefoot friars in the pastures to see whether Brother Edvin had returned—she would have liked so much to meet him. But she didn't know how properly to approach one of the monks or to broach the topic. And now she had so little money left that she didn't know whether she could afford a mass; maybe she would have to settle for offering a thick wax candle.

Suddenly they heard a terrible roar from countless voices out at the paddock on the shore—it was as if a storm were passing over the swarm of people gathered down there. And then the whole crowd came rushing up toward them, shrieking and hollering. Everyone was running in wild terror, and several people screamed to Haakon and the maidens that the leopards were loose.

They raced back toward the bridge, and they heard people shouting to each other that a cage had tipped over and two leopards had escaped; someone also mentioned a snake. The closer they came to the bridge, the greater the crowd. A baby fell from a woman's arms right in front of them, and Haakon stood over the little one to protect him. A moment later Kristin and Ingebjørg caught a glimpse of the old man far off to one side, holding the child in his arms, and then they lost sight of him.

At the narrow bridge the mob surged forward so fiercely that the maidens were forced out into a field. They saw people running along the riverbank; young men jumped into the water and began to swim, but the older people leaped into the moored boats, which became instantly overloaded.

Kristin tried to make Ingebjørg listen to her; she screamed that they should run over to the Minorites' cloister. The gray-cowled monks had come rushing over and were trying to gather the terrified people. Kristin was not as frightened as her friend, and they saw nothing of the wild animals, but Ingebjørg had completely lost her head. The swarms of people surged forward again, and then were driven back from the bridge because a large crowd of men who had gone to the nearest farms to arm themselves was now headed back, some on horseback, some running. When Ingebjørg was almost trampled by a horse, she gave a shriek and took off up the hill toward the forest. Kristin had never imagined that Ingebjørg could run so fast—she was reminded of a hunted boar —and she ran after her so that they wouldn't become separated.

They were deep inside the forest before Kristin managed to stop Ingebjørg on a small pathway which seemed to lead down toward the road to Trælaborg. They paused for a moment to catch their breath. Ingebjørg was sniffling and crying, and she said she didn't dare go back alone through the town and all the way out to the convent.

Kristin didn't think it a good idea either, with so much commotion in the streets; she thought they should find a house where they might hire a boy to accompany them home. Ingebjørg recalled a bridle path to Trælaborg farther down near the shore, and she was certain that along the path were several houses. So they followed the path downhill.

Distressed as they both were, it seemed to them that they walked for a long time before they finally saw a farm in the middle of a field. In the courtyard they found a group of men sitting at a table beneath some ash trees, drinking. A woman went back and forth, bringing pitchers out to them. She gave the two maidens in convent attire a surprised and annoyed look, and none of the men seemed to want to accompany them when Kristin explained their need. But finally two young fellows stood up and said they would escort the girls to Nonneseter if Kristin would pay them an *ørtug*.[2]

She could tell from their speech that they weren't Norwegian, but they seemed to be decent men. She thought their demand shamefully exorbitant, but Ingebjørg was scared out of her wits and she didn't think they should walk home alone so late in the day, so she agreed.

No sooner had they come out onto the forest path than the men drew aside and began talking to each other. Kristin was upset by this, but she didn't want to show her apprehension, so she spoke to them calmly, told them about the leopards, and asked them where they were from. She also looked around, pretending that at any minute she expected to meet the servants who had been escorting them; she talked about them as if they were a large group. Gradually the men said less and less, and she understood very little of their language anyway.

After a while Kristin noticed that they were not headed the way she had come with Ingebjørg; the path led in a different direction, more to the north, and she thought they had already gone much too far. Deep inside her, terror was smoldering, but she dared not let it slip into her thoughts. She felt oddly strengthened having Ingebjørg along; the girl was so foolish that Kristin realized she would have to handle things for both of them. Under her cloak she pulled out the reliquary cross that her father had given her, clasped her hand around it, and prayed with all her heart that they might meet up with someone soon, as she tried to gather her courage and pretend that nothing was wrong.

A moment later she saw that the path led out onto a road, and at that spot there was a clearing. The bay and the town lay far below them. The men had led them astray, either willfully or because they were not familiar with the paths. They were high up on the slope and far north of Gjeita Bridge, which Kristin could see. The road they had reached seemed to lead in that direction.

Then she stopped, took out her purse, and began to count out the ten *penninger* into her hand.

"Now, good sirs," she said, "we no longer need your escort. We know the way from here. We give you thanks for your trouble, and here is your payment, as we agreed. God be with you, good friends."

The men looked at each other for a moment, quite foolishly, so that Kristin was almost about to smile. But then one of them said with an ugly leer that the road down to the bridge was a desolate one; it would not be advisable for them to go alone.

"No one would be so malicious or so stupid as to want to stop two maidens, especially two dressed in convent attire," replied Kristin. "We prefer to go alone," and then she handed them the money.

The man grabbed hold of her wrist, stuck his face close to hers, and said something about a "Kuss" and a "Beutel." Kristin understood that they would be allowed to go unharmed if she would give him a kiss and her purse.

She remembered Bentein's face close to hers, just like this, and for a moment fear seized her; she felt nauseated and sick. But she pressed her lips together, calling upon God and the Virgin Mary in her heart—and at that moment she heard hoofbeats on the path coming from the north.

Then she struck the man in the face with her coin purse so that he stumbled, and she shoved him in the chest so that he toppled off the path and tumbled down into the woods. The other German grabbed her from behind, tore the purse out of her hand, and tugged at the chain around her neck, breaking it. She was just about to fall, but she seized hold of the man, attempting to get her cross back. He tried to pull away; the robber had now heard someone approaching too. Ingebjørg screamed loudly, and the horsemen on the path came racing as fast as they could. They emerged from the thickets; there were three of them. Ingebjørg ran toward them, shrieking, and they jumped down from their horses. Kristin recognized the gentleman from Didrek's loft; he drew his sword, grabbed the German she was struggling with by the scruff of his neck, and struck him with the flat of the blade. His men ran after the other one, seized him, and beat him with all their might.

Kristin leaned against the rock face. Now that it was over she was shaking, but what she felt most was astonishment that her prayer had been answered so quickly. Then she noticed Ingebjørg. The girl had thrown back her hood, letting her cloak fall loosely over her shoulders, and she was arranging her thick blonde braids on her breast. Kristin burst out laughing at the sight. She sank down and had to cling to a tree because she couldn't hold herself up; it was as if she had water instead of marrow in her bones, she felt so weak. She trembled and laughed and cried.

The gentleman came over to her and cautiously placed his hand on her shoulder.

"No doubt you have been more frightened than you dared show," he said, and his voice was pleasant and kind. "But now you must get hold of yourself; you acted so bravely while the danger lasted."

Kristin could only nod. He had beautiful bright eyes, a thin, tan face, and coal-black hair that was cropped short across his forehead and behind his ears.

Ingebjørg had managed to arrange her hair properly at last; she came over and thanked the stranger with many elegant words. He stood there with his hand on Kristin's shoulder as he spoke to the other maiden.

"We'll take these birds along to town so they can be thrown in the dungeon," he said to his men who were holding the two Germans, who said they belonged to the Rostock ship. "But first we must escort the maidens back to their convent. I'm sure you can find some straps to tie them up with. . . ."

"Do you mean the maidens, Erlend?" asked one of the men.

They were young, strong, and well-dressed boys, and they were both flushed after the fight.

Their master frowned and was about to give a sharp reply. But Kristin put her hand on his sleeve.

"Let them go, kind sir!" She gave a small shudder. "My sister and I would be most reluctant to have this matter talked about."

The stranger looked down at her, bit his lip, and nodded as he gazed at her. Then he gave each of the prisoners a blow on the back of the neck with the flat of his blade so that they fell forward. "Get going," he said, giving them a kick, and they took off as fast as they could. The gentleman turned back to the maidens and asked them if they would like to ride.

Ingebjørg allowed herself to be lifted up into Erlend's saddle, but it turned out that she couldn't stay in it; she slipped down again at once. He gave Kristin a questioning look, and she told him that she was used to riding a man's saddle.

He grasped her around the knees and lifted her up. She felt a thrill pass through her, sweet and good, because he held her away from himself so carefully, as if he were afraid to get too close to her. Back home they had never paid attention if they pressed her too close when they helped her onto her horse. She felt so strangely honored.

The knight—as Ingebjørg called him, even though he wore silver spurs[3]—offered the other maiden his hand, and his men leaped onto their horses. Ingebjørg now wanted them to go north, around the town and along the foot of the Ryen hills and the Marte outcrop, not through the streets. Her excuse was that Sir Erlend and his men were fully armed, weren't they? The knight replied somberly that the ban against bearing weapons was not so strictly enforced for those who were traveling, or for all the people in town who were now hunting wild beasts. Kristin realized full well that Ingebjørg wanted to take the longest and least traveled road in order to talk more with Erlend.

"This is the second time we have delayed you this evening, sir," said Ingebjørg.

Erlend replied gravely, "It doesn't matter; I'm going no farther than to Gerdarud tonight—and it stays light all night long."

Kristin was so pleased that he neither teased nor jested but spoke to her as he would to an equal, or more than that. She thought of Simon; she had never met any other young men of the courtly class. But this man was probably somewhat older than Simon.

They made their way down into the valley below the Ryen hills and up along the stream. The path was narrow, and the young leafy bushes flicked wet, fragrant branches at Kristin. It was a little darker down there, the air was chill, and the foliage was wet with dew along the streambed.

They moved slowly, and the hooves of the horses sounded muffled against the damp, grass-covered path. Kristin swayed in the saddle; behind her she could hear Ingebjørg talking, and the stranger's dark, calm voice. He didn't say much, answering as if preoccupied—as if he were feeling the same as she was, thought Kristin. She felt so strangely drowsy, but safe and content now that all the events of the day had slipped away.

It was like waking up as they emerged from the forest, out onto the slopes below the Marte outcrop. The sun had gone down and the town and the bay lay below them in clear, pallid light. The Aker ridges were limned with bright yellow beneath the pale blue sky. Sounds carried a long way in the quiet of the evening, as if they were coming from the depths of the cool air. From somewhere along the road came the screech of a wagon wheel, and dogs barked to each other from farms on opposite sides of the town. But in the forest behind them birds chirped and sang at the top of their voices now that the sun had gone down.

Smoke drifted through the air as dry grass and leaves were burned, and in the middle of a field a bonfire flared red; the great fiery rose made the clarity of the night seem dim.

They were riding between the fences of the convent's fields when the stranger spoke to Ingebjørg again. He asked her what she thought would be best: Should he escort her to the door and ask to speak with Fru Groa, so that he could tell her how this had all come about? But Ingebjørg thought they should sneak in through the church; then they might be able to slip into the convent without being noticed. They had been gone much too long. Perhaps Sister Potentia had forgotten them because of the visit from her kinsmen.

It didn't occur to Kristin to wonder why it was so quiet in the square in front of the west entrance of the church. Usually there was a great hubbub in the evening as people from the neighboring area came to the nuns' church. And all around stood houses where many of the lay servants and corrodians lived. This was where they said farewell to Erlend. Kristin paused to pet his horse; it was black, with a handsome head and gentle eyes. She thought it looked like Morvin, the horse she had ridden back home when she was a child.

"What's the name of your horse, sir?" she asked as the animal turned his head and snuffled at the man's chest.

"Bajard," he said, looking at Kristin over the horse's neck. "You ask the name of my horse, but not mine?"

"I would indeed like to know your name, sir," she replied, with a little bow.

"Erlend Nikulaussøn is my name," he said.

"Then we must thank you, Erlend Nikulaussøn, for your good assistance tonight," replied Kristin, giving him her hand.

Suddenly her face flushed bright red; she pulled her hand halfway out of his grasp.

"Fru Aashild Gautesdatter at Dovre—is she your kinswoman?" she asked.

She saw with surprise that he too turned blood red. He let go of her hand abruptly and replied, "She is my mother's sister. It's true that I am Erlend Nikulaussøn of Husaby." He gave Kristin such a strange look that she grew even more confused, but she pulled herself together.

"I should have thanked you with better words, Erlend Nikulaussøn, but I don't know what to say to you."

Then he bowed, and she thought she should say goodbye, even though she would have preferred to talk with him longer. At the entrance to the church she turned around, and when she saw that Erlend was still standing next to his horse, she raised her hand and waved.

Inside the convent great fear and commotion reigned. Haakon had sent a messenger home on horseback while he himself walked through the town searching for the maidens, and servants had been sent out to help him. The nuns had heard that the wild animals had supposedly killed and devoured two children in town. This turned out to be a rumor, and the leopard—there was only one—

had been captured well before vespers by several men from the king's castle.

Kristin stood with her head bowed and kept silent as the abbess and Sister Potentia vented their anger on the maidens. She seemed to be asleep inside. Ingebjørg wept and spoke in their defense: they had gone out with Sister Potentia's permission, after all, with the proper escort, and they were not to blame for what had happened afterward.

But Fru Groa told them to stay in the church until the clock struck midnight and try to turn their thoughts to spiritual matters and thank God, who had saved their lives and honor. "God has clearly shown you the truth about the world," she said. "Wild beasts and the Devil's servants threaten His children every step of the way, and there is no salvation unless you cleave to Him with entreaties and prayers."

She gave each of them a lit candle and told them to go with Sister Cecilia Baardsdatter, who often sat in the church alone, praying into the night.

Kristin placed her candle on the altar of Saint Laurentius and knelt down on the prayer bench. She stared steadily into the flame as she said her *Pater noster* and *Ave Maria*. Gradually the glow of the taper seemed to envelop her, shutting out everything else surrounding her and the candle. She felt her heart open up, brimming over with gratitude and promises and love for God and His gentle Mother—she felt them so near. She had always known that they saw her, but on this night she *felt* that it was so. She saw the world as if in a vision: a dark room into which a beam of sunlight fell, with dust motes tumbling in and out, from darkness to light, and she felt that now she had finally moved into the sunbeam.

She thought she would gladly have stayed in the quiet night-dark church forever—with the few tiny specks of light like golden stars in the night, the sweet fragrance of old incense, and the warm smell of burning wax. With herself resting inside her own star.

This sense of joy seemed to vanish when Sister Cecilia silently approached and touched her shoulder. Curtseying before the altar, the three women slipped out of the small south entrance into the convent courtyard.

Ingebjørg was so sleepy that she got into bed without talking.

Kristin was relieved; she was reluctant to be disturbed, now that she was thinking so clearly. And she was glad they had to keep their shifts on at night—Ingebjørg was so fat and sweated heavily.

Kristin lay awake for a long time, but the deep current of sweetness which had borne her as she knelt in the church would not return. And yet she still felt its warmth inside her; she fervently thanked God, and she sensed a feeling of strength in her spirit as she prayed for her parents and her sisters and for the soul of Arne Gyrdsøn.

Father, she thought. She felt such a longing for him, for all they had had together before Simon Darre had entered their lives. A new tenderness for Lavrans welled up inside her, as if there were a presentiment of maternal love and maternal sorrows in her love for her father that night. She was dimly aware that there was much in life that he had not received. She thought of the old black wooden church at Gerdarud, where at Eastertide she had seen the graves of her three little brothers and her grandmother—her father's own mother, Kristin Sigurdsdatter—who had died as she gave birth to him.

What could Erlend Nikulaussøn be doing at Gerdarud? She could not fathom it.

She wasn't conscious of giving any more thought to him that night, but the whole time the memory of his thin, dark face and his quiet voice had hovered somewhere in the shadows, just beyond the radiance of her soul.

When Kristin woke up the next morning, the sun was shining in the dormitory, and Ingebjørg told her that Fru Groa herself had sent word to the lay sisters that they should not be awakened for matins. They had permission to go over to the cookhouse now to have some food. Kristin felt warm with joy at the kindness of the abbess. It was as if the whole world had been good to her.

## CHAPTER 3

THE FARMERS' GUILD at Aker was dedicated to Saint Margareta, and every year began its meeting on the twentieth of July, which was Saint Margareta's Day. On that day the brothers and sisters would gather with their children, guests, and servants at Aker Church to attend mass at the Saint Margareta altar. Afterward they would go to the guild hall, which stood near Hofvin Hospice; there they would drink for five days.

But because both Aker Church and Hofvin Hospice belonged to Nonneseter, and since many of the Aker peasants were tenant farmers of the convent, the custom had arisen for the abbess and several of the eldest sisters to honor the guild by attending the celebrations on the first day. And the young maidens of the convent who were there to be educated but who were not going to enter the order were allowed to go along and dance in the evening; and for this celebration they would wear their own clothes and not their convent attire.

So there was a great commotion in the young novices' dormitory on the evening before Saint Margareta's Day. Those maidens who were to attend the banquet rummaged through their chests and laid out their finery, while the others looked on and moped. Some of the girls had set small pots on the hearth and were boiling water to make their skin soft and white. Others were brewing something that they rubbed in their hair; afterward, when they had wound strands of their hair tightly around leather straps, they would have wavy and curly tresses.

Ingebjørg took out all that she owned of finery, but she couldn't decide what to wear. Not her best leaf-green velvet dress, anyway; it was too costly and too elegant to wear to such a farmers' guild. But a thin little maiden who was not going along—Helga was her name, and she had been given to the convent as a child—pulled

Kristin aside and whispered that Ingebjørg would of course wear the green dress and her pink silk shift.

"You've always been kind to me, Kristin," said Helga. "It's most improper for me to get involved in such things, but I'm going to tell you anyway. The knight who escorted you home on that evening in the spring—I have both seen and heard that Ingebjørg has talked to him since then. They have spoken to each other in church, and he has waited for her up along the fenced road when she goes to visit Ingunn at the corrodians' house. But it's you that he asks for, and Ingebjørg has promised to bring you out there with her. I'll wager that you've never heard about this before, have you?"

"It's true that Ingebjørg has never mentioned this to me," said Kristin. She pursed her lips so the other maiden wouldn't see the smile that threatened to appear. So that's the kind of girl Ingebjørg was. "I expect she realizes that I'm not the type to run off to meetings with strange men behind house corners and fences," she said haughtily.

"Then I could have spared myself the trouble to tell you this news, since it would have been more proper for me not to mention it," said Helga, offended; and the two parted.

But all evening Kristin had to try not to smile whenever anyone looked at her.

The next day Ingebjørg dawdled for a long time, wearing only her shift. Kristin finally realized that the other maiden was not going to get dressed until she herself was done.

Kristin didn't say a word, but she laughed as she went over to her chest and took out her golden-yellow silk shift. She had never worn it before, and it felt so soft and cool as it slid over her body. It was beautifully trimmed with silver and blue and brown silk at the neck and across the part of the bodice that would be visible above the neckline of her dress. There were also matching sleeves. She pulled on her linen stockings and tied the ribbons of the dainty blue-violet shoes, which Haakon had fortunately managed to bring home on that tumultuous day. Ingebjørg looked at her.

Then Kristin laughed and said, "My father has always taught me that we should not show contempt for our inferiors, but you are no doubt so grand that you won't want to dress up for peasants and tenant farmers."

Her face as red as a berry, Ingebjørg dropped the woolen shift from her white hips and put on the pink silk one. Kristin slipped her best velvet dress over her head; it was violet-blue and cut deep across the bodice, with slit sleeves and cuffs that trailed almost to the ground. She wrapped the gilded belt around her waist and slung her gray squirrel cloak over her shoulders. Then she spread out her thick blond hair over her shoulders and placed the circlet studded with roses on her forehead.

She noticed that Helga was watching them. Then she took from her chest a large silver clasp. It was the one she had worn on her cloak the night that Bentein had confronted her on the road, and she had never wanted to wear it since. She went over to Helga and said softly, "I realize that you meant to show me kindness yesterday; you must believe I know that." And she handed the clasp to Helga.

Ingebjørg was also quite beautiful when she had finished dressing, wearing her green gown with a red silk cloak over her shoulders and her pretty, curly hair falling loose. They had been in a race to outdress each other, thought Kristin and laughed.

The morning was cool and fresh with dew when the procession wound its way from Nonneseter, heading west toward Frysja. The haying season was almost over in that area, but along the fences grew clusters of bluebells and golden Maria-grass. The barley in the fields had sprouted spikes and rippled pale silver with a sheen of faint rose. In many places where the path was narrow and led through the fields, the grain brushed against people's knees.

Haakon walked in front, carrying the convent's banner with the image of the Virgin Mary on blue silk cloth. Behind him walked the servants and corrodians, and then came Fru Groa and four old nuns on horseback, followed by the young maidens on foot; their colorful, secular feast attire shimmered and fluttered in the sun. Several corrodian women and a few armed men brought up the rear of the procession.

They sang as they walked across the bright meadows, and whenever they met others on the side roads, the people would step aside and greet them respectfully. All across the fields small groups of people were walking and riding, heading toward the church from every house and farm. In a little while they heard behind them hymns sung by deep male voices, and they saw the cloister banner from Hovedø rise up over a hill. The red silk cloth gleamed in the sun, bobbing and swaying with the footsteps of the man who was bearing it.

The mighty, sonorous voice of the bells drowned out the neighs and whinnies of the stallions as they came over the last hill to the church. Kristin had never seen so many horses at one time—a surging, restless sea of glossy equine backs surrounded the green in front of the entrance to the church. People dressed for the celebration were standing, sitting, and lying on the slope, but everyone stood up in greeting when the Maria banner from Nonneseter was carried in amongst them, and they all bowed deeply to Fru Groa.

It looked as if more people had come than the church could hold, but an open space closest to the altar had been reserved for the people from the convent. A moment later the Cistercian monks from Hovedø came in and went up to the choir, and then song resounded throughout the church from the throats of men and boys.

During the mass, when everyone had risen, Kristin caught sight of Erlend Nikulaussøn. He was tall, and his head towered above those around him. She saw his face from the side. He had a high, narrow forehead and a large, straight nose; it jutted out like a triangle from his face and was strangely thin, with fine, quivering nostrils. There was something about it that reminded Kristin of a skittish, frightened stallion. He was not as handsome as she thought she had remembered him; the lines in his face seemed to extend so long and somberly down to his soft, small, attractive mouth—oh yes, he was handsome after all.

He turned his head and saw her. She didn't know how long they continued to stare into each other's eyes. Then her only thought was for the mass to be over; she waited expectantly to see what would happen next.

As everyone began to leave the crowded church, there was a great crush. Ingebjørg pulled Kristin along with her, backward into the throng; they were easily separated from the nuns, who were the first to leave. The girls were among the last to approach the altar with their offering and then exit from the church.

Erlend was standing outside, right next to the door, between the priest from Gerdarud and a stout, red-faced man wearing a magnificent blue velvet surcoat. Erlend was dressed in silk but in dark colors—a long, brown-and-black patterned surcoat and a black cape interwoven with little yellow falcons.

They greeted each other and walked across the slope toward the spot where the men's horses were tethered. As they exchanged words about the weather, the beautiful mass, and the great crowd of people in attendance, the fat, ruddy-faced gentleman—he wore golden spurs and his name was Sir Munan Baardsøn—offered his hand to Ingebjørg. He seemed to find the maiden exceedingly attractive. Erlend and Kristin fell behind; they walked along in silence.

There was a great hubbub on the church hill as people began to ride off. Horses jostled past each other and people shouted, some of them angry, some of them laughing. Many of them rode in pairs—men with their wives behind them or children in front on the saddle—and young boys leaped up to ride with a friend. They could already see the church banners, the nuns, and the priest far below them.

Sir Munan rode past; Ingebjørg was sitting in front of him, in his arms. They both shouted and waved.

Then Erlend said, "My men are both here with me. They could take one of the horses and you could have Haftor's—if you would prefer that?"

Kristin blushed as she replied, "We're so far behind the others already, and I don't see your men, so . . ." Then she laughed and Erlend smiled.

He leaped into the saddle and helped her up behind him. At home Kristin often sat sideways behind her father after she grew too old to sit astride the horse's loins. And yet she felt a little shy and uncertain as she placed one of her hands over Erlend's shoulder; with the other hand she supported herself against the horse's back. Slowly they rode down toward the bridge.

After a while Kristin felt that she ought to speak since he did not, and she said, "It was unexpected, sir, to meet you here today."

"Was it unexpected?" asked Erlend, turning his head around toward her. "Hasn't Ingebjørg Filippusdatter brought you my greeting?"

"No," said Kristin. "I haven't heard of any greeting. She has never mentioned you since that day when you came to our aid back in May," she said slyly. She wanted Ingebjørg's duplicity to come to light.

Erlend didn't turn around, but she could hear in his voice that he was smiling when he spoke again.

"And what about the little black-haired one—the novitiate—I can't remember her name. I even paid her a messenger's fee to give you my greetings."

Kristin blushed, but then she had to laugh. "Yes, I suppose I owe it to Helga to tell you that she earned her pay," she said.

Erlend moved his head slightly, and his neck came close to her hand. Kristin shifted her hand at once to a place farther out on his shoulder. Rather uneasy, she thought that perhaps she had shown greater boldness than was proper, since she had come to this feast after a man had, in a sense, arranged to meet her there.

After a moment Erlend asked, "Will you dance with me tonight, Kristin?"

"I don't know, sir," replied the maiden.

"Perhaps you think it might not be proper?" he asked. When she didn't answer, he went on. "It could be that it's not. But I thought perhaps you might not think it would do any harm if you took my hand tonight. And by the way, it has been eight years since I took part in a dance."

"Why is that, sir?" asked Kristin. "Is it because you are married?" But then it occurred to her that if he were a married man, it would not have been seemly for him to arrange this rendezvous with her. So she corrected herself and said, "Perhaps you have lost your betrothed or your wife?"

Erlend turned around abruptly and gave her a peculiar look.

"Me? Hasn't Fru Aashild . . ." After a moment he asked, "Why did you blush when you heard who I was that evening?"

Kristin blushed again but did not reply.

Then Erlend went on. "I would like to know what my aunt has told you about me."

"Nothing more than that she praised you," said Kristin hastily. "She said you were handsome and so highborn that . . . she said that compared to a lineage such as yours and hers, we were of little consequence, my ancestors and I."

"Is she still talking about such things, there, where she now resides?" said Erlend with a bitter laugh. "Well, well, if it comforts her . . . And she has said nothing else about me?"

"What else would she say?" asked Kristin. She didn't know why she felt so strange and anxious.

"Oh, she might have said . . . ," replied Erlend in a low voice, his head bowed, "she might have said that I had been excommunicated and had to pay dearly for peace and reconciliation."

Kristin said nothing for a long time. Then she said quietly, "I've heard it said that there are many men who are not masters of their fortunes. I've seen so little of the world. But I would never believe of you, Erlend, that it was for any . . . ignoble . . . matter."

"God bless you for such words, Kristin," said Erlend. He bent his head and kissed her wrist so fervently that the horse gave a start beneath them. When the animal was once again walking calmly, he said with great ardor, "Won't you dance with me tonight, Kristin? Later I'll tell you everything about my circumstances—but tonight let's be happy together."

Kristin agreed, and they rode for a while in silence.

But a short time later Erlend began asking about Fru Aashild, and Kristin told him everything she knew; she had much praise for her.

"Then all doors are not closed to Bjørn and Aashild?" asked Erlend.

Kristin replied that they were well liked and that her father and many others thought that most of what had been said of the couple was untrue.

"What did you think of my kinsman, Munan Baardsøn?" asked Erlend with a chuckle.

"I didn't pay much heed to him," said Kristin, "and it didn't seem to me that he was much worth looking at anyway."

"Didn't you know that he's her son?" asked Erlend.

"Fru Aashild's son?" said Kristin in astonishment.

"Yes, the children couldn't take their mother's fair looks, since they took everything else," said Erlend.

"I didn't even know the name of her first husband," said Kristin.

"They were two brothers who married two sisters," said Erlend. "Baard and Nikulaus Munansøn. My father was the older one; Mother was his second wife, but he had no children by his first wife. Baard, who married Aashild, wasn't a young man either, and apparently they never got on well. I was a child when it all happened, and they kept as much from me as they could. But she left the country with Herr Bjørn and married him without the counsel of her kinsmen—after Baard was dead. Then people wanted to annul their marriage. They claimed that Bjørn had slept with her while her first husband was still alive and that they conspired together to get rid of my father's brother. But they couldn't find any proof of this, and they had to let the marriage stand. But they had to give up all their possessions. Bjørn had killed their nephew too—the nephew of my mother and Aashild, I mean."

Kristin's heart was pounding. At home her parents had taken strict precautions to keep the children from hearing impure talk. But things had occurred in their village, too, that Kristin had heard about—a man who lived in concubinage with a married woman. That was adultery, one of the worst of sins. They were also to blame for the husband's violent death, and then it was a case for excommunication and banishment. Lavrans had said that no woman had to stay with her husband if he had been with another man's wife. And the lot of offspring from adultery could never be improved, even if the parents were later free to marry. A man could pass on his inheritance and name to his child by a prostitute or a wandering beggar woman, but not to his child from adultery—not even if the mother was the wife of a knight.

Kristin thought about the dislike she had always felt toward Herr Bjørn, with his pallid face and his slack, corpulent body. She couldn't understand how Fru Aashild could always be so kind and amenable toward the man who had lured her into such shame; to think that such a gracious woman could have allowed herself to be fooled by him. He was not even nice to her; he let her toil with all the work on the farm. Bjørn did nothing but drink ale. And yet Aashild was always so gentle and tender when she spoke to her husband. Kristin wondered whether her father knew about this, since he had invited Herr Bjørn into their house. Now that she thought about it, it seemed odd to her that Erlend would speak in this manner of his close kinsmen. But he probably thought that she knew about it already.

"It would please me," said Erlend after a moment, "to visit her, my Aunt Aashild, sometime—when I journey north. But is he still a handsome man, my kinsman Bjørn?"

"No," said Kristin. "He looks like a mound of hay that has lain on the ground all winter long."

"Ah yes, it must wear on a man," said Erlend with the same bitter smile. "Never have I seen a more handsome man—that was twenty years ago, and I was only a small boy back then—but I have never seen his equal."

A short time later they reached the hospice. It was an enormous and grand estate with many buildings of both stone and wood: a hospital, an almshouse, a guest inn for travelers, the chapel, and the rectory. There was a great tumult in the courtyard, for food was being prepared for the banquet in the hospice's cookhouse, and the poor and the sick guild members were also to be served the very best on that day.

The guild hall was beyond the gardens of the hospice, and people were heading that way through the herb garden, for it was quite famous. Fru Groa had brought in plants that no one in Norway had ever heard of before and, besides that, all the plants that usually grew in such gardens seemed to thrive better in hers—flowers and cooking herbs and medicinal herbs. She was the most skilled woman in all such matters, and she had even translated herbals from Salerno into the Norwegian language. Fru Groa had been particularly friendly toward Kristin ever since she noticed that the maiden knew something of the art of herbs and wanted to know more about it.

So Kristin pointed out to Erlend what plants were growing in the beds on both sides of the green lane as they walked. In the noonday sun there was a hot, spicy fragrance of dill and celery, onions and roses, southernwood and wallflowers. Beyond the shadeless, sun-baked herb garden, the rows of fruit trees looked enticingly cool; red cherries gleamed in the dark foliage, and apple trees bowed their branches, weighted down by green fruit.

Surrounding the garden was a hedge of sweetbriar. There were still some roses left—they looked no different from other hedge roses, but the petals smelled of wine and apples in the heat of the sun. People broke off twigs and pinned them to their clothing as they passed. Kristin picked several roses too, tucking them into the circlet at her temples. She held one in her hand, and after a moment

Erlend took it from her, without saying a word. He carried it for a while and then stuck it into the filigree brooch on his chest. He looked self-conscious and embarrassed, and did it so clumsily that he scratched his fingers and drew blood.

In the banquet loft several wide tables had been set up: one for the men and one for the women along the walls. In the middle of the floor there were two tables where the children and the young people sat together.

At the women's table Fru Groa sat in the high seat; the nuns and most of the wives of high standing sat along the wall, and the unmarried women sat on the opposite bench, with the maidens from Nonneseter closest to the head of the table. Kristin knew that Erlend was looking at her, but she didn't dare turn her head even once, either when they were standing or after they sat down. Not until they rose and the priest began to read the names of the deceased guild brothers and sisters did she cast a hasty glance toward the men's table. She caught a glimpse of him as he stood near the wall, behind the burning candle on the table. He was looking at her.

The meal lasted a long time with all of the toasts in honor of God, the Virgin Mary, and Saint Margareta, Saint Olav, and Saint Halvard, interspersed with prayers and hymns.

Kristin could see through the open door that the sun had gone down; the sound of fiddles and songs could be heard from out on the green, and the young people had already left the tables when Fru Groa said to the young daughters that now they might go out to play for a while, if they so pleased.

Three red bonfires were burning on the green; around them moved the chains of dancers, now aglow, now in silhouette. The fiddlers were sitting on stacks of chests, bowing the strings of their instruments; they were playing and singing a different tune in each circle. There were far too many people to form only one dance. It was nearly dusk already; to the north the crest of the forested ridges stood coal-black against the yellowish green sky.

People were sitting under the gallery of the loft, drinking. Several men leaped up as soon as the six maidens from Nonneseter came down the stairs. Munan Baardsøn ran up to Ingebjørg and dashed off with her, and Kristin was seized by the wrist—it was Erlend; she already knew his touch. He gripped her hand so tightly that their rings scraped against each other and bit into their flesh.

He pulled her along to the farthest bonfire, where many children were dancing. Kristin took a twelve-year-old boy by the hand, and Erlend had a tiny, half-grown maiden on his other side.

No one was singing in their circle just then—they walked and swayed from side to side, in time with the sound of the fiddle. Then someone shouted that Sivord the Dane should sing a new ballad for them. A tall, fair man with enormous fists stepped in front of the chain of dancers and performed his song:

They are dancing now at Munkholm
across the white sand.
There dances Ivar Herr Jonsøn
taking the Queen's hand.
Do you know Ivar Herr Jonsøn?

The fiddle players didn't know the tune; they plucked a little on the strings, and the Dane sang alone. He had a beautiful, strong voice.

Do you remember, Danish Queen,
that summer so clear
when you were led out of Sweden
and to Denmark here.

When you were led out of Sweden
and to Denmark here
with a golden crown so red
and on your cheek a tear.

With a golden crown so red
and on your cheek a tear.
Do you remember, Danish Queen,
the first man you held dear!

The fiddlers played along once more, and the dancers hummed the newly learned tune and joined in with the refrain.

And are you, Ivar Herr Jonsøn,
my very own man,
then tomorrow from the gallows
you shall surely hang!

And it was Ivar Herr Jonsøn
but he did not quail,
he sprang into the golden boat,
clad in coat of mail.

May you be granted, Danish Queen,
as many good nights
as do fill the vault of heaven
all the stars so bright.

May you be granted, Danish King,
life so fraught with cares
as the linden tree has leaves
and the hart has hairs.
Do you know Ivar Herr Jonsøn?

It was late at night, and the bonfires were mere mounds of glowing embers that grew dimmer and dimmer. Kristin and Erlend stood hand in hand beneath the trees by the garden fence. Behind them the noise of the revelers had died out; a few young boys were humming and leaping around the ember mounds, but the fiddlers had gone off to bed and most of the people had left. Here and there a woman walked around in search of her husband, toppled by ale somewhere outdoors.

"I wonder where I've left my cloak," whispered Kristin. Erlend put his arm around her waist and wrapped his cape around both of them. Walking close together, they went into the herb garden.

A remnant of the day's hot, spicy scent wafted toward them, muted and damp with the coolness of the dew. The night was quite dark, the sky hazy gray with clouds above the treetops. But they sensed that others were in the garden.

Erlend pressed the maiden to him once and asked in a whisper, "You're not afraid, are you Kristin?"

Suddenly she vaguely remembered the world outside this night —it was madness. But she was so blissfully robbed of all power. She leaned closer to the man and whispered faintly; she didn't know herself what she said.

They reached the end of the path; there was a stone fence along the edge of the woods. Erlend helped her up. As she was about to jump down to the other side, he caught her and held her in his arms for a moment before he set her down in the grass.

She stood there with her face raised and received his kiss. He placed his hands at her temples. She thought it so wonderful to feel his fingers sinking into her hair, and then she put her hands up to his face and tried to kiss him the way he had kissed her.

When he placed his hands on her bodice and stroked her breasts, she felt as if he had laid her heart bare and then seized it; gently he parted the folds of her silk shift and kissed the place in between—heat rushed to the roots of her heart.

"You I could never hurt," whispered Erlend. "Don't ever weep a single tear for my sake. I never thought a maiden could be as good as you are, my Kristin. . . ."

He pulled her down into the grass under the bushes; they sat with their backs against the stone fence. Kristin said not a word, but when he stopped caressing her, she raised her hand and touched his face.

After a moment Erlend asked, "Are you tired, dear Kristin?" And when she leaned against his chest, he wrapped his arms around her and whispered, "Sleep, Kristin, sleep here with me."

She slipped deeper and deeper into the darkness and the warmth and the joy at his chest.

When she woke up, she was lying stretched out on the grass with her cheek against the brown silk of his lap. Erlend was still sitting with his back against the stone fence; his face was gray in the gray light, but his wide-open eyes were so strangely bright and beautiful. She saw that he had wrapped his cape all around her; her feet were wonderfully warm inside the fur lining.

"Now you have slept on my lap," he said, smiling faintly. "May God reward you, Kristin. You slept as soundly as a child in her mother's arms."

"Haven't you slept, Herr Erlend?" asked Kristin, and he smiled down into her newly awakened eyes.

"Perhaps someday the night will come when you and I dare to fall asleep together—I don't know what you will think once you have considered that. I have kept vigil here in the night. There is still so much between us, more than if a naked sword had lain between you and me. Tell me, will you have affection for me after this night is over?"

"I will have affection for you, Herr Erlend," said Kristin. "I will have affection for you as long as you wish—and after that I will love no one else."

"Then may God forsake me," said Erlend slowly, "if ever a woman or maiden should come into my arms before I dare to possess you with honor and in keeping with the law. Repeat what I have said," he implored her.

Kristin said, "May God forsake me if I ever take any other man into my arms, for as long as I live on this earth."

"We must go now," said Erlend after a moment. "Before everyone wakes up."

They walked along the outside of the stone fence, through the underbrush.

"Have you given any thought to what should happen next?" asked Erlend.

"You must decide that, Erlend," replied Kristin.

"Your father," he said after a pause. "Over in Gerdarud they say that he's a kind and just man. Do you think he would be greatly opposed to breaking the agreement he has made with Andres Darre?"

"Father has so often said that he would never force any of his daughters," said Kristin. "The main concern is that our lands would fit so well together. But I'm certain that Father would not want me to lose all joy in the world for that reason." She had a sudden inkling that it might not be quite as simple as that, but she pushed it aside.

"Then maybe this will be easier than I thought last night," said Erlend. "God help me, Kristin—I can't bear to lose you. Now I will never be happy if I can't have you."

They parted among the trees, and in the dim light of dawn Kristin found the path to the guest house where everyone from Nonneseter was sleeping. All the beds were full, but she threw her cloak over some straw on the floor and lay down in her clothes.

When she woke up, it was quite late. Ingebjørg Filippusdatter was sitting on a bench nearby, mending a fur border that had torn loose from her cloak. She was full of chatter, as always.

"Were you with Erlend Nikulaussøn all night long?" she asked. "You ought to be a little more careful about that young man, Kristin. Do you think Simon Andressøn would like it if you befriended him?"

Kristin found a basin and began to wash herself. "And what about your betrothed? Do you think he would like it that you danced with Munan the Stump last night? But we have to dance with anyone who invites us on such an evening; and Fru Groa gave us permission, after all."

Ingebjørg exclaimed, "Einar Einarssøn and Sir Munan are friends, and besides, he's married and old. And he's ugly too, but amiable and courteous. Look what he gave me as a souvenir of the night." And she held out a gold buckle which Kristin had seen on Sir Munan's hat the day before. "But that Erlend—well, the ban was lifted from him this past Easter, but they say that Eline Ormsdatter has been staying at his manor at Husaby ever since. Sir Munan says that he has fled to Sira Jon at Gerdarud because he's afraid that he'll fall back into sin if he sees her again."

Kristin, her face white, went over to the other girl.

"Didn't you know that?" asked Ingebjørg. "That he lured a woman from her husband somewhere up north in Haalogaland? And that he kept her at his estate in spite of the king's warning and the archbishop's ban? They have two children together too. He had to flee to Sweden, and he has had to pay so many fines that Sir Munan says he'll end up a pauper if he doesn't mend his ways soon."

"Oh yes, you can be sure that I knew all about it," said Kristin, her face rigid. "But that's all over now."

"Yes, that's what Sir Munan said, that it's been over between them so many times before," replied Ingebjørg thoughtfully. "It won't affect you—you're going to marry Simon Darre, after all. But that Erlend Nikulaussøn is certainly a handsome man."

The company from Nonneseter was going to leave that same day, after the midafternoon prayers. Kristin had promised Erlend to meet him at the stone fence where they had sat during the night, if she could find a way to come.

He was lying on his stomach in the grass, with his head on his arms. As soon as he saw her, he leaped up and offered her both of his hands as she was about to jump down.

She took them, and they stood for a moment, hand in hand.

Then Kristin said, "Why did you tell me that story about Herr Bjørn and Fru Aashild yesterday?"

"I can see that you know," replied Erlend, abruptly letting go of her hands. "What do you think of me now, Kristin?

"I was eighteen years old back then," he continued vehemently. "It was ten years ago that the king, my kinsman, sent me on the journey to Vargøy House, and then we spent the winter at Steigen. She was married to the judge Sigurd Saksulvsøn. I felt sorry for her because he was old and unbelievably ugly. I don't know how it happened; yes, I was fond of her too. I told Sigurd to demand what he wanted in fines; I wanted to do right by him—he's a decent man in many ways—but he wanted things to proceed according to the law, and he took the case to the *ting*. I was to be branded for adultery with the woman in whose house I had been a guest, you see.

"My father got wind of it, and then King Haakon found out too. And he . . . he banished me from his court. And if you need to know the whole story: there's nothing left between Eline and me except the children, and she cares very little for them. They're at Østerdal, on a farm that I own there. I've given the farm to Orm, the boy. But she doesn't want to be with them. I suppose she expects that Sigurd can't live forever, but I don't know what she wants.

"Sigurd took her back, but she says she was treated like a dog and a slave on his farm. So she asked me to meet her in Nidaros. I was not faring much better at Husaby with my father. I sold everything I could get my hands on and fled with her to Halland; Count Jacob has been a kind friend to me. What else could I do? She was carrying my child. I knew that so many men had managed to escape unscathed from such a relationship with another man's wife—if they were rich, that is. But King Haakon is the sort of man who treats his own most sternly. We were separated from each other for a year, but then my father died, so she came back.

And then other things happened. My tenants refused to pay their land rent or to speak to my envoys because I had been excommunicated. I retaliated harshly, and then a case was brought against me for robbery, but I had no money to pay my house servants. You can see that I was too young to deal sensibly with these difficulties, and my kinsmen refused to help me—except for Munan, who did as much as he dared without angering his wife.

"So now you know, Kristin, that I have compromised much, both my land and my honor. You would certainly be much better served if you stayed with Simon Andressøn."

Kristin put her arms around his neck.

"We will stand by what we swore to each other last night, Erlend—if you feel as I do."

Erlend pulled her close, kissed her, and then said, "You must also have faith that my circumstances are bound to change. Now no one in the world has power over me except you. Oh, I thought about so many things last night as you lay asleep in my lap, my fair one. The Devil cannot have so much power over a man that I would ever cause you sorrow or harm, you who are the most precious thing in my life."

## CHAPTER 4

DURING THE TIME he lived at Skog, Lavrans Bjørgulfsøn had given property to Gerdarud Church for requiems to be held for the souls of his parents on the anniversaries of their deaths. His father Bjørgulf Ketilsøn's death date was the thirteenth of August, and this year Lavrans had made arrangements for his brother to bring Kristin out to his estate so that she could attend the mass.

She was afraid that something might happen to prevent her uncle from keeping his promise. She thought she had noticed that Aasmund was not particularly fond of her. But on the day before the mass was to be held, Aasmund Bjørgulfsøn arrived at the convent to get his niece. Kristin was told to dress in secular attire, but dark and simple in appearance. People had begun to remark that the sisters of Nonneseter spent a great deal of time outside the convent, and the bishop had therefore decreed that the young daughters who were not to become nuns should not wear anything resembling convent garb when they went to visit their kinsmen—then the populace would not mistake them for novices or nuns of the order.

Kristin was in a joyous mood as she rode along the road with her uncle, and Aasmund became more cheerful and friendly toward her when he noticed that the maiden was an affable companion. Otherwise, Aasmund was rather dejected; he said it seemed likely that a campaign[1] was about to be launched in the fall and that the king would sail with his army to Sweden to avenge the vile deed that had been perpetrated against his brother-in-law and his niece's husband. Kristin had heard about the murder of the Swedish dukes and thought it an act of the worst cowardice, although all such affairs of the realm seemed so distant to her. No one talked much about such things back home in the valley. But she also remembered that her father had participated in the campaign against

Duke Eirik at Ragnhildarholm and Konungahella. Aasmund explained everything that had happened between the king and the dukes. Kristin didn't understand much of what he said, but she paid close attention to what her uncle told her about the betrothals that had been agreed upon and then broken by the king's daughters. It gave her some comfort to hear that it was not the same in all places as it was back home in the villages, where an arranged betrothal was considered almost as binding as a marriage. So she gathered her courage, told her uncle about her adventures on the evening before the Vigil of Saint Halvard, and asked him whether he knew Erlend of Husaby. Aasmund gave Erlend a good report, saying that he had acted unwisely, but that his father and the king were mostly to blame. He said they had behaved as if the boy had been the horn of the Devil himself because he had landed in such a predicament. The king was much too pious, and Sir Nikulaus was angry because Erlend had wasted so much good property, so they had both thundered about adultery and the fires of hell.

"Any able-bodied young man has to have a certain amount of defiance in him," said Aasmund Bjørgulfsøn. "And the woman was exceedingly beautiful. But you have no reason to have anything to do with Erlend, so pay no heed to his affairs."

Erlend did not attend the mass as he had promised Kristin he would, and she thought more about this than about the word of God. But she felt no remorse over it. She merely had the odd feeling of being a stranger to everything to which she had previously felt herself bound.

She tried to console herself; Erlend probably thought it best that no one who had authority over her should find out about their friendship. She could understand this herself. But she had longed to see him with all her heart, and she wept when she went to bed that evening in the loft where she slept with Aasmund's small daughters.

The next day she headed up toward the woods with the youngest of her uncle's children, a little maiden six years old. When they had gone some distance, Erlend came running after them. Kristin knew who it was before she even saw him.

"I've been sitting up here on the hill looking down at the farmyard all day long," he said. "I was sure that you'd find some chance to slip away."

"Do you think I've come out here to meet you?" said Kristin with a laugh. "And aren't you afraid to be wandering in my uncle's woods with your dogs and bow?"

"Your uncle has given me permission to hunt here for a short time," said Erlend. "And the dogs belong to Aasmund—they found me up here this morning." He patted the dogs and picked up the little girl. "You remember me, don't you, Ragndid? But you mustn't say that you've talked to me, and then I'll give you this." He took out a little bundle of raisins and handed it to the child. "I had intended it for you," he told Kristin. "Do you think this child can keep quiet?"

Both of them spoke quickly and laughed. Erlend was wearing a short, snug brown tunic, and he had a small red silk cap pressed down onto his black hair; he looked so young. He laughed and played with the child, but every once in a while he would take Kristin's hand, squeezing it so hard it hurt.

He talked about the rumors of the campaign with joy. "Then it will be easier for me to win back the friendship of the king. Everything will be easier then," he said fervently.

At last they sat down in a meadow some distance up in the woods. Erlend had the child on his lap. Kristin sat at his side. He was playing with her fingers in the grass. He put into her hand three gold rings tied together with a string.

"Later on," he whispered to her, "you shall have as many as you can fit on your fingers.

"I'll wait for you here in this field every day at this time, for as long as you are at Skog," he said as they parted. "Come when you can."

The next day Aasmund Bjørgulfsøn, along with his wife and children, left for Gyrid's ancestral estate at Hadeland. They had become alarmed by the rumors of the campaign. The people around Oslo were still filled with terror ever since Duke Eirik's devastating incursion[2] into the region some years before. Aasmund's old mother was so frightened that she decided to seek refuge at Nonneseter; she was too frail to travel with the others. So Kristin would stay at Skog with the old woman, whom she called Grandmother, until Aasmund returned from Hadeland.

Around noontime, when the servants on the farm were resting, Kristin went up to the loft where she slept. She had brought along some clothing in a leather bag, and she hummed as she changed her clothes.

Her father had given her a dress made of thick cotton fabric from the East; it was sky-blue with an intricate red flower pattern. This is what she put on. She brushed and combed out her hair, tying it back from her face with red silk ribbons. She wrapped a red silk belt tightly around her waist and slipped Erlend's rings onto her fingers, all the while wondering whether he would find her beautiful.

She had let the two dogs that had been up in the forest with Erlend sleep in the loft with her at night. Now she enticed them to come with her. She sneaked around the buildings and took the same path up through the outlying fields that she had used the day before.

The forest meadow lay empty and still in the glare of the noonday sun. There was a hot fragrance coming from the spruce trees that surrounded it on all sides. The blazing sun and the blue sky seemed strangely close and harsh against the treetops.

Kristin sat down in the shade at the edge of the clearing. She wasn't disappointed at Erlend's absence. She was sure that he would come, and she felt a peculiar joy at being allowed to sit there alone, the first to arrive.

She listened to the soft buzz of insects across the yellow, scorched grass. She plucked off several dry, spice-scented flowers that she could reach without moving more than her hand. She twirled them between her fingers and sniffed at them; with her eyes wide open she sank into a kind of trance.

She didn't move when she heard a horse approaching from the forest. The dogs growled and raised their hackles; then they bounded up across the meadow, barking and wagging their tails. Erlend jumped down from his horse at the edge of the forest and let it go with a slap on its loins. Then he ran down toward Kristin with the dogs leaping around him. He grabbed their snouts with his hands and walked toward her between the two animals, which were elk-gray and wolflike. Kristin smiled and reached out her hand without getting up.

Once, as she was looking down at his dark-brown head lying in her lap between her hands, a memory abruptly rose up before her. It stood there, clear and distant, the way a house far off on the slope of a ridge can suddenly emerge quite clearly from the dark clouds as it is struck by a ray of sunshine on a turbulent day. And her heart suddenly seemed filled with all of the tenderness that Arne Gyrdsøn had once wanted, back when she hardly even understood his words. Anxiously she drew the man to her, pressing his face against her breast, kissing him as if she were afraid that he might be taken from her. And when she looked at his head lying in her embrace, she thought it was like having a child in her arms. She hid his eyes with her hand and sprinkled little kisses over his mouth and cheek.

The sun had disappeared from the meadow. The intense color above the treetops had deepened to a dark blue, spreading over the entire sky. There were small copper-red streaks in the clouds, like smoke from a fire. Bajard came toward them, gave a loud whinny, and then stood motionless, staring. A moment later the first lightning flashed, followed at once by thunder, not far away.

Erlend stood up and took the reins of the horse. There was an old barn at the bottom of the meadow, and that's where they headed. He tethered Bajard to some planks just inside the door. In the back of the barn was a mound of hay, and there Erlend spread out his cape. They sat down with the dogs at their feet.

Soon the rain had formed a curtain in front of the doorway. The wind rushed through the forest and the rain lashed against the hillside. A moment later they had to move farther inside because of a leak in the roof.

Every time there was lightning and thunder, Erlend would whisper, "Aren't you afraid, Kristin?"

"A little," she would whisper back and then press closer to him.

They had no idea how long they sat there. The storm passed over quite quickly, and they could still hear the thunder far away, but the sun was shining outside the door in the wet grass, and fewer and fewer glittering drops were falling from the roof. The sweet smell of hay grew stronger in the barn.

"I have to go now," said Kristin.

And Erlend replied, "I suppose you do." He put his hand on her foot. "You'll get wet. You must ride, and I'll walk. Out of the forest . . ." He gave her such a strange look.

Kristin was trembling—she thought it was because her heart was pounding so hard—and her hands were clammy and cold. When he kissed the bare skin above her knee, she tried powerlessly to push him away. Erlend raised his face for a moment, and she was suddenly reminded of a man who had once been given food at the convent—he had kissed the bread they handed to him. She sank back into the hay with open arms and let Erlend do as he liked.

She was sitting bolt upright when Erlend lifted his head from his arms. Abruptly he propped himself up on his elbow.

"Don't look like that, Kristin!"

His voice etched a wild new pain into Kristin's soul. He wasn't happy—he was distressed too.

"Kristin, Kristin . . ."

And a moment later he asked, "Do you think I lured you out here to the woods because I wanted this from you, to take you by force?"

She stroked his hair but didn't look at him.

"I wouldn't call it force. No doubt you would have let me go as I came if I had asked you to," she said softly.

"I'm not sure of that," he replied, hiding his face in her lap.

"Do you think I will forsake you?" he asked fervently. "Kristin—I swear on my Christian faith—may God forsake me in my last hour if I fail to be faithful to you until I die."

She couldn't say a word; she merely caressed his hair, over and over.

"Now, surely, it must be time for me to go home," she said at last, and she felt as if she were waiting with dread for his reply.

"I suppose it is," he said gloomily. He stood up quickly, went over to his horse, and began to untie the reins.

Then Kristin stood up too—slowly, feeling faint and shattered. She didn't know what she had expected him to do—perhaps help her up onto his horse and take her along with him so that she could avoid going back to the others. Her whole body seemed to be aching with astonishment—that this was the iniquity that all the songs were about. And because Erlend had done this to her, she felt as if she had become his possession, and she couldn't imagine how she could live beyond his reach anymore. She was going to have to leave him now, but she could not conceive of doing so.

Down through the woods he walked, leading the horse and holding Kristin's hand in his, but they could think of nothing to say to each other.

When they had gone so far that they could see the buildings of Skog, he said farewell.

"Kristin, don't be sad. Before you know it the day will come when you'll be my wife."

But her heart sank as she spoke.

"Then you have to leave me?" she asked fearfully.

"As soon as you've left Skog," he said, and his voice sounded more vibrant all at once. "If there's no campaign, then I'll speak to Munan. He's been urging me for a long time to get married; I'm certain he'll accompany me and speak to your father on my behalf."

Kristin bowed her head. For every word he spoke, the time that lay before her seemed longer and more impossible to imagine—the convent, Jørundgaard—it was as if she were floating in a stream that was carrying her away from everything.

"Do you sleep alone in the loft, now that your kinsmen have gone?" asked Erlend. "If so, I'll come and talk to you tonight. Will you let me in?"

"Yes," murmured Kristin. And then they parted.

The rest of the day Kristin sat with her grandmother, and after the evening meal she helped the old woman into bed. Then she went up to the loft where she slept. There was a small window in the room, and Kristin sat down on the chest that stood beneath it; she had no desire to go to bed.

She had to wait for a long time. It was pitch dark outside when she heard the quiet footsteps on the gallery. He tapped on the door with his cape wrapped around his knuckles, and Kristin stood up, drew back the bolt, and let Erlend in.

She noticed that he was pleased when she threw her arms around his neck and pressed herself against him.

"I was afraid you'd be angry with me," he said.

Some time later he said, "You mustn't grieve over this sin. It's not a great one. God's law is not the same as the law of the land in this matter. Gunnulv, my brother, once explained it all to me. If two people agree to stand by each other for all eternity and then lie with each other, they are married before God and cannot break their vows without committing a great sin. I would tell you the word in Latin if I could remember it—I knew it once."

Kristin wondered what could have been the reason for Erlend's brother to speak of this, but she brushed aside the nagging fear that it might have been about Erlend and someone else. And she sought solace in his words.

They sat next to each other on the chest. Erlend put his arm around Kristin, and now she felt warm and secure—at his side was the only place she would ever feel safe and protected again.

From time to time Erlend would say a great deal, speaking elatedly. Then he would fall silent for long periods, simply caressing her. Without knowing it, Kristin was gathering up from all he said every little thing that might make him more attractive and dear to her, and that would lessen his blame in all she knew about him that was not good.

Erlend's father, Sir Nikulaus, was so old when his children were born that he had neither the patience nor the ability to raise them himself. Both sons had grown up in the home of Sir Baard Petersøn of Hestnæs. Erlend had no siblings other than his brother Gunnulv, who was one year younger and a priest at Christ Church. "I love him more dearly than anyone, except for you."

Kristin asked Erlend whether Gunnulv looked like him, but he laughed and said they were quite different in both temperament and appearance. Gunnulv was abroad, studying. This was the third year he had been gone, but twice he had sent letters home; the last one arrived the year before, when he was about to leave Sancta Genoveva in Paris and head for Rome. "Gunnulv will be happy when he comes home and finds me married," said Erlend.

Then he talked about the vast inheritance he had acquired from his parents. Kristin realized that he hardly knew himself how his affairs now stood. She was quite familiar with her father's land dealings, but Erlend's dealings had been of the opposite kind. He had sold and scattered, mortgaged and squandered his property, especially during the past few years as he had tried to separate from his mistress, thinking that with time his wild life would be forgotten and his kinsmen would take him back. He had believed that in the end he would be named sheriff of half of Orkdøla county, just as his father had been.

"But now I have no idea how things will finally go," he said. "Maybe I'll end up on a farm on some scruffy slope like Bjørn Gunnarsøn, and I'll have to carry out the dung on my back the way slaves used to do in the past because I own no horses."

"God help you," said Kristin, laughing. "Then I'd better come with you. I think I know more about peasant ways than you do."

"But I don't imagine that you've ever carried a dung basket," he said, laughing too.

"No, but I've seen how they spread out the muck, and I've sown grain almost every year back home. My father usually plows the closest fields himself, and then he lets me sow the first section because I'll bring him luck . . ." The memory painfully pierced her heart, and she said hastily, "And you'll need a woman to bake and brew the weak ale and wash out your only shirt and do the milking. You'll have to lease a cow or two from the nearest wealthy farmer."

"Oh, thank God I can hear you laugh a little once again," said Erlend, taking her onto his lap so that she lay in his arms like a child.

During the six nights before Aasmund Bjørgulfsøn returned home, Erlend came up to the loft to be with Kristin each evening.

On the last night he seemed just as unhappy as she was; he said many times that they would not be parted from each other a day longer than was necessary.

Finally he said in a subdued voice, "If things should go so badly that I cannot return here to Oslo before winter—and you happen to be in need of a friend's help—then you can safely turn to Sira Jon here at Gerdarud; we've been friends since childhood. And Munan Baardsøn you can also trust."

Kristin could only nod. She realized that he was talking about the same thing that had been on her mind every single day, but

Erlend didn't mention it again. Then she was silent too, not wanting to show him how sick at heart she felt.

The other times he had left her as the hour grew late, but on this last night he pleaded earnestly to be allowed to lie down and sleep with her for a while.

Kristin was afraid, but Erlend said defiantly, "You should realize that if I'm discovered here in your chamber, I know how to defend myself."

She wanted so badly to keep him with her a little longer, and she was incapable of refusing him anything.

But she was worried that they might sleep too long. So for most of the night she sat up, leaning against the headboard, dozing a little now and then, not always conscious of when he was actually caressing her and when she had simply dreamed it. She kept one hand on his chest, where she could feel the beat of his heart, and turned her face toward the window so she could watch for the dawn outside.

Finally she had to wake him. She threw on some clothes and walked out onto the gallery with him. He leaped over the railing on the side of the house facing another building. Then he disappeared around the corner. Kristin went back inside and crawled into bed again; then she let herself go and wept for the first time since she had become Erlend's possession.

## CHAPTER 5

At Nonneseter the days passed as they had before. Kristin spent her time in the dormitory and the church, the weaving room, the library, and the refectory. The nuns and the convent servants harvested the crops of the herb garden and orchard, Holy Cross Day arrived in the fall with its procession, and then came the time of fasting before Michaelmas. Kristin was astonished that no one seemed to notice anything different about her. But she had always been quiet in the company of strangers, and Ingebjørg Filippusdatter, who was her companion day and night, managed to talk enough for both of them.

So no one noticed that her thoughts were far away from everything around her. Erlend's mistress. She told herself this: now she was Erlend's mistress. It was as if she had dreamed it all—the evening of Saint Margareta's Day, the time in the barn, the nights in her bedchamber at Skog. Either she had dreamed all that or she was dreaming now. But one day she would have to wake up; one day it would all come out. Not for a moment did she doubt that she was carrying Erlend's child.

But she couldn't really imagine what would happen to her when this came to light—whether she would be thrown into a dark cell or be sent home. Far off in the distance she glimpsed the faint images of her father and mother. Then she would close her eyes, dizzy and sick, submerged by the imagined storm, trying to steel herself to bear the misfortune, which she thought would inevitably end with her being swept into Erlend's arms for all eternity—the only place where she now felt she had a home.

So in this sense of tension there was just as much anticipation as there was terror; there was sweetness as well as anguish. She was unhappy, but she felt that her love for Erlend was like a plant that had been sown inside her, and for every day that passed it sprouted a new and even lusher abundance of flowers, in spite of her misery. She had experienced the last night that he had slept with her as a delicate and fleeting sweetness, and a passion and joy awaited her in his embrace which she had never known before. Now she trembled at the memory; it felt to her like the hot, spicy gust from the sun-heated gardens. Wayside bastard—those were the words that Inga had flung at her. She reached out for the words and held them tight. Wayside bastard—a child that had been conceived in secret in the woods or meadows. She remembered the sunshine and the smell of the spruce trees in the glade. Every new, trickling sensation, every quickened pulse in her body she took to be the unborn child, reminding her that now she had ventured onto new paths; and no matter how difficult they might be to follow, she was certain that in the end they would lead her to Erlend.

She sat between Ingebjørg and Sister Astrid, embroidering on the great tapestry with the knights and birds beneath the twining leaves. All the while she was thinking that she would run away once her condition could no longer be concealed. She would walk along the road, dressed as a poor woman, with all the gold and silver she owned knotted into a cloth in her hand. She would pay for a roof over her head at a farm somewhere in an isolated village. She would become a servant woman, carrying water buckets on a yoke across her shoulders. She would tend to the stables, do the baking and washing, and suffer curses because she refused to name the father of her child. Then Erlend would come and find her.

Sometimes she imagined that he would come too late. Snow-white and beautiful, she would be lying in the poor peasant bed. Erlend would lower his head as he stepped through the doorway. He was wearing the long black cape he had worn when he came to her on those nights at Skog. The farm woman had led him to the room where she lay. He sank down and took her cold hands in his, his eyes desperate with grief. "Is this where you are, my only joy?" Then, bowed with sorrow, he would leave, with his infant son pressed to his breast inside the folds of his cape.

No, that's not how she wanted things to end. She didn't want to die, and Erlend must not suffer such a sorrow. But she was so despondent, and it helped to think such things.

Then all of a sudden it became chillingly clear to her—the child was not something she had merely imagined, it was something inevitable. One day she would have to answer for what she had done, and she felt as if her heart had stopped in terror.

But after some time had passed, she realized it was not as certain as she had thought that she was with child. She didn't understand why this did not make her happy. It was as if she had been lying under a warm blanket, weeping; now she had to get up and step into the cold. Another month passed, then another. Finally she was convinced—she had escaped that misfortune. Freezing and empty, she now felt more unhappy than ever, and in her heart a tiny bitterness toward Erlend was brewing. Advent was approaching and she had not heard a word, either about him or from him; she had no idea where he was.

And now she felt she could no longer endure the anguish and uncertainty; it was as if a bond between them had been broken. Now she was truly frightened. Something might happen and she would never see him again. She was separated from everything she had been bound to in the past, and the bond between them was such a fragile one. She didn't think that he would forsake her, but so many things might happen. She couldn't imagine how she would be able to stand the day-to-day uncertainty and agony of this waiting time any longer.

Sometimes she would think about her parents and sisters. She longed for them, but with the feeling that she had lost them for good.

And occasionally in church, and at other times as well, she would feel a fervent yearning to become part of it all, this community with God. It had always been part of her life, and now she stood outside with her unconfessed sin.

She told herself that this separation from her home and family and Christianity was only temporary. But Erlend would have to lead her back by the hand. When Lavrans consented to the love between her and Erlend, then she would be able to go to her father as she had before; and after she and Erlend were married, they would make confession and atone for their offense.

She began looking for evidence that other people, like herself, were not without sin. She paid more attention to gossip, and she took note of all the little things around her which indicated that not even the sisters in the convent were completely holy and unworldly. There were only small things—under Fru Groa's guidance Nonneseter was, in the eyes of the outside world, exactly as a holy order of nuns ought to be. The nuns were zealous in their service to God, diligent, and attentive to the poor and the sick. Confinement to the cloister was not so strictly enforced that the sisters could not receive visits from their friends and kinsmen in the parlatory; nor were they prevented from returning these visits in the town if the occasion so warranted. But no nun had ever brought shame upon the order through her actions in all the years that Fru Groa had been in charge.

Kristin had now developed an alert ear for all the small disturbances within the convent's walls: little complaints and jealousies and vanities. Other than nursing, no nun would lend a hand with the rough housework; they all wanted to be learned and skilled women. Each one tried to outshine the other, and those sisters who did not have talent for such refined occupations gave up and drifted through the hours as if in a daze.

Fru Groa herself was both learned and wise. She kept a vigilant eye on the conduct and industry of her spiritual daughters, but she paid little heed to the welfare of their souls. She had always been friendly and kind toward Kristin and seemed to favor her above the other young daughters, but that was because Kristin was well trained in book learning and needlework and was diligent and quiet. Fru Groa never expected replies from the sisters. On the other hand, she enjoyed talking to men. They came and went in her parlatory: landholders and envoys associated with the convent, predicant brothers from the bishop, and representatives from the cloister at Hovedø, with which she was involved in a legal matter. She had her hands full tending to the convent's large estates, the accounts, sending out clerical garb, and taking in and then sending off books to be copied. Not even the most ill-tempered person could find anything improper about Fru Groa's behavior. She simply liked to talk about those things that women seldom knew anything about.

The prior, who lived in a separate building north of the church, seemed to have no more will than the reed pen or switch of the abbess. Sister Potentia, for the most part, ruled the house. She was primarily intent on maintaining the customs that she had observed in the distinguished German convents where she had lived during her novitiate. Her former name was Sigrid Ragnvaldsdatter, but she had changed her name when she assumed the habit of the order, as was the custom in other countries. She was also the one who had decided that the pupils who were only at Nonneseter for a short time should also wear the attire of young novices.

Sister Cecilia Baardsdatter was not like the other nuns. She walked around in silence, her eyes downcast. She always replied meekly and humbly, acted as everyone's maidservant, preferred to take on the roughest tasks, and fasted more often than was prescribed—as much as Fru Groa would allow. And in church she would kneel for hours after the evening hymn or go there long before matins.

But one evening, after she had spent the whole day at the creek washing clothes along with two lay sisters, she suddenly began to sob loudly at the supper table. She threw herself onto the stone floor, crawled on her knees among the sisters, and beat her breast. With burning cheeks and streaming tears she begged them to forgive her. She was the worst sinner of them all—she had been stone-hard with arrogance all her days. It was arrogance and not humility or gratitude for the death of Christ the Savior that had sustained her when she was tempted in the world; she had fled to the convent not because she loved a man's soul but because she had loved her own pride. She had served her sisters with arrogance, she had drunk vanity from her water goblet, and she had spread her bare bread thick with conceit while the sisters drank ale and ate butter on their bread.

From all this Kristin understood that not even Cecilia Baardsdatter was completely pure of heart. An unlit tallow candle that has hung from the ceiling and turned filthy with soot and cobwebs—that was how she compared her loveless chastity.

Fru Groa herself went over and lifted up the sobbing young woman. Sternly she said that as punishment for her outburst Cecilia would move from the sisters' dormitory into the abbess's own bed and stay there until she had recovered from this fever.

"And then, Sister Cecilia, you will sit in my chair for eight days. We will ask your advice in spiritual matters and show you such respect because of your godly conduct that you will grow sated from the tribute of sinful people. Then you must judge whether this is worth so much struggle, and decide either to live by the rules as the rest of us do or to continue the trials that no one demands of you. Then you can contemplate whether all the things that you say you do now so that we might look up to you, henceforward you will do out of love of God and so that He might look upon you with mercy."

And so it was. Sister Cecilia lay in the abbess's room for two weeks; she had a high fever, and Fru Groa nursed the nun herself. When she had recovered, for eight days she had to sit at the abbess's side in the place of honor both in church and at home, and everyone served her. She wept the whole time, as if she were being beaten. Afterward she was much gentler and happier. She continued to live in almost the same manner as before, but she would blush like a bride if anyone looked at her, whether she was sweeping the floor or walking alone to church.

This episode with Sister Cecilia aroused in Kristin a strong yearning for peace and reconciliation with everything from which she had come to feel herself cut off. She thought about Brother Edvin, and one day she gathered her courage and asked Fru Groa for permission to visit the barefoot friars to see a friend of hers there.

She could tell that Fru Groa was not pleased; there was little friendship between the Minorites and the other cloisters of the diocese. And the abbess was no more favorably disposed when she heard who Kristin's friend was. She said that this Brother Edvin was an unreliable man of God, always roaming about the country seeking alms in other dioceses. In many places the peasantry considered him a holy man, but he didn't seem to realize that the first duty of a Franciscan monk was obedience to his superiors. He had heard the confessions of outlaws and those who had been excommunicated; he had baptized their children and sung them into their graves without asking for permission. And yet his sin was as much due to lack of understanding as it was to defiance, and he had patiently borne the reprimands which had been imposed on him because of these matters. The Church had treated him with forbearance because he was skilled at his craft; but even in the execution of his art he had come into conflict with others. The bishop's master painters in Bergen refused to allow him to work in their diocese.

Kristin was bold enough to ask where this monk with the un-Norwegian name had come from. Fru Groa was in a mood to talk. She said that he was born in Oslo, but his father was an Englishman, Rikard the Armormaster, who had married a farmer's daughter from the Skogheim district, and they had taken up residence in Oslo. Two of Edvin's brothers were respected armorers in town. But Edvin, the eldest of the armormaster's sons, had been a restless soul all his days. He had no doubt felt an attraction for the monastic life since early childhood; he had joined the gray monks at Hovedø as soon as he reached the proper age. They sent him to a cloister in France to be educated; he had excellent abilities. From there he managed to win permission to leave the Cistercian order and enter the order of the Minorites instead. And when the brothers arbitrarily decided to build their church out in the fields to the east, against the orders of the bishop,[1] Brother Edvin had been one of the worst and most obstinate among them—he had even used a hammer to strike one of the men sent by the bishop to stop the work and had almost killed him.

It had been a long time since anyone had talked at such length with Kristin. When Fru Groa dismissed her, the young maiden bent down and kissed the abbess's hand, respectfully and fervently, and tears sprang at once into her eyes. But Fru Groa, who saw that Kristin was crying, thought it was from sorrow—and so she said that perhaps one day she would be allowed to go out to visit Brother Edvin after all.

And several days later Kristin was told that some of the convent's servants had to go over to the king's castle, so at the same time they could accompany her out to the brothers in the fields.

Brother Edvin was home. Kristin had not imagined that she would be so happy to see anyone other than Erlend. The old man sat and stroked her hand as they talked, thanking her for coming. No, he hadn't been to her part of the country since that night he had stayed at Jørundgaard, but he had heard that she was to marry, and he offered her his congratulations. Then Kristin asked him to go over to the church with her.

They had to go out of the cloister and around to the main entrance; Brother Edvin didn't dare lead her across the courtyard. He seemed in general quite timid and afraid to do anything that might offend. He had grown terribly old, thought Kristin.

And when she had placed her offering on the altar for the priest of the church and then asked Edvin to hear her confession, he grew quite frightened. He didn't dare; he had been strictly forbidden to listen to confessions.

"Perhaps you've heard about it," he said. "I didn't think that I could deny these poor souls the gifts that God has bestowed on me so freely. But I was supposed to exhort them to seek reconciliation at the proper place. . . . Well then. But you, Kristin, you will have to confess to the prior at the convent."

"There is something that I cannot confess to the prior," said Kristin.

"Do you think it would benefit you if you confess to me something that you wish to conceal from your proper confessor?" said the monk more sternly.

"If you cannot hear my confession," said Kristin, "then you can let me talk to you and ask your advice about what is on my mind."

The monk looked around. The church was empty at the moment. He sat down on a chest that stood in the corner. "You must remember that I cannot absolve you, but I will advise you and I will keep silent as if you had spoken in confession."

Kristin stood before him and said, "You see, I cannot become Simon Darre's wife."

"As to this matter, you know I cannot advise you otherwise than the prior would," said Brother Edvin. "Disobedient children bring God no joy, and your father has done his best for you—you must realize that."

"I don't know what your advice will be when you hear the rest," said Kristin. "The situation is such that Simon is too good to gnaw on the bare branch from which another man has broken off the blossom."

She looked directly at the monk. But when she met his eye and noticed how the dry, wrinkled old face suddenly changed and became filled with grief and horror, something seemed to break inside her; the tears poured out, and she tried to throw herself to her knees. But Edvin pulled her vehemently back.

"No, no, sit down here on the chest with me. I cannot hear your confession." He moved aside to make room for her.

Kristin continued to cry.

He stroked her hand and said softly, "Do you remember that morning, Kristin, when I saw you for the first time on the stairs of Hamar Cathedral? I once heard a legend, when I was abroad, about a monk who could not believe that God loved all of us wretched, sinful souls. An angel came and touched his sight so that he saw a stone at the bottom of the sea, and under the stone lived a blind, white, naked creature. And the monk stared at the creature until he began to love it because it was so small and pitiful. When I saw you sitting there, so tiny and pitiful inside that huge stone building, then I thought it was reasonable that God should love someone like you. You were lovely and pure, and yet you needed protection and help. I thought I saw the whole church, with you inside it, lying in the hand of God."

Kristin said softly, "We have bound ourselves to each other with the most solemn of oaths—and I have heard that such an agreement consecrates us before God just as much as if our parents had given us to each other."

But the monk replied with despair, "I see, Kristin, that someone has been telling you of the canonical law without fully understanding it. You could not promise yourself to this man without sinning against your parents; God placed them above you before you met him. And won't it also be a sorrow and a shame for this man's kinsmen if they learn that he has seduced the daughter of a man who has carried his shield with honor all these years? And you were also betrothed. I see that you do not think you have sinned so greatly—and yet you dare not confess this to your parish priest. And if you think you are as good as married to this man, why don't you wear the linen wimple instead of going around bareheaded among the young maidens, with whom you have so little in common now? For now your thoughts must be on other things than theirs are."

"I don't know what I'm thinking about," said Kristin wearily. "It's true that all my thoughts are with this man, whom I yearn for. If it weren't for Father and Mother, then I would gladly pin up my hair on this very day—I wouldn't care if they called me a paramour, if only I could be called his."

"Do you know whether this man's intentions are such that you might be his with honor someday?" asked Brother Edvin.

Then Kristin told him about everything that had happened between Erlend Nikulaussøn and herself. And as she talked, she seemed to have forgotten that she had ever doubted the outcome of the whole matter.

"Don't you see, Brother Edvin," she continued, "we couldn't control ourselves. God help me, if I met him here outside the church, after I leave you, I would go with him if he asked me to. And you should know that I have now seen that other people have sinned as we have. When I was back home I couldn't understand how anything could have such power over the souls of people that they would forget all fear of sin, but now I have seen so much that if one cannot rectify the sins one has committed out of desire or anger, then heaven must be a desolate place. They say that you too once struck a man in anger."

"That's true," said the monk, "and it is only through God's mercy that I am not called a murderer. That was many years ago. I was a young man back then, and I didn't think I could tolerate the injustice that the bishop wished to exercise against us poor brothers. King Haakon—he was the duke at that time—had given us the land for our building, but we were so poor that we had to do the work on our church ourselves, with the help of a few workmen who lent a hand more for their reward in heaven than for what we were able to pay them. Perhaps it was arrogance on the part of the mendicant monks that we wanted to build our church with such splendor; but we were as happy as children in the meadows, singing hymns as we chiseled and built walls and toiled. May God bless Brother Ranulv. He was a master builder, a skilled stonemason; I think God Himself had granted this man all his knowledge and skills. I was cutting altarpieces from stone back then. I had finished one of Saint Clara, with the angels leading her to the church of Saint Francis early Christmas morning. It had turned out beautifully, and we all rejoiced over it. Then those cowardly devils tore down the walls, and the stones toppled and crushed my altarpieces. I lunged at a man with a hammer; I couldn't control myself.

"Yes, I see that you're smiling, Kristin. But don't you realize how badly things stand with you now? For you would rather hear about other people's frailties than about the deeds of decent people, which might serve as an example for you."

As Kristin was about to leave, Brother Edvin said, "It's not easy to advise you. If you were to do what's right, then you would bring sorrow to your parents and shame upon your entire lineage. But you must try to win release from your promise to Simon Andressøn. Then you must wait patiently for the joy that God will send you. Do penance in your heart as best you can—and do not let this Erlend tempt you to sin more often, but ask him lovingly to seek reconciliation with your kinsmen and with God.

"I cannot absolve you of your sin," said Brother Edvin as they parted. "But I will pray for you with all my heart."

Then he placed his thin old hands on Kristin's head and said a prayer of blessing and peace for her in farewell.

## CHAPTER 6

AFTERWARD Kristin could not remember everything that Brother Edvin had said to her. But she left him with a strange feeling of clarity and serene peace in her soul.

Before, she had struggled with a hollow and secret fear, trying to defy it: her sin had not been so great. Now she felt that Edvin had shown her clearly and lucidly that she had indeed sinned, that such and such were her sins, and that she would have to take them upon her shoulders and try to bear them with patience and dignity. She strove to think of Erlend without impatience, in spite of the fact that he had sent no word and she missed his caresses. She simply had to be faithful and full of kindness toward him. She thought about her parents and promised herself that she would repay all their love after they had first recovered from the sorrow that she was going to cause them by breaking with the Dyfrin people. And she thought most about Brother Edvin's advice that she should not seek solace by looking at the failings of others; she felt herself growing humble and kind, and soon realized how easy it was for her to win the friendship of others. At once she felt consoled that it was not so difficult, after all, to get along with people—and then she thought that it shouldn't be so difficult for her and Erlend either.

Up until the day when she gave Erlend her promise, she had always tried diligently to do everything that was right and good, but she had done everything at the bidding of other people. Now she felt that she had grown up from maiden to woman. This was not just because of the passionate, secret caresses she had received and given. She had not merely left her father's guardianship and subjected herself to Erlend's will. Brother Edvin had impressed on her the responsibility of answering for her own life, and for Erlend's as well, and she was willing to bear this burden with grace and dignity. So she lived among the nuns during the Christmas season; during the beautiful services and amidst the joy and peace, she no doubt felt herself unworthy, but she consoled herself with the belief that the time would soon come when she would be able to redeem herself again.

But on the day after New Year's, Sir Andres Darre arrived unexpectedly at the convent together with his wife and all five children. They were going to spend the last part of the Christmas holidays with friends and kinsmen in town, and they came to ask Kristin to join them at the place where they were staying for several days.

"I've been thinking, my daughter, said Fru Angerd, "that you probably wouldn't mind seeing some new faces by now."

The Dyfrin people were staying in a beautiful house that was part of an estate near the bishop's citadel. Sir Andres's nephew owned it. There was a large room where the servants slept and a magnificent loft room with a brick fireplace and three good beds. Sir Andres and Fru Angerd slept in one of the beds, along with their youngest son, Gudmund, who was still a child. Kristin and their two daughters, Astrid and Sigrid, slept in the second bed. And in the third slept Simon and his older brother, Gyrd Andressøn.

All of Sir Andres's children were good-looking—Simon the least so, and yet people still considered him handsome. And Kristin noticed even more than when she had been at the Dyfrin manor the year before that both his parents and his four siblings listened closely to Simon and did everything he wished. All his kinsmen loved each other heartily but agreed without rancor to place Simon foremost.

These people led a joyful and happy life, going to one of the churches each day to make their offerings, meeting to drink among friends each evening, and allowing the young to play and dance. Everyone showed Kristin the greatest kindness, and no one seemed to notice how little joy she felt.

At night, when the candles were put out in the loft and everyone had gone to bed, Simon would get up and come over to where the maidens lay. He would sit for a while on the edge of the bed, speaking mostly to his sisters, but in the dark he would sneak his hand up to Kristin's breast and let it stay there. She would lie there, sweating with indignation.

Now that her sense for such matters was so much keener, she realized there were many things that Simon was both too proud and too shy to say to her, once he noticed that she didn't want to go into such topics. And she felt a strange, bitter anger toward him because it seemed to her that he was trying to make himself seem a better man than the one who had taken her—even though he had no idea of the other man's existence.

But one evening when they had been out dancing at another estate, Astrid and Sigrid stayed behind and were going to sleep with a foster sister. Late that night, when the people from Dyfrin had gone to bed in the loft, Simon came over to Kristin's bed and climbed in; he lay on top of the furs.

Kristin pulled the covers up to her chin and crossed her arms tightly over her chest. After a moment Simon reached out his hand to touch her breasts. She felt the silk embroidery at his wrists, so she realized that he had not undressed.

"You're just as shy in the dark as in the daylight, Kristin," said Simon with a chuckle. "Surely you'll let me hold your hand, won't you?" he asked, and Kristin gave him her fingertips.

"Don't you think we might have a few things to talk about, now that we have the chance to be alone for a little while?" he said. And Kristin thought that now she would be able to speak. So she agreed. But then she could not utter a word.

"Can I come under the furs?" he asked again. "It's cold in the room." And he slipped in between the furs and the woolen blanket she had over her. He crooked one arm behind her head, but in such a way that he did not touch her. And they lay there like that for a while.

"You're not an easy person to woo, either," said Simon after a pause, and then laughed in resignation. "I promise you I won't so much as kiss you, if you don't want me to. But surely you can talk to me, can't you?"

Kristin moistened her lips with the tip of her tongue, but she still remained silent.

"It seems to me that you're lying here trembling," Simon continued. "Is it because you have something against me, Kristin?"

She didn't think that she could lie to Simon, so she said, "No," but nothing more.

Simon lay there a little longer, trying to get a conversation started. But finally he laughed again and said, "I see that you think I should be satisfied with this—that you have nothing against me—for tonight, at least, and that I should even be happy. It's strange how proud you are too. But you must give me a kiss, all the same; then I'll go and not plague you any longer."

He took his kiss, sat up, and set his feet on the floor. Kristin thought that now she would manage to tell him what had to be said—but he had already left her bed, and she could hear him getting undressed.

The next day Fru Angerd was not as friendly toward Kristin as she usually was. The young maiden realized that she must have heard something and felt that the betrothed girl had not received her son in the manner that his mother felt she should have.

Later in the afternoon Simon mentioned that he was thinking of trading for a horse that was owned by one of his friends. He asked Kristin whether she would like to go along and watch. She said yes, and they went into town together.

The weather was clear and beautiful. It had snowed a little during the night, but now the sun was shining, and it was still so cold that the snow squeaked under their feet. Kristin enjoyed getting out in the cold and walking, so when Simon had found the horse that he was thinking of, she talked to him about it in the most lively manner; she had some knowledge of horses, since she had always spent so much time with her father. And this one was a fine animal: a mouse-gray stallion with narrow black stripes along his back and a short, clipped mane. He was well built and spirited, but quite small and slight.

"He won't last long under a fully-armed man," said Kristin.

"No, but that's not what I had in mind, either," said Simon.

He led the horse out to the open area behind the farm, let him run and walk, rode the animal himself, and then had Kristin ride him too. They stayed outdoors in the white pasture for a long time.

Finally, as Kristin was feeding bread to the horse from her hand,

Simon leaned against the animal with his arm over his back and said suddenly, "It seems to me, Kristin, that you and my mother have been rather cross with each other."

"I haven't meant to be cross with your mother," she said, "but I can't find much to say to Fru Angerd."

"You don't seem to find much to say to me, either," said Simon. "I won't force myself on you, Kristin, before the time comes. But things can't go on like this; I never get a chance to talk to you."

"I have never been talkative," said Kristin. "I know that myself, and I don't expect you to think it a great loss if things don't work out between us."

"You know what I think about that subject," replied Simon, looking at her.

Kristin blushed as red as blood. And she was startled to find that she was not averse to Simon Darre's wooing.

After a moment he said, "Is it Arne Gyrdsøn, Kristin, that you think you can't forget?" Kristin stared at him. Simon continued, and his voice was kind and understanding, "I won't blame you for that. You grew up as siblings, and barely a year has passed. But you can depend on this: I want only what's best for you."

Kristin's face had grown quite pale. Neither of them spoke as they walked through town in the twilight. At the end of the street, in the greenish blue sky, the crescent of the new moon hung with a bright star in its embrace.

One year, thought Kristin, and she could hardly remember when she had last given Arne a thought. It gave her a fright—maybe she was a loose, vile woman. A year since she had seen him lying on the bier in the death chamber, when she thought she would never be happy again. She whimpered silently in fear at the inconstancy of her own heart and at the transitory nature of all things. Erlend, Erlend—would he forget her? But worse yet was that she might ever forget him.

Sir Andres and his children went to the great Christmas celebration at the king's castle. Kristin saw all the finery and splendor, and they were also invited into the hall where King Haakon sat with Fru Isabel Bruce, the widow of King Eirik. Sir Andres went forward to greet the king, while his children and Kristin remained behind. She thought of everything that Fru Aashild had told her, and she remembered that the king was Erlend's close kinsman—their fathers' mothers had been sisters. And she was Erlend's wife by seduction; she had no right to stand here, especially not among these good, fine people, the children of Sir Andres.

Suddenly she saw Erlend Nikulaussøn. He had stepped forward in front of Queen Isabel and was standing there with his head bowed and his hand on his breast while she spoke a few words to him. He was wearing the brown silk surcoat that he had worn to their banquet rendezvous. Kristin stepped behind Sir Andres's daughters.

When Fru Angerd, some time later, escorted the three maidens over to the queen, Kristin could not see Erlend anywhere, but she didn't dare raise her eyes from the floor. She wondered if he was standing somewhere in the hall; she thought she could feel his eyes on her. But she also thought that everyone was staring at her, as if they could tell that she was standing there like a liar with the gold wreath on her hair, which fell loosely over her shoulders.

He was not in the hall where the young people were served dinner and where they danced after the tables had been cleared away. Kristin had to dance with Simon that evening.

Along one wall stood a built-in table, and that's where the king's servants set ale and mead and wine all night long. Once when Simon took Kristin over there and drank a toast to her, she saw that Erlend was standing quite close to her, behind Simon. He looked at her, and Kristin's hand shook as Simon gave her the goblet and she raised it to her lips. Erlend whispered fiercely to the man who was with him—a tall, heavyset, but handsome older man, who shook his head dismissively with an angry expression. In the next moment Simon led Kristin back to the dance.

She had no idea how long that dance lasted; the ballad seemed endless and every moment was tedious and painful with longing and unrest. At last it was over, and Simon escorted her over to the table for drinks again.

One of his friends approached and spoke to him, leading him away a few paces, over to a group of young men. Then Erlend stood before her.

"I have so much I want to say to you," he whispered. "I don't know what to say first. In Christ's name, Kristin, how are things with you?" he asked hastily, for he noticed that her face had turned as white as chalk.

She couldn't see him clearly; it was as if there was running water between their faces. He picked up a goblet from the table, drank from it, and handed it to Kristin. She thought it was much too heavy, or that her arm had been pulled from its socket; she couldn't manage to raise it to her lips.

"Is that how things stand—that you'll drink with your betrothed but not with me?" asked Erlend softly. But Kristin dropped the goblet and swooned forward into his arms.

When she woke up she was lying on a bench with her head in the lap of a maiden she didn't know. They had loosened her belt and the brooch on her breast. Someone was slapping her hands, and her face was wet.

She sat up. Somewhere in the circle of people around her she saw Erlend's face, pale and ill. She felt weak herself, as if all her bones had melted, and her head felt huge and hollow. But somewhere in her mind a single thought, clear and desperate, shone—she had to talk to Erlend.

Then she said to Simon Darre, who was standing close by, "It must have been too hot for me. There are so many candles burning in here, and I'm not accustomed to drinking so much wine."

"Are you all right now?" asked Simon. "You frightened everyone. Perhaps you would like me to take you home?"

"I think we should wait until your parents leave," said Kristin calmly. "But sit down here. I don't feel like dancing anymore." She patted the cushion beside her. Then she stretched out her other hand to Erlend.

"Sit down here, Erlend Nikulaussøn. I didn't have a chance to give you my full greeting. Ingebjørg was just saying lately that she thought you had forgotten all about her."

She saw that he was having a much more difficult time composing himself than she was. It cost her great effort to hold back the tender little smile that threatened to appear on her lips.

"You must thank the maiden for still remembering me," he said, stammering. "And here I was so afraid that she had forgotten *me*."

Kristin hesitated for a moment. She didn't know what message she could bring from the flighty Ingebjørg that would be interpreted correctly by Erlend. Then bitterness rose up inside her for all those months of helplessness, and she said, "Dear Erlend, did you think that we maidens would forget the man who so magnificently defended our honor?"

She saw that he looked as if she had struck him. And she regretted it at once when Simon asked what she meant. Kristin told him of her adventure with Ingebjørg out in the Eikaberg woods. She noticed that Simon was not pleased. Then she asked him to go in search of Fru Angerd, to see if they would be leaving soon. She was tired after all. When he had gone, she turned to look at Erlend.

"It's odd," he said in a low voice, "how resourceful you are—I wouldn't have thought it of you."

"I've had to learn to conceal things, as you might well imagine," she said somberly.

Erlend breathed heavily. He was still quite pale.

"Is that it?" he whispered. "But you promised to go to my friends if that should come about. God knows, I've thought about you every single day, about whether the worst had happened."

"I know what you mean by the worst," replied Kristin tersely. "You needn't worry about that. It seems worse to me that you would not send me a word of greeting. Can't you understand that I'm living there with the nuns like some strange bird?" She stopped because she could feel the tears rising.

"Is that why you're with the Dyfrin people now?" he asked. Then she grew so full of despair that she couldn't answer.

She saw Fru Angerd and Simon appear in the doorway. Erlend's hand lay on his knee, close to her own, but she could not touch it.

"I have to talk to you," he said fiercely. "We haven't said a word to each other of what we should have talked about."

"Come to the mass at the Maria Church after the last day of the Christmas season," Kristin said hastily, as she stood up and stepped forward to meet the others.

Fru Angerd was quite loving and kind toward Kristin on the way home, and she helped the maiden into bed herself. Kristin didn't have a chance to speak to Simon until the following day.

Then he said, "How is it that you would agree to convey messages between this Erlend and Ingebjørg Filippusdatter? You should not lend a hand in this matter, if they have some secret business between them."

"I don't think there's anything behind it," said Kristin. "She's just a chatterbox."

"I thought you would have been more sensible," said Simon, "than to venture into the woods and out onto roads alone with that magpie." But Kristin reminded him with some fervor that it was not their fault they had gone astray. Simon didn't say another word.

The next day the Dyfrin people escorted her back to the convent before setting off for home themselves.

Erlend came to vespers at the convent church every day for a week, but Kristin didn't have the chance to exchange a single word with him. She felt as if she were a hawk that sat chained to a roost with a hood pulled over its eyes. She was also unhappy about every word they had said to each other at their last meeting; that was not the way it was supposed to have been. It didn't help that she told herself it had happened so suddenly for both of them that they hardly knew what they were saying.

But one afternoon, at dusk, a beautiful woman who looked like the wife of a townsman appeared in the parlatory. She asked for Kristin Lavransdatter and said that she was the wife of a clothing merchant. Her husband had just arrived from Denmark with some fine cloaks, and Aasmund Bjørgulfsøn wished to give one of them to his niece, so the maiden was to go with her to select it herself.

Kristin was allowed to accompany the woman. She thought it unlike her uncle to want to give her a costly gift, and peculiar that he would send a stranger to get her.

At first the woman said little, replying only briefly to Kristin's questions, but when they had walked all the way into town, she suddenly said, "I don't want to fool you, lovely child that you are. I'm going to tell you how things truly stand so you can decide for yourself. It wasn't your uncle who sent me, but a man—maybe you can guess his name, and if you can't, then you shouldn't come with me. I have no husband, and I have to make a living for myself and mine by keeping an inn and serving ale. So I can't be too afraid of either sin or servants—but I will not let my house be used for purposes of deceiving you within my walls."

Kristin stopped, her face flushed. She felt strangely hurt and ashamed on Erlend's behalf.

The woman said, "I will accompany you back to the convent, Kristin, but you must give me something for my trouble. The knight promised me a large reward, but I was also beautiful once, and I too was deceived. And then you can remember me in your prayers tonight. They call me Brynhild Fluga."

Kristin took a ring from her finger and gave it to the woman.

"That was kind of you, Brynhild, but if the man is my kinsman Erlend Nikulaussøn, then I have nothing to fear. He wants me to reconcile him with my uncle. You will not be blamed—but thank you for warning me."

Brynhild Fluga turned away to hide her smile.

She led Kristin through the alleys behind Clement's Church and north toward the river. A few small, isolated farms were situated on the bank. They walked between several fences, and there came Erlend to meet them. He glanced around and then took off his cape and wrapped it around Kristin, pulling the hood forward over her face.

"What do you think of this ruse?" he asked quickly, in a low voice. "Do you think I've done wrong? But I had to talk to you."

"It won't do much good for us to think about what's right and what's wrong," said Kristin.

"Don't talk like that," implored Erlend. "I take the blame. Kristin, I've longed for you every day and every night," he whispered close to her ear.

A shudder passed through her as she briefly met his glance. She felt guilty because she had been thinking about something besides her love for him when he looked at her in that way.

Brynhild Fluga had gone on ahead. When they reached the inn, Erlend asked Kristin, "Do you want to go into the main room, or should we talk upstairs in the loft?"

"As you please," replied Kristin.

"It's cold up there," said Erlend softly. "We'll have to get into the bed." Kristin merely nodded.

The instant he had closed the door behind them, she was in his arms. He bent her this way and that like a wand, blinding her and smothering her with kisses, as he impatiently tore both cloaks off her and tossed them to the floor. Then he lifted the girl in the pale convent dress in his arms, pressing her to his shoulder, and carried her over to the bed. Frightened by his roughness and by her own sudden desire for this man, she put her arms around him and buried her face in his neck.

It was so cold in the loft that they could see their own breath like a cloud of smoke in front of the little candle standing on the table. But there were plenty of blankets and furs on the bed, covered by a great bearskin, which they pulled all the way up over their faces.

She didn't know how long she had lain like that in his arms when Erlend said, "Now we must talk about those things that have to be discussed, my Kristin. I don't dare keep you here long."

"I'll stay here the whole night if you want me to," whispered Kristin.

Erlend pressed his cheek to hers.

"Then I would not be much of a friend to you. Things are bad enough already, but I won't have people gossiping about you because of me."

Kristin didn't reply, but she felt a twinge of pain. She didn't understand how he could say such a thing, since he was the one who had brought her here to Brynhild Fluga's house. She didn't know how she knew it, but she realized that this was not a good place. And he had expected that everything would proceed just as it did, for he had a cup of mead standing inside the bed drapes.

"I've been thinking," continued Erlend, "that if there's no other alternative, then I'll have to take you away by force, to Sweden. Duchess Ingebjørg received me kindly this autumn and spoke of the kinship between us. But now I'm paying for my sins—I've fled the country before, you know—and I don't want you to be mentioned as that other one's equal."

"Take me home to Husaby with you," said Kristin quietly. "I can't bear to be separated from you and to live with the maidens in the convent. Surely both your kinsmen and mine will be reasonable enough that they'll allow us to be together and become reconciled with them."

Erlend hugged her tight and moaned, "I can't take you to Husaby, Kristin."

"Why can't you?" she asked in a whisper.

"Eline came back this fall," he said after a moment. "I can't make her leave the farm," he continued angrily, "not unless I carry her by force out to the sleigh and drive her away myself. And I don't think I could do that—she brought both of our children home with her."

Kristin felt as if she were sinking deeper and deeper. In a voice that was brittle with fear she said, "I thought you had parted from her."

"I thought so too," replied Erlend curtly. "But she apparently heard in Østerdal, where she was living, that I was thinking of marriage. You saw the man I was with at the Christmas banquet—that was my foster father, Baard Petersøn of Hestnæs. I went to him when I returned from Sweden; I visited my kinsman, Heming Alvsøn, in Saltvik too. I told them that I wanted to get married now and asked them to help me. That must be what Eline heard.

"I told her to demand whatever she wanted for herself and the children. But they don't expect Sigurd, her husband, to survive the winter, and then no one can prevent us from living together.

"I slept in the stables with Haftor and Ulv, and Eline slept in the house in my bed. I think my men had a good laugh behind my back."

Kristin couldn't say a word.

After a moment Erlend went on, "You know, on the day when our betrothal is formally celebrated, she'll have to realize that it will do her no good—that she has no power over me any longer.

"But it will be bad for the children. I hadn't seen them in a year—they're good-looking children—and there's little I can do to secure their situation. It wouldn't have helped them much even if I had been able to marry their mother."

Tears began to slide down Kristin's cheeks.

Then Erlend said, "Did you hear what I said? That I have spoken to my kinsmen? And they were pleased that I want to marry. Then I told them that it was you I wanted and no one else."

"And weren't they pleased about that?" asked Kristin at last, timidly.

"Don't you see," said Erlend gloomily, "that there was only one thing they could say? They cannot and they will not ride with me to speak with your father until this agreement between you and

Simon Andressøn has been dissolved. It hasn't made things any easier for us, Kristin, that you have celebrated Christmas with the Dyfrin people."

Kristin broke down completely and began to sob quietly. She had no doubt felt that there was something unwise and ignoble about her love, and now she realized that the blame was hers.

She shivered with cold as she got out of bed a short time later and Erlend wrapped both cloaks around her. It was now completely dark outside, and Erlend accompanied her to Clement's churchyard; then Brynhild escorted her the rest of the way to Nonneseter.

## CHAPTER 7

THE FOLLOWING WEEK Brynhild Fluga came with word that the cloak was now finished, and Kristin went with her and was with Erlend in the loft room as before.

When they parted he gave her a cloak, "so you have something to show at the convent," he said. It was made of blue velvet interwoven with red silk, and Erlend asked her whether she noticed that they were the same colors as the dress she had worn on that day in the forest. Kristin was surprised that she could be so happy over what he said; she felt as if he had never given her greater joy than with those words.

But now they could no longer use this excuse to meet, and it was not easy to think of something else. Erlend went to vespers at the convent church, and several times after the service Kristin went on an errand up to the corrodians' farms; they stole a few words with each other up along the fences in the dark of the winter evening.

Then Kristin thought of asking Sister Potentia for permission to visit several palsied old women, charity cases of the convent, who lived in a house out in a field some distance away. Behind the house was a shed where the women kept a cow. Kristin offered to tend to the animal for them when she visited, and then she would let Erlend come in while she worked.

She noticed with some surprise that in spite of Erlend's joy at being with her, a tiny scrap of bitterness had settled in his mind that she had been able to think up this excuse.

"It was not to your best advantage that you became acquainted with me," he said one evening. "Now you've learned to use these kinds of secret ruses."

"*You* should not be blaming me for that," replied Kristin dejectedly.

"It's not you that I blame," said Erlend at once, embarrassed.

"I never thought," she went on, "that it would be so easy for me to lie. But what must be done can be done."

"That's not always true," said Erlend in the same voice as before. "Do you remember this past winter, when you couldn't tell your betrothed that you wouldn't have him?"

Kristin didn't reply, but merely stroked his face.

She never felt so strongly how much she loved Erlend as when he said such things that made her feel dejected or surprised. And she was glad that she could take the blame for everything that was disgraceful or ignoble about their love. If she had had the courage to speak to Simon as she should have, then they could have progressed a long way in settling these matters. Erlend had done all that he could when he had spoken of marriage to his kinsmen. This is what she told herself whenever the days at the convent grew long and dreary. Erlend had wanted to make everything right and proper. With tender little smiles she would think about him as he looked whenever he described their wedding. She would ride to the church dressed in silk and velvet, and she would be led to the bridal bed with the tall golden crown on her hair, which would be spread out over her shoulders—her lovely, beautiful hair, he said, running her braids through his fingers.

"But for you it won't be the same as if you had never possessed me," Kristin once said thoughtfully when he had spoken of such things.

Then he had pulled her ardently to him.

"Don't you think I can remember the first time I celebrated Christmas, or the first time I saw the mountainsides turn green back home after winter? Oh, of course I'll remember the first time I had you, and every time after that. But to possess you, that's like perpetually celebrating Christmas or hunting birds on the green slopes."

Joyfully she crept closer in his arms.

Not that she for a moment believed that things would go as Erlend so confidently expected. Kristin thought that a judgment day was sure to befall them before long. It was impossible for things to continue to go so well. But she was not particularly afraid. She was much more frightened that Erlend might have to travel north before the matter could be settled, and she would have to stay behind, separated from him. He was over at the fortress on Akersnes right now; Munan Baardsøn was there while the Royal Treasurer was in Tunsberg, where the king lay deathly ill. But one day Erlend would no doubt have to return home to see to his property. She refused to admit that this frightened her because he would be going home to Husaby where his mistress was waiting for him. But she was less afraid of being caught in sin with Erlend than of standing up alone and telling Simon, and her father as well, what was in her heart.

And so she almost wished that some punishment would befall her, and soon. For now she had no thoughts for anything but Erlend. She longed for him in the daytime and she dreamed of him at night. She felt no repentance, but she consoled herself with the thought that the day would come when she would have to pay dearly for everything they had taken in secret. And during those brief evening hours when she could be together with Erlend in the poor women's cowshed, she would throw herself into his arms so ardently, as if she had paid with her soul to be his.

But time passed, and it looked as if Erlend was to have the good fortune that he was counting on. Kristin noticed that no one at the convent ever suspected her, although Ingebjørg had discovered that she met with Erlend. But Kristin could see that the other girl never thought it was anything more than a little amusement she was allowing herself. That a betrothed maiden of good family would dare to break the agreement that her kinsmen had made was something that would never occur to Ingebjørg. And for a moment fear raced through Kristin once more; perhaps this was something completely unheard of, this situation she had landed in. And then she wished again that she would be found out, so that it could be brought to an end.

Easter arrived. Kristin couldn't understand what had happened to the winter; each day that she had not seen Erlend had been as long as a dismal year, and the long gloomy days had become linked together into endless weeks. But now it was spring and Easter, and it seemed to her as if they had just celebrated Christmas. She asked Erlend not to seek her out during the holidays; and it seemed to Kristin that he acquiesced to all her wishes. It was just as much her fault as his that they had sinned against the strictures of Lent.

But she wanted them to observe the Easter holiday—even though it hurt not to see him. He might have to leave quite soon; he hadn't said anything about it, but she knew that the king was now dying, and she thought that this might cause some change in Erlend's position.

This was how matters stood for Kristin, when, a few days after Easter, she was summoned down to the parlatory to speak with her betrothed.

As soon as Simon came toward her and put out his hand, she realized that something was wrong. His face was not the same as usual; his small gray eyes weren't laughing, and they were untouched by his smile. Kristin couldn't help noticing that it suited him to be a little less jovial. And he looked quite handsome in the traveling clothes he wore: a long, blue, tight-fitting outer garment that men called a *cote-hardie*, and a brown shoulder-cape with a hood, which he had thrown back. His light brown hair was quite curly from the raw, damp air.

They sat and talked for a while. Simon had been at Formo during Lent, and he was over at Jørundgaard almost daily. They were all well there. Ulvhild was as healthy as anyone could expect. Ramborg was home now; she was charming and lively.

"The time is almost over, the year that you were supposed to spend here at Nonneseter," said Simon. "They're probably preparing everything for our betrothal feast at your home."

Kristin didn't reply as Simon continued.

"I told Lavrans that I would ride to Oslo to speak with you about it."

Kristin looked down and said quietly, "Things are such, Simon, that I would prefer to speak with you in private about this matter."

"I too have felt that this would be necessary," replied Simon Andressøn. "I was going to ask that you obtain Fru Groa's permission for us to walk in the garden together."

Kristin stood up abruptly, and slipped soundlessly out of the room. A short time later she returned, accompanied by one of the nuns with a key.

A door from the parlatory opened onto the herb garden, which lay beyond the buildings on the west side of the convent. The nun unlocked the door, and they stepped out into a fog so dense that they could see only a few steps in front of them amidst the trees. The closest trunks were black as coal; beads of moisture clung to every branch and twig. Small patches of new snow were melting on the wet soil, but beneath the bushes tiny white and yellow lilies had already sprouted flowers, and it smelled fresh and cool from the violet-grass.

Simon led her to the nearest bench. He sat down, leaning forward slightly with his elbows propped on his knees. Then he looked up at her with an odd little smile.

"I almost think I know what you want to tell me," he said. "There's another man that you like better than me?"

"That is true," replied Kristin softly.

"I think I know his name too," said Simon, his voice more harsh. "Is it Erlend Nikulaussøn of Husaby?"

After a moment Kristin said in a low voice, "So this has come to your attention?"

Simon hesitated before he answered.

"Surely you can't think me so stupid that I wouldn't notice anything when we were together at Christmastime? I couldn't say anything then, because my father and mother were present. But this is the reason that I wanted to come here alone this time. I don't know whether it's wise of me to speak of this matter, but I thought that we ought to talk of such things before we are joined in marriage.

"But as it happened, when I arrived here yesterday, I met my kinsman, Master Øistein. And he spoke of you. He said that he saw you walking across Clement's churchyard one evening, and that you were with a woman they call Brynhild Fluga. I swore a sacred oath that he must have been mistaken. And if you tell me that it's untrue, I will take you at your word."

"The priest was right," replied Kristin stubbornly. "You forswore yourself, Simon."

He sat in silence for a moment before he spoke again.

"Do you know who this Brynhild Fluga is, Kristin?" When she shook her head, he said, "Munan Baardsøn set her up in a house here in town after he was married—she sells wine illegally and other such things."

"Do you know her?" asked Kristin derisively.

"I've never been inclined to become a monk or a priest," said

Simon, turning red. "But I know that I have never acted unjustly toward a maiden or another man's wife. Don't you realize that it's not the conduct of an honorable man to allow you to go out at night in such company?"

"Erlend did not seduce me," said Kristin, blushing and indignant. "And he has promised me nothing. I set my heart on him though he did nothing to tempt me. I loved him above all men from the first moment I saw him."

Simon sat there, playing with his dagger, tossing it from one hand to the other.

"These are strange words to be hearing from one's betrothed," he said. "This does not bode well for us now, Kristin."

Kristin took a deep breath. "You would be poorly served to take me for your wife, Simon."

"Almighty God knows that this seems to be so," said Simon Andressøn.

"Then I trust that you will support me," said Kristin, meek and timid, "so that Sir Andres and my father will retract this agreement between us?"

"Oh, is that what you think?" said Simon. He was silent for a moment. "God only knows whether you truly understand what you're saying."

"I do," Kristin told him. "I know that the law is such that no one can force a maiden into a marriage against her will; then she can bring her case before the *ting*."

"I think it's before the bishop," said Simon, smiling harshly. "But I've never had any reason to look into what the law says about such matters. And don't think you'll have any need to do so either. You know I won't demand that you keep your promise if you're so strongly opposed to it. But don't you realize . . . it's been two years since our betrothal was agreed upon, and you've never said a word against it until now, when everything is being prepared for the betrothal banquet and the wedding. Have you thought about what it will mean if you step forward and ask for the bond to be broken, Kristin?"

"You wouldn't want me now, anyway," said Kristin.

"Yes, I would," replied Simon curtly. "If you think otherwise, you had better think again."

"Erlend Nikulaussøn and I have promised ourselves on our

Christian faith," she said, trembling, "that if we cannot be joined in marriage, then neither of us will ever take a husband or a wife."

Simon was silent for a long time. Then he said wearily, "Then I don't understand what you meant, Kristin, when you said that he had neither seduced you nor promised you anything. He has lured you away from the counsel of all your kinsmen. Have you thought about what kind of husband you'll have if you marry a man who took another man's wife as his mistress? And now he wants to take as his wife another man's betrothed."

Kristin swallowed her tears, whispering in a thick voice, "You're saying this to hurt me."

"Do you think I want to hurt you?" asked Simon softly.

"This is not how things would have been if you . . . ," Kristin said hesitantly. "You were never asked, either, Simon. It was your father and mine who decided on this marriage. It would have been different if you had chosen me yourself."

Simon drove his dagger into the bench so that it stood upright. After a moment he pulled it out and tried to slip it back into its scabbard. But it refused to go in because the tip was bent. Then he went back to fumbling with it, tossing it from one hand to the other.

"You know very well . . . ," he said, his voice low and shaking. "You know that you would be lying if you tried to pretend that I didn't . . . You know quite well what I wanted to talk to you about, many times, but you received me in such a way that I wouldn't have been a man if I had mentioned it afterward, not if they tried to draw it out of me with burning tongs.

"At first I thought it was the dead boy. I thought I should give you some time . . . you didn't know me. . . . I thought it would be harmful to you, such a short time after. Now I see that you didn't need long to forget . . . and now . . . now . . . now . . ."

"No," said Kristin quietly. "I understand, Simon. I can't expect you to be my friend any longer."

"Friend!" Simon gave an odd little laugh. "Are you in need of my friendship now?"

Kristin blushed.

"You're a man now," she said softly. "And old enough. You can decide on your own marriage."

Simon gave her a sharp look. Then he laughed as he had before.

"I see. You want me to say that I'm the one who . . . I should take the blame for this breach of promise?

"If it's true that you are set in your decision—if you dare and are determined to press your case—then I will do it," he said softly. "To my family back home and before all your kinsmen—except one. You will have to tell your father the truth, such as it is. If you wish, I will take your message to him and make it as easy for you as I can. But Lavrans Bjørgulfsøn must know that I would never go against a promise that I have made to him."

Kristin gripped the edge of the bench with both hands; this affected her more strongly than everything else Simon Darre had said. Pale and frightened, she glanced up at him.

Simon stood up.

"We must go in now," he said. "I think we're both freezing, and the sister is waiting for us with the key. I'll give you a week to think things over. I have some business here in town. I'll come back to talk to you before I leave, but I doubt you'll want to see me before then."

## CHAPTER 8

So that was finally settled, Kristin told herself. But she felt exhausted, drained, and sick with yearning for Erlend's arms.

She lay awake most of the night, and she decided to do what she had never before dared—she would send a message to Erlend. It wasn't easy to find someone who could carry out this errand for her. The lay sisters never went out alone, and she couldn't think of anyone she knew who would do it. The men who did the farm work were older and seldom came near the nuns' residence except to speak with the abbess. So Olav was the only one. He was a half-grown boy who worked in the gardens. He had been Fru Groa's foster son ever since he was found one morning as a newborn infant on the steps of the church. People said his mother was one of the lay sisters. She was supposed to become a nun, but after she had sat in the dark cell for six months—for gross disobedience, it was said, and that was after the child was found—she was given lay-sister garb, and since then she had worked in the farmyard. During the past months Kristin had often thought about Sister Ingrid's fate, but she had never had the chance to talk to her. It was risky to count on Olav; he was only a child, and Fru Groa and all the nuns talked to him and teased him whenever they saw him. But Kristin thought she had very little left to lose. And a couple of days later, when Olav was about to go into town one morning, Kristin asked him to take her message out to Akersnes, telling Erlend to find some excuse so they could meet alone.

That same afternoon Ulv, Erlend's own servant, appeared at the speaking gate. He said he was Aasmund Bjørgulfsøn's man and had been sent by his master to ask whether Aasmund's niece might come into town for a while, because he didn't have time to come up to Nonneseter himself. Kristin thought this would never work; but when Sister Potentia asked her whether she knew the messenger, she said yes. So she went with Ulv over to Brynhild Fluga's house.

Erlend was waiting for her in the loft. He was nervous and tense, and Kristin realized at once that he was again afraid of the one thing that he seemed to fear most.

She always felt a pang in her heart that he should be so terrified that she might be carrying a child, when they couldn't seem to stay away from each other. So anxious was she feeling that evening that she said as much to him, quite angrily. Erlend's face turned dark red; he lay his head on her shoulder.

"You're right," he said. "I should try to leave you alone, Kristin, and not keep testing your luck in this way. If you want me to . . ."

She threw her arms around him and laughed, but he clasped her tightly around the waist and pressed her down onto a bench; then he sat down on the other side of the table. When she reached her hand across to him, he impetuously kissed her palm.

"I've been trying harder than you have," he said fiercely. "If you only knew how important I think it is for both of us that we be married with full honor."

"Then you should not have taken me," said Kristin.

Erlend hid his face in his hands.

"No, I wish to God that I hadn't done you this wrong," he said.

"Neither one of us wishes that," said Kristin with a giddy laugh. "And as long as I can be reconciled and make peace in the end with my family and with God, then I won't grieve if I have to be wed wearing the wimple of a married woman. As long as I can be with you, I often think that I could even do without peace."

"You're going to bring honor back to my manor," said Erlend. "I'm not going to pull you down into my disgrace."

Kristin shook her head. Then she said, "You'll be glad to hear that I have spoken to Simon Andressøn—and he's not going to bind me to the agreements that were made for us before I met you."

Erlend was jubilant, and Kristin had to tell him everything, although she kept to herself the derogatory words that Simon had spoken about Erlend. But she did mention that he refused to let Lavrans think he was the one to blame.

"That's reasonable," said Erlend curtly. "They like each other, your father and Simon, don't they? Lavrans will like me less."

Kristin took these words to mean that Erlend understood she would still have a difficult path ahead of her before they had settled everything, and she was grateful for that. But he didn't return to this topic. He was overjoyed and said he had been afraid she wouldn't have the courage to speak to Simon.

"I can see that you're fond of him, in a way," he said.

"Does it matter to you," asked Kristin, "after all that you and I have been through, that I realize Simon is both a just and capable man?"

"If you had never met me," said Erlend, "you could have enjoyed good days with him, Kristin. Why do you laugh?"

"Oh, I'm thinking about something that Fru Aashild once said," replied Kristin. "I was only a child back then. But it was something about good days being granted to sensible people, but the grandest of days are enjoyed by those who dare to act unwisely."

"God bless Aunt Aashild for teaching you that," said Erlend, taking her onto his lap. "It's strange, Kristin, but I haven't noticed that you were ever afraid."

"Haven't you ever noticed?" she asked, pressing herself to him.

He set her on the edge of the bed and took off her shoes, but then he pulled her back over to the table.

"Oh no, Kristin—now things look bright for both of us. I wouldn't have acted toward you as I have," he said, stroking her hair over and over, "if it hadn't been for the fact that every time I saw you, I thought it was so unlikely that they would ever give me such a fine and beautiful wife. Sit down here and drink with me."

At that moment there was a pounding on the door, as if someone were striking it with the hilt of a sword.

"Open the door, Erlend Nikulaussøn, if you're in there!"

"It's Simon Darre," said Kristin softly.

"Open up, man, in the name of the Devil—if you *are* a man!" shouted Simon, striking the door again.

Erlend went over to the bed and took his sword down from the peg. He looked around in bewilderment. "There's no place here for you to hide—except in the bed . . ."

"It wouldn't make things any better if I did that," said Kristin. She had stood up and spoke quite calmly, but Erlend saw that she was trembling. "You'll have to open the door," she said in the same voice. Simon was hammering on the door again.

Erlend went over and drew back the bolt. Simon stepped inside, holding a drawn sword in his hand, but he stuck it back into its scabbard at once.

For a moment the three of them stood there without saying a word. Kristin was shaking, and yet in those first few moments she felt an oddly sweet excitement—deep inside her something rose up, sensing this fight between two men—and she exhaled slowly: here was the culmination to those endless months of silent waiting and longing and fear. She looked from one man to the other, their faces pale, their eyes shining; then her excitement collapsed into an unfathomable, freezing despair. There was more cold contempt than indignation or jealousy in Simon Darre's eyes, and she saw that Erlend, behind his obstinate expression, was burning with shame. It dawned on her how other men would judge him—he who had allowed her to come to him in such a place—and she realized that it was as if he had been struck in the face; she knew that he was burning to pull out his sword and fall upon Simon.

"Why have you come here, Simon?" she shouted loudly, sounding frightened.

Both men turned toward her.

"To take you home," said Simon. "You shouldn't be here."

"You no longer have any right to command Kristin Lavransdatter," said Erlend furiously. "She is mine now."

"No doubt she is," said Simon coarsely. "And what a lovely bridal house you've brought her to." He stood there for a moment, breathing hard. Then he regained control over his voice and continued calmly, "But as things stand right now, I'm still her betrothed—until her father can come to get her. And until then I intend to defend with both the point and the edge of my sword as much of her honor as can be protected—in the judgment of other people."

"You don't need to do that; I can do it myself." Erlend again turned as red as blood under Simon's gaze. "Do you think I would allow myself to be threatened by a whelp like you?" he bellowed, putting his hand on the hilt of his sword.

Simon put his hands behind his back.

"I'm not so timid that I'm afraid you'll think I'm afraid of you," he said in the same tone as before. "I shall fight you, Erlend Nikulaussøn, you can bet the Devil on that, if you do not ask Kristin's father for her hand within a reasonable time."

"I won't do it at your bidding, Simon Andressøn," said Erlend angrily; crimson washed over his face again.

"No, do it to right the wrong you have done to so young a wife," replied Simon, unperturbed. "That will be better for Kristin."

Kristin screamed shrilly, tormented by Erlend's pain. She stamped on the floor.

"Go now, Simon, go! What right do you have to meddle in our affairs?"

"I have already told you," replied Simon. "You'll have to put up with me until your father has released us from each other."

Kristin broke down completely.

"Go, go, I'll come right away. Jesus, why are you tormenting me like this, Simon? You can't think it's worth it for you to worry about my affairs."

"It's not for your sake I'm doing this," replied Simon. "Erlend, won't you tell her that she has to come with me?"

Erlend's face quivered. He touched her shoulder.

"You have to go now, Kristin. Simon Darre and I will talk about this some other time."

Kristin rose obediently. She fastened her cloak around her. Her shoes stood next to the bed; she remembered them, but didn't have the courage to put them on with Simon watching.

Outside the fog had descended again. Kristin rushed along with her head bowed and her hands clutching at her cloak. Her throat was bursting with suppressed sobs; wildly she wished that there was some place she could go to be alone, to weep and weep. The worst, the very worst she still had ahead of her. She had experienced something new that night, and now she was writhing from it—how it felt to see the man she had given herself to humiliated.

Simon was at her elbow as she dashed through the narrow alleys and across the streets and the open squares where the buildings had vanished; they could see nothing but the fog. Once, when she stumbled over something, he gripped her arm and stopped her from falling.

"Don't run so fast," he said. "People are staring at us. How you're trembling," he said in a gentler tone. Kristin was silent and kept walking.

She slipped on the muck of the road, she was soaking wet, and her feet were ice cold. The hose she wore were made of leather, but quite thin; she could feel them starting to split open, and the mud seeped in to her naked feet.

They reached the bridge across the convent creek and walked more slowly up the slope on the other side.

"Kristin," said Simon suddenly, "your father must never hear of this."

"How did you know that I was . . . there?" Kristin asked.

"I came to talk to you," replied Simon tersely. "Then I heard about the servant sent by your uncle. I knew that Aasmund was at Hadeland. The two of you aren't very good at inventing ruses. Did you hear what I just said?"

"Yes," replied Kristin. "I was the one who sent word to Erlend that we should meet at the Fluga house. I knew the woman."

"Then shame on you! But you couldn't have known what kind of woman she is—and he . . . Now listen," said Simon sternly. "If it *is* possible to conceal it, then you should conceal from Lavrans what you have thrown away. And if you cannot, then you must try to spare him the worst of the shame."

"You certainly show great concern for my father," said Kristin, trembling. She tried to speak defiantly, but her voice was about to break with tears.

Simon walked on a short distance. Then he stopped—she caught a glimpse of his face as they stood out there alone in the fog. She had never seen him look that way before.

"I've noticed it every time I've been out to visit your home," he said. "You, his women, have so little understanding of the kind of man Lavrans is. Trond Gjesling says that he doesn't keep you all in line. But why should Lavrans bother with such things when he was born to rule over *men*? He had the makings of a *chieftain*, he was someone men would have followed, gladly; but these are not the times for such men. My father knew him at Baagahus. And so it has ended with him living up there in the valley, almost like a peasant. He was married off much too young; and your mother, with that temperament of hers, was not the one to make it any easier for him to lead such a life. It's true that he has many friends, but do you think that any one of them can measure up to him? His sons he was not allowed to keep; it was you daughters who were to continue the lineage after him. Will he now have to endure the day when he sees that one is without health and another is without honor?"

Kristin clasped her hands to her heart. She felt that she had to hold on to it to make herself as hard as she needed to be.

"Why are you telling me this?" she whispered after a moment. "You neither want to possess me nor marry me anymore."

"That . . . I do not," said Simon uncertainly. "God help me, Kristin. I remember you on that night in the loft at Finsbrekken. But may the Devil take me alive if I ever trust a maiden by her eyes again!

"Promise me this, that you will not see Erlend until your father arrives," he said as they stood at the gate.

"I won't promise that," said Kristin.

"Then *he* will make me this promise," said Simon.

"I won't meet him," replied Kristin quickly.

"That poor little dog I once sent you," said Simon before they parted. "You must let your sisters have him—they're so fond of him—if you don't mind seeing him in the house, that is.

"I'm heading north tomorrow morning," he said, taking her hand in farewell as the sister keeping the gate looked on.

Simon Darre walked down toward the town. He struck at the air with his clenched fist as he walked, muttering in a low voice and cursing at the mist. He swore to himself that he wasn't sorry about *her*. Kristin was like something he had believed to be pure gold, but when he saw it up close, it was merely brass and tin. White as a snowflake, she had knelt and put her hand into the flame; that was a year ago. This year she was drinking wine with an excommunicated rogue in Fluga's loft. The Devil take it, no! It was because of Lavrans Bjørgulfsøn, who was sitting up there at Jørundgaard and believed . . . Never would it have occurred to Lavrans that they might betray him in this way. Now he would have to bring Lavrans the message himself and be an accomplice in lying to this man. That was why his heart was burning with grief and rage.

Kristin had not intended to keep her promise to Simon Darre, but she managed to exchange only a few words with Erlend, one evening up on the road.

She stood there holding his hand, strangely submissive, while he talked about what had happened up in Brynhild's loft the last time they had met. He would speak to Simon Andressøn some other time. "If we had fought up there, news of it would have spread all over town," said Erlend angrily. "He knew that quite well, that Simon."

Kristin could see how the incident had made him suffer. She had also been thinking about it constantly ever since. There was no escaping the fact that in this situation, Erlend was left with even less honor than she was. And she felt that now they were truly one flesh; she would have to answer for everything he did, even when she disliked his conduct, and she would feel it on her own hand when Erlend so much as scratched his skin.

Three weeks later Lavrans Bjørgulfsøn came to Oslo to get his daughter.

Kristin was both afraid and sick at heart when she went to the parlatory to meet her father. The first thing that struck her as she watched him conversing with Sister Potentia was that he didn't look the same as she remembered him. Perhaps he had not actually changed since they parted a year ago, but over the years she had always seen him as the young, vigorous, and handsome man she had been so proud to have as her father when she was small. Each winter and each summer that had passed up there at home had no doubt marked him and made him age, just as they had seen her develop into a grown-up young woman—but she had not noticed it. She hadn't noticed that his hair had paled in some spots and had acquired a rusty reddish sheen at his temples, the way blond hair goes gray. His cheeks had become dry and thin so that the muscles of his face extended like cords to his mouth; his youthful white and pink complexion had grown uniformly weather-beaten. His back was not bowed, and yet his shoulder blades curved in a different manner beneath his cape. His step was light and steady as he came toward her with his hand outstretched, but these were not the same limber, brisk movements of the past. All of these things had probably been present the year before, but Kristin simply hadn't noticed. Perhaps there was a slight touch of something else—a touch of dejection—that made her see these things now. She burst into tears.

Lavrans put his arm around her shoulder and held his hand to her cheek.

"Now, now, try to calm yourself, child," he said gently.

"Are you angry with me, Father?" she asked softly.

"Surely you must realize that I am," he replied, but he kept on caressing her cheek. "But you also know full well that you needn't be afraid of me," he said sadly. "No, you must calm down now, Kristin; aren't you ashamed to be acting this way?" She was crying so hard that she had to sit down on a bench. "We're not going to speak of these matters here where people are coming and going," he said, sitting down next to her and taking her hand. "Aren't you going to ask me about your mother? And your sisters?"

"What does Mother say about all this?" asked his daughter.

"Oh, you can imagine what she thinks—but we're not going to talk about that here," he said again. "Otherwise she's fine." And then he began to tell her all about everyone back home, until Kristin gradually grew calmer.

But she felt as if the tension only grew worse as her father refused to say anything about her breach of promise. He gave her money to distribute among the poor at the convent and gifts for the lay sisters; he himself gave generously to the convent and to the sisters, and no one at Nonneseter had any other thought than that Kristin was now going home to celebrate her betrothal and her marriage. They both ate the last meal at Fru Groa's table in the abbess's room, and the abbess gave Kristin the best report.

But all this finally came to an end. She said her last goodbyes to the sisters and her friends at the convent gate. Lavrans escorted her to her horse and lifted her into the saddle. It was so strange to be riding with her father and the men from Jørundgaard down to the bridge, along the road on which she had crept in the dark; it was odd to be riding so nobly and freely through the streets of Oslo. She thought about the magnificent wedding procession that Erlend had spoken of so often. Her heart grew heavy; it would have been easier if he had taken her with him. There was still a long time remaining for her to be one person in secret and another in public with other people. But then her gaze fell on her father's aging, somber face, and she tried to convince herself that Erlend was right after all.

There were other travelers at the hostel. In the evening they all ate together in a small room with an open hearth where there were only two beds. Lavrans and Kristin were to sleep there, for they were the foremost guests at the inn. The others left when it grew late, saying a friendly good night and then dispersing to find a place to sleep. Kristin thought about the fact that she was the one who had sneaked up to Brynhild Fluga's loft and allowed Erlend to take her in his arms. Sick with sorrow and the fear that she might never be his, she felt that she no longer belonged here, among these people.

Her father was sitting over on the bench, looking at her.

"We're not going to Skog this time?" Kristin asked, to break the silence.

"No," replied Lavrans. "I've had enough of listening to your uncle for a while—about why I don't use force against you," he explained when she looked at him.

"Yes, I would force you to keep your word," he said after a moment, "if only Simon hadn't said that he did not want an unwilling wife."

"*I* have never given Simon my word," said Kristin hastily. "You always said before that you would never force me into a marriage."

"It would not be force if I demanded that you keep to an agreement that has been known to everyone for such a long time," replied Lavrans. "For two winters people have called you betrothed, and you never said a word of protest or showed any unwillingness until the wedding day was set. If you want to hide behind the fact that the matter was postponed last year, so that you have never given Simon your promise, I would not call that honorable conduct."

Kristin stood there, gazing into the fire.

"I don't know which looks worse," her father continued. "People will either say that you have cast Simon out or that you have been abandoned. Sir Andres sent me a message . . ." Lavrans turned red as he said this. "He was angry with the boy and begged me to demand whatever penalties I might find reasonable. I had to tell him the truth—I don't know whether the alternative would have been any better—that if there were penalties to be paid, we were the ones to do so. We both share the shame."

"I can't see that the shame is so great," murmured Kristin. "Since Simon and I both agree."

"Agree!" Lavrans seized upon the word. "He didn't hide the fact that he was unhappy about it, but he said that after the two of you had talked he didn't think anything but misery would result if he demanded that you keep the agreement. But now you must tell me why you have made this decision."

"Didn't Simon say anything about it?" asked Kristin.

"He seemed to think," said her father, "that you had given your affections to another man. Now you must tell me how things stand, Kristin."

Kristin hesitated for a moment.

"God knows," she said quietly, "I realize that Simon would be good enough for me—more than that. But it's true that I have come to know another man, and then I realized that I would never have another joyous moment in my life if I had to live with Simon—not if he possessed all the gold in England. I would rather have the other man even if he owned no more than a single cow."

"You can't expect me to give you to a servant," said her father.

"He is my equal and more," replied Kristin. "He has enough of both possessions and land, but I simply meant that I would rather sleep with him on bare straw than with any other man in a silk bed."

Her father was silent for a moment.

"It's one thing, Kristin, that I would not force you to take a man you don't want—even though only God and Saint Olav know what you might have against the man I had promised you to. But it's another matter whether the man you have now set your heart on is the sort that I would allow you to marry. You're young and have little experience . . . and setting his sights on a maiden who is betrothed is not something a decent man would normally do."

"That's not something a person can help," said Kristin vehemently.

"Oh yes, he can. But this much you have to realize—that I will not offend the Dyfrin people by betrothing you again as soon as you turn your back on Simon—and least of all to a man who might seem more distinguished or who is richer. You must tell me who this man is," he said after a moment.

Kristin clasped her hands tight, breathing hard. Then she said hesitantly, "I can't do that, Father. Things are such that if I cannot have this man, then you can take me back to the convent and leave me there for good—then I don't think I can live any longer. But it wouldn't be right for me to tell you his name before I know whether he has as good intentions toward me as I do toward him. You . . . you mustn't force me to tell you who he is until . . . until it becomes clear whether he intends to ask you for my hand through his kinsmen."

Lavrans was silent for a long time. He could not be displeased that his daughter acted in this manner. At last he said, "Then let it be so. It's reasonable that you would prefer not to give his name, since you don't know his intentions."

After a moment he said, "You must go to bed now, Kristin." He came over to her and kissed her.

"You have caused much sorrow and anger with this notion of yours, my daughter, but you know that your welfare is what I have most at heart. God help me, I would feel the same no matter what you did. He and His gentle Mother will help us to turn this to the best. Go now and sleep well."

After he had gone to bed, Lavrans thought he heard the faint sound of sobbing from the other bed where his daughter lay, but he pretended to be asleep. He didn't have the heart to tell her that he now feared the old gossip about her and Arne and Bentein would be dug up again. But it weighed heavily on his mind that there was little he could do to prevent the child's good reputation from being sullied behind his back. And the worst thing was that he thought she might have brought this upon herself by her own thoughtlessness.

PART III

# LAVRANS BJØRGULFSØN

## CHAPTER 1

KRISTIN CAME HOME during the loveliest time of the spring. The Laag River raced in torrents around the farm and the fields; through the young leaves of the alder thickets the stream glittered and sparkled white with silver flashes. The glints of light seemed to have voices, singing along with the rush of the current; when dusk fell, the water seemed to flow with a more muted roar. The thunder of the river filled the air over Jørundgaard day and night, so that Kristin thought she could feel the very timbers of the walls quivering with the sound, like the sound box of a zither.

Thin tendrils of water shone on the mountain slopes, which were shrouded in a blue mist day after day. The heat steamed and trembled over the land; the spears of grain hid the soil in the fields almost completely, and the grass in the meadows grew deep and shimmered like silk when the wind blew across it. There was a sweet scent over the groves and hills, and as soon as the sun went down, a strong, fresh, sharp fragrance of sap and young plants streamed forth; the earth seemed to heave a great sigh, languorous and refreshed. Trembling, Kristin remembered how Erlend had released her from his embrace. Every night she lay down, sick with longing, and each morning she awoke, sweating and exhausted from her own dreams.

It seemed incomprehensible to her that everyone at home could avoid saying a word about the one thing that was in her thoughts. But week after week went by, and they were silent about her breach of promise to Simon and did not question what she had on her mind. Her father spent a great deal of time in the woods now that the spring plowing was done. He visited his tar-burners, and he took along his hawk and dogs and was gone for days. When he came home, he would speak to his daughter in just as friendly a manner as he always had; but he seemed to have so little to say to her, and he never asked her to come along when he went out riding.

Kristin had dreaded coming home to her mother's reproaches, but Ragnfrid didn't say a word, and to Kristin that felt even worse. For his ale feast on Saint Jon's Day each year, Lavrans Bjørgulfsøn distributed to the poor people of the village all the meat and food that was saved in the house during the last week of fasting. Those who lived closest to Jørundgaard usually came in person to receive the alms. Great hospitality was shown, and Lavrans and his guests and the entire household would gather around these poor folk, for some of them were old people who knew many sagas and ballads. Then they would sit in the hearth room and pass the time drinking ale and engaging in friendly conversation, and in the evening they would dance in the courtyard.

This year Saint Jon's Day was cold and overcast, but no one complained about it because the farmers of the valley were beginning to fear a drought. No rain had fallen since the Vigil of Saint Halvard, and there was so little snow on the mountains that in the past thirteen years people couldn't remember seeing the river so low at midsummer.

Lavrans and his guests were in a good mood when they went down to greet the poor folk in the hearth room. The people were sitting around the table eating milk porridge and drinking stout. Kristin went back and forth to the table, serving the old and the sick.

Lavrans greeted his guests and asked them if they were satisfied with the food. Then he went over to welcome a poor old peasant man who had been moved to Jørundgaard that very day. The man's name was Haakon, and he had been a soldier under old King Haakon and had taken part in the king's last expedition to Scotland. Now he was impoverished and nearly blind. People had offered to build a cottage for him, but he preferred to be taken from farm to farm, since he was received everywhere as an honored guest. He was unusually knowledgeable and had seen so much of the world.

Lavrans stood with his hand on his brother's shoulder; Aasmund Bjørgulfsøn had come to Jørundgaard as a guest. He too asked Haakon whether he was satisfied with the food.

"The ale is good, Lavrans Bjørgulfsøn," said Haakon. "But a slut must have made the porridge for us today. Overly bedded cooks make overly boiled porridge, as the saying goes, and this porridge is scorched."

"It's a shame for me to give you burned porridge," said Lavrans. "But I hope that the old saying isn't always true, because it was my daughter herself who made the porridge." He laughed and asked Kristin and Tordis to hurry and bring in the meat dishes.

Kristin dashed outside and over to the cookhouse. Her heart was pounding—she had caught a glimpse of her uncle's face when Haakon was talking about the cook and the porridge.

Late that evening she saw her father and uncle talking for a long time as they walked back and forth in the courtyard. She was dizzy with fear, and it was no better the next day when she noticed that her father was taciturn and morose. But he didn't say a word to her.

He said nothing after his brother left either. But Kristin noticed that he wasn't talking to Haakon as much as usual, and when their time was up for housing the old man, Lavrans didn't offer to keep him longer but let him move on to the next farm.

There were plenty of reasons for Lavrans Bjørgulfsøn to be unhappy and gloomy that summer, because there were signs it would be a bad harvest in the village. The landowners called a *ting* to discuss how they were going to face the coming winter. By late summer it was already clear to most people that they would have to slaughter their livestock or drive a large part of their cattle to market in the south in order to buy grain for people to eat in the winter. The year before had not been a good year for grain, so supplies of old grain were smaller than normal.

One morning in early autumn Ragnfrid went out with all three of her daughters to see to some linen she had spread out to bleach. Kristin praised her mother's weaving skill. Then Ragnfrid began stroking Ramborg's hair.

"This is for your wedding chest, little one."

"Mother," said Ulvhild, "will I have a chest too, if I go to a cloister?"

"You know that you'll have no smaller dowry than your

sisters," said Ragnfrid. "But you won't need the same kinds of things. And you know that you can stay with your father and me for as long as we live . . . if that's what you want."

"And by the time you go to the convent," said Kristin, her voice quavering, "it's possible, Ulvhild, that I will have been a nun for many years."

She glanced at her mother, but Ragnfrid was silent.

"If I could have married," said Ulvhild, "I would never have turned away from Simon. He was kind, and he was so sad when he said goodbye to all of us."

"You know your father has said we shouldn't talk about this," said Ragnfrid.

But Kristin said stubbornly, "Yes, I know he was sadder to part with all of you than with me."

Her mother said angrily, "He wouldn't have had much pride if he had shown you his sorrow. You didn't deal fairly with Simon Andressøn, my daughter. And yet he asked us not to threaten you or curse you."

"No, he probably thought he had cursed me so much that no one else needed to tell me how wretched I was," said Kristin in the same manner as before. "But I never noticed that Simon was particularly fond of me until he realized that I held another man dearer than I held him."

"Go on home," said Ragnfrid to the two younger ones. She sat down on a log lying on the ground and pulled Kristin down by her side. "You know very well," she began, "that it has always been thought more proper and honorable for a man not to speak too much of love to his betrothed—or to sit alone with her or show too much feeling."

"I'd be amazed," said Kristin, "if young people in love didn't forget themselves once in a while, instead of always keeping in mind what their elders regard as proper."

"Take care, Kristin," said her mother, "that you do keep it in mind." She was silent for a moment. "I think it's probably true that your father is afraid you have thrown your love away on a man to whom he is unwilling to give you."

"What did my uncle say?" asked Kristin after a moment.

"Nothing except that Erlend of Husaby has better lineage than reputation," her mother said. "Yes, he did ask Aasmund to put in a good word for him with Lavrans. Your father wasn't pleased when he heard about it."

But Kristin sat there beaming. Erlend had spoken to her uncle. And here she had been so miserable because he hadn't sent any word.

Then her mother spoke again. "Now, Aasmund did mention something about a rumor going around Oslo that this Erlend had been hanging around the streets near the convent and that you had gone out and talked to him by the fence."

"Is that so?" said Kristin.

"Aasmund advised us to accept this offer, you see," said Ragnfrid. "But then Lavrans grew angrier than I've ever seen him before. He said that a suitor who took such a path to his daughter would find him with his sword in hand. The manner in which we dealt with the Dyfrin people was dishonorable enough, but if Erlend had lured you into taking to the roads with him in the dark—and while you were living in a convent, at that—then Lavrans would take it as a sure sign that you would be better served to lose such a husband."

Kristin clenched her fists in her lap. The color came and went in her face. Her mother put her arm around her waist, but Kristin wrenched herself loose and screamed, beside herself with outrage, "Leave me be, Mother! Or maybe you'd like to feel whether I've grown thicker around the middle."

The next moment she was on her feet, holding her hand to her cheek. In confusion she stared down at her mother's furious face. No one had struck her since she was a child.

"Sit down," said Ragnfrid. "Sit down," she repeated so that her daughter obeyed. The mother sat in silence for a moment. When she spoke, her voice was unsteady.

"I've always known, Kristin, that you've never been very fond of me. I thought it might be because you didn't think I loved you enough—not the way your father loves you. I let it pass. I thought that when the time came for you to have children yourself, then you would realize . . .

"Even when I was nursing you, whenever Lavrans came near, you would always let go of my breast and reach out to him and laugh so the milk ran out of your mouth. Lavrans thought it was funny, and God knows I didn't begrudge him that. I didn't begrudge you either that your father would play and laugh whenever he saw you. I felt so sorry for you, poor little thing, because I couldn't help weeping all the time. I worried more about losing you than I rejoiced at having you. But God and the Virgin Mary know that I loved you no less than Lavrans did."

Tears ran down over Ragnfrid's cheeks, but her face was quite calm and her voice was too.

"God knows that I never resented him or you because of the affection you shared. I thought that I had not given him much happiness during the years we had lived together, and I was glad that he had you. And I also thought that if only my father Ivar had treated me that way . . .

"There are many things, Kristin, that a mother should teach her daughter to watch out for. I didn't think it was necessary with you, since you've been your father's companion all these years; you ought to know what is proper and right. What you just mentioned—do you think I would believe that you would cause Lavrans such sorrow?

"I just want to say that I wish you would find a husband you could love. But then you must behave sensibly. Don't let Lavrans get the idea that you have chosen a troublemaker or someone who doesn't respect the peace and honor of women. For he would never give you to such a man—not even if it were a matter of protecting you from public shame. Then Lavrans would rather let steel be the judge between him and the man who had ruined your life."

And with that her mother rose and left her.

## CHAPTER 2

ON SAINT BARTHOLOMEW'S DAY, the twenty-fourth of August, the grandson of blessed King Haakon was acclaimed at the Hauga *ting*. Among the men who were sent from northern Gudbrandsdal was Lavrans Bjørgulfsøn. He had been one of the king's men since his youth, but in all those years he had seldom spent any time with the king's retainers, and he had never tried to use for his own benefit the good name he had won in the campaign against Duke Eirik. He was not very keen on going to the *ting* of acclamation either, but he couldn't avoid it. The tribunal officials from Norddal had also been given the task of attempting to buy grain in the south and send it by ship to Raumsdal.

The people in the villages were despondent and worried about the approaching winter. The peasants also thought it a bad sign that yet another child was to be king of Norway. Old people remembered the time when King Magnus died and his sons were children.

Sira Eirik said, "*Vae terrae, ubi puer rex est*. In plain Norwegian it means: there's no peace at night for the rats on the farm when the cat is young."

Ragnfrid Ivarsdatter managed the farm while her husband was away, and both she and Kristin were glad to have their minds and hands full of cares and work. Everyone in the village was struggling to gather moss in the mountains and to cut bark because there was so little hay and almost no straw, and even the leaves that were collected after midsummer were yellow and withered. On Holy Cross Day, when Sira Eirik carried the crucifix across the fields, there were many in the procession who wept and loudly entreated God to have mercy on men and beasts.

One week after Holy Cross Day, Lavrans Bjørgulfsøn came home from the *ting*.

It was long past everyone's bedtime, but Ragnfrid was still sitting in her weaving room. She had so much to do these days that she often worked into the night at her weaving and sewing. And Ragnfrid always felt so happy in that building. It was thought to be the oldest one on the farm; they called it the women's house, and people said it had stood there since heathen times. Kristin and the maid named Astrid were with Ragnfrid, spinning wool next to the open hearth.

They had been sitting there, sleepy and silent, for a while when they heard the hoofbeats of a single horse; a man came riding at great speed into the wet courtyard. Astrid went to the entryway to look outside. She returned at once, followed by Lavrans Bjørgulfsøn.

Both his wife and daughter saw at once that he was quite drunk. He staggered and grabbed hold of the smoke vent pole as Ragnfrid removed his soaking wet cape and hat and unfastened his scabbard belt.

"What have you done with Halvdan and Kolbein?" she asked apprehensively. "Did you leave them behind along the road?"

"No, I left them behind at Loptsgaard," he said, laughing a bit. "I had such an urge to come home. I couldn't rest before I did. They went to bed down there, but I took Guldsvein and raced homeward.

"Go and find me some food, Astrid," he said to the maid. "Bring it over here so you won't have to walk so far in the rain. But be quick; I haven't eaten since early this morning."

"Didn't you have any food at Loptsgaard?" asked his wife in surprise.

Lavrans sat down on a bench and rocked back and forth, chuckling.

"There was food enough, but I didn't feel like eating while I was there. I drank with Sigurd for a while, but then I thought I might just as well come home at once instead of waiting till morning."

Astrid brought ale and food; she also brought dry shoes for her master.

Lavrans fumbled as he tried to unfasten his spurs but he kept lurching forward.

"Come over here, Kristin," he said, "and help your father. I know you'll do it with a loving heart—yes, a loving heart—today at least."

Kristin obeyed and knelt down. Then he put his hands on either side of her head and tilted her face up.

"You know very well, my daughter, that I want only what is best for you. I wouldn't cause you sorrow unless I saw that I was saving you from many sorrows later on. You're still so young, Kristin. You only turned seventeen this year, three days after Saint Halvard's Day. You're seventeen . . ."

Kristin had finished her task. Somewhat pale, she got up and sat down on her stool by the hearth again.

The intoxication seemed to wear off to some extent as Lavrans ate. He answered questions from his wife and the servant girl about the *ting*. Yes, it had been magnificent. They had bought grain and flour and malt, some in Oslo and some in Tunsberg. They were imported goods—could have been better, but could have been worse too. Yes, he had met many kinsmen and acquaintances and brought greetings from them all. He simply sat there, the answers dripping from him.

"I talked to Sir Andres Gudmundsøn," he said when Astrid had gone. "Simon has celebrated his betrothal to the young widow at Manvik. The wedding will be at Dyfrin on Saint Andreas's Day. The boy made the decision himself this time. I tried to avoid Sir Andres in Tunsberg, but he sought me out. He wanted to tell me that he was absolutely certain that Simon saw Fru Halfrid for the first time around midsummer this year. He was afraid I'd think that Simon was planning on this wealthy marriage when he broke off with us." Lavrans sat for a moment, laughing mirthlessly. "You see, this honorable man was terribly afraid that we'd think something like that of his son."

Kristin sighed with relief. She thought that this was what her father was so upset about. Maybe he had been hoping all along that it would still take place—the marriage between Simon Andressøn and herself. At first she had been afraid that he had inquired about her behavior down south in Oslo.

She stood up and said goodnight. Then her father told her to stay a while.

"I have some other news," said Lavrans. "I might have kept it from you, Kristin, but it's better that you hear it. Here it is: That man you have set your heart on, you must try to forget."

Kristin had been standing with her arms at her sides and her head bowed. Now she raised her head and looked into her father's face. Her lips moved, but she couldn't manage a single audible word.

Lavrans turned away from his daughter's gaze; he threw out his hand.

"You know I wouldn't be against it if I sincerely believed that it would be to your benefit," he said.

"What news have you heard on this journey, Father?" asked Kristin, her voice steady.

"Erlend Nikulaussøn and his kinsman Sir Munan Baardsøn came to me in Tunsberg," replied Lavrans. "Sir Munan asked me for your hand on Erlend's behalf, and I told him no."

Kristin stood in silence for a moment, breathing heavily.

"Why won't you give me to Erlend Nikulaussøn?" she asked.

"I don't know how much you know about this man you want for your husband," said Lavrans. "If you don't know the reason yourself, it won't be pleasant for you to hear it from my lips."

"Is it because he was excommunicated and outlawed?" asked Kristin in the same tone as before.

"Do you know what it was that caused King Haakon to drive his close kinsman from his court? And do you know that he was banned by the Church in the end because he defied the archbishop's decree? And that he did not leave the country alone?"

"Yes," said Kristin. Her voice grew uncertain. "I know too that he was eighteen years old when he met her—his mistress."

"That's how old I was when I was married," said Lavrans. "When I was young, we reckoned that from a man's eighteenth birthday he could answer for himself and be responsible for his own welfare and that of others."

Kristin stood in silence.

"You called her his mistress, that woman he has lived with for ten years and who has borne him children," said Lavrans after a moment. "I would regret the day I sent my daughter off with a husband who had lived openly with a mistress for years on end before he married. But you know it was more than merely living in sin."

"You weren't so harsh to judge Fru Aashild and Herr Bjørn," said Kristin quietly.

"Yet I cannot say I would willingly join families with them," replied Lavrans.

"Father," said Kristin, "have you and Mother been so without sin all your lives that you dare judge Erlend so harshly?"

"God knows," replied Lavrans sternly, "that I judge no man to be a greater sinner than I am myself. But one cannot expect me to give my daughter to any man who wishes to ask for her, just because we all need God's mercy."

"You know that's not what I meant," said Kristin hotly. "Father, Mother, you were both young once. Don't you remember that it's not easy to guard yourself against the sin that love provokes?"

Lavrans turned blood-red.

"No," he said curtly.

"Then you don't know what you're doing," screamed Kristin in despair, "if you separate Erlend Nikulaussøn and me!"

Lavrans sat down on the bench again.

"You're only seventeen years old, Kristin," he continued. "It might be that the two of you are more fond of each other than I thought. But he's not so young a man that he shouldn't have realized . . . If he were a good man, then he wouldn't have approached such a young, immature child as you with words of love. He seems to have considered it trivial that you were promised to someone else.

"But I will not betroth my daughter to a man who has two children with another man's true wife. Don't you realize that he has children?

"You're too young to understand that such an injustice breeds endless quarrels and strife among kinsmen. The man cannot abandon his own offspring; neither can he claim them. It will be difficult for him to find a way to present his son in society, or to marry off his daughter to anyone other than a servant boy or a smallholder. And his children would not be made of flesh and blood if they didn't despise you and your children. . . .

"Don't you see, Kristin? Sins like this . . . God may forgive such sins more readily than many others, but they damage a lineage so severely that it can never be redeemed. I was thinking about Bjørn and Aashild myself. There stood that Munan, her son. He was dripping with gold and he sits on the King's council. He and his brothers control the inheritance from their mother, and yet he hasn't visited Aashild in her poverty in all these years. Yes, this was the man that your friend chose as his spokesman.

"No, I say, no! You shall never be part of that family as long as my head is above ground."

Kristin covered her face with her hands and burst into tears. "Then I'll pray to God night and day, night and day, to take me away from here if you won't change your mind!"

"It's useless to discuss this any more tonight," said her father, aggrieved. "You may not believe it, but I must watch over you in such a way that I can answer for the consequences. Go to bed now, child."

He held out his hand to her, but she refused to acknowledge it and went sobbing out of the room.

The parents sat for a moment in silence.

Then Lavrans said to his wife, "Would you mind bringing some ale over here? No, bring some wine. I'm tired."

Ragnfrid did as he asked. When she returned with the tall goblet, her husband was sitting with his face in his hands. He looked up, and then stroked his hands over the wimple covering her head and down along her arms.

"Poor thing, now you've gotten wet. Drink a toast to me, Ragnfrid."

She placed the goblet to her lips.

"No, drink *with* me," said Lavrans vehemently, pulling his wife down onto his lap. Reluctantly she yielded to him.

Lavrans said, "You'll stand behind me in this matter, won't you, my wife? It will be best for Kristin if she realizes from the very start that she must put this man out of her mind."

"It will be hard for the child," said Ragnfrid.

"Yes, I know that," replied Lavrans.

They sat in silence for a while, and then Ragnfrid asked, "What does he look like, this Erlend of Husaby?"

"Oh," said Lavrans, hesitating, "he's a handsome fellow—in a way. But he doesn't look as if he were much good for anything but seducing women."

They were silent again for a while, and then Lavrans went on, "He has handled the great inheritance he received from Sir Nikulaus in such a way that it is much reduced. I haven't struggled and striven to protect my children for a son-in-law like that."

Ragnfrid paced the floor nervously.

Lavrans went on, "I was most displeased by the fact that he tried to bribe Kolbein with silver—he was supposed to carry a secret letter from Erlend to Kristin."

"Did you look at the letter?" asked Ragnfrid.

"No, I didn't want to," said Lavrans crossly. "I tossed it back to Sir Munan and told him what I thought of such behavior. He had put his seal on it too; I don't know what to make of such childish pranks. Sir Munan showed me the seal—said it was King Skule's privy seal that Erlend had inherited from his father. He thought I ought to realize that it's a great honor that they would ask for my daughter. But I don't think that Sir Munan would have presented this matter on Erlend's behalf with such great warmth if he hadn't realized that, with this man, the power and honor of the Husaby lineage—won in the days of Sir Nikulaus and Sir Baard—are now in decline. Erlend can no longer expect to make the kind of marriage that was his birthright."

Ragnfrid stopped in front of her husband.

"I don't know whether you're right about this matter or not, my husband. First I ought to mention that, in these times, many a man on the great estates has had to settle for less power and honor than his father before him. You know quite well yourself that it's not as easy for a man to gain wealth, whether from the land or through commerce, as it was before."

"I know, I know," interrupted her husband impatiently. "All the more reason to handle with caution what one *has* inherited."

But his wife continued. "There is also this: It doesn't seem to me that Kristin would be an unequal match for Erlend. In Sweden your lineage is among the best; your grandfather and your father bore the title of knight in this country. My distant ancestors were barons, son after father for many hundreds of years down to Ivar the Old; my father and my grandfather were sheriffs of the county. It's true that neither you nor Trond has acquired a title or land from the Crown. But I think it could be said that things are no different for Erlend Nikulaussøn than for the two of you."

"It's not the same thing," said Lavrans vehemently. "Power and a knight's title lay just within reach for Erlend, and he turned his back on them for the sake of whoring. But I see now that you're against me too. Maybe you think, like Aasmund and Trond, that it's an honor for me that these noblemen want my daughter to be one of their kinswomen."

"I told you," said Ragnfrid rather heatedly, "that I don't think you need to be so offended and afraid that Erlend's kinsmen will think they're condescending in this matter. But don't you realize one thing above all else? That gentle, obedient child had the courage to stand up to us and reject Simon Darre. Haven't you noticed that Kristin has not been herself since she came back from Oslo? Don't you see that she's walking around as if she had just stepped out from the spell of the mountain? Don't you realize that she loves this man so much that if you don't give in, a great misfortune may befall us?"

"What do you mean by that?" asked Lavrans, looking up sharply.

"Many a man greets his son-in-law and does not know it," said Ragnfrid.

Her husband seemed to stiffen; he slowly turned white in the face.

"And you are her mother!" he said hoarsely. "Have you . . . have you seen . . . such certain signs . . . that you dare accuse your own daughter of this?"

"No, no," said Ragnfrid quickly. "I didn't mean what you think. But no one can know what may have happened or is going to happen. Her only thought is that she loves this man. That much I've seen. She may show us someday that she loves him more than her honor—or her life!"

Lavrans leaped up.

"Have you taken leave of your senses? How can you think such things of our good, beautiful child? Nothing much can have happened to her there, with the nuns. I know she's no milkmaid who gives up her virtue behind a fence. You must realize that she can't have seen this man or spoken to him more than a few times. She'll get over him. It's probably just the whim of a young maiden. God knows it hurts me dearly to see her grieving so, but you know that this *has* to pass with time!

"Life, you say, and honor. Here at home on my own farm I can surely protect my own daughter. And I don't believe any maiden of good family and with an honorable and Christian upbringing would part so easily with her honor, or her life. No, this is the kind of thing people write ballads about. I think when a man or a maiden is tempted to do something like that, they make up a ballad about it, which helps them, but they refrain from actually doing it. . . .

"Even you," he said, stopping in front of his wife. "There was another man you would rather have had, back when the two of us were married. What kind of situation do you think you'd have been in if your father had let you make up your own mind?"

Now it was Ragnfrid's turn to grow pale as death.

"Jesus and Maria! Who told you . . ."

"Sigurd of Loptsgaard said something about it, right after we moved here to the valley," said Lavrans. "But give me an answer to my question. Do you think you would have been happier if Ivar had given you to that man?"

His wife stood with her head bowed low.

"That man," she said almost inaudibly, "didn't want *me*." A shudder seemed to pass through her body; she struck at the air with a clenched fist.

Then her husband gently placed his hands on her shoulders.

"Is *that* it?" he said, overcome, and a profound and sorrowful amazement filled his voice. "Is *that* it? For all these years . . . have you been harboring sorrow for *him*, Ragnfrid?"

She was shaking, but she did not answer.

"Ragnfrid?" he said in the same tone of voice. "But after Bjørgulf died . . . and when you . . . when you wanted me to be toward you—in a way that I couldn't . . . Were you thinking about the other man then?" he whispered, frightened and confused and tormented.

"How can you think such things?" she whispered, on the verge of tears.

Lavrans leaned his forehead against his wife's and turned his head gently from side to side.

"I don't know. You're so strange, everything you said tonight . . . I was afraid, Ragnfrid. I don't understand women very well."

Ragnfrid smiled wanly and put her arms around his neck.

"God knows, Lavrans . . . I begged you because I loved you more than is good for a human soul. And I hated the other man so much that I knew it made the Devil happy."

"I have loved you, dear wife, with all my heart," said Lavrans tenderly, kissing her. "Do you know that? I thought we were so happy together—weren't we, Ragnfrid?"

"You are the best husband," she said with a little sob, pressing herself against him.

Ardently he embraced her.

"Tonight I want to sleep with you, Ragnfrid. And if you would be toward me the way you were in the old days, then I wouldn't be . . . such a fool."

His wife stiffened in his arms and pulled away a little.

"It's fasting time," she said quietly, her voice strangely hard.

"So it is." Her husband chuckled. "You and I, Ragnfrid, we have observed all the fast days and have tried to live by God's commandments in all things. And now it almost seems to me . . . that we might have been happier if we had had more to regret."

"Don't talk that way," implored his wife in despair, holding his temples in her gaunt hands. "You know that I don't want you to do anything except what you think is right."

He pulled her to him once more. He gasped aloud as he said, "God help her. God help us all, my Ragnfrid.

"I'm tired," he said, releasing her. "You should go to bed now too, shouldn't you?"

He stood by the door, waiting as she put out the fire in the hearth, blew out the little iron lamp by the loom, and pinched the wick. Together they walked through the rain over to the main house.

Lavrans already had his foot on the stairs up to the loft when he turned back to his wife, who was still standing in the door to the entryway. He pulled her fervently to him one last time and kissed her in the darkness. Then he made the sign of the cross over his wife's face and went upstairs.

Ragnfrid threw off her clothes and crept into bed. She lay still for a while, listening to her husband's footsteps overhead in the loft room; then the bed creaked up there and silence fell. Ragnfrid crossed her thin arms over her withered breasts. Yes, God help her. What kind of woman was she? What kind of mother was she? She would soon be old. And yet she was just the same. She no longer begged the way she had when they were young, when she had threatened and raged against this man who closed himself off, shy and modest, when she grew ardent—who turned cold when she wanted to give him more than his husband's right. That's the way things were, and that's how she had gotten with child, time after time—humiliated, furious with shame because she couldn't be content with his lukewarm, married man's love. Then, when she was pregnant and in need of kindness and tenderness, he had had so much to give. Whenever she was sick or tormented, her husband's tireless, gentle concern for her fell like dew on her hot soul. He willingly took on all her troubles and bore them, but there was something of his own that he refused to share. She had loved her children so much that it felt as though her heart were cut out of her each time she lost one of them. God, God, what kind of woman was she, who in the midst of her suffering was capable of tasting that drop of sweetness when he took on her sorrow and laid it close to his own?

Kristin. She would gladly have walked through fire for her daughter; they wouldn't believe it, neither Lavrans nor the child, but it was true. And yet she felt an anger toward her that was close to hatred right now. It was to forget his own sorrow over the child's sorrow that Lavrans had wished tonight that he could have given in to his wife.

Ragnfrid didn't dare get up, for she didn't know whether Kristin might be lying awake over in the other bed. But she got soundlessly to her knees, and with her forehead leaning against the footboard of the bed, she tried to pray—for her daughter, for her husband, and for herself. As her body gradually grew stiff with the cold, she set out once more on one of her familiar night journeys, trying to break a path to a peaceful home for her heart.

## CHAPTER 3

HAUGEN LAY HIGH up on the slope on the west side of the valley. On this moonlit night the whole world was white. Wave after wave of white mountains arched beneath the bluish, washed-out sky with few stars. Even the shadows cast across the snowy surfaces by rounded summits and crests seemed strangely light and airy, for the moon was sailing so high.

Down toward the valley the forest, laden white with snow and frost, stood enclosing the white slopes around the farms with intricate patterns of fences and buildings. But at the very bottom of the valley the shadows thickened into darkness.

Fru Aashild came out of the cowshed, pulled the door shut behind her, and paused for a moment in the snow. The whole world was white, and yet it was still more than three weeks until the beginning of Advent. The cold of Saint Clement's Day would herald the real arrival of winter. Well, it was all part of a bad harvest year.

The old woman sighed heavily, standing outdoors in the desolation. Winter again, and cold and loneliness. Then she picked up the milk pail and the lantern and walked toward the house, gazing around once more.

Four black spots emerged from the forest halfway down the slope. Four men on horseback. There was the flash of a spear point in the moonlight. They were making their way across with difficulty. No one had come here since the snowfall. Were they heading this way?

Four armed men. It was unlikely that anyone with a legitimate reason for visiting her would travel in such company. She thought about the chest containing Bjørn's and her valuables. Should she hide in the outbuilding?

She looked out across the wintry landscape and wilderness around her. Then she went into the house. The two old dogs that had been lying in front of the fireplace beat their tails against the floorboards. Bjørn had taken the younger dogs along with him to the mountains.

She blew at the coals in the hearth and laid on some wood. She filled the iron pot with snow and hung it over the fire. She strained some milk into a wooden cask and carried it to the storeroom near the entryway.

Aashild took off her filthy, undyed homespun dress that stank of sweat and the cowshed and put on a dark blue one. She exchanged the rough muslin kerchief for a white linen wimple which she draped around her head and throat. She took off her fleecy leather boots and put on silver-buckled shoes.

Then she set about putting the room in order. She smoothed out the pillows and furs on the bed where Bjørn had been sleeping during the day, wiped off the long table, and straightened the cushions on the benches.

Fru Aashild was standing in front of the fireplace, stirring the evening porridge, when the dogs gave warning. She heard the horses in the yard, the men coming into the gallery, and a spear striking the door. Aashild lifted the pot from the fire, straightened her dress, and, with the dogs at her side, stepped forward and opened the door.

Out in the moonlit courtyard three young men were holding four frost-covered horses. The man standing in the gallery shouted joyfully, "Aunt Aashild, is that you opening the door yourself? Then I must say '*Ben trouvé!*'"

"Nephew—is that you? Then I must say the same! Come inside while I show your men to the stable."

"Are you alone on the farm?" asked Erlend. He followed along as she showed the men where to go.

"Yes, Herr Bjørn and his man went out with the sleigh. They were going to see about bringing back some supplies we have stored on the mountain," said Fru Aashild. "And I have no servant girl," she added, laughing.

Soon afterward the four young men were seated on the outer bench with their backs against the table, watching the old woman quietly bustling about and putting out food for them. She spread a cloth on the table and set down a single lighted candle; she brought butter, cheese, a bear thigh, and a tall stack of fine, thin pieces of flatbread. She brought ale and mead from the cellar beneath the room, and then she served up the porridge in a beautiful wooden trencher and invited them to sit down and begin.

"It's not much for you young fellows," she said with a laugh. "I'll have to cook another pot of porridge. Tomorrow you'll have better fare—but I close up the cookhouse in the winter except when I'm baking or brewing. There are only a few of us here on the farm, and I'm starting to get old, my kinsman."

Erlend laughed and shook his head. He noticed that his men showed the old woman more courtesy and respect than he had ever seen them show before.

"You're a strange woman, Aunt. Mother was ten years younger than you, but the last time we visited, she looked older than you do tonight."

"Yes, youth fled quickly enough from Magnhild," said Fru Aashild softly. "Where are you coming from now?" she asked after a while.

"I've been spending some time on a farm up north in Lesja," said Erlend. "I've rented lodgings there. I don't know whether you can guess why I've come here to these parts."

"You mean whether I know that you've asked for the hand of Lavrans Bjørgulfsøn's daughter here in the south, at Jørundgaard?" asked Fru Aashild.

"Yes," said Erlend. "I asked for her in proper and honorable fashion, and Lavrans Bjørgulfsøn stubbornly said no. Since Kristin and I refuse to let anything part us, I know of no other way than to take her away by force. I have . . . I've had a scout here in the village, and I know that her mother is supposed to be at Sundbu until some time after Saint Clement's Day and that Lavrans is out at the headland with the other men to bring in the winter provisions for Sil."

Fru Aashild sat in silence for a moment.

"You'd better give up that idea, Erlend," she said. "I don't think the maiden would follow you willingly, and you wouldn't use force, would you?"

"Oh yes she will. We've talked about this many times. She's begged me many times to carry her away."

"Did Kristin . . . !" said Fru Aashild. Then she laughed. "That's no reason for you to count on the maiden coming with you when you show up to take her at her word."

"Oh yes it is," said Erlend. "And now I was thinking, Aunt, that you should send an invitation to Jørundgaard for Kristin to come and visit you—for a week or so while her parents are away. Then we could reach Hamar before anyone notices that she's gone," he explained.

Fru Aashild replied, still laughing a little, "Did you also think about what we should say—Herr Bjørn and I—when Lavrans comes to call us to account for his daughter?"

"Yes," said Erlend. "We were four armed men, and the maiden was willing."

"I won't help you with this," said his aunt sternly. "Lavrans has been a faithful friend to us for many years. He and his wife are honorable people, and I won't participate in betraying them or shaming her. Leave the maiden in peace, Erlend. It's also about time that your kinsmen heard of other exploits from you than that you were slipping in and out of the country with stolen women."

"We need to talk alone, Aunt," said Erlend abruptly.

Fru Aashild took a candle, went into the storeroom, and shut the door behind them. She sat down on a cask of flour; Erlend stood with his hands stuck in his belt looking down at her.

"You can also tell Lavrans Bjørgulfsøn that Sira Jon in Gerdarud married us before we continued on to stay with Duchess Ingebjørg Haakonsdatter in Sweden."

"I see," said Fru Aashild. "Do you know whether the duchess will receive you when you arrive there?"

"I spoke with her in Tunsberg," said Erlend. "She greeted me as her dear kinsman and thanked me for offering her my service, either here or in Sweden. And Munan has promised to give me letters to her."

"Then you know," said Fru Aashild, "that even if you can find a priest to marry you, Kristin will relinquish all right to property and inheritance from her father. And her children will not be legitimate heirs. It's uncertain whether she will be considered your wife."

"Maybe not here in this country. That's also why I want to head for Sweden. Her forefather, Laurentius Lagmand, was never married to the maiden Bengta in any other way; they never received her brother's blessing. And yet she was considered his wife."

"There were no children," said Fru Aashild. "Do you think my sons would keep their hands off their inheritance from you if Kristin were left a widow with children and there was any doubt that they were born legitimate?"

"You do Munan an injustice," replied Erlend. "I know little of your other children. You have no reason to be kind to them, that I know. But Munan has always been my loyal kinsman. He would like to see me married; he spoke with Lavrans on my behalf. Otherwise, by law, I can sue for the inheritance and the good name of whatever children we may have."

"With that you will brand their mother as your mistress," said Fru Aashild. "But I don't think that meek priest, Jon Helgesøn, would dare risk trouble with his bishop in order to marry you against the law."

"I confessed to him this summer," said Erlend, his voice muted. "He promised then to marry us if all other means were exhausted."

"I see," replied Fru Aashild. "Then you have taken a grave sin upon yourself, Erlend. Kristin was happy at home with her father and mother. A good marriage with a handsome and honorable man of good family was arranged for her."

"Kristin told me herself," said Erlend, "that you said she and I might suit each other well. And that Simon Andressøn was no fit husband for her."

"Oh, never mind what I said or didn't say," snapped his aunt. "I've said so much in my time. I don't think you could have had your way with Kristin so easily. You couldn't have met very often. And I wouldn't think she was easy to win over, that maiden."

"We met in Oslo," said Erlend. "Afterward she was staying with her uncle in Gerdarud. She came out to the woods to meet me." He looked down and said quite softly, "I had her alone to myself out there."

Fru Aashild sprang up. Erlend bowed his head even lower.

"And after that . . . was she friends with you?" asked his aunt in disbelief.

"Yes." Erlend's smile was wan and quivering. "We were friends after that. And she didn't resist very strongly; but she is without blame. That was when she wanted me to take her away; she didn't want to go back to her kinsmen."

"But you refused?"

"Yes, I wanted to attempt to win her as my wife with her father's consent."

"Was this long ago?" asked Fru Aashild.

"It was a year ago, on Saint Lavrans's Day," replied Erlend.

"You haven't made much haste to ask for her hand," said his aunt.

"She wasn't free of her previous betrothal," said Erlend.

"And since then you haven't come too close to her?" asked Aashild.

"We made arrangements so that we could meet several times." Once again that quavering smile flitted across his face. "At a place in town."

"In God's name," said Fru Aashild. "I'll help the two of you as much as I can. I see that it will be much too painful for Kristin to stay here with her parents with something like this on her conscience. There's nothing else, is there?" she asked.

"Not that I know of," said Erlend curtly.

After a pause, Fru Aashild asked, "Have you thought about the fact that Kristin has friends and kinsmen all along this valley?"

"We must travel in secrecy as best we can," said Erlend. "That's why it's important for us to get away quickly, so we can put some distance behind us before her father comes home. You have to lend us your sleigh, Aunt."

Aashild shrugged her shoulders. "Then there's her uncle at Skog. What if he hears you're celebrating a wedding with his brother's daughter in Gerdarud?"

"Aasmund has spoken with Lavrans on my behalf," said Erlend. "He can't be an accomplice, that's true, but he'll probably look the other way. We'll go to the priest at night and keep on traveling by night. I imagine that Aasmund will probably tell Lavrans afterward that it's improper for a God-fearing man like him to part us once we've been married by a priest. Rather, he ought to give us his blessing so that we will be legally married. You must tell Lavrans the same thing. He can state his own conditions for a reconciliation with us and demand whatever penalties he deems reasonable."

"I don't think Lavrans Bjørgulfsøn will be easy to advise in this matter," said Fru Aashild. "God and Saint Olav know that I do not like this business, nephew. But I realize that this is your last recourse if you are to repair the harm you have done to Kristin. Tomorrow I will ride to Jørundgaard myself if you'll lend me one of your men, and I can get Ingrid to the north to look after my livestock."

Fru Aashild arrived at Jørundgaard the following evening just as the moonlight broke away from the last glow of the day. She saw how pale and hollow-cheeked Kristin had become when the girl came out to the courtyard to receive her guest.

Fru Aashild sat next to the hearth and played with the two younger sisters. Secretly she watched Kristin with searching eyes as the maiden set the table. She was thin and silent. She had always been quiet, but it was a different kind of silence that had come over her now. Fru Aashild could imagine all the tension and stubborn defiance that lay behind it.

"You've probably heard," said Kristin, coming over to her, "about what happened here this fall?"

"Yes, that my sister's son has asked for your hand?"

"Do you remember," said Kristin, "that you once said he and I might suit each other well? Except that he was much too rich and of too good a family for me?"

"I hear that Lavrans is of another mind," said Aashild dryly. There was a sparkle in Kristin's eye, and she smiled a little. She'll do, thought Fru Aashild. As little as she liked it, she would oblige Erlend and give him the help he had asked for.

Kristin made up her parents' bed for the guest, and Fru Aashild asked the young woman to sleep with her. After they lay down and the main room was quiet, Fru Aashild explained her errand.

Her heart grew strangely heavy when she saw that this child did not seem to give a thought to the sorrow she would cause her parents. Yet I lived in sorrow and torment with Baard for more than twenty years, thought Aashild. But that's probably the way it is for all of us. Kristin didn't even seem to have noticed how Ulvhild's health had declined that autumn. Aashild thought it unlikely that Kristin would see her little sister alive again. But she said nothing of this. The longer Kristin could hold on to this wild joy and keep up her courage, the better it would be for her.

Kristin got up, and in the darkness she collected her jewelry in a small box, which she brought over to the bed.

Then Fru Aashild said to her, "It still seems to me, Kristin, a better idea for Erlend to ride over here when your father comes home, admit openly that he has done you a great wrong, and place his case in Lavrans's hands."

"Then I think Father would kill Erlend," said Kristin.

"Lavrans wouldn't do that if Erlend refused to draw his sword against his father-in-law," replied Aashild.

"I don't want Erlend to be humiliated like that," said Kristin. "And I don't want Father to know that Erlend touched me before he asked for my hand with honor and respect."

"Do you think Lavrans will be less angry when he hears that you've fled the farm with him?" asked Aashild. "And do you think it will be any easier for him to bear? According to the law you'll be nothing more than Erlend's mistress as long as you live with him without your father's consent."

"This is a different matter," said Kristin, "since he tried to win me as his wife but could not. I will not be considered his mistress."

Fru Aashild was silent. She thought about having to meet Lavrans Bjørgulfsøn when he returned home and found out that his daughter had stolen away.

Then Kristin said, "I see that you think me a bad daughter, Fru Aashild. But ever since Father came back from the *ting*, every day here at home has been torture for him as well as for me. It's best for everyone if this matter is finally settled."

They set off from Jørundgaard early the next day and reached Haugen at a little past the hour of midafternoon prayers. Erlend met them in the courtyard, and Kristin threw herself into his arms without regard for Erlend's manservant, who had accompanied Fru Aashild and herself. Inside the house she greeted Bjørn Gunnarsøn and then Erlend's two other men as if she knew them well. Fru Aashild could see no sign that she was either shy or afraid. And later, when they were sitting at the table and Erlend presented his plan, Kristin joined in and suggested what road they should take. She said they should ride from Haugen the following night so late that they would arrive at the gorge as the moon went down, then travel in darkness through Sil until they had passed Loptsgaard. From there they should go along the Otta River to the bridge, and then on the west side of the Otta and Laag by back roads as far as the horses could carry them. They would rest during the day at one of the spring huts there on the slopes, she said, "for as far as the law of the Holledis *ting* reaches, we might run into people who know me."

"Have you thought about fodder for the horses?" asked Fru Aashild. "You can't take feed from people's spring huts in a year like this—if there's any there at all—and you know no one has any to sell here in the valley this year."

"I've thought of that," said Kristin. "You must lend us fodder and provisions for three days. That's also the reason why we shouldn't travel in a large group. Erlend will have to send Jon back to Husaby. In Trøndelag it's been a better year, and it should be possible to get some supplies over the mountain before Christmas. There are some poor people south of the village that I'd like you to give some alms to, from Erlend and me, Fru Aashild."

Bjørn uttered a strangely mirthless guffaw. Fru Aashild shook her head.

But the manservant Ulv lifted his sharp, swarthy face and looked at Kristin with a particularly sly smile. "There's never anything left over at Husaby, Kristin Lavransdatter, neither in a good year nor a bad one. But maybe things will be different when you manage the household. From your speech it sounds like you're the wife Erlend needs."

Kristin nodded calmly at the man and continued hastily. They would have to keep away from the main road as much as possible. And it didn't seem advisable for them to travel via Hamar. Erlend objected that that was where Munan was waiting—there was the matter of the letter for the duchess.

"Ulv will have to leave us at Fagaberg and ride to Sir Munan while we head west toward Lake Mjøsa and ride across country and by back roads via Hadeland down to Hakedal. From there a desolate road goes south to Margretadal; I've heard my uncle speak of it. It's not advisable for us to ride through Raumarike while the great wedding is taking place at Dyfrin," she said with a laugh.

Erlend came over and put his arm around her shoulders, and she leaned back against him, not caring about all the people who were sitting there watching.

Fru Aashild said acidly, "Anyone might think you had eloped before."

And Herr Bjørn guffawed again.

A little later Fru Aashild stood up to go to the cookhouse and prepare some food. She had started the fire out there because Erlend's men would be sleeping in the cookhouse that night. She asked Kristin to come along, "because I want to be able to swear to Lavrans Bjørgulfsøn that the two of you were never alone for a single minute in my house," she said crossly.

Kristin laughed and went out with Aashild. Erlend at once came sauntering after them, pulled up a three-legged stool to the hearth and sat down. He kept getting in the women's way. He grabbed Kristin every time she came near him as she bustled and flew around. Finally he pulled her down onto his knee.

"It's probably true what Ulv said, that you're the wife I need."

"Oh yes," said Aashild, both laughing and annoyed, "she will certainly serve you well. She's the one risking everything in this venture; you're not risking much."

"That's true," said Erlend, "but I've shown my willingness to go to her along the proper paths. Don't be so angry, Aunt Aashild."

"I have every right to be angry," she said. "No sooner do you get your affairs in order than you put yourself in a position where you have to run away from everything with a woman."

"You must remember, Aunt," said Erlend, "that it has always been true that it's not the worst men who get themselves into trouble for the sake of a woman. That's what all the sagas say."

"Oh, God help us," said Aashild. Her face grew soft and young. "I've heard that speech before, Erlend." She took his head in her hands and ruffled his hair.

At that moment Ulv Haldorsøn tore open the door and shut it at once behind him.

"A guest has arrived at the farm, Erlend—the one person you would least want to see, I think."

"Is it Lavrans Bjørgulfsøn?" asked Erlend, jumping up.

"Unfortunately not," said the man. "It's Eline Ormsdatter."

The door was opened from the outside; the woman who entered shoved Ulv aside and stepped into the light. Kristin looked over at

Erlend. At first he seemed to wither and collapse; then he straightened up, his face dark red.

"Where the Devil did you come from? What do you want here?"

Fru Aashild stepped forward and said, "Come with us up to the house, Eline Ormsdatter. We have enough courtesy on this farm that we don't receive our guests in the cookhouse."

"I don't expect Erlend's kin to greet me as a guest, Fru Aashild," said the woman. "You asked where I came from? I come from Husaby, as you well know. I bring you greetings from Orm and Margret; they are well."

Erlend didn't reply.

"When I heard that you had asked Gissur Arnfinsøn to raise money for you, and that you were heading south again," she went on, "I thought you would probably visit your kinsmen in Gudbrandsdal this time. I knew that you had made inquiries about the daughter of their neighbor."

She looked at Kristin for the first time and met the girl's eyes. Kristin was very pale, but she gazed at the other woman with a calm and searching expression.

Kristin was as calm as a rock. From the moment she heard who had arrived, she realized that it was the thought of Eline Ormsdatter that she had been constantly fleeing from, that she had tried to drown it out with defiance and restlessness and impatience. The whole time she had been striving not to think about whether Erlend had freed himself completely from his former mistress. Now she had been overtaken, and it was futile to fight it anymore. But she did not try to avoid it.

She saw that Eline Ormsdatter was beautiful. She was no longer young, but she was lovely, and at one time she must have been radiantly beautiful. She had let her hood fall back; her forehead was round and smooth, her cheekbones jutted out slightly—but it was still easy to see that once she had been quite striking. Her wimple covered only the back of her head; as she spoke, Eline tucked the shiny gold, wavy hair in front under the cloth. Kristin had never seen a woman with such big eyes; they were dark brown, round, and hard, but beneath the narrow, coal-black eyebrows and the long eyelashes her eyes were strangely beautiful next to her golden hair. Her skin and lips were chapped from the ride in the cold, but this did not detract from her appearance; she was much too beautiful for that. The heavy traveling clothes enshrouded her figure, but she wore them and carried herself as only a woman can who bears the most confident pride in the splendor of her own body. She was not quite as tall as Kristin, but she had such a bearing that she seemed taller than the slim, small-boned girl.

"Has she been with you at Husaby the whole time?" Kristin asked quietly.

"I haven't been at Husaby," said Erlend brusquely, his face flushing again. "I've been at Hestnæs for most of the summer."

"Here is the news I wanted to bring you, Erlend," said Eline. "You no longer need to seek lodgings with your kinsmen and test their hospitality while I keep house for you. This autumn I became a widow."

Erlend stood motionless.

"I wasn't the one who asked you to come to Husaby to keep house last year," he said with difficulty.

"I heard that everything was going downhill there," said Eline. "I still had enough good feelings toward you from the old days, Erlend, that I thought I should look out for your well-being—though God knows you haven't treated me or our children very kindly."

"I've done what I could for the children," said Erlend, "and you know full well that it was for their sake that I allowed you to stay at Husaby. You can't say that you did either them or me any good," he added, smiling spitefully. "Gissur could manage quite well without your help."

"Yes, you've always trusted Gissur," said Eline, laughing softly. "But the fact is, Erlend—now I am free. If you wish, you can keep the promise you once gave me."

Erlend was silent.

"Do you remember," said Eline, "the night I gave birth to your son? You promised then that you would marry me when Sigurd died."

Erlend pushed back his hair, wet with sweat.

"Yes, I remember," he said.

"Will you keep your word now?" asked Eline.

"No," said Erlend.

Eline Ormsdatter looked over at Kristin, smiled slightly, and nodded. Then she turned back to Erlend.

"That was ten years ago, Eline," he said. "Since that day we have lived together year in and year out like two people condemned to Hell."

"That's not entirely true," she said with the same smile.

"It's been years since there was anything else," said Erlend, exhausted. "It wouldn't help the children. And you know . . . you know that I can hardly stand to be in the same room with you anymore," he almost screamed.

"I didn't notice that when you were home this summer," said Eline with a telling smile. "We weren't enemies then. Not all the time."

"If you think that meant we were friends, go ahead and think so," said Erlend wearily.

"Are you just going to stand here?" said Fru Aashild. She ladled some porridge into two large wooden trenchers and handed one of them to Kristin. The girl took it. "Take it over to the house. Here, Ulv, take the other one. Put them on the table; we must have supper no matter how things stand."

Kristin and the servant went out with the dishes of food. Fru Aashild said to the others, "Come along, you two; it does no good for you to stand here barking at each other."

"It's best for Eline and me to talk this out with each other now," said Erlend.

Fru Aashild said no more and left.

Over in the house Kristin put the food on the table and brought up ale from the cellar. She sat down on the outer bench, erect as a candlestick, her face calm, but she did not eat. Bjørn and Erlend's men didn't have much appetite either. Only Bjørn's man and the servant who had come with Eline ate anything. Fru Aashild sat down and ate a little porridge. No one said a word.

Finally Eline Ormsdatter came in alone. Fru Aashild offered her a place between Kristin and herself; Eline sat down and ate something. Every once in a while the trace of a secret smile flitted across her face, and she would glance at Kristin.

After a while Fru Aashild went out to the cookhouse.

The fire had almost gone out. Erlend was sitting on the three-legged stool near the hearth, huddled up with his head on his arms.

Fru Aashild went over and put her hand on his shoulder. "God forgive you, Erlend, for the way you have handled things."

Erlend looked up. His face was tear-streaked with misery.

"She's with child," he said and closed his eyes.

Fru Aashild's face flamed up; she gripped his shoulder hard. "Whose is it?" she asked bluntly and with contempt.

"Well, it isn't mine," said Erlend dully. "But you probably won't believe me. No one will. . . ." He collapsed once more.

Fru Aashild sat down in front of him at the edge of the hearth. "You must try to pull yourself together, Erlend. It's not so easy to believe you in this matter. Do you swear that it's not yours?"

Erlend lifted his haggard face. "As truly as I need God's mercy. As truly as I hope that . . . that God has comforted Mother in Heaven for all that she had to endure down here. I have *not* touched Eline since the first time I saw Kristin!" He shouted so that Fru Aashild had to hush him.

"Then I don't see that this is such a misfortune. You must find out who the father is and pay him to marry her."

"I think it's Gissur Arnfinsøn, my foreman at Husaby," said Erlend wearily. "We talked about it last fall—and since then too. Sigurd's death has been expected for some time. Gissur was willing to marry her when she became a widow if I would give her a sufficient dowry."

"I see," said Fru Aashild.

Erlend went on. "She swears that she won't have him. She will name me as the father. If I swear that I'm not . . . do you think anyone will believe that I'm not swearing falsely?"

"You'll have to dissuade her," said Fru Aashild. "There's no other way out. You must go home with her to Husaby tomorrow. And then you must stand firm and arrange this marriage between your foreman and Eline."

"You're right," said Erlend. Then he bent forward and sobbed aloud.

"Don't you see, Aunt . . . What do you think Kristin will believe?"

That night Erlend slept in the cookhouse with the servants. In the house Kristin slept with Fru Aashild in her bed, and Eline Ormsdatter slept in the other one. Bjørn went out to sleep in the stable.

The next morning Kristin followed Fru Aashild out to the cowshed. While Fru Aashild went to the cookhouse to make breakfast, Kristin carried the milk up to the house.

A candle was burning on the table. Eline was dressed and sitting on the edge of the bed. Kristin greeted her quietly, got out a basin, and strained the milk.

"Would you give me some milk?" asked Eline. Kristin took a wooden ladle and handed it to the woman. She drank greedily and looked over the rim at Kristin.

"So you're Kristin Lavransdatter, the one who has robbed me of Erlend's affections," she said, handing the ladle back.

"You're the one who should know whether there were any affections to rob," replied the young maiden.

Eline bit her lip. "What will you do," she said, "if Erlend grows tired of you and one day offers to marry you to his servant? Would you obey Erlend in that too?"

Kristin didn't answer.

Then the other woman laughed and said, "You obey him in everything, I imagine. What do you think, Kristin—shall we throw the dice for our man, we two mistresses of Erlend Nikulaussøn?" When she received no reply, she laughed again and said, "Are you so simple-minded that you don't deny you're a kept woman?"

"To you I don't feel like lying," said Kristin.

"It wouldn't do you much good anyway," replied Eline in the same tone of voice. "I know that boy. I can imagine that he probably rushed at you like a black grouse the second time you were together. And it's too bad for you, pretty child that you are."

Kristin's cheeks grew pale. Sick with loathing she said quietly, "I don't want to talk to you."

"Do you think he'll treat you any better than he did me?" Eline continued.

Then Kristin replied sharply, "I won't complain about Erlend, no matter what he does. I was the one who took the wrong path, and I won't moan and feel sorry for myself even if it leads me out over the scree."

Eline was silent for a moment. Then she said, flushed and uncertain, "I was a maiden too, when he took me, Kristin—even though I had been the old man's wife for seven years. But you probably can't understand what a wretched life that was."

Kristin started to tremble violently. Eline gazed at her. Then she took a little horn out of her traveling box which stood at her side on the step of the bed.

She broke the seal and said quietly, "You are young and I am old, Kristin. I know it's useless for me to fight against you—now it's your turn. Will you drink with me, Kristin?"

Kristin didn't move. Then the other woman put the horn to her lips. Kristin noticed that she did not drink.

Eline said, "You might at least do me the honor of drinking to me—and promise that you won't be a harsh stepmother to my children."

Kristin took the horn. At that moment Erlend opened the door. He stood there, looking from one woman to the other.

"What's this?" he asked.

Then Kristin replied, and her voice was shrill and wild. "We're drinking to each other, your two mistresses."

He grabbed her wrist and snatched away the horn. "Be quiet," he said harshly. "You shall not drink with her."

"Why not?" said Kristin in the same voice as before. "She was just as pure as I was when you seduced her."

"She's said that so often that she believes it herself," replied Erlend. "Do you remember when you made me go to Sigurd with that lie, Eline, and he produced witnesses that he had caught you with another man?"

Pale with disgust, Kristin turned away. Eline's face had flushed dark red. Then she said spitefully, "Even so, that girl isn't going to turn into a leper if she drinks with me."

Furious, Erlend turned toward Eline—and then his face suddenly grew rigid and the man gasped in horror.

"Jesus!" he said almost inaudibly. He grabbed Eline by the arm.

"Then drink to *her*," he said, his voice harsh and quavering. "Drink first, and then she'll drink with you."

Eline wrenched herself away with a gasp. She fled backward across the room, the man after her.

"Drink," he said. He pulled his dagger out of his belt and followed her with it in his hand. "Taste the drink you've made for Kristin." He grabbed Eline by the arm, dragged her over to the table, and forced her to bend toward the horn.

Eline screamed once and hid her face in her arm.

Erlend released her and stood there shaking.

"It was a hell with Sigurd," shrieked Eline. "You . . . you promised—but you've treated me even worse, Erlend!"

Then Kristin stepped forward and grabbed the horn. "One of us must drink—you can't keep both of us."

Erlend took the horn from her and flung her across the room so she fell to the floor over by Fru Aashild's bed. He forced the drink to Eline Ormsdatter's mouth. Standing with one knee on the bench next to her and his hand on her head, he tried to force her to drink.

She fumbled under his arm, snatched the dagger from the table, and stabbed at the man. The blow didn't seem to cut much but his clothes. Then she turned the point on herself, and immediately fell sideways into his arms.

Kristin got up and came over to them. Erlend was holding Eline; her head hung back over his arm. The death rattle came almost at once; she had blood in her throat and it was running out of her mouth. She spat out a great quantity and said, "I had intended . . . that drink . . . for you . . . for all the times . . . you betrayed me."

"Go get Aunt Aashild," said Erlend in a low voice. Kristin stood motionless.

"She's dying," said Erlend.

"Then she'll fare better than we will," replied Kristin. Erlend looked at her, and the despair in his eyes softened her. She left the room.

"What is it?" asked Fru Aashild when Kristin called her away from the cookhouse.

"We've killed Eline Ormsdatter," said Kristin. "She's dying."

Fru Aashild set off at a run. But Eline breathed her last as she stepped through the door.

Fru Aashild had laid out the dead woman on the bench; she wiped the blood from her face and covered it with a linen cloth. Erlend stood leaning against the wall behind the body.

"Do you realize," said Fru Aashild, "that this was the worst thing that could have happened?"

She had put branches and kindling into the fireplace; now she placed the horn in the middle and blew on it till it flared up.

"Can you trust your men?" she asked.

"Ulv and Haftor, I think I can. I don't know Jon very well, or the man who came with Eline."

"You realize," said Fru Aashild, "that if it comes out that you and Kristin were here together, and that you were alone with Eline when she died, then you might as well have let Kristin drink Eline's brew. And if there's any talk of poison, people will remember what *I* have been accused of in the past. Did she have any kinsmen or friends?"

"No," said Erlend in a subdued voice. "She had no one but me."

"Even so," said Fru Aashild, "it'll be difficult to cover this up and remove the body without the deepest suspicion falling on you."

"She must be buried in consecrated ground," said Erlend, "if it costs me Husaby to do it. What do you say, Kristin?"

Kristin nodded.

Fru Aashild sat in silence. The more she thought about it, the more impossible it seemed to find a solution. In the cookhouse sat four men; could Erlend bribe all of them to keep quiet? Could any of them, could Eline's man, be paid to leave the country? That would always be risky. And at Jørundgaard they knew that Kristin had been here. If Lavrans found out about it, she couldn't imagine what he might do. They would have to take the body away. The mountain road to the west was unthinkable now; there was the road to Raumsdal or across the mountain to Nidaros or south down the valley. And if the truth came out, it would never be believed—even if it were accepted.

"I have to discuss this with Bjørn," she said, standing up and going out.

Bjørn Gunnarsøn listened to his wife's account without changing expression and without taking his eyes off Erlend.

"Bjørn," said Aashild desperately, "someone has to swear that he saw her lay hands on herself."

The life slowly darkened in Bjørn's eyes; he looked at his wife, and his mouth twisted into a crooked smile.

"You mean that someone should be me?"

Fru Aashild clasped her hands and raised them toward him. "Bjørn, you know what it means for these two. . . ."

"And you think it's all over for me anyway?" he asked slowly. "Or do you think there's enough left of the man I once was that I'll dare to swear falsely to save this boy from going under? I, who was dragged under myself . . . all those years ago. Dragged under, I say," he repeated.

"You say this because I'm old now," whispered Aashild.

Kristin burst into sobs that cut through the room. Rigid and silent, she had been sitting in the corner near Aashild's bed. Now she began to weep out loud. It was as if Fru Aashild's voice had torn open her heart. This voice, heavy with memories of the sweetness of love, seemed to make Kristin fully realize for the first time what the love between her and Erlend had been. The memory of burning, passionate happiness washed over everything else, washed away the cruel despairing hatred from the night before. She felt only her love and her will to survive.

All three of them looked at her. Then Herr Bjørn went over, put his hand under her chin, and gazed down at her. "Kristin, do you say that she did it herself?"

"Every word you've heard is true," said Kristin firmly. "We threatened her until she did it."

"She had planned a worse fate for Kristin," said Aashild.

Herr Bjørn let go of the girl. He went over to the body, lifted it onto the bed where Eline had slept the night before, and laid it close to the wall with the blankets pulled over it.

"You must send Jon and the man you don't know back to Husaby with the message that Eline will accompany you to the south. Have them ride off around noon. Tell them that the women are asleep in here; they'll have to eat in the cookhouse. Then speak to Ulv and Haftor. Has she threatened to do this before? Can you bring witnesses forward if anyone asks about this?"

"Everyone who has been at Husaby during the last years we lived together," said Erlend wearily, "can testify that she threatened to take her own life—and sometimes mine too—whenever I talked about leaving her."

Bjørn laughed harshly. "I thought so. Tonight we'll dress her in traveling clothes and put her in the sleigh. You'll have to sit next to her—"

Erlend swayed where he stood. "I can't do that."

"God only knows how much of a man there will be left of *you* when you take stock of yourself twenty years from now," said Bjørn. "Do you think you can drive the sleigh, then? I'll sit next to her. We'll have to travel by night and on back roads until we reach Fron. In this cold no one will know how long she's been dead. We'll drive to the monks' hostel at Roaldstad. There you and I will testify that the two of you came to words in the back of the sleigh. It's well attested that you haven't wanted to live with her since the ban was lifted from you and that you have asked for the hand of a maiden who is your equal. Ulv and Haftor must keep their distance during the whole journey so that they can swear, if necessary, that she was alive the last time they saw her. You can get them to do that, can't you? At the monks' hostel you can have her placed in a casket; and then you must negotiate with the priests for peace in the grave for her and peace of the soul for yourself.

"I know it's not pleasant, but you haven't handled matters so that it could be pleasant. Don't stand there like a child bride who's about to swoon away. God help you, my boy—I suppose you've never tried feeling the edge of a knife at your throat, have you?"

A biting wind was coming down off the mountain. Snow was blowing, fine and silvery, from the drifts up toward the moon-blue sky as the men prepared to set off.

Two horses were hitched up, one in front of the other. Erlend sat in the front of the sleigh. Kristin went over to him.

"This time, Erlend, you must take the trouble to send me word about how the journey goes and where you end up."

He squeezed her hand so hard she thought the blood would burst from her fingernails.

"Do you still dare stand by me, Kristin?"

"Yes, I still do," she said, and after a moment, "We both bear the blame for this deed. I urged you on because I wanted her dead."

Fru Aashild and Kristin stood and watched them go. The sleigh dipped down and rose up over the drifts. It vanished in a hollow, to appear farther down on a white meadow. But then the men passed into the shadow of a slope and disappeared for good.

The two women were sitting in front of the fireplace, their backs to the empty bed; Fru Aashild had taken out the bedclothes and straw. They both knew that it was standing there empty, gaping at them.

"Do you want us to sleep in the cookhouse tonight?" Fru Aashild asked.

"It makes no difference where we sleep," said Kristin.

Fru Aashild went outside to look at the weather.

"No, it doesn't matter whether a storm blows in or a thaw comes; they won't get far before the truth comes out," said Kristin.

"It always blows here at Haugen," replied Fru Aashild. "There's no sign of a break in the weather."

Then they sat in silence again.

"You mustn't forget what fate she had intended for the two of you," said Fru Aashild.

Kristin said softly, "I keep thinking that in her place I might have wanted to do the same."

"You would never have wanted to cause another person to become a leper," said Fru Aashild staunchly.

"Do you remember, Aunt, you once told me that it's a good thing when you don't dare do something if you don't think it's right. But it's not good when you think something's not right because you don't dare do it."

"You didn't dare because it was a sin," said Fru Aashild.

"No, I don't think so," said Kristin. "I've done many things that I thought I would never dare do because they were sins. But I didn't realize then that the consequence of sin is that you have to trample on other people."

"Erlend wanted to mend his ways long before he met you," replied Aashild vehemently. "It was over between those two."

"I know that," said Kristin, "but she probably never had reason to believe that Erlend's plans were so firm that she wouldn't be able to change them."

"Kristin," pleaded Fru Aashild fearfully, "you won't give up Erlend now, will you? The two of you can't be saved unless you save each other."

"That's hardly what a priest would say," said Kristin, smiling coldly. "But I know that I won't let go of Erlend—even if I have to trample on my own father."

Fru Aashild stood up.

"We might as well keep ourselves busy instead of sitting here like this," she said. "It would probably be useless for us to try to go to bed."

She brought the butter churn from the storeroom, carried in some basins of milk, and filled it up; then she took up her position to churn.

"Let me do that," begged Kristin. "I have a younger back."

They worked without talking. Kristin stood near the storeroom door and churned, and Aashild carded wool over by the hearth. Not until Kristin had strained out the churn and was forming the butter did she suddenly say, "Aunt Aashild—aren't you ever afraid of the day when you have to face God's judgment?"

Fru Aashild stood up and went over to stand in front of Kristin in the light.

"Perhaps I'll have the courage to ask the one who created me, such as I am, whether He will have mercy on me when the time comes. For I have never asked for His mercy when I went against His commandments. And I have never asked God or man to return one *penning* of the fines I've had to pay here in my earthly home."

A moment later she said quietly, "Munan, my eldest son, was twenty years old. Back then he wasn't the way I know him to be now. They weren't like that then, those children of mine . . ."

Kristin replied softly, "And yet you've had Herr Bjørn by your side every day and every night all these years."

"Yes," said Aashild, "that I have."

A little later Kristin was done with forming the butter. Then Fru Aashild said that they ought to try lying down for a while.

In the dark bed she put her arm around Kristin's shoulder and pulled the girl's head toward her. And it wasn't long before she could hear by her even and quiet breathing that Kristin was asleep.

## CHAPTER 4

THE FROST HUNG ON. In every stable of the village the starving animals lowed and complained, suffering from the cold. But the people were already rationing the fodder as best they could.

There was not much visiting done during the Christmas season that year; everyone was staying at home.

At Christmas the cold grew worse; each day felt colder than the one before. People could hardly remember such a harsh winter. And while no more snow fell, even up in the mountains, the snow that had fallen on Saint Clement's Day froze as hard as stone. The sun shone in a clear sky, now that the days were growing lighter. At night the northern lights flickered and sputtered above the mountain ridges to the north; they flickered over half the sky, but they didn't bring a change in the weather. Once in a while it would cloud over, sprinkling a little dry snow, but then the clear skies and biting cold would return. The Laag murmured and gurgled lazily beneath the bridges of ice.

Each morning Kristin would think that now she could stand it no longer; that she wouldn't be able to make it through the day, because each day felt like a duel between her father and herself. And was it right for them to be so at odds with each other right now, when every living thing, every person and beast in the valleys, was enduring a common trial? But when evening came she had made it through after all.

It was not that her father was unfriendly. They never spoke of what lay between them, but Kristin could feel that in everything he left unsaid he was steadfastly determined to stand by his refusal.

And she burned with longing for his affection. Her anguish was even greater because she knew how much else her father had to bear; and if things had been as they were before, he would have talked to her about his concerns. It's true that at Jørundgaard they were better prepared than most other places, but even here they felt the effects of the bad year, every day and every hour. In the winter Lavrans usually spent time breaking and training his foals, but this year, during the autumn, he had sold all of them in the south. His daughter missed hearing his voice out in the courtyard and watching him tussle with the lanky, shaggy two-year-old horses in the game that he loved so much. The storerooms, barns, and bins on the farm had not been emptied after the harvest of the previous year, but many people came to Jørundgaard asking for help, either as a purchase or a gift, and no one asked in vain.

Late one evening a very old man, dressed in furs, arrived on skis. Lavrans spoke to him out in the courtyard, and Halvdan took food to him in the hearth room. No one on the farm who had seen him knew who he was, but it was assumed that he was one of the people who lived in the mountains; perhaps Lavrans had run into him out there. But Kristin's father didn't speak of the visit, nor did Halvdan.

Then one evening a man arrived with whom Lavrans Bjørgulfsøn had had a score to settle for many years. Lavrans went out to the storeroom with him. But when he returned to the house, he said, "Everyone wants me to help them. And yet here on my farm you're all against me. Even you, wife," he said angrily to Ragnfrid.

Then Ragnfrid lashed out at Kristin.

"Do you hear what your father is saying to me? I'm not against you, Lavrans. You know full well, Kristin, what happened south of here at Roaldstad late in the fall, when he traveled through the valley in the company of that other whoremonger, his kinsman from Haugen—she took her own life, that unfortunate woman he had enticed away from all her kinsmen."

Her face rigid, Kristin replied harshly, "I see that you blame him as much for the years when he was striving to get out of sin as for those when he was living in it."

"Jesus Maria," cried Ragnfrid, clasping her hands together. "Look what's become of you! Won't even this make you change your mind?"

"No," said Kristin. "I haven't changed my mind."

Then Lavrans looked up from the bench where he was sitting with Ulvhild.

"Nor have I, Kristin," he said quietly.

* * *

But Kristin knew in her heart that in some way she had changed—if not her decision, then her outlook. She had received word of the progress of that ill-fated journey. It had gone easier than anyone could have expected. Whether it was because the cold had settled in his wound or for some other reason, the knife injury which Erlend had received in his chest had become infected. He lay ill at the hostel in Roaldstad for a long time, and Herr Bjørn tended to him during those days. But because Erlend had been wounded, it was easier to explain everything else and to make others believe them.

When he was able to continue, he transported the dead woman in a coffin all the way to Oslo. There, with Sira Jon's intervention, he found a gravesite for her in the cemetery of Nikolaus Church, which lay in ruins. Then he had confessed to the Bishop of Oslo himself, who had enjoined him to travel to the Shrine of the Holy Blood in Schwerin. So now he had left the country.

There was no place to which *she* could make a pilgrimage to seek redemption. Her lot was to stay here, to wait and worry and try to endure her opposition to her parents. A strange, cold winter light fell over all her memories of her meetings with Erlend. She thought about his ardor—in love and in sorrow—and it occurred to her that if she had been able to seize on all things with equal abruptness and plunge ahead at once, then afterward they might seem of less consequence and easier to bear. Sometimes she thought that Erlend might give her up. She had always had a slight fear that it could become too difficult for them, and he would lose heart. But she would not give him up—not unless he released her from all promises.

And so the winter wore on. And Kristin could no longer fool herself; she had to admit that now the most difficult trial awaited all of them, for Ulvhild did not have long to live. And in the midst of her bitter sorrow over her sister, Kristin realized with horror that her own soul had been led astray and was corrupted by sin. For as she witnessed the dying child and her parents' unspeakable grief, she thought of only one thing: if Ulvhild dies, how will I be able to endure facing my father without throwing myself down before him, to confess everything and to beg him to forgive me and to do with me what he will.

* * *

The Lenten fast was upon them. People were slaughtering the small animals they had hoped to save before the livestock perished on its own. And people were falling ill from living on fish and the scant and wretched portions of grain. Sira Eirik released the entire village from the ban against consuming milk. But no one had even a drop of milk.

Ulvhild was confined to bed. She slept alone in the sisters' bed, and someone watched over her every night. Sometimes Kristin and her father would both sit with her. On one such night Lavrans said to his daughter, "Do you remember what Brother Edvin said about Ulvhild's fate? I thought at the time that maybe this was what he meant. But I put it out of my mind."

During those nights he would occasionally talk about one thing or another from the time when the children were small. Kristin would sit there, pale and miserable, understanding that behind his words, her father was pleading with her.

One day Lavrans had gone out with Kolbein to seek out a bear's lair in the mountain forest to the north. They returned home with a female bear on a sled, and Lavrans was carrying a little bear cub, still alive, inside his tunic. Ulvhild smiled a little when he showed it to her. But Ragnfrid said that this was no time to take in that kind of animal, and what was he going to do with it now?

"I'm going to fatten it up and then tie it to the bedchamber of my maidens," said Lavrans, laughing harshly.

But they couldn't find the kind of rich milk that the bear cub needed, and so several days later Lavrans killed it.

The sun had grown so strong that occasionally, in the middle of the day, the eaves would begin to drip. The titmice clung to the timbered walls and hopped around on the sunny side; the pecking of their beaks resounded as they looked for flies asleep in the gaps between the wood. Out across the meadows the snow gleamed, hard and shiny like silver.

Finally one evening clouds began to gather in front of the moon. In the morning they woke up at Jørundgaard to a whirl of snow that blocked their view in all directions.

On that day it became clear that Ulvhild was going to die.

The entire household had gathered inside, and Sira Eirik had come. Many candles were burning in the room. Early that evening, Ulvhild passed on, calmly and peacefully, in her mother's arms.

Ragnfrid bore it better than anyone could have expected. The parents sat together, both of them weeping softly. Everyone in the room was crying. When Kristin went over to her father, he put his arm around her shoulders. He noticed how she was trembling and shaking, and then he pulled her close. But it seemed to her that he must have felt as if she had been snatched farther away from him than her dead little sister in the bed.

She didn't know how she had managed to endure. She hardly remembered why she was enduring, but, lethargic and mute with pain, she managed to stay on her feet and did not collapse.

Then a couple of planks were pulled up in the floor in front of the altar of Saint Thomas, and a grave was dug in the rock-hard earth underneath for Ulvhild Lavransdatter.

It snowed heavily and silently for all those days the child lay on the straw bier; it was snowing as she was laid in the earth; and it continued to snow, almost without stop, for an entire month.

For those who were waiting for the redemption of spring, it seemed as if it would never come. The days grew long and bright, and the valley lay in a haze of thawing snow while the sun shone. But frost was still in the air, and the heat had no power. At night it froze hard; great cracking sounds came from the ice, a rumbling issued from the mountains, and the wolves howled and the foxes yipped all the way down in the village, as if it were midwinter. People scraped off bark for the livestock, but they were perishing by the dozens in their stalls. No one knew when it would end.

Kristin went out on such a day, when the water was trickling in the furrows of the road and the snow glistened like silver across the fields. Facing the sun, the snowdrifts had become hollowed out so that the delicate ice lattice of the crusted snow broke with the gentle ring of silver when she pressed her foot against it. But wherever there was the slightest shadow, the air was sharp with frost and the snow was hard.

She walked up toward the church. She didn't know why she was going there, but she felt drawn to it. Her father was there.

Several farmers—guild brothers—were holding a meeting in the gallery, that much she knew.

Up on the hill she met the group of farmers as they were leaving. Sira Eirik was with them. The men were all on foot, walking in a dark, fur-wrapped cluster, nodding and talking to each other; they returned her greeting in a surly manner as she passed.

Kristin thought to herself that it had been a long time since everyone in the village had been her friend. Everyone no doubt knew that she was a bad daughter. Perhaps they knew even more about her. Now they probably all thought that there must have been some truth to the old gossip about her and Arne and Bentein. Perhaps she was in terrible disrepute. She lifted her chin and walked on toward the church.

The door stood ajar. It was cold inside the church, and yet a certain warmth streamed toward her from this dim brown room, with the tall columns soaring upward, lifting the darkness up toward the crossbeams of the roof. There were no lit candles on the altars, but a little sunshine came in through the open door, casting a faint light on the paintings and vessels.

Up near the Saint Thomas altar she saw her father on his knees with his head resting on his folded hands, which were clutching his cap against his chest.

Shy and dispirited, Kristin tiptoed out and stood on the gallery. Framed by the arch of two small pillars, which she held on to, she saw Jørundgaard lying below, and beyond her home the pale blue haze over the valley. In the sun the river glinted white with water and ice all through the village. But the alder thicket along its bank was golden brown with blossoms, the spruce forest was spring-green even up by the church, and tiny birds chittered and chirped and trilled in the grove nearby. Oh yes, she had heard birdsong like that every evening after the sun set.

And now she felt the longing that she thought had been wrung out of her, the longing in her body and in her blood; it began to stir now, feeble and faint, as if it were waking up from a winter's hibernation.

Lavrans Bjørgulfsøn came outside and closed the church door behind him. He went over and stood near his daughter, looking out from the next arch. She noticed how the winter had ravaged her father. She didn't think that she could bring this up now, but it tumbled out of her all the same.

"Is it true what Mother said the other day, that you told her . . . if it had been Arne Gyrdsøn, then you would have relented?"

"Yes," said Lavrans without looking at her.

"You never said that while Arne was alive," replied Kristin.

"It was never discussed. I could see that the boy was fond of you, but he said nothing . . . and he was young . . . and I never noticed that you thought of him in that way. You couldn't expect me to *offer* my daughter to a man who owned no property." He smiled fleetingly. "But I was fond of the boy," he said softly. "And if I had seen that you were pining with love for him . . ."

They remained standing there, staring straight ahead. Kristin sensed her father looking at her. She struggled to keep her expression calm, but she could feel how pale she was. Then her father came over to her, put both arms around her, and hugged her tight. He tilted her head back, looked into his daughter's face, and then hid it against his shoulder.

"Jesus Christus, little Kristin, are you so unhappy?"

"I think I'm going to die from it, Father," she said against his chest.

She burst into tears. But she was crying because she had felt in his caress and seen in his eyes that now he was so worn out with anguish that he could no longer hold on to his opposition. She had won.

In the middle of the night she woke up when her father touched her shoulder in the dark.

"Get up," he said quietly. "Do you hear it?"

Then she heard the singing at the corners of the house—the deep, full tone of the moisture-laden south wind. Water was streaming off the roof, and the rain whispered as it fell on soft, melting snow.

Kristin threw on a dress and followed her father to the outer door. Together they stood and looked out into the bright May night. Warm wind and rain swept toward them. The sky was a heap of tangled, surging rain clouds; there was a seething from the woods, a whistling between the buildings. And up on the mountains they heard the hollow rumble of snow sliding down.

Kristin reached for her father's hand and held it. He had called her and wanted to show her this. It was the kind of thing he would have done in the past, before things changed between them. And now he was doing it again.

When they went back inside to lie down, Lavrans said, "The stranger who was here this week carried a letter to me from Sir Munan Baardsøn. He intends to come here this summer to visit his mother, and he asked whether he might seek me out and speak with me."

"How will you answer him, my father?" she whispered.

"I can't tell you that now," replied Lavrans. "But I will speak to him, and then I must act in such a way that I can answer for myself before God, my daughter."

Kristin crawled into bed beside Ramborg, and Lavrans went over and lay down next to his sleeping wife. He lay there, thinking that if the flood waters rose high and suddenly, then few farms in the village would be as vulnerable as Jørundgaard. There was supposed to be a prophecy about it—that one day the river would take the farm.

## CHAPTER 5

SPRING ARRIVED ABRUPTLY. Several days after the frost broke, the village lay brown and black beneath the torrents of rain. Water rushed down the mountain slopes, and the river swelled and lay like a leaden-gray lake at the bottom of the valley, with small flooded groves at the edge of the water and a sly, gurgling furrow of current. At Jørundgaard the water reached far into the fields. And yet everywhere the damage was much less than people had feared.

The spring farm work was late that year, and everyone sowed their sparse seeds with prayers to God that He might spare them from the night frost until harvest time. And it looked as if He would heed their prayers and lighten their burden a little. June came with favorable weather, the summer was good, and everyone began to hope that in time the traces of the bad year would be erased.

The hay harvesting was over when one evening four men came riding toward Jørundgaard. Two gentlemen and their two servants: Sir Munan Baardsøn and Sir Baard Petersøn of Hestnes.

Ragnfrid and Lavrans ordered the table to be set in the high loft and beds to be made up in the loft above the storehouse. But Lavrans asked the gentlemen to wait to set forth their purpose until the following day, after they had rested from their journey.

Sir Munan did most of the talking during the meal, directing much of the conversation toward Kristin, speaking to her as if they were well acquainted. She noticed that her father was not pleased by this. Sir Munan was thickset, with a ruddy face—an ugly and garrulous man with a rather foolish manner. People called him Munan the Stump or Munan the Prancer. But in spite of the impression he made, Fru Aashild's son was still a sensible and capable man who had been the Crown's envoy in several matters and who doubtless had some influence on those who counseled the governance of the kingdom. He lived on his mother's ancestral property in the Skogheim district. He was quite wealthy and he had made a rich marriage. Fru Katrin, his wife, was peculiarly ugly and she seldom opened her mouth, but her husband always spoke of her as if she were the wisest of women. In jest people called Fru Katrin the "resourceful woman with the lovely voice." They seemed to get on well together and treated each other with affection, even though Sir Munan was notorious for his wayward behavior, both before and after his marriage.

Sir Baard Petersøn was a handsome and stately old man, although he was rather portly and heavy of limb. His hair and beard were somewhat faded now, but there was still as much gold in them as there was white. Ever since the death of King Magnus Haakonsøn he had lived quietly, managing his vast properties at Nordmøre. He was a widower after the death of his second wife, and he had many children, who were all said to be handsome, well-mannered, and well-to-do.

The following day Lavrans and his guests went up to the loft to talk. Lavrans asked his wife to join them, but she refused.

"This must lie solely in your hands," said Ragnfrid. "You know that it would be the greatest sorrow for our daughter if this matter could not be resolved, but I see that there is much to be said against this marriage."

Sir Munan presented a letter from Erlend Nikulaussøn. Erlend proposed that Lavrans should decide on all of the conditions if he would agree to the betrothal of his daughter Kristin. Erlend himself was willing to have his properties appraised and his income examined by impartial men, and to offer Kristin such betrothal and wedding gifts that she would own a third of his possessions, in addition to whatever she brought to the marriage herself, and all inheritances that she might acquire from her kinsmen if she should become a widow with no children surviving the father. Furthermore, he offered to allow Kristin to manage with full authority her part of the property, both that which she brought into the marriage and that which she was given by him. But if Lavrans preferred other conditions for the division of property, then Erlend would be willing to hear his views and to act accordingly. There was only one condition to which Kristin's kinsmen would have to bind themselves: if they acquired guardianship over any children that he and she might have, they must never try to revoke the gifts that he had given to his children by Eline Ormsdatter. They must recognize as valid the claim that these properties had been separated from his possessions before he entered into the marriage with Kristin Lavransdatter. Finally, Erlend offered to hold the wedding with all appropriate splendor at his manor at Husaby.

It was then Lavrans's turn to speak, and he said, "This is a handsome offer. I see that it is your kinsman's fervent desire to come to an agreement with me. I also realize that he has asked you, Sir Munan, for a second time to come on such an errand to me—a man of no great import outside this village—and a gentleman such as you, Sir Baard, to take the trouble to make this journey on his behalf. But now I must tell you in regard to Erlend's offer that my daughter has not been raised to manage properties and riches herself, and I have always intended to give her to a man in whose hands I could confidently place the maiden's welfare. I don't know whether Kristin is capable of handling such responsibility or not, but I hardly think that she would thrive by doing so. She is placid and compliant in temperament. One of the reasons that I bore in mind when I opposed the marriage was this: that Erlend has shown a certain imprudence in several areas. Had she been a domineering, bold, and headstrong woman, then the situation would have been quite different."

Sir Munan burst out laughing and said, "My dear Lavrans, are you complaining that the maiden is not headstrong enough?"

And Sir Baard said with a little smile, "It seems to me that your daughter has demonstrated that she is not lacking in will. For two years she has stood by Erlend, in spite of your wishes."

Lavrans said, "I know that quite well, and yet I know what I'm talking about. It has been hard for her during the time she has defied me, and she won't be happy with a husband for long unless he can rule her."

"The Devil take me," said Sir Munan. "Then your daughter must be quite unlike all the women I have known, for I've never found a single one who didn't prefer to rule over both herself and her husband."

Lavrans shrugged his shoulders and didn't reply.

Then Baard Petersøn said, "I can imagine, Lavrans Bjørgulfsøn, that now you are even less in favor of this marriage between your daughter and my foster son since the woman he was with came to such an end. But you should know that it has now come to light that the wretched woman had let herself be seduced by another man, the foreman of Erlend's farm at Husaby. Erlend knew about this when he journeyed with her through the valley; he had offered to provide her with a proper dowry if the man would marry her."

"Are you sure this is true?" asked Lavrans. "And yet I don't know whether it makes the situation any better. It must be bitter for a woman of good family to arrive on the arm of the landowner, only to leave with the farm hand."

Munan Baardsøn put in, "I see, Lavrans Bjørgulfsøn, that your strongest objection to my cousin is that he has had this unfortunate trouble with Sigurd Saksulvsøn's wife. And it's true that it was ill advised. But in the name of God, man, you must remember—there he was, a young boy in the same house with a young and beautiful wife, and she had a cold and useless old husband, and the nights last half the year up there. I don't think much else could have been expected, unless Erlend had actually been a holy man. It can't be denied that Erlend has never had any monk flesh in him, but I don't imagine that your lovely young daughter would be grateful if you gave her to a monk. It's true that Erlend conducted himself foolishly, and even worse later on. But this matter must finally be considered closed. We, his kinsmen, have striven to help set the boy on his feet again. The woman is dead, and Erlend has done everything within his power for her body and soul. The Bishop of Oslo himself has redeemed him from his sin, and now he has come home, cleansed by the Holy Blood in Schwerin. Do you intend to be harsher than the Bishop of Oslo and the archbishop or whoever it is down there who presides over the precious blood?

"My dear Lavrans, it's true that pure living is an admirable thing, but it's hardly within the powers of a grown man unless he is particularly blessed by God. By Saint Olav—you should keep in mind that the holy king himself was not given that blessing until the end of his life on earth. It was evidently God's will that he should first produce the capable boy-king Magnus, who repelled the heathens' invasion of the north. King Olav did not have that son by his queen, and yet he sits among the highest of saints in Heaven. Yes, I can see that you think this improper talk . . ."

Sir Baard interrupted, "Lavrans Bjørgulfsøn, I didn't like this matter any better than you when Erlend first came to me and said that he had set his heart on a maiden who was betrothed. But I have since realized that there is such a strong love between these two young people, it would be a great sin to separate their affections. Erlend was with me at the Christmas feast that King Haakon held for his men. That's where they met, and as soon as they saw each other, your daughter fainted and lay as if dead for a long time—and I could see that my foster son would rather lose his own life than lose her."

Lavrans sat in silence for a moment before he replied.

"Yes, that sort of thing sounds so beautiful when we hear it in a courtly tale from the southern lands. But we are not in Bretland,[1] and surely you would demand more of a man you intend to take as a son-in-law than that he had made your daughter swoon with love before everyone's eyes."

The other two didn't speak, and then Lavrans continued, "I think, good sirs, that if Erlend Nikulaussøn had not so greatly diminished both his property and his reputation, then you would not be sitting here, asking so earnestly for a man of my circumstances to give my daughter to him. But I won't have it said about Kristin that she was honored by coming to Husaby through marriage to a man belonging to this country's best lineage—after that man had disgraced himself so badly that he could neither expect a better match nor maintain his family's distinction."

He stood up abruptly and paced back and forth across the floor.

But Sir Munan jumped up. "No, Lavrans, if you're going to talk about bringing shame upon oneself, then by God you should know that you're being much too proud—"

Sir Baard cut him off. He went over to Lavrans and said, "And proud you are, Lavrans. You're like those landowners in the past we've heard about, who refused to accept titles from the kings because their sense of pride could not tolerate hearing people say that they owed anything to anyone but themselves. I must tell you that if Erlend had possessed all the honor and wealth that the boy was born with, I would still not consider it disparaging to myself when I asked a man of good lineage and good circumstances to give his daughter to my foster son, if I could see that it would break the hearts of these two young people to be kept apart. Especially," he said softly, placing his hand on the other man's shoulder, "if things were such that it was best for the health of both their souls if they were allowed to marry."

Lavrans shook off Baard's hand. His face grew stony and cold. "I don't know what you mean, sir."

The two men looked at each other for a moment. Then Sir Baard said, "I mean that Erlend has told me that they have sworn themselves to each other with the most solemn of oaths. Perhaps you think you have the authority to release your child, since she has sworn without your consent. But you cannot release Erlend. And I can't see that there is anything standing in the way except your pride—and your abhorrence of sin. But in this it seems to me that you wish to be harsher than God Himself, Lavrans Bjørgulfsøn!"

Lavrans answered somewhat uncertainly, "You may be right in what you say, Sir Baard. But I have mainly opposed this marriage because Erlend seemed to me an unreliable man to whom I would not want to entrust my daughter."

"I think I can vouch for my foster son now," said Baard in a subdued tone of voice. "He loves Kristin so much that if you give her to him, I am convinced he will conduct himself in such a manner that you will have no cause to complain of your son-in-law."

Lavrans didn't reply at once.

Then Sir Baard said imploringly, holding out his hand, "In God's name, Lavrans Bjørgulfsøn, give your consent!"

Lavrans gave his hand to Sir Baard. "In God's name."

Ragnfrid and Kristin were called to the loft, and Lavrans told them of his decision. Sir Baard graciously greeted the two women. Sir Munan shook Ragnfrid's hand and spoke courteously to her, but he greeted Kristin in the foreign manner with kisses, and he took his time about it. Kristin noticed that her father was looking at her as he did this.

"How do you like your new kinsman, Sir Munan?" he asked with derision when he was alone with her for a moment that evening.

Kristin gave her father an imploring look. Then he stroked her face several times and said nothing more.

When Sir Baard and Sir Munan had gone to bed, the latter said, "What wouldn't I give to see the face of this Lavrans Bjørgulfsøn if he ever learned the truth about his precious daughter. Here you and I had to beg on our knees for Erlend to win a woman as his wife whom he has had with him up at Brynhild's inn so many times."

"You keep quiet about that," replied Sir Baard bitterly. "It was the worst thing Erlend could have done when he enticed the child to such a place. And never let Lavrans get word of this; it will be best for everyone if those two can be friends."

It was agreed that the betrothal celebration would be held that same autumn. Lavrans said that he could not offer a grand banquet because the previous year had been so bad in the valley; but he would, on the other hand, host the wedding and hold it at Jørundgaard with all appropriate splendor. He mentioned again the bad year as his reason for demanding that the betrothal period should last a year.

## CHAPTER 6

THE BETROTHAL CELEBRATION was postponed for various reasons. It didn't take place until the New Year, but Lavrans agreed that the wedding needn't be delayed because of that. It would be held immediately following Michaelmas, as had been originally agreed.

So Kristin continued to live at Jørundgaard as Erlend's properly acknowledged betrothed. Along with her mother she went over the dowry that had been assembled for her and strove to add even more to the piles of bed linen and clothing, for Lavrans wanted nothing to be spared now that he had given his daughter to the master of Husaby.

Kristin was surprised that she didn't feel happier. But in spite of all the activity, there was no real joy at Jørundgaard.

Her parents missed Ulvhild deeply—she knew that. But she also realized that this was not the only reason they were so silent and somber. They were kind to her, but when they spoke of her betrothed, she could see that they had to force themselves to do so. And they did it to please her and to be kind; they did not do it out of any desire to speak of Erlend themselves. They were not any happier about the husband she had chosen now that they had come to know the man. Erlend was also silent and reserved during the brief time he was at Jørundgaard for the betrothal celebration—and it could not have been any other way, thought Kristin. He knew that her father had only reluctantly given his consent.

Even she and Erlend had hardly exchanged more than a few words alone. And it had been awkward and strange for them to sit together in full view of everyone; they had had little to talk about because they had shared so many secrets. A slight fear began to stir inside her—faint and dim, but always present—that perhaps, in some way, it might be difficult for them when they were finally married, because they had been too close to each other in the beginning and then had been separated for far too long.

But she tried to push this thought aside. Erlend was supposed to stay with them at Jørundgaard during Whitsuntide. He had asked Lavrans and Ragnfrid whether they would have any objections if he came to visit, and Lavrans had hesitated a moment but then replied that he would welcome his son-in-law, Erlend could be assured of that.

During Whitsuntide they would be able to take walks together, and they would talk as they had in the old days; then it would surely go away, this shadow that had come between them during the long separation, when they had each struggled and borne everything alone.

At Easter Simon Andressøn and his wife were at Formo. Kristin saw them in church. Simon's wife was standing quite close to her.

She must be much older than he is, thought Kristin—almost thirty. Fru Halfrid was short and delicate and thin, but she had an unusually lovely face. Even the pale brown color of her hair, which billowed from under her wimple, seemed so gentle, and her eyes were full of gentleness too; they were large and gray with a sprinkling of tiny glints of gold. Every line of her face was fine and pure; but her complexion was a pale gray, and when she opened her mouth, it was apparent that she did not have good teeth. She didn't look strong, and she was also said to be sickly. Kristin had heard that she had already miscarried several times. She wondered how Simon felt about this wife.

The people from Jørundgaard and from Formo had greeted each other across the church hill several times, though they had not spoken. But on the third day Simon came to church without his wife. Then he came over to Lavrans, and they talked together for a while. Kristin heard them mention Ulvhild. Afterward he spoke to Ragnfrid. Ramborg, who was with her mother, said quite loudly, "I remember you. I know who you are."

Simon lifted up the child and swung her around. "It was nice of you not to forget me, Ramborg." Kristin he greeted only from a short distance away. And her parents didn't mention the meeting again.

But Kristin thought a great deal about it. It had been strange to see Simon Darre as a married man. So many things from the past came alive once more: she remembered her own blind and submissive love for Erlend back then. Now it was somehow different. She wondered whether Simon had told his wife how the two of them had parted. But she knew that he wouldn't have done that, "for my father's sake," she thought with derision. She felt so oddly destitute to be still unmarried and living at home with her parents. But they were betrothed; Simon could see that they had forced their will through. Whatever else Erlend might have done, he had remained faithful to *her*, and she had been neither reckless nor frivolous.

One evening in early spring Ragnfrid wanted to send a message south to Old Gunhild, the widow who sewed fur pelts. The evening was so beautiful that Kristin asked if she could go. In the end she was given permission because all the men were busy.

It was after sunset, and a fine white frosty mist rose up toward the golden-green sky. With every hoofbeat Kristin heard the brittle sound of evening ice as it shattered and then dispersed with a rattling sound. But in the twilight, from the thickets along the road, came a jubilant birdsong, soft and full of spring.

Kristin rode briskly down the road without thinking about much of anything, simply feeling how good it was to be outside alone. She rode with her gaze fixed on the new moon, which was about to sink behind the mountain ridge on the other side of the valley. She almost fell off her horse when the animal abruptly swerved to the side and then reared up.

She saw a dark body curled up at the edge of the road. At first she was afraid. The dire fear of meeting someone alone out on the road never left her. But she thought it might be a wanderer who had fallen ill, so when she had regained control of her horse, she turned around and rode back as she called out, "Is anyone there?"

The bundle stirred a bit and a voice said, "I think it must be you, Kristin Lavransdatter."

"Brother Edvin?" she asked softly. She almost thought it was a phantom or some kind of deviltry that was trying to fool her. But she went over to him, and it was the old man after all, but he couldn't get up without help.

"My dear Father, are you out here wandering at this time of year?" she asked in astonishment.

"Praise be to God for sending you this way tonight," said the monk. Kristin noticed that he was shivering all over. "I was on my way north to visit you, but I could go no farther tonight. I almost thought it was God's will that I should lie here and die on the roads where I've roamed and slept all my life. But I would have liked to receive absolution and the last rites. And I wanted to see you again, my daughter."

Kristin helped the monk up onto her horse and then led it by the bridle as she supported him. In between his protests that she was getting her feet wet in the icy slush, he moaned softly in pain.

He told her that he had been at Eyabu since Christmas; some wealthy farmers in the village had promised during the bad year to furnish their church with new adornments. But his work had gone slowly; he had been ill during the winter. There was something wrong with his stomach that made him vomit blood, and he couldn't tolerate food. He didn't think he had long to live, so he was headed home to his cloister; he wanted to die there, among his brothers. But he had set his mind on coming north through the valley one last time, and so he had accompanied the monk from Hamar when he traveled north to become the new resident priest at the pilgrim hostel in Roaldstad. From Fron he had gone on alone.

"I heard that you were betrothed," he said, "to that man. . . . And then I had such a yearning to see you. I felt so anguished that our meeting in the church at the cloister should be our last. It's been weighing so heavy on my heart, Kristin, that you had strayed from the path of peace."

Kristin kissed the monk's hand and said, "I don't understand, Father, what I have done to deserve your willingness to show me such great love."

The monk replied quietly, "I have often thought, Kristin, that if it had been possible for us to meet more often, you might have become my spiritual daughter."

"Do you mean you would have guided me so that I turned my heart to the convent life?" asked Kristin. After a pause she went on. "Sira Eirik impressed on me that if I couldn't win my father's consent to marry Erlend, then I would have to enter a holy sisterhood and do penance for my sins."

"I have often prayed that you might have a yearning for the convent life," said Brother Edvin, "but not since you told me what you know. I wish that you could have come to God with your wreath, Kristin."

When they reached Jørundgaard, Brother Edvin had to be carried inside and put to bed. They put him in the old winter house, in the hearth room, and made him as comfortable as they could. He was very ill, and Sira Eirik came and tended to him with medicaments for his body and soul. But the priest said that the old man was suffering from cancer, and that he didn't have long to live. Brother Edvin himself thought that when he had regained some of his strength he would head south again and try to make it back to his cloister. Sira Eirik told the others that he didn't believe this was likely.

Everyone at Jørundgaard felt that great peace and joy had come to them with the monk. People went in and out of the hearth room all day long, and it was never difficult to find someone willing to keep vigil over the sick man at night. They flocked around him, as many as could find the time to sit and listen when Sira Eirik came and read to the dying man from the holy books; and they talked with Brother Edvin about spiritual matters. And even though much of what he said was vague and obscure, as was his manner of speaking, the people seemed to draw strength and comfort for their souls, because everyone could see that Brother Edvin was filled with his love for God.

But the monk also wanted to hear about everything else; he asked for news from the villages and wanted Lavrans to tell him about the bad year. Some people had seized upon evil counsel in that time of adversity and had sought out the sort of help that Christian men must shun. A short way into the mountains west of the valley, there was a place with great white stones that were shaped like the secret parts of human beings, and some men had fallen to sacrificing boars and cats before this monstrosity. Sira Eirik had then taken several of the most pious and brave of the farmers out there one night, and they had smashed the stones flat. Lavrans had gone along and could testify that they were completely smeared with blood, and there were bones and the like lying all around. Up in Heidal people had apparently made an old woman sit outside on a buried stone and recite ancient incantations on three Thursday nights in a row.

One night Kristin was sitting alone with Brother Edvin.

Around midnight he woke up and seemed to be suffering great pain. Then he asked Kristin to read to him from the book about the miracles of the Virgin Mary, which Sira Eirik had lent to him.

Kristin wasn't used to reading aloud, but she sat down on the step of the bed and put the candle next to her. She placed the book on her knees and read as best she could.

After a while she noticed that the sick man was lying in bed with his teeth clamped tight, and he had clenched his emaciated hands into fists from the pain.

"You're suffering badly, dear Father," said Kristin with dismay.

"It seems that way to me now. But I know it's because God has made me into a child again, and is tossing me up and down.

"I remember a time when I was small—I was four winters old—and I ran away from home and headed into the forest. I got lost and was out there for many days and nights. My mother was with the people who found me, and when she lifted me up into her arms, I remember that she bit me on the back of the neck. I thought it was because she was angry with me, but later I understood otherwise.

"Now I'm longing for home, away from this forest. It is written: 'Forsake all things and follow me.' But there has been far too much here in this world that I didn't have the heart to forsake."

"You, Father?" said Kristin. "I've always heard everyone say that you were a model of pure living and poverty and humility."

The monk chuckled.

"Ah, young child, you probably think there's nothing else that entices in the world save sensual pleasure and wealth and power. I must tell you that these are small things that are found along the side of the road—but I, I have loved the roads themselves. It was not the small things of the world that I loved but the entire world. God in His mercy allowed me to love Sister Poverty and Sister Celibacy even in my youth, and that was why I thought that with these lay sisters I could walk in safety. And so I have wandered and roamed, wishing that I could travel all the roads of the world.

And my heart and my thoughts have wandered and roamed too—I fear that I have often gone astray in my thoughts about the darkest of things. But now that's over, little Kristin. Now I want to go back to my home and put aside all my own thoughts and listen to the clear words of the guardian about what I should believe, and think about my sins and about God's mercy."

A little while later he fell asleep. Kristin sat down near the hearth and tended the fire. But toward morning, when she was also about to doze off, Brother Edvin suddenly said to her from the bed, "I'm glad, Kristin, that this matter between Erlend Nikulaussøn and you has come to a good end."

Then Kristin burst into tears.

"We have done so much wrong to come this far. And worst of all is this gnawing at my heart that I have caused my father such great sorrow. He's not happy about this either. And yet he doesn't know . . . if he knew everything, then he would surely withdraw all his affection from me."

"Kristin," said Brother Edvin gently, "don't you understand, child, that this is why you must never tell him, and why you must not cause him any more sorrow? Because he would never demand penance from you. Nothing you do could ever change your father's heart toward you."

A few days later Brother Edvin was feeling so much better that he wanted to head south. Since he had set his heart on this, Lavrans had a kind of stretcher made that was hung between two horses, and in this manner he carried the sick man as far south as Lidstad. There Brother Edvin was given new horses and a new escort, and in this way he was taken as far as Hamar. There he died in the monastery of the Dominican brothers and was buried in their church. Later the barefoot friars demanded that the body be delivered to them, because many people in the villages considered him a holy man and called him Saint Even. The farmers in the outlying districts and valleys as far north as Nidaros prayed to him. And thus there was a long dispute between the two cloisters over his body.

Kristin didn't hear of this until much later. But she grieved deeply when she parted with the monk. It seemed to her that he alone knew her whole life—he had known the foolish child that she had been under her father's care, and he had known of her secret life with Erlend. So he was like a clasp, she thought, which bound everything she had loved to all that now filled her heart. She was now quite cut off from the person she had been—the time when she was a maiden.

## CHAPTER 7

As SHE TESTED the lukewarm brew in the vats, Ragnfrid said, "I think it's cool enough that we can put in the yeast."

Kristin had been sitting inside the brewhouse door, spinning, while she waited for the liquid to cool. She set the spindle on the doorstep, unwrapped the blanket from around the bucket with the dissolved yeast, and measured out a portion.

"Shut the door first," said her mother, "so there won't be any draft. You're acting as if you're asleep, Kristin," she added, annoyed.

Kristin slowly poured the yeast into the brewing vats as Ragnfrid stirred.

Geirhild Drivsdatter invoked the name of Hatt, but it was Odin who came and helped her with the brewing; in return he demanded what was between her and the vat. This was a saga that Lavrans had once told Kristin when she was little.

What was between her and the vat . . . Kristin felt ill and dizzy from the heat and the sweet, spicy steam in the dark, close brewhouse.

Out in the courtyard Ramborg was dancing in a circle with a group of children and singing:

> The eagle sits in the highest hall
> flexing his golden claw . . .

Kristin followed her mother out to the little entryway, which was filled with empty ale kegs and all kinds of implements. From there a door led out to a strip of ground between the back wall of the brewhouse and the fence surrounding the barley field. A swarm of pigs jostled each other, biting and squealing as they fought over the tepid, discarded mash.

Kristin shaded her eyes with her hand from the glaring noonday sun. Her mother glanced at the scuffling pigs and said, "We won't be able to get by with fewer than eighteen reindeer."

"Do you think we'll need so many?" asked her daughter, distracted.

"Yes, we must serve game with the pork each day," replied her mother. "And we'll only have enough fowl and hare to serve the guests in the high loft. You must remember that close to two hundred people will be coming here, with their servants and children, and the poor must be fed as well. And even though you and Erlend will leave on the fifth day, some of the guests will no doubt stay on for the rest of the week—at least.

"Stay here and tend to the ale, Kristin," said Ragnfrid. "I have to go and cook dinner for your father and the haymakers."

Kristin went to get her spinning and then sat down in the back doorway. She tucked the distaff with the wool under her arm, but her hands sank into her lap, holding the spindle.

Beyond the fence the tips of the barley glinted like silver and silk in the sun. Above the rush of the river, she heard now and then the sound of the scythes in the meadows out on the islet; occasionally the iron would strike against stone. Her father and the servants were working hard to put the worst of the mowing season behind them. There was so much to do for her wedding.

The smell of the tepid mash and the rank breath of the pigs . . . she suddenly felt nauseated again. And the noontime heat made her so faint and weak. White-faced, her spine rigid, she sat there waiting for the sensation to pass; she didn't want to be sick again.

She had never felt this way before. It would do no good for her to try to console herself with the thought that it wasn't yet certain—that she might be mistaken. What was between her and the vat . . .

Eighteen reindeer. Close to two hundred wedding guests. People would have something to laugh about then, when they heard that all the commotion was for the sake of a pregnant woman who had to be married off in time.

Oh no! She tossed aside her spinning and leaped to her feet. With her forehead pressed against the wall of the brewhouse she vomited into the thicket of nettles that grew in abundance there.

Brown caterpillars were swarming over the nettles; the sight of them made her feel even sicker.

Kristin rubbed her temples, wet with sweat. Oh no, surely that was enough.

They were going to be married on the second Sunday after Michaelmas, and then their wedding would be celebrated for five days. That was more than two months away. By then her mother and the other women of the village would be able to see it. They were always so wise about such matters; they could always tell when a woman was with child months before Kristin could see how they knew. Poor thing, she has grown so pale. . . . Impatiently Kristin rubbed her hands against her cheeks, for she could feel that they were wan and bloodless.

In the past she had so often thought that this was bound to happen one day. And she had not been terribly afraid of it. But it wouldn't have been the same back then, when they could not and would not be allowed to marry in the proper fashion. It was considered . . . yes, it was thought to be shameful in many ways, and a sin too. But if it was a matter of two young people who *refused* to be forced from each other, that was something everyone would remember, and they would speak of the two with compassion. *She* would not have been ashamed. But when it happened to those who were betrothed, then everyone merely laughed and teased them mercilessly. She realized herself that it was laughable. Here they were brewing ale and making wine, slaughtering and baking and cooking for a wedding that would be talked about far and wide—and she, the bride, felt ill at the mere smell of food and crept behind the outbuildings, in a cold sweat, to throw up.

Erlend. She clenched her teeth in anger. He should have spared her this. She had not been willing. He should have remembered how it had been before, when everything had been uncertain for her, when she had had nothing to hold on to except his love; then she had always, always gladly yielded to his wishes. He should have left her alone this time, when she tried to refuse because she thought it improper for them to steal something in secret after her father had placed their hands together in the sight of all their kinsmen. But he had taken her, partly by force, but with laughter and with caresses too, so she had been unable to show him that she was serious in her refusal.

Kristin went inside to tend to the ale, and then came back and stood leaning over the fence. The grain swayed faintly, glinting in the light breeze. She couldn't remember ever seeing the crops so dense and lush as this year. She caught a glimpse of the river in the distance, and she heard her father's voice shouting; she couldn't distinguish his words, but the workers out on the islet were laughing.

What if she went to her father and told him? It would be better to forgo all this trouble, to marry her to Erlend quietly, without a church wedding and grand feast—now that it was a matter of her acquiring a wife's name before it became apparent to everyone that she was already carrying Erlend's child.

Erlend would be ridiculed too, just as much as she would be, or more. He was not a young boy, after all. But he was the one who wanted this wedding, he wanted to see her as a bride wearing silk and velvet and a high golden crown; he wanted *that*, but he also wanted to possess her during all those sweet, secret hours. She had acquiesced to everything. She would continue to do as he wanted in this matter too.

And in the end, no doubt, he would realize that no one could have both. He who had talked of the great Christmas celebration he would hold at Husaby during the first year she was his wife on the manor—then he would show all his kinsmen and friends and the people of the villages far and wide what a beautiful wife he had won. Kristin smiled spitefully. Christmas this year would hardly be a fitting occasion for that.

It would happen around Saint Gregor's Day. Her thoughts seemed to swirl in her head whenever she told herself that sometime close to Saint Gregor's Day she would give birth to a child. She was a little frightened by it too; she remembered her mother's shrill screams, which had rung out over the farm for two days when Ulvhild had come into the world. Over at Ulvsvold two young women had died, one after the other, in childbirth; and Sigurd of Loptsgaard's first two wives had died too. And her own grandmother, for whom she was named.

But fear was not what she felt most. These past years, when she realized again that she was still not pregnant, she had thought that perhaps this was to be their punishment, hers and Erlend's—that she would continue to be barren. They would wait and wait in vain for what they had feared before; they would hope so futilely, just as they had feared so needlessly. Until at last they would realize that one day they would be carried out from his ancestral estate and vanish. His brother was a priest, after all, and the children that Erlend already had could never inherit from him. Munan the Stump and his sons would come in and take their place, and Erlend would be erased from the lineage.

She pressed her hand hard against her womb. It was there—between her and the fence, between her and the vat. Between her and the whole world—Erlend's legitimate son. She had tried everything she had heard Fru Aashild once speak of, with blood from her right and left arm. She was carrying a son, whatever fate he might bring her. She remembered her brothers who had died and her parents' sorrowful faces whenever they mentioned them; she remembered all those times when she had seen them in despair over Ulvhild, and the night she died. And she thought about all the sorrow she herself had caused them, and about her father's care-worn face. And yet this was not the end of the grief she would bring to her father and mother.

And yet, and yet. Kristin rested her head on her arm lying along the fence; the other hand she kept pressed against her womb. Even if this brought her new sorrows, even if it caused her own death, she would still rather die giving Erlend a son than have them both die someday, with the buildings standing empty and with the grain in their fields swaying for strangers.

Someone came into the front room. The ale! thought Kristin. I should have looked at it long ago. She straightened up—and then Erlend stooped as he came out of the doorway and stepped forward into the sunlight, beaming with joy.

"So this is where you are," he said. "And you don't even take a step to meet me?" he asked. He came over and embraced her.

"Beloved, have you come to visit?" she asked, astonished.

He must have just dismounted from his horse; he still had his cape over his shoulders and his sword at his side. He was unshaven, filthy, and covered with dust. He was wearing a red surcoat, which draped from the neckline and was slit up the sides almost to his arms. As they went through the brewhouse and across the courtyard, his clothes fluttered around him so that his thighs were visible clear up to his waist. It was odd; she had never noticed before that he walked slightly crooked. Before she had only seen that he had long, slender legs and narrow ankles and small, well-shaped feet.

Erlend had brought a full escort along with him: five men and four spare horses. He told Ragnfrid that he had come to get Kristin's household goods. Wouldn't it be a comfort for her to find her things at Husaby when she arrived? And since the wedding was to take place so late in the fall, it might be more difficult to transport everything then. And wouldn't it be more likely to suffer damage from sea water on the ship? The abbot at Nidarholm had offered to send everything now with the Laurentius cloister's ship; they expected to set sail from Veøy around Assumption Day. That was why he had come to convey her things through Raumsdal to the headland.

He sat in the doorway to the cookhouse and drank ale and talked while Ragnfrid and Kristin plucked the wild ducks that Lavrans had brought home the day before. The mother and daughter were alone at home; the women servants were all out in the meadows, raking. He looked so happy; he was so pleased with himself for coming on such a sensible errand.

Her mother left, and Kristin tended to the birds on the spit. Through the open door she caught a glimpse of Erlend's men lying in the shade across the courtyard, passing the basin of ale among them. He sat on the stoop, chatting and laughing. The sun shone brightly on his bare, soot-black hair; she noticed that there were several gray streaks in it. Well, he would soon be thirty-two, after all, but he acted like a brash young man. She knew that she wouldn't tell him about her trouble; there would be time enough for that when he realized it himself. A good-humored tenderness coursed through her heart, over the hard little anger that lay at the bottom, like a glittering river over stones.

She loved him more than anything; it filled her heart, even though she always saw and remembered everything else. How out of place this courtier seemed amidst the busy farm work, wearing his elegant red surcoat, silver spurs on his feet, and a belt studded with gold. She also noticed that her father didn't come up to the farm, even though her mother had sent Ramborg down to the river with word of the guest who had arrived.

Erlend came over to Kristin and put his hands on her shoulders.

"Can you believe it?" he said, his face radiant. "Doesn't it seem strange to you—that all these preparations are being made for *our* wedding?"

Kristin gave him a kiss and pushed him aside. She poured fat over the birds and told him not to get in her way. No, she wouldn't tell him.

Lavrans didn't come up to the farm until the haymakers did, around suppertime. He wasn't dressed much differently from the workmen, in an undyed, knee-length homespun tunic and ankle-length leggings of the same fabric. He was barefoot and carried his scythe over his shoulder. The only thing that distinguished his attire from that of the servants was a shoulder collar of leather for the hawk that was perched on his left shoulder. He was holding Ramborg's hand.

Lavrans greeted his son-in-law heartily enough and asked his forgiveness for not coming earlier. They had to push as hard as they could to get the farm work done because he had to make a journey into town between the haying season and the harvest. But when Erlend presented the reason for his visit at the supper table, Lavrans became quite cross.

It was impossible for him to do without any of his wagons or horses right now. Erlend replied that he had brought along four extra horses himself. Lavrans thought there would be at least three cartloads. Besides, the maiden would have to keep all her clothing at Jørundgaard. And the bed linen that Kristin would be taking with her would be needed at the farm during the wedding for all the guests they would have to house.

"Never mind," said Erlend. Surely they would find a way to transport everything in the fall. But he had been so pleased, and he thought it sounded so sensible, when the abbot had suggested that Kristin's things might travel with the monastery's ship. The abbot had reminded him of their kinship. "That's something they're all remembering now," said Erlend with a smile. His father-in-law's disapproval did not seem to affect him in the least.

And so it was decided that Erlend should borrow a wagon and take a cartload of those things that Kristin would need most when she arrived at her new home.

The next day they were busy with the packing. Ragnfrid thought that both the large and the small looms could be sent along now; she wouldn't have time to weave anything else before the wedding. The mother and daughter cut off the weaving that was on the loom. It was an undyed homespun fabric, but of the finest and softest wool, with tufts of black wool woven in to form a pattern. Kristin and her mother rolled up the cloth and placed it in a leather bag. Kristin thought it would be good for swaddling clothes, and it would be pretty with red or blue ribbons around it.

The sewing chest that Arne had once made for her could also go along. Kristin took from her box all the things that Erlend had given her over time. She showed her mother the blue velvet cape with the red pattern that she was going to wear in the bridal procession. Her mother turned it this way and that, feeling the fabric and the fur lining.

"This is a most costly cloak," said Ragnfrid. "When did Erlend give this to you?"

"He gave it to me while I was at Nonneseter," her daughter told her.

Kristin's bridal chest, which her mother had been adding to ever since she was little, was repacked. It was carved in panels, and on each there was a leaping deer or a bird sitting amidst the foliage. Ragnfrid placed Kristin's bridal gown in one of her own chests. It was not quite done; they had been sewing on it all winter long. It was made of scarlet silk and cut in such a fashion that it would fit snugly to her body. Kristin thought that now it would be much too tight across her breasts.

Toward evening the load was all packed and tied under the wagon's cover. Erlend would leave early the next morning.

He stood with Kristin, leaning over the farm gate, looking north, where the bluish-black smudge of a storm cloud filled the valley. Thunder rumbled from the mountains, but to the south the meadows and the river lay in dazzling yellow sunlight.

"Do you remember the storm on that day in the forest near Gerdarud?" he asked softly, playing with her fingers.

Kristin nodded and tried to smile. The air was so heavy and sultry; her head was aching and she was sweating with every breath she took.

Lavrans came over to them at the gate and talked about the

weather. It seldom did any harm down here in the village, but God only knew whether it would bring trouble to the cattle and horses up in the mountains.

It was as black as night up behind the church on the hill. A flash of lightning revealed a group of horses, crowding together restlessly, on the meadow outside the church gate. Lavrans didn't think they belonged there in the valley—the horses were more likely from Dovre and had been wandering in the mountains up beneath Jetta. He shouted over the thunder that he had a mind to go up and see to them, to find out whether there were any of his among them.

A terrible bolt of lightning ripped through the darkness up there. Thunder crashed and roared so they could hear nothing else. The horses raced across the grass beneath the ridge. All three of them crossed themselves.

Then more lightning flashed; the sky seemed about to split in half, and a tremendous snow-white bolt of lightning hurtled down toward them. All three were thrown against each other; they stood there with their eyes closed, blinded, and noticed a smell like scorched stone—and then the crash of thunder exploded in their ears.

"Saint Olav, help us," murmured Lavrans.

"Look at the birch, look at the birch!" cried Erlend. The huge birch out in the field seemed to wobble, and then a heavy limb broke off and dropped to the ground, leaving a long gash in the trunk.

"I think it's burning. Jesus Christus! The church roof is on fire!" shouted Lavrans.

They stood there and stared. No . . . yes, it was! Red flames were flickering out of the shingles beneath the ridge turret.

Both men set off running, back across the farmyard. Lavrans tore open all the doors to the buildings, yelling to those inside. Everyone came rushing out.

"Bring axes, bring axes—the felling axes," he shouted. "And the pickaxes!" He raced over to the stables. A moment later he reemerged, leading Guldsvein by his mane. He leaped up onto the unsaddled horse and tore off toward the north. He had the big broadaxe in his hand. Erlend rode right behind him, and all the other men followed. Some were on horseback, but others couldn't control the frightened animals and gave up and set off running.

Behind them came Ragnfrid and the women of the farm with basins and buckets.

No one seemed to notice the storm any longer. In the flash of the lightning they saw people come streaming from the buildings farther down in the village. Sira Eirik was already running up the hill, followed by his servants. Horse hooves thundered across the bridge below, and several farm hands raced past. They all turned their pale, terrified faces toward the burning church.

A light wind was blowing from the southeast. The fire was firmly entrenched in the north wall; on the west side the entrance was already blocked. But it had not yet seized the south side or the apse.

Kristin and the women from Jørundgaard entered the churchyard south of the church, at a place where the gate had collapsed.

The tremendous red blaze lit up the grove north of the church and the area where posts had been erected for tying up the horses. No one could approach the spot because of the heat. Only the cross stood there, bathed in the glow of the flames. It looked as if it were alive and moving.

Through the roaring and seething of the fire they could hear the crash of axes against the staves of the south wall. There were men on the gallery, slashing and chopping, while others tried to tear down the gallery itself. Someone shouted to the women from Jørundgaard that Lavrans and a few other men had followed Sira Eirik into the church. They had to break an opening in the wall—little tongues of fire were playing here and there among the shingles on the roof. If the wind changed or died down altogether, the flames would engulf the whole church.

Any thought of extinguishing the blaze was futile; there was no time to form a chain down to the river, but at Ragnfrid's command, the women took up positions and passed water from the small creek running along the road to the west; at least there was a little water to throw on the south wall and on the men who were toiling there. Many of the women were sobbing as they worked, out of fear and anguish for those who had gone inside the burning building, and out of sorrow for their church.

Kristin stood at the very front of the line of women, throwing the water from the buckets. She stared breathlessly at the church, where they had both gone inside, her father and Erlend.

The posts of the gallery had been torn down and lay in a heap of wood amid pieces of shingle from the gallery's roof. The men were chopping at the stave wall with all their might; a whole group had lifted up a timber and was using it as a battering ram.

Erlend and one of his men came out of the small south door of the choir; they were carrying between them the large chest from the sacristy, the chest that Eirik usually sat on when he heard confession. Erlend and the servant tipped the chest out into the churchyard.

Kristin didn't hear what he shouted; he ran back, up onto the gallery again. He was as lithe as a cat as he dashed along. He had thrown off his outer garments and was dressed only in his shirt, pants, and hose.

The others took up his cry—the sacristy and choir were burning. No one could go from the nave up to the south door anymore; the fire was now blocking both exits. A couple of staves in the wall had been splintered, and Erlend had picked up a fire axe and was slashing and hacking at the wreckage of the staves. They had smashed a hole in the side of the church, while other people were shouting for them to watch out—the roof might collapse and bury them all inside the church. The shingled roof was now burning briskly on this side too, and the heat was becoming unbearable.

Erlend leaped through the hole and helped to bring Sira Eirik out. The priest had his robes full of holy vessels from the altars.

A young boy followed with his hand over his face and the tall processional cross held out in front of him. Lavrans came next. He had closed his eyes against the smoke, staggering under the heavy crucifix he held in his arms; it was much taller than he was.

People ran forward and helped them move down to the churchyard. Sira Eirik stumbled, fell to his knees, and the altar vessels rolled across the slope. The silver dove opened, and the Host fell out. The priest picked it up, brushed it off, and kissed it as he sobbed loudly. He kissed the gilded man's head which had stood above the altar with a scrap of Saint Olav's hair and nails inside.

Lavrans Bjørgulfsøn was still standing there, holding the crucifix. His arm lay across the arms of the cross, and he was leaning his head on the shoulder of Christ. It looked as if the Savior were bending his beautiful, sad face toward the man to console him.

The roof had begun to collapse bit by bit on the north side of the church. A blazing roof beam shot out and struck the great bell in the low tower near the churchyard gate. The bell rang with a deep, mournful tone, which faded into a long moan, drowned out by the roar of the fire.

No one had paid any attention to the weather during all the tumult. The whole event had not taken much time, but no one was aware of that either. Now the thunder and lightning were far away, to the south of the valley. The rain, which had been falling for a while, was now coming down harder, and the wind had ceased.

But suddenly it was as if a sail of flames had been hoisted up from the foundation. In a flash, and with a shriek, the fire engulfed the church from one end to the other.

Everyone dashed away from the consuming heat. Erlend was suddenly at Kristin's side and urging her down the hill. His body reeked with the stench of the fire; she pulled away a handful of singed hair when she stroked his head and face.

They couldn't hear each other's voices above the roaring of the flames. But she saw that his eyebrows had been scorched right off, he had burns on his face, and his shirt was burned in places too. He laughed as he pulled her along after the others.

Everyone followed behind the weeping old priest and Lavrans Bjørgulfsøn, carrying the crucifix.

At the edge of the churchyard, Lavrans leaned the cross against a tree, and then sank down onto the wreckage of the gate. Sira Eirik was already sitting there; he stretched out his arms toward the burning church.

"Farewell, farewell, Olav's church. God bless you, my Olav's church. God bless you for every hour I have spent inside you, singing and saying the mass. Olav's church, good night, good night."

Everyone from the parish wept loudly along with him. The rain was pouring down on the people, huddled together, but no one thought of leaving. It didn't look as if the rain were damping the heat in the charred timbers; fiery pieces of wood and smoldering shingles were flying everywhere. A moment later the ridge turret fell into the blaze with a shower of sparks rising up behind it.

Lavrans sat with one hand covering his face; his other arm lay across his lap, and Kristin saw that his sleeve was bloody from the shoulder all the way down. Blood was running along his fingers. She went over and touched his arm.

"I don't think it's serious. Something fell on my shoulder," he said, looking up. He was so pale that even his lips were white. "Ulvhild," he whispered with anguish as he gazed at the inferno.

Sira Eirik heard him and placed a hand on his shoulder.

"It will not wake your child, Lavrans. She will sleep just as soundly with the fire burning over her resting place," he said. "She has not lost the home of her soul, as the rest of us have this evening."

Kristin hid her face against Erlend's chest. She stood there, feeling his arms around her. Then she heard her father ask for his wife.

Someone said that out of terror a woman had started having labor pains; they had carried her down to the parsonage, and Ragnfrid had gone along.

Kristin was suddenly reminded of what she had completely forgotten ever since they realized that the church was on fire: she shouldn't have looked at it. There was a man south of the village who had a red splotch covering half his face. They said he was born that way because his mother had looked at a fire while she was carrying him. Dear Holy Virgin Mary, she prayed in silence, don't let my unborn child be harmed by this.

The next day a village *ting* was to be convened on the church hillside. The people would decide on how to rebuild the church.

Kristin sought out Sira Eirik up at Romundgaard before he left for the *ting*. She asked the priest whether he thought she should take this as an omen. Perhaps it was God's will that she should tell her father she was unworthy to stand beneath the bridal crown, and that it would be more fitting for her to be married to Erlend Nikulaussøn without a wedding feast.

But Sira Eirik flew into a rage, his eyes flashing with fury.

"Do you think God cares so much about the way you sluts surrender and throw yourselves away that He would burn down a beautiful and honorable church for your sake? Rid yourself of your pride and do not cause your mother and Lavrans a sorrow from which they would scarcely recover. If you do not wear the crown with honor on your wedding day, it will be bad enough for you; but you and Erlend are in even greater need of this sacrament as you are joined together. Everyone has his sins to answer for; no doubt that is why this misfortune has been brought upon us all. Try to better your life, and help us to rebuild this church, both you and Erlend."

Kristin thought to herself that she had not yet told him of the latest thing that had befallen her—but she decided to let it be.

She went to the *ting* with the men. Lavrans attended with his arm in a sling, and Erlend had numerous burns on his face. He looked so ghastly, but he only laughed. None of the wounds was serious, and he said that he hoped they wouldn't disfigure him on his wedding day. He stood up after Lavrans and promised to give to the church four marks of silver, and to the village, on behalf of his betrothed and with Lavrans's consent, a section of Kristin's property worth one mark in land tax.

Erlend had to stay at Jørundgaard for a week because of his wounds. Kristin saw that Lavrans seemed to like his son-in-law better after the night of the fire; the men now seemed to be quite good friends. Then she thought that perhaps her father might be so pleased with Erlend Nikulaussøn that he would be more forbearing and not take it as hard as she had feared when one day he realized that they had sinned against him.

## CHAPTER 8

THAT YEAR was an unusually good one in all the valleys of the north. The hay was abundant, and it was all safely harvested. Everyone returned home from the mountain pastures with fattened livestock and great quantities of butter and cheese—and they had been mercifully free of predators that year. The grain stood so high that few people could remember ever seeing it look so fine. The crops ripened well and were bounteous, and the weather was the best it could be. Between Saint Bartholomew's Day and the Feast of the Birth of Mary, during the time when frosty nights were most likely, it rained a little and the weather was warm and overcast, but after that the harvest month proceeded with sunshine and wind and mild, hazy nights. By the week after Michaelmas, most of the grain had been brought in throughout the valley.

At Jørundgaard they were toiling and preparing for the great wedding. For the past two months Kristin had been so busy from morning to night, every single day, that she had had little time to worry about anything but her work. She could see that her breasts had grown heavier, and that her small pink nipples had turned brown and were as tender as wounds every morning when she had to get out of bed in the cold. But the pain passed as soon as she warmed up from her work, and then she thought only of what she had to do before nightfall. Sometimes when she straightened up to stretch out her back and paused to rest for a moment, she would notice that what she was carrying in her womb was growing heavy. But she was still just as slender and trim in appearance. She smoothed her hands over her long, fine hips. No, she didn't want to worry about it now. At times she would suddenly think, with a prickling sense of longing, that in a month or two she would be able to feel life inside her. By that time she would be at Husaby.

Maybe Erlend would be pleased. She closed her eyes and bit down on her betrothal ring—she saw Erlend's face, pale with emotion, when he stood up in the high loft and spoke the betrothal vows in a loud, clear voice:

"As God is my witness, along with these men who stand before me, I, Erlend Nikulaussøn, promise myself to Kristin Lavransdatter in accordance with the laws of God and men, on such conditions as have been presented to these witnesses who stand here with us. That I shall possess you as my wife, and you shall possess me as your husband as long as we both shall live, that we shall live together in matrimony with all such communion as God's laws and the laws of the land acknowledge."

She was running errands across the courtyard, going from building to building, and she stopped for a moment. The mountain ash was full of berries this year; it would be a snowy winter. And the sun was shining over the pale fields, where the sheaves of grain stood piled on poles. If only the weather would hold until the wedding.

Lavrans held firm to his intention that his daughter should be married in a church. It was therefore decided that this would take place in the chapel at Sundbu. On Saturday the bridal procession would ride over the mountains to Vaage. They would stay the night at Sundbu and the neighboring farms, and then ride back on Sunday after the wedding mass. On the same evening, after vespers, when the Sabbath was over, the wedding would be celebrated and Lavrans would give his daughter away to Erlend. And after midnight the bride and groom would be escorted to bed.[1]

On Friday, in the afternoon, Kristin was standing on the gallery of the high loft, watching the travelers who came riding from the north, past the burned church on the hill. It was Erlend with all his groomsmen. She strained to distinguish him from the others. They were not allowed to see each other; no man could see her until she was led out in the morning, wearing her bridal clothes.

At the place where the road turned toward Jørundgaard, several women pulled away from the group. The men continued on toward Laugarbru, where they would spend the night.

Kristin went downstairs to welcome the guests. She felt so tired after her bath, and her scalp ached terribly; her mother had rinsed her hair in a strong lye solution to give it a bright sheen for the next day.

Fru Aashild Gautesdatter slipped down from her saddle into Lavrans's arms. How lissome and young she keeps herself, thought Kristin. Her daughter-in-law Katrin, Sir Munan's wife, almost looked older than she did; she was tall and stout, her eyes and skin colorless. It's strange, thought Kristin, that she's ugly and he's unfaithful, and yet people say that they get on well together. Two of Sir Baard Petersøn's daughters had also come, one of them married, the other not. They were neither ugly nor beautiful; they looked trustworthy and kind, but seemed quite reserved with strangers. Lavrans thanked them courteously for their willingness to honor this wedding and for making the long journey so late in the fall.

"Erlend was raised by our father when he was a boy," said the older sister, and she stepped forward to greet Kristin.

Then two young men came trotting briskly into the courtyard. They leaped from their horses and ran laughing toward Kristin, who dashed into the house and hid. They were Trond Gjesling's young sons, handsome and promising boys. They brought with them the bridal crown from Sundbu in a chest. Trond and his wife wouldn't come to Jørundgaard until Sunday after the mass.

Kristin had fled to the hearth room, and Fru Aashild had followed. She placed her hands on Kristin's shoulders and pulled her face down to her own for a kiss.

"I'm glad that I shall see this day," said Fru Aashild.

She noticed as she held Kristin's hands how gaunt they had become. She saw that the bride had also grown thin, but her bosom was full. All the lines of her face had become leaner and more delicate than before; in the shadow of her thick, damp hair her temples seemed slightly hollowed. Her cheeks were no longer round, and her fresh complexion had faded. But Kristin's eyes had grown much larger and darker.

Fru Aashild kissed her again.

"I see you've had much to struggle with, Kristin," she said. "I'll give you something to drink tonight so you'll be rested and fresh in the morning."

Kristin's lips began to quiver.

"Hush," said Fru Aashild, patting her hand. "I'm looking forward to dressing you in your finery—no one will ever see a lovelier bride than you shall be tomorrow."

Lavrans rode over to Laugarbru to dine with his guests who were staying there.

The men could not praise the food enough; a better Friday supper could not be had even in the richest cloister. There was rye-flour porridge, boiled beans, and white bread. And the fish that was served was trout, both salted and fresh, and long strips of dried halibut.

Gradually, as they helped themselves to the ale, the men became more and more boisterous and their teasing of the bridegroom became more and more vulgar. All of Erlend's groomsmen were much younger than he was; his own peers and friends had all become married men long ago. Now the men joked about the fact that he was so old and would lie in the bridal bed for the first time. Some of Erlend's older kinsmen, who were still rather sober, were afraid that with each new word uttered the talk might shift to subjects that would be better left untouched. Sir Baard of Hestnæs kept an eye on Lavrans. He was drinking heavily, but it didn't look as if the ale was making him any happier as he sat there in the high seat; his face grew more and more tense as his gaze grew stonier. But Erlend, who was sitting to the right of his father-in-law, parried the teasing merrily and laughed a good deal; his face was red and his eyes sparkled.

Suddenly Lavrans bellowed, "That wagon, son-in-law—while I think of it, what did you do with the wagon that you borrowed from me this past summer?"

"Wagon?" said Erlend.

"Don't you remember that you borrowed a wagon from me last summer? God knows it was a good wagon. I'll probably never see a better one, because I was here myself when it was built on this farm. You promised and you swore, as I can testify before God. And my house servants can verify that you promised you would bring it back to me, but you haven't kept your word."

Some of the guests shouted that this was nothing to talk about right now, but Lavrans pounded on the table and swore that he would find out what Erlend had done with his wagon.

"Oh, it's probably still at the farm on the headland, where we took the boat out to Veøy," said Erlend indifferently. "I didn't think it was so important. You see, Father-in-law, it was a long and arduous journey with the cartload through the valleys, so by the time we reached the fjord, none of my men had a mind to travel the whole way back with the wagon and then over the mountains north to Nidaros. So I thought it could wait for the time being. . . ."

"No, may the Devil seize me right here where I'm sitting if I've ever heard the likes of this," Lavrans interrupted him. "What kind of people do you employ in your household? Is it you or your men who decide where they will or will not go?"

Erlend shrugged his shoulders.

"It's true that many things have not been as they should be in my home. The wagon will be sent back south to you when Kristin and I journey that way. My dear Father-in-law," he said with a smile, putting out his hand, "you must know that now everything will be different, and I will be too, now that Kristin will be coming home as my wife. The matter of the wagon was unfortunate. But I promise you, this will be the last time you shall have reason to complain about me."

"Dear Lavrans," said Baard Petersøn, "reconcile yourself with him over this paltry matter. . . ."

"A paltry matter or a great one . . ." began Lavrans. But then he stopped himself and shook hands with Erlend.

Soon afterward he left, and the guests at Laugarbru went to find their beds for the night.

On Saturday before noon the women and maidens were busy in the old loft. Some were making up the bridal bed, while others were helping the bride to finish dressing.

Ragnfrid had chosen this building for the bridal house because it was the smallest of the lofts—they could house many more guests in the new loft over the storeroom—and it was the bedchamber they had used themselves in the summertime, when Kristin was small, before Lavrans had built the high loft house, where they now lived both summer and winter. But the old storehouse was undoubtedly also the loveliest building on the farm, ever since Lavrans had had it rebuilt; it had been in a state of disrepair when they moved to Jørundgaard. It was now decorated with the most beautiful carvings both inside and out, and the loft was not large, so it was easier to adorn it with tapestries and weavings and pelts.

The bridal bed had been made ready with silk-covered pillows, and lovely blankets had been hung all around as draperies; over the furs and woolen blankets had been spread an embroidered silk coverlet. Ragnfrid and several women were hanging tapestries up on the timbered walls and placing cushions on the benches.

Kristin was sitting in an armchair that had been carried up to the loft. She was wearing her scarlet bridal gown. Large brooches held it together at her breast and closed the yellow silk shift at the neck; golden armbands gleamed on the yellow silk sleeves. A gilded silver belt had been wrapped three times around her waist, and around her neck and on her bosom lay necklace upon necklace—and on top of them all lay her father's old gold chain with the large reliquary cross. Her hands, which lay in her lap, were heavy with rings.

Fru Aashild was standing behind her chair, brushing out Kristin's thick, golden-brown hair.

"Tomorrow you will wear it loose for the last time," she said with a smile, winding around Kristin's head the red and green silk cords that would support the crown. Then the women gathered around the bride.

Ragnfrid and Gyrid of Skog brought over from the table the great bridal crown of the Gjesling family. It was completely gilded; the tips alternated between crosses and cloverleaves, and the circlet was set with rock crystals.

They pressed it down onto the bride's head. Ragnfrid was pale, and her hands shook as she did this.

Kristin slowly rose to her feet. Jesus, how heavy it was to bear all that silver and gold. Then Fru Aashild took her by the hand and led her forward to a large water basin, while the bridesmaids threw open the door to let in the sun and brighten up the loft.

"Look at yourself now, Kristin," said Fru Aashild, and Kristin bent over the basin. She saw her own face rise up, white, from the water; it came so close that she could see the golden crown above. So many light and dark shadows played all around her reflection—there was something she was just about to remember—and suddenly she felt as if she would faint away. She gripped the edge of the basin. Then Fru Aashild placed her hand on top of hers and dug in her nails so hard that Kristin came to her senses.

The sound of *lur* horns[2] came from the bridge. People shouted from the courtyard that now the bridegroom had arrived with his entourage. The women led Kristin out onto the gallery.

The courtyard was swarming with horses, magnificently bridled, and people in festive dress; everything glittered and gleamed in the sun. Kristin stared past everything, out toward the valley. Her village lay bright and still beneath a thin, hazy-blue mist, and out of the mist towered the mountains, gray with scree and black with forests, and the sun poured its light down into the basin of the valley from a cloudless sky.

She hadn't noticed it before, but all the leaves had fallen from the trees, and the groves shone silver-gray and naked. Only the alder thicket along the river still had a little faded green in the crowns of the trees, and a few birches held on to some pale yellow leaves at the very tips of their branches. But the trees were almost bare, except the mountain ash, which was still shining with brownish-red foliage surrounding the blood-red berries. In the still, warm day the acrid smell of autumn rose up from the ash-colored blanket of fallen leaves spread all around.

If not for the mountain ash trees, it might have been springtime—except for the silence, because it was autumn-quiet, so quiet. Every time the *lur* horns ceased, no sound was heard from the village but the clinking of bells from the fallow and harvested fields where the cattle were grazing.

The river was small and low, and it flowed so quietly; it was nothing more than tiny currents trickling between the sandbars and the heavy shoals of white stones worn smooth. No streams rushed down the slopes; it had been such a dry autumn. There were glints of moisture all over the fields, but it was only the dampness that always seeped up from the earth in the fall, no matter how hot the day or how clear the sky.

The throng of people down in the courtyard parted to make way for the bridegroom's entourage. The young groomsmen rode forward. There was a ripple of excitement among the women on the gallery.

Fru Aashild was standing next to the bride.

"Be strong now, Kristin," she said. "It won't be long before you are safely under the wimple of a married woman."

Kristin nodded helplessly. She could feel how terribly pale her face was.

"I'm much too pale a bride," she murmured.

"You are the loveliest bride," replied Aashild. "And there's Erlend—it would be hard to find a more handsome pair than the two of you."

Erlend rode forward beneath the gallery. He leaped from his horse, agile and unhampered by the heavy drapery of his clothing. Kristin thought he was so handsome that her whole body ached.

He was dressed in dark attire: a silk surcoat, pale brown interwoven with a black-and-white pattern, ankle-length and slit at the sides. Around his waist he wore a gold-studded belt and on his left hip a sword with gold on the hilt and scabbard. Over his shoulders hung a heavy, dark-blue velvet cape, and on his black hair he wore a black French silk cap which was shirred like wings at the sides and ended in two long streamers, one of which was draped across his chest from his left shoulder and then thrown back over the other.

Erlend greeted his bride, went over to her horse, and stood there with his hand on the saddlebow as Lavrans climbed the stairs. Kristin felt so odd and dizzy faced with all this splendor; her father seemed a stranger in the formal green velvet surcoat that reached to his ankles. But her mother's face was ashen white beneath the wimple she wore with her red silk dress. Ragnfrid came over and placed the cloak around her daughter.

Then Lavrans took the bride's hand and led her down to Erlend, who lifted her up onto her horse and then mounted his own. They sat there, side by side, in front of the bridal loft as the procession began to pass through the farm gates: first the priests, Sira Eirik and Sira Tormod from Ulvsvold, and a Brother of the Cross from Hamar who was a friend of Lavrans. Next came the groomsmen and the maidens, two by two. And then it was time for Erlend and Kristin to ride forward. After them followed the bride's parents, kinsmen, friends, and guests in long lines, riding between the fences out to the village road. A long stretch of the road was strewn with clusters of mountain ash berries, spruce boughs, and the last white chamomile blossoms of the autumn. People stood along the road as the procession passed, greeting it with cheers.

On Sunday just after sundown the mounted procession returned to Jørundgaard. Through the first patches of twilight the bonfires shone red from the courtyard of the bridal farm. Musicians and fiddlers sang and played their drums and fiddles as the group rode toward the warm red glow.

Kristin was about to collapse when Erlend lifted her down from her horse in front of the gallery to the high loft.

"I was so cold crossing the mountain," she whispered. "I'm so tired." She stood still for a moment; when she climbed the stairway to the loft, she swayed on every step.

Up in the high loft the frozen wedding guests soon had the warmth restored to their bodies. It was hot from all the candles burning in the room, steaming hot food was served, and wine and mead and strong ale were passed around. The din of voices and the sounds of people eating droned in Kristin's ears.

She sat there, unable to get warm. Her cheeks began to burn after a while, but her feet refused to thaw out and shivers of cold ran down her spine. All the heavy gold forced her to lean forward as she sat in the high seat at Erlend's side.

Every time the bridegroom drank a toast to her, she had to look at the red blotches and patches that were so evident on his face now that he was warming up after the ride in the cold air. They were the marks of the burns from that summer.

A terrible fear had come over her the evening before, while they were at dinner at Sundbu, when she felt the vacant stare of Bjørn Gunnarsøn on her and Erlend—eyes that did not blink and did not waver. They had dressed Herr Bjørn in knight's clothing; he looked like a dead man who had been conjured back to life.

That night she shared a bed with Fru Aashild, who was the bridegroom's closest kinswoman.

"What's the matter with you, Kristin?" asked Fru Aashild a little impatiently. "You must be strong now and not so despondent."

"I'm thinking about all the people we have hurt so that we could live to see this day," said Kristin, shivering.

"It wasn't easy for you two either," said Fru Aashild. "Not for Erlend. And I imagine it's been even harder for you."

"I'm thinking about those helpless children of his," said the bride in the same tone as before. "I wonder whether they know that their father is celebrating his wedding today. . . ."

"Think about your own child," said Fru Aashild. "Be glad that you're celebrating your wedding with the one who is the father."

Kristin lay still for a while, helplessly dizzy. It was so pleasant to hear it mentioned—what had occupied her mind every single day for three months or more, though she hadn't been able to breathe a word about it to a living soul. But this helped her for only a moment.

"I'm thinking about the woman who had to pay with her life because she loved Erlend," she whispered, trembling.

"You may have to pay with your own life before you're half a year older," said Fru Aashild harshly. "Be happy while you can.

"What should I say to you, Kristin?" the old woman continued, in despair. "Have you lost all your courage? The time will come soon enough when the two of you will have to pay for everything that you've taken—have no fear of that."

But Kristin felt as if one landslide after another were ravaging her soul; everything was being torn down that she had built up since that terrifying day at Haugen. During those first days she had simply thought, wildly and blindly, that she had to hold out, she had to hold out one day at a time. And she *had* held out until things became easier—quite easy, in the end, when she had cast off all thoughts except one: that now their wedding would take place at last, Erlend's wedding at last.

She and Erlend knelt together during the wedding mass, but it was all like a hallucination: the candles, the paintings, the shining vessels, the priests dressed in linen albs and long chasubles. All those people who had known her in the past seemed like dream images as they stood there filling the church in their unfamiliar festive garb. But Herr Bjørn was leaning against a pillar and looking at them with his dead eyes, and she thought that the other dead one must have come back with him, in his arms.

She tried to look up at the painting of Saint Olav—he stood there, pink and white and handsome, leaning on his axe, treading his own sinful human form underfoot—but Herr Bjørn drew her eyes. And next to him she saw Eline Ormsdatter's dead countenance; she was looking at them with indifference. They had trampled over her in order to get here, and she did not begrudge them that.

She had risen up and cast off all the stones that Kristin had striven so hard to place over the dead. Erlend's squandered youth, his honor and well-being, the good graces of his friends, the health of his soul—the dead woman shook them all off. "He wanted me and I wanted him, you wanted him and he wanted you," said Eline. "I had to pay, and he must pay, and you must pay when your time comes. When the sin is consummated it will give birth to death."

Kristin felt that she was kneeling with Erlend on a cold stone. He knelt with the red, singed patches on his pale face. She knelt beneath the heavy bridal crown and felt the crushing, oppressive weight in her womb—the burden of sin she was carrying. She had played and romped with her sin, measuring it out as if in a child's game. Holy Virgin—soon it would be time for it to lie fully formed before her, looking at her with living eyes, revealing to her the brands of her sin, the hideous deformity of sin, striking hatefully with misshapen hands at his mother's breast. After she had borne her child, after she had seen the marks of sin on him and loved him the way she had loved her sin, then the game would be played to the end.

Kristin thought: What if she screamed now so that her voice pierced through the song and the deep, droning male voices and reverberated out over the crowd? Would she then be rid of Eline's face? Would life appear in the dead man's eyes? But she clenched her teeth together.

Holy King Olav, I call to you. Among all those in Heaven, I beg you for help, for I know that you loved God's righteousness above all else. I beseech you to protect the innocent one who is in my womb. Turn God's anger away from the innocent, turn it toward me. Amen, in the precious name of the Lord.

"My children are innocent," said Eline, "yet there is no room for them in a land where Christian people live. Your child was conceived out of wedlock just as my children were. You can no more demand justice for your child in the land you have strayed from than I could demand it for mine."

Holy Olav, I beg for mercy nevertheless, I beg for compassion for my son. Take him under your protection, then I will carry him to your church in my bare feet. I will bring my golden crown to you and place it on your altar, if you will help me. Amen.

Her face was as rigid as stone, she was trying so hard to keep herself calm, but her body trembled and shuddered as she knelt there and was married to Erlend.

And now Kristin sat beside him in the high seat at home and sensed everything around her as a mere illusion in the delirium of fever.

There were musicians playing on harps and fiddles in the high loft; singing and music came from the room below and from out in the courtyard. A reddish glow from the fire outside was visible whenever servants came through the door, carrying things back and forth.

Everyone stood up around the table; she stood between her father and Erlend. Her father announced in a loud voice that now he had given his daughter Kristin to Erlend Nikulaussøn as his wife. Erlend thanked his father-in-law and all the good people who had gathered to honor him and his wife.

Then they told Kristin to sit down, and Erlend placed his wedding gifts in her lap. Sira Eirik and Sir Munan Baardsøn unrolled documents and read off a list of their property. The groomsmen stood by with spears in hand, pounding the shafts on the floor now and then during the reading and whenever gifts or moneybags were placed on the table.

The tabletops and trestles were removed. Erlend led her out onto the floor and they danced. Kristin thought: Our bridesmaids and groomsmen are much too young for us. Everyone who grew up with us has moved away from this region; how can it be that we have come back here?

"You seem so strange, Kristin," whispered Erlend as they danced. "I'm afraid for you, Kristin. Aren't you happy?"

They went from building to building and greeted their guests. All the rooms were filled with many candles, and people were drinking and singing and dancing everywhere. Kristin felt as though everything was so unfamiliar at home, and she had lost all sense of time;

the hours and the images flowed around each other, oddly disconnected.

The autumn night was mild. There were fiddlers in the courtyard too, and people dancing around the bonfire. They shouted that the bride and groom must also do them the honor, so Kristin danced with Erlend in the cold, dew-laden courtyard. That seemed to wake her up a little and her head felt clearer.

Out in the darkness a light band of fog hovered over the rushing river. The mountains stood pitch black against the star-strewn sky.

Erlend led her away from the dance and crushed her to him in the darkness beneath an overhanging gallery.

"I haven't even told you that you're beautiful, so beautiful and so lovely. Your cheeks are as red as flames." He pressed his cheek against hers as he spoke. "Kristin, what's the matter?"

"I'm just so tired, so tired," she whispered in reply.

"Soon we'll go in and sleep," said the bridegroom, looking up at the sky. The Milky Way had swung around and was stretching almost due north and south. "Do you know we've never spent a whole night together except that one time when I slept with you in your bedchamber at Skog?"

Some time later Sira Eirik shouted across the courtyard that now it was Monday, and then the women came to lead the bride to bed. Kristin was so tired that she hardly had the energy to resist, as she was supposed to do for the sake of propriety. She let herself be led out of the loft by Fru Aashild and Gyrid of Skog. The groomsmen stood at the foot of the stairs with burning tapers and drawn swords; they formed a circle around the group of women and escorted Kristin across the courtyard, up to the old loft.

The women removed her wedding finery, piece by piece, and laid it aside. Kristin noticed that at the foot of the bed was draped the violet-blue velvet dress that she would wear the next day, and on top of it lay a long, finely pleated, snow-white linen cloth. This was the wimple that married women wore and that Erlend had brought for her; tomorrow she would bind up her hair in a bun and fasten the cloth over it. It looked so fresh and cool and reassuring.

Finally she stood before the bridal bed, in her bare feet, bare-armed, dressed only in the ankle-length, golden-yellow silk shift. They had placed the crown on her head again; the bridegroom would take it off when the two of them were alone.

Ragnfrid placed her hands on her daughter's shoulders and kissed her cheek; the mother's face and hands were strangely cold, but she felt sobs bursting deep inside her breast. Then she threw back the covers of the bed and invited the bride to sit down. Kristin obeyed and leaned back on the silk pillows propped up against the headboard; she had to tilt her head slightly forward because of the crown. Fru Aashild pulled the covers up to Kristin's waist, placed the bride's hands on top of the silk coverlet, and arranged her shining hair, spreading it out over her breast and her slender, naked arms.

Then the men led the bridegroom into the loft. Munan Baardsøn removed Erlend's gold belt and sword; when he hung it up on the wall above the bed, he whispered something to the bride. Kristin didn't understand what he said, but she did her best to smile.

The groomsmen unlaced Erlend's silk clothing and lifted the long, heavy garment over his head. He sat down in the high-backed armchair, and they helped him take off his spurs and boots.

Only once did the bride dare to look up and meet his eyes.

Then everyone wished the couple good night. The wedding guests left the loft. Last to leave was Lavrans Bjørgulfsøn, who closed the door to the bridal chamber.

Erlend stood up and tore off his underclothes and threw them onto the bench. He stood before the bed, took the crown and silk ribbons from Kristin's hair, and placed them over on the table. Then he came back and climbed into bed. And kneeling beside her on the bed, he took her head in his hands, pressing it to his hot, naked chest as he kissed her forehead all along the red band that the crown had made.

She threw her arms around him and sobbed loudly. Sweet and wild, she felt that now it would all be chased away—the terror, the ghostly visions—now, at last, it was just the two of them again. He raised her face for a moment, looked down at her, and stroked her face and her body with his hand, strangely quick and rough, as if he were tearing away a covering.

"Forget," he begged in an ardent whisper, "forget everything, my Kristin—everything except that you're my wife, and I'm your husband."

With his hand he put out the last flame and threw himself down next to her in the dark; he was sobbing too.

"I never believed, never in all these years, that we would live to see this day."

Outside in the courtyard the noise died out, little by little. Weary from the ride earlier in the day and bleary with drink, the guests wandered around a while longer for the sake of propriety, but more and more of them began to slip away to find the places where they would sleep.

Ragnfrid escorted the most honored guests to their beds and bade them good night. Her husband, who should have been helping her with this, was nowhere to be found.

Small groups of youths, mostly servants, were the only ones remaining in the dark courtyard when she finally slipped away to find her husband and take him along to bed. She had noticed that Lavrans had grown exceedingly drunk as the evening wore on.

At last she stumbled upon him as she was walking stealthily outside the farmyard, looking for him. He was lying face down in the grass behind the bathhouse.

Fumbling in the dark, she recognized him—yes, it was him. She thought he was sleeping, and she touched his shoulder, trying to pull him up from the ice-cold ground. But he wasn't asleep—at least not completely.

"What do you want?" he asked, his voice groggy.

"You can't stay here," said his wife. She held on to him, for he was reeling as he stood there. With her other hand she brushed off his velvet clothes. "It's time for us to go to bed too, husband." She put her hand under his arm and led the staggering man up toward the farm. They walked along behind the farmyard buildings.

"*You* didn't look up, Ragnfrid, when you sat in the bridal bed wearing the crown," he said in the same voice. "Our daughter was less modest than you were; her eyes were not shy as she looked at her bridegroom."

"She has waited for him for three and a half years," said the mother quietly. "After that I think she would dare to look up."

"No, the Devil take me if they've waited!" shouted the father, and his wife hushed him, alarmed.

They were standing in the narrow lane between the back of the latrine and the fence. Lavrans slammed his fist against the lower timber of the outhouse.

"I put you here to suffer ridicule and shame, you timber. I put you here so the muck would devour you. I put you here as punishment because you struck down my pretty little maiden. I should have put you above the door of my loft and honored and thanked you with decorative carvings because you saved her from shame and from sorrow—for you caused my Ulvhild to die an innocent child."

He spun around, staggered against the fence, and collapsed against it with his head resting on his arms as he sobbed uncontrollably, with long deep moans in between.

His wife put her arms around his shoulders.

"Lavrans, Lavrans." But she could not console him. "Husband."

"Oh, I never, never, never should have given her to that man. God help me—I knew it all along—he has crushed her youth and her fair honor. I refused to believe it, no, I could not believe such a thing of Kristin. But I knew it all the same. Even so, she is too good for that weak boy, who has shamed both her and himself. I shouldn't have given her to him, even if he had seduced her ten times, so that now he can squander more of her life and happiness."

"What else was there to do?" said Ragnfrid in resignation. "You could see for yourself that she was already his."

"Yes, but I didn't need to make such a great fuss to give Erlend what he had already taken himself," said Lavrans. "It's a fine husband she has won, my Kristin." He yanked at the fence. Then he wept some more. Ragnfrid thought he had grown a bit more sober, but now the drink took the upper hand again.

As drunk as he was and as overcome with despair, she didn't think she could take him up to the hearth room where they were supposed to sleep—it was filled with guests. She looked around. Nearby was a small barn where they kept the best hay for the horses during the spring farm work. She walked over and peered inside; no one was there. Then she led her husband inside and shut the door behind them.

Ragnfrid piled the hay up all around and then placed their capes over both of them. Lavrans continued to weep off and on, and occasionally he would say something, but it was so confused that she couldn't understand him. After a while she lifted his head into her lap.

"My dear husband, since they feel such love for each other, maybe everything will turn out better than we expect. . . ."

Lavrans, who now seemed more clearheaded, replied, gasping, "Don't you see? He now has complete power over her; this man who could never restrain himself. She will find it difficult to oppose anything that her husband wishes—and if she is forced to do so one day, then it will torment her bitterly, that gentle child of mine.

"I don't understand any longer why God has given me so many great sorrows. I have striven faithfully to do His will. Why did He take our children from us, Ragnfrid, one after the other? First our sons, then little Ulvhild, and now I have given the one I love most dearly, without honor, to an unreliable and imprudent man. Now we have only the little one left. And it seems to me unwise to rejoice over Ramborg until I see how things may go for her."

Ragnfrid was shaking like a leaf. Then she touched her husband's shoulder.

"Lie down," she begged him. "Let's go to sleep." And with his head in his wife's arms Lavrans lay quietly for a while, sighing now and then, until finally he fell asleep.

It was still pitch dark in the barn when Ragnfrid stirred; she was surprised she had slept at all. She put out her hand. Lavrans was sitting up with his hands clasped around his knees.

"Are you already awake?" she asked, astonished. "Are you cold?"

"No," he replied, his voice hoarse, "but I can't sleep anymore."

"Is it Kristin you're thinking about?" asked Ragnfrid. "It may turn out better than we think, Lavrans," she told him again.

"Yes, that's what I'm thinking about," said her husband. "Well, well. Maiden or wife, at least she lay in the bridal bed with the one she had given her love to. Neither you nor I did that, my poor Ragnfrid."

His wife gave a deep, hollow moan. She threw herself down next to him in the hay. Lavrans placed his hand on her shoulder.

"But I *could* not," he said with fervor and anguish. "No, I *could* not . . . act toward you the way you wanted me to—back when we were young. I'm not the kind of man . . ."

After a moment Ragnfrid murmured, in tears, "We have lived well together all the same, Lavrans—all these years."

"So I too have believed," he replied gloomily.

His thoughts were tumbling and racing through his mind. That one naked glance which the groom and bride had cast at each other, the two young faces blushing with red flames—he thought it so brazen. It had stung him that she was his daughter. But he kept on seeing those eyes, and he struggled wildly and blindly against tearing away the veil from something in his own heart which he had never wanted to acknowledge—there he had concealed a part of himself from his own wife when she had searched for it.

He had not been able to, he interrupted himself harshly. In the name of the Devil, he had been married off as a young boy; he had not chosen her himself. She was older than he was. He had not desired her. He had not wanted to learn this from her—how to love. He still grew hot with shame at the thought of it—that she had wanted him to love her when he had not wanted that kind of love from her. That she had offered him everything that he had never asked for.

He had been a good husband to her; he believed that himself. He had shown her all the respect he could, given her full authority, asked her advice about everything, been faithful to her; and they had had six children. He had simply wanted to live with her without her always trying to seize what was in his heart—and what he refused to reveal.

He had never loved anyone. What about Ingunn, Karl's wife at Bru? Lavrans blushed in the darkness. He had always visited them when he traveled through the valley. He had probably never spoken to the woman alone even *once*. But whenever he saw her—if he merely thought of her—he felt something like that first smell of the earth in the spring, right after the snow had gone. Now he realized: it could have happened to him too . . . he could have loved someone too.

But he had been married so young, and he had grown wary. Then he found that he thrived best out in the wilderness—up on the mountain plateaus, where every living creature demands wide-open space, with room enough to flee. Wary, they watch every stranger that tries to sneak up on them.

Once a year the animals of the forest and in the mountains would forget their wariness. Then they would rush at their females. But he had been given his as a gift. And she had offered him everything for which he had never wooed her.

But the young ones in the nest . . . they had been the little warm spot in his desolation, the most profound and sweetest pleasure of his life. Those small blonde girls' heads beneath his hand . . .

Married off—that was what had happened to him, practically unconsulted. Friends . . . he had many, and he had none. War . . . it had been a joy, but there was no more war; his armor was hanging up in the loft, seldom used. He had become a farmer. But he had had daughters; everything he had done in his life became dear to him because he had done it to provide for those tender young lives that he held in his hands. He remembered Kristin's tiny two-year-old body on his shoulder, her flaxen soft hair against his cheek. Her little hands holding on to his belt while she pressed her hard, round forehead against his shoulder blades when he went riding with her sitting behind him on the horse.

And now she had those ardent eyes, and she had won the man she wanted. She was sitting up there in the dim light, leaning against the silk pillows of the bed. In the glow of the candle she was all golden—golden crown and golden shift and golden hair spread over her naked golden arms. Her eyes were no longer shy.

The father moaned with shame.

And yet it seemed that his heart had burst with blood—for what he had never had. And for his wife, here at his side, to whom he had been unable to give himself.

Sick with compassion, he reached for Ragnfrid's hand in the dark.

"Yes, I thought we lived well together," he said. "I thought you were grieving for our children. And I thought you had a melancholy heart. I never thought that it might be because I wasn't a good husband to you."

Ragnfrid was trembling feverishly.

"You have always been a good husband, Lavrans."

"Hm . . ." Lavrans sat with his chin resting on his knees. "And yet you might have done better if you had been married as our daughter was today."

Ragnfrid sprang up, uttering a low, piercing cry. "You know! How did you find out? How long have you known?"

"I don't know what you're talking about," said Lavrans after a moment, his voice strangely dispirited.

"I'm talking about the fact that I wasn't a maiden when I became your wife," replied Ragnfrid, and her voice was clear and resounding with despair.

After a moment Lavrans said, in the same voice as before, "I never knew of this until now."

Ragnfrid lay down in the hay, shaking with sobs. When the spell had passed she raised her head. A faint gray light was beginning to seep in through the holes in the wall. She could dimly see her husband as he sat there with his hands clasped around his knees, as motionless as if he were made of stone.

"Lavrans—speak to me," she whimpered.

"What do you want me to say?" he asked, not moving.

"Oh, I don't know. You should curse me—strike me . . ."

"It's a little late for that now," replied her husband; there was the shadow of a scornful smile in his voice.

Ragnfrid wept again. "No, I didn't think I was deceiving you, so deceived and betrayed did I feel myself. No one spared me. They brought you . . . I saw you only three times before we were married. I thought you were only a boy, so pink and white . . . so young and childish."

"That I was," said Lavrans, and his voice seemed to acquire more resonance. "And that's why I would have thought that you, who were a woman, you would have been more afraid of . . . of deceiving someone who was so young that he didn't realize . . ."

"I began to think that way later on," said Ragnfrid, weeping. "After I came to know you. Soon the time came when I would have given my soul twenty times over if I could have been without blame toward you."

Lavrans sat silent and motionless.

Then his wife continued, "You're not going to ask me anything?"

"What good would that do now? It was the man who . . . we

met his funeral procession at Feginsbrekka, when we were carrying Ulvhild to Nidaros."

"Yes," said Ragnfrid. "We had to step off the road, into the meadow. I watched them carry his bier past, with priests and monks and armed men. I heard that he had been granted a good death—reconciled with God. As we stood there with Ulvhild's litter between us I prayed that my sin and my sorrow might be placed at his feet on that last day."

"Yes, no doubt you did," said Lavrans, and there was that same shadow of scorn in his quiet voice.

"You don't know everything," said Ragnfrid, cold with despair. "Do you remember when he came out to visit us at Skog that first winter after we were married?"

"Yes," said her husband.

"When Bjørgulf was struggling with death . . . Oh, no one had spared me. He was drunk when he did it to me—later he said that he had never loved me, he didn't want me, he told me to forget about it. My father didn't know about it; he didn't deceive you—you must never believe that. But Trond . . . my brother and I were the dearest of friends back then, and I complained to him. He tried to threaten the man into marrying me—but he was only a boy, so he lost the fight. Later he advised me not to speak of it and to take you. . . ."

She sat in silence for a moment.

"When he came out to Skog . . . a year had passed, and I didn't think much about it anymore. But he came to visit. He said that he regretted what he had done, that he would have taken me then if I hadn't been married, that he was fond of me. So he said. God must judge whether he spoke the truth. After he left . . . I didn't dare go out on the fjord; I didn't dare because of the sin, not with the child. And by then I had . . . by then I had begun to love you so!" She uttered a cry, as if in the wildest torment. Her husband turned his head toward her.

"When Bjørgulf was born," Ragnfrid went on, "oh, I thought I loved him more than my own life. When he lay there, struggling with death, I thought: If he perishes, I will perish too. But I did *not* ask God to spare the boy's life."

Lavrans sat for a long time before he asked, his voice heavy and dead, "Was it because I wasn't his father?"

"I didn't know whether you were or not," said Ragnfrid, stiffening.

For a long time both of them sat there, as still as death.

Then the husband said fervently, "In the name of Jesus, Ragnfrid, why are you telling me this—now?"

"Oh, I don't know." She wrung her hands so hard that her knuckles cracked. "So that you can take vengeance on me. Chase me away from your manor . . ."

"Do you think that would help me?" His voice was shaking with scorn. "What about our daughters?" he said quietly. "Kristin, and the little one?"

Ragnfrid said nothing for a moment.

"I remember how you judged Erlend Nikulaussøn," she murmured. "So how will you judge me?"

A long icy shiver rippled through the man's body, releasing some of his stiffness.

"You have now . . . we have now lived together . . . for almost twenty-seven years. It's not the same thing as with a man who's a stranger. I can see that you have suffered the greatest anguish."

Ragnfrid collapsed into sobs at his words. She tried to reach out for his hand. He didn't move, but sat as still as a dead man. Then she wept louder and louder, but her husband sat motionless, staring at the gray light around the door. Finally she lay there as if all her tears had run out. Then he gave her arm a fleeting caress. And she began to cry again.

"Do you remember," she said in between her sobs, "that man who once visited us while we were at Skog? The one who knew the old ballads? Do you remember the one about a dead man who had come back from the land of torment and told his son the legend of what he had seen? He said that a great clamor was heard from the depths of Hell, and unfaithful wives ground up earth for their husbands' food. Bloody were the stones that they turned, bloody hung their hearts from their breasts . . ."

Lavrans said nothing.

"For all these years I have thought of those words," said Ragnfrid. "Each day I felt as if my heart were bleeding, for I felt as if I were grinding up earth for your food."

Lavrans didn't know why he answered the way he did. His chest felt empty and hollow, like a man whose heart and lungs had been ripped out through his back. But he placed his hand, heavy and weary, on his wife's head and said, "Earth has to be ground up, my Ragnfrid, before the food can grow."

When she tried to take his hand to kiss it, he pulled it abruptly away. Then he looked down at his wife, took her hand, placed it on his knee, and leaned his cold, rigid face against it. And in this manner they sat there together, without moving and without speaking another word.

# II: THE WIFE

In memory of my father

Ingvald Undset

PART I

# THE FRUIT OF SIN

## CHAPTER 1

ON THE EVE of Saint Simon's Day, Baard Petersøn's ship anchored at the spit near Birgsi. Abbot Olav of Nidarholm had ridden down to the shore himself to greet his kinsman Erlend Nikulaussøn and to welcome the young wife he was bringing home. The newly married couple would be the guests of the abbot and spend the night at Vigg.

Erlend led his deathly pale and miserable young wife along the dock. The abbot bantered about the wretchedness of the sea voyage; Erlend laughed and said that his wife was no doubt longing to sleep in a bed that stood firmly next to a wall. And Kristin tried to smile, but she was thinking that she would not go willingly on board a ship again for as long as she lived. She felt ill if Erlend merely came close to her, so strongly did he smell of the ship and the sea—his hair was completely stiff and tacky with salt water. He had been quite giddy with joy the entire time they were on board ship, and Sir Baard had laughed. Out there at Møre, where Erlend had grown up, the boys were constantly out in the boats, sailing and rowing. They had felt some sympathy for her, both Erlend and Sir Baard, but not as much as her misery warranted, thought Kristin. They kept saying that the seasickness would pass after she got used to being on board. But she had continued to feel wretched during the entire voyage.

The next morning she felt as if she were still sailing as she rode up through the outlying villages. Up one hill and down the next, carried over steep moraines of clay, and if she tried to fix her eyes up ahead on the mountain ridge, she felt as if the whole countryside was pitching, rising up like waves, and then tossed up against the pale blue-white of the winter morning sky.

A large group of Erlend's friends and neighbors had arrived at Vigg that morning to accompany the married couple home, so they set off in a great procession. The horses' hooves rang hollowly, for the earth was now as hard as iron from black frost. Steam enveloped the people and the horses; rime covered the animals' bodies as well as everyone's hair and furs. Erlend looked as white-haired as the abbot, his face glowing from the morning drink and the biting wind. Today he was wearing his bridegroom's clothing; he looked so young and happy that he seemed radiant, and joy and wild abandon surged in his beautiful, supple voice as he rode, calling to his guests and laughing with them.

Kristin's heart began quivering so strangely, from sorrow and tenderness and fear. She was still feeling sick after the voyage; she had that terrible burning in her breast that now appeared whenever she ate or drank even the smallest amount. She was bitterly cold; and lodged deep in her soul was that tiny, dull, mute anger toward Erlend, who was so free of sorrow. And yet, now that she saw with what naive pride and sparkling elation he was escorting her home as his wife, a bitter remorse began trickling inside her, and her breast ached with pity for him. Now she wished she hadn't held to her own obstinate decision but had told Erlend when he visited them in the summer that it would not be fitting for their wedding to be celebrated with too much grandeur. And yet she had doubtless wished he might see for himself that they would not be able to escape their actions without humiliation.

But she had also been afraid of her father. And she had thought that after their wedding was celebrated, they would be going far away. She wouldn't see her village again for a long time—not until all talk of her had long since died out.

Now she realized that this would be much worse. Erlend had mentioned the great homecoming celebration that he would hold at Husaby, but she hadn't envisioned that it would be like a second wedding feast. And these guests—they were the people she and Erlend would live among; it was their respect and friendship that they needed to win. These were the people who had witnessed Erlend's foolishness and misfortune all these years. Now he believed that he had redeemed himself in their opinion, that he could take his place among his peers by right of birth and fortune. But he would be ridiculed everywhere, here in the villages, when it became apparent that he had taken advantage of his own lawfully betrothed bride.

The abbot leaned over toward Kristin.

"You look so somber, Kristin Lavransdatter. Haven't you recovered from your seasickness yet? Or are you longing for your mother, perhaps?"

"Oh, yes, Father," said Kristin softly. "I suppose I'm thinking of my mother."

They had reached Skaun. They were riding high up along the mountainside. Beneath them, on the valley floor, the leafless forest stood white and furry with frost; it glittered in the sunlight, and there were glints from a little blue lake down below. Then they emerged from the evergreen grove. Erlend pointed ahead.

"There you can see Husaby, Kristin. May God grant you many happy days there, my wife!" he said warmly.

Spread out before them were vast acres, white with rime. The estate stood on what looked like a wide ledge midway up the mountain slope. Closest to them was a small, light-colored stone church, and directly to the south stood all the buildings; they were both numerous and large. Smoke was swirling up from the smoke vents. The bells began to chime from the church and people came streaming out toward them from the courtyard,[1] shouting and waving. The young men in the bridal procession clanged their weapons against each other—and with much banging and clattering and joyous commotion the group raced toward the manor of the newly married man.

They stopped in front of the church. Erlend lifted his bride down from her horse and led her to the door, where an entire crowd of priests and clerics stood waiting to receive them. It was bitterly cold inside, and the daylight seeped in through the small arched windows in the nave, making the glow of the tapers in the choir pale.

Kristin felt abandoned and afraid when Erlend let go of her hand and went over to the men's side while she joined the group of unfamiliar women, dressed in their holiday finery. The service was very beautiful. But Kristin was freezing, and it seemed as if her prayers were blown back to her when she tried to ease her heart and lift it upwards. She thought it was probably not a good omen that it was Saint Simon's Day—since he was the patron saint of the man whom she had treated so badly.

From the church they walked in procession down toward the manor; first the priests and then Kristin and Erlend, hand in hand, followed by the guests, two by two. Kristin was so distracted that she didn't notice much of the estate. The courtyard was long and narrow; the buildings stood in two rows along the south and north sides. They were massive and set close together, but they seemed old and in disrepair.

The procession stopped at the door to the main house, and the priests blessed it with holy water. Then Erlend led Kristin inside, through a dark entryway. On her right a door was thrown open to brilliant light. She ducked through the doorway and stood next to Erlend in his hall.

It was the largest room she had ever seen on any man's estate. There was a hearthplace in the middle of the floor, and it was so long that fires were burning at both ends. And the room was so wide that the crossbeams were supported by carved pillars. It seemed to Kristin more like the interior of a church or a king's great hall than the hall of a manor. At the east end of the house, where the high seat[2] stood in the middle of the bench along the wall, enclosed beds had been built into the walls between the pillars.

And so many candles were now burning in the room—on the tables, which groaned with precious vessels and platters, and in brackets attached to the walls. As was the custom in the old days, weapons and shields hung between the draped tapestries. The wall behind the high seat was covered with velvet, and that was where a man now hung Erlend's gold-chased sword and his white shield with the leaping red lion.

Serving men and women had taken the guests' outer garments from them. Erlend took his wife by the hand and led her forward to the hearthplace; the guests formed a semicircle behind them. A heavyset woman with a gentle face stepped forward and shook out Kristin's wimple, which had wrinkled a bit under her cloak. As the woman stepped back to her place, she bowed to the young couple and smiled. Erlend bowed and smiled in return and then looked down at his wife. At that moment his face was so handsome. And once again Kristin's heart seemed to sink—she felt such pity for him. She knew what he was now thinking; he saw her standing there in his hall with the long, snow-white wimple of a married woman spread out over her scarlet wedding gown. That morning she had been forced to wind a long woven belt tightly around her stomach and waist under her clothing before she could get the gown to fit properly. And she had rubbed her cheeks with a red salve that Fru Aashild had given her. While she was doing this, she had thought with indignation and sadness that Erlend didn't seem to look at her much, now that he had won her—since he hadn't yet noticed her condition. Now she bitterly regretted that she hadn't told him before.

As the couple stood there, hand in hand, the priests walked around the room, blessing the house and the hearth, the bed and the table.

Then a servant woman brought the keys of the house over to Erlend. He hung the heavy key ring on Kristin's belt—and as he did this he looked as if he wanted to kiss her at the same time. A man brought a large drinking horn, ringed in gold, and Erlend put it to his lips and drank to her.

"Health and happiness on your estate, my wife!"

And the guests shouted and laughed as she drank with her husband and then threw the rest of the wine into the hearth fire.

Then the musicians began to play as Erlend Nikulaussøn led his lawful wife to the high seat and the banquet guests sat down at the table.

On the third day the guests began to leave, and by the fifth day, just before mid-afternoon prayers, the last ones had departed. Then Kristin was alone with her husband at Husaby.

The first thing she did was to ask the servants to remove all the bedclothes from the bed, to wash them and the surrounding walls with lye, and to carry out the straw and burn it. Then she had the bed filled with fresh straw and on top she spread the bedclothes that she had brought with her to the estate. It was late at night before the work was done. But Kristin said that this should be done with all the beds on the farm, and all the furs were to be steamed in the bathhouse. The maids would have to start first thing in the morning and do as much as they could before the sabbath. Erlend shook his head and laughed—what a wife she was! But he was quite ashamed.

Kristin had not slept much on the first night, even though the priests had blessed her bed. On top were spread silk-covered pillows, a linen sheet, and the finest blankets and furs, but underneath lay filthy, rotting straw; there were lice in the bedclothes and in the magnificent black bear pelt that lay on top.

Many things she had noticed during those days. Behind the costly tapestries which covered the walls, the soot and the dirt had not been washed from the timbers. There was an abundance of food for the feast, but much of it was spoiled or ill-prepared. And they had lit the fires with raw, wet wood that offered hardly any heat and filled the room with smoke.

Poor management she had seen everywhere when, on the second day, she walked around with Erlend to look at the estate. There would be empty stalls and storerooms after the celebration was over; the flour bins were almost swept clean. And she couldn't understand how Erlend planned to feed all the horses and so much livestock with what was left of the straw and hay; there was not even enough fodder for the sheep.

But there was a loft half-filled with flax, and nothing had been done with it—it seemed to be a large part of several years' harvest. And a storeroom full of ancient, unwashed, and stinking wool, some in sacks and some lying loose all around. When Kristin put her hand into the wool, tiny brown worm eggs spilled out of it—moths and maggots had gotten into the wool.

The cattle were feeble, gaunt, scabrous, and chafed; never had she seen so many old animals in one place. Only the horses were beautiful and well cared for. But none of them was a match for Guldsvein or Ringdrott, the stallion that her father now owned. Sløngvanbauge, the horse that he had given her from home, was the most splendid horse in Husaby's stables. She couldn't resist putting her arm around his neck and pressing her face against his coat when she went over to him. And the gentry of Trøndelag[3] looked at the horse and praised his strong, stout legs, his deep chest and high neck, his small head and broad flanks. The old man from Gimsar swore by both God and the Fiend that it was a great sin that they had gelded the horse—what a battle horse he might have been. Then Kristin had to boast a little about his sire, Ringdrott. He was much bigger and stronger; there wasn't another stallion that could compete with him; her father had even tested him against the most celebrated horses all the way north to this parish. Lavrans had given these horses the unusual names—Ringdrott and

Sløngvanbauge—because they were golden in color and had markings that were like reddish-gold rings. The mother of Ringdrott had strayed from the other mares one summer up near the Boar Range, and they thought that a bear had taken her, but then she came back to the farm late in the fall. And the foal she bore the following year had surely not been bred by a stallion belonging to anyone aboveground. So they burned sulfur and bread over the foal, and Lavrans gave the mare to the church, to be even safer. But the foal had grown so magnificent that he now said he would rather lose half his estate than Ringdrott.

Erlend laughed and said, "You don't talk much, Kristin, but when you talk about your father, you're quite eloquent!"

Kristin abruptly fell silent. She remembered her father's face when she was about to ride off with Erlend and he lifted her onto her horse. Lavrans had put on a happy expression because there were so many people around them, but Kristin saw his eyes. He stroked her arm and took her hand to say farewell. At that time her main thought had been that she was glad to be leaving. Now she thought that for as long as she lived, she would feel a sting in her soul whenever she remembered her father's eyes on that day.

Then Kristin Lavransdatter set about organizing and managing her household. She was up before dawn each morning, even though Erlend protested and pretended that he would keep her in bed by force; no one expected a newly married woman to be running from one building to another long before the light of day.

When she saw into what a sorry state everything had fallen and how much she would have to tend to, then the thought shot through her mind, hard and clear: if she had committed a sin to come to this place, so be it—but it was also a sin to make use of God's gifts as was done here. Shame was deserved by those who had been in charge before, along with all of those who had allowed Erlend's manor to decline so badly. There had not been a proper foreman at Husaby for the past two years; Erlend himself had been away from home much of the time, and besides, he had little knowledge of how to run the estate. So it was only to be expected that his envoys farther out in the countryside cheated him, as Kristin suspected they did, or that the servants at Husaby worked only as much as they pleased and whenever and in whatever manner it suited each of them. It would not be easy now for her to restore order to things.

One day she talked about this with Ulf Haldorssøn, Erlend's personal servant. They should be done with the threshing, at least of the grain on their own land—and there wasn't much of it—before it was time for the slaughtering.

Ulf said, "You know, Kristin, that I'm not a farmer. We were to be Erlend's weapons bearers, Haftor and I—and I am no longer practiced in farming ways."

"I know that," said the mistress. "But as things stand, Ulf, it won't be easy for me to manage this winter, newly arrived as I am in this northern region and unfamiliar with our people. It would be kind of you to help me and advise me."

"I can see, Kristin, that you won't have an easy time this winter," said the man. He looked at her with a little smile—that odd smile he always wore whenever he spoke to her or to Erlend. It was impudent and mocking, and yet there was in his bearing both kindness and a certain esteem for her. And she didn't feel that she had the right to be offended when Ulf assumed a more familiar attitude toward her than might otherwise be fitting. She and Erlend had allowed this man to be a witness to their improper and sinful behavior; now she saw that he also knew in what condition she found herself. That was something she would have to bear. She saw that Erlend too tolerated whatever Ulf said or did, and the man did not show much respect for his master. But they had been friends in their childhood; Ulf was from Møre, the son of a smallholder who lived near Baard Petersøn's estate. He used the familiar form of address when he spoke to Erlend, as he now did with her—but that was more the custom among people up north than back home in her village.

Ulf Haldorssøn was quite a striking man, tall and dark, with handsome eyes, but his speech was ugly and coarse. Kristin had heard terrible things about him from the maids on the farm. When he went into town he would drink ferociously, reveling and carousing in the houses that stood along the alleyways; but when he was home at Husaby, he was the most steadfast of men, the most capable, the hardest worker, and the wisest. Kristin had taken a liking to him.

"It would not be easy for any woman to come to this estate, after all that has gone on here," he said. "And yet, I believe, Mistress Kristin, that you will fare better here than most women might. You're not the kind to sit down and whimper and complain; instead, you think of protecting the inheritance here for your descendants, when no one else gives any thought to that. And you know full well that you can count on me; I'll help you as much as I can. You must remember that I'm unaccustomed to farming ways. But if you will seek my counsel and allow me to advise you, then we should be able to make it through this winter, after a fashion."

Kristin thanked Ulf and went inside the house.

Her heart was heavy with fear and anguish, but she struggled to free herself. Part of her worry was that she didn't understand Erlend—he still didn't seem to notice anything. But the other part, and this was worse, was that she couldn't feel any life in the child she was carrying. She knew that at twenty weeks it should begin to move; now it was more than three weeks past that time. At night she would lie in bed and feel this burden which was growing and becoming heavier but which continued to be as dull and lifeless as ever. And hovering in her thoughts was all that she had heard about children who were born lame, with hardened sinews; about creatures that came to light without limbs, that had almost no human form. Before her closed eyes passed images of tiny infants, hideously deformed; one horrific sight melted into another that was even worse. In the south of Gudbrandsdal, at Lidstad, they had a child—well, it must be full grown by now. Her father had seen it, but he would never speak of it; she noticed that he grew distressed if anyone even mentioned it. She wondered how it looked . . . Oh, no. Holy Olav, pray for me! She must believe firmly in the beneficence of the Holy King. She had given her child into his care, after all. With patience she would suffer for her sins and place her faith, with all her soul, in help and mercy for the child. It must be the Fiend himself who was tempting her with these loathsome sights in order to lure her into despair. But it was worse at night. If a child had no limbs, if it was lame, then the mother would doubtless feel no sign of life. Half-asleep, Erlend noticed that his wife was uneasy. He folded her tighter into his arms and buried his face in the hollow of her neck.

But in the daytime Kristin acted as if nothing was wrong. And each morning she would dress carefully, to hide from the house servants a little while longer that she was not walking alone.

It was the custom at Husaby that after the evening meal the servants would retire to the buildings where they slept. Then she and Erlend would sit alone in the hall. In general the customs here on the manor were more as they had been in the old days, back when people had thralls to do the housework. There was no permanent table in the hall, but each morning and evening a large plank was placed on trestles and then set with dishes, and after the meal it was hung back up on the wall. For the other meals everyone took their food over to the benches and sat there to eat. Kristin knew that this had been the custom in the past. But nowadays, when it was hard to find men to serve at the table and everyone had to be content with maids to do the work indoors, it was no longer practical—the women didn't want to waste their strength by lifting the heavy tables. Kristin remembered her mother telling her that at Sundbu they had a permanent table when she was eight winters old, and the women thought this a great advantage in every way. Then they no longer had to go out to the women's house with their sewing but could sit in the main room and cut and clip, and it looked so fine to have candlesticks and a few lovely vessels always standing there. Kristin thought that in the summer she would ask Erlend to put a table along the north wall.

That's where it stood at home, and her father had his high seat at the head of the table. But at Jørundgaard the beds stood along the wall to the entryway. At home her mother sat at the end of the outer bench so that she could go back and forth and keep an eye on the food being served. Only when there were guests did Ragnfrid sit at her husband's side. But here the high seat was in the middle beneath the east gable, and Erlend always wanted Kristin to sit with him. At home her father always offered God's servants a place in the high seat if they were guests at Jørundgaard, and he and Ragnfrid would serve them while they ate and drank. But Erlend refused to do so unless they were of high rank. He had little love for priests or monks—they were costly friends, he said. Kristin thought about what her father and Sira Eirik always said when people complained about the avarice of clerics: every man forgets the sinful pleasure he has enjoyed when he has to pay for it.

She asked Erlend about life at Husaby in the old days. But he knew very little. Such and such he had heard, if he remembered rightly—but he couldn't recall exactly. King Skule had owned the manor and built it up, presumably intending to make Husaby his home when he donated Rein manor to the convent. Erlend was exceedingly proud that he was descended from the duke, as he always called the king, and from Bishop Nikulaus. The bishop was the father of his grandfather, Munan Biskopssøn. But Kristin thought that he knew less about these men than she did from her own father's stories. At home things were different. Neither her father nor her mother boasted of the power or prestige of their deceased ancestors. But they often spoke of them, holding out the good they knew about them as an example and telling of their faults and the evil that had resulted as a warning. And they knew amusing little tales—about Ivar Gjesling the Elder and his enmity with King Sverre, about Dean Ivar's sharp and witty replies, about Haavard Gjesling's tremendous girth, and about Ivar Gjesling the Younger's wondrous luck in hunting. Lavrans told of his grandfather's brother who abducted the Folkung maiden from Vreta cloister; about his grandfather, the Swedish knight Ketil; and about his grandmother, Ramborg Sunesdatter, who always longed for her home in Västergötaland and who one day drove her sleigh through the ice of Lake Vänern when she was visiting her brother at Solberga. He told of his father's skill with weapons and of his inexpressible sorrow at the death of his young first wife, Kristin Sigurdsdatter, who died in childbed, giving birth to Lavrans. And he read from a book about his ancestor, the Holy Fru Elin of Skøvde, who was blessed to become God's martyr. Lavrans had often said that he and Kristin should make a pilgrimage to the grave of the holy widow. But nothing had ever come of it.

In her fear and need, Kristin tried to pray to this holy woman to whom she was bound by blood. She prayed to Saint Elin for her child and kissed the cross that her father had given her; inside was a scrap of the holy saint's shroud. But Kristin was afraid of Saint Elin, now that she had shamed her lineage so terribly. When she prayed to Saint Olav and Saint Thomas for their intercession, she often felt that her laments reached living ears and sympathetic hearts. Her father loved these two martyrs of righteousness above all the other saints, even more than Saint Lavrans himself, whose name he bore, and whose feast day in late summer he always honored with a great banquet and rich alms. Kristin's father had seen Saint Thomas in his dreams one night when he lay wounded outside of Baagahus. No one could describe how loving and venerable he was in appearance, and Lavrans himself had not been able to utter anything but "Lord, Lord!" But the radiant bishop had tenderly touched the man's wound and promised him life and vigor so that he would once again see his wife and daughter, as he had prayed for. And yet at that time not a soul had believed that Lavrans Bjørgulfsøn would live through the night.

Well, Erlend had said. One heard so many things. Nothing like that had ever happened to him, and it wasn't likely to, either. He had never been a pious man like Lavrans.

Then Kristin asked about the people who had attended their homecoming feast. Erlend had little to say about them either. It occurred to Kristin that her husband did not resemble the people here in the countryside. Many of them were handsome; blond and ruddy-hued, with round, hard heads; strong and stocky in build. Many of the old men were immensely fat. Erlend looked like a strange bird among his guests. He was a head taller than most of the men, thin and lean, with slender limbs and fine joints. And he had black, silken hair and a tan complexion, but pale blue eyes beneath coal black brows and shadowy black lashes. His forehead was high and narrow, his temples hollowed; his nose was a little too big and his mouth a little too small and weak for a man. And yet he was handsome; Kristin had never seen a man who was half as handsome as Erlend. Even his soft, quiet voice was unlike the husky voices of the others.

Erlend laughed and said that his lineage was not from around here, except for his paternal great-grandmother, Ragnrid Skulesdatter. People said that he was much like his mother's father, Gaute Erlendssøn of Skogheim. Kristin asked him what he knew of this man. But he knew almost nothing.

One evening Erlend and Kristin were undressing. Erlend couldn't unfasten the strap on his shoe, so he cut it off, and the knife sliced into his hand. He bled heavily and cursed fiercely. Kristin took a cloth out of her linen chest. She was wearing only her shift. Erlend put his other arm around her waist as she bandaged his hand.

Suddenly he looked down into her face with horror and confusion—and flushed bright red himself. Kristin bowed her head.

Erlend withdrew his arm. He said nothing, and so Kristin walked quietly away and climbed into bed. Her heart thudded hollowly and hard against her ribs. Now and then she cast a glance at her husband. He had turned his back to her, slowly taking off one garment after the other. Then he came over and lay down.

Kristin waited for him to speak. She waited so long that her heart seemed to stop beating and just stood still, quivering in her breast.

But Erlend didn't say a word. And he didn't take her into his arms.

At last he hesitantly placed his hand on her breast and pressed his chin against her shoulder so that the stubble of his beard prickled her skin. When he still said nothing, Kristin turned over to face the wall.

She felt as if she were sinking and sinking. He had not one word to offer her—now that he knew she had been carrying his child these long, difficult days. Kristin clenched her teeth in the dark. She would not beg him. If he remained silent, then she would be silent too, even if it lasted until the day she gave birth. Resentment surged up inside her. But she lay absolutely still next to the wall. Erlend too lay still in the dark. Hour after hour they lay there this way, and each one knew that the other was not asleep. Finally Kristin heard by his regular breathing that Erlend had dozed off. Then she allowed her tears to fall as they would, from sorrow and hurt and shame. This, she felt, she would never be able to forgive him.

For three days Erlend and Kristin went about in this manner—he seemed like a wet dog, thought the young wife. She was burning and stony with anger, becoming wild with bitterness whenever she felt him give her a searching look but then swiftly shift his glance if she turned her eyes toward his.

On the morning of the fourth day Kristin was sitting in the main house when Erlend appeared in the doorway, dressed for riding. He said that he was going west to Medalby and asked whether she wanted to accompany him to visit the manor; it was part of her wedding-morning gift. Kristin assented, and Erlend himself helped her to put on the fur-lined boots and the black cloak with sleeves and silver clasps.

Out in the courtyard stood four saddled horses, but Erlend told Haftor and Egil to stay home and help with the threshing. Then he helped his wife into the saddle. Kristin realized that Erlend was now planning to speak about the matter which lay unspoken between them. Yet he said nothing as they slowly rode off, southward, toward the forest.

It was now nearly the end of the slaughtering month, but still no snow had fallen in the parish. The day was fresh and beautiful; the sun had just come up, and it glittered and sparkled on the white frost everywhere, on the fields and on the trees. They rode across Husaby's land. Kristin saw that there were few cultivated acres or stubble fields, but mostly fallow land and old meadows, tufted with grass, moss-covered, and overgrown with alder saplings. She mentioned this.

Her husband replied merrily, "Don't you know, Kristin—you who know so well how to tend and manage farms—that it does no good to grow grain this close to a trading port? You gain more by trading butter and wool for grain and flour from the foreign merchants."

"Then you should have traded the goods that are lying in your lofts and have rotted long ago," said Kristin. "I also know that the law says that every man who leases land must sow grain on three parts but let the fourth part lie fallow. And surely the estate of the master should not be worse tended than the farms of his leaseholders—that's what my father always said."

Erlend laughed a bit and said, "I have never asked about the law in that regard. As long as I receive what is my due, my tenants can run their farms as they see fit, and I will run Husaby in the manner that seems to me best and most suitable."

"Do you think yourself wiser then," said Kristin, "than our deceased ancestors and Saint Olav and King Magnus, who established these laws?"

Erlend laughed again and said, "I hadn't given any thought to that. What a devilish good grasp you have of our country's laws and regulations, Kristin."

"I have some understanding of these matters," said Kristin, "because Father often asked Sigurd of Loptsgaard to recite laws for us when he came to visit and we sat at home in the evening. Father thought it was beneficial for the servants and the young people to have some knowledge of such things, and so Sigurd would recount one passage or another."

"Sigurd . . ." said Erlend. "Oh, yes, now I remember. I saw him at our wedding. He was the toothless old man with the long drooping nose who slobbered and wept and patted you on the breast. He was still dead drunk in the morning when everyone came up to us and watched as I put the linen wimple of a married woman on your head."

"He has known me for as long as I can remember," said Kristin crossly. "He used to take me on his lap and play with me when I was a little maiden."

Erlend laughed again. "That was an odd kind of amusement—that you had to sit and listen to the old man chanting the law, passage by passage. Lavrans is unlike any other man in every way. Usually it is said that if the tenant knew the full law of the land and the stallion knew his strength, then the Devil would be a knight. . . ."

Kristin gave a shout and struck her horse on the flank. Erlend threw his wife an angry and astonished look as she rode away from him.

Suddenly he spurred his horse. Jesus, the ford in the river—it was impossible to cross there now, the earth had slid away recently. Sløngvanbauge took longer strides when he noticed another horse chasing him. Erlend was deathly afraid—how she was racing down the steep slopes. He bounded past her through the copsewood and doubled back on the road where it flattened out for a short stretch to make her stop. When he came up alongside her, he saw that Kristin herself had grown a little scared.

Erlend leaned over toward his wife and struck her a ringing blow beneath the ear; Sløngvanbauge leaped sideways, startled, and reared up.

"Well, you deserved that," said Erlend, his voice shaking, after the horses had calmed down and they once again rode side by side. "The way you rushed off like that, senseless with fury . . . You frightened me."

Kristin held her hand to her head so that he couldn't see her face. Erlend wished that he hadn't hit her. But he repeated, "Yes, you scared me, Kristin—to dash off like that! And to do so *now . . .* ," he said softly.

Kristin didn't reply, nor did she look at him. But Erlend felt that she was less angry than before, when he had mocked her home. He was greatly surprised by this, but he saw that it was so.

They arrived at Medalby, and Erlend's leaseholder came out and wanted to show them into the main house. But Erlend thought they first ought to inspect the buildings, and Kristin should come along. "She owns the farm now, and she has a better understanding of such things than I do, Stein," he said with a laugh. Several farmers were there too, who were to act as witnesses, and some of them were also Erlend's tenants.

Stein had come to the farm on the last turnover day[4] and since then he had been begging the master to come up and see the condition that the buildings were in when he took over, or to send an envoy in his stead. The farmers testified that not one building had been without leaks, and those that were now in a state of collapse had been that way when Stein arrived. Kristin saw that it was a good farm, but it had been poorly maintained. She saw that this Stein was a capable man, and Erlend was also very amenable and promised him some reductions in his land rent until he was able to repair the buildings.

Then they went into the main house where the table was set with good food and strong ale. The leaseholder's wife asked Kristin's forgiveness for not coming out to greet her. But her husband would not allow her to step out under open sky until she had been to church after giving birth.[5] Kristin greeted the woman kindly, and then she had to go over to the cradle to see the child. It was the couple's first, and it was a son, twelve nights old, big and strong.

Then Erlend and Kristin were led to the high seat, and everyone sat down and ate and drank for a good long time. Kristin was the one who talked most during the meal; Erlend didn't say much, nor did the farmers, and yet Kristin noticed that they seemed to like her.

Then the child woke up, at first whimpering but then shrieking so terribly that the mother had to put him to her breast to calm his cries. Kristin glanced over at the two of them several times, and when the boy had had enough, she took him from the woman and held him in her arms.

"Look, husband," she said, "don't you think he's a handsome and fine young fellow?"

"That he is," said Erlend, not looking in her direction.

Kristin sat and held the child for a while before she gave him back to his mother.

"I will send a gift over here to your son, Arndis," she said. "For he's the first child I've held in my arms since I came up here to the north."

Flushed and defiant, with a little smile Kristin cast a glance at her husband and then at the farmers sitting along the bench. A few of them showed a slight twitch at the corner of the mouth, but then they stared straight ahead, their faces stiff and solemn. After a moment a very old man stood up; he had been drinking heavily. Now he lifted the ladle out of the ale bowl, placed it on the table, and raised the large vessel.

"So let us drink to that, mistress; that the next child you hold in your arms will be the new master of Husaby!"

Kristin stood up and accepted the heavy bowl. First she offered it to her husband. Erlend barely touched it with his lips, but Kristin took a long, deep drink.

"Thank you for that greeting, Jon of Skog," she said with a cheery nod, her eyes twinkling. Then she sent the bowl around.

Kristin could see that Erlend was red-faced and quite angry. She herself merely felt such a foolish urge to laugh and be merry. A short time later Erlend wanted to leave, and so they set off on their way home.

They had been riding for a while without speaking when Erlend suddenly burst out, "Do you think it's necessary to let even our tenants know that you were carrying a child when you were wed? You can wager your soul with the Devil that talk about the two of us will soon be flying through all the villages along the fjord."

Kristin didn't reply at first. She stared into the distance over her horse's head, and she was now so white in the face that Erlend grew frightened.

"I will never forget for as long as I live," she said at last, without looking at him, "that those were the first words you greeted him with, this son of yours that I carry under my belt."

"Kristin!" said Erlend, his voice pleading. "My Kristin," he implored when she said nothing and refused to look at him. "Kristin!"

"Sir?" she replied coldly and courteously, without turning her head.

Erlend cursed so that sparks flew; he spurred his horse and raced ahead along the road. But a few minutes later he came riding back toward her.

"This time I was almost so furious," he said, "that *I* was going to ride away from *you*."

Kristin said calmly, "Then you might have had to wait a good long time before I followed you to Husaby."

"The things you say!" said her husband, resigned.

Once again they rode for some time without talking. In a while they reached a place where a small path led up over a ridge. Erlend said to his wife, "I was thinking that we could ride home this way, over the heights—it will take a little longer, but I've wanted to travel up this way with you for some time."

Kristin nodded indifferently.

After a while Erlend said that now it would be better for them to walk. He tied their horses to a tree.

"Gunnulf and I had a fortress up here on the ridge," he said. "I'd like to see whether there's anything left of our castle."

He took Kristin's hand. She didn't resist, but walked with her eyes downcast, looking at where she set her feet. It wasn't long before they were up on the heights. Beyond the bare, frost-covered forest, in the crook of the little river, Husaby lay on the mountain slope directly across from them, looming big and grand with the stone church and all its massive buildings, surrounded by the broad acres, and the dark forested ridge behind.

"Mother used to come up here with us," said Erlend softly. "Often. But she would always sit and stare off to the south, toward the Dovre Range. I suppose she was always yearning, night and day, to be far away from Husaby. Or she would turn toward the north and gaze out at the gap in the slopes—there where you can see blue in the distance; those are the mountains on the other side of the fjord. Not once did she look at the farm."

Erlend's voice was tender and beseeching. But Kristin neither spoke nor looked at him. Then he went over and kicked at the frozen heath.

"No, there's probably nothing left here of Gunnulf's and my fortress. And it was a long time ago, after all, that we played up here, Gunnulf and I."

He received no answer. Right below where they stood was a small frozen pond. Erlend picked up a stone and threw it. The hollow was frozen solid so that only a tiny white star appeared on the black mirror. Erlend picked up another stone and threw it harder—then another and another. Now he was throwing them in utter fury, and in the end he would have splintered the ice with a vengeance. But then he caught sight of his wife's face—she stood there, her eyes dark with contempt, smiling scornfully at his childishness.

Erlend spun around, but all at once Kristin grew deathly pale and her eyes fell shut. She stood there with her hands stretched out and groping, swaying as if she were about to faint—then she grabbed hold of a tree trunk.

"Kristin—what is it?" Erlend asked in fear.

She didn't answer but stood as if she were listening to something. Her gaze was remote and strange.

Now she felt it again. Deep within her womb it felt as if a fish was flicking its tail. And again the whole world seemed to reel around her, and she felt dizzy and weak, but not as much as the first time.

"What's the matter?" asked Erlend.

She had waited so long for this—she hardly dared to acknowledge the great fear in her soul. She could not speak of it—not now, when they had been fighting all day long. Then *he* said it.

"Was it the child moving inside you?" he asked gently, touching her shoulder.

Then she cast off all her anger toward him, pressed herself against the father of her child, and hid her face on his chest.

Some time later they walked back down to the place where their horses were tied. The short day was almost over; behind them in the southwest the sun was sinking behind the treetops, red and dull in the frosty haze.

Erlend carefully tested the buckles and straps of the saddle before he lifted his wife up onto her horse. Then he went over and untied his own. He reached under his belt for the gloves he had put there, but he found only one. He looked around on the ground.

Then Kristin couldn't resist and said, "It will do you no good to look for your glove here, Erlend."

"You might have said something to me if you saw me lose it—no matter how angry you were with me," he replied. They were the gloves that Kristin had sewn for him and given to him as one of his betrothal presents.

"It fell out of your belt when you hit me," said Kristin very quietly, her eyes downcast.

Erlend stood next to his horse with his hand on the saddlebow. He looked embarrassed and unhappy. But then he burst out laughing.

"Never would I have believed, Kristin—during all the time I was courting you, rushing around and begging my kinsmen to speak on my behalf and making myself so meek and pitiful in order to win you—that you could be such a witch!"

Then Kristin laughed too.

"No, then you probably would have given up long ago—and it certainly would have been in your own best interest."

Erlend took a few steps toward her and placed his hand on her knee.

"Jesus help me, Kristin—have you ever heard it said of me that I did anything that was in my own best interest?"

He pressed his face down in her lap and then looked up with sparkling eyes into his wife's face. Flushed and happy, Kristin bowed her head, trying to hide her smile and her eyes from Erlend.

He grabbed hold of her horse's harness and let his own horse follow behind; and in this manner he escorted her until they reached the bottom of the ridge. Every time they looked at each other he would laugh and she would turn her face away to hide that she was laughing too.

"So," he said merrily as they came out onto the road again, "now we'll ride home to Husaby, my Kristin, and be as happy as two thieves!"

## CHAPTER 2

On Christmas Eve the rain poured down and the wind blew hard. It was impossible to use sleighs, and so Kristin had to stay home when Erlend and the servants rode off for the evening mass at Birgsi Church.

She stood in the doorway of the main house and watched them go. The pine torches they carried shone red against the dark old buildings, reflected in the icy surface of the courtyard. The wind seized the flames and flattened them out sideways. Kristin stood there as long she could hear the faint sound of their passage in the night.

Inside the hall there were candles burning on the table. The remains of the evening meal were scattered about—lumps of porridge in dishes, half-eaten pieces of bread, and fishbones floating in puddles of spilt ale. The serving maids who were to stay at home had all fallen asleep on the straw spread out on the floor. Kristin was alone with them at the manor, along with an old man named Aan. He had served at Husaby since the time of Erlend's grandfather; now he lived in a little hut down by the lake but he liked to come up to the farm in the daytime to putter around, in the belief that he was working very hard. Aan had fallen asleep at the table that evening, and Erlend and Ulf had laughingly carried him over to a corner and spread a blanket over him.

Back home at Jørundgaard the floor would now be thickly strewn with rushes, for the entire household would sleep together in the main house during the holiday nights. Before they left for church they used to clear away the remains of the meal eaten after their fast, and Kristin's mother and the maids would set the table as beautifully as they could with butter and cheeses, heaps of thin, light bread, chunks of glistening bacon, and the thickest joints of cured mutton. The silver pitchers and horns of mead stood there gleaming. And her father himself would place the ale cask on the bench.

Kristin turned her chair around to face the hearth—she didn't want to look at the loathsome table. One of the maids was snoring so loudly that it was awful to hear.

That was also one of the things that she didn't care for about Erlend. At home on his estate he ate in a manner that was so repugnant and slovenly, pawing through the dishes for good bits of food, hardly bothering to wash his hands before he came to the table. And he let the dogs jump up onto his lap and gulp down food along with him while everyone ate. So it was only to be expected that the servants had no table manners. Back home she had been constrained to eat delicately and slowly. It would not be proper, said her mother, for the master's family to wait while the servants ate, and those who had toiled and labored should have time to eat their fill.

"Here, Gunna," Kristin called softly to the big yellow bitch that lay with a whole cluster of pups against the draft stone by the hearth. She was such an ill-tempered animal, and that's why Erlend had named her after the old mistress of Raasvold.

"You poor wretch," whispered Kristin, petting the dog who had come over and put her head on Kristin's knee. Her backbone was as sharp as a scythe, and her teats almost swept the floor. The pups were literally eating their mother up. "Oh, yes, my poor wretch."

Kristin leaned her head against the back of the chair and looked up at the soot-covered rafters. She was tired.

No, she had not had an easy time of it these past few months that she had spent at Husaby. She had talked with Erlend a little on the evening of the day they had gone to Medalby. Then she realized that he thought she was angry with him because he had brought this upon her.

"I do remember," he said in a low voice, "that day in the spring when we went walking in the woods north of the church. I do remember that you asked me to leave you alone. . . ."

Kristin was pleased that he had told her this. Otherwise she often wondered about all the things that Erlend seemed to have forgotten.

But then he said, "And yet I would not have believed it of you, Kristin, that you could walk around bearing such a secret rancor toward me, and still act so gentle and happy. For you must have known long ago how things stood with you. And I believed that you were as bright and honest as the rays of the sun."

"Oh, Erlend," she said sadly. "You of all people in the world should know best that I have followed forbidden paths and acted falsely toward those who have trusted me most." But she wanted so much for him to understand. "I don't know whether you recall, my dear, but in the past you have behaved toward me in a manner that some might not call proper. And God and the Virgin Mary know that I didn't bear you any grudge, nor did I love you any less."

Erlend's face grew tender.

"So I thought," he said quietly. "But you know too that I have striven all these years to rectify the harm I have done. I consoled myself that in the end I would be able to reward you, for you were so faithful and patient."

Then she said to him, "No doubt you have heard about my grandfather's brother and the maiden Bengta, who fled from Sweden against the wishes of her kinsmen. God punished them by refusing to give the couple a child. Haven't you ever feared, during all these years, that He might punish us in that way too?"

She added, her voice quavering and soft, "You can understand, my Erlend, that I was not very happy this summer when I first became aware of it. And yet I thought . . . I thought that if you should die before we were married, I would rather be left behind with your child than alone. I thought that if I should die in childbirth . . . it was still better than if you had no lawful son who could take your high seat after you, when you must leave this earth."

Erlend replied vehemently, "Then I would think my son was too dearly bought if he should cost you your life. Don't talk like that, Kristin." A little later he said, "Husaby is not so dear to me. Especially since I realized that Orm can never inherit my ancestral property after me."[1]

"Do you care more for *her* son than for mine?" Kristin then asked.

"*Your* son . . . ," Erlend gave a laugh. "Of him I know nothing more than that he will arrive half a year or so before he should. Orm I have loved for twelve years."

Some time later Kristin asked, "Do you ever long for these children of yours?"

"Yes," said her husband. "In the past I often went over to see them in Østerdal, where they are living."

"You could go there now, during Advent," said Kristin quietly.

"You wouldn't be averse to it?" asked Erlend happily.

Kristin said that she would find it reasonable. Then he asked whether she would be against it if he brought the children back home for Christmas. "You will have to see them sometime, after all." And again she had replied that this too seemed reasonable to her.

While Erlend was away, Kristin worked hard to prepare for Christmas. It distressed her greatly to be living among these unfamiliar men and servant women now—she had to take a firm grip on herself whenever she dressed or undressed in the presence of the two maids, whom Erlend had ordered to sleep with her in the hall. She had to remind herself that she would never have dared to sleep alone in the large house—where another had slept with Erlend before her.

The serving women on the estate were no better than could be expected. Those farmers who kept close watch over their daughters did not send them to serve on an estate where the master had lived openly with a concubine and had placed such a woman in charge. The maids were lazy and not in the habit of obeying their mistress. But some of them soon came to like the fact that Kristin was putting the house in good order and personally lent a hand with their work. They grew talkative and joyful when she listened to them and answered them gently and cheerfully. And each day Kristin showed her house servants a kind and calm demeanor. She reprimanded no one, but if a maid refused her orders, then the mistress would act as if the girl did not understand what was asked of her and would quietly show her how the work was to be done. This was how Kristin had seen her father behave toward new servants who grumbled, and no man had tried twice to disobey Lavrans of Jørundgaard.

In this manner they would have to make it through the winter. Later she would see about getting rid of those women she disliked or could not bring around.

There was one type of work that Kristin didn't dare take up unless she was free from the eyes of these strangers. But in the morning, when she was alone in the hall, she would sew the clothing for her child—swaddling clothes of soft homespun, ribbons of red and green fabric from town, and white linen for the christening garments. As she sat there with her sewing, her thoughts would tumble between fear and then faith in the holy friends of humankind, to whom she had prayed for intercession. It was true that the child lived and moved inside her so that she had no peace, night or day. But she had heard about children who were born with a pelt where they should have had a face, with their heads turned around backwards, or their toes where their heels should have been. And she pictured Svein, who was purple over half his face because his mother had inadvertently looked at a fire.[2]

Then Kristin would cast aside her sewing and go over to kneel before the image of the Virgin Mary and say seven *Ave Maria*s. Brother Edvin had said that the Mother of God felt an equal joy every time she heard the angel's greeting, even if it came from the lips of the most wretched sinner. And it was the words *Dominus tecum* that most cheered Mary's heart; that was why Kristin always said them three times.

This always helped her for a while. She knew of many people, both men and women, who paid scant honor to God or to His Mother and who kept the commandments poorly—but she hadn't seen that they gave birth to misshapen children because of it. Often God was so merciful that He did not visit the sins of the parents upon their poor children, although every once in a while He had to show people a sign that He could not perpetually tolerate their evil. But surely it would not be *her* child . . .

Then she called in her heart upon Saint Olav.[3] He was the one she had heard so much about that it was as though she had known him while he lived in Norway and had seen him here on this earth. He was not tall, quite stout, but straight-backed and fair, with the gold crown and shining halo on his golden curls, and a curly red beard on his firm, weatherbeaten, and intrepid face. But his deep-set and blazing eyes looked straight through everyone; those who had strayed did not dare look into them. Kristin didn't dare either. She lowered her gaze before his eyes, but she was not afraid. It was more as if she were a child and had to lower her eyes before her father's glance when she had done something wrong. Saint Olav looked at her, sternly but not harshly—she had promised to better her life, after all. She longed so fervently to go to Nidaros[4] and kneel down before his shrine: Erlend had promised her this, when they came north—that they would go there very soon. But the journey had been postponed. And now Kristin realized that he was reluctant to travel with her; he was ashamed and afraid of gossip.

One evening when she was sitting at the table with her servants, one of the maids, a young girl who helped in the house, said, "I was wondering, Mistress, whether it wouldn't be better if we started sewing swaddling clothes and infant garments before we set up the loom that you're talking about. . . ."

Kristin pretended not to hear and kept on talking about wool dyeing.

Then the girl continued, "But perhaps you have brought such garments from home?"

Kristin smiled faintly and then turned back to the others. When she glanced at the maid a little while later, she was sitting there bright red in the face and peering anxiously at her mistress. Kristin smiled again and spoke to Ulf across the table. Then the young girl began to weep. Kristin laughed a bit, and the maid cried harder and harder until she was sniffing and snuffling.

"Stop that now, Frida," Kristin finally said calmly. "You hired on here as a grown-up serving maid; you shouldn't behave as if you were a little child."

The maid whimpered. She hadn't meant to be impertinent, and Kristin mustn't be angry.

"No," said Kristin, smiling again. "Eat your food now and stop crying. The rest of us have no more sense, either, than what God has granted us."

Frida jumped up and ran out, sobbing loudly.

Later, when Ulf Haldorssøn stood talking to Kristin about the work that had to be done the next day, he laughed and said, "Erlend should have married you ten years ago, Kristin. Then his affairs would have been in a better state today, in every respect."

"Do you think so?" she asked, smiling as before. "Back then I was nine winters old. Do you think Erlend would have been capable of waiting for a child bride for years on end?"

Ulf laughed and went out.

But at night Kristin would lie in bed and weep with loneliness and humiliation.

Then Erlend came home during the week before Christmas, and Orm, his son, rode at his father's side. Kristin felt a stab in her heart when Erlend led the boy forward and told him to greet his stepmother.

He was the most handsome child. This was how she had thought *he* would look, the son that she carried. Sometimes, when she dared to be happy, to believe that her child would be born healthy and well-formed, and to think ahead about the boy who would grow up at her knee, then it was like this she pictured him—just like his father.

Orm was perhaps a little small for his age, and slight, but handsomely built, with fine limbs and a lovely face, his complexion and hair dark, but with big blue eyes and a soft red mouth. He greeted his stepmother courteously, but his expression was hard and cold. Kristin had not had the chance to talk with the boy further. But she sensed his eyes on her, wherever she walked or stood, and she felt as if her body and gait grew even more heavy and clumsy when she knew the boy was staring at her.

She didn't notice Erlend talking much with his son, but she realized that it was the boy who held back. Kristin told her husband that Orm was handsome and looked intelligent. Erlend had not brought his daughter along; he thought Margret was too young to make the long journey in the winter. She was even more lovely than her brother, he said proudly when Kristin asked about the little maiden—and much more clever; she had her foster parents wrapped around her little finger. She had wavy golden hair and brown eyes.

Then she must look much like her mother, thought Kristin. And she couldn't help the feeling of envy that burned inside her. She wondered whether Erlend loved his daughter the way her father had loved her. His voice had sounded so tender and warm when he spoke of Margret.

Kristin stood up and went over to the main door. It was so dark and heavy with rain outside that there seemed to be no moon or stars. But she thought it must soon be midnight. She picked up a lantern from the entryway, went inside, and lit it. Then she threw on her cloak and went out into the rain.

"In Christ's name," she whispered, crossing herself three times as she stepped out into the night.

At the upper end of the courtyard stood the priest's house. It was empty now. Ever since Erlend had been released from the ban of excommunication, there had not been a private cleric at Husaby; now and then one of the assistant priests from Orkedal would come over to say mass, but the new priest who had been assigned to the church was abroad with Master Gunnulf; they were apparently friends from school. They had been expected home this past summer, but now Erlend thought they wouldn't return until after spring. Gunnulf had had a lung ailment in his youth, so he would be unlikely to travel during the winter.

Kristin let herself into the cold, deserted house and found the key to the church. Then she paused for a moment. It was very slippery, pitch dark, windy, and rainy. It was reckless of her to go out at night, and especially on Christmas Eve, when all the evil spirits were in the air. But she refused to give up—she had to go to the church.

"In the name of God, the Almighty, I here proceed," she whispered aloud. Lighting her way with the lantern, Kristin set her feet down where stones and tufts of grass stuck up from the icy ground. In the darkness the path to the church seemed exceedingly long. But at last she stood on the stone threshold in front of the door.

Inside it was piercingly cold, much colder than out in the rain. Kristin walked forward toward the chancel and knelt down before the crucifix, which she glimpsed in the darkness above her.

After she had said her prayers and stood up, she stopped for a moment. She seemed to expect something to happen to her. But nothing did. She was freezing and scared in the desolate, dark church.

She crept up toward the altar and shone her light on the paintings. They were old, ugly, and stern. The altar was bare stone. She knew that the cloths, books, and vessels lay locked up in a chest.

In the nave a bench stood against the wall. Kristin went over and sat down, placing the lantern on the floor. Her cloak was wet, and her feet were wet and cold. She tried to pull one leg up underneath her, but the position was uncomfortable. So she wrapped the cloak tightly around her and struggled to focus her thoughts on the fact that now it was once again the holy midnight hour when Christ was born to the Virgin Mary in Bethlehem.

*Verbum caro factum est et habitavit in nobis.*[5]

Kristin remembered Sira Eirik's deep, pure voice. And Audun, the old deacon, who never attained a higher position. And their church back home where she had stood at her mother's side and listened to the Christmas mass. Every single year she had heard it. She tried to recall more of the holy words, but she could only think about their church and all the familiar faces. In front, on the men's side, stood her father, staring with remote eyes into the dazzling glow of candles from the choir.

It was so incomprehensible that their church was no more. It had burned to the ground. She burst into tears at the thought. And here she was, sitting alone in the dark on this night when all Christian people were gathered in happiness and joy in God's house. But perhaps that was as it should be, that tonight she was shut out from the celebration of the birth of God's son to a pure and innocent maiden.

Her parents were no doubt at Sundbu this Christmas. But there would be no mass in the chapel tonight; she knew that on Christmas Eve those who lived at Sundbu always attended the service at the main church in Ladalm.

This was the first time, for as far back as Kristin could remember, that she was not at the Christmas mass. She must have been quite young the first time her parents took her along. She could recall that she was bundled up in a fur-lined sack, and her father had carried her in his arms. It was a terribly cold night, and they were riding through a forest—the pine torches shone on fir trees heavy with snow. Her father's face was dark red, and the fur border on his hood was chalk-white with frost. Now and then he would bend forward and nip the end of her nose and ask her whether she could feel it. Then, laughing, he would shout over his shoulder to her mother that Kristin's nose hadn't frozen off yet. That must have been while they were still living at Skog; she couldn't have been more than three winters old. Her parents were quite young back then. Now she remembered her mother's voice on that night—clear and happy and full of laughter—when she called out to her husband and asked about the child. Yes, her mother's voice had been young and fresh.

Bethlehem. In Norwegian it means the place of bread. For that was where the bread which will nourish us for eternal life was given to the people.

It was at the mass on Christmas Day that Sira Eirik stepped forward to the pulpit and explained the gospels in the language of his own country.

In between the masses everyone would sit in the banquet hall north of the church. They had brought ale with them and passed it around. The men slipped out to the stables to see to the horses. But on vigil nights, in the summertime before a holy day, the congregation would gather on the church green, and then the young people would dance among the servants.

And the blessed Virgin Mary wrapped her son in swaddling clothes. She placed him in the straw of the manger from which the oxen and asses ate. . . .

Kristin pressed her hands against her sides.

Little son, my own sweet child, my own son. God will have mercy on us for the sake of His own blessed Mother. Blessed Mary, you who are the clear star of the sea,[6] the crimson dawn of eternal life who gave birth to the sun of the whole world—help us! Little child, what is it tonight? You're so restless. Can you feel beneath my heart that I am so bitterly cold?

It was on the Children's Day last year, the fourth day of Christmas, when Sira Eirik preached about the innocent children whom the cruel soldiers had slaughtered in their mothers' arms. But God had chosen these young boys to enter into the hall of heaven before all other blood witnesses. And it would be a sign that such belong to the Kingdom of Heaven. And Jesus picked up a little boy and put him among them. Unless you create yourselves in their image, you cannot enter into the hall of heaven, dear brothers and sisters. So let this be a solace to every man and woman who mourns a young child's death. . . .

Then Kristin had seen her father's eyes meet her mother's across the church, and she withdrew her gaze, because she knew that this was not meant for her.

That was last year. The first Christmas after Ulvhild's death. Oh, but not *my* child! Jesus, Maria. Let me keep my son!

Her father had not wanted to ride in the races on Saint Stefan's Day last year, but the men begged him until he finally agreed. The course extended from the church hill at home, down to the confluence of the two rivers near Loptsgaard; that's where they joined up with the men from Ottadal. She remembered her father racing past on his golden stallion. He stood up in his stirrups and bent low over the horse's neck, shouting and urging the animal on, with the whole group thundering behind.

But last year he had come home early, and he was completely sober. Normally on that day the men would return home late, tremendously drunk, because they had to ride into every farm courtyard and drink from the bowls brought out to them, to honor Christ and Saint Stefan, who first saw the star in the east as he drove King Herod's foals to the River Jordan for water. Even the horses were given ale on that day, for they were supposed to be wild and reckless. On Saint Stefan's Day the farmers were allowed to race their horses until vespers—it was impossible to make the men think or talk of anything but horses.

Kristin could remember one Christmas when they held the great drinking feast at Jørundgaard. And her father had promised a priest who was among the guests that he would be given a young red stallion, son of Guldsvein, if he could manage to swing himself up onto the animal as it ran around unsaddled in the courtyard.

That was a long time ago—before the misfortune with Ulvhild occurred. Her mother was standing in the doorway with the little sister in her arms, and Kristin was holding onto her dress, a bit scared.

The priest ran after the horse and grabbed the halter, leaping so that his ankle-length surcoat swirled around him, and then he let go of the wild, rearing beast.

"Foal, foal—whoa, foal. Whoa, son!" he cried out. He hopped and he danced like a billy goat. Her father and an old farmer stood with their arms around each other's necks, the features of their faces completely dissolved in laughter and drunkenness.

Either the priest must have won Rauden or else Lavrans gave the foal to him all the same, for Kristin remembered that he rode away from Jørundgaard on the horse. By that time they were all sober enough; Lavrans respectfully held the stirrup for him, and the priest blessed them with three fingers in farewell. He was apparently a cleric of high standing.

Oh yes. It was often quite merry at home during the Christmas season. And then there were the Christmas masqueraders. Kristin's father would sling her up onto his back, his tunic icy and his hair wet. To clear their heads before they went to vespers, the men threw ice water over each other down by the well. They laughed when the women voiced their disapproval of this. Kristin's father would take her small, cold hands and press them against his forehead, which was still red and burning hot. This was out in the courtyard, in the evening. A new white crescent moon hung over the mountain ridge in the watery-green air. Once when he stepped into the main house with her, Kristin hit her head on the doorframe so she had a big bump on her forehead. Later she sat on his lap at the table. He lay the blade of his dagger against her bruise, fed her tidbits of food, and let her drink mead from his goblet. Then she wasn't afraid of the masqueraders who stormed into the room.

"Oh Father, oh Father. My dear, kind father!"

Sobbing loudly, Kristin now hid her face in her hands. Oh, if only her father knew how she felt on this Christmas Eve!

When she walked back across the courtyard, she saw that sparks were rising up from the cookhouse roof. The maids had set about preparing food for the churchgoers.

It was gloomy in the hall. The candles on the table had burned out, and the fire in the hearth was barely smoldering. Kristin put more wood on and blew at the embers. Then she noticed that Orm was sitting in her chair. He stood up as soon as his stepmother saw him.

"My dear—" said Kristin. "Didn't you go with your father and the others to mass?"

Orm swallowed hard a couple of times. "I guess he forgot to wake me. Father told me to lie down for a while in the bed on the south wall. He said he would wake me. . . ."

"That's too bad, Orm," said Kristin.

The boy didn't reply. After a moment he said, "I thought you went with them after all. I woke up and was alone here in the hall."

"I went over to the church for a little while," said Kristin.

"Do you dare to go out on Christmas Eve?" asked the boy. "Don't you know that the spirits of the dead could come and seize you?"[7]

"I don't think it's only the evil spirits that are out tonight," she said. "Christmas Eve must be for all spirits. I once knew a monk who is now dead and standing before God, I think, because he was pure goodness. He told me . . . Have you ever heard about the animals in the stable and how they talked to each other on Christmas Eve? They could speak Latin back then. And the rooster crowed: *'Christus natus est!'* No, now I can't remember the whole thing. The other animals asked 'Where?' and the goat bleated, *'Betlem, Betlem,'* and the sheep said, *'Eamus, eamus.'* "

Orm smiled scornfully.

"Do you think I'm such a child that you can comfort me with tales? You should offer to take me on your lap and put me to your breast."

"I told the story mostly to comfort myself, Orm," said Kristin quietly. "I would have liked to go to mass too."

Now she couldn't stand to look at the littered table any longer. She went over, swept all the scraps into a trencher and set it on the floor for the dog. Then she found the whisk made of sedge under the bench and scrubbed off the tabletop.

"Would you come with me over to the western storehouse, Orm? To get bread and salted meat. Then we'll set the table for the holy day," said Kristin.

"Why don't you let your maidservants do that?" asked the boy.

"This is the way I was taught by my father and mother," replied the young mistress. "That at Christmastime no one should ever ask anyone else for anything, but we all should strive to do our utmost. Whoever serves the others most during the holidays is the most blessed."

"But you're asking me," said Orm.

"That's a different matter—you're the son here on the estate."

Orm carried the lantern and they walked across the courtyard together. Inside the storehouse Kristin filled two trenchers with Christmas food. She also took a bundle of large tallow candles.

While they were working, the boy said, "That must be a peasant custom, what you mentioned a moment ago. For I've heard he's nothing more than a homespun farmer, Lavrans Bjørgulfsøn."

"Who did you hear that from?" asked Kristin.

"From Mother," said Orm. "I heard her say it all the time to Father when we were living here at Husaby before. She said he could see that not even a gray-clad farmer would give his daughter's hand in marriage to him."

"It must have been pleasant here at Husaby back then," said Kristin curtly.

The boy didn't reply. His lips quivered.

Kristin and Orm carried the filled trenchers back to the hall, and she set the table. But she had to go back over to the storehouse for food once again.

Orm took the trencher and said, a little awkwardly, "I'll go over there for you, Kristin. It's so slippery in the courtyard."

She stood outside the door and waited until he returned.

Then they sat down near the hearth, Kristin in the armchair and the boy on a three-legged stool nearby. After a moment Orm Erlendssøn said softly, "Tell me another story while we sit here, my stepmother."

"A story?" asked Kristin, her voice equally quiet.

"Yes, a tale or some such—that would be suitable on Christmas Eve," said the boy shyly.

Kristin leaned back in her chair and wrapped her thin hands around the animal heads on the armrests.

"That monk I mentioned—he had also been to England. And he said there is a region where wild rosebushes grow that bloom with white blossoms on Christmas night. Saint Joseph of Arimathea[8] put ashore in that area when he was fleeing from the heathens, and there he stuck his staff into the ground and it took root and flowered. He was the first to bring the Christian faith to Bretland. The name of the region is Glastonbury—now I remember. Brother Edvin had seen the bushes himself. King Arthur, whom you've no doubt heard stories of, was buried there in Glastonbury with his queen. He was one of the seven most noble defenders of Christendom.

"They say in England that Christ's Cross was made of alderwood. But we burned ash during Christmas at home, for it was the ash tree that Saint Joseph, the stepfather of Christ, used when he needed to light a fire for the Virgin Mary and the newborn Son of God. That's something else that Father heard from Brother Edvin."

"But very few ash trees grow up north here," said Orm. "They used them all up for spear poles in the olden days, you know. I don't think there are any ash trees here on Husaby's land other than the one standing east of the manor gate, and Father can't chop that one down, because the spirit of the first owner lives underneath.[9] But you know, Kristin, they have the Holy Cross in Romaborg; so they must be able to find out whether it was made of alderwood."

"Well," said Kristin, "I don't know whether it's true. For you know it's said that the cross was made from a shoot of the tree of life, which Seth was allowed to take from the Garden of Eden and bring home to Adam before he died."

"Yes," said Orm. "But then tell me . . ."

Some time later Kristin said to the boy, "Now you should lie down for a while, kinsman, and sleep. It will be a long time yet before the churchgoers return."

Orm stood up.

"We have not yet toasted each other as kinsmen, Kristin Lavransdatter." He went over and took a drinking horn from the table, drank to his stepmother, and handed her the vessel.

She felt as if ice water were running down her back. She couldn't help remembering that time when Orm's mother wanted to drink with her. And the child inside her womb began to thrash violently. What's going on with him tonight? wondered the mother. It seemed as if her unborn son felt everything that she felt, was cold when she was cold, and shrank in fear when she was frightened. But then I mustn't be so weak, thought Kristin. She took the horn and drank with her stepson.

When she handed it back to Orm, she gently stroked his dark hair. No, I'm certainly not going to be a harsh stepmother to you, she thought. You handsome, handsome son of Erlend.

She had fallen asleep in her chair when Erlend came home and tossed his frozen mittens onto the table.

"Are you back already?" said Kristin, astonished. "I thought you would stay for the daytime mass."

"Oh, two masses will last me for a long time," said Erlend as Kristin picked up his icy cape. "Yes, the sky is clear now, so the frost has set in."

"It was a shame that you forgot to wake Orm," said his wife.

"Was he sad about it?" asked Erlend. "I didn't actually forget," he went on in a low voice. "But he was sleeping so soundly, and I thought . . . You can well believe that people stared enough because I came to church without you. I didn't want to step forward with the boy at my side on top of that."

Kristin said nothing, but she felt distressed. She didn't think Erlend had handled this very well.

## CHAPTER 3

THEY DID NOT have many guests at Husaby that Christmas. Erlend didn't want to travel to any of the places where he was invited; he stayed home on his manor and was in a bad humor.

As it turned out, he took this act of fate more to heart than his wife could know. He had boasted so much of his betrothed, ever since his kinsmen had won Lavrans's assent at Jørundgaard. This was the last thing Erlend had wanted—for anyone to believe that he considered her or her kinsmen to be lesser than his own people. No, everyone must know that he held it to be an honor and a distinction when Lavrans Bjørgulfsøn betrothed him to his daughter. Now people would say that Erlend had not considered the maiden much more than a peasant child, since he had dared to offend her father in such a manner, by sleeping with the daughter before she had been given to him in marriage. At his wedding, Erlend had urged his wife's parents to come to Husaby in the summer to see how things were on his estate. He wanted to show them that it was not to paltry circumstances that he had brought their daughter. But he had also looked forward to traveling around and being seen in the company of these gracious and dignified in-laws; he realized that Lavrans and Ragnfrid could hold their own among the most esteemed of people, wherever they might go. And ever since the time when he was at Jørundgaard and the church burned down, Erlend had thought that Lavrans was rather fond of him, in spite of everything. Now it was unlikely that the reunion between Erlend and his wife's kinsmen would be pleasant for either party.

It angered Kristin that Erlend so often took his ill temper out on Orm. The boy had no children of his own age to play with, so he was frequently peevish and in the way; he also got into a good deal of mischief. One day he took his father's French crossbow without permission, and something broke in the lock. Erlend was very angry; he struck Orm on the ear and swore that the boy would not be allowed to touch a bow again at Husaby.

"It wasn't Orm's fault," said Kristin without turning around. She was sitting with her back to the two, sewing. "The spring was bent when he took it, and he tried to straighten it out. You can't be so unreasonable to refuse to allow this big son of yours to use a single bow out of all those you have on the estate. Why don't you give him one of the bows from up in the armory?"

"You can give him a bow yourself, if you feel like it," said Erlend furiously.

"I'll do that," replied Kristin in the same tone as before. "I'll speak to Ulf about it the next time he goes to town."

"You must go over and thank your kind stepmother, Orm," said Erlend, his voice derisive and angry.

Orm obeyed. And then he fled out the door as fast as he could. Erlend stood there for a moment.

"You did that mostly to annoy me, Kristin," he said.

"Yes, I know I'm a witch. You've said that before," replied his wife.

"Do you also remember, my sweet," said Erlend sadly, "that I didn't mean it seriously that time?"

Kristin neither answered nor looked up from her sewing. Then Erlend left, and afterwards she sat there and cried. She was fond of Orm, and she thought Erlend was often unreasonable toward his son. But the fact was that her husband's taciturn and aggrieved demeanor now tormented her so that she would lie in bed and weep half the night. And then she would walk around with an aching head the next day. Her hands had become so gaunt that she had to slip several small silver rings from her childhood days onto her fingers after her betrothal and wedding rings to keep them from falling off while she slept.

On the Sunday before Lent, late in the afternoon, Sir Baard Peterson arrived unexpectedly at Husaby with his daughter, a widow, and Sir Munan Baardsøn and his wife. Erlend and Kristin went out to the courtyard to bid the guests welcome.

As soon as Sir Munan caught sight of Kristin, he slapped Erlend on the shoulder.

"I see that you've known how to treat your wife, kinsman, so that she is thriving on your estate. You're not so thin and miserable now as you were at your wedding, Kristin. And you have a much healthier color too," he laughed, for Kristin had turned as red as a rosehip.

Erlend did not reply. Sir Baard wore a dark expression, but the two women seemed neither to hear nor see a thing; they greeted their hosts formally and with courtesy.

Kristin had ale and mead brought over to the hearth while they waited for the food. Munan Baardsøn talked without stopping. He had letters for Erlend from the duchess—she was inquiring what had become of him and his bride: whether he was now married to the same maiden that he had wanted to carry off to Sweden. It was hellish traveling now, in midwinter—up through the valleys and by ship to Nidaros. But he was on the king's business, so it would do no good to grumble. He had stopped by to see his mother at Haugen and he brought them greetings from her.

"Were you at Jørundgaard?" Kristin ventured.

No, for he had heard that they had gone to a wake at Blakarsarv. A terrible event had occurred. The mistress, Tora, Ragnfrid's kinswoman, had fallen from the storeroom gallery and had broken her back, and it was her husband who had inadvertently pushed her out. It was one of those old storerooms without a proper gallery; there were merely several floorboards placed on top of the posts at the second-story level. They had been forced to tie up Rolv and keep watch over him night and day ever since the accident occurred. He wanted to lay hands on himself.

Everyone sat in silence, shivering. Kristin didn't know these kinsmen well, but they had come to her wedding. She felt suddenly strange and weak—everything went black before her eyes. Munan was sitting across from her and he leaped to his feet. When he stood over her, his arm around her shoulder, he looked so kind. Kristin realized that it was perhaps not so odd for Erlend to be fond of this cousin of his.

"I knew Rolv when we were young," he said. "People felt sorry for Tora Guttormsdatter—they said he was wild and hard-hearted. But now you can see that he cared for her. Oh yes, many a man may boast and pretend that he'd like to be rid of his spouse, but most men know full well that a wife is the worst thing they can lose—"

Baard Petersøn stood up abruptly and went over to the bench against the wall.

"May God curse my tongue," said Sir Munan in a low voice. "I can never remember to keep my mouth shut either. . . ."

Kristin didn't know what he meant. The dizziness was gone now, but she had such an unpleasant feeling; they all seemed so peculiar. She was glad when the servants brought in the food.

Munan looked at the table and rubbed his hands.

"I didn't think we'd be disappointed if we came to visit you, Kristin, before we have to gnaw on Lenten food. How have you managed to put together such delicious platters in such a short time? One would almost think you had learned to conjure from your mother. But I see that you're quick to set forth everything a wife should offer to please her husband."

They sat down at the table. Velvet cushions had been placed for the guests on the inner benches on either side of the high seat. The servants sat on the outer bench, with Ulf Haldorssøn in the middle, right across from Erlend.

Kristin chatted quietly with the women guests and tried to conceal how ill at ease she felt. Every once in a while Munan Baardsøn would interrupt with words that were meant to tease, and it was always about how Kristin was already moving so slowly. She pretended not to hear.

Munan was an unusually stout man. His small, shapely ears were set deep in the ruddy, fat flesh above his neck, and his belly got in his way when he sat down at the table.

"Yes, I've often wondered about the resurrection of the body," he said. "Whether I'm going to rise up with all this fat that I've put on when that day arrives. You'll be slim-waisted again soon enough, Kristin—but it's much worse for me. You may not believe it, but I was just as slender in the belt as Erlend over there when I was twenty winters old."

"Stop it now, Munan," begged Erlend softly. "You're upsetting Kristin."

"All right then, if that's what you want," replied Munan. "You must be proud now, I can well imagine—presiding over your own table, sitting in the high seat with your wedded wife beside you. And God Almighty knows that it's about time, too—you're plenty old enough, my boy! Of course I'll keep my mouth shut, since that's what you want. But nobody ever told *you* . . . to speak or keep still—back when you were sitting at *my* table. You were often a guest in my house and stayed a long time, and I don't think I ever noticed that you weren't welcome.

"But I wonder whether Kristin dislikes it so much that I tease her a little. What do you say, my fair kinswoman? You weren't as timid in the past. I've known Erlend from the time he was only so high, and I think I can venture to say that I've wished the boy well all his days. Quick and boyish you are, Erlend, with a sword in your hand, whether on horseback or on board ship. But I'll ask Saint Olav to cleave me in half with his axe on the day when I see you stand up on your long legs, look man or woman freely in the eye, and answer for what you have done in your thoughtlessness. No, my dear kinsman, then you will hang your head like a bird in a trap and call on God and your kinsmen to help you out of trouble. And you're such a sensible woman, Kristin, that I imagine you know this. I think you need to laugh a little now; no doubt you've seen enough this winter of shameful memories and sorrows and regrets."

Kristin sat there, her face deep red. Her hands were trembling, and she didn't dare glance at Erlend. Fury was boiling inside her—here sat the women guests and Orm and the servants. So this was the kind of courtesy shown by Erlend's rich kinsmen. . . .

Then Sir Baard said so quietly that only those sitting closest could hear him, "I don't think this is something to banter about—that Erlend has behaved in this way before his marriage. I vouched for you, Erlend, to Lavrans Bjørgulfsøn."

"Yes, and that was devilishly unwise of you, my foster father," said Erlend loudly and fervently. "I can't understand that you could be so foolish. For you know me well."

But Munan was completely intractable.

"Now I'm going to tell you why I think this is so funny. Do you remember what you said to me, Baard, when I came to you and said that we had to help Erlend to achieve this marriage? No, I *am* going to talk about it; Erlend should know what you thought about me. This is the way it stands between them, I said, and if he doesn't win Kristin Lavransdatter, only God and the Virgin Mary know what madness will result. Then you asked me if that was the real reason I wanted him to marry the maiden he had seduced, because I thought perhaps she was barren since she had managed to escape for so long. But I think you know me, all of you; you know that I'm a faithful kinsman to my kin. . . ." And he broke into tears of emotion.

"As God is my witness along with all holy men: never have I coveted your property, kinsman—because otherwise there is only Gunnulf between me and Husaby. But I said to you, Baard, as you know—to Kristin's firstborn son I would give my gold-encrusted dagger with its walrus-tusk sheath. Here, take it," he shouted, sobbing, and he tossed the magnificent weapon across the table to her. "If it's not a son this time, then it'll be one next year."

Tears of shame and anger were pouring down Kristin's hot cheeks. She struggled fiercely not to break down. But the two women guests sat and ate as calmly as if they were used to such commotion. And Erlend whispered that she should take the dagger "or Munan will just keep on all night."

"Yes, and I'm not going to hide the fact," Munan went on, "that I wish your father could see, Kristin, that he was too quick to defend your soul. So arrogant Lavrans was—we weren't good enough for him, Baard and I, and you were much too delicate and pure to tolerate a man like Erlend in your bed. He talked as if he didn't believe that you could stand to do anything in the nighttime hours except sing in the nuns' choir. I said to him, 'Dear Lavrans,' I said, 'your daughter is a beautiful and healthy and lively young maiden, and the winter nights are long and cold here in this country. . . .' "

Kristin pulled her wimple over her face. She was sobbing loudly and tried to get up, but Erlend pulled her back down in her seat.

"Try to get hold of yourself," he said vehemently. "Don't pay any attention to Munan—you can see for yourself that he's dead drunk."

She sensed that Fru Katrin and Fru Vilborg thought it pitiable that she didn't have better command of herself. But she couldn't stop her tears.

Baard Petersøn said furiously to Munan, "Shut your rotten trap. You've been a swine all your days—but even so, you can spare an ill woman from that filthy talk of yours."

"Did you say swine? Yes, I do have more bastard children than you do, be that as it may. But one thing I've never done—and

Erlend hasn't either—we've never paid another man to be the child's father for us."

"Munan!" shouted Erlend, springing to his feet. "Now I demand peace here in my hall!"

"Oh, demand peace in your backside! My children call the man 'father' who sired them—in my swinish life, as you call it!" Munan pounded the table so the cups and small plates danced. "Our sons don't go around as servants in the house of our kinsmen. But here sits your son across the table from you, and he's sitting on the servants' bench. That seems to me the worst of all shame."

Baard leaped up and threw his goblet into the other man's face. The two fell upon each other so the table plank tipped onto its side, and food and vessels slid into the laps of those sitting on the outer bench.

Kristin sat there white-faced, with her mouth agape. Once she stole a glance at Ulf—the man was laughing openly, crudely and maliciously. Then he tipped the table plank back into place and shoved it against the two combatants.

Erlend leaped up onto the table. Kneeling in the middle of the mess, he seized hold of Munan's arms, then grabbed him under the armpits and hauled him up next to him; he turned bright red in the face from the effort. Munan managed to give Baard a kick so that the old man began to bleed from the mouth—then Erlend flung Munan over the table and out onto the floor. He jumped down after him, and stood there huffing like a bellows.

The other man got to his feet and rushed at Erlend, who slipped under his arms a couple of times. Then he fell on Munan and held him entangled in the grip of his long, supple limbs. Erlend was as agile as a cat, but Munan held his ground; strong and bulky, he refused to be forced to the floor. They whirled around and around the room while the serving women shrieked and screamed, and none of the men made a move to separate them.

Then Fru Katrin stood up, heavy and fat and slow; she stepped onto the table as calmly as if she were walking up the storehouse stairs.

"Stop that now," she said in her husky, sated voice. "Let go of him, Erlend! It was wrong, husband—to speak that way to an old man and close kinsman."

The men obeyed her. Munan stood meekly and let his wife wipe his bloody nose with her wimple. She told him to go to bed, and he followed docilely when she led him away to the bed on the south wall. His wife and one of his servants pulled the clothes off him, toppled him into the bed, and closed the door.

Erlend had walked over to the table. He leaned past Ulf, who was still sitting as he had before.

"Foster father," said Erlend unhappily. He seemed to have completely forgotten his wife. Sir Baard sat and rocked his head back and forth, and the tears were dripping down his cheeks.

"He didn't have to become a servant, Ulf didn't," were the words that came out, but his sobs lodged, gasping, in his chest. "You could have taken the farm after Haldor, you know that's what I intended. . . ."

"It wasn't a very good farm that you gave Haldor; you bought a cheap husband for your wife's serving maid," said Ulf. "He fixed it up and managed it well, and it seemed to me reasonable that my brothers should take it over after their father. That's one thing. But I had no desire to end up as a farmer, either—and least of all up on the slope, staring down at the Hestnes courtyard. It seemed to me that I heard every day that Paal and Vilborg were going around saying vicious things about how you gave much too grand a gift to your bastard son."

"I offered to help you, Ulf," said Baard, weeping. "When you wanted to go out traveling with Erlend. I told you everything as soon as you were old enough to understand. I begged you to return to your father."

"I call the man my father who looked after me when I was small. That man was Haldor. He was good to Mother and to me. He taught me to ride a horse and to fight with a sword—the way a farmer wields his club, I remember Paal once said."

Ulf flung the knife he was holding so that it clattered across the table. Then he got to his feet, picked up the knife, wiped it on the back of his thigh, and stuck it in its sheath. He turned to Erlend. "Put an end to this feast now and send the servants to bed! Can't you see that your wife is still not used to the banquet customs we have in our family?"

And with that he left the hall.

Sir Baard stared after him. He seemed so pitifully old and frail as he sat slumped among the velvet cushions. His daughter, Vilborg, and one of his servants helped Baard to his feet and escorted him out.

Kristin sat alone in the high seat, weeping and weeping. When Erlend touched her, she angrily struck his hand aside. She swayed a few times as she walked across the floor, but she replied with a curt "no" when her husband asked if she was ill.

She detested these closed beds. Back home they simply had tapestries hung up facing the room, and thus it was never hot or stuffy. But now it was worse than ever . . . it was so hard for her to breathe. She thought that the hard lump pressing on her all the way up under her ribcage must be the child's head; she imagined him lying with his little black head burrowed in amongst the roots of her heart. He was suffocating her, as Erlend had done before when he pressed his dark-haired head to her breast. But tonight there was no sweetness in the thought.

"Will you never stop your crying?" asked her husband, trying to ease his arm under her shoulder.

He was quite sober. He could tolerate a great deal of liquor, but he usually drank very little. Kristin thought that never in all eternity would this have happened back at her home—never had she heard people fling slanderous words at each other or rip open something that would be better left unsaid. As many times as she had seen her father reeling from intoxication and the hall full of drunken guests, there was *never* a time when he couldn't keep order in his own house. Peace and good will reigned right up until everyone tumbled off the benches and fell asleep in joy and harmony.

"My dearest wife, don't take this so hard," implored Erlend.

"And Sir Baard!" she burst into tears. "Shame on such behavior—this man who spoke to my father as if he were bearing God's message. Yes, Munan told me about it at our betrothal banquet."

Erlend said softly, "I know, Kristin, that I have reason to cast down my eyes before your father. He's a fine man—but my foster father is no worse. Inga, the mother of Paal and Vilborg, lay paralyzed and ill for six years before she died. That was before I came to Hestnes, but I've heard about it. Never has a husband tended to an ailing wife in a more faithful or loving manner. But it was during that time that Ulf was born."

"Then it was an even greater sin—with his sick wife's maid."

"You often act so childish that it's impossible to talk to you," said Erlend in resignation. "God help me, Kristin, you're going to be twenty this spring—and several winters have passed since you had to be considered a grown-up woman."

"Yes, it's true that *you* have the right to scoff at me for that."

Erlend moaned loudly.

"You know yourself that I didn't mean it like that. But you lived all that time at Jørundgaard and listened to Lavrans—so splendid and manly he is, but he often talks as if he were a monk and not a grown man."

"Have you ever heard of any monk who has had six children?" she said, offended.

"I've heard of that man, Skurda-Grim, and he had seven," said Erlend in despair. "The former abbot at Holm . . . No, Kristin, Kristin, don't cry like that. In God's name, I think you've lost your senses."

Munan was quite subdued the next morning. "I didn't think you would take my ale-babble so much to heart, young Kristin," he said somberly, stroking her cheek. "Or I would have kept better watch on my tongue."

He said to Erlend that it must be strange for Kristin with the boy being there. It would be best to send Orm away for the time being. Munan offered to take him in for a while. Erlend approved, and Orm wanted to go with Munan. But Kristin missed the child deeply; she had grown fond of her stepson.

Now she once again sat alone with Erlend in the evenings, and there was not much companionship in him. He would sit over by the hearth, say a few words now and then, take a drink from the ale bowl, and play with his dogs. He would go over to the bench and stretch out—and then he would go to bed, asking a couple of times whether she was coming soon, and then he'd fall asleep.

Kristin sat and sewed. Her breathing was audible, shallow and heavy. But it wouldn't be long now. She couldn't even remember how it felt to be light and slim in the waist—or how to tie her shoes without strain and effort.

Now that Erlend was asleep she no longer tried to hold back her tears. There was not a sound in the hall except the firewood collapsing in the hearth and the dogs stirring. Sometimes she wondered what they had talked about before, she and Erlend. But then they hadn't talked much—they had had other things to do in those brief, stolen hours together.

At this time of year her mother and the maids used to sit in the weaving room in the evenings. Then her father and the men would come to join them and sit down with their work—they would repair leather goods and farm tools and make carvings out of wood. The little room would be crowded with people; conversation flowed quietly and easily among them. Whenever somebody went over to drink from the ale keg, before he hung up the ladle he would always ask whether anyone else would like some—that was the custom.

Then someone would recite a short saga—perhaps about giants in the past who had fought with grave-barrow ghosts and giantesses. Or her father, as he whittled, would recount those tales of knights that he had heard read aloud in Duke Haakon's hall when he was a page in his youth. Strange and beautiful names: King Osantrix, Titurel the knight; Sisibe, Guinevere, Gloriana, and Isolde were the names of the queens. But on other evenings they told bawdy tales and ribald sagas until the men were roaring with laughter and her mother and the maids would shake their heads and giggle.

Ulvhild and Astrid would sing. Ragnfrid had the loveliest voice of all, but they had to plead before they could get her to sing. Lavrans didn't need such persuasion—and he could play his harp so beautifully.

Then Ulvhild would put down her distaff and spindle and press her hands behind her hips.

"Is your back tired now, little Ulvhild?" asked her father, taking her onto his lap. Someone would bring a board game and Ulvhild and her father would move the markers around until it was time for bed. Kristin remembered her little sister's golden locks flowing over her father's brownish-green homespun sleeve. He held the weak little back so tenderly.

Her father's big, slender hands with a heavy gold ring on each little finger . . . They had both belonged to his mother. He had said that the one with the red stone, her wedding ring, Kristin would inherit from him. But the one that he wore on his right hand, with a stone that was half blue and half white, like the emblem on his shield—that one Sir Bjørgulf had ordered made for his wife when she was with child, and it was to be given to her when she had borne him a son. For three nights Kristin Sigurdsdatter had worn the ring; then she tied it around the boy's neck, and Lavrans said that he would wear it to his grave.

Oh, what would her father say when he heard the news about her? When it spread throughout the villages back home, and he had to realize that wherever he went, to church or to the *ting*[1] or to a meeting, every man would be laughing behind his back because he had allowed himself to be fooled? At Jørundgaard they had adorned a wanton woman with the Sundbu crown on her flowing hair.

"People are no doubt saying of me that I can't keep my children in check." She remembered her father's face whenever he said that; he meant to be stern and somber, but his eyes were merry. She had misbehaved in some small way—spoken to him uninvited while guests were present or some such. "And you, Kristin, you don't have much fear of your father, do you?" Then he would laugh, and she laughed along with him. "Yes, but that's not right, Kristin." And neither of them knew *what* was not right—that she didn't have the proper terror of her father, or that it was impossible for him to remain serious when he had to scold her.

It was as if the unbearable fear that something would be wrong with her child diminished and faded away the more trouble and torment Kristin had from her body. She tried to think ahead—to a month from now; by then her son would have already been born. But it didn't seem real to her. She simply yearned more and more for home.

Once Erlend asked Kristin if she wanted him to send for her mother. But she told him no—she didn't think her mother could stand to travel so far in the winter. Now she regretted this. And she regretted that she had said no to Tordis of Laugarbru, who had been so willing to accompany her north and lend a hand during the first winter she was to be mistress. But she felt ashamed before Tordis. Tordis had been Ragnfrid's maid at home at Sundbu and had accompanied her to Skog and then back to the valley. When Tordis married, Lavrans had made her husband a foreman at Jørundgaard because Ragnfrid couldn't bear to be without her beloved maid. Kristin had not wanted to bring along any of the maids from home.

Now it seemed to her terrible that she would have no familiar face above her when her time came to kneel on the floor.[2] She was frightened—she knew so little about what went on at childbirth. Her mother had never spoken to her of it and had never wanted young maidens to be present when she helped a woman give birth. It would only frighten the young, she said. It could certainly be dreadful; Kristin remembered when her mother had Ulvhild. But Ragnfrid said it was because she had inadvertently crawled under a fence—she had given birth to her other children with ease. But Kristin remembered that she herself had been thoughtless and had walked under a rope on board ship.

But that didn't always cause harm—she had heard her mother and other women speak of such things. Ragnfrid had a reputation back home in the village for being the best midwife, and she never refused to go and help, no matter if it was a beggar or the poorest man's seduced daughter, or if the weather was such that three men had to accompany her on skis and take turns carrying her on their backs.

But it was completely unthinkable that an experienced woman like her mother hadn't realized what was wrong with her this past summer, when she was feeling so wretched. It suddenly occurred to Kristin: but then . . . then it was certain that her mother would come, even though they hadn't sent for her! Ragnfrid would never stand for a stranger helping her daughter through the struggle. Her mother was coming—she was probably on her way north right now. Oh, then she could ask for her mother's forgiveness for all the pain she had caused her. Her own mother would support her, she would kneel at her own mother's knees when she gave birth to her child. Mother is coming, Mother is coming. Kristin sobbed with relief, covering her face with her hands. Yes, Mother; forgive me, Mother.

This thought, that her mother was on her way to be with her, became so entrenched in Kristin's mind that one day she thought she could sense that her mother would arrive that very day. In the early morning she put on her cloak and went out to meet her on the road which leads from Gauldal to Skaun. No one noticed her leave the estate.

Erlend had ordered timber to be brought for the improvement of the buildings, so the road was good, but walking was still difficult for her. She was short of breath, her heart pounded, and she had a pain in both sides—it felt as if the taut skin would burst apart after she had walked a short while. And most of the road passed through dense forest. She was afraid, but there had been no word of wolves in the area that winter. And God would protect her, since she was on her way to meet her mother, to fall down before her and beg forgiveness—and she could not stop walking.

She reached a small lake where there were several farms. At the spot where the road led out onto the ice, she sat down on a log. She sat there for a while, walked a little farther when she began to freeze, and waited for many hours. But at last she had to turn back and head for home.

The next day she wandered along the same road. But when she crossed the courtyard of one of the small farms near the lake, the farmer's wife came running after her.

"In God's name, mistress, you mustn't do that!"

When the other woman spoke, Kristin grew so frightened herself that she didn't dare move. Trembling, her eyes wide with fear, she stared at the farmer's wife.

"Through the woods—just think if a wolf caught your scent. Other terrible things could happen to you, too. How can you do something so foolish?"

The farmer's wife put her arm around the young mistress and supported her; she looked into Kristin's gaunt face with the yellowish, brown-flecked skin.

"You must come into our house and rest for a while. Then someone from here will escort you home," said the farmer's wife as she led Kristin indoors.

It was a cramped and impoverished house, and there was great disarray inside; many little children were playing on the floor. Their mother sent them out to the cookhouse, took her guest's cloak, seated her on a bench, and pulled off her snowy shoes. Then she wrapped a fur around Kristin's feet.

No matter how much Kristin begged the woman not to trouble herself, the farmer's wife continued to dish up food and ale from the Christmas cask. All the while the woman thought: So that's how things are at Husaby! She was a poor man's wife; they had little help on the farm, and usually none at all; but Øistein had never allowed her to walk alone outside the courtyard fence when she was with child—yes, even if she was just going out to the cowshed after dark, someone would have to keep watch for her. But the richest mistress in the parish could go out and risk the most hideous death, and not a Christian soul was looking out for her—even though the servants were falling over each other at Husaby and did no work. It must be true then what people said, that Erlend Nikulaussøn was already tired of his marriage and cared nothing for his wife.

But she chatted with Kristin the whole time and urged her to eat and drink. And Kristin was thoroughly ashamed, but she had a craving for food such as she had not felt before—not since the spring. This kind woman's food tasted so good. And the woman laughed and said that the gentry's women probably were created no different from other people. If a woman couldn't stand to look at food at home, someone else's food could often make her almost greedy, even if it was poor and coarse fare.

Her name was Audfinna Andunsdatter, and she was from Updal, she said. When she noticed that it put her guest at ease, she began to talk about her home and her village. And before Kristin knew it, her own tongue was loosened, and she was talking about her own home and her parents and her village. Audfinna could see that the young woman's heart was almost bursting with homesickness, so she stealthily prodded Kristin to keep talking. Hot and giddy from the ale, Kristin talked until she was laughing and crying at the same time. All that she had futilely tried to sob out of her heart during the lonely evening hours at Husaby, now was gradually released as she spoke to this kind farmer's wife.

It was quite dark above the smoke vent, but Audfinna wanted Kristin to wait for Øistein or her sons to return from the woods so they could accompany her. Kristin fell silent and grew drowsy, but she sat there smiling, her eyes shining—she hadn't felt this way since she had to come to Husaby.

Then a man tore open the door, shouting: Had they seen any sign of the mistress? Then he noticed her and went back outside. A moment later Erlend's tall figure ducked through the doorway. He set down the axe he was carrying and leaned back against the wall. He had to put his hands behind him to support himself, and he could not speak.

"You have feared for your wife?" asked Audfinna, going over to him.

"Yes, I'm not ashamed to admit it." Erlend pushed back his hair. "No man has ever been as frightened as I was tonight. When I heard that she had gone through the woods . . ."

Audfinna told him how Kristin had happened to come there. Erlend took the woman's hand.

"I will never forget this—either you or your husband," he said.

Then he went over to where his wife was sitting, stood next to her, and placed his hand on the back of her neck. He didn't say a word to her, but he stood there like that for as long as they remained in the house.

Now they all came inside, the servants from Husaby and men from the nearest farms. Everyone looked as if they could use something fortifying to drink, so Audfinna served ale all around before they left.

The men set off on skis across the fields, but Erlend had given his to a servant; he walked along, holding Kristin under his cape, and headed down the slope. It was quite dark now, but a starry night.

Then they heard it from the forest behind them—a long, drawn-out howl that grew and grew in the night. It was the howl of the wolf—and there were several of them. Shivering, Erlend stopped and let Kristin go. She sensed that he crossed himself while he gripped the axe in his other hand. "If you were now . . . oh, no!" He pulled her to him so hard that she whimpered.

The skiers out in the field turned around and made their way back toward the two as fast as they could. They slung the skis over their shoulders and closed around her in a tight group with spears and axes. The wolves followed them all the way to Husaby—so close that once or twice they caught a glimpse of the beasts in the dark.

When the men entered the hall at home, many of them were gray or white in the face. "That was the most horrifying . . ." said one man, and he at once threw up into the hearth. The frightened maids put their mistress to bed. She could eat nothing. But now that the terrible, sickening fear was over, in an odd way she thought it was good to see that everyone had been so scared on her behalf.

When they were alone in the hall, Erlend came over and sat on the edge of the bed.

"Why did you do that?" he whispered. And when she didn't reply, he said even more softly, "Do you so regret that you came to my manor?"

It took a moment before she realized what he meant.

"Jesus, Maria! How can you think something like that!"

"What did you mean that time when you said—when we were at Medalby, and I was going to ride away from you—that I would have had to wait a good long time before you followed me to Husaby?" he asked in the same tone of voice.

"Oh, I spoke in anger," said Kristin quietly, embarrassed. And now she told him why she had gone out these past few days. Erlend sat quite still and listened to her.

"I wonder when the day will come when you'll think of Husaby here with me as your home," he said, bending toward her in the dark.

"Oh, that time is probably no more than a week away," whispered Kristin, laughing uncertainly. When he lay his face next to hers, she threw her arms around his neck and returned his ardent kisses.

"That's the first time you've ventured to embrace me since I struck you," said Erlend in a low voice. "You hold a grudge for a long time, my Kristin."

It occurred to her that this was the first time, since the night when he realized that she was with child, that she dared to caress him without his asking.

But after that day, Erlend was so kind to her that Kristin regretted every hour that she had spent feeling angry toward him.

## CHAPTER 4

Saint Gregor's Day came and went, and Kristin had thought that surely her time would have come by then. But now it would soon be the Feast of the Annunciation, and she was still on her feet.

Erlend had to go to Nidaros for the mid-Lenten *ting;* he said he would certainly be home on Monday evening, but by Wednesday morning he had still not returned. Kristin sat in the hall and didn't know what to do with herself—she felt as if she couldn't bear to start on anything.

Sunlight came flooding down through the smoke vent, and she sensed that outdoors it must be an almost springlike day. Then she stood up and threw a cloak around her shoulders.

One of the maids had mentioned that if a woman carried a child too long, then a good remedy was to let the bridal horse eat grain from her lap. Kristin paused for a moment in the doorway—in the dazzling sunshine the courtyard looked quite brown with glistening rivulets that had washed shiny, icy stripes through the horse manure and dirt. The sky arched bright and silky-blue above the old buildings, and the two dragon figureheads which were carved into the gables of the eastern storehouse glistened against the sky with the remnants of ancient gilding. Water dripped and trickled off the roofs, and smoke whirled and danced in the little, warm gusts of wind.

She walked over to the stable and went inside, filling her skirt with oats from the grain chest. The smell of the stable and the sound of the horses stirring in the dark did her good. But there were people in the stable, so she didn't have the nerve to do what she had come for.

She went out and threw the grain to the chickens that were strutting around in the courtyard, sunning themselves. Absentmindedly she watched Tore, the stableboy, who was grooming and brushing the gray gelding, which was shedding heavily. Once in a while she would close her eyes and turn her wan, house-pale face up toward the sun.

As Kristin was standing like that, three men rode into the courtyard. The one in front was a young priest she didn't know. As soon as he saw Kristin, he jumped down from his saddle and came straight over to her with his hand outstretched.

"I doubt you had intended to do me this honor, mistress, of standing outside to receive me," he said, smiling. "But I thank you for it all the same. For you must certainly be my brother's wife, Kristin Lavransdatter?"

"Then you must be Master Gunnulf, my brother-in-law," she replied, blushing crimson. "Well met, sir! And welcome home to Husaby!"

"Thank you for your kind greeting," said the priest. He bent down to kiss her cheek in the manner which she knew was the custom abroad, when kinsmen meet. "I hope I find you well, Erlend's wife!"

Ulf Haldorssøn came out and told a servant to take the guests' horses. Gunnulf greeted Ulf heartily.

"Are you here, kinsman? I had expected to find you now a married and settled man."

"No, I won't be marrying until I have to choose between a wife and the gallows," said Ulf with a laugh, and the priest laughed too. "I've made the Devil as firm a promise to live unwed as you have promised the same to God."

"Well, then you'll be safe, no matter which way you turn, Ulf," replied Master Gunnulf, laughing. "Since you'll do well the day you break the promise that you've given. But then it is also said that a man should keep his word, even if it's to the Devil himself.

"Isn't Erlend home?" he asked, surprised. He offered Kristin his hand as they turned to go into the main house.

To hide her shyness, Kristin busied herself among the servant women and tended to the setting of the table. She invited Erlend's learned brother to sit in the high seat, but since she didn't want to sit there with him, he moved down to the bench next to her.

Now that he was sitting at her side, Kristin saw that Master Gunnulf must be at least half a head shorter than Erlend, but he was much heavier. He was stronger and stockier in build and limbs, and his broad shoulders were perfectly straight. Erlend's shoulders drooped a bit. Gunnulf wore dark clothing, very proper for a priest, but his ankle-length surcoat, which came almost up to the neckband of his linen shirt, was fastened with enameled buttons; from his woven belt hung his eating utensils in a silver sheath.

She glanced up at the priest's face. He had a strong, round head and a lean, round face with a broad, low forehead, somewhat prominent cheekbones, and a finely rounded chin. His nose was straight and his ears small and lovely, but his mouth was wide, and his upper lip protruded slightly, overshadowing the little patch of red made by his lower lip. Only his hair looked like Erlend's—the thick fringe around the priest's shaved crown was black with the luster of dry soot and it looked as silky-soft as Erlend's hair. Otherwise he was not unlike his cousin Munan Baardsøn—now Kristin could see that it might be true after all that Munan had been handsome in his youth. No, it was his Aunt Aashild whom he resembled—now she saw that he had the same eyes as Fru Aashild: amber-colored and bright beneath narrow, straight black eyebrows.

At first Kristin was a little shy of this brother-in-law who had been educated in so many fields of knowledge at the great universities of Paris and Italy. But little by little she lost her embarrassment. It was so easy to talk to Gunnulf. It didn't seem as if he were talking about himself—least of all that he wanted to boast about his learning. But before she knew it, he had told her about so many things that Kristin felt she had never before realized what a vast world there was outside Norway. She forgot about herself and everything around her as she sat and looked up into the priest's round, strong-boned face with the bright and delicate smile. He had crossed one leg over the other under his surcoat, and he sat there with his white, powerful hands clasped around his ankle.

Later in the afternoon, when Gunnulf came into the room to join her, he asked whether they might play a board game. Kristin had to tell him that she didn't think there were any board games in the house.

"Aren't there?" asked the priest in surprise. He went over to Ulf.

"Do you know, Ulf, what Erlend has done with Mother's gold board game? The amusements that she left behind—surely he hasn't let anyone have them?"

"They're in a chest up in the armory," said Ulf. "It's more likely that he didn't want anyone who once lived here on the estate to take them. Shall we go and get the chest, Gunnulf?"

"Yes, Erlend can't have anything against that," said the priest.

A little while later the two men came back with a large, carved chest. The key was in the lock, so Gunnulf opened it. On top lay a zither and another stringed instrument, the like of which Kristin had never seen before. Gunnulf called it a psaltery; he ran his fingers over the strings, but it was badly out of tune. There were also twists of silk, embroidered gloves, silken scarves, and three books with metal clasps. Finally, the priest found the board game; it was checked, with white and gilt tiles, and the markers were made of walrus tusk, white and golden.

Not until then did Kristin realize that in all the time she had been at Husaby, she hadn't seen a single amusement of this type that people might use to pass the time.

Kristin now had to admit to her brother-in-law that she wasn't very clever at board games, nor was she much good at playing the zither. But she was eager to take a look at the books.

"Ah, have you learned to read books, Kristin?" asked the priest, and she could tell him rather proudly that she had already learned to do so as a child. And at the convent she had won praise for her skill in reading and writing.

The priest stood over her, smiling, as she paged through the books. One of them was a courtly tale about Tristan and Isolde,[1] and the other was about holy men—she looked up Saint Martin's story.[2] The third book was in Latin and was particularly beautiful, printed with great, colorful initial letters.

"Our ancestor, Bishop Nikulaus, owned this book," said Gunnulf.

Kristin read half-aloud:

*Averte faciem tuam a peccatis meis*
*et omnes iniquitates meas dele.*
*Cor mundum crea in me, Deus*
*et spiritum rectum innova in visceribus meis.*

*Ne projicias me a facie tua*
*et Spiritum Sanctum tuum ne auferas a me.*[3]

"Can you understand it?" asked Gunnulf, and Kristin nodded and said that she understood a little. The words were familiar enough that it seemed strange to her that they should appear before her right now. Her face contorted and tears rose up. Then Gunnulf set the stringed instrument on his lap and said he was tempted to try to tune it.

As they sat there they heard horses out in the courtyard, and a moment later Erlend rushed into the hall, beaming with joy. He had heard who had arrived. The brothers stood with their hands on each other's shoulders; Erlend asking questions and not waiting for the replies. Gunnulf had been in Nidaros for two days, so it was a wonder they hadn't met there.

"It's odd," said Erlend. "I thought the whole clergy of Christ Church would have turned out in procession to meet you when you returned home—so wise and exceedingly learned as you now must be."

"How do you know they didn't do just that?" said his brother with a laugh. "I've heard that you never venture too close to Christ Church when you're in town."

"No, my boy—I don't get too close to my Lord the Archbishop if I can avoid it. He once singed my hide," laughed Erlend insolently. "How do you like your brother-in-law, my sweet? I see you've already made friends with Kristin, brother. She thinks very little of our other kinsmen. . . ."

Not until they were about to sit down to eat that evening did Erlend realize he was still wearing his cape and fur cap and his sword at his belt.

That was the merriest evening Kristin had spent at Husaby. Erlend cajoled his brother into sitting in the high seat with her, while he himself sliced off food for him and replenished his goblet. The first time he drank a toast to Gunnulf, he got down on one knee and tried to kiss his brother's hand.

"Health and happiness, sir! We must learn to show the archbishop the proper respect, Kristin—yes, of course, you'll be the archbishop someday, Gunnulf!"

It was late when the house servants left the hall, but the two brothers and Kristin remained behind, sitting over their drink. Erlend was seated atop the table with his face turned toward his brother.

"Yes, I thought about that during my wedding," he said, pointing to his mother's chest, "and that Kristin should have it. And yet I forget things so quickly, while you forget nothing, my brother. But I think Mother's ring has come to grace a fair hand, don't you?" He placed Kristin's hand on his knee and twisted her betrothal ring around.

Gunnulf nodded. He placed the psaltery on Erlend's lap. "Sing now, brother. You used to sing so beautifully and play so well."

"That was many years ago," said Erlend more somberly. Then he ran his fingers over the strings.

Olav the king, Harald's son,
rode out in the thick woods,
found a tiny footprint there—
and so the news is great.

Then said he, Finn Arnessøn,
riding before the band:
Fair must be so small a foot,
clad in scarlet hose.

Erlend smiled as he sang, and Kristin looked up at the priest a little shyly—to see whether the ballad of Saint Olav and Alvhild might displease him. But Gunnulf sat there smiling too, and yet she suddenly felt certain that it was not because of the ballad but because of Erlend.

"Kristin doesn't have to sing; you must be short of breath now, my dear," Erlend said, caressing her cheek. "But *you* can. . . ." He handed the stringed instrument to his brother.

It could be heard in the priest's playing and in his voice that he had learned well in school.

North over the mountains rode the king—
He heard the dove lament bitterly:
"The hawk took my sweetheart away from me!"

Then he rode so far and wide
The hawk flew over the countryside.

Into a garden the hawk then flew,
Where it blossoms ever anew.
In that garden there is a hall,
Draped with purple over all.

There lies a knight, seeping blood,
He is our Lord so fine and good.

Beneath the blue scarlet he does lie
And etched atop: *Corpus domini.*

"Where did you learn that ballad?" asked Erlend.

"Oh. Some fellows were singing it outside the hostel where I was staying in Canterbury," said Gunnulf. "And I was tempted to turn it into Norwegian. But it doesn't work so well. . . ." He sat there strumming a few notes on the strings.

"Well, brother, it's long past midnight. Kristin must need to go to bed. Are you tired, my wife?"

Kristin looked up at the men timidly; she was very pale.

"I don't know . . . But I don't think I should sleep in the bed in here."

"Are you ill?" they both asked, bending toward her.

"I don't know," she replied in the same voice. She pressed her hands to her flanks. "It feels so strange in the small of my back."

Erlend leaped up and headed for the door. Gunnulf followed. "It's shameful that you haven't yet brought the women here who will help her," he said. "Is it long before her time?"

Erlend turned bright red.

"Kristin said she didn't need anyone but her maids. They've borne children themselves, some of them." He tried to laugh.

"Have you lost your senses?" Gunnulf stared at him. "Even the poorest wench has servant women and neighbors with her when she takes to childbed. Should your wife crawl into a corner to hide and give birth like a cat? No, brother, so much a man you must be that you bring to Kristin the foremost women of the parish."

Erlend bowed his head, blushing with shame.

"You speak the truth, brother. I will ride down to Raasvold myself, and I'll send men to the other farms. You must stay with Kristin."

"Are you going away?" asked his wife, frightened, when she saw Erlend put on his outer garments.

He went over to Kristin and put his arms around her.

"I'm going to bring back the noblest women for you, my Kristin. Gunnulf will stay with you while the maids get ready for you in the little house," he said, kissing her.

"Couldn't you send word to Audfinna Audunsdatter?" she pleaded. "But not until morning—I don't want her to be wakened from her sleep for my sake—she has so much work to do, I know."

Gunnulf asked his brother who Audfinna was.

"It doesn't seem to me proper," said the priest. "The wife of one of your leaseholders—"

"Kristin must have whatever she wants," said Erlend. And as Gunnulf accompanied him out and Erlend waited for his horse, he told the priest how Kristin had come to meet the farmer's wife. Gunnulf bit his lip and looked pensive.

Now there was noise and commotion on the estate; men rode off and servant women came running in to ask how their mistress was faring. Kristin said there was nothing to worry about yet, but they were to make everything ready in the little house. She would send word when she wanted to be escorted there.

Then she sat alone with the priest. She tried to talk calmly and cheerfully with him as she had before.

"You're not afraid then?" he asked with a little smile.

"Yes, of course, I'm afraid!" She looked up into his eyes—her own were dark and frightened. "Can you tell me, brother-in-law, whether they were born here at Husaby—Erlend's other children?"

"No," replied the priest quickly. "The boy was born at Hunehals, and the maiden over at Strind, on an estate that he once owned there." A moment later he asked, "Is that it? Has the thought of that other woman here with Erlend tormented you?"

"Yes," said Kristin.

"It would be difficult for you to judge Erlend's behavior in this dealing with Eline," said the priest somberly. "It wasn't easy for Erlend to know what to do. It was never easy for Erlend to know what was right. Ever since we were children, our mother thought whatever Erlend did was right, and our father thought it was wrong. But he has probably told you so much about our mother that you know all about this."

"I can only recall that he has mentioned her two or three times," said Kristin. "But I understood that he did love her. . . ."

Gunnulf said softly, "I doubt there has ever been such a love between a mother and her son. Mother was much younger than my father. But then that whole trouble with Aunt Aashild happened. Our uncle Baard died, and it was said . . . well, you know about this, don't you? Father thought the worst and said to Mother . . . Erlend once flung his knife at Father; he was only a young boy. He rushed at Father more than once in Mother's defense when he was growing up.

"When Mother fell ill, he parted with Eline Ormsdatter. Mother grew sick with sores and scabs on her skin, and Father said it was leprosy.[4] He sent her away—tried to threaten her into taking a corrody[5] with the sisters at the hospice. Then Erlend went to get Mother and took her to Oslo—they stayed with Aashild too; she's a good healer. And the king's French doctor also said that she was not leprous. King Haakon received Erlend kindly then, and bade him seek out the grave of the holy King Erik Valdemarssøn—the king's grandfather. Many people found cures for their skin afflictions there.

"Erlend journeyed to Denmark with Mother, but she died on board his ship, south of Stad. When Erlend brought her home—well, you must remember that Father was very old, and Erlend had been a disobedient son all his days. When Erlend came to Nidaros with Mother's body, Father was staying at our town estate, and he refused to allow Erlend inside until he determined whether the boy had been infected, as he said. Erlend got on his horse and rode off, not resting until he arrived at the manor where Eline was staying with his son. After that he stood by her, in spite of everything, in spite of the fact that he had grown weary of her; and that's how he happened to bring her here to Husaby and put her in charge when he became owner of the estate. She had such a hold on him, and she said that if he deserted her after this, then he deserved to be struck by leprosy himself.

"But it must be time for your women to tend to you, Kristin." He looked down into the young, gray face that was rigid with fear and anguish.

But when he stood up to move toward the door, she cried loudly after him, "No, no, don't leave me!"

"It will soon be over," the priest consoled her, "since you are already so ill."

"That's not it!" She gripped his arm hard. "Gunnulf!"

He thought he had never seen such terror in anyone's face.

"Kristin—you should remember that this is no worse for you than for other women."

"But it is, it is." She pressed her face against the priest's arm. "For now I know that Eline and her children should be sitting here. He had promised her fidelity and marriage before I became his paramour."

"You know about that?" said Gunnulf calmly. "Erlend himself didn't know any better back then. But you must understand that he could not keep that promise; the archbishop would never have given his consent for those two to marry. You mustn't think that your marriage isn't valid. You are Erlend's rightful wife."

"Oh, I gave up all right to walk this earth long before then. And yet it's worse than I imagined. Oh, if only I might die and this child would never be born. I don't think I dare look at what I've been carrying."

"May God forgive you, Kristin—you don't know what you're saying! Would you wish for your child to die stillborn and unbaptized?"

"Yes, for that which I've carried under my heart may already belong to the Devil! It cannot be saved. Oh, if only I had drunk the potion that Eline offered me—that might have been atonement for all the sins we've committed, Erlend and I. Then this child would never have been conceived. Oh, I've thought this whole time, Gunnulf, that when I saw what I had fostered inside me, then I would come to realize that it would have been better for me to drink the leprosy potion that she offered me—rather than drive to her death the woman to whom Erlend had first bound himself."

"Kristin," said the priest, "you've lost your senses. You weren't the one who drove that poor woman to her death. Erlend *couldn't* keep the promise that he'd given her when he was young and knew little of law and justice. He could never have lived with her without sin. And she herself allowed another man to seduce her, and Erlend wanted to marry her to him when he heard of it. The two of you were not to blame for her taking her own life."

"Do you want to know how it happened that she took her life?" Kristin was now so full of despair that she spoke quite calmly. "We were together at Haugen, Erlend and I, when she arrived. She had brought along a drinking horn, and she wanted me to drink with her. I now see that she probably intended it for Erlend, but when she found me there with him, she wanted me to . . . I realized it was treachery—I saw that she didn't drink any herself when she put the horn to her lips. But I wanted to drink and I didn't care whether I lived or died when I found out that she had been with him here at Husaby the whole time. Then Erlend came in—he threatened her with his knife: 'You must drink first.' She begged and begged, and he was about to let her go. Then the Devil took hold of me; I grabbed the horn—'One of us, your two mistresses,' I said—I egged Erlend on—'You can't keep both of us,' I said. And so it was that she killed herself with Erlend's knife. But Bjørn and Aashild found a way to conceal what had happened."

"So Aunt Aashild took part in this concealment," said Gunnulf harshly. "I see . . . she played you into Erlend's hands."

"No," said Kristin vehemently. "Fru Aashild pleaded with us. She begged Erlend and she begged me so that I don't understand how I dared defy her—to step forward in as honorable a manner as was still possible, to fall at my father's feet and implore him to forgive us for what we had done. But I didn't dare. I argued that I was afraid that Father would kill Erlend—but oh, I knew full well that Father would never harm a man who put himself and his case into his hands. I argued that I was afraid he would suffer such sorrow that he would never be able to hold his head high again. But I have since shown that I was not so afraid to cause my father sorrow. You can't know, Gunnulf, what a good man my father is—no one can realize it who doesn't know him, how kind he has been to me all my days. Father has always been so fond of me. I don't want him to find out that I behaved shamelessly while he thought I was living with the sisters in Oslo and learning everything that was right and just. I even wore the clothing of a lay sister as I met with Erlend in cowsheds and lofts in town."

She looked up at Gunnulf. His face was pale and hard as stone.

"Do you see now why I'm frightened? She who took him in when he arrived, infected with leprosy . . ."

"Wouldn't you have done the same?" the priest asked gently.

"Of course, of course, of course." A shadow of that wild, sweet smile of the past flickered across the woman's ravaged face.

"But Erlend wasn't infected," said Gunnulf. "No one except Father ever thought that Mother died of leprosy."

"But I must be like a leper in God's eyes," said Kristin. She rested her face on the priest's arm which she was gripping. "Such as I am, infected with sins."

"My sister," said the priest softly, placing his other hand on her wimple. "I doubt that you are so sinful, young child, that you have forgotten that just as God can cleanse a person's flesh of leprosy, He can also cleanse your soul of sin."

"Oh, I don't know," she sobbed, hiding her face on his arm. "I don't know—and I don't feel any remorse, Gunnulf. I'm afraid, and yet . . . I was afraid when I stood at the church door with Erlend and the priest married us. I was afraid when I went inside for the wedding mass with him, with the golden crown on my flowing hair, for I didn't dare speak of shame to my father, with all my sins unatoned for; I didn't even dare confess fully to my parish priest. But as I went about here this winter and saw myself growing more hideous for each day that passed—then I was even more frightened, for Erlend did not act toward me as he had before. I thought about those days when he would come to me in my chamber at Skog in the evenings. . . ."

"Kristin," the priest tried to lift her face, "you mustn't think about this now! Think about God, who sees your sorrow and your remorse. Turn to the gentle Virgin Mary, who takes pity on every sorrowful—"

"Don't you see? I drove another human being to take her own life!"

"Kristin," the priest said sternly. "Are you so arrogant that you think yourself capable of sinning so badly that God's mercy is not great enough? . . ."

He stroked her wimple over and over.

"Don't you remember, my sister, when the Devil tried to tempt Saint Martin? Then the Fiend asked Saint Martin whether he dared believe it when he promised God's mercy to all the sinners whose confessions he heard. And the bishop answered, 'Even to you I promise God's forgiveness at the very instant you ask for it—if only you will give up your pride and believe that His love is greater than your hatred.' "

Gunnulf continued to stroke the head of the weeping woman. All the while he thought: Was *this* the way that Erlend had behaved toward his young bride? His lips grew pale and grim at the thought.

Audfinna Audunsdatter was the first of the women to arrive. She found Kristin in the little house; Gunnulf was sitting with her, and a couple of maids were bustling about the room.

Audfinna greeted the priest with deference, but Kristin stood up and went toward her with her hand outstretched.

"I must give you thanks for coming, Audfinna. I know it's not easy for your family to be without you at home."

Gunnulf had given the woman a searching look. Now he too stood up and said, "It was good of you to come so quickly. My sister-in-law needs someone she can trust to be with her. She's a stranger here, young and inexperienced."

"Jesus, she's as white as her linen wimple," whispered Audfinna. "Do you think, sir, that I might give her a sleeping potion? She needs to rest a while before it gets much worse."

She set to work, quietly and efficiently, inspecting the bed that the servant women had prepared on the floor, and telling them to bring more cushions and straw. She put small stone vessels of herbs on the fire to heat. Then she proceeded to loosen all the ribbons and ties on Kristin's clothing, and finally she pulled out all the pins from the ill woman's hair.

"I've never seen anything so lovely," she said when the cascading, silky, golden-brown mane tumbled down around the pale face. She had to laugh. "It certainly hasn't lost much of either fullness or sheen, even though you went bareheaded a little longer than was proper."

She settled Kristin comfortably among the cushions on the floor and covered her with a blanket.

"Drink this now, and you won't feel the pains as much—and see if you can sleep a little now and then."

Gunnulf was ready to leave. He went over and bent down toward Kristin.

"You will pray for me, Gunnulf?" she implored him.

"I will pray for you until I see you with your child in your arms—and after that too," he said as he tucked her hand back under the covers.

Kristin lay there, dozing. She felt almost content. The pain in her loins came and went, came and went—but it was unlike anything she had ever felt before, so that each time it was over, she wondered whether she had just imagined it. After the anguish and dread of the early morning hours, she felt as if she were already beyond the worst fear and torment. Audfinna walked about quietly, hanging up the infant clothes, blankets, and furs to warm at the hearth—and stirring her pots a little so the room smelled of spices. Finally Kristin slept between each wave of pain; she thought she was back home in the brewhouse at Jørundgaard and was supposed to help her mother dye a large woven fabric—probably because of the steam from the ash bark and nettles.

Then the neighbor women arrived, one after another—wives from the estates in the parish and in Birgsi. Audfinna withdrew to her place with the maids. Toward evening, Kristin began to suffer terrible pain. The women told her to walk around as long as she could bear it. This tormented her greatly; the house was now crowded with women, and she had to walk around like a mare that was for sale. Now and then she had to let the women squeeze and touch her body all over, and then they would confer with each other. At last Fru Gunna from Raasvold, who was in charge of things, said that now Kristin could lie down on the floor. She divided up the women: some to sleep and some to keep watch. "This isn't going to pass quickly—but go ahead and scream, Kristin, when it hurts, and don't pay any mind to those who are sleeping. We're all here to help you, poor child," she said, gentle and kind, patting the young woman's cheek.

But Kristin lay there biting her lips to shreds and crushing the corners of the blanket in her sweaty hands. It was suffocatingly hot, but they told her that was as it should be. After each wave of pain, the sweat poured off her.

At times she would lie there thinking about food for all these women. She fervently wanted them to see that she kept good order in her house. She had asked Torbjørg, the cook, to put whey in the water for boiling the fresh fish. If only Gunnulf wouldn't regard this as breaking the fast. Sira Eirik had said that it wasn't, for whey was not milk, and the fish broth would be thrown out. They mustn't be allowed to taste the dried fish that Erlend had brought home in the fall, spoiled and full of mites that it was.

Blessed Virgin Mary—will it be long before you help me? Oh, how it hurts, it hurts, it hurts. . . .

She was trying to hold out a little longer, before she gave in and screamed.

Audfinna sat next to the hearth and tended the pots of water. Kristin wished that she dared ask her to come over and hold her hand. There was nothing she wouldn't give to hold on to a familiar and kind hand right now. But she was ashamed to ask for it.

The next morning a bewildered silence hovered over Husaby. It was the day before the Feast of the Annunciation and the farm work was supposed to be finished by mid-afternoon prayers, but the men were distracted and somber, and the frightened maids were careless with their chores. The servants had grown fond of their young mistress, and it was said that things were not going well for her.

Erlend stood outside in the courtyard, talking to his smith. He tried to keep his thoughts on what the man was saying. Then Fru Gunna came rushing over to him.

"There's no progress with your wife, Erlend—we've tried everything we know. You must come. It might help if she sits on your lap. Go in and change into a short tunic. But be quick; she's suffering greatly, your poor young wife!"

Erlend had turned blood-red. He remembered he had heard that if a woman was having trouble delivering a child she had conceived in secrecy, then it might help if she were placed on her husband's knee.

Kristin was lying on the floor under several blankets; two

women were sitting with her. The moment that Erlend came in, he saw her body convulse and she buried her head in the lap of one of the women, rocking it from side to side. But she didn't utter a single whimper.

When the pain had passed, she looked up with wild, frightened eyes, her cracked, brown lips gasping. All trace of youth and beauty had vanished from the swollen, flushed red face. Even her hair was matted together with bits of straw and wool from the fur of a filthy hide. She looked at Erlend as if she didn't immediately recognize him. But when she realized why the women had sent for him, she shook her head vigorously.

"It's not the custom where I come from . . . for men to be present when a woman is giving birth."

"It's sometimes done here in the north," said Erlend quietly. "If it can lessen the pain a little for you, my Kristin, then you must—"

"Oh!" When he knelt beside her she threw her arms around his waist and pressed herself to him. Hunched over and shaking, she fought her way through the pain without a murmur.

"May I have a few words with my husband alone?" she said when it was over, her breathing rapid and harsh. The women withdrew.

"Was it when she was suffering the agony of childbirth that you promised her what she told me—that you would marry her when she was widowed . . . that night when Orm was born?" whispered Kristin.

Erlend gasped for air, as if he had been struck deep in the heart. Then he vehemently shook his head.

"I was at the castle that night; my men and I had guard duty. It was when I came back to our hostel in the morning and they put the boy in my arms. . . . Have you been lying here thinking about this, Kristin?"

"Yes." Again she clung to him as the waves of pain washed over her. Erlend wiped away the sweat that poured down her face.

"Now you know," he said, when she lay quiet once more. "Don't you want me to stay with you, as Fru Gunna says?"

But Kristin shook her head. And finally the women had to let Erlend go.

But then it seemed as if her power to endure was broken. She screamed in wild terror of the pain that she could feel approaching, and begged pitifully for help. And yet when the women talked of bringing her husband back, she screamed "No!" She would rather be tortured to death.

Gunnulf and the cleric who was with him walked over to the church to attend evensong. Everyone on the estate went along who was not tending to the woman giving birth. But Erlend slipped out of the church before the service was over and walked south toward the buildings.

In the west, above the ridges on the other side of the valley, the sky was a yellowish-red. The twilight of the spring evening was about to descend, clear and bright and mild. A few stars appeared, white in the light sky. A little wisp of fog drifted over the bare woods down by the lake, and there were brown patches where the fields lay open to the sun. The smell of earth and thawing snow filled the air.

The little house was at the westernmost edge of the courtyard, facing the hollow of the valley. Erlend went over and stood for a moment behind the wall. The timbers were still warm from the sun as he leaned against them. Oh, how she screamed. . . . He had once heard a heifer shrieking in the grip of a bear —that was up at their mountain pasture, and he was only a half-grown boy. He and Arnbjørn, the shepherd boy, were running south through the forest. He remembered the shaggy creature that stood up and became a bear with a red, fiery maw. The bear broke Arnbjørn's spear in half with its paw. Then the servant threw Erlend's spear, as he stood there paralyzed with terror. The heifer lay there still alive, but its udder and thigh had been gnawed away.

My Kristin, oh, my Kristin. Lord, for the sake of Your blessed Mother, have mercy. He rushed back to the church.

The maids came into the hall with the evening meal. They didn't set up the table, but placed the food near the hearth. The men took bread and fish over to the benches, sat down in their places, not speaking and eating little; no one seemed to have an appetite. No one came to clear away the dishes after the meal, and none of the men got up to go to bed. They stayed sitting there, staring into the hearth fire, without talking.

Erlend had hidden himself in a corner near the bed; he couldn't bear to have anyone see his face.

Master Gunnulf had lit a small oil lamp and set it on the arm of the high seat. He sat on the bench with a book in his hands, his lips moving gently, soundless and unceasing.

At one point Ulf Haldorssøn stood up, walked forward to the hearth, and picked up a piece of soft bread; he rummaged around among the pieces of firewood and selected one. Then he went over to the corner near the doorway where old man Aan was sitting. The two of them fiddled with the bread, hidden behind Ulf's cape. Aan whittled and cut the piece of wood. The men cast a glance in their direction now and then. In a little while Ulf and Aan got up and left the hall.

Gunnulf watched them go, but said nothing. He took up his prayers once more.

Once a young boy toppled off the bench, falling to the floor in his sleep. He got up and looked around in bewilderment. Then he sighed softly and sat down again.

Ulf Haldorssøn and Aan quietly came back in and returned to the places where they had sat before. The men looked at them, but no one said a word.

Suddenly Erlend jumped up. He strode across the floor toward his servants. He was hollow-eyed, and his face was as gray as clay.

"Doesn't anyone know what to do?" he asked. "You, Aan," he whispered.

"It didn't help," replied Ulf, his voice equally quiet.

"It could be that she's not meant to keep this child," said Aan, wiping his nose. "Then neither sacrifices nor runes can help. It's a shame for you, Erlend, that you should lose this good wife so soon."

"Oh, don't talk as if she were already dead," implored Erlend, broken and in despair. He went back to his corner and threw himself down on the enclosed bed with his head near the foot-board.

Later a man went outside and then came back in.

"The moon is up," he said. "It will soon be morning."

A few minutes later Fru Gunna came into the hall. She sank down onto the beggar's bench near the door. Her gray hair was disheveled, her wimple had slid back onto her shoulders.

The men stood up and slowly moved over to her.

"One of you must come and hold her," she said, weeping. "We have no more strength. You must go to her, Gunnulf. There's no telling how this will end."

Gunnulf stood up and tucked his prayer book inside his belt pouch.

"You must come too, Erlend," said the woman.

A raw and broken howl met him in the doorway. Erlend stopped and shivered. He caught a glimpse of Kristin's contorted, unrecognizable face among the sobbing women. She was on her knees, and they were supporting her.

Over by the door several servant women were kneeling at the benches; they were praying loudly and steadily. He threw himself down next to them and hid his head in his arms. She screamed and screamed, and each time he felt himself freeze with incredulous horror. It couldn't possibly be like this.

He ventured a glance in her direction. Now Gunnulf was sitting on a stool in front of her and holding her under the arms. Fru Gunna was kneeling at her side, with her arms around Kristin's waist, but Kristin was fighting her, frightened to death, and trying to push the other woman away.

"Oh no, oh no, let me go—I can't do it—God, God, help me . . ."

"God will help you soon, Kristin," said the priest each time. A woman held a basin of water, and after each wave of pain he would take a wet cloth and wipe the sick woman's face—along the roots of her hair and in between her lips, from which saliva was dripping.

Then she would rest her head in Gunnulf's arms and doze off for a moment, but the torment would instantly tear her out of her sleep again. And the priest continued to say, "Now, Kristin, you will have help soon."

No one had any idea what time of night it was anymore. The dawn was already a gray glare in the smoke vent.

Then, after a long, mad howl of terror, everything fell silent. Erlend heard the women rushing around; he didn't want to look up. Then he heard someone weeping loudly and he cringed again, not wanting to know.

Then Kristin shrieked once more—a piercing, wild cry of lament that didn't sound like the insane, inhuman animal cries of before. Erlend leaped up.

Gunnulf was bending down and holding on to Kristin, who was still on her knees. She was staring with deathly horror at something that Fru Gunna was holding in a sheepskin. The raw and dark red shape looked like nothing more than the entrails from a slaughtered beast.

The priest pulled her close.

"Dear Kristin—you have given birth to as fine and handsome a son as any mother should thank God for—and he's breathing!" said Gunnulf fiercely to the weeping women. "He's breathing—God would not be so harsh as not to hear us."

And as the priest spoke, it happened. Through the exhausted, confused mind of the mother tumbled, hazily recalled, the sight of a bud she had seen in the cloister garden—something from which red, crinkled wisps of silk emerged and spread out to become a flower.

The shapeless lump moved—it whimpered. It stretched out and became a very tiny, wine-red infant in human form. It had arms and legs and hands and feet with fully formed fingers and toes. It flailed and hissed a bit.

"So tiny, so tiny, so tiny he is," she cried in a thin, broken voice and then burst into laughing sobs. The women around her began to laugh and wipe their tears, and Gunnulf gave Kristin into their arms.

"Roll him in a trencher so he can scream better," said the priest as he followed the women carrying the newborn son over to the hearth.

When Kristin awoke from a long faint, she was lying in bed. Someone had removed the dreadful, sweat-soaked garments, and a feeling of warmth and healing was blessedly streaming through her body. They had placed small pouches of warm nettle porridge on her and wrapped her in hot blankets and furs.

Someone hushed her when she tried to speak. It was quite still in the room. But through the silence came a voice that she couldn't quite recognize.

"Nikulaus, in the name of the Father, the Son, and the Holy Ghost . . ."

There was the sound of water trickling.

Kristin propped herself up on her elbow to take a look. Over by the hearth stood a priest in white garb, and Ulf Haldorssøn was lifting a kicking, red, naked child out of the large brass basin; he handed him to the godmother, and then took the lit taper.

She had given birth to a child, and he was screaming so loudly that the priest's words were almost drowned out. But she was so tired. She felt numb and wanted to sleep.

Then she heard Erlend's voice; he spoke quickly and with alarm.

"His head—he has such a strange head."

"He's swollen up," said the woman calmly. "And it's no wonder—he had to fight hard for his life, this boy."

Kristin shouted something. She felt as if she were suddenly awake, to the very depths of her heart. This was her son, and he had fought for his life, just as she had.

Gunnulf turned around at once and laughed; he seized the tiny white bundle from Fru Gunna's lap and carried it over to the bed. He placed the boy in his mother's arms. Weak with tenderness and joy she rubbed her face against the little bit of red, silky-soft face visible among the linen wrappings.

She glanced up at Erlend. Once before she had seen his face look this haggard and gray—she couldn't remember when, her head felt so dizzy and strange, but she knew that it was good she had no memory of it. And it was good to see him standing there with his brother; the priest had his hand on Erlend's shoulder. An immeasurable sense of peace and well-being came over her as she looked at the tall man wearing alb and stole; the round, lean face beneath the black fringe of hair was strong, but his smile was pleasant and kind.

Erlend drove his dagger deep into the wall timber behind the mother and child.

"That's not necessary now," said the priest with a laugh. "The boy has been baptized, after all."

Kristin suddenly remembered something that Brother Edvin

once said. A newly baptized child was just as holy as the holy angels in heaven. The sins of the parents were washed from the child, and he had not yet committed any sins of his own. Fearful and cautious, she kissed the little face.

Fru Gunna came over to them. She was worn out and exhausted and angry at the father, who had not had the sense to offer a single word of thanks to all the women who had helped. And the priest had taken the child from her and carried him over to his mother. She should have done that, both because she had delivered the woman and because she was the godmother of the boy.

"You haven't yet greeted your son, Erlend, or held him in your arms," she said crossly.

Erlend lifted the swaddled infant from the mother's arms—for a moment he lay his face close.

"I don't think I'm going to be properly fond of you, Naakkve, until I forget what terrible suffering you caused your mother," he said, and then gave the boy back to Kristin.

"By all means give him the blame for that," said the old woman, annoyed. Master Gunnulf laughed, and then Fru Gunna laughed with him. She wanted to take the child and put him in his cradle, but Kristin begged to keep him with her for a while. A moment later she fell asleep with her son beside her—vaguely noticing that Erlend touched her, cautiously, as if he were afraid to hurt her, and then she was sound asleep again.

## CHAPTER 5

IN THE MORNING of the tenth day after the child's birth, Master Gunnulf said to his brother when they were alone in the hall, "It's about time now, Erlend, for you to send word to your wife's kinsmen about how things are with her."

"I don't think there's any haste with that," replied Erlend. "I doubt they will be overly glad at Jørundgaard when they hear that there's already a son here on the manor."

"Don't you think Kristin's mother would have realized last fall that her daughter was unwell?" Gunnulf asked. "She must be worried by now."

Erlend didn't say a word in reply.

But later in the day, as Gunnulf was sitting in the little house and talking to Kristin, Erlend came in. He was wearing a fur cap on his head, a short, thick homespun coat, long pants, and furry boots. He bent down to his wife and patted her cheek.

"So, dear Kristin—do you have any greetings you wish to send to Jørundgaard? I'm heading there now to bring word of our son."

Kristin blushed bright red. She looked both frightened and happy.

"It's no more than your father would demand of me," said Erlend somberly, "that I bring the news myself."

Kristin lay in silence for a moment.

"Tell them at home," she said softly, "that I have yearned every day since I left home to fall at Father's and Mother's feet to beg their forgiveness."

A few minutes later, Erlend left. Kristin didn't think to ask how he would travel. But Gunnulf went out to the courtyard with his brother. Next to the doorway of the main house stood Erlend's skis and a staff with a spear point.

"You're going to ski there?" asked Gunnulf. "Who's going with you?"

"Nobody," replied Erlend, laughing. "You should know best of all, Gunnulf, that it's not easy for anyone to keep up with me on skis."

"This seems reckless to me," said the priest. "There are many wolves in the mountain forests this year, they say."

Erlend merely laughed and began to strap on his skis. "I was thinking of heading up through the Gjeitskar pastures before it gets dark. It will be light for a long time yet. I can make it to Jørundgaard on the evening of the third day."

"The path from Gjeitskar to the road is uncertain, and there are bad patches of fog there too. You know it's unsafe up in the mountain pastures in the wintertime."

"You can lend me your flint," said Erlend in the same tone of voice, "in case I should need to throw mine away—at some elf woman if she demands such courtesies of me as would be unseemly for a married man. Listen, brother, I'm doing now what you said I should do—going to Kristin's father to ask him to demand whatever penances from me that he finds reasonable. Surely you can allow me to decide this much, that I myself choose how I will travel."

And with that Master Gunnulf had to be content. But he sternly commanded the servants to conceal from Kristin that Erlend had set off alone.

To the south the sky arched pale yellow over the blue-tinged snowdrifts of the mountains on the evening when Erlend came racing down past the churchyard, making the snow crust creak and shriek. High overhead hovered the crescent moon, shining white and dewy in the twilight.

At Jørundgaard dark smoke was swirling up from the smoke vents against the pale, clear sky. The sound of an axe rang out cold and rhythmic in the stillness.

At the entrance to the courtyard a pack of dogs started barking loudly at the approaching man. Inside the courtyard a group of shaggy goats ambled around, dark silhouettes in the clear dusk. They were nibbling at a heap of fir boughs in the middle of the courtyard. Three winter-clad youngsters were running among them.

The peace of the place made an oddly deep impression on Erlend. He stood there, irresolute, and waited for Lavrans, who was coming forward to greet the stranger. His father-in-law had been over by the woodshed, talking to a man splitting rails for a fence. Lavrans stopped abruptly when he recognized his son-in-law; he thrust the spear he was holding hard into the snow.

"Is that *you?*" he asked in a low voice. "Alone? Is there . . . is something . . . ?" And a moment later he said, "How is it that you've come here like this?"

"Here's the reason." Erlend pulled himself together and looked his father-in-law in the eye. "I thought I could do no less than to come here myself to bring you the news. Kristin gave birth to a son on the morning of the Feast of the Annunciation.

"And yes, she is doing well now," he added quickly.

Lavrans stood in silence for a moment. He was biting down hard on his lip—his jaw trembled and quivered faintly.

"That was news indeed!" he said then.

Little Ramborg had come over to stand at her father's side. She looked up, her face flaming red.

"Be quiet," said Lavrans harshly, even though the maiden hadn't uttered a word but had merely blushed. "Don't stand here—go away."

He didn't say anything more. Erlend stood leaning forward, with his left hand gripping his staff. His eyes were fixed on the snow. He had stuck his right hand inside his tunic.

Lavrans pointed. "Have you injured yourself?"

"A little," said Erlend. "I slipped down a slope yesterday in the dark."

Lavrans touched his wrist and pressed it cautiously. "I don't think there are any bones broken," he said. "You can tell her mother yourself." He started for the house as Ragnfrid came out into the courtyard. She looked in amazement at her husband; then she recognized Erlend and quickly walked over to him.

She listened without speaking as Erlend, for the second time, presented his message. But her eyes filled with tears when Erlend said at the end, "I thought you might have noticed something before she left here in the fall—and that you might be worried about her now."

"It was kind of you, Erlend," she said uncertainly. "For you to think of that. I think I've been worried every day since you took her away from us."

Lavrans came back.

"Here is some fox fat—I see that you've frozen your cheek, son-in-law. You must stay for a while in the entryway, so Ragnfrid can attend to it and thaw you out. How are your feet? You must take off your boots so we can see."

When the servants came in for the evening meal, Lavrans told them the news and ordered special foreign ale to be brought in so they could celebrate. But there was no real merriment about the occasion—the master himself sat at the table with a cup of water. He asked Erlend to forgive him, but this was a promise he had made during his youth, to drink water during Lent. And so the servants sat there quietly, and the conversation lagged over the good ale. Once in a while the children would go over to Lavrans; he put his arm around them when they stood at his knee, but he gave absentminded answers to their questions. Ramborg replied curtly and sharply when Erlend tried to tease her; she would show that she didn't like this brother-in-law of hers. She was now eight winters old, lively and lovely, but she bore little resemblance to her sisters.

Erlend asked who the other children were. Lavrans told him the boy was Haavard Trondssøn, the youngest child at Sundbu. It was so tedious for him over there among his grown-up siblings; at Christmastime he had decided to go home with his aunt. The maiden was Helga Rolvsdatter. Her kinsmen had been forced to take the children from Blakarsarv home with them after the funeral; it wasn't good for them to see their father the way he was now. And it was nice for Ramborg that she had these foster siblings. "We're getting old now, Ragnfrid and I," said Lavrans. "And she's more wild and playful, this one here, than Kristin was." He stroked his daughter's curly hair.

Erlend sat down next to his mother-in-law, and she asked him about Kristin's childbirth. The son-in-law noticed that Lavrans was listening to them, but then he stood up, went over, and picked up his hat and cape. He would go over to the parsonage, he said, to ask Sira Eirik to come and join them for a drink.

* * *

Lavrans walked along the well-trodden path through the fields toward Romundgaard. The moon was about to sink behind the mountains now, but thousands of stars still sparkled above the white slopes. He hoped the priest would be at home—he could no longer stand to sit there with the others.

But when he turned down the lane between the fences near the courtyard, he saw a small candle coming toward him. Old Audun was carrying it, and when he sensed there was someone in the road, he rang his tiny silver bell. Lavrans Bjørgulfsøn threw himself down on his knees in the snowdrift at the side of the road.

Audun walked past with his candle and bell, which rang faintly and gently. Behind him rode Sira Eirik. With his hands he lifted the Host vessel high as he came upon the kneeling man, but he did not turn his head; he rode silently past as Lavrans bowed down and raised his hands in greeting to his Savior.

That was the son of Einar Hnufa with the priest—it must be nearing the end for the old man now. Ah well. Lavrans said his prayers for the dying man before he stood up and walked back home. The meeting with God in the night had nevertheless strengthened and consoled him a great deal.

When they had gone to bed, Lavrans asked his wife, "Did you know anything about this—that things were such with Kristin?"

"Didn't you?" said Ragnfrid.

"No," replied her husband so curtly that she could tell he must have been thinking of it all the same.

"I was indeed fearful for a time this past summer," said the mother hesitantly. "I could see that she took no pleasure in her food. But as the days passed, I thought I must have been mistaken. She seemed so happy during all the time we were preparing for her wedding."

"Well, she certainly had good reason for *that,*" said the father with some disdain. "But that she said nothing to you. . . . You, her own mother . . ."

"Yes, you think of that now when she's gone astray," said Ragnfrid bitterly. "But you know quite well that Kristin has never confided in me."

Lavrans said no more. A little later he bade his wife sleep well and then lay down quietly. He realized that sleep would not come to him for some time.

Kristin, Kristin—his poor little maiden.

Not with a single word had he ever referred to what Ragnfrid had confessed to him on the night of Kristin's wedding. And in all fairness she couldn't say he had made her feel it was on his mind. He had been no different in his demeanor toward her—rather, he had striven to show her even more kindness and love. But it was not the first time this winter he had noticed the bitterness in Ragnfrid or seen her searching for some hidden offense in the innocent words he had spoken. He didn't understand it, and he didn't know what to do about it—he would simply have to accept it.

"Our Father who art in Heaven . . ." He prayed for Kristin and her child. Then he prayed for his wife and for himself. Finally, he prayed for the strength to tolerate Erlend Nikulaussøn with a patient spirit for as long as he was forced to have his son-in-law there on his estate.

Lavrans would not allow his daughter's husband to set off for home until they saw how his wrist was healing. And he refused to let Erlend go back alone.

"Kristin would be pleased if you came with me," said Erlend one day.

Lavrans was silent for a moment. Then he voiced many objections. Ragnfrid would undoubtedly not like to be left alone on the farm. And once he had journeyed so far north, it would be difficult to return in time for spring planting. But in the end he set off with Erlend. He took no servant along—he would travel home by ship to Raumsdal. There he could hire horses to carry him south through the valley; he knew people everywhere along the way.

They talked little as they skied, but they got along well together. It was a struggle for Lavrans to keep up with his companion; he didn't want to admit that his son-in-law went too fast for him. But Erlend took note of this and at once adapted his pace to his father-in-law's. He went to great lengths to charm his wife's father—and he had that quiet, gentle manner whenever he wished to win someone's friendship.

On the third evening they sought shelter in a stone hut. They had had bad weather and fog, but Erlend seemed to be able to find his way just as confidently. Lavrans noticed that Erlend had an astoundingly accurate knowledge of all signs and tracks, in the air and on the ground, and of the ways of animals and their habits—and he always seemed to know where he was. Everything that Lavrans, experienced in the mountains as he was, had learned by observing and paying attention and remembering, the other man seemed to intuit quite blindly. Erlend laughed at this, but it was simply something he knew.

They found the stone hut in the dark, exactly at the moment Erlend had predicted. Lavrans recalled one such night when he had dug himself a shelter in the snow only an arrow's shot away from his own horse shed. Here the snow had drifted up over the hut and they had to break their way in through the smoke vent. Erlend covered the opening with a horsehide that was lying in the hut, fastening it with sticks of firewood, which he stuck in among the roof beams. With a ski he cleared away the snow that had blown inside and managed to build a fire in the hearth from the frozen wood lying about. He pulled out three or four grouse from under the bench—he had put them there on his way south. He packed them in earth from the floor where it had thawed out around the hearth and then threw the bundles into the embers.

Lavrans stretched out on the earthen bench, which Erlend had prepared for him as best he could, spreading out their knapsacks and capes.

"That's what soldiers do with stolen chickens, Erlend," he said with a laugh.

"Yes, I learned a few things when I was in the Earl's service," said Erlend, laughing too.

Now he was alert and lively, not silent and rather sluggish the way his father-in-law had most often seen him. As he sat on the floor in front of Lavrans, he started telling stories about the years when he served Earl Jacob in Halland.[1] He had been head of the castle guard, and he had patrolled the coast with three small ships. Erlend's eyes shone like a child's—he wasn't boasting, he merely let the words spill out. Lavrans lay there looking down at him.

He had prayed to God to grant him patience with this man, his daughter's husband. Now he was almost angry with himself because he was more fond of Erlend than he wanted to be. He thought about that night when their church burned down and he had taken a liking to his son-in-law. It was not that Erlend lacked manhood in his lanky body. Lavrans felt a stab of pain in his heart. It was a pity about Erlend; he could have been fit for better things than seducing women. But nothing much had come of that except boyish pranks. If only times had been such that a chieftain could have taken this man in hand and put him to use . . . but as the world was now, when every man had to depend on his own judgment about so many things . . . and a man in Erlend's circumstances was supposed to make decisions for himself and for the welfare of many other people. And this was Kristin's husband.

Erlend looked up at his father-in-law. He grew somber too. Then he said, "I want to ask one thing, Lavrans. Before we reach my home, I'd like you to tell me what is in your heart."

Lavrans was silent.

"You must know," said Erlend in the same tone of voice, "that I would gladly fall at your feet in whatever manner you wish and make amends in whatever way you deem a fitting punishment for me."

Lavrans looked down into the younger man's face; then he smiled oddly.

"That might be difficult, Erlend—for me to decide and for you to do. But now you must make a proper gift to the church at Sundbu and to the priests, whom you have also deceived," he said adamantly. "I will speak no more of this! And you cannot blame it on your youth. It would have been much more honorable, Erlend, if you had fallen at my feet *before* you held your wedding."

"Yes," said Erlend. "But at the time I didn't know how things stood, or that it would come to light that I had offended you."

Lavrans sat up.

"Didn't you know, when you were wed, that Kristin . . ."

"No," said Erlend, looking crestfallen. "We were married for almost two months before I realized it."

Lavrans gave him a look of surprise but said nothing.

Then Erlend spoke again, his voice low and unsteady, "I'm glad that you came with me, Father-in-law. Kristin has been so melancholy all winter—she has hardly said a word to me. Many times it seemed to me that she was unhappy, both with Husaby and with me."

Lavrans replied somewhat coldly and harshly, "That's no doubt the way things are with most young wives. Now that she's well again, you two will probably be just as good friends as you were before." And he smiled a little mockingly.

But Erlend sat and stared into the glowing embers. He suddenly understood with certainty—but he had realized it from the moment he first saw the tiny red infant face pressed against Kristin's white shoulder. It would never be the same between them, the way it had been before.

When Kristin's father stepped inside the little house, she sat up in bed and held out her hands toward him. She threw her arms around his shoulders and wept and wept, until Lavrans grew quite alarmed.

She had been out of bed for some time, but then she learned that Erlend had set off for Gudbrandsdal alone, and when he failed to return home for days on end, she grew so anxious that she developed a fever. And she had to go back to bed.

It was apparent that she was still weak—she wept at everything. The new manor priest,[2] Sira Eiliv Serkssøn, had arrived while Erlend was away. He had taken it upon himself to visit the mistress now and then to read to her, but she wept over such unreasonable things that soon he didn't know what he dared let her hear.

One day when her father was sitting with her, Kristin wanted to change the child herself so that he could see how handsome and well-formed the boy was. He lay naked on the swaddling clothes, kicking on the wool coverlet in front of his mother.

"What kind of a mark is that on his chest?" asked Lavrans.

Right over his heart the child had several little blood-red flecks; it looked as if a bloody hand had touched the boy there. Kristin had been distressed by it too, the first time she saw this mark. But she had tried to console herself, and she said now, "It's probably just a fire mark—I put my hand to my breast when I saw the church was burning."

Her father gave a start. Well. He hadn't known how long—or how much—she had kept to herself. And he couldn't understand that she had had the strength—his own child, and from him . . .

* * *

"I don't think you're truly fond of my son," Kristin said to her father many times, and Lavrans would laugh a bit and say of course he was. He had also placed an abundance of gifts both in the cradle and in the mother's bed. But Kristin didn't think anyone cared enough for her son—least of all Erlend. "Look at him, Father," she would beg. "Did you see he was laughing? Have you ever seen a more beautiful child than Naakkve, Father?"

She asked this same thing over and over. Once Lavrans said, as if in thought, "Haavard, your brother—our second son—was a very handsome child."

After a moment Kristin asked in a timid voice, "Was he the one who lived the longest of my brothers?"

"Yes. He was two winters old. Now you mustn't cry again, my Kristin," he said gently.

Neither Lavrans nor Gunnulf Nikulaussøn liked the fact that the boy was called Naakkve; he had been baptized Nikulaus. Erlend maintained that it was the same name, but Gunnulf disagreed; there were men in the sagas who had been called Naakkve since heathen times. But Erlend still refused to use the name that his father had borne. And Kristin always called the boy by the name Erlend had spoken when he first greeted their son.

In Kristin's view there was only one person at Husaby, aside from herself, who fully realized what a splendid and promising child Naakkve was. That was the new priest, Sira Eiliv. In that way, he was nearly as sensible as she was.

Sira Eiliv was a short, slight man with a little round belly, which gave him a somewhat comical appearance. He was exceedingly nondescript; people who had spoken to him many times had trouble recognizing the priest, so ordinary was his face. His hair and complexion were the same color—like reddish-yellow sand—and his round, watery blue eyes were quite dull. In manner he was subdued and diffident, but Master Gunnulf said that Sira Eiliv was so learned that he could have attained high standing if only he had not been so unassuming. But he was far less marked by his learning than by pure living, humility, and a deep love for Christ and his Church.

He was of low birth, and although he was not much older than

Gunnulf Nikulaussøn, he seemed almost like an old man. Gunnulf had known him ever since they went to school together in Nidaros, and he always spoke of Eiliv Serkssøn with great affection. Erlend didn't think it was much of a priest they had been given at Husaby, but Kristin immediately felt great trust and affection for him.

Kristin continued to live in the little house with her child, even after she had made her first visit back to church. That was a bleak day for Kristin. Sira Eiliv escorted her through the church door, but he didn't dare give her the body of Christ. She had confessed to him, but for the sin that she had committed when she became implicated in another person's ill-fated death, she would have to seek absolution from the archbishop. That morning when Gunnulf had sat with Kristin, her spirit in anguish, he had impressed upon her heart that as soon as she was out of any physical danger, she must rush to seek redemption for her soul. As soon as she had regained her health, she must keep her promise to Saint Olav. Now that he, through his intercession, had brought her son, healthy and alive, into the light and to the baptismal font, she must walk barefoot to his grave and place there her golden crown, the honored adornment of maidens, which she had guarded so poorly and unjustly worn. And Gunnulf had advised her to prepare for the journey with solitude, prayers, reading, meditation, and even fasting, although with moderation for the sake of the nursing child.

That evening as she sat in sorrow after going to church, Gunnulf had come to her and given her a *Pater noster* rosary. He told her that in countries abroad, cloister folk and priests were not the only ones who used these kinds of beads to help them with their devotions. This rosary was extremely beautiful; the beads were made of a type of yellow wood from India that smelled so sweet and wondrous they might almost serve as a reminder of what a good prayer ought to be—a sacrifice of the heart and a yearning for help in order to live a righteous life before God. In between there were beads of amber and gold, and the cross was painted with a lovely enamel.

Erlend would give his young wife a look full of longing whenever he met her out in the courtyard. She had never been as beautiful as she was now—tall and slender in her simple, earth-brown dress of undyed homespun. The coarse linen wimple covering her hair, neck, and shoulders merely showed even more how glowing and pure her complexion had become. When the spring sun fell on her face, it was as if the light were seeping deep into her flesh, so radiant she was—her eyes and lips were almost transparent. When he went into the little house to see the child, she would lower her great pale eyelids if he glanced at her. She seemed so modest and pure that he hardly dared touch her hand with his fingers. If she had Naakkve at her breast, she would pull a corner of her wimple over the tiny glimpse of her white body. It seemed as if they were trying to send his wife away from him to heaven.

Then he would joke, half-angrily, with his brother and father-in-law as they sat in the hall in the evening—just men. Husaby had practically become a collegial church. Here sat Gunnulf and Sira Eiliv; his father-in-law could be considered a half-priest, and now they wanted to turn him into one too. There would be three priests on the estate. But the others laughed at him.

During the spring Erlend Nikulaussøn supervised much of the farming on his manor. That year all the fences were mended and the gates were put up in good time; the plowing and spring farm work were done early and properly, and Erlend purchased excellent livestock. At the new year he had been forced to slaughter a great many animals, but this was not a bad loss, as old and wretched as they were. He set the servants to burning tar and stripping off birch bark, and the farm's buildings were put in order and the roofs repaired. Such things had not been done at Husaby since old Sir Nikulaus had had his full strength. And he also sought advice and support from his wife's father—people knew that. Amidst all this work Erlend would visit friends and kinsmen in the villages along with Lavrans and his brother, the priest. But now he traveled in a suitable manner, with a couple of fit and proper servants. In the past, Erlend had been in the habit of riding around with an entire entourage of undisciplined and rowdy men. The gossip, which had for so long seethed with indignation at Erlend Nikulaussøn's shameless living and the disarray and decline at Husaby, now died down to a good-natured teasing. People smiled and said that Erlend's young wife had achieved a great deal in six months.

Shortly before Saint Botolv's Day, Lavrans Bjørgulfsøn left for

Nidaros, accompanied by Master Gunnulf. Lavrans was to be the priest's guest for several days while he visited Saint Olav's shrine and the other churches in town before starting his journey south to return home. He parted from his daughter and her husband with love and kindness.

## CHAPTER 6

KRISTIN WAS TO go to Nidaros three days after the Selje Men's Feast Day. Later in the month the frenzy and tumult in town would have already started as Saint Olav's Day neared, and before that time the archbishop was not in residence.

The evening before, Master Gunnulf came to Husaby, and very early the next morning he went with Sira Eiliv to the church for matins. The dew, gray as a pelt, covered the grass as Kristin walked to church, but the sun was gilding the forest at the top of the ridge, and the cuckoo was singing on the grassy mountainside. It looked as if she would have beautiful weather for her journey.

There was no one in the church except Erlend and his wife and the priests in the illuminated choir. Erlend looked at Kristin's bare feet. It must be ice cold for her to be standing on the stone floor. She would have to walk twenty miles with no escort but her prayers. He tried to lift his heart toward God, which he had not done in many years.

Kristin was wearing an ash-gray robe with a rope around her waist. Underneath he knew that she wore a shift of rough sackcloth. A homespun cloth, tightly bound, hid her hair.

As they came out of the church into the morning sunshine, they were met by a maidservant carrying the child. Kristin sat down on a pile of logs. With her back to her husband she let the boy nurse until he had had his fill before she started off. Erlend stood motionless a short distance away; his cheeks were pale and cold with strain.

The priests came out a little while later; they had taken off their albs in the sacristy. They stopped in front of Kristin. A few minutes later Sira Eiliv headed down toward the manor, but Gunnulf helped her tie the child securely onto her back. Around her neck hung a bag holding the golden crown, some money, and a little bread and salt. She picked up her staff, curtseyed deeply before the priest, and then began walking silently north along the path leading up into the forest.

Erlend stayed behind, his face deathly white. Suddenly he started running. North of the church there were several small hills with scraggly grass slopes and shrubs of juniper and alpine birch that had been grazed over; goats usually roamed there. Erlend raced to the top. From there he would be able to see her for a little while longer, until she disappeared into the woods.

Gunnulf slowly followed his brother. The priest looked so tall and dark in the bright morning light. He too was very pale.

Erlend was standing with his mouth half-open and tears streaming down his white cheeks. Abruptly he bent forward and dropped to his knees; then he threw himself down full length on the scruffy grass. He lay there sobbing and sobbing, tugging at the heather with his long tan fingers.

Gunnulf stood quite still. He stared down at the weeping man and then gazed out toward the forest where the woman had disappeared.

Erlend raised his head off the ground. "Gunnulf—was it necessary for you to compel her to do this? Was it necessary?" he asked again. "Couldn't *you* have offered her absolution?"

The other man did not reply.

Then Erlend spoke again. "I made my confession and offered penance." He sat up. "I bought for *her* thirty masses and an annual mass for her soul and burial in consecrated ground; I confessed my sin to Bishop Helge and I traveled to the Shrine of the Holy Blood in Schwerin. Couldn't that have helped Kristin a little?"

"Even though you have done that," said the priest quietly, "even though you have offered God a contrite heart and been granted full reconciliation with Him, you must realize that year after year you will still have to strive to erase the traces of your sin here on earth. The harm you did to the woman who is now your wife when you dragged her down, first into impure living and then into blood guilt—you cannot absolve her of that, only God can do so. Pray that He holds His hand over her during this journey when you can neither follow her nor protect her. And do not forget, brother, for as long as you both shall live, that you watched your wife leave your estate in this manner—for the sake of your sins more than for her own."

A little later Erlend said, "I swore by God and my Christian faith before I stole her virtue that I would never take any other wife, and she promised that she would never take any other husband for as long as we both should live. You said yourself, Gunnulf, that this was then a binding marriage before God; whoever later wed another would be living in sin in His eyes. So it could not have been impure living that Kristin was my . . ."

"It was not a sin that you lived with her," said the priest after a moment, "if it could have been done without breaking other laws. But you drove her into sinful defiance against everyone God had put in charge of this child—and then you brought the shame of blood upon her. I told you this too, back when we talked of this matter. That's why the Church has created laws regarding marriage, why banns must be announced, and why we priests must not marry man and maiden against the will of their kinsmen." He sat down, clasped his hands around one knee, and stared out across the summer-bright landscape, where the little lake glinted blue at the bottom of the valley. "Surely you must realize that, Erlend. You had sown a thicket of brambles around yourself, with nettles and thorns. How could you draw a young maiden to you without her being cut and flayed bloody?"

"You stood by me more than once, brother, during that time when I was with Eline," said Erlend softly. "I have never forgotten that."

"I don't think I would have done so," replied Gunnulf, and his voice quavered, "if I had imagined that you would have the heart to behave in such a manner toward a pure and delicate maiden—and a mere child compared to you."

Erlend said nothing.

Gunnulf asked him gently, "That time in Oslo—didn't you ever think about what would happen to Kristin if she became with child while she was living in the convent? And was betrothed to another man? Her father a proud and honorable man—and all her kinsmen of noble lineage, unaccustomed to bearing shame."

"Of course I thought about it." Erlend had turned his face away. "Munan promised to take care of her—and I told her that too."

"Munan! Would you deign to speak to a man like Munan of Kristin's honor?"

"He's not the sort of man you think," said Erlend curtly.

"But what about our kinswoman Fru Katrin? For surely you didn't intend for him to take Kristin to any of his other estates, where his paramours live. . . ."

Erlend slammed his fist against the ground, making his knuckles bleed.

"The Devil himself must have a hand in it when a man's wife goes to his brother for confession!"

"She hasn't confessed to me," said the priest. "Nor am I her parish priest. She told me her laments during her bitter fear and anguish, and I tried to help her and give her such advice and solace as I thought best."

"I see." Erlend threw back his head and looked up at his brother. "I know that I shouldn't have done it; I shouldn't have allowed her to come to me at Brynhild's inn."

The priest sat speechless for a moment.

"At Brynhild Fluga's?"

"Yes, didn't she tell you that when she told you all the rest?"

"It will be hard enough for Kristin to say such things about her lawful husband in confession," said the priest after a pause. "I think she would rather die than speak of it anywhere else."

He fell silent and then said harshly and vehemently, "If you felt, Erlend, that you were her husband before God and the one who should protect and guard her, then I think your behavior was even worse. You seduced her in groves and in barns, you led her across a harlot's threshold. And finally up to Bjørn Gunnarssøn and Fru Aashild . . ."

"You mustn't speak of Aunt Aashild that way," said Erlend in a low voice.

"You've said yourself that you thought our aunt caused the death of our father's brother—she and that man Bjørn."

"It makes no difference to me," said Erlend forcefully. "I'm fond of Aunt Aashild."

"Yes, so I see," said the priest. A crooked, mocking little smile appeared on his lips. "Since you were ready to leave her to face Lavrans Bjørgulfsøn after you carried off his daughter. It seems as if you think that your affection is worth paying dearly for, Erlend."

"Jesus!" Erlend hid his face in his hands.

But the priest continued quickly, "If only you had seen the torment of your wife's soul as she trembled in horror of her sins, unconfessed and unredeemed—as she sat there, about to give birth to your child, with death standing at the door—so young a child herself, and so unhappy."

"I know, I know!" Erlend was shaking. "I know she lay there thinking about this as she suffered. For Christ's sake, Gunnulf, say no more. I'm your brother, after all!"

But he continued without mercy.

"If I had been a man like you and not a priest, and if I had led astray so young and good a maiden, I would have freed myself from that other woman. God help me, but I would have done as Aunt Aashild did to her husband and then burned in Hell forever after, rather than allow my innocent and dearest beloved to suffer such things as you have done."

Erlend sat in silence for a moment, trembling.

"You say that you're a priest," he said softly. "Are you such a *good* priest that you have never sinned—with a woman?"

Gunnulf did not look at his brother. Blood flushed red across his face.

"You have no right to ask me that, but I will answer you all the same. He who died for us on the cross knows how much I need his mercy. But I tell you, Erlend—if on the whole round disk of this earth he had not one servant who was pure and unmarked by sin, and if in his holy Church there was not a single priest who was more faithful and worthy than I am, miserable betrayer of the Lord that I am, then the Lord's commandments and laws are what we can learn from this. His Word cannot be defiled by the mouth of an impure priest; it can only burn and consume our own lips—although perhaps you can't understand this. But you know as well as I, along with every filthy thrall of the Devil that He has bought with His own blood—God's law cannot be shaken nor His honor diminished. Just as His sun is equally mighty, whether it shines above the barren sea and desolate gray moors or above these fair lands."

Erlend had hidden his face in his hands. He sat still for a long time, but when he spoke his voice was dry and hard.

"Priest or no priest—since you're not such a strict adherent of pure living—don't you see . . . Could you have done that to a woman who had slept in your arms and borne you two children? Could you have done to her what our aunt did to her husband?"

The priest didn't answer at first. Then he said with some scorn, "You don't seem to judge Aunt Aashild too harshly."

"But it can't be the same for a man as for a woman," said Erlend. "I remember the last time they were here at Husaby, and Herr Bjørn was with them. We sat near the hearth, Mother and Aunt Aashild, and Herr Bjørn played the harp and sang for them. I stood at his knee. Then Uncle Baard called to her—he was in bed, and he wanted her to come to bed too. He used words that were vulgar and shameless. Aunt Aashild stood up and Herr Bjørn did too. He left the room, but before he did, they looked at each other. Later, when I was old enough to understand, I thought . . . that it might be true after all. I had begged for permission to light the way for Herr Bjørn over to the loft where he was going to sleep, but I didn't dare, and I didn't dare sleep in the hall, either. I ran outside and went to sleep with the men in the servants' house. By Jesus, Gunnulf—it can't be the same for a man as it was for Aashild that evening. No, Gunnulf—to kill a woman who . . . unless I caught her with another man . . ."

And yet that was exactly what he had done. But Gunnulf wouldn't dare mention *that* to his brother.

Then the priest asked coldly, "Wasn't it true that Eline had been unfaithful to you?"

"Unfaithful!" Erlend abruptly turned to face his brother, furious. "Do you think I should have blamed her for taking up with Gissur, after I had told her so often that it was over between us?"

Gunnulf bowed his head.

"No. No doubt you're right," he said, his voice weary and low.

But having won that small concession, Erlend flared up. He threw back his head and looked at the priest.

"You take so much notice of Kristin, Gunnulf. The way you've been hanging about her all spring—almost more than is decent for a brother and a priest. It's as if you didn't want her to be mine. If things hadn't been the way they were with her when you first met, people might even think . . ."

Gunnulf stared at him. Provoked by his brother's gaze, Erlend jumped to his feet. Gunnulf stood up too. When he continued to stare, Erlend lashed out at him with his fist. The priest grabbed his wrist. He tried to charge at Gunnulf, but his brother stood his ground.

Erlend grew meek at once. "I should have remembered that you're a priest," he said softly.

"Well, you have nothing to repent on that account," said Gunnulf with a little smile. Erlend stood there rubbing his wrist.

"Yes, you always had such devilishly strong hands."

"This is the way it was when we were boys." Gunnulf's voice grew oddly tender and gentle. "I've thought about that often during the years I was away from home—about when we were boys. We often fought, but it never lasted long, Erlend."

"But now," said the other man sorrowfully, "it can never be the same as when we were boys, Gunnulf."

"No," murmured the priest. "I suppose it can't."

They stood in silence for a long time. Finally Gunnulf said, "I'm going away now, Erlend. I'll go down to bid Eiliv farewell, and then I'm leaving. I'm heading over to visit the priest in Orkedal; I won't go to Nidaros while *she* is there." He gave a small smile.

"Gunnulf! I didn't mean . . . Don't leave me this way."

Gunnulf didn't move. He breathed hard several times and then he said, "There's one thing I want to tell you, Erlend—since you now know that I know everything about you. Sit down."

The priest sat down in the same position as before. Erlend stretched out in front of him, lying with one hand propped under his chin and looking up at his brother's strangely tense and rigid face. Then he smiled.

"What is it, Gunnulf? Are you about to confess to me?"

"Yes," said his brother softly. But then he fell silent for a long time. Erlend noticed that his lips moved once, and he clasped his hands tighter around his knee.

"What is it?" He gave him a fleeting smile. "It can't be that you—that some fair woman out there in the southern lands . . ."

"No," said the priest. His voice had a peculiar gruff tone. "This is not about love. Do you know, Erlend, how it happened that I was promised to the priesthood?"

"Yes. When our brothers died and they thought they were going to lose us too . . ."

"No," said Gunnulf. "They thought Munan had regained his health, and Gaute was not ill at all; he didn't die until the next winter. But you lay in bed and were suffocating, and that's when Mother promised that I would serve Saint Olav if he would save your life."

"Who told you that?" asked Erlend after a moment.

"Ingrid, my foster mother."

"Well, I would have been an odd gift to offer to Saint Olav," said Erlend, with a laugh. "He would have been poorly served by me. But you've told me, Gunnulf, that you were pleased even as a boy to be called to the priesthood."

"Yes," said the priest. "But it was not always so. I remember the day you left Husaby along with Munan Baardsøn to journey to our kinsman, the king, to join his service. Your horse danced beneath you, and your new weapons gleamed and shone. I would never bear weapons. You were handsome, my brother. You were only sixteen winters old, and I had already noticed long ago that women and maidens were fond of you."

"All that glory was short-lived," said Erlend. "I learned to cut my nails straight across, to swear on the name of Jesus with every other word, and to resort to my dagger to defend myself when I wielded a sword. Then I was sent north and met *her*—and was banished with shame from the king's retinue, and our father closed his door to me."

"And you left the country with a beautiful woman," said Gunnulf in the same low voice. "We heard at home that you had become a chief of guards at Earl Jacob's castle."

"Well, it wasn't as grand as it seemed back home," said Erlend, laughing.

"You and Father were no longer friends. But he had so little regard for me that he didn't even bother to quarrel with me. Mother loved me, that I know—but she found me less worthy than you. I felt it the most when you left the country. You, brother, were the only one who had any real love for me. And God knows you were my dearest friend on earth. But back when I was young and ignorant, I would sometimes think you had been given so much more than I had. Now I've told you, Erlend."

Erlend lay with his face against the ground.

"Don't go, Gunnulf," he begged.

"I must," said the priest. "Now we've told each other far too much. May God and the Virgin Mary grant that we meet again at a better time. Farewell, Erlend."

"Farewell," said Erlend, but did not look up.

When Gunnulf, wearing traveling clothes, stepped out of the priest's house several hours later, he saw a man riding south across the fields toward the forest. He had a bow slung over his shoulder and three dogs were running alongside his horse. It was Erlend.

In the meantime Kristin was walking briskly along the forest path over the ridge. The sun was now high, and the tops of the fir trees shone against the summer sky, but inside the woods it was still cool and fresh with the morning. A fragrant smell filled the air from spruce boughs, the marshy earth, and the twinflowers that covered the ground everywhere, in bloom with pairs of tiny pink, bell-shaped blossoms. And the path, overgrown with grass, was damp and soft and felt good under her feet. Kristin walked along, saying her prayers; now and then she would look up at the small white, fair-weather clouds swimming in the blue above the treetops.

The whole time she found herself thinking about Brother Edvin. This is how he had walked and walked, year in and year out, from early spring until late in the fall. Over mountain paths, through dark ravines and white snowdrifts. He rested in the mountain pastures, drank from the creeks, and ate from the bread that milkmaids and horse herdsmen brought out to him. Then he would bid them live well and God's peace and bestow blessings on both them and the livestock. Through rustling mountain meadows the monk would hike down into the valley. Tall and stoop-shouldered, with his head bowed, he wandered the main roads past manors and farms—and everywhere he went, he would leave behind his loving prayers of intercession for everyone, like good weather.

Kristin didn't meet a living soul, except for a few cows now and then—there were mountain pastures on the ridge. But it was a clearly marked path, with log bridges across the marshes. Kristin was not afraid; she felt as if the monk were walking invisibly at her side.

Brother Edvin, if it's true that you are a holy man, if you now stand before God, then pray for me!

Lord Jesus Christ, Holy Mary, Saint Olav. She longed to reach the destination of her journey. She longed to cast off the burden of years of concealed sins, the weight of church services and masses which she had stolen, unconfessed and unredeemed. She longed to be absolved and free—just as she had longed to be released from her burden this past spring when she was carrying the child.

He was sleeping soundly, safe on his mother's back. He didn't wake up until she had walked through the woods down to the farms of Snefugl and could look out across Budvik and the arm of the fjord at Saltnes. Kristin sat down in an outlying field, pulled the bundle with the child around into her lap, and loosened her robe at the breast. It felt good to hold him to her breast; it felt good to sit down; and a blessed warmth coursed through her whole body as she felt her stone-hard breasts bursting with milk empty out as he nursed.

The countryside below her lay silent and baking in the sun, with green pastures and bright fields amidst dark forest. A little smoke drifted up from the rooftops here and there. The hay harvesting had begun in a few places.

She traveled by boat from Saltnes Sand over to Steine. Then she was in completely unfamiliar regions. The road through Bynes went past farms for a while; then she reached the woods again, but there was no longer such a great distance between human dwellings. She was very tired. But then she thought about her parents—they had walked barefoot all the way from Jørundgaard at Sil, through Dovre, and on to Nidaros, carrying Ulvhild on a litter between them. She must not think that Naakkve was so heavy on her back.

And yet her head itched terribly from the sweat under her thick homespun wimple. Around her waist, where the rope held her clothing close to her body, her shift had rubbed on her skin so that it felt quite raw.

After a while there were others on the road. Now and then people would ride past her. She caught up with a farmer's cart taking goods to town; the heavy wheels jolted and jounced over roots and stones, screeching and creaking. Two men were driving a beast to slaughter. They glanced at the young woman pilgrim because she was so beautiful; otherwise people were used to such wayfarers in these parts. At one place several men were building a house a short distance from the road; they shouted to her, and an old man came running to offer her some ale. Kristin curtseyed, took a drink, and thanked the man with such words as poor people usually said to her when she gave them alms.

A little while later she had to rest again. She found a small green hill along the road with a trickling creek. Kristin placed the child on the grass; he woke up and cried loudly, so she hurried distractedly through the prayers she had meant to say. Then she picked up Naakkve, held him on her lap, and loosened the swaddling clothes. He had sullied his underclothes, and she had little to change him with; so she rinsed the cloths and spread them out to dry on a bare rock in the sun. She wrapped the outer garments loosely around the boy. He seemed to like this, and lay there kicking as he drank from his mother's breast. Kristin gazed happily at his fine, rosy limbs and pressed one of his hands between her breasts as she nursed him.

Two men rode past at a fast trot. Kristin glanced up briefly—it was a nobleman and his servant. But suddenly the man reined in his horse, leaped from the saddle, and walked back to where she was sitting. It was Simon Andressøn.

"Perhaps you won't be pleased that I stopped to greet you?" he asked. He stood there holding his horse and looking down at her. He was wearing traveling clothes, with a sleeveless leather vest over a light-blue linen tunic; he wore a small silk cap on his head, and his face was rather flushed and sweaty. "It's strange to see you—but perhaps you'd rather not speak to me?"

"Surely you should know . . . How are you, Simon?" Kristin tucked her bare feet under the hem of her skirts and tried to take the child from her breast. But the boy screamed, opening his mouth to suckle, so she had to let him nurse again. She pulled the robe over her breast as best she could and sat with her eyes lowered.

"Is it yours?" asked Simon, pointing to the child. "That was a foolish question," he laughed. "It's a son, isn't it? He's blessed with good fortune, Erlend Nikulaussøn!" He tied his horse to a tree, and now he sat down on a rock not far from Kristin. He placed his sword between his knees and sat with his hands on the hilt, poking at the dirt with the point of the scabbard.

"It was unexpected to meet you here in the north, Simon," said Kristin, just for something to say.

"Yes," said Simon. "I haven't had business in this part of the country before."

Kristin recalled that she had heard something—at the welcome celebration for her at Husaby—about the youngest son of Arne Gjavvaldssøn of Ranheim being betrothed to Andres Darre's youngest daughter. So she asked him whether that's where he had been.

"You know about it?" asked Simon. "Well, I suppose it must have been talked about all through these parts."

"So it's true," said Kristin, "that Gjavvald is to marry Sigrid?"

Simon looked up abruptly, pressing his lips together.

"I see you don't know everything, after all."

"I haven't been beyond the courtyard of Husaby all winter," said Kristin. "And I've seen few people. I heard there was talk of this marriage."

"You might as well hear it from my lips, then—the news will doubtless reach here soon enough." He sat in silence for a moment. "Gjavvald died three days before Winter Night.[1] He fell off his horse and broke his back. Do you remember before you reach Dyfrin how the road heads east of the river and there's a steep drop-off? No, you probably don't. We were on our way to their betrothal celebration; Arne and his sons had come by ship to Oslo." Then Simon fell silent.

"She must have been happy, Sigrid—because she was going to marry Gjavvald," said Kristin, shy and timid.

"Yes," said Simon. "And she had a son by him—on the Feast Day of the Apostles this spring."

"Oh, Simon!"

Sigrid Andresdatter, with the brown curls framing her small round face. Whenever she laughed, deep dimples appeared in her cheeks. The dimples and the small, childish white teeth—Simon had them too. Kristin remembered that when she grew less kindly inclined toward her betrothed, these things seemed to her unmanly, especially after she had met Erlend. They were much alike, Sigrid and Simon; but in her case it seemed charming that she was so plump and quick to laughter. She was fourteen winters old back then. Kristin had never heard such merry laughter as Sigrid's. Simon was always teasing his youngest sister and joking with her; Kristin could see that of all his siblings, he was most fond of her.

"You know that Father loved Sigrid best," said Simon. "That's why he wanted to see whether she and Gjavvald would like each other before he made this agreement with Arne. And they did—in my mind a little more than was proper. They always had to sit close whenever they met, and they would steal looks at each other and laugh. That was last summer at Dyfrin. But they were so young. No one could have imagined this. And our sister Astrid—you know she was betrothed when you and I . . . Well, *she* voiced no objections; Torgrim is very wealthy and kind, and in a certain way . . . but he finds fault with everyone and everything, and he thinks he suffers from all the ailments and troubles that anyone can name. So all of us were happy when Sigrid seemed so pleased with the man chosen for her.

"And then we brought Gjavvald's body to the manor. Halfrid, my wife, arranged things so that Sigrid would come home with us to Mandvik. And then it came out that Sigrid wasn't left alone when Gjavvald died."

They were silent for a while. Then Kristin said softly, "This has not been a joyful journey for you, Simon."

"No, it hasn't." Then he gave a laugh. "But I've gotten used to traveling on unfortunate business, Kristin. And I was the closest one, after all—Father lacked the courage, and they're living with me at Mandvik, Sigrid and her son. But now he'll have a place in his father's lineage, and I could see from all of them there that he won't be unwelcome, the poor little boy, when he goes to live with them."

"But what of your sister?" asked Kristin, breathlessly. "Where is she to live?"

Simon looked down at the ground.

"Father will take her home to Dyfrin now," he said in a low voice.

"Simon! Oh, how can you have the heart to agree to this?"

"You must realize," he replied without looking up, "that it's a great advantage for the boy, that he'll be part of his father's family from the beginning. Halfrid and I, we would have liked to keep both of them with us. No sister could be more loyal and loving toward another than Halfrid is toward Sigrid. None of our kinsmen has been unkind toward her—you mustn't think that. Not even Father, although this has made him a broken man. But can't you see? It wouldn't be right if any of us objected to the innocent boy gaining inheritance and lineage from his father."

Kristin's child let go of her breast. She quickly drew her garments closed over her bosom and, trembling, hugged the infant close. He hiccupped happily a couple of times and then spit up a little over himself and his mother's hands.

Simon glanced at the two of them and said with an odd smile, "You had better luck, Kristin, than my sister did."

"Yes, no doubt it may seem unfair to you," said Kristin softly, "that I'm called wife and my son was lawfully born. I might have deserved to be left with the fatherless child of a paramour."

"That would seem to me the worst thing I could have heard," said Simon. "I wish you only the best, Kristin," he said even more quietly.

A moment later he asked her for directions. He mentioned that he had come north by ship from Tunsberg. "Now I must continue on and see about catching up with my servant."

"Is it Finn who's traveling with you?" asked Kristin.

"No. Finn is married now; he's no longer in my service. Do you still remember him?" asked Simon, and his voice sounded pleased.

"Is Sigrid's son a handsome child?" asked Kristin, looking at Naakkve.

"I hear that he is. I think one infant looks much like another," replied Simon.

"Then you must not have children of your own," said Kristin, giving a little smile.

"No," he said curtly. Then he bid her farewell and rode off.

When Kristin continued on, she didn't put her child on her back. She carried him in her arms, pressing his face against the hollow of her neck. She could think of nothing else but Sigrid Andresdatter.

Her own father would not have been able to do it. Should Lavrans Bjørgulfsøn ride off to beg for a place and rank for his daughter's bastard child among the father's kinsmen? He would never have been able to do that. And never, never would he have had the heart to take her child away from her—to pull a tiny infant out of his mother's arms, tear him away from her breast while he still had mother's milk on his innocent lips. My Naakkve, no he wouldn't do that—even if it were ten times more just to do so, my father would not have done it.

But she couldn't get the image out of her mind: a group of horsemen vanishing north of the gorge, where the valley grows narrow and the mountains crowd together, black with trees. Cold wind comes in gusts from the river, which thunders over the rocks, icy green and frothing, with deep black pools in between. Whoever throws himself into it would be crushed in the rapids at once. Jesus, Maria.

Then she envisioned the fields back home at Jørundgaard on a light summer night. She saw herself running down the path to the green clearing in the alder grove near the river, where they used to wash clothes. The water rushed past with a loud, monotonous roar along the flat riverbed filled with boulders. Lord Jesus, there is nothing else I can do.

Oh, but Father would not have had the heart to do it. No matter how right it was. If I begged and begged him, begged on my knees: Father, you mustn't take my child from me.

Kristin stood on the hill at Feginsbrekka and looked down at the town lying at her feet in the golden evening sun. Beyond the wide, glittering curve of the river lay brown farm buildings with green sod roofs; the crowns of the trees were dark and domelike in the gardens. She saw light-colored stone houses with stepped gables, churches thrusting their black, shingle-covered backs into the air, and churches with dully gleaming roofs of lead. But above the green landscape, above the glorious town, rose Christ Church so magnificently huge and radiantly bright, as if everything lay prone at its feet. With the evening sun on its breast and the sparkling glass of its windows, with its towers and dizzying spires and gilded weather vanes, the cathedral stood pointing up into the bright summer sky.

All around lay the summer-green land, bearing venerable manors on its hills. In the distance the fjord opened out, shining and wide, with drifting shadows from the large summer clouds that billowed up over the glittering blue mountains on the other side. The cloister island looked like a green wreath with flowers of stone-white buildings, softly lapped by the sea. So many ships' masts out among the islands, so many beautiful houses.

Overcome and sobbing, the young woman sank down before the cross at the side of the road, where thousands of pilgrims had lain and thanked God because helping hands were extended to them on their journey through the perilous and beautiful world.

The bells of the churches and cloisters were ringing for vespers as Kristin entered the courtyard of Christ Church. For a moment she ventured to glance up at the west gable—then she lowered her dazzled eyes.

Human beings could not have done this work on their own. God's spirit had been at work in holy Øistein and the men who built the church after him. *Thy kingdom come, Thy will be done, on earth as it is in heaven.* Now she understood those words. A reflection of the splendor of God's kingdom bore witness through the stones that His will was all that was beautiful. Kristin trembled. Yes, God must surely turn away with scorn from all that was vile—from sin and shame and impurity.

Along the galleries of the heavenly palace stood holy men and women, and they were so beautiful that she dared not look at them. The imperishable vines of eternity wound their way upward, calm and lovely, bursting into flower on spires and towers with stone monstrances. Above the center door hung Christ on the cross; Mary and John the Evangelist stood at his side. And they were white, as if molded from snow, and gold glittered on the white.

Three times Kristin walked around the church, praying. The huge, massive walls with their bewildering wealth of pillars and arches and windows, the glimpse of the roof's enormous slanting surface, the tower, the gold of the spire rising high into the heavens—Kristin sank to the ground beneath her sin.

She was shaking as she kissed the hewn stone of the portal. In a flash she saw the dark carved timber around the church door back home, where as a child she had pressed her lips after her father and mother.

She sprinkled holy water over her son and herself, remembering that her father had done the same when she was small. With the child clasped tightly in her arms, she stepped forward into the church.

She walked as if through a forest. The pillars were furrowed like ancient trees, and into the woods the light seeped, colorful and as clear as song, through the stained-glass windows. High overhead animals and people frolicked in the stone foliage, and angels played their instruments. At an even higher, more dizzying height, the vaults of the ceiling arched upward, lifting the church toward God. In a hall off to the side a service was being held at an altar. Kristin fell to her knees next to a pillar. The song cut through her like a blinding light. Now she saw how deep in the dust she lay.

*Pater noster. Credo in unum Deum. Ave Maria, gratia plena.* She had learned her prayers by repeating them after her father and mother before she could understand a single word, from as far back as she could remember. Lord Jesus Christ. Was there ever a sinner like her?

High beneath the triumphal arch, raised above the people, hung Christ on the cross. The pure virgin, who was his mother, stood looking up in deathly anguish at her innocent son who was suffering the death of a criminal.

And here knelt Kristin with the fruit of her sin in her arms. She hugged the child tight—he was as fresh as an apple, pink and white like a rose. He was awake now, and he lay there looking up at her with his clear, sweet eyes.

Conceived in sin. Carried under her hard, evil heart. Pulled out of her sin-tainted body, so pure, so healthy, so inexpressibly lovely and fresh and innocent. This undeserved beneficence broke her heart in two; crushed with remorse, she lay there with tears welling up out of her soul like blood from a mortal wound.

Naakkve, Naakkve, my child. God visits the sins of the parents upon the children. Didn't I know that? Yes, I did. But I had no mercy for the innocent life that might be awakened in my womb—to be cursed and tormented because of my sin.

Did I regret my sin while I was carrying you inside me, my beloved, beloved son? Oh no, there was no remorse. My heart was hard with anger and evil thoughts at the moment I first felt you move, so small and unprotected. *Magnificat anima mea*

*Dominum. Et exultavit spiritus meus in Deo salutari meo.*[2] That is what she sang, the gentle queen of women, when she was chosen to bear the one who would die for our sins. I didn't think about the one who was the redeemer of my sin and my child's sin. Oh, no, there was no remorse. Instead I made myself pitiful and wretched and begged that the commandments of righteousness be broken, for I could not bear it if God should keep His promise and punish me in accordance with the Word that I have known all my days.

Oh yes, now she knew. She had thought that God was like her own father, that Holy Olav was like her father. All along she had expected, deep in her heart, that whenever the punishment became more than she could bear, then she would encounter not righteousness but mercy.

She wept so hard that she didn't have the strength to rise when the others stood up during the service; she stayed there, collapsed in a heap, holding her child. Near her several other people knelt who did not rise either: two well-dressed farmers' wives with a young boy between them.

She looked up toward the raised chancel. Beyond the gilded, grated door, high up behind the altar, Saint Olav's shrine glistened in the darkness. An ice-cold shiver ran down her back. There lay his holy body, waiting for Resurrection Day. Then the lid would spring open, and he would rise up. With his axe in hand, he would stride through this church. And from the stone floor, from the earth outside, from every cemetery in all of Norway the dead yellow skeletons would rise up; they would be clothed in flesh and would rally around their king. Those who had striven to follow in his bloodied tracks, and those who had merely turned to him for help with the burdens of sin and sorrow and illness to which they had bound themselves and their children, here in this life. They would crowd around their king and ask him to remind God of their need.

"Lord, hear my prayer for these people, whom I love so much that I would rather suffer exile and want and hatred and death than have a single man or maiden grow up in Norway not knowing that you died to save all sinners. Lord, you who bade us go out and make everyone your disciple—with my blood I, Olav Haraldssøn, wrote your gospel in the Norwegian language for these free men, my poor subjects."

Kristin closed her eyes, feeling sick and dizzy. She saw the king's face before her—his blazing eyes pierced the depths of her soul—now she trembled before Saint Olav's gaze.

"North of your village, Kristin, where I rested when my own countrymen drove me from my ancestral kingdom, because they could not keep God's Commandments—wasn't a church built at that spot? Didn't knowledgeable men come there to teach you of God's Word?

"'Thou shalt honor thy father and thy mother. Thou shalt not kill. God visits the sins of the fathers upon the children. I died so that you might learn these teachings. Haven't they been given to you, Kristin Lavransdatter?"

Oh yes, yes, my Lord and King!

Olav's church back home—she saw in her mind the pleasant, brown-timbered room. The ceiling was not so high that it could frighten her. It was unassuming, built in God's honor from dark, tarred wood, in the same way that people constructed their mountain huts and storehouses and cattle sheds. But the timbers had been cut into supple staves, and they were raised and joined to form the walls of God's house. And Sira Eirik taught each year on the church consecration day that in this manner we ought to use the tools of faith to cut and carve from our sinful, natural being a faithful link in the Church of Christ.

"Have you forgotten this, Kristin? Where are the deeds that should bear witness for you on the last day, showing that you were a link in God's church? The good deeds which will bear witness that you belong to God?"

Jesus, her good deeds! She had repeated the prayers that were placed on her lips. She had given out the alms that her father had placed in her hands; she had helped her mother when Ragnfrid clothed the poor, fed the hungry, and tended to the sores of the ill.

But the evil deeds were her own.

She had clung to everyone who offered her protection and support. Brother Edvin's loving admonitions, his sorrow over her sin, his tender intercessionary prayers which she had received—and then she had flung herself into passionate sinful desire as soon as she was beyond the light of his gentle old eyes. She lay down in cowsheds and outbuildings and scarcely felt any shame that she was deceiving the good and honorable Abbess Groa; she had accepted the kind concern of the pious sisters and hadn't even had the wit to blush when they praised her gentle and seemly behavior before her father.

Oh, the worst was thinking about her father. Her father, who had not said a single unkind word when he came to visit this spring.

Simon had concealed the fact that he had caught his betrothed with a man at an inn for wandering soldiers. And she had let him take the blame for her breach of promise, had let him bear the blame before her father.

Oh, but her father, that was the worst. No, her mother, that was even worse. If Naakkve should grow up to show his mother as little love as she had shown her own mother—oh, she couldn't bear it. Her mother, who had given birth to her and nursed her at her breast, kept watch over her when she was sick, washed and combed her hair and rejoiced at its beauty. And the first time that Kristin felt she needed her mother's help and comfort, she had waited for her mother to come, in spite of all her own disdain. "You should know that your mother would have come north to be with you if she had known that it might give you comfort," her father had said. Oh, Mother, Mother, Mother!

She had seen the water from the well back home. It looked so clean and pure when it was in the wooden cups. But her father owned a glass goblet, and when he filled it with water and the sun shone through, the water was muddy and full of impurities.

Yes, my Lord and King, now I see the way I am!

Goodness and love she had accepted from everyone, as if they were her right. There was no end to the goodness and love she had encountered all her days. But the first time someone confronted her, she had risen up like a snake and struck. Her will had been as hard and sharp as a knife when she drove Eline Ormsdatter to her death.

Just as she would have risen up against God Himself if He had placed His righteous hand on the back of her neck. Oh, how could her father and mother bear it? They had lost three young children;

they had watched Ulvhild sicken until she died, after they had striven those long sorrowful years to give the child back her health. But they had borne all these trials with patience, never doubting that God knew what was best for their children. Then she had caused them all this sorrow and shame.

But if there had been anything wrong with her child—if they had taken her child the way they were now taking Sigrid Andresdatter's child from her . . . Oh, *lead us not into temptation, but deliver us from evil.*

She had wandered to the very edge of Hell's abyss. If she should lose her son, after she had thrown herself into the seething rapids, turned away with scorn from any hope of joining the good and dear people who loved her—giving herself into the Devil's power . . .

It was no wonder that Naakkve bore the mark of a bloody hand on his chest.

Oh, Holy Olav, you who heard me when I prayed for you to help my child. I prayed that you would turn the punishment upon me and spare the innocent one. Yes, Lord, I know how I kept my part of the agreement.

Like a wild, heathen animal she had reared up at the first chastisement. Erlend. Not for a moment did she ever believe that he no longer loved her. If she had believed that, then she would not have had the strength to live. Oh no. But she had secretly thought that when she was beautiful again, and healthy and lively—then she would act in such a way that he would have to beg her. It wasn't that he had been unloving during the winter. But she, who had heard ever since she was a girl that the Devil always keeps close to a woman with child and tempts her because she is weak—she had turned a willing ear to the Devil's lies. She had pretended to believe that Erlend didn't care for her because she was ugly and ill, when she noticed that he was distressed because he had made both her and himself the subject of gossip. She had flung his timid and tender words back at him, and when she drove him to say harsh and thoughtless things, she would bring them up later to rebuke him. Jesus, what an evil woman she was—she had been a bad wife.

"Now do you understand, Kristin, that you need help?"

Yes, my Lord and King, now I understand. I am in great need of your support so that I won't turn away from God again. Stay with me, you who are the chieftain of His people, as I step forward with my prayers; pray for mercy for me. Holy Olav, pray for me!

*Cor mundum crea in me, Deus, et Spiritum rectum innova in visceribus meis.*

*Ne projicias me a facie tua.*

*Libera me de sanguinibus, Deus, Deus salutis meæ.*[3]

The service was over. People were leaving the church. The two farmers' wives who were kneeling near Kristin stood up. But the boy between them did not get up. He began moving across the floor by setting his knuckles on the flagstones and hopping along like a fledgling crow. He had tiny legs, bent crooked under his belly. The women walked in such a way as to hide him with their clothes as best they could.

When they were out of sight, Kristin threw herself down and kissed the floor where they had walked past her.

Feeling lost and uncertain, she was standing at the entrance to the chancel when a young priest came out the grated door. He stopped in front of the young woman with the tear-stained face, and Kristin did her best to explain the reason for her journey. At first he didn't understand. Then she pulled out the golden crown and held it out.

"Oh, are you Kristin Lavransdatter, the wife of Erlend of Husaby?" He gave her a rather surprised look; her face was quite swollen from weeping. "Yes, your brother-in-law, Gunnulf, spoke of you, yes he did."

He led her into the sacristy and took the crown; he unwrapped the linen cloth and looked at it. Then he smiled.

"Well, you must realize that there will have to be witnesses and the like. You can't give away such a costly treasure as if it were a piece of buttered *lefse*. But I can keep it for you in the meantime; no doubt you would prefer not to carry it around with you in town.

"Oh, ask Herr Arne if he wouldn't mind coming here," he said to a sexton. "I think that by rights your husband should be present too. But perhaps Gunnulf has a letter from him.

"You wish to speak to the archbishop himself, is that right?

Otherwise there is Hauk Tomassøn, who is the *penitentiarius*. I don't know whether Gunnulf has spoken to Archbishop Eiliv. But you must come here for matins tomorrow, and then you can ask for me after lauds. My name is Paal Aslakssøn. That," and he pointed to the child, "you must leave at the hostel. I seem to remember your brother-in-law saying that you're staying with the sisters at Bakke, is that right?"

Another priest came in, and the two men talked to each other briefly. The first priest then opened a small cupboard in the wall and took out a balance scale and weighed the crown, while the other made a note of it in a ledger. Then they placed the crown in the cupboard and closed the door.

Herr Paal was about to escort Kristin out, but then he asked her whether she would like him to lift her son up to Saint Olav's shrine.

He picked up the boy with the confident, almost indifferent ease of a priest who was used to holding children for baptism. Kristin followed him into the church, and he asked her whether she too would like to kiss the shrine.

I don't dare, thought Kristin, but she accompanied the priest up the stairs to the dais on which the shrine stood. A great, chalk-white light seemed to pass before her eyes as she pressed her lips to the golden chest.

The priest looked at her for a moment, to see whether she might collapse in a faint. But she got to her feet. Then he touched the child's forehead to the sacred shrine.

Herr Paal escorted Kristin to the church door and asked whether she was certain she could find her way to the ferry landing. Then he bade her good night. He spoke the whole time in an even and dry voice, like any other courteous young man in the king's service.

It had started to rain lightly, and a wonderful fragrance wafted blessedly from the gardens and along the street, which, on either side of the worn ruts from the wheel tracks, was as fresh and green as a country courtyard. Kristin sheltered the child from the rain as best she could—he was heavy now, so heavy that her arms were quite numb from carrying him. And he fussed and cried incessantly; he was probably hungry again.

The mother was dead tired from the long journey and from all the weeping and the intense emotions in the church. She was cold, and the rain was coming down harder; the drops splashed on the trees, making the leaves flutter and shake. She made her way down the lanes and came out onto a broad street; from there she could see the rushing river, wide and gray, its surface punctured like a sieve by the falling drops.

There was no ferryboat. Kristin talked to two men who were huddled in a space beneath a warehouse standing on posts at the water's edge. They told her to go out to the sandbanks—there the nuns had a house, and that's where the ferryman was.

Kristin went back up the wide street, wet and tired and with aching feet. She came to a small gray stone church; behind it stood several buildings enclosed by a fence. Naakkve was screaming furiously, so she couldn't go inside the church. But she heard the song from the recessed paneless windows, and she recognized the antiphon: *Lætare, Regina Coeli*—rejoice, thou Queen of Heaven, for he whom you were chosen to bear, has risen, as he promised. Hallelujah!

This was what the Minorites[4] sang after the *completorium*. Brother Edvin had taught her this hymn to the Lord's Mother as Kristin kept vigil over him during those nights when he lay deathly ill in their home at Jørundgaard. She crept out to the churchyard and, standing against the wall with her child in her arms, she repeated his words softly to herself.

"Nothing you do could ever change your father's heart toward you. This is why you must not cause him any more sorrow."

As your pierced hands were stretched out on the cross, O precious Lord of Heaven. No matter how far a soul might stray from the path of righteousness, the pierced hands were stretched out, yearning. Only one thing was needed: that the sinful soul should turn toward the open embrace, freely, like a child who goes to his father and not like a thrall who is chased home to his stern master. Now Kristin realized how hideous sin was. Again she felt the pain in her breast, as if her heart were breaking with remorse and shame at the undeserved mercy.

Next to the church wall there was a little shelter from the rain. She sat down on a gravestone and set about quelling the child's hunger. Now and then she would bend down and kiss his little down-covered head.

She must have fallen asleep. Someone was touching her shoulder. A monk and an old lay brother holding a spade in his hand stood before her. The barefoot brother asked if she was looking for shelter for the night.

The thought raced through her mind that she would much rather stay here tonight with the Minorites, Brother Edvin's brothers. And it was so far to Bakke, and she was nearly collapsing with weariness. Then the monk offered to have the lay servant accompany her to the women's hostel—"and give her a little calamus poultice for her feet; I see that they are sore."

It was stuffy and dark at the women's hostel, which stood outside the fence in the lane. The lay brother brought Kristin water to wash with and a little food, and she sat down near the hearth, trying to soothe her child. Naakkve could no doubt tell from her milk that his mother was worn out and had fasted all day. He fretted and whimpered in between attempts to suckle from her empty breasts. Kristin gulped down the milk that the lay brother brought her. She tried to squirt it from her mouth into the child's, but the boy protested loudly at this new means of being fed, and the old man laughed and shook his head. She would have to drink it her self, and then it would benefit the boy.

Finally the man left. Kristin crept into one of the beds high up beneath the center roof beam. From there she could reach a hatch. There was a foul smell in the hostel—one of the women was in bed with a stomach ailment. Kristin opened the hatch. The summer night was bright and mild, the rain-washed air streamed down on her. She sat in the short bed with her head leaning back against the timbers of the wall; there were few pillows for the beds. The boy was asleep in her lap. She had meant to close the hatch after a moment, but she fell asleep.

In the middle of the night she woke up. The moon, a pale summery honey-gold, was shining down on her and the child and illuminating the opposite wall. At that moment Kristin became aware of a person standing in the midst of the stream of moonlight, hovering between the gable and the floor.

He was wearing an ash-gray monk's cowl; he was tall and stooped. Then he turned his ancient, furrowed face toward her. It was Brother Edvin. His smile was so inexpressibly tender, and a little sly and merry, just as it was when he lived on this earth.

Kristin was not the least bit surprised. Humbly, joyfully, and filled with anticipation, she looked at him and waited for what he would say or do.

The monk laughed and held up a heavy old leather glove toward her; then he hung it on the moonbeam. He smiled even more, nodded to her, and then vanished.

# PART II

# HUSABY

## CHAPTER 1

ONE DAY JUST after New Year's, unexpected guests arrived at Husaby. They were Lavrans Bjørgulfsøn and old Smid Gudleikssøn from Dovre, and they were accompanied by two gentlemen whom Kristin didn't know. But Erlend was very surprised to see his father-in-law in their company—they were Erling Vidkunssøn from Giske and Bjarkøy, and Haftor Graut from Godøy. He hadn't realized that Lavrans knew them. But Sir Erling explained that they had met at Nes; he had served with Lavrans and Smid on the six-man court, which had finally settled the inheritance dispute among Jon Haukssøn's descendants. Then he and Lavrans happened to speak of Erlend; and Erling, who had business in Nidaros, mentioned that he had a mind to pay a visit to Husaby if Lavrans would keep him company and sail north with him.

Smid Gudleikssøn said with a laugh that he had practically invited himself along on the journey. "I wanted to see our Kristin again—the loveliest rose of the north valley. And I also thought that my kinswoman Ragnfrid would thank me if I kept an eye on her husband, to see what kind of decisions he was making with such wise and mighty men. Yes, your father has had other matters on his hands this winter, Kristin, than carousing from farm to farm with us and celebrating the Christmas season until Lent begins. All these years we've been sitting at home on our estates in peace and quiet, with each man tending to his own interests. But now Lavrans wants the men of the valleys who are the king's retainers to ride together to Oslo in the harshest time of the winter—now we're supposed to advise the noblemen of the Council and look after the king's interests. Lavrans says they're handling things so badly for the poor, underaged boy."[1]

Sir Erling looked rather embarrassed. Erlend raised his eyebrows.

"Have you decided to support these efforts, Father-in-law? For the great meeting of the royal retainers?"

"No, no," said Lavrans. "I'm merely going to the meeting, just like the other king's men of the valley, because we have been summoned."

But Smid Gudleikssøn spoke again. It was Lavrans who had persuaded him—and Herstein of Kruke and Trond Gjesling and Guttorm Sneis, as well as others who had not wanted to go.

"Isn't it the custom to invite guests into the house on this estate?" asked Lavrans. "Now we'll see whether Kristin brews ale as good as her mother's." Erlend looked thoughtful, and Kristin was greatly surprised.

"What's this about, Father?" she asked some time later, when he went with her to the little house where she had taken the child in order not to disturb the guests.

Lavrans sat and bounced his grandchild on his knee. Naakkve was now ten months old, big and handsome. He had been allowed to wear a tunic and hose since Christmas.

"I've never heard of you lending your voice to such matters before, Father," she said. "You've always told me that for the country, and for his subjects, it was best for the king to rule, along with those men he called to his side. Erlend says that this attempt is the work of the noblemen in the south; they want to remove Lady Ingebjørg from power, along with those men whom her father appointed to advise her. They want to steal back the power they had when King Haakon and his brother were children. But that brought great harm to the kingdom—you've said so yourself in the past."

Lavrans whispered that she should send the nursemaid away. When they were alone, he asked, "Where did Erlend get this information? Did he hear it from Munan?"

Kristin told him that Orm had brought a letter from Sir Munan when he returned home in the fall. She didn't say that she had read it to Erlend herself—he wasn't very good at deciphering script. But in the letter Munan had complained bitterly that now every man in Norway who bore a coat of arms thought himself better at ruling the kingdom than those men who had stood at King Haakon's side when he was alive, and they presumed to have a better understanding of the young king's welfare than the highborn woman who was his own mother. He had warned Erlend that if there were signs that the Norwegian noblemen had intentions of doing as the Swedes had done in Skara[2] last summer, of plotting against Lady Ingebjørg and her old, trusted advisers, then her kinsmen would stand ready and Erlend should go to meet Munan in Hamar.

"Didn't he mention," asked Lavrans as he tapped his finger under Naakkve's chubby chin, "that I'm one of the men opposed to the unlawful call to arms that Munan has been carrying through the valley, in the name of our king?"

"You!" said Kristin. "Did you meet Munan Baardsøn last fall?"

"Yes, I did," replied Lavrans. "And there was not much agreement between us."

"Did you talk about me?" asked Kristin swiftly.

"No, my dear Kristin," said her father, with a laugh. "I can't recall that your name was mentioned by either of us this time. Do you know whether your husband intends to travel south to meet with Munan Baardsøn?"

"I think so," said Kristin. "Sira Eiliv drafted a letter for Erlend not long ago, and he mentioned that he might soon have to go south."

Lavrans sat in silence for a moment, looking down at the child, who was fumbling with the hilt of his dagger and trying to bite the rock crystal embedded in it.

"Is it true that they want to take the regency away from Lady Ingebjørg?" asked Kristin.

"She's about the same age as you are," replied her father, a slight smile still on his lips. "No one wants to take from the king's mother the honor and power that are her birthright. But the archbishop and some of our blessed king's friends and kinsmen have gathered for a meeting to deliberate how Lady Ingebjørg's power and honor and the interests of the people should best be protected."

Kristin said quietly, "I can see, Father, that you haven't come to Husaby this time just to see Naakkve and me."

"No, that was not the only reason," said Lavrans. Then he laughed. "And I can tell, daughter, that you're not at all pleased!"

He put his hand up to stroke her face, just as he used to do when she was a little girl, any time he had scolded her or teased her.

In the meantime Sir Erling and Erlend were sitting in the armory—that was what the large storehouse was called which stood on the northeast side of the courtyard, right next to the manor gate. It was as tall as a tower, with three stories; on the top floor there was a room with loopholes in the walls for shooting arrows, and that was where all the weapons were stored which were not in daily use on the farm. King Skule had built this structure.

Sir Erling and Erlend were wearing fur capes because it was bitterly cold in the room. The guest walked around looking at the many splendid weapons and suits of armor which Erlend had inherited from his grandfather, Gaute Erlendssøn.

Erling Vidkunssøn was a rather short man, slight in build and yet quite plump, but he carried himself well and with ease. Handsome he was not, although he had well-formed features. But his hair had a reddish tinge, and his eyelashes and brows were white; even his eyes were a very pale blue. That people nevertheless found Sir Erling to be good-looking was perhaps due to the fact that everyone knew he was the wealthiest knight in Norway. But he also had a distinctly winning and modest demeanor. He was exceptionally intelligent, well educated and learned, but because he never tried to boast of his wisdom and always seemed to be willing to listen to others, he had become known as one of the wisest men in the country. He was the same age as Erlend Nikulaussøn, and they were kinsmen, although distant ones, by way of the Stovreim lineage. They had known each other all their lives, but there had never been a close friendship between the two men.

Erlend sat down on a chest and talked about the ship which he had had built in the summer; it was a thirty-two-oar ship, and he deemed it to be a particularly swift sailing ship and easy to steer. He had hired two shipbuilders from the north, and he had personally overseen the work along with them.

"Ships are among the few things I know something about, Erling," he said. "You just wait—it will be a beautiful sight to see *Margygren* cutting through the waves."

"*Margygren*—what a fearfully heathen name you've given your ship, kinsman," said Erling with a little laugh. "Is it your intention to travel south in it?"

"Are you as pious as my wife? She calls it a heathen name, too. She doesn't like the ship much, either, but she's such an inland person—she can't stand the sea."

"Yes, she looks pious and delicate and lovely, your wife," said Sir Erling courteously. "As one might expect from someone of her lineage."

"Yes," said Erlend and laughed. "Not a day passes without her going to mass. And Sira Eiliv, our priest, whom you met, reads to us from the holy books. Reading aloud—that's what he likes best, after ale and sumptuous food. And the poor people come to Kristin for help and advice. I think they would gladly kiss the hem of her skirts; I can scarcely recognize my own servants anymore. She's almost like one of the women described in the holy sagas that King Haakon forced us to sit and listen to as the priest read them aloud—do you remember? Back when we were pages? Things have changed a great deal here at Husaby since you visited us last, Erling."

After a moment he added, "It was odd, by the way, that you were willing to come here that time."

"You mentioned the days when we were pages together," said Erling Vidkunssøn with a smile that became him. "We were friends back then, weren't we? We all expected that you would achieve great things here in Norway, Erlend."

But Erlend merely laughed. "Yes, I expected as much myself."

"Couldn't you sail south with me, Erlend?" asked Sir Erling.

"I was thinking of traveling overland," replied the other man.

"That will be troublesome for you—setting out over the mountains now, in the wintertime," said Sir Erling. "It would be pleasant if you would accompany Haftor and myself."

"I have promised to travel with others," replied Erlend.

"Ah yes, you will join your father-in-law—yes, that seems only fitting."

"Well, no—I don't know these men from the valley who are riding with him." Erlend sat in silence for a moment. "No, I have promised to look in on Munan at Stange," he said quickly.

"You don't need to waste your time looking for Munan there," replied Erling. "He's gone to his estates at Hising, and it might be some time before he comes north again. Has it been a long time since you heard from him?"

"It was around Michaelmas—he wrote to me from Ringabu."

"Well, you know what happened in the valley here last autumn," said Erling. "You don't? Surely you must know that he rode around to the district sheriffs of Lake Mjøsa and all along the valley carrying letters stating that the farmers should pay for provisions and horses for a full campaign[3]—with six farmers for each horse—and that the gentry should send horses but would be allowed to stay at home. Haven't you heard about this? And that the men of the northern valleys refused to pay this war tax when Munan accompanied Eirik Topp to the *ting* in Vaage? And Lavrans Bjørgulfsøn was the one who led the opposition—he demanded that Eirik pursue a lawful course, if anything remained of the lawful taxes, but he called it an injustice against the peasantry to demand war taxes from the farmers to help a Dane in a feud with the Danish king. And yet if our king required the service of his retainers, then he would find them quick enough to respond with good weapons and horses and armed men. But he would not send from Jørundgaard even a goat with a hemp halter unless the king commanded him to ride it himself to the mustering of the army. You truly didn't know about this? Smid Gudleikssøn says that Lavrans had promised his tenants that he would pay the campaign levies for them, if need be."

Erlend sat there stunned.

"Lavrans did that? Never have I heard of my wife's father involving himself in matters other than those concerning his own properties or those of his friends."

"No doubt he seldom does," said Sir Erling. "But this much was clear to me when I was at Nes—when Lavrans Bjørgulfsøn decides to speak about a matter, he receives everyone's full support, for he never speaks without understanding the issue so well that his opinion would be difficult to refute. Now, regarding these events, he has no doubt exchanged letters with his kinsmen in Sweden. Fru Ramborg, his father's mother, and Sir Erngisle's grandfather were the children of two brothers, so Lavrans has strong family ties over there. No matter how quiet his manner, your father-in-law commands power of some consequence in those parishes where people know him—although he doesn't often make use of it."

"Well, now I can understand why you have taken up with him, Erling," said Erlend, laughing. "I was rather surprised that you had become such good friends."

"Why should that surprise you?" replied Erling soberly. "It would be an odd man who would not want to call Lavrans of Jørundgaard his friend. You would be better served, kinsman, to listen to him than to Munan."

"Munan has been like an older brother to me, ever since the day when I left home for the first time," said Erlend, a little heatedly. "He has never failed me whenever I was in trouble. So if he's in trouble now . . ."

"Munan will manage well enough," said Erling Vidkunssøn, his voice still calm. "The letters he carried were written and sealed with the royal seal of Norway—unlawful, but that's not his problem. Oh yes, there's more. That to which he testified and attached his seal when he was a witness to the maiden Eufemia's betrothal[4]—but this cannot be easily revealed without mentioning someone whom we cannot . . . If truth be told, Erlend, I think Munan will save himself without your support—but you may harm yourself if you—"

"It's Lady Ingebjørg that all of you want to depose, I see," said Erlend. "But I've promised our kinswoman to serve her both here and abroad."

"I have too," replied Erling. "And I intend to keep that promise—as does every Norwegian man who has served and loved our lord and kinsman, King Haakon. And she is now best served by being separated from those advisers who counsel so young a woman to the detriment of her son and herself."

"Do you think you're capable of *that?*" asked Erlend, his voice subdued.

"Yes," said Erling Vidkunssøn firmly. "I think we are. And everyone else thinks so too, if they refuse to listen to malicious and slanderous talk." He shrugged his shoulders. "And those of us who are kinsmen of Lady Ingebjørg should be the last to do that."

A servant woman raised the hatch in the floor and said that if it suited them, the mistress would now have the food carried into the hall.

While everyone was sitting at the table, the conversation, such as it was, constantly touched on the great news that was circulating. Kristin noticed that both her father and Sir Erling refused to join in; they brought up news of bride purchases and deaths, inheritance disputes and property trades among family and acquaintances. She grew uneasy but didn't know why. They had business with Erlend—this much she understood. And yet she didn't want to admit this to herself. She now knew her husband so well that she realized Erlend, with all his stubborn-mindedness, was easily influenced by anyone who had a firm hand in a soft glove, as the saying goes.

After the meal, the gentlemen moved over to the hearth, where they sat and drank. Kristin settled herself on a bench, put her needlework frame in her lap, and began twining the threads. A moment later Haftor Graut came over, placed a cushion on the floor, and sat down at Kristin's feet. He had found Erlend's psaltery; he set it on his knee and sat there strumming it as he chatted. Haftor was quite a young man with curly blond hair and the fairest features, but his face was covered with freckles. Kristin quickly noticed that he was exceedingly talkative. He had recently made a rich marriage, but he was bored back home on his estates; that was why he wanted to travel to the gathering of the king's retainers.

"But it's understandable that Erlend Nikulaussøn would want to stay home," he said, laying his head in her lap. Kristin moved away a bit, laughed, and said with an innocent expression that she knew only that her husband was intending to travel south, "for whatever reason that might be. There's so much unrest in the country right now; it's difficult for a simple woman to understand such things."

"And yet it's the simplicity of a woman that's the main cause of it all," replied Haftor, laughing and moving closer. "At least that's what Erling and Lavrans Bjørgulfsøn say—I'd like to know what they mean by that. What do you think, Mistress Kristin? Lady Ingebjørg is a good and simple woman. Perhaps right now she is sitting as you are, twining silk threads with her snow-white fingers and thinking: It would be hard-hearted to refuse the loyal chieftain of her deceased husband some small assistance to improve his lot."

Erlend came and sat down next to his wife so that Haftor had to move over a bit.

"The women chatter about such nonsense in the hostels when their husbands are foolish enough to take them along to the meeting."

"Where I come from, it's said that there's no smoke unless there's fire," said Haftor.

"Yes, we have that saying too," said Lavrans; he and Erling had come over to join them. "And yet I was duped, Haftor, this past winter, when I tried to light my torch with fresh horse droppings." He perched on the edge of the table. Sir Erling at once brought his goblet and offered it to Lavrans with a word of greeting. Then the knight sat down on a bench nearby.

"It's not likely, Haftor," said Erlend, "that up north in Haalogaland you would know what Lady Ingebjørg and her advisers know about the undertakings and enterprises of the Danes. I suspect you might have been short-sighted when you opposed the king's demand for help. Sir Knut[5]—yes, we might as well mention his name since he's the one that we're all thinking about—he seems to me a man who wouldn't be caught unawares. You sit too far away from the cookpots to be able to smell what's simmering inside them. And better to prepare now than regret later, I say."

"Yes," said Sir Erling. "You might almost say that they're cooking for us on the neighboring farm—we Norwegians will soon be nothing more than their wards. They send over the porridge they've made in Sweden and say: Eat this, if you want food! I think our lord, King Haakon, made a mistake when he moved the cookhouse to the outskirts of the farm and made Oslo the foremost royal seat in the land. Before then it was in the middle of the courtyard, if we stay with this image—Bjørgvin[6] or Nidaros—but now the archbishop and chapter[7] rule here alone. What do you think, Erlend? You who are from Trøndelag and have all your property and all your power in this region?"

"Well, God's blood, Erling—if that's what you want: to carry home the cookpot and hang it over the proper hearth, then—"

"Yes," said Haftor. "For far too long we up here in the north have had to settle for smelling the soup cooking while we spoon up cold cabbage."

Lavrans joined in.

"As things stand, Erlend, I would not have presumed to be spokesman for the people of the district back home unless I had letters in my possession from my kinsman, Sir Erngisle. Then I knew that none of the lawful rulers plans to break the peace or the alliance between the countries, neither in the realm of the Danish king nor in that of our own king."

"If you know who now rules in Denmark, Father-in-law, then you know more than most men," said Erlend.

"One thing I do know. There is one man that nobody wants to see rule, not here nor in Sweden nor in Denmark. That was the purpose of the Swedes' actions in Skara last summer, and that is the purpose of the meeting we will now hold in Oslo—to make clear to everyone who has not yet realized it, that on this matter all sober-minded men are agreed."

By this time they had all drunk so much that they had grown boisterous, except for old Smid Gudleikssøn; he was slumped in his chair next to the hearth.

Erlend shouted, "Yes, you're all so sober-minded that the Devil himself can't trick you. It makes sense that you'd be afraid of Knut Porse. You don't understand, all you good gentlemen, that he's not the kind who can be satisfied with sitting quietly, watching the days drift past and the grass grow as God wills. I'd like to meet that knight again; I knew him when I was in Halland. And I'd have no objections to being in Knut Porse's place."

"That's not something *I* would dare say if my wife could hear me," said Haftor Graut.

But Erling Vidkunssøn had also drunk a good deal. He was still trying to maintain his chivalrous manner, but he finally gave up. "You!" he said, laughing uproariously. "You, kinsman? No, Erlend!" He slapped the other man on the shoulder and laughed and laughed.

"No, Erlend," said Lavrans bluntly, "more is needed for that than a man who is capable of seducing women. If there was no more to Knut Porse than his ability to play the fox in the goose pen, then all of us Norwegian noblemen would be much too lazy to make the effort to leave our manors to chase him off—even if the goose was our own king's mother. But no matter who Sir Knut may lure into committing foolish acts in his behalf, he never commits follies without having some reason for doing so. He has his purpose, and you can be certain that he won't take his eyes off it."

There was a pause in the conversation. Then Erlend spoke, and his eyes glittered.

"Then I would wish that Sir Knut were a Norwegian man!"

The others were silent. Sir Erling drank from his goblet and said, "God forbid. If we had such a man among us here in Norway, then I fear there would be a sudden end to peace in the land."

"Peace in the land!" said Erlend scornfully.

"Yes, peace in the land," replied Erling Vidkunssøn. "You must remember, Erlend, that we knights are not the only ones who live in this country. To you it might seem amusing if an adventurous and ambitious man like Knut Porse should rise up here. In the past, things were such in the world that if a man stirred up a group of rebels, it was always easy for him to win a following among the noblemen. Either they won and acquired titles and land, or their kinsmen won and they were granted a reprieve for both their lives and their estates. Yes, those who lost their lives have been entered in the records, but the majority survived, no matter whether things went one way or the other—that's how it was for *our* fathers. But the farmers and the townspeople, Erlend—the workers who often had to make payments to two masters many times in a single year, but who still had to rejoice each time a band of rebels raced through their villages without burning their farms or slaughtering their cattle—the peasants, who had to endure such intolerable burdens and attacks—I think *they* must thank God and Saint Olav for old King Haakon and King Magnus and his sons, who fortified the laws and secured the peace."

"Yes, I can believe you would think that way." Erlend threw back his head. Lavrans sat and stared at the young man—Erlend was now fully alert. A flush had spread over his dark, fierce face, the sinews of his throat were arched taut in his slender, tan neck. Then Lavrans glanced at his daughter. Kristin had let her needlework sink to her lap, and she was intently following the men's conversation.

"Are you so sure that the farmers and common men think this way and are rejoicing over the new sovereign?" said Erlend. "It's true that they often had difficult times—back when kings and their rivals waged war throughout the land. I know they still remember the time when they had to flee to the mountains with their livestock and wives and children while their farms stood in flames down below in the valley. I've heard them talking about it. But I know they remember something else—that their own fathers were part of the hordes. We weren't alone in the battle for power, Erling. The sons of farmers were part of it too—and sometimes they even won our ancestral estates. When law rules the land, a bastard son from Skidan who doesn't know his own father's name cannot win a baron's widow and her estate, such as Reidar Darre did. His descendant was good enough to be betrothed to your daughter, Lavrans; and now he's married to your wife's niece, Erling! Now law and order rule—and I don't understand how it happens, but I do know that farmers' lands have fallen into our hands, and lawfully so. The more entrenched the law, the more quickly they lose their power and authority to take part in their own affairs or those of the realm. And that, Erling, is something that the farmers know too! Oh, no, don't be too certain, any of you, that the peasants aren't longing for the past when they might lose their farms by fire and force—but they could also win with weapons more than they can win with law."

Lavrans nodded. "There may be some truth in what Erlend says," he murmured.

But Erling Vidkunssøn stood up. "I believe you're right; the peasants remember better the few men who rose up from meager circumstances to become lords—in the time of the sword—than the unspeakable numbers who perished in filthy poverty and wretchedness. And yet none was a sterner master to the commoners than they were. I think it was of them that the saying was first spoken: kinsmen behave worst toward their own. A man must be born to be a master, or he will turn out to be a harsh one. But if he has spent his childhood among servant men and women, then he will have an easier time understanding that without the commoners, we are in many ways helpless children all our days, and that for God's sake as well as our own, we ought to serve them in turn with our knowledge and protect them with our chivalry. Never has it been possible to sustain a kingdom without noblemen who had the ability and the will to secure with their power the rights of those poorer than themselves."

"You could compete in sermonizing with my brother, Erling," said Erlend with a laugh. "But I think the people of Outer Trøndelag liked the gentry better back when we led their sons on military incursions, let our blood run and mingle with theirs across the planks, and split apart rings and divided up the booty with our serving men. Yes, as you can hear, Kristin, sometimes I sleep with one ear open when Sira Eiliv reads aloud from the great books."

"Property that is unlawfully won shall not be handed down to the third heir," said Lavrans Bjørgulfsøn. "Haven't you ever heard that before, Erlend?"

"Of course I've heard that!" Erlend laughed loudly. "But I've never seen it happen."

Erling Vidkunssøn said, "Things are such, Erlend, that few are born to rule, but everyone is born to serve; the proper way to rule is to be your servants' servant."

Erlend clasped his hands behind his neck and stretched, smiling. "I've never thought about that. And I don't think my leaseholders have any favors to thank me for. And yet, strange as it may seem, I think they're fond of me." He rubbed his cheek against Kristin's black kitten, which had jumped up onto his shoulder and was now walking around his neck, purring and with its back arched. "But my wife here—she is the most eager to serve of all women, although you wouldn't have reason to believe me, since the pitchers and mugs are now empty, my Kristin!"

Orm, who had been sitting quietly and listening to the men's conversation, stood up at once and left the room.

"Your wife grew so bored that she fell asleep," said Haftor, smiling. "And the blame is yours—you could have let me talk to her in peace—a man who knows how to speak to women."

"All this talk has no doubt gone on much too long for you, mistress," began Sir Erling contritely, but Kristin answered with a smile.

"It's true, sir, that I haven't understood everything that's been said here this evening, but I will remember it well, and I will have plenty of time to think about it later."

Orm came back with several maids who brought in more ale. The boy walked around, pouring for the men. Lavrans looked sorrowfully at the handsome child. He had tried to start up a conversation with Orm Erlendssøn, but he was a taciturn boy, although he had a striking and noble bearing.

One of the maids whispered to Kristin that Naakkve was awake over in the little house and crying terribly. Kristin then bid the men good night and followed the maids out when they left.

The men started drinking again. Sir Erling and Lavrans exchanged occasional glances, and then the former said, "There is something, Erlend, that I meant to discuss with you. A campaign force will certainly be summoned from the countryside here around the fjord and from Møre. People to the north are afraid that the Russians will return this summer, stronger than before, and they won't be able to handle their defense alone. This is the first benefit for which we can thank the royal union with Sweden—but it wouldn't be right for the people of Haalogaland[8] to profit from it alone. Now, things are such that Arne Gjavvaldssøn is too old and sickly—so there has been talk of making you chieftain of the farmers' ships from this side of the fjord. What would you think of that?"

Erlend pounded one fist into the palm of his other hand. His whole face glowed. "What I would think of it!"

"It's unlikely that a large contingent could be mustered," said Erling, admonishingly. "But perhaps you should find out what the sheriffs think. You're well known in this area—there has been talk among the men on the council that you were perhaps the man who could do something about this matter. There are those who still remember that you won more than a little honor when you were a guardsman for Earl Jacob. I myself recall hearing him say to King Haakon that he had acted unwisely when he dealt so harshly with a capable young man. He said you were destined to be a support to your king."

Erlend snapped his fingers. "You're not thinking of becoming our king, Erling Vidkunssøn! Is that what all of you are plotting?" he asked, laughing boisterously. "To make Erling king?"

Erling said impatiently, "No, Erlend. Can't you tell that now I was speaking in earnest?"

"God help me—were you joking before? I thought you were

speaking in earnest all evening. All right then, let's speak seriously. Tell me about this matter, kinsman."

Kristin was asleep with the child at her breast when Erlend came into the little house. He stuck a pine branch into the embers of the hearth and then let it shine on the two of them for a long time.

How beautiful she was. And he was a handsome child, their son. Kristin was always so sleepy in the evening now. As soon as she lay down and placed the boy close to her, they would both fall asleep. Erlend laughed a bit and tossed the twig back into the hearth. Slowly he undressed.

Northward in the spring with *Margygren* and three or four warships. Haftor Graut with three ships from Haalogaland. But Haftor had no experience; Erlend would be able to command him as he liked. Yes, he realized that he would have to take charge himself because this Haftor did not look either fearful or indecisive. Erlend stretched and smiled in the dark. He was thinking of finding a crew for *Margygren* outside of Møre. But there were plenty of bold and hearty boys both here in the parish and in Birgsi—he would be able to choose from the finest of men.

He had been married little more than a year. Childbirth, penance, and fasting. And now the boy, always the boy, night and day. And yet . . . she was still the same sweet, young Kristin, whenever he could make her forget the priest's words and the greedy suckling child for a brief time.

He kissed her shoulder, but she didn't notice. Poor thing—he would let her sleep. He had so much to think about tonight. Erlend turned away from her and lay staring across the room at the tiny glowing dot in the hearth. He ought to get up and cover the ashes, but he didn't feel like it.

In bits and pieces, memories from his youth came back to him. A quivering ship's prow that paused a scant moment, waiting for the approaching swell; then the sea washing over it. The mighty sound of the storm and the sea. The whole vessel shuddered under the press of the waves, the top of the mast cut a wild arc through the scudding clouds. It was somewhere off the coast of Halland. Overwhelmed, Erlend felt tears fill his eyes. He hadn't realized himself how much these years of idleness had tormented him.

* * *

The next morning Lavrans Bjørgulfsøn and Sir Erling Vidkunssøn were standing at the end of the courtyard, watching some of Erlend's horses that were running loose outside the fence.

"I think," said Lavrans, "that if Erlend is to come to this meeting, then he is of such high position and birth, being the kinsman of the king and his mother, that he must step forward to join the ranks of the foremost men. But I don't know, Sir Erling, whether you feel you can trust that his judgment in these matters won't lead him to the opposing side. If Ivar Ogmundssøn attempts to make a countermove . . . Erlend is also strongly tied to the men who will follow Sir Ivar."

"I think it unlikely that Sir Ivar will do anything," said Erling Vidkunssøn. "And Munan . . ." He gave a slight smile. "He's wise enough to stay away. He knows that otherwise it might become clear to everyone how much or how little influence Munan Baardsøn wields." They both laughed. "The truth is . . . Yes, no doubt you know better than I, Lavrans Lagmanssøn,[9] you who have your ancestors and kinsmen over there, that the Swedish nobles are reluctant to consider our knighthood equal to their own. For that reason it's important that we exclude no man who is among the richest and most highborn. We cannot afford to let a man like Erlend win permission to stay at home, jesting with his wife and tending to his estates—in whatever manner he tends to them," he said when he saw Lavrans's expression.

A smile flickered across Lavrans's face.

"But if you think it unwise to pressure Erlend in order to make him join us, then I will not do so."

"I think, dear sir," said Lavrans, "that Erlend would do more good here in the villages. As you said yourself—we can expect that this war levy will be met with opposition in the districts south of Namdalseid, where the people feel they have nothing to fear from the Russians. It's possible that Erlend might be the man who could change people's minds about these matters in some way."

"He has such a cursed loose tongue," Sir Erling exclaimed.

Lavrans replied with a small smile. "Perhaps that's the language that will appeal more to people than . . . the speech of more insightful men." Again they looked at each other and laughed. "However that may be, he could do more harm if he went to the meeting and spoke too loudly."

"Well, if you cannot restrain him, then . . ."

"No, I can do so only until he meets up with the kind of birds he's used to flying around with; my son-in-law and I are too unlike each other."

Erlend came over to them. "Have you benefited so much from the mass that you need no breakfast?"

"I haven't heard mention of breakfast—I'm as hungry as a wolf, and thirsty." Lavrans stroked a dirty-white horse that he had been examining. "Whoever the man is who tends to your horses, son-in-law, I would drive him off my estate before I sat down to eat, if he was *my* servant."

"I don't dare, because of Kristin," said Erlend. "He has gotten one of her maids with child."

"And do you deem it such a great achievement here in these parts," said Lavrans, raising his eyebrows, "that you now find him irreplaceable?"

"No, but you see," said Erlend, laughing, "Kristin and the priest want them to be married—and they want me to place the man in such a position that he'll be able to support the two of them. The girl refuses and her guardian refuses, and Tore himself is reluctant. But I'm not allowed to drive him off; she's afraid that then he would flee the village. But Ulf Haldorssøn is his overseer, when he's home."

Erling Vidkunssøn walked over toward Smid Gudleikssøn. Lavrans said to his son-in-law, "It seems to me that Kristin is looking a little pale these days."

"I know. Can't you talk to her, Father-in-law?" Erlend said eagerly. "That boy is sucking the marrow out of her. I think she wants to keep him at her breast until the third fast, like some kind of pauper's wife."

"Yes, she is certainly fond of her son," said Lavrans with a slight smile.

"I know." Erlend shook his head. "They can sit there for three hours—Kristin and Sira Eiliv—talking about a rash he has here or there; and for every tooth he gets, they seem to think a great miracle has occurred. I've never heard otherwise but that all children get teeth. And it would be more wondrous if our Naakkve should have none."

## CHAPTER 2

ONE EVENING A year later, toward the end of the Christmas holidays, Kristin Lavransdatter and Orm Erlendssøn arrived quite unexpectedly to visit Master Gunnulf at his residence in Nidaros.

The wind had raged and sleet had fallen all day long, since before noon, but now, late in the evening, the weather had grown worse until it was an actual snowstorm. The two visitors were completely covered in snow when they stepped into the room where the priest was sitting at the supper table with the rest of his household.

Gunnulf asked fearfully whether something was wrong back at the manor. But Kristin shook her head. Erlend was away on a visit in Gelmin, she said in reply to her brother-in-law's queries, but she was so weary that she hadn't felt like going with him.

The priest thought about how she had come all the way into town. The horses that she and Orm had ridden were exhausted; during the last part of the journey they had barely been able to struggle their way through the snowdrifts. Gunnulf sent his two servant women off with Kristin to find dry clothing for her. They were his foster mother and her sister—there were no other women at the priest's house. He attended to his nephew himself. And all the while, Orm talked steadily.

"I think Kristin is ill. I told Father, but he got angry."

She had been so unlike herself lately, said the boy. He didn't know what was wrong. He couldn't remember whether it was her idea or his for them to come here—oh yes, she had mentioned first that she had a great longing to go to Christ Church, and he had said that he would accompany her. So this morning, just as soon as his father had ridden off, Kristin told him she wanted to go today. Orm had agreed, even though the weather was threatening—but he didn't like the look in her eyes.

Gunnulf thought to himself that he didn't like it either, when Kristin returned to the room. She looked terribly thin in Ingrid's black dress; her face was as pale as bast and her eyes were sunken, with dark blue circles underneath. Her gaze was strange and dark.

It had been three months since he had last seen her, when he attended the christening at Husaby. She had looked good then as she lay in bed in her finery, and she said she felt well—the birth had been an easy one. So he had protested when Ragnfrid Ivarsdatter and Erlend wanted to give the child to a foster mother; Kristin cried and begged to be allowed to nurse Bjørgulf herself. The second son had been named after Lavrans's father.

Now the priest asked first about Bjørgulf; he knew that Kristin was not pleased with the wet nurse to whom they had given the child. But she said he was doing well and that Frida was fond of him and took better care of him than anyone had expected. And what about Nikulaus? asked her brother-in-law. Was he still so handsome? A little smile flitted across the mother's face. Naakkve grew more and more handsome every day. No, he didn't talk much, but otherwise he was ahead of his years in every way, and so big. No one would believe he was only in his second winter; even Fru Gunna said as much.

Then Kristin fell silent again. Master Gunnulf glanced at the two of them—his brother's wife and his brother's son—who were sitting on either side of him. They looked weary and sorrowful, and his heart felt uneasy as he gazed at them.

Orm had always seemed melancholy. The boy was now fifteen years old, and he would have been the most handsome of fellows if he hadn't looked so delicate and weak. He was almost as tall as his father, but his body was much too slender and narrow-shouldered. His face resembled Erlend's too, but his eyes were much darker blue, and his mouth, beneath the first downy black mustache, was even smaller and weaker, and it was always pressed tight with a sad little furrow at each corner. Even the back of Orm's thin, tan neck under his curly black hair looked oddly unhappy as he sat there eating, slightly hunched forward.

Kristin had never sat at table with her brother-in-law in his own house. Last year she had come to town with Erlend for the springtime *ting,* and they had stayed at this residence, which Gunnulf had inherited from his father; but at that time the priest was living on the estate of the Brothers of the Cross, substituting for one of the canons. Master Gunnulf was now the parish priest for Steine, but he had a chaplain to assist him while he oversaw the work of copying manuscripts for the churches of the archbishopric while the cantor,[1] Herr Eirik Finssøn, was ill. And during this time he lived in his own house.

The main hall was unlike any of the rooms Kristin was used to. It was a timbered building, but in the middle of the end wall, facing east, Gunnulf had had masons construct a large fireplace, like those he had seen in the countries of the south; a log fire burned between cast andirons. The table stood along one wall, and opposite were benches with writing desks. In front of a painting of the Virgin Mary burned a brass lamp, and nearby stood shelves of books.

This room seemed strange to her, and her brother-in-law seemed strange too, now that she saw him sitting at the table with members of his household—clerics and servant men who looked oddly priestlike. There were also several poor people: old men and a young boy with thin, reddish eyelids clinging like membranes to his empty eye sockets. On the women's bench next to the old housekeepers sat a young woman with a two-year-old child on her lap; she was hungrily gulping down the stew and stuffing her child's mouth so that his cheeks were about to burst.

It was the custom for all priests at Christ Church to give supper to the poor. But Kristin had heard that fewer beggars came to Gunnulf Nikulaussøn than to any of the other priests, and yet—or perhaps this was the very reason—he seated them on the benches next to him in the main hall and received every wanderer like an honored guest. They were served food from his own platter and ale from the priest's own barrels. The poor would come whenever they felt in need of a supper of stew, but otherwise they preferred to go to the other priests, where they were given porridge and weak ale in the cookhouse.

As soon as the scribe had finished the prayers after the meal, the poor guests wanted to leave. Gunnulf spoke gently to each of them, asking whether they would like to spend the night or whether they needed anything else; but only the blind boy remained. The priest implored in particular the young woman with the child to stay and not take the little one out into the night, but she murmured an excuse and hurried off. Then Gunnulf asked a servant to make sure that Blind Arnstein was given ale and a good bed in the guest room. He put on a hooded cape.

"You must be tired, Orm and Kristin, and want to go to bed. Audhild will take care of you. You'll probably be asleep when I return from the church."

Then Kristin asked to go with him. "That's why I've come here," she said, fixing her despairing eyes on Gunnulf. Ingrid lent her a dry cloak, and she and Orm joined the small procession departing from the parsonage.

The bells were ringing as if they were right overhead in the black night sky—it wasn't far to the church. They trudged through deep, wet, new snow. The weather was calm now, with a few snowflakes still drifting down here and there, shimmering faintly in the dark.

Dead tired, Kristin tried to lean against the pillar she was standing next to, but the stone was icy cold. She stood in the dark church and stared up at the candles in the choir. She couldn't see Gunnulf up there, but he was sitting among the priests, with a candle beside his book. No, she would not be able to speak to him, after all.

Tonight it seemed to her that there was no help to be found anywhere. Back home Sira Eiliv admonished her because she brooded so much over her everyday sins—he said this was the temptation of pride. She should simply be diligent with her prayers and good deeds, and then she wouldn't have time to dwell on such matters. "The Devil is no fool; he'll realize that he will lose your soul in the end, and he won't feel like tempting you as much."

She listened to the antiphony and remembered the nuns' church in Oslo. There she had raised her poor little voice with others in the hymn of praise—and down in the nave stood Erlend, wrapped in a cape up to his chin, and the two of them thought only of finding a chance to speak to each other in secret.

And she had thought that this heathen and burning love was not so terrible a sin. They couldn't help themselves—and they were both unmarried. It was at most a transgression against the laws of men. Erlend wanted to escape from a terrible life of sin, and she imagined that he would have greater strength to free himself from the old burden if she put her life and her honor and her happiness into his hands.

The last time she knelt here in this church she had fully realized that when she said such things in her heart she had been trying to deceive God with tricks and lies. It was not because of their virtue but because of their good fortune that there were still commandments they had not broken, sins they had not committed. If she had been another man's wife when she met Erlend . . . she would not have been any more sparing of his salvation or his honor than she was of the man she had so mercilessly spurned. It seemed to her now that there was nothing that wouldn't have tempted her back then, in her ardor and despair. She had felt her passion temper her will until it was sharp and hard like a knife, ready to cut through all bonds—those of kinship, Christianity, and honor. There was nothing inside her except the burning hunger to see him, to be near him, to open her lips to his hot mouth and her arms to the deadly sweet desire which he had taught her.

Oh, no. The Devil was probably not so convinced that he was going to lose her soul. But when she lay here before, crushed with sorrow over her sins, over the hardness of her heart, her impure life, and the blindness of her soul . . . then she had felt the saintly king take her in under his protective cloak. She had gripped his strong, warm hand; he had pointed out to her the light that is the source of all strength and holiness. Saint Olav turned her eyes toward Christ on the cross—see, Kristin: God's love. Yes, she had begun to understand God's love and patience. But she had turned away from the light again and closed her heart to it, and now there was nothing in her mind but impatience and anger and fear.

How wretched, wretched she was. Even she had realized that a woman like herself would need harsh trials before she could be cured of her lack of love. And yet she was so impatient that she felt her heart would break with the sorrows that had been imposed on her. They were small sorrows, but there were many of them, and she had so little patience. She glanced at her stepson's tall, slender figure over on the men's side of the church.

She couldn't help it. She loved Orm as if he were her own child; but it was impossible for her to be fond of Margret. She had tried and tried and even commanded herself to like the child, ever since that day last winter when Ulf Haldorssøn brought her home to Husaby. She thought it was dreadful; how could she feel such ill will and anger toward a little maiden only nine years old? And she knew full well that part of it was because the child looked so fearfully like her mother Eline. She couldn't understand Erlend; he was simply proud that his little golden-haired daughter with the brown eyes was so pretty. The child never seemed to arouse any bad memories in the father. It was as if Erlend had completely forgotten the mother of these children. But it wasn't *only* because Margret resembled the other woman that Kristin lacked affection for her stepdaughter. Margret would not tolerate anyone instructing her; she was arrogant and treated the servants badly. She was dishonest too, and she fawned over her father. She didn't love him the way Orm did; she would snuggle up to Erlend with affection and caresses only because she wanted something. And Erlend showered her with gifts and gave in to the maiden's every whim. Orm wasn't fond of his sister, either—that much Kristin had noticed.

Kristin suffered because she felt so harsh and mean since she couldn't watch Margret's behavior without feeling indignant and censorious. But she suffered even more from observing and listening to the constant discord between Erlend and his eldest son. She suffered most of all because she realized that Erlend, deep in his heart, felt a boundless love for the boy—and he treated Orm unjustly and with severity because he had no idea what to do with his son or how he might secure his future. He had given his bastard children property and livestock, but it seemed unthinkable that Orm would ever be fit to be a farmer. And Erlend grew desperate when he saw how frail and weak Orm was; then he would call his son rotten and rage at him to harden himself. He would spend hours with his son, training him in the use of heavy weapons that the boy couldn't possibly handle, urging him to drink himself sick in the evenings, and practically breaking the boy on dangerous and exhausting hunting expeditions. In spite of all this, Kristin saw the fear in Erlend's soul; she realized that he was often wild with sorrow because this fine and handsome son of his was suited for only one position in life—and there his birth stood in the way. And Kristin had come to understand how little patience Erlend possessed whenever he felt concern or compassion for someone he loved.

She saw that Orm realized this too. And she saw that the young boy's soul was split: Orm felt love and pride for his father, but also contempt for Erlend's unfairness when he allowed his child to suffer because he was faced with worries which he himself, and not the boy, had caused. But Orm had grown close to his young stepmother; with her he seemed to breathe easier and feel freer. When he was alone with her, he was able to banter and laugh, in his own quiet way. But Erlend was not pleased by this; he seemed to suspect that the two of them were sitting in judgment of his conduct.

Oh, no, it wasn't easy for Erlend; and it wasn't so strange that he was sensitive when it came to those two children. And yet . . .

She still trembled with pain whenever she thought about it.

The manor had been filled with guests the week before. When Margret came home, Erlend had furnished the loft which was at the far end of the hall, above the next room and the entry hall—it was to be her bower, he said. And there she slept with the servant girl whom Erlend had ordered to keep watch over and serve the maiden. Frida also slept there along with Bjørgulf. But since they had so many Christmas guests, Kristin had made up beds for the young men in this loft room; the two maids and the infant were to sleep in the servant women's house. But because she thought Erlend might not like it if she sent Margret off to sleep with the servants, she had made up a bed for her on one of the benches in the hall, where the women and maidens were sleeping. It was always difficult to get Margret up in the morning. On that morning Kristin had woken her many times, but she had lain back down, and she was still asleep after everyone else was up. Kristin wanted to clean the hall and put things in order; the guests must be given breakfast—and so she lost all patience. She yanked the pillows from under Margret's head and tore off the covers. But when she saw the child lying there naked on the sheet made of hides, she took her own cloak from her shoulders and placed it over Margret. It was a garment made from plain, undyed homespun; she only wore it when she went back and forth to the cookhouse and the storerooms, tending to the food preparation.

At that moment Erlend came into the room. He had been sleeping in a chamber above a storeroom with several other men, since Fru Gunna was sharing Kristin's bed. And he flew into a rage. He grabbed Kristin by the arm so hard that the marks from his fingers were still on her skin.

"Do you think my daughter should be lying on straw and homespun cloth? Margit is mine, even though she may not be yours. What's not good enough for your own children is good enough for her. But since you've mocked the innocent little maiden in the sight of these women, then you must rectify matters before their eyes. Put back the covers that you took from Margit."

It so happened that Erlend had been drunk the night before, and he was always bad-tempered the following day. And no doubt he thought the women must have been gossiping among themselves when they saw Eline's children. And he grew sensitive and testy about their reputation. And yet . . .

Kristin had tried to talk to Sira Eiliv about it. But he couldn't help her with this matter. Gunnulf had told her that she need not mention the sins to which she had confessed and repented before Eiliv Serkssøn became her parish priest unless she thought that he should know about them in order to judge and advise her. So there were many things she had never told him, even though she felt that by not doing so she would seem, in Sira Eiliv's eyes, to be a better person than she was. But it was so good for her to have the friendship of this kind and pure-hearted man. Erlend made fun of her, but she gained such comfort from Sira Eiliv. With him she could talk as much as she liked about her children; the priest was willing to discuss with her all the small bits of news that bored Erlend and drove him from the room. The priest got on well with children, and he understood their small troubles and illnesses. Erlend laughed at Kristin when she went to the cookhouse herself to prepare special dishes, which she would send over to the parsonage. Sira Eiliv was fond of good food and drink, and it amused Kristin to spend time on such matters and to try out what she had learned from her mother or seen at the convent. Erlend didn't care what he ate as long as he was always served meat if it wasn't a time for fasting. But Sira Eiliv would come over to talk and thank her, praising her skill after she had sent him grouse on a spit, wrapped in the best bacon, or a platter of reindeer tongues in French wine and honey. And he gave her advice about her garden, obtaining cuttings for her from Tautra, where his brother was a monk, and from the Olav monastery, whose prior was a good friend of his. And he also read to her and could recount so many wonderful things about life out in the world.

But because he was such a good and pious man, it was often difficult to speak to him about the evil she saw in her own heart. When she confessed to him how embittered she felt at Erlend's behavior that day with Margret, he had impressed upon her that she must bear with her husband. But he seemed to think that Erlend alone had committed an offense when he spoke so unjustly to his wife—and in the presence of strangers. Kristin doubtless agreed with him. And yet deep in her heart she felt a complicity which she could not explain and which caused her great pain.

Kristin looked up at the holy shrine, which glittered a dull gold in the dim light behind the high altar. She had been so certain that if she stood here again, something would happen—a redemption of her soul. Once more a living fount would surge up into her heart and wash away all the anguish and fear and bitterness and confusion that filled her.

But no one had any patience for her tonight. Haven't you learned yet, Kristin—to lift your self-righteousness to the light of God's righteousness, your heathen and selfish passion to the light of love? Perhaps you do not *want* to learn it, Kristin.

But the last time she knelt here she had held Naakkve in her arms. His little mouth at her breast warmed her heart so well that it was like soft wax, easy for the heavenly love to shape. And she *did* have Naakkve; he was playing back home in the hall, so lovely and sweet that her breast ached at the mere thought of him. His soft, curly hair was now turning dark—he was going to have black hair like his father. And he was so full of life and mischief. She made animals for him out of old furs, and he would throw them into the air and then chase after them, racing with the young dogs. And it usually ended with the fur bear falling into the hearth fire and burning up, with smoke and a foul smell. Naakkve would howl, hopping up and down and stomping, and then he would bury his head in his mother's lap—that's where all of his adventures still ended. The maids fought for his favor; the men would pick him up and toss him up to the ceiling whenever they came into the room. If the boy saw Ulf Haldorssøn, he would run over and cling to the man's leg. Ulf sometimes took him along out to the farmyard. Erlend would snap his fingers at his son and set him on his shoulder for a moment, but he was the one person at Husaby who paid the least attention to the boy. And yet he *was* fond of Naakkve. Erlend *was* glad that he now had two lawfully born sons.

Kristin's heart clenched tight.

They had taken Bjørgulf away from her. He whimpered whenever she tried to hold him, and Frida would put him to her own breast at once. His foster mother kept a jealous watch over the boy. But Kristin would refuse to let the new child go. Her mother and Erlend had said that she should be spared, and so they took her newborn son away and gave him to another woman. She felt an almost vengeful joy when she thought that their only accomplishment was that she would now be having a third child before Bjørgulf was even eleven months old.

She didn't dare speak of this to Sira Eiliv. He would merely think that she was resentful because now she would have to go through all of that again so soon. But that wasn't it.

She had come home from her pilgrimage with a deep dread in her soul—never would that wild desire have power over her again. Until the end of summer she lived alone with her child in the old house, weighing in her mind the words of the archbishop and Gunnulf's speech, vigilantly praying and repenting, diligently working to put the neglected farm in order, to win over her servants with kindness and concern for their welfare, eager to help and serve all those around her as far as her hands and her power might reach. A cool and wondrous peace descended upon her. She sustained herself with thoughts of her father, she sustained herself with prayers to the holy men and women Sira Eiliv read to her about, and she pondered their steadfastness and courage. And tender with joy and gratitude, she remembered Brother Edvin, who had appeared before her in the moonlight on that night. She had understood his message when he smiled so gently and hung his glove on the moonbeam. If only she had enough faith, she would become a good woman.

When their first year of marriage came to an end, she had to move back in with her husband. Whenever she felt doubtful, she would console herself that the archbishop himself had impressed upon her that in her life with her husband she should show her new change of heart. And she strove zealously to tend to his welfare and his honor. Erlend himself had said: "And so it has happened after all, Kristin—you have brought honor back to Husaby." People showed her great kindness and respect; everyone seemed willing to forget that she had begun her marriage a little impetuously. Whenever the women gathered, they would seek out her advice; people praised her housekeeping at the manor, she was summoned to assist with weddings and with births on the great estates, and no one made her feel that she was too young or inexperienced or a newcomer to the region. The servants would remain sitting in the hall until late into the evening, just as they did back home at Jørundgaard—they all had something to ask their mistress about. She felt a rush of exhilaration that people were so kind to her and that Erlend was proud of her.

Then Erlend took charge of the men called up for duty on the ships south of the fjord. He dashed around, riding or sailing, and he was busy with people who came to see him and letters that had to be sent. He was so young and handsome, and so happy—the listless, dejected look that she had often seen come over him in the past seemed to have been swept away. He sparkled with alertness, like the morning. He had little time left over for her now; but she grew dizzy and wild whenever he came near her with his smiling face and those adventure-loving eyes.

She had laughed with him at the letter that had come from Munan Baardsøn. The knight had not attended the gathering of the king's retainers himself, but he ridiculed the entire meeting and especially the fact that Erling Vidkunssøn had been appointed leader of the realm. But first Erling had probably given himself new titles—no doubt he would want to be called regent now. Munan also wrote about her father:

> The mountain wolf from Sil crept under a rock and sat there mutely. I mean that your father-in-law took lodgings with the priests at Saint Laurentius Church and did not let his fair voice be heard at the discussions. He had in his possession letters bearing the seals of Sir Erngisle and Sir Karl Turessön; if they haven't yet been worn out it's because the

parchment was tougher than the soles of Satan's shoes. You should also know that Lavrans gave eight marks of pure silver to Nonneseter. Apparently the man realized that Kristin was not as docile when she was there as she should have been.

Kristin felt a stab of pain and shame at this, but she had to laugh along with Erlend. For her the winter and spring had passed in exhilarating merriment and happiness, with now and then a squall for Orm's sake—Erlend couldn't decide whether he should take the boy north with him. It ended with an outburst during Easter. One night Erlend wept in her arms: he didn't dare take his son on board for fear that Orm wouldn't be able to hold his own during a war. She had comforted him and herself—and the youth. Perhaps the boy would grow stronger over the years.

On the day she rode with Erlend to the anchorage at Birgsi, she couldn't feel either fearful or sad. She was almost intoxicated with him and with his joy and high spirits.

At that time she didn't know she was already carrying another child. When she felt unwell she had thought . . . Erlend was so exuberant, there had been so much commotion and drinking at home, and Naakkve was sucking the strength out of her. When she felt the new life stir inside her, she was . . . She had been looking forward to the winter, to traveling to town and around the valley with her bold and handsome husband; she was young and beautiful herself. She had planned to wean the boy by autumn; it was troublesome always having to take him and the nursemaid along wherever she went. She was certain that in this Russian campaign Erlend would prove fit for something other than ruining his name and his property. No, she had not been glad, and she told this to Sira Eiliv. Then the priest had reprimanded her quite sternly for her unloving and worldly disposition. And all summer long she had tried to be happy and to thank God for the new child she was to have, and for the good reports she heard about Erlend's courageous actions in the north.

Then he returned home just before Michaelmas. And she saw that he was not pleased when he realized what was to come. He said as much that evening.

"I thought that when I finally had you, it would be like celebrating Christmas every day. But now it seems that there will be mostly long periods of fasting."

Every time she thought about this, the blood would rush to her face, just as hot as on that evening when she turned away from him, flushing deep red and shedding no tears. Erlend had tried to make amends with love and kindness. But she couldn't forget it. The fire inside her, which all her tears of remorse had been unable to extinguish and all her fear of sin could not smother—it was as if Erlend had stomped it out with his foot when he said those words.

Late that night they sat in front of the fireplace in Gunnulf's house—the priest and Kristin and Orm. A jug of wine and a few small goblets stood at the edge of the hearth. Master Gunnulf had suggested several times that his guests ought to seek rest. But Kristin begged to stay sitting there a little longer.

"Do you remember, brother-in-law," she said, "that I once told you that the priest back home at Jørundgaard counseled me to enter a cloister if Father would not give his consent for Erlend to marry me?"

Gunnulf glanced involuntarily at Orm. But Kristin said with a wry little smile, "Do you think this grown-up boy doesn't know that I'm a weak and sinful woman?"

Master Gunnulf replied softly, "Did you feel a yearning for the life of a nun back then, Kristin?"

"No doubt God would have opened my eyes once I had decided to serve Him."

"Perhaps He thought that your eyes needed to be opened so you would learn that you ought to serve Him wherever you are. Your husband, children, and the servants at Husaby need to have a faithful and patient servant woman of God living among them and tending to their welfare.

"Of course the maiden who makes the best marriage is the one who chooses Christ as her bridegroom and refuses to give herself to a sinful man. But the child who has already done wrong . . ."

" 'I wish that you could have come to God with your wreath,' " whispered Kristin. "That's what he said to me, Brother Edvin Rikardssøn, the monk I've often told you about. Do you feel the same way?"

Gunnulf Nikulaussøn nodded. "And yet many a woman has

pulled herself up from a life of sin with such strength that we dare pray for her intercession. But this happened more often in the past, when she was threatened with torture and fire and glowing tongs if she called herself a Christian. I have often thought, Kristin, that back then it was easier to tear oneself away from the bonds of sin, when it could be done forcefully and all at once. And yet we humans are so corrupt—but courage is by nature present in the heart of many, and courage is what often drives a soul to seek God. The torments have incited just as many people to faithfulness as they have frightened others into apostasy. But a young, lost child who is torn from sinful desire even before she has learned to understand what it has brought upon her soul—a child placed in an order of nuns among pure maidens who have given themselves up to watch over and pray for those who are asleep out in the world . . .

"I wish it would soon be summer," he said suddenly and stood up.

The other two looked at him in amazement.

"Oh, I happened to think about when the cuckoo was singing on the slopes in the morning back home at Husaby. First we would hear the one on the ridge to the east, behind the buildings, and then the other would reply from far off, in the woods close to By. It sounded so lovely out across the lake in the stillness of the morning. Don't you think it's beautiful at Husaby, Kristin?"

"The cuckoo in the east is the cuckoo of sorrow," said Orm Erlendssøn quietly. "Husaby seems to me the fairest manor in the world."

The priest placed his hands on his nephew's narrow shoulders for a moment.

"I thought so too, kinsman. It was my father's estate for me too. The youngest son stands no closer to inheriting the ancestral farm than you do, dear Orm!"

"When Father was living with my mother, you were the closest heir," said the young boy in the same quiet voice.

"We're not to blame, Orm—my children and I," said Kristin sorrowfully.

"You must have noticed that I bear you no rancor," he replied softly.

"It's such an open, wide landscape," said Kristin after a moment. "You can see so far from Husaby, and the sky is so . . . so vast. Where I come from, the sky is like a roof above the mountain slopes. The valley lies sheltered, round and green and fresh. The world seems just the right size—neither too big nor too small." She sighed and her hands began fidgeting in her lap.

"Was his home there—the man your father wanted you to marry?" asked the priest, and Kristin nodded.

"Do you ever regret that you refused to have him?" he then asked, and she shook her head.

Gunnulf went over and pulled a book from the shelf. He sat down near the fire again, opened the clasps, and began turning the pages. But he didn't read; he sat with the open book on his lap.

"When Adam and his wife had defied God's will, then they felt in their own flesh a power that defied *their* will. God had created them, man and woman, young and beautiful, so that they would live together in marriage and give birth to other heirs who would receive the gifts of His goodness: the beauty of the Garden of Eden, the fruit of the tree of life, and eternal happiness. They didn't need to be ashamed of their bodies because as long as they were obedient to God, their whole body and all of their limbs were under the command of their will, just as a hand or a foot is."

Blushing blood-red, Kristin folded her hands under her breast. The priest bent toward her slightly; she felt his strong amber eyes on her lowered face.

"Eve stole what belonged to God, and her husband accepted it when she gave him what rightfully was the property of their Father and Creator. They wanted to be His equal—and they noticed that the first way in which they became His equal was this: Just as they had betrayed His dominion over the great world, so too was their dominion betrayed over the small world, the soul's house of flesh. Just as they had forsaken their Lord God, the body would now forsake its master, the soul.

"Then these bodies seemed to them so hideous and hateful that they made clothes to cover them. First a short apron of fig leaves. But as they became more and more familiar with their own carnal nature, they drew the clothes up over their heart and their back, which is unwilling to bend. Until today, when men dress themselves in steel all the way to their fingertips and toes and hide their faces behind the grids of their helmets. In this way unrest and deceit have grown in the world."

"Help me, Gunnulf," begged Kristin. She was white to the very edge of her lips. "I don't know my own will."

"Then say: Thy will be done," replied the priest softly. "You know you must open your heart to His love. Then you must love Him once more with all the power of your soul."

Kristin abruptly turned to face her brother-in-law.

"You can't know how much I loved Erlend. And my children!"

"Dear sister—all other love is merely a reflection of the heavens in the puddles of a muddy road. You will become sullied too if you allow yourself to sink into it. But if you always remember that it's a reflection of the light from that other home, then you will rejoice at its beauty and take good care that you do not destroy it by churning up the mire at the bottom."

"Yes, but as a priest, Gunnulf, you have promised God that you would shun these . . . difficulties."

"As you have too, Kristin—when you promised to forsake the Devil and his work. The Devil's work is what begins in sweet desire and ends with two people becoming like the snake and the toad, snapping at each other. That's what Eve learned, when she tried to give her husband and her descendants what belonged to God. She brought them nothing but banishment and the shame of blood and death, which entered the world when brother killed brother in that first small field, where thorns and thistles grew among the heaps of stones around the patches of land."

"Yes, but you're a priest," she said in the same tone of voice. "You're not subjected to the daily trial of trying to agree patiently with the will of another." And she broke into tears.

The priest said with a little smile, "About that matter there is disagreement between body and soul in every mother's child. That's why marriage and the wedding mass were created—so that man and woman would be given help in their lives: married folk and parents and children and house servants as loyal and helpful companions on the journey toward the house of peace."

Kristin said quietly, "It seems to me that it would be easier to watch over and pray for those who are asleep out in the world than to struggle with one's own sins."

"That may be," said the priest sharply. "But you mustn't believe, Kristin, that there has ever been a priest who has not had to guard himself against the Fiend at the same time as he tried to protect the lambs from the wolf."

Kristin said in a quiet and timid voice, "I thought that those who live among the holy shrines and possess all the prayers and powerful words . . ."

Gunnulf leaned forward, tended to the fire, and then sat with his elbows on his knees.

"It was almost exactly six years ago that we arrived in Rome, Eiliv and I, along with two Scottish priests whom we had met in Avignon. We journeyed the whole way on foot.

"We arrived in the city just before Lent. That's when people in the southern countries hold great celebrations and feasts—they call it *carnevale*. The wine, both red and white, flows in rivers from the taverns, and people dance late into the night, and there are torches and bonfires in the open marketplaces. It is springtime in Italy then, and the flowers are blooming in the meadows and gardens. The women adorn themselves with blossoms and toss roses and violets down to the people strolling along the streets. They sit up in the windows, with silk and satin tapestries hanging from the ledge over the stone walls. All buildings are made from stone down there, and the knights have their castles and strongholds in the middle of town. There are apparently no town statutes or laws about keeping the peace in the city—the knights and their men fight in the streets, making the blood run.

"There was such a castle on the street where we were staying, and the knight who ruled it was named Ermes Malavolti. Its shadow stretched over the entire narrow lane where our hostel stood, and our room was as dark and cold as the dungeon in a stone fortress. When we went out we often had to press ourselves up against the wall as he rode past with silver bells on his clothing and a whole troop of armed men. Muck and filth would splash up from the horses' hooves, because in that country people simply throw all their slops and offal outdoors. The streets are cold and dark and narrow like clefts in a mountain—quite unlike the green lanes of our towns. In the streets during *carnevale* they hold races—they let the wild Arabian horses race against each other."

The priest sat in silence for a moment, then he continued.

"This Sir Ermes had a kinswoman living at his house. Isota was her name, and she might have been Isolde the Fair One herself.

Her complexion and hair were as light as honey, but her eyes were no doubt black. I saw her several times at a window. . . .

"But outside the city the land is more desolate than the most desolate heaths in this country, and nothing lives there but deer and wolves; and the eagles scream. And yet there are towns and castles in the mountains all around, and out on the green plains you can see traces everywhere that people once lived in this world. Great flocks of sheep graze there now, along with herds of white oxen. Herdsmen with long spears follow them on horseback; they are dangerous folk for wayfarers to meet, for they will kill and rob them and throw their bodies into pits in the ground.

"But out on these green plains are the pilgrim churches."

Master Gunnulf paused for a moment.

"Perhaps this land seems so inexpressibly desolate because the city is nearby—the one that was the queen of the entire heathen world and then became Christ's betrothed. The guards have abandoned the city, which in the teeming din of the feasting seems like an abandoned woman. The revelers have settled into the castle where the husband is absent, and they have lured the mistress into joining their carousing, with their merriment and spilling of blood and strife.

"But underground there are splendors that are more precious than all the splendors on which the sun shines. That's where the graves of the holy martyrs are, dug into the very rock, and there are so many that the thought of them can make you dizzy. When you remember how numerous they are—the tortured witnesses who have suffered death for the sake of Christ—then it seems as if every speck of dust that is whirled up by the hooves of the revelers' horses must be holy and worthy of worship."

The priest pulled out a thin chain from under his robe and opened the little silver cross hanging from it. Inside was something black that looked like tinder-moss, and a tiny green bone.

"One day we were down in those catacombs all day long, and we said our prayers in caves and oratories where the first disciples of Saint Peter and Saint Paul once gathered for mass. Then the monks who owned the church into which we had descended gave us these sacred relics. This is a piece of the sponge which the pious maidens used to wipe up the martyr blood so that it would not be lost, and this is a knuckle from the finger of a holy man—but only

God knows his name. Then all four of us vowed that every day we would invoke this holy man, whose honor is unknown to any human. And we chose this nameless martyr as a witness so that we might never forget how completely unworthy we are of God's reward or the honors of men, and always remember that nothing in this world is worthy of desire except His mercy."

Kristin kissed the cross with deference and handed it to Orm, who did the same.

Then Gunnulf said suddenly, "I want to give you this relic, kinsman."

Orm sank down on one knee and kissed his uncle's hand. Gunnulf hung the cross around the boy's neck.

"Wouldn't you have a mind to see these places, Orm?"

The boy's face lit up with a smile. "Yes, I now know that someday I will go there."

"Have you ever had a mind to become a priest?" asked his uncle.

"Yes," replied the boy. "Whenever Father curses these weak arms of mine. But I don't know whether he would like me to be a priest. And then there's that other matter, as you know," he murmured.

"Dispensation can be sought for your birth," said the priest calmly. "Perhaps we might journey south together sometime, Orm, you and I."

"Tell me more, Uncle," Orm implored.

"That I will." Gunnulf put his hands on the armrests of his chair and stared into the fire.

"As I wandered there, seeing nothing but reminders of the tortured witnesses and thinking of the intolerable torments they had borne in the name of Jesus, a terrible temptation came over me. I thought about the way the Savior had hung nailed to the cross all those hours. But his disciples had suffered inexpressible torments for many days. Women watched their children tortured to death before their very eyes; delicate young maidens had their flesh raked from their bones with iron combs; young boys were forced to confront beasts of prey and enraged oxen. Then it occurred to me that many of these people had suffered more than Christ himself.

"I pondered this until I felt that my heart and mind would burst. But finally I received the light that I had prayed and begged for. And I realized that just as they had suffered, so should we all have the courage to suffer. Who would be so foolish not to accept pain and torment if this was the way to a faithful and steadfast bridegroom who waits with open arms, his breast bloody and burning with love.

"But he loved humankind. And that's why he died as the bridegroom who has gone off to rescue his bride from the robbers' hands. And they bind him and torture him to death, but he sees his sweetest friend sitting at the table with his executioners, bantering with them and mocking his pain and his loyal love."

Gunnulf Nikulaussøn hid his face in his hands.

"Then I realized that this mighty love sustains everything in the world—even the fire in Hell. For if God wanted to, He could take our souls by force; then we would be completely powerless in His grasp. But since He loves us the way the bridegroom loves the bride, He will not force her; if she won't embrace Him willingly, then He must allow her to flee and to shun Him. I have also thought that perhaps no soul is lost for all eternity. For I think every soul must desire this love, but it seems too dearly bought to let go of every other precious possession for the sake of this love alone. When the fire has consumed all other will that is rebellious and hostile to God, then at last the will toward God, even if it was no bigger in a person than one nail in a whole house, shall remain inside the soul, just as the iron remains in a burned-out ruin."

"Gunnulf—" Kristin rose halfway to her feet. "I'm afraid."

Gunnulf looked up, pale, with blazing eyes.

"I was also afraid. For I understood that the torment of God's love will never end as long as men and maidens are born on this earth, and that He must be afraid of losing their souls—as long as He daily and hourly surrenders his body and his blood on thousands of altars and there are those who reject the sacrifice.

"And I was afraid of myself because I, an impure man, had served at his altar, said mass with impure lips, and held up the Host with impure hands. And I felt that I was like the man who led his beloved to a place of shame and betrayed her."

He caught Kristin in his arms when she fainted, and he and Orm carried the unconscious woman over to the bed.

After a while she opened her eyes; she sat up and covered her face with her hands. She burst into tears and uttered a wild and plaintive cry, "I can't, Gunnulf, I can't—when you talk like that, then I realize that I can never . . ."

Gunnulf took her hand. But she turned away from the man's pale and agitated face.

"Kristin. You cannot settle for anything less than the love that is between God and the soul.

"Kristin, look around at what the world is like. You who have given birth to two children—have you never thought about the fact that every child who is born is baptized in blood, and the first thing a person breathes on this earth is the smell of blood? Don't you think that as their mother you should put all your effort into one thing? To ensure that your sons do not fall back on that first baptismal pact with the world but instead hold on to the other pact, which they affirmed with God at the baptismal font."

She sobbed and sobbed.

"I'm afraid of you," she said again. "Gunnulf, when you talk like that, then I realize I'll never be able to find my way to peace."

"God will find you," said the priest quietly. "Stay calm and do not flee from Him who has been seeking you before you even existed in your mother's womb."

He sat in silence for a moment near the edge of the bed. Then he asked calmly and evenly whether he should wake Ingrid and ask the woman to come and help her undress. Kristin shook her head.

He made the sign of the cross over her three times. He bade Orm good night and went into the alcove where he slept.

Orm and Kristin undressed. The boy seemed deeply absorbed in his own thoughts. After Kristin was in bed, he came over to her. He looked at her tear-stained face and asked whether he should sit with her until she fell asleep.

"Oh, yes . . . oh, no, Orm, you must be tired, you who are so young. It must be very late."

Orm stood there a little longer.

"Don't you think it's strange," he said suddenly. "Father and Uncle Gunnulf—they're so unlike each other—and yet they're alike in a certain way."

Kristin lay there, thinking to herself, Yes, perhaps. They're unlike any other men.

A moment later she was asleep, and Orm went over to the other bed. He took off the rest of his clothes and crept under the covers. There was a linen sheet underneath and linen cases on the pillows. With pleasure the boy stretched out on the smooth, cool bed. His heart was pounding with excitement at these new adventures which his uncle's words had pointed out to him. Prayers, fasts, everything he had practiced because he had been taught to do so, suddenly seemed new to him—weapons in a glorious war for which he longed. Perhaps he would become a monk—or a priest—if he could obtain dispensation because he had been born of adultery.

Gunnulf's bed was a wooden bench with a sheet made from a hide spread over a little straw and a single, small pillow; he had to stretch himself out full length to sleep. The priest took off his surcoat, lay down wearing his undergarments, and pulled the thin homespun blanket over himself.

He left the little candlewick burning that was twined around an iron stake.

His own words had oppressed him with fear and uneasiness.

He felt faint with longing for that time—would he ever again find that nuptial joy in his heart that had filled him all spring long in Rome? Together with his three brothers he had wandered in the sunshine across the green, flower-starred meadows. He grew weak and trembled when he saw how beautiful the world was—and then to know that all of this was nothing compared to the riches of that other life. And yet this world greeted them with a thousand small joys and sweet reminders of the bridegroom. The lilies in the field and the birds in the sky reminded them of his words; he had spoken of donkeys like the ones they saw and of wells like the stone-lined cisterns they passed. They received food from the monks at the churches they visited, and when they drank the blood-red wine and broke off the golden crust from the bread made of wheat, all four priests from the barley lands understood why Christ had honored wine and wheat, which were purer than all other foodstuffs that God had given humankind, by manifesting himself in their likeness during the holy communion.

During that spring he had not felt any uneasiness or fear. He had felt himself released from the temptations of the world to such an extent that when he sensed the warm sun on his skin, then everything he had pondered before with such anguish seemed so easy to comprehend. How this body of his could be cleansed by fire to become the transfigured form . . . Feeling light and released from the demands of the earth, he needed no more sleep than the cuckoo, dozing in the spring nights. His heart sang in his breast; his soul felt like a bride in the arms of the bridegroom.

He realized full well that this would not last. No man could live on earth in this manner for long. And he had received each hour of that bright springtime like a pledge—a merciful promise that would strengthen his endurance when the skies darkened over him and the road led down into a dark ravine, through roaring rivers and cold snowdrifts.

But it wasn't until he returned to Norway that the uneasiness seized hold of his mind.

There were so many things. There was his wealth. The great inheritance from his father—and the richly endowed benefice.[2] There was the path he envisioned before him. His place in the cathedral chapter; he knew it was intended for him—provided he didn't renounce everything he owned, enter the friars' order, take the vows of a monk, and submit to their rules. That was the life he desired—with half his heart.

And then when he grew old enough and hardened enough in the battle . . . In the kingdom of Norway there were people who lived like utter heathens or were led astray by the false teachings which the Russians put forward in the name of Christianity—the Finns and the other half-wild peoples,[3] who were constantly on his mind. Wasn't it God who had awakened in him this desire to journey to their villages, bringing the Word and the Light?

But he pushed aside these thoughts with the excuse that he had to obey the archbishop. And Lord Eiliv counseled him against it. Lord Eiliv had talked to him and listened to him and shown him clearly that he was speaking to the son of his old friend, Sir Nikulaus of Husaby. "But you are not capable of moderation, you who are descended from the daughters of Skogheims-Gaute, whether it be good or bad, whatever you have set your mind to." The salvation of the Finns weighed heavily on the archbishop's heart as well—but they had no need of a spiritual teacher who wrote and spoke Latin as well as his own language, who was no less knowledgeable about the law than about *Aritmetica* and *Algorismus*. Gunnulf had acquired his learning in order to use it, hadn't he? "But it is unclear to me whether you have the gift to talk with the poor and simple people up there in the north."

Oh, that sweet spring when his learning seemed to him no more venerable than the learning that every little maiden acquires from her mother—how to spin and brew and bake and milk—the training that every child needs to tend to his place in the world.

He had complained to the archbishop about the uneasiness and fear that came over him whenever he thought about his riches and how much he enjoyed being wealthy. For the needs of his own body he required little; he himself lived like a poor monk. But he liked to see many people sitting at his table; he liked to forestall the needs of the poor with his gifts. And he loved his horses and his books.

Lord Eiliv spoke somberly about the honors of the Church. Some were called to honor it with a stately and dignified demeanor, while others were called to show the world a voluntary poverty; wealth was nothing in itself. He reminded Gunnulf of those archbishops and prelates and priests who had been forced to suffer attacks, banishment, and offenses by kings in the past because they asserted the right of the Church. Time after time they had shown that if it was required of Norwegian clergymen, they would renounce everything to follow God. And God Himself would give the sign if it should be required—if only they all kept this firmly in sight, then they need not be afraid that wealth might become an enemy of the soul.

All this time Gunnulf noticed that the archbishop was not pleased that he thought and pondered so much on his own. It seemed to Gunnulf that Lord Eiliv Kortin and his priests were like men who were adding more and more bricks to their house. The honor of the Church and the power of the Church and the right of the Church. God knew that Gunnulf could be just as zealous as any other priest about matters of the Church; he was not one to avoid the work of hauling stones or carrying mortar for the building. But they seemed to be afraid of entering the house and resting inside. They seemed to be afraid of going astray if they thought too much.

That was not what *he* feared. It was impossible for a man to succumb to heresy if he kept his eye steadfastly fixed on the cross and unceasingly surrendered himself to the protection of the Holy Virgin. That was not the danger for him.

The danger was the unquenchable longing in his soul to win the favor and friendship of others.

He who had felt in the depths of his being that God loved him; to God his soul was as dear and precious as all other souls on earth.

But here at home it rose up in him again: the memory of everything that had tormented him during his childhood and youth. That his mother had not been as fond of him as she was of Erlend. That his father hadn't wanted to pay any attention to him, the way he had constantly paid attention to Erlend. Later, when they lived with Baard at Hestnes, it was Erlend who was praised and Erlend who did wrong—Gunnulf was merely the brother. Erlend, Erlend was the chieftain for all the young boys, Erlend was the one the serving maids cursed at and then laughed at just the same. And Erlend was the one he himself loved above all others on earth. If only Erlend would be fond of him; but he could never be satisfied with the love Erlend gave him. Erlend was the only one who cared for him—but Erlend cared for so many.

And now he saw the way his brother handled everything that had fallen to his lot. God alone must know how it would end with the riches of Husaby; there was gossip enough in Nidaros about Erlend's imprudent management. To think he took so little notice, when God had given him four handsome children; and they *were* handsome, even the children he had begotten in his dissolute days. Erlend perceived this not as a gift of grace but as something that was simply as it should be.

And finally he had won the love of a pure, delicate young maiden of good family. Gunnulf thought about the way Erlend had dealt with her; he could no longer respect his brother after he found that out. He grew impatient with himself when he noticed traits he had in common with his brother. Erlend, as old as he was, would turn pale or blush crimson as easily as a half-grown maiden, and Gunnulf would rage because he felt the blood coming and going just as easily in his own face. They had inherited this from their mother; a single word could make her change color.

Now Erlend assumed it was no more than reasonable that his

wife was a good woman, a mirror for all wives—in spite of the fact that year after year he had tried to corrupt this young child and lead her astray. But Erlend didn't even seem to imagine that things might be otherwise; he was now married to the woman whom he had trained in sensual pleasures, betrayal, and dishonesty. He didn't seem to think it was something he should honor his wife for—that in spite of her fall, she was still truthful and faithful, modest and good.

And yet, when the news arrived this past summer and autumn about Erlend's actions in the north . . . Then he had yearned for only *one* thing: to be with his brother. Erlend, the king's military protector in Haalogaland; and he, the preacher of God's words in the desolate, half-heathen districts near the Gandvik Sea[4] . . .

Gunnulf stood up. On one wall of the alcove hung a large crucifix, and in front of it, on the floor, lay a big slab of stone.

He knelt down on the stone and stretched out his arms to either side. He had hardened his body to tolerate this position, and he could remain like this for hours, as motionless as stone. With his eyes fastened on the crucifix, he waited for the solace that would come when he was able to focus all his attention on his contemplation of the cross.

But the first thought that now came to him was this: Should he part with this image? Saint Francis and his friars had crosses which they carved themselves from a couple of tree branches. He ought to give away this beautiful rood—he could give it to the church at Husaby. Peasants, children, and women who went there for mass might gain strength from such a visible display of the Savior's loving gentleness during his suffering. Simple souls like Kristin. For him it shouldn't be necessary.

Night after night he had knelt here with his senses closed off and his limbs numb, until he saw the vision. The hill with the three crosses against the sky. The cross in the middle, which was meant to bear the king of heaven and earth, shook and trembled; it bent like a tree in a storm, in fear of bearing the much too precious burden, the sacrifice for all the sins of the world. The lord of the storm tents forced it, the way a knight forces his defiant stallion; the chieftain of heaven carried it into battle. Then that miracle occurred which was the key to ever deeper miracles. The blood that ran down from the cross in redemption for all sins and penance for all sorrows—that was the visible sign. With this first miracle the eye of the soul could be opened to contemplate those still hidden—God, who came down to earth and became the son of a virgin and brother to the human kin, who lay waste to Hell and who, with the released souls that were his spoils of war, stormed toward the dazzling sea of light from which the world was born and which sustains the earth. It was toward that unfathomable and eternal depth of light that his thoughts were drawn, and there they perished in the light, vanishing like a flock of birds into the radiance of an evening sky.

Not until the bells of the church rang for matins did Gunnulf get up. There was not a sound as he walked through the main hall—they were both asleep, Kristin and Orm.

Out in the dark courtyard the priest paused for a moment. But none of the servants appeared to accompany him to church. He didn't require them to attend more than two services a day. But Ingrid, his foster mother, almost always went with him to matins. This morning she was evidently still asleep too. Well, she had been up late the night before.

All that day the three kinsmen spoke little to each other, and then only about unimportant things. Gunnulf looked tired, but he kept up his bantering just the same. "How foolish we were last night. We sat here so mournfully, like three fatherless children," he said once. Many funny little things went on in Nidaros, with the pilgrims and such, which the priests often jested about among themselves. An old man from Herjedal had come to offer prayers on behalf of his fellow villagers, but he managed to mix them all up—and he later realized that things would have looked bad in his village if Saint Olav had taken him at his word.

Late that evening Erlend arrived, soaking wet. He had come to Nidaros by ship, and now the wind was blowing hard again. He was furious and fell upon Orm at once with angry words.

Gunnulf listened for a while and said, "When you speak to Orm in that manner, Erlend, you sound like our father—the way he used to speak to you."

Erlend abruptly fell silent. Then he shouted, "But I know I

never acted so senselessly when I was a boy—running off from the manor in a snowstorm, a woman who is ill and a whelp of a boy! There's not much else to boast of about Orm's manhood, but you can see that he's not afraid of his father!"

"You weren't afraid of Father either," replied his brother with a smile.

Orm stood before his father without saying a word and tried to look indifferent.

"Well, you can go now," said Erlend. "I'm tired of the whole lot at Husaby. But one thing I know—this summer Orm will go north with me, then I'll make something of this pampered lamb of Kristin's. He's no bumbler, either," he said eagerly to his brother. "He has a sure aim, I can tell you that. And he's not afraid; but he's always surly and morose, and it seems as if he has no marrow in his bones."

"If you often rage at your son the way you did just now, then it's not so strange that he would be morose," said the priest.

Erlend's mood shifted; he laughed and said, "I often had to suffer much worse from Father—and God knows I didn't grow morose from that. It could very well be . . . but now that I've come here, we should celebrate Christmas, since it's Christmastime, after all. Where's Kristin? What was it she had to talk to you about again that she would . . ."

"I don't think there was anything she wanted to talk to me about," said the priest. "She had a mind to attend mass here during Christmas."

"It seems to me that she could have made do with what we have at home," said Erlend. "But it's hard for her—all her youth is being stripped from her in this way." He rammed one fist against the other. "I don't understand why our Lord should think we need a new son every year."

Gunnulf looked up at his brother.

"Well . . . I have no idea what our Lord thinks you may need. But what Kristin no doubt needs most is for you to be kind to her."

"Yes, I suppose she does," murmured Erlend.

The next day Erlend went to morning mass with his wife. They set off for Saint Gregor's Church; Erlend always attended mass there when he was in Nidaros. The two of them went alone, and in the lane where the snow lay piled up in drifts, heavy and wet, Erlend led his wife by the hand, in a refined and courtly fashion. He hadn't said a word to her about her flight, and he had been kind toward Orm after his first outburst.

Kristin walked along, pale and silent, with her head bowed slightly; the ankle-length, black fur cloak with the silver clasps seemed to weigh heavily on her frail, thin body.

"Would you like me to ride back home with you? Then Orm can travel home by ship," her husband said. "I suppose you would prefer not to travel across the fjord."

"No, you know I'm reluctant to journey by ship."

The weather was calm and mild now—every once in a while mounds of heavy wet snow would slide down off the trees. The sky hung low and dark-gray over the white town. There was a watery, greenish-gray sheen to the snow; the timbered walls of the houses, the fences, and the tree trunks looked black in the damp air. Never, thought Kristin, had she seen the world look so cold and faded and pale.

## CHAPTER 3

KRISTIN SAT WITH Gaute on her lap and stared into the distance from the hill north of the manor. It was such a lovely evening. Below, the lake lay glistening and still, reflecting the mountain ridges, the buildings of By, and the golden clouds in the sky. The strong smell of leaves and earth rose up after the rainfall earlier in the day. The grass in the meadows must be knee-deep by now, and the fields were covered with spears of grain.

Sounds traveled a long way on such an evening. Now the pipes and drums and fiddles began playing down on the green near Vinjar; they sounded so splendid up on the hill.

The cuckoo fell silent for long periods, but then it would cry out a few notes, far away in the woods to the south. And birds whistled and warbled in all the groves around the farm—but sporadic and quiet, because the sun was still high.

The livestock were bellowing and their bells were ringing as they returned home from the pasture across from the farmyard gate.

"Now Gaute will soon have his milk," she cooed to the infant, lifting him up. The boy lay as he usually did, with his heavy head resting on his mother's shoulder. Now and then he would press closer, and Kristin took this as a sign that he understood her endearing words and chatter.

She walked down toward the buildings. Outside the main hall Naakkve and Bjørgulf were leaping around, trying to entice a cat down from the roof where it had taken refuge. Then the boys took up the broken dagger which belonged to both of them and went back to digging a hole in the earthen floor of the entryway.

Dagrun came into the hall carrying a basin of goat milk, and Kristin let Gaute drink ladle after ladle of the warm liquid. The boy grunted crossly when the servant woman spoke to him; when she tried to take him away, he struck out at her and hid his face on his mother's breast.

"But it seems to me that he's getting better," said the milkmaid.

Kristin cupped the little face in her hand; it was yellowish-white, like tallow, and his eyes were always tired. Gaute had a big, heavy head and thin, frail limbs. He had turned two years old on the eighth day after Saint Lavrans's Day, but he still couldn't stand on his own, he had only five teeth, and he couldn't speak a word.

Sira Eiliv said that it wasn't rickets; and neither the alb nor the altar books had helped. Everywhere the priest went he would ask advice about this illness that had overtaken Gaute. Kristin knew that he mentioned the child in all his prayers. But to her he could only say that she must patiently submit to God's will. And she should let him have warm goat milk.

Her poor little boy. Kristin hugged him and kissed him after the woman had left. How handsome, how handsome he was. She thought she could see that he took after her father's family—his eyes were dark gray and his hair as pale as flax, thick and silky soft.

Now he began to whimper again. Kristin stood up and paced the floor as she held him. Small and weak though he was, he still grew heavy after a while. But Gaute refused to leave his mother's arms. So she walked back and forth in the dim hall, carrying the boy and lulling him to sleep.

Someone rode into the courtyard. Ulf Haldorssøn's voice echoed between the buildings. Kristin went over to the entryway door with the child in her arms.

"You'll have to unsaddle your own horse tonight, Ulf. All the men have gone off to the dance. It's a shame you should have to be troubled with this, but I'm afraid it can't be helped."

Ulf muttered with annoyance, but he unsaddled the horse. Naakkve and Bjørgulf swarmed around him and wanted to ride the horse over in the pasture.

"No, Naakkve, you must stay with Gaute—play with your brother so he doesn't cry while I'm in the cookhouse," said Kristin.

The boy frowned unhappily. But then he got down on all fours, roaring and butting at his little brother whom Kristin had put down on a cushion near the entryway door. She bent down and stroked Naakkve's hair. He was so good to his younger brothers.

When Kristin came back to the hall holding the big trencher in her hands, Ulf Haldorssøn was sitting on the bench, playing with the children. Gaute liked to be with Ulf as long as he didn't see his mother—but now he began crying at once and reached out for her. Kristin put down the trencher and picked Gaute up.

Ulf blew on the foam of the newly tapped ale, took a swallow, and then began taking food from the small bowls on the trencher. "Are all of your maidservants out tonight?"

Kristin said, "There are fiddles and drums and pipes—a group of musicians arrived from Orkedal after the wedding. And you know that as soon as they heard about them . . . They're young girls, after all."

"You let them run around too freely, Kristin. I think you're most afraid that it'll be hard to find a wet nurse this autumn."

Kristin involuntarily smoothed down her gown over her slender waist. She had blushed dark red at the man's words.

Ulf laughed harshly. "But if you keep carrying around Gaute this way, then things may go as they did last year. Come here to your foster father, my boy, and I'll give you some food from my plate."

Kristin didn't reply. She set her three small sons in a row on the bench along the opposite wall, brought the basin of milk porridge, and pulled over a little stool close by. There she sat, feeding the boys, although Naakkve and Bjørgulf grumbled—they wanted spoons so they could feed themselves. The oldest was now four, and the other would soon be three years old.

"Where's Erlend?" asked Ulf.

"Margret wanted to go to the dance, and so he went with her."

"It's good he understands he should keep a watchful eye on that maiden of his," said Ulf.

Again Kristin did not reply. She undressed the children and put them to bed—Gaute in the cradle and the other two in her own bed. Erlend had resigned himself to having them there after she recovered from her long illness the year before.

When Ulf had eaten his fill, he stretched out on the bench. Kristin pushed the chair carved from a tree stump over to the cradle, got her basket of wool, and began to wind up balls of yarn for her loom as she gently and quietly rocked the cradle.

"Shouldn't you go to bed?" she asked once without turning her head. "Aren't you tired, Ulf?"

The man got up, poked at the fire a bit, and came over to Kristin. He sat down on the bench across from her. Kristin saw that he was not as spent from carousing as he usually was whenever he had been in Nidaros for a few days.

"You don't even ask about news from town, Kristin," he said, looking at her as he leaned forward with his elbows on his knees.

Her heart began pounding with fear. She could see from the man's expression and manner that again there was news that wasn't good. But she said with a gentle and calm smile, "You must tell me, Ulf—have you heard anything?"

"Yes, well . . ." But first he took out his traveling bag and unpacked the things he had brought from town for her. Kristin thanked him.

"I understand that you've heard some news in Nidaros," she said after a while.

Ulf looked at the young mistress; then he turned his gaze to the pale, sleeping child in the cradle.

"Does he always sweat like this?" he asked softly, gently pushing back the boy's damp, dark hair. "Kristin—when you were betrothed to Erlend . . . the document that was drawn up regarding the ownership of both your possessions—didn't it state that you should manage with full authority those properties which he gave you as betrothal and wedding gifts?"

Kristin's heart pounded harder, but she said calmly, "It's also true, Ulf, that Erlend has always asked my advice and sought my consent in all dealings with those properties. Is this about the sections of the estate in Verdal that he has sold to Vigleik of Lyng?"

"Yes," said Ulf. "He has bought a ship called *Hugrekken* from Vigleik. So now he's going to maintain two ships. And what do you gain in return, Kristin?"

"Erlend's share of Skjervastad and two plots of land in Ulfkelstad—each taxed by one month's worth of food—and what he owns of Aarhammar," she said. "Surely you didn't think Erlend would sell that estate without my permission or without repaying me?"

"Hmm . . ." Ulf sat in silence for a moment. "And yet your income will be reduced, Kristin. Skjervastad—that was where Erlend obtained hay this past winter and in return he released the farmer from the land tax for the next three years."

"Erlend was not to blame because we had no dry hay last year. I know, Ulf, you did everything you could, but with all the misery we had here last summer—"

"He sold more than half of Aarhammar to the sisters at Rein back when he was preparing to flee the country with you." Ulf laughed. "Or pledged it as security, which amounts to the same thing, in Erlend's case. Free of war levies—the entire burden rests on Audun, who oversees the farm which you will now call your own."

"Can't he lease the land from the convent?" asked Kristin.

"The nuns' tenant farmer on the neighboring estate has leased it," said Ulf. "It's difficult and risky for leaseholders to manage when lands are split up the way Erlend is bent on doing."

Kristin was silent. She knew he was right.

"Erlend is working quickly," said Ulf, "to increase his lineage and to destroy his property."

When she didn't reply, Ulf went on, "You will soon have *many* children, Kristin Lavransdatter."

"But none I would give up," she said, with a slight quaver in her voice.

"Don't be so fearful for Gaute—I'm sure he'll grow strong over time," said Ulf softly.

"It must be as God wills, but it's difficult to wait."

He could hear the concealed suffering in the mother's voice; a strange sense of helplessness came over the ponderous, gloomy man.

"It's of such little avail, Kristin. You have accomplished much here at Husaby, but if Erlend is now going to set off with two ships . . . I have no faith that there will be peace in the north, and your husband has so little cunning; he doesn't know how to turn to his advantage what he has gained in the past two years. Bad years they have been, and you have been constantly ill. If things should continue in this way, you'll be brought to your knees in the end, and as such a young woman. I've helped you as best I could here on the estate, but this other matter, Erlend's lack of prudence—"

"Yes, God knows you have," she interrupted him. "You've been the best of kinsmen toward us, Ulf my friend, and I can never fully thank you or repay you."

Ulf stood up, lit a candle at the hearth, and set it in the candlestick on the table; he stood there with his back turned to Kristin. She had let her hands sink into her lap as they talked, but now she began winding up the yarn and rocking the cradle with her foot again.

"Can't you send word to your parents back home?" he asked. "So that Lavrans might journey north in the fall along with your mother when she comes to help you?"

"I hadn't thought of troubling my mother this fall. She's getting older, and it happens much too often now that I must lie down in the straw to give birth. I can't ask her to come every time." Her smile looked a bit strained.

"Do it this time," said Ulf. "And ask your father to come along, so you can seek his advice on these matters."

"I will not ask my father's advice about this," she said quietly but firmly.

"What about Gunnulf then?" asked Ulf after a moment. "Can't you speak to him?"

"It's not proper to disturb him with such things now," said Kristin in the same tone of voice.

"Do you mean because he has entered a monastery?" Ulf laughed scornfully. "I've never noticed that monks had less understanding about managing estates than other people."

When she didn't answer, he said, "But if you won't seek advice from anyone, Kristin, then you must speak to Erlend. Think of your sons, Kristin!"

She sat in silence for a long time.

"You who are so good toward our children, Ulf," she said at last. "It would seem to me more reasonable if you married and had your own worries to tend to—than that you should stay here, tormenting yourself . . . with Erlend's and my troubles."

Ulf turned to face her. He stood with his hands gripping the edge of the table behind him and looked at Kristin Lavransdatter. She was still straight-backed and slender and beautiful as she sat there. Her gown was made of dark, hand-dyed woolen cloth, but she wore a fine, soft linen wimple around her calm, pale face. The belt from which her ring of keys hung was adorned with small silver roses. On her breast glittered two chains with crosses, the larger one on gilded links which hung almost to her waist; that one had been given to her by her father. On top lay the thin silver chain with the little cross which Orm had given to his stepmother, asking her to wear it always.

So far she had recovered from each childbirth looking just as lovely as ever—only a little quieter, with heavier responsibilities on her young shoulders. Her cheeks were thinner, her eyes a little darker and more somber beneath the wide, white forehead, and her lips were a little less red and full. But her beauty would soon be worn away before many more years had passed if things continued in this fashion.

"Don't you think, Ulf, that you would be happier if you settled down on your own farm?" she continued. "Erlend told me that you've bought three more plots of land at Skjoldvirkstad—you will soon own half the estate. And Isak has only the one child—Aase is both beautiful and kind, a capable woman, and she seems to like you—"

"And yet I don't want her if I have to marry her," sneered the man crudely and laughed. "Besides, Aase Isaksdatter is too good for . . ." His voice changed. "I've never known any other father but my foster father, Kristin, and I think it's my fate not to have any other children but foster children."

"I'll pray to the Virgin Mary that you'll have better fortune, kinsman."

"I'm not so young, either. Thirty-five winters, Kristin," he laughed. "It wouldn't take many more than that and I could be your father."

"Then you must have begun your sinful ways early," replied Kristin. She tried to make her voice sound merry and light-hearted.

"Shouldn't you go to sleep now?" Ulf asked.

"Yes, soon—but you must be tired too, Ulf. You should go to bed."

The man quietly bade her good night and left the room.

Kristin took the candlestick from the table and shone the light on the two sleeping boys in the enclosed bed. Bjørgulf's eyelashes were not festering—thank God for that. The weather would stay fine for a while yet. As soon as the wind blew hard or the weather forced the children to stay inside near the hearth, his eyes would grow inflamed. She stood there a long time, gazing at the two boys. Then she went over and bent down to look at Gaute in his cradle.

They had been as healthy as little fledglings, all three of her sons—until the sickness had come to the region last summer. A fever had carried off children in homes all around the fjord; it was a terrible thing to see and to hear about. She had been allowed to keep hers—all her own children.

For five days she had sat near the bed on the south wall where they lay, all three of them, with red spots covering their faces and with feverish eyes that shunned the light. Their small bodies were burning hot. She sat with her hand under the coverlet and patted the soles of Bjørgulf's feet while she sang and sang until her poor voice was no more than a whisper.

Shoe, shoe the knight's great horse.
How are we to shoe it best?
Iron shoes will pass the test.

Shoe, shoe the earl's great horse.
How are we to shoe it best?
Silver shoes will pass the test.

Shoe, shoe the king's great horse.
How are we to shoe it best?
Golden shoes will pass the test.

Bjørgulf was less sick than the others, and more restless. If she stopped singing for even a minute, he would throw off the coverlets at once. Gaute was then only ten months old; he was so ill that she didn't think he would survive. He lay at her breast, wrapped in blankets and furs, and had no strength to nurse. She held him with one arm as she patted the soles of Bjørgulf's feet with her other hand.

Now and then, if all three of them happened to fall asleep for a while, she would stretch out on the bed beside them, fully dressed.

Erlend came and went, looking helplessly at his three small sons. He tried to sing to them, but they didn't care for their father's fine voice—they wanted their mother to sing, even though she didn't have the voice for it.

The servant women would come in, wanting their mistress to rest; the men would come in to inquire about the boys; and Orm tried to play with his young brothers. At Kristin's advice, Erlend had sent Margret over to Østerdal, but Orm wanted to stay—he was grown up now, after all. Sira Eiliv sat at the children's bedside whenever he wasn't out tending to the sick. Through work and worry the priest had shed all the corpulence he had acquired at Husaby; it grieved him greatly to see so many fair young children perish. And some grownups had died too.

By the evening of the sixth day, all the children were so much better that Kristin promised her husband to undress and go to bed that night. Erlend offered to keep watch along with the maids and to call Kristin if need be. But at the supper table she noticed that Orm's face was bright red and his eyes were shiny with fever. He said it was nothing, but he jumped up abruptly and rushed out. When Erlend and Kristin went out to him, they found him vomiting in the courtyard.

Erlend threw his arms around the youth.

"Orm, my son. Are you ill?"

"My head aches," complained the boy, and he let his head sink heavily onto his father's shoulder.

That night they kept vigil over Orm. Most of the time he lay there muttering in delirium—then screaming loudly and flailing his long arms about, seeming to see hideous things. What he said they could not understand.

In the morning Kristin collapsed. It turned out that she must have been with child again; now it went very badly for her, and afterwards she lay as if immersed in a deathlike sleep; later she was seized by a terrible fever. Orm had been in the grave for more than two weeks before she learned of her stepson's death.

At the time she was so weak that she couldn't properly grieve. She felt so bloodless and faint that nothing seemed to reach her—she was content to lie in bed, only half-alive. There had been a dreadful time when the women hardly dared touch her or tend to her cleanliness, but that had all merged with the confusion of the fever. Now it felt good to submit to the care of others. Around her bed hung many fragrant wreaths of mountain flowers which were meant to keep the flies away—the people from the mountain pastures had sent them, and they smelled especially sweet whenever there was rain in the air. One day Erlend brought the children to her. She saw that they were haggard from their illness, and that Gaute didn't recognize her, but even that didn't trouble her. She merely sensed that Erlend seemed always to be at her side.

He went to mass every day, and he knelt at Orm's grave to pray. The cemetery was next to the parish church at Vinjar, but some of the infants in the family had been given a resting place inside the manor church at Husaby—Erlend's two brothers and one of Munan Biskopssøn's little daughters. Kristin had often felt sorry for these little ones who lay so alone under the flagstones. Now Orm Erlendssøn had his final resting place among these children.

While the others feared for Kristin's life, processions of beggars on their way to Nidaros just before Saint Olav's Day began to pass through the region. They were mostly the same wandering men and women who had made the journey the year before; the pilgrims in Nidaros were always generous to the poor, since intercessions of this kind were considered particularly powerful. And they had learned to travel by way of Skaun during the years since Kristin had settled at Husaby. They knew that there on the estate they would be given shelter, alms, and an abundance of food before they continued on. This time the servants wanted to send them away because the mistress was ill. But when Erlend, who had been up north the last two summers, heard that his wife was accustomed to receiving the beggars so kindly, he ordered that they should be given food and lodging, just as they had before. And in the morning he himself tended to the wanderers, helping the servants to pour the ale and bring in food for them; he gave them alms as he quietly asked for their prayers of intercession for his wife. Many of the beggars wept when they heard that the gentle young woman lay close to death.

All of this Sira Eiliv had told Kristin when she began to regain her health. Not until Christmastime was she strong enough to take up her keys again.

Erlend had sent word to her parents as soon as she fell ill, but at the time they were in the south, attending a wedding at Skog. Later they came to Husaby; she was better by then, but so tired that she had little energy to talk to them. What she wanted most was simply to have Erlend at her bedside.

Weak and pale and always cold, she would cling to his healthy body. The old fire in her blood had gone. It had disappeared so completely that she could no longer remember how it felt to love in that way, but with it had also vanished the worry and bitterness from the past few years. She felt that things were better now, even though the sorrow over Orm's death lay heavily on both of them, and even though Erlend didn't realize how frightened she was for little Gaute. But things were so good between them. She saw that he had feared terribly that he might lose her.

And so it was difficult and painful for her to speak to him, to touch on matters that might destroy the peace and joy they now shared.

She was standing outside in the bright summer night, in front of the entrance to the main house, when the servants returned from the dance. Margret was clinging to her father's arm. She was dressed and adorned in a fashion that would have been more suited to a wedding feast than to a dance out on the green, where all manner of folk came together. But her stepmother had stopped interfering in the maiden's upbringing. Erlend could do as he pleased in raising his own daughter.

Erlend and Margret were both thirsty, so Kristin brought ale for them. The girl sat and talked with them for a while; she and her stepmother were good friends now that Kristin no longer attempted to instruct her. Erlend laughed at everything his daughter said about the dance. But finally Margret and her maid went up to the loft to sleep.

Erlend continued roaming around the hall; he stretched, yawned, but claimed he wasn't tired. He ran his fingers through his long black hair.

"There wasn't time for it after we were in the bathhouse. Because of the dance. I think you'll have to cut my hair, Kristin; I can't walk around like this during the holy days."

Kristin protested that it was too dark, but Erlend laughed and pointed to the vent hole in the ceiling; it was already daylight again. Then she relit the candle, told him to sit down, and draped a cloth around his shoulders. As she worked, he squirmed from the tickling, and laughed when the scissors came too close to his neck.

Kristin carefully gathered up the hair clippings and burned them in the hearth; she shook out the cloth over the fire as well. Then she combed Erlend's hair straight down from his scalp and snipped here and there, wherever the ends weren't quite even.

Erlend grabbed her hands tightly as she stood behind him, placed them at his throat, and smiled as he tilted his head back to look up at her.

But then he let her go, saying, "You're tired." And he stood up with a little sigh.

Erlend sailed to Bjørgvin right after Midsummer. He was disconsolate because his wife was again unable to travel with him. She smiled wearily; all the same, she wouldn't have been able to leave Gaute.

And so Kristin was once again alone at Husaby in the summer. But she was glad that this year she wouldn't give birth until Saint Matthew's Day; it would be difficult both for her and for the women who would attend her if it occurred during the harvest season.

She wondered whether it would always be this way. Times were different now than when she was growing up. She had heard her father speak of the Danish war, and she remembered when he was away from home during the campaign against Duke Eirik. That was how he got the terrible scars on his body. But back home in the valleys, war had still seemed so far away, and no doubt most people thought it would never return. It was mostly peaceful, and her father was home, managing his estates, and thinking about and caring for all of them.

Nowadays there was always unrest—everyone talked about wars and campaigns and the ruling of the kingdom. In Kristin's mind it all merged with her image of the sea and the coast, which she had seen only once since she had moved north. From the coast they sailed and to the coast they came—men whose heads were full of ideas and plans and counterplots and deliberations; clergymen and laymen. To these men belonged Erlend, by virtue of his high birth and his wealth. But she felt that he stood partially outside their circles.

She pondered and thought about this. What was it that caused her husband to have such a position? How did his peers truly regard him?

When he was simply the man she loved, she had never asked about such things. She could see that he was short-tempered and impetuous and rash, that he had a particular penchant for acting unwisely. But back then she had found excuses for everything, never troubling to think about what his temperament might bring upon them both. When they had won her father's consent to marry, everything would be different—that was how she had consoled herself. Gradually it dawned on her that it was from the moment a child was born to them that she began to think about things. What kind of man was Erlend, whom people called irresponsible and imprudent, a man whom no one could trust?

But she had trusted him. She remembered Brynhild's loft, she remembered how the bond between him and that other woman had finally been severed. She remembered his conduct after she had become his lawful bride. But he had stood by her in spite of all the humiliations and rejections; and she had seen that he did not want to lose her for all the gold on earth.

She thought about Haftor of Godøy. He was always following her around, speaking words of nonsense and affection whenever they met, but she had never cared for his attentions. That must be his way of jesting. She didn't think it was more than that; she had been fond of the handsome and boisterous man, and she was still fond of him. But to think that anyone would act that way in mere jest—no, she didn't understand it.

She had met Haftor Graut again at the royal banquets in Nidaros, and he sought out her company there too, just as he usually did. One evening he convinced her to go into a loft room, and she lay down with him on a bed that stood there. Back home in Gudbrandsdal she would never have thought of doing such a thing—there it was not a banquet custom for men and women to slip away, two by two. But here everyone did it; no one seemed to find it improper—it was apparently common practice among knights in other countries. When they first entered the room, Fru Elin, the wife of Sir Erling, was lying on the other bed with a

Swedish knight; Kristin could hear that they were talking about the king's earache. The Swede looked pleased when Fru Elin wanted to get up and go back to the hall.

When Kristin realized that Haftor was quite serious about the intentions behind his request as they lay there and talked, she was so astonished that she failed to be either frightened or suitably indignant. They were both married, after all, and they both had children with their spouses. She had never truly believed that such things actually went on. In spite of all she herself had done and experienced—no, she hadn't believed that such things happened. Haftor had always been merry and affectionate and full of laughter. She couldn't say that what he wanted was to try to seduce her; he hadn't been serious enough for that. And yet he wanted her to commit the worst of sins.

He got off the bed the minute she told him to go. He had turned submissive, but he seemed more surprised than ashamed. And he asked in utter disbelief: Did she truly think that married people were never unfaithful? But she must know that few men could admit to never having a paramour. Women were perhaps a little better than the men, and yet . . .

"Did you believe everything the priests preach about sin and the like even back when you were a young maiden?" he asked. "Then I don't understand, Kristin Lavransdatter, how Erlend ever managed to have his way with you."

Then he had looked into her eyes—and her eyes must have spoken, although she wouldn't have discussed this matter with Haftor for any amount of gold. But his voice rang with amazement as he said, "I thought that was only something they wrote about—in ballads."

Kristin had not mentioned this episode to anyone, not even Erlend. He was fond of Haftor. And of course it was dreadful that some people could behave as recklessly as Haftor Graut, but she couldn't see that it was any concern of hers. And he hadn't attempted to be overly familiar toward her since then. Now whenever they met, he would simply sit and stare at her with obvious astonishment in his sea-blue eyes.

No, if Erlend behaved rashly, it was not in that fashion, at any rate. And was he truly so imprudent? she wondered. She saw that people were startled by things he said, and afterwards they would put their heads together to talk. There was often much that was truthful and just in the opinions that Erlend Nikulaussøn expressed. The problem was that he never saw what the other men never allowed to slip from view: the cautious hindsight with which they kept an eye on each other. Intrigue, Erlend called it, and then he would laugh insolently, which seemed to provoke people at first but eventually won them over. They would laugh too, slap him on the shoulder, and say that he could be sharp-witted enough, but short-sighted.

Then he would undo his own words with raucous and impudent banter. And people tolerated a great deal of this sort of behavior from Erlend. His wife was dimly aware of why everyone put up with his reckless talk, and it made her feel humiliated. For Erlend would yield as soon as he encountered any man who held firm to his own opinion; even if he understood no more than that this opinion was foolish, Erlend would nevertheless relinquish his own view on the matter. But he covered his retreat with disrespectful gossip about the man. And people were satisfied that Erlend had this cowardice of spirit—reckless as he was with his own welfare, adventurous, and boldly enamored of any danger that could be faced with armed force. All the same, they had no need to worry about Erlend Nikulaussøn.

The year before, toward the end of winter, the regent had come to Nidaros, and he had brought the young king along with him. Kristin attended the grand feast at the king's palace. With quiet dignity, wearing a silk wimple and with all her best jewelry adorning her red bridal gown, she had sat there among the most highborn women at the banquet. With alert eyes she studied her husband's conduct among the men, watching and listening and pondering—just as she watched and listened and pondered wherever she went with Erlend, and wherever she noticed that people were talking about him.

And she had learned several things. Sir Erling Vidkunssøn was willing to risk every effort to assert the right of the Norwegian Crown north to the Gandvik Sea, to defend and protect Haalogaland. But the Council and the knights opposed him and were reluctant to support any endeavor that might help. The archbishop himself and the clergy of the archdiocese were not unwilling to offer financial support—this she knew from Gunnulf—but otherwise the men of the Church all over the country were opposed to the war, even though it was against the enemies of God: heretics and heathens. And the noblemen were working against the regent, at least here in Trøndelag. They had grown accustomed to disregarding the words of the law books and the rights of the Crown, and they were not pleased that Sir Erling so sternly invoked the spirit of his blessed kinsman King Haakon in these matters. But it was not for these reasons that Erlend refused to allow himself to be used, as Kristin now understood that the regent had intended to use her husband. For Erlend it was simply because the other man's somber and dignified demeanor bored him, so he took revenge by lightly ridiculing his powerful kinsman.

Kristin now thought she understood Sir Erling's attitude toward Erlend. On the one hand, he had felt a certain affection for Erlend ever since their youth; no doubt he thought that if he could win the support of the noble and fearless master of Husaby, who also had some experience in the art of war from the days when he served Earl Jacob—at any rate more than most of the other men who had stayed at home—then it would be of benefit to both Erling Vidkunssøn's plans and to Erlend's welfare. But that's not how things had turned out.

For two summers Erlend had stayed out at sea until late autumn, patrolling the waters off the long northern coast and chasing off pirate vessels with the four small ships that bore his banner. One day he had arrived in search of fresh provisions at a new Norwegian settlement far north in Tana just as the Karelians[1] were in the process of plundering it. With the handful of men he had brought ashore, he captured eighteen of the pirates and hanged them from the roof beam in the half-burned barn. He cut down a troop of Russians attempting to flee into the mountains; he vanquished and burned several enemy ships somewhere out among the distant skerries. Rumors of his speed and boldness spread through the north; his men from Outer Trøndelag and Møre loved their chieftain for his toughness and his willingness to share in all the toil and travails of his crew. He had won friends among the peasants and the young sons on the estates of the chieftains up north in Haalogaland, where people had almost grown accustomed to having to defend their own coasts alone.

But even so, Erlend was of no help to the regent and his plans for a great crusade north. In Trøndelag people boasted of Erlend's exploits in the Russian campaign—if talk turned to this subject, they would point out that he was one of their own. Yes, it had turned out that the young boys from the fjord possessed a fair share of good old-fashioned valor. But no matter what Erlend of Husaby said or did, it was not enough to impress grown-up and sensible men.

Kristin saw that Erlend continued to be counted among the young, even though he was a year older than the regent. She realized that this suited many, because then his words and actions could be disparaged as those of a young and reckless man. People liked him, humored him, and boasted of him—but he was never considered a fully entitled man. And she saw how willingly he accepted the role that his peers wanted him to play.

He spoke in favor of the Russian war; he talked about the Swedes who shared the Norwegian king. But they refused to acknowledge the Norwegian lords and knights as noblemen, equal with their own. In other countries, for as long as the world had existed, had anyone ever heard of demanding payment of war levies from noblemen in any other form than having them ride their own horses and bear their own shields into battle? Kristin knew this was much the same thing her father had said that time at the *ting* in Vaage, and Lavrans had also mentioned it to Erlend when his son-in-law had not wanted to oppose Munan Baardsøn's plans. No, Erlend now said—and he would allude to his father-in-law's powerful kinsmen in Sweden—he knew full well how the Swedish noblemen regarded the Norwegians. "And if we don't show them what we're capable of, we'll soon be considered nothing more than wards of the Swedes."

And people agreed that there was some truth to this. But then they would go back to talking about the regent. Sir Erling had his own reasons for lamenting what went on in the north. One year the Karelians had burned down Bjarkøy in defiance of his overseer and persecuted his leaseholders. But Erlend would change his tone and jest—Erling Vidkunssøn wasn't thinking of his own affairs, he was sure of that. Sir Erling was such a noble and refined and distinguished knight; they couldn't have found a better man to serve as leader for all of them. By God, Erling was as honorable and venerable as the most beautiful golden initial capital at the beginning of the book of law. People laughed, less impressed with Erlend's praise of the regent's integrity than with Erlend's comparing him to a gilded letter.

No, they didn't take Erlend seriously—not now, when he was in some ways respected. But back in the days when he was young and stubborn and desperate, when he lived with his concubine and refused to send her away in spite of the king's command and excommunication from the Church—back then they did take him seriously, turning away from him in bitter fury at his ungodly and disgraceful life. Now it was all forgiven and forgotten, and Kristin realized that it was partly out of gratitude for this that her husband so willingly acquiesced and behaved in the way people wanted him to behave. He must have suffered bitterly during that time when he was banished from the company of his peers in Norway. But the problem was, it made her think of her father, when he released incompetent men from their obligations or debts with a mere shrug of his shoulders. It was a Christian duty to bear with those who could not conduct themselves properly. Was it in this manner that Erlend had been forgiven the sins of his youth?

But Erlend *had* paid the consequences for his actions when he was living with Eline. He had answered for his sins right up until the moment when he met Kristin and she eagerly followed him into new sin. Was she then the one who . . .

No. Now she was afraid of her own thoughts.

And she tried to block out of her mind all the worries about things she could not change. She wanted only to think about matters in which she could do something with her compassion. Everything else she would have to place in God's hands. God had helped her in every instance when her own hard work could do some good. Husaby had now been transformed into a prosperous farm, as it had been in the past—in spite of the bad years. Three healthy and handsome sons He had given her, and each year He had granted her new life whenever she was faced with death in childbirth. He had allowed her to recover her full health after each convalescence. She had been permitted to keep all three of her small sons the year before, when illness took the lives of so many fair children in the region. And Gaute—Gaute *would* regain his health, that she firmly believed.

It must be as Erlend had said: It was necessary for him to lead his life and maintain his estates in as costly a fashion as he did. Otherwise he wouldn't be able to assert himself among his peers and win the rights and revenues that were his birthright under the Crown. She would have to believe that he understood this better than she did.

It was senseless to think that things might have been better in some ways for him—and even for her—back when he was living tangled up in sin with that other woman. In glimpses of memory she saw his face from that time, ravaged with sorrow, contorted with passion. No, no, things were fine as they were now. He was merely a little too carefree and thoughtless.

Erlend returned home just before Michaelmas. He had hoped to find Kristin confined to bed, but she was still on her feet. She came to meet him out on the road. Her gait was terribly cumbersome this time—but she had Gaute in her arms, as usual; the two older sons came running ahead of her.

Erlend jumped down from his horse and lifted the boys onto the saddle. Then he took his youngest son from his wife so he could carry him. Kristin's pale, worn face lit up when Gaute wasn't frightened by his father; he must have recognized him, after all. She asked nothing about her husband's travels, but talked only about Gaute's four new teeth which had made him so sick.

Then the boy started to scream; he had scraped his cheek bloody on the filigree brooch on his father's chest. He wanted to go back to his mother, and she wanted to take him, no matter how much Erlend protested.

Not until evening, when they were sitting alone in the hall and the children were asleep, did Kristin ask her husband about his journey to Bjørgvin—as if she only then happened to think about it.

Erlend glanced furtively at Kristin. His poor wife—she looked so miserable. He began to tell her all kinds of news. Erling had asked him to send his greetings and give her this—it was a bronze dagger, corroded with verdigris. They had found it in a heap of stones out at Giske; it was supposed to be beneficial to place such a thing in the cradle in case it was rickets that had stricken Gaute.

Kristin wrapped up the dagger again, awkwardly rose from her chair, and went over to the cradle. She put the bundle under the bedclothes with everything else that lay there: a stone axe found buried in the ground, the musk gland of a beaver, a cross made from daphne twigs, old silver, flint, roots of a Mariahand orchid, and an Olav's Beard fern.

"Lie down now, dear Kristin," Erlend said tenderly. He came over and pulled off her shoes and stockings. All the while he talked.

Haakon Ogmundssøn had come back, and peace with the Russians and Karelians had been concluded and sealed. Erlend himself would have to travel north this fall. For it was certain that calm would not be restored at once, and a man was needed at Vargøy who knew the region. He would be given full authority as the king's officer in command at the fortress up there, which had to be better secured so that peace could be defended at the new border markers.

Erlend looked up into his wife's face with excitement. She seemed a bit alarmed—but she didn't ask many questions, and it was clear that she had little understanding of what his news meant. He saw how tired she was, so he spoke no more about this matter but remained sitting on the edge of her bed for a while.

He understood the gravity of what he had taken on. Erlend laughed quietly to himself as he took his time undressing. There would be no sitting back with his silver belt around his belly, holding feasts for friends and kinsmen, and filing his nails straight and clean as he dispatched his vassals and lieutenants here and there—the way the king's commanders of the castles did here in the south of Norway. And the castle at Vargøy was quite a different sort of fortress.

Finns, Russians, Karelians, and mixed breeds of all kinds—troll rabble, conjurers, heathen dogs, the Devil's own precious lambs who had to be taught to pay taxes to the Norwegian emissaries and to leave the Norwegian settlements in peace, which were spread out with as much distance between each other as from Husaby all the way to Møre. Peace—perhaps the king's peace would be possible up there someday, but in his lifetime there would be peace only when the Devil attended mass. And he would have his own roughnecks to keep in check too. Especially toward the spring, when they began to grow despondent from the darkness and the cold and the hellish roar of the sea—when the flour and butter and liquor were in short supply, and they began fighting over their women, and life on the island grew unbearable. Erlend had witnessed some of this when he was there as a young boy with Gissur Galle. No, he wouldn't be lying about idle!

Ingolf Peit, who was now in charge, was able enough. But Erling was right: A man from the knighthood should take control of things up there—not until then would anyone realize that it was the Norwegian king's firm intention to assert his power over the land. Ha, ha—in that territory he would be like a needle in a coverlet. Not a single Norwegian settlement until as far south as Malang.

Ingolf was a capable fellow, but only as long as he had someone in command over him. He would put Ingolf in charge of his ship *Hugrekken*. *Margygren* was the most splendid of ships; that much he had now learned. Erlend laughed softly and happily. He had told Kristin so often before, this was one mistress she would have to put up with.

He was awakened by one of the children crying in the dark. Over by the bed on the opposite wall, he could hear Kristin stirring and speaking gently—it was Bjørgulf who was complaining. Sometimes the boy woke up in the night and couldn't open his festering eyes; then his mother would moisten them with her tongue. Erlend had always been repelled by the sight of this.

Kristin was softly humming. The thin, weak sound of her voice annoyed him.

Erlend remembered what he had been dreaming. He was walking along a shore somewhere; it was low tide, and he was leaping from stone to stone. In the distance the sea was glistening and pale, lapping at the seaweed; it was like a silent, cloudy summer evening, with no sun. At the mouth of the silvery fjord he saw the ship anchored, black and sleek, rocking gently on the waves. There was an ungodly, delicious smell of sea and kelp.

His heart grew sick with longing. Now in the darkness of the night, as he lay here in the guest bed and listened to the monotonous sound of the lullaby gnawing at his ear, he felt how strong his longing was. To be away from this house and the swarms of children who filled it, away from talk of farming matters and servants and tenants and children—and from his anguished concern for her, who was always ill and whom he always had to pity.

Erlend clasped his hands over his heart. It felt as if it had stopped; it merely lay there, shivering with fright inside his breast. He longed to be away from her. When he thought about what she would have to endure, as weak and frail as she now was—and he knew that it could happen at any hour—he felt as if he would suffocate from fear. But if he should lose Kristin . . . He didn't know how he would be able to live without her. But he didn't feel able to live *with* her, either, not now. He wanted to flee from everything and breathe freely—as if it were a matter of life itself for him.

Jesus, my Savior—oh, what kind of man was he! He realized it now, tonight. Kristin, my sweet, my dearest wife—the only time he had known deep, heartfelt joy with her was when he was leading her astray.

He who had been so convinced on that day when he was given Kristin to have and to hold before God and man that everything bad would be driven from his life so completely that he would forget it had ever existed.

He must be the kind of man who couldn't tolerate anything truly good or pure to be near him. Because Kristin . . . Ever since she had emerged from the sin and impurity into which he had led her, she had been like an angel from God's heaven. Kind and faithful, gentle, capable, deserving of respect. She had returned honor to Husaby. She had become once again the person she had been on that summer night, when the pure young maiden had crept under his cape there in the convent garden; and he had thought when he felt that slender young body against his side: The Devil himself wouldn't dare harm this child or cause her sorrow.

Tears streamed down Erlend's face.

It must be true, what the priests had told him, that sin ate up a man's soul like rust—for he could find no rest or peace here with his sweet beloved. He longed to be away from her and everything that was hers.

He had wept himself almost to sleep when he sensed that she was up and pacing the floor, quietly humming and singing.

Erlend sprang out of bed, stumbled in the dark over a child's shoes on the floor, and went right over to his wife and took Gaute from her. The boy started screaming, and Kristin said crossly, "I had almost lulled him to sleep!"

The father shook the crying child, gave him a few slaps on the bottom—and when the boy shrieked even louder, he hushed him so harshly that Gaute fell silent with fear. Nothing like that had ever happened to him before.

"It's time for you to use what good sense you have, Kristin." His fury robbed him of all power as he stood there, startled and naked and freezing in the pitch-dark room with a sobbing child in his arms. "There has to be an end to this, I tell you—what do you have nursemaids for? The children will sleep with them; you can't keep on this way."

"Won't you allow me to have my children with me during the time I have left?" replied his wife, her voice low and plaintive.

Erlend refused to acknowledge what she meant.

"During the time you have left, you need *rest*. Go to bed now, Kristin," he implored her more calmly.

He took Gaute with him to bed. He hummed to him for a while, and in the dark he found his belt lying on the step of the bed. The little silver medallions adorning it clinked and clattered as the boy played with the belt.

"The dagger isn't in it, is it?" asked Kristin anxiously from her bed, and Gaute began howling again when he heard his mother's voice. Erlend hushed him and made the belt clink—at last the child stopped crying and grew calm.

Perhaps it would be unwise to wish for this poor little boy to grow to adulthood—it was not certain that Gaute possessed all his wits.

Oh no, oh no. Blessed Virgin Mary, he didn't mean that. He didn't wish death for his own little son. No, no. Erlend held the child close in his arms and pressed his face to the soft, fine hair.

Their handsome sons. But he grew so weary of listening to them all day long; of stumbling over them whenever he came home. He couldn't understand how three small children could be everywhere at once on such a large estate. But he remembered how furious he had been with Eline because she showed no interest in their children. He must be an unreasonable man, for he was also resentful that he no longer saw Kristin without children clinging to her.

When he held his lawfully born sons in his arms he never felt the same way he had when they gave him Orm to hold for the first time. Oh Orm, Orm, my son. He had been so tired of Eline by then—sick and tired of her stubbornness and her vehemence and her uncontrollable ardor. He had seen that she was too old for him. And he had begun to realize what this madness would eventually cost him. But he hadn't felt that he could send her away—not after she had given up everything for his sake. The boy's birth had given him a reason to tolerate the mother, it seemed to him. He had been so young when he became Orm's father, and he hadn't fully understood the child's position, since the mother was another man's lawful wife.

Sobs overcame him once more, and he held Gaute tighter. Orm—he had never loved any of his children the way he loved that boy; he missed him terribly, and he bitterly regretted every harsh and impatient word he had ever said to him. Orm couldn't have known how much his father loved him. Bitterness and despair had gradually seized Erlend as it became abundantly clear that Orm would never be considered his lawful son, that he would never be able to inherit his father's coat of arms. And Erlend felt jealousy too because he saw his son draw closer to his stepmother than to him, and it seemed to him that Kristin's calm, gentle kindness toward the boy was a form of reproach.

Then came those days and nights that Erlend could not bear to remember. Orm lay on his bier in the loft, and the women came to tell him that they didn't think Kristin would live. They dug a grave for Orm over in the church, and they asked whether Kristin should be buried there too. Or should she be taken instead to Saint Gregor's Church to be laid to rest beside his parents?

Oh . . . He held his breath in fear. Behind him lay an entire lifetime of memories from which he had fled, and he couldn't bear to think of it. Now, tonight, he understood. He could forget about it to some extent from day to day. But he couldn't protect himself from the memories turning up at some moment such as this—and then it felt as if all courage had been conjured out of him.

Those days at Haugen—he had almost succeeded in forgetting about them entirely. He hadn't been back to Haugen since that night when he drove off, and he hadn't seen Bjørn or Aashild again after his wedding. And now . . . He thought about what Munan had told him—it was said that their spirits had come back. Haugen was so haunted that the buildings stood deserted; no one wanted to live there, even if they were given the farm free.

Bjørn Gunnarssøn had possessed a type of courage that Erlend knew he himself would never have. His hand had been steady when he stabbed his wife—right through the heart, said Munan.

It would be two years this winter since Bjørn and Fru Aashild died. People had not seen smoke coming from the buildings at Haugen for nearly a week; finally several men gathered their courage and went over there. Herr Bjørn was lying in bed with his throat cut; he was holding his wife's body in his arms. On the floor next to the bed lay his bloody dagger.

Everyone knew what had happened, and yet Munan Baardsøn and his brother managed to have the two buried in consecrated ground. Perhaps they had fallen victim to robbers, people said, although the chest containing Bjørn's and Aashild's valuables had not been touched. And the bodies were untouched by mice or rats—in fact, those kinds of vermin never came to Haugen, and people took this as a sign of the woman's sorcery skills.

Munan Baardsøn had been terribly distressed by his mother's death. He had set off on a pilgrimage to Santiago de Compostela[2] at once.

Erlend remembered the morning following his own mother's death. They were anchored in Moldøy Sound, but the fog was so white and thick that only occasionally could they catch a glimpse of the mountain ridge towering above them. But there was a muffled echo from the hollow sound of the boat being rowed to shore with the priest. Erlend stood in the bow and watched them rowing away from the ship. Everything he came near was wet with fog; beads of moisture covered his hair and clothing. And the priest and his acolyte, who were strangers to Erlend, sat in the bow of the boat, their shoulders hunched as they bent over the holy vessels they held on their laps. They looked like hawks in the rain. The slap of the oars and the scrape of the oarlocks and the echo from the mountain continued to resound long after the boat had been spirited away by the fog.

On that day Erlend had also vowed to make a pilgrimage. He had only had one thought back then: that he be allowed to see his mother's lovely, sweet face again, the way it had been before, with its soft, smooth, light tan complexion. Now she lay dead belowdecks, with her face ravaged by the terrible sores that ruptured and seeped little drops of clear fluid whenever she had tried to smile at him.

He was not to blame for the way his father had received him. Nor for the fact that he had turned to someone who was outcast, like himself. But then Erlend had pushed the pilgrimage from his mind, and he had refused to think any more about his mother. As painful as her life had been here on earth, she must now be in that place of peace—and there was not much peace for him, after he took up with Eline again.

Peace—he had known it only once in his life; on that night when he sat behind the stone wall near the woods of Hofvin and held Kristin as she slept on his lap—the safe, tender, undisturbed sleep of a child. He hadn't been able to hold out for long before he shattered her tranquillity. And it wasn't peace that he found with her later on, and he had no peace with her now. And yet he saw that everyone else in his home did find peace in the presence of his young wife.

Now he longed only to go away to that strife-torn place. He yearned madly and wildly for that remote promontory and for the thundering sea surrounding the forelands of the north, for the endless coastline and the enormous fjords which could conceal all manner of traps and deceptions, for the people whose language he understood only slightly, for their sorcery and inconstancy and cunning, for war and the sea, and for the singing of weapons, both his own and his men's.

At last Erlend fell asleep, and then woke up again—what was it he had dreamed? Oh yes. That he was lying in a bed with a black-haired Finnish girl on either side of him. Something half-forgotten that had happened to him back when he was up north with Gissur. A wild night when they had all been drunk and reeling. He couldn't recall much more of the whole night than the rank, wild-beast smell of the women.

And now here he lay with his sick little son in his arms and dreamed of such things. He was so shocked at himself that he didn't dare try to sleep anymore. And he couldn't bear to lie awake in bed. He must truly be fated to unhappiness. Rigid with anguish he lay motionless and felt the clench of his heart in his breast, while he longed for the redemption of dawn.

He persuaded Kristin to stay in bed the next day. He didn't think he could stand to see her so miserable, dragging herself around the house. He sat with her and played with her hand. She had had the loveliest arms—slim and yet so plump that the small, delicate bones were hardly visible in the slender joints. Now they stood out like knots on her gaunt forearm, and the skin underneath was bluish-white.

Outside it stormed and rained so hard that water gushed down the slopes. Erlend came out of the armory later in the day and heard Gaute screaming and crying from somewhere in the courtyard. He found his small sons in the narrow passageway between two of the buildings, sitting directly under the dripping eaves. Naakkve was clutching the youngest boy while Bjørgulf was trying to force-feed him a worm—he had a whole fistful of pink worms, twisting and squirming.

The boys looked crestfallen as their father scolded them. It was Old Aan, they said, who had mentioned that Gaute's teeth would come in with no trouble if they could get him to take a bite of a live worm.

They were soaked through from head to toe, all three of them. Erlend bellowed for the nursemaids, who came rushing out—one from the workroom and the other from the stable. Their master cursed them roundly, stuffed Gaute under his arm like a piglet, and then chased the other two ahead of him into the hall.

A little while later, dry and content in their best blue tunics, the boys sat in a row on the step of their mother's bed. Erlend had brought a stool over, and he chattered nonsense and fussed over his sons, hugging them close and laughing in order to drive out the remnants of the nighttime terror from his mind. But Kristin smiled happily because Erlend was playing with their children. Erlend told them that he had a Finnish witch; she was two hundred winters old, and so wizened that she was no bigger than this. He kept her in a leather pouch in the big chest that stood in his boathouse. Oh yes, he gave her food, all right; every Christmas he gave her the thigh of a Christian man—that was enough to last her the whole year. And if they weren't nice and quiet and didn't stop plaguing their mother, who was ill, then he would put them in the pouch too.

"Mother is sick because she's carrying our sister," said Naakkve, proud that he knew about such matters.

Erlend pulled the boy by the ears down onto his knee.

"Yes, and after she's born, this sister of yours, I'm going to let my old Finnish woman work her magic on all three of you and turn you into polar bears so you can go padding around in the wild forest, but my daughter will inherit all that I own."

The children shrieked and tumbled into their mother's bed. Gaute didn't understand, but he yelled and scrambled up there too, after his brothers. Kristin complained—Erlend shouldn't tease them so horribly. But Naakkve toppled off the bed again; in an ecstasy of laughter and fright he rushed at his father, hung on to his belt, and bit at Erlend's hands, while he shouted and cheered.

Erlend didn't get the daughter he had wished for this time, either. His wife gave birth to two big, handsome sons, but they almost cost Kristin her life.

Erlend had them baptized; one of them was named after Ivar Gjesling and the other after King Skule. His name had otherwise not been continued in their family; Fru Ragnrid had said that her father was a man fated to misfortune, and no one should be named for him. But Erlend swore that none of his sons bore a prouder name than the youngest.

It was now so late in the autumn that Erlend had to journey north as soon as Kristin was out of the worst danger. And he felt in his heart that it was just as well that he left before she was out of bed again. Five sons in five years—that should be enough, and he didn't want to have to worry that she would die in childbirth while he sat up north at Vargøy.

He could see that Kristin had thought much the same. She no longer complained that he was going to leave her behind. She had accepted each child that came as a precious gift from God, and the suffering as something to which she had to submit. But this time the experience had been so appallingly difficult that Erlend could tell that all courage seemed to have been stripped from her. She lay in bed listlessly, her face yellow as clay, staring at the two little bundles at her side; and her eyes were not as happy as they had been with the others.

Erlend sat beside her and went over the entire trip north in his mind. It would doubtless be a hard sea voyage so late in the fall—and strange to arrive there for the long nights. But he felt such an unspeakable yearning. This last bout of fear for his wife had completely broken all resistance in his soul—helplessly he surrendered to his own longing to flee from home.

## CHAPTER 4

ERLEND NIKULAUSSØN SERVED as the king's military commander and chieftain at the fortress of Vargøy for almost two years. In all that time he never ventured farther south than to Bjarkøy, when he and Sir Erling Vidkunssøn once arranged a meeting there. During the second summer Erlend was away, Heming Alfssøn finally died, and Erlend was appointed sheriff of Orkdøla county in his place. Haftor Graut traveled north to succeed him at Vargøy.

Erlend was a happy man when he sailed south in the autumn, several days after the Feast of the Birth of Mary. This was the redress he had been seeking all these years—to become sheriff of the region as his father had once been. Not that this had been a goal which he had ever worked to achieve. But it had always seemed to him that this was what he needed in order to assume the standing which he rightfully deserved—both in his own eyes and those of his peers. Now it no longer mattered that he was considered somewhat different from the men who were bench sitters—there was no longer anything awkward about his special position.

And he longed for home. It had been more peaceful in Finnmark than he had expected. Even the first winter took its toll on him; he sat idle in the castle and could do nothing about repairing the fortress. It had been well restored seventeen years before, but now it had fallen into terrible disrepair.

Then came spring and summer with great activity and commotion—meetings at various places along the fjords with the Norwegian and half-Norwegian tax collectors and with spokesmen for the peoples of the inland plains. Erlend sailed here and there with his two ships and enjoyed himself immensely. On the island the buildings were repaired and the castle fortified. But the following year, peace still prevailed.

Haftor would no doubt see to it that troubles commenced soon enough. Erlend laughed. They had sailed together almost as far as Trjanema, and there Haftor had found himself a Sami woman from Kola[1] whom he had taken with him. Erlend had spoken to him sternly. He had to remember that it was important for the heathens to realize that the Norwegians were the masters. And he would have to conduct himself so as not to provoke anyone unnecessarily, considering the small group of men he had with him. He shouldn't intervene if the Finns fought and killed each other; they were to be granted that pleasure without interference. But act like a hawk over the Russians and the Kola people, or whatever that rabble was called. And leave the women alone—for one thing, they were all witches; and for another, there were plenty who would offer themselves willingly. But the Godøy youth would just have to take care of himself, until he learned.

Haftor wanted to get away from his estates and his wife. Erlend now wanted to go back home to his. He felt a blissful longing for Kristin and Husaby and his home district and all his children—for everything that was back home with Kristin.

At Lyngsfjord he got word of a ship with several monks on board; they were supposedly Dominican friars from Nidaros who were heading north to try to plant the true faith among heathens and heretics in the border territories.

Erlend felt certain that Gunnulf was among them. And three nights later he was indeed sitting alone with his brother in a sod hut that belonged to a little Norwegian farm near the shore where they had found each other.

Erlend felt strangely moved. He had attended mass and had taken communion with his crew for the first time since he had come north, except when he was at Bjarkøy. The church at Vargøy was without a priest; a deacon lived at the castle, and he had made an effort to observe the holy days for them, but otherwise the Norwegians in the north had found little help for their souls. They had to console themselves with the thought that they were part of a kind of crusade, and surely their sins would not be judged so severely.

Erlend sat talking to Gunnulf about this, and his brother listened with an odd, remote smile on his thin, compressed lips. It looked as if he were constantly sucking on his lower lip, the way a person often does when he is thinking hard about something and is on the verge of understanding but has not yet achieved full clarity in his mind.

It was late at night. All the other people on the farm were asleep in the shed; the brothers knew that they were now the only ones awake. And they were both struck by the strange circumstance that the two of them should be sitting there alone.

The muffled and muted sound of the storm and the roaring sea reached them through the sod walls. Now and then gusts of wind would blow in, breathe on the embers of the hearth, and make the flame of the oil lamp flicker. There was no furniture in the hut; the brothers were sitting on the low earthen bench which ran along three sides of the room, and between them lay Gunnulf's writing board with ink horn, his quill pen, and a rolled-up parchment. Gunnulf had been writing down a few notes as his brother told him about meetings and Norwegian settlements, about navigation markers and weather indications and words in the Sami language—everything Erlend happened to think of. Gunnulf was piloting the ship himself; it was named *Sunnivasuden,* for the friars had chosen Saint Sunniva[2] as the patron saint for their endeavor.

"As long as you don't suffer the same fate as the martyred Selje men," said Erlend, and Gunnulf again gave him a little smile.

"You call me restless, Gunnulf," Erlend continued. "Then what should we call you? First you wander around in the southern lands for all those years, and then you've barely returned home before you give up your benefice and prebends[3] to go off to preach to the Devil and his offspring up north in Velliaa. You don't know their language and they don't know yours. It seems to me that you're even more inconstant than I am."

"I own neither manors nor kinsmen to answer for," said the monk. "I have now freed myself from all bonds, but you have bound yourself, brother."

"Yes, well . . . I suppose the man who owns nothing is free."

Gunnulf replied, "A man's possessions own him more than he owns them."

"Hmm. No, by God, I might concede that Kristin owns me. But I won't agree that the manor and the children own me too."

"Don't think that way, brother," said Gunnulf softly. "For then you might easily lose them."

"No, I refuse to be like those other old men, up to their chins in the muck of their land," said Erlend, laughing, and his brother smiled with him.

"I've never seen fairer children than Ivar and Skule," he said. "I think you must have looked like them at that age—it's no wonder our mother loved you so much."

Both brothers rested a hand on the writing board, which lay between them. Even in the faint light of the oil lamp it was possible to see how unlike the hands of these two men were. The monk's fingers bore no rings; they were white and sinewy, shorter and stubbier than the other man's fingers, and yet they looked much stronger—even though the palm of Erlend's fist was now as hard as horn and a blue-white scar from an arrow wound furrowed the dark skin from his wrist all the way up his sleeve. But the fingers of Erlend's slender, tanned hand were dry and knotty-jointed like tree branches, and they were completely covered with rings of gold and precious stones.

Erlend had an urge to take his brother's hand, but he was too embarrassed to do so; instead, he drank a toast to him, grimacing at the bad ale.

"And you think that Kristin has now regained her full health?" Erlend continued.

"Yes, she had blossomed like a rose when I was at Husaby in the summer," said the monk with a smile. He paused for a moment and then said somberly, "I ask this of you, brother—think more about the welfare of Kristin and your children than you have done in the past. Abide by her advice and agree to the decisions she and Eiliv have made; they're only waiting for your consent to conclude them."

"I'm not greatly in favor of these plans you speak of," said Erlend with some reluctance. "And now my position will be quite different."

"Your lands will gain in value if you consolidate your property more," replied the monk. "Kristin's plans seemed sensible when she explained them to me."

"And there isn't another woman in all of Norway who offers advice more freely than she does," said Erlend.

"But in the end you're the one who commands. And you now command Kristin too, and can do as you please," Gunnulf said, his voice strangely weak.

Erlend laughed softly from deep in his throat, then stretched and yawned. Suddenly somber, he said, "You have also counseled her, my brother. And at times your advice may well have come between our friendship."

"Do you mean the friendship between you and your wife, or the friendship between the two of us?" the monk asked hesitantly.

"Both," replied Erlend, as if the thought had just now occurred to him.

"It isn't usually necessary for a laywoman to be so pious," he continued in a lighter tone of voice.

"I have counseled her as I thought best. As it *was* best," Gunnulf corrected himself.

Erlend looked at the monk dressed in the rough, grayish-white friar's robes, with the black cowl thrown back so that it lay in thick folds around his neck and over his shoulders. The crown of his head was shaved so that only a narrow fringe of hair now remained, encircling his round, gaunt, pallid face; but his hair was no longer thick and black as it had been in Gunnulf's younger days.

"Well, you aren't as much my brother anymore as you are the brother of all men," said Erlend, surprising himself by the great bitterness in his own voice.

"That's not true—although it ought to be."

"So help me God, I think that's the real reason that you want to go up there to the Finns!"

Gunnulf bowed his head. His amber eyes smoldered.

"To some extent that's true," he said swiftly.

They spread out the furs and coverlets they had brought with them. It was too cold and raw in the room for them to undress, so they bade each other good night and lay down on the earthen bench, which was quite low to the floor to escape the smoke from the hearth.

Erlend lay there thinking about the news he had received from home. He hadn't heard much during the past years—two letters from his wife had reached him, but they had been outdated by the time they arrived. Sira Eiliv had written them for her. Kristin could write, and she had a beautiful hand, but she was never eager to do so, because she didn't think it quite proper for an uneducated woman.

She would no doubt become even more pious now that they had acquired a holy relic in the neighboring village, and it was from a man whom she had known while he was alive. And Gaute had now won release from his illness there, and Kristin herself had recovered her full health after having been weak ever since giving birth to the twins. Gunnulf said that the friars of Hamar had finally been forced to give Edvin Rikardssøn's body back to his brothers in Oslo, and they had now written down everything about Brother Edvin's life and about the miracles he was said to have performed, both during his lifetime and after death. It was their intention to send these writings to the Pope in an attempt to have the monk proclaimed a saint. Several brothers from Gauldal and Medaldal had journeyed south to bear witness to the wonders that Brother Edvin had achieved with his prayers of intercession in the parishes and with a crucifix he had carved; it was now at Medalhus. They had vowed to build a small church on Vatsfjeld, the mountain where he had spent several summers, living a hermit's existence, and where a mountain spring had become endowed with healing powers. And the brothers were given a hand from his body to enshrine in the church.

Kristin had contributed two silver bowls and the large cloak clasp with blue stones which she had inherited from her grandmother, Ulvhild Haavardsdatter, so that Tiedeken Paus in Nidaros could fashion a silver hand for Brother Edvin's bones. And she had been to Vatsfjeld with Sira Eiliv and her children and a great entourage when the archbishop consecrated the church at Midsummer the year after Erlend had departed for the north.

Afterwards, Gaute's health quickly improved; he had learned to walk and talk, and he was now like any other child his age. Erlend stretched out his limbs. That was the greatest joy they had been granted—that Gaute was now well. He would donate some land to the church. Gunnulf had told him that Gaute was blond, with a fair complexion, like his mother. If only he had been a little maiden, then he would have been named Magnhild. Yes, he was also longing for his handsome sons now.

Gunnulf Nikulaussøn lay there thinking about the spring day three years ago when he rode toward Husaby. On the way he met a man from the manor. The mistress was not at home, he had said; she was tending to a woman who was ill.

He was riding along a narrow, grass-covered road between old split-rail fences. Young, leafy trees covered the slopes, from the top all the way down to the swollen river rushing through the ravine below. He rode into the sun, and the tender green leaves glittered like golden flames on the branches, but inside the forest the shadows were already spreading, cool and deep, across the grassy floor.

Gunnulf reached a place where he could catch a glimpse of the lake, with a reflection of the dark opposite shore and the blue of the sky, and an image of the great summer clouds constantly merging and dispersed by the ripples. Far below the road was a small farm on green, flower-strewn slopes. A group of women wearing white wimples stood outside in the courtyard, but Kristin was not among them.

A little farther away he saw her horse; it was walking around in the pasture with several others. The road dipped down into a hollow of green shadows ahead of him, and where it curved up over the next rise in the hills, he saw her standing next to the fence beneath the foliage, listening to the birds singing. He looked at her slim, dark figure, leaning over the fence, facing the woods; there was a gleam of white from her wimple and her arm. He reined in his horse and rode toward her slowly, step by step. But when he drew closer, he saw that it was the slender stump of an old birch tree standing there.

The next evening, when his servants sailed his ship into Nidaros, the priest himself was at the helm. He felt his heart beating in his chest, steadfast and newborn. Now nothing could deter his purpose.

He now knew that what had held him back in life was the unquenchable longing he had carried with him ever since childhood. He wanted to win the love of others. To do so he had been kindhearted, gentle, and good-natured toward the poor; he had let his wisdom shine, but with moderation and humility, among the priests of the town so that they would like him; he had been submissive toward Lord Eiliv Kortin because the archbishop was friends with his father, and he knew how Lord Eiliv wanted people to behave. He had been loving and gentle toward Orm, in order to win the boy's affection away from his moody father. And Gunnulf had been stern and demanding toward Kristin because he saw what she needed: to encounter something that would not give way when she reached for help, something that would not lead her astray when she came, ready to follow.

But now he realized that he had sought to win her trust for himself more than he had tried to strengthen her faith in God.

Erlend had found expression for it this evening: Not as much my brother anymore as the brother of all men. This was the detour he would have to take before his brotherly love could benefit anyone at all.

Two weeks later he had divided up his possessions among his kinsmen and the Church and donned the robes of a friar. And now, this spring, when everyone was profoundly troubled by the terrible misfortune that had befallen the country—lightning had struck Christ Church in Nidaros and partially destroyed Saint Olav's shrine—Gunnulf had won the support of the archbishop for his old plan. Together with Brother Olav Jonssøn, who was an ordained priest like himself, and three younger monks—one from Nidaros and two from the order in Bjørgvin—he was now headed north to bring the light of the Word to the lost heathens who lived and died in darkness within the boundaries of a Christian land.

Christ, you who were crucified! Now I have given up everything that could bind me. And I have placed myself in your hands, if you would find my life worthy enough to be freed from its servitude to Satan. Take me so that I may feel that I am your slave, for then I will possess you in return.

Then someday, once again, his heart would crow and sing in his chest, as it did when he walked across the green plains at Romaborg, from pilgrim church to pilgrim church: "I am my Beloved's, and to Him belongs my desire."

The two brothers lay there, each on his own bench in the little hut, and let their thoughts lull them to sleep. A tiny ember smoldered in the hearth between them. Their thoughts took them farther and farther away from each other. And the following day one of them headed north, and the other south.

Erlend had promised Haftor Graut to go out to Godøy and take his sister south with him. She was married to Baard Aasulfssøn of Lensvik, who was also one of Erlend's kinsmen, but distantly related.

On the first morning, as *Margygren* cut through the waters of

Godøy Sound with its sails billowing against the blue mountains in the fine breeze, Erlend was standing on the raised afterdeck of the ship. Ulf Haldorssøn had the helm. Then Fru Sunniva came up to them. The hood of her cloak was draped over her shoulders, and the wind was blowing her wimple back from her curly, sun-yellow hair. She had the same sea-blue, gleaming eyes as her brother, and like him she had a fair complexion, but with many freckles, which also covered her small, plump hands.

From the first evening Erlend saw her at Godøy—their eyes met, and then they looked away, both of them smiling secretively—he was convinced that she knew him, and he knew her. Sunniva Olavsdatter—he could take her with his bare hands, and she was waiting for him to do so.

Now, as he stood with her hand in his—he had helped her up onto the deck—he happened to look into Ulf's coarse, dark face. No doubt Ulf knew it too. Erlend felt oddly ashamed under the other man's gaze. He suddenly remembered everything that this kinsman and weaponsbearer had witnessed—every mad prank that Erlend had gotten caught up in, ever since his youth. Ulf didn't need to look at him so scornfully. Erlend consoled himself that he hadn't intended to come any closer to this woman than honor and virtue permitted. He was old enough by now, and wise from his mistakes; he could be allowed north to Haalogaland without getting himself tangled up in some foolishness with another man's wife. He had a wife himself now. He had been faithful to Kristin from the very first time he saw her and to this day. No reasonable man would count those few incidents that had occurred up north. But otherwise he hadn't even looked at another woman—in that way. He knew . . . with a Norwegian woman, and even worse, with one of their peers . . . no, he would never have a moment's peace in his heart if he betrayed Kristin in that way. But this voyage south with her on board—it might easily prove risky.

It helped somewhat that they had stormy weather along the way, so he had other things to do than banter with the woman. They had to seek harbor in Dynøy and wait a few days. While they were anchored there, something happened that made Fru Sunniva seem less enticing to him.

Erlend and Ulf and a couple of the servants slept in the same cabin where she and her maids slept. One morning he was there alone, and Fru Sunniva had not yet gotten up. Then she called to him, saying that she had lost a gold ring in her bed. He had to agree to come and help her look for it. She was crawling around in bed on her knees, wearing only her shift. Now and then they would bump into each other, and every time they would both get a devilish glint in their eyes. Then she grabbed hold of him. And it's true that his behavior had not been overly proper, either; time and place were both against him. But she was so bold and disgracefully willing that he grew suddenly cold. Blushing with shame, he turned away from that face, which had dissolved with laughter and wantonness. He tore himself away without further explanation and left; then he sent in Fru Sunniva's maidservants to her.

No, by Satan, he was not some young pup who allowed himself to be caught in the bedstraw. It was one thing to seduce—but to be seduced was something else entirely. But he had to laugh; here he stood, having fled from a beautiful woman like Joseph the Hebrew. Yes, strange things happened both at sea and on land.

No, Fru Sunniva. No, he had to think of one woman—a woman that he knew. She had come to meet him in a hostel for wandering soldiers—and she came with as much chasteness and dignity as a royal maiden going to mass. In groves and in barns she had been his. God forgive him—he had forgotten her birthright and her honor; and she had forgotten them for his sake, but she hadn't been able to fling them away. Her lineage was evident in her, even when she did not think of it.

God bless you, dear Kristin. So help me, God—I will keep the promise that I made to you in secret and at the church door, or I will never be a man. So be it.

Then Erlend had Fru Sunniva put ashore at Yrjar where she had kinsmen. And best of all, she didn't seem overly angry when they parted. There had been no need for him to bow his head with a somber expression, like a monk; they had chased each other out over the oarlocks, as the saying goes. In parting, Erlend gave her several costly furs for a cloak, and she promised that one day he would see her wearing that cloak. They would surely meet again. Poor thing, her husband was sickly and no longer young.

But Erlend was glad to come home to his wife with nothing on his conscience that he would have to conceal from her, and he was proud of his own newly tested steadfastness. He was quite giddy and wild with longing for Kristin. She was the sweetest and loveliest rose and lily—and she was his!

Kristin came out to the skerries to meet him when Erlend anchored at Birgsi. Fishermen had brought word to Vigg that *Margygren* had been seen near Yrjar. She had brought along her two eldest sons and Margret, and back home at Husaby a feast was being prepared for friends and kinsmen to celebrate Erlend's homecoming.

She had grown so beautiful that it took Erlend's breath away when he saw her. But she had changed. The girlish demeanor which had returned each time she had recovered from a childbirth—the frail and delicate nunlike face beneath the wimple of a married woman—was now gone. She was a blossoming young woman and mother. Her cheeks were round and a healthy pink, framed by the white wimple; her breasts were high and firm, covered with glittering chains and brooches. Her hips were rounder and wider, soft beneath the belt bearing her ring of keys and the gilded sheath holding her scissors and knife. Oh yes, she had grown even more lovely. She didn't look as if she might be easily carried off to heaven as she had before. Even her large, slender hands had grown fuller and whiter.

They stayed at Vigg that night, in the abbot's house. And this time it was a young, flushed, and happy Kristin, gentle and glowing with joy, who rode with Erlend to the celebration at Husaby when they set off for home the next day.

There were so many important matters that she had to speak with her husband about when he came home. There were hundreds of things about the children, about her worries for Margret, and about her plans to set the estates back on their feet. But all this was swallowed up in the festivities.

They went from one banquet to another, and she accompanied the new sheriff on his rounds. Erlend now had more men serving at Husaby. Messages and letters flew between him and his subordinates and envoys. Erlend was full of high spirits and merriment. Why shouldn't he be a capable sheriff? He who had beat his head against nearly every barrier of Norwegian law and Christian commandment. Such things were well learned and not easily forgotten. The man was quick-witted and he had been taught well in his youth. Now all this became apparent in him again. He grew accustomed to reading letters himself, and he had acquired an Icelander as his scribe. In the past, Erlend had put his seal on everything that was read aloud to him, barely casting a glance at even a single line—this is what Kristin had discovered during the two years in which she had become familiar with all the papers she found in his chests of letters.

Now a certain recklessness came over her, which she had never felt before. She grew livelier and more talkative when she was among other people—for she sensed that she was beautiful now, and she felt completely healthy and well for the first time since she had been married. And in the evening, when she and Erlend lay together in a strange bed in the loft of one of the great estates or in a farmer's house, they would laugh and whisper and jest about the people they had met and the news they had heard. Erlend was more rash in his speech than ever, and people seemed to like him even better than before.

Kristin could see it in their own children. They would grow flustered with delight whenever their father occasionally took notice of them. Naakkve and Bjørgulf now spent all their time with such things as bows and spears and axes. Every once in a while their father would stop on his way across the courtyard, glance at them, and then correct whatever they were doing. "Not like that, my son—you should hold it like this." And then he would shift the grip of the boy's small fist and place his fingers in the proper position. Then they would be filled with zeal.

The two eldest sons were inseparable. Bjørgulf was the biggest and strongest of the children, as tall as Naakkve, who was a year and a half older, but stouter. Bjørgulf had tightly curled, raven black hair; his small face was broad but handsome, his eyes dark blue. One day Erlend asked Kristin anxiously whether she knew that Bjørgulf saw poorly out of one eye—he also had a slight squint. Kristin said she didn't think there was anything wrong and that he'd probably grow out of it. As things had turned out, this child was the one she had given the least attention; he had been born when she was worn out from caring for Naakkve, and Gaute had followed soon afterwards. He was the hardiest of the children, no doubt also the smartest, but taciturn. Erlend was more fond of this son than the others.

Although he wouldn't admit it to himself, Erlend bore some ill will toward Naakkve because the boy had arrived so inopportunely and because he was named for his grandfather. And Gaute was not as he'd expected. The boy had a large head, which was understandable, since for two years it seemed as if only his head had grown—and now his limbs had to catch up. His wits were good enough, but he spoke very slowly because if he talked fast he would slur his words or stutter, and then Margret would make fun of him. Kristin had a great weakness for the boy, even though Erlend could see that in some ways the eldest son was her favorite child. But Gaute had been so frail, and he looked a bit like Kristin's father, with his flaxen hair and dark gray eyes. And he was always clinging to his mother. He was a rather solitary child, between the two oldest ones, who always stuck together, and the twins, who were still so little that they kept close to their foster mothers.

Kristin had less time for her children now, and she had to do as the other women did and let the serving maids look after them; but the two oldest sons preferred to follow the men around on the farm. She no longer brooded over them with that old, sickly tenderness, but she played and laughed with them more, whenever she had time to gather them around her.

At the beginning of the New Year, they received a letter at Husaby under the seal of Lavrans Bjørgulfsøn. It had been written in his own hand and sent with the priest of Orkedal, who had been traveling in the south, so it was two months old. The biggest news in the letter was that Lavrans had betrothed Ramborg to Simon Andressøn of Formo. The wedding would take place on Holy Cross Day in the spring.

Kristin was surprised beyond words. But Erlend said he had thought this might happen—ever since he had heard that Simon Darre had become a widower and had settled on his estate at Sil after old Sir Andres Gudmundssøn had died.

## CHAPTER 5

SIMON DARRE HAD accepted it as only proper when his father had arranged the marriage with Lavrans Bjørgulfsøn's daughter for him. It had always been the custom in his family for the parents to make these decisions. He was pleased when he saw that his betrothed was so beautiful and charming. And he had always thought that he would be good friends with the woman his father had chosen for him. He and Kristin were well-suited in age and wealth and birth. Lavrans may have come from a somewhat better lineage, but Simon's father was a knight and had been close to King Haakon, while Lavrans had always lived quietly on his estates. And Simon had never seen married couples not get on well together, as long as they were equals.

Then came that evening in the loft at Finsbrekken, when the people tried to torment the innocent young child. From that moment he knew that he felt greater affection for his betrothed than was merely expected of him. He didn't dwell on this—he was happy. He could see that the maiden was modest and shy, but he didn't give this much thought either. Then came that time in Oslo, when he was forced to think about these things—and then the night in Fluga's loft.

He had been faced with something he had never imagined could happen in this world—not between honorable people of good family, and not in these times. Blinded and confused, he had staggered his way out of the betrothal, although his demeanor had been cool and calm and steady as he talked over these matters with his father and hers.

Then he had found himself outside the traditions of his family, and so he did what was also unheard of in his lineage: Without even consulting his father, he had courted the rich young widow of Mandvik. It dazzled him when he realized that Fru Halfrid was fond of him. She was much wealthier and more highborn than Kristin; she was the niece of Baron Tore Haakonssøn of Tunsberg and the widow of Sir Finn Aslakssøn. And she was beautiful, with such a gracious and noble bearing that compared to her, the women in his circle were little more than peasant women, he thought. The Devil take him if he wouldn't show everyone that he could win the noblest wife; she was even more resplendent with wealth and other possessions than that man from Trønder who had lured Kristin into shame. And a widow—that was good and proper; then he knew where he stood. By Satan, he would never trust a maiden again.

He had learned that it was not as simple to live in this world as he had thought back home at Dyfrin. There his father ruled over everything, and his views were always right. Simon had been one of the king's retainers, and he had served as a page for a while; he had also been taught by his father's resident priest at home. At times he would find what his father said a bit old-fashioned. Occasionally he would voice his opposition, but it was only meant in jest, and it was taken as such. "What a quick wit Simon has," laughed his father and mother and siblings, who never spoke against Sir Andres. But everything was done as his father commanded, and Simon himself thought this reasonable.

During the years he was married to Halfrid Erlingsdatter and lived at Mandvik, he learned a little more each day that life could be more complicated and difficult than Sir Andres Gudmundssøn had ever dreamed.

Simon could never have imagined that he would not be happy with such a wife as he had now won. Deep in his soul he felt a painful sense of amazement whenever he looked at his wife, as she moved about the house all day long, so lovely, with her gentle eyes, and her mouth so sweet as long as it was closed. He had never seen any other woman wear gowns and jewelry with such grace. But in the dark gloom of the night his aversion to her stripped him of all youth and vigor. She was sickly, her breath was tainted, and her caresses plagued him. And yet she was so kind that he felt a desperate sense of shame, but he still could not overcome his dislike of her.

They hadn't been married long before he realized that she would never give him a healthy, living child. He could see that she herself grieved over this even more than he did. The pain he felt was like knives in his heart whenever he thought of *her* fate in this matter. One way or another he had heard that she was this way because Sir Finn had kicked and struck her so badly that she had miscarried many times while she was married to him. He had been insanely jealous of his beautiful young wife. Her kinsmen wanted to take her away from him, but Halfrid felt that it was a Christian wife's duty to stay with her lawful husband, no matter how he behaved.

But as long as Simon had no children with her, he would feel all his days that it was *her* land they lived on and *her* riches that he managed. He managed sensibly and carefully, but during those years there rose up in his soul a longing for Formo, his grandmother's ancestral estate, which he had always been destined to inherit after his father. He began to feel that he belonged north in Gudbrandsdal even more than at Romerike.

People continued to call Halfrid "the knight's wife," as they had during the time of her first husband. And this made Simon feel even more as if he were merely her advisor at Mandvik.

Then one day, Simon and his wife were sitting alone in the hall. One of the maids had just come in on some errand. Halfrid stared after her as she left.

"I'm not sure," she said, "but I'm afraid that Jorunn is with child this summer."

Simon was holding a crossbow on his lap, adjusting the locking device. He adjusted the crank, sighted down the spring assembly, and said without looking up, "Yes, and it's mine."

His wife didn't reply. When he finally looked up at her, she was sitting there sewing, going about her work just as steadily as he had been doing his.

Simon was truly sorry. Sorry he had offended his wife in this manner, and sorry he had taken up with this girl, regretting that he had now assumed the burden of fatherhood. He was far from certain that it was actually his—Jorunn had loose ways. And he had never really liked her; she was ugly, but she was quick-witted and amusing to talk to. And she was the one who had always sat up to wait for him whenever he came home late the winter before. He had spoken rashly because he expected his wife to berate and denounce him. That was foolish of him; he should have known that Halfrid would consider herself above such conduct. But now it was done, and he wouldn't retreat from his own words. He would have to put up with being called father of his maid's child, whether he was or not.

Halfrid didn't mention the matter until a year later; then she asked Simon one day whether he knew that Jorunn was to be married over at Borg. Simon knew this quite well, since he himself had given her a dowry. Where was the child to live? his wife wanted to know. With the mother's parents, where she now was, replied Simon.

Then Halfrid said, "It seems to me that it would be more proper for your daughter to grow up here on your manor."

"On *your* manor, you mean?" asked Simon.

A slight tremor flickered across his wife's face.

"You know full well, dear husband, that as long as we both live, you are the one who rules here at Mandvik," she said.

Simon went over and placed his hands on his wife's shoulders.

"If it's true, Halfrid, that you think you can stand to see that child here with us, then I owe you great thanks for your generosity."

But he didn't like it. Simon had seen the girl several times—she was a rather unattractive child, and he couldn't see that she looked like him or anyone else in his family. He was even less inclined to believe that he was the father. And he had resented it deeply when he heard that Jorunn had the child baptized Arngjerd, after his mother, without asking his permission. But he would have to let Halfrid do as she wished. She brought the child to Mandvik, found a foster mother for her, and saw to it that the girl lacked for nothing. If she caught sight of the child, she would often take her onto her lap and chat with her, kindly and lovingly. And gradually, as Simon saw more of the child, he grew fond of the little maiden—he had great affection for children. Now he also thought he could see some resemblance between Arngjerd and his father. It was possible that Jorunn had been wise enough to restrain herself after the master had come too close to her. If so, then Arngjerd was indeed his daughter, and what Halfrid had persuaded him to do was honorable and right.

After they had been married for five years, Halfrid bore her husband a fully formed son. She was radiant with joy, but soon after the birth she fell ill, and it quickly became clear to everyone that she would die. And yet she was without fear, the last time that she had her full wits about her for a moment. "Now you will sit here, Simon, master of Mandvik, and rule over the estate for your lineage and mine," she told her husband.

After that her fever rose so sharply that she was no longer aware of anything, and so she did not have to suffer the grief, while she was still in this world, of hearing that the boy had died one day before his mother. And no doubt in that other home she would not feel sorrow over such things, but would be glad that she had their Erling with her, thought Simon.

Later, Simon remembered that on the night when the two bodies were laid out in the loft, he had stood leaning over the fence next to a field down by the sea. It was just before Midsummer, and the night was so bright that the glow of the full moon was barely visible. The water was gleaming and pale, rippling and lapping along the shore. Simon had slept no more than an hour at a time, off and on, since the night the boy was born. That seemed to him very long ago now, and he was so tired that he scarcely felt able to grieve.

He was then twenty-seven years old.

In the middle of the summer, after the inheritance had been settled,[1] Simon turned over Mandvik to Stig Haakonssøn, Halfrid's cousin. He left for Dyfrin and stayed there all winter.

Old Sir Andres lay in bed, suffering from dropsy and numerous ailments and pains; he was approaching the end now, and he complained a great deal. Life had not been so easy for him in the long run, either. Things had not gone as he had wished and expected for his handsome and promising children. Simon sat with his father and tried hard to adopt the calm and lighthearted tone from the past, but the old man moaned incessantly. Helga Saksesdatter, whom Gyrd had married, was so refined that there was no end to the unreasonable demands she could dream up—Gyrd didn't even dare belch in his own manor without asking his wife for permission. And then there was Torgrim, who was always whining about his stomach. Sir Andres would never have given his daughter to Torgrim if he had known the man was so loathsome that he was incapable of either living or dying. Astrid would have no joy from her youth or her wealth as long as her husband was alive. Sigrid wandered around the estate, broken and grieving—all smiles and merriment had deserted her, that good daughter of his. And she had borne that child, while Simon had none. Sir Andres wept, miserable and old and ill. Gudmund had refused all of the marriages suggested by his father, who had grown so old and frail that he had let the boy wear him down.

But the misfortunes had begun when Simon and that foolish maiden had defied their parents. And Lavrans was to blame—as bold a man as he was among men, his knees buckled before his womenfolk. No doubt the girl had sobbed and screamed, and he at once relented and sent word to that gilded whoremaster from Trøndelag who couldn't even wait until he and his bride were married. But if Lavrans had been master of his house, then he, Andres Darre, would have shown that he could teach a beardless whelp sensible behavior. Kristin Lavransdatter—she certainly had children enough. A healthy, squirming son every eleventh month, he had heard.

"It's going to be costly, Father," said Simon, laughing. "Their inheritance will be divided up many times." He picked up Arngjerd and set her on his lap. She had just come toddling into the room.

"Well, that one there won't cause your inheritance to be divided up into too many parts after you—whoever does inherit it," said Sir Andres crossly. He was fond of his son's daughter in his own way, but it infuriated him that Simon had a bastard child. "Have you thought of marrying anew, Simon?"

"You must let Halfrid grow cold in her grave first, Father," said Simon, stroking the child's pale hair. "I'll probably marry again, but there's no reason to make haste."

Then he picked up his crossbow and skis and set off for the forest to find some respite. With his dogs at his side he tracked elk through the mountain pass and shot wood grouse in the treetops. At night he slept in the forest hut belonging to Dyfrin, thinking that it felt good to be alone.

There was the sound of skis scraping outside in the pass; the dogs leaped up, and other dogs responded from outdoors. Simon threw open the door to the moon-blue night, and Gyrd came in, slender and tall, handsome and silent. He now looked younger than Simon, who had always been rather stout and had grown a good deal heavier during those years at Mandvik.

The brothers sat with the sack of provisions between them, eating and drinking and staring into the hearth.

"I suppose you know," said Gyrd, "that Torgrim will make a great deal of noise and ruckus when Father is gone. And he has won Gudmund's support. And Helga's. They will not grant Sigrid the full rights of a sister with us."

"I realize that. But she must be given her share as a sister; you and I should be able to force them to agree, brother."

"It would be best if Father himself saw to this matter before he dies," said Gyrd.

"No, let Father die in peace," replied Simon. "You and I will manage to protect our sister, so they don't rob her because she has suffered such misfortune."

So the heirs of Sir Andres Darre parted in bitter enmity after his death. Gyrd was the only one Simon said farewell to when he left home, and now he knew that Gyrd wouldn't have many pleasant days with that wife of his. Sigrid moved to Formo with Simon; she would keep house for him, and he in turn would manage her properties.

He rode into his own estate on a grayish-blue day as the snow was melting, when the alder trees along the Laag River were brown with buds. As he was about to cross the threshold of the main house with Arngjerd in his arms, Sigrid Andresdatter asked, "Why are you smiling like that, Simon?"

"Was I smiling?"

He had been thinking that this was a different kind of homecoming than what he had once dreamed of—when he would one day settle down here on his grandmother's estate. A seduced sister and a paramour's child—these were now his companions.

During that first summer he saw little of the people at Jørundgaard; he diligently avoided them.

But on the Sunday after the Feast of the Birth of Mary in the fall, he happened to be standing next to Lavrans Bjørgulfsøn in church, and so the two of them had to give each other the traditional kiss after Sira Eirik had prayed for the peace of the Holy Church to be bountiful among them. And when Simon felt the older man's thin, dry lips on his cheek and heard him whisper the prayer of peace, he was strangely moved. He realized that Lavrans meant more by this than if he were simply obeying the ritual of the Church.

He hastened outside after the mass was done, but over by the horses he again ran into Lavrans, who invited him to come to Jørundgaard for dinner. Simon replied that his daughter was sick and that his sister was sitting with her. Lavrans then prayed that God might heal the child and shook his hand in farewell.

Several days later they had been working hard at Formo to bring in the harvest because the weather looked threatening. Most of the grain had been brought in by evening, when the first showers opened up. Simon ran across the courtyard in the downpour; great bands of bright sunshine broke through the clouds and lit up the main building and the mountain wall beyond. Then he caught sight of a little maiden standing in front of the door in the rain and the sunlight. She had his favorite dog with her. The dog pulled loose and leaped at Simon, dragging along a woven woman's belt, which was tied to his collar.

He saw that the girl came from highborn family. She was bareheaded and wore no cloak, but her wine-red dress was made from foreign cloth, and it was embroidered across the breast and fastened with a gilded brooch. A silken cord held her rain-dark hair back from her brow. The girl had a lively little face with a broad forehead, a sharp chin, and big, shining eyes. Her cheeks were flaming red, as if she had been running hard.

Simon knew who the maiden must be and greeted her by name: Ramborg.

"What might be the reason for you honoring us with this visit?"

It was the dog, she told Simon, as she followed him into the house and out of the rain. The dog had gotten into the habit of running off to Jørundgaard; now she was bringing him back. Oh yes, she knew it was his dog; she had seen the animal running alongside when he rode.

Simon scolded her a bit because she had come alone. He said he would have horses saddled and escort her home himself. But first she must have some food. Ramborg ran at once over to the bed where little Arngjerd lay ill; both the child and Sigrid were pleased with their guest, for Ramborg was both lively and merry. She wasn't like her sisters, thought Simon.

He rode with Ramborg as far as the manor gate and was then about to turn around when he met Lavrans, who had just learned that the child was not with her foster sisters at Laugarbru. He was on his way out with his servants to look for her—he was quite worried. Now Simon had to come inside, and as soon as he sat down in the hall of the main house, his shyness left him and he soon felt at home with Ragnfrid and Lavrans. They sat up late over their ale, and since the weather had grown quite fierce, he accepted their invitation to stay the night.

There were two beds in the hall. Ragnfrid made up one of them nicely for the guest, and then she asked where Ramborg should sleep—with her parents or in the other building?

"No, I want to sleep in my own bed," said the child. "Can't I sleep with you, Simon?" she begged.

Her father said that their guest should not be bothered with children in his bed, but Ramborg continued to insist that she wanted to sleep with Simon. Finally Lavrans said sternly that she was too big to share a bed with a strange man.

"No, I'm not, Father," she protested. "I'm not too big, am I, Simon?"

"You're too little," said Simon, laughing. "Offer to sleep with me five years from now and I certainly won't say no. But by then you'll no doubt want a different sort of man than a hideous, fat old widower, little Ramborg!"

Lavrans didn't seem pleased by the jest; he told her sharply to keep quiet now and go lie down in her parents' bed.

But Ramborg shouted, "Now you have asked for me, Simon Darre, so my father could hear you!"

"So be it," replied Simon with a laugh. "But I'm afraid he would refuse me, Ramborg."

After that day the people of Formo and Jørundgaard were constantly together. Ramborg went over to the neighboring estate as often as she had the chance, tending to Arngjerd as if the child were one of her dolls, following Sigrid around and helping with household chores, sitting on Simon's lap when they were in the main house. He fell into the habit of teasing and chattering with the maiden as he had in the old days when she and Ulvhild were like sisters to him.

Simon had lived in the valley for two years when Geirmund Hersteinssøn of Kruke asked for the hand of Sigrid Andresdatter. The family of Kruke was an old lineage, but even though some of the men had served in the retinues of kings, they had never won fame outside their own district. Yet it was the best marriage Sigrid could expect to make, and she was quite willing to marry Geirmund. Her brothers made the arrangements, and Simon was to hold his sister's wedding on his estate.

One evening just before the wedding, when they were rushing about making preparations for the feast, Simon said in jest that he didn't know how things would go with his household after Sigrid left. Then Ramborg said, "You'll have to manage as best you can for two more years, Simon. At fourteen a maiden reaches a marriageable age, and then you can bring me home."

"No, *you* I wouldn't want," said Simon with a laugh. "I don't trust my ability to harness a wild maiden like you."

"It's the ponds with still water that have deceptive bottoms, my father says," replied Ramborg. "I may be wild, but my sister was meek and quiet. Have you forgotten Kristin, Simon Andressøn?"

Simon jumped up from the bench, took the maiden in his arms, and raised her to his chest. He kissed her throat so hard that he left a little red mark. Horrified and astounded by his own actions, he let her go; then he grabbed Arngjerd, tossed her in the air, and hugged her in the same way so as to hide his feelings. He ran about, chasing the girls, the half-grown maiden and the little one, so that they fled up onto the tables and along the benches, until finally he lifted them up onto the crossbeam nearest the door and then ran outside.

They almost never mentioned Kristin at Jørundgaard when he was within earshot.

Ramborg Lavransdatter grew up to be a lovely maiden. The local gossips were busy marrying her off. One time it was Eindride Haakonssøn of the Valders-Gjeslings. They were third cousins but Lavrans and Haakon were both so wealthy that they should be able to send a letter to the Pope in Italy and obtain dispensation.[2]

That would finally put an end to some of the old legal disputes that had continued ever since the old Gjeslings had sided with Duke Skule, and King Haakon had taken the Vaage estate away from them and given it to Sigurd Eldjar. Ivar Gjesling the Younger had, in turn, acquired Sundbu through marriage and the exchange of properties, but these matters had caused an endless number of quarrels and disagreements. Lavrans himself laughed at the whole thing; whatever compensation he might be able to claim for his wife wasn't worth the parchment and wax he had used up on this matter—not to mention the toil and traveling. But he had been embroiled in the dispute ever since he had become a married man, so he couldn't give it up.

But Eindride Gjesling celebrated his marriage to another maiden, and the people at Jørundgaard didn't seem overly troubled by this. They were invited to the banquet, and Ramborg told everyone proudly when she came home that four men had spoken to Lavrans about her, either on their own behalf or for kinsmen. Lavrans had told them he wouldn't agree to any betrothal for his daughter until she was old enough to have some say in the matter herself.

And that's how things stood until the spring of the year when Ramborg was fourteen winters old. One evening she was out in the cowshed at Formo with Simon, looking at a new calf. It was white with a brown patch, and Ramborg thought the patch looked very much like a church. Simon was sitting on the edge of the grain bin, the maiden was leaning on his knees, and he was tugging at her braids.

"It looks as if you will soon be riding in a bridal procession to church, Ramborg!"

"You know quite well that my father wouldn't refuse you if you asked for my hand," she said. "I'm old enough now that I could be married this year."

Simon gave a little start, but he tried to laugh.

"Are you talking about that foolishness again?"

"You know it's not foolishness," said the girl, looking up at him with her big eyes. "I've known for a long time that what I want is to move over here to Formo with you. Why have you kissed me and held me on your lap so often for all these years if you didn't want to marry me?"

"Certainly I would like to marry you, dear Ramborg. But I've never thought that such a young, beautiful maiden would be intended for me. I'm seventeen years older than you; no doubt you haven't thought about how you would end up with an old, bleary-eyed, big-bellied husband while you were a woman in the best of her years."

"These *are* my best years," she said, her face radiant. "And besides, you're not so decrepit, Simon!"

"But I'm ugly too. You'd soon grow tired of kissing me!"

"You have no reason to think that," she replied, laughing again as she tilted her face up toward him for a kiss. But he didn't kiss her.

"I won't take advantage of your imprudence, my sweet. Lavrans wants to take you with him to the south this summer. If you haven't changed your mind when you return, then I will thank God and Our Lady for better fortune than I had ever expected—but I will not bind you to this, fair Ramborg."

He took his dogs, his spear, and his bow and went up into the mountains that same evening. There was still a great deal of snow on the high plateau. He went to his hut to get a pair of skis and then stayed out by the lake south of the Boar Range and hunted reindeer for a week. But on the night he headed back toward the village, he grew uneasy and afraid again. It would be just like Ramborg to have said something to her father all the same. As he crossed the meadow near Jørundgaard's mountain hut, he saw smoke and sparks coming from the roof. He thought Lavrans himself might be there, so he went over to the hut.

From the other man's demeanor Simon thought he had guessed right. But they sat and talked about the bad summer the year before and about when might be a good time to move the livestock up to the mountain pastures; about the hunting and about Lavrans's new falcon, which was sitting on the floor, flapping its wings over the entrails of the birds roasting on a spit over the fire. Lavrans had come up to see to his horse shed in Ilmandsdal; it was reported to have collapsed, according to several people from Alvdal who had passed through earlier that day. The two men spent most of the evening in this fashion.

Then Simon finally said, "I don't know whether Ramborg has

said anything to you about a matter which we discussed one evening?"

Lavrans said slowly, "I think you should have spoken to me first, Simon. You might imagine what kind of answer you would have received. Yes, well—I can understand how it happened that you mentioned it first to the maiden—and it will make no difference. I'm happy to give my child into the hands of a good man."

Then there's not much more to say, thought Simon. And yet it was strange—here he sat, a man who had never intended to come too close to any virtuous maiden or woman, and now he was bound on his honor to marry a girl he did not truly want. But he made an attempt.

"It's not true, Lavrans, that I've been courting your daughter behind your back. I thought I was so old that she wouldn't consider it anything but brotherly affection from the past if I talked with her so often. And if you think I'm too old for her, I wouldn't be surprised nor would I allow it to end the friendship between us."

"I've met few men I would rather see take a son's place than you, Simon," replied Lavrans. "And I would rather give Ramborg away myself. You know who would be the man to arrange her marriage after I'm gone." That was the first time any mention was made between them of Erlend Nikulaussøn. "In many ways my son-in-law is a better man than I took him for when I first met him. But I don't know whether he's the right person to make a wise decision about a young maiden's marriage. And I can tell that this is what Ramborg wants herself."

"She thinks so now," said Simon. "But she's hardly more than a child, and I don't intend to press you, if you think we should wait a little longer."

"And I," said Lavrans with a slight frown, "do not intend to force my daughter upon you—you mustn't believe that."

"*You* should know," said Simon quickly, "that there is not another maiden in all of Norway I would rather have than Ramborg. If truth be told, Lavrans, my good fortune seems much too great if I'm to have such a fair, young, and good bride, who is rich and descended from the best lineage. And you as my father-in-law," he added, a little self-consciously.

Lavrans chuckled with embarrassment. "You know how I feel

about you. And you will deal with my child and her inheritance in such a way that her mother and I will never have cause to regret this arrangement."

"That I promise you, with the help of God and all the saints," said Simon.

Then they shook hands. Simon remembered the first time he had secured such an arrangement by clasping Lavrans's hand. His heart felt small and pained in his breast.

But Ramborg *was* a better match than he could have expected. There were only the two daughters to divide up the inheritance after Lavrans's death. He would step into the role of son with the man whom he had always respected and loved above all others he knew. And Ramborg was indeed young and sweet and lively.

Surely he must have acquired the wisdom of a grown man by now. Had he actually thought he could win Kristin as a widow even though he couldn't have her as a maiden? After the other man had enjoyed her youth—and with a dozen stepsons of his lineage? No, then he deserved to have his brothers declare him incapable and refuse to let him handle his own affairs. Erlend would live to be as old as the stone of the mountain—that type of fellow always did.

So now they would be called brothers-in-law. They hadn't seen each other since that night in the house in Oslo. Well, no doubt it would be even more uncomfortable for Erlend than for him to be reminded of that.

He would be a good husband to Ramborg, with no deceptions. And yet it was possible that the child had lured him into a trap.

"You're sitting there laughing?" said Lavrans.

"Was I laughing? It was just something that struck me . . ."

"You must tell me what it is, Simon, so I can laugh too."

Simon Andressøn fixed his small, sharp eyes on the other man's face.

"I was thinking about . . . women. I wonder whether any woman respects the laws and beliefs of men as we do among ourselves—when she or her own kind can win something by stepping over them. Halfrid, my first wife . . . Well, I haven't spoken of this to a single Christian soul before you, Lavrans Bjørgulfsøn, and I will never speak of it again. She was such a good and pious and virtuous woman that I don't think she has ever had an equal.

I've told you about what she did when Arngjerd was born. But back when we realized how things stood with Sigrid—well, Halfrid wanted us to hide my sister and she would pretend that she herself was with child and then present Sigrid's child as her own. In that way we would have an heir and the child would be cared for, and Sigrid could live with us and wouldn't have to be separated from her son. I don't think Halfrid realized that this would have been a betrayal of her own kinsmen."

After a moment Lavrans said, "Then you could have stayed at Mandvik, Simon."

"Yes." Simon Darre laughed harshly. "And perhaps with just as much right as many other men occupy lands they call their ancestral estates. Since we have nothing more to rely on in such matters except the honor of women."

Lavrans pulled the hood over the falcon's head and lifted the bird onto his wrist.

"This is a strange topic of conversation for a man who is thinking of marriage," he said quietly. There was a hint of displeasure in his voice.

"Of course no one would think such things of *your* daughters," replied Simon.

Lavrans looked down at his falcon, scratching it with a twig.

"Not even about Kristin?" he whispered.

"No," said Simon firmly. "She didn't deal with me kindly, but I never found that she was untruthful. She told me honestly and openly that she had met another man whom she cared for more than me."

"When you so willingly let her go," said Lavrans softly, "that was not because you had heard . . . any rumors about her?"

"No," said Simon in the same firm voice. "I never heard rumors about Kristin."

It was agreed that the betrothal would be celebrated that very summer and the wedding would take place during Easter of the following year, after Ramborg had turned fifteen.

Kristin had not seen Jørundgaard since the day she rode away as a bride, and that was eight winters ago. Now she returned with a great entourage: her husband, Margret, five sons, nursemaids, serving men and women, and horses carrying their traveling goods. Lavrans had ridden out to meet them and found them at Dovre. Kristin no longer cried as easily as she had in her youth, but when she saw her father riding toward them, her eyes filled with tears. She reined in her horse, slipped down from the saddle, and ran to greet her father; when she reached him, she grabbed his hand and kissed it humbly. Lavrans at once jumped down from his horse and took his daughter in his arms. Then he shook hands with Erlend, who had done as the others had and came to meet his father-in-law on foot, with respectful words of greeting.

The next day Simon came over to Jørundgaard to see his new kinsmen. Gyrd Darre and Geirmund of Kruke were with him, but their wives had stayed behind at Formo. Simon was going to hold the wedding at his own estate, so there was much work for the women to do.

It turned out that when they met, Simon and Erlend greeted each other openly and without restraint. Simon kept his feelings in check, and Erlend was so unabashed and merry that the other man thought he must have forgotten where they had last met. Then Simon gave Kristin his hand. The two of them were more uncertain, and their eyes barely met for more than a moment.

Kristin thought his looks had faded a good deal. In his youth, Simon had been quite handsome, even though he was much too stout and his neck was too thick. His steel-gray eyes had seemed small under his full eyelids, his mouth was too little, and his dimples were too big in his round, childish face. But he had had a healthy complexion and a broad, milky-white forehead under his beautiful, curly, light-brown hair. His hair was still curly, and just as thick and nut-brown, but his whole face was now reddish-brown; he had lines under his eyes, heavy jowls, and a double chin. He had become heavyset, and he had a noticeable belly. He didn't look like a man who would take time to lie down on the edge of the bed in the evening to whisper to his betrothed. Kristin felt sorry for her young sister; she was so lively and lovely and childishly happy about her marriage. On the very first day she showed Kristin all the chests containing her dowry and Simon's betrothal gifts. And she said she had heard from Sigrid Andresdatter about a gilded chest that was up in the bridal loft at Formo; there were twelve costly wimples inside, and this was what her husband was going to give her on their first morning. Poor little thing, she had no idea what marriage was like. It was too bad that Kristin hardly knew her little sister; Ramborg had been to Husaby twice, but there she was always sullen and unfriendly. She didn't care for Erlend or for Margret, who was the same age.

Simon thought to himself that he had expected—perhaps even hoped—that Kristin would look more careworn than she did, after having so many children. But she was glowing with youth and health, her posture was still erect, and her bearing just as lovely, although her step was a little firmer than before. She was the most beautiful mother with her five handsome small sons.

She was wearing a homemade gown of rust-brown wool with dark-blue birds woven into the cloth; Simon remembered standing next to her loom while she sat and worked on that cloth.

There was some commotion when they were about to sit down at the table in the loft of the main house. Skule and Ivar began screaming; they wanted to sit between their mother and foster mother, as they usually did. Lavrans didn't think it proper for Ramborg to sit farther down than her sister's servant woman and children, so he invited his daughter to sit in the high seat next to him, since she would soon be leaving home.

The small sons from Husaby were unruly and seemed to have no table manners. They had barely started eating before the little blond boy ducked under the table and popped up on the cushion next to Simon's knee.

"Can I look at that odd sheath you have on your belt, kinsman Simon?" he asked. The boy spoke slowly and solemnly. It was the large silver-studded sheath holding a spoon and two knives that he had caught sight of.

"Yes, you may, kinsman. And what is your name, cousin?"

"My name is Gaute Erlendssøn, cousin." He put the scrap of bacon he was holding onto the lap of Simon's silver-gray Flemish surcoat, pulled a knife out of the sheath, and examined it carefully. Then he took the knife that Simon was eating with, and the spoon, and put them all back in place so he could see how the sheath looked when everything was inside. He was quite earnest, and his fingers and face were very greasy. Simon smiled at the eager expression on the small, handsome face.

A few minutes later the two oldest boys came over to the men's bench too. The twins toppled under the table and began rolling around between everyone's feet; then they went over to the dogs near the fire. There was little peace for the adults as they ate their supper. Their mother and father reprimanded the boys and told them to sit quietly, but the children paid them no mind. And their parents kept laughing at them and seemed not to take their mischievous behavior too seriously—not even when Lavrans, in a rather sharp voice, told one of his men to take the whelps down to the room below so people in the hall could hear themselves speak.

Everyone from Husaby was to sleep in the loft of the main house, and after the meal, while more ale was being brought in for the men, Kristin and her maids took the children over to a corner of the hall to undress them. They had gotten so dirty while eating that their mother wanted to wash them up a bit. But the youngest boys refused to be washed, and the older ones splashed the water, and then all of them started rushing around the hall as the maids pulled one piece of clothing after another off them. Finally they were all put into one bed, but they continued to yell and play and shove each other, laughing and shrieking. Pillows and coverlets and sheets were hurled this way and that, making dust fly, and the smell of chaff filled the whole room. Kristin laughed and explained calmly that they were so high-spirited from being in a strange place.

Ramborg accompanied her betrothed outside and walked with him for a short distance between the fences in the spring night. Gyrd and Geirmund had ridden on ahead while Simon stopped to say good night. He had already put his foot in the stirrup when he turned back to the maiden, took her in his arms, and held the delicate child so close that she whimpered happily.

"God bless you, dear Ramborg—you're so fine and so fair—much too fine and fair for me," he murmured into her mass of curls.

Ramborg stood watching Simon as he rode off into the misty moonlight. She rubbed her arm—he had gripped her so hard that it hurt. Dizzy with joy, she thought: Now there were only three days left until she would be married to him.

Lavrans stood next to Kristin at the children's bedside and watched her tucking in her small sons. The eldest were already big boys with lanky bodies and slender, lean limbs; but the two smallest ones were chubby and rosy, with folds in their skin and dimples at their joints. Lavrans thought it a lovely sight to see them lying there, pink and warm, their thick hair damp with sweat, breathing quietly as they slept. They were healthy, beautiful boys—but never had he seen such poorly behaved children as his grandsons. Luckily Simon's sister and sister-in-law hadn't been present tonight. But he wasn't the one to speak to Kristin about discipline. Lavrans gave a small sigh and then made the sign of the cross over the small boys' heads.

Then Simon Andressøn celebrated his wedding to Ramborg Lavransdatter, and it was magnificent and grand in every way. The bride and bridegroom looked happy, and it seemed to many that Ramborg was more lovely on her wedding day than her sister had been—perhaps not as striking as Kristin, but much happier and gentler. Everyone could see in the bride's clear, innocent eyes that she wore the golden crown of her Gjesling ancestors with full honor on that day.

And full of joy and pride, with her hair pinned up, she sat in the armchair in front of the bridal bed as the guests came upstairs to greet the young couple on the first morning. With laughter and bold teasing, they watched as Simon placed the wimple of a married woman over his young wife's head. Cheers and the clanging of weapons filled the room as Ramborg stood up, straight-backed and flushed beneath the white wimple, and gave her husband her hand.

It was not often that two noble children from the same district were married—when all the branches of the lineage were studied, it was often found that the kinship was too close. So everyone considered this wedding to be a great and joyous occasion.

## CHAPTER 6

ONE OF THE first things Kristin noticed at home was that all the carvings of old men's heads which sat carved above the crossbeams on the building gables were now gone. They had been replaced by spires with foliage and birds, and there was a gilded weather vane atop the new house. The old posts on the high seat in the hearth room had also been replaced with new ones. The old ones had been carved to look like two men—rather hideous, but they had apparently been there since the house was built, and the servants used to polish them with fat and wash them with ale before the holy days. On the new posts her father had carved two men with crosses on their helmets and shields. They weren't meant to be Saint Olav himself, Lavrans said, for he didn't think it would be proper for a sinful man to have images of the saint in his house, except those he knelt in front of to say his prayers. But they could very well be two of Olav's men. Lavrans had chopped up and burned all the old carvings himself. The servants didn't dare. It was with some reluctance that he still allowed them to take food out to the great stone at Jørund's grave on the evening before holy days; Lavrans conceded that it would be a shame to take away from the original owner of the estate something he had grown accustomed to receiving for as long as anyone had lived on the land. He died long before Christianity came to Norway, so it wasn't his fault that he was a heathen.

People didn't like these changes that Lavrans Bjørgulfsøn had made. That was fine for him, since he could afford to buy his security elsewhere. And it seemed to be equally powerful, because he continued to have the same good fortune with his farming as before. But there was some talk that the spirits might take their revenge when the estate was taken over by a master who was less pious and not as generous about everything that belonged to the

Church. And it was easier for poor folk to give the ancestors what they were used to receiving instead of stirring up strife with them by siding too much with the priests.

Otherwise it was rather uncertain how things would go with the friendship between Jørundgaard and the parsonage after Sira Eirik was gone. The priest was old now and in poor health, and he had been forced to bring in a curate to assist him. At first he had talked to the bishop about his grandson Bentein Jonssøn; but Lavrans had also had a word with the bishop, who had been his friend in the past. People thought this unfair. No doubt the young priest had been overly importunate toward Kristin Lavransdatter on that evening, and he may have even frightened the girl; but it was also possible that she herself might have been to blame for the young man's boldness. It had later turned out that she was not as shy as she seemed to be. But Lavrans had always believed his daughter to be good, and he treated her as if she were a holy shrine.

After that there was a coldness between Sira Eirik and Lavrans for some time. But then Sira Solmund arrived, and he was immediately embroiled in a dispute with the parish priest over a piece of land and whether it belonged to the parsonage or to Eirik himself. Lavrans had the best grasp of any man in the district about land purchases and such matters back to ancient times, and it was his testimony that determined the outcome. Since then, he and Sira Solmund had not been friends. But it might be said that Sira Eirik and Audun, the old deacon, practically lived at Jørundgaard now, for they went over there every day to sit with Lavrans and complain of all the injustices and troubles they had to endure from the new priest; and they were waited on as if they were bishops.

Kristin had heard a little about this from Borgar Trondssøn of Sundbu; his wife came from Trøndelag, and he had been a guest at Husaby several times. Trond Gjesling had been dead for a few years now. But this was not considered a great loss, since he had been like an intruder in the ancient lineage—surly, avaricious, and sickly. Lavrans was the only one who had any patience with Trond, for he pitied his brother-in-law and even more Gudrid, his wife. Now they were both gone, and all four of their sons lived together on the estate. They were intrepid, promising, and handsome men; people thought them a good replacement for the father. There was great friendship between these men and the master of

Jørundgaard. Lavrans rode to Sundbu a couple of times each year to join them in hunting on the slopes of Vestfjeld. But Borgar said that it seemed completely unreasonable the way Lavrans and Ragnfrid were now worrying themselves with penances and devotions.

"He gulps down water during fasts just as eagerly as always, but your father doesn't speak to the ale bowls with the same heartiness he used to show in the past," said Borgar. No one could understand the man—it was unthinkable that Lavrans might have some secret sin to repent. As far as people could tell, he had lived as Christian a life as any child of Adam, apart from the saints.

Deep inside Kristin's heart, a foreboding began to stir about why her father was always striving so hard to come closer to God. But she didn't dare think about it too much.

She didn't want to acknowledge how changed her father was. It wasn't that he had aged excessively: he was still slim, with an erect and noble bearing. His hair was quite gray now, but it wasn't overly noticeable, since he had always been so fair. And yet . . . Kristin's memory was haunted by the image of the young and radiantly handsome man—the fresh roundness of his cheeks in the narrow face, the pure blush of his skin under the sheen of tan, and the crimson fullness of his lips with the deep corners. Now his muscular body had withered to bone and sinew, his face was brown and sharp, as if carved out of wood, and his cheeks were flat and gaunt, with a knot of muscle at the corners of his mouth. Well, he was no longer a young man—and yet he wasn't very old, either.

He had always been quiet, sober-minded, and pensive, and Kristin knew that even in childhood he had obeyed the Christian commandments with particular zeal. He loved the holy mass and prayers spoken in Latin, and he regarded the church as the place where he felt the most joy. But everyone had sensed a daring courage and zest for life flowing calmly in this quiet man's soul. Now it seemed as if something had ebbed out of him.

Since she had come home, she hadn't seen him drunk except on one occasion—an evening during the wedding celebration at Formo. Then he had staggered a bit and slurred his words, but he hadn't been especially merry. She thought back to her childhood, to the banquets and great ale drinking on feast days, when her father would roar with laughter and slap his thighs at every jest—offering to fight or wrestle with any man renowned for his physical strength, trying out horses, and leaping into dance, but laughing most at himself when he was unsteady on his feet, and lavishly handing out gifts, brimming over with good will and kindness toward everyone. She understood that her father needed this sort of exhilaration from time to time, amidst the constant work, the strict fasts he kept, and the sedate home life with his own people, who saw him as their best friend and supporter.

She also saw that her husband never had this need to get drunk because he put so few restrictions on himself, no matter how sober he might be. He regularly gave in to his impulses, without brooding over right or wrong or what was considered good and proper behavior for sensible people. Erlend was the most moderate man she had ever met when it came to strong liquor. He drank in order to quench his thirst and for the sake of camaraderie, but otherwise he didn't particularly care for it.

Lavrans Bjørgulfsøn had now lost his old sense of enjoyment for the ale bowls. He no longer had that craving inside him that needed to be released through revelry. It had never occurred to him before to drown his sorrows in drunkenness, and it didn't occur to him now—he had always thought that a man ought to bring his joy to the drinking table.

He had turned elsewhere with his sorrows. There was an image that had always hovered dimly in his daughter's memory: Lavrans on the night when the church burned down. He stood beside the crucifix he had rescued, holding on to the cross and supporting himself with it. And without thinking it through, Kristin had the feeling that what had changed Lavrans was partly his fear for the future of herself and her children with the husband she had chosen, along with the awareness of his own powerlessness.

This knowledge secretly gnawed at her heart. And she had returned home to Jørundgaard, worn out by the tumult of the previous winter and by her own rashness in accepting Erlend's nonchalance. She knew he was wasteful and always would be, and he had no idea how to manage his properties, which were slowly but constantly diminishing under his control. She had been able to get him to agree to a few things which she and Sira Eiliv had advised, but she didn't have the heart to speak to him about such matters time and again. And it was tempting simply to be happy with him now. She was tired of arguing and fighting with everything both outside and inside her own soul. But she was also the kind of person who was made anxious and weary by such heedless behavior.

Here at home she had expected to rediscover the peace from her childhood, under the protection of her father.

No, she felt so uneasy. Erlend now had a good income from his position as sheriff, but he also lived with greater ostentation, with more servants and an entourage befitting a chieftain. And he had begun to shut her out of everything that didn't concern their domestic life together. She realized that he didn't want to have her watchful eyes on what he was doing. With other men he would talk willingly about all he had seen and experienced up north—to her he never said a word. And there were other things as well. He had met with Lady Ingebjørg, the king's mother, and Sir Knut Porse several times over the past few years. But it had never been opportune for Kristin to accompany him. Now Sir Knut was a duke in Denmark, and King Haakon's daughter had bound herself to him in marriage. This had aroused bitter indignation in the souls of many Norwegian men; measures had been taken against the king's mother which Kristin did not understand. And the bishop in Bjørgvin had secretly sent several chests to Husaby. They were now on board *Margygren,* and the ship was anchored at Nes. Erlend had been given boxes of letters and was to sail to Denmark later in the summer. He wanted Kristin to go along with him, but she refused. She could see that Erlend moved among these noble people as an equal and a dear kinsman, and this worried her—it wasn't safe with such an impetuous man as Erlend. But she didn't dare travel with him; she wouldn't be able to advise him in these matters, and she didn't want to run the risk of consorting with people among whom she, a simple wife, could not assert herself. And she was also afraid of the sea. For her, seasickness was worse than the most difficult childbirth.

So she spent the days at Jørundgaard with her soul shivering and uneasy.

One day she went with her father to Skjenne. There she saw again the strange treasure which they kept on the estate. It was a spur of the purest gold, shaped in a bulky and old-fashioned style, with peculiar ornamentation. She, like every other child in the area, knew where it had come from.

It was soon after Saint Olav had brought Christianity to the valley that Audhild the Fair of Skjenne was lured into the mountain. The villagers carried the church bell up onto the slopes and rang it for the maiden. On the third evening she came walking across the meadow, adorned with so much gold that she glittered like a star. Then the rope broke, the bell tumbled down the scree, and Audhild had to return to the mountain.

But many years later, twelve warriors came to the priest—this was the first priest here at Sil. They wore golden helmets and silver coats of mail, and they rode dark-brown stallions. They were the sons of Audhild and the mountain king, and they asked that their mother might be given a Christian funeral and be buried in consecrated ground. She had tried to maintain her faith and observe the holy days of the Church inside the mountain, and this was her earnest prayer. But the priest refused. And people said that because of this, he himself had no peace in the grave. On autumn nights he could be heard walking through the grove north of the church, weeping with remorse at his own cruelty. That same night Audhild's sons had gone to Skjenne to bring greetings from their mother to her old parents who still lived there. The next morning the golden spur was found in the courtyard. And the sons doubtless continued to regard the Skjenne men as their kin, for they always had exceptional good fortune in the mountains.

Lavrans said to his daughter as they rode home in the summer night, "The sons of Audhild repeated Christian prayers that their mother had taught them. They couldn't mention the name of God or Jesus, but they said the Lord's Prayer and credo like this: 'I believe in the Almighty, I believe in the only begotten Son, I believe in the mightiest Spirit.' And then they said: 'Hail to the Lady, you who are the most blessed of women—and blessed is the fruit of your womb, the solace of all the earth.' "

Kristin timidly glanced up at her father's gaunt, weatherbeaten face. In the bright summer night it seemed more ravaged with sorrows and worries than she had ever seen it.

"You've never told me that before," she said softly.

"Haven't I? Well, I may have thought it would give you more melancholy thoughts than your years could bear. Sira Eirik says that it is written according to Saint Paul the Apostle that humankind is not alone in sighing with agony."

One day Kristin was sitting and sewing at the top of the stairs leading up to the high loft when Simon came riding into the courtyard and stopped just below where she sat, although he didn't see her. Her parents both came out of the house. No, Simon wouldn't dismount; Ramborg had merely asked him to find out, when he was passing this way, whether they had sent the sheep that had been her pet lamb up to the mountain pastures. She wanted to bring it to Formo.

Kristin saw her father scratching his head. Ramborg's sheep. Yes, well . . . He gave an exasperated laugh. It was a shame, but he had hoped she would have forgotten about it. He had given each of his two eldest grandsons a little axe, and the first thing they had used them for was to kill Ramborg's sheep.

Simon laughed. "Yes, those Husaby boys, they're rascals all right."

Kristin ran down the loft stairs and unfastened the silver scissors from her belt.

"You can give these to Ramborg, as compensation for my sons killing her sheep. I know she's wanted to have these scissors ever since she was a child. No one must say that my sons . . ." She had spoken in anger, but now she fell silent. She had noticed her parents' faces—they were giving her a look of dismay and astonishment.

Simon didn't take the scissors; he felt embarrassed. Then he caught sight of Bjørgulf and rode over to him, leaning down to lift the boy up into the saddle in front of him.

"I hear you've been making raids around the countryside—now you're my prisoner, and tomorrow your parents can come over to see me and we'll negotiate the ransom."

And with that he gave a laugh and a wave and rode off with the boy wriggling and laughing in his arms. Simon had become great friends with Erlend's sons. Kristin remembered that he had always had a way with children; her younger sisters had loved him dearly.

Oddly enough it made her cross that he should be so fond of children and take pleasure in playing with them when her own husband had little interest in listening to children's prattle.

The next day, when they were at Formo, Kristin realized that Simon had not won any favors with his wife by bringing this guest home with him.

"No one should expect Ramborg to care much for children yet," said Ragnfrid. "She's hardly more than a child herself. Things will be different when she's older."

"No doubt you're right." Simon and his mother-in-law exchanged a look and a little smile.

Ah, thought Kristin. Well, it had already been two months since the wedding.

Distressed and agitated as Kristin now was, she took her feelings out on Erlend. He had accepted this stay at his wife's ancestral estate with the satisfaction and pleasure of a righteous man. He was good friends with Ragnfrid and made it known that he had a deep fondness for his wife's father. And Lavrans, in turn, seemed to have affection for his son-in-law. But Kristin had now become so sensitive and wary that she saw in her father's kindness toward Erlend much of the same tolerant tenderness that Lavrans had always shown toward every living creature he felt was less able to take care of itself. His love for his other son-in-law was different; he treated Simon as a friend and equal. And even though Erlend was much closer in age to his father-in-law than Simon was, it was Lavrans and Simon who addressed each other in the informal manner. Ever since Erlend had become betrothed to Kristin, Lavrans had addressed Erlend informally, while Erlend had continued to use the more formal mode. It was up to Lavrans to change this, but he had never offered to do so.

Simon and Erlend got along well whenever they were together, but they didn't seek out each other's company. Kristin still felt a secret shyness toward Simon Darre—because of what he knew about her, and even more because she knew that he was the one whose conduct had been honorable, while Erlend had acted with shame. It made her furious when she realized that Erlend could forget even this. And so she wasn't always amenable toward her husband. If Erlend was in a mood to bear her irritability with good humor and gentleness, it would annoy her that he wasn't taking her words seriously. On some other day he might have little patience, and then his temper would flare, but she would respond with bitterness and coldness.

One evening they were sitting in the hearth room at Jørundgaard. Lavrans always felt most comfortable in this building, especially in weather that was rainy and oppressive, as it was on that day. In the main building, up in the hall, the ceiling was flat and the smoke from the fireplace could be bothersome. But in the hearth room the smoke would rise up to the central beam in the pitched roof, even when they had to close the smoke vent because of the weather.

Kristin sat near the hearth, sewing. She was feeling out of sorts and bored. Right across from her was Margret, dozing over her needlework and yawning now and then. The children were noisily running about the room. Ragnfrid was at Formo, and most of the servants were elsewhere. Lavrans sat in the high seat, with Erlend at his elbow, at the end of the outer bench. They had a chessboard between them and they were moving the pieces in silence, after much reflection. Once, when Ivar and Skule were tugging on a puppy, trying to tear it in half, Lavrans stood up and took the poor howling animal away from them. He didn't say a word, but simply sat down to his game again with the dog on his lap.

Kristin went over to them and stood with one hand on her husband's shoulder, watching the game. Erlend was a much less skilled chess player than his father-in-law, so he was most often the loser when they took out the board in the evening, but he bore this with gentle equanimity. This evening he was playing especially badly. Kristin stood there castigating him, and not in a particularly kind or sweet way.

Finally Lavrans said rather harshly, "Erlend can't keep his thoughts on the game when you're standing here bothering him. What do you want, anyway, Kristin? You've never understood board games!"

"No, you don't seem to think I understand much at all."

"There's one thing I see that you don't understand," said her father sharply, "and that's the proper way for a wife to speak to her husband. It would be better if you went and reined in your sons—they're behaving worse than a pack of Christmas trolls."

Kristin went over and set her children in a row on a bench and then sat down next to them.

"Be quiet now, my sons," she said. "Your grandfather doesn't want you to play in here."

Lavrans glanced at his daughter but didn't speak. A little later the foster mothers came in, and Kristin left with her maids and Margret to put the children to bed.

Erlend said after a moment, when he and Lavrans were alone, "I would have wished, Father-in-law, that you hadn't reprimanded Kristin in that way. If it gives her some comfort to carp at me when she's in a bad temper, then . . . It does no good to talk to her, and she won't stand for anyone saying a word against her children."

"And what about you?" said Lavrans. "Do you intend to allow your sons to grow up so ill-behaved? Where were the maids who are supposed to watch and tend to the children?"

"In the servants' house with your men, I would think," said Erlend, laughing and stretching. "But I don't dare say a word to Kristin about her serving maids. Then she flies into a fury and tells me that she and I have never been examples for anyone."

The following day Kristin was picking strawberries in the meadow south of the farm when her father called to her from the smithy door and asked her to come over to him.

Kristin went, though rather reluctantly. It was probably Naakkve again—that morning he had left a gate open, and the cows had wandered into a barley field.

Lavrans pulled a glowing iron from the forge and set it on the anvil. His daughter sat down to wait, and for a long time there was no sound other than the pounding of the hammer against the glowing piece of iron and the ringing reply of the anvil. Finally Kristin asked her father what he wanted to say to her.

The iron was now cold. Lavrans put down his tongs and hammer and came over to Kristin. With soot on his face and hair, his clothing and hands blackened, and garbed as he was in the big leather apron, Lavrans looked much sterner than usual.

"I called you over here, my daughter, because I want to tell you this. Here on my estate you will show your husband the respect that is proper for a wife. I refuse to hear my daughter speaking the way you did to Erlend last night."

"This is something new, Father, for you to think Erlend is a man worthy of people's respect."

"He's *your* husband," said Lavrans. "I didn't force you to arrange this marriage. You should remember that."

"You're such warm friends," replied Kristin. "If you had known him back then the way you know him now, then you might well have done so."

Lavrans looked down at her, his face somber and sad.

"Now you're speaking rashly, Kristin, and saying things that are untrue. I didn't try to force you when you wanted to cast off the man to whom you were lawfully betrothed, even though you know I was very fond of Simon."

"No, but Simon didn't want me either."

"Oh, he was much too high-minded to demand his rights when you were unwilling. But I don't know whether he would have been so against it in his heart if I had done as Andres Darre wanted. He said we should pay no attention to the whims of you two young people. And I wonder whether the knight might have been right—now that I see you can't live in a seemly fashion with the husband you insisted on winning."

Kristin gave a loud and ugly laugh.

"Simon! You would never have been able to threaten Simon into marrying the woman he had found with another man in such a house."

Lavrans gasped for air. "House?" he repeated involuntarily.

"Yes, what you men call a house of sin. The woman who owned it was Munan's paramour. She warned me herself not to go there. I told her I was going to meet a kinsman—I didn't know he was *her* kinsman." She gave another laugh, wild and harsh.

"Silence!" said her father.

He stood there for a moment. A tremor flickered across his countenance—a smile that made his face blanch. She thought suddenly of the foliage on the mountain slope which turns white when gusts of wind twist each leaf around—patches of pale and glittering light.

"A man can learn a great deal without asking."

Kristin broke down as she sat there on the bench, supporting herself on one elbow, with her other hand covering her eyes. For the first time in her life she was afraid of her father—deathly afraid.

He turned away from her, picked up the hammer, and put it back in its place next to the others. Then he gathered up the files and small tools and went about putting them back on the cross-beam between the walls. He stood with his back to his daughter; his hands were shaking violently.

"Have you never thought about the fact, Kristin, that Erlend kept silent about this?" Now he was standing in front of her, looking down into her pale, frightened face. "I told him no, quite firmly, when he came to me in Tunsberg with his rich kinsmen and asked for your hand. I didn't know then that *I* was the one who should have thanked *him* for wanting to redeem my daughter's honor. Many a man would have told me so.

"Then he came again and courted you with full honor. Not all men would have been so persistent in winning a wife who was . . . who was . . . what you were back then."

"I don't think any man would have dared say such a thing to you."

"Erlend has never been afraid of cold steel." A great weariness suddenly came over Lavrans's face, and his voice lost all vigor and resonance. But then he spoke again, quietly and deliberately.

"As bad as this is, Kristin—it seems to me even worse that you speak of it now that he's your husband and the father of your sons.

"If things were as you say, then you knew the worst about him before you insisted on entering into marriage with him. And yet he was willing to pay as dearly for you, as if you had been an honest maiden. He has granted you much freedom to manage and rule; you must do penance for your sin by ruling sensibly and make up for Erlend's lack of caution—that much you owe to God and your children.

"I myself have said, and others have said the same, that Erlend doesn't seem to be capable of much else than seducing women. You are also to blame for this being said, according to your own testimony. But since then he has shown he is capable of other things—your husband has won a good name for himself through courage and swiftness in battle. It's no small benefit for your sons that their father has acquired a reputation for his boldness and skill with weapons. That he is . . . incautious . . . you must realize this better than anyone. It would be best for you to redeem your shame by honoring and helping the husband whom you yourself have chosen."

Kristin was bending forward, with her head in her hands. Now she looked up, her face pale and despairing. "It was cruel of me to tell you this. Oh . . . Simon begged me . . . It was the only thing he asked of me—that I should spare you from knowing the worst."

"Simon asked you to spare me?" Kristin heard the pain in her father's voice. And she realized it was also cruel of her to tell him that a stranger saw fit to remind her to spare her own father.

Then Lavrans sat down beside her, took her hand in both of his, and placed it on his knee.

"Yes, it was cruel, my Kristin," he said gently and sadly. "You are good to everyone, my dear child, but I have also realized that you can be cruel to those you love too dearly. For the sake of Jesus, Kristin, spare me the need to be so worried for you—that your impetuous spirit might bring more sorrow upon you and yours. You struggle like a colt that has been tied up in the stable for the first time, whenever your heartstrings are bound."

Sobbing, she sank against her father, and he held her tight in his arms. They sat there for a long time in that manner, but Lavrans said no more. Finally he lifted her face.

"You're covered in soot," he said with a little smile. "There's a cloth over in the corner, but it will probably just make you blacker. You must go home and wash; everyone can see that you've been sitting on the blacksmith's lap."

Gently he pushed her out the door, closed it behind her, and stood there for a moment. Then he staggered a few steps over to the bench, sank down onto it, and leaned his head back against the timbers of the wall with his contorted face tilted upward. With all his might he pressed a fist against his heart.

It never lasted long. The shortness of breath, the black dizziness, the pain that radiated out into his limbs from his heart, which shuddered and struggled, giving a few fierce thuds and then quivering quietly again. His blood hammered in the veins of his neck.

It would pass in a few minutes. It always did after he sat still for a while. But it was happening more and more often.

Erlend had called his crews to a meeting at Veøy on the eve of Saint Jacob's Day, but then he stayed on at Jørundgaard a while longer to accompany Simon on a hunt for a vicious bear that had killed some of the livestock in the mountain pastures. When Erlend returned from the hunting expedition, there was a message for him. Some of his men had gotten into trouble with the townspeople, and he had to hurry north to win their release. Lavrans had business up there too, and so he decided to ride along with his son-in-law.

It was already nearing the end of Saint Olav's Day by the time they reached the island. Erling Vidkunssøn's ship was anchored offshore, and they met the regent at vespers in Saint Peter's Church. He went back to the monastery with them, where Lavrans had taken lodgings. There he dined with them, sending his men down to the ship for some particularly good French wine, which he had brought along from Nidaros.

But the conversation waned as they sat drinking. Erlend was lost in his own thoughts; his eyes sparkled as they always did when he was out on some new adventure, but he seemed distracted as the others talked. Lavrans merely sipped at his wine, and Sir Erling had fallen silent.

"You look tired, kinsman," Erlend said to him.

Yes, they had encountered stormy weather near Husastadvik the night before; he hadn't gotten any sleep.

"And now you'll have to ride swiftly if you're going to reach Tunsberg by Saint Lavrans's Day. I doubt you'll have much peace or comfort there either. Is Master Paal with the king now?"

"Yes. Are you thinking of coming to Tunsberg?"

"If I did, it would have to be to ask the king whether he'd like to send filial greetings to his mother." Erlend laughed. "Or whether Bishop Audfinn wants to send word to Lady Ingebjørg."

"Many are surprised that you're heading for Denmark, just as the chieftains are gathering for a meeting in Tunsberg," said Sir Erling.

"Yes, isn't it odd how people are always surprised by me? Maybe I have a mind to see some of the folk customs I haven't seen since I was last in Denmark—maybe even participate in a tournament. And our kinswoman has invited me, after all. No one else in her lineage here in Norway wants anything to do with her now, except Munan and myself."

"Munan . . ." Erling frowned. Then he laughed and said, "Is there so much life left in the old boar? I'd almost thought he wouldn't have the energy to move his bulk about anymore. So Duke Knut is organizing a tournament, is he? And is Munan going to join in the jousting?"

"Yes—it's too bad, Erling, you can't come along to see it." And Erlend laughed as well. "I can see you fear that Lady Ingebjørg has invited us to this christening-ale so that we might brew a different kind of ale and invite her in. But you know very well that I'm too heavy-footed and too lighthearted to be used in making secret plans. And from Munan you've yanked out every tooth."

"Oh no, we're not afraid of secret plans from those quarters, either. Ingebjørg Haakonsdatter must have realized by now that she squandered all rights in her own country when she married Knut Porse. It would be unwise for her to set foot inside the door here after giving her hand to that man, when we don't want to see even his little finger within our boundaries."

"Yes, it was clever of you to separate the boy from his mother," said Erlend gloomily. "He's still only a child—and now all of us Norwegian men have reason to hold our heads up high when we think about the king whom we have sworn to protect."

"Be quiet!" said Erling Vidkunssøn in a low, dejected voice. "That's . . . surely that's not true."

But the other two could see from his face that he knew it was true. Although King Magnus Eirikssøn might still be a child, he had already been infected by a sin which was unseemly to mention among Christian men. A Swedish cleric, who had been assigned to guide his book learning while he was in Sweden, had led him astray in an unmentionable manner.

Erlend said, "People are whispering on every estate and in every house around us in the north that Christ Church burned because our king is unworthy to sit in Saint Olav's seat."

"In God's name, Erlend—I tell you it's not certain this is true!

And we must believe that the child, King Magnus, is innocent in God's eyes. He can surely redeem himself. And you say that *we* have separated him from his mother? I say that God punishes the mother who deserts her child the way Ingebjørg has deserted her son—and do not put your trust in such a woman, Erlend. Keep in mind that these are treacherous people you're now setting off to meet!"

"I think they've been admirably loyal toward each other. But you speak as if letters from Christ himself were floating down into the lap of your robe every day—that must be why you've decided that you dare to be so bold as to provoke a fight with the highest authorities of the Church."

"Now you must stop, Erlend. Talk about things that you understand, my boy, but otherwise keep quiet." Sir Erling got to his feet; they were both standing up now, angry and red in the face.

Erlend grimaced with disgust.

"If an animal has been mistreated, we kill it and toss the corpse into a waterfall."

"Erlend!" The regent gripped the edge of the table with both hands. "You have sons yourself . . ." he said softly. "How can you say such a thing? And you'd better watch your tongue, Erlend. Think before you speak in that place where you're now going. And think about it twenty times over before you do anything."

"If that's how you act, you who rule over the affairs of the kingdom, then it doesn't surprise me that everything has gone awry. But I don't think you need to be afraid," Erlend sneered. "I doubt that I'll do anything. But what a splendid thing it has become to live in this country. . . .

"Well, you have to set out early in the morning. And my father-in-law is tired."

The other two men remained sitting there, without speaking, after Erlend had bid them good night. He was going to sleep aboard his ship. Erling Vidkunssøn sat and turned his goblet around and around in his hand.

"Are you coughing?" he asked, just for something to say.

"Old men catch cold easily. We have so many ailments, dear sir, which you young men know nothing about," said Lavrans with a smile.

They sat in silence again. Until Erling Vidkunssøn said, as if to himself, "Yes, everyone thinks the same—that it doesn't bode well for this kingdom. Six years ago in Oslo, I thought it was clear that there was a firm desire to support the Crown—among the men who are born to this task by virtue of their lineage. I . . . was counting on that."

"I think back then your perception was correct, sir. But you yourself said that we're accustomed to rallying around our king. This time he's merely a child—and he spends half his time in another country."

"Yes. Sometimes I think . . . nothing is so bad that it's not good for something. In the past, when our kings frolicked around like stallions—then there were enough fine colts to choose from; our countrymen simply had to select the one who was the best fighter."

Lavrans gave a laugh. "Yes, well . . ."

"We spoke three years ago, Lavrans Lagmanssøn, when you returned from your pilgrimage to Skøvde and had paid a visit to your kinsmen in Götaland."

"I remember, sir, that you honored me by seeking me out."

"No, no, Lavrans, you need not be so formal." A little impatiently, Erling threw out his hands. "It was as I said," he continued gloomily. "There's no one here who can unite the nobles of this country. Whoever has the greatest hunger forces his way forward—there's still some food in the trough. But those who might attempt to win power and wealth in an honorable manner, as was done in the time of our fathers, are not the ones who come forward now."

"That seems to be true. But honor follows the banner of the chieftains."

"Then men must think that my banner carries with it little honor," said Erling dryly. "You have avoided everything that might have won you renown, Lavrans Lagmanssøn."

"I've done so ever since I became a married man, sir. And that was at a young age; my wife was sickly and had little tolerance for the company of others. And it looks as if our lineage will not continue to thrive here in Norway. My sons died young, and only one of my brother's sons has lived to be a man."

Lavrans regretted that he had come to speak of this matter. Erling Vidkunssøn had endured great sorrow of his own. His daughters were healthy children and had grown to adulthood, but he too had only been allowed to keep a single son, and the boy was said to be in poor health.

But Sir Erling merely said, "And you have no close kinsmen from your mother's lineage, either, as I recall."

"No, no closer than the children of my grandfather's sister. Sigurd Lodinssøn had only two daughters, and they both died giving birth to their first child—and my aunt took hers to the grave with her."

They sat in silence again for a while.

"Men like Erlend," said the regent in a low voice. "They're the most dangerous kind. Men who think a little farther than their own interests, but not far enough. Don't you think Erlend is just like an indolent youth?" He slid his wine goblet around on the table with annoyance. "But he's intelligent, isn't he? And of good family, and courageous? But he never wants to listen to any matter long enough to understand it fully. And if he bothers to hear a man out, he forgets the first part before the discussion comes to an end."

Lavrans glanced over at the other man. Sir Erling had aged a great deal since he had last seen him. He looked careworn and weary; he seemed to have shrunk in his chair. He had fine, clear features, but they were a little too small, and he had a pallid complexion, as he always had. Lavrans felt that this man—even though he was a knight with integrity, who was wise and willing to serve without deceit, never sparing himself—fell somewhat short in every way as a leader. If he had been a head taller, he might have won full support more easily.

Lavrans said quietly, "Sir Knut is also clever enough that he would realize—if they're contemplating any kind of incursion down there—that he wouldn't have much use for Erlend in any secret council."

"You're rather fond of this son-in-law of yours, aren't you, Lavrans?" said the other man, almost crossly. "If truth be told, you have no reason to love him."

Lavrans sat running his finger through a puddle of spilled wine on the table. Sir Erling noticed that his rings were quite loose on his fingers now.

"Do *you?*" Lavrans looked up with a little smile. "And yet I think that you too are fond of him!"

"Well . . . God knows . . . But I swear to you, Lavrans, Sir Knut has plenty of things going through his mind right now. He's the father of a son who is the grandson of King Haakon."

"Even Erlend must realize that the child's father has much too broad a back for that poor young nobleman ever to get around it. And his mother has all the people of Norway against her because of this marriage."

A little while later Erling Vidkunssøn stood up and strapped on his sword. Lavrans had politely taken his guest's cape from the hook and was holding it in his hands, when he suddenly swayed and was about to collapse, but Sir Erling caught him in his arms. With difficulty he carried the man, who was heavy and tall, over to the bed. It wasn't a stroke, but Lavrans lay there with his lips pale blue, his limbs weak and limp. Sir Erling raced across the courtyard to wake up the hostel priest.

Lavrans felt quite embarrassed when he came to himself again. Yes, it was a weakness that occurred now and then, ever since an elk hunt two winters before, when he had gotten lost in a blizzard. That was evidently what it took for a man to learn that his body was no longer youthful, and he smiled apologetically.

Sir Erling waited until the monk had bled the ill man, although Lavrans begged him not to take the trouble, because he would have to leave so early in the morning.

The moon was high, shining above the mountains of the mainland; the water lay black below, but out on the fjord the light glinted like flecks of silver. Not a wisp came from the smoke-vent holes; the grass on the rooftops glittered like dew in the moonlight. Not a soul was on the one short street of the town as Sir Erling swiftly walked the few paces down to the king's fortress, where he was to sleep. He looked strangely fragile and small in the moonlight, with his black cape wrapped tightly around him, shivering slightly. A couple of weary servants, who had sat up waiting for him, tumbled out of the courtyard with a lantern. The regent took the lantern and sent his men off to bed; then he shivered a little again as he climbed the stairs to his chamber up in the loft room.

## CHAPTER 7

JUST AFTER SAINT Bartholomew's Day Kristin set off on the journey home in the company of a large entourage of children, servants, and possessions. Lavrans rode with her as far as Hjerdkinn.

They went out into the courtyard to talk, he and his daughter, on the morning when he was to head back south. Sunlight sparkled over the mountains; the marshes were already crimson, and the slopes were yellow like gold from the alpine birches. Up on the plateau, lakes alternately glittered and then darkened as shadows from the big, glossy, fair-weather clouds passed overhead. They billowed up incessantly, and then sank down between distant clefts and gaps amid all the gray-domed mountains and blue peaks, with patches of new snow and old snowdrifts, which encircled the view far into the distance. The small grayish-green fields of grain belonging to the travelers' hostel looked so strange in color against the brilliant autumn hues of the mountains.

The wind was blowing, sharp and brisk. Lavrans pulled up the hood of Kristin's cloak which had blown back around her shoulders, smoothing out the corners of her linen wimple with his fingertips.

"It seems to me your cheeks have grown so pale and thin back home on my manor," he said. "Haven't we taken good care of you, Kristin?"

"Yes, you have. That's not why . . ."

"And it's a wearisome journey for you with all the children," said her father.

"Yes, well . . . It's not because of those five that I have pale cheeks." She gave him a fleeting smile, and when her father cast a startled and inquiring glance at her, she nodded and smiled again.

Lavrans looked away, but after a moment he said, "If I understand rightly how matters stand, then perhaps it will be some time before you return to Gudbrandsdal?"

"Well, we won't let eight years pass this time," she said in the same tone of voice. Then she caught a glimpse of his face. "Father! Oh, Father!"

"Hush, hush, my daughter." Involuntarily he gripped her arm to stop her as she tried to throw her arms around him. "No, Kristin."

He took her hand firmly in his and set off walking beside her. They had come some distance away from the buildings and were now wandering along a small path through the yellow birch forest, paying no attention to where they were going. Lavrans jumped over a little creek cutting across the path, and then turned around to offer his daughter a helping hand.

She saw, even from that slight movement, that he was no longer agile or spry. She had noticed before but refused to acknowledge it. He no longer sprang in and out of the saddle as nimbly as he once had; he didn't race up the stairs or lift heavy things as easily as he had in the past. He carried his body more rigidly and carefully—as if he bore some slumbering pain within and was moving quietly so as not to arouse it. His blood pulsed visibly in the veins of his neck when he came home after riding his horse. Sometimes she noticed a swelling or puffiness under his eyes. She remembered one morning when she came into the main house, and he was lying on the bed, half-dressed, with his bare legs draped over the footboard; her mother was kneeling in front of him, rubbing his ankles.

"If you're going to grieve for every man who is felled by age, then you'll have much to cry about, child," Lavrans said in a calm and quiet voice. "You have big sons yourself now, Kristin. It shouldn't surprise you to see that your father will soon be an old man. Whenever we parted in my younger days, we didn't know any better back then than we do now, whether we're destined to meet again here on this earth. And I might live for a long time yet; it must be as God wills, Kristin."

"Are you ill, Father?" she asked in a toneless voice.

"Certain frailties always come with age," her father replied lightly.

"You're not old, Father. You're only fifty-two."

"My own father didn't live this long. Come and sit down here with me."

There was a sort of grass-covered shelf beneath the rock face which leaned out over the stream. Lavrans unfastened his cape, folded it up, and pulled his daughter down to sit beside him. The creek gurgled and trickled over the stones in front of them, rocking a willow branch that was lying in the water. Lavrans sat with his eyes fixed on the blue-and-white mountain far beyond the autumn-tinged plateau.

"You're cold, Father," said Kristin. "Take my cloak." She undid the clasp, and then he pulled a corner of the cloak around his shoulders, so it covered both of them. He slipped his arm around her waist.

"You must know, my Kristin, that it's an unwise person who weeps at another's passing. Christ will protect you better than I—no doubt you have heard this said. I put all my faith in God's mercy. It's not for long that friends are parted. Although at times it may seem so to you now, while you're young. But you have your children and your husband. When you reach my age, then you'll think it's been no time at all since you saw those of us who have departed, and you'll be surprised when you count the winters that have passed to see how many there have been. It seems to me now that it wasn't long ago that I was a boy myself—and yet it's been so many years since you were that little blonde maiden who followed me everywhere I went. You followed your father so lovingly. May God reward you, my Kristin, for all the joy you have given me."

"Yes, but if He should reward me as I rewarded you . . ." Then she sank to her knees in front of her father, took his wrists, and kissed his hands, hiding her face in them. "Oh, Father, my dear father. No sooner was I a grown maiden than I rewarded your love by causing you the most bitter sorrow."

"No, no, child. You mustn't weep like this." He pulled his hands away and then lifted her up to sit beside him as before.

"I've also had great joy from you during these years, Kristin. I've seen handsome and promising children growing up at your knee; you've become a capable and sensible wife. And I've seen that you've grown more and more accustomed to seeking help where it can best be found, whenever you're in some difficulty. Kristin, my most precious gold, do not weep so hard. You might harm the one you carry under your belt," he whispered. "Do not grieve so!"

But he could not console her. Then he took his daughter in his arms and lifted her onto his lap so he was holding her as he had when she was small. Her arms were clasped around his neck, and her face was pressed to his shoulder.

"There is one thing I have never told another mother's child except for my priest, but now I'll tell it to you. During the time of my youth—back home at Skog and in the early years when I was one of the king's retainers—I thought of entering a monastery as soon as I was old enough, although I hadn't made any kind of promise, not even in my own heart, and many things pulled me in the opposite direction. But whenever I was out fishing on Botn Fjord and heard the bells ringing from the brothers' cloister on Hovedø, then I would think that I was drawn most strongly there.

"When I was sixteen winters old, Father had a coat of mail made for me from Spanish steel plates covered in silver. Rikard, the Englishman in Oslo, made it. And I was given my sword—the one I've always used—and the armor for my horse. It wasn't as peaceful back then as it was during your childhood; we were at war with the Danes, so I knew I would soon have use for my splendid weapons. And I didn't want to lay them aside. I consoled myself with the thought that my father wouldn't want his eldest son to become a monk, and I had no wish to defy my parents.

"But I chose this world myself, and whenever things went against me, I tried to tell myself that it would be unmanly to complain about the fate I had chosen. For I've realized more and more with each year that I've lived: There is no worthier work for the person who has been graced with the ability to see even a small part of God's mercy than to serve Him and to keep vigil and to pray for those people whose sight is still clouded by the shadow of worldly matters. And yet I must tell you, my Kristin, that it would be hard for me to sacrifice, for the sake of God, that life which I have lived on my estates, with its care of temporal things and its worldly joys, with your mother at my side and with all of you children. So a man must learn to accept, when he produces offspring from his own body, that his heart will burn if he loses them or if the world goes against them. God, who gave them souls, is the one who owns them—not I."

Sobs shook Kristin's body; her father began rocking her in his arms as if she were a small child.

"There were many things I didn't understand when I was young. Father was fond of my brother Aasmund too, but not in the same way as he loved me. It was because of my mother, you see—he never forgot her, but he married Inga because that was what his father wanted. Now I wish I could still go to my stepmother here on earth and beg her to forgive me for not respecting her goodness."

"But you've often said, Father, that your stepmother never did much for you, either good or bad," said Kristin in between sobs.

"Yes, God help me, I didn't know any better. Now it seems to me a great thing that she didn't hate me and never spoke an unkind word to me. How would you like it, Kristin, to see your stepson favored above your own son, constantly and in everything?"

Kristin was somewhat calmer now. She lay with her face turned so that she could look out at the mountain meadow. It grew dark from an enormous gray-blue cloud passing in front of the sun; several yellow rays pierced through, and the water of the creek glinted sharply.

Then she broke into tears again.

"Oh, no—Father, my father. Will I never see you again in this life?"

"May God protect you, Kristin, my child, so that we might meet again on that day, all of us who were friends in this life . . . and every human soul. Christ and the Virgin Mary and Saint Olav and Saint Thomas will keep you safe all your days." He took her face in his hands and kissed her on the lips. "May God have mercy on you. May God grant you light in the light of this world and in the great light beyond."

Several hours later, as Lavrans Bjørgulfsøn rode away from Hjerdkinn, his daughter walked alongside his horse. His servant was already a good distance ahead, but Lavrans continued on slowly, step by step. It hurt him to see her tear-stained and despairing face. This was also the way she had sat the whole time inside the guesthouse, as he ate and talked with her children, bantering with them and taking them onto his lap, one after the other.

Lavrans said softly, "Do not grieve any more for whatever you might regret toward *me*, Kristin. But remember it when your children are grown and you don't think they behave toward you or their father in a way you consider reasonable. And remember too what I told you about my youth. You're loyal in your love for them, that I know, but you're most stubborn when you love most, and there is obstinacy in those boys of yours—that much I've seen," he said with a little smile.

At last Lavrans said that she had to turn around and go back. "I don't want you to walk alone any farther away from the buildings." They had reached a hollow between small hills, with birch trees at the bottom and heaps of stones on the slopes.

Kristin threw herself against her father's foot in the stirrup. She ran her fingers over his clothing and his hand and his saddle, and along the neck and flank of his horse; she pressed her head here and there, weeping and uttering such deep, pitiful moans that her father thought his heart would break to see her in such terrible sorrow.

He jumped down from his horse and took his daughter in his arms, holding her tight for the last time. Again and again he made the sign of the cross over her and gave her into the care of God and the saints. Finally he said that now she would have to let him go.

And so they parted. But after he had gone some distance, Kristin saw that her father reined in his horse, and she realized that he was weeping as he rode away from her.

She ran into the birch grove, raced through it, and began scrambling up the lichen-gold scree on the nearest hillside. But it was rocky and difficult to climb, and the little hill was higher than she thought. At last she reached the top, but by that time he had disappeared among the hills. She lay down on the moss and bearberries growing on the ridge, and there she stayed, sobbing, with her face buried in her arms.

Lavrans Bjørgulfsøn arrived home at Jørundgaard late in the evening. A feeling of warmth passed through him when he saw that someone was still awake in the hearth room—there was a faint flicker of firelight behind the tiny glass window facing the gallery. It was in this building that he always felt most at home.

Ragnfrid was alone inside, sitting at the table with clothes to be mended in front of her. A tallow candle in a brass candlestick stood nearby. She got up at once, greeted him, put more wood on the hearth, and then went to get food and drink. No, she had sent the maids off to bed long ago; they had had a hard day, but now enough barley bread had been baked to last until Christmas. Paal and Gunstein had gone off into the mountains to gather moss. While they were talking about moss . . . Would Lavrans like to have for his winter surcoat the cloth that was dyed with moss or the one that was heather green? Orm of Moar had come to Jørundgaard that morning, wanting to buy some leather rope. She had taken the ropes hanging in the front of the shed and said he could have them as a gift. Yes, Orm's daughter was a little better now; the injury to her leg had knit together nicely.

Lavrans answered her questions and nodded while he and his servant ate and drank. But he was quickly done with eating. He stood up, wiped his knife on the back of his thigh, and picked up a spool of thread that lay at Ragnfrid's place. The thread had been wound around a stick with a bird carved into both ends—one of them had a slightly broken tail. Lavrans smoothed out the rough part and whittled it down so the bird had a stump of a tail. Once, long ago, he had made many of these thread spools for his wife.

"Are you going to mend them yourself?" he asked, looking down at her sewing. It was a pair of his leather hose; Ragnfrid was patching the inner side of the thighs, where they were worn from the saddle. "That's hard work for your fingers, Ragnfrid."

"Hmm." His wife placed the pieces of the leather edge to edge and poked holes in them with an awl.

The servant bade them good night and left. The husband and wife were alone. Lavrans stood near the hearth, warming himself, with one foot up on the edge and his hand on the smoke-vent pole. Ragnfrid glanced over at him. Then she noticed that he wasn't wearing the little ring with the rubies—his mother's bridal ring. He saw that she had noticed.

"Yes, I gave it to Kristin," he said. "I always meant it to be hers, and I thought she might as well have it now."

Then one of them said to the other that they ought to go to bed. But Lavrans stayed where he was, and Ragnfrid sat and sewed. They exchanged a few words about Kristin's journey, about the work that had to be done on the farm, about Ramborg and about

Simon. Then they mentioned again that they should probably go to bed, but neither of them moved.

Finally Lavrans took off the gold ring with the blue-and-white stone from his right hand and went over to his wife. Shy and embarrassed, he took her hand and put on the ring; he had to try several times before he found a finger it would fit. He put it on her middle finger, in front of her wedding ring.

"I want you to have this now," he said in a low voice, without looking at her.

Ragnfrid sat motionless, her cheeks blood red.

"Why are you doing this?" she whispered at last. "Do you think I begrudge our daughter her ring?"

Lavrans shook his head and gave a little smile. "I think you know why I'm doing this."

"You've said in the past that you wanted to have this ring in the grave with you," she said in the same tone of voice. "And no one but you was to wear it."

"And that's why you must never take it off, Ragnfrid. Promise me that. After you, I want no one else to wear it."

"Why are you doing this?" she repeated, holding her breath.

Her husband looked down into her face.

"This spring it was thirty-four years ago that we were married. I was an under-aged boy; during all of my manhood you have been at my side, whenever I suffered grief and whenever things went well. May God help me, I had such little understanding of how many troubles you had to bear in our life together. But now it seems to me that all of my days I felt it was good that you were here.

"I don't know whether you believed that I had more love for Kristin than for you. It's true that she was my greatest joy, and she caused me the greatest sorrow. But you were mother to them all. Now I think leaving you behind will hurt me the most, when I go.

"And that's why you must never give my ring to anyone else—not even to one of our daughters; tell them they must not take it from you.

"Perhaps you may think, wife, that you've had more sorrow than joy with me; things did go wrong for us in some ways. And yet I think we have been faithful friends. And this is what I have thought: that afterwards we will meet again in such a manner that all the wrongs will no longer separate us; and the friendship that we had, God will build even stronger."

Ragnfrid lifted her pale, furrowed face. Her big, sunken eyes burned as she looked up at her husband. He was still holding her hand; she looked at it, lying in his, slightly raised. The three rings gleamed next to each other: on the bottom her betrothal ring, next her wedding ring, and on top his ring.

It seemed so strange to her. She remembered when he put the first one on her finger; they were standing in front of the smoke-vent pole in the hall back home at Sundbu, their fathers with them. He was pink and white, his cheeks were round, hardly more than a child—a little bashful as he took a step forward from Sir Bjørgulf's side.

The second ring he had put on her finger in front of the church door in Gerdarud, in the name of the Trinity, under the hand of the priest.

With this last ring, she felt as if he were marrying her again. Now that she would soon sit beside his lifeless body, he wanted her to know that with this ring he was committing to her the strong and vital force that had lived in this dust and ashes.

Her heart felt as if it were breaking in her breast, bleeding and bleeding, young and fierce. From grief over the warm and ardent love which she had lost and still secretly mourned; from anguished joy over the pale, luminous love which drew her to the farthest boundaries of life on this earth. Through the great darkness that would come, she saw the gleam of another, gentler sun, and she sensed the fragrance of the herbs in the garden at world's end.

Lavrans set his wife's hand back in her lap and sat down on the bench a short distance away, with his back against the table and one arm resting along the top. He did not look at her, but stared into the hearth fire.

And yet her voice was quiet and calm when she once again spoke.

"I did not know, my husband, that you had such affection for me."

"I do," he replied, his voice equally calm.

They sat in silence for a while. Ragnfrid moved her sewing from her lap onto the bench beside her. After a time she said softly, "What I told you that night—have you forgotten that?"

"I doubt that any man on this earth could forget such words. And it's true that I myself have felt that things were no better between us after I heard them. But God knows, Ragnfrid, I tried so hard to conceal from you that I gave that matter so much thought."

"I didn't realize you thought so much about it."

He turned toward her abruptly and stared at his wife.

Then Ragnfrid said, "I am to blame that things grew worse between us, Lavrans. I thought that if you could be toward me exactly the same as before that night—then you must have cared even less for me than I thought. If you had been a stern husband toward me afterwards, if you had struck me even once when you were drunk—then I would have been better able to bear my sorrow and my remorse. But when you took it so lightly . . ."

"Did you think I took it lightly?"

The faint quaver in his voice made her wild with longing. She wanted to bury herself inside him, down in the depths of the emotions that could make his voice ripple with tension and strain.

She exclaimed in fury, "If only you had taken me in your arms even once, not because I was the lawful, Christian wife they had placed at your side, but as the wife you had yearned for and fought to win. Then you couldn't have behaved toward me as if those words had not been said."

Lavrans thought about what she had said. "No . . . then . . . I don't think I could have. No."

"If you had been as fond of your betrothed as Simon was of our Kristin . . ."

Lavrans didn't reply. After a moment, as if against his will, he said softly and fearfully, "Why did you mention *Simon?*"

"I suppose because I couldn't compare you to that other man," Ragnfrid said, confused and frightened herself although she tried to smile. "You and Erlend are too unlike each other."

Lavrans stood up, took a few steps, feeling uneasy. Then he said in an even quieter voice, "God will not forsake Simon."

"Have you never thought that God had forsaken you?" asked his wife.

"No."

"What did you think that night as we sat in the barn, when you found out at the very same moment that Kristin and I—the two people you held dearest and loved the most faithfully—we had both betrayed you as much as we possibly could?"

"I don't think I thought much about it," replied her husband.

"But later on," continued his wife, "when you kept thinking about it, as you say you did . . ."

Lavrans turned away from her. She saw a blush flood his sunburned neck.

"I thought about all the times I had betrayed Christ," he said in a low voice.

Ragnfrid stood up, hesitating a moment before she dared go over and place her hands on her husband's shoulders. When he put his arms around her, she pressed her forehead against his chest. He could feel her crying. Lavrans pulled her closer and rested his face against her hair.

"Now, Ragnfrid, we will go to bed," he said after a moment.

Together they walked over to the crucifix, knelt, and made the sign of the cross. Lavrans said the evening prayers, speaking the language of the Church in a low, clear voice, and his wife repeated the words after him.

Then they undressed. Ragnfrid lay down on the inner side of the bed; the headboard was now much lower because lately her husband had been plagued with dizziness. Lavrans shoved the bolt on the door closed, scraped ashes over the fire in the hearth, blew out the candle, and climbed in beside her. In the darkness they lay with their arms touching each other. After a moment they laced their fingers together.

Ragnfrid Ivarsdatter thought it seemed like a new wedding night, and a strange one. Happiness and sorrow flowed into each other, carrying her along on waves so powerful that she felt her soul beginning to loosen its roots in her body. Now the hand of death had touched her too—for the first time.

This was how it had to end—when it had begun as it did. She remembered the first time she saw her betrothed. At that time Lavrans was pleased with her—a little shy, but willing enough to have affection for his bride. Even the fact that the boy was so radiantly handsome had irritated her. His hair hung so thick and glossy and fair around his pink-and-white, downy face. Her heart burned with anguish at the thought of another man, who was not handsome nor young nor gentle like milk and blood; she was dying with longing to sink into his embrace and drive her knife into his throat. And the first time her betrothed tried to caress her . . . They were sitting together on the steps of a loft back home, and he reached out to take one of her braids. She leaped to her feet, turned her back on him, white with anger, and left.

Oh, she remembered that nighttime journey, when she rode with Trond and Tordis through Jerndal to Dovre, to the woman who was skilled in sorcery. She had fallen to her knees, pulling off rings and bracelets and putting them on the floor in front of Fru Aashild; in vain she had begged for a remedy so her bridegroom might not have his will with her. She remembered the long journey with her father and kinsmen and bridesmaids and the entourage from home, down through the valley, out across the flat countryside, to the wedding at Skog. And she remembered the first night—and all the nights afterwards—when she received the clumsy caresses of the newly married boy and acted cold as stone, never concealing how little they pleased her.

No, God had not forsaken her. In His mercy, He had heard her cries for help when she called on Him, as she sank more and more into her misery—even when she called without believing she would be heard. It felt as if the black sea were rushing over her; now the waves lifted her toward a bliss so strange and so sweet that she knew it would carry her out of life.

"Talk to me, Lavrans," she implored him quietly. "I'm so tired."

Her husband whispered, "*Venite ad me, omnes qui laborate et onerati estis. Ego reficiam vos*[1]—the Lord has said."

He slipped one arm under her shoulder and pulled her close to his side. They lay there for a moment, cheek to cheek.

Then she said softly, "Now I have asked the Mother of God to answer my prayer that I need not live long after you, my husband."

His lips and his lashes brushed her cheek in the darkness like the wings of a butterfly.

"My Ragnfrid, my Ragnfrid."

## CHAPTER 8

Kristin stayed home at Husaby during the autumn and winter with no wish to go anywhere; she blamed this on the fact that she was unwell. But she was simply tired. She had never felt so tired before in all her life. She was tired of merriment and tired of sorrow, and most of all tired of brooding.

It would be better after she had this new child, she thought; and she felt such a fierce longing for it. It was the child that would save her. If it was a son and her father died before he was born, he would bear her father's name. And she thought about how dearly she would love this child and nurse him at her own breast. It had been such a long time since she had had an infant, and she wept with longing whenever she thought about holding a tiny child in her arms again.

She gathered her sons around her as she had in the past and tried to bring a little more discipline and order to their upbringing. She felt that in this way she was acting in accordance with her father's wishes, and it seemed to give her soul some peace. Sira Eiliv had now begun to teach Naakkve and Bjørgulf reading and Latin, and Kristin often sat in the parsonage when the children went there for lessons. But they weren't very eager pupils, and all the boys were unruly and wild except for Gaute, and so he continued to be his mother's lap-child, as Erlend called him.

Erlend had returned home from Denmark in high spirits around All Saints' Day. He had been received with the greatest honor by the duke and by his kinswoman, Lady Ingebjørg. They had thanked him heartily for his gifts of furs and silver; he had ridden in a jousting tournament and hunted stag and deer. And when they parted, Sir Knut had given him a coal-black Spanish stallion, while Lady Ingebjørg had sent kind greetings along with two silver greyhounds for his wife. Kristin thought these foreign dogs looked sly and treacherous, and she was afraid they would harm her children. And people all around were talking about the Castilian horse. Erlend looked good on the back of the long-legged, elegantly built horse, but animals like that were not suited to this country, and only God knew how the stallion would manage in the mountains. In the meantime, wherever he went in his district, Erlend would buy the most splendid of black mares, and he now had a herd that was beautiful in appearance, at any rate. Erlend Nikulaussøn usually gave his horses refined, foreign names, such as Belkolor and Bajard, but he said that this stallion was so magnificent that it didn't need any further adornment, and he named it simply Soten.[1]

Erlend was greatly annoyed that his wife refused to accompany him anywhere. He couldn't see that she was ill; she neither swooned nor vomited this time, and it was not even visible that she was with child. And by constantly sitting indoors, brooding and worrying over his misdeeds, she had grown weary and pale. It was during the Christmas season that fierce quarrels erupted between them. But this time Erlend didn't come and apologize for his bad temper, as he had in the past. Until now, whenever they had disagreements, he had always believed that he was to blame. Kristin was good, she was always right; if he felt uncomfortable and bored at home, then it must be because it was his nature to grow weary of what was good and right if he had too much of it. But this summer he had noticed more than once that his father-in-law had sided with him and seemed to think Kristin was lacking in wifely gentleness and tolerance. It occurred to him that she was overly sensitive about petty matters and reluctant to forgive him for minor offenses which he had committed with no ill intent. He would always beg her forgiveness after taking time to reflect, and she would say that she forgave him. But afterwards he could see that it was simply stored away, not forgotten.

So Erlend spent much time away from home, and now he often took his daughter Margret along with him. The maiden's upbringing had always been a source of disagreement between him and his wife. Kristin had never said a word about it, but Erlend knew quite well what she, and others, thought. He had treated Margret in all respects as his lawful child, and whenever she accompanied her father and stepmother everyone received her as if she were. At Ramborg's wedding she had been one of the bridesmaids, wearing a golden wreath on her flowing hair. Many of the women didn't approve, but Lavrans had persuaded them, and Simon had also said that no one should voice any objection to Erlend or say a word about it to the maiden. The lovely child was not to blame for her unfortunate birth.

But Kristin knew that Erlend planned to marry Margret to a man of noble lineage. He thought that with his present position, he could succeed in arranging it, even though the maiden had been conceived in adultery and it would be difficult to gain for her a position that was firm and secure. It might have been possible if people had been convinced that Erlend was capable of preserving and increasing his power and wealth. But although he was well-liked and respected in many ways, no one truly believed that the prosperity at Husaby would last. So Kristin was afraid that it would be difficult for him to carry out his plans for Margret. Even though she was not particularly fond of Margret, Kristin felt sorry for the maiden and dreaded the day when the girl's arrogant spirit might be broken—if she had to settle for a match that was much poorer than what her father had taught her to expect, and for circumstances that were quite different from what she had grown up with.

Then, around Candlemas, three men came from Formo to Husaby; they had skied over the mountains to bring Erlend troubling news from Simon Andressøn. Simon wrote that their father-in-law was ill, and that he was not expected to live long. Lavrans wanted to ask Erlend to come to Sil, if he could; he wanted to speak to both of his sons-in-law about how everything should be arranged after his death.

Erlend cast surreptitious glances at his wife. She was heavy with child now; her face was thin and quite pale. And she looked so unhappy, as if she might cry at any moment. Now he regretted his behavior toward her that winter; her father's illness came as no surprise to her, and if she had been carrying such a secret sorrow, he would have to forgive her for being unreasonable.

Alone he would be able to travel to Sil quite swiftly, if he skied over the mountains. But if he had to take along his wife, it would be a slow and difficult journey. And then he would have to wait until after the weapons-*ting*[2] during Lent, and call meetings with his deputies first. There were also several meetings and *tings* that he would have to attend himself. Before they could leave, it would be dangerously close to the time when she would give birth—and Kristin couldn't stand the sea, even when she was feeling well. But he didn't dare think about her not being allowed to see her father before he died. That evening, after they had gone to bed, he asked his wife whether she dared make the journey.

He felt rewarded as she wept in his arms, grateful and full of remorse for her unkindness toward him that winter. Erlend grew gentle and tender, as he always did whenever he had caused a woman sorrow and then was forced to see her struggle with her grief before his eyes. And he gave in to Kristin's proposal with reasonable patience. He said at once that he wouldn't take the children along. But Kristin replied that Naakkve was old enough now, and it would be good for him to witness his grandfather's passing. Erlend said no. Then she thought that Ivar and Skule were too young to be left in the care of the servant women. No, said Erlend. And Lavrans had grown so fond of Gaute. No, said Erlend again. It would be difficult enough, as things now stood with her—for Ragnfrid to have a nursemaid on the estate while she was tending to her husband on his sickbed, and for them to bring the newborn home again. Either Kristin would have to leave the child with foster parents on one of Lavrans's farms, or she would have to stay at Jørundgaard until summer; but he would have to travel home before then. He went over all the plans, again and again, but he tried to make his voice calm and convincing.

Then it occurred to him that he ought to bring a few things from Nidaros that his mother-in-law might need for the funeral feast: wine and wax, wheat flour and Paradise grains and the like. But at last they made their departure, reaching Jørundgaard on the day before Saint Gertrud's Day.

But this homecoming was much different for Kristin than she had imagined.

She had to be grateful that she was given the chance to see her father again. When she thought about his joy at her arrival and how he had thanked Erlend for bringing her, then she was happy. But this time she felt shut out from so many things, and it was a painful feeling.

It was less than a month before she would give birth, and

Lavrans forbade her from lifting a hand to tend to him. She wasn't allowed to keep watch over him at night with the others, and Ragnfrid wouldn't hear of her offering the slightest help in spite of all the work to be done. She sat with her father during the day, but they were seldom alone together. Almost daily, guests would come to the manor; friends who wanted to see Lavrans Bjørgulfsøn one last time before he died. This pleased her father, although it made him quite weary. He would talk in a merry and hearty voice to everyone—women and men, poor and rich, young and old—thanking them for their friendship and asking for their prayers of intercession for his soul, and hoping that God might allow them to meet on the day of rejoicing. At night, when only his close family was with him, Kristin would lie in bed in the high loft, staring into the darkness, unable to sleep because she was thinking about her father's passing and about the impetuousness and wickedness of her own heart.

The end was coming quickly for Lavrans. He had held on to his strength until Ramborg gave birth to her child and Ragnfrid no longer needed to be at Formo so often. He had also had his servants take him over there one day so he could see his daughter and granddaughter. The little maiden had been christened Ulvhild. But then he took to his bed, and it was unlikely he would ever get up again.

Lavrans lay in the hall of the high loft. They had made up a kind of bed for him on the high-seat bench, for he couldn't bear to have his head raised; then he would grow dizzy at once and suffer fainting spells and heart spasms. They didn't dare bleed him anymore; they had done it so often during the fall and winter that he was now quite lacking in blood, and he had little desire for food or drink.

The handsome features of his face were now sharp, and the tan had faded from his once-fresh complexion; it was sallow like bone, and bloodless and pale around his lips and eyes. The thick blond hair with streaks of white was now untrimmed, lying withered and limp against the blue-patterned expanse of the pillow. But what had changed him most was the rough, gray beard now covering the lower half of his face and growing on his long, broad neck, where the sinews stood out like thick cords. Lavrans had always been meticulous about shaving before every holy day. His body was so gaunt that it was little more than a skeleton. But he said he felt fine as long as he lay flat and didn't move. And he was always cheerful and happy.

They slaughtered and brewed and baked for the funeral feast; they took out the bedclothes and mended them. Everything that could be done ahead of time was done now, so that there would be quiet when the last struggle came. It cheered Lavrans considerably to hear about these preparations. His last banquet would be far from the poorest to be held at Jørundgaard; in an honorable and worthy manner he was to take leave of his guardianship of the estate and his household. One day he wanted to have a look at the two cows that would be included in the funeral procession, to be given to Sira Eirik and Sira Solmund, and so they were led into the house. They had been fed extra fodder all winter long and were as splendid and fat as cows in the mountain pastures around Saint Olav's Day, even though the valley was now in the midst of the spring shortages. He laughed the hardest every time one of the cows relieved itself on the floor.

But he was afraid his wife was going to wear herself out. Kristin had considered herself a diligent housewife, and that was her reputation back home in Skaun, but she now thought that compared to her mother she was completely incompetent. No one understood how Ragnfrid managed to accomplish everything she did—and yet she never seemed to be absent for very long from her husband's side; she also helped to keep watch at night.

"Don't think of me, husband," she would say, putting her hand in his. "After you're gone, you know that I'll take a rest from all these toils."

Many years before, Lavrans Bjørgulfsøn had purchased his resting place at the friars' monastery in Hamar, and Ragnfrid Ivarsdatter would accompany his body there and then stay on. She would live on a corrody in a manor owned by the monks in town. But first the coffin would be carried to the church here at home, with splendid gifts for the church and the priests; Lavrans's stallion would follow behind with his armor and weapons, and Erlend would then redeem them by paying forty-five marks of silver. One of his sons would be given the armor, preferably the child Kristin now carried, if it was a son. Perhaps there would be another Lavrans at Jørundgaard sometime in the future, said the ill man with a smile. On the journey south through Gudbrandsdal, the coffin would be carried into several more churches and stay there overnight; these would be remembered in Lavrans's testament with gifts of money and candles.

One day Simon mentioned that his father-in-law had bedsores, and he helped Ragnfrid to lift the sick man and tend to him.

Kristin was in despair over her jealous heart. She could hardly bear to see her parents on such familiar terms with Simon Andressøn. He felt at home at Jørundgaard in a way that Erlend never had. Almost every day his huge, sorrel-colored horse would be tied to the courtyard fence, and Simon would be sitting inside with Lavrans, wearing his hat and cape. He wasn't intending to stay long. But a short time later he would appear in the doorway and yell to the servants to put his horse in the stable after all. He was acquainted with all of her father's business affairs; he would get out the letter box and take out deeds and documents. He took care of chores for Ragnfrid, and he talked to the overseer about the management of the farm. Kristin thought to herself that her greatest desire had been for her father to be fond of Erlend, but the first time Lavrans had taken his side against her, she had responded at once in the worst possible manner.

Simon Andressøn was deeply grieved that he would soon be parted from his wife's father. But he felt such joy at the birth of his little daughter. Lavrans and Ragnfrid spoke often of little Ulvhild, and Simon could answer all their questions about the child's welfare and progress. And here too Kristin felt jealousy sting her heart—Erlend had never taken that kind of interest in their children. At the same time, it seemed to her a bit laughable when this man with the heavy, reddish-brown face who was no longer young would sit and talk so knowledgeably about an infant's stomachaches and appetite.

One day Simon brought a sleigh to take her south to see her sister and niece.

He had rebuilt the old, dark hearth house, where the women of Formo had gone for hundreds of years whenever they were going to give birth. The hearth had been thrown out and replaced with a stone fireplace, with a finely carved bed placed snugly against one side. On the opposite wall hung a beautiful carved image of the Mother of God, so that whoever lay in the bed could see it.

Flagstones had been laid down, and a glass pane was put in the window; there were lovely, small pieces of furniture and new benches. Simon wanted Ramborg to have this house as her women's room. Here she could keep her things and invite other women in; and whenever there were banquets at the manor, the women could retire to this house if they grew uneasy when the men became overwhelmed by drink late in the evening.

Ramborg was lying in bed, in honor of her guest. She had adorned herself with a silk wimple and a red gown trimmed across the breast with white fur. She had silk-covered pillows behind her back and a flowered, velvet coverlet on top of the bedclothes. In front of the bed stood Ulvhild Simonsdatter's cradle. It was the old Swedish cradle that Ramborg Sunesdatter had brought to Norway, the same one in which Kristin's father and grandfather, and she herself and all her siblings had slept. According to custom, she, as the eldest daughter, should have had the cradle as part of her dowry, but it had never been mentioned at the time she was married. She thought that her parents had purposely forgotten about the cradle. Didn't they think the children she and Erlend would have were worthy to sleep in it?

After that, she refused to go back to Formo, saying that she didn't have the strength.

And Kristin did feel ill, but this was from sorrow and her anguished soul. She couldn't hide from herself that the longer she stayed at home, the more painful it felt. That was just her nature: it hurt her to see that now, as her father approached his death, it was his wife who was closest to him.

She had always heard people praise her parents' life together as an exemplary marriage, beautiful and noble, with harmony, loyalty, and good will. But she had felt, without thinking too closely about it, that there was something that kept them apart—some indefinable shadow that made their life at home subdued, even though it was calm and pleasant. Now there was no longer any shadow between her parents. They talked to each other calmly and quietly, mostly about small, everyday matters; but Kristin sensed there was something new in their eyes and in the tone of their voices. She could see that her father missed his wife whenever she was somewhere else. If he managed to convince her to take a rest, he would lie in bed, fidgeting and waiting; when Ragnfrid came back, it was as if she brought peace and joy to the ill man. One day Kristin heard them talking about their dead children, and yet they looked happy. When Sira Eirik came over to read to Lavrans, Ragnfrid would always sit with them. Then he would take his wife's hand and lie there, playing with her fingers and twisting her rings around.

Kristin knew that her father loved her no less than before. But she had never noticed until now that he loved her mother. And she could see the difference between the love of a husband for the wife he had lived with all his life, during good days and bad—and his love for the child who had shared only his joys and had received his greatest tenderness. And she wept and prayed to God and Saint Olav for help—for she remembered that tearful, tender farewell with her father on the mountain in the autumn, but surely it couldn't be true that she now wished it had been the last.

On Summer Day[3] Kristin gave birth to her sixth son. Five days later she was already out of bed, and she went over to the main house to sit with her father. Lavrans was not pleased by this; it had never been the custom on his estate for a woman who had recently given birth to go outdoors under open sky until the first time she went to church. She must at least agree not to cross the courtyard unless the sun was up. Ragnfrid listened as Lavrans talked about this.

"I was just thinking, husband," she said, "that your women have never been very obedient; we've usually done whatever we wanted to do."

"And you've never realized that before?" asked her husband, laughing. "Well, your brother Trond isn't to blame, at any rate. Don't you remember that he used to call me spineless because I always let all of you have your way?"

When the next mass was celebrated, Ramborg went to church for the first time after giving birth, and afterwards she paid her first visit to Jørundgaard. Helga Rolvsdatter came with her; she was also a married woman now. And Haavard Trondssøn of Sundbu had come to see Lavrans, too. These three young people were all the same age, and for three years they had lived together like siblings at Jørundgaard. The other two had looked up to

Haavard, and he had been the leader in all their games because he was a boy. But now the two young wives with the white wimples made him feel quite clearly that they were experienced women with husbands and children and households to manage, while he was merely an immature and foolish child. Lavrans found this greatly amusing.

"Just wait until you have a wife of your own, Haavard, my foster son. Then you will truly be told how little you know," he said, and all the men in the room laughed and agreed.

Sira Eirik came daily to visit the dying man. The old parish priest's eyesight was now failing, but he could still manage to read just as easily the story of Creation in Norwegian and the gospels and psalms in Latin, because he knew those books so well. But several years earlier, down in Saastad, Lavrans had acquired a thick volume, and it was passages from this book that he wanted to hear. Sira Eirik couldn't read it because of his bad eyes, so Lavrans asked Kristin to try to read from the book. And after she grew accustomed to it, she managed to read beautifully and well. It was a great joy for her that now there was something she could do for her father.

The book contained what seemed to be dialogues between Fear and Courage, between Faith and Doubt, Body and Soul. There were also stories of saints and many accounts of men who, while still alive, were swept away in spirit and who witnessed the torments of the abyss, the trials of fiery purgatory, and the salvation of Heaven. Lavrans now spoke often of the purgatory fire, which he expected to enter soon, but he showed no sign of fear. He hoped for great solace from the prayers of intercession offered by his friends and the priests; and he consoled himself that Saint Olav and Saint Thomas would give him strength for the last trial, as he felt they had given him strength here in life. He had always heard that the person who firmly believed would never for a moment lose sight of the salvation toward which the soul was moving, through the fiery blaze. Kristin thought her father seemed to be looking forward to it, as if it were a test of manhood. She vaguely remembered from her childhood the time when the king's retainers from the valley set off on a campaign against Duke Eirik.[4] Now she thought that her father seemed eager for his death, in the same way he had been eager for battle and adventure back then.

One day she said that she thought her father had endured so many trials in this life that surely he would be spared from the worst of them in the next. Lavrans replied that it didn't seem that way to him; he had been a rich man, he was descended from a splendid lineage, and he had won friends and prosperity in the world. "My greatest sorrows were that I never saw my mother's face, and that I lost my children—but soon they will no longer be sorrows. And the same is true of other things that have grieved me in my life—they are no longer sorrows."

Ragnfrid was often in the room while Kristin read. Strangers were also present, and now Erlend wanted to sit and listen too. Everyone found joy in what she read, but Kristin grew dejected and distressed. She thought about her own heart, which fully understood what was right and wrong, and yet it had always yearned for what was not righteous. And she was afraid for her little child; she could hardly sleep at night for fear that he would die unbaptized. Two women had to keep constant vigil over her, and yet she was still afraid to fall asleep. Her other children had all been baptized before they were three days old, but they had decided to wait this time, because the boy was big and strong, and they wanted to name him after Lavrans. But in the valley people strictly abided by the custom that children not be named for anyone who was still alive.

One day when Kristin was sitting with her father and holding the child on her lap, Lavrans asked her to unwrap the swaddling clothes. He had still not seen more than the infant's face. She did as he asked and then placed the child in her father's arms. Lavrans stroked the small, rounded chest and took one of the tiny, plump hands in his own.

"It seems strange, kinsman, that one day you will wear my coat of mail. Right now you wouldn't fill up more space than a worm in a hollow nutshell; and this hand will have to grow big before it can grip the hilt of my sword. Looking at a lad like this, it almost seems God's will that we not bear arms. But you won't have to grow very old, my boy, before you long to take them up. There are so few men born of women who have such a love for God that they would forswear the right to carry weapons. I did not have it."

He lay quietly, looking at the infant.

"You carry your children under a loving heart, my Kristin. The boy is fat and big, but you're pale and thin as a reed; your mother said it was always that way after you gave birth. Ramborg's daughter is small and thin, but Ramborg is blossoming like a rose," he said, laughing.

"And yet it seems strange to me that she doesn't want to nurse the child herself," said Kristin.

"Simon is also against it. He says he wouldn't reward her for the gift by wearing her out in that way. You must remember that Ramborg was not even sixteen, and she had barely grown out of her own childhood shoes when her daughter was born. And she has never known a moment of ill health before. It's not so strange that she would have little patience. You were a grown woman when you were married, my Kristin."

Suddenly Kristin was overcome by violent sobs; she hardly knew what she was crying about. But it was true: She had loved her children from the first moment she held them in her womb; she had loved them even as they had tormented her with anguish, weighing her down and spoiling her looks. She had loved their small faces from the first moment she saw them, and loved them every single hour as they grew and changed, becoming young men. But no one had loved them as she had or rejoiced along with her. It was not in Erlend's nature. He was fond of them, of course, but he had always thought that Naakkve came too early, and that each son afterwards was one too many. She recalled what she had thought about the fruit of sin during the first winter she lived at Husaby; she realized she had tasted its bitterness, although not as much as she had feared. Things had gone wrong between her and Erlend back then and apparently could never be rectified.

Kristin hadn't been close to her mother. Her sisters were mere children when she was already a grown maiden, and she had never had companions to play with. She was brought up among men; she was able to be gentle and soft because there had always been men around to hold up protective and shielding hands between her and everything else in the world. Now it seemed reasonable to her that she gave birth only to sons—boys to nurse with her blood and at her breast, to love and protect and care for until they were old enough to join the ranks of men. She remembered that she had heard of a queen who was called the Mother of Boys. She must have had a wall of watchful men around her when she was a child.

"What is it now, Kristin?" asked her father quietly after a while.

She couldn't tell him any of this; when she stopped crying enough to talk, she said, "Shouldn't I grieve, Father, when you are lying here . . . ?"

Finally, when Lavrans pressed her, she told him of her fears for the unbaptized child. Then he at once ordered the boy to be taken to church the next time mass was celebrated; he said he didn't think it would cause his death any sooner than God willed it.

"And besides, I've been lying here long enough," he said with a laugh. "Wretched deeds accompany our arrival and our departure, Kristin. In sickness we are born and in sickness we die, except for those who die in battle. That seemed to me the best kind of death when I was young: to be killed on the battlefield. But a sinful man has need of a sickbed, and yet I don't think my soul will be any better healed if I lie here longer."

And so the boy was baptized on the following Sunday and was given his grandfather's name. Kristin and Erlend were bitterly criticized for this in the outlying villages. Lavrans Bjørgulfsøn told everyone who came to visit that it was done on his orders; he refused to have a heathen in his house when death came to the door.

Lavrans now began to worry that his death would come in the middle of the spring farm work, which would be a great hardship for many people who wanted to honor him by escorting his funeral procession. But two weeks after the child was baptized, Erlend came to Kristin in the old weaving room where she had been sleeping since giving birth. It was late in the morning, past breakfast time, but she was still in bed because the boy had been restless. Erlend was deeply distressed, but he said in a calm and loving voice that now she must get up and go to her father. Lavrans had suffered terrible convulsions and heart spasms at daybreak, and since then he lay drained of all strength. Sira Eirik was with him now, and had just heard his confession.

It was the fifth day after the Feast of Saint Halvard. It was raining lightly but steadily. When Kristin went out into the courtyard, she noticed in the gentle southern wind the earthy smell of newly plowed and manured fields. The countryside was brown in the spring rain, the sky was pale blue between the high mountains, and the mist was drifting by, halfway up the slopes. The ringing of little bells came from the groves of trees along the swollen gray river; herds of goats had been let out, and they were nibbling at the bud-covered branches. This was the kind of weather that had always filled her father's heart with joy. The cold of winter was over for both people and livestock, the animals were finally released from their dark, narrow stalls and scanty fodder.

Kristin saw at once from her father's face that death was now very near. The skin around his nostrils was snowy white, but bluish under his eyes and at his lips; his hair had separated into sweaty strings lying on his broad, damp forehead. But he had his full wits about him and spoke clearly, although slowly and in a weak voice.

The servants approached the bed, one by one, and Lavrans gave his hand to each of them, thanking them for their service, telling them to live well and asking for forgiveness if he had ever offended them in any way; and he asked them to remember him with a prayer for his soul. Then he said goodbye to his kinsmen. He told his daughters to bend down so he could kiss them, and he asked God and all the saints to bless them. They wept bitterly, both of them; and young Ramborg threw herself into her sister's arms. Holding on to each other, Lavrans's two daughters went back to their place at the foot of their father's bed, and the younger one continued to weep on Kristin's breast.

Erlend's face quivered and the tears ran down his face when he lifted Lavrans's hand to kiss it, as he quietly asked his father-in-law to forgive him for the sorrows he had caused him over the years. Lavrans said he forgave him with all his heart, and he prayed that God might be with him all his days. There was a strange, pale light in Erlend's handsome face when he silently moved away to stand at his wife's side, hand in hand with her.

Simon Darre did not weep, but he knelt down as he took his father-in-law's hand to kiss it, and he held on to it tightly as he stayed on his knees a moment longer. "Your hand feels warm and good, son-in-law," said Lavrans with a faint smile. Ramborg turned to her husband when he went to her, and Simon put his arm around her thin, girlish shoulders.

Last of all, Lavrans said goodbye to his wife. They whispered a few words to each other that no one else could hear, and exchanged a kiss in everyone's presence, as was now proper when death was in the room. Then Ragnfrid knelt in front of her husband's bed, with her face turned toward him; she was pale, silent, and calm.

Sira Eirik stayed with them after he had anointed the dying man with oil and given him the viaticum. He sat near the headboard and prayed; Ragnfrid was now sitting on the bed. Several hours passed. Lavrans lay with his eyes half-closed. Now and then he would move his head restlessly on the pillow and pick at the covers with his hands, breathing heavily and groaning from time to time. They thought he had lost his voice, but there was no death struggle.

Dusk came early, and the priest lit a candle. Everyone sat quietly, watching the dying man and listening to the dripping and trickling of the rain outside the house. Then the sick man grew agitated, his body trembled, his face turned blue, and he seemed to be fighting for breath. Sira Eirik put his arm under Lavrans's shoulders and lifted him into a sitting position as he supported his head against his chest and held up the cross before his face.

Lavrans opened his eyes, fixed his gaze on the crucifix in the priest's hand, and said softly, but so clearly that almost everyone in the room could hear him:

*"Exsurrexi, et adhuc sum tecum."*[5]

Several more tremors passed over his body, and his hands fumbled with the coverlet. Sira Eirik continued to hold him against his chest for a moment. Then he gently laid his friend's body down on the bed, kissing his forehead and smoothing back his hair, before he pressed his eyelids and nostrils closed; then he stood up and began to say a prayer.

Kristin was allowed to join the vigil and keep watch over the body that night. They had laid Lavrans out on his bier in the high loft, since that was the biggest room and they expected many people to come to the death chamber.

Her father seemed to her inexpressibly beautiful as he lay in the glow of the candles, with his pale, golden face uncovered. They had folded down the cloth that hid his face so that it wouldn't become soiled by the many people who came to view the body. Sira Eirik and the parish priest from Kvam were singing over him; the latter had arrived that evening to say his last farewell to Lavrans, but he had come too late.

By the following day guests already began riding into the courtyard, and then, for the sake of propriety, Kristin had to take to her bed since she had not yet been to church. Now it was her turn to have her bed adorned with silk coverlets and the finest pillows in the house. The cradle from Formo was borrowed, and there lay the young Lavrans; all day long people came in to see her and the child.

She heard that her father's body continued to look beautiful—it had merely yellowed a bit. And no one had ever seen so many candles brought to a dead man's bier.

On the fifth day the funeral feast began, and it was exceptionally grand in every way. There were more than a hundred strange horses at the manor and at Laugarbru; even Formo housed some of the guests. On the seventh day the heirs divided up the estate, amicably and with friendship; Lavrans himself had made all the arrangements before his death, and everyone carefully abided by his wishes.

The next day the body, which now lay in Olav's Church, was to begin the journey to Hamar.

The evening before—or rather, late that night—Ragnfrid came into the hearth room where her daughter lay in bed with her child. Ragnfrid was very tired, but her face was calm and clear. She asked her serving women to leave.

"All the houses are full, but I'm sure you can find a corner to sleep in. I have a mind to sit with my daughter myself on this last night that I'll spend on my estate."

She took the child from Kristin's arms and carried him over to the hearth to get him ready for the night.

"It must be strange for you, Mother, to leave this manor where you've lived with my father all these years," said Kristin. "I don't see how you can stand to do it."

"I could stand it much less to stay here," replied Ragnfrid, rocking little Lavrans in her arms, "and not see your father going about among the buildings.

"I've never told you how we happened to move to this valley and ended up living here," she continued after a moment. "When word came that Ivar, my father, was expected to breathe his last, I was unable to travel; Lavrans had to go north alone. I remember the weather was so beautiful on the evening he left—back then he liked to ride late, when it was cool, and so he set off for Oslo in the evening. It was just before Midsummer. I followed him out to the place where the road from the manor crosses the church road—do you remember the spot where there are several big flat rocks and barren fields all around? The worst land at Skog, and always arid; but that year the grain stood high in the furrows, and we talked about that. Lavrans was on foot, leading his horse, and I was holding you by the hand. You were four winters old.

"When we reached the crossroads, I wanted you to run back to the farm buildings. You didn't want to, but then your father told you to see if you could find five white stones and lay them out in a cross in the creek below the spring—that would protect him from the trolls of Mjørsa Forest when he sailed past. Then you set off running."

"Is that something people believe?" asked Kristin.

"I've never heard of it, either before or since. I think your father made it up right then. Don't you remember how he could think up so many things when he was playing with you?"

"Yes. I remember."

"I walked with him through the woods, all the way to the dwarf stone. He told me to turn around, and then he accompanied me back to the crossroads. He laughed and said I should know he couldn't very well allow me to walk alone through the forest, especially after the sun was down. As we stood there at the crossroads, I put my arms around his neck. I was so sad that I couldn't travel home with him. I had never felt comfortable at Skog, and I was always longing to go north to Gudbrandsdal. Lavrans tried to console me, and at last he said, 'When I return and you're holding my son in your arms, you can ask me for whatever you wish, and if it's within my power to give it to you, then you will not have asked in vain.' And I replied that I would ask that we might move up here and live on my ancestral estate. Your father wasn't pleased, and he said, 'Couldn't you have thought of something bigger to ask for?' He laughed a little, and I thought this was something he would never agree to, which seemed to me only reasonable. But as you know, Sigurd, your youngest brother, lived less than an hour. Halvdan baptized him, and after that the child died.

"Your father came home early one morning. The evening before, he had asked in Oslo how things stood at home, and then he set off for Skog at once. I was still keeping to my bed; I was so full of grief that I didn't have the strength to get up, and I thought I would prefer never to get up again. God forgive me—when they brought you in to me, I turned to the wall and refused to look at you, my poor little child. But then Lavrans said, as he sat on the edge of my bed, still wearing his cape and sword, that now we would try to see if things might be better for us living here at Jørundgaard, and that's how we came to move from Skog. But now you can see why I don't want to live here any longer, now that Lavrans is gone."

Ragnfrid brought the child and placed him on his mother's breast. She took the silk coverlet, which had been spread over Kristin's bed during the day, folded it up, and laid it aside. Then she stood there for a moment, looking down at her daughter and touching the thick, dark-blonde braids which lay between her white breasts.

"Your father asked me often whether your hair was still thick and beautiful. It was such a joy to him that you didn't lose your looks from giving birth to so many children. And you made him so happy during the last few years because you had become such a capable wife and looked so healthy and lovely with all your fair young sons around you."

Kristin tried to swallow back her tears.

"He often told me, Mother, that you were the best wife—he told me to tell you that." She paused, embarrassed, and Ragnfrid laughed softly.

"Lavrans should have known that he didn't need anyone else to tell me of his good will toward me." She stroked the child's head and her daughter's hand which was holding the infant. "But perhaps he wanted . . . It's not true, my Kristin, that I have ever envied your father's love for you. It's right and proper that you should have loved him more than you loved me. You were such a sweet and lovely little maiden—I could hardly believe that God would let me keep you. But I always thought more about what I had lost than what I still had."

Ragnfrid sat down on the edge of the bed.

"They had other customs at Skog than I was used to back home. I can't remember that my father ever kissed me. He kissed my mother when she lay on her bier. Mother would kiss Gudrun during the mass, because she stood next to her, and then my sister would kiss me; otherwise that was not something we ever did.

"At Skog it was the custom that when we came home from church, after taking the *corpus domini,* and we got down from our horses in the courtyard, then Sir Bjørgulf would kiss his sons and me on the cheek, while we kissed his hand. Then all the married couples would kiss each other, and we would shake hands with all the servants who had been to the church service and ask that everyone might benefit from the sacrament. They did that often, Lavrans and Aasmund; they would kiss their father on the hand when he gave them gifts and the like. Whenever he or Inga came into the room, the sons would always get to their feet and stand there until asked to sit down. At first these seemed to me foolish and foreign ways.

"Later, during the years I lived with your father when we lost our sons, and all those years when we endured such great anguish and sorrow over our Ulvhild—then it seemed good that Lavrans had been brought up as he had, with gentler and more loving ways."

After a moment Kristin murmured, "So Father never saw Sigurd?"

"No," replied Ragnfrid, her voice equally quiet. "Nor did I see him while he was alive."

Kristin lay in silence; then she said, "And yet, Mother, it seems to me that there has been much good in your life."

The tears began to stream down Ragnfrid Ivarsdatter's pale face.

"God help me, yes. It seems that way to me, too."

A little later she carefully picked up the infant, who had fallen asleep at his mother's breast, and placed him in the cradle. She fastened Kristin's shift with the little silver brooch, caressed her daughter's cheek, and told her to go to sleep now.

Kristin put out her hand. "Mother . . ." she implored.

Ragnfrid bent down, gathered her daughter into her arms, and kissed her many times. She hadn't done that in all the years since Ulvhild died.

It was the most beautiful springtime weather on the following day, as Kristin stood behind the corner of the main house looking out toward the slopes beyond the river. There was a verdant smell in the air, the singing of creeks released everywhere, and a green sheen over all the groves and meadows. At the spot where the road went along the mountainside above Laugarbru, a blanket of winter rye shimmered fresh and bright. Jon had burned off the saplings there the year before and planted rye on the cleared land.

When the funeral procession reached that spot, she would be able to see it best.

And then the procession emerged from beneath the scree, across from the fresh new acres of rye.

She could see all the priests riding on ahead, and there were also vergers among the first group, carrying the crosses and tapers. She couldn't see the flames in the bright sunlight, but the candles looked like slender white streaks. Two horses followed, carrying her father's coffin on a litter between them, and then she recognized Erlend on the black horse, her mother, Simon and Ramborg, and many of her kinsmen and friends in the long procession.

For a moment she could faintly hear the singing of the priests above the roar of the Laag, but then the tones of the hymn died away in the rush of the river and the steady trickling of the springtime streams on the slopes. Kristin stood there, gazing off into the distance, long after the last packhorse with the traveling bags had disappeared into the woods.

PART III

# ERLEND NIKULAUSSØN

## CHAPTER 1

RAGNFRID IVARSDATTER LIVED less than two years after her husband's death; she died early in the winter of 1332. It's a long way from Hamar to Skaun, so they didn't hear of her death at Husaby until she had already been in the ground more than a month. But Simon Andressøn came to Husaby during Whitsuntide; there were a few things that needed to be agreed upon among kinsmen about Ragnfrid's estate. Kristin Lavransdatter now owned Jørundgaard, and it was decided that Simon would oversee her property and collect payments from her tenants. He had managed his mother-in-law's properties in the valley while she lived in Hamar.

Just then Erlend was having a great deal of trouble and vexation with several matters that had occurred in his district. During the previous autumn, Huntjov, the farmer at Forbregd in Updal, had killed his neighbor because the man had called his wife a sorceress. The villagers bound the murderer and brought him to the sheriff; Erlend put him in custody in one of his lofts. But when the cold grew worse that winter, he allowed the man to move freely among his servant men. Huntjov had been one of Erlend's crew members on *Margygren* on the voyage north, and at that time he had displayed great courage. When Erlend submitted his report regarding Huntjov's case and asked that he be allowed to remain in the country,[1] he also presented the man in the most favorable light. When Ulf Haldorssøn offered a guarantee that Huntjov would appear at the proper time for the *ting* at Orkedal, Erlend permitted the farmer to go home for the Christmas holy days. But then Huntjov and his wife went to visit the innkeeper in Drivdal who was their kinsman, and on the way there, they disappeared. Erlend thought they had perished in the terrible storm that had raged at the time, but many people said they had fled; now the sheriff's men could go whistling after them. And then new charges were brought against the man who had vanished. It was said that several years earlier, Huntjov had killed a man in the mountains and buried the body under a pile of rocks—a man whom Huntjov claimed had wounded his mare in the flank. And it was revealed that his wife had indeed practiced witchcraft.

Then the priest of Updal and the archbishop's envoy set about investigating these rumors of sorcery. And this led to shameful discoveries about the way in which people observed Christianity in many parts of Orkdøla county. This occurred mostly in the remote regions of Rennabu and Updalsskog, but an old man from Budvik was also brought before the archbishop's court in Nidaros. Erlend showed so little zeal for this matter that people began talking about it. There was also that old man named Aan, who had lived near the lake below Husaby and practically had to be considered one of Erlend's servants. He was skilled in runes and incantations, and it was said that he had several images in his possession to which he offered sacrifices. But nothing of the kind was found in his hut after his death. Erlend himself, along with Ulf Haldorssøn, had been with the old man when he died; people said that no doubt they had destroyed one thing or another before the priest arrived. Yes, now that people happened to think about it, Erlend's own aunt had been accused of witchcraft, adultery, and the murder of her husband—although Fru Aashild Gautesdatter had been much too wise and clever and had too many powerful friends to be convicted of anything. Then people suddenly remembered that in his youth Erlend had lived a far from Christian life and had defied the laws of the Church.

The result of all this was that the archbishop summoned Erlend Nikulaussøn to Nidaros for an interview. Simon accompanied his brother-in-law to town; he was going to Ranheim to get his sister's son, for the boy was supposed to travel home with him to Gudbrandsdal to visit his mother for a while.

It was a week before the Frosta *ting*[2] was to be held, and Nidaros was full of people. When the brothers-in-law arrived at the bishop's estate and were shown into the audience hall, many Brothers of the Cross were there, as well as several noble gentlemen, including the judge of the Frosta *ting*, Harald Nikulaussøn; Olav Hermanssøn, judge in Nidaros; Sir Guttorm Helgessøn, the sheriff of Jemtland; and Arne Gjavvaldssøn, who at once came over to Simon Darre to give him a hearty greeting. Arne drew Simon over to a window alcove, and they sat down there together.

Simon felt ill at ease. He hadn't seen the other man since he was at Ranheim ten years before, and even though everyone had treated him exceedingly well, the purpose of that journey had left a scar on his soul.

While Arne boasted of young Gjavvald, Simon kept an eye on his brother-in-law. Erlend was speaking to the royal treasurer, whose name was Sir Baard Peterssøn, but he was not related to the Hestnes lineage. It could not be said that Erlend's conduct was lacking in courtesy, and yet his manner seemed overly free and unrestrained as he stood there talking to the elderly gentleman while he rocked back and forth on his heels, with his hands clasped behind his back. As usual, he was wearing garments that were dark in color, but magnificent: a violet-blue *cote-hardi*[3] that fit snugly to his body, with slits up the sides; a black shoulder collar with the cowl thrown back to reveal the gray silk lining; a silver-studded belt; and high red boots that were laced tightly around his calves, displaying the man's handsome, slim legs and feet.

In the sharp light coming through the glass windows of the stone building, it was evident that Erlend Nikulaussøn now had quite a bit of gray hair at his temples. Around his mouth and under his eyes the fine, tanned skin was now etched with wrinkles, and there were creases on the long, handsome arch of his throat. And yet he looked quite young among the other gentlemen, although he was by no means the youngest man in the room. But he was just as slim and slender, and he carried his body in the same loose, rather careless fashion as he had in his youth. And when the royal treasurer left him, Erlend's gait was just as light and supple as he began pacing around the hall, with his hands still clasped behind his back. All the other men were sitting down, occasionally conversing with each other in low, dry voices. Erlend's light step and the ringing of his small silver spurs were all too audible.

Finally one of the younger men told him with annoyance to sit down, "And stop making so much noise, man!"

Erlend came to an abrupt halt and frowned—then he turned to face the man who had spoken and said with a laugh, "Where were you out drinking last night, Jon my friend, since your head is so tender?" Then he sat down. When Judge Harald came over to him, Erlend got to his feet and waited until the other man had taken a seat, but then he sank down next to the judge, crossed one leg over the other, and sat with his hands clasped around his knee while they talked.

Erlend had told Simon quite openly about all the troubles he had endured because the murderer and his sorceress wife had escaped from his hands. But no man could possibly look more carefree than Erlend as he sat discussing the case with the judge.

Then the archbishop came in. He was escorted to his high seat by two men who propped cushions around him. Simon had never seen Lord Eiliv Kortin before. He looked old and frail and seemed to be freezing even though he wore a fur cape and a fur-trimmed cap on his head. When his turn came, Erlend escorted his brother-in-law over to the archbishop, and Simon fell to one knee as he kissed Lord Eiliv's ring. Erlend, too, kissed the ring with respect.

He behaved very properly and respectfully when he at last stood before the archbishop, after Lord Eiliv had talked with the other gentlemen for some time about various matters. But he answered the questions put to him by one of the canons in a rather light-hearted manner, and his demeanor seemed casual and innocent.

Yes, he had heard the talk about sorcery for many years. But as long as no one had come to him as enforcer of the law, he couldn't very well be responsible for investigating all such gossip that flew among the womenfolk in a parish. Surely it was the priest who should determine whether there were any grounds for pressing charges.

Then he was asked about the old man who had lived at Husaby and was said to possess magic skills.

Erlend gave a little smile. Yes, well, Aan had boasted of this himself, but Erlend had never seen proof of his abilities. Ever since his childhood he had heard Aan talk about three women whom he called Hærn and Skøgul and Snotra, but he had never taken this for anything but storytelling and jest. "My brother Gunnulf and our priest, Sira Eiliv, talked to him many times about this matter, but apparently they never found any cause to accuse him, since they never did so. After all, the man came to church for every mass and he knew his Christian prayers." Erlend had never had much faith in Aan's sorcery, and after he had witnessed something of the spells and witchcraft of the Finns in the north, he had come to realize that Aan's purported skills were mere foolishness.

Then the priest asked whether it was true that Erlend himself had once been given something by Aan—something that would bring him luck in *amor?*

Yes, replied Erlend swiftly and openly, with a smile. He must have been fifteen at the time, for it was about twenty-eight years ago. A leather pouch with a small white stone inside and several dried pieces that must have come from some animal. But he hadn't had much faith in that kind of thing even back then. He gave it away the following year, when he was serving at the king's castle for the first time. It happened in a bathhouse up in town; he had rashly shown the talismans to several other, younger boys. Later, one of the king's retainers came to him, wanting to purchase the pouch, and Erlend had exchanged it for a fine shaving knife.

He was asked who this gentleman might be.

At first Erlend refused to say. But the archbishop himself urged him to speak. Erlend looked up with a roguish glint in his blue eyes.

"It was Sir Ivar Ogmundssøn."

Everyone's face took on a peculiar expression. Old Sir Guttorm Helgessøn uttered several odd snorts. Even Lord Eiliv tried to restrain a smile.

Then Erlend dared to say, with lowered eyes and biting his lip, "My Lord, surely you would not disturb that good knight with this ancient matter. As I said, I didn't have much faith in it myself—and I've never noticed that it made any difference to any of us that I gave those charms to him."

Sir Guttorm doubled over with a bellow, and then the other men gave in, one after the other, and roared with laughter. The archbishop chuckled and coughed and shook his head. It was well known that Sir Ivar had always had more desire than luck in certain matters.

After a while one of the Brothers of the Cross regained his composure enough to remind them that they had come here to discuss serious issues. Erlend asked rather sharply whether anyone had accused him of anything and whether this was an interrogation;

he had assumed he had simply been invited to an interview. The discussion was then continued, but it was greatly disrupted by the fact that Guttorm Helgessøn sat there incessantly snickering.

The next day, as the brothers-in-law rode home from Ranheim, Simon brought up the subject of the interview. Simon said that Erlend seemed to take it terribly lightly—and yet he thought he could see that many of the noblemen would have blamed something on him if they could.

Erlend said he knew that's what they would have liked, if it was within their power. For here in the north, most men now sided with the chancellor—except for the archbishop; in him, Erlend had a true friend. But Erlend's actions in all matters were taken in accordance with the law; he always consulted with his scribe, Kløng Aressøn, who was exceptionally knowledgeable about the law. Erlend was now speaking somberly, and he smiled only briefly as he said that doubtless no one had expected him to have such a good grasp of his business affairs as he now had—neither his dear friends around the countryside nor the gentlemen of the Council. But he was no longer certain that he wanted the position of sheriff, if other conditions should apply than those he had been granted while Erling Vidkunssøn represented the king. His own situation was now such, especially since the death of his wife's parents, that he no longer needed to secure the favor of those who had risen to power after the king had been proclaimed of age. Yes, that rotten boy might as well be declared of age now rather than later; he wasn't going to become any more manly if they kept him hidden. Then they would know even sooner what he was concealing behind his shield—or how much the Swedish nobles controlled him. The people would learn the truth: that Erling had been right, after all. It would cost the Norwegians dearly if King Magnus tried to put Skaane[4] under the Swedish Crown—and it would immediately lead to war with the Danes the moment *one* man, whether Danish or German, seized power there. And the peace in the north, which was supposed to be enforced for ten years . . . Half of that time had now passed, and it was uncertain whether the Russians would adhere to the treaty much longer. Erlend had not much faith in it, nor did Erling. No, Chancellor Paal was a learned man and in many respects sensible too—perhaps. But all the gentlemen of the Council, who had chosen him as their leader, had little more combined wit than his horse Soten. But now they were rid of Erling, for the time being. And until things changed, Erlend would just as soon step aside too. But surely Erling and his friends would want Erlend to maintain his power and prosperity up here in the north. He didn't know what he should do.

"It seems to me that now you've learned to sing Sir Erling's tune," Simon Darre couldn't help remarking.

Erlend replied that this was true. He had stayed at Sir Erling's estate the summer before, when he was in Bjørgvin, and he now knew the man much better. It was evident that, above all else, Erling wanted to maintain peace in the land. But he wanted the Norwegian Crown to have the peace of the lion—which meant that no one should be allowed to break off a tooth or cut off a claw from their kinsman King Haakon's lion. Nor should the lion be required to become the hunting dog for the people of some other country. And now Erling was also determined to bring to an end the old quarrels between the Norwegians and Lady Ingebjørg. Now that she had been left a widow by Sir Knut, it was only desirable for her to have some control over her son again. It was no doubt true that she felt such great love for the children she had borne to Knut Porse that she seemed to have almost forgotten her eldest son—but things would surely be different when she saw him again. And Lady Ingebjørg could have no reason to wish for King Magnus to interfere in the unrest occurring in Skaane, because it was under the authority of his half-brothers.

Simon thought Erlend sounded quite well-informed. But he wondered about Erling Vidkunssøn. Did the former regent think that Erlend Nikulaussøn was capable of making decisions in such matters? Or was Erling merely grasping for any possible support? The knight from Bjarkøy would be unlikely to give up his power. He could never be accused of having used it for his own benefit, but his great wealth made this unnecessary. Everyone said that over the years he had become more and more obstinate and single-minded; and by the time the other men of the Council gradually started to oppose him, he had grown so belligerent that he hardly deigned to listen to anyone else's opinion.

It was like Erlend for him finally to climb aboard Erling Vidkunssøn's ship with both feet, so to speak, as soon as the winds were against it. It was uncertain whether either Sir Erling or Erlend himself would benefit, now that he seemed to have joined forces wholeheartedly with his wealthy kinsman. And yet Simon had to admit that no matter how reckless Erlend's words might be about both people and events, what he had said did not seem entirely foolish.

But that evening he was quite wild and boisterous. Erlend was now staying at Nikulausgaard, which his brother had given to him when he joined the friars. Kristin was there too, along with their two eldest boys, their youngest son, and Erlend's daughter Margret.

Late in the evening a large group of people came to visit them, including many of the gentlemen who had been at the meeting with the archbishop the previous morning. Erlend laughed and talked loudly as they sat drinking at the table after supper. He had taken an apple from a bowl and had cut and carved it with his knife; then he rolled it across the table into the lap of Fru Sunniva Olavsdatter, who sat opposite him.

The woman sitting next to Sunniva wanted to look at it, and she reached for the apple. But Sunniva refused to give it up, and the two women pushed and tugged at each other with much shrieking and laughter. Then Erlend cried that Fru Eyvor should have an apple from him too. Before long he had tossed apples to every woman there, and he claimed to have carved love-runes into all of them.

"You're going to be worn out, my boy, if you try to redeem all those pledges," one of the men shouted.

"Then I'll have to forget about redeeming them—I've done that before," replied Erlend, and there was more laughter.

But the Icelander Kløng had taken a look at one of the apples and exclaimed that they weren't runes but just meaningless cuts. He would show them how runes should be carved.

Then Erlend shouted that he shouldn't do that. "Or else they'll tell me I have to tie you up, Kløng, and I can't get along without you."

During all the commotion Erlend's and Kristin's youngest son had come padding into the hall. Lavrans Erlendssøn was now a little more than two years old and an exceptionally attractive child, plump and fair, with silky, fine blond curls. The women on the outer bench all wanted to hold the boy at once; they sent him from lap to lap, caressing him freely, for by now they were all giddy and wild. Kristin, who was sitting against the wall in the high seat next to her husband, asked to be given the child; he began fretting and wanted to go to his mother, but it did no good.

Suddenly Erlend leaped across the table and picked up the boy, who was now howling because Fru Sunniva and Fru Eyvor were tugging at him and fighting over him. The father took the boy in his arms, speaking soothing words. When the child kept on crying, he began humming and singing as he held him and paced back and forth in the dim light of the hall. Erlend seemed to have completely forgotten about his guests. The child's little blond head lay on his father's shoulder beneath the man's dark hair, and every once in a while Erlend would touch his parted lips to the small hand resting on his chest. He continued in this way until a serving maid came in who was supposed to watch the child and should have put him to bed long ago.

Then some of the guests shouted that Erlend should sing them a ballad for a dance; he had such a fine voice. At first he declined, but then he went over to his young daughter who was sitting on the women's bench. He put his arm around Margret and escorted her out to the floor.

"You must come with me, my Margret. Take your father's hand for a dance!"

A young man stepped forward and took the maiden's hand. "Margit promised to dance with me tonight," he said. But Erlend lifted his daughter into his arms and set her down on the other side of him.

"Dance with your wife, Haakon. I never danced with anyone else when I was so newly married as you are."

"Ingebjørg says she doesn't want to . . . and I did promise Haakon to dance with him, Father," said Margret.

Simon Darre had no wish to dance. He stood next to an old woman for a while and watched; now and then his gaze fell on Kristin. While her servants cleared away the dishes, wiped the table, and brought in more liquor and walnuts, Kristin stood at the end of the table. Then she sat down near the fireplace and talked to a priest who was one of the guests. After a while Simon sat down near them.

They had danced to one or two ballads when Erlend came over

to his wife. "Come and dance with us, Kristin," he begged, holding out his hand.

"I'm tired," she said, looking up for a moment.

"You ask her, Simon. She can't refuse to dance with you."

Simon rose halfway and held out his hand, but Kristin shook her head. "Don't ask me, Simon. I'm so tired. . . ."

Erlend stood there for a moment, looking as if he were embarrassed. Then he went back to Fru Sunniva and took her hand in the circle of dancers as he shouted to Margit that now she should sing for them.

"Who is that dancing next to your stepdaughter?" asked Simon. He thought he didn't much care for that fellow's face, even though he was a stalwart and boyish-looking young man with a healthy, tan complexion, fine teeth, and sparkling eyes, but they were set too close to his nose and he had a large, strong mouth and chin, although his face was narrow across the brow. Kristin told him it was Haakon Eindridessøn of Gimsar, the grandson of Tore Eindridessøn, the sheriff of Gauldøla county. Haakon had recently married the lovely little woman who was sitting on the lap of Judge Olav—he was her godfather. Simon had noticed her because she looked a little like his first wife, although she was not as beautiful. When he now heard that there was kinship between them, he went over and greeted Ingebjørg and sat down to talk to her.

After a while the dancing broke up. The older folks sat down to drink, but the younger ones continued to sing and frolic out on the floor. Erlend came over to the fireplace along with several elderly gentlemen, but he was still absentmindedly leading Fru Sunniva by the hand. The men sat down near the fire, but there was no room for Sunniva, so she stood in front of Erlend and ate the walnuts he cracked in his hands for her.

"You're an unchivalrous man, Erlend," she said suddenly. "There you sit while I have to stand."

"Then sit down," said Erlend with a laugh, pulling her down onto his lap. She struggled against him, laughing and shouting to his wife to come and see how her husband was treating her.

"Erlend just does that to be kind," replied Kristin, laughing too. "My cat can't rub against his leg without him picking her up and putting her in his lap."

Erlend and Fru Sunniva remained sitting there as before, feigning nonchalance, but they had both turned crimson. He held his arm lightly around her, as if he hardly noticed she was sitting there, while he and the men talked about the enmity between Erling Vidkunssøn and Chancellor Paal which was so much on everyone's mind. Erlend said that Paal Baardsøn had displayed his attitude toward Erling in quite a womanish way—as they could judge for themselves:

"Last summer a young country boy had come to the gathering of the chieftains to offer his services to the king. Now this poor boy from Vors was so eager to learn courtly customs and manners that he tried to embellish his speech with Swedish words—it was French back when I was young, but today it's Swedish. So one day the boy asks someone how to say *traakig,* which happens to mean 'boring' in Norwegian. Sir Paal hears this and says: '*Traakig,* my friend, that's what Sir Erling's wife, Fru Elin, is.' The boy now thinks this means beautiful or noble, because that's what she is, and apparently the poor fellow hadn't had much opportunity to hear the woman *talk.* But one day Erling meets him on the stairs outside the hall, and he stops and speaks kindly to the youth, asking him whether he liked being in Nidaros, and such things, and then he tells him to give his greetings to his father. The boy thanks him and says it will please his father greatly when he returns home with greetings 'from you, kind sir, and your boring wife.' Whereupon Erling slaps him in the face so the boy tumbles backwards down three or four steps until a servant catches him in his arms. Now there's a great commotion, people come running, and the matter is finally cleared up. Erling was furious at being made a laughingstock, but he feigned indifference. And the only response from the chancellor was that he laughed and said he should have explained that '*traakig*' was what the regent was—then the boy couldn't have misunderstood."

Everyone agreed that such behavior on the part of the chancellor was undignified, but all of them laughed a great deal. Simon listened in silence, sitting with his chin resting on his hand. He thought this was a peculiar way for Erlend to show his friendship for Erling Vidkunssøn. The story made it quite clear that Erling must be a little unbalanced if he could believe that a youth, freshly arrived from the countryside, would dare stand on the stairs to the king's palace and ridicule him to his face. Erlend could hardly be expected to remember Simon's former relationship as the brother-in-law of Fru Elin and Sir Erling.

"What are you thinking about, Kristin?" he asked. She was sitting quietly, her back straight, with her hands crossed on her lap.

She replied, "Right now I'm thinking about Margret."

Late that night, as Erlend and Simon were tending to a chore out in the courtyard, they scared off a couple standing behind the corner of the house. The nights were as light as day, and Simon recognized Haakon of Gimsar and Margret Erlendsdatter. Erlend stared after them; he was quite sober, and the other man could see that he wasn't pleased. But Erlend said, as if in excuse, that the two had known each other since childhood and they had always teased each other. Simon thought that even if this meant nothing, it was still a shame for Haakon's young wife, Ingebjørg.

The next day young Haakon came over to Nikulausgaard on an errand, and he asked for Margit.

Then Erlend furiously exclaimed, "My daughter is not *Margit* to you. And if you didn't say everything you wanted to say yesterday, then you'll have to forget about telling it to her."

Haakon shrugged his shoulders, but when he left, he asked them to give his greetings to *Margareta*.

The people from Husaby stayed in Nidaros for the *ting,* but Simon took little pleasure in this. Erlend was often bad-tempered when he stayed at his estate in town, because Gunnulf had granted the hospital, which stood on the other side of the orchard, the right to use any of the buildings that faced in its direction, and also rights to part of the garden. Erlend wanted to buy these rights back from the hospital. He didn't like seeing the patients in the garden or courtyard; many of them were also hideous in appearance, and he was afraid they would infect his children. But he couldn't reach an agreement with the monks who were in charge of the hospital.

And there was Margret Erlendsdatter. Simon knew that people gossiped about her a good deal and that Kristin took this to heart, but her father seemed not to care. Erlend seemed certain that he could protect his maiden and that the talk meant nothing. And yet he said to Simon one day that Kløng Aressøn would like to marry his daughter, and he didn't quite know how to handle this matter.

He had nothing against the Icelander except that he was the son of a priest; he didn't want it to be said of Margret's children that they bore the taint of both parents' birth. Otherwise Kløng was a likeable man, good-humored, clever, and very learned. His father, Sira Are, had raised him himself and taught him well; he had hoped his son would become a priest and had even taken steps to obtain dispensation for him, but then Kløng refused to take the vows. It seemed as if Erlend intended to leave the matter unsettled. If no better match presented itself, then he could always give the maiden to Kløng Aressøn.

And yet Erlend had already had such a good offer for his daughter that there was a great deal of talk about his arrogance and imprudence, when he allowed that match to slip away. It was the grandson of Baron Sigvat of Leirhole—Sigmund Finssøn was his name. He wasn't wealthy, because Finn Sigvatssøn had had eleven surviving children. Nor was he altogether young; he was about the same age as Erlend, but a respected and sensible man. And yet Margret would have been wealthy enough because of the properties Erlend had given her when he married Kristin Lavransdatter, along with all the jewelry and costly possessions he had given the child over the years, as well as the dowry he had agreed upon with Sigmund. Erlend had also been overjoyed to have such a suitor for his daughter born of adultery. But when he came home and told Margret about this bridegroom, the maiden protested that she wouldn't have him because Sigmund had several warts on one of his eyelids, and she claimed this made her feel such revulsion for him. Erlend bowed to her wishes. When Sigmund became indignant and began talking of a breach of agreement, Erlend responded angrily and told the man that he should realize all agreements were made on the condition that the maiden was willing. His daughter would not be forced into a bridal bed. Kristin agreed with her husband on this matter; he shouldn't force the girl. But she thought Erlend ought to have had a serious discussion with his daughter and made her realize that Sigmund Finssøn was such a good match that Margret couldn't possibly expect to find any better, considering her birth. But Erlend grew terribly angry with his wife, simply because she had dared to broach the subject with him. All of this Simon had heard about at Ranheim. There they predicted that things could not possibly end well. Erlend might be a powerful man now, and the maiden was certainly lovely, but it had done her no good for her father to spoil her and encourage her stubbornness and arrogance for all these years.

After the Frosta *ting*, Erlend went home to Husaby with his wife, children, and Simon Darre, who now had his sister's son, Gjavvald Gjavvaldssøn, with him. He was afraid that the reunion, which Sigrid had been yearning for with inexpressible joy, would not turn out well. Sigrid now lived at Kruke in good circumstances; she had three handsome children with her husband, and Geirmund was as good a man as could be found on this earth. He was the one who had spoken to his brother-in-law about bringing Gjavvald south so that Sigrid might see him, for the child was always on her mind. But Gjavvald had grown accustomed to living with his grandparents, and the old couple loved the child beyond measure, giving him everything he wanted and humoring his every whim; and things were not the same at Kruke as at Ranheim. Nor was it to be expected that Geirmund would be pleased to have his wife's bastard son come visiting and then behave like a royal child, even bringing along his own servant—an elderly man whom the boy ruled and tyrannized. The man didn't dare say a word against any of Gjavvald's unreasonable demands. But for Erlend's sons, it was cause for celebration when Gjavvald came to Husaby. Erlend didn't think his sons should have any less than the grandson of Arne Gjavvaldssøn did, and so Naakkve and Bjørgulf were given all the things they told him the boy possessed.

Now that Erlend's oldest sons were big enough to accompany him and go out riding with him, he paid more attention to the boys. Simon noticed that Kristin wasn't entirely pleased by this; she thought that what they learned among his men was not all good. And it was usually about the children that unkind words most often erupted between the couple. Even though they might not have an outright quarrel, they were much closer to it than Simon thought was proper. And it seemed to him that Kristin was most to blame. Erlend could be quick-tempered, but she often spoke as if she harbored a deep, hidden rancor toward him. That was the case one day when Kristin brought up several complaints about Naakkve. Erlend replied that he would have a serious talk with the boy. But after another remark from his wife, he exclaimed angrily that he wasn't about to give the boy a beating in front of the servants.

"No, it's too late for that now. If you had done it when he was younger, he would listen to you now. But back then you never paid the slightest attention to him."

"Oh yes, I did. But surely it was reasonable that I left him in your keeping when he was small—and besides, it's no job for a man to hand out beatings to little boys who aren't even in breeches yet."

"That's not what you thought last week," said Kristin, her voice scornful and bitter.

Erlend didn't reply but stood up and left the room. And Simon thought it was unkind of his wife to speak to him in this manner. Kristin was referring to something that had happened the week before. Erlend and Simon had come riding into the courtyard when little Lavrans ran toward them with a wooden sword in his hand. As he raced past his father's horse, he rashly struck the animal across the leg with his sword. The horse reared up, and the boy was suddenly lying under its feet. Erlend backed away, yanked the horse to the side, and threw his reins to Simon. His face was white with dread as he lifted the child up in his arms. But when he saw that the boy was unharmed, he put him over his arm, took the wooden sword, and gave Lavrans a beating on his bare bottom—the boy was not yet wearing breeches. In those first heated moments, he didn't realize how hard he was striking, and Lavrans was still walking around with black and blue marks. But afterwards Erlend tried all day to make amends with the boy, who sulked and clung to his mother, hitting and threatening his father. Later that evening, when Lavrans was settled in his parents' bed where he usually slept because his mother still nursed him during the night, Erlend sat next to him for hours. Every once in a while he would stroke the sleeping child a bit as he gazed down at him. He told Simon that this was the boy he loved most of all his sons.

When Erlend set off for the summer *tings*, Simon headed home. He raced south along Gauldal, making the sparks fly from his horse's hooves. Once, as they rode more slowly up several steep slopes, his men laughingly asked him whether he was trying to cover three days' journey in two. Simon laughed in reply and said that was indeed his intention, "because I'm longing to reach Formo."

That was how he always felt whenever he had been away from his estate for long; he loved his home and always felt great joy when he could turn his horse homeward. But this time it seemed he had never longed so much to return to his valley and manor and his young daughters—yes, he even yearned for Ramborg. To be truthful, he thought it unreasonable to feel this way, but up there at Husaby he had been so uneasy that now he thought he knew firsthand how cattle could sense in their bodies that a storm was brewing.

## CHAPTER 2

All summer long Kristin thought of little else but what Simon had told her about her mother's death.

Ragnfrid Ivarsdatter had died alone; no one had been near as she drew her last breath except a servant woman, who was asleep. And it helped very little that Simon had said she was well prepared for her death. It was like the providence of God that several days earlier Ragnfrid had felt such a longing for the body of the Savior that she made her confession and was given communion by the priest of the cloister, who was her confessor. It was true that she had been granted a good death. Simon saw her body and said he thought it a wondrous sight—she had grown so beautiful in death. She was a woman of nearly sixty, and for many years her face had been greatly lined and wrinkled, and yet now it was completely changed; her face was youthful and smooth, and she looked just like a young woman asleep. She had been laid to rest at her husband's side; there they had also brought Ulvhild Lavransdatter's remains shortly after her father's death. On top of the graves a large slab of stone had been placed, divided in two by a beautifully carved cross. On a winding banner a long Latin verse had been written, composed by the prior of the cloister, but Simon couldn't remember it properly, for he understood little of that language.

Ragnfrid had lived in her own house on the estate in town where the corrodians of the cloister resided; she had a small room with a lovely loft room above. There she lived alone with a poor peasant woman who had taken lodgings with the brothers in return for a small payment, provided she would lend a hand to one of the wealthier women lodgers. But during the past half year, it had been Ragnfrid who had served the other woman, because the widow, whose name was Torgunna, had been unwell. Ragnfrid tended to her with great love and kindness.

On the last evening of her life, she had attended evensong in the cloister church, and afterwards she went into the cookhouse of the estate. She made a hearty soup with several restorative herbs and told the other women there that she was going to give the soup to Torgunna. She hoped the woman would feel well enough the next day so that they could both attend matins. That was the last time anyone saw the widow of Jørundgaard alive. Neither she nor the peasant woman came to matins or to the next service. When some of the monks in the choir noticed that Ragnfrid didn't come to the morning mass either, they were greatly surprised—she had never before missed three services in a day. They sent word to town, asking whether the widow of Lavrans Bjørgulfsøn was ill. When the servants went up to the loft, they found the soup bowl standing untouched on the table. In the bed, Torgunna was sleeping sweetly against the wall. But Ragnfrid Ivarsdatter lay on the edge with her hands crossed over her breast—dead and already nearly cold. Simon and Ramborg went to her funeral, which was very beautiful.

Now that there were so many people in the Husaby household and Kristin had six sons, she could no longer manage to take part in all the individual chores that had to be done. She had to have a housekeeper to assist her. The mistress of the manor would usually sit in the hall with her sewing. There was always someone who needed clothing—Erlend, Margret, or one of the boys.

The last time she had seen her mother, Ragnfrid was riding behind her husband's bier, on that bright spring day while she herself stood in the meadow outside Jørundgaard and watched her father's funeral procession setting off across the green carpet of winter rye beneath the hillside scree.

Kristin's needle flew in and out as she thought about her parents and their home at Jørundgaard. Now that everything had become memories, she seemed to see so much that she hadn't noticed when she was in the midst of it all—when she took for granted her father's tenderness and protection, as well as the steady, quiet care and toil of her silent, melancholy mother. She thought about her own children; she loved them more than the blood of her own heart, and there was not a waking hour when she wasn't thinking about them. And yet there was much in her soul that she brooded over more—her children she could love without brooding. While she lived at Jørundgaard, she had never thought otherwise than that her parents' whole life and everything they did was for the sake of her and her sisters. Now she seemed to realize that great currents of both sorrow and joy had flowed between these two people, who had been given to each other in their youth by their fathers, without being asked. And she knew nothing of this except that they had departed from her life together. Now she understood that the lives of these two people had contained much more than love for their children. And yet that love had been strong and wide and unfathomably deep; while the love she gave them in return was weak and thoughtless and selfish, even back in her childhood when her parents were her whole world. She seemed to see herself standing far, far away—so small at that distance of time and place. She was standing in the flood of sunlight streaming in through the smoke vent in the old hearth house back home, the winter house of her childhood. Her parents were standing back in the shadows, and they seemed to tower over her, as tall as they had been when she was small. They were smiling at her, in the way she now knew one smiles at a little child who comes and pushes aside dark and burdensome thoughts.

"I thought, Kristin, that once you had children of your own, then you would better understand. . . ."

She remembered when her mother said those words. Sorrowfully, the daughter thought that she still didn't understand her mother. But now she was beginning to realize how much she didn't understand.

That fall Archbishop Eiliv died. At about the same time, King Magnus had the terms changed for many of the sheriffs in the land, but not for Erlend Nikulaussøn. When he was in Bjørgvin during the last summer before the king came of age, Erlend had received a letter stating that he should be granted one fourth of the income collected from bail paid by criminals, from fines for the crime of letter-breaching,[1] and from forfeitures of property. There had been much talk about his acquisition of such rights toward the end of a regency. Erlend had a vast income because he now owned a great deal of land in the county and usually stayed on his own estates when he traveled around his district, but he permitted his leaseholders to buy their way out of their obligation to house and feed him. It's true that he took in little in land taxes, and the upkeep of his manor was costly; in addition to his household servants, he never had fewer than twelve armed men with him at Husaby. They rode the best horses and were splendidly outfitted, and whenever Erlend traveled around his district, his men lived like noblemen.

This matter was mentioned one day when Judge Harald and the sheriff of Gauldøla county were visiting Husaby. Erlend replied that many of these men had been with him when he lived up north. "Back then we shared whatever conditions we found there, eating dried fish and drinking bitter ale. Now these men whom I clothe and feed know that I won't begrudge them white bread and foreign ale. And if I tell them to go to Hell when I get angry, they know that I don't mean for them to set off on the journey without me in the lead."

Ulf Haldorssøn, who was now the head of Erlend's men, later told Kristin that this was true. Erlend's men loved him, and he had complete command of them.

"You know yourself, Kristin, that no one should rely too heavily on what Erlend says; he must be judged by what he does."

It was also rumored that in addition to his household servants, Erlend had men throughout the countryside—even outside Orkdøla county—who had sworn allegiance to him on the hilt of his sword. Finally a letter from the Crown arrived regarding this matter, but Erlend replied that these men had been part of his ship's crew and they had been bound to him by oath ever since that first spring when he sailed north. He was then commanded to release the men at the next *ting* he held to announce the verdicts and decisions of the Law *ting;* and he was to summon to the meeting those men who lived outside the county and pay for their journey himself. He did summon some of his old crew members from outside Møre to the *ting* at Orkedal—but no one heard that he released them or any other men who had served him in his position as chieftain. For the time being the matter was allowed to languish, and as the autumn wore on, people stopped talking about it altogether.

Late that fall Erlend journeyed south and spent Christmas at the court of King Magnus, who was residing in Oslo that year. Erlend was annoyed that he couldn't persuade his wife to come with him, but Kristin had no courage for the difficult winter journey, and she stayed at Husaby.

Erlend returned home three weeks after Christmas, bringing splendid gifts for his wife and all his children. He gave Kristin a silver bell so she could ring for her maids; to Margret he gave a clasp of solid gold, which was something she didn't yet own, although she had all sorts of silver and gilded jewelry. But when the women were putting away these costly gifts in their jewelry chests, something got caught on Margret's sleeve.

The girl quickly removed it and hid it in her hand as she said to her stepmother, "This belonged to my mother—that's why Father doesn't want me to show it to you."

But Kristin's face had turned even more crimson than the maiden's. Her heart pounded with fear, but she knew that she *had* to speak to the young girl and warn her.

After a moment she said in a quiet and uncertain voice, "That looks like the gold clasp that Fru Helga of Gimsar used to wear to banquets."

"Well, many gold things look much the same," replied the maiden curtly.

Kristin locked her chest and stood with her hands resting on top so that Margret wouldn't see how they were shaking.

"Dear Margret," she said softly and gently, but then she had to stop while she gathered all her strength.

"Dear Margret, I have often bitterly regretted . . . My happiness has never been complete, even though my father forgave me with all his heart for the sorrows I caused him. You know that I sinned greatly against my parents for the sake of your father. But the longer I live and the more I come to understand, the harder it is for me to remember that I rewarded their kindness by causing them sorrow. Dear Margret, your father has been good to you all your days . . ."

"You don't have to worry, Mother," replied the girl. "I'm not your lawful daughter; you don't have to worry that I might put on your filthy shift or step into your shoes . . ."

Her eyes flashing with anger, Kristin turned to face her stepdaughter. But then she gripped the cross she wore around her neck tightly in her hand and bit back the words she was about to speak.

She took this matter to Sira Eiliv that very evening after vespers, and she looked in vain for some sign in the priest's face. Had a misfortune already occurred, and did he know about it? She thought about her own misguided youth; she remembered Sira Eirik's face, which gave nothing away as he lived side by side with her and her trusting parents, with her sinful secret locked inside his heart—while she remained mute and callous to his stern entreaties and admonitions. And she remembered when she showed her own mother gifts that Erlend had given her in Oslo; that was after she had been lawfully betrothed to him. Her mother's expression was steady and calm as she picked up the items, one by one, looked at them, praised them, and then laid them aside.

Kristin was deathly afraid and anguished, and she kept a vigilant eye on Margret. Erlend noticed that something was troubling his wife, and one evening after they had gone to bed, he asked whether she might be with child again.

Kristin lay in silence for a moment before she replied that she thought she was. And when her husband lovingly took her in his arms without another word, she didn't have the heart to tell him that something else was causing her sorrow. But when Erlend whispered to her that this time she must try and give him a daughter, she couldn't manage a reply but lay there, rigid with fear, thinking that Erlend would find out soon enough what kind of joy a man had from his daughters.

Several nights later everyone at Husaby had gone to bed slightly drunk and with their stomachs quite full because it was the last few days before Lent began; for this reason, they all slept heavily. Late that night little Lavrans woke up in his parents' bed, crying and demanding sleepily to nurse at his mother's breast. But they were trying to wean him. Erlend woke up, grunting crossly. He picked up the boy, gave him some milk from a cup that stood on the step of the bed, and then lay the child back down on the other side of him.

Kristin had fallen into a deep slumber again when she suddenly realized that Erlend was sitting up in bed. Only half awake, she asked what was wrong. He hushed her in a voice that she didn't recognize. Soundlessly he slipped out of bed, and she saw that he was pulling on a few clothes. When she propped herself up on one elbow, he pressed her back against the pillows with one hand as he bent over her and took down his sword, which hung over the headboard.

He moved as quietly as a lynx, but she saw that he was going over to the ladder which led up to Margret's chamber above the entry hall.

For a moment Kristin lay in bed completely paralyzed with fear. Then she sat up, found her shift and gown, and began hunting for her shoes on the floor beside the bed.

Suddenly a woman's scream rang out from the loft—loud enough to be heard all over the estate. Erlend's voice shouted a word or two, and then Kristin heard the clang of swords striking each other and the stomp of feet overhead—then the sound of a weapon falling to the floor and Margret screaming in terror.

Kristin was on her knees, huddled next to the hearth. She scraped away the hot ashes with her bare hands and blew on the embers. When she had lit a torch and lifted it up with trembling hands, she saw Erlend in the darkness above. He leaped down from the loft, not bothering with the ladder, holding his drawn sword in his hand, and then dashed out the main door.

The boys were peering out from the dark on all sides of the room. Kristin went over to the enclosed bed on the north wall where the three eldest slept and told them to lie down and shut the door. Ivar and Skule were sitting on the bench, blinking at the light, frightened and bewildered. She told them to climb up into her bed, and then she shut them inside too. Then she lit a candle and went out into the courtyard.

It was raining. For a moment, as the light of her candle was reflected in the glistening, ice-covered ground, she saw a crowd standing outside the door to the next building: the servants' hall where Erlend's men slept. Then the flame of her candle was blown out, and for a moment the night was pitch-dark, but then a lantern emerged from the servants' hall, and Ulf Haldorssøn was carrying it.

He bent down over a dark body curled up on the wet patches of ice. Kristin knelt down and touched the man. It was young Haakon of Gimsar, and he was either senseless or dead. Her hands were at once covered with blood. With Ulf's help she straightened out his body and turned him over. The blood was gushing out of his right arm, where his hand had been lopped off.

Involuntarily Kristin glanced at the window hatch of Margret's chamber as it slammed shut in the wind. She couldn't discern any face up there, but it was quite dark.

As she knelt in the rain puddles, clamping her hand as tight as she could around Haakon's wrist to stop the spurting blood, she was aware of Erlend's men standing half-dressed all around her. Then she noticed Erlend's gray, contorted face. With a corner of his tunic he wiped off his bloody sword. He was naked underneath and his feet were bare.

"One of you . . . find me something to bind this with. And you, Bjørn, go and wake up Sira Eiliv. We'll carry him over to the parsonage." She took the leather strap that they gave her and wrapped it around the stump of the man's arm.

Suddenly Erlend said, his voice harsh and wild, "Nobody touch him! Let the man lie where he fell!"

"You must realize, husband, we can't do that," said Kristin calmly, although her heart was pounding so loud that she thought she would suffocate.

Erlend rammed the tip of his sword hard against the ground.

"Yes—she's not your flesh and blood—you've made that quite clear to me every single day, for all these years."

Kristin stood up and whispered quietly to him, "And yet for her sake I want this to be concealed—if it can be done. You men . . ." she turned to the servants who were standing around them. "If you're loyal to your master, you won't speak of this until he has told you how this quarrel with Haakon arose."

All the men agreed. One of them dared step forward and explained: They had been awakened by the sound of a woman screaming, as if she were being taken by force. And then someone ran along their roof, but he must have slipped on the icy surface. They heard a scrambling noise and then a thud on the ground. But Kristin told the man to be silent. At that moment Sira Eiliv came running.

When Erlend turned on his heel and went inside, his wife ran after him and tried to force her way past him. When he headed for the ladder to the loft, she sprang in front of him and grabbed him by the arm.

"Erlend—what will you do to the child?" she gasped, looking up into his wild, gray face.

Without replying, he tried to fling her aside, but she held on tight.

"Wait, Erlend, wait—your child! You don't know . . . The man was fully clothed," she cried urgently.

He gave a loud wail before he answered. She turned as pale as a corpse with horror—his words were so raw and his voice unrecognizable with desperate anguish.

Then she wrestled mutely with the raging man. He snarled and gnashed his teeth, until she managed to catch his eye in the dim light.

"Erlend—let me go to her first. I haven't forgotten the day when I was no better than Margret. . . ."

Then he released her and staggered backwards against the wall to the next room; he stood there, shaking like a dying beast. Kristin went to light a candle, then came back and went past him up to Margret in her bedchamber.

The first thing the candlelight fell on was a sword lying on the floor not far from the bed, and the severed hand beside it. Kristin tore off the wimple which she, without thinking, had wrapped loosely over her flowing hair before she went out to the men in the courtyard. Now she dropped it over the hand lying on the floor.

Margret was huddled up on the pillows at the headboard, staring at Kristin's candle, wide-eyed and terrified. She was clutching the bedclothes around her, but her white shoulders shone naked under her golden curls. There was blood all over the room.

The strain in Kristin's body erupted into violent sobs; it was such a terrible sight to see that fair young child amidst such horror.

Then Margret screamed loudly, "Mother—what will Father do to me?"

Kristin couldn't help it: In spite of her deep sympathy for the girl, her heart seemed to shrink and harden in her breast. Margret didn't ask what her father had done to Haakon. For an instant she saw Erlend lying on the ground and her own father standing over him with the bloody sword, and she herself . . . But Margret hadn't budged. Kristin couldn't stem her old feeling of scornful displeasure toward Eline's daughter as Margret threw herself against her, trembling and almost senseless with fear. She sat down on the bed and tried to soothe the child.

That was how Erlend found them when he appeared on the ladder. He was now fully dressed. Margret began screaming again and hid her face in her stepmother's arms. Kristin glanced up at her husband for a moment; he was calm now, but his face was pale and strange. For the first time he looked his age.

But she obeyed him when he said calmly, "You must go downstairs now, Kristin. I want to speak to my daughter alone." Gently she laid the girl down on the bed, pulled the covers up to her chin, and went down the ladder.

She did as Erlend had done and got properly dressed—there would be no more sleep at Husaby that night—and then she set about reassuring the frightened children and servants.

The next morning, in a snowstorm, Margret's maid left the manor in tears, carrying her possessions in a sack on her back. The master had chased her out with the harshest words, threatening to flay her bloody because she had sold her mistress in such a fashion.

Then Erlend interrogated the other servants. Hadn't any of the maids suspected anything when all autumn and winter Ingeleiv kept coming to sleep with them instead of with Margret in her chamber? And the dogs had been locked up with them too. But all of them denied it, which was only to be expected.

Finally, he took his wife aside to speak to her alone. Sick at heart and deathly tired, Kristin listened to him and tried to counter his injustice with meek replies. She didn't deny that she had been worried; but she didn't tell him that she had never spoken to him of her fears because she received nothing but ingratitude every time she attempted to counsel him or Margret about the maiden's best interests. And she swore by God and the Virgin Mary that she had never realized or even imagined that this man might come to Margret up in the loft at night.

"You!" said Erlend scornfully. "You said yourself that you remember the time when you were no better than Margret. And the Lord God in Heaven knows that every day, in all these years we've lived together, you've made certain I would see how you remember the injustice I did to you—even though your desire was as keen as mine. And it was your father, not I, who caused much of the unhappiness when he refused to give you to me as my wife. I was willing enough to rectify the sin from the very outset. When you saw the Gimsar gold . . ." He grabbed his wife's hand and held it up; the two rings glittered which Erlend had given her while they were together at Gerdarud. "Didn't you know what it meant? When all these years you've worn the rings I gave you after you let me take your honor?"

Kristin was faint with weariness and sorrow; she whispered, "I wonder, Erlend, whether you even remember that time when you won my honor. . . ."

Then he covered his face with his hands and flung himself down on the bench, his body writhing and convulsing. Kristin sat down some distance away; she wished she could help her husband. She realized that this misfortune was even harder for him to bear because he himself had sinned against others in the same way as they had now sinned against him. And he, who had never wanted to take the blame for any trouble he might have caused, couldn't possibly bear the blame for this unhappiness—and there was no one else but her for him to fault. But she wasn't angry as much as she was sad and afraid of what might happen next.

Every once in a while she would go up to see to Margret. The girl lay in bed, motionless and pale and staring straight ahead. She had still not asked about Haakon's fate. Kristin didn't know if this was because she didn't dare or because she had grown numb from her own misery.

That afternoon Kristin saw Erlend and Kløng the Icelander walking together through the snowdrifts over to the armory. But only a short time later Erlend returned alone. Kristin glanced up for a moment when he came into the light and walked past her—but then she didn't dare turn her gaze toward the corner of the room where he had retreated. She had seen that he was a broken man.

Later, when she went over to the storeroom to get something, Ivar and Skule came running to tell their mother that Kløng the

Icelander was going to leave that evening. The boys were sad, because the scribe was their good friend. He was packing up his things right now; he wanted to reach Birgsi by nightfall.

Kristin could guess what had happened. Erlend had offered his daughter to the scribe, but he didn't want a maiden who had been seduced. What this conversation must have been like for Erlend . . . she felt dizzy and ill and refused to think any more about it.

The following day a message came from the parsonage. Haakon Eindridessøn wanted to speak to Erlend. Erlend sent back a reply that he had nothing more to say to Haakon. Sira Eiliv told Kristin that if Haakon lived, he would be greatly crippled. In addition to losing his hand, he had also gravely injured his back and hips when he fell from the roof of the servants' hall. But he wanted to go home, even in this condition, and the priest had promised to find a sleigh for him. Haakon now regretted his sin with all his heart. He said that the actions of Margret's father were fully justified, no matter what the law might say; but he hoped that everyone would do their best to hush up the incident so that his guilt and Margret's shame might be concealed as much as possible. That afternoon he was carried out to the sleigh, which Sira Eiliv had borrowed at Repstad, and the priest rode with him to Gauldal.

The next day, which was Ash Wednesday, the people of Husaby had to go to the parish church at Vinjar. But at vespers Kristin asked the curate to let her into the church at Husaby.

She could still feel the ashes on her head as she knelt beside her stepson's grave and said the *Pater noster* for his soul.

By now there was probably not much left of the boy but bones beneath the stone. Bones and hair and a scrap of the clothing he had been laid to rest in. She had seen the remains of her little sister when they dug up her grave to take her body to her father in Hamar. Dust and ashes. She thought about her father's handsome features; about her mother's big eyes in her lined face, and Ragnfrid's figure which continued to look strangely young and delicate and light, even though her face seemed old so early. Now they lay under a stone, falling apart like buildings that collapse when the people have moved away. Images swirled before her eyes: the charred remains of the church back home, and a farm in Silsaadal which they rode past on their way to Vaage—the buildings were deserted and caving in. The people who worked the fields didn't dare go near after the sun went down. She thought about her own beloved dead—their faces and voices, their smiles and habits and demeanor. Now that they had departed for that other land, it was painful to think about their figures; it was like remembering your home when you knew it was standing there deserted, with the rotting beams sinking into the earth.

She sat on the bench along the wall of the empty church. The old smell of cold incense kept her thoughts fixed on images of death and the decay of temporal things. And she didn't have the strength to lift up her soul to catch a glimpse of the land where *they* were, the place to which all goodness and love and faith had finally been moved and now *endured*. Each day, when she prayed for the peace of their souls, it seemed to her unfair that she should pray for those who had possessed more peace in their souls here on earth than she had ever known since she became a grown woman. Sira Eiliv would no doubt say that prayers for the dead were always good—good for oneself, since the other person had already found peace with God.

But this did not help her. It seemed to her that when her weary body was finally rotting beneath a gravestone, her restless soul would still be hovering around somewhere nearby, the way a lost spirit wanders, moaning, through the ruined buildings of an abandoned farm. For in her soul sin continued to exist, like the roots of a weed intertwined in the soil. It no longer blossomed or flared up or smelled fragrant, but it was still there in the soil, pale and strong and alive. In spite of all the tenderness that welled up inside her when she saw her husband's despair, she didn't have the will to silence the inner voice that asked, hurt and embittered: How can you speak that way to *me*? Have you forgotten when I gave you my faith and my honor? Have you forgotten when I was your beloved friend? And yet she understood that as long as this voice spoke within her, she would continue to speak to him as if *she* had forgotten.

In her thoughts she threw herself down before Saint Olav's shrine, she reached for Brother Edvin's moldering bones over in the church at Vatsfjeld, she held in her hands the reliquaries containing the tiny remnants of a dead woman's shroud and the splinters of bone from an unknown martyr. She reached for protection to the small scraps which, through death and decay, had preserved a little of the power of the departed soul—like the magical powers residing in the rusted swords taken from the burial mounds of ancient warriors.

On the following day Erlend rode to Nidaros with only Ulf and one servant to accompany him. He didn't return to Husaby during all of Lent, but Ulf came to get his armed men and then left to meet him at the mid-Lenten *ting* in Orkedal.

Ulf drew Kristin aside to tell her that Erlend had arranged with Tiedeken Paus, the German goldsmith in Nidaros, for Margret to marry his son Gerlak just after Easter.

Erlend came home for the holy day. He was quite calm and composed now, but Kristin thought she could tell that he would never recover from this misfortune the way he had recovered from so much else. Perhaps this was because he was no longer young, or because nothing had ever humiliated him so deeply. Margret seemed indifferent to the arrangements her father had made on her behalf.

One evening when Erlend and Kristin were alone, he said, "If she had been my lawful child—or her mother had been an unmarried woman—I would never have given her to a stranger, as things now stand with her. I would have granted shelter and protection to both her and any child of hers. That's the worst of it—but because of her birth, a lawful husband can offer her the best protection."

As Kristin made all the preparations for the departure of her stepdaughter, Erlend said one day in a brusque voice, "I don't suppose you're well enough to travel to town with us?"

"If that's what you wish, I will certainly go with you," said Kristin.

"Why should I wish it? You've never taken a mother's place for her before, and you don't need to do so now. It's not going to be a festive wedding. And Fru Gunna of Raasvold and her son's wife have promised to come, for the sake of kinship."

And so Kristin stayed at Husaby while Erlend was in Nidaros to give his daughter to Gerlak Tiedekenssøn.

## CHAPTER 3

THAT SUMMER, JUST before Saint Jon's Day, Gunnulf Nikulaussøn returned to his monastery. Erlend was in town during the Frosta *ting;* he sent a message home, asking his wife whether she would care to come to Nidaros to see her brother-in-law. Kristin wasn't feeling very well, but she went all the same. When she met Erlend, he told her that his brother's health seemed completely broken. The friars hadn't had much success with their endeavors up north at Munkefjord. They never managed to have the church they had built consecrated, because the archbishop couldn't travel north during a time of such unrest. Finally they ended up with no bread or wine, candles or oil for the services, but when Brother Gunnulf and Brother Aslak sailed for Vargøy for supplies, the Finns cast their spells and the ship sank. They were stranded on a skerry for three days, and afterwards neither of them regained his full health. Brother Aslak died a short time later. They had suffered terribly from scurvy during Lent, for they had no flour or herbs to eat along with the dried fish. Then Bishop Haakon of Bjørgvin and Master Arne, who was in charge of the cathedral chapter while Lord Paal was at the Curia to be ordained as archbishop, instructed the monks who were still alive to return home; the priests at Vargøy were to tend to the flocks at Munkefjord for the time being.

Although she was not unprepared, Kristin was still shocked when she saw Gunnulf Nikulaussøn again. She went with Erlend over to the monastery the next day, and they were escorted into the interview room. The monk came in. His body was bent over, his fringe of hair was now completely gray, and the skin under his sunken eyes was wrinkled and dark brown. But his smooth, pale complexion was flecked with leaden-colored spots, and she noticed that his hand was covered with the same spots when he thrust it out from the sleeve of his robe to take her hand. He smiled, and she saw that he had lost several teeth.

They sat down and talked for a while, but it seemed as if Gunnulf had also forgotten how to speak. He mentioned this himself before they left.

"But you, Erlend, you are just the same—you don't seem to have aged at all," he said with a little smile.

Kristin knew that she looked miserable at the moment, while Erlend was so handsome as he stood there, tall and slender and dark and well-dressed. And yet Kristin knew in her heart that he too had been greatly changed. It was odd that Gunnulf couldn't see it; he had always been so sharp-sighted in the past.

One day late in the summer Kristin was up in the clothing loft, and Fru Gunna of Raasvold was with her. She had come to Husaby to help Kristin when she once again gave birth. They could hear Naakkve and Bjørgulf singing down in the courtyard as they sharpened their knives—a lewd and vulgar ballad which they sang at the top of their lungs.

Their mother was beside herself with rage as she went downstairs to speak to her sons in the harshest words. She wanted to know who had taught the boys the song—it must have been in the servants' hall, but who among the men would teach children such a song? The boys refused to answer. Then Skule appeared beneath the loft steps; he told his mother she might as well stop asking, because they had learned the ballad from listening to their father sing it.

Fru Gunna joined in: Had they no fear of God that they would sing such a song? Especially now that they couldn't be sure, when they went to bed at night, whether they might be motherless before the roosters crowed? Kristin didn't reply but went quietly back into the house.

Later, after she had taken to her bed to rest, Naakkve came into the room to see her. He took his mother's hand but did not speak, and then he began to weep softly. She talked to him gently, jesting and begging him not to grieve or cry. She had made it through six times before; surely she would make it through the seventh. But the boy wept harder and harder. Finally she allowed him to crawl into the bed between her and the wall, and there he lay, sobbing, with his arms around her neck and his head pressed to his mother's breast. But she couldn't get him to tell her what he was crying about, even though he stayed with her until the servants began carrying in the evening meal.

Naakkve was now twelve years old. He was big for his age and tried to affect a manly and grown-up bearing, but he had a gentle soul, and his mother could sometimes see that he was very childish. But he was old enough to understand the misfortune that had befallen his half-sister; Kristin wondered whether he could also see that his father was different afterwards.

Erlend had always been the kind of man who could say the worst things when his temper was aroused, but in the past he had never said an unkind word to anyone except in anger, and he had been quick to make amends when his own good humor was restored. Nowadays he could say harsh and ugly things with a cold expression on his face. Before, he used to curse and swear fiercely, but to some extent he had put aside this bad habit when he saw that it bothered his wife and offended Sira Eiliv, for whom he had gradually developed great respect. But he had never been rude or spoken in a vulgar manner, and he had never approved when other men talked that way. In that sense, he was much more modest than many a man who had lived a purer life. As much as it offended Kristin to hear such a song on the lips of her innocent sons, especially in her present condition, and then to hear they had learned it from their father, there was something else that gave her an even more bitter taste in her mouth. She realized that Erlend was still childish enough to think that he could counter cruelty with cruelty since, after suffering the shame of his daughter, he had now begun to use foul words and speak in an offensive manner.

Fru Gunna had told her that Margret had given birth to a stillborn son shortly before Saint Olav's Day. She also knew that Margret already seemed to have found ample consolation; she got on well with Gerlak, and he was kind to her. Erlend went to see his daughter whenever he was in Nidaros, and Gerlak always made a great fuss over his father-in-law, although Erlend was not particularly willing to accept this man as his kinsman. But Erlend had not once mentioned his daughter at Husaby since she had left the manor.

Kristin gave birth to another son; he was baptized Munan, after

Erlend's grandfather. During the time she lay in the little house, Naakkve came to see his mother daily, bringing her berries and nuts he had picked in the woods, or wreaths he had woven from medicinal herbs. Erlend returned home when the new child was three weeks old. He often sat with his wife and tried to be gentle and loving—and this time he didn't complain that the infant was not a maiden or that the boy was weak and frail. But Kristin said very little in response to his warm words; she was silent and pensive and despondent, and this time she was slow to recover her health.

All winter long Kristin was ailing, and it seemed unlikely that the child would survive. The mother had little thought for anything but the poor infant. For this reason she listened with only half an ear to all the talk of the great news that was heard that winter. King Magnus had fallen into the worst financial straits through his attempts to win sovereignty over Skaane, and he had demanded assistance and taxes from Norway. Some of the noblemen of the Council seemed willing enough to support him in this matter. But when the king's envoys came to Tunsberg, the royal treasurer was away, and Stig Haakonssøn, who was the chieftain of Tunsberg Fortress, barred the king's men from entering and made ready to defend the stronghold with force. He had few men of his own, but Erling Vidkunssøn, who was his uncle through marriage and was at home on his estate at Aker, sent forty armed men to the fortress while he himself sailed west. At about the same time the king's cousins, Jon and Sigurd Haftorssøn, threatened to oppose the king because of a court ruling that had gone against some of their men.

Erlend laughed at all this and said the Haftorssøns had shown their youth and stupidity in this matter. Discontent with King Magnus was not rampant in Norway. The noblemen were demanding that a regent be placed in charge of the kingdom and that the royal seal be given to a Norwegian man for safekeeping, since the king, because of his dealings in Skaane, seemed to want to spend most of his time in Sweden. The townsmen and the clergy of the towns had become frightened by rumors of the king's loans from the German city-states. The insolence of the Germans and their disregard for Norwegian laws and customs were already more than could be tolerated. And now it was said that the king had promised them even greater rights and freedoms in Norwegian towns, and this would make it impossible to bear for the Norwegian traders, who already had difficult conditions. Among the peasantry the rumor of King Magnus's secret sin still held sway, and many of the parish priests in the countryside and the wandering monks were agreed about at least one thing: They believed this was the reason that Saint Olav's Church in Nidaros had burned. The farmers also blamed this sin for the many misfortunes that had befallen one village after another over the past few years: sickness in the livestock, blight in the crops, which brought illness and disease to both people and beasts, and poor harvests of grain and hay. Erlend said that if the Haftorssøns had been wise enough to hold their peace a little longer and acquire a reputation for amenable and chieftainlike conduct, then people might have remembered that they too were grandsons of King Haakon.

Eventually this unrest died down, but the result was that the king appointed Ivar Ogmundssøn as lord chancellor in Norway. Erling Vidkunssøn, Stig Haakonssøn, the Haftorssøns, and all their supporters were threatened with charges of treason. Then they yielded and came to make peace with the king. There was a powerful man from the Uplands whose name was Ulf Saksesøn; he had taken part in the Haftorssøns' opposition, and he did not make peace with the king but came instead to Nidaros after Christmas. He spent a good deal of time with Erlend in town, and from him the people of the north heard about the matters, as Ulf perceived them. Kristin had a great dislike for this man; she didn't know him, but she knew his sister Helga Saksesdatter, who was married to Gyrd Darre of Dyfrin. She was beautiful but exceedingly arrogant, and Simon didn't care for her either, although Ramborg got along well with her. Soon after the beginning of Lent, letters arrived for the sheriffs stating that Ulf Saksesøn was to be declared an outlaw at the *tings*, but by that time he had already sailed away from Norway in midwinter.

That spring Erlend and Kristin were staying at their town estate during Easter, and they had brought their youngest son, Munan, with them because there was a sister at the Bakke convent who was so skilled in healing that every sick child she touched regained health, as long it was not God's wish for the child to die.

One day shortly after Easter, Kristin came home from the convent with the infant. The manservant and maid who had accompanied her came with her into the house. Erlend was alone, lying on one of the benches. After the manservant left, and the women had taken off their cloaks, Kristin sat near the hearth with the child while the maid heated some oil which the nun had given them. Then Erlend asked from his place on the bench what Sister Ragnhild had said about the boy. Kristin replied brusquely to his questions as she unwrapped the swaddling clothes; finally she stopped talking altogether.

"Are things so bad with the boy, Kristin, that you don't want to tell me?" he asked with some impatience.

"You've asked the same things before, Erlend," replied his wife in a cold voice. "And I've answered you many times. But since you care so little about the boy that you can't remember from one day to the next . . ."

"It has also happened to me, Kristin," said Erlend as he stood up and went over to her, "that I've had to give you the same answer two or three times to some question you've asked me because you didn't bother to remember what I'd said."

"It was probably not about such important matters as the children's health," she said in the same cold voice.

"But it wasn't about petty things, either, this past winter. They were matters that weighed heavily on my mind."

"That's not true, Erlend. It's been a long time since you talked to me about those things that were most on your mind."

"Leave us now, Signe," said Erlend to the maid. His brow was flushed red as he turned to his wife. "I know what you're referring to. But I won't speak to you about that as long as your maid might hear me—even though you're such good friends with her that you think it a small matter for her to be present when you start a quarrel with your husband and say I'm not speaking the truth."

"One learns least from the people one lives with," said Kristin curtly.

"It's not easy to understand what you mean by that. I've never spoken unkindly to you in the presence of strangers or forgotten to show you honor and respect in front of our servants."

Kristin burst into an oddly desolate and quavering laugh.

"You forget so well, Erlend! Ulf Haldorssøn has lived with us all these years. Don't you remember when you had him and Haftor bring me to you in the bedchamber of Brynhild's house in Oslo?"

Erlend sank down onto the bench, staring at his wife with his mouth agape.

But she continued, "You never thought it necessary to conceal from your servants all that was improper or disrespectful here at Husaby, or anywhere else—whether it was something shameful for yourself or for your wife."

Erlend stayed where he was, looking at her aghast.

"Do you remember that first winter of our marriage? I was carrying Naakkve, and as things stood, it seemed likely that it would be difficult for me to demand obedience and respect from my household. Do you remember how you supported me? Do you remember when your foster father visited us with women guests we didn't know, and his maids and serving men, and our own servants, sat across the table from us? Do you remember how Munan pulled from me every shred of dignity I might use to hide behind, and you sat there meekly and dared not stop his speech?"

"Jesus! Have you been brooding about this for fifteen years?" Then he looked up at her—his eyes seemed such a strange pale blue, and his voice was faltering and helpless. "And yet, my Kristin—it doesn't seem to me that the two of us say unkind or harsh words to each other. . . ."

"No," said Kristin, "and that's why it cut even deeper into my heart that time during the Christmas celebration when you railed at me because I had spread my cape over Margret, while women from three counties stood around and listened."

Erlend did not reply.

"And yet you blame me for the way things went with Margret, but every time I tried to reprimand her with even a single word, she would run to you, and you would tell me sternly to leave the maiden in peace—she was yours and not mine."

"Blame you? No, I don't," Erlend said with difficulty, struggling hard to speak calmly. "If one of our children had been a daughter, then you might have better understood how this matter of my daughter . . . it stabs a father to the very marrow."

"I thought I showed you this spring that I understood," said his wife softly. "I only had to think of my own father. . . ."

"All the same, this was much worse," said Erlend, his voice still calm. "I was an unmarried man. This man . . . was married. I was not bound. At least," he corrected himself, "I wasn't bound in such a way that I couldn't free myself."

"And yet you didn't free yourself," said Kristin. "Don't you remember how it came about that you were freed?"

Erlend leaped to his feet and slapped her face. Then he stood staring at her in horror. A red patch appeared on her white cheek, but she sat rigid and motionless, her eyes hard. The child began to cry in fright; she rocked him gently in her arms, hushing him.

"That . . . was a vile thing to say, Kristin," said her husband uncertainly.

"The last time you struck me," she answered in a low voice, "I was carrying your child under my heart. Now you hit me as I hold your son on my lap."

"Yes, we keep having all these children," he shouted impatiently.

They both fell silent. Erlend began swiftly pacing back and forth. She carried the child over to the alcove and put him on the bed; when she reappeared in the alcove doorway, he stopped in front of her.

"I . . . I shouldn't have struck you, my Kristin. I wish I hadn't done it. I'll probably regret it for as long as I regretted it the first time. But you . . . you've told me before that you think I forget things too quickly. But you never forget—not a single injustice I might have done you. I've tried . . . tried to be a good husband to you, but you don't seem to think that worth remembering. You . . . you're so beautiful, Kristin . . ." He gazed after her as she walked past him.

Oh, his wife's quiet and dignified bearing was as lovely as the willowy grace of the young maiden had been; she was wider in the bosom and hips, but she was also taller. She held herself erect, and her neck bore the small, round head as proudly and beautifully as ever. Her pale, remote face with the dark-gray eyes stirred and excited him as much as her round, rosy child's face had stirred and excited his restless soul with its wondrous calm. He went over and took her hand.

"For me, Kristin, you will always be the most beautiful of women, and the most dear."

She allowed him to hold her hand but didn't squeeze his in return. Then he flung it aside; rage overcame him once again.

"You say I've forgotten. That may not always be the worst of sins. I've never pretended to be a pious man, but I remember what I learned from Sira Jon when I was a child, and God's servants have reminded me of it since. It's a sin to brood over and dwell on the sins we have confessed to the priest and repented before God, receiving His forgiveness through the hand and the words of the priest. And it's not out of piety, Kristin, that you're constantly tearing open these old sins of ours—you want to hold the knife to my throat every time I oppose you in some way."

He walked away and then came back.

"Domineering . . . God knows that I love you, Kristin, even though I can see how domineering you are, and you've never forgiven me for the injustice I did to you or for luring you astray. I've tolerated a great deal from you, Kristin, but I will no longer tolerate the fact that I can never have peace from these old misfortunes, nor that you speak to me as if I were your thrall."

Kristin was trembling with fury when she spoke.

"I've never spoken to you as if you were my thrall. Have you *ever* heard me speak harshly or in anger to anyone who might be considered lesser than me, even if it was the most incompetent or worthless of our household servants? I know that before God I am free of the sin of offending His poor in either word or deed. But you're supposed to be my *lord;* I'm supposed to obey and honor you, bow to you and lean on you, next to God, in accordance with God's laws, Erlend! And if I've lost patience and talked to you in a manner unbefitting a wife speaking to her husband—then it's because many times you've made it difficult for me to surrender my ignorance to your better understanding, to honor and obey my husband and lord as much as I would have liked. And perhaps I had expected that you . . . perhaps I thought I could provoke you into showing me that you were a man and I was only a poor woman. . . .

"But you needn't worry, Erlend. I will not offend you again with my words, and from this day forward, I will never forget to speak to you as gently as if you were descended from thralls."

Erlend's face had flushed dark red. He raised his fist at her, then turned swiftly on his heel, grabbed his cape and sword from the bench near the door, and rushed out.

It was sunny outside, with a piercing wind. The air was cold, but glistening particles of thawing ice sprayed over him from the building eaves and from the swaying tree branches. The snow on the rooftops gleamed like silver, and beyond the black-green, forested slopes surrounding the town, the mountain peaks sparkled icy blue and shiny white in the sharp, dazzling light of the wintry spring day.

Erlend raced through the streets and alleyways—fast but aimless. He was boiling inside. She was wrong, it was clear that *she* had been wrong from the very beginning, and he was right. He had allowed himself to be provoked and struck her, undercutting his position, but she was the one who was wrong. Now he had no idea what to do with himself. He had no wish to visit any acquaintances, and he refused to go back home.

There was a great tumult in town. A large trading ship from Iceland—the first of the spring season—had put in at the docks that morning. Erlend wandered west through the lanes and emerged near Saint Martin's Church; he headed down toward the wharves. There were already shrieks and clamor coming from the inns and alehouses, even though it was early afternoon. In his youth Erlend could have gone into such places himself, along with friends and companions. But now people would stare, wide-eyed, and afterwards they would wear out their gums gossiping if the sheriff of Orkdøla county, who had a residence in town and ale, mead, and wine in abundance in his own home, should go into an inn and ask for a taste of their paltry ale. But that was truly what he wished for most—to sit and drink with the smallholders who had come to town and with the servants and seamen. No one would make a fuss if these fellows gave their women a slap in the face; it would do them good. How in fiery Hell was a man to rule his wife if he couldn't beat her because of her high birth and his own sense of honor. The Devil himself couldn't compete with a woman through words. She was a witch—but so beautiful. If only he could beat her until she gave in.

The bells began to ring from all the churches in town, calling the people to vespers. The sounds tumbled in the spring wind, hovering over him in the turbulent air. No doubt she was on her way to Christ Church now, that holy witch. She would complain to God and the Virgin Mary and Saint Olav that she had been struck in the face by her husband. Erlend sent his wife's guardian saints a greeting of sinful thoughts as the bells resounded and tolled and clanged. He headed toward Saint Gregor's Church.

The graves of his parents lay in front of Saint Anna's altar in the north aisle of the nave. As Erlend said his prayers, he noticed that Fru Sunniva Olavsdatter and her maid had entered the church portal. When he finished praying, he went over to greet her.

In all the years he had known Fru Sunniva, things had always been such between them that they could banter and jest quite freely whenever they met. On this evening, as they sat on the bench and waited for evensong to begin, he grew so bold that several times she had to remind him that they were in church, with people constantly coming in.

"Yes, yes," said Erlend, "but you're so lovely tonight, Sunniva! It's wonderful to banter with a woman who has such gentle eyes."

"You're not worthy enough, Erlend Nikulaussøn, for me to look at you with gentle eyes," she said, laughing.

"Then I'll come and banter with you after it grows dark," replied Erlend in the same tone of voice. "When the mass is over, I'll escort you home."

At that moment the priests entered the choir, and Erlend went over to the south nave to join the other men.

When the service came to an end, he left the church through the main door. He saw Fru Sunniva and her maid a short distance down the street. He thought it best he didn't accompany her and go right home instead. Just then a group of Icelanders from the trading ship appeared in the street, staggering and clinging to each other, and seemed intent on blocking the way of the two women. Erlend ran after them. As soon as the seamen saw a gentleman with a sword on his belt approaching, they stepped aside and made room for the women to pass.

"I think it would be best if I escorted you home, after all," said Erlend. "There's too much unrest in town tonight."

"What do you think, Erlend? As old as I am . . . And yet perhaps it doesn't displease me if a few men still find me pretty enough to try to block my passage. . . ."

There was only one answer that a courteous man could give.

He returned to his own residence at dawn the next morning, pausing for a moment outside the bolted door to the main building, frozen, dead tired, heartsick, and dejected. Should he pound on the door to wake the servants and then slip inside to crawl into bed next to Kristin, who lay there with the child at her breast? No. He had with him the key to the eastern storehouse loft; that's where he kept some possessions that were in his charge. Erlend unlocked the door, pulled off his boots, and spread some homespun fabric and empty sacks on top of the straw in the bed. He wrapped his cape around him, crept under the sacks, and was fortunate enough to fall asleep and forget everything, exhausted and confused as he was.

Kristin was pale and weary from a sleepless night as she sat down to breakfast with her servants. One of the men said he had asked the master to come to the table—he was sleeping in the east loft—but Erlend told him to go to the Devil.

Erlend was supposed to go to Elgeseter after the morning service to be a witness to the sale of several estates. Afterwards he managed to excuse himself from the meal in the refectory, and to slip away from Arne Gjavvaldssøn, who had also declined to stay and drink with the brothers but wanted Erlend to come home to Ranheim with him.

Later he regretted that he had parted company with the others, and he was filled with dread as he walked home alone through town—now he would have to think about what he had done. For a moment he was tempted to go straight down to Saint Gregor's Church; he had promised to make confession to one of the priests whenever he was in Nidaros. But if he did it again, after he had confessed, it would be an even greater sin. He had better wait for a while.

Sunniva must think he was little better than a chicken she had caught with her bare hands. But no, the Devil take him if he'd ever thought a woman would be able to teach him so many new things—here he was walking around and gasping with astonishment at what he had encountered. He had imagined himself to be rather experienced in *ars amoris,* or whatever the learned men called it. If he had been young and green, he would probably have felt quite cocky and thought it splendid. But he didn't like that woman—that wild woman. He was sick of her. He was sick of *all* women except his own wife—and he was sick of her as well! By the Holy Cross, he had been so married to her that he had grown pious himself, because he had believed in her piety. But what a handsome reward he had been given by his pious wife for his faithfulness and love—witch that she was! He remembered the sting of her spiteful words from the evening before. So she thought he acted as if he were descended from thralls. . . . And that other woman, Sunniva, no doubt thought he was inexperienced and clumsy because he had been caught off guard and showed some surprise at her skills in love. Now he would show her that he was no more a saint than she was. He had promised her to come to Baardsgaard that night, and he might as well go. He had committed the sin—he might as well enjoy the pleasure that it offered.

He had already broken his vows to Kristin, and she herself was to blame, with her spiteful and unreasonable behavior toward him. . . .

He went home and wandered through the stables and outbuildings, looking for something to complain about; he quarreled with the priest's servant from the hospital because she had brought malt into the drying room, even though he knew that his own servants had no use for the grain-drying house while they were in Nidaros. He wished that his sons were with him; they would have been good company. He wished he could go back home to Husaby at once. But he had to stay in Nidaros and wait for letters to arrive from the south; it was too risky to receive such letters at his own home in the village.

The mistress of the house didn't come to the evening meal. She was lying in bed in the alcove, said her maid Signe, with a reproachful look at her master. Erlend replied harshly that he hadn't asked about her mistress. After the servants had left the room, he went into the alcove. It was oppressively dark. Erlend bent over Kristin on the bed.

"Are you crying?" he asked very softly, for her breathing sounded so strange. But she answered brusquely that she wasn't.

"Are you tired? I'm about to go to bed too," he murmured.

Kristin's voice quavered as she said, "Then I would rather, Erlend, that you went to bed in the same place where you slept last night."

Erlend didn't reply. He went out and then returned with the candle from the hall and opened up his clothes chest. He was already dressed suitably enough to go out wherever he liked, for he was wearing the violet-blue *cote-hardi* because he had been to Elgeseter in the morning. But now he took off these garments, slowly and deliberately, and put on a red silk shirt and a mouse-gray, calf-length velvet tunic with small silver bells on the points of the sleeves. He brushed his hair and washed his hands, all the while keeping his eyes on his wife. She was silent and didn't move. Then he left without bidding her good night. The next day he openly returned home to the estate at breakfast time.

This went on for a week. Then one evening, when Erlend came back home after going up to Hangrar on business, he was told that Kristin had set off for Husaby that morning.

He was already quite aware that no man had ever had less pleasure from a sin than he was having from his dealings with Sunniva Olavsdatter. In his heart he was so unbearably tired of that demented woman—sick of her even as he played with her and caressed her. He had also been reckless; it must be known all over town and throughout the countryside by now that he had been spending his nights at Baardsgaard. And it was not worth having his reputation sullied for Sunniva's sake. Occasionally he also wondered whether there might be consequences. After all, the woman had a husband, such as he was, decrepit and sickly. He pitied Baard for being married to such a wanton and foolish woman; Erlend was hardly the first to tread too close to the man's honor. And Haftor . . . but when he took up with Sunniva he hadn't remembered that she was Haftor's sister; he didn't think of this until it was too late. The situation was as bad as it could possibly be. And now he realized that Kristin knew about it.

Surely she wouldn't think of bringing a charge against him before the archbishop, seeking permission to leave him. She had Jørundgaard to flee to, but it would be impossible for her to travel over the mountains at this time of year; even more so if she wanted to take the children along, and Kristin would never leave them behind. He reassured himself that she wouldn't be able to travel by ship with Munan and Lavrans so early in the spring. No, it would be unlike Kristin to seek help from the archbishop against him. She had reason to do so, but he would willingly stay away from their bed until she understood that he felt true remorse. Kristin would never allow this matter to become a public case. Yet he realized it had been a long time since he could be certain what his wife might or might not do.

That night he lay in his own bed, letting his thoughts roam. It occurred to him that he had acted with even greater folly than he had first thought when he entered into this miserable affair, now that he was involved in the greatest plans.

He cursed himself for still being such a fool over a woman that she could drive him to this. He cursed both Kristin and Sunniva. By Devil, he was no more besotted with women than other men; he had gotten involved with fewer of them than most of the men he knew. But it was as if the Fiend himself were after him; he couldn't come near a woman without landing in mire up to his armpits.

It had to be stopped now. Thank the Lord he had other matters on his hands. Soon, very soon, he would receive Lady Ingebjørg's letters. Well, he couldn't avoid trouble with women in this matter either, but that must be God's punishment for the sins of his youth. Erlend laughed out loud in the dark. Lady Ingebjørg would have to see that what they had told her about the situation was true. The question was whether it would be one of her sons or the sons of her unlawful sister whom the Norwegians supported to oppose King Magnus. And she loved the children she had borne to Knut Porse in a way she had never loved her other children.

Soon, very soon . . . then it would be the sharp wind and the salty waves that would fill his embrace. God in Heaven, it would be good to be soaked through by the sea swells and feel the fresh wind seep into his marrow—to be quit of women for a good long time.

Sunniva. Let her think what she would. He wouldn't go back there again. And Kristin could go off to Jørundgaard if she liked. It might be safest and best for her and the children to be far away in Gudbrandsdal this summer. Later on he would no doubt make amends with her again.

The following morning he rode up toward Skaun. He decided he wouldn't have any peace until he knew what his wife intended to do.

She received him politely, her demeanor gentle and cool, when he arrived at Husaby later in the day. Unless he asked her a question, she said not a word, not even anything unkind, and she didn't object when later that evening he came over and tentatively lay down in their bed. But when he had lain there for a while, he hesitantly tried to put his hand on her breast.

Kristin's voice shook, but Erlend couldn't tell if it was from sorrow or bitterness, when she whispered, "Surely you're not so lowly a man, Erlend, that you will make this even worse for me. I cannot start a quarrel with you, since our children are sleeping all around. And since I have seven sons by you, I would rather our servants didn't see that I know I'm a woman who has been betrayed."

Erlend lay there in silence for a long time before he dared reply.

"Yes, may God have mercy on me, Kristin—I have betrayed you. I wouldn't have . . . wouldn't have done it if I had found it easier to bear those vicious words you said to me in Nidaros. I haven't come home to beg your forgiveness, for I know this would be too much to ask of you right now."

"I see that Munan Baardsøn spoke the truth," replied his wife. "The day will never come when you will stand up and take the blame for what you have done. You should turn to God and seek redemption from Him. You need to ask His forgiveness more than you need to ask mine."

"Yes, I know that," said Erlend bitterly. And then they said no more. The next morning he rode back to Nidaros.

He had been in town several days when Fru Sunniva's maid came to speak to him in Saint Gregor's Church one evening. Erlend thought he ought to talk to Sunniva one last time and told the girl to keep watch that night; he would come the same way as before.

He had to creep and climb like a chicken thief to reach the loft where they always met. This time he felt sick with shame that he had made such a fool of himself—at his age and in his position. But in the beginning it had amused him to carry on like a youth.

Fru Sunniva received him in bed.

"So you've finally come, at this late hour?" she laughed and yawned. "Hurry up, my friend, and come to bed. We can talk later about where you've been all this time."

Erlend didn't know what to do or how to tell her what was on his mind. Without thinking, he began to unfasten his clothing.

"We've both been reckless, Sunniva—I don't think it advisable that I stay here tonight. Surely Baard must be expected home sometime?" he said.

"Are you afraid of my husband?" teased Sunniva. "You've seen for yourself that Baard didn't even prick up his ears when we flirted right in front of him. If he asks me whether you've been spending time here at the manor, I'll just convince him that it's the same old nonsense. He trusts me much too well."

"Yes, he does seem to trust you too well," laughed Erlend, digging his fingers into her fair hair and her firm, white shoulders.

"Do you think so?" She gripped his wrist. "And do you trust your own wife? I was still a shy and virtuous maiden when Baard won me. . . ."

"We'll keep *my* wife out of this," said Erlend sharply, releasing her.

"Why is that? Does it seem to you less proper for us to talk about Kristin Lavransdatter than about Sir Baard, my husband?"

Erlend clenched his teeth and refused to answer.

"You must be one of those men, Erlend," said Sunniva scornfully, "who thinks you're so charming and handsome that a woman can hardly be blamed if her virtue is like fragile glass to you—when usually she's as strong as steel."

"I've never thought that about you," replied Erlend roughly.

Sunniva's eyes glittered. "What did you want with me then, Erlend? Since you have married so well?"

"I told you not to mention my wife."

"Your wife or my husband."

"You were always the one who started talking about Baard, and you were the worst to ridicule him," said Erlend bitterly. "And if you didn't mock him in words . . . I'd like to know how dearly you held his honor when you took another man in your husband's place. *She* is not diminished by my misdeeds."

"Is that what you want to tell me—that you still love Kristin even though you like me well enough to want to play with me?"

"I don't know how well I like you . . . You were the one who showed your affection for me."

"And Kristin doesn't care for your love?" she sneered. "I've seen how tenderly she looks at you, Erlend. . . ."

"Be silent!" he shouted. "Perhaps she knew how worthless I

was," he said, his voice harsh and hateful. "You and I might be each other's equal."

"Is that it?" threatened Sunniva. "Am I supposed to be the whip you use to punish your wife?"

Erlend stood there, breathing hard. "You could call it that. But you put yourself willingly into my hands."

"Take care," said Sunniva, "that the whip doesn't turn back on you."

She was sitting up in bed, waiting. But Erlend made no attempt to argue or to make amends with his lover. He finished getting dressed and left without saying another word.

He wasn't overly pleased with himself or with the way he had parted with Sunniva. There was no honor in it for him. But it didn't matter now; at least he was rid of her.

## CHAPTER 4

DURING THAT SPRING and summer they saw little of the master at home at Husaby. On those occasions when he did return to his manor, he and his wife behaved with courtesy and friendliness toward each other. Erlend didn't try in any way to breach the wall that she had now put up between them, even though he would often give her a searching look. Otherwise, he seemed to have much to think about outside his own home. And he never inquired with a single word about the management of the estate.

This was something his wife mentioned when, shortly after Holy Cross Day, he asked her whether she wanted to accompany him to Raumsdal. He had business to tend to in the Uplands; perhaps she would like to take the children along, spend some time at Jørundgaard, visit kinsmen and friends in the valley? But Kristin had no wish to do so, under any circumstances.

Erlend was in Nidaros during the Law *ting* and afterwards out in Orkedal. Then he returned home to Husaby but immediately began preparations for a journey to Bjørgvin. The *Margygren* was anchored out at Nidarholm, and he was only waiting for Haftor Graut, who was supposed to sail with him.

Three days before Saint Margareta's Day, the hay harvesting began at Husaby. It was the finest weather, and when the workers went back out into the meadows after the midday rest, Olav the overseer asked the children to come along.

Kristin was up in the clothing chamber, which was on the second story of the armory. The house was built in such a fashion that an outside stair led up to this room and the exterior gallery running along the side; projecting over it was the third floor, which could be reached only by means of a ladder through a hatchway inside the clothing chamber. It was standing open because Erlend was up in the weapons loft.

Kristin carried the fur cape that Erlend wanted to take along on his sea voyage out to the gallery and began to shake it. Then she heard the thunder of a large group of horsemen, and a moment later she saw men come riding out of the forest on Gauldal Road. An instant later, Erlend was standing at her side.

"Is it true what you said, Kristin, that the fire went out in the cookhouse this morning?"

"Yes, Gudrid knocked over the soup kettle. We'll have to borrow some embers from Sira Eiliv."

Erlend looked over at the parsonage.

"No, he can't get mixed up in this. . . . Gaute," he called softly to the boy dawdling under the gallery, picking up one rake after another, with little desire to go out to the hay harvesting. "Come up the stairs, but stop at the top or they'll be able to see you."

Kristin stared at her husband. She'd never seen him look this way before. A taut, alert calm came over his voice and face as he peered south toward the road, and over his tall, supple body as he ran inside the loft and came back at once with a flat package wrapped in linen. He handed it to the boy.

"Put this inside your shirt, and pay attention to what I tell you. You must safeguard these letters—it's more important than you can possibly know, my Gaute. Put your rake over your shoulder and walk calmly across the fields until you reach the alder thickets. Keep to the bushes down by the woods—you know the place well, I know you do—and then sneak through the densest underbrush all the way over to Skjoldvirkstad. Make sure that things are calm at the farm. If you notice any sign of unrest or strange men around, stay hidden. But if you're sure it's safe, then go down and give this to Ulf, if he's home. If you can't put the letters into his own hand and you're sure that no one is near, then burn them as soon as you can. But take care that both the writing and the seals are completely destroyed, and that they don't fall into anyone's hands but Ulf's. May God help us, my son—these are weighty matters to put into the hands of a boy only ten winters old; many a good man's life and welfare . . . Do you understand how important this is, Gaute?"

"Yes, Father. I understand everything you said." Gaute lifted his small, fair face with a somber expression as he stood on the stairs.

"If Ulf isn't home, tell Isak that he has to set off at once for Hevne and ride all night—he must tell them, and he knows who I mean, that I think a headwind has sprung up here, and that I fear my journey has now been cursed. Do you understand?"

"Yes, Father. I remember everything you've told me."

"Go then. May God protect you, my son."

Erlend dashed up to the weapons loft and was about to close the hatchway, but Kristin was already halfway through the opening. He waited until she had climbed up, then shut the hatch and ran over to a chest and took out several boxes of letters. He tore off the seals and stomped them to bits on the floor; he ripped the parchments into shreds and wrapped them around a key and tossed the whole thing out the window to the ground, where it landed in the tall nettles growing behind the building. With his hands on the windowsill, Erlend stood and watched the small boy who was walking along the edge of the grain field toward the meadow where the rows of harvest workers were toiling with scythes and rakes. When Gaute disappeared into the little grove of trees between the field and the meadow, Erlend pulled the window closed. The sound of hoofbeats was now loud and close to the manor.

Erlend turned to face his wife.

"If you can retrieve what I threw outside just now . . . let Skule do it, he's a clever boy. Tell him to fling it into the ravine behind the cowshed. They'll probably be watching you, and maybe the older boys as well. But I don't think they would search you. . . ." He tucked the broken pieces of seal inside her bodice. "They can't be recognized anymore, but even so . . ."

"Are you in some kind of danger, Erlend?" Kristin asked. As he looked down at her face, he threw himself into her open arms. For a moment he held her tight.

"I don't know, Kristin. We'll find out soon enough. Tore Eindridessøn is riding in the lead, and I saw that Sir Baard is with them. I don't expect that Tore is coming here for any good purpose."

Now the horsemen had entered the courtyard. Erlend hesitated for a moment. Then he kissed his wife fervently, opened the hatchway, and ran downstairs. When Kristin came out onto the gallery, Erlend was standing in the courtyard below, helping the royal treasurer, an elderly and ponderous man, down from his saddle. There were at least thirty armed men with Sir Baard and the sheriff of Gauldøla county.

As Kristin walked across the courtyard, she heard the latter man say, "I bring you greetings from your cousins, Erlend. Borgar and Guttorm are enjoying the king's hospitality in Veøy, and I think that Haftor Toressøn has already paid a visit to Ivar and the young boy at home at Sundbu by this time. Sir Baard seized Graut yesterday morning in town."

"And now you've come here to invite me to the same meeting of the royal retainers, I can see," said Erlend with a smile.

"That is true, Erlend."

"And no doubt you'll want to search the manor? Oh, I've taken part in this kind of thing so many times that I should know how it goes. . . ."

"But you've never had such great matters as high treason on your hands before," said Tore.

"No, not until now," said Erlend. "And it looks as if I'm playing with the black chess pieces, Tore, and you have me checkmated—isn't that so, kinsman?"

"We're looking for the letters that you've received from Lady Ingebjørg Haakonsdatter," said Tore Eindridessøn.

"They're in the chest covered with red leather, up in the weapons loft. But they contain little except such greetings as loving kinsmen usually send to each other; and all of them are old. Stein here can show you the way. . . ."

The strangers had dismounted, and the servants of the estate had now come swarming into the courtyard.

"There was much more than that in the one we took from Borgar Trondssøn," said Tore.

Erlend began whistling softly. "I suppose we might as well go into the house," he said. "It's getting crowded out here."

Kristin followed the men into the hall. At a sign from Tore, a couple of the armed guards came along.

"You'll have to surrender your sword, Erlend," said Tore of Gimsar when they came inside. "As a sign that you're our prisoner."

Erlend slapped his flanks to show that he carried no other weapon than the dagger at his belt.

But Tore repeated, "You must hand over your sword, as a sign—"

"Well, if you want to do this formally . . ." said Erlend, laughing a bit. He went over and took down his sword from the peg, holding it by the sheath and offering the hilt to Tore Eindridessøn with a slight bow.

The old man from Gimsar loosened the fastenings, pulled the sword all the way out, and stroked the blade with a fingertip.

"Was it this sword, Erlend, that you used . . . ?"

Erlend's blue eyes glittered like steel; he pressed his lips together into a narrow line.

"Yes. It was with this sword that I punished your grandson when I found him with my daughter."

Tore stood holding the sword; he looked down at it and said in a threatening tone, "You who were supposed to uphold the law, Erlend—you should have known then that you were going farther than the law would follow you."

Erlend threw back his head, his eyes blazing and fierce. "There is a law, Tore, that cannot be subverted by sovereigns or *tings*, which says that a man must protect the honor of his women with the sword."

"You've been fortunate, Erlend Nikulaussøn, that no man has ever used that law against you," replied Tore of Gimsar, his voice full of malice. "Or you might have needed as many lives as a cat."

Erlend's response was infuriatingly slow.

"Isn't the present undertaking serious enough that you would think it inopportune to bring up those old charges from my youth?"

"I don't know whether Baard of Lensvik would consider them old charges." Rage surged up inside Erlend and he was about to reply, but Tore shouted, "You ought to find out first, Erlend, whether your paramours are so clever that they can read, before you run around on your nightly adventures with secret letters in your belt. Just ask Baard who it was that warned us you were planning treachery against your king, to whom you've sworn loyalty and who granted you the position of sheriff."

Involuntarily Erlend pressed a hand to his breast—for a moment he glanced at his wife, and the blood rushed to his face. Then Kristin ran forward and threw her arms around his neck. Erlend looked down into her face—he saw nothing but love in her eyes.

"Erlend—husband!"

The royal treasurer had remained largely silent. Now he went over to the two of them and said softly, "My dear mistress, perhaps it would be best if you took the children and the serving women with you into the women's house and stayed there as long as we're here at the manor."

Erlend let go of his wife with one last squeeze of his arm around her shoulder.

"It would be best, my dear Kristin. Do as Sir Baard advises."

Kristin stood on her toes and offered Erlend her lips. Then she went out into the courtyard and collected her children and serving women from among the crowd, taking them with her into the little house. There was no other women's house at Husaby.

They sat there for several hours; the composure of their mistress kept the frightened group more or less calm. Then Erlend entered, bearing no weapons and dressed for travel. Two strangers stood guard at the door.

He shook hands with his eldest sons and then lifted the smallest ones into his arms, while he asked where Gaute was. "Well, you must give him my greetings, Naakkve. He must have gone off into the woods with his bow the way he usually does. Tell him he can have my English longbow after all—the one I refused to give him last Sunday."

Kristin pulled him to her without speaking a word.

Then she whispered urgently, "When are you coming back, Erlend, my friend?"

"When God wills it, my wife."

She stepped back, struggling not to break down. Normally he never addressed her in any other way except by using her given name; his last words had shaken her to the heart. Only now did she fully understand what had happened.

At sunset Kristin was sitting up on the hill north of the manor.

She had never before seen the sky so red and gold. Above the opposite ridge stretched an enormous cloud; it was shaped like a bird's wing, glowing from within like iron in the forge, and gleaming brightly like amber. Small golden shreds like feathers tore away and floated into the air. And far below, on the lake at the bottom of the valley, spread a mirror image of the sky and the cloud and the ridge. Down in the depths the radiant blaze was flaring upward, covering everything in sight.

The grass in the meadows had grown tall, and the silky tassels of the straw shone dark red beneath the crimson light from the sky; the barley had sprouted spikes and caught the light on the young, silky-smooth awn. The sod-covered rooftops of the farm buildings were thick with sorrel and buttercups, and the sun lay across them in wide bands. The blackened shingles of the church roof gleamed darkly, and its light-colored stone walls were becoming softly gilded.

The sun broke through from beneath the cloud, perched on the mountain rim, and lit up one forested ridge after another. It was such a clear evening; the light opened up vistas to small hamlets amidst the spruce-decked slopes. She could make out mountain pastures and tiny farms in among the trees that she had never been able to see before from Husaby. The shapes of huge mountains rose up, reddish-violet, in the south toward Dovre, in places that were usually covered by haze and clouds.

The smallest bell down in the church began to ring, and the church bell at Vinjar answered. Kristin sat bowed over her folded hands until the last notes of the ninefold peal died away.

Now the sun was behind the ridge; the golden glow paled and the crimson grew softer and pinker. After the ringing of the bells had ceased, the rustling sound from the forest swelled and spread again; the tiny creek trickling through the leafy woods down in the valley sounded louder. From the pasture nearby came the familiar clinking of the livestock bells; a flying beetle buzzed halfway around her and then disappeared.

She sent a last sigh after her prayers; an appeal for forgiveness because her thoughts had been elsewhere while she prayed.

The beautiful large estate lay below her on the hillside, like a jewel on the wide bosom of the slope. She gazed out across all the land she had owned along with her husband. Thoughts about the manor and its care had filled her soul to the brim. She had worked and struggled. Not until this evening did she realize how much she had struggled to put this estate back on its feet and keep it going—how hard she had tried and how much she had accomplished.

She had accepted it as her fate, to be borne with patience and a straight back, that this had fallen to her. Just as she had striven to be patient and steadfast no matter what life presented, every time she learned she was carrying yet another child under her breast—again and again. With each son added to the flock she recognized that her responsibility had grown for ensuring the prosperity and secure position of the lineage. Tonight she realized that her ability to survey everything at once and her watchfulness had also grown with each new child entrusted to her care. Never had she seen it so clearly as on this evening—what destiny had demanded of her and what it had given her in return with her seven sons. Over and over again joy had quickened the beat of her heart; fear on their behalf had rent it in two. They were her children, these big sons with their lean, bony, boy's bodies, just as they had been when they were small and so plump that they barely hurt themselves when they tumbled down on their way between the bench and her knee. They were hers, just as they had been back when she lifted them out of the cradle to her milk-filled breast and had to support their heads, which wobbled on their frail necks the way a bluebell nods on its stalk. Wherever they ended up in the world, wherever they journeyed, forgetting their mother—she thought that for her, their lives would be like a current in her own life; they would be one with her, just as they had been when she alone on this earth knew about the new life hidden inside, drinking from her blood and making her cheeks pale. Over and over she had endured the sinking, sweat-dripping anguish when she realized that once again her time had come; once again she would be pulled under by the groundswell of birth pains—until she was lifted up with a new child in her arms. How much richer and stronger and braver she had become with each child was something that she first realized tonight.

And yet she now saw that she was the same Kristin from Jørundgaard, who had never learned to bear an unkind word because she had been protected all her days by such a strong and gentle love. In Erlend's hands she was still the same . . .

Yes. Yes. Yes. It was true that all this time she had remembered, year after year, every wound he had ever caused her—even though she had always known that he never wounded her the way a grown person intends harm to another, but rather the way a child strikes out playfully at his companion. Each time he offended her, she had tended to the memory the way one tends to a venomous sore. And with each humiliation he brought upon himself by acting on any impulse he might have—it struck her like the lash of a whip against her flesh, causing a suppurating wound. It wasn't true that she willfully or deliberately harbored ill feelings toward her husband; she knew she wasn't usually narrow-minded, but with him she was. If Erlend had a hand in it, she forgot nothing—and even the smallest scratch on her soul would continue to sting and bleed and swell and ache if he was the one to cause it.

About him she would never be wiser or stronger. She might strive to seem capable and fearless, pious and strong in her marriage with him—but in truth, she wasn't. Always, always there was the yearning lament inside her: She wanted to be his Kristin from the woods of Gerdarud.

Back then she would have done everything she knew was wrong and sinful rather than lose him. To bind Erlend to her, she had given him all that she possessed: her love and her body, her honor and her share of God's salvation. And she had given him anything else she could find to give: her father's honor and his faith in his child, everything that grown and clever men had built up to protect an innocent little maiden if she should fall. She had set her love against their plans for the welfare and progress of her lineage, against their hopes for the fruit of their labors after they themselves lay buried. She had put at risk much more than her own life in this game, in which the only prize was the love of Erlend Nikulaussøn.

And she had won. She had known from the first time he kissed her in the garden of Hofvin until he kissed her today in the little house, before he was escorted from his home as a prisoner—Erlend loved her as dearly as his own life. And if he had not counseled her well, she had known from the first moment she met him how he had counseled himself. If he had not always treated her well, he had nonetheless treated her better than he did himself.

Jesus, how she had won him! She admitted it to herself tonight; she had driven him to break their marriage vows with her own coldness and poisonous words. She now admitted to herself that even during those years when she had looked on his unseemly flirting with that woman Sunniva with resentment, she had also felt, in the midst of her rancor, an arrogant and spiteful joy. No one knew of any obvious stain on Sunniva Olavsdatter's reputation, and yet Erlend talked and jested with her like a hired man with an alehouse maid. About Kristin he knew that she could lie and betray those who trusted her most, that she could be willingly lured to the worst of places—and yet he had trusted her, he had honored her as best he could. As easily as he forgot his fear of sin, as easily as he had finally broken his promise to God before the church door—he had still grieved over his sins against her, he had struggled for years to keep his promises to her.

She had chosen him herself. She had chosen him in an ecstasy of passion, and she had chosen him again each day during those difficult years back home at Jørundgaard—his impetuous passion in place of her father's love, which would not allow even the wind to touch her harshly. She had refused the destiny that her father had wished for her when he wanted to put her into the arms of a man who would have safely led her onto the most secure paths, even bending down to remove every little pebble that she might tread upon. She had chosen to follow the other man, whom she knew traveled on dangerous paths. Monks and priests had pointed out remorse and repentance as the road home to peace, but she had chosen strife rather than give up her precious sin.

So there was only one thing left for her; she could not lament or complain over whatever might now befall her at this man's side. It made her dizzy to think how long ago she had left her father. But she saw his beloved face and remembered his words on that day in the smithy when she stabbed the last knife into his heart; she remembered how they talked together up on the mountain that time when she realized that death's door stood open behind her father. It was shameful to complain about the fate she had chosen herself. Holy Olav, help me, so that I do not now prove myself unworthy of my father's love.

Erlend, Erlend . . . When she met him in her youth, life became for her like a roiling river, rushing over cliffs and rocks. During these years at Husaby, life had expanded outward, becoming wide and spacious like a lake, mirroring everything around her. She remembered back home when the Laag overflowed in the spring, stretching wide and gray and mighty along the valley floor, carrying with it drifting logs; and the crowns of the trees that stood rooted to the bottom would rock in the water. In the middle appeared small, dark, menacing eddies, where the current ran rough and wild and dangerous beneath the smooth surface. Now she knew that her love for Erlend had rushed like a turbulent and dangerous current through her life for all these years. Now it was carrying her outward—she didn't know where.

Erlend, dear friend!

Once again Kristin spoke the words of a prayer to the Virgin into the red of the evening. Hail Mary, full of grace! I dare not ask you for more than one thing—I see that now. Save Erlend, save my husband's life!

She looked down at Husaby and thought about her sons. Now, as the manor lay swathed in the evening light like a dream vision that might be whirled away, as her fear for the uncertain fate of her children shook her heart, she remembered this: She had never fully thanked God for the rich fruits her toils had borne over the years, she had never fully thanked Him for giving her a son seven times.

From the vault of the evening sky, from the countryside beneath her gaze came the murmur of the mass intoned as she had heard it thousands of times before, in the voice of her father, who had explained the words to her when she was a child and stood at his knee: Then Sira Eirik sings the *Præfatio* when he turns toward the altar, and in Norwegian it means:

> Truly it is right and just, proper and redemptive that we always and everywhere should thank Thee, Holy Lord, Almighty Father, eternal God. . . .

When she lifted her face from her hands, she saw Gaute coming up the hillside. Kristin sat quietly and waited until the boy stood before her; then she reached out to take his hand. There was grassy meadow all around and not a single place to hide anywhere near the rock where she sat.

"How have you carried out your father's errand, my son?" she asked him softly.

"As he asked me to, Mother. I made my way to the farm without being seen. Ulf wasn't home, so I burned what Father had given me in the hearth. I took it out of the wrapping." He hesitated for a moment. "Mother—there were nine seals on it."

"My Gaute." His mother put her hands on the boy's shoulders and looked into his face. "Your father has had to place important matters in your hands. If you don't know what else to do, but you feel you need to speak of this to someone, then tell your mother what's troubling you. But it would please me most if you could keep silent about this altogether, son!"

The fair complexion beneath the straight, flaxen hair, the big eyes, the full, firm red lips—he looked so much like her father now. Gaute nodded. Then he placed his arm around his mother's shoulders. With painful sweetness Kristin noticed that she could lean her head against the boy's frail chest; he was so tall now that as he stood there and she sat beside him, her head reached to just above his heart. It was the first time she had leaned for support against this child.

Gaute said, "Isak was home alone. I didn't show him what I was carrying, just told him I had something that needed to be burned. Then he made a big fire in the hearth before he went out and saddled his horse."

Kristin nodded. Then he released her, turned to face her, and asked in a childish voice full of fear and awe, "Mother, do you know what they're saying? They're saying that Father . . . wants to be *king*."

"That sounds most unlikely, child," she replied with a smile.

"But he comes from the proper lineage, Mother," said the boy, somber and proud. "And it seems to me that Father might be better at it than most other men."

"Hush." She took his hand again. "My Gaute . . . you should realize, after Father has shown such trust in you . . . You and all the rest of us must neither think nor speak, but guard our tongues well until we learn more and can judge whether we ought to speak, and in what way. I'm going to ride to Nidaros tomorrow, and if I can talk to your father alone for a moment, I'll tell him that you have carried out his errand well."

"Take me with you, Mother!" begged the boy earnestly.

"We must not let anyone think you're anything but a thoughtless child, Gaute. You will have to try, little son, to play and be as happy as you can at home—in that way you will serve him best."

Naakkve and Bjørgulf walked slowly up the hill. They came over to their mother and stood there, looking so young and strained and distraught. Kristin saw that they were still children enough to turn to their mother at this anxious time—and yet they were so close to being men that they wanted to console or reassure her, if they could find some way to do so. She reached out a hand to each of the boys. But neither of them said very much.

After a while they headed back home; Kristin walked with one hand on the shoulder of each of her eldest sons.

"Why are you looking at me that way, Naakkve?" she said. But the boy blushed, turned his head away, and did not reply.

He had never before thought about how his mother looked. It had been years ago that he began comparing his father to other men—his father was the most handsome of men, with the bearing most like a chieftain. His mother was the mother who had more and more children; they grew up and left the hands of women to join the life and companionship and fighting and friendship of the group of brothers. His mother had open hands through which everything they needed flowed; his mother had a remedy for almost every ill; his mother's presence at the manor was like the fire in the hearth. She created life at home the way the fields around Husaby created the year's crops; life and warmth issued from her as they did from the beasts in the cowshed and the horses in the stable. The boy had never thought to compare her to other women.

Tonight he suddenly saw it: She was a proud and beautiful woman. With her broad, pale forehead beneath the linen wimple, the even gaze of her steel-gray eyes under the calm arch of her brows, with her heavy bosom and her long, slender limbs. She held her tall figure as erect as a sword. But he could not speak of this; blushing and silent, he walked beside her, with her hand on the nape of his neck.

Gaute followed along behind. Bjørgulf was also gripping the back of his mother's belt, and the older boy began grumbling because his brother was treading on his heels. They started shoving and pushing at each other. Their mother told them to hush and put an end to their quarreling—but her somber expression softened into a smile. They were still just children, her sons.

She lay awake that night; she had Munan sleeping at her breast and Lavrans lay between her and the wall.

Kristin tried to take stock of her husband's case.

She couldn't believe that it was truly dangerous. Erling Vidkunssøn and the king's cousins at Sudrheim had been charged with treason against their king and country—but they were still here in Norway, as secure and rich as ever, although they might not stand as high in the king's favor as before.

No doubt Erlend had become involved in some unlawful activities in the service of Lady Ingebjørg. Over all these years he had maintained his friendship with his highborn kinswoman. Kristin knew that five years back, when he visited her in Denmark, he had done her some unlawful service that had to be kept secret. Now that Erling Vidkunssøn had taken up Lady Ingebjørg's cause and was trying to acquire for her control of the property she owned in Norway—it was conceivable that Erling had sent her to Erlend, or that she herself had turned to the son of her father's cousin after the friendship had cooled between Erling and the king. And then Erlend had handled the matter recklessly.

Yet if that was true, it was hard to understand how her kinsmen at Sundbu could have been involved in this.

It could only end with Erlend coming to a full reconciliation with the king, if he had done nothing more than act overzealously in service of the king's mother.

High treason. She had heard about the downfall of Audun Hugleikssøn; it had happened during her father's youth. But they were terrifying misdeeds that Audun had been charged with. Her father said it was all a lie. The maiden Margret Eiriksdatter had died in the arms of the bishop of Bjørgvin, but Audun took no part in the crusade, so he could not have sold her to the heathens. Maiden Isabel was thirteen years old, but Audun was more than fifty when he brought her home to be King Eirik's bride. It was shameful for a Christian to pay any heed at all to such rumors as there were about that bridal procession. Her father refused to allow the ballads about Audun to be sung at home on his manor. And yet there were unheard-of things said about Audun Hestakorn. He had supposedly sold all of King Haakon's military power to the French king and promised to sail to his aid with twelve hundred warships—and for that he had received seven barrels of gold in payment. But it had never been fully explained to the peasants of the country why Audun Hugleikssøn had to die on the gallows at Nordnes.

His son fled the country; people said he had taken service in the army of the French king. The granddaughters of the Aalhus knight, Gyrid and Signe, had left their grandfather's execution site with his stable boy. They were to live like poor peasant wives somewhere in a mountain village in Haddingjadal.

It was a good thing, after all, that she and Erlend did not have daughters. No, she was not going to think about such matters. It was so unlikely that Erlend's case should have a worse outcome than . . . than that of Erling Vidkunssøn and the Haftorssøns.

Nikulaus Erlendssøn of Husaby. Oh, now she too felt that Husaby was the most beautiful manor in all of Norway.

She would go to Sir Baard and find out all she could. The royal treasurer had always been her friend. Judge Olav, as well—in the past. But Erlend had gone too far, that time when the judge decided against him in the case of his estate in town. And Olav had taken to heart the misfortune with his goddaughter's husband.

They had no close kinsmen, neither she nor Erlend—no matter how extensive their lineage might be. Munan Baardsøn no longer had great influence. He had been charged with unlawful deeds when he was sheriff of Ringerike; he was too eager in his attempts to further the position of his many children in the world—he had four from his marriage and five outside of it. And he had apparently declined greatly since Fru Katrin had died. Inge of Ry county, Julitta and her husband, Ragnrid who was married to a Swede—Erlend knew little of them. They were the remaining children of Herr Baard and Fru Aashild. There had never been friendship between Erlend and the Hestnes people since the death of Sir Baard Petersøn; Tormod of Raasvold had grown senile; and his children with Fru Gunna were all dead and his grandchildren underage.

Kristin herself had no other kinsmen in Norway from her father's lineage than Ketil Aasmundssøn of Skog and Sigurd Kyrning, who was married to her uncle's oldest daughter. The second daughter was a widow, and the third was a nun. All four of the men of Sundbu seemed to be involved in the case. Lavrans had become such foes with Erlend Eldjarn over the inheritance after Ivar Gjesling's death that they had refused to see each other ever again, so Kristin did not know her aunt's husband or his son.

The ailing monk at the friars' monastery was Erlend's only close kinsman. And the one who stood closest to Kristin in the world was Simon Darre, since he was married to her only sister.

Munan woke up and began to whimper. Kristin turned over in bed and placed the child to her other breast. She couldn't take him with her to Nidaros, as uncertain as everything now stood. Perhaps this would be the last drink the poor child would ever have from his own mother's breast. Perhaps this was the last time in this world that she would lie in bed holding a little infant . . . so good, so good . . . If Erlend was condemned to death . . . Blessed Mary, Mother of God, if she had ever for an hour or a day been impatient because of the children that God had granted to her . . . Was this to be the last kiss she ever received from a little mouth, sweet with milk?

## CHAPTER 5

Kristin went to the king's palace the next evening, as soon as she arrived in Nidaros. Where are they holding Erlend? she wondered as she looked around at the many stone buildings. She seemed to be thinking more about how Erlend might be faring than about what she needed to find out. But she was told that the royal treasurer was not in town.

Her eyes were stinging from the long boat trip in the glittering sunshine, and her breasts were bursting with milk. After the servants who slept in the main house had fallen asleep, she got out of bed and paced the floor all night.

The next day she sent Haldor, her personal servant, over to the king's palace. He came back shocked and distressed.

His uncle, Ulf Haldorssøn, had been taken prisoner on the fjord as he attempted to reach the monastery on the island of Holm. The royal treasurer had not yet returned.

This news also frightened Kristin terribly. Ulf had not lived at Husaby during the past year but had served as the sheriff's deputy, residing for the most part at Skjoldvirkstad, a large share of which he now owned. What kind of matter could this be when so many men seemed to be involved? She couldn't stop herself from thinking the worst, ill and exhausted as she now was.

By the morning of the third day, Sir Baard had still not returned home. And a message that Kristin had tried to send to her husband was not allowed through. She thought about seeking out Gunnulf at the monastery, but decided against it. She paced the floor at home, back and forth, again and again, with her eyes half-closed and burning. Now and then she felt as if she were walking in her sleep, but as soon as she lay down, fear and pain would seize hold of her and she would have to get up again, wide awake, and walk to make it bearable.

Shortly after mid-afternoon prayers Gunnulf Nikulaussøn came to see her. Kristin walked swiftly toward the monk.

"Have you seen Erlend? Gunnulf, what are they accusing him of?"

"The news is troubling, Kristin. No, they won't allow anyone near Erlend—least of all any of us from the monastery. They think that Abbot Olav knew about his undertakings. He borrowed money from the brothers, but they swear they knew nothing about what he intended to use it for when they placed the cloister's seal on the document. And Abbot Olav refuses to give any explanation."

"Yes, but what is it all about? Was it the duchess who lured Erlend into this?"

Gunnulf replied, "It seems instead that they had to press hard before she would agree. Someone . . . has seen drafts of a letter, which Erlend and his friends sent to her in the spring; it's not likely to fall into the hands of the authorities unless they can threaten Lady Ingebjørg to part with it. And they haven't found any drafts. But according to both the reply letter and the letter from Herr Aage Laurisen, which they seized from Borgar Trondssøn in Veøy, it seems certain enough that she did receive such a missive from Erlend and the men who have joined forces with him in this plan. For a long time she clearly seemed to fear sending Prince Haakon to Norway; but they persuaded her that no matter what the outcome might be, King Magnus would not possibly harm the child, since they are brothers. Even if Haakon Knutssøn did not win the Crown in Norway, he would be no worse off than before. But these men were willing to risk their lives and their property to put him on the throne."

For a long time Kristin sat in utter silence.

"I understand. These are more serious matters than what came between Sir Erling or the Haftorssøns and the king."

"Yes," said Gunnulf in a subdued voice. "Haftor Olavssøn and Erlend were supposedly sailing to Bjørgvin. But they were actually heading for Kalundborg, and they were to bring Prince Haakon back with them to Norway while King Magnus was abroad courting his bride."

After a moment the monk continued in the same tone of voice. "It must be . . . nearly a hundred years since any Norwegian has dared attempt such a thing: to overthrow the man who was king by right of succession and replace him with an opposing king."

Kristin sat and stared straight ahead; Gunnulf could not see her face.

"Yes. The last men who dared undertake this game were your ancestors and Erlend's. Back then my deceased kinsmen of the Gjesling lineage were also on the side of King Skule," she said pensively.

She met Gunnulf's searching glance and then exclaimed hotly and fiercely, "I'm merely a simple woman, Gunnulf—I paid little attention when my husband spoke with other men about such matters. I was unwilling to listen when he wanted to discuss them with me. God help me, I don't have the wits to understand such weighty topics. But foolish woman that I am, with knowledge of nothing more than my household duties and rearing children—even I know that justice had much too long a road to travel before any grievance could find its way to the king and then back again to the villages. I too have seen that the peasants of this country are faring worse and must endure more hardships now than when I was a child, and blessed King Haakon was our lord. My husband . . ." She took several quick, shuddery breaths. "My husband took up a cause that was so great that none of the other chieftains in all the land dared raise it. I see that now."

"That he did." The monk clasped his hands tightly together. His voice was hardly more than a whisper. "Such a great cause that many will think it very grave that he brought about its downfall himself . . . and in this way . . ."

Kristin cried out and leaped to her feet. She moved with such force that the pain in her breast and arms brought the sweat pouring from her body. Agitated and dizzy with fever, she turned to Gunnulf and shouted loudly, "Erlend is not to blame . . . it just happened . . . it was his misfortune . . ."

She threw herself to her knees and pressed her hands on the bench; she lifted her blazing, desperate face to the monk.

"You and I, Gunnulf . . . you, his brother, and I, his wife for thirteen years, we shouldn't blame Erlend now that he's a poor prisoner, with his life perhaps in danger."

Gunnulf's face quivered. He looked down at the kneeling woman. "May God reward you, Kristin, for accepting things in this manner." Again he wrung his emaciated hands. "God . . . may God grant Erlend life and such circumstances that he might repay your loyalty. May God turn this evil away from you and your children, Kristin."

"Don't talk like that!" She straightened her back as she knelt, and looked up into the monk's eyes. "No good has come of it, Gunnulf, whenever you have taken on Erlend's affairs or mine. No one has judged him more harshly than you—his brother and God's servant."

"Never have I judged Erlend more harshly than . . . than was necessary." His pale face had grown even paler. "I've never loved anyone on earth more than my brother. That is no doubt why . . . They stung me as if they were my own sins, sins that I had to repent myself, when Erlend dealt with you so badly. And then there is Husaby. Erlend alone must carry on the lineage which is also mine. And I have put most of my inheritance into his hands. Your sons are the men who are closest to me by blood. . . ."

"Erlend has *not* dealt with me badly! I was no better than him! Why are you talking to me this way, Gunnulf? You were never my confessor. Sira Eiliv never blamed my husband—he admonished *me* for my sins whenever I complained of my difficulties to him. He was a better priest than you are; he's the one God has placed over me, he's the one I must listen to, and he has never said that I suffered unjustly. I will listen to him!"

Gunnulf stood up when she did. Pale and distressed, he murmured, "What you say is true. You must listen to Sira Eiliv."

He turned to go, but she gripped his hand tightly. "No, don't leave me like this! I remember, Gunnulf . . . I remember when I visited you here on this estate, back when it belonged to you. And you were kind to me. I remember the first time I met you—I was in great need and anguish. I remember you spoke to me in Erlend's defense; you couldn't know . . . You prayed and prayed for my life and my child's. I know that you meant us well, and that you loved Erlend. . . .

"Oh, don't speak harshly of Erlend, Gunnulf! Who among us is pure before God? My father grew fond of him, and our children love their father. Remember that he found me weak and easy to sway, but he led me to a good and honorable place. Oh, yes, Husaby is beautiful. On the night before I left, it was so lovely; the sunset was magnificent that evening. We've spent many a good day there, Erlend and I. No matter how things go, no matter what happens, he is still my husband—my husband, whom I love."

Gunnulf leaned both hands on his staff, which he always carried now whenever he left the monastery.

"Kristin . . . Do not put your faith in the red of the sunset and in the . . . love that you remember, now that you fear for his life.

"I remember, when I was young—only a subdeacon. Gudbjørg, whom Alf of Uvaasen later married, was serving at Siheim then. She was accused of stealing a gold ring. It turned out that she was innocent, but the shame and the fear shook her soul so fiercely that the Fiend seized power over her. She went down to the lake and was about to sink into the water. She has often told us of this afterwards: that the world seemed to her such a lovely red and gold, and the water glistened and felt wondrously warm. But as she stood out there in the lake, she spoke the name of Jesus and made the sign of the cross—and then the whole world grew gray and cold, and she saw where she was headed."

"Then I won't say his name." Kristin spoke quietly; her bearing was rigid and erect. "If I thought that, then I would be tempted to betray my lord when he is in need. But I don't think it would be the name of Christ but rather the name of the Devil that would bring this about. . . ."

"That's not what I meant. I meant . . . May God give you strength, Kristin, that you may have the will to do this, to bear your husband's faults with a loving spirit."

"You can see that's what I'm doing," she said in the same voice as before.

Gunnulf turned away from her, pale and trembling. He drew his hand over his face.

"I must go home now. It's easier . . . at home it's easier for me to collect myself—to do what I can for Erlend and for you. God . . . May God and all the saints protect my brother's life and freedom. Oh, Kristin . . . You mustn't ever think that I don't love my brother."

But after he had left, Kristin thought everything seemed much worse. She didn't want the servants in the room with her; she paced back and forth, wringing her hands and moaning softly. It was already late in the evening when people came riding into the courtyard. A moment later, as the door was thrown open, a tall, stout man wearing a traveling cloak appeared in the twilight; he walked toward her with his spurs ringing and his sword trailing behind. When she recognized Simon Andressøn, Kristin broke into loud sobbing and ran toward him with outstretched arms, but she shrieked in pain when he embraced her.

Simon let her go. She was standing with her hands on his shoulders and her forehead leaning against his chest, weeping inconsolably. He put his hands lightly on her hips.

"In God's name, Kristin!" There was a sense of deliverance in the very sound of his dry, warm voice and in the vital male smell about him: of sweat, road dust, horses, and leather harnesswork. "In God's name, it's much too soon to lose all hope and courage. Surely there must be a way . . ."

After a while she regained her composure enough to ask his forgiveness. She was feeling quite wretched because she had been forced to take the youngest child from her breast so suddenly.

Simon heard how she had been faring the last three days. He shouted for her maid and asked angrily whether there wasn't a single woman on the estate who had enough wits to see what was wrong with the mistress. But the maid was an inexperienced young girl, and Erlend's foreman of his Nidaros manor was a widower with two unmarried daughters. Simon sent a man to town to find a woman skilled in healing, but he begged Kristin to lie down and rest. When she felt a little better he would come in and talk to her.

While they waited for the woman to arrive, Simon and his man were given food in the hall. As they ate, he talked to Kristin, who was undressing in the alcove. Yes, he had ridden north as soon as he heard what had happened at Sundbu. He had come here, while Ramborg went to stay with the wives of Ivar and Borgar. They had taken Ivar to Mjøs Castle, but they allowed Haavard to remain free, although he had to promise to stay in the village. It was said that Borgar and Guttorm had been fortunate enough to flee; Jon of Laugarbru had ridden out to Raumsdal to hear the news and would send word to Nidaros. Simon had reached Husaby around midday, but he hadn't stayed long. The boys were fine, but Naakkve and Bjørgulf had begged him earnestly to bring them along.

Kristin had regained her calm and courage when Simon, late that evening, came to sit at her bedside. She lay there with the feeling of pleasant exhaustion which follows great suffering, and looked at her brother-in-law's heavy, sunburned face and his small, piercing eyes. It was a great comfort to her that he had come. Simon grew quite somber when he heard more details of the matter, and yet his words were full of hope.

Kristin lay in bed, staring at the elkskin belt around his portly middle. The large, flat buckle made of copper and chased with silver, its only decoration a filigreed "A" and "M" which stood for *Ave Maria;* the long dagger with the gilded silver mountings and the large rock crystals on the hilt; the pitiful little table knife with its cracked horn hilt which had been repaired with a band of brass—all these things had been part of her father's everyday attire ever since she was a child. She remembered when Simon received them; it was right before her father died, and he wanted to give Simon his best gilded belt with enough silver to have extra plates made so that his son-in-law could wear it. But Simon asked for the other belt instead, and when Lavrans said that now he was cheating himself, Simon replied that the dagger was a costly item. "Yes, and then there's the knife," said Ragnfrid with a little smile, and both men laughed and said: "Yes indeed, the knife." Her father and mother had had so many quarrels over that knife. Ragnfrid had complained every day at having to look at that ugly little knife on her husband's belt. But Lavrans swore that she would never succeed in parting him from it. "I've never drawn this knife against you, Ragnfrid—and it's the best one in all of Norway for cutting butter, as long as it's warm."

Kristin now asked to see the knife, and she lay in bed, holding it in her hands for a moment.

"I wish that I might own this knife," she pleaded softly.

"Yes, I can well believe that. I'm glad it's mine; I wouldn't sell it for even twenty marks of silver." With a laugh Simon grabbed her wrist and took back the knife. His small, plump hands always felt so good—warm and dry.

A short time later he bade her good night, picked up the candle, and went into the main room. She heard him kneel down before the cross, then stand up and drop his boots onto the floor. A few minutes later he climbed heavily into the bed against the north wall. Then Kristin sank into a deep, sweet sleep.

She didn't wake up until quite late the next morning. Simon Andressøn had left hours earlier, and he had asked the servants to tell her to stay calm and remain at the estate.

He didn't return until almost time for mid-afternoon prayers; he said at once, "I bring you greetings from Erlend, Kristin. I was allowed to speak to him."

He saw how young her face became, soft and full of anguished tenderness. Then he held her hand in his as he talked. He and Erlend hadn't been able to say much to each other, because the man who had escorted Simon up to the prisoner never left the room. Judge Olav had won Simon permission for this meeting, because of the kinship that had existed between them while Halfrid was alive. Erlend sent loving greetings to Kristin and the children; he had asked about all of them, but most about Gaute. Simon thought that in a few days Kristin would surely be allowed to see her husband. Erlend had seemed calm and in good spirits.

"If I had gone with you today, they would have let me see him too," she said quietly.

But Simon thought he had been granted permission because he came alone. "Although it might be easier for you in many ways, Kristin, to gain concessions if a man steps forward in your behalf."

Erlend was being held in a room in the east tower, facing the river—one of the finer chambers, although it was small. Ulf Haldorssøn was supposedly sitting in the dungeon; Haftor in a different chamber.

Cautiously and hesitantly, as he tried to discern how much she could bear, Simon recounted what he had been able to learn in town. When he saw that she understood fully what had happened, he didn't hide that he too thought it a dangerous matter. But everyone he had spoken to said that Erlend would never have ventured to plan such an undertaking and carry it out as far as he had without being certain that he had a majority of the knights and gentry behind him. And since the ranks of the malcontent noblemen were so great, it wasn't expected that the king would dare deal harshly with their chieftain; he would have to allow Erlend to be reconciled with him in some way.

Kristin asked in a low voice, "Where does Erling Vidkunssøn stand in all this?"

"I think that's something that many a man would like to know," said Simon.

He didn't tell Kristin, nor had he told any of the men he talked to, but he thought it unlikely that Erlend would have a large group of men behind him who had bound themselves to support him with their lives and property in such a perilous undertaking. And certainly they would never have chosen him as chieftain; all his peers knew that Erlend was unreliable. It was true that he was the kinsman of Lady Ingebjørg and the pretender to the throne. He had enjoyed both power and respect in the last few years, he was more experienced in war than most of his peers, and he had a reputation for being able to recruit and lead soldiers. Even though he had acted unwisely so many times, he could still present his arguments in such a good and convincing manner that it was almost possible to believe he had finally learned caution from his misdeeds. Simon thought it likely that there were some who knew of Erlend's plan and had urged him on, but he would be surprised if they had bound themselves so closely that they couldn't now retreat; Erlend would be left standing with no one to back him.

Simon thought he could see that Erlend himself expected little else, and he seemed prepared to have to pay dearly for his risky game. "When cows are stuck in the mire, whoever owns them has to pull them out by the tail," he had said with a laugh. Otherwise Erlend had not been able to say much in the presence of the third man.

Simon wondered why the reunion with his brother-in-law had upset him so greatly. Perhaps it was the small, confining tower room where Erlend had invited him to take a seat on the bed, which stretched from one wall to the other and filled half the room, or Erlend's slender, dignified form as he stood at the small slit in the wall which allowed in light. Erlend looked unafraid, his eyes alert, unclouded by either fear or hope. He was a vigorous, cool, and manly figure now that all the constraining webs of flirtations and foolishness over women had been swept away from him. And yet it was women and his dealings in love that had landed him there, along with all his bold plans, which came to an end before he had even brought them to light. But Erlend didn't seem to be thinking about that. He stood there like a man who had risked the most daring of ventures and lost, and then knew how to bear the defeat in a manly and stalwart fashion.

And his surprised and joyous gratitude when he saw his brother-in-law suited him well.

Simon had said, "Do you remember, brother-in-law, that night we kept watch at our father-in-law's bedside? We shook hands, and Lavrans placed his hand on top. We promised each other and him that all our days we would stand together as brothers."

"Yes." Erlend's smile lit up his face. "Yes, Lavrans probably never thought that you would ever be in need of *my* help."

"It was more likely," said Simon unperturbed, "that he meant *you,* in your circumstances, might be of support to *me,* and not that you should need *my* help."

Erlend smiled again. "Lavrans was a wise man, Simon. And as strange as it may sound, I know he was fond of me."

Simon thought that God knew it might indeed seem strange, but now he himself—in spite of all he knew about Erlend and in spite of everything the other man had done to him—couldn't help feeling a brotherly tenderness toward Kristin's husband. Then Erlend had asked about her.

Simon told him how he had found her: ill and very frightened for her husband. Olav Hermanssøn had promised to seek permission for her to come to see him as soon as Sir Baard returned home.

"Not before she's well," said Erlend quickly, his voice fearful. An odd, almost girlish blush spread across his tan, unshaven face. "That's the only thing I fear, Simon—that I won't be able to bear it when I see her!"

But after a moment he said calmly, "I know you will stand steadfast at her side if she is to be widowed this year. They won't be poor, at any rate—she and the children—with her inheritance from Lavrans. And then she'll have you close at hand when she goes to live at Jørundgaard."

The day after the Feast of the Birth of Mary, the lord chancellor, Ivar Ogmundssøn, arrived in Nidaros. A court was now appointed, consisting of twelve of the king's retainers from the northern districts, to decide Erlend Nikulaussøn's case. Sir Finn

Ogmundssøn, the lord chancellor's brother, was chosen to present the charges against him.

In the meantime, during the summer, Haftor Olavssøn of Godøy had killed himself, using the little dagger that every prisoner was allowed to keep to cut up his food. Imprisonment had apparently taken such a toll on Haftor that he hadn't had his full wits about him. When Erlend heard of this, he told Simon that at least now he wouldn't have to worry about what Haftor might say. And yet he was clearly shaken.

Gradually it became a habit for the guard to leave the room on an errand whenever Simon or Kristin was visiting Erlend. Both of them realized, and mentioned it to each other, that Erlend's first and foremost thought was to make it through the court case without revealing his accomplices. One day he said this quite openly to Simon. He had promised every man who had conspired with him that he would rather cut off his own hand than reveal anything, if it came to that; "and I have never yet betrayed anyone who has put their trust in me." Simon stared at the man. Erlend's eyes were blue and clear; it was obvious that he truly believed this about himself.

The king's envoys had not succeeded in tracking down anyone else who had taken part in Erlend's plot other than the two brothers, Greip and Torvard Toressøn of Møre. And they refused to admit to knowing anything but that Erlend and several other men planned to persuade Lady Ingebjørg to allow Prince Haakon Knutssøn to be educated in Norway. Later the chieftains would propose to King Magnus that it would be of benefit to both of his kingdoms if he gave his half-brother sovereignty in Norway.

Borgar and Guttorm Trondssøn had been fortunate enough to escape from the king's castle at Veøy. No one knew how, but people guessed that Borgar had been helped by a woman. He was very handsome and quite impetuous. Ivar of Sundbu was still being held in Mjøs Castle; the brothers had apparently kept young Haavard out of their plans.

At the same time the meeting of the retainers was being held at the king's palace, the archbishop convened a *concilium* at his estate. Simon was a man with many friends and acquaintances, and so he could report to Kristin what was happening. Everyone thought that Erlend would be banished and would have to forfeit his properties to the king. Erlend also thought this was how things would turn out, and he was in good spirits; he was planning to go to Denmark. As things now stood in that country, there were always opportunities open for a man who was fit and skilled with weapons, and Lady Ingebjørg would surely embrace his wife as her kinswoman and keep her at her side with the proper honors. Simon would have to take care of the children, although Erlend wanted to take his two eldest sons with him.

Kristin hadn't been outside of Nidaros for a single day in all this time, nor had she seen her children, except for Naakkve and Bjørgulf. They had come riding up to the estate one evening alone. Their mother kept them with her for several days, but then she sent them to Raasvold, where Fru Gunna had taken in the younger boys.

This was in accordance with Erlend's wishes. And she was afraid of the thoughts that might rise up in her mind if she should see her sons around her, hear their questions, and try to explain matters to them. She struggled to push aside all thoughts and memories of her marriage years spent at Husaby, which had been so rich that now they seemed to her like a great calm—the way there is a kind of calm over the waves of the sea if viewed from high enough up a mountain ridge. The swells that surge after each other seem eternal, melding into one; that was the way life had rippled through her soul during that vast span of years.

Now things were once again the way they had been in her youth, when she had put her faith in Erlend, defying everyone and everything. Once again her life had become one long waiting from hour to hour, in between the times when she was allowed to see her husband, to sit at his side on the bed in the tower room of the king's palace, and to talk with him calmly—until they happened to be alone for a few moments. Then they would throw themselves into each other's arms with endless, passionate kisses and wild embraces.

At other times she would sit in Christ Church for hours on end. She would sink to her knees and stare up at Saint Olav's golden shrine behind the gratings of the choir. Lord, I am his wife. Lord, I stood by him when I was his, in sin and iniquity. By the grace of God, we two unworthy souls were joined together in holy marriage. Branded by the flames of sin, bowed by the burdens of sin, we came together at the portals of God's house; together we received the Savior's Host from the hand of the priest. Should I now complain if God is testing my faith? Should I now think about anything else but that I am his wife and he is my husband for as long as we both shall live?

On the Thursday before Michaelmas the meeting of the royal retainers was held and sentence was pronounced over Erlend Nikulaussøn of Husaby. He was found guilty of attempting to steal land and subjects from King Magnus, of inciting opposition to the king throughout the country, and of attempting to bring into Norway mercenary forces from abroad. After looking into similar cases from the past, the judges found that Erlend Nikulaussøn should forfeit his life and his property at the hands of King Magnus.

Arne Gjavvaldssøn brought the news to Simon Darre and Kristin Lavransdatter at Nikulausgaard. He had been present at the meeting.

Erlend had not tried to prove his innocence. In a clear, firm voice he had acknowledged his intentions: With these undertakings he had sought to force King Magnus Eirikssøn to grant the Crown of Norway to his young half-brother, Prince Haakon Knutssøn Porse. Erlend had spoken eloquently, thought Arne. He had talked about the great hardships that had befallen his countrymen because for the past few years the king had spent little time within Norway's boundaries and had never seemed willing to appoint representatives who could rule justly and exercise royal authority. Because of the king's actions in Skaane, and because of the extravagance and inability to handle money matters shown by those men he listened to most, the people had been subjected to great burdens and poverty. And they never felt safe from new demands for aid and taxes above what was normally expected. Since the Norwegian knights and noblemen had far fewer rights and freedom than the Swedish knighthood, it was difficult for the former to compete with the latter. And it was only reasonable that the young and imprudent man, King Magnus Eirikssøn, should listen more to his Swedish lords and love them better, since they had more wealth and thus a greater ability to support him with men who were both armed and experienced in war.

Erlend and his allies had thought they could sense such strong feelings among the majority of their countrymen—the gentry, farmers, and townsmen in the north and west of Norway—that they were certain of finding full support if they could produce a royal rival who was as closely related to our dear lord, the blessed King Haakon, as the king who was now in power. Erlend had expected that his countrymen would rally around the plan to persuade King Magnus to allow his brother to assume the throne here, but Prince Haakon would have to swear to maintain peace and brotherhood with King Magnus, to protect the kingdom of Norway in accordance with the ancient land boundaries, to assert the rights of God's Church, to enforce the laws and customs of the land according to ancient tradition, along with the rights and freedoms of the peasants and townsmen, as well as to fend off any incursion of foreigners into the realm. It had been the intention of Erlend and his friends to present this plan to King Magnus in a peaceful manner. And yet it had always been the right of Norwegian farmers and chieftains in the past to reject any king who attempted to rule unlawfully.

As to the actions of Ulf Saksesøn in England and Scotland, Erlend said that Ulf's sole purpose had been to win favor there for Prince Haakon, if God should grant that he became king. No other Norwegian man had taken part in these endeavors except for Haftor Olavssøn of Godøy—may God have mercy on his soul—the three sons of his kinsman Trond Gjesling of Sundbu, and Greip and Torvard Toressøn of the Hatteberg lineage.

Erlend's speech had made a deep impression, said Arne Gjavvaldssøn. But in the end, when he mentioned that they had expected support from men of the Church, he then referred to the old rumors from the days when King Magnus was growing up, and that had been unwise, thought Arne. The archbishop's representative had responded sharply: Archbishop Paal Baardsøn, both now and when he was chancellor, felt great love for King Magnus because of his godly temperament, and people wanted to forget that these rumors had ever existed about their king. Now he was about to marry a maiden, the daughter of the Earl of Namur . . . so even if there had ever been any truth to the rumors, Magnus Eirikssøn had now completely turned away from such interests.

Arne Gjavvaldssøn had shown Simon Andressøn the greatest friendship while he was in Nidaros. It was also Arne who now reminded Simon that Erlend had the right to appeal this sentence as having been unlawfully decided. According to the law books, the charge against Erlend had to be brought by one of his peers, but Sir Finn of Hestbø was a knight, while Erlend was a nobleman, but not a knight. Arne thought it was possible that a new court would find that Erlend could not be sentenced to a harsher punishment than banishment.

In terms of what Erlend had proposed, about the kind of sovereignty which he thought would serve the country best . . . that had sounded fine indeed. And everyone knew where the man was who would like to take the helm and steer that course while the new king was underage. Arne scratched the gray stubble of his beard and gave Simon a sidelong glance.

"No one has heard from Erling Vidkunssøn or spoken to him all summer?" asked Simon, also keeping his voice low.

"No. Well, I've heard he says he's fallen out of favor with the king and is keeping out of all such matters. But it's been years since he could stand to sit at home for such a long time and listen to Fru Elin chattering. And people say his daughters are just as beautiful and just as foolish as their mother."

Erlend had listened to his sentence with a steadfast, calm expression, and he had greeted the gentlemen of the royal retinue in just as courteous, open, and splendid a manner when he was led out as when he had been escorted in. He was calm and cheerful when Kristin and Simon were allowed to talk to him the following day. Arne Gjavvaldssøn was with them, and Erlend said that he would take Arne's advice.

"I could never persuade Kristin here to come with me to Denmark before," he said, putting an arm around his wife's waist. "And I always had such a desire to journey out into the world with her. . . ." A tremor seemed to pass over his features, and suddenly he pressed an ardent kiss to her pale cheek, without concern for the two men who stood looking on.

Simon Andressøn set off for Husaby to make arrangements for Kristin's personal possessions to be moved to Jørundgaard. He had also advised her to send the children to Gudbrandsdal at the same time.

Kristin said, "My sons will not leave their father's estate until they are driven from it."

"I wouldn't wait for that, if I were you," said Simon. "They're young; they can't fully understand these things. It would be better if you let them leave Husaby believing that they are merely going to visit their aunt and see their mother's property in the valley."

Erlend said that Simon was right about this. But in the end only Ivar and Skule traveled with their uncle south. Kristin didn't have the heart to send the two youngest boys so far away from her. When Lavrans and Munan were brought to her at the estate in town and she saw that the smallest didn't even recognize her, she broke down. Simon hadn't seen her shed a single tear since the first evening he arrived in Nidaros; now she wept and wept over Munan, who squirmed and wriggled in the crush of his mother's arms, wanting to go to his foster mother. And she wept over little Lavrans, who crept up into his mother's lap and put his arms around her neck and cried because she was crying. Now she would keep the two youngest with her, along with Gaute, who didn't want to go with Simon. She also thought it ill-advised to let the child out of her sight, since he had to bear a burden that was much too heavy for his age.

Sira Eiliv had brought the children to Nidaros. He had asked the archbishop for leave from his church and permission to visit his brother in Tautra; this was gladly granted to Erlend Nikulaussøn's house priest. Now he said that Kristin couldn't stay in town with so many children to care for, and he offered to take Naakkve and Bjørgulf out to the monastery.

On the last evening before the priest and the two boys were to depart—Simon had already left with the twins—Kristin made her confession to the pious and pure-hearted man who had been her spiritual father all these years. They sat together for hours, and Sira Eiliv impressed upon her heart that she must be humble and obedient toward God; patient, faithful, and loving toward her husband. She knelt before the bench where he sat. Then Sira Eiliv stood up and knelt at her side, still wearing the red stole which was a symbol of the yoke of Christ's love; he prayed long and fervently, without words. But she knew he was praying for the father and mother and the children and all the servants whose salvation he had striven so faithfully to encourage all these years.

The next day Kristin stood on the shore of Bratør and watched the lay brothers from Tautra set sail in the boat that would carry away the priest and her two eldest sons. On her way home she went over to the Minorites' church and stayed there until she felt strong enough to venture back to her own residence. And in the evening, when the two youngest were asleep, she sat with her spinning and told Gaute stories until it was his bedtime too.

## CHAPTER 6

ERLEND WAS HELD at the king's palace until almost Saint Clement's Day. Then messages and letters arrived stating that he was to be taken under safe conduct to meet with King Magnus. The king intended to celebrate Christmas at Baagahus that year.

Kristin grew terribly frightened. With unspeakable effort she had accustomed herself to feigning a calm demeanor while Erlend sat in prison, condemned to death. Now he would be taken far away to an uncertain fate. Much was said about the king, and among the circle of men who stood closest to him, her husband had no friends. Ivar Ogmundssøn, who was now the chieftain of the castle at Baagahus, had spoken the harshest words regarding Erlend's treason. And he was supposedly further enraged at having heard once again some disrespectful remarks which Erlend had made about him.

But Erlend was in good spirits. Kristin could see that he didn't take their imminent separation lightly, but the long imprisonment had now begun to wear him down; he eagerly seized upon the prospect of a long sea voyage and seemed almost indifferent to everything else.

In a matter of three days everything was arranged, and Erlend sailed with Sir Finn's ship. Simon had promised to return to Nidaros before Advent, after he had taken care of some obligations at home. If there was any news before then, he had asked Kristin to send word to him, and he would come at once. Now she decided to travel south to visit him, and from there she would go to see the king—to fall at his feet and beg for mercy for her husband. She would gladly give all she possessed in return for his life.

Erlend had sold and mortgaged every part of his residence in Nidaros to various buyers; Nidarholm cloister now owned the main house, but Abbot Olav had written a kind letter to Kristin, offering her the use of the house for as long as she needed it. She was living there alone with one maid and Ulf Haldorssøn—who had been released because they hadn't been able to prove anything against him—and his nephew, Haldor, who was Kristin's personal servant.

She sought Ulf's counsel, and at first he was rather doubtful. He thought it would be a difficult journey for her through the Dovre Range; a great deal of snow had fallen in the mountains. But when he saw the anguish of her soul, he advised her to go. Fru Gunna took the two youngest children out to Raasvold, but Gaute refused to be parted from his mother, and she didn't dare let the boy out of her sight up there in the north.

The weather was so severe when they came south to the Dovre Range that they followed Ulf's advice to leave their horses behind at Drivstuen and borrowed skis, prepared to spend the next night out in the open if need be. Kristin hadn't had skis on her feet since she was a child, so it was difficult for her to make progress, even though the men supported her as best they could. They reached no farther that day than halfway over the mountain, between Drivstuen and Hjerdkinn. When it began to grow dark, they had to seek shelter in a birch grove and dig themselves into the snow. At Toftar they managed to hire some horses, but there they ran into fog, and when they had descended partway into the valley, rain set in. When they rode into the courtyard of Formo several hours after dark, the wind was howling around the corners of the buildings, the river was roaring, and a great rushing and droning came from the forested slopes. The courtyard was a soggy mire, muffling the sound of the horses' hooves. As the Sabbath had already begun at this hour on Saturday evening, there was no sign of life on the large estate, and neither the servants nor the dogs seemed to have noticed their arrival.

Ulf pounded on the door to the main house with his spear; a serving man opened the door. A moment later Simon himself was standing in the entryway, broad and dark against the light behind him, holding a child in his arms. He pushed back the barking dogs. He gave a shout when he recognized his wife's sister, set the child down, and then pulled Kristin and Gaute inside as he helped them out of their soaked outer garments.

It was splendidly warm in the room, but the air seemed oppressive because it was a hearth room with a flat ceiling beneath the loft hall. And it was full of people; children and dogs were swarming from every corner. Then Kristin caught sight of both of her own small sons, their faces ruddy and warm and gleeful, behind the table on which a lighted candle stood. The two boys came forward and greeted their mother and brother a bit awkwardly; Kristin could see that they had arrived in the midst of everyone's merriment and fun. And the room was in great disarray. She stepped on crunching nutshells at every turn—they were scattered all over the floor.

Simon sent his servants off to do chores, and the room was emptied of people—neighbors and their attendants, as well as most of the children and dogs. While he asked questions and listened to her replies, Simon fastened his shirt and tunic, which were open wide, revealing his bare, hairy chest. The children had brought him to such a state, he said apologetically. He was terribly disheveled; his belt was twisted around, his clothes and hands were dirty, his face was covered with soot, and his hair was full of straw and dust.

A few minutes later two serving women came in to take Kristin and Gaute over to Ramborg's women's house. A fire had been started in the fireplace, and several maids busily lit the candles, made up the beds, and helped her and the boy into dry clothes, while others set the table with food and drink. A half-grown maiden with silk-wrapped braids brought Kristin a frothy bowl of ale. The girl was Simon's eldest daughter, Arngjerd.

Then Simon came into the room. He had tidied himself up and now looked more as Kristin was used to seeing him, handsomely and splendidly dressed. He was leading his little daughter by the hand, and Ivar and Skule followed.

Kristin asked about her sister, and Simon replied that Ramborg had accompanied the Sundbu women down to Ringheim; Jostein had come to get his daughter, Helga, and then he wanted Dagny and Ramborg to come along too. He was such a merry, kind old man, and he had promised to take good care of the three young wives. Ramborg might stay there all winter. She was expecting a child around Saint Matthew's Day, and Simon had thought he might have to be away from home that winter, so she would be better off with her young kinswomen. No, it made no difference to the housekeeping here at Formo whether she was home or not, laughed Simon. He had never demanded that young Ramborg trouble herself with all that toil.

As to Kristin's plans, Simon said at once that he would travel south with her. He had so many kinsmen there, as well as his father's friends and his own from the past, that he hoped to be able to serve her better than he had in Nidaros. And there it would be easier for him to determine whether it would be wise for her to pay a visit to the king himself. He could be ready to travel in three or four days.

They attended mass together the next day, which was Sunday, and afterwards they visited Sira Eirik at his home at Romundgaard. The priest was old now. He received Kristin kindly and seemed very saddened by her troubling fate. Then they went over to Jørundgaard.

The buildings looked the same, and the rooms held the same beds, benches, and tables. It was now her property, and it seemed most likely that her sons would grow up here; this was also where she herself would one day lie down and close her eyes. But never had she felt so clearly as at this moment that life in this home had depended on her father and mother. No matter what they had struggled with in private, from them had streamed warmth, help, peace, and security to everyone else who lived there.

Uneasy and dejected as she now felt, it made her weary to listen to Simon talk about his own affairs: his manor and his children. She knew she was being unreasonable; he was willing to do all he could to help her. She realized how good it was of him to agree to leave his home during the Christmas season, and to be away from his wife, as things now stood. No doubt he was thinking a great deal about whether he might have a son. He had only the one child with Ramborg, even though they had been married six years. Kristin couldn't expect that he should take Erlend's and her misfortune so much to heart that he would forget all the joy he had from his own life. But it was strange to be there with him; he seemed so happy and warm and secure in his own home.

Without thinking, Kristin had assumed that Ulvhild Simonsdatter would be like her own little sister, for whom the child had been named—fair and fragile and pure. But Simon's little daughter was round and plump, with cheeks like apples and lips as red as a berry, lively gray eyes that looked like her father's in his youth, and lovely brown curls. Simon had the greatest love for his pretty, merry child, and he was proud of her bright chatter.

"Even though this girl is so hideous and wicked and naughty," he said, putting his hands around her chest and tumbling her around as he lifted her up into the air. "I think she must be a changeling that the trolls up here in the hills left in the cradle for her mother and me—such an ugly and loathsome child she is." Then he set her down abruptly and hastily made the sign of the cross over her three times, as if he were frightened by his own imprudent words.

Arngjerd, the daughter born of his maid, was not beautiful, but she looked kind and sensible, and Simon took her with him whenever he could. He was constantly praising her cleverness. Kristin had to look at everything in Arngjerd's marriage chest, at all she had spun and woven and stitched as part of her dowry.

"When I place the hand of my daughter into the hand of a faithful husband," said Simon as he gazed after the child, "it will be one of the happiest days of my life."

To spare expenses and so that the journey might proceed faster, Kristin was to take along no maids, nor any servant other than Ulf Haldorssøn. Two weeks before Christmas they left Formo, accompanied by Simon Andressøn and his two young, vigorous men.

When they arrived in Oslo, Simon learned at once that the king would not be coming to Norway—he would apparently celebrate Christmas in Stockholm. Erlend was being held in the castle at Akersnes; the chieftain was away, so for the time being it would be impossible for any of them to see him. But the deputy royal treasurer, Olav Kyrning, promised to let Erlend know that they had come to town. Olav was quite friendly toward Simon and Kristin because his brother was married to Ramborg Aasmundsdatter of Skog, which made him distantly related to the daughters of Lavrans.

Ketil of Skog came to town and invited them to spend Christmas with him, but Kristin had no wish for noisy feasting as matters now stood for Erlend. And then Simon too refused to go, no matter how earnestly she begged him. Simon and Ketil knew each other, but Kristin had only met her uncle's son once since he had grown up.

Kristin and Simon had taken lodgings at the same residence where she had once been the guest of his parents, back when the two of them were betrothed, but this time they were staying in a different building. There were two beds in the main room; Kristin slept in one of them, Simon and Ulf slept in the other. The servants bedded down in the stable.

On Christmas Eve Kristin wanted to attend midnight mass at Nonneseter's church; she said it was because the sisters sang so beautifully. All five of them decided to go. The night was starry and clear, mild and lovely; it had snowed a little in the evening, so it was quite bright. When the bells began to ring from the churches, people came streaming out of all the houses, and Simon had to give Kristin his hand. Now and then he would cast a sidelong glance at her. She had grown terribly thin in the autumn, but her tall, erect figure seemed to have regained some of its maidenly softness and quiet grace. Her pale face had assumed the expression from her youth of calm and gentleness, which hid a deep, tense wariness. She had taken on an oddly phantomlike resemblance to the young Kristin from that Christmastime so long ago. Simon gripped her hand hard, unaware that he was doing so until she squeezed his fingers in return. He looked up. She smiled and nodded, and he understood that she had interpreted the pressure of his hand as a reminder that she must remain brave—and now she was trying to show him that she would.

When the holy days were over, Kristin went out to the convent and asked to be allowed to pay her respects to the abbess and to those sisters who were still living there since she had left. She then spent a little time in the abbess's parlatory. Afterwards she went into the church. She realized that there was nothing for her to gain inside the walls of the convent. The sisters had received her kindly, but she saw that for them she was merely one of the many young maidens who had spent a year there. If they had heard any talk about her distinguishing herself from the rest of the young daughters in any way, and not for the better, they made no mention of it. But that year at Nonneseter, which loomed so large in her own life, meant so little in the life of the cloister. Her father had bought for himself and his family a place in the convent's prayers of intercession for their souls. The new abbess, Fru Elin, and the sisters said that they would pray for her and for her husband's salvation. But

Kristin saw that she had no right to force her way in and disturb the nuns with her visits. Their church stood open to her, as it did to everyone; she could stand in the north aisle and listen to the singing of the pure women's voices from the choir; she could look around the familiar room, at the altars and pictures. And when the sisters left the church through the door to the convent courtyard, she could go up and kneel before the gravestone of Abbess Groa Guttormsdatter and think about the wise, powerful, and dignified mother whose words she had neither understood nor heeded. She had no other rights in this women's residence for Christ's servants.

At the end of the holy days, Sir Munan came to see Kristin. He said he had just learned that she was in Oslo. He greeted her heartily, as he did Simon Andressøn and Ulf, whom he kept calling his kinsman and dear friend. He thought it would be difficult for them to win permission to see Erlend; he was being kept under tight guard. Munan himself had not succeeded in gaining access to his cousin. But after the knight had ridden off, Ulf said with a laugh that he thought Munan probably hadn't tried very hard—he was so deathly afraid of being mixed up in the case that he hardly dared hear mention of it. Munan had aged greatly; he was quite bald and gaunt, and his skin hung loosely on his large frame. He was living out at Skogheim, with one of his unlawful daughters, who was a widow. Munan would have liked to be rid of her because none of his other children, lawful or unlawful, would come near him as long as this half-sister was managing his household. She was a domineering, avaricious, and sharp-tongued woman. But Munan didn't dare ask her to leave.

Finally, around New Year's, Olav Kyrning obtained permission for Kristin and Simon to see Erlend. It was again Simon's lot to escort the sorrowful wife to these heartbreaking meetings. The guards were much more careful here than they were in Nidaros not to let Erlend speak to anyone without the chieftain's men being present.

Erlend was calm, as before, but Simon could see that the situation was now beginning to wear him down. He never complained; he said he suffered no privations and was treated as well as was allowed, but he admitted that the cold bothered him a good deal; there was no hearth fire in the room. And there was little he could do to keep himself clean—although, he jested, if he hadn't had the lice to fight with, the time might have passed much more slowly out there.

Kristin too was calm—so calm that Simon held his breath with fear, waiting for the day when she would completely fall apart.

King Magnus was making his royal tour of Sweden, and there was little prospect that he would return to his homeland anytime soon, or that there would be any change in Erlend's situation.

On Saint Gregor's Day Kristin and Ulf Haldorssøn had been to church at Nonneseter. On their way home, as they crossed the bridge over the convent creek, she did not take the road to their hostel, which lay near the bishop's citadel; instead, she turned east toward the lane near Saint Clement's Church and headed along the narrow alleyways between the church and the river.

The day was hazy and gray, and a thaw had set in, so their footwear and the hems of their cloaks grew quickly soaked and heavy from the yellow mud near the river. They reached the fields along the riverbank. Once their eyes met. Ulf laughed softly and a kind of smirk appeared on his lips, but his eyes were sad; Kristin gave him an odd, sickly smile.

A moment later they were standing on the ridge of a hill; the earth had given way out here sometime before, and the farm now lay right below the hill—so close to the dirty-yellow slope, covered with tufts of black, dried weeds, that the rank stench from the pigsty, which they were looking down at, rose up toward them. Two fat sows were wallowing around in the dark muck. The riverbank was only a narrow strip here; the gray, murky current of the river, filled with careening ice floes, ran right up to the dilapidated buildings with the faded rooftops.

As they stood there, a man and a woman came walking over to the fenced area and looked at the pigs; the man leaned over and scratched one of the sows with the haft of the silver-chased, thin-bladed axe he was using as a staff. It was Munan Baardsøn himself, and the woman was Brynhild Fluga. He looked up and noticed them. He stood there gaping, until Kristin shouted a merry greeting down to him.

Sir Munan began to bellow with laughter.

"Come down and have a hot ale in this vile weather," he called.

On their way down to the farmyard fence, Ulf told Kristin that Brynhild Jonsdatter no longer kept an inn or an alehouse. She had been in trouble several times and was finally threatened with flogging, but Munan had come to her rescue and vouched for her; she promised to stop all her unlawful activities. And her sons now held such positions that, for their sake, their mother had to think about improving her reputation. After the death of his wife, Munan Baardsøn had taken up with Brynhild again and was often over at Flugagaard.

He met them at the gate.

"All four of us are kinsmen, after a fashion," he chuckled. He was slightly drunk, but not overly so. "You're a good woman, Kristin Lavransdatter, pious but not at all haughty. Brynhild is now an honorable and respectable woman too. And I was an unmarried man when I produced the two sons we have together—and they're the most splendid of all my children. That's what I've told you every single day in all these years, Brynhild. I'm more fond of Inge and Gudleik than any of my other children. . . ."

Brynhild was still beautiful, but her skin was sallow and looked as if it would be clammy to the touch, thought Kristin—the way it does after standing over a pot of grease all day long. But her house was well-kept, the food and drink she set on the table were excellent, and the crockery was pleasing and clean.

"Yes, I drop by over here whenever I have business in Oslo," said Munan. "A mother likes to hear news of her sons, you see. Inge writes to me himself, because he's a learned man, Inge—a bishop's envoy has to be, you know. . . . I found him a good match too: Tora Bjarnesdatter from Grjote. Do you think many men could have acquired such a woman for their bastard son? So we sit here and talk about that, and Brynhild brings in the food and ale for me, just like in the old days, when she wore my keys at Skogheim. It's hard to sit out there now and think about my blessed wife . . . So I ride over here to find some solace—when Brynhild here has a mind to grant me a little kindness and warmth."

Ulf Haldorssøn was sitting with his chin in his hand and gazing at the mistress of Husaby. Kristin sat and listened, answering quietly and gently and courteously—just as calm and refined as if she were a guest at one of the grand estates back home in Trøndelag.

"Well, Kristin Lavransdatter, you won honor and the name of wife," said Brynhild Fluga, "even though you came willingly enough to meet Erlend up in my loft. But I was called a wanton and loose woman all my days; my stepmother sold me into the hands of that man there—I bit and fought, and the scratches from my fingernails marked his face before he had his way with me."

"Are you going to bring that up again?" fretted Munan. "You know full well . . . I've told you so many times before . . . I would have let you go in peace if you had behaved properly and begged me to spare you, but you rushed at my face like a wildcat before I had even stepped inside the door."

Ulf Haldorssøn chuckled to himself.

"And I've treated you well ever since," said Munan. "I gave you everything you wanted . . . and our children . . . well, they're in a better and more secure position than those poor sons of Kristin. May God protect the poor boys, the way Erlend has left things for his children! I think that must be more important to a mother's heart than the name of wife—and you know how many times I wished that you had been highborn so that I might marry you—I've never liked any other woman as much as you, even though you were seldom gentle or kind to me . . . and the wife I did have, may God reward her. I've established an altar for my Katrin and me in our church, Kristin—I've thanked God and Our Lady every day for my marriage. . . . no man has had things better. . . ." He sniffed and began to cry.

A little later Ulf Haldorssøn said they would have to leave. He and Kristin didn't exchange a single word on the way home. But outside the main door, she took Ulf's hand.

"Ulf—my kinsman and my friend!"

"If it would help," he said quietly, "I would gladly go to the gallows in Erlend's place—for his sake and for yours."

In the evening, a little before bedtime, Kristin was sitting alone in the room with Simon. Suddenly she began to tell him where she had been that day. She recounted the conversation they had had out there.

Simon was sitting on a small stool a short distance away. Bending forward slightly, with his arms resting on his thighs and his hands hanging down, he sat and gazed up at her with a peculiar, searching look in his small, sharp eyes. He didn't say a word, and not a muscle twitched in his heavy, broad face.

Then Kristin mentioned that she had told her father everything, and what his response had been.

Simon sat in the same position, without moving. But after a while he said calmly, "That was the only request I have ever made of you in all the years we've known each other . . . if I remember right . . . that you should . . . but if you couldn't keep that to yourself to spare Lavrans, then . . ."

Kristin's body trembled violently. "Yes. But . . . Oh, Erlend, Erlend, Erlend!"

At her wild cries, the man leaped to his feet. Kristin had flung herself forward, and with her head in her arms she was rocking from side to side, calling to Erlend over and over in between the quavering, racking sobs that seemed to be wrung from her body, filling her mouth with moans that welled up and spilled out.

"Kristin, in the name of Jesus!"

When he grasped her arms and tried to console her, she threw her full weight against his chest and put her arms around his neck, as she continued to weep and call out her husband's name.

"Kristin—calm yourself. . . ." He crushed her in his arms but saw that she took no notice; she was crying so hard that she couldn't stand on her own. Then he lifted her in his arms—held her tight for a moment, and then carried her over to the bed and laid her down.

"Calm yourself," he again implored, his voice stifled and almost threatening. He placed his hands over her face, and she took hold of his wrists and arms and then clung to him.

"Simon . . . Simon . . . oh, he must be saved. . . ."

"I'll do what I can, Kristin. But now you *must* calm yourself!" Abruptly he turned away, walked to the door, and went out. He shouted so loudly that his voice echoed between the buildings; he called for the serving maid Kristin had hired in Oslo. She came running, and Simon told her to go in to her mistress. A moment later the girl came back out—her mistress wanted to be left alone, she fearfully told Simon; he hadn't moved from the spot where he stood.

He nodded and went over to the stable, staying there until his servant Gunnar and Ulf Haldorssøn came out to give the horses their evening fodder. Simon began talking with them and then went with Ulf back to the main house.

Kristin saw little of her brother-in-law the following day. But after mid-afternoon prayers, as she sat and sewed on a garment she was going to take to her husband, Simon came dashing into the room. He didn't speak to her or look at her; he merely threw open his traveling chest, filled his silver goblet with wine, and left. Kristin stood up and followed. Outside the main door stood a stranger, still holding the reins of his horse. Simon took a gold ring off his finger, tossed it into the goblet, and drank a toast to the messenger.

Kristin guessed what the news was and shouted joyfully, "You've been given a son, Simon!"

"Yes." He slapped the messenger on the shoulder as the man uttered his thanks and tucked the goblet and ring under his belt. Then Simon put his arm around the waist of his wife's sister and spun her around. He looked so happy that Kristin had to put her hands on his shoulders; then he kissed her full on the mouth and laughed loudly.

"I see it will be the Darre lineage, after all, that will live on at Formo after you're gone, Simon," she said joyously.

"So be it . . . if God wills."

When Kristin asked him if they should go to evensong together, he replied, "No, tonight I want to go alone."

That evening he told Kristin he had heard that Erling Vidkunssøn was supposed to be at his manor, Aker, near Tunsberg. Earlier in the day Simon had booked passage on a ship down the fjord; he wanted to talk to Sir Erling about Erlend's case.

Kristin said very little. They had mentioned this possibility before, but avoided discussing it further—whether Sir Erling had known about Erlend's endeavor or not. Simon said he would seek Erling Vidkunssøn's counsel—ask him what he thought of Kristin's plan that Simon should accompany her to meet with Lavrans's powerful kinsmen in Sweden, to ask the help of friends and kin.

Then she said, "But you have received such great news, brother-in-law, that it seems to me it would be more reasonable for you to postpone this journey to Aker and first travel to Ringheim, to see Ramborg and your son."

He had to turn away, he felt so weak. He had been waiting for this—whether Kristin would show some sign that she understood how he longed to see his son. But when he had regained mastery of his feelings, he said with some embarrassment, "I've been thinking, Kristin, that God will perhaps grant the boy better health if I can be patient and rein in my longing to see him until I've helped Erlend and you a little more in this matter."

The next day Simon went out and bought rich and splendid gifts for his wife and son, as well as for all the women who had been at Ramborg's side when she gave birth. Kristin took out a beautiful silver spoon she had inherited from her mother; this was for the infant, Andres Simonssøn. But to her sister she sent the heavy gilded silver chain, which Lavrans had once given her in her childhood along with the reliquary cross. The cross she now moved to the chain Erlend had given her as a betrothal present. The following day, around noon, Simon set sail.

In the evening the ship anchored off an island in the fjord. Simon stayed on board, lying in a sleeping bag made of pelts, with several homespun blankets spread on top; he looked up at the starry skies, where the images seemed to rock and sway as the ship pitched on the sleepily gliding swells. The water sloshed and the ice floes scraped and hammered against the sides of the vessel. It was almost pleasant to feel the cold seeping deeper and deeper into his body. It was soothing. . . .

And yet he was now certain that as bad as things had been, they would never be so again. Now that he had a son. It was not that he thought he would love the boy more than he did his daughters. But this was different. As joyful as the small maidens could make him feel whenever they came to their father with their games and laughter and chatter, and as wonderful as it felt to have them sitting on his lap with their soft hair beneath his chin—a man could not claim the same position in the succession of men among his kin if his estate and property and the memory of his deeds in this world should be transferred on the hand of his daughter to some other lineage. But now that he dared to hope—if only God would allow this infant boy to grow up—that son would follow father at Formo: Andres Gudmundssøn, Simon Andressøn, Andres Simonssøn. Then it was clear that he must be for Andres what his own father had been for him: a man of integrity, both in his secret thoughts and in his actions.

Sometimes he felt he didn't have the strength to continue. If only he had seen a single sign that she understood. But Kristin behaved toward him as if they were actual siblings: considerate of his welfare, kind and loving and gentle. And he didn't know how long it could last: living together in the same house in this manner. Didn't she ever think about the fact that he couldn't forget? Even though he was now married to her sister, he could still never forget that they had once been betrothed to live together as man and wife.

But now he had a son. Whenever he said his prayers, he had always shied away from adding any of his own words, whether wishes or words of gratitude. But Christ and Mary knew full well what he meant when he had said double the number of *Pater nosters* and *Ave Marias* lately. He would continue to do so as long as he was away from home. And he would show his gratitude in an equally fitting and generous manner. Then perhaps he would receive help on this journey, as well.

In truth, he thought it unreasonable to expect to make any gains from this meeting. Relations between Erling and the king were now quite cold. And no matter how powerful and proud the former regent might be, no matter how little he needed to fear the young king—who was in a much more difficult position than Norway's wealthiest and most highborn man—it was still unlikely that he would want to provoke King Magnus even more by speaking on Erlend Nikulaussøn's behalf and drawing suspicion upon himself that he might have known about Erlend's treasonous plans. Even if Erling had taken part in them—yes, even if he was behind the whole undertaking, prepared to intervene and allow himself to be placed in charge of the realm as soon as there was once again an underaged king in the land—he would not feel bound to take any risks to help the man who had ruined the entire plan for the sake of a shameful love affair. This was something Simon almost forgot whenever he was together with Erlend and Kristin, for the two of them seemed hardly to remember it anymore. But it was true that Erlend himself was to blame for the whole endeavor resulting in nothing more than misfortune for him and the good men who had been exposed by his foolish philandering.

He must try every recourse to help her and her husband. And now he began to hope. Perhaps God and the Virgin Mary or some of the saints, whom he had always honored with offerings and alms, would support him in this undertaking too.

He arrived at Aker quite late the following evening. An overseer on the estate met him and sent servants on ahead, some with the horses and some to escort Simon's man over to the servants' hall. The overseer himself went up to the loft where the knight was sitting and drinking. A moment later Sir Erling came out onto the gallery and stood there as Simon climbed the stairs. Then he welcomed his guest courteously enough and led him into the chamber where Stig Haakonssøn of Mandvik was sitting with a very young man who was Erling's only son, Bjarne Erlingssøn.

Simon was received in a friendly fashion; the servants took his outer garments and brought in food and drink. But he could see that the men had guessed why he had come—or at least Erling and Stig had—and he noticed their reticence. When Stig began to talk about how rare it was to see Simon in that part of the country, and how he wasn't exactly wearing down the doorstep of his former kinsmen—he hadn't even been farther south than to Dyfrin since Halfrid died—then Simon replied, "No, not until this winter." But he had been in Oslo for several months now with his wife's sister, Kristin Lavransdatter, who was married to Erlend Nikulaussøn.

At that they all fell silent. Then Sir Erling asked politely about Kristin and about Simon's wife and siblings, and Simon asked about Fru Elin and Erling's daughters, and Stig's health, and news from Mandvik and old neighbors there.

Stig Haakonssøn was a stout, dark-haired man a few years older than Simon, the son of Halfrid Erlingsdatter's half-brother, Sir Haakon Toressøn, and the nephew of Erling Vidkunssøn's wife, Elin Toresdatter. He had lost his position as sheriff of Skidu and his command of the castle at Tunsberg two winters earlier when he fell out of favor with the king, but otherwise he lived well enough at Mandvik, although he was a widower with no children. Simon knew him quite well and had been on good terms with him, as he was with all the kinsmen of his first wife—although the friendship had never been overly warm. He knew what they had all thought about Halfrid's second marriage: Sir Andres Gudmundssøn's younger son might be both well positioned and of good lineage, but he was not an equal marriage match for Halfrid Erlingsdatter, and he was ten years younger than she was. They couldn't understand why she had set her heart on this young man, but they allowed her to do as she wished, since she had suffered so unbearably with her first husband.

Simon had met Erling Vidkunssøn only a couple of times before, and then he had always been in the company of Fru Elin and uttered hardly a sound; no one needed to say more than "yes," or "ah," whenever she was in the room. Sir Erling had aged quite a bit since that time. He had grown stouter, but he still had a handsome and stately figure for he carried himself exceedingly well and it suited him that his pale, reddish-gold hair had now turned a gleaming, silvery gray.

Simon had never met the young Bjarne Erlingssøn before. He had grown up near Bjørgvin in the house of a clergyman who was Erling's friend—within the family it was said that this was because the father didn't want his son living out there at Giske amidst all the prattling of the women. Erling himself didn't spend any more time at home than he had to, but he didn't dare take the boy along with him on his frequent journeys because Bjarne had suffered poor health in his childhood, and Erling Vidkunssøn had lost two other sons when they were small.

The boy looked exceptionally handsome as he sat with the light behind him and his face turned in profile. Thick, black, curly hair cascaded over his forehead; his big eyes were dark, his nose was large, with a graceful curve, his lips were firm and delicate, his chin well-shaped. He was also tall, broad-shouldered, and slim. But when Simon was about to sit down at the table to eat, the servant moved the candle, and then he saw that the skin of Bjarne's throat was completely eaten away by scrofulous scars—they spread out to both sides, all the way up to his ears and under his chin: dead, shiny white patches of skin, purplish stripes, and swollen knots. And Bjarne had the habit of suddenly pulling up the hood of the round, fur-trimmed velvet shoulder collar which he wore even inside the house—pulling it up to his ears. After a few minutes it would grow too hot for him, and he would let it fall back, only to pull it up again. He didn't seem aware that he was doing this. After a while Simon felt his own hands grow restless from watching him, even though he tried to avoid looking in his direction.

Sir Erling hardly took his eyes off his son, although he too seemed unaware that he was sitting with his gaze fixed on the boy. Erling Vidkunssøn's face showed little emotion, and there was no particular expression in his pale-blue eyes; but behind that somewhat vague and watery glance there seemed to lie endless years of worry and care and love.

Then the three older men conversed, politely but in a desultory fashion, while Simon ate, and the young man sat there fidgeting with his hood. Afterwards all four of them drank for a proper length of time, and then Sir Erling asked Simon if he was weary from his journey, and Stig invited him to share his bed. Simon was glad to postpone talking about the purpose of his visit. This first evening at Aker had left him quite dejected.

The next day, when he finally spoke of it, Sir Erling replied in much the way Simon had expected. He said that King Magnus had never willingly listened to him, but he had noticed that the moment Magnus Eirikssøn became old enough to have an opinion, it had been his view that Erling Vidkunssøn wouldn't have anything more to say to him after he came of age. And ever since the dispute had been settled between Erling and his friends on one side and the king on the other, he had neither heard from nor spoken to the king or the king's friends. If he spoke on Erlend's behalf to King Magnus, it would be of little benefit to the man. And he was aware that many people in the country thought he had been behind Erlend's undertaking in some way. Simon could believe him or not, but neither he nor his friends had known anything about what was being planned. But if this matter had come to light in a different fashion, or if these adventuresome young daredevils had carried through their plot and failed—then he might have stepped forward and tried to mediate. But because of the way things had gone, he didn't think anyone could reasonably demand him to stand up and reinforce the people's suspicions that he had been playing two games.

But he advised Simon to appeal to the Haftorssøns. They were the king's cousins, and when they weren't quarreling with him, they managed to maintain a certain friendship. And as far as Erling could see, the men Erlend was protecting were more likely to be found among the Haftorssøns' circles, as well as among the younger noblemen.

As everyone knew, the king's wedding was to be celebrated in Norway that summer. It might provide a fitting opportunity for King Magnus to show mercy and leniency toward his enemies. And the king's mother and Lady Isabel would no doubt attend the festivities. Simon's mother had been Queen Isabel's handmaiden when she was young, after all; perhaps Simon should appeal to her, or perhaps Erlend's wife ought to fall to her knees before the king's bride and Lady Ingebjørg Haakonsdatter with her prayers for their intercession.

Simon thought it would have to be the last resort, for Kristin to kneel before Lady Ingebjørg. If she had realized what was honorable, Lady Ingebjørg would have long ago stepped forward to gain Erlend's release from his troubles. But when Simon had once mentioned this to Erlend, he had simply laughed and said that Lady Ingebjørg always had so many troubles and worries of her own, and no doubt she was angry because it now seemed unlikely that her most beloved child would ever win the title of king.

## CHAPTER 7

In early spring Simon Andressøn traveled north to Toten to see his wife and infant son and accompany them home to Formo. He stayed there for some time to tend to his own affairs.

Kristin didn't want to leave Oslo. And she didn't dare give in to her burning, urgent longing to see her three sons who were back home in Gudbrandsdal. If she was going to continue to endure the life she was now living from day to day, she couldn't think about her children. And she did manage to endure; she seemed calm and brave. She talked and listened to strangers and accepted advice and encouragement. But she had to hold on to the thought of Erlend—only Erlend! In those moments when she failed to hold her thoughts tight in the grasp of her will, other images and pictures would race through her mind: Ivar standing in the woodshed at Formo with Simon and waiting expectantly as his uncle searched for a split piece of wood for him, bending down to heft each one in his hand. Gaute's fair, boyish face, full of manly determination as he struggled through the snowdrifts on that gray wintry day in the mountains last fall. His skis slipped backwards, and he slid some distance down the steep slope, sinking deep into the snow. For a moment his face seemed about to crumple; he was an exhausted, helpless child. Her thoughts would wander to her youngest sons: Munan must be able to walk and even talk a little by now. Was he just as sweet as the others had been at his age? Lavrans had probably forgotten her by now. And the two oldest boys out at the monastery at Tautra. Naakkve, Naakkve . . . her firstborn . . . How much did the two older sons understand? What were they thinking about? And how was Naakkve, still a child, coping with the fact that now nothing in his life would be the way that she and he and everyone else had imagined it would be?

Sira Eiliv had sent her a letter, and she had reported to Erlend what it said about their sons. Otherwise they never spoke of their children. They didn't talk about the past or the future anymore. Kristin would bring him some piece of clothing or a plate of food; he would ask her how she had fared since they last met, and they would sit on the bed holding hands. Sometimes they would be left alone for a moment in the small, cold and filthy, stench-filled room. Then they would cling to each other with mute, passionate caresses, hearing but paying no attention to Kristin's maid laughing with the castle guards outside on the stairs.

There would be plenty of time, either after he was taken from her or after he came back to her, for thinking about all the children and their changed circumstances—and about everything else in her life besides her husband. She didn't want to lose a single hour of the time they had together, and she didn't dare think about her reunion with the four sons she had left behind up north. For this reason she accepted Simon Andressøn's offer to travel alone to Nidaros; along with Arne Gjavvaldssøn, he would see to her interests in the settling of the estate. King Magnus would not be made richer by acquiring Erlend's property; his debts were much greater than he himself had thought, and he had raised money that was sent to Denmark and Scotland and England. Erlend shrugged his shoulders and said with a faint smile that he didn't expect to be compensated for that.

So Erlend's situation was largely unchanged when Simon Andressøn returned to Oslo around Holy Cross Day in the fall. But he was horrified to see how exhausted they both looked, Kristin and his brother-in-law; and he felt strangely weak and sick at heart when they both still had enough composure to thank him for coming at that time of year, when he could least be spared from his own estates. But now people were gathering in Tunsberg, where King Magnus had come to wait for his bride.

A little later in the month Simon managed to book himself passage on a ship with several merchants who were planning to sail there in a week's time. One morning a stranger arrived with the request that Simon Andressøn should trouble himself to come to Saint Halvard's Church at once. Olav Kyrning was waiting for him there.

The deputy royal treasurer was in a terribly agitated state. He was in charge of the castle while the treasurer was in Tunsberg.

The previous evening a group of gentlemen had arrived and shown him a letter with King Magnus's seal on it, saying that they were to investigate Erlend Nikulaussøn's case. He had ordered the prisoner to be brought to them. The three men were foreigners, apparently Frenchmen; Olav didn't understand their language, but this morning the royal priest had spoken to them in Latin. They were supposedly kinsmen of the maiden who was to be Norway's queen—what a promising start this was! They had interrogated Erlend in the harshest manner . . . had brought along some kind of rack and several men who knew how to use such things. Today Olav had refused to allow Erlend to be taken out of his chamber and had put him under heavy guard. He would take responsibility for it, because this was not lawful—such conduct had never been heard of before in Norway!

Simon borrowed a horse from one of the priests at the church and rode at once back to Akersnes with Olav.

Olav Kyrning glanced a little anxiously at the other man's grim face, which was flooded with furious waves of crimson. Now and then Simon would make a wild and violent gesture, not even aware of it himself—but the borrowed horse would start, rear up, and rebel beneath the rider.

"I can see you're angry, Simon," said Olav Kyrning.

Simon hardly knew what was foremost in his mind. He was so furious that he felt spells of nausea overtake him. The blind and desperate feeling that surged up inside him, driving him to the utmost rage, was a form of shame—a man who was defenseless, without weapon or protection, who had to tolerate the hands of strangers in his clothes, strangers searching his body . . . It was like hearing about the rape of women. He grew dizzy with the desire for revenge and the need to spill blood to retaliate. No, such had never been the custom in Norway. Did they want Norwegian noblemen to grow used to tolerating such things? That would never happen!

He was sick with horror at what he would now see. Fear of the shame he would bring upon the other man by seeing him in such a state overwhelmed all other feelings as Olav Kyrning unlocked the door to Erlend's prison cell.

Erlend was lying flat on the floor, his body placed diagonally from one corner of the room to the other; he was so tall that this was the only way he could find enough room to stretch out full length. Some straw and pieces of clothing had been placed underneath him, on top of the floor's thick layer of filth. His body was covered all the way up to his chin with his dark-blue, fur-lined cape so that the soft, grayish-brown marten fur of the collar seemed to blend with the curly black tangle of the beard that Erlend had grown while in prison.

His lips were pale next to his beard; his face was snowy white. The large, straight triangle of his nose seemed to protrude much too far from his hollowed cheeks; his gray-flecked hair lay in lank, sweaty strings, swept back from his high, narrow forehead. At each temple was a large purple mark, as if something had clamped or held him there.

Slowly, with great difficulty, Erlend opened his big pale-blue eyes and attempted to smile when he recognized the men. His voice was odd-sounding and husky. "Sit down, brother-in-law . . ." He turned his head toward the empty bed. "I've learned a few new things since we last met. . . ."

Olav Kyrning bent over Erlend and asked him if he wanted anything. When he received no answer—probably because Erlend had no strength to reply—he pulled the cape aside. Erlend was wearing only linen pants and a ragged shirt. The sight of the swollen and discolored limbs shocked and enraged Simon like some indecent horror. He wondered whether Erlend felt the same way—a shadow of a blush passed over his face as Olav gently rubbed his arms and legs with a cloth he had dipped in a basin of water. And when he replaced the cape, Erlend straightened it out with a few small movements of his limbs and by drawing it all the way up to his chin, so that he was completely covered.

"Well," said Erlend. Now he sounded a bit more like himself, and the smile was stronger on his pale lips. "Next time it will be worse. But I'm not afraid. No one needs to be afraid . . . they won't get anything out of me . . . not that way."

Simon could tell that he was speaking the truth. Torture was not going to force a word out of Erlend Nikulaussøn. He could do and say anything in anger and on impulse, but he would never let himself be budged even a hand's breadth by violence. Simon realized that the shame and indignation he felt on the other man's behalf was not something Erlend felt himself—instead, he was filled with a stubborn joy at defying his tormenter and a confident faith in his ability to resist. He who had always yielded so pitifully when confronted by a strong will, who might have shown cruelty himself in a moment of fear, now displayed his valor when he, in this cruel situation, sensed an opponent who was weaker than he was.

But Simon snarled through clenched teeth, "Next time . . . will never come! What do you say, Olav?"

Olav shook his head, but Erlend said with a trace of the old impudent boldness in his voice, "If only I could believe that . . . as firmly as you do! But these men will hardly . . . be satisfied with this . . ." He noticed the twitching of Simon's muscular, heavy face. "No, Simon . . . brother-in-law!" Erlend tried to raise himself up on one elbow; in pain he uttered a stifled moan and then sank back in a faint.

Olav and Simon tended to him. When the fainting spell had passed, Erlend lay still with his eyes open wide; he spoke more somberly.

"Don't you see . . . how much is at stake . . . for King Magnus? To find out . . . which men he shouldn't trust . . . farther than he can see them. So much unrest . . . and discontent . . . as we've had here . . ."

"Well, if he thinks this will quell the discontent, then—" said Olav Kyrning angrily.

But Erlend said in a soft, clear voice, "I've handled this matter in such a way . . . that few will consider it important how I'm treated. I know that myself."

The two men blushed. Simon hadn't thought that Erlend understood this—and neither of them had ever referred to Fru Sunniva. Now he exclaimed in despair, "How could you be so foolish and reckless!"

"I can't understand it either . . . now," said Erlend honestly. "But—how in hell was I to know that she could read! She seemed so uneducated."

His eyes closed again; he was about to faint once more. Olav Kyrning murmured that he would get something and left the room. Simon bent over Erlend, who was again lying there with half-open eyes.

"Brother-in-law . . . did . . . did Erling Vidkunssøn support you in this matter?"

Erlend shook his head and smiled. "No, by Jesus. We thought either he wouldn't have the courage to join us . . . or else he would want to control the whole thing. But don't ask me, Simon . . . I don't want to tell . . . anyone. Then I know that I won't talk . . ."

Suddenly Erlend whispered his wife's name. Simon bent over him; he expected Erlend to ask him to bring Kristin to him. But he said hastily, as if in a feverish breath, "She mustn't find out about this, Simon. Tell her the king has sent word that no one is to be allowed to see me. Take her out to Munan—at Skogheim. Do you hear me? These Frenchmen . . . or Moors . . . new friends of our king . . . they won't stop yet. Get her out of Oslo before the news spreads through town! Simon?"

"Yes," he replied, although he had no idea how he would manage it.

Erlend lay still for a moment with his eyes closed. Then he said with a sort of smile, "I was thinking last night . . . about the time she gave birth to our eldest son. She was no better off than I am now—judging by how she wailed. And if she could bear it seven times . . . for the sake of our pleasure . . . then surely I can too."

Simon was silent. The involuntary qualms he felt about life revealing to him its last secrets of suffering and desire seemed not to trouble Erlend in the least. He wrestled with the worst and with the sweetest, as innocently as a naive young boy whose friends have taken him to a house of sin, drunken and full of curiosity.

Erlend rolled his head back and forth impatiently.

"These flies are the worst . . . I think they're the Devil himself."

Simon took off his cap and swatted vigorously at the swarms of blue-black flies so that they rose up in great clouds, buzzing noisily. And all those that were knocked senseless to the floor, he furiously trampled in the dirt. It wouldn't help much because the window hole in the wall stood wide open. The previous winter there had been a wooden shutter with a skin-covered opening. But it had made the room very dark.

He was still busily flailing at the flies when Olav Kyrning came back with a priest who was carrying a drinking goblet. The priest put his hand under Erlend's head to support him as he drank. Much of the liquid ran down into his beard and along his neck, but he lay as calm and unconcerned as a child when the priest wiped him off with a rag.

Simon felt as if his whole body was in ferment—his blood was pulsing hard in his neck beneath his ears, and his heart was pounding in an odd and restless fashion. He stood in the doorway for a moment, staring at the tall body stretched out under the cape. A feverish flush was now passing in waves over Erlend's face. He lay there with his eyes half-open and glittering, but he gave his brother-in-law a smile, a shadow of his peculiar, boyish smile.

The following day, as Stig Haakonssøn of Mandvik was sitting at the breakfast table with his guests, Sir Erling Vidkunssøn and his son Bjarne, they heard the hoofbeats of a lone horse out in the courtyard. A moment later the door of the building was flung open and Simon Andressøn stepped swiftly toward them. He wiped his face on his sleeve; he was spattered with mud all the way up to his neck after the ride.

The three men sitting at the table rose to their feet to greet the new arrival with small exclamations that were part welcome and part surprise. Simon didn't greet them but stood there leaning on the hilt of his sword with both hands. He said, "I bring you strange news—they have taken Erlend Nikulaussøn and stretched him on the rack—some foreigners that the king has sent to interrogate him. . . ."

The men shouted and then crowded around Simon Andressøn. Stig pounded a fist into the palm of his other hand. "What did he tell them?"

At the same time both he and Bjarne Erlingssøn involuntarily turned to face Sir Erling. Simon burst into laughter; he roared and roared.

Then he sank down onto the chair that Bjarne Erlingssøn pulled out for him, accepted the ale bowl the young man offered him, and drank greedily.

"Why are you laughing?" asked Sir Erling sternly.

"I was laughing at Stig." Simon was leaning slightly forward, with his hands resting on the thighs of his mud-covered breeches. He gave a few more bursts of laughter. "I had thought . . . All of us here are the sons of great chieftains . . . I expected you to be so angry that such a thing could be done to one of our peers that your first response would be to ask how this could possibly happen.

"I can't say that I know exactly what the law is about such matters. Ever since my lord King Haakon died, I've been content with the idea that I owed his successor my service if he should ask for it, both in war and in peace; otherwise I've lived quietly on my manor. But now I can only think that this case against Erlend Nikulaussøn has been unlawfully handled. His fellow noblemen have passed judgment on him, but I don't know by what right they condemned him to death. Then a reprieve and safe conduct were granted to him until he could meet with his kinsman, King Magnus, to see whether the king might allow Erlend to be reconciled with him. But since then the man has been imprisoned in the tower at Akers Castle for nearly a year, and the king has been abroad almost all that time. Letters have been dispatched, but nothing has come of it. And now he sends over these louts, who are neither Norwegian nor the king's retainers, and who attempt to interrogate Erlend with conduct that is unheard of toward any Norwegian man with the rights of a royal retainer—while peace reigns in the land, and Erlend's kinsmen and peers are gathering in Tunsberg to celebrate the royal wedding. . . .

"What do you think of all this, Sir Erling?"

"I think . . ." Erling sat down on the bench across from him. "I think you have told us clearly and bluntly how this matter now stands, Simon Darre. As I see it, the king can only do one of three things: He can allow Erlend to appeal the sentence that was handed down in Nidaros. Or he can appoint a new court of royal retainers and have the case against Erlend brought by a man who does not bear the title of knight, and then they will sentence Erlend to exile, with the proper time allowed for him to leave the realms of King Magnus. Or he will have to permit Erlend to be reconciled with him. And that would be the wisest solution of all.

"It seems to me that this case is now so clear, that whoever you present it to in Tunsberg will assist you and support you. Jon Haftorssøn and his brother are there. Erlend is their kinsman, just as he is the king's. The Ogmundssøns will realize that injustice in this matter would be folly. You should seek out the commander of the royal retinue first; ask him and Sir Paal Eirikssøn to call a meeting of the retainers who are now in town and who seem most suited to handle this case."

"Won't you and your kinsmen go with me, sir?" asked Simon.

"We don't intend to join the festivities," said Erling curtly.

"The Haftorssøns are young, Sir Paal is old and feeble, and the others . . . You know yourself, sir, that they have some power, being in the king's favor and such, but . . . what importance do they have compared to you, Erling Vidkunssøn? You, sir, have held more power in this country than any other chieftain since . . . I don't know when. Behind you, sir, stand the ancient families that the people of this country have known, man after man, for as far back as the legends tell us of bad times and good times in our villages. In your father's lineage—what is Magnus Eirikssøn or the sons of Haftor of Sudrheim compared to you? Is their wealth worth mentioning compared to yours? This advice you have given me—it will take time, and the Frenchmen are already in Oslo, and you can bet that they will not yield. It's clear that the king is attempting to rule Norway according to foreign customs. I know that abroad there's a tradition for the king to ignore the law when he so chooses, if he can find amenable men among the knighthood to support him. Olav Kyrning has sent letters to those noblemen he could find to join him, and the bishop has promised to write as well. But you could end this dispute and unrest at once, Erling Vidkunssøn, by seeking out King Magnus. You are the foremost descendant of all the old noblemen here in Norway; the king knows that all the others would stand behind you."

"I can't say that I've noticed that in the past," said Erling bitterly. "You speak with great fervor on behalf of your brother-in-law, Simon. But don't you understand that I can't do it *now?* If I do, people would say . . . that I step forward the minute pressure is put on Erlend and it's feared he might not be able to hold his tongue."

There was silence for a moment. Then Stig asked again, "Has Erlend . . . talked?"

"No," replied Simon impatiently. "He has kept silent. And I think he'll continue to do so. Erling Vidkunssøn," he implored, "he's your kinsman—you were friends."

Erling took a few deep, heavy breaths.

"Yes. Simon Andressøn, do you fully understand exactly *what* Erlend Nikulaussøn has brought upon himself? He wanted to dissolve the royal union with the Swedes—this form of rule that has never been tested before—which seems to bring more and more hardship and difficulty to Norway for each year that passes. He wanted to go back to the old, familiar rule, which we know brings good fortune and prosperity. Don't you see that this was the plan of a wise and bold man? And don't you see that now it would be difficult for anyone else to take up this plan after him? He has ruined the chances of the sons of Knut Porse—and there are no other men of royal lineage the people can rally around. You might argue that if Erlend had carried out his intentions and brought Prince Haakon here to Norway, then he would have played right into my hands. Other than deliver the boy into the country, these . . . young fellows . . . wouldn't have been able to do much without the intervention of sober-minded men who could handle all the rest that needed to be done. That's how it is—I can vouch for it. God knows I've reaped few rewards; rather, I've had to set aside the care of my own estates for the ten years I've endured unrest and toil, strife and torment without end—a few men in this country have understood as much, and I've had to be satisfied with that!" He pounded his hand hard against the table. "Don't you understand, Simon, that the man who took such great plans onto his shoulders—and no one knows how important they might have been to the welfare of all of us here in Norway, and to our descendants for many years to come—he set them all aside, along with his breeches, on the bed of a wanton woman. God's blood! It could be he deserves to pay the same penance Audun Hestakorn did!"

He grew calmer.

"Otherwise I have no reason to begrudge Erlend his release, and you mustn't think I'm not angry about what you have told us. I think if you follow my advice, you'll find plenty of men who will support you in this matter. But I don't think I can help you enough by joining you that I would approach the king uninvited for the sake of this cause."

Simon got to his feet stiffly and arduously. His face was gray-streaked with fatigue. Stig Haakonssøn came over and put his arm around his shoulders. Now he would have food; he hadn't wanted any servants in the room before they finished talking. But now he ought to regain his strength with food and drink, and then rest. Simon thanked him, but he wanted to continue on his way shortly, if Stig would lend him a fresh horse, and if he would give his servant, Jon Daalk, lodging for the night. Simon had been forced to ride on ahead of his man the night before because his horse couldn't keep up with Digerbein. Yes, he had been traveling almost all night; he thought he knew the road to Mandvik so well, but he had lost his way a couple of times.

Stig asked him to stay until the next day; then he would go with him at least part of the way. Well, he might even accompany him as far as Tunsberg.

"There's no reason for me to stay here any longer. I just want to go over to the church. Since I'm here on the estate, I want to say a prayer at Halfrid's grave, at least."

The blood rushed and roared through his exhausted body; the pounding of his heart was deafening. He felt as if he might collapse; he was only half awake. But he heard his own voice saying evenly and calmly, "Won't you go over there with me, Sir Erling? Of all her kinsmen, I know she was most fond of you."

He didn't look at the other man, but he could sense him stiffen. After a moment he heard through the rushing and ringing sound of his own blood the clear and courteous voice of Erling Vidkunssøn.

"I'll gladly do so, Simon Darre. It's miserable weather," he said as he buckled on the belt with his sword and threw a thick cape around his shoulders. Simon stood as still as a rock until the other man was ready. Then they went out the door.

Outside, the autumn rain was pouring down, and the fog was drifting in so thick from the sea that they could barely see more than a couple of horse-lengths into the fields and the yellow leafy groves on either side of the path. It was not far to the church. Simon went to get the key from the chaplain at the parsonage nearby; he was relieved to see that new people had come since the days when he lived there, so he could avoid a long chat.

It was a small stone church with only one altar. Distractedly Simon looked at the same pictures and adornments he had seen so many hundreds of times before as he knelt down a short distance from Erling Vidkunssøn near the white marble gravestone; he said his prayers, crossing himself at the proper times, without fully taking notice.

Simon didn't understand how he'd been able to do it. But now he was in the thick of it all. What he should say, he wasn't sure—but no matter how sick with fear and shame he felt, he knew he would attempt it all the same.

He remembered the white, ill face of the aging woman lying in the dim light of the bed, and her lovely, gentle voice on that afternoon when he sat at her bedside and she told him. It was a month before the child was due, and she expected that it would take her life—but she was willing and happy to pay so dearly for their son. That poor boy who now lay under the stone in a little coffin at his mother's shoulder. No, no man could do what he intended. . . .

But he thought of Kristin's white face. She knew what had happened, when he returned from Akersnes that day. Pale and calm, she spoke of it and asked him questions; but he had looked into her eyes for one brief moment, and he didn't dare meet them again. Where she was now or what she was doing, he didn't know. Whether she was at the hostel or with her husband, or whether they had persuaded her to go out to Skogheim . . . he had left it in the hands of Olav Kyrning and Sira Ingolf. He lacked the strength to do more, and he didn't think he could waste any time.

Simon didn't realize that he was hiding his face in his hands. Halfrid . . . it's not a question of sin or shame, my Halfrid. And yet . . . What she had told her husband—about her sorrow and her love, which had made her stay with that old devil. One day he had even killed the child she carried under her heart, but she stayed because she didn't want to tempt her beloved friend.

Erling Vidkunssøn was kneeling with no expression on his colorless, finely shaped face. He held his hands in front of his chest, with the palms pressed together; from time to time he would cross himself with a quiet, tender, and graceful gesture, and then put his fingertips together as before.

No. It was too terrible for any man to do. Not even for Kristin's sake could he do *that*. They stood up together, bowed to the altar, and walked back through the church. Simon's spurs rang faintly with every step he took on the flagstone floor. They had still not said a word to each other since leaving the manor, and Simon had no idea what might happen next.

He locked the church door, and Erling Vidkunssøn walked on ahead across the cemetery. Under the little roof of the churchyard gate, he stopped. Simon joined him, and they stood there for a while before heading back out into the pouring rain.

Erling spoke calmly and evenly, but Simon sensed the stifled, boundless rage that was menacing deep inside the other man; he didn't dare look up.

"In the name of the Devil, Simon Andressøn! What do you mean by . . . referring to . . . that?"

Simon couldn't say a word.

"If you think you can threaten me so that I'll do what you want because you've heard some false rumors about events that supposedly occurred, back when you were hardly weaned from your mother's breast . . ." His fury was snarling closer to the surface now.

Simon shook his head. "I thought, sir, that if you remembered the woman who was better than the purest gold, then you might have pity for Erlend's wife and children."

Sir Erling looked at him. He didn't reply but began to scrape moss and lichen off the stones of the churchyard wall. Simon swallowed and then moistened his lips with his tongue.

"I hardly know what I was thinking, Erling. Perhaps if you remembered the woman who endured all those terrible years, with no solace or help except from God alone, then you might want to help many other people—because you can! Since you couldn't help her . . . Have you ever regretted riding away from Mandvik on that day and leaving Halfrid behind in the hands of Sir Finn?"

"But I didn't do that!" Erling's voice was now scathing. "Because I know that *she* never . . . but I don't think *you* can understand that! For if you fully understood for a single moment how proud she was, that woman who became *your* wife . . ." He laughed angrily. "Then you would never have done this. I don't know how much you know—but I'll gladly tell you this: Haakon was ill at the time, and so they sent *me* to bring her home to her kinsmen. She and Elin had grown up together like sisters; they were almost the same age, although Elin was her father's sister. We had . . . it so happened that whenever she came home from Mandvik, we were forced to meet quite often. We would sit and talk, sometimes all night long, on the gallery to the Lindorm chamber. Every word that was spoken she and I can both defend before God on Judgment Day. Then maybe *He* can tell us why it had to be so.

"And yet God rewarded her piety in the end. He gave her a good husband as consolation for the one she had had before. Such a young whelp you were . . . lying with her serving maids on her own estate . . . and making her raise your bastard children." He flung far away the ball of moss he had crushed in his hand.

Simon stood motionless and mute. Erling scraped off another patch of moss and tossed it aside.

"I did what *she* asked me to do. Have you heard enough? There was no other way. Wherever else we might have met in the world, we would have had . . . we would have had . . . Adultery is not a nice word. The shame of blood is much worse."

Simon gave a stiff little nod. He could see that it would be laughable to say what he was thinking. Erling Vidkunssøn had been in his early twenties, handsome and refined; Halfrid had loved him so much that she would have gladly kissed his footprints in the dewy grass of the courtyard on that spring morning. Her husband was an aging, portly, loathsome farmer. What about Kristin? It would never occur to her now to think there was any danger to anyone's salvation if she lived together with her brother-in-law on the same estate for twenty years. That was something Simon had learned well enough by now.

Then he said quietly, almost meekly, "Halfrid didn't want the innocent child her maid had conceived with her husband to suffer in this world. *She* was the one who begged me to do right by her as best I could. Oh, Erling Vidkunssøn—for the sake of Erlend's poor wife . . . She's grieving herself to death. I didn't think I could leave any stone unturned while I searched for help for her and all her children."

Erling stood leaning against the gatepost. His face was just as calm as always, and his voice was courteous and cool when he spoke again.

"I liked her, Kristin Lavransdatter, the few times I've met her. She's a beautiful and dignified woman. And as I've told you many times now, Simon Andressøn, I'm certain you'll win support if you follow my advice. But I don't fully understand what you mean by this . . . strange notion. You can't mean that because I had to let my uncle decide my marriage, underaged as I was back then, and the maiden I loved most was already betrothed when we met . . . And Erlend's wife is not as innocent as you say. Yes, you're married to her sister, that's true; but *you* are the one, not I, who has caused us to have this . . . strange conversation . . . and so you'll have to tolerate that I mention this. I remember there was plenty of talk about it when Erlend married her; it was against Lavrans Bjørgulfsøn's will and advice that the marriage was arranged, but the maiden thought more of having her own way than of obeying her father or guarding her honor. Yes, she might well be a good woman all the same—but she *was* allowed to marry Erlend, and no doubt they've had their share of joy and pleasure. I don't think Lavrans ever had much joy from that son-in-law; *he* had chosen another man for his daughter. When she met Erlend she was already betrothed, that much I know." He suddenly fell silent, glanced at Simon for a moment, and then turned his face away in embarrassment.

Burning red with shame, Simon bowed his head, but he said in a low, firm voice, "Yes, she was betrothed to me."

For a moment they stood there, not daring to look at each other. Then Erling tossed away the last ball of moss, turned on his heel, and stepped out into the rain. Simon stayed where he was, but when the other man had gone some distance into the fog, he turned and signaled to him impatiently.

Then they walked back, just as silently as they had come. They had almost reached the manor when Sir Erling said, "I'll do it, Simon Andressøn. You'll have to wait until tomorrow; then we can travel together, all four of us."

Simon looked up at the other man. His face was contorted with shame and grief. He wanted to thank him, but he couldn't. He had to bite his lip hard because his jaw was trembling so violently.

As they entered the hall, Erling Vidkunssøn touched Simon's shoulder, as if by accident. But both of them knew that they dared not look at each other.

The next day, as they were preparing for the journey, Stig Haakonssøn wanted to lend Simon some clothes—he hadn't brought any with him. Simon looked down at himself. His servant had brushed and cleaned his garments, but they were still badly soiled from the long ride in the foul weather. But he gave a slap to his thighs.

"I'm too fat, Stig. And I won't be invited to the banquet anyway."

Erling Vidkunssøn stood with his foot up on the bench as his son attached his gilded spur; Erling seemed to want to keep his servants away as much as possible that day. The knight gave an oddly cross laugh.

"I suppose it wouldn't do any harm if it looked as if Simon Darre had spared nothing in the aid of his brother-in-law, coming right in from the road with his bold and pleasing words. He has a finely tailored tongue, this former kinsman of ours, Stig. There's only one thing I fear—that he won't know when to stop."

Simon's face was dark red, but he didn't reply. In everything that Erling had said to him since the day before, he had noticed this scornful mocking, as well as a strangely reluctant kindness, and a firm will to see this matter through to the end, now that he had taken it on.

Then they set off north from Mandvik: Sir Erling, his son, and Stig, along with ten handsomely outfitted and well-armed men. Simon, with his one servant, thought that he should have had the sense to arrive better attired and with a more impressive entourage. Simon Darre of Formo shouldn't have to ride with his former kinsmen like some smallholder who had sought their support in his helpless position. But he was so weary and broken by what he had done the day before that he now felt almost indifferent to whatever outcome this journey might bring.

Simon had always claimed that he put no faith in the ugly rumors about King Magnus. He was not so saintly a man that he couldn't stand some vulgar jesting among grown men. But when people put their heads together, muttering and shuddering over dark and secret sins, Simon would grow uneasy. And he thought it unseemly to listen to or believe such things about the king, when he was a member of his retinue.

Yet he was surprised when he stood before the young sovereign. He hadn't seen Magnus Eirikssøn since the king was a child, but he had expected there would be something womanish, weak, or unhealthy about him. But the king was one of the most handsome young men Simon had ever set eyes on—and he had a manly and regal bearing, in spite of his youth and slender build.

He wore a surcoat patterned in light blue and green, ankle-length and voluminous, cinched around his slim waist with a gilded belt. He carried his tall, slender body with complete grace beneath the heavy garment. King Magnus had straight, blond hair framing his handsomely shaped head, although the ends of his locks had been artfully curled so they billowed around the staunch, wide column of his neck. The features of his face were delicate and charming, his complexion fresh, with red cheeks and a faint golden tinge from the sun; he had clear eyes and an open expression. He greeted his men with a polite bearing and pleasant courtesy. Then he placed his hand on Erling Vidkunssøn's sleeve and led him several steps away from the others, as he thanked him for coming.

They talked for a moment, and Sir Erling mentioned that he had a particular request to make of the king's mercy and good will. Then the royal servants set a chair for the knight before the king's throne, showed the other three men to seats somewhat farther away in the hall, and left the room.

Without even thinking, Simon had assumed the bearing and demeanor he had learned in his youth. He had relented and agreed to borrow from Stig a brown silk garment so that his attire was no different from what the other men wore. But he sat there feeling as if he were in a dream. He was and yet he was not the same man as that young Simon Darre, the alert and courtly son of a knight who had carried towels and candles for King Haakon in the Oslo castle an endless number of winters ago. He was and was not Simon the owner of Formo who had lived a free and merry life in the valley for all these years—largely without sorrows, although he had always known that within him resided that smoldering ember; but he turned his thoughts away from this. A stifled, ominous sense of revolt rose up inside the man—he had never willfully sinned or caused any trouble that he knew of, but fate had fanned the blaze, and he had to struggle to keep his composure while he was being roasted over a slow fire.

He rose to his feet along with all the others; King Magnus had stood up.

"Dear kinsmen," he said in his young, fresh voice. "Here is how I view this matter. The prince is my brother, but we have never attempted to share a royal retinue—the same men cannot serve us both. Nor does it sound as if this was Erlend's intention, although for a while he might continue as sheriff under my rule, even after becoming one of Haakon's retainers. But those of my men who would rather join my brother Haakon will be released from my service and be permitted to try their fortune at his court.

Who *they* might be—that's what I intend to find out from Erlend's lips."

"Then, my Lord King," said Erling, "you must try to reach agreement with Erlend Nikulaussøn regarding this matter. You must keep the promise of safe conduct which you have made, and grant your kinsman an interview."

"Yes, he is my kinsman and yours, and Sir Ivar persuaded me to promise him safe conduct. But he did not keep his promise to *me,* nor did he remember our kinship." King Magnus gave a small laugh and then placed his hand on Erling's arm once more. "Dear friend, my kinsmen seem to live by the saying we have here in Norway: that a kinsman is the worst enemy of his kin. I am quite willing to show mercy to my kinsman, Erlend of Husaby, for the sake of God and Our Lady and my betrothed; I will grant him his life and property and lift the sentence of banishment if he will be reconciled with me; or I will allow him proper time to leave my kingdoms if he wishes to join his new lord, Prince Haakon. This same mercy I will show to any man who has conspired with him—but I want to know which of my men residing in this country have served their lord falsely. What do you have to say, Simon Andressøn? I know that your father was my grandfather's faithful supporter, and that you yourself served King Haakon with honor. Do you think I have the right to investigate this matter?"

"I think, my Lord King . . ." Simon stepped forward and bowed again, "that as long as Your Grace rules in accordance with the laws and customs of the land, with benevolence, then you will never find out who these men might be who tried to resort to lawlessness and treason. For as soon as the people see that Your Grace intends to uphold the laws and traditions established by your ancestors, then surely no man in this kingdom would think of breaking the peace. Instead, they will hold their tongues and acknowledge what for a time it may have been difficult to believe—that you, my Lord, in spite of your youth, can rule two kingdoms with wisdom and power."

"That is so, Your Majesty," added Erling Vidkunssøn. "No man in this country would think of refusing you allegiance over something which you lawfully command."

"No? Then you think that Erlend may not have incited betrayal and high treason—if we look closer at the case?"

For a moment Sir Erling seemed at a loss for a reply, when Simon spoke.

"You, my Lord, are our king—and every man expects that you will counter lawlessness with law. But if you pursue the path that Erlend Nikulaussøn has embarked upon, then men might step forward to state their names, which you are now pressing so hard to discover, or other men might begin to wonder about the true nature of this case—for it will be much discussed if Your Grace proceeds as you have warned, against a man as well-known and highborn as Erlend Nikulaussøn."

"What do you mean by that, Simon Andressøn?" said the king sharply, and his face turned crimson.

"Simon means," interjected Bjarne Erlingssøn, "that Your Grace might be poorly served if people began to ask why Erlend was not allowed the privilege of personal security, which is the right of every man except thieves and villains. They might even begin to think about King Haakon's other grandsons. . . ."

Erling Vidkunssøn swiftly turned to face his son with a furious expression.

But the king asked dryly, "Don't you consider traitors to be villains?"

"No one will *call* him that, if he wins support for his plans," replied Bjarne.

For a moment they all fell silent. Then Erling Vidkunssøn said, "Whatever Erlend is called, my Lord, it would not be proper for you to disregard the law for his sake."

"Then the law needs to be changed in this case," said the king vehemently, "if it is true that I have no power to obtain information about how the people intend to show their loyalty to me."

"And yet you cannot proceed with a change in the law before it has been enacted without exerting excessive force against the people—and from ancient times the people have had difficulty in accepting excessive force from their kings," said Sir Erling stubbornly.

"I have my knights and my royal retainers to support me," replied Magnus Eirikssøn with a boyish laugh. "What do you say to this, Simon?"

"I think, my Lord . . . it may turn out that this support cannot be counted on, judging by the way the knights and nobles in Denmark and Sweden have dealt with their kings when the people had no power to support the Crown against the nobles. But if Your Grace is considering such a plan, then I would ask you to release me from your service—for then I would rather take my place among the peasants."

Simon spoke in such a calm and composed manner that the king at first seemed not to understand what he had said. Then he laughed.

"Are you threatening me, Simon Andressøn? Do you want to cast down your gauntlet before me?"

"As you wish, my Lord," said Simon just as calmly as before, but he took his gloves from his belt and held them in his hand. Then the young Bjarne leaned over and took them.

"These are not proper wedding gloves for Your Grace to buy!" He held up the thick, worn riding gloves and laughed. "If word gets out, my Lord, that you have demanded such gloves, you might receive far too many of them—and for a good price!"

Erling Vidkunssøn gave a shout. With an abrupt movement he seemed to sweep the young king to one side and the three men to the other; he urged them toward the door. "I must speak to the king alone."

"No, no, I want to talk to Bjarne," called the king, running after them.

But Sir Erling shoved his son outside along with the others.

For some time they roamed around the castle courtyard and out on the slope—no one said a word. Stig Haakonssøn looked pensive, but held his tongue, as he had all along. Bjarne Erlingssøn walked around with a little, secretive smile on his lips the whole time. After a while Sir Erling's armsbearer came out and said that his master requested they wait for him at the hostel—their horses stood ready in the courtyard.

And so they waited at the hostel. They avoided discussing what had happened. Finally they fell to talking about their horses and dogs and falcons. By late that evening, Stig and Simon ended up recounting amorous adventures. Stig Haakonssøn had always had a good supply of such tales, but Simon discovered that whenever he began to tell some remembered story, Stig would take over, saying that either the event had happened to him or it had recently occurred somewhere near Mandvik—even though Simon recalled hearing the tale in his childhood, told by servants back home at Dyfrin.

But he laughed and roared along with Stig. Once in a while he felt as if the bench were swaying under him—he was afraid of something but didn't dare think about what it might be. Bjarne Erlingssøn laughed quietly as he drank wine, gnawed on apples, and fidgeted with his hood; now and then he would tell some little anecdote—and they were always the worst of the lot, but so wily that Stig could not understand them. Bjarne said that he had heard them from the priest at Bjørgvin.

Finally Sir Erling arrived. His son went to meet him, to take his outer garments. Erling turned angrily to the youth.

"You!" He threw his cape into Bjarne's arms. Then a trace of a smile, which he refused to acknowledge, flitted across the father's face. He turned to Simon and said, "Well, now you must be content, Simon Andressøn! You can rest assured that the day is not far off when you will be sitting together in peace and comfort on your neighboring estates—you and Erlend—along with his wife and all their sons."

Simon's face had turned a shade more pale as he stood up to thank Sir Erling. He realized what the fear was that he hadn't dared face. But now there was nothing to be done about it.

About fourteen days later Erlend Nikulaussøn was released. Simon, along with two men and Ulf Haldorssøn, rode out to Akersnes to bring him home.

The trees were already nearly bare, for there had been a strong wind the week before. Frost had set in—the earth rang hard beneath the horses' hooves, and the fields were pale with rime as the men rode in toward town. It looked like snow; the sky was overcast and the daylight was dreary and a chilly gray.

Simon noticed that Erlend dragged one leg a bit as he came out to the castle courtyard, and his body seemed stiff and clumsy as he mounted his horse. He was also very pale. He had shaved off the beard, and his hair was trimmed and neat; the upper part of his face was now a sallow color, while the lower part was white with bluish stubble. There were deep hollows under his eyes. But he was a handsome figure in the long, dark-blue surcoat and cap, and as he bade farewell to Olav Kyrning and handed out gifts of money to the men who had guarded him and brought him food in prison, he looked like a chieftain who was parting with the servants at a wedding feast.

As they rode off, he seemed at first to be freezing; he shivered several times. Then a little color crept into his cheeks, and his face brightened—as if sap and vitality were welling up inside him. Simon thought it was no easier to break Erlend than a willow branch.

They reached the hostel, and Kristin came out to meet her husband in the courtyard. Simon tried to avert his eyes, but he could not.

They took each other's hands and exchanged a few words, their voices quiet and clear. They handled this meeting under the eyes of the servants in a manner that was graceful and seemly enough. Except that they flushed bright red as they gazed at each other for a moment, and then they both lowered their eyes. Erlend once again offered his wife his hand, and together they walked toward the loft room, where they would stay while they were in Oslo.

Simon turned toward the room which he and Kristin had shared up until now. Then she turned around on the lowest step to the loft room and called to him with a strange resonance in her voice.

"Aren't you coming, brother-in-law? Have some food first—and you too, Ulf!"

Her body seemed so young and soft as she stood there with her hip turned slightly, looking back over her shoulder. As soon as she arrived in Oslo, she had begun fastening her wimple in a different manner than before. Here in the south only the wives of smallholders wore the wimple in the old-fashioned way she had worn it ever since she was married: tightly framing her face like a nun's wimple, with the ends crossed in front so her neck was completely hidden, and the folds draped along the sides and over her hair, which was knotted at the nape of her neck. In Trøndelag it was considered a sign of piety to wear the wimple in this manner, which Archbishop Eiliv had always praised as the most seemly and chaste style for married women. But in order to fit in, Kristin had adopted the fashion of the south, with the linen cloth placed smoothly on her head and hanging straight back, so that her hair in front was visible, and her neck and shoulders were free. And another part of the style was to have the braids simply pinned up so they couldn't be seen under the edge of the wimple, with the cloth fitted softly to the shape of her head. Simon had seen this before and thought it suited her—but he had never noticed how young it made her look. And her eyes were shining like stars.

Later in the day a great many people arrived to bring greetings to Erlend: Ketil of Skog, Markus Torgeirssøn, and later that evening Olav Kyrning himself, along with Sira Ingolf and Herr Guttorm, a priest from Saint Halvard's Church. By the time the two priests arrived, it had begun to snow, a fine, dry powder, and they had lost their way in a field and wandered into some burdock bushes—their clothing was full of burrs. Everyone busily fell to picking the burdocks from the priests and their servants. Erlend and Kristin were helping Herr Guttorm; every now and then they would blush as they jested with the priest, their voices strangely unsteady and quavering when they laughed.

Simon drank a good deal early in the evening, but it didn't make him merry—only a little more sluggish. He heard every word that was said, his hearing unbearably sharp. The others soon began speaking openly—none of them supported the king.

After a while he felt so strangely weary of it all. They sat there spouting foolish chatter, in loud and heated voices. Ketil Aasmundssøn was quite a simpleton, and his brother-in-law Markus was not much more clever himself; Olav Kyrning was a right-minded and sensible man, but short-sighted. And to Simon the two priests didn't seem any more intelligent. Now they were all sitting there listening to Erlend and agreeing with him—and he grew more and more like the man he had always been: brash and impetuous. Now he had taken Kristin's hand and placed it on his knee; he was sitting there playing with her fingers—and they sat close together, so their shoulders touched. Now she blushed bright red; she couldn't take her eyes off him. When he put his arm around her waist, her lips trembled and she had trouble pressing them closed.

Then the door flew open, and Munan Baardsøn stepped in.

"At last the mighty ox himself arrives," shouted Erlend, jumping up and going to greet him.

"May God and the Virgin Mary help us—I don't think you're troubled in the least, Erlend," said Munan, annoyed.

"And do you think it would do any good to whine and weep now, kinsman?"

"I've never seen anything like it—you've squandered all your wealth. . . ."

"Well, I was never the kind of man who would go to Hell with a bare backside merely to save my breeches from being burned," said Erlend, and Kristin laughed softly, looking flustered.

Simon leaned over the table and rested his head on his arms. If only they would think he was so drunk that he'd fallen asleep—he just wanted to be left alone.

Nothing was any different than he'd expected—or at least ought to have expected. She wasn't either. Here she sat, the only woman among all these men, as gentle and modest, comfortable and confident as ever. That's how she had been back then—when she betrayed him—shameless or innocent, he wasn't sure. Oh, no, that wasn't true either . . . she hadn't been confident at all, she hadn't been shameless—she hadn't been calm behind that calm demeanor. But the man had bewitched her; for Erlend's sake she would gladly walk on searing stones—and she had trampled on Simon as if she thought he was nothing more than a cold stone.

And here he lay, thinking foolishness. She had wanted to have her way and thought of nothing else. Let them have their joy—it made no difference to him. He didn't care if they produced seven more sons; then there would be fourteen to divide up the inheritance from Lavrans Bjørgulfsøn's estate. It didn't look as if he would have to worry about his own children; Ramborg wasn't as quick to give birth as her sister. And one day his descendants would be left with power and wealth after his death. But it made no difference to him—not this evening. He wanted to keep on drinking, but he knew that tonight God's gifts would have no hold on him. And then he would have to lift his head and perhaps be pulled into the conversation.

"Well, you probably think you would have made a good regent, don't you?" said Munan scornfully.

"No, you should know that we intended that position for you," laughed Erlend.

"In God's name, watch your tongue, man."

The others laughed.

Erlend came over and touched Simon's shoulder.

"Are you sleeping, brother-in-law?" Simon looked up. Erlend was standing before him with a goblet in his hand. "Drink with me, Simon. To you I owe the most gratitude for saving my life—which is dear to me, even such as it is, my man! You stood by me like a brother. If you hadn't been my brother-in-law, I would have surely lost my head. Then you could have had my widow. . . ."

Simon leaped to his feet. For a moment they stood there staring at each other. Erlend grew sober and pale; his lips parted in a gasp.

Simon knocked the goblet out of the other man's hand with his fist; the mead spilled out. Then he turned on his heel and left the room.

Erlend stayed where he was. He wiped his hand and wrist on the fabric of his surcoat without realizing that he was doing so, then looked around—the others hadn't noticed. With his foot he pushed the goblet under the bench, then stood there a moment before following after his brother-in-law.

Simon Darre was standing at the bottom of the stairs. Jon Daalk was leading his horses from the stable. He didn't move when Erlend came down to stand beside him.

"Simon! Simon . . . I didn't know. I didn't know what I was saying!"

"Now you do."

Simon's voice was toneless. He stood stock-still, without looking at the other man.

Erlend glanced around him helplessly. A pale sliver of the moon shone through the veil of clouds; small, hard bits of snow were falling. Erlend shivered in the cold.

"Where . . . where are you going?" he asked uncertainly, looking at the servant and horses.

"To find myself another inn," said Simon curtly. "You know full well that I can't stay *here*."

"Simon!" Erlend exclaimed. "Oh, I don't know what I would give to have those words unsaid!"

"As would I," replied the other man in the same voice.

The door to the loft opened. Kristin stepped out onto the gallery with a lantern in her hand; she leaned over and shone the light on them.

"Is that where you are?" she asked in her clear voice. "What are you doing outdoors?"

"I thought I should see to my horses—as it's the custom for polite people to say," replied Simon, laughing up at her.

"But . . . you've taken your horses out!" she said merrily.

"Yes, a man can do strange things when he's been drinking," said Simon in the same manner as before.

"Well, come back up here now!" she called, her voice bright and joyful.

"Yes. At once." She went inside, and Simon shouted to Jon to put the horses back in the stable. Then he turned to Erlend, who was standing there, his expression and demeanor oddly numb. "I'll come inside in a few minutes. We must try to pretend it was never said, Erlend—for the sake of our wives. But this much you might realize: that you were the last man on earth I wanted . . . to know about . . . this. And don't forget that I'm not as forgetful as you are!"

The door above them opened again; the guests came swarming out, and Kristin was with them; her maid carried the lantern.

"Well, it's getting late," teased Munan Baardsøn, "and I think these two must be longing for bed. . . ."

"Erlend. Erlend. Erlend." Kristin had flung herself into his arms as soon as they were alone inside the loft. She clung tightly to him. "Erlend, you look sad," she whispered fearfully, with her half-parted lips against his mouth. "Erlend?" She pressed both of her hands to his temples.

He stood there for a moment with his arms limply clasped around her. Then, with a soft moaning sound in his throat, he crushed her to him.

Simon walked over to the stable; he was going to tell Jon something, but halfway there he forgot what it was. For a moment he stood in front of the stable door and looked up at the hazy moonlight and the snow drifting down—now bigger flakes were beginning to fall. Jon and Ulf came out and closed the door behind them, and then the three men walked together over to the building where they would sleep.

# III: THE CROSS

PART I

# HONOR AMONG KIN

## CHAPTER 1

DURING THE SECOND year that Erlend Nikulaussøn and Kristin Lavransdatter lived at Jørundgaard, Kristin decided to spend the summer up in the mountain pastures.

She had been thinking about this ever since winter. At Skjenne it had long been the custom for the mistress herself to stay in the mountain pastures; in the past a daughter from the manor had once been lured into the hills, and afterward her mother insisted on living in the mountains each summer. But in many ways they had their own customs at Skjenne; people in the region were used to it and expected as much.

But elsewhere it wasn't customary for the women of the gentry on the large estates to go up to the pastures. Kristin knew that if she did so, people would be surprised and would gossip about it.

In God's name, then, let them talk. No doubt they were already talking about her and her family.

Audun Torbergssøn owned nothing more than his weapons and the clothes on his back when he was wed to Ingebjørg Nikulausdatter of Loptsgaard. He had been a groom for the bishop of Hamar. It was back when the bishop came north to consecrate the new church that Ingebjørg suffered the misfortune. Nikulaus Sigurdssøn took it hard at first, swearing by God and man that a stable-boy would never be his son-in-law. But Ingebjørg gave birth to twins, and people said with a laugh that Nikulaus evidently thought it would be too much to support them on his own. He allowed his daughter to marry Audun.

This happened two years after Kristin's wedding. It had not been forgotten, and people probably still thought of Audun as a stranger to the region; he was from Hadland, of good family, but his lineage had become quite impoverished. And the man himself was not well liked in Sil; he was obstinate, hardheaded, and slow to forget either bad or good, but he was a most enterprising farmer, with a fair knowledge of the law. In many ways Audun Torbergssøn was now a respected man in the parish and a man with whom people were loath to become foes.

Kristin thought about Audun's broad, tanned face with the thick, curly red hair and beard and those sharp, small blue eyes of his. He looked like many other men she had seen; she had seen such faces among their servants at Husaby, among Erlend's men and ship's crew.

She sighed. It must be easier for such a man to assert himself as he sat there on his wife's ancestral estate since he had never ruled over anything else.

All winter and spring Kristin spent time talking to Frida Styrkaarsdatter, who had come with them from Trøndelag and was in charge of all her other maids. Again and again she would tell the woman that such and such was the way they did things here in the valley during the summer, this was what the haymakers were used to getting, and this was how things were done at harvest time. Surely Frida must remember how Kristin had done things the year before. For she wanted everything on the manor to be just as it was during Ragnfrid Ivarsdatter's time.

But to come right out and say that she would not be there on the farm during the summer, that was hard for her to do. She had been the mistress of Jørundgaard for two winters and a summer, and she knew that if she went up to the mountain pastures now, it would be the same as running away.

She realized that Erlend was in a terribly difficult position. Ever since the days when he sat on his foster mother's knee, he had never known anything other than that he was born to command and rule over everything and everyone around him. And if the man had allowed himself to be ruled and commanded by others, at least he had never been aware of this himself.

He couldn't possibly feel the way he outwardly seemed. He must be unhappy here. She herself . . . Her father's estate at the bottom of the quiet, closed-in valley, the flat fields along the curve of the gleaming river through the alder woods, the farms on the cultivated land far below at the foot of the mountain, and the steep slopes above, with the gray clefts against the sky overhead, pale slides of scree and the spruce forest and leafy woods clambering upward through the meadows from the valley—no, this no longer seemed to her the most beautiful and safest home in the world. It felt closed off. Surely Erlend must think that it was ugly and confining and unpleasant.

But no one could tell anything from his appearance except that he seemed content.

On the day when they let out the livestock at Jørundgaard, she finally managed to speak of it, in the evening as they ate their supper. Erlend was picking through the fish platter in search of a good piece; in surprise he sat there with his fingers in the dish while he stared at his wife. Then Kristin added quickly that it was mostly because of the throat ailment that was rampant among the children in the valley. Munan wasn't strong; she wanted to take him and Lavrans along with her up to the mountains.

Well, said Erlend. In that case it would be advisable for Ivar and Skule to go with her too.

The twins leaped up from the bench. During the rest of the meal they both chattered at once. They wanted to go with Erling, who would be camping north among the Gray Peaks with the sheep. Three years before, the sheepherders from Sil had caught a poacher and killed him near his stone hut in the Boar Range; he was a man who had been banished to the forest from Østerdal. As soon as the servants got up from the table, Ivar and Skule brought into the hall all the weapons they owned and sat down to tinker with them.

A little later that evening Kristin set off southward with Simon Andressøn's daughters and her own sons Gaute and Lavrans. Arngjerd Simonsdatter had been at Jørundgaard most of the winter. The maiden was now fifteen years old, and one day during Christmas at Formo, Simon had mentioned that Arngjerd ought to learn something more than what they could teach her at home; she was just as skilled as the serving maids. Kristin had then offered to take the girl home with her and teach her as best she could, for she could see that Simon dearly loved his daughter and worried a great deal about her future. And the child needed to learn other ways than those practiced at Formo. Since the death of his wife's parents Simon Andressøn was now one of the richest men in the region.

He managed his properties with care and good sense, and he oversaw the farm work at Formo with zeal and intelligence. But indoors things were handled poorly; the serving women were in charge of everything. Whenever Simon noticed that the disarray and slovenliness in the house had surpassed all bounds, he would hire one or two more maids, but he never spoke of such things to his wife and seemed neither to wish nor to expect that she should pay more attention to the housekeeping. It was almost as if he didn't yet consider her to be fully grown up, but he was exceedingly kind and amenable toward Ramborg and was constantly showering her and the children with gifts.

Kristin grew fond of Arngjerd after she got to know her. The maiden was not pretty, but she was clever, gentle, good-hearted, nimble-fingered, and diligent. When the young girl accompanied her around the house or sat by her side in the weaving room in the evenings, Kristin often thought that she wished one of her own children had been a daughter. A daughter would spend more time with her mother.

She was thinking about that on this evening as she led Lavrans by the hand and looked at the two children, Gaute and Arngjerd, who were walking ahead of her along the road. Ulvhild was running about, stomping through the brittle layer of nighttime ice on the puddles of water. She was pretending to be some kind of animal and had turned her red cloak around so that the white rabbit fur was on the outside.

Down in the valley in the dusk the shadows were deepening across the bare brown fields. But the air of the spring evening seemed sated with light. The first stars were sparkling, wet and white, high up in the sky, where the limpid green was turning blue, moving toward darkness and night. Above the black rim of the mountains on the other side of the valley a border of yellow light still lingered, and its glow lit up the scree covering the steep slope that towered above them as they walked. At the very top, where the snowdrifts jutted out over the ridges, the snow glistened, and underneath glittered the glaciers, which gave birth to the streams rushing and splashing everywhere down through the scree. The sound of water completely filled the air of the countryside; from below reverberated the loud roar of the river. And the singing of birds came from the groves and leafy shrubbery on all sides.

Once Ulvhild stopped, picked up a stone, and threw it toward the sound of the birds. Her big sister grabbed her arm, and she walked on calmly for a while. But then she tore herself away and ran down the hill until Gaute shouted after her.

They had reached the place where the road headed into the forest; from the thickets came the ringing of a steel bow. Inside the woods snow lay on the ground, and the air smelled cold and fresh. A little farther on, in a small clearing, stood Erlend with Ivar and Skule.

Ivar had taken a shot at a squirrel; the arrow was stuck high up in the trunk of a fir tree, and now he was trying to get it down. He pitched stone after stone at it; the huge mast tree resonated when he struck the trunk.

"Wait a minute. I'll try to see if I can shoot it down for you," said his father. He shook his cape back over his shoulders, placed an arrow in his bow, and took aim rather carelessly in the uncertain light among the trees. The string twanged; the arrow whistled through the air and buried itself in the tree trunk right next to the boy's. Erlend took out another arrow and shot again; one of the two arrows sticking out of the tree clattered down from branch to branch. The shaft of the other one had splintered, but the point was still embedded in the tree.

Skule ran into the snow to pick up the two arrows. Ivar stood and stared up at the treetop.

"It's mine—the one that's still up there, Father! It's buried up to the shaft. That was a powerful shot, Father!" Then he proceeded to explain to Gaute why he hadn't hit the squirrel.

Erlend laughed softly and straightened his cape. "Are you going to turn back now, Kristin? I'm setting off for home; we're planning to go after wood grouse early in the morning, Naakkve and I."

Kristin told him briskly no, that she wanted to accompany the maidens to their manor. She wanted to have a few words with her sister tonight.

"Then Ivar and Skule can go with Mother and escort her home if I can stay with you, Father," said Gaute.

Erlend lifted Ulvhild Simonsdatter up in his arms in farewell. Because she was so pretty and pink and fresh, with her brown curls under the white fur hood, he kissed her before he set her back down and then turned and headed for home with Gaute.

Now that Erlend had nothing else to occupy him, he was always in the company of a few of his sons. Ulvhild took her aunt's hand and walked on a bit; then she started running again, rushing in between Ivar and Skule. Yes, she was a beautiful child, but wild and unruly. If they had had a daughter, Erlend would have no doubt taken her along and played with her too.

At Formo Simon was alone in the house with his little son when they came in. He was sitting in the high seat[1] in the middle of the long table, looking at Andres. The child was kneeling on the outer bench and playing with several old wooden pegs, trying to make them stand on their heads on the table. As soon as Ulvhild saw this, she forgot about greeting her father. She climbed right up onto the bench next to her brother, grabbed him by the back of the neck, and pounded his face against the table while she screamed that they were *her* pegs; Father had given them to *her*.

Simon stood up to separate the children; then he happened to knock over a little pottery dish standing near his elbow. It fell to the floor and shattered.

Arngjerd crawled under the table and gathered up the pieces. Simon took them from her and looked at them, greatly dismayed. "Your mother is going to be angry." It was a pretty little flower-painted dish made of shiny white ceramic that Sir Andres Darre had brought home from France. Simon explained that Helga had inherited it, but she had given it to Ramborg. The women considered it a great treasure. At that moment he heard his wife out in the entryway, and he hid his hands, holding the pottery shards, behind his back.

Ramborg came in and greeted her sister and nephews. She took off Ulvhild's cloak, and the maiden ran over to her father and clung to him.

"Look how fine you are today, Ulvhild. I see that you're wearing your silver belt on a workday." But he couldn't hug the child because his hands were full.

Ulvhild shouted that she had been visiting her aunt Kristin at Jørundgaard; that was why Mother had dressed her so nicely in the morning.

"Yes, your mother keeps you dressed so splendid and grand;

they could set you up on the shrine on the north side of the church, the way you look," said Simon, smiling. The only work Ramborg ever did was to sew garments for her daughter; Ulvhild was always magnificently clothed.

"Why are you standing there like that?" Ramborg asked her husband.

Simon showed her the pottery pieces. "I don't know what you're going to say about this—"

Ramborg took them from him. "You didn't have to stand there looking like such a fool because of this."

Kristin felt ill at ease as she sat there. It was true that Simon had looked quite ridiculous as he stood there hiding the broken pieces in such a childish manner, but Ramborg didn't need to mention it.

"I expected you to be mad because your dish was broken," said her husband.

"Yes, you always seem to be so afraid that something will make me mad—and something so frivolous," replied Ramborg. And the others saw that she was close to tears.

"You know quite well, Ramborg, that's not the only way I act," said Simon. "And it's not just frivolous things either . . ."

"I wouldn't know," replied his wife in the same tone of voice. "It has never been your habit, Simon, to talk to me about important matters."

She turned on her heel and walked toward the entryway. Simon stood still for a moment, staring after her. When he sat down, his son Andres came over and wanted to climb onto his father's lap. Simon picked him up and sat there with his chin resting on the child's head, but he didn't seem to be listening to the boy's chatter.

After a while Kristin ventured, a little hesitantly, "Ramborg isn't so young anymore, Simon. Your oldest child is already seven winters old."

"What do you mean?" asked Simon, and it seemed to her that his voice was unnecessarily sharp.

"I mean nothing more than that . . . perhaps my sister thinks you find her too young to . . . maybe if you could try to let her take charge of things more here on the estate, together with you."

"*My* wife takes charge of as much as she likes," replied Simon heatedly. "I don't demand that she do more than she wants to do, but I've never refused to allow Ramborg to manage anything here at Formo. If you think otherwise, then it's because you don't know—"

"No, no," said Kristin. "But it has seemed to me, brother-in-law, that now and then you don't consider Ramborg to be any older than when you married her. You should remember, Simon—"

"*You* should remember—" he set the child down and jumped to his feet—"that Ramborg and I came to an agreement; you and I never could." His wife came into the room at that moment, carrying a container of ale for the guests. Simon quickly went over to her and placed his hand on her shoulder. "Did you hear that, Ramborg? Your sister is standing here saying that she doesn't think you're happy with your lot." He laughed.

Ramborg looked up; her big dark eyes glittered strangely. "Why is that? I got what I wanted, just as you did, Kristin. If we two sisters can't be happy, then I don't know . . ." And she too laughed.

Kristin stood there, flushed and angry. She refused to accept the ale bowl. "No, it's already late; time for us to head back home now." And she looked around for her sons.

"Oh no, Kristin!" Simon took the bowl from his wife and drank a toast. "Don't be angry. You shouldn't take so much to heart every word that falls between the closest kin. Sit down for a while and rest your feet and be good enough to forget it if I've spoken to you in any way that I shouldn't have."

Then he said, "I'm tired," and he stretched and yawned. He asked how far they had gotten with the spring farm work at Jørundgaard. Here at Formo they had plowed up all the fields north of the manor road.

Kristin left as soon as she thought it was seemly. No, Simon didn't need to accompany her, she said when he picked up his hooded cape and axe; she had her big sons with her. But he insisted and also asked Ramborg to walk along with them, at least up through the fenced fields. She didn't usually agree to this, but tonight she went with them all the way up to the road.

Outdoors the night was black and clear with glittering stars. The faint, warm and pleasant smell of newly manured fields gave a springtime odor to the night frost. The sound of water was everywhere in the darkness around them.

Simon and Kristin walked north; the three boys ran on ahead. She could sense that the man at her side wanted to say something, but she didn't feel like making it easier for him because she was still quite furious. Of course she was fond of her brother-in-law, but there had to be a limit to what he could say and then brush aside afterward—as merely something between kinsmen. He had to realize that because he had stood by them so loyally during their troubles, it wasn't easy for her when he grew quick-tempered or rude. It was difficult for her to take him to task. She thought about the first winter, not long after they had arrived in the village. Ramborg had sent for her because Simon lay in bed with boils in his throat and was terribly ill. He suffered from this ailment now and then. But when Kristin arrived at Formo and went in to see the man, he refused to allow her to touch him or even look at him. He was so irate that Ramborg, greatly distressed, begged her sister's forgiveness for asking her to come. Simon had not been any kinder toward her, she said, the first time he fell ill after they were married and she tried to nurse him. Whenever he had throat boils, he would retreat to the old building they called the Sæmund house, and he couldn't stand to have anyone near him except for a horrid, filthy, and lice-ridden old man named Gunstein, who had served at Dyfrin since before Simon was born. Later Simon would no doubt come to see his sister-in-law to make amends. He didn't want anyone to see him when he was ill like that; he thought it such a pitiful shortcoming for a full-grown man. Kristin had replied, rather crossly, that she didn't understand—it was neither sinful nor shameful to suffer from throat boils.

Simon accompanied her all the way up to the bridge, and as they walked, they exchanged only a few words about the weather and the farm work, repeating things they had already said back at the house. Simon said good night, but then he asked abruptly, "Do you know, Kristin, how I might have offended Gaute that the boy should be so angry with me?"

"Gaute?" she said in surprise.

"Yes, haven't you noticed? He avoids me, but if he can't help meeting me, he barely opens his mouth when I speak to him."

Kristin shook her head. No, she hadn't noticed, "unless you said something in jest and he took it wrong, child that he is."

He heard in her voice that she was smiling; then he laughed a bit and said, "But I can't remember anything of the sort."

And with that he again bade her good night and left.

It was completely quiet at Jørundgaard. The main house was dark, with the ashes raked over the fire in the hearth. Bjørgulf was awake and said that his father and brothers had left some time ago.

Over in the master's bed Munan was sleeping alone. Kristin took him in her arms after she lay down.

It was so difficult to talk about it to Erlend when he didn't seem to realize himself that he shouldn't take the older boys and run off with them into the woods when there was more than enough work to be done on the estate.

That Erlend himself should walk behind a plow was not something she had ever expected. He probably wouldn't be able to do a proper job of it either. And Ulf wouldn't like it much if Erlend interfered in the running of the farm. But her sons could not grow up in the same way as their father had been allowed to do, learning to use weapons, hunting animals, and amusing himself with his horses or poring over a chessboard with a priest who would slyly attempt to cajole the knight's son into acquiring a little knowledge of Latin and writing, of singing and the playing of stringed instruments. She had so few servants on the estate because she thought that her sons should learn even as children that they would have to become accustomed to farm work. It now looked doubtful that there would be any knighthood for Erlend's sons.

But Gaute was the only one of the boys who had any inclination for farming. Gaute was a hard worker, but he was thirteen years old, and it could only be expected that he would rather go with his father when Erlend came and invited him to come along.

It was difficult to talk to Erlend about this because it was Kristin's firm resolve that her husband should never hear from her a single word that he might perceive as a criticism of his behavior or a complaint over the fate that he had brought upon himself and his sons. That meant it wasn't easy to make the father understand that his sons had to get used to doing the work themselves on their estate. If only Ulf would speak of it, she thought.

When they moved the livestock from the spring pastures up to Høvringen, Kristin went along up to the mountains. She didn't want to take the twins with her. They would soon be eleven years old, and they were the most unruly and willful of her children; it was even harder for her to handle them because the two boys stuck together in everything. If she managed to get Ivar alone, he was good and obedient enough, but Skule was hot-tempered and stubborn. And when the brothers were together, Ivar said and did everything that Skule demanded.

## CHAPTER 2

ONE DAY EARLY in the fall Kristin went outside about the time of midafternoon prayers. The herdsman had said that a short distance down the mountainside, if she followed the riverbed, there was supposed to be an abundance of mulleins on a cleared slope.

Kristin found the spot, a steep incline baking in the direct glare of the sun; it was the very best time for picking the flowers. They grew in thick clumps over the heaps of stones and around the gray stubble. Tall, pale yellow stalks, richly adorned with small open stars. Kristin set Munan to picking raspberries in among some brushwood from which he wouldn't be able to escape without her help; she told the dog to stay with him and keep watch. Then she took out her knife and began cutting mulleins, constantly casting an eye at the little child. Lavrans stayed at her side and cut flowers too.

She was always fearful for her two small children in the mountains. Otherwise she was not afraid of the people up there anymore. Many had already gone home from the pastures, but she was thinking of staying until after the Feast of the Birth of Mary. It was pitch black at night now, and vile when the wind blew hard—vile if they had to go outside late at night. But the weather had been so fine up in the heights, while down below, the countryside was parched this year and the grazing was poor. The men would have to stay up in the mountains during both the late fall and winter, but her father had said that he had never noticed anyone haunting their high pastures during the winter.

Kristin stopped under a solitary spruce tree in the middle of the hillside; she stood with her hands wrapped around the heavy weight of the flower stalks that were draped over her arm. From here she could look northward and see halfway to Dovre. In many places the grain was gathered in shocks in the fields.

The hillsides were yellow and sun-scorched over there too. But it was never truly green here in the valley, she thought, not as green as in Trøndelag.

Yes, she longed for the home they had had there: the manor that stood so high and magnificent on the broad breast of the ridge, with fields and meadows spreading out all around, extending below to the cluster of leafy woods that sloped down toward the lake at the bottom of the valley. The vast view across low, forested hills that undulated, wave upon wave, south toward the Dovre Range. And the lush meadows so thick and tall in the summer, red with crimson flowers beneath the red evening sky, the second crop of hay so succulent and green in the autumn.

Yes, sometimes she even felt a longing for the fjord. The skerries of Birgsi, the docks with the boats and ships, the boathouses, the smell of tar and fishing nets and the sea—all those things she had disliked so much when she first went north.

Erlend must be longing for that smell, and for the sea and the sea wind.

She missed everything that she had once found so wearisome: all the housekeeping, the scores of servants, the clamor of Erlend's men as they rode into the courtyard with clanging weapons and jangling harnesses, the strangers who came and went, bringing them great news from all over the land and gossip about people in the town and countryside. Now she realized how quiet her life had become when all this had been silenced.

Nidaros with its churches and cloisters and banquets at the great estates in town. She longed to walk through the streets with her own servingman and maid accompanying her, to climb the loft stairs to the merchants' shops, to choose and reject wares, to step aboard the boats on the river to buy goods: English linen hats, elegant shawls, wooden horses with riders that would thrust out their lances if you pulled a string. She thought about the meadows outside town near Nidareid where she used to walk with her children, looking at the trained dogs and bears of the wandering minstrels, buying gingerbread and walnuts.

And there were times when she longed to dress in her finery again. A silk shift and a delicate, fine wimple. The sleeveless surcoat made of pale blue velvet that Erlend had bought for her the winter before the misfortune befell them. It was edged with marten fur along the deep cut of the bodice and around the wide armholes, which reached all the way down to her hips, revealing the belt underneath.

And occasionally she longed for . . . oh no, she should be sensible and be happy about *that*—happy as long as she was free from having any more children. When she fell ill this autumn after the great slaughtering . . . It was best that it happened that way. But she had wept a little, those first few nights afterward.

It seemed an eternity since she had held an infant. Munan was only four winters old, but she had been forced to give him into the care of strangers before he was even a year. When he came back to her, he could already walk and talk, and he didn't know her.

Erlend. Oh, Erlend. Deep in her heart she knew that he wasn't as nonchalant as he seemed. This man who was always restless, now he seemed always so calm. Like a stream that finally runs up against a steep cliff and lets itself be diverted, trickling out into the peat to become a calm pool with marshlands all around. He wandered about Jørundgaard, doing nothing, and then he would find one or another of his sons to keep him company in his idleness. Or he would go out hunting with them. Once in a while he would go off to tar and repair one of the fishing boats they kept at the lake. Or he would set about breaking in one of the young colts, although he never had much success; he was far too impatient.

He kept to himself and pretended not to notice that no one sought out his company. His sons followed their father's example. They were not well liked, these outsiders who had been driven to the valley by misfortune and who still went about like proud strangers, never inquiring about the customs of the region or its people. Ulf Haldorssøn was outright despised. He was openly scornful of the inhabitants of the valley, calling them stupid and old-fashioned; people who hadn't grown up near the sea weren't proper folks at all.

As for Kristin herself . . . She knew that she didn't have many friends here in her own valley either. Not anymore.

She straightened her back in the peat-brown homespun dress, shading her eyes with her hand against the golden flood of afternoon sunlight.

To the north she caught a glimpse of the valley along the pale green ribbon of the river and then the crush of mountainous shapes, one after the other, grayish yellow with scree and moss-covered plateaus; toward the center, snowdrifts and clouds melded into one another in the passes and ravines. Right across from her the Rost Range jutted out its knee, closing off the valley. The Laag River had to bend its course; a distant roar reached her from the river, which cut deep through the rocky cliffs below and tumbled in a roiling froth from ledge to ledge. Just beyond the mossy slopes at the top of the range towered the two enormous Blue Peaks, which her father had compared to a woman's breasts.

Erlend must think this place hemmed in and hideous, find it difficult to breathe.

It was a little farther to the south, on this same hillside, but closer to the familiar slopes, that she had seen the elf maiden when she was a small child.

A gentle, soft, pretty child with lush silken hair framing her round, pink-and-white cheeks. Kristin closed her eyes and turned her sunburned face up toward the flood of light. A young mother, her breasts bursting with milk, her heart churned up and fecund like a newly plowed field after the birth of her child—yes. But with someone like herself there should be no danger: They wouldn't even try to lure her inside.[1] No doubt the mountain king would find the bridal gold ill suited to such a gaunt and worn-out woman. The wood nymph would have no desire to place her child at Kristin's withered teats. She felt hard and dry, like the spruce root under her foot that curved around stones and clung to the ground. Abruptly she dug her heel into the root.

The two little boys who had come over to their mother rushed to do as she did, kicking the tree root with all their might and then asking eagerly, "Why are you doing that, Mother?"

Kristin sat down, placed the mulleins in her lap, and began tearing off the open blossoms to put in the basket.

"Because my shoe was pinching my toes," she replied so much later that the boys had forgotten what they had asked. But this didn't bother them; they were used to the way their mother seemed not to listen when they spoke to her or the way she would wake up and give an answer after they had long forgotten their own question.

Lavrans helped tear off the flowers; Munan wanted to help too, but he merely shredded the tufts. Then Kristin took the mulleins away from him without a word, showing no anger, completely absorbed in her own thoughts. After a while the boys began playing and fighting with the bare stalks that she had cast aside.

They were making a loud ruckus next to her knee. Kristin looked at the two small, round heads with brown hair. They still looked much alike; their hair was the same light brown color, but from various faint little traits and hastily glimpsed signs, their mother could tell they would grow up to be quite different. Munan was going to look like his father; he had those pale blue eyes and such silky hair, which curled in thick, soft tendrils on his narrow head. It would grow as dark as soot with time. His little face was still so round in the chin and cheeks that it was a pleasure to cup her hands around its tender freshness; his face would become thin and lean when he grew older. He would also have the high, narrow forehead with hollowed temples and the straight, jutting triangle of a nose that was narrow and sharp across the ridge with thin, flaring nostrils, just as Naakkve already had and the twins clearly showed signs of having too.

Lavrans had had flaxen, curly hair as fine as silk when he was small. Now it was the color of a hazelnut, but it gleamed like gold in the sun. It was quite straight and still soft enough, although somewhat coarser and heavier than before, close and thick when she buried her fingers in it. Lavrans looked like Kristin; he had gray eyes and a round face with a broad forehead and a softly rounded chin. He would probably retain his pink-and-white complexion long after he became a man.

Gaute too had that fresh coloring; he looked so much like her father, with a long, full face, iron-gray eyes, and pale blond hair.

Bjørgulf was the only one in whom she could see no resemblance. He was the tallest of her sons, with broad shoulders and heavy, strong limbs. Curly locks of raven-black hair fell low over his broad white forehead; his eyes were blue-black but oddly without luster, and he squinted badly when he looked up. She didn't know when he had actually started doing this, because he was the child to whom she had always paid the least attention. They took him away from her and gave him to a foster mother right after his birth. Eleven months later she had Gaute, and Gaute had been in poor health during the first four years of his life. After the birth of the twins she had gotten out of bed, still ailing and with a pain in her back, and resumed caring for the older child, carrying him around and tending to him. She barely had time to look at the two new children except when Frida brought her Ivar, who was crying and thirsty. And Gaute would lie there screaming while she sat and nursed the infant. She hadn't had the strength . . . Blessed Virgin Mary, you know that I *couldn't* manage to pay more attention to Bjørgulf. And he preferred to keep to himself and do things alone, solitary and quiet as he always had been; he never seemed to like it when she caressed him. She had thought he was the strongest of her children; a young, stubborn, dark bull is how she thought of him.

Gradually she realized that his eyesight was quite poor. The monks had done something for his eyes when he and Naakkve were at Tautra, but it hadn't seemed to help.

He continued to be taciturn; it did no good for her to try to draw Bjørgulf closer. She saw that he was just the same with his father. Bjørgulf was the only one of their sons who didn't warm to Erlend's attention the way a meadow receives the sunlight. Only toward Naakkve was Bjørgulf any different, but when Kristin tried to talk to Naakkve about his brother, he refused to say anything. She wondered whether Erlend had any better luck in those quarters, since Naakkve's love for Erlend was so great.

Oh no, Erlend's offspring readily bore witness to who their father was. She had seen that child from Lensvik when she was in Nidaros the last time. She had met Sir Baard in the Christ Church courtyard. He was coming out the door, accompanied by many men and women and servants; a maid carried the swaddled infant. Baard Aasulfssøn greeted Kristin with a nod of his head, silent and courteous, as they walked past her. His wife was not with him.

She had seen the child's face, just a single glance. But that was enough. He looked like the tiny infant faces that she had held to her own breast.

Arne Gjavvaldssøn was with her, and he couldn't keep from talking—that's just the way he was. Sir Baard's other heirs were not pleased when the child was born the previous winter. But Baard had had him baptized Aasulf. Between Erlend Nikulaussøn and Fru Sunniva there had never been any other friendship than what everyone knew; that's what Baard claimed never to doubt. Indiscreet and reckless as Erlend was, he had probably let too much slip when he was bantering with Sunniva, and it was nothing more than her duty to warn the king's envoys when she became suspicious. But if they had been *too* friendly, then Sunniva must have also known that her brother was involved in Erlend's plans. When Haftor Graut took his own life and forfeited his salvation in prison, she was greatly distraught. No one could know how much she blamed herself during that time. Sir Baard had placed his hand on the hilt of his sword and stared at everyone as he spoke of this, said Arne.

Arne had also mentioned the matter to Erlend. One day when Kristin was up in one of the lofts, the men were standing beneath the gallery, unaware that she could hear their conversation. The Lensvik knight was overjoyed about the son his wife had given birth to the winter before; he never doubted that he himself was the father.

"Yes, well, Baard must know best about that," Erlend had replied. She knew that tone of voice of his; now he would be standing there with lowered eyes and a little smile tugging at the corner of his mouth.

Sir Baard bore such rancor toward his kinsmen who would have been his heirs if he had died childless. But people were now saying this was unfair. "Well, the man himself must know best," said Erlend again.

"Yes, yes, Erlend, but that boy is going to inherit more than the seven sons you have with your wife."

"I will provide for *my* seven sons, Arne."

Then Kristin went downstairs; she couldn't bear to hear them talk anymore about this subject. Erlend was a little startled when he saw her. Then he went over and took her hand, standing behind her so that her shoulder touched his body. She understood that as he stood there, gazing down at her, he was repeating without words what he had just affirmed, as if he wanted to give her strength.

Kristin became aware that Munan was staring up at her a bit anxiously. She had apparently smiled, though not in a pleasant way. But when his mother looked down at him, the boy smiled back, hesitant and uncertain.

Impetuously she pulled him onto her lap. He was little, little, still so little, her youngest . . . not too big to be kissed and caressed by his mother. She winked one eye at him; he wanted to wink back, but try as he might, *both* his eyes kept winking. His mother laughed loudly, and then Munan laughed too, chortling as Kristin hugged him in her arms.

Lavrans had been sitting with the dog on his lap. They both turned toward the woods to listen.

"It's Father!" First the dog and then the boy bounded down the steep slope.

Kristin stayed where she was for a moment. Then she stood up and walked forward to the precipice. Now they appeared on the path below: Erlend, Naakkve, Ivar, and Skule. They shouted greetings up to her, merry and boisterous.

Kristin greeted them in return. Were they on their way up to get the horses? No, Erlend replied. Ulf planned to send Sveinbjørn after them that evening. He and Naakkve were off to hunt reindeer, and the twins had wanted to come along to see her.

She didn't reply. She had realized this even before she asked. Naakkve had a dog on a tether; he and his father were dressed in gray-and-black dappled homespun tunics that were hard to see against the scree. All four were carrying bows.

Kristin asked about news from the manor, and Erlend chatted as they climbed upward. Ulf was in the midst of the grain harvesting. He seemed pleased enough, but the hay was stunted, and the grain in the rest of the fields had ripened too early in the drought; it was falling off the stalks. And the oats would soon be ready to harvest; Ulf said they would have to work fast. Kristin walked along, nodding, without saying a word.

She went to the cowshed herself to do the milking. She usually enjoyed the time she sat in the dark next to the bulging flank of the cow, smelling the sweet breath of the milk as it reached her nose. A spurting sound echoed from the darkness where the milkmaid and herdsman were milking. It created such a calm feeling: the strong, warm smell of the shed, the creaking sounds of the osier door hasps, horns butting against wood, a cow shifting her hooves in the soft muck of the floor and swatting her tail at the flies. The wagtails that had made their nests inside during the summer were gone now.

The cows were restless tonight. Bluesides set her foot down in the milk pail. Kristin gave her a slap and scolded her. The next cow began acting refractory as soon as Kristin moved over to her side. She had sores on her udder. Kristin took off her wedding ring and milked the first spurts through the ring.

She heard Ivar and Skule down by the gate. They were shouting and throwing stones at the strange bull that always followed her cows in the evening. They had offered to help Finn milk the goats in the pen, but they had soon grown bored.

A little later, when Kristin walked up the hill, they were teasing the pretty white calf that she had given to Lavrans, who was standing nearby and whimpering. She put down her pails, seized the two boys by the shoulder and flung them aside. They should leave the calf alone if their brother, who was its owner, told them to do so.

Erlend and Naakkve were sitting on the doorstep. They had a fresh cheese between them, and they were eating sliver after sliver as they fed some to Munan, who was standing between Naakkve's knees. He had put her horsehair sieve on the little boy's head, saying that now Munan would be invisible, because it wasn't really a sieve but a wood nymph's hat. All three of them laughed, but as soon as Naakkve saw his mother, he handed her the sieve, stood up, and took the milk pails from her.

Kristin lingered in the dairy shed. The upper half of the door stood open to the outer room of the hut; they had put plenty of wood on the hearth. In the warm flickering glow, they sat around the fire and ate: Erlend, the children, her maid, and the three herdsmen.

By the time she came in they had finished eating. She saw that the two youngest had been put to bed on the bench along the wall; they were already asleep. Erlend had crawled up into the bed. She stumbled over his outer garments and boots and picked them up as she walked past and then went outside.

The sky was still light, with a red stripe above the mountains to the west. Several dark wisps of clouds hovered in the clear air. It looked as if they would have fair weather the next day too, since it was so calm and biting cold now that night had begun to fall. No wind, but an icy gust from the north, a steady breath from the bare gray slopes. Above the hills to the southeast the moon was rising, nearly full, huge, and still a pale crimson in the slight haze that always lingered over the marshes in that direction.

Somewhere up on the plateau the strange ox was bellowing and carrying on. Otherwise it was so quiet that it hurt—only the roar of the river from below their pasture, the little trickling creek on the slope, and a languid murmuring in the woods—a rustling through the boughs as they moved, paused for a moment, and then moved again.

She busied herself with some milk pans and trenchers that stood next to the wall of the hut. Naakkve and the twins came out, and their mother asked them where they were going.

They were going to sleep in the barn; there was such a foul smell in the dairy shed from all the cheeses and butter and from the goats that slept inside.

Naakkve didn't go to the barn at once. His mother could still see his pale gray figure against the green darkness of the hayfield down at the edge of the woods. A little later the maid appeared in the doorway; she gave a start when she saw her mistress standing near the wall.

"Shouldn't you go to bed now, Astrid? It's getting late."

The maid muttered that she just had to go behind the cowshed. Kristin waited until she saw the girl go back inside. Naakkve was now in his sixteenth year. It was some time ago that his mother had begun keeping an eye on the serving maids on the manor whenever they flirted with the handsome and lively young boy.

Kristin walked down to the river and knelt on a rock protruding out over the water. Before her the river flowed almost black into a wide pool with only a few rings betraying the current, but a short distance above, it gushed white in the darkness with a great roar and cold gusts of air. By now the moon had risen so high that it shone brightly; it glittered here and there on a dewy leaf. Its rays caught on a ripple in the stream.

Erlend called her name from right behind her. She hadn't heard him come down the slope. Kristin dipped her arm in the icy water and fished up a couple of milk pans weighted with stones that were being rinsed by the river. She got to her feet and followed her husband back, with both her hands full. They didn't speak as they clambered upward.

Inside the hut Erlend undressed completely and climbed into bed. "Aren't you coming to bed soon, Kristin?"

"I'm just going to have a little food first." She sat down on her stool next to the hearth with some bread and a slice of cheese in her lap. She ate slowly, staring at the embers, which gradually grew dark in the stone-rimmed hollow in the floor.

"Are you asleep, Erlend?" she whispered as she stood up and shook out her skirt.

"No."

Kristin went over and drank a ladleful of curdled milk from the basin in the corner. Then she went back to the hearth, lifted a stone, and laid it down flat, sprinkling the mullein blossoms on top to dry.

But then she could find no more tasks to do. She undressed in the dark and lay down in the bed next to Erlend. When he put his arms around her, she felt weariness wash over her whole body like a cold wave; her head felt empty and heavy, as if everything inside it had sunk down and settled like a knot of pain in the back of her neck. But when he whispered to her, she dutifully put her arms around his neck.

She woke up and didn't know what time of night it was. But through the transparent hide[2] stretched over the smoke vent she could see that the moon must still be high.

The bed was short and cramped so they had to lie close to each other. Erlend was asleep, breathing quietly and evenly, his chest moving faintly as he slept. In the past she used to move closer to his warm, healthy body when she woke up in the night and grew frightened that he was breathing so silently. Back then she thought it so blissfully sweet to feel his breast rise and fall as he slept at her side.

After a while she slipped out of bed, got dressed in the dark, and crept out the door.

The moon was sailing high over the world. The moss glistened with water, and the rocky cliffs gleamed where streams had trickled during the day—now they had turned to ice. Up on the plateaus frost glittered. It was bitterly cold. Kristin crossed her arms over her breasts and stood still for a moment.

Then she set off along the creek. It murmured and gurgled with the tiny sounds of ice crystals breaking apart.

At the top of the meadow a huge boulder rose up out of the earth. No one ever went near it unless they had to, and then they would be certain to cross themselves. People poured cream under it whenever they went past. Otherwise she had never heard that anyone had ever witnessed anything there, but such had been the custom in that pasture ever since ancient times.

She didn't know what had come over her that she would leave the house this way, in the middle of the night. She stopped at the boulder and set her foot in a crevice. Her stomach clenched tight, her womb felt cold and empty with fear, but she refused to make the sign of the cross. Then she climbed up and sat on top of the rock.

From up there she could see a long, long way. Far into the ugly bare mountains in the moonlight. The great dome near Dovre rose up, enormous and pale against the pale sky. Snowdrifts gleamed white in the pass on the Gray Peaks. The Boar Range glistened with new snow and blue clefts. The mountains in the moonlight were more hideous than she could have imagined; only a few stars shone here and there in the vast, icy sky. She was frozen to the very marrow and bone; terror and cold pressed in on her from all sides. But defiantly she stayed where she was.

She refused to get down and lie in the pitch dark next to the warm, slumbering body of her husband. She could tell that for her there would be no more sleep that night.

As sure as she was her father's daughter, her husband would never hear his wife reproach his actions. For she remembered what she had promised when she beseeched the Almighty God and all the saints in heaven to spare Erlend's life.

That was why she had come out into this troll night to breathe when she felt about to suffocate.

She sat there and let the old, bitter thoughts rise up like good friends, countering them with other old and familiar thoughts—in feigned justification of Erlend.

He had certainly never demanded this of her. He had not asked her to bear any of the things she had taken upon her own shoulders. He had merely conceived seven sons with her. "I will provide for *my* seven sons, Arne." God only knew what Erlend had meant by those words. Maybe he meant nothing; it was simply something he had said.

Erlend hadn't asked her to restore order to Husaby and his other estates. He hadn't asked her to fight with her life to save him. He had borne it like a chieftain that his property would be dispersed, that his life was at stake, and that he would lose everything he owned. Stripped and empty-handed, with chieftainlike dignity and calm he had accepted the misfortune; with chieftainlike calm and dignity he lived on her father's manor like a guest.

And yet everything that was in her possession lawfully belonged to her sons. They lawfully owned her sweat and blood and all her strength. But then surely she and the estate had the right to make claims on them.

She hadn't needed to flee to the mountain pastures like some kind of poor leaseholder's wife. But the situation was such at home that she felt pressed and hemmed in from all sides—until she felt as if she couldn't breathe. Then she had felt the need to prove to herself that she *could* do the work of a peasant woman. She had toiled and labored every hour and every day since she had arrived at the estate of Erlend Nikulaussøn as his bride—and realized that *someone* there would have to fight to protect the inheritance of the one she carried under her heart. If the father couldn't do it, then *she* must. But now she needed to be certain. For that matter, she had demonstrated before to her nursemaids and servant women that there wasn't any kind of work she wasn't capable of doing with her own hands. It was a good day up here if she didn't feel an ache in her flanks from standing and churning. It felt good in the morning when she would go along to let out the cattle; the animals had grown fat and glossy in the summer. The tight grip on her heart eased when she stood in the sunset and called to the cows coming home. She liked to see food growing under her own hands; it felt as if she were reaching down into the very foundation from which the future of her sons would be rebuilt.

Jørundgaard was a good estate, but it was not as good as she had thought. And Ulf was a stranger here in the valley; he made mistakes, and he grew impatient. As people saw it in the region, they always had plenty of hay at Jørundgaard. They had the hay meadows along the river and out on the islands, but it wasn't *good* hay, not the kind that Ulf was used to in Trøndelag. He wasn't used to having to gather so much moss and foliage, heath and brushwood as they did here.

Her father had known every patch of his land; he had possessed all the farmer's knowledge about the whims of the seasons and the way each particular strip of field handled rain or drought, windy summers or hot summers; about livestock that he himself had bred, raised, foddered, and sold from, generation after generation—the very sort of knowledge that was needed here. She did not have that kind of knowledge of her estate. But she would acquire it, and her sons would too.

And yet Erlend had never demanded this of her. He hadn't married her in order to lead her into toil and travail. He had married her so she could sleep in his arms. Then, when her time came, the child lay at her side, demanding a place on her arm, at her breast, in her care.

Kristin moaned through clenched teeth. She was shivering with cold and anger.

"*Pactum serva*—in Norwegian it means 'keep thy faith.' "

That was back when Arne Gjavvaldssøn and his brother Leif of Holm had come to Husaby to take her possessions and the children's belongings to Nidaros. This too Erlend had left for her to handle; he had taken lodgings at the monastery at Holm. She was staying at their residence in town—now owned by the monks—and Arne Gjavvaldssøn was with her, helping her in word and deed. Simon had sent him letters about it.

Arne could not have been more zealous if he had been trying to salvage the goods for himself. On the evening he arrived in town with everything, he wanted both Kristin and Fru Gunna of Raasvold, who had come to Nidaros with the two small boys, to come out to the stable. Seven splendid horses—people wanted to be fair with Erlend Nikulaussøn, and they agreed to Arne's claim that the five oldest boys each owned a horse and that one belonged to the mistress herself and one to her personal servant. He could testify that Erlend had given the Castilian, his Spanish stallion, to his son Nikulaus, even though this had been done mostly in jest. Not that Arne thought much of the long-legged animal, but he knew that Erlend was fond of the stallion.

Arne thought it a shame to lose the magnificent armor with the great helmet and gold-chased sword; it was true that these things were of real use only in a tournament, but they were worth a great deal of money. But he had managed to keep Erlend's coat of mail made of black silk with the embroidered red lion. And he had demanded his English armor for Nikulaus; it was so splendid that Arne didn't think its equal could be found in all of Norway—at least to those who knew how to *see*—although it was in disrepair. Erlend had used his weapons far more than most sons of noblemen at the time. Arne caressed each piece: the helmet, shoulder collar, the leather arm and leg coverings, the steel gloves made of the finest plates, the corselet and skirt made of rings, so light and comfortable and yet so strong. And the sword . . . It had only a plain steel hilt, and the leather of the handle was worn, but the likes of such a blade were rarely seen.

Kristin sat and held the sword across her lap. She knew that Erlend would embrace it like a much-loved betrothed; it was the only one he had used of all the swords he owned. He had inherited it in his early youth from Sigmund Torolfssøn, who had been his bedmate when he first joined the king's retainers. Only once had Erlend ever mentioned this friend of his to Kristin. "If God had not been so hasty to take Sigmund away from this world, many things would have doubtless been different for me. After his death I was so unhappy at the royal palace that I managed to beg permission from King Haakon to go north with Gissur Galle that time. But then I might never have won you, my dear; then I probably would have been a married man for many years before you were a grown maiden."

From Munan Baardsøn she had heard that Erlend nursed his friend day and night, the way a mother cares for her child, getting no more sleep than short naps at the bedside of the ailing man during that last winter when Sigmund Torolfssøn lay vomiting up bits of his heart's blood and lungs. And after Sigmund was buried at Halvard Church, Erlend had constantly visited his grave, lying prostrate on the gravestone to grieve. But to Kristin he had mentioned the man only once. She and Erlend had arranged to meet several times in Halvard Church during that sinful winter in Oslo. But he had never told her that his dearest friend from his youth lay buried there. She knew he had mourned his mother in the same way, and he had been quite frantic with grief when Orm died. But he never spoke of them. Kristin knew that he had gone into town to see Margret, but he never mentioned his daughter.

Up near the hilt she noticed that some words had been etched into the blade. Most of them were runes, which she couldn't read; nor could Arne. But the monk picked up the sword and studied it for a moment. "*Pactum serva*," he said finally. "In Norwegian it means 'keep thy faith.' "

Arne and his brother Leif talked about the fact that a large part of Kristin's properties in the north, Erlend's wedding gifts to her, had been mortgaged and dispersed. They wondered whether there was any way to salvage part of them. But Kristin refused. Honor was the most important thing to salvage; she didn't want to hear of any disputes over whether her husband's dealings had been lawful. And she was deadly tired of Arne's chatter, no matter how well intentioned it was. That evening, when he and the monk bade her good night and went to their sleeping chambers, Kristin had thrown herself to her knees before Fru Gunna and buried her head in her lap.

After a moment the old woman lifted her face. Kristin looked up. Fru Gunna's face was heavy, yellowish, and stout, with three deep creases across her forehead, as if shaped out of wax; she had pale freckles, sharp and kind blue eyes, and a sunken, toothless mouth shadowed by long gray whiskers. Kristin had had that face above her so many times. Fru Gunna had been at her side each time she gave birth, except when Lavrans was born and she was at home to attend her father's deathbed.

"Yes, yes, my daughter," said the woman, putting her hands at Kristin's temples. "I've given you help a few times when you had to sink to your knees, yes, I have. But in this trouble, my Kristin, you must kneel down before the Mother of God and ask her to help you through."

Oh, she had already done that too, thought Kristin. She had said her prayers and read some of the Gospels every Saturday; she had observed the fast days as Archbishop Eiliv had enjoined her to do when he granted her absolution; she gave alms and personally served every wanderer who asked for shelter, no matter how he might look. But now she no longer felt any light inside her when she did so. She knew that the light outside did exist, but it felt as if shutters had closed her off inside. That must be what Gunnulf had spoken of: spiritual drought. Sira Eiliv said that was why no soul should lose courage; remain faithful to your prayers and good deeds, the way the farmer plows and spreads manure and sows. God would send the good weather for growing when it was time. But Sira Eiliv had never managed a farm himself.

She had not seen Gunnulf during that time. He was living north in Helgeland, preaching and collecting gifts for the monastery. Well, yes, that was one of the knight's sons from Husaby, while the other . . .

But Margret Erlendsdatter came to visit Kristin several times at the town residence. Two maids accompanied the merchant's wife. She was beautifully dressed and glittering with jewelry. Her father-in-law was a goldsmith, so they had plenty of jewelry at home. She seemed happy and content, although she had no children. She had received her inheritance from her father just in time. God only knew if she ever gave any thought to that poor cripple Haakon, out at Gimsar. He could barely manage to drag himself around the courtyard on two crutches, Kristin had heard.

And yet she thought that even back then she had not had bitter feelings toward Erlend. She seemed to realize that for Erlend, the worst was still ahead when he became a free man. Then he had taken refuge with Abbot Olav. Tend to the moving or show himself in Nidaros now—that was more than Erlend Nikulaussøn could bear.

Then came the day when they sailed across Trondheim Fjord, on the Laurentius boat, the same ship on which Erlend had transported all the belongings she had wanted to bring north with her after they had won permission to marry.

A still day in late autumn; a pale, leaden gleam on the fjord; the whole world cold, restless, white-ribbed. The first snow blown into streaks along the frozen acres, the chill blue mountains white-striped with snow. Even the clouds high overhead, where the sky was blue, seemed to be scattered thin like flour by a wind high up in the heavens. Heavy and sluggish, the ship pulled away from the land, the town promontory. Kristin stood and watched the white spray beneath the cliffs, wondering if she was going to be seasick when they were farther out in the fjord.

Erlend stood at the railing close to the bow with his two eldest sons beside him. The wind fluttered their hair and capes.

Then they looked across Kors Fjord, toward Gaularos and the skerries of Birgsi. A ray of sunlight lit up the brown and white slope along the shore.

Erlend said something to the boys. Then Bjørgulf abruptly turned on his heel, left the railing, and walked toward the stern of the ship. He fumbled along, using the spear that he always carried and used as a staff, as he made his way between the empty rowing benches and past his mother. His dark, curly head was bent low over his breast, his eyes squinting so hard they were nearly closed, his lips pressed tight. He walked under the afterdeck.

Kristin glanced forward at the other two, Erlend and his eldest son. Then Nikulaus knelt, the way a page does to greet his lord; he took his father's hand and kissed it.

Erlend tore his hand away. Kristin caught a glimpse of his face, pale as death and trembling, as he turned his back to the boy and walked away, disappearing behind the sail.

They put in at a port down by Møre for the night. The sea swells were more turbulent; the ship tugged at its ropes, rising and pitching. Kristin was below in the cabin where she was to sleep with Erlend and the two youngest children. She felt sick to her stomach and couldn't find a proper foothold on the deck, which rose and fell beneath her feet. The skin-covered lantern swung above her head, its tiny light flickering. And she stood there struggling with Munan, trying to get him to pee in between the planks. Whenever he woke up, groggy with sleep, he would both pee and soil their bed, raging and screaming and refusing to allow this strange woman, his mother, to help him by holding him over the floor. Then Erlend came below.

She couldn't see his face when he asked in a low voice, "Did you see Naakkve? His eyes were just like yours, Kristin." Erlend drew in a breath, quick and harsh. "That's the way your eyes looked on that morning out by the fence in the nuns' garden—after you had heard the worst about me—and you pledged me your trust."

That was the moment when she felt the first drop of bitterness rise up in her heart. God protect the boy. May he never see the day when he realizes that he has placed his trust in a hand that lets everything run through its fingers like cold water and dry sand.

A few moments ago she thought she heard distant hoofbeats somewhere on the mountain heights to the south. Now she heard them again, closer. Not horses running free, but a single horse and rider; he rode sharply over the rocky slopes beneath the hillside.

Fear seized her, icy cold. Who could be traveling about so late? Dead men rode north under a waning moon; didn't she hear the other horsemen accompanying the first one, riding far behind? And yet she stayed sitting where she was; she didn't know if this was because she was suddenly bewitched or because her heart was so stubborn that night.

The rider was coming toward her; now he was fording the river beneath the slope. She saw the glint of a spearpoint above the willow thickets. Then she scrambled down from the boulder and was about to run back to the hut. The rider leaped from his horse, tied it to the gatepost, and threw his cape over its back. He came walking up the slope; he was a tall, broad man. Now she recognized him: it was Simon.

When he saw her coming to meet him in the moonlight, he seemed to be just as frightened as she had been before.

"Jesus, Kristin, is that you? Or . . . How is it that you're out at this time of night? Were you waiting for me?" he asked abruptly, as if in great dread. "Did you have a premonition of my journey?"

Kristin shook her head. "I couldn't sleep. Brother-in-law, what is it?"

"Andres is so ill, Kristin. We fear for his life. So we thought . . . We know you are the most practiced woman in such matters. You must remember that he's the son of your own sister. Will you agree to come home with me to tend to him? You know that I wouldn't come to you in this manner if I didn't think the boy's life was in peril," he implored her.

He repeated these words inside the hut to Erlend, who sat up in bed, groggy with sleep and quietly surprised. He tried to comfort Simon, speaking from experience. Such young children grew easily feverish and jabbered deliriously if they caught the least cold; perhaps it was not as dangerous as it looked.

"You know full well, Erlend, that I would not have come to get

Kristin at such an hour of the night if I hadn't clearly seen that the child is lying there, struggling with death."

Kristin had blown on the embers and put on more wood. Simon sat and stared into the fire, greedily drinking the milk she offered him but refusing to eat any food. He wanted to head back down as soon as the others arrived. "If you are willing, Kristin." One of his men was following behind with a widow who was a servant at Formo, an able woman who could take over the work up here while she was away. Aasbjørg was most capable, he said again.

After Simon had lifted Kristin up into the saddle, he said, "I'd prefer to take the shortcut to the south if you're not averse to it."

Kristin had never been on that part of the mountain, but she knew there was supposed to be a path down to the valley, cutting steeply across the slope opposite Formo. She agreed, but then his servant would have to take the other road and ride past Jørundgaard to get her chest and the pouches of herbs and bulbs. He should wake up Gaute; the boy knew best about these things.

At the edge of a large marsh they were able to ride side by side, and Kristin asked Simon to tell her again about the boy's illness. The children of Formo had had sore throats around Saint Olav's Day, but they had quickly recovered. The illness had come over Andres suddenly, while he seemed in the best of health—in the middle of the day, three days before. Simon had taken him along, and he was going to ride on the grain sledge down to the fields. But then Andres complained that he was cold, and when Simon looked at the boy, he was shivering so hard that his teeth were rattling in his mouth. Then came the burning fever and the coughing; he vomited up such quantities of loathsome brown matter and had such pain in his chest. But he couldn't tell them much about where it hurt most, the poor little boy.

Kristin tried to reassure Simon as best she could, and then she had to ride behind him for a while. Once he turned around to ask whether she was cold; he wanted her to take his cape over her cloak.

Then he spoke again of his son. He had noticed that the boy wasn't strong. But Andres had grown much more robust during the summer and fall; his foster mother thought so too. The last few days before he fell ill he had acted a little strange and skittish. "Scared," he had said when the dogs leaped at him, wanting to play. On the day when the fever seized him, Simon had come home in the first rays of dawn with several wild ducks. Usually the boy liked to borrow the birds his father brought home and play with them, but this time Andres screamed loudly when his father swung the bundle toward him. Later he crept over to touch the birds, but when he got blood on his hands, he grew quite wild with terror. And now, this evening, he lay whimpering so terribly, unable to sleep or rest, and then he screamed something about a hawk that was after him.

"Do you remember that day in Oslo when the messenger arrived? You said, 'It will be your descendant who will live on at Formo after you're gone.' "

"Don't talk like that, Simon. As if you think you will die without a son. Surely God and His gentle Mother will help. It's unlike you to be so disheartened, brother-in-law."

"Halfrid, my first wife, said the same thing to me after she gave birth to our son. Did you know that I had a son with her, Kristin?"

"Yes. But Andres is already in his third year. It's during the first two years that it's the most difficult to protect a child's life." But even to her these words seemed to offer little help. They rode and rode; the horses plodded up a slope, nodding and casting their heads about so the harnesses jangled. Not a sound in the frosty night except the sound of their own passage and occasionally the rush of water as they crossed a stream, and the moon shining on everything. The scree and the rocky slopes glistened as hideously as death as they rode along beneath the cliffs.

Finally they reached a place where they could look down into the countryside. The moonlight filled the whole valley; the river and marshes and lake farther south gleamed like silver; the fields and meadows were pale.

"Tonight there's frost in the valley too," said Simon.

He dismounted and walked along, leading Kristin's horse down the hillside. The path was so steep in many places that she hardly dared look ahead. Simon supported her by keeping his back against her knee, and she held on by putting one hand behind on the horse's flank. A stone would sometimes roll from under the horse's hooves, tumbling downward, pausing for a moment, and then continuing to roll, loosening more on the way and carrying them along.

Finally they reached the bottom. They rode across the barley fields north of the manor, between the rime-covered shocks of grain. There was an eerie rustling and clattering in the aspen trees above them in the silent, bright night.

"Is it true," asked Simon, wiping his face with his sleeve, "that you had no premonition?"

Kristin told him it was true.

He went on, "I've heard that it does happen; a premonition can appear if a person yearns strongly for someone. Ramborg and I talked about it several times, that if you had been home, you might have known—"

"None of you has entered my thoughts all this time," said Kristin. "You must believe me, Simon." But she couldn't see it gave him much solace.

In the courtyard a couple of servants appeared at once to take their horses. "Things are just as you left them, Simon—not any worse," one of them said quickly. He had glanced up at the master's face. Simon nodded. He walked ahead of Kristin toward the women's house.

Kristin could see that there was indeed grave danger. The little boy lay alone in the large, fine bed, moaning and gasping, ceaselessly tossing his head from side to side on the pillows. His face was fiery hot and dark red; he lay with his glistening eyes partially open, struggling to breathe. Simon stood holding Ramborg's hand, and all the women of the estate who had gathered in the room crowded around Kristin as she examined the boy.

But she spoke as calmly as she could and comforted the parents as best she could. It was probably lung fever. But this night would soon be over without any turn for the worse; it was the nature of this illness that it usually turned on the third or sixth or ninth night before the rooster crowed. She told Ramborg to send all the servingwomen to bed except for two, so that she would always have rested maids to help her. When the servant returned from Jørundgaard with her healing things, she brewed a sweat-inducing potion for the boy and then lanced a vein in his foot so the fluids would be drawn away from his chest.

Ramborg's face blanched when she saw her child's blood. Simon put his arm around her, but she pushed her husband away and sat down on a chair at the foot of the bed. There she stayed, staring at Kristin with her big dark eyes while her sister tended to the child.

Later in the day, when the boy seemed to be a little better, Kristin persuaded Ramborg to lie down on a bench. She arranged pillows and blankets around the young woman and sat near her head, stroking her forehead gently. Ramborg took Kristin's hand.

"You only wish us well, don't you?" she asked with a moan.

"Why shouldn't I wish you well, sister? The two of us, living here in our village once again, the only ones remaining of our kinsmen . . ."

Ramborg uttered several small, stifled sobs from between her tightly pressed lips. Kristin had seen her young sister cry only once, when they stood at their father's deathbed. Now a few swift little tears rose up and trickled down her cheeks. Ramborg lifted Kristin's hand and stared at it. It was big and slender, but reddish brown now, and rough.

"And yet it's more beautiful than mine," she said. Ramborg's hands were small and white, but her fingers were short and her nails square.

"Yes, it is," she said, almost angrily when Kristin shook her head and laughed lightly. "And you're still more lovely than I have ever been. Our father and mother loved you more than me, all their days. You caused them sorrow and shame; I was docile and obedient and set my sights on the man they most wanted me to marry. And yet they loved you more."

"No, sister. They were just as fond of you. Be happy, Ramborg, that you never gave them anything but joy; you cannot know how heavy the other is to bear. But they were younger back when I was young; perhaps that was why they talked to me more."

"Yes, I think everybody was younger back when you were young," said Ramborg, and sighed again.

A short time later she fell asleep. Kristin sat and looked at her. She had known her sister so little; Ramborg was a child when she herself was wed. It seemed to her that in some ways her sister had remained a child. As she sat beside her ill son she looked like a child, a pale, scared child who was trying stubbornly to fend off terror and misfortune.

Sometimes an animal would stop growing if it had young ones too soon. Ramborg was not even sixteen when she gave birth to her daughter, and ever since she had never seemed to grow properly again; she continued to be slender and small, lacking in vigor and fertility. She had given birth only to the one boy since then, and he was oddly weak—with a handsome face, fair and fine, but so pitifully frail and small. He had learned to walk late, and he still talked so poorly that only those who were with him every day could understand any of his chatter. He was also so shy and peevish with strangers that Kristin had hardly even touched her nephew until now. If only God and Holy Olav would grant her the joy to save this poor small boy, she would thank them for it all her days. The mother was such a child herself that she wouldn't be able to bear losing him. And Kristin realized that for Simon Darre it would also be terribly difficult to bear if his only son were taken from him.

That she had become deeply fond of her brother-in-law became most apparent to her now as she saw how much he was suffering from fear and grief. No doubt she could understand her own father's great love for Simon Andressøn. And yet she wondered whether he might have done wrong by Ramborg when he was in such haste to arrange this marriage. For as she gazed down at her little sister, she thought that Simon must be both too old and much too somber and steadfast to be the husband of this young child.

## CHAPTER 3

THE DAYS PASSED, and Andres remained ill in bed; there were no great changes, either for the worse or for the better. The worst thing was that he got almost no sleep. The boy would lie with his eyes half open, seeming not to recognize anyone, his thin little body racked by coughs, gasping for breath, the fever rising and falling. One evening Kristin had given him a soothing drink, and then calm descended on him, but after a while she saw that the child had turned pale blue and his skin felt cold and clammy. Quickly she poured warm milk down his throat and placed heated stones at the soles of his feet. Then she didn't dare give him any more sleeping potions; she realized that he was too young to tolerate them.

Sira Solmund came and brought the sacred vessels from the church to him. Simon and Ramborg promised prayers, fasts, and alms if God would hear them and grant their son his life.

Erlend stopped by one day; he declined to get down from his horse and go inside, but Kristin and Simon came out to the courtyard to talk to him. He gave them a look of great distress. And yet that expression of his had always annoyed Kristin in an oddly vague and unclear way. No doubt Erlend felt aggrieved whenever he saw anyone either sad or ill, but he seemed mostly perplexed or embarrassed; he looked genuinely bewildered when he felt sad for someone.

After that, either Naakkve or the twins would come to Formo each day to ask about Andres.

The sixth night brought no change, but later the following day the boy seemed a little better; he was not quite as feverish. Simon and Kristin were sitting alone with him around midday.

The father pulled out a gilded amulet he wore on a string around his neck under his clothing. He bent down over the boy, dangling the amulet before his eyes and then putting it in the child's hand, closing the small fingers around it. But Andres didn't seem to take any notice.

Simon had been given this amulet when he himself was a child, and he had worn it ever since; his father had brought it back from France. It had been blessed at a cloister called Mont Saint Michel, and it bore a picture of Saint Michael with great wings. Andres liked to look at it, Simon explained softly. But the little boy thought it was a rooster; he called the greatest of all the angels a rooster. At long last Simon had managed to teach the boy to say "angel." But one day when they were out in the courtyard, Andres saw the rooster screeching at one of the hens, and he said, "The angel's mad now, Father."

Kristin looked up at the man with pleading eyes; it cut her to the heart to listen to him, even though Simon was speaking in such a calm and even voice. And she was so worn out after keeping vigil all these nights; she realized that it would not be good for her to begin weeping now.

Simon stuck the amulet back inside his shirt. "Ah, well. I will give a three-year-old ox to the church on the eve of Saint Michael's Day every autumn for as long as I live if he will wait a little longer to come for this soul. He'd be no more than a bony chicken on the balance scale, Andres, as small as he is—" But when Simon tried to laugh, his voice broke.

"Simon, Simon!" she implored.

"Yes, things will happen as they must, Kristin. And God Himself will decide; surely He knows best." The father said no more as he stood gazing down at his son.

On the eighth night Simon and one of the maids kept watch as Kristin dozed on a bench some distance away. When she woke up, the girl was asleep. Simon sat on the bench with the high back, as he had on most nights. He was sitting with his face bent over the bed and the child.

"Is he sleeping?" whispered Kristin as she came forward.

Simon raised his head. He ran his hand over his face. She saw that his cheeks were wet, but he replied in a calm, quiet voice, "I don't think that Andres will have any sleep, Kristin, until he lies under the turf in consecrated ground."

Kristin stood there as if paralyzed. Slowly her face turned pale beneath the tan until it was white all the way to her lips.

Then she went back to her corner and picked up her outer garments.

"You must arrange things so that you are alone in here when I come back." She spoke as if her throat and mouth were parched. "Sit with him, and when you see me enter, don't say a word. And never speak of this again—not to me or to anyone else. Not even to your priest."

Simon got to his feet and slowly walked over to her. He too had grown pale.

"No, Kristin!" His voice was almost inaudible. "I don't dare . . . for you to do this thing. . . ."

She put on her cloak, then took a linen cloth from the chest in the corner, folded it up, and hid it in her bodice.

"But *I* dare. You understand that no one must come near us afterward until I call; no one must come near us or speak to us until he wakes up and speaks himself."

"What do you think your father would say of this?" he whispered in the same faint voice. "Kristin . . . don't do it."

"In the past I have done things that my father thought were wrong; back then it was merely to further my own desire. Andres is *his* flesh and blood too—my own flesh, Simon—my only sister's son."

Simon took in a heavy, trembling breath; he stood with his eyes downcast.

"But if you don't want me to make this last attempt . . ."

He stood as before, with his head bowed, and did not reply. Then Kristin repeated her question, unaware that an odd little smile, almost scornful, had appeared on her white lips. "Do you not want me to go?"

He turned his head away. And so she walked past him, stepped soundlessly out the door, and closed it silently behind her.

It was pitch dark outside, with small gusts of wind from the south making all the stars blink and flicker uneasily. She had reached no farther than the road up between the fences when she felt as if she had stepped into eternity itself. An endless path both behind her and up ahead. As if she would never emerge from what she had entered into when she walked out into this night.

Even the darkness was like a force she was pressing against. She plodded through the mud; the road had been churned up by the carts carrying unthreshed grain, and now it was thawing in the south wind. With every footstep she had to pull herself free from the night and the raw chill that clung to her feet, swept upward, and weighted down the hems of her garments. Now and then a falling leaf would drift past her, as if something alive were touching her in the dark—gentle but confident of its superior power: Turn back.

When she came out onto the main road, it was easier to walk. The road was covered with grass, and her feet did not get stuck in the mire. Her face felt as rigid as stone, her body tensed and taut. Each step carried her mercilessly toward the forest grove through which she would have to pass. A feeling rose up inside her like an inner paralysis: She couldn't possibly walk through that patch of darkness. But she had no intention of turning around. She couldn't feel her body because of her terror, yet all the while she kept moving forward, as if in her sleep, steadily stepping over stones and roots and puddles of water, unconsciously careful not to stumble or break her steady stride and thus allow fear to overwhelm her.

Now the spruce trees rustled closer and closer in the night; she stepped in among them, still as calm as a sleepwalker. She sensed every sound and hardly dared blink because of the dark. The drone of the river, the heavy sighing of the firs, a creek trickling over stones as she walked toward it, passed by it, and then continued on. Once a rock slid down the scree, as if some living creature were moving about up there. Sweat poured from her body, but she did not venture either to slow or to speed her step because of it.

Kristin's eyes had now grown so accustomed to the dark that when she emerged from the woods, she could see much better; a glint came from the ribbon of the river and from the water on the marshes. The fields became visible in the blackness; the clusters of buildings looked like clumps of earth. The sky was also beginning to lighten overhead; she could feel it, although she didn't dare look up at the black peaks towering above. But she knew that it would soon be time for the moon to rise.

She tried to remind herself that in four hours it would be daytime; people would be setting about their daily chores on all the farms throughout the countryside. The sky would grow pale with dawn; the light would rise over the mountains. Then it wouldn't seem far to go; in the daylight it wasn't far from Formo to the church. And by then she would have returned home long ago. But it was clear that she would be a different person.

She knew that if it had been one of her own children, she would not have dared make this last attempt. To turn away God's hand when He reached out for a living soul. When she kept watch over her own ill children, back when she was young and her heart bled with tenderness, when she thought she would collapse in anguish and torment, she had tried to say: Lord, you love them better than I do, let thy will be done.

But now on this night she was walking along, defying her own terror. This child who was not her own—she *would* save him, no matter what fate she was saving him for. . . .

Because you too, Simon Darre, acquiesced when the dearest thing you possessed on earth was at stake; you agreed to more than anyone can accept with full honor.

Do you not want me to go? He hadn't been man enough to answer. Deep in her heart she knew that if the child died, Simon would have the strength to bear this too. But she had struck at the only moment when she ever saw him on the verge of breaking down; she had seized hold of that moment and carried it off. She would share that secret with him, the knowledge that she had also witnessed *him* when he once stood unsteady on his feet.

For he had learned too much about her. She had accepted help from the man she had spurned every time it was a matter of saving the one she had chosen. This suitor whom she had cast aside—he was the man she had turned to each time she needed someone to protect her love. And never had she asked for Simon's help in vain. Time after time he had stepped forward, covering her with his kindness and his strength.

So she was undertaking this nighttime errand to rid herself of a little of the debt; until that hour, she hadn't fully realized how heavy a burden it was.

Simon had forced her to see at last that he was the strongest: stronger than she was and stronger than the man to whom she had chosen to give herself. No doubt she had realized this from the moment all three of them met, face-to-face, in that shameful place in Oslo. And yet she had refused to accept it then: that such a plump-cheeked, stout, and gaping young man could be stronger than . . .

Now she was walking along, not daring to call on a good and holy name; she took upon herself this sin in order to . . . She didn't know what. Was it revenge? Revenge because she had been forced to see that he was more noble-minded than the two of them?

But now you too understand, Simon, that when the life of the one you love more than your own heart is at stake . . . Then the poor person grasps for anything, anything.

The moon had risen over the mountain ridge as she walked up the hill to the church. Again she felt as if she had to overcome a new wave of terror. The moonlight lay like a delicate spiderweb over the tar-timbered edifice. The church itself looked terrifying and ominously dark beneath the thin veil. Out on the green she saw the cross, but for the first time she didn't dare approach to kneel before the blessed tree. She crept over the churchyard wall at the place where she knew the sod and stone were the lowest and most easily breached.

Here and there a gravestone glistened like water down in the tall, dewy grass. Kristin walked straight across the cemetery to the graves of the poor, which lay near the south wall.

She went over to the burial place of a poor man who had been a stranger in the parish. One winter the man had frozen to death on the mountainside. His two motherless daughters had been taken in by one farm after another,[1] until Lavrans Bjørgulfsøn had offered to keep them and bring them up, for the sake of Christ. When they were full grown and had turned out well, Kristin's father had found honorable, hardworking husbands for them and married them off with cows and calves and sheep. Ragnfrid had given them bedding and iron pots. Now both women were well provided for, as befitted their station. One of them had been Ramborg's maid, and Ramborg had carried the woman's child to be baptized.

So you must grant me a bit of the turf covering you, Bjarne, for Ramborg's son. Kristin knelt down and pulled out her dagger.

Drops of ice cold sweat prickled her brow and upper lip as she dug her fingers under the dew-drenched sod. The earth resisted . . . it was only roots. She sliced through them with the dagger.

In return, the ghost must be given gold or silver that had been passed down through three generations. She slipped off the little gold ring with the rubies that had been her grandmother's betrothal ring.

The child is my father's descendant.

She pushed the ring as far down into the earth as she could, wrapped the piece of sod in the linen cloth, and then spread peat and leaves over the spot where she had removed it.

When she stood up, her legs trembled under her, and she had to pause for a moment before she could turn around. If she looked under her arm right now, she would be able to see them.

She felt a terrible tugging inside her, as if they would force her to do so. All the dead who had known her before in this world. Is that you, Kristin Lavransdatter? Are you coming here in this way?

Arne Gyrdsøn lay buried outside the west entrance. Yes, Arne, you may well wonder—I was not like this, back when you and I knew each other.

Then she climbed over the wall again and headed down the slope.

The moon was now bright over the countryside. Jørundgaard lay out on the plain; the dew glittered in the grass on all the rooftops. She stared in that direction, almost listlessly. She felt as if she herself were dead to that home and all the people there; the door was closed to her, to the woman who had wandered past, up along the road on this night.

The mountains cast their shadows over her nearly the whole way back. The wind was blowing harder now; one gust of wind after another came straight toward her. Withered leaves blew against her, trying to send her back to the place she had just left.

Nor did she believe that she was walking along unaccompanied. She heard the steady sound of stealthy footsteps behind her. Is that you, Arne?

Look back, Kristin, look under your arm, it urged her.

And yet she didn't feel truly afraid anymore. Just cold and numb, sick with desire to give up and sink down. After this night she could never be afraid of anything else in the world.

Simon was sitting in his usual place at the head of the bed, leaning over the child, when she opened the door and stepped inside. For a brief moment he looked up; Kristin wondered if she had grown as worn out and haggard and old as he had during these days. Then Simon bowed his head and hid his face with his arm.

He staggered a bit as he got to his feet. He turned his face away from her as he walked past and over to the door, his head bowed, his shoulders slumped.

Kristin lit two candles and set them on the table. The boy opened his eyes slightly and looked up, his gaze strangely unseeing; he whimpered a bit and tried to turn his head toward the light. When Kristin straightened out his little body, the way a corpse is laid out, he tried to change position, but he seemed too weak to move.

Then she covered his face and chest with the linen cloth and placed the strip of sod on top.

At that moment the terror seized her again, like a great sea swell.

She had to sit down on the bed. The window was right above the short bench, and she didn't dare sit with her back to it. Better to look them in the eyes if anyone should be standing outside and looking in. She pulled the high-backed chair over to the bed and sat down facing the windowpane. The stifling black of the night pressed against it; one of the candles was reflected in the glass. Kristin fixed her eyes on it, clutching the arms of the chair so that her knuckles grew white; now and then her arms trembled. She couldn't feel her own legs, as chilled and wet as they were. She sat there with her teeth chattering from horror and cold, and the sweat ran like ice water down her face and back. She sat without moving, merely casting now and then a quick glance at the linen cloth, which faintly rose and fell with the child's breath.

Finally the pale light of dawn appeared in the windowpane. The rooster crowed shrilly. Then she heard men out in the courtyard. They were heading for the stable.

She slumped against the back of the chair, shuddering as if with convulsions, and tried to find a position for her legs so they wouldn't twitch and jerk around from the shaking.

There was a strong movement under the linen cloth. Andres pushed it away from his face, whimpering crossly. He seemed partially conscious since he grunted at Kristin when she jumped to her feet and leaned over him.

She grabbed the cloth and sod, rushed over to the fireplace, and stuffed twigs and wood inside it; then she threw the ghostly goods into the fresh, crackling fire. She had to stand still for a moment, holding on to the wall. The tears poured down Kristin's face.

She took a ladleful of milk from the little pot that stood near the hearth and carried it over to the child. Andres had fallen asleep again. He seemed to be slumbering peacefully now.

Then she drank the milk herself. It tasted so good that she had to gulp down two or three more ladlefuls of the warm drink.

Still, she didn't dare speak; the boy hadn't yet said a comprehensible word. But she sank to her knees next to the foot of the bed and recited mutely to herself:

> Convertere, Domine, aliquantulum; et deprecare super servos tuos. Ne ultra memineris iniquitatis nostræ: ecce respice; populus tuus omnes nos.[2]

Yes, yes, yes. This was a terrible thing she had done. But he was their only son. While she herself had seven! Shouldn't she try *everything* to save her sister's only son?

All the thoughts she had had during the night—they were merely ramblings of the night. She had done it only because she couldn't stand to see this child die in her hands.

Simon—the man who had never failed her. The one who had been loyal and good toward every child she had ever known and most of all toward herself and her own. And this son whom he loved above all else—shouldn't she use every measure to save the boy's life? Even if it was a sin?

Yes, it was sinful, but let the punishment fall on me, God. That poor, beautiful, innocent son of Simon and Ramborg. God would not allow Andres to be punished.

She went back and leaned over the bed, breathing on the tiny, waxen hand. She didn't dare kiss it; he mustn't be wakened.

So fair and blameless.

It was during the nights of terror when they were left alone at Haugen that Fru Aashild had told her about it—told her about her own errand to the cemetery at Kongunahelle. "That, Kristin, was surely the most difficult task I have ever undertaken." But Bjørn Gunnarssøn was not an innocent child when he lay there after Aashild Gautesdatter's cousins had come too close to his heart with their swords. He had slain one man before he was brought down himself, and the other man never regained his vigor after the day he exchanged blows with Herr Bjørn.

Kristin stood at the window and looked out into the courtyard. Servants were moving from building to building, going about the day's chores. Several young calves were roaming about the yard; they were so lovely.

Many different thoughts rise up in the darkness—like those gossamer plants that grow in the lake, oddly bewitching and pretty as they bob and sway; but enticing and sinister, they exert a dark pull as long as they're growing in the living, trickling mire. And yet they're nothing but slimey brown clumps when the children pull them into the boat. So many strange thoughts, both terrifying and enticing, grow in the night. It was probably Brother Edvin who once said that those condemned to Hell had no wish to give up their torment: hatred and sorrow were their pleasures. That was why Christ could never save them. Back then this had sounded to her like wild talk. An icy shiver ran through her; now she was beginning to understand what the monk had meant.

She leaned over the bed once more, breathing in the smell of the little child. Simon and Ramborg were not going to lose him. Even though she had done it out of a need to prove herself to Simon, to show him that she could do something other than take from him. She had needed to take a risk on his behalf, to repay him.

Then she knelt again, repeating over and over as much as she could remember from the prayer book.

That morning Simon went out and sowed winter rye in the newly plowed field south of the grove. He had decided he must act as if this were merely reasonable, because the work on the estate had to continue as usual. The serving maids had been greatly surprised when he went in to them during the night to tell them that Kristin wanted to be alone with the boy until she sent word. He said the same to Ramborg when she got up: Kristin had requested that no one should go near the women's house that day.

"Not even you?" she asked quickly, and Simon said no. That was when he went out to get the seed box.

But after the midday meal he stayed up at the manor; he didn't have the heart to go far from the buildings. And he didn't like the look in Ramborg's eyes. A short time after the noonday rest it happened. He was standing down by the grain barn when he saw his wife racing across the courtyard. He rushed after her. Ramborg threw herself at the door to the women's house, pounding on it with her fists and screaming shrilly for Kristin to open up.

Simon put his arms around her, speaking gently. Then she bent down as fast as lightning and bit him on the hand. He saw that she was like a raging beast.

"He's *my* child! What have the two of you done to my son?"

"You know full well that your sister wouldn't do anything to Andres except what might do him good." When he put his arms around her again, Ramborg struggled and screamed.

"Come now, Ramborg," said her husband, making his voice stern. "Aren't you ashamed in front of our servants?"

But she kept on screaming. "He's mine—that much I know. You weren't with us when I gave birth to him, Simon," she shouted. "We weren't so precious to you back then."

"You know what I had on my hands at the time," replied her husband wearily. He dragged her across to the main house; he had to use all his strength.

After that he didn't dare leave her side. Ramborg gradually calmed down, and when evening came, she obediently allowed her maids to help her undress.

Simon stayed up. His daughters were asleep over in their bed, and he had sent the servingwomen away. Once when he stood up and walked across the room, Ramborg asked from her bed where he was going; her voice sounded wide awake.

"I was thinking of lying down with you for a while," he said after a moment. He took off his outer garments and shoes and then crawled under the blanket and woolen coverlet. He put his arm around his wife's shoulders. "I realize, my Ramborg, that this has been a long and difficult day for you."

"Your heart is beating so hard, Simon," she said a little later.

"Well, I'm afraid for the boy too, you know. But we must wait patiently until Kristin sends us word."

He sat up abruptly in bed, propping himself up on one elbow. In bewilderment he stared at Kristin's white face. It was right above his own, glistening wet with tears in the candlelight; her hand was on his chest. For a moment he thought . . . But this time he wasn't merely dreaming. Simon threw himself back against the headboard, and with a stifled moan he covered his face with his arm. He felt sick; his heart was hammering inside him, furious and hard.

"Simon, wake up!" Kristin shook him again. "Andres is calling for his father. Do you hear me? It was the first thing he said." Her face was beaming with joy as her tears fell steadily.

Simon sat up, rubbing his face several times. Surely he hadn't spoken in confusion when she woke him. He looked up at Kristin, who was standing next to the bed with a lantern in her hand.

Quietly, so as not to wake Ramborg, he crept out of the room with her. The loathsome nausea was still lodged in his chest. He felt as if something were about to burst inside him. Why couldn't he stop having that dreadful dream? He who in his waking hours struggled and struggled to drive all such thoughts from his mind. But when he lay asleep, powerless and defenseless, he would have that dream, which the Devil himself must have sent. Even now, while she sat and kept watch over his deathly ill son, he dreamed like some kind of demon.

It was raining, and Kristin had no idea what time of night it might be. The boy had been half conscious, but he hadn't spoken. And it was only when night came and she thought he was sleeping comfortably and soundly that she dared lie down for a moment to rest—with Andres in her arms so she would notice if he stirred. Then she had fallen asleep.

The boy looked so tiny as he lay alone in the bed. He was terribly pale, but his eyes were clear, and his face lit up with a smile when he saw his father. Simon dropped to his knees beside the bed, but when he reached out to lift the small body into his embrace, Kristin grabbed him by the arm.

"No, no, Simon. He's soaked with sweat, and it's cold in here." She pulled the covers tighter around Andres. "Lie down next to him instead, while I send word for a maid to keep watch. I'll go back to the main house now and get into bed with Ramborg."

Simon crept under the covers. There was a warm hollow where she had lain and the faint, sweet scent of her hair on the pillowcase. Simon quietly uttered a moan, and then he gathered up his little son and pressed his face against the child's damp, soft hair. Andres had become so small that he felt like nothing in Simon's arms, but he lay there contentedly, occasionally saying a word or two.

Then he began tugging and poking at the opening of his father's shirt; he stuck his clammy little hand inside and pulled out the amulet. "The rooster," he said happily. "There it is."

On the day of Kristin's departure, as she made ready to leave, Simon came to see her in the women's house and handed her a little wooden box.

"I thought this was something you might like to have."

Kristin knew from the carving that it was the work of her father. Inside, wrapped in a soft piece of glove leather, was a tiny gold clasp set with five emeralds. She recognized it at once. Lavrans had worn it on his shirt whenever he wanted to look particularly fine.

She thanked Simon, but then she turned blood red. She suddenly remembered that she had never seen her father wear this clasp since she had come home from the convent in Oslo.

"When did Father give this to you?" She regretted the question the moment she asked it.

"He gave it to me as a farewell gift one time when I was leaving the estate."

"This seems to me much too great a gift," she said softly, looking down.

Simon chuckled and replied, "You're going to need many such things, Kristin, when the time comes for you to send out all your sons with betrothal gifts."

Kristin looked at him and said, "You know what I mean, Simon—those things that my father gave you . . . You know that I'm as fond of you as if you had been his own son."

"Are you?" He placed the back of his hand against her cheek and gave it a fleeting caress as he smiled, an odd little smile, and spoke as if to a child, "Yes, yes, Kristin. I know that."

## CHAPTER 4

LATER THAT FALL Simon Andressøn had business with his brother at Dyfrin. While he was there, a suitor was proposed for his daughter Arngjerd.

The matter was not settled, and Simon felt rather uneasy and apprehensive as he rode northward. Perhaps he ought to have agreed; then the child would have been well provided for, and he could stop all his worrying about her future. Perhaps Gyrd and Helga were right. It was foolish of him not to seize hold with both hands when he received such an offer for this daughter of his. Eiken was a bigger estate than Formo, and Aasmund himself owned more than a third of it; he would never have thought of proposing his son as a suitor for a maiden of such birth as Arngjerd—of lowly lineage and with no kin on her mother's side—if Simon hadn't held a mortgage on a portion of the estate worth three marks in taxes. The family had been forced to borrow money from both Dyfrin and the nuns in Oslo when Grunde Aasmundssøn happened to slay a man for the second time. Grunde grew wild when he was drunk, although he was otherwise an upright and well-meaning fellow, said Gyrd, and surely he would allow himself to be guided by such a good and sensible woman as Arngjerd.

But the fact was that Grunde was not many years younger than Simon himself. And Arngjerd was young. And the people at Eiken wanted the wedding to take place as early as spring.

It hung on like a bad memory in Simon's mind; he tried not to think of it if he could avoid it. But now that Arngjerd's marriage had come under discussion, it kept cropping up. He had been an unhappy man on that first morning when he woke up at Ramborg's side. Certainly he had been no more giddy or bold than a bridegroom ought to be when he went to bed—although it had made him feel strange and reckless to see Kristin among the bride's attendants, and Erlend, his new brother-in-law, was among the men who escorted him up to the loft. But when he woke up the next morning and lay there looking at his bride, who was still asleep, he had felt a terrible, painful shame deep in his heart—as if he had mistreated a child.

And yet he knew that he could have spared himself this sorrow. But *she* had laughed when she opened her big eyes.

"Now you're *mine*, Simon." She ran her hands over his chest. "My father is your father, and my sister is your sister." And he grew cold with anguish, for he wondered whether she knew that his heart had given a start at her words.

Otherwise he was quite content with his marriage—this much he firmly believed. His wife was wealthy, of distinguished lineage, young and lively, beautiful and kind. She had borne him a daughter and a son, and that was something a man valued after he had tried living among riches without producing any children who could keep the estate together after the parents were gone. Two children, and their position was assured. He was so rich that he could even obtain a good match for Arngjerd.

He would have liked to have another son; yes, he wouldn't be sad if one or two more children were born on Formo. But Ramborg was probably happy as long as she was spared all that. And that was worth something too. For he couldn't deny that things were much more comfortable at home when Ramborg was in good humor. He might well have wished that she had a more even temperament. He didn't always know how he stood with his wife. And more attention could have been paid to the housekeeping in his home. But no man should dare expect to have all his bowls filled to the brim, as the saying goes. This is what Simon kept telling himself as he rode homeward.

Ramborg was to travel to Kruke during the week before Saint Clement's Day; it always cheered her up to get away from home for a while.

God only knew how things would go over there this time around. Sigrid was now carrying her eighth child. Simon had been shocked when he paid a visit to his sister on his way south; she didn't look as if she could stand much more.

He had offered four thick wax tapers to the ancient image of the Virgin Mary at Eyabu, which was supposed to be particularly powerful in effecting miracles, and he had promised many gifts if Sigrid made it through with her life and her health. How things would go with Geirmund and all their children if the mother died and left them behind . . . No, he couldn't think about that.

They lived together so well, Sigrid and Geirmund. Never had she heard an unkind word from her husband, she said; never had he left anything undone that he thought might please her. When he noticed that Sigrid was wasting away with longing for the child she had borne in her youth with Gjavvald Arnessøn, he had asked Simon to bring the boy to visit so the mother could spend some time with him. But Sigrid had reaped only sorrow and disappointment from the reunion with that spoiled, rich man's son. Since then Sigrid Andresdatter had clung to her husband and the children she had with him, the way a poor, ailing sinner clings to her priest and confession.

Now she seemed fully content in many ways. And Simon understood why. Few men were as pleasant to be with as Geirmund. He had such a fine voice that even if he was only talking about the narrow-hoofed horse that had been foisted upon him, it was almost like listening to harp music.

Geirmund Hersteinssøn had always had a strange and ugly face, but in the past he had been a strong man, with a handsome build and limbs, the best bowman and hunter, and better than most in all sports. Three years ago he had become a cripple, after he returned to the village from a hunting expedition, crawling on his hands and one knee, with the other leg crushed and dragging behind him. Now he couldn't walk across the room without a cane, and he couldn't mount a horse or hobble around the steep slopes of the fields without help. Misfortune constantly plagued him, such an odd and eccentric man as he was, and ill prepared for safeguarding his property or welfare. Anyone who had the heart for it could fool him in trade or business dealings. But he was clever with his hands, an able craftsman in both wood and iron, and a wise and skilled speaker. And when this man took his harp on his lap, Geirmund could make people laugh or cry with his singing and playing. It was almost like listening to the knight in Geirmund's song who could entice the leaves from the linden tree and the horn from the lively cattle with his playing.

Then the older children would take up the refrain and sing along with their father. They were more lovely to hear than the chiming of all the bells in the bishop's Hamar. The next youngest child, Inga, could walk if she held on to the bench, although she had not yet learned to talk. But she would hum and sing all day long, and her tiny voice was so light and delicate, like a little silver bell.

They lived crowded together in a small, dark old hearth house: the man and his wife, the children, and the servants. The loft, which Geirmund had talked of building all these years, would now probably never be built. He had barely managed to put up a new barn to replace the one that had burned the previous year. But the parents couldn't bear to part with a single one of their many children. Every time he visited Kruke, Simon had offered to take some of them in and raise them; Geirmund and Sigrid had thanked him but declined.

Simon sometimes thought that perhaps she was the one among his siblings who had found the best life, after all. Although Gyrd did say that Astrid was quite pleased with her new husband; they lived far south in Ry County, and Simon hadn't seen them since their wedding. But Gyrd had mentioned that the sons of Torgrim were constantly quarreling with their stepfather.

And Gudmund was very happy and content. But if that was man's happiness, then Simon thought it would not be a sin to thank God that their father hadn't lived to see it. As soon as it could be decently permitted after Andres Darre's death, Gudmund had celebrated his wedding to the widow whom his father wouldn't allow him to marry. The knight of Dyfrin thought that since he had sought out young, rich, and beautiful maidens of distinguished families and unblemished reputation for his two eldest sons, and this had led to little joy for either Gyrd or Simon, then it would mean pure misery for Gudmund if his father allowed him to follow his own foolish wishes. Tordis Bergsdatter was much older than Gudmund, moderately wealthy, and she had had no children from her first marriage. But afterward she had given birth to a daughter by one of the priests at the Maria Church in Oslo, and people said that she had been much too amenable toward other men as well—including Gudmund Darre, as soon as she became acquainted with him. She was as ugly as a troll, and much too rude and coarse in speech for a woman, thought Simon. But she was lively and witty, intelligent and good-natured. He knew that he would have been fond of Tordis himself, if only she hadn't married into their lineage. Now Gudmund was flourishing, and it was dreadful to witness; he was almost as stout and portly as Simon. And that was not Gudmund's nature; in his youth he had been slender and handsome. He had grown so flabby and indolent that Simon felt an urge to give the boy a thrashing every time he saw him. But it was true that Gudmund had been a cursed simpleton all his days. And the fact that his children took their wits from their mother but their looks from him was at least one bit of luck in this misfortune. And yet Gudmund was thriving.

So Simon didn't need to fret as much as he did over his brother. And in some ways it was probably also needless for him to lament on Gyrd's behalf. But each time he went home to his father's manor and saw how things now stood there, he felt so dreadfully overwhelmed that his heart ached when he left.

The wealth of the estate had increased; Gyrd's brother-in-law, Ulf Saksesøn, now enjoyed the king's full favor and grace, and he had drawn Gyrd Andressøn into the circle of men who possessed the most power and advantages in the realm. But Simon didn't care for the man and saw that Gyrd apparently didn't either. Reluctantly and with little joy, Gyrd of Dyfrin followed the course that his wife and her brother had set for him in order to have some peace in his house.

Helga Saksesdatter was a witch. But it was Gyrd's two sons who caused him to look as careworn as he did. Sakse, the older one, must be sixteen winters old by now. Nearly every night his personal servant had to heave the whelp into bed, dead drunk. He had already ruined his mind and his health with liquor; no doubt he would drink himself to death before he reached the age of a man. It would be no great loss; Sakse had acquired an ugly reputation in the region for coarseness and insolence, in spite of his youth. He was his mother's favorite. Gyrd loved Jon, his younger son, better. He also had more of the temperament needed for him to bring honor to his lineage, if only he hadn't been . . . Well, he was a bit misshapen, with hunched shoulders and a crooked back. And he had some kind of inner stomach complaint and was unable to tolerate any food other than gruel and flat bread.

* * *

Simon Andressøn had always taken secret refuge in a feeling of community with his family whenever his own life seemed to him . . . well, troublesome, or whatever he might call it. When he met with adversity, it bothered him less if he could remember the good fortune and well-being of his siblings. If only things had been the same at Dyfrin as during his father's time, when peace, contentment, and prosperity reigned, then Simon thought there would have been much to ease his secret distress. He felt as if the roots of his own life were intertwined with those of his brothers and sisters, somewhere deep down in the dark earth. Every blow that struck, every injury that ate away at the marrow of one of them was felt by all.

He and Gyrd, at any rate, had felt this way, at least in the past. Now he wasn't so sure that Gyrd felt the same anymore.

He had been most fond of his older brother and of Sigrid. He remembered when they were growing up: He could sit and feel such joy for his youngest sister that he had to do *something* to show it. Then he would pick a quarrel with her, tease and needle her, pull on her braids, and pinch her arm—as if he couldn't show his affection for her in any other way without feeling ashamed. He had to tease her so that without embarrassment he could give her all the treasures he had stashed away; he could include the little maiden in his games when he built a millhouse at the creek, built farms for her, and cut willow whistles for the little girls in the springtime.

The memory of that day when he learned the full extent of her misfortune was like a brand scorched onto his mind. All winter long he had seen the way Sigrid was grieving herself into the grave over her dead betrothed, but he didn't know any more than that. Then one Sunday in early spring he was standing on the gallery at Mandvik, feeling cross with the women for not appearing. The horses were in the courtyard, outfitted with their church saddles, and the servants had been waiting a long time. Finally he grew angry and went into the women's house. Sigrid was still in bed. Surprised, he asked whether she was ill. His wife was sitting on the edge of the bed. A tremor passed over her gentle, withered face as she looked up.

"Ill she is indeed, the poor child. But even more than that, I think she's frightened . . . of you and your kinsmen . . . and how you will take the news."

His sister shrieked loudly, throwing herself headlong into Halfrid's arms and clinging to her, wrapping her thin, bare arms around her sister-in-law's waist. Her scream pierced Simon to the heart, so he thought it would stop and be drained of all blood. Her pain and her shame coursed through him, robbing him of his wits; then came the fear, and the sweat poured out. Their father—what would he do with Sigrid now?

He was so frightened as he struggled through the thawing muck on the journey home to Raumarike that at last the servant, who was traveling with him and knew nothing of the matter, began joking about the way Simon constantly had to get down from his horse. He had been a full-grown married man for many years, and yet he was so terrified at the thought of the meeting with his father that his stomach was in upheaval.

Then his father had barely uttered a word. But he had fallen apart, as if his roots had been chopped in half. Sometimes when he was about to doze off, Simon would recall that image and be wide awake at once: his father sitting there, rocking back and forth, with his head bowed to his chest, and Gyrd standing beside him with his hand on the arm of the high seat, a little paler than usual, his eyes downcast.

"God be praised that she wasn't here when this came out. It's a good thing she's staying with you and Halfrid," Gyrd had said when the two of them were alone.

That was the only time Simon heard Gyrd say anything that might indicate he didn't put his wife above all other women.

But he had witnessed how Gyrd seemed to fade and retreat ever since he had married Helga Saksesdatter.

During the time he was betrothed to her Gyrd had never said much, but each time he caught sight of his bride, Gyrd had looked so radiantly handsome that Simon had felt uneasy when he glanced at his brother. He had seen Helga before, Gyrd told Simon, but he had never spoken to her and could not have imagined that her kinsmen would give such a rich and beautiful bride to him.

Gyrd Darre's splendid good looks in his youth had been something that Simon regarded as a kind of personal honor. He was handsome in a particularly appealing way, as if everyone must see that goodness, gentility, and a courageous and noble heart resided in this fine, quiet young man. Then he was wed to Helga Saksesdatter, and it was as if nothing more ever came of him.

He had always been taciturn, but the two brothers were constantly together, and Simon managed to talk enough for both of them. Simon was garrulous, well liked, and considered sensible. For drinking bouts and bantering, for hunting and skiing expeditions, and for all manner of youthful amusements, Simon had countless friends, all equally close and dear. His older brother went along, saying little but smiling his lovely, somber smile, and the few words he did say seemed to count all the more.

Now Gyrd Andressøn was as silent as a locked chest.

The summer when Simon came home and told his father that he and Kristin Lavransdatter had agreed that they both wished to have the agreement retracted which had been made on their behalf . . . back then Simon knew that Gyrd understood most of what lay behind this matter: that Simon loved his betrothed, but there was some reason why he had given up his right, and this reason was such that Simon felt scorched inside with rancor and pain. Gyrd had quietly urged his father to let the matter drop. But to Simon he had never hinted with a single word that he understood. And Simon thought that if he could possibly have greater affection for his brother than he had felt all his days, it was then, because of his silence.

Simon *tried* to be happy and in good spirits as he rode north toward home. Along the way he stopped in to visit his friends in the valley, greeting them and drinking merrily. And his friends saddled up their horses to accompany him to the next manor, where other friends lived. It was so pleasant and easy to ride when there was frost but no snow.

He rode the last part of the journey in the twilight. The flush of the ale had left him. His men were wild and raucous, but their master seemed to have run dry of laughter and banter; he must be tired.

Then he was home. Andres tagged after his father, wherever he stood or walked. Ulvhild hovered around the saddlebags; had he brought any presents home for her? Arngjerd brought in ale and food. His wife sat down next to him as he ate, chattering and asking for news. When the children had gone to bed, Simon took Ramborg on his knee as he passed on greetings to her and spoke of kinsmen and acquaintances.

He thought it shameful and unmanly if he could not be content with such a life as he had.

The next day Simon was sitting in the Sæmund house when Arngjerd came over to bring him food. He thought it would be just as well to speak to her of the suitor while they were alone, and so he told his daughter about his conversation with the men from Eiken.

No, she was not very pretty, thought her father. He looked up at the young girl as she stood before him. Short and stocky, with a small, plain, pale face; her grayish blond hair was blotchy in color, hanging down her back in two thick braids, but over her forehead it fell in lank wisps in her eyes, and she had a habit of constantly brushing her hair back.

"It must be as you wish, Father," she said calmly when he was done speaking.

"Yes, I know that you're a good child, but what do you think about all this?"

"I have nothing to say. You must decide about this matter, dear Father."

"This is how things stand, Arngjerd: I would like to grant you a few more free years, free from childbirth and cares and responsibilities—all those things that fall to a woman's lot as soon as she is married. But I wonder if perhaps you might be longing to have your own home and to take charge yourself?"

"There is no need for haste on my account," said the girl with a little smile.

"You know that if you moved to Eiken through marriage, you would have your wealthy kinsmen nearby. Bare is the brotherless back." He noticed the glint in Arngjerd's eyes and her fleeting smile. "I mean Gyrd, your uncle," he said quickly, a little embarrassed.

"Yes, I know you didn't mean my kinswoman Helga," she said, and they both laughed.

Simon felt a warmth in his soul, in gratitude to God and the Virgin Mary, and to Halfrid, who had made him acknowledge this daughter as his own. Whenever he and Arngjerd happened to laugh together in this way, he needed no further proof of his paternity.

He stood up and brushed off some flour that she had on her sleeve. "And the suitor—what do you think of the man?" he asked.

"I like him well enough, the little that I've seen of him. And one shouldn't believe everything one hears. But you must decide, Father."

"Then we'll do as I've said. Aasmund and Grunde can wait a while longer, and if they're of the same mind when you're a little older . . . Otherwise, you must know, my daughter, that you may decide on your marriage yourself, insofar as you have the sense to choose in your own best interest. And your judgment is sound enough, Arngjerd."

He put his arms around her. She blushed when her father kissed her, and Simon realized that it had been a long time since he had done this. He was usually not the kind of man who was afraid to embrace his wife in the light of day or to banter with his children. But it was always done in jest, and Arngjerd . . . It suddenly dawned on Simon that his young daughter was probably the only person at Formo with whom he sometimes spoke in earnest.

He went over and pulled the peg out of the slit in the south wall. Through the small hole he gazed out across the valley. The wind was coming from the south, and big gray clouds were piling up where the mountains converged and blocked out the view. When a ray of sun broke through, the brilliance of all the colors deepened. The mild weather had licked away the sallow frost; the fields were brown, the fir trees blue-black, and high on the mountain crests the light gleamed with a golden luster where the bare slopes began, covered with lichen and moss.

Simon felt as if he could glean a singular power from the autumn wind outside and the shifting radiance over the countryside. If they had a lasting thaw for All Saints' Day, there would be mill water in the creeks, at least until Christmas. And he could send men into the mountains to gather moss. It had been such a dry fall; the Laag was a meager, small stream running through the fish traps made of yellow gravel and pale stones.

Up in the north end of the valley only Jørundgaard and the parsonage had millhouses on the river. He had little desire to ask permission to use the Jørundgaard mill. No doubt everyone in the region would be taking their grain there, since Sira Eirik charged a mill fee. And people thought he gained too good an idea of how much grain they had; he was so greedy about demanding tithes. But Lavrans had always allowed people to grind their grain at his mill without charge, and Kristin wanted things to continue in the same way.

If he so much as thought of her, his heart would begin trembling, sick and anguished.

It was the day before both Saint Simon's Day and the Feast of Saint Jude, the day when he always used to go to confession. It was to search his soul, to fast and to pray, that he was sitting there in the Sæmund house while the house servants were doing the threshing in the barn.

It took no time at all to go over his sins: He had cursed; he had lied when people asked about matters that were not their concern; he had shot a deer long after he had seen by the sun that the Sabbath had begun on a Saturday evening; and he had gone hunting on Sunday morning when everyone else in the village was at mass.

What had happened when the boy lay ill—that was something he must not and dared not mention. But this was the first time in his life that he reluctantly kept silent about a sin before his parish priest.

He had thought much about it and suffered terribly over it in his heart. Surely this must be a great sin, whether he himself had used sorcery to heal or had directly lured another person into doing so.

But he wasn't able to feel remorse when he thought about the fact that otherwise his son would now be lying in the ground. He felt fearful and dejected and kept watch to see if the child had changed afterward. He didn't think he could discern anything.

He knew it was true of many kinds of birds and wild animals. If human hands touched the eggs or their young, the parents wanted no more to do with them but would turn away from their offspring. A man who had been granted the light of reason by God could not do the same. For Simon the situation had become such that when he held his son, he almost felt as if he couldn't let the child out of his hands because he had grown so fearful for Andres. Sometimes he could understand why the heathen dumb beasts felt such loathing for their young because they had been *touched.* He too felt as if his child had been in some way infected.

But he had no regrets, did not wish that it hadn't happened. He merely wished it had been someone other than Kristin. It was difficult enough for him that they lived in the same region.

Arngjerd came in to ask for a key. Ramborg didn't think she had gotten it back after her husband had used it.

There was less and less order to the housekeeping on the manor. Simon remembered giving the key back to his wife; that was before he journeyed south.

"Well, I'm sure I'll find it," said Arngjerd.

She had such a nice smile and wise eyes. She wasn't truly ugly either, thought her father. And her hair was lovely when she wore it loose, so thick and blond, for holy days and feasts.

The daughter of Erlend's paramour had been pretty enough, and nothing but trouble had come of it.

But Erlend had had that daughter with a fair and highborn woman. Erlend had probably never even glanced at a woman like Arngjerd's mother. He had sauntered jauntily through the world, and beautiful, proud women and maidens had lined up to offer him love and adventure.

Simon's only sin of that kind—and he didn't count the boyish pranks when he was at the king's court—might have had a little more grandeur to it when he finally decided to betray his good and worthy wife. And he hadn't paid her any more heed, that Jorunn; he couldn't even remember how it happened that he first came too near the maid. He had been out carousing with friends and acquaintances a good deal that winter, and when he came home to his wife's estate, Jorunn would always be waiting there, to see that he got into bed without causing any accidents with the hearth.

It had been no more splendid an adventure than that.

He had deserved even less that the child should turn out so well and bring him such joy. But he shouldn't dwell on such thoughts now, when he was supposed to be thinking about his confession.

It was drizzling when Simon walked home from Romundgaard in the dark. He cut across the fields. In the last faint glimmer of daylight the stubble shone pale and wet. Over by the old bathhouse wall something small and white lay shining on the slope. Simon went over to have a look. It was the pieces of the French bowl that had been broken in the spring; the children had set a table made from a board placed across two stones. Simon struck at it with his axe and it toppled over.

He regretted his action at once, but he didn't like being reminded of that evening.

As if to make amends for the fact that he had kept silent about a sin, he had talked to Sira Eirik about his dreams. It was also because he needed to ease his heart—at least from *that*. He had been ready to leave when it suddenly occurred to him that he needed to talk about it. And this old, half-blind priest had been his spiritual father for more than twelve years.

So he went back and knelt again before Sira Eirik.

The priest sat motionless until Simon had finished talking. Then he spoke, his powerful voice now sounding old and veiled from inside the eternal twilight: It was not a sin. Every limb of the struggling church had to be tested in battle with the Fiend; that's why God allowed the Devil to seek out a man with many kinds of temptations. As long as the man did not cast aside his weapons, as long as he refused to forsake the Lord's banner or, fully alert and aware, refused to surrender to the visions with which the impure spirit was trying to bewitch him, then the sinful impulses were not a sin.

"No!" cried Simon, ashamed at the sound of his own voice.

He had *never* surrendered. He was tormented, tormented, tormented by them. Whenever he woke up from these sinful dreams, he felt as if he himself had been violated in his sleep.

Two horses were tied to the fence when he entered the courtyard. It was Soten, who belonged to Erlend Nikulaussøn, and Kristin's horse. He called for the stableboy. Why hadn't they been led inside? Because the visitors had said it wasn't necessary, replied the boy sullenly.

He was a young lad who had taken a position with Simon now that he was home; before, he had served at Dyfrin. There everything was supposed to be done according to courtly custom; that's what Helga had demanded. But if this fool Sigurd thought he could grumble at his master here at Formo because Simon preferred to jest and banter with his men and didn't mind a bold reply from a servant, then the Devil would . . . Simon was about to scold the boy roundly, but he refrained; he had just come from confession after all. Jon Daalk would have to take the newcomer in hand and teach him that good peasant customs were just as acceptable as the refined ways at Dyfrin.

He merely asked in a relatively calm voice whether Sigurd was fresh out of the mountains this year and told him to put the horses inside. But he was angry.

The first thing he saw as he entered the house was Erlend's laughing face. The light from the candle on the table shone directly on him as he sat on the bench and fended off Ulvhild, who was kneeling beside him and trying to scratch him or whatever she was doing. She was flailing her hands at the man's face and laughing so hard that she hiccupped.

Erlend sprang to his feet and tried to push the child aside, but she gripped the sleeve of his tunic and hung on to his arm as he walked across the room, erect and light-footed, to greet his brother-in-law. She was nagging him for something; Erlend and Simon could barely get a word in.

Her father ordered her, rather harshly, to go out to the cookhouse with the maids; they had just finished setting the table. When the maiden protested, he took her hard by the arm and tore her away from Erlend.

"Here!" Ulvhild's uncle took a lump of resin out of his mouth and stuck it into hers. "Take it, Ulvhild, my little plum cheeks! That daughter of yours," he said to his brother-in-law with a laugh as he gazed after the maiden, "is not going to be as docile as Arngjerd!"

Simon hadn't been able to resist telling his wife how well Arngjerd had handled the marriage matter. But he hadn't intended for her to tell the people of Jørundgaard. And it was unlike Ramborg to do so; he knew that she had little affection for Erlend. He didn't like it. He didn't like the fact that Ramborg had spoken of this matter, or that she was so capricious, or that Ulvhild, little girl though she was, seemed so charmed by Erlend—just as all women were.

He went over to greet Kristin. She was sitting in the corner next to the hearth wall with Andres on her lap. The boy had grown quite fond of his aunt during the time she nursed him when he was recovering from his illness the previous fall.

Simon realized that there must be some purpose for this visit since Erlend had come too. He was not one to wear out the doorstep at Formo. Simon couldn't deny that Erlend had handled the difficult situation admirably—considering how things had turned out between the brothers-in-law. Erlend avoided Simon as much as he could, but they met as often as necessary so that gossip wouldn't spread about enmity between kinsmen, and then they always behaved like the best of friends. Erlend was quiet and a bit reticent whenever they were together but still displayed a free and unfettered manner.

When the food had been brought to the table and the ale set out, Erlend spoke, "I think you're probably wondering about the reason for my visit, Simon. We're here to invite you and Ramborg to a wedding at our manor."

"Surely you must be jesting? I didn't think you had anyone of marrying age on your estate."

"That depends on how you look at it, brother-in-law. It's Ulf Haldorssøn."

Simon slapped his thigh.

"Next I'll expect my plow oxen to produce calves at Christmastime!"

"You shouldn't call Ulf a plow ox," said Erlend with a laugh. "The unfortunate thing is that the man has been far too bold . . ."

Simon whistled.

Erlend laughed again and said, "Yes, you can well imagine that I didn't believe my own ears when they came to the estate yesterday—the sons of Herbrand of Medalheim—and demanded that Ulf should marry their sister."

"Herbrand Remba's? But they're nothing but boys; their sister can't be old enough that Ulf would . . ."

"She's twenty winters old. And Ulf is closer to fifty. Yes." Erlend had turned somber. "You realize, Simon, that they must consider him a poor match for Jardtrud, but it's the lesser of two evils if she marries him. Although Ulf is the son of a knight and a well-to-do man; he doesn't need to earn his bread on another man's estate, but he followed us here because he would rather live with his kinsmen than on his own farm at Skaun . . . after what happened. . . ."

Erlend fell silent for a moment. His face was tender and handsome. Then he continued.

"Now we, Kristin and I, intend to celebrate this wedding as if he were our brother. That's why Ulf and I will ride south in the coming week to Musudal to ask for her hand at Medalheim. For the sake of appearances, you understand. But I thought of asking you a favor, brother-in-law. I remember, Simon, that I owe you a great deal. But Ulf is not well liked here in the villages. And you are so highly respected; few men are your equal . . . while I myself . . ." He shrugged his shoulders and laughed a little. "Would you be willing, Simon, to ride with us and act as spokesman on Ulf's behalf? He and I have been friends since we were boys," pleaded Erlend.

"That I will, brother-in-law!" Simon had turned crimson; he felt oddly embarrassed and powerless at Erlend's candid speech. "I will gladly do anything I can to honor Ulf Haldorssøn."

Kristin had been sitting in the corner with Andres; the boy wanted his aunt to help him undress. Now she came forward into the light, holding the half-naked child, who had his arms around her neck.

"That's kind of you, Simon," she said softly, holding out her hand. "For this we all thank you."

Simon lightly clasped her hand for a moment.

"Not at all, Kristin. I have always been fond of Ulf. You should know that I do this gladly." He reached up to take his son, but Andres pretended to fret, kicking at his father with his little bare feet, laughing and clinging to Kristin.

Simon listened to the two of them as he sat and talked to Erlend about Ulf's money matters. The boy suddenly started giggling; she knew so many lullabies and nursery rhymes, and she laughed too, a gentle, soft cooing sound from deep in her throat. Once he glanced in their direction and saw that she had made a kind of stairway with her fingers, and Andres's fingers were people walking up it. At last she put him in the cradle and sat down next to Ramborg. The sisters chatted to each other in hushed voices.

It was true enough, he thought as he lay down that night: He had always been fond of Ulf Haldorssøn. And ever since that winter in

Oslo when they had both struggled to help Kristin, he had felt himself bound to the man with a kind of kinship. He never thought that Ulf was anything but his equal, the son of a nobleman. The fact that he had no rights from his father's family because he had been conceived in adultery meant only that Simon was even more respectful in his dealings with Ulf. Somewhere in the depths of his own heart there was always a prayer for Arngjerd's well-being. But otherwise this was not a good situation to get involved with: a middle-aged man and such a young child. Well, if Jardtrud Herbrandsdatter had strayed when she was at the *ting*[1] last summer, it was none of his concern. He had done nothing to offend these people, and Ulf was the close kinsman of his brother-in-law.

Unasked, Ramborg had offered to help Kristin by overseeing the table at the wedding. He thought this kind of her. When it mattered, Ramborg always showed what lineage she was from. Yes indeed, Ramborg was a good woman.

## CHAPTER 5

THE DAY AFTER Saint Catherine's Day, Erlend Nikulaussøn celebrated the wedding of his kinsman in a most beautiful and splendid fashion. Many good people had gathered; Simon Darre had seen to that. He and his wife were exceedingly well liked in all the surrounding villages. Both priests from the Olav Church were in attendance, and Sira Eirik blessed the house and the bed. This was considered a great honor since nowadays Sira Eirik only said mass on the high holy days and performed other priestly duties only for those few who had been coming to him for confession for many years. Simon Darre read aloud the document detailing Ulf's betrothal and wedding gifts to his bride, and Erlend gave an admirable speech to his kinsman at the table. Ramborg Lavransdatter oversaw the serving of the food along with her sister, and she was also present to help the bride undress in the loft.

And yet it was not a truly joyous wedding. The bride was from an old and respected family there in the valley; her kinsmen and neighbors could not possibly think she had won an equal match since she had to make do with an outsider and one who had served on another man's estate, even though it belonged to a kinsman. Neither Ulf's birth, as the son of a wealthy knight and his maid, nor his kinship with Erlend Nikulaussøn seemed to impress the sons of Herbrand as any great honor.

Apparently the bride herself was not content either, considering how she had behaved. Kristin sounded quite despondent when she spoke to Simon about this. He had come to Jørundgaard to take care of some matters several weeks after the wedding. Jardtrud was urging her husband to move to his property at Skaun. Weeping, she had said within Kristin's earshot that the worst thing she could imagine was that her child should be called the son of a servant. Ulf had not replied. The newly married couple lived in the building known as the foreman's house because Jon Einarssøn had lived there before Lavrans bought all of Laugarbru and moved him out there. But this name displeased Jardtrud. And she resented keeping her cows in the same shed as Kristin's; no doubt she was afraid that someone might think she was Kristin's servingwoman. That was reasonable enough, thought Kristin. She would have a shed built for the foreman's house if Ulf didn't decide to take his wife and move to Skaun. But perhaps that might be best after all. He was no longer so young that it would be easy for him to change the way he lived; perhaps it would be less difficult for him in a new place.

Simon thought she might be right about that. Ulf was greatly disliked in the region. He spoke scornfully about everything there in the valley. He was a capable and hardworking farmer, but he was unaccustomed to so many things in that part of the country. He took on more livestock in the fall than he could manage to feed through the winter, and when the cows languished or he ended up having to slaughter some of the starving beasts toward spring, he would grow angry and blame the fact that he was unused to the meager ways of the region, where people had to scrape off bark for fodder as early as Saint Paal's Day.

There was another consideration: In Trøndelag the custom had gradually developed between the landowner and his tenants that he would demand as lease payment the goods that he needed most—hay, skins, flour, butter, or wool—even though certain goods or sums had been specified when the lease was settled. And it was the landowner or his envoys who recalculated the worth of one item in replacement for another, completely arbitrarily. But when Ulf made these demands upon Kristin's leaseholders around the countryside, people called them injurious and grievously unlawful, as they were, and the tenants complained to their mistress. She took Ulf to task as soon as she heard of the matter, but Simon knew that people blamed not only Ulf but Kristin Lavransdatter as well. He had tried to explain, wherever talk of this arose, that Kristin hadn't known about Ulf's demands and that they were based on customs of the man's own region. Simon feared this had done little good, although no one had said as much to his face.

For this reason he wasn't sure whether he should wish for Ulf to stay or to leave. He didn't know how Kristin would handle things without her diligent and loyal helper. Erlend was completely incapable of managing the farmwork, and their sons were far too young. But Ulf had turned much of the countryside against her, and now there was this: He had seduced a young maiden from a wealthy and respected family in the valley. God only knew that Kristin was already struggling hard enough, as the situation now stood.

And they were in difficult straits, the people of Jørundgaard. Erlend was no better liked than Ulf. If Erlend's overseer and kinsman was arrogant and surly, the master himself, with his gentle and rather indolent manner, was even more irksome. Erlend Nikulaussøn probably had no idea that he was turning people against him; he seemed unaware of anything except that, rich or poor, he was the same man he had always been, and he wouldn't dream that anyone would call him arrogant for that very reason. He had plotted to incite a group of rebels against his king even though he was Lord Magnus's kinsman, vassal, and retainer; then he himself had caused the downfall of the plan through his own foolish recklessness. But he evidently never thought that he might be branded a villain in anyone's eyes because of these matters. Simon couldn't see that Erlend gave much thought to anything at all.

It was hard to figure the man out. If one sat and conversed with Erlend, he was far from stupid, thought Simon, but it was as if he could never take to heart the wise and splendid things he often said. It was impossible to remember that this man would soon be old; he could have had grandchildren long ago. Upon closer study, his face was lined and his hair sprinkled with gray, yet he and Nikulaus looked more like brothers than father and son. He was just as straight-backed and slender as when Simon had seen him for the first time; his voice was just as young and resonant. He moved among others with the same ease and confidence, with that slightly muted grace to his manner. With strangers he had always been rather quiet and reserved; letting others seek him out instead of seeking their company himself, during times of both prosperity and adversity. That no one sought his company now was something that Erlend didn't seem to notice. And the whole circle of noblemen and landowners all along the valley, intermarried and closely related with each other as they were, resented the way this haughty Trøndelag chieftain, who had been cast into their midst by misfortune, nevertheless considered himself too highborn and noble to seek their favor.

But what had caused the most bad blood toward Erlend Nikulaussøn was the fact that he had drawn the men of Sundbu into misfortune along with him. Guttorm and Borgar Trondssøn had been banished from Norway, and their shares of the great Gjesling estates, as well as their half of the ancestral manor, had been seized by the Crown. Ivar of Sundbu had to buy himself reconciliation with King Magnus. The king gave the confiscated properties—not without demanding compensation, it was said—to Sir Sigurd Erlendssøn Eldjarn. Then the youngest of the sons of Trond, Ivar and Haavard, who had not known of their brothers' treasonous plans, sold their shares of the Vaage estates to Sir Sigurd, who was their cousin as well as the cousin of the daughters of Lavrans. Sigurd's mother, Gudrun Ivarsdatter, was the sister of Trond Gjesling and Ragnfrid of Jørundgaard. Ivar Gjesling moved to Ringheim at Toten, a manor that he had acquired from his wife. His children would do well to live where they had inheritance and property rights from their mother's family. Haavard still owned a great deal of property, but it was mostly in Valdres, and with his marriage he had now come into possession of large estates in the Borge district. But the inhabitants of Vaage and northern Gudbrandsdal thought it the greatest misfortune that the ancient lineage of landowners had lost Sundbu, where they had lived and ruled the countryside for as far back as people could remember.

For a short time Sundbu had been in the hands of King Haakon Haakonssøn's loyal retainer Erlend Eldjarn of Godaland at Agder. The Gjeslings had never been warm friends with King Sverre or his noblemen, and they had sided with Duke Skule when he rallied the rebels against King Haakon.[1] But Ivar the Younger had won Sundbu back in an exchange of properties with Erlend Eldjarn and had given his daughter Gudrun to him in marriage. Ivar's son, Trond, had not brought honor of any kind to his lineage, but his four sons were handsome, well liked, and intrepid men, and people took it hard when they lost their ancestral estate.

Before Ivar moved away from the valley, an accident occurred that made people even more sorrowful and indignant about the fate of the Gjeslings. Guttorm was unmarried, but Borgar's young wife had been left behind at Sundbu. Dagny Bjarnesdatter had always been a little slow-witted, and she had openly shown that she loved her husband beyond all measure. Borgar Trondssøn was handsome but had rather loose ways. The winter after he had fled from the land, Dagny fell through a hole in the ice of Vaage Lake and drowned. It was called an accident, but people knew that grief and longing had robbed Dagny of the few wits she had left, and everyone felt deep pity for the simple, sweet, and pretty young woman who had met with such a terrible end. That's when the rancor became widespread toward Erlend Nikulaussøn, who had brought such misfortune upon the best people of the region. And then everybody began to gossip about how he had behaved when he was to marry the daughter of Lavrans Lagmandssön. She too was a Gjesling, after all, on her mother's side.

The new master of Sundbu was not well liked, even though no one had anything specific to say against Sigurd himself. But he was from Egde, and his father, Erlend Eldjarn, had quarreled with everyone in this part of the land with whom he had had any dealings. Kristin and Ramborg had never met this cousin of theirs. Simon had known Sir Sigurd in Raumarike; he was the close kinsman of the Haftorssøns, and they in turn were close kinsmen of Gyrd Darre's wife. But as complicated as matters now were, Simon avoided meeting Sir Sigurd as much as possible. He never had any desire to go to Sundbu anymore. The Trondssøns had been his dear friends, and Ramborg and the wives of Ivar and Borgar used to visit each other every year. Sir Sigurd Erlendssøn was also much older than Simon Andressøn; he was a man of almost sixty.

Things had become so tangled up because Erlend and Kristin were now living at Jørundgaard that although the marriage of their overseer could not be called important news, Simon Darre thought it was enough to make the situation even more vexed. Usually he would not have troubled his young wife if he was having any difficulties or setbacks. But this time he couldn't help discussing these matters a bit with Ramborg. He was both surprised and pleased when he saw how sensibly she spoke about them and how admirably she tried to do all that she could to help.

She went to see her sister at Jørundgaard much more often than she had before, and she gave up her sullen demeanor with Erlend. On Christmas Day, when they met on the church hill after the mass, Ramborg kissed not only Kristin but her brother-in-law as well. In the past she had always fiercely mocked these foreign customs of his: the fact that he used to kiss his mother-in-law in greeting and the like.

It suddenly occurred to Simon when he saw Ramborg put her arms around Erlend's neck that he might do the same with his wife's sister. But then he realized that he couldn't do it after all. He had never been in the habit of kissing the wives of his kinsmen; his mother and sisters had laughed at him when he suggested trying it when he came home after he had been at court, in service as a page.

For the Christmas banquet at Formo, Ramborg seated Ulf Haldorssøn's young wife in a place of honor, showing both of them such respect as was seemly toward a newly married couple. And she went to Jørundgaard to be with Jardtrud when she gave birth.

That took place a month after Christmas—two months too soon, and the boy was stillborn. Then Jardtrud flew into a fury. If she had known that things might go this way, she would never have married Ulf. But now it was done and could not be helped.

What Ulf Haldorssøn thought about the matter, no one knew. He didn't say a word.

During the week before Mid-Lent, Erlend Nikulaussøn and Simon Andressøn rode south together to Kvam. Several years before Lavrans died, he and a few other farmers had purchased a small estate in the village there. Now the original owners of the manor wanted to buy it back, but it was rather unclear how things had been handled in the past as far as offering the land to the heirs,[2] or whether the kinsmen of the sellers had claimed their rights in lawful fashion. When Lavrans's estate had been settled after his death, his share in this farm had been excluded, along with several other small properties that might involve legal proceedings over proof of ownership. The two sisters then divided up the income from them. That was why both of Lavrans's sons-in-law were now appearing on behalf of their wives.

A good number of people had gathered, and because the tenant's wife and children lay sick in bed in the main house, the men had to make do with meeting in an old outbuilding on the farm. It was drafty and in terrible disrepair; everyone kept on his fur cape. Each man placed his weapons within reach and kept his sword on his belt; no one had a desire to stay any longer than necessary. But they would at least have a bite to eat before they parted, and so at the time of midafternoon prayers, when the discussion was over, the men took out their bags of provisions and sat down to eat, with the packets lying next to them on the benches or in front of them on the floor. There was no table in the building.

The parish priest of Kvam had sent his son, Holmgeir Moisessøn, in his stead. He was a devious and untrustworthy young man, whom few people liked. But his father was greatly admired, and his mother had belonged to a respected family. Holmgeir was a tall and strong fellow, hot-blooded and quick to turn on people, so no one wished to quarrel with the priest's son. There were also many who thought him an able and witty speaker.

Simon hardly knew him and didn't like his looks. He had a long, narrow face with pale freckles and a thin upper lip, which made his big yellow front teeth gleam like a rat's. But Sira Moises had been Lavrans's good friend, and for a time the son had been raised at Jørundgaard, partly as a servant and partly as a foster son, until his father had acknowledged him as his own.[3] For this reason Simon was always friendly when he met Holmgeir Moisessøn.

Now Holmgeir had rolled a stump over to the hearth and was sitting there, sticking slices of meat—roasted thrush with pieces of bacon—on his dagger and heating them in the fire. He had been ill and had been granted fourteen days' indulgence, he told the others, who were chewing on bread and frozen fish as the fragrant smell of Holmgeir's meat rose up to their noses.

Simon was in a bad humor—not truly angry but slightly dejected and embarrassed. The whole property matter was difficult to sort out, and the documents he had received from his father-in-law were very unclear; and yet when he left home, he thought that he understood them. He had compared them with other documents, but now when he heard the statements of the witnesses and saw the other evidence that was put forth, he realized that his view of the matter wouldn't hold up. But none of the other men had any better grasp of it—particularly not the sheriff's envoy, who was also present. It was suggested that the case would have to be brought up before a *ting*. Then Erlend suddenly spoke and asked to see the documents.

Up to that moment he had sat and listened, almost as if he had no interest in the matter. Now he seemed to wake up. He carefully read through all the documents, a few of them several times. Then he explained the situation, clearly and briefly: Such and such were the provisions of the lawbooks, and in such a way they could be interpreted. The vague and clumsy phrases in the documents had to mean either this or that. If the case were brought before a *ting*, it would be decided in either this or that manner. Then he proposed a solution with which the original owners might be satisfied but which was not entirely to the detriment of the present owners.

Erlend stood up as he spoke, with his left hand resting lightly on the hilt of his sword, his right hand carelessly holding the stack of documents. He acted as if he were the one in charge of the meeting, although Simon could see that he wasn't aware of this himself. He was used to standing up and speaking in this manner when he used to hold sheriff *tings* in his county. When he turned to one of the others to ask if something was so and if the man understood what he was explaining, he spoke as if he were interrogating a witness—not without courtesy and yet as if it were his place to ask the questions and the other man's place to answer. When he was done speaking, he handed the documents to the envoy as if the man could be his servant and sat down. While the others discussed the matter and Simon also stated his opinion, Erlend listened, but in such a fashion as if he had no stake in the case. His replies were curt, clear, and instructive if anyone happened to address him, but all the while he scraped his fingernail on some grease spots that had appeared on his tunic, straightened his belt, picked up his gloves, and seemed to be waiting rather impatiently for the conversation to come to an end.

The others agreed to the arrangement that Erlend had proposed, and it was one that Simon could be tolerably satisfied with; he would have been unlikely to win anything more from a court case.

But he had fallen into a bad mood. He knew full well that it was childish of him to be cross because his brother-in-law had understood the matter while he had not. It was reasonable that Erlend should be better able to interpret the word of law and decipher confusing documents, since for years it had been his role to explain the statutes to people and settle disputes. But it had come upon Simon quite unexpectedly. The night before at Jørundgaard, when he talked to Erlend and Kristin about the meeting, Erlend hadn't mentioned any opinion; he seemed to listen with only half an ear. Yes, it was clear that Erlend would be better versed in the law than ordinary farmers, but it was as if the law were no concern of his as he sat there and counseled the others with friendly indifference. Simon had a vague feeling that in some way Erlend had never respected the law as a guide in his own life.

It was also strange that he could stand up in that manner, completely untroubled. He had to be aware that this made the others think about who and what he had been and what his situation now was. Simon could feel the others thinking about this; some probably resented this man, who never seemed to care what other people thought of him. But no one said anything. When the blue-frozen clerk who had come with the envoy sat down and put the writing board on his lap, he addressed all his questions to Erlend, and Erlend spelled things out for him as he sat holding a few pieces of straw, which he had picked up from the floor, twining them around his long tan fingers and weaving them into a ring. When the clerk was finished, he handed the calfskin to Erlend, who tossed the straw ring into the hearth, took the letter, and read it half aloud:

" 'To all men who see or hear this document, greetings from God and from Simon Andressøn of Formo, Erlend Nikulaussøn of Jørundgaard, Vidar Steinssøn of Klaufastad, Ingemund and Toralde Bjørnssøn, Bjørn Ingemundssøn of Lundar, Alf Einarssøn, Holmgeir Moisessøn . . .'

"Do you have the wax ready?" he asked the clerk, who was blowing on his frozen fingers. " 'Let it be known that in the year of our Lord, one thousand three hundred and thirty-eight winters, on the Friday before Mid-Lent Sunday, we met at Granheim in the parish of Kvam . . .'

"We can take the chest that's standing in the alcove, Alf, and use it as a table." Erlend turned to the envoy as he gave the document back to the scribe.

Simon remembered how Erlend had been when he was in the

company of his peers up north. Easy and confident enough; he wasn't lacking in that regard. Impetuous and rash in his speech, but always with something slightly ingratiating about his manner. He was not in the least indifferent to what others thought of him if he considered them his peers or kinsmen. On the contrary, he had doubtless put great effort into winning their approval.

With an oddly fierce sense of bitterness, Simon suddenly felt allied with these farmers from here in the valley—men whom Erlend respected so little that he didn't even wonder what they might think of him. He had done it for Erlend's sake. For his sake Simon had parted with the circles of the gentry and well-to-do. It was all very well to be the rich farmer of Formo, but he couldn't forget that he had turned his back on his peers, kinsmen, and the friends of his youth. Because he had assumed the role of a supplicant among them, he no longer had the strength to meet them, hardly had the strength to think of it at all. For this brother-in-law of his he had as good as denied his king and departed from the ranks of royal retainers. He had revealed to Erlend something that he found more bitter than death to recall whenever it entered his thoughts. And yet Erlend behaved toward him as if he had understood nothing and remembered nothing. It didn't seem to trouble the fellow at all that he had wreaked havoc with another man's life.

At that moment Erlend said to him, "We should see about leaving, Simon, if we want to make it back home tonight. I'll go out and see to the horses."

Simon looked up, feeling a strange ill will at the sight of the other man's tall, handsome figure. Under the hood of his cape Erlend wore a small black silk cap that fit snugly to his head and was tied under his chin. His lean dark face with the big pale blue eyes sunk deep in the shadow of his brow looked even younger and more refined under that cap.

"And pack up my bag in the meantime," he said from the door as he went out.

The other men had continued to talk about the case. It was quite peculiar, said one of them, that Lavrans hadn't been able to arrange things better; the man usually knew what he was doing. He was the most experienced of farmers in all matters regarding the purchase and sale of land.

"It's probably my father who is to blame," said Holmgeir, the priest's son. "He said as much this morning. If he had listened to Lavrans back then, everything would have been plain and clear. But you know how Lavrans was. . . . Toward priests he was always as amenable and submissive as a lamb."

Even so, Lavrans of Jørundgaard had always guarded his own welfare, said someone else.

"Yes, and no doubt he thought he was doing so when he followed the priest's advice," said Holmgeir, laughing. "That can be the wise thing to do, even with earthly matters—as long as you're not eyeing the same patch that the Church has set its sights on."

Lavrans had been a strangely pious man, thought Vidar. He had never spared either property or livestock with regard to the Church or the poor.

"No," said Holmgeir thoughtfully. "Well, if I'd been such a rich man, I too might have had a mind to pay out sums for the peace of my soul. But I wouldn't have given away my goods with both hands, the way he did, and then walk around with red eyes and white cheeks every time I'd been to see the priest to confess my sins. And Lavrans went to confession every month."

"Tears of remorse are the fair gifts of grace from the Holy Spirit, Holmgeir," said old Ingemund Bjørnssøn. "Blessed is he who can weep for his sins here in this world; all the easier it will be for him to enter the other. . . ."

"Then Lavrans must have been in Heaven long ago," said Holmgeir, "considering the way he fasted and disciplined his flesh. I've heard that on Good Friday he would lock himself in the loft above the storeroom and lash himself with a whip."

"Hold your tongue," said Simon Andressøn, trembling with bitterness; his face was blood red. Whether Holmgeir's remark was true or not, he didn't know. But when he was cleaning up his father-in-law's belongings, he had found a small, oblong wooden box in the bottom of his book chest, and inside lay a silk whip that the cloisters called a flagellum. The braided strips of leather bore dark spots, which might have been blood. Simon had burned it, with a feeling of sad reverence. He realized that he had come upon something in the other man's life that Lavrans had never wanted a living soul to see.

"I don't think he would talk about such things to his servants, in any case," said Simon when he trusted himself to speak.

"No, it's just something that people have made up," replied Holmgeir. "Surely he didn't have such sins to repent that he would need to—" The man gave a little sneer. "If I had lived as blameless and Christian a life as Lavrans Bjørgulfsøn, and been married to a mournful woman like Ragnfrid Ivarsdatter, I think I would have wept for the sins that I *hadn't* committed—"

Simon leaped up and struck Holmgeir in the mouth so the man tumbled back toward the hearth. His dagger fell to the floor, and in the next instant he grabbed it and tried to stab the other man. Simon shielded himself with his arm holding his cape as he seized Holmgeir's wrist with his other hand and tried to wrest the dagger away. In the meantime the priest's son aimed a number of blows at his face. Simon then gripped him by both arms, but the young man sank his teeth into Simon's hand.

"You dare to bite me, you dog!" Simon let go, took several steps back, and pulled his sword from its sheath. He fell upon Holmgeir so that his young body arched back, with a few inches of steel buried in his chest. A moment later Holmgeir's body slipped from the sword point and fell heavily, halfway in the hearth fire.

Simon flung his sword away and was about to lift Holmgeir out of the blaze when he saw Vidar's axe raised to strike right above his head. He ducked and lunged to the side, seized hold of his sword again, and just managed to fend off the blade of the envoy, Alf Einarssøn; he whirled around and again had to shield himself from Vidar's axe. Out of the corner of his eye he saw behind him that the Bjørnssøns and Bjørn of Lunde were aiming spears at him from the other side of the hearth. He then drove Alf in front of him over to the opposite wall but sensed that Vidar was coming for him from behind. Vidar had dragged Holmgeir out of the fire; they were cousins, those two. And the louts from Lunde were approaching from around the hearth. He stood exposed on all sides, and in the midst of it all, even though he had more than enough to do to save his life, he felt a vague, unhappy sense of surprise that the men were all against him.

At the next moment Erlend's sword flashed between the Lunde men and Simon. Toralde reeled aside and fell against the wall. Quick as lightning, Erlend shifted his sword to his left hand and struck Alf's weapon away so that it slid with a clatter across the floor, while with his right hand he grabbed the shaft of Bjørn's spear and pressed it downward.

"Get outside," he told Simon, breathing hard and shielding his brother-in-law from Vidar. Simon ground his teeth together and raced across the room toward Bjørn and Ingemund. Erlend was at his side, screaming over the tumult and clanging of swords: "Get outside! Do you hear me, you fool? Head for the door—we have to get out!"

When Simon realized that Erlend meant for both of them to go out, he began moving backward, still fighting, toward the door. They ran through the entryway, and then they were out in the courtyard, Simon a few steps farther away from the building, and Erlend right in front of the door with his sword half raised and his face turned toward those who were swarming after them.

For a moment Simon felt blinded; the winter day was so dazzling bright and clear. Under the blue sky the mountains arched white-gold in the last rays of the sun; the forest was weighted down with snow and frost. The expanse of fields glittered and gleamed like gemstones.

He heard Erlend say, "It will not make amends for the misfortune if more deaths occur. We should use our wits, good sirs, so there is no more bloodshed. Things are bad enough as they are, with my brother-in-law having slain a man."

Simon stepped to Erlend's side.

"You killed my cousin without cause, Simon Andressøn," said Vidar of Klaufastad, who was standing in front of the others in the doorway.

"It was not entirely without cause that he fell. But you know, Vidar, that I won't refuse to pay the penance for this misfortune I've brought upon you. All of you know where you can find me at home."

Erlend talked a little more to the farmers. "Alf, how did it happen?" He went indoors with the other men.

Simon stayed where he was, feeling strangely numb. Erlend came back after a moment. "Let's go now," he said as he headed for the stable.

"Is he dead?" asked Simon.

"Yes. And Alf and Toralde and Vidar all have wounds, but none is serious. Holmgeir's hair was singed off the back of his head." Erlend had spoken in a somber voice, but now he abruptly burst out laughing. "*Now* it certainly smells like a damn roasted thrush in there, you'd better believe me! How the Devil could all of you get into such a quarrel in such a short time?" he asked in astonishment.

A half-grown boy was holding their horses. Neither of the men had brought his own servant along on this journey.

Both were still carrying their swords. Erlend picked up a handful of hay and wiped the blood from his. Simon did the same. When he had rubbed off the worst of it, he stuck his sword back in its sheath. Erlend cleaned his sword very thoroughly and then polished it with the hem of his cape. Then he made several playful little thrusts into the air and smiled, fleetingly, as if at a memory. He tossed the sword high up, caught it by the hilt, and stuck it back in its sheath.

"Your wounds . . . We should go up to the house, and I'll bandage them for you."

Simon said they were nothing. "But you're bleeding too, Erlend!"

"It's nothing dangerous, and my skin heals fast. I've noticed that heavyset people always take longer to heal. And with this cold . . . and we have such a long way to ride."

Erlend got some salve and cloths from the tenant farmer and carefully tended to the other man's wounds. Simon had two flesh wounds right next to each other on the left side of his chest; they bled a great deal at first, but they weren't serious. Erlend had been slashed on the thigh by Bjørn's spear. That would make it painful to ride, said Simon, but his brother-in-law laughed. It had barely made a scratch through his leather hose. He dabbed at it a bit and then wrapped it tightly against the frost.

It was bitterly cold. Before they reached the bottom of the hill on which the farm stood, their horses were covered with rime and the fur trim on the men's hoods had turned white.

"Brrr." Erlend shivered. "If only we were home! We'll have to ride over to the manor down here and report the slaying."

"Is that necessary?" asked Simon. "I spoke to Vidar and the others after all . . ."

"It would be better if you did so," said Erlend. "You should report the news yourself. Don't let them have anything to hold against you."

The sun had slipped behind the ridge now; the evening was a pale grayish blue but still light. They rode along a creek, beneath the branches of birch trees that were even more shaggy with frost than the rest of the forest. There was a stink of raw, icy fog in the air, which could make a man's breath stick in his throat. Erlend grumbled impatiently about the long period of cold they had had and about the chill ride that lay before them.

"You're not getting frostbite on your face, are you, brother-in-law?" He peered anxiously under Simon's hood. Simon rubbed his hand over his face; it wasn't frostbitten, but he had grown quite pale as he rode. It didn't suit him, because his large, portly face was weather-beaten and ruddy, and the paleness appeared in gray blotches, which made his complexion look unclean.

"Have you ever seen a man spreading manure with his sword the way Alf did?" asked Erlend. He burst out laughing at the memory and leaned forward in his saddle to imitate the gesture. "What a splendid envoy he is! You should have seen Ulf playing with his sword, Simon—Jesus, Maria!"

Playing . . . Well, now he'd seen Erlend Nikulaussøn playing at that game. Over and over again he saw himself and the other men tumbling around the hearth, the way farmers chop wood or toss hay. And Erlend's slender, lightning-swift figure among them, his gaze alert and his wrist steady as he danced with them, quick-witted and an expert swordsman.

More than twenty years ago he himself had been considered one of the foremost swordsmen among the youth of the royal retainers, when they practiced out on the green. But since then he hadn't had much opportunity to use his knightly skills.

And here he was now, riding along and feeling sick at heart because he had killed a man. He kept seeing Holmgeir's body as it fell from his sword and sank into the fire; he heard the man's abrupt, strangled death cry in his ears and saw, again and again, images of the brief, furious battle that followed. He felt dejected, pained, and confused; they had turned on him suddenly, all those men with whom he had sat and felt a sense of belonging. And then Erlend had come to his aid.

He had never thought himself a coward. He had hunted down six bears during the years he had lived at Formo, and twice he had put his life at risk in the most reckless manner. With only the thin trunk of a pine tree between him and a raging, wounded female, with no other weapon than his spearpoint on a shaft a scant hand's breadth long . . . The tenseness of the game had not disturbed his steadiness of thought, action, or instinct. But now, in that outbuilding . . . he didn't know if he had been afraid, but he certainly had been confused, unable to think clearly.

When he was back home after the bear hunt, with his clothes thrown on haphazardly, with his arm in a sling, feverish, his shoulder stiff and torn, he had merely felt an overwhelming joy. Things might have gone worse; how much worse, he didn't dwell on. But now he kept thinking about it, ceaselessly: how everything might have ended if Erlend hadn't come to his aid just in time. He hadn't been afraid, but he had such a peculiar feeling. It was the expressions on the faces of the other men . . . and Holmgeir's dying body.

He had never killed a man before.

Except for the Swedish horseman he had felled . . . It was during the year when King Haakon led an incursion into Sweden to avenge the murder of the dukes.[4] Simon had been sent out on a scouting mission; he had taken along three men, and he was to be their chieftain. How bold and cocky he was. Simon remembered that his sword had gotten stuck in the steel helmet of the horseman so that he had to pry and wriggle it loose. There was a nick in the blade when he looked at it the next morning. He had always thought about that incident with pride, and there had been eight Swedes. He had gotten a taste of war at any rate, and that wasn't the lot of everyone who joined the king's men that year. When daylight came, he saw that blood and brains had splattered over his coat of mail; he tried to look modest and not boastful as he washed it off.

But it did no good to think about that poor devil of a horseman now. No, that was not the same thing. He couldn't get rid of a terrible feeling of remorse about Holmgeir Moisessøn.

There was also the fact that he owed Erlend his life. He didn't yet know what import this would have, but he felt as if everything would be different, now that he and Erlend were even.

In that way they were even at least.

The brothers-in-law had been riding in near silence. Once Erlend said, "It was foolish of you, Simon, not to think of getting out right from the start."

"Why is that?" asked Simon rather brusquely. "Because you were outside?"

"No . . ." There was the hint of a smile in Erlend's voice. "Well, because of that too. I hadn't thought about that. But through that narrow door they couldn't follow you more than one at a time. And it's always astounding how quickly people regain their senses when they come out under the open sky. It seems to me a miracle that there weren't more deaths."

A few times Erlend inquired about his brother-in-law's wounds. Simon said he hardly noticed them, even though they were throbbing terribly.

They reached Formo late that evening, and Erlend went inside with his brother-in-law. He had advised Simon to send the sheriff a report of the incident the very next day in order to arrange for a letter of reprieve[5] as soon as possible. Erlend would gladly compose the letter for Simon that night since the wounds on his chest would no doubt hamper his writing hand. "And tomorrow you must keep to your bed; you may have a little wound fever."

Ramborg and Arngjerd were waiting up for them. Because of the cold, they had settled on the bench on the warm side of the hearth, tucking their legs underneath them. A board game lay between them; they looked like a couple of children.

Simon had barely uttered a few words about what had happened before his young wife flew to his side and threw her arms around his neck. She pulled his face down to hers and pressed her cheek against his. And she crushed Erlend's hands so tightly that he laughingly said he had never thought Ramborg could have such strong fingers.

She begged her husband to spend the night in the main house so that she could keep watch over him. She implored him, almost in tears, until Erlend offered to stay and sleep with Simon if she would send a man north to Jørundgaard to take word. It was too late for him to ride home anyway, "and a shame for Kristin to sit up so late in this cold. She waits up for me too; you're both good wives, you daughters of Lavrans."

While the men ate and drank, Ramborg sat close to her husband. Simon patted her arm and hand; he was both a little embarrassed and greatly touched that she showed so much concern and love for him. Simon was sleeping in the Sæmund house during Lent, and when the men went over there, Ramborg went with them and put a large kettle of honey-ale to warm near the hearthstone.

The Sæmund house was an ancient little hearth building, warm and snug; the timbers were so roughly hewn that there were only four beams to each wall. Right now it was cold, but Simon threw a great armful of resinous pine onto the fire and chased his dog up into the bed. The animal could lie there and warm it up for them. They pulled the log chair and the high-backed bench all the way up to the hearth and made themselves comfortable, for they were frozen to the bone after their ride, and the meal in the main house had only partially thawed them.

Erlend wrote the letter for Simon. Then they proceeded to undress. Simon's wound began to bleed again when he moved his arms too much, so his brother-in-law helped him pull the outer tunic over his head and take off his boots. Erlend limped a bit from his wounded leg; it was stiff and tender after the ride, he said, but it was nothing. Then they sat down near the fire again, half dressed. The room had grown pleasantly warm, and there was still plenty of ale in the kettle.

"I can see that you're taking this much too hard," Erlend said once. They had been dozing and staring into the fire. "He was no great loss to the world, that Holmgeir."

"That's not what Sira Moises will think," said Simon quietly. "He's an old man and a good priest."

Erlend nodded somberly.

"It's a bad thing to have made enemies with such a man. Especially since he lives so near. And you know that I often have business in that parish."

"Yes, well . . . This kind of thing can happen so easily—to any of us. They'll probably sentence you to a fine of ten or twelve marks of gold. And you know that Bishop Halvard is a stern master when he has to hear the confession of an assailant, and the boy's father is one of his priests. But you'll get through whatever is required."

Simon did not reply.

Erlend continued. "No doubt I'll have to pay fines for the injuries." He smiled to himself. "And I own no other piece of Norwegian land than the farm at Dovre."

"How big of a farm *is* Haugen?" asked Simon.

"I don't remember exactly; it says in the deed. But the people who work the land harvest only a small amount of hay. No one wants to live there; I've heard that the buildings are in great disrepair. You know what people say: that the dead spirits of my aunt and Herr Bjørn haunt the place.

"But I know that I will win thanks from my wife for what I did today. Kristin is fond of you, Simon—as if you were her own brother."

Simon's smile was almost imperceptible as he sat there in the shadows. He had pushed the log chair back a bit and had put his hand up to shield his eyes from the heat of the flames. But Erlend was as happy as a cat in the heat. He sat close to the hearth, leaning against a corner of the bench, with one arm resting along its back and his wounded leg propped up on the opposite side.

"Yes, she had such charming words to say about it one day this past fall," said Simon after a moment. There was an almost mocking ring to his voice.

"When our son was ill, she showed that she was a loyal sister," he said somberly, but then that slightly jesting tone was back. "Well, Erlend, we have kept faith with each other the way we swore to do when we gave our hands to Lavrans and vowed to stand by each other as brothers."

"Yes," said Erlend, unsuspecting. "I'm glad for what I did today too, Simon, my brother-in-law." They both fell silent for a while. Then Erlend hesitantly stretched out his hand to the other man. Simon took it. They clasped each other's fingers tightly, then let go and huddled back in their seats, a little embarrassed.

Finally Erlend broke the silence. For a long time he had been sitting with his chin in his hand, staring into the hearth, where only a tiny flame now flickered, flaring up, dancing a bit, and playing over the charred pieces of wood, which broke apart and collapsed with brittle little sighs. Soon there would be only black coals and glowing embers left of the fire.

Erlend said quite softly, "You have treated me so magnanimously, Simon Darre, that I think few men are your equal. I . . . I haven't forgotten . . ."

"Silence! You don't know, Erlend . . . Only God in Heaven knows everything that resides in a man's mind," whispered Simon, frightened and distraught.

"That's true," said Erlend in the same quiet and somber tone of voice. "We all need Him to judge us . . . with mercy. But a man must judge a man by what he *does*. And I . . . I . . . May God reward you, brother-in-law!"

Then they sat in dead silence, not daring to move for fear of being shamed.

Suddenly Erlend let his hand fall to his knee. A fiery blue ray of light flashed from the stone on the ring he wore on his right index finger. Simon knew that Kristin had given it to Erlend when he was released from the prison tower.

"But you must remember, Simon," he said in a low voice, "the old saying: Many a man is given what was intended for another, but no one is given another man's fate."

Simon raised his head sharply. Slowly his face flushed blood red; the veins at his temples stood out like dark, twisted cords.

Erlend glanced at him for a moment but quickly withdrew his eyes. Then he too turned crimson. A strangely delicate and girlish blush spread over his tan skin. He sat motionless, embarrassed and confused, with his little, childish mouth open.

Simon stood up abruptly and went over to the bed.

"You'll want to take the outside edge, I presume." He tried to speak calmly and with nonchalance, but his voice quavered.

"No, I'll let you decide," said Erlend numbly. He got to his feet. "The fire?" he asked, flustered. "Should I cover the ashes?" He began raking the hearth.

"Finish that and then come to bed," said Simon in the same tone. His heart was pounding so hard that he could barely talk.

In the dark Erlend, soundless as a shadow, slipped under the covers on the outer edge of the bed and lay down, as quiet as a forest creature. Simon thought he would suffocate from having the other man in his bed.

## CHAPTER 6

EVERY YEAR DURING Easter week Simon Andressøn held an ale feast for the people of the village. They came to Formo on the third day after mass and stayed until Thursday.

Kristin had never particularly enjoyed these banquets with their bantering and pleasantry. Both Simon and Ramborg seemed to think that the more commotion and noise there was, the better. Simon always invited his guests to bring along their children, their servants, and the children of their servants—as many as could be spared from home. On the first day everything proceeded in a quiet and orderly manner; only the gentry and the elders would converse, while the youth listened and ate and drank, and the little children kept mostly to a different building. But on the second day, from early in the morning on, the host would urge the lively young people and the children to drink and make merry, and before long the teasing would grow so wild and unrestrained that the women and maidens would slip away to the corners and stand there in clusters, giggling and ready to flee. But many of the more high-standing wives would seek out Ramborg's women's house, which was already occupied by the mothers who had rescued the youngest children from the tumult of the main building.

One game that was a favorite among the men was pretending to hold a *ting*. They would read summons documents, present grievances, proclaim new laws and modify old ones, but they always twisted the words around and said them backward. Audun Torbergssøn could recite King Haakon's letter to the merchants of Bjørgvin:[1] what they could charge for men's hose and for leather soles on a woman's shoes, about the men who made swords and big and small shields. But he would mix up the words until they were all jumbled and sheer babble. This game always ended with the men not having any idea what they were saying. Kristin remembered from her childhood that her father would never allow the jesting to turn to ridicule of anything related to the Church or divine services. But otherwise Lavrans thought it great fun when he and his guests would compete by jumping up on the tables and benches while they merrily shouted all manner of coarse and unseemly nonsense.

Simon was usually most fond of games in which a man was blindfolded and had to search through the ashes for a knife, or two people had to bob for pieces of gingerbread in a big bowl of ale. The other guests would try to make them laugh, and the ale would spray all around. Or they were supposed to use their teeth to dig a ring out of a flour bin. The hall would soon take on the look of a pigsty.

But this year they had such surprisingly glorious spring weather for Easter. On Wednesday by early morning it was already sunny and warm, and right after breakfast everyone went out to the courtyard. Instead of making a noisy ruckus, the young people played with balls, or shot at targets or had tugs-of-war with a rope. Later they played the stag game or the woodpile dance,[2] and afterward they persuaded Geirmund of Kruke to sing and play his harp. Soon everyone, both young and old, had joined the dance. Snow still covered the fields, but the alder trees were brown with buds, and the sun shone warm and lovely on all the bare slopes. When the guests came outside after supper, there were birds singing everywhere. Then they made a bonfire in the field beyond the smithy, and they sang and danced until late into the night. The next morning everyone stayed in bed a long time and left the banquet manor much later than usual. The guests from Jørundgaard were normally the last to depart, but this time Simon persuaded Erlend and Kristin to stay until the following day. Those from Kruke were to stay at Formo until the end of the week.

Simon had accompanied the last of his guests up to the main road. The evening sun was shining so beautifully on his estate, spread out over the hillside. He was warm and in high spirits from the drinking and noise of the feast. He walked back between the fences, homeward to the calm and pleasant goodwill that prevails when a small circle of close kin remains after a great banquet. He felt so light of heart and happier than he had been for a long time.

Down in the field near the smithy they had lit another bonfire:

Erlend's sons, Sigrid's older children, Jon Daalk's sons, and his own daughters. Simon leaned over the fence for a moment to watch. Ulvhild's scarlet feast day gown gleamed and rippled in the sun. She ran back and forth, dragging branches over to the fire, and suddenly she was stretched out full length on the ground! Her father shouted merrily, but the children didn't hear him.

In the courtyard two serving maids were tending to the smallest of the children. They were sitting against the wall of the women's house, basking in the sun. Above their heads the evening light gleamed like molten gold on the small glass windowpane. Simon picked up little Inga Geirmundsdatter, tossed her high in the air, and then held her in his arms. "Can you sing for your uncle today, pretty Inga?" Then her brother and Andres both fell upon Simon, wanting to be tossed up in the air too.

Whistling, he climbed the stairs to the great hall in the loft. The sun was shining into the room so splendidly; they had let the door stand open. A wondrous calm reigned over everyone. At the end of the table Erlend and Geirmund were bent over the harp, on which they were putting new strings. They had the mead horn standing near them on the table. Sigrid was in bed, nursing her youngest son. Kristin and Ramborg were sitting with her, and a silver mug stood on a footstool between the sisters.

Simon filled his own gilded goblet to the brim with wine, went over to the bed, and drank a toast to Sigrid. "I see that all have quenched their thirst, except you, my sister!"

Laughing, she propped herself up on her elbow and accepted the goblet. The infant began howling crossly at being disturbed.

Simon sat down on the bench, still whistling softly, and listened with half an ear to what the others were saying. Sigrid and Kristin were talking about their children; Ramborg was silent, fiddling with a windmill that belonged to Andres. The men at the table were strumming the harp, trying it out; Geirmund picked out a melody on the harp and sang along. They both had such charming voices.

After a while Simon went out to the gallery, leaned against the carved post, and gazed out. From the cowshed came the eternally hungry lowing. If this weather held on for a time, perhaps the spring shortages wouldn't last as long this year.

Kristin was approaching. He didn't have to turn around; he recognized her light step. She stepped forward and stood at his side in the evening sun.

So fair and graceful, she had never seemed to him more beautiful. And all of a sudden he felt as if he had somehow been lifted up and were swimming in the light. He let out a long breath. Suddenly he thought: It was simply good to be alive. A rich and golden bliss washed over him.

She was his own sweet love. All the troubled and bitter thoughts he had had seemed nothing more than half-forgotten foolishness. My poor love. If only I could comfort you. If only you could be happy again. I would gladly give up my life if it would help you.

Oh yes, he could see that her lovely face looked older and more careworn. She had an abundance of fine, little wrinkles under her eyes, and her skin had lost its delicate hue. It had become coarser and tan from the sun, but she was pale under the tan. And yet to him she would surely always be just as beautiful. Her big gray eyes, her fine, calm mouth, her round little chin, and her steady, subdued demeanor were the fairest he knew on earth.

It was a pleasure to see her once again dressed in a manner befitting a highborn woman. The thin little silk wimple covered only half of her golden brown tresses; her braids had been pinned up so they peeked out in front of her ears. There were streaks of gray in her hair now, but that didn't matter. And she was wearing a magnificent blue surcoat made of velvet and trimmed with marten fur. The bodice was cut so low and the sleeve holes so deep that the garment clung to her breast and shoulders like the narrow straps of a bridle. It looked so lovely. Underneath there was a glimpse of something sand yellow, a gown that fit snugly to her body, all the way up to her throat and down to her wrists. It was held closed with dozens of tiny gilded buttons, which touched him so deeply. God forgive him—all those little golden buttons gave him as much joy as the sight of a flock of angels.

He stood there and felt the strong, steady beat of his own heart. Something had fallen away from him—yes, like chains. Vile, hateful dreams—they were just phantoms of the night. Now he could see the love he felt for her in the light of day, in full sunlight.

"You're looking at me so strangely, Simon. Why are you smiling like that?"

The man gave a quiet, merry laugh but did not reply. Before them stretched the valley, filled with the golden warmth of the evening sun. Flocks of birds warbled and chirped metallically from the edge of the woods. Then the full, clear voice of the song thrush rang out from somewhere inside the forest. And here she stood, warmed by the sun, radiant in her brilliant finery, having emerged from the dark, cold house and the rough, heavy clothing that smelled of sweat and toil. My Kristin, it's good to see you this way again.

He took her hand, which lay before him on the railing of the gallery, and lifted it to his face. "The ring you're wearing is so lovely." He turned the gold ring on her finger and then put her hand back down. It was reddish and rough now, and he didn't know how he could ever make amends to it—so fair it had once been, her big, slender hand.

"There's Arngjerd and Gaute," said Kristin. "The two of them are quarreling again."

Their voices could be heard from underneath the loft gallery, shrill and angry. Now the maiden began shouting furiously, "Go ahead and remind me of that. It seems to me a greater honor to be called my father's bastard daughter than to be the lawful son of yours!"

Kristin spun on her heel and ran down the stairs. Simon followed and heard the sound of two or three slaps. She was standing under the gallery, clutching her son by the shoulder.

The two children had their eyes downcast; they were red-faced, silent, and defiant.

"I see you know how to behave as a guest. You do us such honor, your father and me."

Gaute stared at the ground. In a low, angry voice he said to his mother, "She said something . . . I don't want to repeat it."

Simon put his hand under his daughter's chin and tilted her face up. Arngjerd turned even brighter red, and her eyes blinked under her father's gaze.

"Yes," she said, pulling away from him. "I reminded Gaute that his father was a condemned villain and traitor. But before that he called you . . . He said that you, Father, were the traitor, and that it was thanks to Erlend that you were now sitting here, safe and rich, on your own manor."

"I thought you were a grown-up maiden by now. Are you going to let childish chatter provoke you so that you forget both your manners and honor among kin?" Angrily he pushed the girl away, turned toward Gaute, and asked calmly, "What do you mean, Gaute, my friend, that I betrayed your father? I've noticed before that you're cross with me. Now tell me: What do you mean?"

"You know what I mean!"

Simon shook his head.

Then the boy shouted, his eyes flashing with bitterness, "The letter they tortured my father on the rack for, trying to make him say who had put their seal on it—I saw that letter myself! I was the one who took it and burned it."

"Keep silent!" Erlend broke in among them. His face was deathly white, all the way to his lips; his eyes blazed.

"No, Erlend. It's better that we clear up this matter now. Was my name mentioned in that letter?"

"Keep silent!" Furiously Erlend seized Gaute by the shoulder and chest. "I trusted you. You, my son! It would serve you right if I killed you now."

Kristin sprang forward, as did Simon. The boy tore himself loose and took refuge with his mother. Beside himself with rage, he screamed furiously as he hid behind Kristin's arm, "I picked it up and looked at the seals before I burned it, Father! I thought the day might come when I could serve you by doing so. . . ."

"May God curse you!" A brief dry sob racked Erlend's body.

Simon too had turned pale and then dark red in the face, out of shame for his brother-in-law. He didn't dare look in Erlend's direction; he thought he would suffocate from the other's humiliation.

Kristin stood as if bewitched, still holding her arms protectively around her son. But one thought followed another, in rapid succession.

Erlend had had Simon's private seal in his possession for a short time during that spring. The brothers-in-law had jointly sold Lavrans's dock warehouse at Veøy to the cloister on Holm. Erlend had mentioned that this was probably unlawful, but surely no one would question it. He had shown her the seal and said that Simon should have had a finer one carved. All three brothers had acquired a copy of their father's seal; only the inscriptions were different. But Gyrd's was much more finely etched, said Erlend.

Gyrd Darre . . . Erlend had brought her greetings from him after both of his last journeys to the south. She remembered being surprised that Erlend had visited Gyrd at Dyfrin. They had met only once, at Ramborg's wedding. Ulf Saksesøn was Gyrd Darre's brother-in-law; Ulf had been part of the plot. . . .

"You were mistaken, Gaute," said Simon in a low, firm voice.

"Simon!" Unawares, Kristin gripped her husband's hand. "Keep in mind . . . there are other men than yourself who bear that emblem on their seal."

"Silence! Will you too—" Erlend tore himself away from his wife with a tormented wail and raced across the courtyard toward the stable. Simon set off after him.

"Erlend . . . Was it my brother?"

"Send for the boys. Follow me home," Erlend shouted back to his wife.

Simon caught up with him in the stable doorway and grabbed him by the arm. "Erlend, was it Gyrd?"

Erlend didn't reply; he tried to wrench his arm away. His face looked oddly stubborn and deathly pale.

"Erlend, answer me. Did my brother join you in that plan?"

"Perhaps you too would like to test your sword against mine?" Erlend snarled, and Simon could feel the other man's body trembling as they struggled.

"You know I wouldn't." Simon let go and sank back against the doorframe. "Erlend, in the name of Christ, who suffered death for our sakes: Tell me if it's true!"

Erlend led Soten out, and Simon had to step aside from the doorway. An attentive servant brought his saddle and bridle. Simon took them and sent the man away. Then Erlend took them from Simon.

"Erlend, surely you can tell me *now*! You can tell *me*!" He didn't know why he was begging as if for his very life. "Erlend, answer me. On the wounds of Christ, I beseech you. Tell me, man!"

"You can keep on thinking what you thought before," said Erlend in a low and cutting voice.

"Erlend, I didn't think . . . anything."

"I *know* what you thought." Erlend swung himself into the saddle. Simon grabbed the harness; the horse shifted and pranced uneasily.

"Let go, or I'll run you down," said Erlend.

"Then I'll ask Gyrd. I'll ride south tomorrow. By God, Erlend, you have to tell me. . . ."

"Yes, I'm sure *he* will give you an answer," said Erlend scornfully, spurring the stallion so that Simon had to leap aside. Then Erlend galloped off from the estate.

Halfway up the courtyard Simon met Kristin. She was wearing her cloak. Gaute walked at her side, carrying their clothing sack. Ramborg followed her sister.

The boy glanced up for a moment, frightened and confused. Then he withdrew his gaze. But Kristin fixed her big eyes directly on Simon's face. They were dark with sorrow and anger.

"Could you truly believe that of Erlend? That he would betray you in such a manner?"

"I didn't believe anything," said Simon vehemently. "I thought the boy was just babbling nonsense and foolishness."

"No, Simon, I don't want you to come with me," said Kristin quietly.

He saw that she was unspeakably offended and grieved.

That evening, when Simon was alone with his wife in the main house, as they undressed and their daughters were already asleep in the other bed, Ramborg suddenly asked, "Didn't you know anything about this, Simon?"

"No. Did you?" he asked tensely.

Ramborg came over and stood in the glow of the candle standing on the table. She was half undressed, in her shift and laced bodice; her hair fell in loose curls around her face.

"I didn't know, but I had a feeling. . . . Helga was so strange . . ." Her features twisted into an odd sort of smile, and she looked as if she were freezing. "She talked about how new times would be coming to Norway. The great chieftains would acquire the same rights here as in other lands." Ramborg gave a crooked, almost contorted smile. "They would be called knights and barons again.

"Later, when I saw that you took up their affairs with such zeal, and you were away from home almost a whole year . . . and didn't even feel that you could come north to be with me at Ringheim when I was staying on a stranger's estate, about to give birth to your child . . . I thought perhaps you knew that it concerned others than Erlend."

"Ha! Knights and barons!" Simon gave an angry laugh.

"Then was it merely for Kristin's sake that you did it?"

He saw that her face was pale, as if from frostbite; it was impossible to pretend that he didn't understand what she meant. Out of spite and despair, he exclaimed, "Yes."

Then he thought that she must have gone mad, and he was mad too. Erlend was mad; they had all lost their wits that day. But now there had to be an end to it.

"I did it for your sister's sake, yes," he said soberly. "And for the sake of the children who had no other man closer in family or kinship to protect them. And for Erlend's sake, since we should be as loyal to each other as brothers. So don't start behaving foolishly, for I've seen more than enough of that here on the estate today," he bellowed, and flung the shoe he had just taken off against the wall.

Ramborg went over and picked it up; she looked at the timber it had struck.

"It's shameful that Torbjørg didn't think of it herself, to wash off the soot in here before the feast. I forgot to mention it to her." She wiped off the shoe. It was Simon's best, with a long toe and red heel. She picked up its mate and put both of them into his clothes chest. But Simon noticed that her hands were shaking badly as she did so.

Then he went over and took her in his arms. She twined her thin arms around her husband as she trembled with stifled sobs and whispered to him that she was so tired.

Seven days later Simon and his servant rode through Kvam, heading north. They fought their way through a blizzard of great wet snowflakes. At midday they arrived at the small farm on the public road where there was an alehouse.

The proprietress came out and invited Simon to come into their home; only commoners were shown into the tavern. She shook out his outer garment and hung it up to dry on the wall peg near the hearth as she talked. Such awful weather . . . hard on the horses . . . and he must have had to ride the whole way around . . . it wasn't possible to go across Lake Mjøsa now, was it?

"Oh yes, if a man was sick enough of his life . . ."

The woman and her children standing nearby all laughed agreeably. The older ones went about their chores, bringing in wood and ale, while the younger ones huddled together near the door. They usually received a few *penninger* from Simon, the master of Formo, whenever he stayed there, and if he was bringing home treats for his own children from Hamar, he would often give them a tidbit too. But today he didn't seem to notice them.

He sat on the bench, leaning forward, with his hands hanging over his knees, staring into the hearth fire, and replied with a word or two to the woman's incessant chatter. Then she mentioned that Erlend Nikulaussøn happened to be at Granheim. It was the day on which the ancestral owners were to place the first payment in the hands of the former owners. Should she send one of the children over to his brother-in-law with a message so that they could ride home together?

No, said Simon. She could give him a little food, and then he would lie down and sleep for a while.

He would see Erlend in good time. What he had to say he wanted to say in front of Gaute. But he would prefer not to speak of the matter more than once.

His servant, Sigurd, had sought refuge in the cookhouse while the woman prepared the food. Yes, it had been a wearisome journey, and his master had been like an angry bull almost the whole way. Normally Simon Andressøn liked to hear whatever news from his home district his servants could glean while they were at Dyfrin. He usually had one or more people from Raumerike in his service. Folks would come to him to ask for work whenever he was home, for he was known as a well-liked and generous man who was merry and not high-handed with his servants. But on this journey about the only answer that he, Sigurd, had received from his master was "Keep silent!"

He had apparently had a great quarrel with his brothers; he hadn't even stayed the night at Dyfrin. They had taken lodgings on a tenant farm farther out in the countryside. Sir Gyrd—yes, for he could tell her that the king had made his master's brother a knight at Christmastime—well, Sir Gyrd had come out to the courtyard and warmly entreated Simon to stay, but Simon had given his brother a curt reply. And they had roared and bellowed and shouted, all those gentlemen up in the high loft—Sir Ulf Saksesøn and Gudmund Andressøn had been on the estate as well—so that everyone was terribly frightened. God only knew what it was that had made them foes.

Simon came past the cookhouse, paused for a moment, and peered inside. Sigurd announced quickly that he would get an awl and a strap to make proper repairs to the harness that had been torn in the morning.

"Do they have those kinds of things in the cookhouse on this farm?" Simon flung over his shoulder as he left. Sigurd shook his head and nodded to the woman when Simon had disappeared from sight.

Simon pushed his plate aside but stayed seated. He was so tired that he could hardly even get up. At last he got to his feet and threw himself onto the bed, still wearing his boots and spurs, but then thought better of it. It was a good, clean bed for the house of a commoner. He sat up and pulled off his boots. Stiff and worn out as he was, surely he would be able to sleep now. He was soaked through and freezing, but his face burned after the long ride in the storm.

He crawled under the coverlet, twisting and turning the pillows; they smelled so strangely of fish. Then he stretched out, half reclining, propped up on one elbow.

His thoughts began circling again. He had been thinking and thinking these past few days, the way an animal plods around a tether.

Even if Erling Vidkunssøn had known that the welfare of Gyrd and Gudmund Darre might also be at stake if Erlend Nikulaussøn had been broken and talked . . . well, that didn't make it any worse that Simon had seized upon all means to win the help of the Bjarkø knight. Quite the opposite. Surely a man was obligated to stand by his own brothers, even to the death if need be. But he still wished that he knew whether Erling had known about it. Simon weighed the matter for and against. Erling couldn't possibly have been entirely ignorant that a rebellion was brewing. But what exactly had he known? Gyrd and Ulf, at any rate, didn't seem to know whether the man was aware of their complicity. But Simon remembered that Erling had mentioned the Haftorssøns and had advised him to seek their help, for it was most likely their friends who would need to be afraid. The Haftorssøns were cousins of Ulf Saksesøn and Helga. The nose is right next to the eyes!

But even if Erling Vidkunssøn believed that he was also thinking of his own brothers, surely that didn't make what he had done any worse. And Erling might have realized that he knew nothing about his brothers' peril. Besides, he had said himself that . . . He remembered he had told Stig that he didn't think they could torture Erlend into talking.

They might still have reason to fear Erlend's tongue. He had kept silent through the torture and imprisonment, but he was the kind of man who might let it slip out afterward through some chance remark. It would be just like him.

And yet . . . Simon thought this was the one thing he could be certain that Erlend would never do. He was as silent as a rock every time the conversation touched on the matter, precisely because he was afraid of being lured into some slip of the tongue. Simon understood that Erlend had a fierce, almost childish terror of breaching a promise. Childish because the fact that he had given away the whole plan to his lover clearly did not seem to Erlend to have tarnished his honor in any significant way. He apparently thought that such could happen to the best of men. As long as he himself held his tongue, he considered his shield unblemished and his promise unbroken. And Simon had noticed that Erlend was sensitive about his honor, as far as his own understanding of honor and reputation went. He had nearly lost his wits from desperation and anger at the mere thought that any of his fellow conspirators might be exposed—even now, so much later and in such a manner that it couldn't possibly make any difference to the men whom he had protected with his life, as well as with his honor and his property. All because of a child talking to the closest kinsman of these men.

Erlend wanted to handle it in such a way that if things went wrong, he would be the one to pay the price for all of them. That's what he had vowed on the crucifix to every man who had joined him in the plot. But to think that grown-up, sensible men would put their faith in such an oath, when it was not entirely within

Erlend's control . . . Now that Simon had learned everything about the plan, he thought it was the greatest foolishness he had ever heard. Erlend had been willing to let his body be torn apart, limb from limb, in order to keep his sworn oath. All the while the secret lay in the hands of a ten-year-old boy; Erlend himself had seen to that. And it was evidently no thanks to him that Sunniva Olavsdatter didn't know more than she did. Could anyone ever make sense of such a man?

If, for a moment, he had believed . . . well, what Erlend and his wife thought he had believed. . . . God only knew how close to the truth such a thought was when Gaute started talking about seeing his seal on the treasonous letter. The two of them might remember that he knew a few things about Erlend Nikulaussøn so that he, more than most other men, had little reason to believe the best of that gentleman. But they had probably forgotten long ago how he had once come upon them and witnessed the depths of their shamelessness.

So there was little reason for him to lie here, berating himself like a dog because he had wrongly accused Erlend in his mind. God knew it was not because he wanted to think ill of his brother-in-law; it only made him unhappy to have such thoughts. He was fully aware that it was a wildly foolish notion; he would have realized at once, even without Kristin's words, that things *couldn't* have happened that way. As quickly as the suspicion occurred to him—that Erlend might have misused his seal—he had dismissed it. No, Erlend couldn't possibly have done that. Erlend had never in his life committed a dishonorable act that had been thought out in advance or with some specific purpose in mind.

Simon tossed and turned in bed, moaning. They had made him half mad with all this madness. He felt so tormented when he thought about how Gaute had gone around for years, believing this of him. But it was unreasonable for him to take it so hard. Even though he was fond of the boy, fond of all of Kristin's sons, they were still hardly more than children. Did he need to be so concerned about how they might judge him?

To think he could be so furious with rage when he thought about the men who had placed their hands on the hilt of Erlend's sword and sworn to follow their chieftain. If they were such sheep to allow themselves to be dazzled by Erlend's persuasive and bold manner and to believe that he was a suitable chieftain, then it was only to be expected that they would behave like frightened sheep when the whole venture went awry. And yet he felt dazed when he thought about what he had learned at Dyfrin: that so *many* men had dared entrust the peace of the land and their own welfare into Erlend's hands. Even Haftor Olavssøn and Borgar Trondssøn! But not *one* of them had the courage to step forward and demand of the king that Erlend should be granted an honorable reconciliation and a reprieve for his ancestral estates. There were so many of them that if they had joined forces, it could easily have been accomplished. Apparently there was less wisdom and courage among the noblemen of Norway than he had thought.

Simon was also angry because he had been entirely kept out of these plans. Not that they would have been able to enlist *him* in such a foolhardy enterprise. But that both Erlend and Gyrd had gone behind his back and concealed everything . . . Surely he was just as good a nobleman as any of the others, and not without some influence in the regions where people knew him.

In some ways he agreed with Gyrd. Considering the manner in which Erlend had squandered his position as chieftain, the man couldn't reasonably demand that his fellow conspirators should step forward and declare their allegiance with him. Simon knew that if he had found Gyrd alone, he would not have ended up parting with his brothers in such a fashion. But there sat that knight, Sir Ulf, stretching out his long legs in front of him and talking about Erlend's lack of sense—after it was all over! And then Gudmund spoke up. In the past neither Gyrd nor Simon had let their younger brother take a position against them. But ever since he had married the priest's paramour, who then became his own paramour, the boy had grown so swaggering and cocky and independent. Simon had sat there glaring fiercely at Gudmund. He spoke so arrogantly and his round, red face looked so much like a child's backside that Simon's hands itched to give it a swat. In the end he hardly knew what he was saying to the three men.

And now he had broken with his brothers. He felt as if he would bleed to death when he thought about it, as if bonds of flesh and blood had been severed. He was the poorer for it. Bare is the brotherless back.

But however things now stood, in the midst of the heated exchange of words he had suddenly realized—he didn't know exactly why—that Gyrd's closed and stony demeanor wasn't solely due to the fact that he was hard pressed to find any peace at home. In a flash Simon saw that Gyrd still loved Helga; that was what made him so strangely fettered and powerless. And in some secretive, incomprehensible way, this aroused his fury over . . . well, over life itself.

Simon hid his face in his hands. Yes, in that sense they had been good, obedient sons. It had been easy for Gyrd and him to feel love for the brides whom his father announced he had chosen for them. The old man had made a long, splendid speech to them one evening, and afterward they had both sat there feeling abashed. About marriage and friendship and faithfulness between honorable, noble spouses; in the end their father even mentioned prayers of intercession and masses. It was too bad their father hadn't given them advice on how to forget as well—when the friendship was broken and the honor dead and the faithfulness a sin and a secret, disgraceful torment, and there was nothing left of the bond but the bleeding wound that would never heal.

After Erlend was released, an odd feeling of calm came over Simon—if only because a man can't continue to endure the kind of pain he had suffered during that time in Oslo. Either something happens, or it gets better of its own accord.

Simon had not been pleased when Kristin moved to Jørundgaard with her husband and all their children so that he had to see them more often and keep up their friendship and kinship. But he consoled himself that it would have been much worse if he had been forced to live with her in a fashion that is unbearable for a man: to live with a woman he loves when she is not his wife or his kinswoman by blood. He chose to ignore what had occurred between his brother-in-law and himself on that evening when they celebrated Erlend's release from the tower. Erlend had probably understood only half of it and surely hadn't given it much thought. Erlend had such a rare talent for forgetting. And Simon had his own estate, a wife whom he loved, and his children.

He had found some semblance of peace with himself. It was not his fault that he loved his wife's sister. She had once been his betrothed, and he was not the one who had broken his promise. Back when he had set his heart on Kristin Lavransdatter, it had simply been his duty to do so, because he thought she was intended to be his wife. The fact that he married her sister . . . that was Ramborg's doing, and her father's. Lavrans, as wise a man as he was, hadn't thought to ask whether Simon had forgotten. But he knew that he couldn't have stood to be asked that question by Lavrans.

Simon wasn't good at forgetting. He was not to blame for that. And he had never spoken a single word that he ought to have withheld. But he couldn't help it if the Devil plagued him with impulses and dreams that violated the bonds of blood; he had never willingly indulged in sinful thoughts of love. And he had always behaved like a loyal brother toward her and her kin. Of that he was certain.

At last he had managed to be tolerably content with his lot.

But only as long as he knew that he was the one who had served those two: Kristin and the man she had chosen in his stead. They had always been in need of his support.

Now this had changed. Kristin had risked her life and soul to save the life of his son. It felt as if all the old wounds had opened up ever since he allowed that to happen.

Later he became indebted to Erlend for his own life.

And then, in return, he had affronted the man—not intentionally, and only in his thoughts, but still . . .

*"Et dimitte nobis debita nostra, sicut et nos dimittibus debitoribus nostris."* It was strange that the Lord hadn't also taught them to pray: *"sicut et nos dimittibus creditoribus nostris."* He didn't know whether this was proper Latin; he had never been particularly good at the language. But he knew that in some way he had always been able to forgive his debtors. It seemed much harder to forgive anyone who had bound a debt around *his* neck.

But now they were even: he and those two. He felt all the old resentments, which he had trampled underfoot for years, rip open and come to life.

He could no longer shove Erlend aside in his thoughts as a foolish chatterer who couldn't see or learn or remember or ponder anything at all. Now the other man weighed on his mind precisely because no one knew *what* Erlend saw or thought or remembered; he was completely unfathomable.

Many a man is given what was intended for another, but no one is given another man's fate.

How truly spoken.

Simon had loved his young betrothed. If he had won her, he would certainly have been a contented man; surely they would have lived well together. And she would have continued to be as she was when they first met: gentle and seemly, intelligent enough that a man would gladly seek her counsel even on important matters, a bit headstrong about petty things, but otherwise amenable, accustomed as she was to accepting from her father's hands guidance and support and protection. But then that man had seized hold of her: a man incapable of restraining himself, who had never offered protection to anything. He had ravaged her sweet innocence, broken her proud calm, destroyed her womanly soul, and forced her to stretch and strain to the utmost every faculty she possessed. She had to defend her lover, the way a tiny bird protects its nest with a trembling body and shrill voice when anyone comes too close. It had seemed to Simon that her lovely, slender body was created to be lifted up and fervently shielded by a man's arms. He had seen it tense with wild stubbornness, as her heart pounded with courage and fear and the will to fight, and she battled for her husband and children, the way even a dove can turn fierce and fearless if she has young ones.

If he had been her husband, if she had lived with his honorable goodwill for fifteen winters, he was certain that she would have stood up to defend him too if he had landed in misfortune. With shrewdness and courage she would have stood by his side. But he would never have seen that stony face she turned toward him on the evening in Oslo when she told him that she had been over to take a look around in that house. He would never have heard her scream his own name in such desperate need and distress. And it was not the honorable and just love of his youth that had answered in his heart. The ardor that rose up and cried out toward her wild spirit . . . he would never have known that such feeling could reside in his own heart if things had happened between them as their fathers had intended.

Her expression, as she walked past him and went out into the night to find help for his child . . . She would not have dared to take those measures if she had not been Erlend's wife and had grown accustomed to acting fearlessly, even when her heart trembled with anguish. Her tear-streaked smile when she woke him up and said the boy was calling for his father . . . A smile of such heartbreaking sweetness was possible only for someone who knew what it meant both to lose a battle and to win.

It was Erlend's wife whom he loved—the way he loved her now. But that meant his love was sinful, and that was why things stood as they did and why he was unhappy. He was so unhappy that sometimes he felt only a great astonishment that he was the one this had befallen, and he could see no way out of his distress.

When he trampled on his own honor and noble decorum and reminded Erling Vidkunssøn of things that no honorable man would have imagined that he knew, he had done it not for his brothers or kinsmen but for her alone. It was for her sake that he had dared plead with the other man, just like the lepers who begged at the church doors in town, displaying their hideous sores.

He had thought that someday he would tell her about it. Not everything, not how deeply he had humbled himself. But after they had both grown old, he thought that he would say to Kristin: I helped you as best I could because I remembered how sincerely I loved you, back when I was your betrothed.

But there was one thing he didn't dare touch on with his thoughts. Had Erlend said anything to Kristin? Yes, he had thought that one day she should hear it from his own lips: I never forgot that I loved you when we were young. But if she already knew, and if she had learned it from her husband . . . No, then he didn't think he could go on.

He had intended to tell only her . . . someday, a long time from now. Then he thought about that moment when he had revealed it himself, when Erlend unwittingly happened to see what he thought he had hidden in the most secret part of his soul. And Ramborg knew—although he didn't understand how she had found out.

His own wife . . . and her husband—they both knew.

Simon gave a wild, stifled scream and abruptly flung himself onto the other side of the bed.

May God help him! Now he was the one who lay here, flayed naked, violated, bleeding with torment and trembling with shame.

The proprietress peeked around the door and met Simon's feverish, dry, and sharply glittering eyes from the bed. "Didn't you sleep? Erlend Nikulaussøn was just riding past with two men; no doubt two of his sons were traveling with him." Simon mumbled something in reply, angry and incomprehensible.

He wanted to give them a good head start. But he too would soon have to see about setting off for home.

As soon as Simon entered the main house at Formo and took off his outer garments, Andres would seize hold of his leather cap and try it on. While the boy straddled the bench and rode off to see his uncle at Dyfrin, the big cap would slip down, first over his small nose and then back over his lovely blond curls. But it did little good for Simon to try to remember such things now. God only knew when the boy would be visiting his uncle at Dyfrin again.

Instead the memory of his other son rose up: Halfrid's child. The tiny, pale blue body of an infant. He had seen little of the boy during the few days he lived; he had to sit at the bedside of the dying mother. If the child had survived, or if he had lived longer than his mother, then Simon would have kept Mandvik. Then he probably would have looked for a new wife there in the south. Occasionally he might have come north to the valley to see to his estate up here. Then surely he would have . . . not *forgotten* Kristin; she had led him into much too strange a dance for him to do that. By the Devil, a man should be allowed to remember it as a peculiar adventure: that he had been forced to rescue his betrothed, a highborn young maiden, reared in Christian and seemly behavior, from a house of ill repute and another man's bed. But then he wouldn't have been able to think of her in such a way that it troubled him and robbed the taste from everything good that life had to offer.

His son Erling . . . He would have been fourteen winters old by now. When Andres one day reached so near the age of a man, he himself would be old and feeble.

Oh, yes, Halfrid . . . You weren't very happy with me, were

you? I'm not entirely without blame that things have gone as they have for me.

Erlend Nikulaussøn might well have had to pay with his life for his impetuousness. And Kristin would now be living as a widow at Jørundgaard.

And he himself might have then regretted that he was a married man. Nothing seemed so foolish anymore that he didn't think himself capable of it.

The wind had died down, but great wet flakes of springtime snow were still falling when Simon rode out of the alehouse courtyard. And now, toward evening, birds began whistling and warbling in the grove of trees, defying the snowfall.

Just as a gash in the skin can reopen from too sudden a movement, a fleeting memory caused him pain. Not long ago, at his Easter banquet, several guests were standing outside, basking in the midday sun. High above them in the birch tree sat a robin, whistling into the warm blue air. Geirmund came limping around the corner of the house, dragging himself along with his cane, his other hand resting on the shoulder of his oldest son. He looked up, stopped, and imitated the bird. The boy also pursed his lips and whistled. They could mimic nearly all the birdsongs. Kristin was standing a short distance away, with several other women. Her smile had been so charming as she listened.

Now, toward sunset the clouds began to disperse in the west, tumbling golden over the white mountain slopes, filling the passes and small valleys like gray mist. The river gleamed dully like brass; the dark currents, free of ice, rushed around the rocks in the riverbed, and on each rock lay a little white pillow of new snow.

They made slow progress on the weary horses through the heavy snow. It was a milky white night with a full moon, which peeked out from the drifting haze and clouds as Simon rode down the slopes to the Ula River. When he had crossed the bridge and reached the flat expanses of pine forest, through which the winter road passed, the horses began moving faster. They knew they were approaching the stable. Simon patted Digerbein's steaming wet neck. He was glad this journey would soon be over. Ramborg had probably gone to bed long ago.

At the place where the road turned sharply and emerged from

the woods, there stood a small house. He was nearly upon it when he noticed that men on horseback were stopped in front of the door. He heard Erlend's voice shout, "Then it's agreed that you'll come to visit the day after Sunday? Can I tell my wife as much?"

Simon called out a greeting. It would seem much too strange not to stop and continue on in their company, but he told Sigurd to ride on ahead. Then he rode over to join them; it was Naakkve and Gaute. Erlend was just stepping out of the entryway.

They greeted each other again, the three others in a somewhat strained fashion. Simon could see their faces, although not very clearly in the fading light. He thought their expressions seemed uncertain—both tense and begrudging at the same time. So he said at once, "I've come from Dyfrin, my brother-in-law."

"Yes, I heard that you had traveled south." Erlend stood with his hand on the saddlebow, his eyes downcast. "You've made good time," he added, as if the silence were uncomfortable.

"No, wait a bit," said Simon to the young boys who were about to ride off. "You should hear this too. It was my brother's seal that you saw on the letter, Gaute. And I know you must think they showed poor loyalty to your father, both he and the other gentlemen who had affixed their seals on the letter to Prince Haakon, which your father was to carry to Denmark."

The boy looked down in silence.

Erlend said, "There was one thing you probably didn't think about, Simon, when you went to see your brother. I paid dearly for the safety of Gyrd and the others who joined me; it cost me all I owned except for my reputation as a loyal man who keeps his word. Now Gyrd Darre must think that I couldn't save even my reputation."

Shamefully Simon bowed his head. He hadn't thought about that.

"You might have told me this, Erlend, when I said that I was going to Dyfrin."

"You must have seen for yourself that I was so desperate and furious that I was beyond thinking or reasoning when I rode away from your manor."

"I wasn't particularly levelheaded myself, Erlend."

"No, but I thought you might have had time to come to your senses during the long ride. And I couldn't very well ask you not to talk to your brother without revealing things I had sworn a sacred oath to conceal."

Simon fell silent for a moment. At first he thought that Erlend was right. But then it occurred to him: No, Erlend was being quite unreasonable. Was he supposed to submit to having Kristin and the boys think so ill of him? He mentioned this rather vehemently.

"I have never uttered a word about this, kinsman—not to my mother or to my brothers," said Gaute, turning his handsome, fair face toward his uncle.

"But in the end they found out about it just the same," replied Simon obstinately. "I thought, after everything that happened on that day at my estate, we needed to clear up the matter. And I don't understand why it should take your father so unawares. You're still not much older than a child, my Gaute, and you were so young when you were mixed up in this . . . secret plot."

"Surely I should be able to trust my own son," replied Erlend angrily. "And I had no other choice when I needed to save the letter. I either had to give it to Gaute or let the sheriff find it."

Simon thought it pointless to discuss the matter any further. But he couldn't resist saying, "I wasn't happy when I heard what the boy has been thinking of me these past four years. I've always been fond of you, Gaute."

The boy urged his horse forward a few paces and stretched out his hand; Simon saw that his face had darkened, as if he were blushing.

"You must forgive me, Simon!"

Simon clasped the boy's hand. At times Gaute looked so much like his grandfather that Simon felt strangely moved. He was rather bowlegged and slight in build, but he was an excellent rider, and on the back of a horse he was as handsome a youth as any father could want.

All four of them began riding north; the boys were in front, and when they were beyond earshot, Simon continued.

"You must understand, Erlend . . . I don't think you can rightfully blame me for seeking out my brother and asking him to tell me the truth about this matter. But I know that you had reason to be angry with me, both you and Kristin. Because as soon as this strange news came out . . ." He fumbled for words. "What Gaute said about my seal . . . I can't deny that I thought . . . I know both of you believed that I thought . . . what I should have had sense enough to realize was unthinkable. So I can't deny that you have reason to be angry," he repeated.

The horses splashed through the slushy snow. It took a moment before Erlend replied, and then his voice sounded gentle and subdued. "I don't know what else you could have thought. It was almost inevitable that you should believe—"

"Oh, no. I should have known it wasn't possible," Simon interrupted, sounding aggrieved. After a moment he asked, "Did you think that I knew about my brothers? That I tried to help you for their sake?"

"No!" said Erlend in surprise. "I realized you couldn't possibly know. I knew that *I* hadn't said anything. And I thought I could safely rely on your brothers not to talk." He laughed softly. Then he grew somber and said gently, "I knew you did it for the sake of our father-in-law and because you're a good man."

Simon rode on in silence for a while.

"I imagine you must have been bitterly angry," he then said.

"Well . . . when I had time to think about it . . . I didn't see that there was any other way you could interpret things."

"What about Kristin?" asked Simon, his voice even lower.

"Kristin!" Erlend laughed again. "You know she won't stand for anyone censuring me—except for herself. She seems to think she can handle that well enough all alone. It's the same with our children. God save me if I should chastise them with a single word! But you can rest assured that I've brought her around."

"You have?"

"Yes, well . . . with time I'll manage to convince her. You know that once Kristin gives it some thought, she's the sort of person who will remember you've shown us such loyal friendship that . . ."

Simon, agitated and distraught, felt his heart trembling. He found it unbearable. The other man seemed to think that they could now dismiss this matter from their minds. In the pale moonlight Erlend's face looked so genuinely peaceful. Simon's voice quavered with emotion as he spoke again. "Forgive me, Erlend, but I don't see how I could have believed—"

"I told you I understand it." The other broke in rather impatiently. "It seems to me that you couldn't have thought anything else."

"If only those two foolish children had never spoken," said Simon heatedly.

"Yes. Gaute has never received such a beating before in his life. And the whole thing started because they were quarreling about their ancestors: Reidar Birkebein and King Skule and Bishop Nikolas." Erlend shook his head. "But let's not think about this anymore, kinsman. It's best if we forget about it as soon as we can."

"I can't do that!"

"But, Simon!" This was spoken in reproach, with mild astonishment. "It's not worth it to take this so seriously."

"I can't—don't you understand? I'm not as good a man as you are."

Erlend gave him a bewildered look. "I don't know what you mean."

"I'm not as good a man as you are. I can't so easily forgive those I have wronged."

"I don't know what you mean," repeated Erlend in the same tone of voice.

"I mean . . ." Simon's face was contorted with pain and desperation. His voice was low, as if he were stifling an urge to scream out the words. "I mean that I've heard you speaking kindly of Judge Sigurd of Steigen, the old man whose wife you stole. I've seen how you loved Lavrans with all the love of a son. And I've never noticed that you bore any grudge toward me because you . . . enticed my betrothed away from me. I'm not as noble-minded as you think, Erlend. I'm not as noble-minded as you are. I . . . I do bear a grudge toward the man whom I have wronged."

His cheeks flecked with white from the strain, Simon stared into the eyes of his companion. Erlend had listened to him with his mouth agape.

"I've never realized this until now! Do you *hate* me, Simon?" he whispered, overwhelmed.

"Don't you think I have reason to do so?"

Unawares, both men had reined in their horses. They sat and stared at each other. Simon's small eyes glittered like steel. In the hazy white light of the night, he saw that Erlend's lean features were twitching as if something had broken inside him: an awakening. He looked up from beneath half-closed lids, biting his quivering lower lip.

"I can't bear to see you anymore," said Simon.

"But that was twenty years ago, man!" exclaimed Erlend, overcome and confused.

"Yes. But don't you think she's . . . worth thinking about for twenty years?"

Erlend pulled himself erect in the saddle. He met Simon's eyes with a steady, open gaze. The moonlight lit a blue-green spark in his big, pale blue eyes.

"Yes, yes, I do. May God bless her!"

For a moment he sat motionless. Then he spurred his horse and galloped off through the puddles so the water sprayed up behind him. Simon held Digerbein back; he was almost thrown to the ground because he reined in the horse so sharply. He waited there at the edge of the woods, struggling with the restless animal, for as long as he could hear hoofbeats in the slush.

Remorse had overwhelmed him as soon as he said it. He felt regret and shame, as if in senseless anger he had struck the most defenseless of creatures—a child or a delicate, gentle, and witless beast. His hatred felt like a shattered lance; he was shattered himself from the confrontation with the man's foolish innocence. That bird of misfortune, Erlend Nikulaussøn, understood so little that he seemed both helpless and without guile.

Simon swore and cursed to himself as he rode. Without guile . . . The man was well past forty; it was about time that he could handle a conversation man to man. If Simon had wounded himself, then by the Devil it should be considered worth the price if for once he had managed to strike Erlend a blow.

Now he was riding home to her. May God bless her, Simon thought ruefully. And so it was over: the plodding around in that sibling love. The two of them over there, and he and his family. He would never have to meet Kristin Lavransdatter again.

The thought took his breath away. Just as well, by the Devil. If your eye offends you, then pluck it out, said the priests. He told himself that the main reason he had done this was to escape the sister-brother love with Kristin. He couldn't bear it anymore.

He had only one wish now: that Ramborg would not be awake when he came home.

But when he rode in among the fences, he saw someone wearing a dark cloak standing beneath the aspen trees. The white of her wimple gleamed.

She said that she had been waiting for him ever since Sigurd returned home. The maids had gone to bed, so Ramborg herself ladled up the porridge that stood on the edge of the hearth, keeping warm. She placed bacon and bread on the table and brought in newly tapped ale.

"Shouldn't you go to bed now, Ramborg?" asked her husband as he ate.

Ramborg did not reply. She went over to her loom and began threading the colorful little balls of wool in and out of the warp. She had set up the loom for a tapestry before Christmas, but she hadn't made much progress yet.

"Erlend rode past, heading north, some time ago," she said, with her back turned. "From what Sigurd said, I thought you would be riding together."

"No, it didn't turn out that way."

"Erlend had a greater longing for his bed than you did?" She laughed a little. When she received no answer, she said again, "I suppose he always longs to be home with Kristin when he has been away."

Simon was silent for a good while before he replied, "Erlend and I did not part as friends."

Ramborg turned around abruptly. Then he told her what he had learned at Dyfrin and about the first part of the conversation with Erlend and his sons.

"It seems to me rather unreasonable that you should quarrel over such a matter when you've been able to remain friends until now."

"Perhaps, but that's how things went. And it will take too long to discuss the whole matter tonight."

Ramborg turned back to her loom and busied herself with her work.

"Simon," she said suddenly, "do you remember a story that Sira

Eirik once told us . . . from the Bible? About a maiden named Abishag the Shunammite?"[3]

"No."

"Back when King David was old and his vigor and manhood were beginning to fade—" Ramborg began, but Simon interrupted her.

"My Ramborg, it's much too late at night; this is no time to start telling sagas. And now I do remember the story about the woman you mentioned."

Ramborg pushed up the reed of the loom and fell silent for a while. Then she spoke again. "Do you remember the saga my father knew—about the handsome Tristan and fair Isolde and dark Isolde?"

"Yes, I remember." Simon pushed his plate aside, wiped the back of his hand across his mouth, and got up. He went over to stand in front of the fireplace. With one foot resting on the edge, his elbow on his knee, and his chin in his hand, he stared into the fire, which was about to die out inside the stone-lined hollow. From the loom over in the corner came Ramborg's voice, fragile-sounding and close to tears.

"When I listened to those stories, I always thought that men like King David and Sir Tristan . . . It seemed to me so foolish, and cruel, that they didn't love the young brides who offered them their maidenhood and the love of their hearts with gentleness and seemly graciousness but preferred instead such women as Fru Bathsheba or fair Isolde, who had squandered themselves in other men's arms. I thought that if I had been a man, I wouldn't have been so lacking in pride . . . or so heartless." Overcome, she fell silent. "It seems to me the most terrible fate: what happened to Abishag and poor Isolde of Bretland." Abruptly she turned around, walked quickly across the room, and stood before her husband.

"What is it, Ramborg?" Simon reluctantly asked in a low voice. "I don't know what you mean by all this."

"Yes, you do," she replied fiercely. "You're a man just like that Tristan."

"I find it hard to believe"—he tried to laugh—"that I should be compared with the handsome Tristan. And the two women you mentioned . . . If I remember right, they lived and died as pure maidens, untouched by their husbands." He looked at his wife. The little triangle of her face was pale, and she was biting her lip.

Simon set his foot down, straightened up, and put both hands on her shoulders.

"My Ramborg, you and I have two children," he said softly.

She didn't reply.

"I've done my best to show you my gratitude for that gift. I thought . . . I've tried to be a good husband to you."

When she didn't speak, he let her go, went over to a bench, and sat down. Ramborg followed and stood before him, looking down at her husband: his broad thighs in the wet, muddy hose, his stout body, his heavy reddish-brown face. Her lip curled with displeasure.

"You've grown so ugly over the years, Simon."

"Well, I've never thought myself to be a handsome man," he said calmly.

"But I'm young and pretty. . . ." She sat down on his lap, the tears pouring from her eyes as she held his head in her hands. "Simon, look at me. Why can't you reward me for this? Never have I wanted to belong to anyone but you. It's what I dreamed of ever since I was a little maiden: that my husband would be a man like you. Do you remember how we were once allowed to follow along with you, both Ulvhild and I? You were going with Father to the west pasture, to look at his foals. You carried Ulvhild over the creek, and Father was going to lift me up, but I cried that I wanted you to carry me too. Do you remember?"

Simon nodded. He remembered paying a great deal of attention to Ulvhild because he thought it so sad that the lovely child was crippled. Of the youngest daughter he had no memory, except that he knew there was a girl younger than Ulvhild.

"You had the most beautiful hair. . . ." Ramborg ran her fingers through the lock of wavy light-brown hair that fell over her husband's forehead. "And there's still not a single streak of gray. Erlend's hair will soon be as much white as black. And I always loved to see the deep dimples in your cheeks when you smiled . . . and the fact that you had such a merry voice."

"Yes, no doubt I looked a little better back then than I do now."

"No," she whispered fiercely. "When you look at me tenderly . . . Do you remember the first time I slept in your arms? I was in bed, whimpering over a toothache. Father and Mother were asleep, and it was dark in the loft, but you came over to the bench where we lay, Ulvhild and I, and asked me why I was crying. You told me to hush and not wake the others; then you lifted me in your arms. You lit a candle and cut a splinter of wood and then poked at my gums around the aching tooth until you drew blood. Then you said a prayer over the splinter, and the tooth didn't hurt anymore. And I was allowed to sleep in your bed, and you held me in your arms."

Simon placed his hand on her head, pressing it to his shoulder. Now that she spoke of it, he remembered. It was when he had come to Jørundgaard to tell Lavrans that the bond between him and Kristin had to be broken. He had slept very little that night. And now he recalled that he had gotten up to tend to little Ramborg, who lay fretting over a toothache.

"Have I ever behaved toward you in such a way, my Ramborg, that you thought it right to say that I didn't love you?"

"Simon . . . don't you think I might deserve that you loved me more than Kristin? She was wicked and dishonest toward you, while I have stayed with you like a little lapdog all these years."

Gently Simon lifted her off his lap, stood up, and took her hands in his.

"Speak no more of your sister, Ramborg—not in that manner. I wonder whether you even realize what you're saying. Don't you think that I fear God? Can you believe that I would be so unafraid of shame and the worst of sins, or that I wouldn't think of my children and all my kinsmen and friends? I'm your husband, Ramborg. Don't forget that, and don't talk of such things to me."

"I know you haven't broken any of God's commandments or breached any laws or code of honor."

"Never have I spoken a word to your sister or touched her with my hand in any way that I cannot defend on the Day of Judgment. This I swear before God and the apostle Saint Simon."

Ramborg nodded silently.

"Do you think your sister would have treated me as she has all these years if she thought, as you do, that I love her with sinful desire? Then you don't know Kristin."

"Oh, she has never thought about whether any man might desire her, except for Erlend. She hardly notices that the rest of us are flesh and blood."

"Yes, what you say is probably true, Ramborg," replied Simon calmly. "But then you must realize how senseless it is for you to torment me with your jealousy."

Ramborg pulled her hands away.

"I didn't mean to do so, Simon. But you've never loved me the way you love her. She is still always in your thoughts, but you seldom think of me unless you see me."

"I'm not to blame, Ramborg, if a man's heart is created in such a fashion that whatever is inscribed on it when it's young and fresh is carved deeper than all the runes that are later etched."

"Haven't you ever heard the saying that a man's heart is the first thing to come alive in his mother's womb and the last thing to die inside him?" replied Ramborg quietly.

"No . . . Is there such a saying? That might well be true." Lightly he caressed her cheek. "But if we're going to get any sleep tonight, we should go to bed now," he said wearily.

Ramborg fell asleep after a while. Simon slipped his arm out from under her neck, moved over to the very edge of the bed, and pulled the fur covers all the way up to his chin. His shirt was soaked through at the shoulder from her tears. He felt a bitter sympathy for his wife, but at the same time he realized with renewed bewilderment that he could no longer treat her as if she were a blind and inexperienced child. Now he had to acknowledge that Ramborg was a full-grown woman.

Gray light appeared in the windowpane; the May night was fading. He was dead tired, and tomorrow was the Sabbath. He wouldn't go to church in the morning, even though he might need to. He had once promised Lavrans that he would never miss a mass without an exceedingly good reason. But it hadn't helped him much to keep that promise during all these years, he thought bitterly. Tomorrow he was not going to ride to mass.

PART II

# DEBTORS

## CHAPTER 1

KRISTIN DID NOT hear a full account of what had happened between Erlend and Simon. Her husband told her and Bjørgulf what Simon had said about his journey to Dyfrin, and he said that afterward they had exchanged words and ended up parting as foes. "I can't tell you any more than that."

Erlend was rather pale, his expression firm and resolute. She had seen him look that way only a few times before, in all the years she had been married to him. She knew that this was something he would refuse to discuss any further.

She had never liked it when Erlend countered her questions with that expression. God only knew she didn't consider herself more than a simple woman; she would have preferred to avoid taking responsibility for anything but her own children and her household duties. And yet she had been forced to deal with so many things that seemed to her more appropriate concerns for a man to handle. But Erlend had thought it quite reasonable to let them rest on her shoulders. So it didn't suit him to act so overbearing and to rebuff her when she wanted to know about things that he had undertaken on his own that would affect the welfare of them all.

She took this enmity between Erlend and Simon Darre greatly to heart. Ramborg was her only sister. And when she thought about losing Simon's companionship, she realized for the first time how fond she had become of this man and how much gratitude she owed him. His loyal friendship had been the best support she had in her difficult situation.

She knew that now people would be talking about this all over the countryside: that the folks of Jørundgaard had quarreled with Simon of Formo too. Simon and Ramborg were liked and respected by everyone. But most people regarded Kristin, her husband, and her sons with suspicion and ill will; this was something she had noticed long ago. Now they would be so alone.

Kristin felt as if she would sink into the earth from sorrow and shame on that first Sunday when she arrived at the green in front of the church and saw Simon standing a short distance away, among a group of farmers. He greeted her and her family with a nod, but it was the first time he didn't come over to shake hands and talk with them.

Ramborg did come over to her sister and took her hand. "It's dreadful that our husbands have fallen into discord, but you and I need not quarrel because of that." She stood on her toes to kiss Kristin so that everyone in the churchyard could see it. Kristin wasn't sure why, but she seemed to sense that Ramborg was not as sad as she might have been. She had never liked Erlend; God only knew whether she had set her husband against him, intentionally or not.

And yet Ramborg always came over to greet her sister whenever they met at church. Ulvhild asked in a loud voice why her aunt didn't come south to visit them anymore; then she ran over to Erlend, to cling to him and his oldest sons. Arngjerd stood quietly at her stepmother's side, took Kristin's hand, and looked embarrassed. Simon and Erlend, along with his sons, vigilantly avoided each other.

Kristin greatly missed her sister's children as well. She had grown fond of the two maidens. One day when Ramborg brought her son to mass, Kristin kissed Andres after the service and then burst into tears. She loved this tiny, frail boy so dearly. She couldn't help it, but now that she no longer had any small children of her own, it was a comfort to her to look after this little nephew from Formo and pamper him whenever his parents brought him along to Jørundgaard.

From Gaute she learned a little more about the matter because he told her what words were spoken between Erlend and Simon on that night when they met at Skindfeld-Gudrun's hut. The longer Kristin thought about it, the more it seemed to her that Erlend was most at fault. She had felt bitter toward Simon because he ought to have known his kinsman well enough to realize that Erlend would not have betrayed and deceived his brother in any dishonorable way, no matter how many strange things he might do out of recklessness or on impulse. And whenever Erlend saw what he had done, he usually behaved like a skittish stallion that has torn its reins loose and become wild with fright at what is dragging along behind.

But Erlend never seemed to understand that sometimes other people needed to protect their own interests in the face of the mischief that he had such a rare talent for stirring up. Then Erlend would fail to guard his tongue or watch how he behaved. She remembered from her own experience, back when she was still young and tender; time after time she had felt as if he were trampling on her heart with his reckless behavior. He had driven away his own brother. Even before Gunnulf entered the monastery, he had withdrawn from them, and she knew that Erlend was to blame. He had so often offended his pious and worthy brother, even though Gunnulf had never done anything but good for Erlend, as far as she knew. Now he had pushed Simon away, and when she wanted to know what had caused this animosity between him and their only friend, Erlend merely gave her a stubborn look and said he couldn't tell her.

She could see that he had told Naakkve more.

Kristin felt dismayed and uneasy when she noticed that Erlend and her eldest son would fall silent or change the topic of their conversation as soon as she came near, and this was not a rare occurrence.

Gaute and Lavrans and Munan kept closer to their mother than Nikulaus had ever done, and she had always talked more to them than to him. And yet she still felt that of all her children, her firstborn son was in some sense closest to her heart. After she had returned to live at Jørundgaard, memories of the time when she bore this son under her heart and gave birth to him became strangely vivid and alive. For she noticed in so many ways that the people of Sil had not forgotten the sins of her youth. It was almost as if they felt she had tarnished the honor of the entire region when she, daughter of the man who was regarded as their chieftain, had gone astray. They had not forgiven her, or the fact that she and Erlend had added mockery to Lavrans's sorrow and shame when they fooled him into giving away a seduced maiden with the grandest wedding that had ever been seen in Gudbrandsdal.

Kristin didn't know whether Erlend realized that people had begun gossiping about these old subjects again. If he did, he probably paid them no mind. He considered her neighbors no more than homespun farmers and fools, every one of them. And he taught his sons to think the same. It pained her soul to know that these people who had wished her so well back when she was Lavrans Bjørgulfsøn's pretty daughter, the rose of the northern valley, now despised Erlend Nikulaussøn and his wife and judged them harshly. She didn't plead with them; she didn't weep because she had become a stranger among them. But it hurt nevertheless. And it seemed as if even the steep mountains surrounding the valley that had sheltered her childhood now looked differently at her and her home: black with menace and stone-gray with a fierce determination to subdue her.

Once she had wept bitterly. Erlend knew about it, and he had had little patience with her back then. When he discovered that she had walked alone for many months with the burden of his child under her frightened, sorrowful heart, he did not take her in his arms and console her with tender and loving words. He was bitter and ashamed that it would come out how dishonorably he had acted toward Lavrans. But he hadn't thought about how much more difficult it would be for her on that day when she stood in disgrace before her proud and loving father.

And Erlend had not greeted his son with much joy when she finally brought the child into the light of life. That moment when her soul was released from endless anguish and dread and torment and she saw the hideous, shapeless fruit of her sin come alive under the fervent prayers of the priest and become the most beloved and healthy of children, then it felt as if her heart would melt with humble joy, and even the hot, defiant blood of her body turned to sweet, white, innocent milk. Yes, with God's help the boy would doubtless become a man, Erlend had said as she lay in bed, wanting him to rejoice with her over this precious treasure, which she could hardly bear to let out of her arms when the women wanted to tend to the child. He loved the children he had by Eline Ormsdatter—that much she had both seen and sensed—but when she carried Naakkve over to Erlend and tried to place him in his father's arms, Erlend wrinkled his nose and asked what he was supposed to do with this infant who leaked from both ends. For years Erlend would only grudgingly look at his eldest, lawfully born son, unable to forget that Naakkve had come into the world at an inopportune time. And yet the boy was such a handsome and good and promising child that any father would rejoice to see such a son grow up to succeed him.

From the time he was quite little, Naakkve loved his father so dearly that it was wondrous to behold. His whole small, fair face would light up like the sun whenever his father took him on his knee for a moment and spoke a few words to him or he was allowed to hold his father's hand to cross the courtyard. Steadfastly Naakkve had courted his father's favor during that time when Erlend was more fond of all his other children than the eldest. Bjørgulf was his father's favorite when the boys were small, and occasionally Erlend would take his sons along to the armory when he went up there. That was where all the armor and weapons were kept that were not in daily use at Husaby. While his father talked and bantered with Bjørgulf, Naakkve would sit quietly on top of a chest, simply breathing with happiness because he was allowed to be there.

But as time passed and Bjørgulf's poor eyesight meant that he could not accompany Erlend as readily as his other sons, and Bjørgulf also grew more taciturn and withdrawn, things changed. Erlend began to seem almost a little embarrassed in the boy's presence. Kristin wondered whether Bjørgulf, in his heart, blamed his father for destroying their well-being and taking his sons' future with him when he fell—and whether Erlend knew or guessed as much. However that might be, Bjørgulf was the only one of Erlend's sons who did not seem to look up to him with blind love and boundless pride at calling him Father.

One morning the two smallest boys noticed that Erlend was reading from the prayer book and fasting on bread and water. They asked him why he was doing this since it wasn't a fast day. Erlend replied that it was because of his sins. Kristin knew that these fast days were part of the penance that had been imposed upon Erlend for breaking his marriage vows with Sunniva Olavsdatter, and she knew that her oldest sons were aware of this.

Naakkve and Gaute seemed untroubled by it, but she happened to glance at Bjørgulf at that moment. The boy was sitting at the table, squinting nearsightedly at his bowl of food and chuckling to himself. Kristin had seen Gunnulf smile that way several times when Erlend was being most boastful. She didn't like it.

Now it was Naakkve whom Erlend always wanted to take along. And the youth seemed to come alive, as if all his roots were attached to his father. Naakkve served his father the way a young page serves his lord and chieftain. He took care of his father's horse himself and kept his harnesswork and weapons in order. He fastened Erlend's spurs on his feet and brought his hat and cape when Erlend was going out. He filled his father's goblet and served him slices of meat at the table, sitting on the bench just to the right of Erlend's seat. Erlend jested a bit over the boy's chivalrous and noble manners, but he was pleased, and he commanded more and more of Naakkve's attention.

Kristin saw that Erlend had now completely forgotten how she had struggled and begged to win from him a scrap of fatherly love for this child. And Naakkve had forgotten the time when she was the one he turned to, seeking solace from all his ills and advice for all his troubles when he was little. He had always been a loving son toward his mother, and he still was in many ways, but she felt that the older the boy became, the farther away he moved from her and her concerns. Naakkve lacked all sense for what she had to cope with. He was never disobliging when she gave him a task to do, but he was oddly awkward and clumsy at anything that might be called farm work. He did the chores without interest or desire and never finished anything. His mother thought that in many ways he was not unlike his deceased half brother, Orm Erlendssøn; he also resembled him in appearance. But Naakkve was strong and healthy, a lively dancer and sportsman, an excellent bowman and tolerably skilled in the use of other weapons, a good horseman and a superb skier. Kristin spoke about this one day to Ulf Haldorssøn, Naakkve's foster father.

Ulf said, "No one has lost more from Erlend's folly than that boy. There is not another youth growing up in Norway today who would make a more splendid horseman and chieftain than Naakkve."

But Kristin saw that Naakkve never gave a thought to what his father had ruined for him.

At that time there was once again great unrest in Norway, and rumors were flying all through the valleys, some of them reasonable and some of them completely unlikely. The noblemen in the south and west of the kingdom as well as in the uplands had grown exceedingly discontented with the rule of King Magnus. It was said they had even threatened to take up arms, rally the peasantry, and force Lord Magnus Eirikssøn to rule in accordance with their wishes and advice; otherwise they would proclaim his cousin, the young Jon Haftorssøn of Sudrheim, their king. His mother, Lady Agnes, was the daughter of the blessed King Haakon Haalegg. Not much was heard from Jon himself, but his brother Sigurd was supposed to be in the vanguard of the entire enterprise, and Bjarne, Erling Vidkunssøn's young son, was also part of it. People said that Sigurd had promised that if Jon became king, he would take one of Bjarne's sisters as his queen because the maidens of Giske were also descended from the ancient Norwegian kings. Sir Ivar Ogmundssøn, who had formerly been one of King Magnus's most ardent supporters, was now said to have joined forces with these young noblemen, as had many others among the wealthiest and most highborn of men. People said that Erling Vidkunssøn himself and the bishop of Bjørgvin stood behind the effort.

Kristin paid little mind to these rumors; she thought bitterly that she and her family were commoners now and the affairs of the realm no longer concerned them. And yet she had talked about this a bit with Simon Andressøn during the previous fall, and she also knew that he had spoken of it to Erlend. But she saw that Simon was loath to discuss such things—partly, no doubt, because he disapproved of his brothers getting involved in such dangerous matters. And Gyrd, at any rate, was being led along by his wife's kinsmen. But Simon also feared that it wouldn't be pleasant for Erlend to hear such talk since he had been born to take his place among men who counseled the rulers of Norway, but now misfortune had shut him out from the company of his peers.

And yet Kristin saw that Erlend spoke of these matters with his sons. One day she heard Naakkve say, "But if these men win out against King Magnus, then surely they can't be so cowardly, Father, that they wouldn't take up your case and force the king to make amends with you."

Erlend laughed.

His son continued, "You were the first to show the way to these men and remind them that it was never the custom among Norwegian nobles in the past to sit back calmly and tolerate injustice from their kings. It cost you your ancestral estates and your position as sheriff. The men who supported you escaped without a scratch. You alone have paid the price for all of them."

"Yes, and that's all the more reason why they would want to forget me," said Erlend with a laugh. "And the archbishopric has acquired Husaby against a loan. I don't think the gentlemen of the council will urge impoverished King Magnus to redeem it."

"The king is your kinsman, as are Sigurd Haftorssøn and most of the other men," replied Naakkve vehemently. "Not without shame can they desert the man who carried his shield with honor to the borderlands of the north and cleared Finnmark and the Gandvik coast[1] of the enemies of God and the Crown. Then they would indeed be miserable cowards."

Erlend gave a whistle. "Son, one thing I can tell you. I don't know how this venture of the Haftorssøns will end, but I would wager my own neck they don't dare show Lord Magnus the naked blade of a Norwegian sword. Talk and compromise are what I think will result, with not a single arrow fired. And those fellows won't exert themselves for my sake, because they know me and realize that I'm not as squeamish about honed steel as some of the others.

"Kinsmen you say . . . Yes, they're your third cousins, both Magnus and those sons of Haftor. I remember them from the time I served at King Haakon's court. It was fortunate that my kinswoman Lady Agnes was the daughter of a king; otherwise she might have found herself out on the wharves, pulling in fish, if a woman like your mother, out of pious mercy, didn't hire her to help out in the cowshed. More than once I've wiped the snouts of those Haftorssøns when they had to appear before their grandfather, and they came racing into the hall as snot-nosed as if they had just crept from their mother's lap. And if I gave them a swat out of loving kinship, to teach them some proper manners, they would shriek like stuck pigs. I hear they've made men of these Sudrheim changelings at last. But if you expect to receive the help of kinsmen from those quarters, you'd be looking for solace in the backside of a dog."

Later Kristin said to Erlend, "Naakkve is so young, my dear husband. Don't you think it's unwise to speak so openly about such matters with him?"

"You speak so gently, my dear wife," replied Erlend with a smile, "that I see you wish to rebuke me. When I was Naakkve's age, I was headed north to Vargøy for the first time. If Lady Ingebjørg had remained loyal to me," he exclaimed vehemently, "I would have sent Naakkve and Gaute to serve her. In Denmark there might have been a future for two intrepid adventurers skilled with weapons."

"When I gave birth to these children," said Kristin bitterly, "I didn't think that our sons would seek their living in a foreign land."

"You know I didn't intend that either," said Erlend. "But man proposes, God disposes."

Then Kristin told herself that it wasn't simply that she felt a stab in her heart every time she noticed that Erlend and her sons, now that they were getting older, acted as if their concerns were beyond the comprehension of a woman. But she feared Erlend's reckless tongue; he never remembered that his sons were little more than children.

And yet as young as the boys were—Nikulaus was now seventeen winters old, Bjørgulf would be sixteen, and Gaute would turn fifteen in the fall—all three had a certain way with women that made their mother uneasy.

Admittedly nothing had happened that she could point to. They didn't run after women, they were never coarse or discourteous in speech, and they didn't like it when the servant men told vulgar stories or brought filthy rumors back to the manor. But Erlend too had always been very chivalrous and seemly; she had seen him blush at words over which both her father and Simon laughed heartily. But at the time she had vaguely felt that the other two laughed the way peasants laugh at tales about the Devil, while learned men, who know better his ferocious cunning, have little affection for such jests.

Even Erlend could not be called guilty of the sin of running after women; only people who didn't know the man would think he had loose ways, meaning that he had lured women to himself and then deliberately led them astray. She never denied that Erlend had had his way with her without resorting to seductive arts and without using deceit or force. And she was certain that it was not Erlend who had done the seducing in the case of the two married women with whom he had sinned. But when loose women approached him with bold and provocative manners, she had seen him turn into an inquisitive youth; an air of concealed and impetuous frivolity would come over the man.

With anguish she thought she could see that the sons of Erlend took after their father in this regard. They always forgot to think about how others would judge them before they acted, although afterward they would take what was said to heart. And when women greeted them with smiles and gentleness, they didn't become shy or sullen or awkward, as did most young boys their age. They would smile back and talk and behave as freely and easily as if they had been at the king's court and were familiar with royal customs. Kristin feared they would get mixed up in some misfortune or trouble out of sheer innocence. She thought the wealthy wives and daughters, as well as the poor servingwomen, were all much too flirtatious with these handsome boys. But like other young men, they would grow furious afterward if anyone teased them about a woman. Frida Styrkaarsdatter was particularly fond of doing this. She was a foolish woman, in spite of her age; she wasn't much younger than her mistress, and she had given birth to two bastard children. She had had difficulty even finding the father of the younger child. But Kristin had offered the poor thing a protective hand. Because Frida had nursed Bjørgulf and Skule with such care and affection, the mistress was quite indulgent toward this serving maid, even though she was annoyed that the woman was always talking to the boys about young maidens.

Kristin now thought it would be best if she could marry off her sons at a young age, but she knew this wouldn't be easy. The men whose daughters would be equal matches for Naakkve and Bjørgulf by birth and blood would not think her sons wealthy enough. And the condemnation and royal enmity their father had brought down upon himself would stand in the way if the boys tried to improve their lot through service with greater noblemen. With bitterness she thought about the days when Erlend and Erling Vidkunssøn had spoken of a marriage between Naakkve and one of the lord's daughters.

She knew of one or another young maiden now growing up in the valleys who might be suitable: wealthy and of good lineage, although for several generations their forefathers had refrained from serving at the king's court and had stayed home in their parishes. But she couldn't bear the thought that Erlend might be refused if they should make an offer to one of these landowners. In this situation Simon Darre would have been the best spokesman, but now Erlend had deprived them of his help.

She didn't think any of her sons had a desire to serve the Church, except perhaps Gaute or Lavrans. But Lavrans was still so young. And Gaute was the only one of the boys who gave her any real help with the estate.

Storms and snow had wreaked havoc with the fences that year, and the snowfall before Holy Cross Day had delayed the repairs, so the workers had to press hard to finish in time. For this reason, Kristin sent Naakkve and Bjørgulf off one day to mend the fence around a field up near the main road.

In midafternoon Kristin went out to see how the boys were handling the unaccustomed chore. Bjørgulf was working over by the lane leading to the manor; she stopped for a while to talk with him. Then she continued northward. There she saw Naakkve leaning over the fence and talking to a woman on horseback who had stopped at the side of the road, right next to the rails. He stroked the horse and then grabbed the girl's ankle, moving his hand, as if carelessly, up her leg under her clothing.

The maiden was the first to notice Kristin. She blushed and said something to Naakkve. Quickly he pulled his hand away and looked a little abashed. The girl was about to ride off, but Kristin called out a greeting and then talked to the maiden for a moment, asking about her kinswoman. The young girl was the niece of the mistress of Ulvsvold and had recently arrived for a visit. Kristin pretended that she hadn't seen anything, talking to Naakkve about the fence after the maiden had gone.

Not long after, Kristin happened to stay at Ulvsvold for two weeks' time because the mistress gave birth to a child and was then quite ill. Kristin was both her neighbor and considered the most capable healer in the region. Naakkve often came over with messages and queries for his mother, and the niece, Eyvor Haakonsdatter, would always find the opportunity to meet and talk with him. Kristin wasn't pleased by this; she had taken a disliking to the maiden and didn't find her beautiful, although she had heard that most men did. She was happy on the day she learned that Eyvor had returned home to Raumsdal.

But she didn't think Naakkve had been particularly fond of Eyvor, especially when she heard that Frida kept chattering about the daughter at Loptsgaard, Aasta Audunsdatter, and teasing Naakkve about her.

One day Kristin was in the brewhouse, boiling a juniper decoction, when she heard Frida once again carrying on about Aasta. Naakkve was with Gaute and their father outside behind the courtyard. They were building a boat that they wanted to take up to the small fishing lake in the mountains. Erlend was a moderately good boatbuilder. Naakkve grew cross, and then Gaute began to tease him too: Aasta might be a suitable match.

"Ask for her hand yourself if that's what you think," said his brother heatedly.

"No, I don't want her," replied Gaute, "because I've heard that red hair and pine forests thrive on meager soil. But you think that red hair is pretty."

"That saying can't be used about women, my son," said Erlend with a laugh. "Those with red hair usually have soft white skin."

Frida laughed uproariously, but Kristin grew angry. She thought this talk too frivolous for such young boys. She also remembered that Sunniva Olavsdatter had red hair, although her friends called it golden.

Then Gaute said, "You should be glad I didn't say anything; I didn't dare, for fear of sin. On the vigil night of Whitsunday you sat with Aasta in the grain tithe barn all the time we were dancing on the church hill. So you must be fond of her."

Naakkve was about to fall upon his brother, but at that moment Kristin came outside. After Gaute had left, she asked her other son, "What was that Gaute said about you and Aasta Audunsdatter?"

"I don't think anything was said that you didn't hear, Mother," replied the boy. His face was red, and he frowned angrily.

Annoyed, Kristin said, "It's unseemly that you young people can't hold a vigil night without dancing and leaping about between services. We never used to do that when I was a maiden."

"But you've told us yourself, Mother, that back when you were young, our grandfather used to sing while the people danced on the church hill."

"Well, not those kinds of ballads and not such wild dancing," said his mother. "And we children stayed properly with our parents; we didn't go off two by two and sit in the barn."

Naakkve was about to make an angry retort. Then Kristin happened to glance at Erlend. He was smiling so slyly as he eyed the plank he was about to cut with an axe. Indignant and dismayed, she went back inside the brewhouse.

But she thought a good deal about what she had heard. Aasta Audunsdatter was not a poor match; Loptsgaard was a wealthy estate, and there were three daughters, but no son. And Ingebjørg, Aasta's mother, belonged to an exceedingly good lineage.

She had never thought that one day the people of Jørundgaard might call Audun Torbergssøn kinsman. But he had suffered a stroke this past winter, and everyone thought he had little time left to live. The girl was seemly and charming in manner, and clever, or so Kristin had heard. If Naakkve had great affection for the maiden, there was no reason to oppose this marriage. They would still have to wait for two more years to hold the wedding, as young as Aasta and Naakkve both were, but then she would gladly welcome Aasta as her son's wife.

On a fine day in the middle of the summer Sira Solmund's sister came to see Kristin to borrow something. The women were standing outside the house to say their farewells when the priest's sister said, "Well, that Eyvor Haakonsdatter!" Her father had driven her from his estate because she was with child, so she had sought refuge at Ulvsvold.

Naakkve had been up in the loft; now he stopped on the lowest step. When his mother caught a glimpse of his face, she was suddenly so overcome that she could hardly feel her own legs beneath her. The boy was crimson all the way up to his ears as he walked away toward the main house.

But Kristin soon understood from the other woman's gossip that things must have been such with Eyvor long before she came to their parish for the first time in the spring. My poor, innocent boy, thought Kristin, sighing with relief. He must be ashamed that he thought well of the girl.

A few nights later Kristin was alone in bed because Erlend had gone out fishing. As far as she knew, Naakkve and Gaute had gone along with him. But she was awakened when Naakkve touched her and whispered that he needed to talk to her. He climbed up and sat at the foot of her bed.

"Mother, I've been out to talk with that poor woman Eyvor tonight. I was sure they were lying about her; I was so certain that I would have held a glowing piece of iron in my hand to prove that she was lying—that magpie from Romundgaard."

Kristin lay still and waited. Naakkve tried to speak firmly, but suddenly his voice threatened to break with emotion and distress.

"She was on her way to matins on the last day of Christmas. She was alone, and the road from their manor passes through the woods for a long stretch. There she met two men. It was still dark. She doesn't know who they were, maybe foresters from the mountains. In the end she couldn't defend herself any longer, the poor young child. She didn't dare tell her troubles to anyone. When her mother and father discovered her misfortune, they drove her from home, with slaps and curses as they pulled her hair. When she told me all this, Mother, she wept so hard that it would have melted a rock in the hills." Naakkve abruptly fell silent, breathing heavily.

Kristin said she thought it the worst misfortune that those villains had escaped. She hoped that God's justice would find them and that for their deeds they might suffer their just deserts on the executioner's block.

Then Naakkve began to talk about Eyvor's father, how rich he was and how he was related to several respected families. Eyvor intended to send the child away to be raised in another parish. Gudmund Darre's wife had given birth to a bastard child by a priest, and there sat Sigrid Andresdatter at Kruke, a good and honored woman. A man would have to be both hardhearted and unfair to pronounce Eyvor despoiled because against her will she had been forced to suffer such shame and misfortune; surely she was still fit to be the wife of an honorable man.

Kristin pitied the girl and cursed her assailants, and in her heart she gave thanks and exulted over what good luck it was that Naakkve would not come of age for three more years. Then she told him gently to bear in mind that he should be careful not to seek out Eyvor in her chamber late at night, as he had just done, or to show himself at Ulvsvold unless he had tasks for the landowner's servants. Otherwise he might unwittingly cause people to gossip even worse about the unfortunate child. It was all well and good to say that those who claimed to doubt Eyvor's word and refused to believe she had landed in this misfortune without blame, wouldn't find him weak in the arms. All the same, it would be painful for the poor girl if there was more talk.

Three weeks later Eyvor's father came to take his daughter home for a betrothal banquet and wedding. She was to marry a good farmer's son from her parish. At first both fathers had opposed the marriage because they were feuding over several sections of land. In the winter the men had reached an agreement, and the two young people were about to be betrothed, but suddenly Eyvor had refused. She had set her heart on another man. Afterward she realized it was too late for her to reject her first suitor. In the meantime she went to visit her aunt in Sil, no doubt thinking that there she would receive help in concealing her shame, because she wanted to marry this new man. But when Hillebjørg of Ulvsvold saw what condition the girl was in, she sent her back to her parents. The rumors were true enough—her father was furious and had struck his daughter several times, and she had indeed fled to Ulvsvold—but now he had come to an agreement with her first suitor, and Eyvor would have to settle for the man, no matter how little she liked it.

Kristin saw that Naakkve took this greatly to heart. For days he went around without saying a word, and his mother felt so sorry for him that she hardly dared cast a glance in his direction. If he met his mother's eye, he would turn bright red and look so ashamed that it cut Kristin to the heart.

Whenever the servants at Jørundgaard started talking about

these events, their mistress would tell them sharply to hold their tongues. That filthy story and that wretched woman were not to be mentioned in her house. Frida was astonished. So many times she had heard Kristin Lavransdatter speak with forbearance and offer help with both hands to a maiden who had fallen into such misfortune. Frida herself had twice found salvation in the compassion of her mistress. But the few words Kristin said about Eyvor Haakonsdatter were as vile as anything a woman might say about another.

Erlend laughed when she told him how badly Naakkve had been fooled. It was one evening when she was sitting out on the green, spinning, and her husband came over and stretched out on the grass at her side.

"No misfortune has come of it," said Erlend. "Rather, it seems to me the boy has paid a small price to learn that a man shouldn't trust a woman."

"Is that so?" said his wife. Her voice quivered with stifled indignation.

"Yes," said Erlend, smiling. "Now you, when I first met you, I thought you were such a gentle maiden that you would hardly even take a bite out of a slice of cheese. As pliable as a silk ribbon and as mild as a dove. But you certainly fooled me, Kristin."

"How do you think things would have gone for all of us if I had been that soft and gentle?" she asked.

"No . . ." Erlend took her hands, and she had to stop working. He looked up at her with a radiant smile. Then he laid his head in her lap. "No, I didn't know, my sweet, what good fortune God was granting me when He set you in my path, Kristin."

But because she constantly had to restrain herself in order to hide her despair at Erlend's perpetual nonchalance, her anger would sometimes overwhelm her when she had to reprimand her sons. Her fists would turn harsh, and her words fierce. Ivar and Skule felt the brunt of it.

They were at the worst age, their thirteenth year, and so wild and willful that Kristin often wondered in utter despair whether any mother in Norway had ever given birth to such rogues. They were handsome, as all her children were, with black, silky soft, and curly hair, blue eyes beneath black brows, and lean, finely shaped faces. They were quite tall for their age, but still narrow-shouldered, with long, spare limbs. Their joints stood out like knots on a sprig of grain. They looked so much alike that no one outside their home could tell them apart, and in the countryside people called them the Jørundgaard swords—but it wasn't meant as a title of honor. Simon had first given them this name in jest because Erlend had presented each of them with a sword, and they never let these small swords out of their grasp except when they were in church. Kristin wasn't pleased with this gift, or with the fact that they were always rushing around with axes, spears, and bows. She feared it would land these hot-tempered boys in some kind of trouble. But Erlend said curtly that they were old enough now to become accustomed to carrying weapons.

She lived in constant fear for these twin sons of hers. When she didn't know where they were, she would secretly wring her hands and implore the Virgin Mary and Saint Olav to lead them back home, alive and unharmed. They went through mountain passes and up steep cliffs where no one had ever traveled before. They plundered eagles' nests and came home with hideous yellow-eyed fledglings hissing inside their tunics. They climbed among the boulders along the Laag and north in the gorge where the river plunged from one waterfall to the next. Once Ivar was nearly dragged to his death by his stirrups; he was trying to ride a half-tame young stallion, and God only knew how the boys had managed to put a saddle on the animal. And by chance, out of simple curiosity, they had ventured into the Finn's hut in Toldstad Forest. They had learned a few words of the Sami language from their father, and when they used them to greet the Finnish witch, she welcomed them with food and drink. They had eaten until they were bursting, even though it was a fast day. Kristin had always strictly enjoined that when the grown-ups were fasting, the children should make do with a small portion of food they didn't care for; it was what her own parents had accustomed her to when she was a child. For once Erlend also took his sons sternly to task. He burned all the tidbits that the Finnish woman had given the boys as provisions, and he strictly forbade them ever to approach even the outskirts of the woods where the Finns lived. And yet it amused him to hear about the boys' adventure. Later he would often tell Ivar and Skule about his travels up north and what he had observed of the ways of those people. And he would talk to the boys in that ugly and heathen language of theirs.

Otherwise Erlend almost never chastised his children, and whenever Kristin complained about the wild behavior of the twins, Erlend would dismiss it with a jest. At home on the estate they got into a great deal of mischief, although they could make themselves useful if they had to; they weren't clumsy-handed like Naakkve. But occasionally, when their mother had given them some chore to do and she went out to see how it was going, she would find the tools lying on the ground and the boys would be watching their father, who might be showing them how seafaring men tied knots.

When Lavrans Bjørgulfsøn painted tar crosses over the door to the livestock stalls or in other such places, he used to add a few flourishes with the brush: drawing a circle around the cross or painting a stroke through each of its arms. One day the twins decided to use one of these old crosses as a target. Kristin was beside herself with fury and despair at such unchristian behavior, but Erlend came to the children's defense. They were so young; they shouldn't be expected to think about the holiness of the cross every time they saw it painted above the door of a shed or on the back of a cow. The boys would be told to go up to the cross on the church hill, kneel down, and kiss it as they said five *Pater nosters* and fifteen *Ave Marias*. It wasn't necessary to call in Sira Solmund for such a reason. But this time Kristin had the support of Bjørgulf and Naakkve. The priest was summoned, and he sprinkled holy water on the wall and reprimanded the two young sinners with great severity.

They fed oxen and goats the heads of snakes to make them more vicious. They teased Munan because he was still clinging to his mother's skirts, and Gaute because he was the one they fought with most often. Otherwise the sons of Erlend stuck together with the greatest brotherly affection. But sometimes Gaute would give them a thrashing if they were too rough. Trying to talk some sense into them was like talking to a wall. And if their mother grew angry, they would stand there stiffly, their fists clenched, as they scowled at her with flashing eyes beneath frowning brows, their faces fiery red with rage. Kristin thought about what Gunnulf had said about Erlend: He had flung his knife at their father and raised his hand against him many times when he was a child. Then she would strike the twins, and strike them hard, because she was frightened. How would things end up for these children of hers if they weren't tamed in time?

Simon Darre was the only one who had ever had any power over the two wild boys. They loved their uncle, and they always complied whenever he chided them, in a friendly and calm manner. But now that they didn't see him anymore, Kristin hadn't noticed that they missed him. Dejected, she thought how faithless a child's heart could be.

But secretly, in her own heart, she knew that she was actually proudest of these two. If only she could break their terrible defiant and wild behavior, she thought that none of their brothers would make more promising men than they would. They were healthy, with good physical abilities; they were fearless, honest, generous, and kind toward all the poor. And more than once they had shown an alacrity and resourcefulness that seemed to her far beyond what might be expected of such young boys.

One evening during the hay harvesting Kristin was up late in the cookhouse when Munan came rushing in, screaming that the old goat shed was on fire. There were no men at home on the manor. Some were in the smithy, sharpening their scythes; some had gone north to the bridge where the young people usually gathered on summer evenings. Kristin grabbed a couple of buckets and set off running, calling to her maids to follow her.

The goat shed was a little old building with a roof that reached all the way down to the ground. It stood in the narrow passageway between the farmyard and the courtyard of the estate, right across from the stable and with other houses built close on either side. Kristin ran onto the gallery of the hearth house and found a broadaxe and a fire hook, but as she rounded the corner of the stable, she didn't see any fire, just a cloud of smoke billowing out of a hole in the roof of the goat shed. Ivar was sitting up on the ridge, hacking at the roof; Skule and Lavrans were inside, pulling down patches of the thatching and then stomping and trampling out the fire. Now they were joined by Erlend, Ulf, and the men who had been in the smithy. Munan had run over to warn them; so the fire was put out in short order. And yet the most terrible of misfortunes might easily have occurred. It was a sultry, still evening, but with occasional gusts of wind from the south, and if the fire had engulfed the goat shed, all the buildings at the north end of the courtyard—the stable, storerooms, and living quarters—would certainly have burned with it.

Ivar and Skule had been up on the stable roof. They had snared a hawk and were going to hang it from the gable when they caught a whiff of fire and saw smoke coming from the roof below them. They leaped to the ground at once, and with the small axes they were carrying they began chopping at the smoldering sod while they sent off Lavrans and Munan, who were playing nearby—one to find hooks and the other to get their mother. Fortunately the rafters and beams in the roof were quite rotten, but it was clear that this time the twins had saved their mother's estate by instantly setting about tearing down the burning roof and not wasting time by first running to get help from the grown-ups.

It was hard to understand how the fire had started, except that Gaute had passed that way an hour before, carrying embers to the smithy, and he admitted that the container had not been covered. A spark had probably flown up onto the tinder-dry sod roof.

But less was said about this than about the quick-wittedness of the twins and Lavrans when Ulf later imposed a fire watch and all the servants kept him company during the night while Kristin had strong ale and mead carried out to them. All three boys had been singed on their hands and feet; their shoes were so burned that they split into pieces. Young Lavrans was only nine years old, so it was hard for him to bear the pain patiently for very long, but from the start he was the proudest of the lot, walking around with his hands wrapped up and taking in the praise of the manor servants.

That night Erlend took his wife in his arms. "My Kristin, my Kristin . . . Don't complain so much about your children. Can't you see, my dear, what good breeding there is in our sons? You always treat these two hearty boys as if you thought their path would lead between the gallows and the execution block. Now it seems to me that you should enjoy some pleasure after all the pain and suffering and toil you've borne through all the years when you constantly carried a child under your belt, with another child at your breast and one on your arm. Back then you would talk of nothing else but those little imps, and now that they've grown up to be both sensible and manly, you walk among them as if you were deaf and dumb, hardly even answering when they speak to you. God help me, but it's as if you love them less now that you no longer have to worry for their sake and these big, handsome sons of ours can give you both help and joy."

Kristin didn't trust herself to answer with a single word.

But she lay in bed, unable to sleep. And toward morning she carefully stepped over her slumbering husband and walked barefoot over to the shuttered peephole, which she opened.

The sky was a hazy gray, and the air was cool. Far off to the south, where the mountains merged and closed off the valley, rain was sweeping over the plateaus. Kristin stood there for a moment, looking out. It was always so hot and stuffy in this loft above the new storeroom where they slept in the summertime. The trace of moisture in the air brought the strong, sweet scent of hay to her. Outside a bird or two chittered faintly in their sleep in the summer night.

Kristin rummaged around for her flint and lit a candle stump. She crept over to where Ivar and Skule were sleeping on a bench. She shone the light on them and touched their cheeks with the back of her hand. They both had a slight fever. Softly she said an *Ave Maria* and made the sign of the cross over them. The gallows and the execution block . . . to think that Erlend could jest about such things . . . he who had come so close. . . .

Lavrans whimpered and murmured in his sleep. Kristin stood bending over her two youngest sons, who were bedded down on a small bench at the foot of their parents' bed. Lavrans was hot and flushed and tossed back and forth but did not wake up when she touched him.

Gaute lay with his milk-white arms behind his head, under his long flaxen hair. He had thrown off all the bedclothes. He was so hot-blooded that he always slept naked, and his skin was such a dazzling white. The tan color of his face, neck, and hands stood out in sharp contrast. Kristin pulled the blanket up around his waist.

It was difficult for her to be angry with Gaute; he looked so much like her father. She hadn't said much to him about the calamity he had nearly brought upon them. As clever and levelheaded as the boy was, she thought that doubtless he would learn from the incident and not forget it.

Naakkve and Bjørgulf slept in the other bed up in the loft. Kristin stood there longer, shining the light on the two sleeping young men. Black down already shadowed their childish, soft pink lips. Naakkve's foot was sticking out from the covers, slender, with a high instep, a deep arch over the sole, and not very clean. And yet, she thought, it wasn't long ago that the foot of this man was so small that she could wrap her fingers around it, and she had crushed it to her breast and raised it to her lips, nibbling on each tiny toe, for they were as rosy and sweet as the blossoms on a bilberry twig.

It was probably true that she didn't pay enough heed to what God had granted her as her lot. The memory of those days when she was carrying Naakkve and the visions of terror she had wrestled with . . . it could pass with fiery heat through her soul. She had been delivered the way a person wakes up to the blessed light of day after terrifying dreams with the oppressive weight of the mare[2] on her breast. But other women had awakened to see that the unhappiness of the day was worse than the very worst they had dreamed. And yet, whenever she saw a cripple or someone who was deformed, Kristin would feel heartsick at the reminder of her own fear for her unborn child. Then she would humble herself before God and Holy Olav with a burning fervor; she would hasten to do good, striving to force tears of true remorse from her eyes as she prayed. But each time she would feel that unthawed discontent in her heart, the fresh surge would cool, and the sobs would seep out of her soul like water in sand. Then she consoled herself that she didn't have the gift of piety she had once hoped would be her inheritance from her father. She was hard and sinful, but surely she was no worse than most people, and like most people, she would have to bear the fiery blaze of that other world before her heart could be melted and cleansed.

And yet sometimes she longed to be different. When she looked at the seven handsome sons sitting at her table or when she made her way up to church on Sabbath mornings as the bells tolled, calling so agreeably to joy and God's peace, and she saw the flock of straight-backed, well-dressed young boys, her sons, climbing the hillside ahead of her . . . She didn't know of any other woman who had given birth to so many children and had never experienced what it was like to lose one. All of them were handsome and healthy, without a flaw in their physical or mental capacities, although Bjørgulf's sight was poor. She wished she could forget her sorrows and be gentle and grateful, fearing and loving God as her father had done. She remembered her father had said that the person who recalls his sins with a humble spirit and bows before the cross of the Lord need never bow his head beneath any earthly unhappiness or injustice.

Kristin blew out the candle, pinched the wick, and returned the stump to its place between the uppermost logs in the wall. She went back over to the peephole. It was already daylight outside, but gray and dead. On the lower rooftops, upon which she gazed, the dirty, sun-bleached grass stirred faintly from a gust of wind; a little, rustling sound passed through the leaves of the birches across from the roof of the high loft building.

She looked down at her hands, holding on to the sill of the peephole. They were rough and worn; her arms were tanned all the way up to her elbows, and her muscles were swollen and as hard as wood. In her youth the children had sucked the blood and milk from her until every trace of maidenly smoothness and fresh plumpness had been sapped from her body. Now each day of toil stripped away a little more of the remnants of beauty that had distinguished her as the daughter, wife, and mother of men with noble blood. The slender white hands, the pale, soft arms, the fair complexion, which she had carefully shielded from sunburn with linen kerchiefs and protected with specially brewed cleansing concoctions . . . She had long ago grown indifferent to whether the sun shone directly on her face, sweaty from work, and turned it as brown as that of a poor peasant woman.

Her hair was the only thing she had left of her girlish beauty. It was just as luxuriant and brown, even though she seldom found time to wash or tend to it. The heavy, tangled braid that hung down her back hadn't been undone in three days.

Kristin pulled it forward over her shoulder, undid the plait, and shook out her hair, which still enveloped her like a cloak and reached below her knees. She took a comb from her chest, and shivering now and then, she sat in her shift beneath the peephole, open to the coolness of the morning, and gently combed out her tangled tresses.

When she was done with her hair and had rebraided it in a

tight, heavy rope, she felt a little better. Then she cautiously lifted the sleeping Munan into her arms, placed him next to the wall in her husband's bed, and then crawled in between them. She held her youngest child in her arms, rested his head against her shoulder, and fell asleep.

She slept late the next morning. Erlend and the boys were already up when she awakened. "I think you've been suckling at your mother's breast when nobody's looking," said Erlend when he saw Munan lying next to his mother. The boy grew cross, ran outside, and crept across the gallery, out onto a carved beam atop the posts holding up the gallery. He would prove he was a man. "Run!" shouted Naakkve from down in the courtyard. He caught his little brother in his arms, turned him upside down, and tossed him to Bjørgulf. The two older boys wrestled with him until he was laughing and shrieking at the same time.

But the following day when Munan cried because his fingers had been stung by the recoil of the bowstring, the twins rolled him up in a coverlet and carried him over to their mother's bed; in his mouth they stuffed a piece of bread so big that the boy nearly choked.

## CHAPTER 2

Erlend's house priest at Husaby had taught his three oldest sons their lessons. They were not very diligent pupils, but all three learned quickly, and their mother, who had been raised with this kind of book learning, kept an eye on them so that the knowledge they gained was not altogether paltry.

During the year that Bjørgulf and Naakkve spent with Sira Eiliv at the monastery on Tautra, they had eagerly suckled at the breasts of Lady Wisdom, as the priest expressed it. Their teacher was an exceedingly old monk who had devoted his life with the zeal of a bee to gleaning knowledge from all the books he came across, both in Latin and in Old Norse. Sira Eiliv was himself a lover of wisdom, but during his years at Husaby he had had little opportunity to follow his inclination for bookish pursuits. For him the time spent with Aslak, the teacher, was like pasture grazing for starved cattle. And the two young boys, who kept close to their own priest while staying with the monks, followed the learned conversations of the men with their mouths agape. Then Brother Aslak and Sira Eiliv found joy in feeding these two young minds with the most delectable honey from the monastery's book treasures, which Brother Aslak had supplemented with many copied versions and excerpts of the most magnificent books. Soon the boys grew so clever that the monk seldom had to speak to them in Norwegian, and when their parents came to get them, both could answer the priest in Latin, fluently and correctly.

Afterward the brothers kept up what they had learned. There were many books at Jørundgaard. Lavrans had owned five. Two of them had been inherited by Ramborg when his estate was settled, but she had never wanted to learn to read, and Simon was not so practiced with written words that he had any desire to read for his own amusement, although he could decipher a letter and compose one himself. So he asked Kristin to keep the books until his children were older. After they were married, Erlend gave Kristin three books that had belonged to his parents. She had received another book as a gift from Gunnulf Nikulaussøn. He had had it copied for his brother's wife from a book about Holy Olav and his miracles, several other saint legends, and the missive the Franciscan monks of Oslo had sent to the pope about Brother Edvin Rikardssøn, seeking to have him recognized as a saint. And finally, Naakkve had been given a prayer book by Sira Eiliv when they parted. Naakkve often read to his brother. He read fluently and well, with a slight lilt to his voice, the way Brother Aslak had taught him; he was most fond of the books in Latin—his own prayer book and one that had belonged to Lavrans Bjørgulfsøn. But his greatest treasure was a big, exceptionally splendid book that had been part of the family inheritance ever since the days of the ancestor who was his namesake, Bishop Nikulaus Arnessøn.

Kristin wanted her younger sons also to acquire learning that would be fitting for men of their birth. But it was difficult to know how this might be done. Sira Eirik was much too old, and Sira Solmund could read only from those books that he used for the church service. Much of what he read he didn't fully understand. On some evenings Lavrans found it amusing to sit with Naakkve and let his brother show him how to form the letters on his wax tablet, but the other three had absolutely no desire to learn such skills. One day Kristin took out a Norwegian book and asked Gaute to see if he could remember anything of what he had learned in his childhood from Sira Eiliv. But Gaute couldn't even manage to spell his way through three words, and when he came across the first symbol that stood for several letters, he closed the book with a laugh and said he didn't feel like playing that game anymore.

This was the reason that Sira Solmund came over to Jørundgaard one evening late in the summer and asked Nikulaus to accompany him home. A foreign knight had come from the Feast of Saint Olav in Nidaros and taken lodgings at Romundgaard, but he spoke no Norwegian. Nor did his soldiers or servants, while the guide who was escorting them spoke only a few words of their language. Sira Eirik was ill in bed. Could Naakkve come over and speak to the man in Latin?

Naakkve was not at all displeased to be asked to act as interpreter, but he feigned nonchalance and went with the priest. He returned home very late, in high spirits and quite drunk. He had been given wine, which the foreign knight had brought along and liberally poured for the priest and the deacon and Naakkve. His name was something like Sir Alland or Allart of Bekelar; he was from Flanders and was making a pilgrimage to various holy shrines in the northern countries. He was exceedingly friendly, and it had been no trouble to talk to him. Then Naakkve mentioned his request. From there the knight was headed for Oslo and then on to pilgrim sites in Denmark and Germany, and now he wanted Naakkve to come with him to be his interpreter, at least while he was in Norway. But he had also hinted that if the youth should accompany him out into the world, then Sir Allart was the man who could make his fortune. Where he came from, it seemed as if golden spurs and necklaces, heavy money pouches, and splendid weapons were simply waiting for a man like young Nikulaus Erlendssøn to come along and take them. Naakkve had replied that he was not yet of age and would need permission from his father. But Sir Allart had still pressed a gift upon him—he had expressly stated that it would in no way bind him—a knee-length, plum-blue silk tunic with silver bells on the points of the sleeves.

Erlend listened to him, saying hardly a word, with an oddly tense expression on his face. When Naakkve was finished, he sent Gaute to get the chest with his writing implements and at once set about composing a letter in Latin. Bjørgulf had to help him because Naakkve was in no condition to do much of anything and his father had sent him off to bed. In the letter Erlend invited the knight to his home on the following day, after prime[1] so they might discuss Sir Allart's offer to take the noble-born young man, Nikulaus Erlendssøn, into his service as his esquire. He asked the knight's forgiveness for returning his gift with the plea that Sir Allart might keep it until Nikulaus, with his father's consent, had been sworn into the man's service in accordance with such customs as prevailed among knights in all the lands.

Erlend dripped a little wax on the bottom of the letter and lightly pressed his small seal, the one on his ring, into it. Then he sent a servant boy off to Romundgaard at once with the letter and the silk tunic.

"Husband, surely you can't be thinking of sending your young son off to distant lands with an unknown foreigner," said Kristin, shivering.

"We shall see. . . ." Erlend smiled quite strangely. "But I don't think it's likely," he added when he noticed her distress. He smiled again and caressed her cheek.

At Erlend's request, Kristin had strewn the floor in the high loft with juniper and flowers, placed the best cushions on the benches, and set the table with a linen cloth and good food and drink in fine dishes and the precious silver-chased animal horns they had inherited from Lavrans. Erlend had shaved carefully, curled his hair, and dressed in a black, richly embroidered ankle-length robe made of foreign cloth. He went to meet his guest at the manor gate, and as they crossed the courtyard together, Kristin couldn't help thinking that her husband looked more like the French knights mentioned in the sagas than did the fat, fair-haired stranger in the colorful and resplendent garments made from velvet and sarcenet. She stood on the gallery of the high loft, beautifully attired and wearing a silk wimple. The Flemish man kissed her hand as she bade him *bienvenu*. She didn't exchange another word with him during all the hours he spent with them. She understood nothing of the men's conversation; nor did Sira Solmund, who had come with his guest. But the priest told the mistress that now he had assuredly made Naakkve's fortune. She neither agreed nor disagreed with him.

Erlend spoke a little French and could fluently speak the kind of German that mercenaries spoke; the discussion between him and the foreign knight flowed easily and courteously. But Kristin noticed that the Flemish man did not seem pleased as things progressed, although he strove to conceal his displeasure. Erlend had told his sons to wait over in the loft of the new storehouse until he sent word for them to join them, but they were not sent for.

Erlend and his wife escorted the knight and the priest to the gate. When their guests disappeared among the fields, Erlend turned to Kristin and said with that smile she found so distasteful, "I wouldn't let Naakkve leave the estate with that fellow even to go south to Breidin."

Ulf Haldorssøn came over to them. He and Erlend spoke a few words that Kristin couldn't hear, but Ulf swore fiercely and spat.

Erlend laughed and slapped the man on the shoulder. "Yes, if I'd been such a country dolt as the good farmers around here . . . But I've seen enough that I wouldn't let my fair young falcons out of my hands by selling them to the Devil. Sira Solmund had no idea, that blessed fool."

Kristin stood with her arms hanging at her sides, the color ebbing and rising in her face. Horror and shame overcame her, making her feel sick; her legs seemed to lose all strength. She had known about such things—as something endlessly remote—but that this unmentionable might venture as close as her own doorstep . . . It was like the last wave, threatening to overturn her storm-tossed, overloaded boat. Holy Mary, did she also need to fear *that* for her sons?

Erlend said with the same loathsome smile, "I already had my doubts last night. Sir Allart seemed to me a little too chivalrous from Naakkve's account. I know that it's not the custom among knights anywhere in the world to welcome a man who is to be taken into service by kissing him on the lips or by giving him costly presents before seeing proof of his abilities."

Shaking from head to toe, Kristin said, "Why did you ask me to strew the floor with roses and cover my table with linen cloths for such a—" And she uttered the worst of words.

Erlend frowned. He had picked up a stone and was keeping an eye on Munan's red cat, which was slithering on its stomach through the tall grass along the wall of the house, heading for the chickens near the stable door. Whoosh! He threw the stone. The cat streaked around the corner, and the flock of hens scattered. He turned to face his wife.

"I thought I could at least have a *look* at the man. If he had been a trustworthy fellow, then . . . But in that case I had to show the proper courtesy. I'm not Sir Allart's confessor. And you heard that he's planning to go to Oslo." Erlend laughed again. "Now it's possible that some of my true friends and dear kinsmen from the past may hear that we're not sitting up here at Jørundgaard shaking the lice from our rags or eating herring and oat *lefse*."

Bjørgulf had a headache and was lying in bed when Kristin came up to the loft at suppertime, and Naakkve said he didn't want to go over to the main house for the evening meal.

"You seem to me morose tonight, son," said his mother.

"How can you think that, Mother?" said Naakkve with a scornful smile. "The fact that I'm a worse fool than other men and it's easier to throw sand in my eyes . . . surely that's nothing to be morose about."

"Console yourself," said his father as they sat down at the table and Naakkve was still too quiet. "No doubt you'll go out into the world and have a chance to try your luck."

"That depends, Father," replied Naakkve in a low voice, as if he intended only Erlend to hear him, "whether Bjørgulf can go with me." Then he laughed softly. "But talk to Ivar and Skule about what you just said. They're merely waiting to reach the proper age before they set off."

Kristin stood up and put on her hooded cloak. She was going to go north to tend to the beggar at Ingebjørg's hut, she told them when they asked. The twins offered to go along and carry her sack, but she wanted to go alone.

The evenings were already quite dark, and north of the church the path passed through the woods and beneath the shadow of Hammer Ridge. There gusts of cold wind always issued from Rost Gorge, and the din of the river brought a trace of moisture to the air. Swarms of big white moths hovered and flitted under the trees, sometimes flying straight at her. The pale glow of the linen around her face and on her breast seemed to draw them in the dark. She swatted them away with her hand as she rushed upward, sliding on the slippery carpet of needles and stumbling over the writhing roots that sprawled across the path she was following.

A certain dream had haunted Kristin for many years. The first time she had it was on the night before Gaute was born, but occasionally she would still wake up, soaked with sweat, her heart hammering as if it would shatter in her chest, and she had dreamed the same thing.

She saw a meadow with flowers, a steep hill deep inside a pine forest that bordered the mound on three sides, dark and dense. At the foot of the slope a small lake mirrored the dim forest and the dappled green of the clearing. The sun was behind the trees; at the top of the hill the last long golden rays of evening light filtered through the boughs, and at the bottom of the lake sun-touched, gleaming clouds swam among the leaves of water lilies.

Halfway up the slope, standing deep in the avalanche of alpine catchflies and globeflowers and the pale green clouds of angelica, she saw her child. It must have been Naakkve the first time she had the dream; back then she had only two, and Bjørgulf was still in the cradle. Later she was never certain which of her children it might be. The little round, sunburned face under the fringe of yellow-brown hair seemed to her to resemble first one and then another of her sons, but the child was always between two and three years old and dressed in the kind of small dark yellow tunic that she usually sewed for her little boys as everyday attire, from homespun wool, dyed with lichen, and trimmed with red ribbon.

Sometimes she seemed to be on the other side of the lake. Or she might not be present at all when it happened, and yet she saw everything.

She saw her little son moving about, here and there, turning his face as he tugged at the flowers. And even though her heart felt the clutch of a dull anguish—a premonition of the evil about to occur—the dream always brought with it first a powerful, aching sweetness as she gazed at the lovely child there in the meadow.

Then she sees emerging from the darkness at the edge of the woods a furry bulk that is alive. It moves soundlessly, its tiny, vicious eyes smoldering. The bear reaches the top of the meadow and stands there, its head and shoulders swaying, as it considers the slope. Then it leaps. Kristin had never seen a bear alive, but she knew bears didn't leap that way. This is not a real bear. It runs like a cat; at the same moment it turns gray, and like a giant light-colored cat it flies with long, soft strides down the hill.

The mother is deathly frightened, but she can't reach the child to protect him; she can't make a sound of warning. Then the boy notices that *something* is there; he turns halfway and looks over his shoulder. With a horrifying, low-pitched cry of terror he tries to run downhill, lifting his legs high in the tall grass the way children do. And his mother hears the tiny crack of sap-filled stalks breaking as he runs through the profusion of blossoms. Now he stumbles over something in the grass, falls headlong, and in the next instant the beast is upon him with its back arched and its head lowered between its front paws. Then she wakes up.

And each time she would lie awake for hours before her attempts to reassure herself did any good. It was only a dream after all! She would draw into her arms her smallest child, who lay between herself and the wall, thinking that if it had been real, she could have done such and such: scared off the animal with a shriek or with a pole. And there was always the long, sharp knife that hung from her belt.

But just as she had convinced herself in this manner to calm down, it would sieze hold of her once again: the unbearable anguish of her dream as she stood powerless and watched her little son's pitiful, hopeless flight from the strong, ruthlessly swift, and hideous beast. Her blood felt as if it were boiling inside her, foaming so that it made her body swell, and her heart was about to burst, for it couldn't contain such a violent surge of blood.

Ingebjørg's hut lay up on Hammer Ridge, a short distance below the main road that led up to the heights. It had stood empty for many years, and the land had been leased to a man who had been allowed to clear space for a house nearby. An ill beggar who had been left behind by a procession of mendicants had now taken refuge inside. Kristin had sent food and clothing and medicine up to him when she heard of this, but she hadn't had time to visit him until now.

She saw that the poor man's life would soon be over. Kristin gave her sack to the beggar woman who was staying with him and then tended to the ill man, doing what little she could. When she heard that they had sent for the priest, she washed his face, hands, and feet so they would be clean to receive the last anointment.

The air was thick with smoke, and a terribly oppressive, foul smell filled the tiny room. When two women from the neighboring household came in, Kristin asked them to send word to Jørundgaard for anything they might need; then she bade them farewell and left. She suddenly had a strange, sick fear of meeting the priest with the *Corpus Domini*, so she took the first side path she encountered.

It was merely a cattle track, she soon realized. And it led her right into the wilderness. The fallen trees with their tangle of roots sticking up frightened her; she had to crawl over them in those places where she couldn't make her way around. Layers of moss slid out from under her feet when she clambered down over large rocks. Spiderwebs clung to her face, and branches swung at her and caught on her clothes. When she had to cross a small creek or she came to a marshy clearing in the woods, it was almost impossible to find a place where she could slip though the dense, wet thickets of leafy shrubs. And the loathsome white moths were everywhere, teeming beneath the trees in the darkness, swarming up in great clouds from the heath-covered mounds when she trod on them.

But at last she reached the flat rocks down by the Laag River. Here the pine forest thinned out because the trees had to twine their roots over barren rocks, and the forest floor was almost nothing but dry grayish-white reindeer moss, which crackled under her feet. Here and there a black, heath-covered mound was visible. The fragrance of pine needles was hotter and drier and sharper than higher up. Here all the branches of the trees always looked yellow-scorched from early spring on. The white moths continued to plague her.

The roar of the river drew her. She walked all the way over to the edge and looked down. Far below, the water shimmered white as it seethed and thundered over the rocks from one pool to the next.

The monotonous drone of the waterfalls resonated through her overwrought body and soul. It kept reminding her of something, of a time that was an eternity ago; even back then she realized that she would not have the strength to bear the fate she had chosen for herself. She had laid bare her protected, gentle girl's life to a ravaging, fleshly love; she had lived in anguish, anguish, anguish ever since—an unfree woman from the first moment she became a mother. She had given herself up to the world in her youth, and the more she squirmed and struggled against the bonds of the world, the more fiercely she felt herself imprisoned and fettered by them. She struggled to protect her sons with wings that were bound by the constraints of earthly care. She had striven to conceal her anguish and her inexpressible weakness from everyone, walking forward with her back erect and her face calm, holding her tongue, and fighting to ensure the welfare of her children in any way she could.

But always with that secret, breathless anguish: If things go badly for them, I won't be able to bear it. And deep in her heart she wailed at the memory of her father and mother. They had borne anguish and sorrow over their children, day after day, until their deaths; they had been able to carry this burden, and it was not because they loved their children any less but because they loved with a better kind of love.

Was this how she would see her struggle end? Had she conceived in her womb a flock of restless fledgling hawks that simply lay in her nest, waiting impatiently for the hour when their wings were strong enough to carry them beyond the most distant blue peaks? And their father would clap his hands and laugh: Fly, fly, my young birds.

They would take with them bloody threads from the roots of her heart when they flew off, and they wouldn't even know it. She would be left behind alone, and all the heartstrings, which had once bound her to this old home of hers, she had already sundered. That was how it would end, and she would be neither alive nor dead.

She turned on her heel, stumbling hastily across the pale, parched carpet of reindeer moss, with her cloak pulled tight around her because it was so unpleasant when it caught on the branches. At last she emerged onto the sparse meadow plains that lay slightly north of the farmers' banquet hall and the church. As she cut across the field, she caught sight of someone in the road. He called out: "Is that you, Kristin?" and she recognized her husband.

"You were gone a long time," said Erlend. "It's almost night, Kristin. I was starting to grow frightened."

"Were you frightened for me?" Her voice sounded more harsh and haughty than she had intended.

"Well, not exactly frightened . . . But I thought I would come out to meet you."

They barely spoke as they walked southward. All was quiet when they entered the courtyard. Some of the horses they kept on the manor were slowly moving along the walls of the main house, grazing, but all the servants had gone to bed.

Erlend headed straight for the storeroom loft, but Kristin turned toward the cookhouse. "I have to see to something," she replied to his query.

He stood leaning over the gallery railing, waiting for his wife, when he saw her come out of the cookhouse with a pine torch in her hand and go over to the hearth house. Erlend waited a moment and then ran down and followed her inside.

She had lit a candle and placed it on the table. Erlend felt an odd, cold shiver of fear pass through him when he saw her standing there with the lone candle in the empty house. Only the built-in furniture remained in the room, and the glow of the flame shimmered over the worn wood, unadorned and bare. The hearth was cold and swept clean, except for the torch, which had been tossed into it, still smoldering. They never used this building, Erlend and Kristin, and it must have been almost half a year since a fire had been lit inside. The air was strangely oppressive; missing was the vital blend of smells from people living there and coming and going; the smoke vent and doors had not been opened in all that time. The place also smelled of wool and hides; several rolled-up skins and sacks, which Kristin had taken from among the goods in the storeroom, were piled up on the empty bed that had belonged to Lavrans and Ragnfrid.

On the table lay a heap of small skeins of thread and yarn—linen and wool to be used for mending—which Kristin had set aside when she did the dyeing. She was going through them now, setting them in order.

Erlend sat down in the high seat at the end of the table. It seemed oddly spacious for the slender man, now that it had been stripped of its cushions and coverings. The two Olav warriors, with their helmets and shields bearing the sign of the cross, that Lavrans had carved into the armrests of the high seat scowled glumly and morosely under Erlend's slim tan hands. No man could carve foliage and animals more beautifully than Lavrans, but he had never been very skilled at capturing human likenesses.

The silence between them was so complete that not a sound was heard except for the hollow thudding out on the green, where the horses were plodding around in the summer night.

"Aren't you going to bed soon, Kristin?" he finally asked.

"Aren't you?"

"I thought I would wait for you," said her husband.

"I don't want to go yet. . . . I can't sleep."

After a moment he asked, "What is weighing so heavily on your heart, Kristin, that you don't think you'll be able to sleep?"

Kristin straightened up. She stood holding a skein of heather-green wool in her hands, tugging and pulling on it with her fingers.

"What was it you said to Naakkve today?" She swallowed a couple of times; her throat felt so parched. "Some piece of advice . . . He didn't think it was much good for him . . . but the two of you talked about Ivar and Skule. . . ."

"Oh . . . that!" Erlend gave a little smile. "I just told the boy . . . I do have a son-in-law, now that I think of it. Although Gerlak wouldn't be as eager to kiss my hands or carry my cape and sword as he used to be. But he has a ship on the sea and wealthy kin both in Bremen and in Lynn. Surely the man must realize that he's obliged to help his wife's brothers. I didn't stint on my gifts when I was a rich man and married my daughter to Gerlak Tiedekenssøn."

Kristin did not reply.

At last Erlend exclaimed vehemently, "Jesus, Kristin, don't just stand there staring like that, as if you had turned to stone."

"I never thought, when we were first married, that our children would have to roam the world, begging food from the manors of strangers."

"No, and the Devil take me, I don't mean for them to beg! But if all seven of them have to grow their own food here on your estates, then it will be a peasant's diet, my Kristin. And I don't think my sons are suited to that. Ivar and Skule look like they'll turn out to be daredevils, and out in the world there is both wheat bread and cake for the man willing to slice his food with a sword."

"You intend your sons to become hired soldiers and mercenaries?"

"I hired on myself when I was young and served Earl Jacob. May God bless him, I say. I learned a few things back then that a man can never learn at home in this country, whether he's sitting in splendor in his high seat with a silver belt around his belly and swilling down ale or he's walking behind a plow and breathing in the farts of the farm horse. I lived a robust life in the earl's service; I say that even though I ended up with that stump chained to my foot when I was no older than Naakkve. But I was allowed to enjoy some of my youth."

"Silence!" Kristin's eyes grew dark. "Wouldn't you think it the most unbearable sorrow if your sons should be lured into such sin and misfortune?"

"Yes, may God protect them from that. But surely it shouldn't be necessary for them to copy all the follies of their father. It *is* possible, Kristin, to serve a noble lord without being saddled with such a burden."

"It is written that he who draws his sword shall lose his life by the sword, Erlend!"

"Yes, I've heard that said, my dear. And yet most of our forefathers, both yours and mine, Kristin, died peacefully and in a Christian manner in their beds, with the last rites and comfort for their souls. You only need think of your own father; he proved in his youth that he was a man who could use his sword."

"But that was during a war, Erlend, at the summons of the king to whom they had sworn allegiance; it was in order to protect their homeland that Father and the others took up their weapons. And yet Father said himself that it was not God's will that we should bear arms against each other—baptized Christian men."

"Yes, I know that. But the world has been this way ever since Adam and Eve ate from the tree—and that was before my time. It's not my fault that we're born with sin inside us."

"What shameful things you're saying!"

Erlend heatedly interrupted her. "Kristin, you know full well that I have never refused to atone and repent for my sins as best I could. It's true that I'm not a pious man. I saw too much in my childhood and youth. My father was such a dear friend of the great lords of the chapter.[2] They came and went at his house like gray pigs: Lord Eiliv, back when he was a priest, and Herr Sigvat Lande, and all the others, and they brought little else with them but quarrels and disputes. They were hardhearted and merciless toward their own bishop; they proved to be no more holy or peaceable even though each day they held the most sacred relics in their hands and lifted up God Himself in the bread and wine."

"Surely we are not to judge the priests. That's what Father always said: It's our obligation to bow before the priesthood and obey them, but their human behavior shall be judged by God alone."

"Yes, well . . ." Erlend hesitated. "I know he said that, and you've also said the same in the past. I know you're more pious than I can ever be. And yet, Kristin, I have difficulty accepting that this is the proper interpretation of God's words: that you should go about storing everything away and never forgetting. He had a long memory too, Lavrans did. No, I won't say anything about your father except that he was pious and noble, and you are too; I know that. But often when you speak so gently and sweetly, as if your mouth were full of honey, I fear that you're thinking mostly about old wrongs, and God will have to judge whether you're as pious in your heart as you are in words."

Suddenly Kristin fell forward, stretched out across the table with her face buried in her arms, and began shrieking. Erlend leaped to his feet. She lay there, weeping with raw, ragged sobs that shuddered down her back. Erlend put his arm around her shoulder.

"Kristin, what is it? What is it?" he repeated, sitting down next to her on the bench and trying to lift her head. "Kristin, don't weep like this. I think you must have lost your senses."

"I'm frightened!" She sat up, wringing her hands together in her lap. "I'm so frightened. Gentle Virgin Mary, help us all. I'm so frightened. What will become of my sons?"

"Yes, my Kristin . . . but you must get used to it. You can't keep hiding them under your skirts. Soon they'll be grown men, all our sons. And you're still acting like a bitch with pups." He sat with his legs crossed and his hands clasped around one knee, looking down at his wife with a weary expression. "You snap blindly at both friend and foe over anything that has to do with your offspring."

Abruptly she got to her feet and stood there for a moment, mutely wringing her hands. Then she began swiftly pacing the room. She didn't say a word, and Erlend sat in silence, watching her.

"Skule . . ." She stopped in front of her husband. "You gave your son an ill-fated name. But you insisted on it. You *wanted* the duke to rise up again in that child."

"It's a fine name, Kristin. Ill fated . . . that can mean many things. When I revived my great-grandfather through my son, I remembered that good fortune had deserted him, but he was still a king, and with better rights than the combmaker's descendants."

"You were certainly proud, you and Munan Baardsøn, that you were close kinsmen of King Haakon Haalegg."

"Yes, you know that Sverre's lineage gained royal blood from my father's aunt, Margret Skulesdatter."

For a long time both husband and wife stood staring into each other's eyes.

"Yes, I know what you're thinking, my fair wife." Erlend went back to the high seat and sat down. With his hands resting on the heads of the two warriors, he leaned forward slightly, giving her a cold and challenging smile. "But as you can see, my Kristin, it hasn't broken me to become a poor and friendless man. You should know that I have no fear that the lineage of my forefathers has fallen along with me from power and honor for all eternity. Good fortune has also deserted me; but if my plan had been carried out, my sons and I would now have positions and seats at the king's right hand, which we, his close kinsmen, are entitled to by birth. For me, no doubt, the game is over. But I see in my sons, Kristin, that they will attain the positions which are their birthright. You don't need to lament over them, and you must not try to bind them to this remote valley of yours. Let them freely make their own way. Then you might see, before you die, that they have once again won a foothold in their father's ancestral regions."

"Oh, how you can talk!" Hot, bitter tears rose up in his wife's eyes, but she brushed them aside and laughed, her mouth contorted. "You seem even more childish than the boys, Erlend! Sitting there and saying . . . when it was only today that Naakkve nearly won the kind of fortune that a Christian man can hardly speak of, if God hadn't saved us."

"Yes, and I was the one lucky enough to be God's instrument this time." Erlend shrugged his shoulders. Then he added in a somber voice, "Such things . . . you needn't fear, my Kristin. If this is what has frightened you from your wits, my poor wife!" He lowered his eyes and said almost timidly, "You should remember, Kristin, that your blessed father prayed for our children, just as he prayed for all of us, morning and night. And I firmly believe that salvation can be found for many things, for the worst of things, in such a good man's prayers of intercession." She noticed that her husband secretly made the sign of the cross on his own chest with his thumb.

But as distressed as she was, this only infuriated her more.

"Is that how you console yourself, Erlend, as you sit in my father's high seat? That your sons will be saved by his prayers, just as they are fed by his estates?"

Erlend grew pale. "Do you mean, Kristin, that I'm not worthy to sit in the high seat of Lavrans Bjørgulfsøn?"

His wife's lips moved, but not a word came.

Erlend rose to his feet. "Do you mean that? For if you do, then as surely as God is above us both, I will never sit here again.

"Answer me," he insisted when she remained standing in silence. A long shudder passed through his wife's body.

"He was . . . a better husband . . . the man who sat there before you." Her words were barely audible.

"Guard your tongue now, Kristin!" Erlend took a few steps toward her.

She straightened up with a start. "Go ahead and strike me. I've endured it before, and I can bear it now."

"I had no intention of . . . striking you." He stood leaning on the table. Again they stared at each other, and his face had that oddly unfamiliar calm she had seen only a few times before. Now it drove her into a rage. She knew she was in the right; what Erlend had said was foolish and irresponsible, but that expression of his made her feel as if she were utterly wrong.

She gazed at him, and feeling sick with anguish at her own words, she said, "I fear that it won't be *my* sons that will thrive once more among your lineage in Trøndelag."

Erlend turned blood red.

"You couldn't resist reminding me of Sunniva Olavsdatter, I see."

"I wasn't the one to mention her name. You did."

Erlend blushed even more.

"Haven't you ever thought, Kristin, that you weren't entirely without blame in that . . . misfortune? Do you remember that evening in Nidaros? I came and stood by your bed. I was terribly meek and sad about having grieved you, my wife. I came to beg your forgiveness for my wrong. You answered me by saying that I should go to bed where I had slept the night before."

"How could I know that you had slept with the wife of your kinsman?"

Erlend was silent for a moment. His face turned white and then red again. Abruptly he turned on his heel and left the room without a word.

Kristin didn't move. For a long time she stood there motionless, with her hands clasped under her chin, staring at the candle.

Suddenly she lifted her head and let out a long breath. For once he had been forced to listen.

Then she became aware of the sound of horse hooves out in the courtyard. She could tell from its gait that a horse was being led out of the stable. She crept over to the door and out onto the gallery and peered from behind the post.

The night had already turned a pale gray. Out in the courtyard stood Erlend and Ulf Haldorssøn. Erlend was holding his horse, and she saw that the animal was saddled and her husband was dressed for travel. The two men talked for a moment, but she couldn't make out a single word. Then Erlend swung himself up into the saddle and began riding north, at a walking pace, toward the manor gate. He didn't look back but seemed to be talking to Ulf, who was striding along next to the horse.

When they had disappeared between the fences, she tiptoed out, ran as soundlessly as she could up to the gate, and stood there listening. Now she could hear that Erlend had let Soten begin trotting along the main road.

A little later Ulf came walking back. He stopped abruptly when he caught sight of Kristin at the gate. For a moment they stood and stared at each other in the gray light. Ulf had bare feet in his shoes and was wearing a linen tunic under his cape.

"What is it?" his mistress asked heatedly.

"Surely you must know, for I have no idea."

"Where was he riding off to?" she asked.

"To Haugen." Ulf paused. "Erlend came in and woke me. He said he wanted to ride there tonight, and he seemed in a great hurry. He asked me to see to it that certain things were sent to him up there later on."

Kristin fell silent for a long time.

"He was angry?"

"He was calm." After a moment Ulf said quietly, "I fear, Kristin . . . I wonder if you might have said what should have been best left unspoken."

"Surely Erlend for once should be able to stand hearing me speak to him as if he were a sensible man," said Kristin vehemently.

They walked slowly down the hill. Ulf turned toward his own house, but she followed him.

"Ulf, kinsman," she implored him anxiously. "In the past you were the one who told me morning and night that for the sake of my sons I had to steel myself and speak to Erlend."

"Yes, but I've grown wiser over the years, Kristin. You haven't," he replied in the same tone of voice.

"You offer me such solace now," she said bitterly.

He placed his hand heavily on the woman's shoulder, but at first he didn't speak. As they stood there, it was so quiet they could both hear the endless roar of the river, which they usually didn't notice. Out across the countryside the roosters were crowing, and the cry of Kristin's own rooster echoed from the stable.

"Yes, I've had to learn to ration out the solace sparingly, Kristin. There's been a cruel shortage of it for several years now. We have to save it up because we don't know how long it might have to last."

She tore herself away from his hand. With her teeth biting her lower lip, she turned her face away. And then she fled back to the hearth house.

The morning was icy cold. She wrapped her cloak tightly around her and pulled the hood up over her head. With her dew-drenched shoes tucked up under her skirts and her crossed arms resting on her knees, she huddled at the edge of the cold hearth to think. Now and then a tremor passed over her face, but she did not cry.

She must have fallen asleep. She started up with an aching back, her body frozen through and stiff. The door stood ajar. She saw that sunlight filled the courtyard.

Kristin went out onto the gallery. The sun was already high;

from the fenced pasture below she could hear the bell of the horse that had gone lame. She looked toward the new storehouse. Then she noticed that Munan was standing up on the loft gallery, peering out from between the posts.

Her sons. It raced through her mind. What had they thought when they woke up and saw their parents' bed untouched?

She ran across the courtyard and up to the child. Munan was wearing only his shirt. As soon as his mother reached him, he put his hand in hers, as if he were afraid.

Inside the loft none of the boys was fully dressed; she realized that no one had woken them. All of them looked quickly at their mother and then glanced away. She picked up Munan's leggings and began helping him to put them on.

"Where's Father?" asked Lavrans in surprise.

"Your father rode north to Haugen early this morning," she replied. She saw that the older boys were listening as she said, "You know he's been talking about it so long, that he wanted to go up there to see to his manor."

The two youngest sons looked up into their mother's face with wide, atonished eyes, but the five older brothers hid their gaze from her as they left the loft.

## CHAPTER 3

THE DAYS PASSED. At first Kristin wasn't worried. She didn't want to ponder over what Erlend might have meant by his behavior—fleeing from home like that in the middle of the night in a fit of rage—or how long he intended to stay north on his upland farm, punishing her with his absence. She was furious at her husband, but perhaps most furious because she couldn't deny that she too had been wrong and had said things she sincerely wished had not been said.

Certainly she had been wrong many times before, and in anger she had often spoken mean and vile words to her husband. But what offended her most bitterly was that Erlend would never offer to forget and forgive unless she first humbled herself and asked him meekly to do so. She didn't think she had let her temper get the better of her very often; couldn't he see that it was usually when she was tired and worn out with sorrows and anguish, which she had tried to bear alone? That was when she could easily lose mastery over her feelings. She thought Erlend might have remembered, after all the years of worry she had borne about the future of their sons, that during the past summer she had twice endured a terrible agony over Naakkve. Her eyes had been opened to the fact that after the burdens and toil of a young mother comes a new kind of fear and concern for the aging mother. Erlend's carefree chatter about having no fear for the future of his sons had angered her until she felt like a wild she-bear or like a bitch with pups. Erlend could go ahead and say that she was like a female dog with her children. She would always be alert and vigilant over them for as long as she had breath in her body.

If, for that reason, he chose to forget that she had stood by him every time it mattered, with all her strength, and that she had been both reasonable and fair, in spite of her anger, when he struck her and when he betrayed her with that hateful, loose woman from Lensvik, then she could do nothing to stop him. Even now, when she thought about it, she couldn't feel much anger or bitterness toward Erlend over the worst of the wrongs he had done her. Whenever she turned on him to complain about *that*, it was because she knew that he regretted it himself; he knew it was a great offense. But she had never been so angry with Erlend—nor was she now—that she didn't feel sorrow for the man himself when she remembered how he struck her or betrayed her, with everything that followed afterward. She always felt that with these outbursts of his unruly spirit he had sinned more against himself and the well-being of his own soul than he had against her.

What continued to vex her were all the small wounds he had caused her with his cruel nonchalance, his childish lack of patience, and even the wild and thoughtless kind of love he gave her whenever he showed that he did indeed love her. And during all those years when her heart was young and tender, when she realized that neither her health nor her strength of will would be sufficient—as she sat with her arms full of such defenseless little children—if their father, her husband, didn't show that he was both capable and loving enough to protect her and the young sons in her arms. It had been such torment to feel her body so weak, her mind so ignorant and inexperienced, and yet not dare rely on the wisdom and strength of her husband. She felt as if she had suffered deep wounds back then, which would never heal. Even the sweet pleasure of lifting up her infant, placing his loving mouth to her breast, and feeling his warm, soft little body in her arms was soured by fear and uneasiness. So small, so defenseless you are, and your father doesn't seem to remember that above all else he needs to keep you safe.

Now that her children had gained marrow in their bones and mettle in their spirits but still lacked the full wisdom of men, now he was luring them away from her. They were whirling away from her, both her husband and all her sons, with that strange, boyish playfulness which she seemed to have glimpsed in all the men she had ever met and in which a somber, fretful woman could never participate.

For her own sake then she felt only sorrow and anger whenever she thought about Erlend. But she grew fearful when she wondered what her sons were thinking.

Ulf had gone up to Dovre with two packhorses and taken Erlend the things he had sent for: clothing and a good many weapons, all four of his bows, sacks of arrowpoints and iron bolts, and three of his dogs. Munan and Lavrans wept loudly when Ulf took the small, short-haired female with the silky soft, drooping ears. It was a splendid foreign animal which the abbot of Holm had given to Erlend. That their father should own such a rare dog seemed, more than anything else, to elevate him above all other men in the eyes of the two young boys. And their father had promised that when the dog had pups, they would each be allowed to choose one from the litter.

When Ulf Haldorssøn returned, Kristin asked him whether Erlend had mentioned when he intended to come back home.

"No," said Ulf. "It looks like he means to settle in up there."

Ulf volunteered little else about his journey to Haugen. And Kristin had no desire to ask.

In the fall, when they moved from the new storeroom into other quarters, her oldest sons said that this winter they wanted to sleep upstairs in the high loft. Kristin granted them permission to do so; she would sleep alone with the two youngest boys in the main room below. On the first evening she said that now Lavrans could sleep in her bed as well.

The boy lay in bed, rolling around with delight and burrowing into the ticking. The children were used to having their beds made up on a bench, with leather sacks filled with straw and furs to wrap around them. But in the beds there was blue ticking to lie on and fine coverlets as well as furs, and their parents had white linen cases on their pillows.

"Is it just until Father comes home that I can sleep here?" asked Lavrans. "Then we'll have to move back to the bench, won't we, Mother?"

"Then you can sleep in the bed with Naakkve and Bjørgulf," replied his mother. "If the boys don't change their minds, that is, and move back downstairs when the weather turns cold." There was a little brick fireplace up in the loft, but it produced more smoke than heat, and the wind and cold were felt much more in the upper story.

As the fall wore on, an uncertain fear crept over Kristin; it grew from day to day, and the strain was difficult to bear. No one seemed to have heard from Erlend or seen him.

During the long, dark autumn nights she would lie awake, listening to the even breathing of the two little boys, noting the swirl of the wind around the corners of the house, and thinking about Erlend. If only he wasn't staying at that particular farm.

She hadn't been pleased when the two cousins had begun talking about Haugen. Munan Baardsøn was visiting them at the hostel in Oslo on one of the last evenings before their departure. Back then Munan had inherited sole ownership of the small manor of Haugen from his mother. Both he and Erlend had been quite drunk and boisterous, and while she sat there feeling tormented by their talk of that place of misfortune, Munan suddenly gave Erlend the farm—so that he wouldn't be entirely bereft of land in Norway. This happened amid much bantering and laughter; they even jested about the rumors that no one could live at Haugen because of the ghosts. The horror that Sir Munan Baardsøn had harbored in his heart ever since the violent death of his mother and her husband up there now seemed to have eased somewhat.

He ended up giving Erlend the deed and documents to Haugen. Kristin couldn't hide her displeasure that he had become the owner of that ignominious place.

But Erlend merely jested, "It's unlikely that either you or I will ever set foot in those buildings—if they're still standing, that is, and haven't collapsed. And surely neither Aunt Aashild nor Herr Bjørn will bring us the land rent themselves. So it shouldn't matter to us if it's true what people say, that they still haunt the place."

The year came to an end, and Kristin's thoughts were always circling around one thing: How was Erlend doing up north at Haugen? She grew so reticent that she barely spoke a word to her children or the servants except when she had to answer their questions. And they were reluctant to address their mistress unless it was absolutely necessary, for she gave such curt and impatient replies when they interrupted and disturbed her restless, anxious brooding. She was so unaware of this herself that when she finally noticed that the two youngest children had stopped asking her about their father or talking about him, she sighed and concluded that children forget so quickly. But she didn't realize how often she had scared them away with her impatient words when she told them to keep quiet and stop plaguing her.

To her oldest sons she said very little.

As long as the hard frost lasted, she could still tell strangers who passed by the manor and asked for her husband that he was up in the mountains trying his luck at hunting. But then a great snowfall descended upon both the countryside and the mountains during the first week of Advent.

Early in the morning on the day before Saint Lucia's Day, while it was still pitch-dark outside and the stars were bright, Kristin came out of the cowshed. She saw by the light of a pine torch stuck in a mound of snow that three of her sons were putting on their skis outside the door of the main house. And a short distance away stood Gaute's gelding with snowshoes under its feet and packs on its back. She guessed where they were headed, so she didn't dare say a word until she noticed that one of the boys was Bjørgulf; the other two were Naakkve and Gaute.

"Are you going out skiing, Bjørgulf? But it's going to be clear today, son!"

"As you can see, Mother, I am."

"Perhaps you'll all be home before the holy day?" she asked helplessly. Bjørgulf was a very poor skier. He couldn't tolerate the brilliance of the snow in his eyes and spent most of the winter indoors. But Naakkve replied that they might be gone for several days.

Kristin went home feeling fearful and uneasy. The twins were cross and sullen, so she realized that they had wanted to go along but their older brothers had refused to take them.

Early on the fifth day, around breakfast time, the three boys returned. They had left before dawn for Bjørgulf's sake, said Naakkve, in order to reach home before the sun came up. The two of them went straight up to the high loft; Bjørgulf looked dead tired. But Gaute carried the bags and packs into the house. He had two handsome pups for the small boys, who at once forgot all about their questions and grievances. Gaute seemed embarrassed but tried not to show it.

"And this," he said as he took something out of a sack, "this Father asked me to give to you."

Fourteen marten pelts, exceedingly beautiful. Kristin took them, greatly confused; she couldn't utter a single word in reply. There were far too many things she wanted to ask, but she was afraid of being overwhelmed if she opened even the smallest part of her heart. And Gaute was so young.

She could only manage to say, "They've already turned white, I see. Yes, we're deep into the winter half of the year now."

When Naakkve came downstairs and he and Gaute sat down to the porridge bowl, Kristin quickly told Frida that she would take food to Bjørgulf up in the loft herself. It occurred to her that she might be able to talk about things with the taciturn boy, who she knew was much more mature in spirit than his brothers.

He was lying in bed, holding a linen cloth over his eyes. His mother hung a kettle of water on the hook over the hearth, and while Bjørgulf propped himself up on his elbow to eat, she boiled a concoction of eyebright and celandine.

Kristin took away the empty food bowl, washed his red and swollen eyes with the concoction, and placed moist linen cloths over them. Then she finally gathered her courage to ask, "Didn't your father say anything about when he intends to come back home to us?"

"No."

"You always say so little, Bjørgulf," replied his mother after a moment.

"That seems to run in the family, Mother." After a pause he continued, "We met Simon and his men north of Rost Gorge. They were headed north with supplies."

"Did you speak to them?" she asked.

"No," he said with a laugh. "There seems to be some kind of sickness between us and our kinsmen that makes it impossible for friendship to thrive."

"Are you blaming me for that?" fumed his mother. "One minute you complain that we talk too little, and the next you say that we can't keep our friends."

Bjørgulf merely laughed again. Then he lifted himself up on his elbow, as if he were listening to his mother's breathing.

"In God's name, Mother, you mustn't cry now. I'm tired and dejected, unaccustomed as I am to traveling on skis. Pay no mind to whatever I say. Of course I know that you're not a woman who's fond of quarrels."

Kristin then left the loft at once. But she no longer dared, for any price, to ask this son what her children thought of these matters.

She would lie in bed, night after night, when the boys had gone up to the loft, listening and keeping watch. She wondered whether they talked to each other when they were alone up there. She could hear the thump of their boots as they dropped them to the floor, the clatter of their knife belts falling. She heard their voices but couldn't make out their words. They talked all at the same time, growing boisterous; it seemed to be half quarrel, half banter. One of the twins shouted loudly; then something was dragged across the floor, making dust sprinkle down from the ceiling into the main room. The gallery door crashed open with a bang, there was a stomping from outside on the gallery, and Ivar and Skule threatened and carried on as they pounded on the door. She heard Gaute's voice, loud and full of laughter. She could tell that he was standing just inside the door; he and the twins had been fighting again, and Gaute had ended up throwing the twins out. Finally she heard Naakkve's grown-up man's voice. He intervened, and the twins came back inside. For a little while longer their chatter and laughter reached her, and then the beds creaked overhead. Gradually silence fell. Then a steady drone interrupted by pauses could be heard—a drone like the sound of thunder deep inside the mountains.

Kristin smiled in the dark. Gaute snored whenever he was especially tired. Her father had done the same. Such similarities pleased her; the sons who took after Erlend in appearance were also like him in that they slept as soundlessly as birds. As she lay in bed, thinking about all the small likenesses that could be recognized in offspring, generation after generation, she had to smile to herself. The painful anguish in her heart loosened its grip for a moment, and the trance of sleep descended, tangling up all the threads of her thoughts as she sank down, first into well-being and then into oblivion.

They were young, she consoled herself. They probably didn't take it so hard.

But one day, shortly after New Year's, the curate Sira Solmund came to see Kristin at Jørundgaard. It was the first time he arrived uninvited, and Kristin welcomed him courteously, even though she had her suspicions at once. And it turned out just as she had thought: He felt it was his duty to inquire whether she and her husband had arbitrarily, and without Church consent, ended their marriage and, if so, which of the spouses was responsible for this unlawful act.

Kristin felt as if her eyes flitted restlessly, and she spoke too swiftly, using far too many words, as she explained to the priest that Erlend thought he should tend to his property up north in Dovre. It had been sorely neglected over the past few years, and the buildings were apparently in ruins. Considering that they had so many children, they needed to look after their welfare—and many other such matters. She gave much too detailed an account of the situation, so that even Sira Solmund, as dull-witted as he was, had to notice that she was feeling uncertain. She talked on and on about what an eager hunter Erlend was; surely the priest must know that. She showed him the marten pelts she had received from her husband, and in her confusion, before she realized it or could reconsider, she gave them to the priest.

Anger overtook her after Sira Solmund had gone. Erlend should have known that if he stayed away in this manner, their priest, being the kind of man he was, would show up to investigate the reason for his absence.

Sira Solmund was a little trifle of a man in appearance; it wasn't easy to guess his age, but he was supposedly about forty winters old. He was not very shrewd and apparently didn't possess an overabundance of learning, but he was an upright, pious, and moral priest. One of his sisters, an aging, childless widow and a wicked gossip, managed his meager household.

He wanted to be seen as a zealous servant of the Church, but he concerned himself mostly with paltry matters and common folk.

He had a timid disposition and was reluctant to meddle with the gentry or take up difficult questions, but once he did so, he grew quite fierce and stubborn.

In spite of this, he was well liked by his parishioners. On the one hand, people respected his quiet and honorable way of living; on the other hand, he was not nearly as avaricious or strict when it came to the rights of the Church or people's obligations as Sira Eirik had been. This was doubtless due to the fact that he was much less bold than the old priest.

But Sira Eirik had loved and respected every man and every child in all the surrounding villages. In the past people often grew angry when the priest strove, with unseemly greed, to secure the fortunes and wealth of the children he had conceived out of wedlock with his housekeeper. During the first years he lived in the parish, the people of Sil had a difficult time tolerating his imperious harshness toward anyone who overstepped the slightest dictate of Church law. He had been a soldier before he took his vows, and he had accompanied the pirate earl, Sir Alf of Tornberg, in his youth. This was all quite evident in his behavior.

But even back then the people had been proud of their priest, for he surpassed nearly all other parish priests in the realm in terms of knowledge, wisdom, physical strength, and courtly manners; he also had the loveliest singing voice. As the years passed and he had to endure the heavy trials God seemed to have placed on His servant because of his willfulness in his youth, Sira Eirik Kaaressøn grew so much in wisdom, piety, and righteousness that his name was now known and respected throughout the entire bishopric. When he journeyed to ecclesiastical meetings in the town of Hamar, he was honored as a father by all the other priests, and it was said that Bishop Halvard wanted to have him moved to a church which would have granted him a noble title and a seat in the cathedral chapter. But Sira Eirik supposedly requested to stay where he was; he gave his age as his excuse, and the fact that his sight had been failing him for many years.

On the main road at Sil, a little south of Formo, stood the beautiful cross carved from soapstone that Sira Eirik had paid to have erected where a rockslide on the slope had taken the lives of both his promising young sons forty years before. Older people in the parish never passed that way without stopping to say a *Pater noster* and *Ave Maria* for the souls of Alf and Kaare.

The priest had married off his daughter with a dowry of property and cattle. He gave her to a handsome farmer's son of good family from Viken. No one had any other thought but that Jon Fis was a good lad. Six years later she had returned home to her father, starving, her health broken, wearing rags and full of lice, holding a child by each hand, and with another one under her belt. The people living in Sil back then all knew, although they never mentioned it, that the children's father had been hanged as a thief in Oslo. The sons of Jon didn't turn out well either, and now all three of them were dead.

While his offspring were still alive, Sira Eirik had greedily sought to adorn and honor his church with gifts. Now it was the church that would doubtless acquire the majority of his fortune and his precious books. The new Saint Olav and Saint Thomas Church in Sil was much larger and more splendid than the old one that had burned down, and Sira Eirik had endowed it with many magnificent and costly adornments. He went to church every day to say his prayers and to reflect, but now he only said mass for the parishioners on high holy days.

It was Sira Solmund who now handled most of the other official priestly duties. But when people had a heavy sorrow, or if their souls were troubled by great difficulties or pangs of conscience, they preferred to seek out their old parish priest, and they all felt that they took home solace from a meeting with Sira Eirik.

One evening in early spring Kristin Lavransdatter went to Romundgaard and knocked on the door of Sira Eirik's house. She didn't know how to bring up the subject she wanted to discuss, so she talked about one thing and another after she had expressed her greetings.

Finally the old man said a little impatiently, "Have you just come here to bring me greetings, Kristin, and to see how I am? If so, that is most kind of you. But it seems to me that you have something on your mind, and if this is true, tell me about it now, and don't waste time with idle talk."

Kristin clasped her hands in her lap and lowered her eyes. "I'm so unhappy, Sira Eirik, that my husband is living up there at Haugen."

"Surely the road isn't any longer," said the priest, "than that you can easily journey up there to talk to him and ask him to return home soon. He can't have so much to do up there on such a small one-man farm that he should need to stay any longer."

"I feel frightened when I think of him sitting alone up there in the winter nights," said Kristin, shivering.

"Erlend Nikulaussøn is old enough and strong enough to look out for himself."

"Sira Eirik . . . you know about everything that happened up there, back in the old days," whispered Kristin, her voice barely audible.

The priest turned his dim old eyes toward her; once they had been coal-black, sharp, and gleaming. He didn't say a word.

"Surely you must have heard what people say," she continued, speaking in the same low voice. "That the dead . . . still haunt the place."

"Do you mean you don't dare seek him out because of that? Or are you afraid the ghosts might break your husband's neck? If they haven't done it by now, Kristin, then no doubt they'll let him stay there in peace." The priest laughed harshly. "It's mostly just ignorance—heathen nonsense and superstition—when people start gossiping about ghosts and the return of dead men. I fear there are stern guards at the door, in that place where Herr Bjørn and Fru Aashild now find themselves."

"Sira Eirik," she whispered, her voice trembling, "do you believe there is no salvation for those two poor souls?"

"God forbid that I should dare judge the limits of His mercy. But I can't imagine that those two could have managed to settle their debts so quickly; all the slates the two of them have had a hand in carving have not yet been presented: her children, whom she abandoned, and the two of you, who took lessons from the wise woman. If I thought that it might help, so that some of the misdeeds she committed could be rectified . . . but since Erlend is living up there, God must not think it would be of any benefit for his aunt to reappear and warn him. For we know that it is through the grace of God and the compassion of Our Lady and the intercessionary prayers of the Church that a poor soul may be allowed to return to this world from the fires of purgatory if his sin is such that it can be absolved with the help of someone who is alive and in this manner shorten his time of torment. Such was the case with the wretched soul who moved the boundary between Hov and Jarpstad, or the farmer in Musudal with the false documents about the millstream. But souls cannot leave the fires of purgatory unless they have a lawful errand. It's mostly nonsense what people say about ghosts and phantoms or the mirages of the Devil, which disappear like smoke if you protect yourself with the sign of the cross and the name of the Lord."

"But what about the blessed ones who are with God, Sira Eirik?" she asked softly.

"You know quite well that the holy ones who are with God can be sent out to bring gifts and messages from Paradise."

"I once told you that I saw Brother Edvin Rikardssøn," she said in the same tone of voice.

"Yes, either it was a dream—and it might have been sent by God or one of his guardian angels—or else the monk is a holy man."

Shivering, Kristin whispered, "My father . . . Sira Eirik, I have prayed so often that I might be allowed to see his face one more time. I long so fervently to see him, Sira Eirik. And perhaps I might be able to tell from his expression what he wants me to do. If my father could give me advice in that way . . ." She had to bite her lip, and she used a corner of her wimple to brush away the tears that had welled up.

The priest shook his head.

"Pray for his soul, Kristin—although I'm convinced that Lavrans and your mother have long ago found solace with those from whom they sought comfort for all the sorrows they endured here on earth. And certainly Lavrans still holds you firmly in his love there too, but your prayers and the masses said for his soul will bind you and all the rest of us to him. How this occurs is one of the secret things that are difficult to fathom, but I have no doubt that this is a better way than if he should be disturbed in his peace to come here and appear before you."

Kristin had to sit still for a moment before she gained enough mastery over herself that she dared speak. But then she told the priest about everything that had happened between Erlend and her on the evening in the hearth house, repeating every word that was said, as best as she could remember.

The priest sat in silence for a long time after she was finished.

Then Kristin clapped her hands together harshly. "Sira Eirik! Do you think I was the one most at fault? Do you think I was so wrong that it wasn't a sin for Erlend to desert me and all our sons in this manner? Do you think it is fair for him to demand that I seek him out, fall to my knees, and take back the words I spoke in anger? Because I *know* that unless I do, he will never return home to us!"

"Do you think you need to call Lavrans back from the other world to ask his advice in this matter?" The priest stood up and placed his hand on the woman's shoulder. "The first time I saw you, Kristin, you were a tiny maiden. Lavrans made you stand between his knees as he crossed your little hands on your breast and told you to say the *Pater noster* for me. You repeated it in a lovely, clear voice, even though you didn't understand a single word. Later you learned the meaning of every prayer in our language; perhaps you've forgotten about that now.

"Have you forgotten that your father taught you and honored you and loved you? He honored the man before whom you are now afraid of humbling yourself. Or have you forgotten how splendid the feast was that he held for the two of you? And then you rode away from his manor like two thieves. Did you take with you Lavrans Bjørgulfsøn's esteem and honor?"

Sobbing, Kristin hid her face in her hands.

"Do you remember, Kristin? Did he ever demand that the two of you should fall to your knees before he thought he could take you back into his fatherly love? Do you think it too harsh a penance for your pride if you have to bow before a man whom you may not have wronged as much as you sinned against your father?"

"Jesus!" Kristin wept in utter despair. "Jesus, have mercy on me."

"I see that you at least remember his name," said the priest. "The name of the one your father strove to follow like a disciple and serve like a loyal knight." He touched the small crucifix that hung above them. "Free of sin, God's son died on the cross to atone for the sins we had committed against him.

"Go home now, Kristin, and think about what I have told you," said Sira Eirik after she had regained some measure of calm.

But during those very days a southerly gale set in with sleet and torrential rains; at times it was so fierce that people could barely cross their own courtyards without the risk of being swept away above all the rooftops; at least that was how it seemed. The roads through the countryside were completely impassable. The spring floods arrived so abruptly and turbulently that people had to move out of the estates that were most vulnerable. Kristin moved most of their belongings up into the loft of the new storehouse, and she was granted permission to put her livestock in Sira Eirik's springtime shed. The shed used at Jørundgaard in the spring was on the other side of the river. It was a dreadful toil in the storm; up in the meadows the snow was as soft as melted butter, and the animals were so wretched. Two of the best calves broke their legs as if they were tender stalks as they walked along.

On the day they moved the livestock Simon Darre suddenly appeared in the middle of the road with four of his servants. They set about lending a hand. In the wind and rain and all the tumult with the cattle that had to be prodded and the sheep and lambs that had to be carried, there was neither peace nor quiet for the kinsmen to talk. But after they returned to Jørundgaard in the evening and Kristin had seated Simon and his men in the main house—everyone who had helped out that day needed some warm ale—he spoke a few words with her. He asked her to go to Formo with the women and children, while he and two of his men would stay behind with Ulf and the boys. Kristin thanked him but said that she wanted to stay on her manor. Lavrans and Munan were already at Ulvsvold, and Jardtrud had gone to stay with Sira Solmund; she had become such good friends with the priest's sister.

Simon said, "People think it's strange, Kristin, that you two sisters never see each other. Ramborg won't be happy if I return home without you."

"I know it looks strange," she told him, "but I think it would look even stranger if we should visit my sister now, when the master of this estate is not home and people know that there's animosity between him and you."

Then Simon said no more, and soon after he and his men took their leave.

The week preceding Ascension Day arrived with a terrible storm, and on Tuesday word spread from farm to farm in the north of the region that the floods had now carried off the bridge up in Rost Gorge, which people crossed when they went up to the Høvring pastures. They began to fear for the big bridge south of the church. It was solidly built of the roughest timbers, with a high arch in the middle, and was supported underneath with thick posts that were sunk into the riverbed. But now the waters were flooding over the bridgeheads where they joined the banks, and beneath the vault of the bridge all kinds of debris that had been brought by the currents from the north were piling up. The Laag had now overflowed the low embankments on both shores, and in one place the water had accumulated across Jørundgaard's fields like in a cove, almost reaching the buildings. There was a hollow in the pastures and in the middle was the roof of the smithy, and the tops of the trees looked like little islands. The barn on the islet had already been swept away.

Very few people attended church from the farms on the east side of the river. They were afraid the bridge would be washed away and they wouldn't be able to get back home. But up on the other shore, on the slope beneath Laugarbru's barn, where there was some shelter from the storm, a dark cluster of people could be glimpsed through the gusts of snow. It was rumored that Sira Eirik had said he would carry the cross over the bridge and set it on the east bank of the river, even if no one dared follow him.

A squall of snow rushed toward the procession of people coming out of the church. The flakes formed slanting streaks in the air. Only a glimmer of the valley was visible: here and there a scrap of the darkening lake where the fields usually lay, the rush of clouds sweeping over the scree-covered slopes and the lobes of forest, and glimpses of the mountain peaks against the billowing clouds high overhead. The air was sated with the clamor of the river, rising and falling, with the roar from the forests, and with the howl of the wind. Occasionally a muffled crash could be heard, echoing the storm's fury from the mountains and the thunder of an avalanche of new snow.

The candles were blown out as soon as they were carried beyond the church gallery. That day fully grown young men had donned the white shirts of choirboys. The wind whipped at their garments. They walked along in a large group, carrying the banner with their hands, gripping the fabric so the wind wouldn't shred it to pieces as the procession leaned forward, struggling across the slope in the wind. But now and then, above the raging of the storm, the sound of Sira Eirik's resonant voice could be heard as he fought his way forward and sang:

*Venite: revertamur ad Dominum; quia ipse cepit & sanabit nos: percutiet, & curabit nos, & vivemus in conspectu ejus. Sciemus sequemurque, ut cognoscamus Dominum. Alleluia.*[1]

Kristin stopped, along with all the other women, when the procession reached the place where the water had overflowed the road, but the white-clad young boys, the deacons, and the priests were already up on the bridge, and almost all the men followed; the water came up to their knees.

The bridge shuddered and shook, and then the women noticed that an entire house was rushing from the north toward the bridge. It churned around and around in the current as it was carried along, partially shattered, with its timbers jutting out, but still managing to stay in one piece. The woman from Ulvsvold clung to Kristin Lavransdatter and moaned loudly; her husband's two nearly grown-up brothers were among the choirboys. Kristin screamed without words to the Virgin Mary, fixing her gaze on the group in the middle of the bridge where she could discern the white-clad figure of Naakkve among the men holding the banner. The women thought they could still hear Sira Eirik's voice, almost drowned out by the din.

He paused at the crest of the bridge and lifted the cross high up as the house struck. The bridge shuddered and swayed; to the people on both shores, it looked as if it had dipped slightly to the south. Then the procession moved on, disappearing behind the curved arch of the bridge and then reappearing on the opposite shore. The wreckage of the house had become tangled up in the heaps of other flotsam caught in the underpinnings of the bridge.

All of a sudden, like a miracle, silvery light began seeping from the windblown masses of clouds; a dull gleam like molten lead spread over the whole expanse of the swollen river. The haze lifted, the clouds scattered, the sun broke through, and as the procession came back over the bridge, the rays glittered on the cross. On the wet white alb of the priest, the crossed stripes of his stole shimmered a wondrous purple. The valley lay gilded and sparkling with moisture, as if at the bottom of a dark blue grotto, for the storm clouds had gathered around the mountain ridges and, brought low by the rays of the sun, had turned the heights black. The haze fled between the peaks, and the great crest above Formo reached up from the darkness, dazzling white with new snow.

She had seen Naakkve walk past. The drenched garments clung to the boys as they sang at the top of their lungs to the sunshine:

> *Salvator mundi, salva nos omnes. Kyrie, eleison, Christe, eleison, Christe, audi nos—.*[2]

The priests with the cross had gone past; the group of farmers followed in their heavy, soaked clothing, but looking around them at the weather with amazed and shining faces as they took up the prayer's refrain: *Kyrie eleison!*

Suddenly she saw . . . She couldn't believe her own eyes, and now it was her turn to grab hold of the woman next to her for support. There was Erlend walking along in the procession; he was wearing a dripping wet coat made of reindeer hide with the hood pulled over his head. But it was him. His lips were slightly parted, and he was crying, *Kyrie eleison,* along with the others. He looked right at her as he walked past. She couldn't properly decipher the expression on his face, but it looked as if he wore a shadow of a smile.

Together with the other women, she joined the procession as it moved up the church hill, calling out with the others as the young boys sang the litany. She was unaware of anything except the wild pounding of her own heart.

During the mass she caught a glimpse of him only once. She

didn't dare stand in her customary place but hid in the darkness of the north nave.

As soon as the service was over, she rushed outdoors. She fled from her maids who had been in church. Outside, the countryside was steaming in the sunshine. Kristin raced home without noticing the sodden state of the road.

She spread a cloth over the table and set a full horn of mead before the master's high seat before she took time to exchange her wet clothes for her Sabbath finery: the dark blue, embroidered gown, silver belt, buckled shoes, and the wimple with the blue border. Then she knelt in the alcove. She couldn't think, she couldn't find the words she sought; over and over again she said the *Ave Maria*: Blessed Lady, dear Lord, son of the Virgin, you know what I want to say.

This went on for a long time. From her maids she heard that the men had gone back to the bridge; with broadaxes and hooks they were trying to remove the tangle of debris that had gotten caught. It was a matter of saving the bridge. The priests had also gone back after they had taken off their vestments.

It was well past midday when the men returned: Kristin's sons, Ulf Haldorssøn, and the three servants—an old man and two youths who had been given refuge on the manor.

Naakkve had already sat down at his place, to the right of the high seat. Suddenly he stood up, stepped forward, and rushed for the door.

Kristin softly called out his name.

A moment later he came back and sat down. The color came and went in his young face; he kept his eyes lowered, and now and then he had to bite his lip. His mother saw that he was struggling hard to master his feelings, but he managed to do so.

Finally the meal came to an end. Her sons, who were seated on the inner bench, rose to their feet and came around the end of the table past the vacant high seat, adjusting their belts as they usually did after they had put their knives back in their sheaths. Then they left the room.

When they had all gone, Kristin followed. In the sunshine, water was now streaming off all the eaves. There wasn't a soul in the courtyard except for Ulf; he was standing on the doorstep to his own house.

His face took on an oddly helpless expression when the mistress approached him. He didn't speak, and so she asked quietly, "Did you talk to him?"

"Only a few words. I saw that he and Naakkve talked."

After a moment he went on, "He was a little worried . . . about all of you . . . when the flooding got this bad. So he decided to head home to see how things were. Naakkve told him how you were handling everything.

"I don't know how he happened to hear about it . . . that you gave away the pelts he sent with Gaute in the fall. He was cross about that. Also when he heard that you had rushed home right after the mass; he thought you would have stayed to talk to him."

Kristin didn't say a word; she turned on her heel and went back inside.

That summer there were constant quarrels and strife between Ulf Haldorssøn and his wife. The son of Ulf's half brother, Haldor Jonssøn, had come to visit his kinsman in the spring, along with his wife; he had been married the year before. It was understood that Haldor would now lease the estate Ulf owned in Skaun and move there on turnover day.[3] But Jardtrud was angry because she thought Ulf had given his nephew conditions that were too good, and she saw that it was the men's intention to ensure for Haldor, perhaps through some kind of agreement, inheritance of the estate after his uncle's death.

Haldor had been Kristin's personal servant at Husaby, and she was very fond of the young man. She also liked his wife, who was a quiet and proper young woman. Shortly after Midsummer the couple had a son, and Kristin lent the wife her weaving house, where the mistresses of the estate used to reside whenever they gave birth. But Jardtrud took offense that Kristin herself should attend the woman as the foremost of the midwives, even though Jardtrud was young and quite inexperienced, unable to offer help with a birth or with caring for a newborn infant.

Kristin was the boy's godmother, and Ulf gave the christening banquet, but Jardtrud thought he lavished too much on it and put too many costly gifts in the cradle and in the mother's bed. To placate his wife somewhat, Ulf gave her several precious items from among his own possessions: a gilded cross on a chain, a fur-lined cape with a large silver clasp, a gold ring, and a silver brooch. But she saw that he refused to present her with a single parcel of land that he owned, aside from what he had given her when they married. Everything else would go to his half siblings if he himself had no offspring. Now Jardtrud lamented that her child had been stillborn, and it seemed unlikely that she would have any more; she was ridiculed throughout the countryside because she talked about this to everyone.

Ulf had to ask Kristin to allow Haldor and Audhild to live in the hearth house after the young wife had gone to church for the first time after giving birth. Kristin gladly consented. She avoided Haldor because she was reminded of so many things that were painful to think about whenever she spoke with her former servant. But she talked a great deal with his wife, for Audhild wanted to help Kristin as much as she could. Toward the end of the summer the child fell gravely ill, and then Kristin stepped in to tend the boy for his young and inexperienced mother.

When the couple journeyed north in the fall, she missed them both, but she missed the child even more. She realized it was foolish, but in recent years she couldn't help feeling some measure of pain because she suddenly seemed to be barren—and yet she wasn't an old woman, not even forty.

It had helped to keep her thoughts off painful matters when she had the childish young wife and her infant to care for and advise. And even though she found it sad to see that Ulf Haldorssøn had not found greater happiness in his marriage, the state of affairs in the foreman's house had also served to divert her thoughts from other things.

After the way Erlend had behaved on Ascension Day, she hardly dared to speculate anymore about how the whole situation might end. The fact that he had appeared in the village and the church in full view of everyone and then had raced northward again without speaking a single word of greeting to his wife seemed to her so heartless that she felt as if she had at last grown completely indifferent toward him.

She had not exchanged a word with Simon Andressøn since the day of the spring floods when he came to help her. She would greet him and often speak a few words to her sister at church. But she had no idea what they thought about her affairs or the fact that Erlend had gone away to Dovre.

On the Sunday before Saint Bartholomew's Day, Sir Gyrd of Dyfrin came to church with the people from Formo. Simon looked immensely happy as he went inside for mass at his brother's side. And Ramborg came over to Kristin after the service, eagerly whispering that she was with child again and expected to give birth around the Feast of the Virgin Mary in the spring.

"Kristin, sister, can't you come home and celebrate with us today?"

Kristin shook her head sadly, patted the young woman's pale cheek, and prayed that God might bring the parents joy. But she said that she couldn't go to Formo.

After the falling-out with his brother-in-law, Simon tried to make himself believe that it was for the best. His position was such that he didn't need to ask how people might judge his actions in everything; he had helped Erlend and Kristin when it mattered, and the assistance he could offer them here in the parish was not so important that he should allow it to make his own life more complicated.

But when he heard that Erlend had left Jørundgaard, it was impossible for Simon to sustain the stubborn, melancholy calm he had striven to display. It was useless to tell himself that no one fully understood what lay behind Erlend's absence; people chattered so much but knew so little. Even so, he couldn't get himself mixed up in this matter. But he was still uneasy. At times he wondered whether he ought to seek out Erlend at Haugen and take back the words he had said when they parted; then he could see about finding some way to return order to the affairs of his brother-in-law and his wife's sister. But Simon never got any farther than thinking about this.

He didn't think anyone could tell from looking at him that his heart was uneasy. He lived as he always had, running his farm and managing his properties; he was merry and drank boldly in the company of friends; he went up to the mountains to hunt when he had time and spoiled his children when he was home. And never was an unkind word spoken between him and his wife. For the servants of the manor it must have looked as if the friendship between Ramborg and him was now better than it had ever been, since his wife was more even-tempered and calm, never exhibiting those fits of capriciousness and childish anger over petty matters. But secretly Simon felt awkward and uncertain in his wife's company; he could no longer make himself treat her as if she were still half a child, teasing and pampering her. He didn't know how he should treat her anymore.

Neither did he know how to take it when she told him one evening that she was again with child.

"I suppose you're not particularly happy about it, are you?" he finally said, stroking her hand.

"But surely *you* are happy, aren't you?" Ramborg pressed close to him, half crying and half laughing. He laughed, a little embarrassed, as he pulled her into his arms.

"I'll be sensible this time, Simon; I won't behave the way I did before. But you must *stay* with me, do you hear me? Even if all your brothers-in-law and all your brothers were to be led off to the gallows, one after the other, with their hands bound, you mustn't leave me!"

Simon laughed sadly. "Where would I go, my Ramborg? Geirmund, that poor creature, isn't likely to get mixed up in any weighty matters, and he's the only one left among my friends and kinsmen that I haven't quarreled with yet."

"Oh . . ." Ramborg laughed too as her tears fell. "That enmity will last only until they need a helping hand and you think you can offer it. I know you too well by now, my husband."

Two weeks later Gyrd Andressøn unexpectedly arrived at the manor. The Dyfrin knight had brought only a single man as an escort.

The meeting between the brothers took place with few words spoken. Sir Gyrd explained that he hadn't seen his sister and brother-in-law at Kruke in all these years, and so he had decided to come north to visit them. Since he was in the valley, Sigrid felt he should also visit Formo. "And I thought, brother, that surely you couldn't be so angry with me that you wouldn't offer me and my servant food and lodging until tomorrow."

"You know I will," said Simon as he stood looking down, his face dark red. "It was . . . noble of you, Gyrd, to come to see me."

The brothers walked through the fields after they had eaten. The grain was starting to turn pale on the slopes facing the sun, down by the river. The weather was so beautiful. The Laag now glittered gently enough, visible as little white flashes amid the alder trees. Big, glossy clouds drifted across the summer sky; sunshine filled the entire basin of the valley, and the mountain on the other side looked light blue and green in the shimmer of heat and the fleeting shadows of the clouds.

A pounding sound came from the pasture behind them as the horses trampled across the dry hillside; the herd came rushing through the alder thickets. Simon leaned over the fence. "Foal, foal . . . Bronstein's getting old, isn't he?" he said as Gyrd's horse poked his head over the rail and nudged his shoulder.

"Eighteen winters." Gyrd stroked the horse. "I thought, kinsman, that this matter . . . It wouldn't be right if it should end the friendship between you and me," he said without looking at his brother.

"It has grieved me every single day," replied Simon softly. "Thank you for coming, Gyrd."

They continued walking along the fence—Gyrd first, with Simon plodding behind. Finally they sank down on the edge of a little yellow-scorched stony embankment. A strong, sweet fragrance came from the small mounds of hay that were scattered about, where the scythe had scraped together short stalks of hay mixed with flowers between the piles of stones. Gyrd spoke of the reconciliation between King Magnus and the Haftorssøns and their followers.

After a moment Simon asked, "Do you think it's out of the question that any of these kinsmen of Erlend Nikulaussøn would be willing to attempt to win full reconciliation for him and clemency from the king?"

"There is not much *I* can do," said Gyrd Darre. "And they have few kind words to say of him, Simon, those who might be able to do something. Oh, I have little desire to talk of this matter *now*. I thought he was a bold and splendid fellow, but the others think he brought his plans to such a bad end. But I'd rather not talk of this now; I know you're so fond of that brother-in-law of yours."

Simon sat gazing out across the silvery white brilliance of the crowns of the trees on the hillside and the sparkling gleam of the river. Surprised, he thought that yes, in a way it was true, what Gyrd had said.

"Except that right now we are foes, Erlend and I," he said. "It's been a long time since we last spoke."

"It seems to me that you've grown quite quarrelsome over the years, Simon," said Gyrd with a laugh.

After a moment he continued, "Haven't you ever thought of moving away from these valleys? We kinsmen could support each other more if we lived closer to each other."

"How can you even think of such a thing? Formo is my ancestral estate . . ."

"Aasmund of Eiken owns part of the manor through inherited rights. And I know that he would not be unwilling to exchange one ancestral property for another. He hasn't yet given up the idea that if he could win your Arngjerd for his Grunde on the terms that he mentioned . . ."

Simon shook his head. "The lineage of our father's mother has resided on this estate ever since Norway was a heathen land. And it is here that I intend for Andres to live when I'm gone. I don't think you have your wits about you, brother. How could I give up Formo!"

"No, that's understandable." Gyrd blushed a little. "I merely thought that perhaps . . . Most of your kinsmen are at Raumarike, along with the friends from your youth; perhaps you might find that you'd thrive better there."

"I'm thriving *here*." Simon had also turned red. "This is the place where I can give the boy a secure seat." He looked at Gyrd, and his brother's fine, furrowed face took on an embarrassed expression. Gyrd's hair was now almost white, but his body was still just as slender and lithe as ever. He shifted rather uneasily; several stones rolled out from the pile of rocks and tumbled down the slope and into the grain.

"Are you going to send the whole scree down into my field?" asked Simon in a stern voice as he laughed. Gyrd leaped to his feet, light and agile, reaching out a hand to his brother, who moved more slowly.

Simon gripped his brother's hand for a moment after he got to his feet. Then he placed his arm around his brother's shoulder. Gyrd did the same, and with their arms loosely resting around each other's shoulders, the brothers slowly walked over the hills toward the manor.

They sat together in the Sæmund house that night; Simon would share a bed with his brother. They had said their evening prayers, but they wanted to empty the ale keg before they went to bed.

"*Benedictus tu in muliebris . . . mulieribus* . . . Do you remember that?" Simon laughed suddenly.

"Yes. It cost me a few blows across the back before Sira Magnus wrung our grandmother's misteachings out of my head." Gyrd smiled at the memory. "And he had a devilishly hard hand too. Do you remember, brother, that time when he sat and scratched the calves of his legs, and he had lifted up the hem of his robe? You whispered to me that if you had had such misshapen calves as Magnus Ketilssøn, you would have become a priest too and always worn full-length surcoats."

Simon smiled. Suddenly he seemed to *see* the boyish face of his brother, about to burst with stifled laughter, his eyes pitifully miserable. They weren't very old back then, and Sira Magnus was cruelly hard-handed whenever he had to reprimand them.

Gyrd had not been terribly clever when they were children. And it wasn't because Gyrd was a particularly wise man that Simon loved him now. But he felt warm with gratitude and tenderness toward his brother as he sat there: for every day of their kinship during almost forty years and for Gyrd, just the way he was—the most loyal and forthright of men.

It seemed to Simon that winning back his brother Gyrd was like gaining a firm foundation for at least one foot. And for such a long time his life had been so unreasonably disjointed and complicated.

He felt a warmth inside every time he thought about Gyrd, who had come to him to make amends for something that Simon himself had provoked when he rode to his brother's estate in anger and with curses. His heart overflowed with gratitude; he had to thank more than Gyrd.

A man such as Lavrans . . . He knew quite well how he would have handled such an event. He could follow his father-in-law as far as he was able, by giving out alms and the like. But he wasn't capable of such things as true contrition or contemplation of the wounds of the Lord, unless he stared zealously at the crucifix—and that was not what Lavrans had intended. Simon couldn't bring forth tears of remorse; he hadn't wept more than two or three times since he was a child, and never when he needed to most, those times when he had committed the worst of sins: with Arngjerd's mother while he was a married man and that killing the previous year. And yet he had felt great regret; he thought that he always sincerely regretted his sins, taking pains to confess and to atone as the priest commanded. He was always diligent in saying his prayers and saw to it that he gave the proper tithes and abundant alms—with particular generosity in honor of the apostle Saint Simon, Saint Olav, Saint Michael, and the Virgin Mary. Otherwise he was content with what Sira Eirik had said: that salvation was to be found in the cross alone and how a man faced or fought with the Fiend was something for God to decide and not the man himself.

But now he felt an urge to show his gratitude to the holy ones with greater fervor. His mother had told him that he was supposedly born on the birthday of the Virgin Mary. He decided that he wanted to show the Lord's Mother his veneration with a prayer he was not usually accustomed to saying. He had once had a beautiful prayer copied out, back when he was at the royal court, and he took out the small piece of parchment.

Now, much later, he feared that it was probably intended more as an appeal to King Haakon than for the sake of God or Mary that he had acquired these small epistles with prayers and learned them while he was among the king's retainers. All the young men did so, for the king was in the habit of quizzing the pages about what they knew of such useful knowledge when he lay in bed at night, unable to sleep.

Oh yes . . . that was so long ago. The king's bedchamber in the stone hall of the Oslo palace. On the little table next to his bed burned a single candle; the light fell across the finely etched, faded, and aging face of the man, resting above the red silken quilts. When the priest had finished reading aloud and taken his leave, the king often picked up the book himself and lay in bed, reading with the heavy volume resting against his propped-up knees. On two footstools over by the brick fireplace sat the pages; Simon nearly always had the watch with Gunstein Ingasøn. It was pleasant in the chamber. The fire burned brightly, giving heat without smoke, and the room seemed so snug with the cross-beamed ceiling and the walls always covered with tapestries. But they would grow sleepy from sitting there in that fashion, first listening to the priest read and then waiting for the king to fall asleep, as he rarely did until close to midnight. When he was sleeping, they were allowed to take turns keeping guard and napping on the bench between the fireplace and the door to the royal Council hall.

Occasionally the king would converse with them; this didn't happen often, but when it did, he was inexpressibly kind and charming. Or he would read aloud from the book a sentence or a few stanzas of a verse that he thought the young men might find useful or beneficial to hear.

One night Simon was awakened by King Haakon calling for him in pitch-darkness. The candle had burned out. Feeling wretched with shame, Simon blew some life into the embers and lit a new candle. The king lay in bed, smiling secretively.

"Does that Gunstein always snore so terribly?"

"Yes, my Lord."

"You share a bed with him in the dormitory, don't you? It might be deemed reasonable if you asked for another bedfellow for a while who makes less noise when he sleeps."

"Thank you, my Lord, but it doesn't bother me, Your Majesty!"

"Surely you must wake up, Simon, when that thunder explodes right next to your ear—don't you?"

"Yes, Your Grace, but then I give him a shove and turn him over a bit."

The king laughed. "I wonder whether you young men realize that being able to sleep so soundly is one of God's great gifts. When you reach my age, Simon my friend, perhaps you will remember my words."

That seemed endlessly far away—still clear, but not as if he were the same man, sitting here now, who had once been that young page.

One day at the beginning of Advent, when Kristin was almost alone on the estate—her sons were bringing home firewood and moss—she was surprised to see Simon Darre come riding into the courtyard. He had come to invite her and her sons to be their guests during Christmas.

"You know quite well, Simon, that we can't do that," she said somberly. "We can still be friends in our hearts, you and Ramborg and I, but as you know, it's not always possible for us to determine what we must do."

"Surely you don't mean that you're going to take this so far that you won't come to your only sister when she has to lie down to give birth."

Kristin prayed that all would go well and bring both of them joy. "But I can't tell you with certainty that I will come."

"Everyone will think it remarkably strange," admonished Simon. "You have a reputation for being the best midwife, and she's your sister, and the two of you are the mistresses of the largest estates in the northern part of the region."

"Quite a few children have been brought into the world on the great manors around here over the past few years, but I've never been asked to come. It's no longer the custom, Simon, for a birth to be considered improperly attended if the mistress of Jørundgaard is not in the room." She saw that he was greatly distressed by her words, and so she continued, "Give my greetings to Ramborg, and tell her that I will come to help her when it's time; but I cannot come to your Christmas feast, Simon."

But on the eighth day of the Christmas season she met Simon as he came to mass without Ramborg. No, she was feeling fine, he said, but she needed to rest and gather her strength, for the next day he was taking her and the children south to Dyfrin. The weather was so good for traveling by sleigh, and since Gyrd had invited them, and Ramborg was so keen on going, well . . .

## CHAPTER 4

On the day after Saint Paal's Day, Simon Darre rode north across Lake Mjøsa, accompanied by two men. A bitter frost had set in, but he didn't think he could stay away from home any longer; the sleighs would have to follow later, as soon as the cold had let up a bit.

At Hamar he met a friend, Vigleik Paalssøn of Fagaberg, and they continued on together. When they reached Lillehammer, they rested for a while at a farm where ale was served. As they sat and drank, several drunken fur peddlers began brawling in the room. Finally Simon stood up, stepped into the thick of things and separated them, but in doing so, he received a knife wound in his right forearm. It was little more than a scratch, so he paid it no mind, although the proprietress of the alehouse insisted on being allowed to bind a cloth around it.

He rode home with Vigleik and stayed the night at his manor. The men shared a bed, and toward morning Simon was awakened because the other man was thrashing in his sleep. Several times Vigleik called out his name, and so Simon woke him up to ask what was wrong.

Vigleik couldn't remember his dream properly. "But it was loathsome, and you were in it. One thing I do remember: Simon Reidarssøn stood in this room and asked you to leave with him. I saw him so clearly that I could have counted every single freckle on his face."

"I wish you could sell me that dream," said Simon, half in jest and half seriously. Simon Reidarssøn was his uncle's son, and they had been good friends when they were growing up, but the other Simon had died at the age of thirteen.

In the morning when the men sat down to eat, Vigleik noticed that Simon hadn't buttoned the sleeve of his tunic around his right wrist. The flesh was red and swollen all the way down to the back of his hand. He mentioned it, but Simon merely laughed.

A little later, when his friend begged him to stay on a few more days and to wait there for his wife—Vigleik couldn't forget his dream—Simon Andressøn replied, almost indignantly, "Surely you haven't had such a bad dream about me that I should keep to my bed because of a mere louse bite?"

Around sunset Simon and his men rode down to Lake Losna. It had been the most beautiful day; now the towering blue and white peaks turned gold and crimson in the twilight, while along the river the groves, heavy with rime, stood furry gray in the shadows. The men had excellent horses and a brisk ride ahead of them across the long lake; tiny bits of ice sprayed up, ringing and clinking beneath the hooves of the horses. A biting wind blew hard against them. Simon was freezing, but in spite of the cold, strange nauseating waves of heat kept washing over him, followed by icy spells that seemed to seep all the way into the marrow of his spine. Now and then he noticed that his tongue was swollen and felt oddly thick at the back of his throat. Even before they had crossed the lake he had to stop and ask one of his men to help him fasten his cape so it would support his right arm.

The servants had heard Vigleik Paalssøn recounting his dream; now they wanted their master to show them his wound. But Simon said it was nothing; it merely stung a bit. "I may have to get used to being left-handed for a few days."

But later that night, when the moon had risen and they were riding high along the ridge north of the lake, Simon realized that his arm might turn out to be rather troublesome after all. It ached all the way up to his armpit, the jolting of the horse caused him great pain, and the blood was hammering in his wounded limb. His head was pounding too, and spasms were shooting up from the back of his neck. He was hot and then cold by turn.

The winter road passed high up along the slope, partway through forest and partway across white fields. Simon gazed at everything: The full moon was sailing brightly in the pale blue sky, having driven all the stars far away; only a few larger ones still dared wander in the distant heavens. The white fields glittered and sparkled; the shadows fell short and jagged across the snow; inside the woods the uncertain light lay in splotches and stripes among the firs, heavy with snow. Simon saw all this.

But at the same time he saw quite clearly a meadow with tufts of ash-brown grass in the sunlight of early spring. Several small spruce trees had sprung up here and there at the edge of the field; they glowed green like velvet in the sun. He recognized this place; it was the pasture near his home at Dyfrin. The alder woods stood beyond the field with its tree trunks a springtime shiny gray and the tops brown with blossoms. Behind stretched the long, low Raumarike ridges, shimmering blue but still speckled white with snow. They were walking down toward the alder thicket, he and Simon Reidarssøn, carrying fishing gear and pike spears. They were on their way to the lake, which lay dark gray with patches of thawing ice, to fish at the open end. His dead cousin walked at his side; he saw his playmate's curly hair sticking out from his cap, reddish in the spring sunlight; he could see every freckle on the boy's face. The other Simon stuck out his lower lip and blew—phew, phew—whenever he thought his namesake was speaking gibberish. They jumped over meandering rivulets and leaped from mound to mound across the trickling snow water in the grassy meadow. The bottom was covered with moss; under the water it churned and frothed a lively green.

He was fully aware of everything around him; the whole time he saw the road passing up one hill and down another, through the woods and over white fields in the glittering moonlight. He saw the slumbering clusters of houses beneath snow-laden roofs casting shadows across the fields; he saw the band of fog hovering over the river in the bottom of the valley. He knew that it was Jon who was riding right behind him and who moved up alongside him whenever they entered open clearings, and yet he happened to call the man Simon several times. He knew it was wrong, but he couldn't help himself, even though he noticed that his servants grew alarmed.

"We must manage to reach the monks at Roaldstad tonight, men," he said once when his mind had cleared.

The men tried to dissuade him; instead they should see about finding lodgings as soon as possible, and they mentioned the nearest parsonage. But their master clung to his plan.

"It will be hard on the horses, Simon." The two men exchanged a glance.

But Simon merely laughed. They would have to manage it for once. He thought about the arduous miles. Pain shot through his whole body as he jolted in the saddle. But he wanted to go home because now he knew that he was fated to die.

Even though his heart was alternately freezing and burning in the winter night, at the same time he felt the mild spring sunshine of the pasture back home, while he and the dead boy kept walking and walking toward the alder thicket.

For brief moments the image would vanish and his head would clear, except that it ached so dreadfully. He asked one of his men to cut open the sleeve on his wounded arm. His face turned white and the sweat poured down when Jon Daalk cautiously slit open his vest and shirt from his wrist up to his shoulder, but he managed to support the swollen limb himself with his left hand. After a while the pain began to ease.

Then the men started discussing whether they should see about sending word back south to Dyfrin once they reached Roaldstad. But Simon had his objections. He didn't want to worry his wife with such a message when it might be unnecessary; a sleigh ride in this bitter cold would be ill advised. Perhaps, when they were home at Formo . . . They should wait and see. He tried to smile at Sigurd to cheer up the young servant, who looked quite frightened and distressed.

"But you can send word to Kristin at Jørundgaard as soon as we reach home. She's so skilled at healing." His tongue felt as thick and stiff as wood as he spoke.

Kiss me, Kristin, my betrothed! At first she would think he was speaking in delirium. No, Kristin. Then she would be surprised.

Erlend had understood. Ramborg had understood. But Kristin . . . She sat there with her sorrow and rancor, and yet as angry and bitter as she now felt toward that man Erlend, she still had no thoughts for anyone else but him. You've never cherished me enough, Kristin, my beloved, that you might consider how difficult it would be for me when I had to be a brother to the woman who was once meant to be my wife.

He hadn't realized it himself back then, when he parted from her outside the convent gate in Oslo: that he would continue to think about her in this way. That he would end up feeling as if nothing he had acquired afterward in life were an equal replacement for what he had lost back then. For the maiden who had been promised to him in his youth.

She would hear this before he died. She would give him one kiss.

I am the one who loved you and who loves you still.

He had once heard those words, and he had never been able to forget them. They were from the Virgin Mary's book of miracles, a saga about a nun who fled from her convent with a knight. The Virgin saved them in the end and forgave them in spite of their sin. If it was a sin that he said this to his wife's sister before he died, then God's Mother would grant him forgiveness for this as well. He had so seldom troubled her by asking for anything. . . .

I didn't believe it myself back then: that I would never feel truly happy or merry again . . .

"No, Simon, it's too great a burden for Sokka if she has to carry both of us . . . considering how far she has had to travel tonight," he said to the person who had climbed up behind him on the horse and was supporting him. "I can see that it's you, Sigurd, but I thought it was someone else."

Toward morning they reached the pilgrims' hostel, and the two monks who were in charge tended to the ill man. After he had revived a little under their care and the feverish daze had abated, Simon Andressøn insisted on borrowing a sleigh to continue northward.

The roads were in good condition; they changed horses along the way, journeyed all night, and arrived at Formo the following morning, at dawn. Simon had lain and dozed under all the covers that someone had spread over him. He felt so weighted down—sometimes he felt as if he were being crushed under heavy boulders—and his head ached terribly. Now and then he seemed to slip away. Then the pain would begin raging inside him again; it felt as if his body were swelling up more and more, growing unimaginably big and about to burst. There was a constant throbbing in his arm.

He tried to walk from the sleigh to the house, with his good arm around Jon's shoulder and Sigurd walking behind to support him. Simon sensed that the faces of the men were gray and grimy with weariness; they had spent two nights in a row in the saddle. He wanted to say something to them about it, but his tongue refused to obey him. He stumbled over the threshold and fell full length into the room—with a roar of pain as his swollen and misshapen arm struck against something. The sweat poured off him as he choked back the moans that rose up as he was undressed and helped into bed.

Not long afterward he noticed that Kristin Lavransdatter was standing next to the fireplace, grinding something with a pestle in a wooden bowl. The sound kept thudding right through his head. She poured something from a small pot into a goblet and added several drops from a glass vial that she took out of a chest. Then she emptied the crushed substance from the bowl into the pot and set it next to the fire. Such a quiet and competent manner she had.

She came over to the bed with the goblet in her hand. She walked with such ease. She was just as straight-backed and lovely as she had been as a maiden—this slender woman with the thin, somber face beneath the linen wimple. The back of his neck was also swollen, and it hurt when she slipped one arm under his shoulders to lift him up. She supported his head against her breast as she held the goblet to his lips with her left hand.

Simon smiled a little, and as she cautiously let his head slip back down to the pillow, he seized hold of her hand with his good one. Her fine, slim woman's hand was no longer soft or white.

"I suppose you can't sew silk with these fingers of yours anymore," said Simon. "But they're good and light—and how pleasantly cool your hand is, Kristin." He placed it on his forehead. Kristin remained standing there until she felt her palm grow warm; then she removed it and gently pressed her other hand against his burning brow, up along the hairline.

"Your arm has a nasty wound, Simon," she said, "but with God's help it will mend."

"I'm afraid that you won't be able to heal me, Kristin, no matter how skilled you are with medicines," said Simon. But his expression was almost cheerful. The potion began to take effect; he felt the pain much less. But his eyes felt so strange, as if he had no control over them. He thought he must be lying there with each eye squinting in opposite directions.

"No doubt things will go with me as they must," he said in the same tone of voice.

Kristin went back to her pots; she spread a paste on some linen cloths and then came over and wrapped the hot bandages around his arm, from the tips of his fingers all the way around his back and across his chest, where the swelling splayed out in red stripes from his armpit. It hurt at first, but soon the discomfort eased. She spread a woolen blanket on top and placed soft down pillows under his arm. Simon asked her what she had put on the bandages.

"Oh, various things—mostly comfrey and swallowwort," said Kristin. "If only it was summer, I could have picked them fresh from my herb garden. But I had a plentiful supply; thanks be to God I haven't needed them earlier this winter."

"What was it you once told me about swallowwort? You heard it from the abbess when you were at the convent . . . something about the name."

"Do you mean that in all languages it has a name that means 'swallow,' all the way from the Greek sea up to the northern lands?"

"Yes, because it blossoms everywhere when the swallows awake from their winter slumber." Simon pressed his lips together more firmly. By then he would have been in the ground for a long time.

"I want my resting place to be here, at the church, if I should die, Kristin," he said. "I'm such a rich man by now that someday Andres will most likely possess considerable power here at Formo. I wonder if Ramborg will have a son after I'm gone, in the spring. I would have liked to live long enough to see two sons on my estate."

Kristin told him she had sent word south to Dyfrin that he was gravely ill—with Gaute, who had ridden off that morning.

"You didn't send that child off alone, did you?" asked Simon with alarm.

There was no one at hand whom she thought could manage to keep up with Gaute riding Rauden, she told him. Simon said it would surely be a difficult journey for Ramborg; if only she wouldn't travel any faster than she could bear. "But I would like to see my children . . ."

Sometime later he began talking about his children again. He mentioned Arngjerd, wondering whether he might have been wrong not to accept the offer from the people of Eiken. But the man seemed too old to him, and he had been afraid that Grunde could turn out to be violent when he was drunk. He had always wanted to place Arngjerd in the most secure of circumstances. Now it would be Gyrd and Gudmund who would decide on her marriage. "Tell my brothers, Kristin, that I sent them my greetings and that they should tend to this matter with care. If you would take her back to Jørundgaard for a while, I would be most grateful, as I lie in my grave. And if Ramborg should remarry before Arngjerd's place is assured, then you must take her in, Kristin. You mustn't think that Ramborg has been anything but kind toward her, but if she should end up with both a stepmother and a stepfather, I'm afraid she would be regarded more as a servant girl than a . . . You remember that I was married to Halfrid when I became her father."

Kristin gently placed her hand on top of Simon's and promised she would do all she could for the maiden. She remembered everything she had seen of how difficult they were situated, those children who had a nobleman for a father and were conceived in adultery. Orm and Margret and Ulf Haldorssøn. She stroked Simon's hand over and over.

"It's not certain that you will die this time, you know, brother-in-law," she said with a little smile. A glimmer of the sweet and tender smile of a maiden could still pass over her thin, stern woman's face. You sweet, young Kristin.

Simon's fever was not as high that evening, and he said the pain was less. When Kristin changed the bandage on his arm, it was not as swollen, but his skin was darker, and when she cautiously pressed it, the marks from her fingers stayed for a moment.

Kristin sent the servants off to bed. She allowed Jon Daalk, who insisted on keeping watch over his master, to lie down on a bench in the room. She moved the chest with the carved back over next to the bed and sat down, leaning against the corner. Simon dozed and slept. Once when he woke up, he noticed that she had found a spindle. She was sitting erect, having stuck the distaff with the wool under her left arm, and her fingers were twining the yarn as the spindle dropped lower and lower beside her long, slender lap. Then she rolled up the yarn and began spinning again as the spindle dropped. He fell asleep watching her.

When he awoke again, toward morning, she was sitting in the same position, spinning. The light from the candle, which she had placed so the bed hangings would shield him, fell directly on her face. It was so pale and still. Her full, soft lips were narrow and pressed tight; she was sitting with her eyes lowered as she spun. She couldn't see that he was lying awake and staring at her in the shadow of the bed hangings. She looked so full of despair that Simon felt as if his heart were bleeding inside him as he lay there looking at her.

She stood up and went over to tend the fire. Without a sound. When she came back, she peeked behind the bed hangings and met his open eyes in the dark.

"How are you feeling now, Simon?" she asked gently.

"I feel fine . . . now."

But he seemed to notice that it felt tender under his left arm too, and under his chin when he moved his head. No, it must be just something he imagined.

Oh, she would never think that she had lost anything by rejecting his love; for that matter, he might as well tell her about it. It wasn't possible for *that* to make her any more melancholy. He wanted to say it to her before he died—at least once: I have loved you all these years.

His fever rose again. And his left arm was hurting after all.

"You must try to sleep some more, Simon. Perhaps you will soon feel better," she said softly.

"I've slept a great deal tonight." He began talking about his children again: the three he had and loved so dearly and the one who was still unborn. Then he fell silent; the pain returned much worse. "Lie down for a while, Kristin. Surely Jon can sit with me for a time if you think it necessary for someone to keep watch."

In the morning, when she took off the bandage, Simon replied calmly to her desperate expression: "Oh no, Kristin, there was already too much festering and poison in my arm, and I was chilled through before I came into your hands. I told you that I didn't think you could heal me. Don't be so sad about it, Kristin."

"You shouldn't have made such a long journey," she said faintly.

"No man lives longer than he is meant to live," replied Simon in the same voice. "I wanted to come home. There are things we must discuss: how everything is to be arranged after I'm gone."

He chuckled. "All fires burn out sooner or later."

Kristin gazed at him, her eyes shiny with tears. He had always had so many proverbs on his lips. She looked down at his flushed red face. The heavy cheeks and the folds under his chin seemed to have sunk, lying in deep furrows. His eyes seemed both dull and glistening, but then clarity and intent returned to them. He looked up at her with the steady, searching glance that had been the most constant expression in his small, sharp, steel-gray eyes.

When daylight filled the room, Kristin saw that Simon's face had grown pinched around the nose. A white streak stretched downward on either side to the corners of his mouth.

She walked over to the little glass-paned window and stood there, swallowing her tears. A golden-green light sparkled and gleamed in the thick coating of frost on the window. Outside, it was no doubt as beautiful a day as the whole week had been.

It was the mark of death. . . . She knew that.

She went back and slid her hand under the coverlet. His ankles were swollen all the way up to his calves.

"Do you want me—do you want me to send for Sira Eirik now?" she asked in a low voice.

"Yes, tonight," replied Simon.

He had to speak of it *before* he confessed and received the last rites. Afterward he must try to turn his thoughts in another direction.

"It's odd that you should be the one who will probably have to tend to my body," said Simon. "And I'm afraid I won't be a particularly handsome corpse."

Kristin forced back a sob. She moved away to prepare another soothing potion.

But Simon said, "I don't like these potions of yours, Kristin. They make my thoughts so muddled."

After a while he asked her to give him a little all the same. "But don't put so much in it that it will make me drowsy. I have to talk to you about something."

He took a sip and then lay waiting for the pain to ease enough that he would have the strength to talk to her clearly and calmly.

"Don't you want us to bring Sira Eirik to you, so he can speak the words that might give you comfort?"

"Yes, soon. But there is something I must say to you first."

He lay in silence for a while. Then he said, "Tell Erlend Nikulaussøn that the words I spoke to him the last time we parted—those words I have regretted every day since. I behaved in a petty and unmanly fashion toward my brother-in-law that night. Give him my greetings and tell him . . . beg him to forgive me."

Kristin sat with her head bowed. Simon saw that she had turned blood red under her wimple.

"You will give this message to your husband, won't you?" he asked.

She gave a small nod.

Then Simon went on. "If Erlend doesn't come to my funeral, you must seek him out, Kristin, and tell him this."

Kristin sat mutely, her face dark red.

"You wouldn't refuse to do what I ask of you, now that I'm about to die, would you?" asked Simon Andressøn.

"No," she whispered. "I will . . . do it."

"It's not good for your sons, Kristin, that there is enmity between their father and mother," Simon continued. "I wonder whether you've noticed how much it torments them. It's hard for those lively boys, knowing that their parents are the subject of gossip in the countryside."

Kristin replied in a harsh, low voice, "Erlend left our sons—not I. First my sons lost their foothold in the regions where they were born into noble lineage and property. If they now have to bear having gossip spread about them here in the valley, which is my home, I am not to blame."

Simon lay in silence for a moment. Then he said, "I haven't forgotten that, Kristin. There is much you have a right to complain about. Erlend has managed poorly for his children. But you must remember, if that plan of his had been carried out, his sons would now be well provided for, and he himself would be among the most powerful knights in the realm. The man who fails in such a venture is called a traitor to his king, but if he succeeds, people speak quite differently. Half of Norway thought as Erlend did back then: that we were poorly served by sharing a king with the Swedes and that the son of Knut Porse was probably made of stronger stuff than that coddled boy, if we could have won over Prince Haakon in his tender years. Many men stood behind Erlend at the time and tugged on the rope along with him; my own brothers did so, and many others who are now called good knights and men with coats of arms. Erlend alone had to fall. And back then, Kristin, your husband showed that he was a splendid and courageous man, even though he may have acted otherwise, both before and since."

Kristin sat in silence, trembling.

"I think, Kristin, that if this is the reason you've said bitter words to your husband, then you must take them back. You should be able to do it, Kristin. Once you held firmly enough to Erlend; you refused to listen to a word of truth about his behavior toward you when he acted in a way I never thought an honorable man would act, much less a highborn gentleman and a chivalrous retainer of the king. Do you remember where I found the two of you in Oslo? You could forgive Erlend for *that,* both at the time and later on."

Kristin replied quietly, "I had cast my lot with his by then. What would have become of me afterward if I had parted my life from Erlend's?"

"Look at me, Kristin," said Simon Darre, "and answer me truthfully. If I had held your father to his promise and chosen to take you as you were . . . If I had told you that I would never remind you of your shame, but I would not release you . . . What would you have done then?"

"I don't know."

Simon laughed harshly. "If I had forced you to celebrate a wedding with me, you would never have taken me willingly into your arms, Kristin, my fair one."

Now her face turned white. She sat with her eyes lowered and did not reply.

He laughed again. "I don't think you would have embraced me tenderly when I climbed into your bridal bed."

"I think I would have taken my knife to bed with me," she whispered in a stifled voice.

"I see you know the ballad about Knut of Borg," said Simon with a bitter smile. "I haven't heard that such a thing ever happened, but God only knows whether *you* might have done it!"

Some time later he went on, "It's also unheard of among Christian people for married folks to part ways of their own free will, as you two have done, without lawful cause and the consent of the bishop. Aren't you ashamed? You trampled on everyone, defied everyone in order to be together. When Erlend was in mortal danger, you thought of nothing but how to save him, and he thought much more about you than about his seven sons or his reputation and property. But whenever you can have each other in peace and security, you're no longer capable of maintaining calm and decency. Discord and discontent reigned between you at Husaby too—I saw it myself, Kristin.

"I tell you, for the sake of your sons, that you must seek reconciliation with your husband. If you are even the slightest bit at fault, then surely it's easier for you to offer Erlend your hand," he said in a somewhat gentler tone.

"It's easier for you than for Erlend Nikulaussøn, sitting up there at Haugen in poverty," he repeated.

"It's not easy for me," she whispered. "I think I've shown that I can do something for my children. I've struggled and struggled for them. . . ."

"That is true," said Simon. Then he asked, "Do you remember that day when we met on the road to Nidaros? You were sitting in the grass, nursing Naakkve."

Kristin nodded.

"Could you have done for that child at your breast what my sister did for her son? Given him away to those who were better able to provide for him?"

Kristin shook her head.

"But ask his father to forget what you may have said to him in anger . . . Do you mean that you're unable to do that for him and your six other fair sons? To tell your husband that the young lads need him to come home to them, to his own manor?"

"I will do as you ask, Simon," said Kristin softly. After a moment she continued, "You have used harsh words to tell me this.

In the past you've also chastised me more sternly than any other man has."

"Yes, but now I can assure this will be the last time." His voice had that teasing, merry ring to it that it used to have. "No, don't weep like that, Kristin. But remember, my sister, that you have made this promise to a dying man." Once again the old, mirthful glint came into his eyes.

"You know, Kristin . . . it's happened to me before that I learned you weren't to be counted on!

"Hush now, my dear," he implored a little later. He had been lying there listening to her piteous, broken sobs. "You should know that I remember you were also a good and loyal sister. We will remain friends to the end, my Kristin."

Toward evening he asked them to send for the priest. Sira Eirik came, heard his confession, and gave him the last oil and viaticum. He took leave of his servants and the sons of Erlend, the five who were home; Kristin had sent Naakkve to Kruke. Simon had asked to see Kristin's children, to bid them farewell.

On that night Kristin again kept vigil over the dying man. Toward morning she dozed off for a moment. She woke up to a strange sound; Simon lay there, moaning softly. It distressed her greatly when she heard this—that *he* should complain, as quietly and pitifully as a miserable, abandoned child, when he thought no one would hear him. She leaned down and kissed his face many times. She noticed that his breath and his whole body smelled sickly and of death. But when daylight came, she saw that his eyes were lively and clear and steadfast.

She could see that he suffered terrible pain when Jon and Sigurd lifted him up in a sheet while she changed his bed, making it as soft and comfortable as she could. He had refused any food for more than a day, but he was very thirsty.

After she had gotten him settled, he asked her to make the sign of the cross over him, saying, "Now I can't move my left arm anymore either."

But whenever we make the sign of the cross over ourselves or over anything that we want to protect with the cross, then we must remember how the cross was made sacred and what it means, and remember that with the suffering and death of the Lord, this symbol was given honor and power.

Simon remembered that he had once heard this read aloud. He wasn't used to thinking about much when he made the sign of the cross over his breast or his houses or possessions. He felt ill prepared and not ready to take leave of this earthly home; he had to console himself that he had prepared himself as best he could in the time he had, through confession, and he had been given the last rites. Ramborg . . . But she was so young; perhaps she would be much happier with a different man. His children . . . May God protect them. And Gyrd would look out for their welfare with loyalty and wisdom. And so he would have to put his trust in God, who judges a man not according to his worth but through His mercy.

Later that day Sigrid Andresdatter and Geirmund of Kruke arrived. Simon then asked Kristin to leave and take some rest, now that she had been keeping watch and tending to him for such a long time. "And soon it will be quite vexing to be around me," he said with a little smile. At that she broke into loud sobs for a moment; then she leaned down and once again kissed his wretched body, which was already starting to decay.

Simon lay in bed quietly. The fever and pain were now much less. He lay there thinking that it couldn't be much longer before he would be released.

He was surprised that he had spoken to Kristin as he had. It was not what he had intended to say to her. But he had not been able to speak of anything else. There were moments when he felt almost annoyed by this.

But surely the festering would soon reach his heart. A man's heart is the first thing to come alive in his mother's womb and the last thing to fall silent. Surely it would soon fall silent inside him.

That night his mind rambled. Several times he screamed loudly, and it was terrible to hear. Other times he lay there, laughing softly and saying his own name, or so Kristin thought. But Sigrid, who sat bending over him, whispered to her that he seemed to be talking about a boy, their cousin, who had been his good friend when they were children. Around midnight he grew calm and seemed to sleep. Then Sigrid persuaded Kristin to lie down for a while in the other bed in the room.

She was awakened by a commotion in the room. It was shortly

before daybreak, and then she heard that the death struggle had begun. Simon had lost his voice, but he still recognized her; she could tell by his eyes. Then it was as if a piece of steel had broken inside them; they rolled up under his eyelids. But for a moment he lay there, still alive, a rattling sound in his throat. The priest had come, and he said the prayers for the dying. The two women sat next to the bed and the entire household was in the room. Just before midday Simon finally breathed his last.

The next day Gyrd Darre came riding into the courtyard at Formo. He had ridden a horse to exhaustion along the way. Down at Breiden he had learned of his brother's death, so at first he seemed quite composed. But when his sister, weeping, threw her arms around his neck, he pulled her close and began to sob like a child himself.

He told them that Ramborg Lavransdatter was at Dyfrin with a newborn son. When Gaute Erlendssøn brought them the message, she had shrieked at once that she knew this would be the death of Simon. Then she fell to the floor with birth pains. The child was born six weeks early, but they hoped he would live.

A magnificent funeral feast was held in Simon Andressøn's honor, and he was buried right next to the cross at the Olav Church. People in the parish were pleased that he had chosen his resting place there. The ancient Formo lineage, which had died out with Simon Sæmundssøn on the male side, had been mighty and grand. Astrid Simonsdatter had made a wealthy marriage; her sons had borne the title of knight and sat on the royal Council, but they had seldom come home to their mother's ancestral manor. When her grandson decided to settle on the estate, people thought it was almost as if the old lineage had been revived. They soon forgot to think of Simon Andressøn as a stranger, and they felt great sorrow that he had died so young, for he was only forty-two winters old.

## CHAPTER 5

WEEK AFTER WEEK passed, and Kristin prepared herself in her heart to take the dead man's message to Erlend. There was no doubt that she would do it, but it seemed to her a difficult task. In the meantime so much had to be done at home on the estates. She went about arguing with herself about postponing it.

At Whitsuntide, Ramborg Lavransdatter arrived at Formo. She had left her children behind at Dyfrin. They were well, she said when Kristin asked about them. The two maidens had wept bitterly and mourned their father. Andres was too young to understand. The youngest, Simon Simonssøn, was thriving, and they hoped he would grow up to be big and strong.

Ramborg went to church to visit her husband's grave a couple of times; otherwise she never left her manor. But Kristin went south to see her as often as she could. She now sincerely wished that she had known her sister better. The widow looked like such a child in her mourning garb. Her body seemed fragile and only half grown in the heavy, dark blue gown; the little triangle of her face was yellow and thin, framed by the linen bands beneath the black woolen veil, which fell in stiff folds from the crown of her head almost to the hem of her skirts. And she had dark circles under her big eyes, the coal-black pupils wide and always staring.

During the hay harvest there was a week's time when Kristin couldn't get away to see her sister. From the harvesters she heard that a guest was visiting Ramborg at Formo: Jammælt Halvardssøn. Kristin remembered that Simon had mentioned this man; he owned an exceedingly large estate not far from Dyfrin, and he and Simon had been friends since childhood.

A week into the harvest the rains came. Then Kristin rode over to see her sister. Kristin sat talking about the terrible weather and about the hay and then asked how things were going at Formo.

All of a sudden Ramborg said, "Jon will have to manage things here; I'm heading south in a few days, Kristin."

"Yes, you must be longing for your children, poor dear," said Kristin.

Ramborg stood up and paced the floor.

"I'm going to tell you something that will surprise you," the young woman said after a moment. "You and your sons will soon be invited to a betrothal feast at Dyfrin. I said yes to Jammælt before he left here, and Gyrd will hold the wedding."

Kristin sat without saying a word. Her sister stood staring at her, pale and dark-eyed.

Finally the older sister spoke, "I see that you won't be left a widow for very long after Simon's death. I thought you mourned him so grievously. But you can make your own decisions now."

Ramborg did not reply. After a moment Kristin asked, "Does Gyrd Darre know that you intend to marry again so soon?"

"Yes." Ramborg began pacing again. "Helga advises me to do so. Jammælt is rich." She laughed. "And Gyrd is such a clever man that he must have seen long ago that our life was so wretched together, Simon's and mine."

"What are you saying! No one else has ever noticed that your life together was wretched," Kristin said after a pause. "I don't think anyone has ever seen anything but friendship and goodwill between the two of you. Simon indulged you in every way, gave you everything you wished for, always kept in mind your youth, and took care that you should enjoy it and be spared toil and travail. He loved his children and showed you every day that he was grateful to you for giving birth to the two of them."

Ramborg smiled scornfully.

Kristin continued fiercely, "If you have any cause to think that your life wasn't good together, then surely Simon is not to blame."

"No," said Ramborg. "I will bear the blame—if *you* do not dare."

Kristin sat there, dumbfounded.

"I don't think you know what you're saying, sister," she replied at last.

"Yes, I do," said Ramborg. "But I can believe that *you* might not know. You've had so little thought for Simon that I'm convinced this may be new to you. You considered him good enough to turn to whenever you needed a helper who would gladly have carried red-hot iron for your sake. But never did you give any thought to Simon Andressøn or ask what it might have cost him. I was allowed to enjoy my youth, yes. With joy and gentleness Simon would lift me up into the saddle and send me off to feasts and merriment; with equal joy and gentleness he would welcome me when I came back home. He would pat me the way he patted his dog or his horse. He never missed me while I was gone."

Kristin was on her feet; she stood quietly next to the table. Ramborg was wringing her hands so the knuckles cracked, pacing back and forth in the room.

"Jammælt . . ." she said in a calmer voice. "I've known for years how he thought of me. I saw it even while his wife was still alive. Not that he ever gave himself away in word or deed—you mustn't think that! He grieved for Simon too and came to me often to console me—that much is true. It was Helga who said to both of us that now it would be fitting if we . . .

"And I don't know what I should wait for. I will never find more consolation or any less than I feel right now. I want to try living with a man who has been silently thinking of *me* for years on end. I know all too well what it feels like to live with a man who is silently thinking about someone else."

Kristin didn't move. Ramborg stopped in front of her, with her eyes flashing. "You know what I say is true!"

Kristin left the room without a word, her head bowed. As she stood in the rain outside in the courtyard, waiting for the servant to bring her horse, Ramborg appeared in the doorway. She stared at her sister with dark and hateful eyes.

Not until the next day did Kristin remember what she had promised Simon if Ramborg should marry again. She rode back to Formo. This was not an easy thing for her to do. And the worst of it was that she knew there was nothing she could say that would give her sister any help or solace. This marriage to Jammælt of Ælin seemed to her a rash decision when Ramborg was in such a state of mind. But Kristin realized that it would do no good for her to object.

Ramborg was sullen and morose and answered her sister curtly. Under no circumstances would she allow her stepdaughter to go to

Jørundgaard. "Things at your estate are not such that I would think it advisable to send a young maiden over there." Kristin replied meekly that Ramborg might be right about that, but she had promised Simon to make the offer.

"If Simon, in his feverish daze, didn't realize that he was offending me when he made this request of you, then surely you should realize that you offend me by mentioning it," said Ramborg, and Kristin had to return home without accomplishing her goal.

The next morning promised good weather. But when her sons came in for breakfast, Kristin told them they would have to bring in the hay without her. She had a mind to set off on a journey, and she might be gone several days.

"I'm thinking of going north to Dovre to find your father," she said. "I intend to ask him to forget the discord that has existed between the two of us, to ask him when he will come home to us."

Her sons blushed; they didn't dare look up, but she could tell they were glad. She pulled Munan into her arms and bent her face down to look at him. "You probably don't even remember your father, do you, little one?"

The boy nodded mutely with sparkling eyes. One by one the other sons cast a glance at their mother. Her face looked younger and more beautiful than they had seen it in many years.

She came out to the courtyard some time later, dressed for travel in her church attire: a black woolen gown trimmed with blue and silver at the neck and sleeves and a black, sleeveless hooded cloak since it was high summer. Naakkve and Gaute had saddled her horse as well as their own; they wanted to go with their mother. She didn't voice any objections. But she said little to her sons as they rode north across Rost Gorge and up toward Dovre. For the most part she was silent and preoccupied; if she spoke to the young lads, it was about other things, not about where they were going.

When they had gone so far that they could look up the slope and glimpse the rooftops of Haugen against the horizon, she asked the boys to turn back.

"You know full well that your father and I have much to talk about, and we would rather discuss things while we're alone."

The brothers nodded; they said goodbye to their mother and turned their horses around.

The wind from the mountains blew cool and fresh against her hot cheeks as she came over the last sharp rise. The sun gilded the small gray buildings, which cast long shadows across the courtyard. The grain was just about to form ears up there; it stood so lovely in the small fields, glistening and swaying in the wind. Tall crimson fireweed in bloom fluttered from all the heaps of stones and up on the crags; here and there the hay had been piled up in stacks. But there wasn't a trace of life on the farm—not even a dog to greet her or give warning.

Kristin unsaddled her horse and led it over to the water trough. She didn't want to let it roam loose, so she took it over to the stable. The sun shone through a big hole in the roof; the sod hung in strips between the beams. And there was no sign that a horse had stood there for quite some time. Kristin tended to the animal and then went back out to the courtyard.

She looked in the cowshed. It was dark and desolate; she could tell by the smell that it must have stood empty for a long time.

Several animal hides were stretched out to dry on the wall of the house; a swarm of blue flies buzzed up into the air as she approached. Near the north gable, earth had been piled up and sod spread over it, so the timbers were completely hidden. He must have done that to keep in the heat.

She fully expected the house to be locked, but the door opened when she touched the handle. Erlend hadn't even latched the door to his dwelling.

An unbearable stench met her as she stepped inside: the rank and pungent smell of hides and a stable. The first feeling that came over her as she stood in his house was a deep remorse and pity. This place seemed to her more like an animal's lair.

Oh yes, yes, yes, Simon—you were right!

It was a small house, but it had been beautifully and carefully built. The fireplace even had a brick chimney so that it wouldn't fill the room with smoke, as the hearths did in the high loft room back home. But when she tried to open the damper to air out the foul smell a bit, she saw that the chimney had been closed off with several flat rocks. The glass pane in the window facing the gallery was broken and stuffed with rags. The room had a wooden floor, but it was so filthy that the floorboards were barely visible. There were no cushions on the benches, but weapons, hides, and old clothing were strewn about everywhere. Scraps of food littered the dirty table. And the flies buzzed high and low.

She gave a start and stood there trembling, unable to breathe, her heart pounding. In that bed over there, in the bed where that *thing* had lain when she was here last . . . Something was lying there now, covered with a length of homespun. She wasn't sure what she thought. . . .

Then she clenched her teeth and forced herself to go over and lift up the cloth. It was only Erlend's armor, with his helmet and shield. They were lying on the bare boards of the bed, covered up.

She glanced at the other bed. That's where they had found Bjørn and Aashild. That's where Erlend now slept. No doubt she too would sleep there in the night.

How must it have been for him to live in this house, to sleep here? Once again all her other feelings were drowned in pity. She went over to the bed; it hadn't been cleaned in a long time. The straw under the hide sheet had been pressed down until it was quite hard. There was nothing else but a few sheepskin blankets and a couple of pillows covered with homespun, so filthy that they stank. Dust and dirt scattered as she touched the bedding. Erlend's bed was no better than that of a stableboy in a stall.

Erlend, who could never have enough splendor around him. Erlend, who would put on silk shirts, velvet, and fine furs if he could find the slightest excuse to do so; who resented having to let his children wear handwoven homespun on workdays; and who had never liked it when she nursed them herself or lent her maids a hand with the housework—like a leaseholder's wife, he said.

Jesus, but he had brought this upon himself.

No, I won't say a word. I will take back everything I said, Simon. You were right. He must not stay here . . . the father of my sons. I will offer him my hand and my lips and ask his forgiveness.

This isn't easy, Simon. But you were right. She remembered his sharp gray eyes, his gaze just as steadfast, almost to the very end. In that wretched body which had begun to decay, his pure, bright spirit had shone from his eyes until his soul was drawn home, the way a blade is pulled back. She knew it was as Ramborg had said. He had loved her all these years.

Every single day in the months since his death she couldn't help thinking about him, and now she saw that she had realized it even before Ramborg spoke. During this time she had been forced to mull over all the memories she had of him, for as far back as she had known Simon Darre. In all these years she had carried false memories of this man who had once been her betrothed; she had tampered with these memories the way a corrupt ruler tampers with the coin and mixes impure ore with the silver. When he released her and took upon himself the blame for the breach of promise, she told herself, and believed it, that Simon Andressøn had turned away from her with contempt as soon as he realized that her honor had been disgraced. She had forgotten that when he let her go, on that day in the nuns' garden, he was certainly not thinking that she was no longer innocent or pure. Even back then he was willing to bear the shame for her inconstant and disobedient disposition; all he asked was that her father should be told that he was not the one who sought to break the agreement.

And there was something else she now knew. When he had learned the worst about her, he stood up to redeem for her a scrap of honor in the eyes of the world. If she could have given her heart to him then, Simon would have still taken her as his wife before the church door, and he would have tried to live with her so she would never feel that he concealed a memory of her shame.

But she still knew that she could never have loved him. She could never have loved Simon Andressøn. And yet . . . Everything that had enraged her about Erlend because he didn't have particular traits—those were the traits that Simon did possess. But she was a pitiful woman who couldn't help complaining.

Simon had given selflessly to the one he loved; no doubt she had believed that she did the same.

But when she received his gifts, without thought or thanks, Simon had merely smiled. Now she realized that he had often been melancholy when they were together. She now knew that he had concealed sorrow behind his strangely impassive demeanor. Then he would toss out some impertinent jest and push it aside, as ready as ever to protect and to help and to give.

She herself had raged, storing away and brooding over every grief, whenever she offered her gifts and Erlend paid them no mind.

Here, in this very room, she had stood and pronounced such bold words: "I was the one who took the wrong path, and I won't complain about Erlend even if it leads me out over the scree." That was what she had said to the woman whom she drove to her death in order to make room for her own love.

Kristin moaned aloud, clasped her hands before her breast, and stood there, rocking back and forth. Yes, she had said so proudly that she would not complain about Erlend Nikulaussøn if he grew tired of her, betrayed her, or even left her.

Yes, but if *that* was what Erlend had done . . . She thought she *would* have been able to stand it. If he had betrayed her once, and that had been the end of it. But he hadn't betrayed her; he had merely failed her again and again and made her life full of anguish and uncertainty. No, he had never betrayed her, nor had he ever made her feel secure. And she could see no end to it all. Here she stood now, about to beg him to come back, to fill her goblet each day with uncertainty and unrest, with expectations, with longings and fear and hope that would be shattered.

She felt now as if he had worn her out. She had neither the youth nor the courage to live with him any longer, and she would probably never grow so old that Erlend couldn't play with her heart. Not young enough to have the strength to live with him; not old enough to have patience with him. She had become a miserable woman; no doubt that was what she had always been. Simon was right.

Simon . . . and her father. They had held on to their loyal love for her, even as she trampled on them for the sake of this man whom she no longer had the strength to endure.

Oh, Simon. I know that never for a minute did you wish vengeance upon me. But I wonder, Simon, if you know in your grave, that now you have been avenged after all.

No, she couldn't bear it any longer; she would have to find something to do. She made up the bed and looked for a dishrag and broom, but they were not to be found anywhere. She glanced into the alcove; now she understood why it smelled like a stable. Erlend had made a stall for his horse in there. But it had been mucked out and cleaned. His saddle and harness, which hung on the wall, were well cared for and oiled, with all the torn pieces mended.

Compassion once more washed away all other thoughts. Did he keep Soten inside because he couldn't bear to be alone in the house?

Kristin heard a sound out on the gallery. She stepped over to the window. It was covered with dust and cobwebs, but she thought she caught a glimpse of a woman. She pulled the rag from the hole and peeked out. A woman was setting down a pail of milk and a small cheese out there. She was middle-aged and lame and wore ugly, tattered clothes. Kristin herself was hardly aware of how much easier she breathed.

She tidied up the room as best she could. She found the inscription that Bjørn Gunnarssøn had carved into a timber of the wall. It was in Latin, so she couldn't decipher the whole thing, but he called himself both *Dominus* and *Miles*, and she read the name of his ancestral estate in Elve County, which he had lost because of Aashild Gautesdatter. In the midst of the splendid carvings on the high seat was his coat of arms with its unicorn and water lilies.

A short time later Kristin heard a horse somewhere outside. She went over to the entryway and peered out.

From the leafy forest across from the farm a tall black stallion emerged, pulling a load of firewood. Erlend walked alongside to guide him. A dog was perched on top of the wood, and several more dogs were running around the sled.

Soten, the Castilian, strained against the harness and pulled the sledful of wood across the grassy courtyard. One of the dogs began barking as it crossed the green. Erlend, who had begun to unfasten the harnesses, noticed from all the dogs that something must be wrong. He took his axe from the load of wood and walked toward the house.

Kristin fled back inside, letting the door fall shut behind her. She crept over to the fireplace and stood there, trembling and waiting.

Erlend stepped inside with his axe in hand and the dogs milling around him on the threshold. They found the intruder at once and began barking furiously.

The first thing she noticed was the rush of blood that flooded his face, so youthful and red. The quick tremor on his fine, soft lips, and his big, deep-set eyes beneath the shadow of his brows.

The sight of him took her breath away. No doubt she saw the old stubble of beard on the lower half of his face, and she saw that his disheveled hair was iron gray. But the color that came and went so swiftly in his cheeks, the way it had when they were young . . . He was just as young and handsome; it was as if nothing had been able to break him.

He was poorly clad. His blue shirt was filthy and tattered; over it he wore a leather vest, scratched and scraped and torn around the eyelets, but it fit snugly and followed pliantly the graceful, strong movements of his body. His tight leather hose was torn at one knee, and the seam was split on the back of the other leg. And yet he had never looked more like the descendant of chieftains and noblemen than he did now. With such calm dignity he carried his slender body with the wide, rather sloping shoulders and the long, elegant limbs. He stood there, his weight resting slightly on one foot, one hand stuck in the belt around his slim waist, the other holding the axe at his side.

He had called the dogs back, and now he stood staring at her, turning red and pale and not saying a word. For a good long time they both were silent. Finally the man spoke, his voice a little uncertain. "So you've come here, Kristin?"

"I wanted to see how you were doing up here," she replied.

"Well, now you've seen it." He glanced around the room. "You can see that I'm tolerably comfortable here; it's good that you happened to come by on a day when everything was tidied up so nicely." He noticed the shadow of a smile on her face. "Or perhaps you're the one who has been cleaning up," he said, laughing softly.

Erlend put down his axe and sat on the outer bench with his back leaning against the table. All of a sudden he grew somber. "You're standing there so . . . there's nothing wrong back home, is there? At Jørundgaard, I mean? With the boys?"

"No." Now she had the chance to present her purpose. "Our sons are thriving and show great promise. But they long so much for you, Erlend. It was my intention . . . I've come here, husband, to ask you to return home to us. We all miss you." She lowered her eyes.

"You look well, Kristin." Erlend gazed at her with a little smile.

Kristin stood there, red-faced, as if he had struck a blow to her ear.

"That's not why—"

"No, I know it's not because you think you're too young and fresh to be left a widow," Erlend said when she broke off. "I don't think any good would come of it if I returned home, Kristin," he added in a more serious tone. "In your hands everything is flourishing at Jørundgaard; I know that. You have good fortune with all your undertakings. And I am quite content with my situation here."

"The boys aren't happy that we . . . are quarreling," she replied softly.

"Oh . . ." Erlend hesitated. "They're so young. I don't think they take it so hard that they won't forget about it when it's time for them to leave their childhood behind. I might as well tell you," he added with a little smile, "that I see them from time to time."

She knew about this, but she felt humiliated by his words, and it seemed as if that was his intention, since he thought she didn't know. Her sons had never realized that she knew. But she replied somberly, "Then you also know that many things at Jørundgaard are not as they should be."

"We never talk about such matters," he said with the same smile. "We go hunting together. But you must be hungry and thirsty." He jumped up. "And here you stand . . . No, sit down in the high seat, Kristin. Yes, sit there, my dear. I won't crowd in next to you."

He brought in the milk and cheese and found some bread, butter, and dried meat. Kristin was hungry and quite thirsty, but she had trouble swallowing her food. Erlend ate in a hasty and careless manner, as had always been his custom when not among guests, and he was soon finished.

He talked about himself. The people who lived at the foot of the hill worked his land and brought him milk and a little food; otherwise he went into the mountains to hunt and fish. But then he mentioned that he was actually thinking about leaving the country, to seek service with some foreign warlord.

"Oh no, Erlend!"

He gave her a swift, searching glance. But she said no more. The light was growing dim in the room. Her face and wimple shone white against the dark wall. Erlend stood up and stoked the fire in the hearth. Then he straddled the outer bench and turned to face her; the red glow of the fire flickered over his body.

To think that he would even consider such a thing. He was almost as old as her father had been when he died. But it was all too likely that he would do it one day: take off on some whim, in search of new adventures.

"Don't you think it's enough?" said his wife heatedly. "Enough that you fled the village, leaving me and your sons behind? Do you have to flee the country to leave us too?"

"If I'd known what you thought of me, Kristin," said Erlend gravely, "I would have left *your* estate much sooner! But I now see that you've had to bear a great deal because of me."

"You know quite well, Erlend . . . You say *my* estate, but you have the rights of a husband over all that is mine." She herself could hear how weak her voice sounded.

"Yes," replied Erlend. "But I know I was a poor master over what I owned myself." He fell silent for a moment. "Naakkve . . . I remember the time before he was born, and you spoke of the child you were carrying, who would take my high seat after me. I now see, Kristin, that it was hard for you. It's best if things stay as they are. And I'm content with my life up here."

Kristin shuddered as she glanced around at the room in the fading light. Shadows now filled every cranny, and the glow from the flames danced.

"I don't understand," she said, on the verge of collapse, "how you can bear this house. You have nothing to occupy your time, and you're all alone. I think you could at least take on a workman."

"You mean that I should run the farm myself?" Erlend laughed. "Oh no, Kristin, you know I'm ill suited to be a farmer. I can never sit still."

"Sit still . . . But surely you're sitting still here . . . during the long winter."

Erlend smiled to himself; his eyes had an odd, remote look to them.

"Yes, in some sense you're right. When I don't have to think about anything but whatever happens to cross my mind and can come and go as I like. And you know that I've always been the kind of person who can fall asleep if there's nothing to keep watch over; I sleep like a hibernating bear whenever the weather isn't good enough to go into the mountains."

"Aren't you ever afraid to be here alone?" whispered Kristin.

At first he gave her a look of incomprehension. Then he laughed. "Because people say this place is haunted? I've never noticed anything. Sometimes I've wished that my kinsman Bjørn would pay me a visit. Do you remember that he once said he didn't think I'd be able to stand to feel the edge of a blade at my throat? I'd like to tell him now that I wasn't particularly frightened when I had the rope around my neck."

A long shiver rippled through Kristin's body. She sat without saying a word.

Erlend stood up. "It must be time for us to go to bed now, Kristin."

Stiff and cold, she watched Erlend remove the coverlet from his armor, spread it over the bed, and tuck it around the dirty pillows. "This is the best I have," he said.

"Erlend!" She clasped her hands under her breast. She searched for something to say, to win a little more time; she was so frightened. Then she remembered the promise she had made.

"Erlend, I have a message to give you. Simon asked me, when he was near the end, to bring you his greetings. Every single day he regretted the words he spoke to you when you last parted. 'Unmanly' he called them, and he asked you to forgive him."

"Simon." Erlend was standing with one hand on the bedpost; he lowered his eyes. "He's the one man I would least like to be reminded of."

"I don't know what came between the two of you," said Kristin. She thought Erlend's words remarkably heartless. "But it would be strange, and unlike Simon, if things were as he said, that he did not treat you justly. Surely he wasn't entirely to blame if this is true."

Erlend shook his head. "He stood by me like a brother when I was in need," he said in a low voice. "And I accepted his help and his friendship, and I never realized that it had always been difficult for him to tolerate me.

"It seems to me that it would have been easier to live in the old days, when two fellows like us could have fought a duel, meeting out on the islet to let the test of weapons decide who would win the fair maiden."

He picked up an old cape from the bench and slung it over his arm.

"Perhaps you'd like to keep the dogs inside with you tonight?"

Kristin had stood up.

"Where are you going, Erlend?"

"Out to the barn to sleep."

"No!"

Erlend stopped, standing there slender and straight-backed and young in the red glow from the dying embers in the fireplace.

"I don't dare sleep alone in this room. I don't dare."

"Do you dare sleep in my arms then?" She caught a glimpse of his smile in the darkness, and she grew faint. "Aren't you afraid that I might crush you to death, Kristin?"

"If only you would." She fell into his arms.

When she woke up, she could see from the windowpane that it was daylight outdoors. Something was weighing down her breast; Erlend was sleeping with his head on her shoulder. He had placed his arm across her body and was gripping her left arm with his hand.

She looked at her husband's iron-gray hair. She looked at her own small, withered breasts. Above and below them she could see the high, curved arch of her ribs under the thin covering of skin. A kind of terror seized hold of her as one memory after another from the night before rose up. In this room . . . the two of them, at their age . . . Horror and shame overwhelmed her as she saw the patches of red on her worn mother arms, on her shriveled bosom. Abruptly she grabbed the blanket to cover herself.

Erlend awoke, raised himself up on one elbow, and stared down at her face. His eyes were coal-black after his slumber.

"I thought . . ." He threw himself down beside her again; a

deep, wild tremor rushed through her at the sound of joy and anguish in his voice. "I thought I was dreaming again."

She opened her lips to his mouth and wrapped her arms around his neck. Never, never had it felt so blessed.

Later that afternoon, when the sunshine was already golden and the shadows lay stretched out across the green courtyard, they set off to get water from the creek. Erlend was carrying the two large buckets. Kristin walked at his side, lithe, straight-backed, and slender. Her wimple had slipped back and lay around her shoulders; her uncovered hair was a gleaming brown in the sun. She could feel it herself as she closed her eyes and lifted her face to the light. Her cheeks had turned red; the features of her face had softened. Each time she glanced over at him she would lower her gaze, overwhelmed, when she saw in Erlend's face how young she was.

Erlend decided that he wanted to bathe. As he walked farther down, Kristin sat on the thick carpet of grass, leaning her back against a rock. The murmuring and gurgling of the mountain stream lulled her into a doze; now and then, when mosquitoes or flies touched her skin, she would open her eyes briefly and swat them away with her hand. Down among the willow thickets, near the deep pool, she caught sight of Erlend's white body. He was standing with one foot up on a rock, scrubbing himself with tufts of grass. Then she closed her eyes again and smiled, weary but happy. She was just as powerless against him as ever.

Her husband came back and threw himself down on the grass in front of her, his hair wet, his red lips cold from the water as he pressed them to her hand. He had shaved and put on a better shirt, although it was not particularly grand either. Laughing, he pointed to his armpit, where the fabric was torn.

"You could have brought me a shirt when you finally decided to come north."

"I'll start sewing a shirt for you as soon as I get home, Erlend," she replied with a smile, caressing his forehead with her hand.

He grabbed hold of it. "Never will you leave here again, my Kristin."

She merely smiled without replying. Erlend pushed himself away so that he could lie down on his stomach. Under the bushes, in a damp, shady spot, grew a cluster of small, white, star-shaped flowers. Their petals had blue veins like a woman's breast, and in the center of each blossom sat a tiny brownish-blue bud. Erlend picked every one of them.

"You who are so clever about such things, Kristin—surely you must know what these flowers are called."

"They're called Friggja grass. No, Erlend . . ." She blushed and pushed away his hand as he tried to slip the flowers into her bodice.

Erlend laughed and gently bit the white petals, one after the other. Then he put all the flowers into her open hands and closed her fingers around them.

"Do you remember when we walked in the garden at Hofvin Hospice, and you gave me a rose?"

Kristin slowly shook her head as she gave him a little smile. "No. But you took a rose from my hand."

"And you let me take it. Just as you let me take you, Kristin. As gentle and pious as a rose. Later on you sometimes scratched me bloody, my sweet." He flung himself into her lap and put his arms around her waist. "Last night, Kristin . . . it did no good. You weren't allowed to sit there demurely and wait."

Kristin bent her head and hid her face against his shoulder.

On the fourth day they had taken refuge up in the birch woods among the foothills across from the farm, for on that day the tenant was bringing in the hay. Without discussing it, Kristin and Erlend had agreed that no one needed to know that she was visiting him. He went down to the buildings a few times to get food and drink, but she stayed among the alpine birches, sitting in the heather. From where they sat, they could see the man and woman toiling to carry home the hay bundles on their backs.

"Do you remember," asked Erlend, "the time you promised me that if I ended up on a smallholder's farm in the mountains, you would come and keep house for me? You wanted to have two cows and some sheep."

Kristin laughed a little and tugged at his hair. "What do you think our boys would think about that, Erlend? If their mother ran away and left them behind in that manner?"

"I think they would be happy to manage Jørundgaard on their own," said Erlend, laughing. "They're old enough now. Gaute is a capable farmer, even as young as he is. And Naakkve is almost a man."

"Oh no . . ." Kristin laughed softly. "It's probably true that he thinks so himself. Well, no doubt all five of them do. But he's still lacking a man's wisdom, that boy."

"If he takes after his father, it's possible that he might acquire it late, or perhaps never at all," replied Erlend. He gave a sly smile. "You think you can hide your children under the hem of your cloak, Kristin. Naakkve fathered a son this summer—you didn't know about that, did you?"

"No!" Kristin sat there, red-faced and horror-stricken.

"Yes, it was stillborn, and the boy is apparently careful not to go over there anymore. It was the widow of Paal's son, here at Haugsbrekken. She said it was his, and I suppose he wasn't without blame, no matter how things stood. Yes, we're getting to be so old, you and I—"

"How can you talk that way after your son has brought upon himself such dishonor and trouble!" It pierced her heart that her husband could speak so nonchalantly and that it seemed to amuse him that she hadn't known anything about it.

"Well, what do you want me to say?" asked Erlend in the same tone of voice. "The boy is eighteen winters old. You can see for yourself that it does little good for you to treat your sons as if they were children. When you move up here with me, we'll have to see about finding him a wife."

"Do you think it will be easy for us to find a suitable match for Naakkve? No, husband, after this I think you must realize that you need to come back home with me and lend a hand with the boys."

Vehemently Erlend propped himself up on his elbow. "I won't do that, Kristin. I'm a stranger here and will always be one in your parish. No one remembers anything about me except that I was condemned as a traitor and betrayer of the king. Didn't you ever think, during the years I've lived here at Jørundgaard, that my presence was an uneasy one? Back home in Skaun I was accustomed to a position of some importance among the people. Even during those days in my youth, when gossip flew about my evil ways and I was banned from the Church, I was still Erlend Nikulaussøn of Husaby! Then came the time, Kristin, when I had the joy of showing the people of the northern regions that I was not entirely debased from the honor of my ancestors. No, I tell you! Here on this little farm I'm a free man; no one glares at my footprints or talks behind my back. Do you hear me, Kristin, my only love? Stay with me! You will never have cause to regret it. Life here is better than it ever was at Husaby. I don't know why it is, Kristin, but I've never been so happy or lighthearted—not as a child or ever since. It was hell while Eline lived with me at Husaby, and you and I were never truly happy together there either. And yet the Almighty God knows that I have loved you every hour and every day that I've known you. I think that manor was cursed; Mother was tormented to death there, and my father was always an unhappy man. But here life is good, Kristin—if only you would stay with me. Kristin . . . As truly as God died on the cross for us, I love you as much today as on that evening when you slept under my cape, the night of Saint Margareta's Day. I sat and looked at you, such a pure and fresh and young and untouched flower you were!"

Kristin said quietly, "Do you remember, Erlend, that you prayed on that night that I would never weep a single tear for your sake?"

"Yes, and God and all the saints in Heaven know that I meant it! It's true that things turned out differently—as surely they must. That's what always happens while we live in this world. But I loved you, both when I treated you badly and when I treated you well. Stay here, Kristin!"

"Haven't you ever thought that it would be difficult for our sons?" she asked in the same quiet voice. "To have people talk about their father, as you admit? All seven of them can't very well run off to the mountains to escape the parish gossip."

Erlend lowered his eyes. "They're young," he said. "Handsome and intrepid boys. They'll figure out how to make their own way. But the two of us, Kristin . . . We don't have many years left before we'll be old. Do you want to squander the time you have remaining when you are beautiful and healthy and meant to rejoice in life? Kristin?"

She looked down to avoid the wild glint in his eyes. After a moment she said, "Have you forgotten, Erlend, that two of our sons are still children? What would you think of me if I left Lavrans and Munan behind?"

"Then you can bring them up here, unless Lavrans would rather stay with his brothers. He's not a little boy anymore. Is Munan still so handsome?" he asked, smiling.

"Yes," said Kristin, "he's a lovely child."

Then they sat in silence for a long time. When they spoke again, it was of other matters.

She woke up in the gray light of dawn the next day, as she had every morning up there. She lay in bed listening to the horses plodding around outside the house. She had her arms wrapped around Erlend's head. The other mornings, when she woke up in the early gray hour, she had been seized by the same anguish and shame as the first time; she had fought to subdue those feelings. The two of them were a married couple who had quarreled and now reconciled; nothing could benefit the children more than that their father and mother became friends once again.

But on this morning she lay there, struggling to remember her sons. For she felt as if she had been bewitched; Erlend had spirited her away and brought her up here, straight from the woods of Gerdarud, where he had taken her into his arms the first time. They were so young; it couldn't be true that she had already borne this man seven sons. She was the mother of tall, grown-up men. But she felt as if she had been lying here in his arms and merely dreamed about those long years they had spent together as husband and wife at Husaby. All his impetuous words resounded and enticed her; dizzy with fear, she felt as if Erlend had swept away her sevenfold burden of responsibility. This is the way it must feel when the young mare is unsaddled up in the mountain pasture. The packs and saddle and bridle are removed, and the wind and air of the mountain plateau stream against her; she is free to graze the fine grass on the heights, free to run as far as she likes across all the slopes.

But at the same time she was already yearning, with a sweet and willing sense of longing, to bear a new burden. She was yearning with a faint, tender giddiness for the one who would now live nearest her heart for nine long months. She had been certain of it, from the first morning she woke up here in Erlend's arms. Her barrenness had left her, along with the harsh, dry, gasping heat in her heart. She was hiding Erlend's child in her womb, and with a strangely gentle feeling of impatience, her soul was reaching out toward the hour when the infant would be brought into the light.

My big sons no longer need me, she thought. They think I'm unreasonable, that I nag them. We'll just be in their way, the little child and I. No, I can't leave here; we must stay here with Erlend. I can't leave.

But when they sat down together to eat breakfast, she mentioned nevertheless that she would have to return home to her children.

It was Lavrans and Munan she was thinking of. They were old enough now that she was embarrassed to imagine them living up here with Erlend and herself, perhaps looking with astonishment at their parents who had become so youthful. But those two couldn't be without her.

Erlend sat and stared at her as she talked about going home. At last he gave her a fleeting smile. "Well . . . if that's what you want, then you must go."

He wanted to accompany her for part of the journey. He rode all the way through Rost Gorge and up to Sil, until they could see a little of the church roof above the tops of the spruce trees. Then he said goodbye. He smiled to the very end, slyly confident.

"You know now, Kristin, that whether you come at night or by day, whether I have to wait for you a short time or a long time, I will welcome you as if you were the Queen of Heaven come down from the clouds to my farm."

She laughed. "I don't dare speak as grandly as that. But you must now realize, my love, that there will be great joy at your manor on the day the master returns to his own home."

He shook his head and chuckled. Smiling, they took leave of each other; smiling, Erlend leaned over as they sat on their horses, side by side, and kissed her many times, and between each kiss, he looked at her with his laughing eyes.

"So we'll see," he said finally, "which of us is more stubborn, my fair Kristin. This is not the last time we will meet; you and I both know that!" As she rode past the church, she gave a little shudder. She felt as if she were returning home from inside the mountain. As if Erlend were the mountain king himself and could not come past the church and the cross on the hill.

She pulled in the reins; she had a great urge to turn around and ride after him.

Then she looked out across the green slopes, down at her beautiful estate with the meadows and fields and the glistening curve of the river winding through the valley. The mountains rose up in a blue shimmer of heat. The sky was filled with billowing summer clouds. It was madness. There, with his sons, was where he belonged. He was no mountain knight; he was a Christian man, no matter how full he was of wild ideas and foolish whims. Her lawful husband, with whom she had endured both good and bad—beloved, beloved, no matter how sorely he had tormented her with his unpredictable impulses. She would have to be forbearing, since she could not live without him; she would have to strive to bear the anguish and uncertainty as best she could. She didn't think it would be long before he followed her—now that they had been together once again.

## CHAPTER 6

SHE TOLD HER sons that their father had to take care of a few things at Haugen before he moved home. No doubt he would come south early in the fall.

She went about her estate, looking young, her cheeks flushed, her face soft and gentle, moving more quickly about her work, although she didn't manage to accomplish nearly as much as she used to with her usual quiet and measured manner. She no longer chastised her sons sharply, as had been her custom whenever they did something wrong or failed to satisfy her demands properly. Now she spoke to them in a jesting manner or let it pass without saying a word.

Lavrans now wanted to sleep with his older brothers up in the loft.

"Yes, I suppose you should be counted among the grown-up boys too, my son." She ran her fingers through the boy's thick, golden-brown hair and pulled him close; he was already so tall that he came up to the middle of her breast. "What about you, Munan? Can you stand to have your mother treat you as a child for a while longer?" In the evenings, after the boy had gone to bed in the main room, he liked to have his mother sit on the bed and pamper him a bit. He would lie there with his head in her lap, chattering more childishly than he allowed himself to do during the day when his brothers could hear him. They would talk about when his father was coming home.

Then he would move over next to the wall, and his mother would spread the covers over him. Kristin would light a candle, pick up her sons' clothes that needed mending, and sit down to sew.

She pulled out the brooch pinned to her bodice and put her hand inside to touch her breasts. They were as round and firm as a young woman's. She pushed up her sleeve all the way to the shoulder and looked at her bare arm in the light. It had grown whiter and fuller. Then she stood up and took a few steps, noticing how softly she walked in her soft slippers. She ran her hands down over her slim hips; they were no longer sharp and dry like a man's. The blood coursed through her body the way sap flows through the trees in the spring. It was youth that was sprouting inside her.

She went to the brewhouse with Frida to pour warm water over the grain for the Christmas malt. Frida had neglected to tend to it in time, and the grain had lain there, swelling until it was completely dry. But Kristin didn't scold the maid; with a slight smile she listened to Frida's excuses. This was the first time that Kristin had failed to take care of it herself.

By Christmas she would have Erlend back home with her. When she sent word to him, he would have to return at once. The man wasn't so rash that he would refuse to relent this time; he had to realize that she couldn't possibly move up to Haugen, far from everyone, when she was no longer walking alone. But she would wait a little more before she sent word—even though it was certain enough—perhaps until she felt some sign of life. The second autumn that they lived at Jørundgaard, she had strayed from the road, as people called a miscarriage. But she had quickly taken solace. She was not afraid that it would happen again this time; it couldn't possibly. And yet . . .

She felt as if she had to wrap her entire body protectively around this tiny, fragile life she carried under her heart, the way a person cups her hands like a shield around a little, newly lit flame.

One day late in the fall Ivar and Skule came and told her they wanted to ride up to see their father. It was fine weather up in the mountains, and they wanted to ask if they could stay with him and go hunting during these days of bare frost.

Naakkve and Bjørgulf were sitting at the chessboard. They paused to listen.

"I don't know," said Kristin. She hadn't given any thought to who should carry her message. She looked at her two half-grown sons. She realized it was foolish, but she couldn't manage to speak of it to them. She could tell them to take Lavrans along and then ask him to talk to his father alone. He was so young that he wouldn't think it strange. And yet . . .

"Your father will soon be coming home," she said. "You might end up delaying him. And soon I'll be sending word to him myself."

The twins sulked. Naakkve looked up from the chess game and said curtly, "Do as our mother says, boys."

During Christmas she sent Naakkve north to Erlend. "You must tell him, son, that I am longing for him so greatly, as all of you must be too!" She didn't mention the other news that had come about; she thought it likely that this grown lad would have noticed it. He would have to decide for himself whether he would speak of it to his father.

Naakkve returned without having seen his father. Erlend had gone to Raumsdal. He must have received word that his daughter and her husband were about to move to Bjørgvin, and that Margret wanted to meet with her father at Veøy.

That was reasonable enough. Kristin lay awake at night, now and then stroking Munan's face as he slept at her side. She was sad that Erlend didn't come for Christmas. But it was reasonable that he should want to see his daughter while he had the chance. She wiped away her tears as they slid down her cheeks. She was so quick to weep, just as she had been when she was young.

Just after Christmas, Sira Eirik died. Kristin had visited him at Romundgaard several times during the fall after he had taken to his bed, and she attended his funeral. Otherwise she never went out among people. She thought it a great loss that their old parish priest was gone.

At the funeral she heard that someone had met Erlend north at Lesja. He was on his way home to his farm. Surely he would come soon.

Several days later she sat on the bench under the little window, breathing on her hand mirror, which she had taken out, and rubbing it shiny so she could study her face.

She had been as suntanned as a peasant woman during the past few years, but now all trace of the sun had vanished. Her skin was white, with round, bright red roses on her cheeks, like in a painting. Her face had not been so lovely since she was a young maiden. Kristin sat and held her breath with wondrous joy.

At last they would have a daughter, as Erlend had wished for so dearly, if it turned out as the wise women said. Magnhild. They would have to break with custom this time and name her after his mother.

Part of a fairy tale she had once heard drifted through her mind. Seven sons who were driven high into the wilderness as outlaws because of an unborn little sister. Then she laughed at herself; she didn't understand why she happened to think about that now.

She took from her sewing chest a shirt of the finest white linen, which she worked on whenever she was alone. She pulled out threads from the neckband and stitched birds and beasts on the loosely woven backing; it was years since she had done such fine embroidery. If only Erlend would come *now*, while it was still making her look beautiful: young and straight-backed, blushing and thriving.

Just after Saint Gregor's Day the weather turned so lovely that it was almost like spring. The snow began to melt, gleaming like silver; there were already bare brown patches on the slopes facing south, and the mountains rose up from the blue haze.

Gaute was standing outside in the courtyard, repairing a sleigh that had fallen apart. Naakkve was leaning against the wall of the woodshed, watching his brother work. At that moment Kristin came from the cookhouse, carrying with both hands a large trough full of newly baked wheat bread.

Gaute glanced up at his mother. Then he threw the axe and wheel hubs into the sleigh, ran after her, and took the trough from her; he carried it over to the storehouse.

Kristin had stopped where she was, her cheeks red. When Gaute came back, she went over to her sons. "I think the two of you should ride up to your father in the next few days. Tell him that he is sorely needed here at home to take over the management from me. I have so little strength now, and I will be in bed in the middle of the spring farm work."

The young boys listened to her, and they too blushed, but she could see that they were full of joy. Naakkve said, feigning nonchalance, "We might as well ride up there today, around midafternoon prayers. What do you think, brother?"

On the following day around noon Kristin heard horsemen out in the courtyard. It was Naakkve and Gaute; they were alone. They stood next to their horses, their eyes on the ground, not saying a word.

"What did your father say?" their mother asked.

Gaute stood leaning on his spear. He kept his eyes downcast.

Then Naakkve spoke. "Father asked us to tell you that he has been waiting for you to come to him every day this winter. And he said that you would be no less welcome than you were last time you saw him."

The color came and went in Kristin's face.

"Didn't you mention to your father . . . that things are such with me that . . . it won't be long before I have another child?"

Gaute replied without looking up, "Father didn't seem to think that was any reason . . . that you shouldn't be able to move to Haugen."

Kristin stood there for a moment. "What did he say?" she then asked, her voice low and sharp.

Naakkve didn't want to speak. Gaute lifted his hand slightly, casting a swift and beseeching glance at his brother. Then the older son spoke after all. "Father asked us to tell you this: You knew when the child was conceived how rich a man he was. And if he hasn't grown any richer since, he hasn't grown any poorer either."

Kristin turned away from her sons and slowly walked back toward the main house. Heavy and weary, she sat down on the bench under the window from which the spring sun had already melted the ice and frost.

It *was* true. She had begged to sleep in his arms—at first. But it wasn't kind of him to remind her of that now. She thought it wasn't kind of Erlend to send her such a reply with their sons.

The spring weather held on. The wind blew from the south, and the rain lasted for a week. The river rose, becoming swollen and thunderous. It roared and rushed down the slopes; the snow plunged down the mountainsides. And then the sunshine returned.

Kristin was standing outside behind the buildings in the grayish blue of the evening. A great chorus of birdsong came from the thicket down in the field. Gaute and the twins had gone up to the mountain pastures; they were in search of blackcock. In the morning the clamor of the birds' mating dance on the mountain slopes could be heard all the way down at the manor.

She clasped her hands under her breast. There was so little time left; she had to bear these last days with patience. She too had doubtless been stubborn and difficult to live with quite often. Unreasonable in her worries about the children . . . For too long, as Erlend had said. Yet it seemed to her that he was being harsh now. But the day would soon arrive when he would have to come to her; surely he knew that too.

It was sunny and rainy by turns. One afternoon her sons called to her. All seven of them were standing out in the courtyard along with all the servants. Above the valley stretched three rainbows. The innermost one ended at the buildings of Formo; it was unbroken, with brilliant colors. The two outer ones were fainter and faded away at the top.

Even as they stood there, staring at this astonishing fair omen, the sky grew dark and overcast. From the south a blizzard of snow swept in. It began snowing so hard that soon the whole world had turned white.

That evening Kristin told Munan the story about King Snjo and his pretty white daughter, whose name was Mjøll, and about King Harald Luva, who was brought up by the Dovre giant inside the mountain north of Dovre. She thought with sorrow and remorse that it was years since she had sat and told stories to her children in this fashion. She felt sorry that she had offered Lavrans and Munan so little pleasure of this kind. And they would soon be big boys. While the others had been small, back home at Husaby, she had spent the evenings telling them stories—often, so often.

She saw that her older sons were listening too. She blushed bright red and came to a stop. Munan asked her to tell them more. Naakkve stood up and moved closer.

"Do you remember, Mother, the story about Torstein Uksafot and the trolls of Høiland Forest? Tell us that one!"

As she talked, a memory came back to her. They had lain down to rest and to have something to eat in the birch grove down by the river: her father and the hay harvesters, both men and women. Her father was lying on his stomach; she was sitting astride him, on the small of his back, and kicking him in the flanks with her heels. It was a hot day, and she had been given permission to go barefoot, just like the grown-up women. Her father was reeling off the members of the Høiland troll lineage: Jernskjold married Skjoldvor; their daughters were Skjolddis and Skjoldgjerd, whom Torstein Uksafot killed. Skjoldgjerd had been married to Skjoldketil, and their sons were Skjoldbjørn and Skjoldhedin and Valskjold, who wed Skjoldskjessa; they gave birth to Skjoldulf and Skjoldorm. Skjoldulf won Skjoldkatla, and together they conceived Skjold and Skjoldketil . . .

No, he had already used that name, cried Kolbjørn, laughing. For Lavrans had boasted that he would teach them two dozen troll names, but he hadn't even made it through the first dozen. Lavrans laughed too. "Well, you have to understand that even trolls revive the names of their ancestors!" But the workers refused to give in; they fined him a drink of mead for them all. And you shall have it, said the master. In the evening, after they went back home. But they wanted to have it at once, and finally Tordis was sent off to get the mead.

They stood in a circle and passed the big drinking horn around. Then they picked up their scythes and rakes and went back to the hay harvesting. Kristin was sent home with the empty horn. She carried it in front of her in both hands as she ran barefoot through the sunshine on the green path, up toward the manor. Now and then she would stop, whenever a few drops of mead had collected in the curve of the horn. Then she would tilt it over her little face and lick the gilded rim inside and out, as well as her fingers, tasting the sweetness.

Kristin Lavransdatter sat still, staring straight ahead. Father! She remembered a tremor passing over his face, a paleness, the way a forest slope grows pale whenever a stormy gust turns the leaves of the trees upside down. An edge of cold, sharp derision in his voice, a gleam in his gray eyes, like the glint of a half-drawn sword. A brief moment, and then it would vanish—into cheerful, good-humored jest when he was young, but becoming more often a quiet, slightly melancholy gentleness as he grew older. Something other than deep, tender sweetness had resided in her father's heart.

She had learned to understand it over the years. Her father's marvelous gentleness was not because he lacked a keen enough perception of the faults and wretchedness of others; it came from his constant searching of his own heart before God, crushing it in repentance over his own failings.

No, Father, I will not be impatient. I too have sinned greatly toward my husband.

On the evening of Holy Cross Day Kristin was sitting at the table with her house servants and seemed much the same as usual. But when her sons had gone up to the high loft to sleep, she quietly called Ulf Haldorssøn to her side. She asked him to go down to Isrid at the farm and ask her to come up to her mistress in the old weaving room.

Ulf said, "You must send word to Ranveig at Ulvsvold and to Haldis, the priest's sister, Kristin. It would be most fitting if you sent for Astrid and Ingebjørg of Loptsgaard to take charge of the room."

"There's no time for that," said Kristin. "I felt the first pangs just before midafternoon prayers. Do as I say, Ulf. I want only my own maids and Isrid at my side."

"Kristin," said Ulf somberly, "don't you see what vile gossip may come of this if you creep into hiding tonight."

Kristin let her arms fall heavily onto the table. She closed her eyes.

"Then let them talk, whoever wants to talk! I can't *bear* to see the eyes of those other women around me tonight."

The next morning her big sons sat in silence, their eyes lowered, as Munan talked on and on about the little brother he had seen in his mother's arms over in the weaving room. Finally Bjørgulf said that he didn't need to talk anymore about *that*.

Kristin lay in bed, merely listening; she felt as if she never slept so soundly that she wasn't listening and waiting.

She got out of bed on the eighth day, but the women who were with her could tell that she wasn't well. She was freezing, and then waves of heat would wash over her. On one day the milk would pour from her breasts and soak her clothes; the next day she didn't have enough to give the child his fill. But she refused to go back to bed. She never let the child out of her arms; she never put him in the cradle. At night she would take him to bed with her; in the daytime she carried him around, sitting at the hearth with him, sitting on her bed, listening and waiting and staring at her son, although at times she didn't seem to see him or to hear that he was crying. Then she would abruptly wake up. She would hold the boy in her arms and walk back and forth in the room with him. With her cheek pressed against his, she would hum softly to him, then sit down and place him to her breast, and sit there staring at him as she had before, her face as hard as stone.

One day when the boy was almost six weeks old, and the mother had not yet taken a single step across the threshold of the weaving room, Ulf Haldorssøn and Skule came in. They were dressed for travel.

"We're riding north to Haugen now, Kristin," said Ulf. "There has to be an end to this matter."

Kristin sat mute and motionless, with the boy at her breast. At first she didn't seem to comprehend. All of a sudden she jumped up, her face flushed blood red. "Do as you like. If you're longing for your proper master, I won't hold you back. It would be best if you drew your earnings now; then you won't need to come back here for them later."

Ulf began cursing fiercely. Then he looked at the woman standing there with the infant clutched to her bosom. He pressed his lips together and fell silent.

But Skule took a step forward. "Yes, Mother, I'm riding up to see Father now. If you're forgetting that Ulf has been a foster father to all of us children, then you should at least remember that you can't command and rule me as if I were a servant or an infant."

"Can't I?" Kristin struck him a blow to the ear so the boy staggered. "I think I can command and rule all of you as long as I give you food and clothing. Get out!" she shrieked, stomping her foot.

Skule was furious. But Ulf said quietly, "It's better this way, my boy, better for her to be unreasonable and angry than to see her sitting and staring as if she had lost her wits to grief."

Gunhild, her maid, came running after them. They were to come at once to see her mistress in the weaving room. She wanted to talk to them and to all her sons. In a curt, sharp voice, Kristin asked Ulf to ride down to Breidin to speak with a man who had leased two cows from her. He should take the twins along with him, and there was no need to return home until the next day. She sent Naakkve and Gaute up to the mountain pastures. She wanted them to go to Illmanddal to see to the horse paddock there. And on their way up they were to stop by to see Bjørn, the tar-burner and Isrid's son, and ask him to come to Jørundgaard that evening. It would do no good for them to object since tomorrow was the Sabbath.

The next morning, as the bells were ringing, the mistress left Jørundgaard, accompanied by Bjørn and Isrid, who carried the child. She had given them good and proper clothing, but for this first church visit after the birth Kristin herself was adorned with so much gold that everyone could see she was the mistress and the other two her servants.

Defiant and proud, she faced the indignant astonishment she felt directed at her from everyone on the church green. Oh yes, in the past she had come to church quite differently on such an occasion, accompanied by the most noble of women. Sira Solmund looked at her with unkind eyes as she stood before the church door with a taper in her hand, but he received her in his customary fashion.

Isrid had retreated into childhood by now and understood very little; Bjørn was an odd and taciturn man, who never interfered in anyone else's affairs. These two were the godmother and godfather.

Isrid told the priest the child's name. He gave a start. He hesitated. Then he pronounced it so loudly that it was heard by the people standing in the nave.

"Erlend. In the name of the Father, the Son, and the Holy Spirit . . ."

A shudder seemed to pass through the entire assembled congregation. And Kristin felt a wild, vindictive joy.

The child had looked quite strong when he was born. But from the very first week Kristin thought she could tell that he was not going to thrive. She herself had felt, at the moment she gave birth, that her heart was collapsing like an extinguished ember. When Isrid showed her the newborn son, she imagined that the spark of life had only an uncertain hold on this child. But she pushed this thought aside; an unspeakable number of times she had already felt as if her heart would break. And the child was plenty big and did not look weak.

But her uneasiness over the boy grew from day to day. He whimpered constantly and had a poor appetite. She often had to struggle for a long time before she could get him to take her breast. When she had finally enticed him to suckle, he would fall asleep almost at once. She couldn't see that he was getting any bigger.

With inexpressible anguish and heartache she thought she saw that from the day he was baptized and received his father's name, little Erlend began to weaken more quickly.

None of her children, no, none of them had she loved as she did this little unfortunate boy. None of them had she conceived in such sweet and wild joy; none had she carried with such happy anticipation. She thought back on the past nine months; in the end she had fought with all her life to hold on to hope and belief. She couldn't bear to lose this child, but neither could she bear to save him.

Almighty God, merciful Queen, Holy Olav. She could feel that this time it would do her no good to fling herself down and beg for her child's life.

Forgive us our sins, as we forgive those who have sinned against us.

She went to church every Sabbath, as was her custom. She kissed the doorpost, sprinkled herself with holy water, sank to her knees before the ancient crucifix above the choir. The Savior gazed down, sorrowful and gentle in his death throes. Christ died to save his murderers. Holy Olav stands before him, perpetually praying for intercession for those who drove him into exile and killed him.

As we forgive those who have sinned against us.

Blessed Mary, my child is dying!

Don't you know, Kristin, that I would rather have carried his cross and suffered his death myself than stand under my son's cross and watch him die? But since I knew that this had to happen to save the sinners, I consented in my heart. I consented when my son prayed: Father, forgive them, for they know not what they do.

As we forgive those who have sinned against us . . .

What you scream in your heart does not become a prayer until you have said your *Pater noster* without deceit.

Forgive us our sins . . . Do you remember how many times your sins were forgiven? Look at your sons over there on the men's side. Look at him standing in front, like the chieftain of that handsome group of youths. The fruit of your sin . . . For nearly twenty years you have seen God grant him greater looks, wisdom, and manliness. See His mercy. Where is your own mercy toward your youngest son back home?

Do you remember your father? Do you remember Simon Darre?

But deep in her heart Kristin felt that she had not forgiven Erlend. She could not, because she would not. She held on to her bowl of love, refusing to let it go, even though it now contained only these last, bitter dregs. The moment when she left Erlend behind, no longer thinking of him even with this corrosive bitterness, then everything that had been between them would be over.

So she stood there during mass and knew that it would be of no benefit to her. She tried to pray: Holy Olav, help me. Work a miracle on my heart so that I might say my prayer without deceit and think of Erlend with God-fearing peace in my soul. But she knew that she did not want this prayer to be heard. Then she felt that it was useless for her to pray to be allowed to keep the child. Young Erlend was on loan from God. Only on one condition could she keep him, and she refused to accept that condition. And it was useless to lie to Saint Olav. . . .

So she kept watch over the ill child. Her tears spilled out; she wept without a sound and without moving. Her face was as gray and stony as ever, although gradually the whites of her eyes and her eyelids turned blood red. If anyone came near her, she would quickly wipe her face and simply sit there, stiff and mute.

And yet it took so little to thaw her heart. If one of her big sons came in, cast a glance at the tiny child, and spoke a few kind and sympathetic words to him, then Kristin could hardly keep from bursting into loud sobs. If she could have talked to her grown-up sons about her anguish over the infant, she knew her heart would have melted. But they had grown shy around her now. Ever since that day when they came home and learned what name she had given their youngest brother, the boys seemed to have drawn closer together and stood so far away from her.

But one day, when Naakkve was looking at the child, he said, "Mother, give me permission . . . to seek out Father and tell him how things stand with the boy."

"It will no longer do any good," replied his mother in despair.

Munan didn't understand. He brought his playthings to the little brother, rejoiced when he was allowed to hold him, and thought he had made the child smile. Munan talked about when his father would come home and wondered what he would think of the new son. Kristin sat in silence, her face gray, and let her soul be torn apart by the boy's chatter.

The infant was now thin and wrinkled like an old man; his eyes were unnaturally big and clear. And yet he had begun to smile at his mother; she would moan softly whenever she saw this. Kristin caressed his small, thin limbs, held his feet in her hands. Never would this child lie there and reach with surprise for the sweet, strange, pale pink shapes that flailed in the air above him, which he didn't recognize as his own legs. Never would these tiny feet walk on the earth.

After she had sat through all the arduous days of the week and kept watch over the dying child, then she would think as she dressed for church that surely she was humble enough now. She had forgiven Erlend; she no longer cared about him. If only she might keep her sweetest, her most precious possession, then she would gladly forgive the man.

But when she stood before the cross, whispering her *Pater noster,* and she came to the words *sicut et nos dimittibus debitoribus nostris,* then she would feel her heart harden, the way a hand clenches into a fist to strike. No!

Without hope, her soul aching, she would weep, for she could not *make* herself do it.

And so Erlend Erlendssøn died on the day before the Feast of Mary Magdalena, a little less than three months old.

## CHAPTER 7

THAT AUTUMN BISHOP Halvard came north through the valley on an official church visit. He arrived in Sil on the day before Saint Matthew's Day. It had been more than two years since the bishop had come that far north, so there were many children who were to be confirmed this time. Munan Erlendssøn was among them; he was now eight years old.

Kristin asked Ulf Haldorssøn to present the child to the bishop; she didn't have a single friend in her home parish whom she could ask to do this. Ulf seemed pleased by her request. And so, when the church bells rang, the three of them walked up the hill: Kristin, Ulf, and the boy. Her other sons had been to the earlier mass—all of them except for Lavrans, who was in bed with a fever. They didn't want to attend this mass because it would be so crowded in the church.

As they walked past the foreman's house, Kristin noticed that many strange horses were tied to the fence outside. Farther along the road they were overtaken by Jardtrud, who was riding with a large entourage and raced past them. Ulf pretended not to see his wife and her kinsmen.

Kristin knew that Ulf had not set foot inside his own house since just after New Year's. Things had apparently gotten worse than usual between him and his wife, and afterward he had moved his clothes chest and his weapons up to the high loft, where he now lived with the boys. Once, in early spring, Kristin had mentioned that it was wrong for there to be such discord between him and his wife. Then he had looked at her and laughed, and she said no more.

The weather was sunny and beautiful. High over the valley the sky was blue between the peaks. The yellow foliage of the birch-covered slopes was beginning to thin out, and in the countryside most of the grain had been cut, although a few acres of pale barley still swayed near the farms, and the second crop of hay stood green and wet with dew in the meadows. There were throngs of people at the church, and a great neighing and whinneying of stallions, because the church stables were full and many had been forced to tie up their horses outside.

A muted, rancorous uneasiness passed through the crowd as Kristin and her escort moved forward. A young man slapped his thigh and laughed but was fiercely hushed by his elders. Kristin walked with measured steps and erect bearing across the green and then entered the cemetery. She paused for a moment at her child's grave and at that of Simon Andressøn. A flat gray stone had been placed on top of it, and on the stone was etched the likeness of a man wearing a helmet and coat of mail, leaning his hands on a big, triangular shield with his coat of arms. Around the edge of the stone were chiseled the words:

*In pace. Simon Armiger. Proles Dom. Andreae Filii Gudmundi Militis Pater Noster.*

Ulf was standing outside the south door; he had left his sword in the gallery.

At that moment Jardtrud entered the cemetery in the company of four men: her two brothers and two old farmers. One of them was Kolbein Jonssøn, who had been Lavrans Bjørgulfsøn's arms bearer for many years. They walked toward the priest's entrance south of the choir.

Ulf Haldorssøn raced over to block their way. Kristin heard them speaking rapidly and vehemently; Ulf was trying to prevent his wife and her escorts from going any farther. People in the churchyard drew nearer; Kristin too moved closer. Then Ulf jumped up onto the stone foundation on which the gallery rested, leaned in, and pulled out the first axe he could reach. When one of Jardtrud's brothers tried to pull it out of his hand, Ulf leaped forward and swung the axe in the air. The blow fell on the man's shoulder, and then people came running and seized hold of Ulf. He struggled to free himself. Kristin saw that his face was dark red, contorted, and desperate.

Then Sira Solmund and a cleric from the bishop's party appeared in the priest's doorway. They exchanged a few words with the farmers. Three men who bore the white shields of the bishop took Ulf away at once, leading him out of the cemetery, while his wife and her escorts followed the two priests into the church.

Kristin approached the group of farmers. "What is it?" she asked sharply. "Why did they take Ulf away?"

"Surely you saw that he struck a man in the cemetery," replied one of them, his voice equally sharp. Everyone moved away from her so that she was left standing alone with her son at the church door.

Kristin thought she understood. Ulf's wife wanted to present a complaint against him to the bishop. By losing mastery of his feelings and breaching the sanctity of the cemetery, he had placed himself in a difficult position. When an unfamiliar deacon came to the door and peered outside, she went over to him, told him her name, and asked whether she might be taken to the bishop.

Inside the church all the sacred objects had been set out, but the candles on the altars were not yet lit. A little sunshine fell through the round windows high overhead and streamed between the dark brown pillars. Many of the congregation had already entered the nave and were sitting on the benches along the wall. In front of the bishop's seat in the choir stood a small group of people: Jardtrud Herbrandsdatter and her two brothers—Geirulv with his arm bandaged—Kolbein Jonssøn, Sigurd Geitung, and Tore Borghildssøn. Behind and on either side of the bishop's carved chair stood two young priests from Hamar, several other men from the bishop's party, and Sira Solmund.

All of them stared as the mistress of Jørundgaard stepped forward and courtsied deeply before the bishop.

Lord Halvard was a tall, stout man with an exceedingly venerable appearance. Beneath the red silk cap his hair gleamed snow-white at his temples, and his full, oval face was a blazing red. He had a strong, crooked nose and heavy jowls, and his mouth was as narrow as a slit, almost without lips, as it cut through his closely trimmed, grayish-white beard. But his bushy eyebrows were still dark above his glittering, coal-black eyes.

"May God be with you, Kristin Lavransdatter," said Lord Halvard. He gave the woman a penetrating look from under his heavy eyebrows. With one of his large, pale old man's hands he grasped the gold cross hanging on his chest; in the other hand, which rested on the lap of his dark violet robes, he held a wax tablet.

"What brings you to seek me out here, Mistress Kristin?" the bishop asked. "Don't you think it would be more fitting if you waited until the afternoon and came to see me at Romundgaard to tell me what is in your heart?"

"Jardtrud Herbrandsdatter has sought you out here, Reverend Father," replied Kristin. "Ulf Haldorssøn has now been in the service of my husband for thirty-five years; he has always been our loyal friend and helper and a good kinsman. I thought I might be able to help him in some way."

Jardtrud uttered a low cry of scorn or indignation. Everyone else stared at Kristin: the parishioners with bitterness, the bishop's party with intent curiosity. Lord Halvard cast a sharp glance around before he said to Kristin, "Are things such that you would venture to defend Ulf Haldorssøn? Surely you must know—" As she attempted to answer, he quickly added, raising one hand, "No one has the right to demand testimony from you in this matter—other than your husband—unless your conscience forces you to speak. Consider it carefully, before you—"

"I was mostly thinking, Lord Bishop, that Ulf let his temper get the better of him, and he took up arms at church; I thought I might aid him in this matter by offering to pay a guarantee. Or," she said with great effort, "my husband will certainly do all he can to help his friend and kinsman in this case."

The bishop turned impatiently to those standing nearby, who all seemed to be seized by strong emotions. "That woman doesn't need to be here. Her spokesman can wait over in the nave. Go over there, all of you, while I speak to the mistress. And send the parishioners outside for the time being, and Jardtrud Herbrandsdatter along with them."

One of the young priests had been busy laying out the bishop's vestments. Now he carefully set the miter with the gold cross on top of the spread-out folds of the cope and went over to speak to the people in the nave. The others followed him. The congregation, along with Jardtrud, left the church, and the verger closed the doors.

"You mentioned your husband," said the bishop, looking at

Kristin with the same expression as before. "Is it true that last summer you sought to be reconciled with him?"

"Yes, my Lord."

"But you were not reconciled?"

"My Lord, forgive me for saying this, but . . . I have no complaints about my husband. I sought you out to speak of this matter regarding Ulf Haldorssøn."

"Did your husband know you were carrying a child?" asked Lord Halvard. He seemed angered by her objection.

"Yes, my Lord," she replied in a low voice.

"How did Erlend Nikulaussøn receive the news?" asked the bishop.

Kristin stood twisting a corner of her wimple between her fingers, her eyes on the floor.

"Did he refuse to be reconciled with you when he heard about this?"

"My Lord, forgive me . . ." Kristin had turned bright red. "Whether my husband Erlend acted one way or another toward me . . . if it would help Ulf's case for him to come here, then I know that Erlend would hasten to his side."

The bishop frowned as he looked at her. "Do you mean out of friendship for this man, Ulf? Or, now that the matter has come to light, will Erlend after all agree to acknowledge the child you gave birth to this spring?"

Kristin lifted her head and stared at the bishop with wide eyes and parted lips. For the first time she began to understand what his words signified.

Lord Halvard gave her a somber look. "It's true, mistress, that no one other than your husband has the right to bring charges against you for this. But surely you must realize that he will bring upon both you and himself a great sin if he takes on the paternity of another man's child in order to protect Ulf. It would be better for all of you, if you have sinned, to confess and repent of this sin."

The color came and went in Kristin's face. "Has someone said that my husband wouldn't . . . that it was not his child?"

The bishop reluctantly replied, "Would you have me believe, Kristin, that you had no idea what people have been saying about you and your overseer?"

"No, I didn't." She straightened up, standing with her head tilted back slightly, her face white under the folds of her wimple. "I pray you, my Reverend Lord and Father—if people have been whispering rumors about me behind my back, then ask them to repeat them to my face!"

"No names have been mentioned," replied the bishop. "That is against the law. But Jardtrud Herbrandsdatter has asked permission to leave her husband and go home with her kinsmen because she accuses him of keeping company with another woman, a married woman, and conceiving a child with her."

For a moment both of them fell silent. Then Kristin repeated, "My Lord, I beg you to show me such mercy that you would demand these men to speak so that I might hear them, to say that *I* am supposed to be this woman."

Bishop Halvard gave her a sharp and piercing look. Then he waved his hand, and the men in the nave approached and stood around his chair. Lord Halvard spoke: "You good men of Sil have come to me today at an inconvenient time, bringing a complaint which by rights should have been presented first to my plenipotentiary. I have acceded to this because I know that you cannot be fully knowledgeable of the law. But now this woman, Mistress Kristin Lavransdatter of Jørundgaard, has come to me with an odd request. She begs me to ask you if you dare say to her face what people have been saying in the parish: that her husband, Erlend Nikulaussøn, is not the father of the child she gave birth to this spring."

Sira Solmund replied, "It has been said on every estate and in every hovel throughout the countryside that the child was conceived in adultery and with blood guilt, by the mistress and her overseer. And it seems to us hardly credible that she did not know of this rumor herself."

The bishop was about to speak, but Kristin said, in a loud and firm voice, "So help me Almighty God, the Virgin Mary, Saint Olav, and the archbishop Saint Thomas, I did not know this lie was being said about us."

"Then it's hard to understand why you felt such a need to conceal the fact that you were with child," said the priest. "You hid from everyone and barely came out of your house all winter."

"It's been a long time since I had any friends among the farmers of this parish; I've had so little to do with anyone here over the past few years. And yet I didn't know until now that everyone seems to be my foe. But I came to church on every Sabbath," she said.

"Yes, and you wrapped yourself up in cloaks and dressed so that no one might see you were growing big under your belt."

"As any woman would do; surely any woman would want to look decent in the company of other people," replied Kristin curtly.

The priest continued, "If the child was your husband's, as you say, then surely you wouldn't have tended to the infant so poorly that you caused him to die of neglect."

One of the young priests from Hamar quickly stepped forward and caught hold of Kristin. A moment later she stood as she had before, pale and straight-backed. She thanked the priest with a nod of her head.

Sira Solmund vehemently declared, "That's what the serving-women at Jørundgaard said. My sister, who has been to the manor, witnessed it herself. The mistress went about with her breasts bursting with milk, so that her clothing was soaked through. But any woman who saw the boy's body can testify that he died of starvation."

Bishop Halvard put up his hand. "That's enough, Sira Solmund. We will keep to the matter at hand, which is whether Jardtrud Herbrandsdatter had any other basis for her claims when she brought her case against her husband than that she had heard rumors, which the mistress here says are lies. And whether Kristin can dispute these rumors. Surely no one would claim that she laid hands on the child . . ."

But Kristin stood there, her face pale, and did not speak.

The bishop said to the parish priest, "But you, Sira Solmund, it was your duty to speak to this woman and let her know what was being said. Haven't you done so?"

The priest blushed. "I have said heartfelt prayers for this woman, that she might willingly give up her stubborn ways and seek remorse and repentance. Her father was not *my* friend," said the priest heatedly. "And yet I know that Lavrans of Jørundgaard was a righteous man and a firm believer. No doubt he might have deserved better, but this daughter of his has brought shame after shame upon him. She was barely a grown maiden before her loose ways caused two boys here in the parish to die. Then she broke her promise and betrothal to a fine and splendid knight's son, whom her father had chosen to be her husband, and forced her own will, using dishonorable means, to win this man, who you, my Lord, know full well was condemned as a traitor and betrayer of the Crown. But I thought that at last her heart would have to soften when she saw how she was hated and scorned—she and all her family—and with the worst of reputations, living there at Jørundgaard, where her father and Ragnfrid Ivarsdatter had enjoyed the respect and love of everyone.

"But it was too much when she brought her son here today to be confirmed, and that man was supposed to present the boy to you when the whole parish knows that she lives with him in both adultery and blood guilt."

The bishop gestured for the other man to be silent.

"How closely related is Ulf Haldorssøn to your husband?" he asked Kristin.

"Ulf's rightful father was Sir Baard Petersøn of Hestnes. He had the same mother as his half brother Gaute Erlendssøn of Skogheim, who was Erlend Nikulaussøn's maternal grandfather."

Lord Halvard turned impatiently to Sira Solmund, "There is no blood guilt; her mother-in-law and Ulf are cousins. It would be a breach of kinship ties and a grave sin if it were true, but you need not make it any worse than that."

"Ulf Haldorssøn is godfather to this woman's eldest son," said Sira Solmund.

The bishop looked at her, and Kristin answered, "Yes, my Lord."

Lord Halvard sat in silence for a while.

"May God help you, Kristin Lavransdatter," he said sorrowfully. "I knew your father in the past; I was his guest at Jørundgaard in my youth. I remember that you were a lovely, innocent child. If Lavrans Bjørgulfsøn had been alive, this would never have happened. Think of your father, Kristin. For his sake, you must put aside this shame and cleanse yourself, if you can."

In a flash the memory came back to her; she recognized the

bishop. A winter's day at sunset . . . a red, rearing colt in the courtyard and a priest with a fringe of black hair around his flaming red face. Hanging on to the halter, splattered with froth, he was trying to tame the wild animal and climb on to its back without a saddle. Groups of drunken, laughing Christmas guests were crowding around, her father among them, red-faced from liquor and the cold, shouting loudly and merrily.

She turned toward Kolbein Jonssøn.

"Kolbein! You who have known me ever since I wore a child's cap, you who knew me and my sisters back home with my father and mother . . . I know that you were so fond of my father that you . . . Kolbein, do you believe such a thing of me?"

The farmer Kolbein looked at her, his face stern and sorrowful. "Fond of your father, you say . . . Yes, we who were his men, poor servants and commoners who loved Lavrans of Jørundgaard and thought he was the kind of man that God wanted a chieftain to be . . .

"Don't ask us, Kristin Lavransdatter, we who saw how your father loved you and how you rewarded his love, what we think you might be capable of doing!"

Kristin bowed her head to her breast. The bishop couldn't get another word out of her; she would no longer answer his questions.

Then Lord Halvard stood up. Next to the high altar was a small door which led to the enclosed section of the gallery behind the apse of the choir. Part of it was used as the sacristy, and part of it was furnished with several little hatches through which the lepers could receive the Host when they stood out there and listened to the mass, separated from the rest of the congregation. But no one in the parish had suffered from leprosy for many years.

"Perhaps it would be best if you waited out there, Kristin, until everyone has come inside for the service. I want to talk to you later, but in the meantime you may go home to your family."

Kristin curtsied before the bishop. "I would rather go home now, venerable Lord, with your permission."

"As you please, Mistress Lavransdatter. May God protect you, Kristin. If you are guilty, then they will plead your defense: God Himself and His martyrs who are the lords of the church here: Saint Olav and Saint Thomas, who died for the sake of righteousness."

Kristin curtsied once more before the bishop. Then she went through the priest's door out into the cemetery.

A small boy wearing a new red tunic stood there all alone, his bearing stiff and erect. Munan tilted his pale child's face up toward his mother for a moment, his eyes big and frightened.

Her sons . . . She hadn't thought about them before. In a flash she saw her flock of boys: the way they had stood at the periphery of her life during the past years, crowding together like a herd of horses in a thunderstorm, alert and wary, far away from her as she struggled through the final death throes of her love. What had they understood, what had they thought, what had they endured as she wrestled with her passion? What would become of them now?

She held Munan's small, scrubbed fist in her hand. The child stared straight ahead; his lips quivered slightly, but he held his head high.

Hand in hand Kristin Lavransdatter and her son walked across the churchyard and out onto the hillside. She thought about her sons, and she felt as if she would break down and collapse on the ground. The throngs of people moved toward the church door, as the bells rang from the nearby bell tower.

She had once heard a saga about a murdered man who couldn't fall to the ground because he had so many spears in his body. She couldn't fall as she walked along because of all the eyes piercing through her.

Mother and child entered the high loft room. Her sons were huddled around Bjørgulf, who was sitting at the table. Naakkve straightened up and stood over his brothers, with one hand on the shoulder of the half-blind boy. Kristin looked at the narrow, dark, blue-eyed visage of her firstborn son, with the soft, downy black beard around his mouth.

"You know about it?" she asked calmly, walking over to the group.

"Yes." Naakkve spoke for all of them. "Gunhild was at church."

Kristin paused for a moment. The other boys turned back to

their eldest brother, until their mother asked, "Did any of you know that such things were being said in the countryside—about Ulf and me?"

Then Ivar Erlendssøn abruptly turned to face her. "Don't you think you would have heard the clamor of our actions if we had? I know *I* couldn't have sat still and let my mother be branded an adulteress—not even if I knew it was true that she *was!*"

Kristin gazed at them sorrowfully. "I wonder, my sons, what you must have thought about everything that has happened here over the last few years."

The boys stood in silence. Then Bjørgulf lifted his face and looked up at his mother with his failing eyes. "Jesus Christus, Mother, what were we supposed to think? This past year and all the other years before that! Do you think it was easy for us to figure out what to think?"

Naakkve said, "Oh yes, Mother. I know I should have talked to you, but you behaved in such a way that made it impossible for us. And when you let our youngest brother be baptized as if you wanted to call our father a dead man—" He broke off, gesturing vehemently.

Bjørgulf continued. "You and Father thought of nothing else but your quarrel. Not about the fact that we had grown up to be men in the meantime. You never paid any heed to anyone who happened to come between your weapons and was dealt bloody wounds."

He had leaped to his feet. Naakkve placed a hand on his shoulder. Kristin saw it was true: The two were grown men. She felt as if she were standing naked before them; she had shamelessly revealed herself to her children.

This was what they had seen most as they grew up: that their parents were getting old, that their youthful ardor was pitifully ill suited to them, and that they had not been able to age with honor and dignity.

Then the voice of a child cut through the silence. Munan shrieked in wild despair, "Mother! Are they coming to take you prisoner, Mother? Are they coming to take Mother away from us now?"

He threw his arms around her and buried his face against her waist. Kristin pulled him close, sank down onto a bench, and gathered the little boy into her arms. She tried to console him. "Little son, little son, you mustn't cry."

"No one can take Mother away from us." Gaute came over and touched his little brother. "Don't cry. They can't do anything to her. You must get hold of yourself, Munan. Rest assured that we will protect our mother, my boy!"

Kristin sat holding the child tightly in her arms; she felt as if he had saved her with his tears.

Then Lavrans spoke, sitting up in bed with the flush of fever on his cheeks. "Well, what are you going to do, brothers?"

"When the mass is over," said Naakkve, "we'll go over to the parsonage and offer to pay a guarantee for our foster father. That's the first thing we'll do. Do you agree, my lads?"

Bjørgulf, Gaute, Ivar, and Skule assented.

Kristin said, "Ulf raised a weapon against a man in the cemetery. And I must do something to clear both his name and mine from these rumors. These are such serious matters, boys, that I think you young men must seek someone else's counsel to decide what should be done."

"Who should we ask for advice?" said Naakkve, a little scornfully.

"Sir Sigurd of Sundbu is my cousin," replied his mother hesitantly.

"Since that has never occurred to him before," said the young man in the same tone of voice, "I don't think it fitting for the sons of Erlend to go begging to him now, when we're in need. What do you say, brothers? Even if we're not legally of age, we can still wield our weapons with skill, all five of us."

"Boys," said Kristin, "using weapons will get you nowhere in this matter."

"You must let us decide that, Mother," replied Naakkve curtly. "But now, Mother, I think you should let us eat. And sit down in your usual place—for the servants' sake," he said, as if he could command her.

She could hardly eat a thing. She sat and pondered . . . She didn't dare ask whether they would now send word to their father. And she wondered how this case would be handled. She knew little of the law in such matters; no doubt she would have to refute the rumors by swearing an oath along with either five or eleven others.[1] If so, it would probably take place at the church of Ullinsyn in Vaagaa. She had kinsmen there on nearly every large estate, from her mother's lineage. If her oath failed, and she had to stand before their eyes without being able to clear herself of this shameful charge . . . It would bring shame upon her father. He had been an outsider here in the valley. But he had known how to assert himself; everyone had respected him. Whenever Lavrans Bjørgulfsøn took up a matter at a *ting* or a meeting, he had always won full support. Still, she knew it was on him that her shame would fall. She suddenly realized how alone her father had stood; in spite of everything, he was alone and a stranger among the people here every time she heaped upon him one more burden of sorrow and shame and disgrace.

She didn't think she could ever feel this way anymore; again and again she had thought her heart would burst into bloody pieces, and now, once again, it felt as if it would break.

Gaute went out to the gallery and looked north. "People are leaving the church," he said. "Shall we wait until they've gone some distance away?"

"No," replied Naakkve. "Let them see that the sons of Erlend are coming. We should get ready now, lads. We had better wear our steel helmets."

Only Naakkve owned proper armor. He left the coat of mail behind, but he put on his helmet and picked up his shield, his sword, and a long lance. Bjørgulf and Gaute put on the old iron hats that boys wore when they practiced sword fighting, while Ivar and Skule had to be content with the small steel caps that peasant soldiers still wore. Their mother looked at them. She had such a shattered feeling in her breast.

"It seems to me ill advised, my sons, for you to arm yourselves in this fashion to go over to the parsonage," she said uneasily. "You shouldn't forget about the peace of the Sabbath and the presence of the bishop."

Naakkve replied, "Honor has grown scarce here at Jørundgaard, Mother. We have to pay dearly for whatever we can get."

"Not you, Bjørgulf," pleaded their mother fearfully, for the weak-sighted boy had picked up a big battleaxe. "Remember that you can't see well, son!"

"Oh, I can see as far as I need to," said Bjørgulf, weighing the axe in his hand.

Gaute went over to young Lavrans's bed and took down their grandfather's great sword, which the boy always insisted on keeping on the wall above his bed. He drew the blade from its scabbard and looked at it.

"You must lend me your sword, kinsman. I think our grandfather would be pleased if we took it along on this venture."

Kristin wrung her hands as she sat there. She felt as if she would scream—with terror and the utmost dread, but also with a power that was stronger than either her torment or her fear. The way she had screamed when she gave birth to these men. Wound after countless wound she had endured in this life, but now she knew that they all had healed; the scars were as tender as raw flesh, but she knew that she would not bleed to death. Never had she felt more alive than she did now.

Blossoms and leaves had been stripped away from her, but she had not been cut down, nor had she fallen. For the first time since she had given birth to the children of Erlend Nikulaussøn, she completely forgot about the father and saw only her sons.

But the sons did not look at their mother, who sat there, pale, with strained and frightened eyes. Munan was still on her lap; he hadn't let go of her even for a moment. The five boys left the loft.

Kristin stood up and stepped out onto the gallery. They emerged from behind the buildings and walked swiftly along the path toward Romundgaard between the pale, swaying acres of barley. Their steel caps and iron hats gleamed dully, but the sun glittered on Naakkve's lance and on the spearpoints of the twins. She stood staring after the five young men. She was mother to them all.

Back inside she collapsed before the chest over which the picture of Mary hung. Sobs tore her apart. Munan began to cry too, and weeping, he crept close to his mother. Lavrans leaped out of bed and threw himself to his knees on the other side of her. She put her arms around both her youngest sons.

Ever since the infant had died, she had wondered why she should pray. Hard, cold, and heavy as stone, she had felt as if she were falling into the gaping maw of Hell. Now the prayers burst from her lips of their own volition; without any conscious will, her soul streamed toward Mary, maiden and mother, the Queen of Heaven and earth, with cries of anguish and gratitude and praise. Mary, Mary, I have so much—I still have endless treasures that can be plundered from me. Merciful Mother, take them into your protection!

There were many people in the courtyard of Romundgaard. When the sons of Erlend arrived, several farmers asked them what they wanted.

"We want nothing from you . . . yet," said Naakkve, smiling slyly. "We have business with the bishop today, Magnus. Later my brothers and I may decide that we want to have a few words with the rest of you too. But today you have no need to fear us."

There was a great deal of shouting and commotion. Sira Solmund came out and tried to forbid the boys to stay, but then several farmers took up their cause and said they should be allowed to make inquiries about this charge against their mother. The bishop's men came out and told the sons of Erlend they would have to leave because food was being served and no one had time to listen to them. But the farmers were not pleased by this.

"What is it, good folks?" thundered a voice overhead. No one had noticed that Lord Halvard himself had come out onto the loft gallery. Now he was standing there in his violet robes, with the red silk cap on his white hair, tall and stout and looking like a chieftain. "Who are these young men?"

He was told that they were Kristin's sons from Jørundgaard.

"Are you the oldest?" the bishop asked Naakkve. "Then I will talk to you. But the others must wait here in the courtyard in the meantime."

Naakkve climbed the steps to the high loft and followed the bishop into the room. Lord Halvard sat down in the high seat and looked at the young man standing before him, leaning on his lance.

"What is your name?"

"Nikulaus Erlendssøn, my Lord."

"Do you think you need to be so well armed, Nikulaus Erlendssøn, in order to speak to your bishop?" asked the other man with a little smile.

Nikulaus blushed bright red. He went over to the corner, put down his weapons and cape, and came back. He stood before the bishop, bareheaded, his face lowered, with one hand clasping the wrist of the other, his bearing easy and free, but seemly and respectful.

Lord Halvard thought that this young man had been taught courtly and noble manners. And he couldn't have been a child when his father lost his riches and honorable position; he must certainly remember the time when he was considered the heir of Husaby. He was a handsome lad as well; the bishop felt great compassion for him.

"Were those your brothers, all those young men who were with you? How many of you are there, you sons of Erlend?"

"There are seven of us still living, my Lord."

"So many young lives involved in this." The bishop gave an involuntary sigh. "Sit down, Nikulaus. I suppose you want to talk to me about these rumors that have come forth about your mother and her overseer?"

"Thank you, Your Grace, but I would prefer to stand."

The bishop looked thoughtfully at the youth. Then he said slowly, "I must tell you, Nikulaus, that I find it difficult to believe that what has been said about Kristin Lavransdatter is true. And no one other than her husband has the right to accuse her of adultery. But then there is the matter of the kinship between your father and this man Ulf and the fact that he is your godfather. Jardtrud has presented her complaint in such a manner that there is much to indicate a lack of honor on your mother's part. Do you know whether it's true what she says: that the man often struck her and that he has shunned her bed for almost a year?"

"Ulf and Jardtrud did not live well together; our foster father was no longer young when he married, and he can be rather stubborn and hot-tempered. Toward myself and my brothers, and toward our father and mother, he has always been the most loyal kinsman and friend. That is the first request I intended to make of you, kind sir: If it is at all possible, that you would release Ulf as a free man against payment of a guarantee."

"You are not yet of lawful age?" asked the bishop.

"No, my Lord. But our mother is willing to pay whatever guarantee you might demand."

The bishop shook his head.

"But my father will do the same, I'm certain of that. It's my intention to ride straight from here to see him, to tell him what has happened. If you would grant him an audience tomorrow . . ."

The bishop rested his chin on his hand and sat there stroking his beard with his thumb, making a faint scraping sound.

"Sit down, Nikulaus," he said, "and we'll be able to talk better." Naakkve bowed politely and sat down. "So then it's true that Ulf has refused to live with his wife?" he continued as if he just happened to remember it.

"Yes, my Lord. As far as I know . . ."

The bishop couldn't help smiling, and then the young man smiled a little too.

"Ulf has been sleeping in the loft with all of us brothers since Christmas."

The bishop sat in silence for a moment. "What about food? Where does he eat?"

"He had his wife pack provisions for him whenever he went into the woods or left the estate." Naakkve's expression grew a little uncertain. "There were some quarrels about that. Mother thought it best for him to take his meals with us, as he did before he was married. Ulf didn't want to do that because he said people would talk if he changed the terms of the agreement which he and Father made when he set up his own household, about the goods that he would be given from the estate. And he didn't think it was right for Mother to provide food for him again without some deductions in what he had been granted. But it was arranged as Mother wanted, and Ulf began taking his meals with us again. The other part was to be figured out later."

"Hmm . . . Otherwise your mother has a reputation for keeping a close eye on her property, and she is an exceedingly enterprising and frugal woman."

"Not with food," said Naakkve eagerly. "Anyone will tell you that—any man or woman who has ever served on our estate. Mother is the most generous of women when it comes to food. In that regard she's no different now from when we were rich. She's never happier than when she can set some special dish on the table, and she makes such an abundance that every servant, right down to the goatherd and the beggar, receives his share of the good food."

"Hmm . . ." The bishop sat lost in thought. "You mentioned that you wanted to seek out your father?"

"Yes, my Lord. Surely that must be the reasonable thing to do?" When the bishop didn't reply, he continued. "We spoke to Father this winter, my brother Gaute and I. We also told him that Mother was with child. But we saw no sign, nor did we hear a single word from his lips, that might indicate he had doubts that Mother had not been as faithful as gold to him or that he was surprised. But Father has never felt at ease in Sil; he wanted to live on his own farm in Dovre, and Mother was up there for a while this summer. He was angry because she refused to stay and keep house for him. He wanted her to let Gaute and me manage Jørundgaard while she moved to Haugen."

Bishop Halvard kept rubbing his beard as he studied the young man.

No matter what sort of man Erlend Nikulaussøn might be, surely he wouldn't have been contemptible enough to accuse his wife of adultery before their young sons.

In spite of everything that seemed to speak against Kristin Lavransdatter, he just didn't believe it. He thought she was telling the truth when she denied knowledge of the suspicions about her and Ulf Haldorssøn. And yet he remembered that this woman had been weak before, when desires of the flesh had beckoned; with loathsome deceit she and this man with whom she now lived in discord had managed to win Lavrans's consent.

When the talk turned to the death of the child, he saw at once that her conscience troubled her. But even if she had neglected her child, she could not be brought before a court of law for that reason. She would have to repent before God, in accordance with the strictures of her confessor. And the child might still be her husband's even if she had cared for it poorly. She couldn't possibly be glad to be burdened with another infant, now that she was no longer young and had been abandoned by her husband, with seven sons already, and in much more meager circumstances than was their birthright. It would be unreasonable to expect that she could have had much love for that child.

He didn't think she was an unfaithful wife, although only God knew what he had heard and experienced in the forty years he had been a priest and listened to confessions. But he believed her.

And yet there was only one way in which he could interpret Erlend Nikulaussøn's behavior in this matter. He had refused to seek out his wife while she was with child, or after the birth, or when the infant died. He must have thought that he was not the father.

What now remained to find out was how the man would act. Whether he would stand up and defend his wife all the same, for the sake of his seven sons, as an honorable man would do. Or whether, now that these rumors were being openly discussed, he would bring charges against her. Based on what the bishop had heard about Erlend of Husaby, he wasn't sure he could count on the man not to do this.

"Who are your mother's closest kinsmen?" he asked.

"Jammælt Halvardssøn of Ælin is married to her sister, the widow of Simon Darre of Formo. She also has two cousins: Ketil Aasmundssøn of Skog and his sister, Ragna, who is married to Sigurd Kyrning. Ivar Gjesling of Ringheim and his brother, Haavard Trondssøn, are the sons of her mother's brother. But all of them live far away."

"What about Sir Sigurd Eldjarn of Sundbu? He and your mother are cousins. In a case like this the knight must step forward to defend his kinswoman, Nikulaus! You must seek him out this very day and tell him about this, my friend!"

Naakkve replied reluctantly, "Honorable Lord, there has been little kinship between him and us. And I don't think, my Lord, that it would benefit Mother's case if this man came to her defense. Erlend Eldjarn's lineage is not well liked here in the villages. Nothing harmed my father more in the eyes of the people than the fact that the Gjeslings had joined him in the plot that cost us Husaby, while they lost Sundbu."

"Yes, Erlend Eldjarn . . ." The bishop laughed a little. "Yes, he had a talent for disagreeing with people; he quarreled with all his kinsmen up here in the north. Your maternal grandfather, who was a pious man and not afraid to give in if it meant strengthening the peace and harmony among kin—even he couldn't manage any better. He and Erlend Eldjarn were the bitterest of foes."

"Yes." Naakkve couldn't help chuckling. "And it wasn't over anything important either: two embroidered sheets and a blue-hemmed towel. Altogether they weren't worth more than two marks. But my grandmother had impressed upon her husband that he must make sure to acquire these things when her father's estate was settled, and Gudrun Ivarsdatter had also spoken of them to her own husband. Erlend Eldjarn finally seized them and hid them away in his traveling bag, but Lavrans took them out again. He felt he had the most right to these things, for it was Ragnfrid who had made them as a young maiden, while she was living at home at Sundbu. When Erlend became aware of this, he struck my grandfather in the face, and then Grandfather threw him to the floor three times and shook him like a pelt. After that they never spoke again, and it was all because of those scraps of fabric; Mother has them at home in her chest."

The bishop laughed heartily. He knew this story well, which had amused everyone greatly when it occurred: that the husbands of the daughters of Ivar should be so eager to please their wives. But he had achieved what he intended: The features of the young man's face had thawed into a smile, and the wary, anguished expression had been driven from his handsome blue-gray eyes for a moment. Then Lord Halvard laughed even louder.

"Oh yes, Nikulaus, they did speak to each other one more time, and I was present. It was in Oslo, at the Christmas banquet, the year before Queen Eufemia died. My blessed Lord King Haakon was talking to Lavrans; he had come south to bring his greetings to his lord and to pledge his loyal service. The king told him that this enmity between the husbands of two sisters was unchristian and the behavior of petty men. Lavrans went over to where Erlend Eldjarn was standing with several other royal retainers and asked him in a friendly manner to forgive him for losing his temper; he said he would send the things to Fru Gudrun with loving greetings from her brother and sister. Erlend replied that he would agree to reconcile if Lavrans would accept the blame before the men standing there and admit that he had acted like a thief and a robber with regard to the inheritance of their father-in-law. Lavrans turned on his heel and walked away—and *that,* I believe, was the last time Ivar Gjesling's sons-in-law ever met on this earth," concluded the bishop, laughing loudly.

"But listen to me, Nikulaus Erlendssøn," he said, placing the palms of his hands together. "I don't know whether it would be wise to make such haste to bring your father here or to set this Ulf Haldorssøn free. It seems to me that your mother *must* clear her name since there has been so much talk that she has sinned. But as matters now stand, do you think it would be easy for Kristin to find the women willing to swear the oath along with her?"

Nikulaus looked up at the bishop; his eyes grew uncertain and fearful.

"But wait a few days, Nikulaus! Your father and Ulf are strangers in the region and not well liked. Kristin and Jardtrud both are from here in the valley, but Jardtrud is from much farther south, while your mother is one of their own. And I've noticed that Lavrans Bjørgulfsøn has not been forgotten by the people. It looks as if they mostly had intended to chastise her because she seemed to them a bad daughter. And yet already I can see that many realize the father would be poorly served by raising such an outcry against his child. They are remorseful and repentant, and soon there will be nothing they wish for more than that Kristin should be able to clear her name. And perhaps Jardtrud will have scant evidence to present when she has a look inside her bag. But it's another matter if her husband goes around turning people against him."

"My Lord," said Naakkve, looking up at the bishop, "forgive me for saying this, but I find this difficult to accept. That we should do nothing for our foster father and that we should not bring our father to stand at Mother's side."

"Nevertheless, my son," said Bishop Halvard, "I beg you to take my advice. Let us not hasten to summon Erlend Nikulaussøn here. But I will write a letter to Sir Sigurd of Sundbu, asking him to come see me at once. What's that?" He stood up and went out on the gallery.

Against the wall of the building stood Gaute and Bjørgulf Erlendssøn, and several of the bishop's men were threatening them with weapons. Bjørgulf struck a man to the ground with a blow of his axe as the bishop and Naakkve came outside. Gaute defended himself with his sword. Some farmers seized hold of Ivar and Skule, while others led away the wounded man. Sira Solmund stood off to the side, bleeding from his mouth and nose.

"Halt!" shouted Lord Halvard. "Throw down your weapons,

you sons of Erlend." He went down to the courtyard and approached the young men, who obeyed at once. "What is the meaning of this?"

Sira Solmund stepped forward, bowed, and said, "I can tell you, Reverend Father, that Gaute Erlendssøn has broken the peace of the Sabbath and struck me, his parish priest, as you can see!"

Then a middle-aged farmer stepped forward, greeted the bishop, and said, "Reverend Father, the boy was sorely provoked. This priest spoke of his mother in such a way that it would be difficult to expect Gaute to listen peaceably."

"Keep silent, priest. I cannot listen to more than one of you at a time," said Lord Halvard impatiently. "Speak, Olav Trondssøn."

Olav Trondssøn said, "The priest tried to rankle the sons of Erlend, but Bjørgulf and Gaute countered his words, calmly enough. Gaute also said what we all know is true: that Kristin was with her husband at Dovre for a time this past summer, and that's when he was conceived, the poor infant who has stirred up all this trouble. But then the priest said the people of Jørundgaard have always had so much book learning—no doubt she knew the story of King David and Bathsheba—but Erlend Nikulaussøn might have been just as cunning as Uriah the knight."[2]

The bishop's face turned as purple as his robes; his black eyes flashed. He looked at Sira Solmund for a moment, but he did not speak to him.

"Surely you must know, Gaute Erlendssøn, that with this deed you have brought the ban of the Church upon your head," he said. Then he ordered the sons of Erlend to be escorted home to Jørundgaard; he sent along two of his men and four farmers, whom the bishop selected from among the most honorable and sensible, to keep guard over them.

"You must go with them as well, Nikulaus," he told Naakkve. "But stay calm. Your brothers have not helped your mother, but I realize they were sorely vexed."

In his heart the bishop of Hamar didn't think that Kristin's sons had harmed her case. He saw that there were already many who held a different opinion of the mistress of Jørundgaard than they had in the morning, when she caused the goblet to overflow by coming to church with Ulf Haldorssøn so that he might be godfather to her son. One of them was Kolbein Jonssøn, so Lord Halvard put him in charge of the guards.

Naakkve was the first to enter the high loft where Kristin was sitting on the bed with Lavrans, holding Munan on her lap. He told her what had happened but put great weight on the fact that the bishop considered her innocent and also thought the younger brothers had been greatly provoked to react as violently as they had. He counseled his mother not to seek out the bishop herself.

Then the four brothers were escorted into the room. Their mother stared at them; she was pale, with an odd look in her eye. In the midst of her deep despair and anguish, she felt again the strange swelling of her heart, as if it might burst. And yet she said calmly to Gaute, "Ill advised was your behavior, son, and you brought little honor to the sword of Lavrans Bjørgulfsøn by drawing it against a crowd of farmers who stood there gnawing on rumors."

"First I drew it against the bishop's armed men," said Gaute indignantly. "But it's true it did little honor to our grandfather that we had to bear arms against anyone for such a reason."

Kristin looked at her son. Then she had to turn away. As much as his words pained her, she had to smile too—like when a child bites his mother's nipple with his first teeth, she thought.

"Mother," said Naakkve, "now I think it best if you go, and take Munan with you. You mustn't leave him alone even for a moment until he is calmer," he said quietly. "Keep him indoors so he doesn't see that his brothers are under guard."

Kristin stood up. "My sons, if you don't think me undeserving, then I would ask that you kiss me before I leave."

Naakkve, Bjørgulf, Ivar, and Skule went over and kissed her. The one who had been banned gave his mother a sorrowful look; when she held out her hand to him, he took a fold of her sleeve and kissed it. Kristin saw that all of them, except for Gaute, were now taller than she was. She straightened up Lavrans's bed a bit, and then she left with Munan.

There were four buildings with lofts at Jørundgaard: the high loft house, the new storeroom—which had been the summer quarters during Kristin's childhood, before Lavrans built the large house—the old storeroom, and the salt shed, which also had a loft. That's where the servingwomen slept in the summer.

Kristin went up to the loft above the new storeroom with Munan. The two of them had slept there ever since the death of the infant. She was pacing back and forth when Frida and Gunhild brought the evening porridge. Kristin asked Frida to see to it that the guardsmen were given ale and food. The maid replied that she had already done so—at Naakkve's bidding—but the men had said they would not accept anything from Kristin since they were at her manor for such a purpose. They had received food and drink from somewhere else.

"Even so, you must have a keg of foreign ale brought to them."

Gunhild, the younger maid, was red-eyed from weeping. "None of the house servants believes this of you, Kristin Lavransdatter; surely you must know that. We always said that we knew it was a lie."

"So you have heard this gossip before?" said her mistress. "It would have been better if you had mentioned it to me."

"We didn't dare because of Ulf," said Frida.

And Gunhild said as she wept, "He warned us to keep it from you. I often thought that I should mention it and beg you to be more wary . . . when you would sit and talk to Ulf until late into the night."

"Ulf . . . so he has known about this?" asked Kristin softly.

"Jardtrud has accused him of it for a long time; that was apparently always the reason that he struck her. One evening during Christmas, about the time when you were growing heavy, we were sitting and drinking with them in the foreman's house. Solveig and Øivind were there too, along with several people from south in the parish. Suddenly Jardtrud said that he was the one who had caused it. Ulf hit her with his belt so the buckle drew blood. Since then Jardtrud has gone around saying that Ulf did not deny it with a single word."

"And ever since people have been talking about this in the countryside?" asked the mistress.

"Yes. But those of us who are your servants have always denied it," said Gunhild in tears.

To calm Munan, Kristin had to lie down next to the boy and take him in her arms, but she did not undress, and she did not sleep that night.

In the meantime, up in the high loft, young Lavrans had gotten out of bed and put on his clothes. Toward evening, when Naakkve went downstairs to help tend to the livestock, the boy went out to the stable. He saddled the red gelding that belonged to Gaute; it was the best horse except for the stallion, which he didn't trust himself to ride.

Several of the men standing guard on the estate came out and asked the boy where he was headed.

"I didn't know that *I* was a prisoner too," replied young Lavrans. "But I don't need to hide it from you. Surely you wouldn't refuse to allow me to ride to Sundbu to bring back the knight to defend his kinswoman."

"It will soon be dark, my boy," said Kolbein Jonssøn. "We can't let this child ride across Vaage Gorge at night. We must speak to his mother."

"No, don't do that," said Lavrans. His lips quivered. "The purpose of my journey is such that I will trust in God and the Virgin Mary to keep watch over me, if my mother is without blame. And if not, then it makes little difference—" He broke off, for he was close to tears.

The man stood in silence for a moment. Kolbein gazed at the handsome, fair-haired child. "Go on then, and may God be with you, Lavrans Erlendssøn," he said, and was about to help the boy into the saddle.

But Lavrans led the horse forward so the men had to step aside. At the big boulder near the manor gate, he climbed up and then flung himself onto the back of Raud. Then he galloped westward, along the road to Vaagaa.

## CHAPTER 8

LAVRANS HAD RIDDEN his horse into a lather by the time he reached the spot where he knew a path led up through the scree and steep cliffs that rise up everywhere on the north side of Silsaa valley. He knew he had to make it to the heights before dark. He didn't know these mountains between Vaagaa, Sil, and Dovre, but the gelding had grazed here one summer, and he had carried Gaute to Haugen many times, although along different paths. Young Lavrans leaned forward and patted the neck of his horse.

"You must find the way to Haugen, Raud, my son. You must carry me to Father tonight, my horse."

As soon as he reached the crest of the mountains and was once again sitting in the saddle, darkness fell quickly. He rode through a marshy hollow; an endless progression of narrow ridges was silhouetted against the ever-darkening sky. There were groves of birches on the valley slopes, and their trunks shone white. Wet clusters of leaves constantly brushed against the horse's chest and the boy's face. Stones were dislodged by the animal's hooves and rolled down into the creek at the bottom of the incline. Raud found his way in the dark, up and down the hillsides, and the trickling of the creek sounded first close and then far away. Once some beast bayed into the mountain night, but Lavrans couldn't tell what it was. And the wind rushed and sang, first stronger, then fainter.

The child held his spear along the neck of his horse, so that the tip pointed forward between the animal's ears. This was bear country, this valley here. He wondered when it would end. Very softly he began to hum into the darkness: "*Kyrie eleison, Christe eleison, Kyrie eleison, Christe eleison.*"

Raud splashed through the shallow crossing of a mountain stream. The sky became even more star-strewn all around; the mountain peaks looked more distant against the blackness of the night, and the wind sang with a different tone in the vast space. The boy let the horse choose his own path as he hummed as much as he could remember of the hymn, "*Jesus Redemptor omnium—Tu lumen et splendor patris,*" interspersed with "*Kyrie eleison.*" Now he could see by the stars that they were riding almost due south, but he didn't dare do anything but trust the horse and let him lead. They were riding over rocky slopes with reindeer moss gleaming palely on the stones beneath him. Raud paused for a moment, panting and peering into the night. Lavrans saw that the sky was growing lighter in the east; clouds were billowing up, edged with silver underneath. His horse moved on, now headed directly toward the rising moon. It must be about an hour before midnight, as far as the boy could tell.

When the moon slipped free of the crests off in the distance, new snow gleamed atop the domes and rounded summits, and drifting wisps of fog turned the passes and peaks white. Lavrans recognized where he was in the mountians. He was on the mossy plateau beneath the Blue Domes.

Soon afterward he found a path leading down into the valley. And three hours later Raud limped into the courtyard of Haugen, which was white with moonlight.

When Erland opened the door, the boy collapsed on the floor of the gallery in a deep faint.

Some time later Lavrans woke up in bed, lying between filthy, rank-smelling fur covers. Light shone from a pine torch that had been stuck in a crack in the wall nearby. His father was standing over him, moistening his face with something. His father was only half dressed, and the boy noticed in the flickering light that his hair was completely gray.

"Mother . . ." said young Lavrans, looking up.

Erlend turned away so his son wouldn't see his face. "Yes," he said after a moment, almost inaudibly. "Is your mother—has she . . . is your mother . . . ill?"

"You must come home at once, Father, and save her. Now they're accusing her of the worst of things. They've taken Ulf and her and my brothers captive, Father!"

Erlend touched the boy's hot face and hands; his fever had flared up again. "What are you saying?" But Lavrans sat up and gave a fairly coherent account of everything that had taken place back home the day before. His father listened in silence, but halfway through the boy's story he began to finish getting dressed. He pulled on his boots and fastened his spurs. Then he went to get some milk and food and brought them over to the child.

"But you can't stay here alone in this house, my son. I will take you over to Aslaug, north of here in Brekken, before I ride home."

"Father." Lavrans grabbed his arm. "No, I want to go home with you."

"You're ill, little son," said Erlend, and the boy couldn't recall ever hearing such a tender tone in his father's voice.

"No, Father . . . I want to go home with you—to Mother. I want to go home to my mother. . . ." Now he was weeping like a small child.

"But Raud is limping, my boy." Erlend took his son on his lap, but he could not console the child. "And you're so tired. . . ." Finally he said, "Well, well . . . Soten can surely carry both of us."

After he had led out the stallion, put Raud inside, and tended to the animal, he said, "You must make sure to remember that someone comes north to take care of your horse . . . and my things."

"Are you going to stay home now, Father?" asked Lavrans joyfully.

Erlend gazed straight ahead. "I don't know. But I have a feeling I won't be back here again."

"Shouldn't you be better armed, Father?" the boy asked, for aside from his sword Erlend had picked up only a small, lightweight axe and was now about to leave the house. "Aren't you even going to take your shield?"

Erlend looked at his shield. The oxhide was so scratched and torn that the red lion against the white field had almost disappeared. He put it back down and spread the covers over it again.

"I'm armed well enough to drive a horde of farmers from my manor," he said. He went outside, closed the door to the house, mounted his horse, and helped the boy climb up behind him.

The sky was growing more and more overcast. By the time they had come partway down the slope, where the forest was quite dense, they were riding in darkness. Erlend noticed that his son was so tired that he could hardly hold on. Then he let Lavrans sit in front of him, and he held the boy in his arms. The young, fair-haired head rested against his chest; of all the children, Lavrans was most like his mother. Erlend kissed the top of his head as he straightened the hood on the boy's cape.

"Did your mother grieve greatly when the infant died this summer?" he asked once, quite softly.

Young Lavrans replied, "She didn't cry after he died. But she has gone up to the cemetery gate every night since. Gaute and Naakkve usually follow her when she leaves, but they haven't dared speak to her, and they don't dare let Mother see that they've been keeping watch over her."

A little later Erlend said, "She didn't cry? I remember back when your mother was young, and she wept as readily as the dew drips from goat willow reeds along the creek. She was so gentle and tender, Kristin, whenever she was with people whom she knew wished her well. Later on she had to learn to be harder, and most often I was the one to blame."

"Gunhild and Frida say that in all the days our youngest brother lived," continued Lavrans, "she cried every minute when she thought no one would see her."

"May God help me," said Erlend in a low voice. "I've been a foolish man."

They rode through the valley floor, with the curve of the river at their backs. Erlend wrapped his cape around the boy as best he could. Lavrans dozed and kept threatening to fall asleep. He sensed that his father's body smelled like that of a poor man. He had a vague memory from his early childhood, while they were living at Husaby, when his father would come from the bathhouse on Saturdays and he would have several little balls in his hands. They smelled so good, and the delicate, sweet scent would cling to his palms and to his clothing during the whole Sabbath.

Erlend rode steadily and briskly. Down on the moors it was pitch-dark. Without thinking about it, he knew at every moment where he was; he recognized the changing sound of the river's clamor, as the Laag rushed through rapids and plunged over falls. Their path took them across flat stretches, where the sparks flew from the horse's hooves. Soten ran with confidence and ease among the writhing roots of pine trees, where the road passed through thick forest; there was a soft gurgling and rushing sound as he raced across small green plains where a meandering rivulet from the mountains streamed across. By daybreak he would be home, and that would be a fitting hour.

The whole time Erlend was doubtless thinking about that moon-blue wintry night long ago when he drove a sleigh down through this very valley. Bjørn Gunnarssøn sat in back, holding a dead woman in his arms. But the memory was pale and distant, just as everything the child had told him seemed distant and unreal: all that had happened down in the village and those mad rumors about Kristin. Somehow his mind refused to grasp it. After he arrived, there would surely be time enough to think about what he should do. Nothing seemed real except the feeling of strain and fear—now that he would soon see Kristin.

He had waited and waited for her. He had never doubted that one day she would come to him—up until he heard what name she had given the child.

Stepping out of the church into the gray light were those people who had been to early mass to hear one of the priests from Hamar preach. The ones who emerged first saw Erlend Nikulaussøn ride past toward home, and they told the others. Some uneasiness and a great deal of talk arose; people headed down the slope and stood in groups at the place where the lane to Jørundgaard diverged from the main road.

Erlend rode into the courtyard as the waning moon sank behind the rim of clouds and the mountain ridge, pale in the dawn light.

Outside the foreman's house stood a group of people: Jardtrud's kinsmen and her friends who had stayed with her overnight. At the sound of horse hooves in the courtyard the men who had been keeping guard in the room under the high loft came outside.

Erlend reined in his horse. He gazed down at the farmers and said in a loud, mocking voice, "Is there a feast being held on my estate and I know nothing about it? Or why are you good folks gathered here at this early hour?"

Angry, dark looks met him from all sides. Erlend sat tall and slender astride the long-legged foreign stallion. Before, Soten's mane had been clipped short, but now it was thick and uncut. The horse was ungroomed and had gray hairs on his head, but his eyes glittered dangerously, and he stomped and shifted uneasily, laying his ears back and tossing his small, elegant head so that flecks of lather sprinkled his neck and shoulders and the rider. The harness-work had once been red and the saddle inlaid with gold; now they were worn and broken and mended. And the man was dressed almost like a beggar. His hair, which billowed from under a simple black woolen hat, was grayish white; a gray stubble grew on his pale, furrowed face with the big nose. But he sat erect, and he was smiling arrogantly down at the crowd of farmers. He looked young, in spite of everything, and like a chieftain. Fierce hatred surged toward this outsider, who sat there, holding his head high and uncowed—after all the grief and shame and misery he had brought upon those whom these people considered their own chieftains.

And yet the farmer who was the first to answer Erlend spoke with restraint. "I see you have found your son, Erlend, so I think you must know that we have not gathered here for any feast. And it seems strange you would jest about such a matter."

Erlend looked down at the child, who was still asleep. His voice grew more gentle.

"The boy is ill; surely you must see that. The news he brought me from here in the parish seemed so unbelievable that I thought he must be speaking in a feverish daze.

"And some of it is nonsense, after all, I see." Erlend frowned as he glanced at the stable door. Ulf Haldorssøn and two other men—one of them his brother-in-law—were at that moment leading out several horses.

Ulf let go of his horse and strode swiftly toward his master.

"Have you finally come, Erlend? And there's the boy—praise be to Christ and the Virgin Mary! His mother doesn't know he was missing. We were about to go out to look for him. The bishop released me on my sworn oath when he heard the child had set off alone for Vaagaa. How is Lavrans?" he asked anxiously.

"Thank God you've found the boy," said Jardtrud, weeping. She had come out into the courtyard.

"Are you here, Jardtrud?" said Erlend. "That will be the first thing I see to: that you leave my estate, you and your cohorts. First we'll drive off this gossiping woman, and then anyone else who has spread lies about my wife will be fined."

"That cannot be done, Erlend," said Ulf Haldorssøn. "Jardtrud is my lawful wife. I don't think either she or I has any desire to stay together, but she will not leave my house until I have placed in the hands of my brothers-in-law her livestock, dowry, betrothal gifts, and wedding gifts."

"Am I not the master of this estate?" asked Erlend, furious.

"You will have to ask Kristin Lavransdatter about that," said Ulf. "Here she comes."

The mistress was standing on the gallery of the new storeroom. Now she slowly came down the stairs. Without thinking, she pulled her wimple forward—it had slipped back off her head—and she smoothed her church gown, which she had worn since the day before. But her face was as motionless as stone.

Erlend rode forward to meet her, at a walking pace. Bending down a bit, he stared with fearful confusion at his wife's gray, dead face.

"Kristin," he implored. "My Kristin. I've come home to you."

She didn't seem to hear or see him. Then Lavrans, who was sitting in his father's arms and had gradually woken up, slid down to the ground. The moment his feet touched the grass, the boy collapsed and he lay in a heap.

A tremor passed over his mother's face. She leaned down and lifted the big boy in her arms, pressing his head against her throat, as if he were a little child. But his long legs hung down limply in front of her.

"Kristin, my dearest love," begged Erlend in despair. "Oh, Kristin, I know I've come to you much too late . . ."

Again a tremor passed over his wife's face.

"It's not too late," she said, her voice low and harsh. She stared down at her son, who lay in a swoon in her arms. "Our last child is already in the ground, and now it's Lavrans's turn. Gaute has been banished by the Church, and our other sons . . . But the two of us still own much that can be ruined, Erlend!"

She turned away from him and began walking across the courtyard with the child. Erlend rode after her, keeping his horse at her side.

"Kristin—Jesus, what can I do for you? Kristin, don't you want me to stay with you now?"

"I don't need you to do anything more for me," said his wife in the same tone of voice. "You cannot help me, whether you stay here or you throw yourself into the Laag."

Erlend's sons had come out onto the gallery of the high loft. Now Gaute ran down and raced toward his mother, trying to stop her.

"Mother," he begged. Then she gave him a look, and he halted in bewilderment.

Several farmers were standing at the bottom of the loft stairs.

"Move aside, men," said the mistress, trying to pass them with her burden.

Soten tossed his head and danced uneasily; Erlend turned the horse halfway around, and Kolbein Jonssøn grabbed the bridle. Kristin hadn't seen what was happening; now she turned to look over her shoulder.

"Let go of the horse, Kolbein. If he wants to ride off, then let him."

Kolbein took a firmer grip and replied, "Don't you see, Kristin, that it's time for the master to stay home on his estate? You at least should realize it," he said to Erlend.

But Erlend struck the man over the hand and urged the stallion forward, so the old man fell. A couple of other men leaped forward.

Erlend shouted, "Get away from here! You have nothing to do with matters concerning me or my wife—and I'm not the master. I refuse to bind myself to a manor like a calf to the stall. I may not own this estate, but neither does this estate own me!"

Kristin turned to face her husband and screamed, "Go ahead and ride off! Ride, ride like the Devil to Hell. That's where you've driven me and cast off everything you've ever owned or been given—"

What occurred next happened so fast that no one properly foresaw it or could prevent it. Tore Borghildssøn and another man grabbed her by the arms. "Kristin, you mustn't speak that way to your husband."

Erlend rode up close to them.

"Do you dare to lay hands on my wife?" He swung his axe and struck at Tore Borghildssøn. The blow fell between his shoulder blades, and the man sank to the ground. Erlend lifted his axe again, but as he raised up in the stirrups, a man ran a spear through him, and it pierced his groin. It was the son of Tore Borghildssøn who did this.

Soten reared up and kicked with his front hooves. Erlend pressed his knees against the animal's sides and leaned forward as he pulled on the reins with his left hand and again raised his axe. But almost at once he lost one of his stirrups, and the blood gushed down over his left thigh. Several arrows and spears whistled across the courtyard. Ulf and Erlend's sons rushed into the throng with axes raised and swords drawn. Then a man stabbed the stallion Erlend was riding, and the animal fell to his knees, whinnying so wildly and shrilly that the horses in the stable replied.

Erlend stood up, his legs straddling the animal. He put his hand on Bjørgulf's shoulder and stepped off. Gaute came up and grabbed his father under the other arm.

"Kill him," he said, meaning the horse, which had now rolled onto his side and lay with his neck stretched out, blood frothing around his jaw, and his mighty hooves flailing. Ulf Haldorssøn complied.

The farmers had retreated. Two men carried Tore Borghildssøn over to the foreman's house, and one of the bishop's men led away his companion, who was wounded.

Kristin had put Lavrans down, since he had now regained his wits; they stood there, clinging to each other. She didn't seem to understand what had taken place; it had all happened so fast.

Her sons began helping their father toward the high loft house, but Erlend said, "I don't want to go in there. I don't want to die where Lavrans died."

Kristin ran forward and threw her arms around her husband's neck. Her frozen face shattered, contorted with sobs, the way ice is splintered when struck by a stone. "Erlend, Erlend!"

Erlend bent his head down so his cheek touched hers, and he stood in that manner for a moment.

"Help me up into the old storeroom, boys," he said. "I want to lie down there."

Hastily Kristin and her sons made up the bed in the old loft and helped Erlend undress. Kristin bandaged his wounds. The blood was gushing in spurts from the gash of the spear in his groin, and he had an arrow wound on the lower left side of his chest, but it was not bleeding much.

Erlend stroked his wife's head. "I'm afraid you won't be able to heal me, my Kristin."

She looked up, despairing. A great shudder passed through her body. She remembered that Simon had said the same thing, and this seemed to her the worst omen, that Erlend should speak the same words.

He lay in bed, supported with pillows and cushions, and with his left leg raised to stop the blood flowing from his groin wound. Kristin sat leaning over him. Then he took her hand. "Do you remember the first night we slept together in this bed, my sweet? I didn't know then that you were already carrying a secret sorrow for which I was to blame. And that was not the first sorrow you had to bear for my sake, Kristin."

She held his hand in both of hers. His skin was cracked, with dirt ingrained around his small, grooved fingernails and in the creases of every joint of his long fingers. Kristin lifted his hand to her breast and then to her lips; her tears streamed over it.

"Your lips are so hot," said Erlend softly. "I waited and waited for you . . . I longed so terribly . . . Finally I thought I should give in; I should come down here to you, but then I heard . . . I thought, when I heard that he had died, that now it would be too late for me to come to you."

Sobbing, Kristin replied, "I was still waiting for you, Erlend. I thought that someday you would have to come to the boy's grave."

"But then you would not have welcomed me as your friend," said Erlend. "And God knows you had no reason to do so either. As sweet and lovely as you are, my Kristin," he whispered, closing his eyes.

She sobbed quietly, in great distress.

"Now nothing remains," said her husband in the same tone as before, "except for us to try to forgive each other as a Christian husband and wife, if you can . . ."

"Erlend, Erlend . . ." She leaned over him and kissed his white face. "You shouldn't talk so much, my Erlend."

"I think I must make haste to say what I have to say," replied her husband. "Where is Naakkve?" he asked uneasily.

He was told that the night before, as soon as Naakkve heard that his younger brother was headed for Sundbu, he had set off after him as fast as his horse would go. He must be quite distraught by now, since he hadn't found the child. Erlend sighed, his hands fumbling restlessly on the coverlet.

His six sons stepped up to the bed.

"No, I haven't handled things well for you, my sons," said their father. He began to cough, in a strange and cautious manner. Bloody froth seeped out of his lips. Kristin wiped it away with her wimple.

Erlend lay quietly for a moment. "Now you must forgive me, if you can. Never forget, my fine boys, that your mother has striven on your behalf every day, during all the years that she and I have lived together. Never has there been any enmity between us except that for which I was to blame because I paid too little mind to your well-being. But she has loved you more than her own life."

"We won't forget," replied Gaute, weeping, "that you, Father, seemed to us all our days the most courageous of men and the noblest of chieftains. We were proud to be called your sons—no less so when fortune forsook you than during your days of prosperity."

"You say this because you understand so little," said Erlend. He gave a brittle, sputtering laugh. "But do not cause your mother the sorrow of taking after me; she has had enough to struggle with since she married me."

"Erlend, Erlend," sobbed Kristin.

The sons kissed their father's hand and cheek; weeping, they turned away and sat down against the wall. Gaute put his arm around Munan's shoulder and pulled the boy close; the twins sat hand in hand. Erlend again placed his hand in Kristin's. His was cold. Then she pulled the covers all the way up to his chin but sat holding his hand in her own under the blankets.

"Erlend," she said, weeping. "May God have mercy on us—we must send word to the priest for you."

"Yes," said Erlend faintly. "Someone must ride up to Dovre to bring Sira Guttorm, my parish priest."

"Erlend, he won't get here in time," she said in horror.

"Yes, he will," said Erlend vehemently. "If God will grant me . . .

For I refuse to receive the last rites from that priest who has been spreading gossip about you."

"Erlend—in the name of Jesus—you must not talk that way."

Ulf Haldorssøn stepped forward and bent over the dying man. "I will ride to Dovre, Erlend."

"Do you remember, Ulf," said Erlend, his voice beginning to sound weak and confused, "the time we left Hestnes, you and I?" He laughed a bit. "And I promised that all my days I would stand by you as your loyal kinsman . . . God save me, kinsman . . . Of the two of us, it was most often you and not I who showed the loyalty of kin, my friend Ulf. I give you . . . thanks . . . for that, kinsman."

Ulf leaned down and kissed the man's bloody lips. "I thank you too, Erlend Nikulaussøn."

He lit a candle, placed it near the deathbed, and left the room.

Erlend's eyes had closed again. Kristin sat staring at his white face; now and then she caressed it with her hand. She thought she could see that he was sinking toward death.

"Erlend," she implored him softly. "In the name of Jesus, let us send word to Sira Solmund for you. God is God, no matter what priest brings Him to us."

"No!" Her husband sat up in bed so that the covers slid down his naked, sallow body. The bandages across his breast and stomach were once again colored with bright red splotches from the fresh blood pouring out. "I am a sinful man. May God bestow on me the grace of His mercy, as much as He will grant me, but I know . . ." He fell back against the pillows and whispered almost inaudibly, "I will not live long enough to be . . . so old . . . and so pious . . . that I can bear . . . to sit calmly in the same room with someone who has told lies about you."

"Erlend, Erlend—think of your soul!"

The man shook his head on the pillows. His eyelids had fallen shut again.

"Erlend!" She clasped her hands; she screamed loudly, in the utmost distress. "Erlend, don't you understand that after the way you have acted toward me, this *has* to be said!"

Erlend opened his big eyes. His lips were pale blue, but a remnant of his youthful smile flickered across his ravaged face.

"Kiss me, Kristin," he whispered. There was a trace of laughter in his voice. "Surely there has been too much else between you and me—besides Christendom and marriage—for it to be possible for us to . . . take leave of each other . . . as a Christian husband and wife."

She called and called his name, but he lay with closed eyes, his face as pale as newly split wood beneath his gray hair. A little blood seeped from the corners of his mouth; she wiped it away, whispering entreaties. When she moved, she could feel her clothes were cold and sticky, wet with the blood that had spattered her when she helped him inside and put him to bed. Now and then a faint gurgling came from Erlend's chest, and he seemed to have trouble breathing; but he did not move again, nor was he aware of anything more as he surely and steadily sank into the torpor of death.

The loft door was abruptly thrown open. Naakkve came rushing in; he flung himself down beside the bed and seized his father's hand as he called his name.

Behind him came a tall, stout gentleman wearing a traveling cape. He bowed to Kristin.

"If I had known, my kinswoman, that you were in need of the help of your kin . . ." Then he broke off as he saw that the man was dying. He crossed himself and went over to the farthest corner of the room. Quietly the Sundbu knight began saying the prayer for the dying, but Kristin seemed not to have even noticed Sir Sigurd's arrival.

Naakkve was on his knees, bending over the bed. "Father! Father! Don't you know me anymore, Father?" He pressed his face against Erlend's hand, which Kristin was holding. The young man's tears and kisses showered the hands of both his parents.

Kristin pushed her son's head aside a little—as if she were suddenly half awake.

"You're disturbing us," she said impatiently. "Go away."

Naakkve straightened up as he knelt there. "Go? But, Mother . . ."

"Yes. Go sit down with your brothers over there."

Naakkve lifted his young face—wet with tears, contorted with grief—but his mother's eyes saw nothing. Then he went over to the bench where his six brothers were already sitting. Kristin paid no attention; she simply stared, with wild eyes, at Erlend's face, which now shone snow-white in the light of the candle.

A short time later the door was opened again. Bearing candles and ringing a silver bell, deacons and a priest followed Bishop Halvard into the loft. Ulf Haldorssøn entered last. Erlend's sons and Sir Sigurd stood up and then fell to their knees before the body of the Lord. But Kristin merely raised her head, and for a moment she turned her tear-filled eyes, seeing nothing, toward those who had arrived. Then she lay back down, the way she was before, stretched out across Erlend's corpse.

PART III

# THE CROSS

## CHAPTER 1

ALL FIRES BURN out sooner or later.

There came a time when these words spoken by Simon Darre resounded once more in Kristin's heart.

It was the summer of the fourth year after Erlend Nikulaussøn's death, and of the seven sons, only Gaute and Lavrans remained with their mother at Jørundgaard.

Two years before, the old smithy had burned down, and Gaute had built a new one north of the farm, up toward the main road. The old smithy had stood to the south of the buildings, down by the river in a low curve of land between Jørund's burial mound and several great heaps of rocks which had apparently been cleared from the fields long ago. Almost every year during the flood season the water would reach all the way up to the smithy.

Now there was nothing left on the site but the heavy, fire-scorched stones that showed where the threshold had been and the brick fireplace. Soft, slender blades of pale green grass were now sprouting from the dark, charred floor.

This year Kristin Lavransdatter had sown a field of flax near the site of the old smithy; Gaute had wanted to put grain in the acres closer to the manor, where the mistresses of Jørundgaard, since ancient times, had always planted flax and cultivated onions. And so Kristin often went out to the far fields to see to her flax. On Thursday evenings she would carry a gift of ale and food to the farmer in the mound.[1] On light summer evenings the lonely fireplace in the meadow looked at times like some ancient heathen altar as it was glimpsed through the grass, grayish white and streaked with soot. On hot summer days, under the baking sun, she would take her basket to the rock heaps at midday to pick raspberries or to gather the leaves of fireweed, which could be used to make cooling drinks for a fever.

The last notes of the church bells' noon greeting to the Mother of God died away in the light-sated air up among the peaks. The countryside seemed to be settling into sleep beneath the flood of white sunlight. Ever since the dew-soaked dawn, scythes had been ringing in the flowery meadows; the scrape of iron against whetstones and the shouting of voices could be heard from every farm, near and far. Now all the sounds of busy toiling fell away; it was time for the midday rest. Kristin sat down on a pile of stones and listened. Only the roar of the river could be heard now, and a slight rustling of the leaves in the grove, along with the faint rubbing and soft buzzing of flies over the meadow, and the clinking bell of a solitary cow somewhere off in the distance. A bird flapped its way, swift and mute, along the edge of the alder thicket; another flew up from a meadow tussock and with a harsh cry perched atop a thistle.

But the drifting blue shadows on the hillsides, the fair-weather clouds billowing up over the mountain ridges and melting into the blue summer sky, the glitter of the Laag's water beyond the trees, the white glint of sunlight on all the leaves—these things she noticed more as silent sounds, audible only to her inner ear, rather than as visible images. With her wimple pulled forward over her brow, Kristin sat and listened to the play of light and shadow across the valley.

All fires burn out sooner or later.

In the alder woods along the marshy riverbank, pockets of water sparkled in the darkness between the dense willow bushes. Star grass grew there, along with tufts of cotton grass and thick carpets of marshlocks with their dusty green, five-pointed leaves and reddish brown flowers. Kristin had picked an enormous pile of them. Many times she had pondered whether this herb might possess useful powers; she had dried it and boiled it and added it to ale and mead. But it didn't seem good for anything. And yet Kristin could never resist going out to the marsh and getting her shoes wet to gather the plant.

Now she stripped all the leaves from the stalks and plaited a wreath from the dark flowers. They had the color of both red wine and brown mead, and in the center, under the knot of red filaments, they were as moist as honey. Sometimes Kristin would plait a wreath for the picture of the Virgin Mary up in the high loft; she had heard from priests who had been to the southern lands that this was the custom there.

Otherwise she no longer had anyone to make wreaths for. Here in the valley the young men didn't wear wreaths on their heads when they went out to dance on the green. In some areas of Trøndelag the men who came home from the royal court had introduced the custom. Kristin thought this thick, dark red wreath would be well suited to Gaute's fair face and flaxen hair or Lavrans's nut-brown mane.

It was so long ago that she used to walk through the pasture above Husaby with the foster mothers and all her young sons on those long, fair-weather days in the summer. Then she and Frida couldn't make wreaths fast enough for all the impatient little children. She remembered when she still had Lavrans at her breast, but Ivar and Skule thought the infant should have a wreath too; the four-year-olds thought it should be made from very tiny flowers.

Now she had only grown-up children.

Young Lavrans was fifteen winters old; he couldn't yet be considered full-grown. But his mother had gradually realized that this son was in some ways more distant from her than all the other children. He didn't purposely shun her, as Bjørgulf had done, and he wasn't aloof, nor did he *seem* particularly taciturn, the way the blind boy was. But he was apparently much quieter by nature, although no one had noticed this when all the brothers were home. He was bright and lively, always seemed happy and kind, and everyone was fond of the charming child without thinking about the fact that Lavrans nearly always went about in silence and alone.

He was considered the handsomest of all the handsome sons of Kristin of Jørundgaard. Their mother always thought that the one she happened to be thinking about at the moment was the most handsome, but she too could see there was a radiance about Lavrans Erlendssøn. His light brown hair and apple-fresh cheeks seemed gilded, sated with sunshine; his big dark gray eyes seemed to be strewn with tiny yellow sparks. He looked much the way she had looked when she was young, with her fair coloring burnished tan by the sun. And he was tall and strong for his age, capable and diligent at any task he was given, obedient to his mother and older brothers, merry, good-natured, and companionable. And yet there was this odd sense of reserve about the boy.

During the winter evenings, when the servants gathered in the weaving room to pass the time with talk and banter as each person was occupied with some chore, Lavrans would sit there as if in a dream. Many a summer evening, when the daily work on the farm was done, Kristin would go out and sit with the boy as he lay on the green, chewing on a piece of resin or twirling a sprig of sorrel between his lips. She would look at his eyes as she spoke to him; he seemed to be shifting his attention back from far away. Then he would smile up at his mother's face and give her a proper and sensible reply. Often the two of them would sit together for hours on the hillside, talking comfortably and with ease. But as soon as she stood up to go inside, it seemed as if Lavrans would let his thoughts wander again.

She couldn't figure out what it was the boy was pondering so deeply. He was skilled enough in sports and the use of weapons, but he was much less zealous than her other sons had been about such things, and he never went out hunting alone, although he was pleased whenever Gaute asked him to go along on a hunt. And he never seemed to notice that women cast tender eyes on this fair young boy. He had no interest in book learning, and the youngest son paid little attention to all the older boys' talk of their plans to enter a monastery. Kristin couldn't see that the boy had given any thought to his future, other than that he would continue to stay there at home all his days and help Gaute with the farm work, as he did now.

Sometimes this strange, aloof creature reminded Kristin Lavransdatter a bit of his father. But Erlend's soft, languid manner had often given way to a boisterous wildness, and Lavrans had none of his father's quick, hot disposition. Erlend had never been far removed from what was going on around him.

Lavrans was now the youngest. Munan had long ago been laid to rest in the grave beside his father and little brother. He died early in the spring, the year after Erlend was killed.

After her husband's death the widow had behaved as if she neither heard nor saw a thing. Stronger than pain or sorrow was the feeling she had of a numbing chill and a dull lassitude in both her body and soul, as if she herself were bleeding to death from his mortal wounds.

Her whole life had resided in his arms ever since that thunder-laden midday hour in the barn at Skog when she gave herself to Erlend Nikulaussøn for the first time. Back then she was so young and inexperienced; she understood so little about what she was doing but strove to hide that she was close to tears because he was hurting her. She smiled, for she thought she was giving her lover the most precious of gifts. And whether or not it was a good gift, she had given him herself, completely and forever. Her maidenly life, which God had mercifully adorned with beauty and health when He allowed her to be born into secure and honorable circumstances, which her parents had protected during all those years as they brought her up with the most loving strictness: With both hands she had given all this to Erlend, and ever since she had lived within his embrace.

So many times in the years that followed she had received his caresses, and stony and cold with anger, she had obediently complied with her husband's will, while she felt on the verge of collapse, ravaged by weariness. She had felt a sort of resentful pleasure when she looked at Erlend's lovely face and healthy, graceful body—at least *that* could no longer blind her to the man's faults. Yes, he was just as young and just as handsome; he could still overwhelm her with caresses that were as ardent as they had been in the days when she too was young. But *she* had aged, she thought, feeling a rush of triumphant pride. It was easy for someone to stay young if he refused to learn, refused to adapt to his lot in life, and refused to fight to change his circumstances in accordance with his will.

And yet even when she received his kisses with her lips pressed tight, when she turned her whole being away from him in order to fight for the future of her sons, she sensed that she threw herself into this effort with the same fiery passion this man had once ignited in her blood. She thought the years had cooled her ardor because she no longer felt desire whenever Erlend had that old glint in his eyes or that deep tone to his voice, which had made her swoon, helpless and powerless with joy, the first time she met him. But just as she had once longed to ease the heavy burden of separation and the anguish of her heart in her meetings with Erlend, she now felt a dull but fervent longing for a goal that would one day be reached when she, at long last, was a white-haired old woman and saw her sons well provided for and secure. Now it was for Erlend's sons that she endured the old fear of the uncertainty that lay ahead. And yet she was tormented with a longing that was like a hunger and a burning thirst—she must see her sons flourish.

And just as she had once given herself to Erlend, she later surrendered herself to the world that had sprung up around their life together. She threw herself into fulfilling every demand that had to be met; she lent a hand with every task that needed to be done in order to ensure the well-being of Erlend and his children. She began to understand that Erlend was always with her when she sat at Husaby and studied the documents in her husband's chest along with their priest, or when she talked to his leaseholders and laborers, or worked alongside her maids in the living quarters and cookhouse, or sat in the horse pasture with the foster mothers and kept an eye on her children on those lovely summer days. She came to realize that she turned her anger on Erlend whenever anything went wrong in the house and whenever the children disobeyed her will; but it was also toward him that her great joy streamed whenever they brought the hay in dry during the summer or had a good harvest of grain in the fall, or whenever her calves were thriving, and whenever she heard her boys shouting and laughing in the courtyard. The knowledge that she belonged to him blazed deep within her heart whenever she laid aside the last of the Sabbath clothes she had sewn for her seven sons and stood rejoicing over the pile of lovely, carefully stitched work she had done that winter. *He* was the one she was sick and tired of one spring evening when she walked home with her maids from the river. They had been washing wool from the last shearing, boiling water in a kettle on the shore and rinsing the wool in the current. And the mistress herself felt a great strain in her back, and her arms were coal-black with dung; the smell of sheep and dirty fat had soaked into her clothes until she thought her body would never be clean, even after three visits to the bathhouse.

But now that he was gone, it seemed to the widow that there was no purpose left to the restless toil of her life. *He* had been cut down, and so she had to die like a tree whose roots have been severed. The young shoots that had sprung up around her lap would now have to grow from their own roots. Each of them was old enough to decide his own fate. The thought flitted through Kristin's mind that if she had realized this before, back when Erlend mentioned it to her . . . Shadowy images of a life with Erlend up at his mountain farm passed through her mind: the two of them youthful again, with the little child between them. But she felt neither regret nor remorse. She had not been able to cut her life away from that of her sons; now death would soon separate them, for without Erlend she had no strength to live. All that had happened and would happen was meant to be. Everything happens as it is meant to be.

Her hair and her skin turned gray; she took little interest in bathing or tending to her clothes properly. At night she would lie in bed thinking about her life with Erlend; in the daytime she would walk about as if in a dream, never speaking to anyone unless addressed first, not seeming to hear even when her young sons spoke to her. This diligent and alert woman did not raise a hand to do any work. Love had always been behind her toil with earthly matters. Erlend had never given her much thanks for that; it was not the way he wanted to be loved. But she couldn't help it; it was her nature to love with great toil and care.

She seemed to be slipping toward the torpor of death. Then the scourge came to the countryside, flinging her sons onto their sickbeds, and the mother woke up.

The sickness was more dangerous for grown-ups than for children. Ivar was struck so hard that no one expected him to live. The youth acquired enormous strength in his fevered state; he bellowed and wanted to get out of bed to take up arms. His father's death seemed to be weighing on his mind. With great difficulty Naakkve and Bjørgulf managed to hold him down. Then it was Bjørgulf's turn to take to his bed. Lavrans lay with his face swollen beyond recognition with festering sores; his eyes glittered dully between narrow slits and looked as if they would be extinguished in a blaze of fever.

Kristin kept vigil in the loft with all three of them. Naakkve and Gaute had had the sickness as boys, and Skule was less ill than his brothers. Frida was taking care of him and Munan downstairs in the main room. No one thought there was any danger for Munan, but he had never been strong, and one evening when they thought he had already recovered, he suddenly fell into a faint. Frida had just enough time to warn his mother. Kristin ran downstairs, and a moment later Munan breathed his last in her arms.

The child's death aroused in her a new, wide-awake despair. Her wild grief over the infant who had died at his mother's breast had seemed red-tinged with the memory of all her crushed dreams of happiness. Back then the storm in her heart had kept her going. And the dire strain, which ended with her seeing her husband killed before her very eyes, left behind such a weariness in her soul that Kristin was convinced she would soon die of grief over Erlend. But that certainty had dulled the sharpness of her pain. She went about feeling the twilight and shadows growing all around her as she waited for the door to open for her in turn.

Over Munan's little body his mother stood alert and gray. This lovely, sweet little boy had been her youngest child for so many years, the last of her sons whom she still dared caress and laugh at when she ought to have been stern and somber, chastising him for his little misdeeds and careless acts. And he had been so loving and attached to his mother. It cut into her living flesh. As bound to life as she still was, it wasn't possible for a woman to die as easily as she had thought, after she had poured her life's blood into so many new young hearts.

In cold, sober despair she moved between the child who lay on his bier and her ill sons. Munan was laid out in the old storeroom, where first the infant and then his father had lain. Three bodies on her manor in less than a year. Her heart was withered with anguish, but rigid and mute, she waited for the next one to die; she expected it, like an inevitable fate. She had never fully understood what she had been given when God bestowed on her so many children. The worst of it was that in some ways she *had* understood. But she had thought more about the troubles, the pain, the anguish, and the strife—even though she had learned over and over again, from her yearning every time a child grew out of her arms, and from her joy every time a new one lay at her breast, that her happiness was inexpressibly greater than her struggles or pain. She had grumbled because the father of her children was such an unreliable man, who gave so little thought to the descendants who would come after him. She always forgot that he had been no different when she broke God's commandments and trampled on her own family in order to win him.

Now he had fallen from her side. And now she expected to see her sons die, one after the other. Perhaps in the end she would be left all alone, a childless mother.

There were so many things she had seen before to which she had given little thought, back when she viewed the world as if through the veil of Erlend's and her love. No doubt she had noticed how Naakkve took it seriously that he was the firstborn son and should be the leader and chieftain of his brothers. No doubt she had also seen that he was very fond of Munan. And yet she was greatly shaken, as if by something unexpected, when she saw his terrible grief at the death of his youngest brother.

But her other sons regained their health, although it took a long time. On Easter Day she was able to go to church with four sons, but Bjørgulf was still in bed, and Ivar was too weak to leave the house. Lavrans had grown quite tall while he was sick in bed, and in other ways it seemed as if the events of the past half year had carried him far beyond his years.

Kristin felt as if she were now an old woman. It seemed to her that a woman was young as long as she had little children sleeping in her arms at night, playing around her during the day, and demanding her care at all times. When a mother's children have grown away from her, then she becomes an old woman.

Her new brother-in-law, Jammælt Halvardssøn, said that the sons of Erlend were still quite young, and she herself was little more than forty years old. Surely she would soon decide to marry again; she needed a husband to help her manage her property and raise her younger sons. He mentioned several good men who he thought would be a noble match for Kristin; she should come to Ælin for a visit in the fall, and then he would see to it that she met these men, and afterward they could discuss the matter at greater length.

Kristin smiled wanly. It was true that she *wasn't* more than forty years old. If she had heard about another woman who had been widowed at such a young age, with so many half-grown children, she would have said the same as Jammælt: The woman should marry again and seek support from a new husband; she might even give him more children. But she herself would not.

It was just after Easter that Jammælt of Ælin came to Jørundgaard, and this was the second time that Kristin met her sister's new husband. She and her sons had not attended either the betrothal feast at Dyfrin or the wedding at Ælin. The two banquets had been held within a short time of each other during the spring when she was carrying her last child. As soon as Jammælt heard of the death of Erlend Nikulaussøn, he had rushed to Sil; in both word and deed he had helped his wife's sister and nephews. As best he could, he took care of everything that had to be done after the master's death, and he handled the case against the killers, since none of Erlend's sons had yet come of age. But back then Kristin had paid no heed to anything happening around her. Even the sentencing of Gudmund Toressøn, who was found to be the murderer of Erlend, seemed to make little impression on her.

This time she talked more with her brother-in-law, and he seemed to her a pleasant man. He was not young; he was the same age as Simon Darre. A calm and steadfast man, tall and stout, with a dark complexion and quite a handsome face, but rather stoop-shouldered. He and Gaute became good friends at once. Ever since their father's death Naakkve and Bjørgulf had grown closer to each other but had withdrawn from all the others. Ivar and Skule told their mother that they liked Jammælt, "but it seems to us that Ramborg could have shown Simon more respect by staying a widow a little longer; this new husband of hers is not his equal." Kristin saw that these two unruly sons of hers still remembered Simon Andressøn. They had allowed him to admonish them both with sharp words and mild jests, even though the two impatient boys refused to hear a word of chastisement from their own parents except with eyes flashing with anger and hands clenched into fists.

While Jammælt was at Jørundgaard, Munan Baardsøn also paid a visit to Kristin. There was now little remaining of the former Sir

Munan the Prancer. He had been a towering and imposing figure in the old days; back then he had carried his bulky body with some amount of grace, so that he seemed taller and more stately than he was. Now rheumatism had crippled him, and his flesh hung on his shriveled body; more than anything he resembled a little goblin, with a bald pate and a meager fringe of lank white hair at the back of his head. Once a thick blue-black beard had darkened his taut, full cheeks and jaw, but now an abundance of gray stubble grew in all the slack folds of his cheeks and throat, which he had a hard time shaving with his knife. He had grown bleary-eyed, he slobbered a bit, and he was terribly plagued by a weak stomach.

He had brought along his son Inge, whom people called Fluga, after his mother. He was already an old man. The father had offered this son a great deal of help in the world; he had found him a rich match and managed to get Bishop Halvard to take an interest in Inge. Munan had been married to the bishop's cousin Katrin. Lord Halvard wanted to help Inge become prosperous so that he wouldn't deplete the inheritance of Fru Katrin's children. The bishop had been given authority over the county of Hedemark, and he had then made Inge Munanssøn his envoy, so he now owned quite a few properties in Skaun and Ridabu. His mother had also bought a farm in those parts; she was now a most pious and charitable woman who had vowed to live a pure life until her death. "Well, she is neither aged nor infirm," said Munan crossly when Kristin laughed. He had doubtless wanted to arrange things so that Brynhild would move in with him and manage his household at his estate in Hamar, but she had refused.

He had so little joy in his old age, Sir Munan complained. His children were full of rancor. Those siblings who had the same mother had joined forces against the others, quarreling and squabbling with their half siblings. Worst of all was his youngest daughter; she had been born to one of his paramours while he was a married man, so she could be given no share of the inheritance. For that reason, she was trying to glean from him all that she could while he was still alive. She was a widow and had settled at Skogheim, the estate which was Sir Munan's only real home. Neither her father nor her siblings could roust her from the place. Munan was deathly afraid of her, but whenever he tried to run off to live with one of his other children, they would torment him with complaints about the greed and dishonest behavior of their other siblings. He felt most comfortable with his youngest, lawfully born daughter, who was a nun at Gimsøy. He liked to stay for a time in the convent's hostel, striving hard to better his soul with penances and prayers under the guidance of his daughter, but he didn't have the strength to stay there for long. Kristin wasn't convinced that Brynhild's sons were any kinder toward their father than his other children, but that was something that Munan Baardsøn refused to admit; he loved them more than all his other offspring.

As pitiful as this kinsman of hers now was, it was during the time spent with him that Kristin's stony grief first began to thaw. Sir Munan talked about Erlend day and night. When he wasn't lamenting over his own trials, he could talk of nothing else but his dead cousin, boasting of Erlend's exploits—particularly about his reckless youth. Erlend's wild boldness as soon as he made his way out into the world, away from his home at Husaby—where Fru Magnhild went about raging over his father while his father raged over his elder son—and away from Hestnes and Sir Baard, his pious, somber foster father. It might have seemed that Sir Munan's chatter would offer an odd sort of consolation for Erlend's grieving widow. But in his own way the knight had loved his young kinsman, and all his days he had thought Erlend surpassed every other man in appearance, courage—yes, even in good sense, although he had never wanted to use it, said Munan earnestly. And even though Kristin had to recall that it surely was not in Erlend's best interest that he had joined the king's retainers at the age of sixteen, with this cousin as his mentor and guide, nevertheless she had to smile with tender sorrow at Munan Baardsøn. He talked so that the spittle flew from his lips and the tears seeped from his old red-rimmed eyes, as he remembered Erlend's sparkling joy and spirit in those days of his youth, before he became tangled up in misfortune with Eline Ormsdatter and was branded for life.

Jammælt Halvardssøn, who was having a serious conversation with Gaute and Naakkve, cast a wondering glance at his sister-in-law. She was sitting on the bench against the wall with that loathsome old man and Ulf Haldorssøn, who Jammælt thought looked so sinister, but she was smiling as she talked to them and served them ale. He hadn't seen her smile before, but it suited her, and her little, low laugh was like that of a young maiden.

Jammælt said that it would be impossible for all six brothers to continue living on their mother's estate. It was not expected that any wealthy man of equal birth would give one of his kinswomen to Nikulaus in marriage if his five brothers settled there with him and perhaps continued to take their food from the manor after they married. And they ought to see about finding a wife for the young man; he was already twenty winters old and seemed to have a hardy disposition. For this reason Jammælt wanted to take Ivar and Skule home with him when he returned south; he would find some way to ensure their future. After Erlend Nikulaussøn had lost his life in such an unfortunate manner, it so happened that the great chieftains of the land suddenly remembered that the murdered man had been one of their peers—by birth and blood meant to surpass most of them, charming and magnanimous in many ways, and in battle a daring chieftain and skilled swordsman. But he had not had fortune on his side. Measures of the utmost severity had been levied against those men who had taken part in the murder of the landowner in his own courtyard. And Jammælt could report that many had asked him about Erlend's sons. He had met the men of Sudrheim during Christmas, and they had mentioned that these young boys were their kinsmen. Sir Jon had asked him to bring his greetings and say that he would receive and treat the sons of Erlend Nikulaussøn as his kin if any of them wanted to join his household. Jon Haftorssøn was now about to marry the maiden Elin, who was Erling Vidkunssøn's youngest daughter, and the young bride had asked whether the sons looked like their father. She remembered that Erlend had visited them in Bjørgvin when she was a child, and she had thought him to be the handsomest of men. And her brother, Bjarne Erlingssøn, had said that anything he could do for Erlend Nikulaussøn's sons, he would do with the most heartfelt joy.

Kristin sat and looked at her twin sons as Jammælt talked. They looked more and more like their father: Silky, fine soot-black hair clung smoothly to their heads, although it curled a bit across their brows and down the back of their slender tan necks. They had thin faces with long, jutting noses and delicate, small mouths with a knot of muscle at each corner. But their chins were blunter and broader and their eyes were darker than Erlend's. And above all else, his eyes were what had made Erlend so astoundingly handsome, his wife now thought. When he opened them in that lean, dark face beneath the pitch-black hair, they were so unexpectedly clear and light blue.

But now there was a glint of steely blue in the eyes of the young boys when Skule replied to his uncle. He was the one who usually spoke for both twins.

"We thank you for this fine offer, kinsman. But we have already spoken with Sir Munan and Inge and sought the advice of our older brothers, and we have come to an agreement with Inge and his father. These men are our closest kin of Father's lineage; we will go south with Inge and intend to stay at his estate this summer and for some time to come."

That evening the boys came downstairs to the main room to speak to Kristin after she had gone to bed.

"We hope that you will understand, Mother," said Ivar Erlendssøn.

"We refuse to beg for the help and friendship of kin from those men who sat in silence and watched our father wrongly suffer," added Skule.

Their mother nodded.

It seemed to her that her sons had acted properly. She realized that Jammælt was a sensible and fair-minded man, and his offer had been well intended, but she was pleased the boys were loyal to their father. And yet she could never have imagined that her sons would one day come to serve the son of Brynhild Fluga.

The twins left with Inge Fluga as soon as Ivar was strong enough to ride. It was very quiet at the manor after they were gone. Their mother remembered that at this time the year before, she lay in bed in the weaving room with a newborn child; it seemed to her like a dream. Such a short time ago she had felt so young, with her soul stirred up by the yearnings and sorrows of a young woman, by hopes and hatreds and love. Now her flock had shrunk to four sons, and in her soul the only thing stirring was an uneasiness for the grown young men. In the silence that descended upon Jørundgaard after the departure of the twins, her fear for Bjørgulf flared up with bright flames.

When guests arrived, he and Naakkve moved to the old hearth house. Bjørgulf would get out of bed in the daytime, but he had still not been outdoors. With deep fear Kristin noticed that Bjørgulf was always sitting in the same spot; he never walked around, he hardly moved at all when she came to see him. She knew that his eyes had grown worse during his last illness. Naakkve was terribly quiet, but he had been that way ever since his father's death, and he seemed to avoid his mother as much as he could.

Finally one day she gathered her courage and asked her eldest son how things now stood with Bjørgulf's eyesight. For a while Naakkve gave only evasive replies, but at last she demanded that her son tell her the truth.

Naakkve said, "He can still make out strong light—" All at once the young man's face lost all color; abruptly he turned away and left the room.

Much later that day, after Kristin had wept until she was so weary that she thought she could trust herself to speak calmly with her son, she went over to the old house.

Bjørgulf was lying in bed. As soon as she came in and sat down on the edge of his bed, she could tell by his face that he knew she had spoken to Naakkve.

"Mother. You mustn't cry, Mother," he begged fearfully.

What she most wanted to do was to fling herself at her son, gather him into her arms, and weep over him, grieving over his harsh fate. But she merely slipped her hand into his under the coverlet.

"God is sorely testing your manhood, my son," she said hoarsely.

Bjørgulf's expression changed, becoming firm and resolute. But it took a moment before he could speak.

"I've known for a long time, Mother, that this was what I was destined to endure. Even back when we were at Tautra . . . Brother Aslak spoke to me about it and said that if things should go in such a way . . .

"The way our Lord Jesus was tempted in the wilderness, he

said. He told me that the true wilderness for a Christian man's soul was when his sight and senses were blocked—then he would follow the footsteps of the Lord out of the wilderness, even if his body was still with his brothers or kinsmen. He read to me from the books of Saint Bernard about such things. And when a soul realizes that God has chosen him for such a difficult test of his manhood, then he shouldn't be afraid that he won't have the strength. God knows my soul better than the soul knows itself."

He continued to talk to his mother in this manner, consoling her with a wisdom and strength of spirit that seemed far beyond his years.

That evening Naakkve came to Kristin and asked to speak with her alone. Then he told her that he and Bjørgulf intended to enter the holy brotherhood and to take the vows of monks at Tautra.

Kristin was dismayed, but Naakkve kept on talking, quite calmly. They would wait until Gaute had come of age and could lawfully act on behalf of his mother and younger siblings. They wanted to enter the monastery with as much property as was befitting the sons of Erlend Nikulaussøn of Husaby, but they also wanted to ensure the welfare of their brothers. From their father the sons of Erlend had inherited nothing of value that was worth mentioning, but the three who were born before Gunnulf Nikulaussøn had entered the cloister owned several shares of estates in the north. He had made these gifts to his nephews when he dispersed his wealth, although most of what he hadn't given to the Church or for ecclesiastical use he had left to his brother. And since Naakkve and Bjørgulf would not demand their full share of the inheritance, it would be a great relief to Gaute, who would then become the head of the family and carry on the lineage, if the two of them were dead to the world, as Naakkve put it.

Kristin felt close to fainting. Never had she dreamed that Naakkve would consider a monk's life. But she did not protest; she was too overwhelmed. And she didn't dare try to dissuade her sons from such a noble and meaningful enterprise.

"Back when we were boys and were staying with the monks up there in the north, we promised each other that we would never be parted," said Naakkve.

His mother nodded; she knew that. But she had thought their

intention was for Bjørgulf to continue to live with Naakkve, even after the older boy was married.

It seemed to Kristin almost miraculous that Bjørgulf, as young as he was, could bear his misfortune in such a manly fashion. Whenever she spoke to him of it, during that spring, she heard nothing but god-fearing and courageous words from his lips. It seemed to her incomprehensible, but it must be because he had realized for many years that this would be the outcome of his failing eyesight, and he must have been preparing his soul ever since the time he had stayed with the monks.

But then she had to consider what a terrible burden this unfortunate child of hers had endured—while she had paid so little heed as she went about absorbed with her own concerns. Now, whenever she had a moment to herself, Kristin Lavransdatter would slip away and kneel down before the picture of the Virgin Mary up in the loft or before her altar in the north end of the church when it was open. Lamenting with all her heart, she would pray with humble tears for the Savior's gentle Mother to serve as Bjørgulf's mother in her stead and to offer him all that his earthly mother had left undone.

One summer night Kristin lay awake in bed. Naakkve and Bjørgulf had moved back into the high loft room, but Gaute was sleeping downstairs with Lavrans because Naakkve had said that the older brothers wanted to practice keeping vigil and praying. She was just about to fall asleep at last when she was awakened by someone walking quietly along the gallery of the loft. She heard a stumbling on the stairs and recognized the blind man's gait.

He must be going out on some errand, she thought, but all the same she got up and began looking for her clothes. Then she heard a door flung open upstairs, and someone raced down the steps, taking them two or three at a time.

Kristin ran to the entryway and out the door. The fog was so thick outside that only the buildings directly across the courtyard could be glimpsed. Up by the manor gate Bjørgulf was furiously struggling to free himself from his brother's grasp.

"Do you lose anything," cried the blind man, "if you're rid of me? Then you'll be released from all your oaths . . . and you won't have to be dead to this world."

Kristin couldn't hear what Naakkve said in reply. She ran barefoot through the soaking wet grass. By this time Bjørgulf had pulled free; suddenly, as if struck down, he fell upon the boulder by the gate and began beating it with his fists.

Naakkve saw his mother and took a few swift steps in her direction. "Go inside, Mother. I can handle this best alone. You *must* go inside, I tell you," he whispered urgently, and then he turned around and went back to lean over his brother.

Their mother remained standing some distance away. The grass was drenched with moisture, water was dripping from all the eaves, and drops were trickling from every leaf; it had rained all day, but now the clouds had descended as a thick white fog. When her sons headed back after a while—Naakkve had taken Bjørgulf by the arm and was leading him—Kristin retreated to the entryway door.

She saw that Bjørgulf's face was bleeding; he must have hit himself on the rock. Involuntarily Kristin pressed her hand to her lips and bit her own flesh.

On the stairs Bjørgulf tried once more to pull away from Naakkve. He threw himself against the wall and shouted, "I curse, I curse the day I was born!"

When she heard Naakkve shut the loft door behind them, Kristin crept upstairs and stood outside on the gallery. For a long time she could hear Bjørgulf's voice inside. He raged and shouted and swore; a few of his vehement words she could understand. Every once in a while she would hear Naakkve talking to him, but his voice was only a subdued murmur. Finally Bjørgulf began sobbing, loudly and as if his heart would break.

Kristin stood trembling with cold and anguish. She was wearing only a cloak over her shift; she stood there so long that her loose, flowing hair became wet with the raw night air. At last there was silence in the loft.

Entering the main room downstairs, she went over to the bed where Gaute and Lavrans were sleeping. They hadn't heard anything. With tears streaming down her face, she reached out a hand in the dark and touched the two warm faces, listening to the boys' measured, healthy breathing. She now felt as if these two were all that she had left of her riches.

Shivering with cold, she climbed into her own bed. One of the dogs lying next to Gaute's bed came padding across the room and jumped up, circling around and then leaning against her feet. The dog was in the habit of doing this at night, and she didn't have the heart to chase him away, even though he was heavy and pressed on her legs so they would turn numb. But the dog had belonged to Erlend and was his favorite—a shaggy coal-black old bearhound. Tonight, thought Kristin, it was good to have him lying there, warming her frozen feet.

She didn't see Naakkve the next morning until at the breakfast table. Then he came in and sat down in the high seat, which had been his place since his father's death.

He didn't say a word during the meal, and he had dark circles under his eyes. His mother followed him when he went back outside.

"How is Bjørgulf now?" she asked in a low voice.

Naakkve continued to evade her eyes, but he replied in an equally low voice that Bjørgulf was asleep.

"Has . . . has he been this way before?" she whispered fearfully.

Naakkve nodded, turned away from her, and went back upstairs to his brother.

Naakkve watched over Bjørgulf night and day, and kept his mother away from him as much as possible. But Kristin saw that the two young men spent many hours struggling with each other.

It was Nikulaus Erlendssøn who was supposed to be the master of Jørundgaard now, but he had no time to tend to the managing of the estate. He also seemed to have as little interest and ability as his father had had. And so Kristin and Gaute saw to everything, for that summer Ulf Haldorssøn had left her too.

After the unfortunate events that ended with the killing of Erlend Nikulaussøn, Ulf's wife had gone home with her brothers. Ulf stayed on at Jørundgaard; he said he wanted to show everyone that he couldn't be driven away by gossip and lies. But he hinted that he had lived long enough at Jørundgaard; he thought he might head north to his own estate in Skaun as soon as enough time had passed so that no one could say he was fleeing from the rumors.

But then the bishop's plenipotentiary began making inquiries into the matter, to determine whether Ulf Haldorssøn had unlawfully spurned his wife. And so Ulf made preparations to leave; he went to get Jardtrud, and they were now setting off together for the north, before the autumn weather made the road through the mountains impassable. He told Gaute that he wanted to join forces with his half sister's husband, who was a swordsmith in Nidaros, and live there, but he would settle Jardtrud at Skjoldvirkstad, which his nephew would continue to manage for him.

On his last evening Kristin drank a toast to him with the gold-chased silver goblet her father had inherited from his paternal grandfather, Sir Ketil the Swede. She asked him to accept the goblet as a keepsake to remember her by. Then she slipped onto his finger a gold ring that had belonged to Erlend; he was to have it in his memory.

Ulf gave her a kiss to thank her. "It's customary among kinsmen," he said with a laugh. "You probably never imagined, Kristin, when we first met, and I was the servant who came to get you to escort you to my master, that we would part in this way."

Kristin turned bright red, for he was smiling at her with that old, mocking smile, but she thought she could see in his eyes that he was sad. Then she said, "All the same, Ulf, aren't you longing for Trøndelag—you who were born and raised in the north? Many a time I too have longed for the fjord, and I lived there only a few years." Ulf laughed again, and then she added quietly, "If I ever offended you in my youth, with my overbearing manner or . . . I didn't know that you were close kin, you and Erlend. But now you must forgive me!"

"No . . . but Erlend was not the one who refused to acknowledge our kinship. I was so insolent in my youth; since my father had ousted me from his lineage, I refused to beg—" He stood up abruptly and went over to where Bjørgulf was sitting on the bench. "You see, Bjørgulf, my foster son . . . your father . . . and Gunnulf, they treated me as a kinsman even back when we were boys—just the opposite of how my brothers and sisters at Hestnes behaved. Afterward . . . to others I never presented myself as Erlend's kinsman because I saw that in that way I could serve him better . . . as well as his wife and all of you, my foster sons. Do you understand?" he asked earnestly, placing his hand on Bjørgulf's face, hiding the extinguished eyes.

"I understand." Bjørgulf's reply was almost stifled behind the other man's fingers; he nodded under Ulf's hand.

"We understand, foster father." Nikulaus laid his hand heavily on Ulf's shoulder, and Gaute moved closer to the group.

Kristin felt strangely ill at ease. They seemed to be speaking of things that she could not comprehend. Then she too stepped over to the men as she said, "Be assured, Ulf, my kinsman, that all of us understand. Never have Erlend and I had a more loyal friend than you. May God bless you!"

The next day Ulf Haldorssøn set off for the north.

Over the course of the winter Bjørgulf seemed to settle down, as far as Kristin could tell. Once again he came to the table for meals with the servants of the house, he went with them to mass, and he willingly and gladly accepted the help and services that his mother so dearly wanted to offer him.

As time passed and Kristin never heard her sons make any mention of the monastery, she realized how unspeakably reluctant she was to give up her eldest son to the life of a monk.

She couldn't help admitting that a cloister would be the best place for Bjørgulf. But she didn't see how she could bear to lose Naakkve in that way. It must be true, after all, that her firstborn was somehow bound closer to her heart than her other sons.

Nor could she see that Naakkve was suited to be a monk. He did have a talent for learned games and a fondness for devotional practices; nevertheless, his mother didn't think he was particularly disposed toward spiritual matters. He didn't attend the parish church with any special zeal. He often missed the services, giving some meager excuse, and she knew that neither he nor Bjørgulf confessed to their parish priest anything but the most ordinary of sins. The new priest, Sira Dag Rolfssøn, was the son of Rolf of Blakarsarv, who had been married to Ragnfrid Ivarsdatter's cousin; for this reason he often visited his kinswoman's estate. He was a young man about thirty years old, well educated and a good cleric, but the two oldest sons never warmed to him. With Gaute, on the other hand, he soon became good friends.

Gaute was the only one of Erlend's sons who had made friends among the people of Sil. But none of the others had continued to be as much an outsider as Nikulaus was. He never had anything to do with the other youths. If he went to the places where young people gathered to dance or meet, he usually stood on the outskirts of the green to watch, asserting by his demeanor that he was too good to take part. But if he was so inclined, he might join in the games unasked, and then everyone saw that he was doing it to show off. He was vigorous, strong, and agile, and it was easy to provoke him to fight. But after he had defeated two or three of the most renowned opponents in the parish, people had to tolerate his presence. And if he wished to dance with a maiden, he paid no heed to her brothers or kinsmen but simply danced with the girl and walked and sat with her alone. No woman ever said no when Nikulaus Erlendssøn requested her company, which did not make people like him any better.

After his brother had gone blind, Naakkve seldom left his side, but if he went out in the evening, he acted no differently from before. For the most part he also gave up his long hunting expeditions, but that fall he had bought himself an exceedingly costly white falcon from the sheriff, and he was as eager as ever to practice his bowmanship and prowess in sports. Bjørgulf had taught himself to play chess blind, and the brothers would often spend an entire day at the chessboard; they were both the most zealous of players.

Then Kristin heard people talking about Naakkve and a young maiden, Tordis Gunnarsdatter from Skjenne. The following summer she was staying up in the mountain pastures. Many times Naakkve was away from home at night. Kristin found out that he had been with Tordis.

The mother's heart trembled and twisted and turned like an aspen leaf on its stem. Tordis belonged to an old and respected family; she herself was a good and innocent child. Naakkve couldn't possibly mean to dishonor her. If the two young people forgot themselves, then he would have to make the girl his wife. Sick with anguish and shame, Kristin realized nevertheless that she would not be overly aggrieved if this should happen. Only two years ago she would never have stood for it if Tordis Gunnarsdatter were to succeed her as the mistress of Jørundgaard. The maiden's grandfather was still alive and lived on his estate with four married sons; she herself had many siblings. She would not be a wealthy bride. And every woman of that lineage had given birth to at least one witless child. The children were either exchanged at birth or possessed by the mountain spirits; no matter how they strove to protect the women in childbed, neither baptism nor sacred incantations seemed to help. There were now two old men at Skjenne whom Sira Eirik had judged to be changelings, as well as two children who were deaf and mute. And the wood nymph had bewitched Tordis's oldest brother when he was seventeen. Otherwise those belonging to the Skjenne lineage were a handsome lot, their livestock flourished, and good fortune followed them, but they were too numerous for their family to have any wealth.

God only knew whether Naakkve could have abandoned his resolve without sinning if he had already promised himself to the service of the Virgin Mary. But a man always had to spend one year as a young brother in the monastery before he was ordained; he could withdraw voluntarily if he realized that he was not meant to serve God in that way. And she had heard that the French countess who was the mother of the great doctor of theology, the friar Sir Thomas Aquinas, had locked her son in with a beautiful, wanton woman in order to shake his resolve when he wanted to retreat from the world. Kristin thought this was the vilest thing she had ever heard, and yet when the woman died, she had reconciled with God. So it must not be such a terrible sin if Kristin now imagined that she would open her arms to embrace Tordis of Skjenne as the wife of her son.

In the autumn Jammælt Halvardssøn came to Formo, and he confirmed the rumors of great news that had also reached the valley. In consultation with the highest leaders of the Church and Norway's Council of knights and noblemen, King Magnus Eirikssøn had decided to divide his realms between the two sons he had fathered with his queen, Lady Blanche. At the meeting of nobles in Vardberg, he had given the younger son, Prince Haakon, the title of king of Norway. Both learned priests and laymen of the gentry had sworn sacred oaths to defend the land under his hand. He was supposed to be a handsome and promising three-year-old child, and he was to be brought up in Norway with four foster mothers, all the most highborn wives of knights, and with two spiritual and two worldly chieftains as his foster fathers when King Magnus and Queen Blanche were in Sweden. It was said that Sir Erling Vidkunssøn and the bishops of Bjørgvin and Oslo were behind this selection of a sovereign, and Bjarne Erlingssøn had presented the matter to the king; Lord Magnus loved Bjarne above all his other Norwegian men. Everyone expected the greatest benefits for the realm of Norway now that they would once again have a king who was reared and lived among them, who would protect the laws and rights and interests of the country instead of squandering his time, energies, and the wealth of the kingdom on incursions in other lands.

Kristin had heard about the selection of a king, just as she had heard about the discord with the German merchants in Bjørgvin and about the king's wars in Sweden and Denmark. But these events had touched her so little—like the echo of thunder from the mountains after a storm had passed over the countryside and was far away. No doubt her sons had discussed these matters with each other. Jammælt's account threw the sons of Erlend into a state of violent agitation. Bjørgulf sat with his forehead resting in his hand so he could hide his blind eyes. Gaute listened with his lips parted as his fingers tightly clenched the hilt of his dagger. Lavrans's breathing was swift and audible, and all of a sudden he turned away from his uncle and looked at Naakkve, sitting in the high seat. The oldest son's face was pale, and his eyes blazed.

"It has been the fate of many a man," said Naakkve, "that those who were his fiercest opponents in life found success on the road he had pointed out to them—but only after they had made him into fodder for the worms. After his mouth was stuffed with earth, the lesser men no longer shrank from affirming the truth of his words."

"That may well be, kinsman," said Jammælt in a placating tone. "You may be right about that. Your father was the first of all men to think of this way out of the foreign lands—with two brothers on the thrones, here and in Sweden. Erlend Nikulaussøn was a deep-thinking, wise, and magnanimous man. I see that. But take care what you now say, Nikulaus. Surely you wouldn't want your words to be spread as gossip that might harm Skule."

"Skule didn't ask my permission to do what he did," said Naakkve sharply.

"No, he probably didn't remember that you had come of age by now," replied Jammælt in the same tone as before. "And I didn't think about it either, so it was with my consent and blessing that he placed his hand on Bjarne's sword and swore allegiance."

"I think he did remember it, but the whelp knew I would never give my consent. And no doubt the Giske men needed this salve for their guilty consciences."

Skule Erlendssøn had joined Bjarne Erlingssøn as one of his loyal men. He had met the great chieftain when he was visiting his aunt at Ælin during Christmas, and Bjarne had explained to the boy that it was largely due to the intercession of Sir Erling and himself that Erlend had been granted his life. Without their support Simon Andressøn would never have been able to accomplish his mission with King Magnus. Ivar was still with Inge Fluga.

Kristin knew that what Bjarne Erlingssøn had said was not entirely untrue—it was in accordance with Simon's own account of his journey to Tunsberg—and yet during all these years she had always thought of Erling Vidkunssøn with great bitterness; it seemed to her that he should have been able to help her husband attain better terms if he had wished to do so. Bjarne hadn't been capable of much back then, as young as he was. But she wasn't pleased that Skule had joined up with this man, and in an odd way it took her breath away that the twins had acted on their own and had set off into the world. They were no more than children, she thought.

After Jammælt's visit the uneasiness of her mind grew so great that she hardly dared think at all. If it was true what the men said—that the prosperity and security of the people of the realm would increase beyond words if this small boy in Tunsberg Castle were now called Norway's king—then they could have been enjoying this turn of events for almost ten years if Erlend hadn't . . . No! She refused to think about *that* when she thought about the dead. But she couldn't help it because she knew that in her sons' eyes their father was magnificent and perfect, the most splendid warrior and chieftain, without faults or flaws. And she herself had thought, during all these years, that Erlend had been betrayed by his peers and wealthy kinsmen; her husband had suffered great injustice. But Naakkve went too far when he said that *they* had made him into fodder for the worms. She too bore her own heavy share of the blame, but it was mostly Erlend's folly and his desperate obstinacy that had brought about his wretched death.

But no . . . all the same, she wasn't pleased that Skule was now in the service of Bjarne Erlingssøn.

Would she ever live to see the day when she was released from the ceaseless torment of anguish and unrest? Oh Jesus, remember the anguish and grief that your own mother bore for your sake; have mercy on me, a mother, and give me comfort!

She felt uneasy even about Gaute. The boy had the makings of the most capable of farmers, but he was so impetuous in his eagerness to restore prosperity to his lineage. Naakkve gave him free rein, and Gaute had his hands in so many enterprises. With several other men of the parish he had now started up the old iron-smelting sites in the mountains. And he sold off far too much; he sold not only the goods from the land leases but also part of the yield from his own estate. All her days Kristin had been used to seeing full storerooms and stalls on her farm, and she grew a little cross with Gaute when he frowned in disapproval at the rancid butter and made fun of the ten-year-old bacon she had hung up. But she wanted to know that on her manor there would never be a shortage of food; she would never have to turn a poor man away unaided if years of drought should strike the countryside. And there would be nothing lacking when the time came for weddings and christening feasts and banquets to be held once again on the old estate.

Her ambitious hopes for her sons had been diminished. She would be content if they would settle down here in her parish. She could combine and exchange her properties in such a fashion that three of them could live on their own estates. And Jørundgaard, along with the portion of Laugarbru that lay on this side of the river, could feed three leaseholders. They might not be circumstances fit for noblemen, but they wouldn't be poor folk either. Peace reigned in the valley; here little was heard about all the unrest among chieftains of the land. If this should be perceived as a decline in the power and prestige of their lineage . . . well, God would be able to further the interests of their descendants if He saw that it would be to their benefit. But surely it would be vain of her to hope that she might see them all gathered around her in this manner. It was unlikely they would settle down so easily, these sons of hers who had Erlend Nikulaussøn as their father.

During this time her soul found peace and solace whenever she let her thoughts dwell on the two children she had laid to rest up in the cemetery.

Every day, over the ensuing years, she had thought of them; as she watched children of the same age grow and thrive, she would wonder how her own would have looked by now.

As she went about her daily chores, just as diligent and hardworking as ever, but reticent and preoccupied, her dead children were always with her. In her dreams they grew older and flourished, and they turned out, in every way, to be exactly as she had wished. Munan was as loyal to his kinsmen as Naakkve, but he was as cheerful and talkative with his mother as Gaute was, and he never worried her with unwise impulses. He was as gentle and thoughtful as Lavrans, but Munan would tell his mother all the strange things he was pondering. He was as clever as Bjørgulf, but no misfortune clouded his way through life, so his wisdom held no bitterness. He was as self-reliant, strong, and bold as the twins, but not as unruly or stubborn.

And she recalled once more all the sweet, merry memories of the loving charm of her children when they were small every time she thought about little Erlend. He stood on her lap, waiting to be dressed. She put her hands around his chubby, naked body, and he reached up with his small hands and face and his whole precious body toward her face and her caresses. She taught him to walk. She had placed a folded cloth across his chest and up under his arms; he hung in this harness, as heavy as a sack, vigorously fumbling backward with his feet. Then he laughed until he was wriggling like a worm from laughter. She carried him in her arms out to the farmyard to see the calves and lambs, and he shrieked with joy at the sow with all her piglets. He leaned his head back and gaped at the doves perched in the stable hayloft. He ran to her in the tall grass around the heaps of stones, crying out at each berry he saw and eating them out of her hand so avidly that her palm was wet from his greedy little mouth.

All the joys of her children she remembered and relived in this dream life with her two little sons, and all her sorrows she forgot.

It was spring for the third time since Erlend had been laid in his grave. Kristin heard no more about Tordis and Naakkve. Neither did she hear anything about the cloister. And her hope grew; she couldn't help it. She was so reluctant to sacrifice her eldest son to the life of a monk.

Right before Saint Jon's Day, Ivar Erlendssøn came home to Jørundgaard. The twins had been young lads in their sixteenth year when they left home. Now Ivar was a grown man, almost eighteen years old, and his mother thought he had become so handsome and manly that she could hardly get her fill of looking at him.

On the first morning Kristin took breakfast up to Ivar as he lay in bed. Honey-baked wheat bread, *lefse,* and ale that she had tapped from the last keg of Christmas brew. She sat on the edge of his bed while he ate and drank, smiling at everything he said. She got up to look at his clothes, turning and fingering each garment; she rummaged through his traveling bag and weighed his new silver brooch in her slender reddish-brown hand; she drew his dagger out of its sheath and praised it, along with all his other possessions. Then she sat down on the bed again, looked at her son, and listened with a smile in her eyes and on her lips to everything the young man told her.

Then Ivar said, "I might as well tell you why I've come home, Mother. I've come to obtain Naakkve's consent for my marriage."

Overwhelmed, Kristin clasped her hands together. "My Ivar! As young as you are . . . Surely you haven't committed some folly!"

Ivar begged his mother to listen. She was a young widow, Signe Gamalsdatter of Rognheim in Fauskar. The estate was worth six marks in land taxes, and most of it was her sole property, which she had inherited through her only child. But she had become embroiled in a lawsuit with her husband's kinsmen, and Inge Fluga had tried to acquire all manner of unlawful benefits for himself if he was to help the widow win justice. Ivar had become indignant and had taken up the woman's defense, accompanying her to the bishop himself, for Lord Halvard had always shown Ivar a fatherly goodwill every time they had met. Inge Munanssøn's actions in the county could not bear close scrutiny, but he had been wise enough to stay on friendly terms with the nobles of the countryside, frightening the peasants into their mouseholes. And he had thrown sand in the bishop's eyes with his great cleverness. It was doubtless for Munan's sake that Lord Halvard had refrained from being too stern. But now things did not look good for Inge, so the cousins had parted with the gravest enmity when Ivar took his horse and rode off from Inge Fluga's manor. Then he had decided to pay a visit at Rognheim, in the south, before he left the region. That was at Eastertime, and he had been staying with Signe ever since, helping her on the estate in the springtime. Now they had agreed that he would marry her. *She* didn't think that Ivar Erlendssøn was too young to be her husband and protect her interests. And the bishop, as he had said, looked on him with favor. He was still much too young and lacking in learning for Lord Halvard to appoint him to any position, but Ivar was convinced that he would do well if he settled at Rognheim as a married man.

Kristin sat fidgeting with her keys in her lap. This was sensible talk. And Inge Fluga certainly deserved no better. But she wondered what that poor old man, Munan Baardsøn, would say about all this.

About the bride she learned that Signe was thirty winters old, from a lowborn and impoverished family, but her first husband had acquired much wealth so that she was now comfortably situated, and she was an honorable, kind, and diligent woman.

Nikulaus and Gaute accompanied Ivar south to have a look at the widow, but Kristin wanted to stay home with Bjørgulf. When her sons returned, Naakkve could tell his mother that Ivar was now betrothed to Signe Gamalsdatter. The wedding would be celebrated at Rognheim in the autumn.

Not long after his arrival back home Naakkve came to see his mother one evening as she sat sewing in the weaving room. He barred the door. Then he said that now that Gaute was twenty years old and Ivar would also come of age by marrying, he and Bjørgulf intended to journey north in the fall and ask to be accepted as novices at the monastery. Kristin said little; they spoke mainly about how they would arrange those things that her two oldest sons would want to take with them from their inheritance.

But a few days later men came to Jørundgaard with an invitation to a betrothal banquet: Aasmund of Skjenne was going to celebrate the betrothal of his daughter Tordis to a good farmer's son from Dovre.

That evening Naakkve came again to see his mother in the weaving room, and once again he barred the door behind him. He sat on the edge of the hearth, poking a twig into the embers. Kristin had lit a small fire since the nights were cold that summer.

"Nothing but feasts and carousing, my mother," he said with a little laugh. "The betrothal banquet at Rognheim and the celebration at Skjenne and then Ivar's wedding. When Tordis rides in her wedding procession, I doubt I'll be riding along; by that time I will have donned cloister garb."

Kristin didn't reply at once. But then, without looking up from her sewing—she was making a banquet tunic for Ivar—she said, "Many probably thought it would be a great sorrow for Tordis Gunnarsdatter if you became a monk."

"I once thought so myself," replied Naakkve.

Kristin let her sewing sink to her lap. She looked at her son; his face was impassive and calm. And he was so handsome. His dark hair brushed back from his white forehead, curling softly behind his ears and along the slender, tan stalk of his neck. His features were more regular than his father's; his face was broader and more solid, his nose not as big, and his mouth not as small. His clear blue eyes were lovely beneath the straight black brows. And yet he didn't *seem* as handsome as Erlend had been. It was his father's animal-like softness and languid charm, his air of inextinguishable youth that Naakkve did not possess.

Kristin picked up her work again, but she didn't go back to sewing. After a moment, as she looked down and tucked in a hem of the cloth with her needle, she said, "Do you realize, Naakkve, that I haven't voiced a single word of objection to your godly plans? I wouldn't dare do so. But you're young, and you know quite well—being more learned than I am—that it is written somewhere that it ill suits a man to turn around and look over his shoulder once he has set his hand to the plow."

Not a muscle moved in her son's face.

"I know that you've had these thoughts in mind for a long time," continued his mother. "Ever since you were children. But back then you didn't understand what you would be giving up. Now that you've reached the age of a man . . . Don't you think it would be advisable if you waited a while longer to see if you have the calling? *You* were born to take over this estate and become the head of your lineage."

"You dare to advise me now?" Naakkve took several deep breaths. He stood up. All of a sudden he slapped his hand to his breast and tore open his tunic and shirt so his mother could see his naked chest where his birthmark, the five little blood-red, fiery specks, shone amid the black hair.

"I suppose you thought I was too young to understand what you were sighing about with moans and tears whenever you kissed me here, back when I was a little lad. I may not have understood, but I could never forget the words you spoke.

"Mother, Mother . . . Have you forgotten that Father died the most wretched of deaths, unconfessed and unanointed? And *you* dare to dissuade us!

"I think Bjørgulf and I know what we're turning away from. It doesn't seem to me such a great sacrifice to give up this estate and marriage—or the kind of peace and happiness that you and Father had together during all the years I can remember."

Kristin put down her sewing. All that she and Erlend had lived through, both bad and good . . . A wealth of memories washed over her. This child understood so little what he was renouncing. With all his youthful fights, bold exploits, careless dealings, and games of love—he was no more than an innocent child.

Naakkve saw the tears well up in his mother's eyes; he shouted, "*Quid mihi et tibi est, mulier.*"[2] Kristin cringed, but her son spoke with violent agitation. "God did not say those words because he felt scorn for his mother. But he chastised her, that pure pearl without blemish or flaw, when she tried to counsel him on how to use the power that he had been given by his Father in Heaven and not by his mother's flesh. Mother, you must not advise me about this; do not venture to do so."

Kristin bent her head to her breast.

After a moment Naakkve said in a low voice, "Have you forgotten, Mother, that you pushed me away—" He paused, as if he didn't trust his own voice. But then he continued, "I wanted to kneel beside you at my father's deathbed, but you told me to go away. Don't you realize my heart wails in my chest whenever I think about that?"

Kristin whispered, almost inaudibly, "Is that why you've been so . . . cold . . . toward me during all these years I've been a widow?"

Her son was silent.

"I begin to understand . . . You've never forgiven me for that, have you, Naakkve?"

Naakkve looked away. "Sometimes . . . I have forgiven you, Mother," he said, his voice faint.

"But not very often . . . Oh, Naakkve, Naakkve!" she cried bitterly. "Do you think I loved Bjørgulf any less than you? I'm his mother. I'm mother to both of you! It was cruel of you to keep closing the door between him and me!"

Naakkve's pale face turned even whiter. "Yes, Mother, I closed the door. Cruel, you say. May Jesus comfort you, but you don't know . . ." His voice faded to a whisper, as if the boy's strength were spent. "I didn't think you should . . . We had to spare you."

He turned on his heel, went to the door, and unbarred it. But then he paused and stood there with his back to Kristin. Finally she softly called out his name. He came back and stood before her with his head bowed.

"Mother . . . I know this isn't . . . easy . . . for you."

She placed her hands on his shoulders. He hid his eyes from her gaze, but he bent down and kissed her on the wrist. Kristin recalled that his father had once done the same, but she couldn't remember when.

She stroked his sleeve, and then he lifted his hand and patted her on the cheek. They sat down again, both of them silent for a time.

"Mother," said Naakkve after a while, his voice steady and quiet, "do you still have the cross that my brother Orm left to you?"

"Yes," said Kristin. "He made me promise never to part with it."

"I think if Orm had known about it, he would have consented to letting me have it. I too will now be without inheritance or lineage."

Kristin pulled the little silver cross from her bodice. Naakkve accepted it; it was warm from his mother's breast. Respectfully he kissed the reliquary in the center of the cross, fastened the thin chain around his neck, and hid the cross inside his clothing.

"Do you remember your brother Orm?" asked his mother.

"I'm not sure. I think I do . . . but perhaps that's just because you always talked so much about him, back when I was little."

Naakkve sat before his mother for a while longer. Then he stood up. "Good night, Mother!"

"May God bless you, Naakkve. Good night!"

He left her. Kristin folded up the wedding tunic for Ivar, put away her sewing things, and covered the hearth.

"May God bless you, may God bless you, my Naakkve." Then she blew out the candle and left the old building.

Some time later Kristin happened to meet Tordis at a manor on the outskirts of the parish. The people there had fallen ill and hadn't been able to bring in the hay, so the brothers and sisters of the Olav guild had gone to lend them a hand. That evening Kristin accompanied the girl part of the way home. She walked along slowly, as an old woman does, and chatted; little by little she turned the conversation so that Tordis found herself telling Naakkve's mother all about what there had been between the two of them.

Yes, she had met with him in the paddock at home, and the summer before, when she was staying up in their mountain pastures, he had come to see her several times at night. But he had never tried to be too bold with her. She knew what people said about Naakkve, but he had never offended her, in either word or deed. But he had lain beside her on top of the bedcovers a few times, and they had talked. She once asked him if it was his intention to court her. He replied that he couldn't; he had promised himself to the service of the Virgin Mary. He told her the same thing in the spring, when they happened to speak to each other. And then she decided that she would no longer resist the wishes of her grandfather and father.

"It would have brought great sorrow upon both of you if he had broken his promise and you had defied your kinsmen," said Kristin. She stood leaning on her rake and looked at the young maiden. The child had a gentle, lovely round face, and a thick braid of the most beautiful fair hair. "God will surely bestow happiness on you, my Tordis. He seems a most intrepid and fine boy, your betrothed."

"Yes, I'm quite fond of Haavard," said the girl, and began to sob bitterly.

Kristin consoled her with words befitting the lips of an old and sensible woman. Inside, she moaned with longing; she so dearly wished she could have called this good, fresh child her daughter.

After Ivar's wedding she stayed at Rognheim for a while. Signe Gamalsdatter was not beautiful and looked both weary and old, but she was kind and gentle. She seemed to have a deep love for her young husband, and she welcomed his mother and brothers as if she thought them to be so high above her that she couldn't possibly honor or serve them well enough. For Kristin it was a new experience to have this woman go out of her way to anticipate her wishes and tend to her comfort. Not even when she was the wealthy mistress of Husaby, commanding dozens of servants, did anyone ever serve Kristin in a way that showed they were thinking of the mistress's ease or well-being. She had never spared herself when she bore the brunt of the work for the benefit of the whole household, and no one else ever thought of sparing her either. Signe's obliging concern for the welfare of her mother-in-law during the days she was at Rognheim did Kristin good. She soon grew so fond of Signe that almost as often as she prayed to God to grant Ivar happiness in his marriage, she also prayed that Signe might never have reason to regret that she had given herself and all her properties to such a young husband.

Right after Michaelmas Naakkve and Bjørgulf headed north for Trøndelag. The only thing she had heard since then was that they had arrived safely in Nidaros and had been accepted as novices by the brotherhood at Tautra.

And now Kristin had lived at Jørundgaard for almost a year with only two of her sons. But she was surprised it wasn't longer than that. On that day, the previous fall, when she had come riding past the church and looked down to see the slopes lying under a blanket of cold, raw fog so that she couldn't make out the buildings of her own estate—she had accompanied her two oldest sons as far as Dovre—then she had thought this was what someone must feel who is riding toward home and knows that the farm lying there is nothing but ashes and cold, charred timbers.

Now, whenever she took the old path home past the site of the smithy—and by now it was almost overgrown, with tufts of yellow bedstraw, bluebells, and sweet peas spilling over the borders of the lush meadow—it seemed almost as if she were looking at a picture of her own life: the weather-beaten, soot-covered old hearth that would never again be lit by a fire. The ground was strewn with bits of coal, but thin, short, gleaming tendrils of grass were springing up all over the abandoned site. And in the cracks of the old hearth blossomed fireweed, which sows its seeds everywhere, with its exquisite, long red tassels.

## CHAPTER 2

SOMETIMES, AFTER KRISTIN had gone to bed, she would be awakened by people entering the courtyard on horseback. There would be a pounding on the door to the loft, and she would hear Gaute greet his guests loudly and joyously. The servants would have to get up and go out. There was a clattering and stomping overhead; Kristin could hear Ingrid's cross voice. Yes, she was a good child, that young maid, and she didn't let anyone get too forward with her. A roar of laughing young voices would greet her sharp and lively words. Frida shrieked; the poor thing, she never grew any wiser. She was not much younger than Kristin, and yet at times her mistress had to keep an eye on her.

Then Kristin would turn over in bed and go back to sleep.

Gaute was always up before dawn the next morning, as usual. He never stayed in bed any longer even if he had been up drinking ale the night before. But his guests wouldn't appear until breakfast time. Then they would stay at the manor all day; sometimes they had trade to discuss, sometimes it was merely a friendly visit. Gaute was most hospitable.

Kristin saw to it that Gaute's friends were offered the best of everything. She wasn't aware that she went about smiling quietly at the hum of youth and merry activity returning to her father's estate. But she seldom talked with the young men, and she saw little of them. What she did see was that Gaute was well liked and happy.

Gaute Erlendssøn was as much liked by commoners as by the wealthy landowners. The case against the men who killed Erlend had brought great misfortune upon their kin, and there were doubtless people on many manors and belonging to many lineages who vigilantly avoided meeting any of the Erlendssøns, but Gaute himself had not a single foe.

Sir Sigurd of Sundbu had taken a keen liking to his young kinsman. This cousin of hers, whom Kristin had never met until fate led him to the deathbed of Erlend Nikulaussøn, had shown her the greatest loyalty of a kinsman. He stayed at Jørundgaard almost until Christmas and did everything he could to help the widow and her fatherless young boys. The sons of Erlend displayed their gratitude in a noble and courteous manner, but only Gaute drew close to him and had spent a great deal of time at Sundbu since then.

When this nephew of Ivar Gjesling eventually died, the estate would pass out of the hands of his lineage; he was childless, and the Haftorssøns were his closest descendants. Sir Sigurd was already quite an old man, and he had endured a terrible fate when his young wife lost her wits during her first childbirth. For nearly forty years now he had been married to this madwoman, but he still went in almost daily to see how she was doing. She lived in one of the best houses at Sundbu and had many maids to look after her. "Do you know me today, Gyrid?" her husband would ask. Sometimes she didn't answer, but other times she said, "I know you well. You're the prophet Isaiah who lives north at Brotveit, beneath Brotveit Peak." She always had a spindle at her side. When she was feeling good, she would spin a fine, even yarn, but when things were bad, she would unravel her own work and strew all over the room the wool that her maids had carded. After Gaute had told Kristin about this, she always welcomed her cousin with the most heartfelt kindness when he came to visit. But she declined to go to Sundbu; she hadn't been there since the day of her wedding.

Gaute Erlendssøn was much smaller in stature than Kristin's other sons. Between his tall mother and lanky brothers he looked almost short, but he was actually of average height. In general Gaute seemed to have grown larger in all respects now that his two older brothers and the twins, who were born after him, had left. Beside them he had always been a quiet figure. People in the region called him an exceedingly handsome man, and he did have a lovely face. With his flaxen yellow hair and big gray eyes so finely set beneath his brow, with his narrow, suitably full countenance, fresh complexion, and beautiful mouth, he looked much like his grandfather Lavrans. His head was handsomely set on his shoulders, and his hands, which were well shaped and rather large, were unusually strong. But the lower half of his body was a little too short, and he was quite bowlegged. For this reason he always wore his clothing long unless, for the sake of his work, he had to put on a short tunic—although at the time it was more and more thought to be elegant and courtly for men to have their banquet attire cut shorter than in the past. The farmers learned of this fashion from traveling noblemen who passed through the valley. But whenever Gaute Erlendssøn arrived at church or at a feast wearing his ankle-length embroidered green Sabbath surcoat, the silver belt around his waist and the great cape with the squirrel-skin lining thrown back over his shoulders, the people of the parish would turn pleased and gentle eyes on the young master of Jørundgaard. Gaute always carried a magnificent silver-chased axe Lavrans Bjørgulfsøn had inherited from his father-in-law, Ivar Gjesling. And everyone thought it splendid to see Gaute Erlendssøn following in the footsteps of his forefathers, even as young as he was, and keeping up the good farming traditions of the past, in his attire, demeanor, and the way he lived.

On horseback Gaute was the handsomest man anyone had ever seen. He was the boldest of riders, and people in the countryside boasted there wasn't a horse in all of Norway that Gaute couldn't manage to tame and ride. When he was in Bjørgvin the year before, he had purportedly mastered a young stallion that no man had ever been able to handle or ride; under Gaute's hands he was so submissive that he could be ridden without a saddle and with a maiden's ribbons as reins. But when Kristin asked her son about this story, he merely laughed and refused to talk about it.

Kristin knew that Gaute was reckless in his dealings with women, and this did not please her, but she thought it was mostly because the women treated the handsome young man much too kindly, and Gaute had an open and charming manner. Surely it was largely banter and foolishness; he didn't take such matters seriously or go about concealing things the way Naakkve had. He came and told his mother himself when he had conceived a child with a young girl over at Sundbu; that had happened two years ago. Kristin heard from Sir Sigurd that Gaute had generously provided the mother with a good dowry, befitting her position, and he wanted to bring the child to Jørundgaard after she had been weaned from her mother's breast. He seemed to be quite fond of his little daughter; he always went to see her whenever he was at Vaagaa. She was the loveliest child, Gaute proudly reported, and he had had her baptized Magnhild. Kristin agreed that since the boy had sinned, it was best if he brought the child home and became her loyal father. She looked forward with joy to having little Magnhild live with them. But then she died, only a year old. Gaute was greatly distressed when he heard the news, and Kristin thought it sad that she had never seen her little granddaughter.

Kristin had always had a difficult time reprimanding Gaute. He had been so miserable when he was little, and later he had continued to cling to his mother more than the other children had. Then there was the fact that he resembled her father. And he had been so steadfast and trustworthy as a child; with his somber and grown-up manner he had walked at her side and often lent her a well-intentioned helping hand that he, in his childish innocence, thought would be of the greatest benefit to his mother. No, she had never been able to be stern with Gaute; when he did something wrong out of thoughtlessness or the natural ignorance of his years, he never needed more than a few gentle, admonishing words, so sensible and wise the boy was.

When Gaute was two years old, their house priest at Husaby, who had a particularly good understanding of childhood illnesses, advised that the boy be given mother's milk again, since no other measures had helped. The twins were newborns, and Frida, who was nursing Skule, had much more milk than the infant could consume. But the maid found the poor boy loathsome. Gaute looked terrible, with his big head and thin, wizened body; he could neither speak nor stand on his own. She was afraid he might be a changeling, even though the child had been healthy and fair-looking up until he fell ill at the age of ten months. All the same, Frida refused to put Gaute to her breast, and so Kristin had to nurse him herself, and he was allowed to suckle until he was four winters old.

Since then Frida had never liked Gaute; she was always scolding him, as much as she dared for fear of his mother. Frida now sat next to her mistress on the women's bench and carried her keys whenever Kristin was away from home. She said whatever she liked to the mistress and her family; Kristin showed her great forbearance and found the woman amusing, even though she was often annoyed with her too. Nevertheless, she always tried to make amends and smooth things over whenever Frida had done something wrong or spoken too coarsely. Now the maid had a hard time accepting that Gaute sat in the high seat and was to be master of the estate. She seemed to consider him no more than a foolish boy; she boasted about his brothers, especially Bjørgulf and Skule, whom she had nursed, while she mocked Gaute's short stature and crooked legs. Gaute took it with good humor.

"Well, you know, Frida, if I had nursed at your breast, I would have become a giant just like my brothers. But I had to be content with my mother's breast." And he smiled at Kristin.

Mother and son often went out walking in the evening. In many places the path across the fields was so narrow that Kristin had to walk behind Gaute. He would stroll along carrying the long-hafted axe, so manly that his mother had to smile behind his back. She had an impetuous, youthful desire to rush at him from behind and pull him to her, laughing and chattering with Gaute the way she had done occasionally when he was a child.

Sometimes they would go all the way down to the place on the riverbank where the washing was done and sit down to listen to the roar of the water rushing past, bright and roiling in the dusk. Usually they said very little to each other. But once in a while Gaute would ask his mother about the old days in the region and about her own lineage. Kristin would tell him what she had heard and seen in her childhood. His father and the years at Husaby were never mentioned on those nights.

"Mother, you're sitting here shivering," Gaute said one evening. "It's cold tonight."

"Yes, and I've grown stiff from sitting on this stone." Kristin stood up. "I'm getting to be an old woman, my Gaute!"

Walking back, she placed her hand on his shoulder for support.

Lavrans was sleeping like a rock in his bed. Kristin lit the little oil lamp; she felt like sitting up for a while to enjoy the sea calm in her own soul. And there was always some task to occupy her hands. Upstairs Gaute was clattering around with something; then she heard him climb into bed. Kristin straightened her back for a moment, smiling a bit at the tiny flame in the lamp. She moved her lips faintly, making the sign of the cross over her face and breast and in the air in front of her. Then she picked up her sewing again.

Bjørn, the old dog, stood up and shook himself, stretching out his front paws full length as he yawned. He padded across the floor to his mistress. As soon as she started petting him, he placed his front paws on her lap. When she spoke to him gently, the dog eagerly licked her face and hands as he wagged his tail. Then Bjørn slunk off again, turning his head to peer at Kristin. Guilt shone in his tiny eyes and was evident in his whole bulky, wiry-haired body, right down to the tip of his tail. Kristin smiled quietly and pretended not to notice; then the dog jumped up onto her bed and curled up at the foot.

After a while she blew out the lamp, pinched the spark off the wick, and tossed it into the oil. The light of the summer night was rising outside the little windowpane. Kristin said her last prayers of the day, silently undressed, and slipped into bed. She tucked the pillows comfortably under her breast and shoulders, and the old dog settled against her back. A moment later she fell asleep.

Bishop Halvard had assigned Sira Dag to the cleric's position in the parish, and from him Gaute had purchased the bishop's tithes for three years hence. He had also traded for hides and food in the region, sending the goods over the winter roads to Raumsdal and from there by ship to Bjørgvin in the spring. Kristin wasn't pleased with these ventures of her son; she herself had always sold her goods in Hamar, because both her father and Simon Andressøn had done so. But Gaute had formed some sort of trade partnership with his kinsman Gerlak Paus. And Gerlak was a clever merchant, with close ties to many of the richest German merchants in Bjørgvin.

Erlend's daughter Margret and her husband had come to Jørundgaard during the summer after Erlend's death. They presented great gifts to the church for his soul. When Margret was a young maiden back home at Husaby, there had been scant friendship between her and her stepmother, and she had cared little for her small half brothers. Now she was thirty years old, with no children from her marriage; now she showed her handsome, grown-up brothers the most loving sisterly affection. And she was the one who arranged the agreement between Gaute and her husband.

Margret was still beautiful, but she had grown so big and fat that Kristin didn't think she had ever seen such a stout woman. But there was all the more room for silver links on her belt, while a silver brooch as large as a small shield fit nicely between her enormous breasts. Her heavy body was always adorned like an altar with the costliest of fabrics and gilded metals. Gerlak Tiedekenssøn seemed to have the greatest love for his wife.

A year earlier Gaute had visited his sister and brother-in-law in Bjørgvin during the spring meetings, and in the fall he traveled over the mountains with a herd of horses, which he sold in town. The journey turned out to be so profitable that Gaute swore he would do it again this autumn. Kristin thought he should be allowed to do as he wished. No doubt he had some of his father's lust for travel in his blood; surely he would settle down as he grew older. When his mother saw that he was aching to get away, she urged him to go. Last year he had been forced to come home through the mountains at the height of winter.

He set off on a beautiful sunny morning right after Saint Bartholomew's Day. It was the time for slaughtering the goats, and the whole manor smelled of cooked goat meat. Everyone had eaten his fill and was feeling content. All summer long they had tasted no fresh meat except on high holy days, but now they had their share of the pungent meat and the strong, fatty broth at both breakfast and supper for many days. Kristin was exhausted and elated after helping with the first big slaughtering of the year and making sausages. She stood on the main road and waved with a corner of her wimple at Gaute's entourage. It was a lovely sight: splendid horses and fresh young men riding along with glittering weapons and jangling harnesses. There was a great thundering as they rode across the high bridge. Gaute turned in his saddle and waved his hat, and Kristin waved back, giving a giddy little cry of joy and pride.

Just after Winter Day[1] rain and sleet swept in over the countryside, with storms and snow in the mountains. Kristin was a little uneasy, for Gaute had still not returned. But she was never as fearful for him as she had been for the others; she believed in the good fortune of this son.

A week later Kristin was coming out of the cowshed late one

evening when she caught sight of several horsemen up by the manor gate. The fog was billowing like white smoke around the lantern she carried; she began walking through the rain to meet the group of dark, fur-clad men. Could it be Gaute? It was unlikely that strangers would be arriving so late.

Then she saw that the rider in front was Sigurd of Sundbu. With the slight stiffness of an old man, he dismounted from his horse.

"Yes, I bring you news from Gaute, Kristin," he said after they had greeted each other. "He arrived at Sundbu yesterday."

It was so dark she couldn't make out his expression. But his voice sounded so strange. And when he walked toward the door of the main house, he told his men to go with Kristin's stableboy to the servants' quarters. She grew frightened when he said nothing more, but when they were alone in the room, she asked quite calmly, "What news do you bring, kinsman? Is he ill, since he hasn't come home with you?"

"No, Gaute is so well that I've never seen him look better. But his men were tired . . ."

He blew at the foam on the ale bowl that Kristin handed to him, then took a swallow and praised the brew.

"Good ale should be given to the one who brings good news," said the mistress with a smile.

"Well, I wonder what you'll say when you've heard all of my news," he remarked rather diffidently. "He did not return alone this time, your son . . ."

Kristin stood there waiting.

"He has brought along . . . well, she's the daughter of Helge of Hovland. He has apparently taken this—this maiden . . . taken her by force from her father."

Kristin still said nothing. But she sat down on the bench across from him. Her lips were narrow and pressed tight.

"Gaute asked me to come here; I suppose he was afraid you wouldn't be pleased. He asked me to tell you the news, and now I've done so," concluded Sir Sigurd faintly.

"You must tell me everything you know about this matter, Sigurd," said Kristin calmly.

Sir Sigurd did as she asked, in a vague and disjointed way, with a great deal of roundabout talk. He himself seemed to be quite horrified by Gaute's action. But from his account Kristin discerned that Gaute had met the maiden in Bjørgvin the year before. Her name was Jofrid, and no, she had not been abducted. But Gaute had probably realized that it would do no good to speak to the maiden's kinsmen about marriage. Helge of Hovland was a very wealthy man and belonged to the lineage known as Duk, with estates all over Voss. And then the Devil had tempted the two young people. . . . Sir Sigurd tugged at his clothing and scratched his head, as if he were swarming with lice.

Then, this past summer—when Kristin thought that Gaute was at Sundbu and was going to accompany Sir Sigurd into the mountain pastures to hunt for two vicious bears—he had actually journeyed over the heights and down to Sogn; Jofrid was staying there with a married sister. Helge had three daughters and no sons. Sigurd groaned in distress; yes, he had promised Gaute to keep silent about this. He knew the boy must be going to see a maiden, but he had never dreamed that Gaute was thinking of doing anything so foolish.

"Yes, my son is going to have to pay dearly for this," replied Kristin. Her face was impassive and calm.

Sigurd said that winter had now set in for good, and the roads were nearly impassable. After the men of Hovland had had time to think things over, perhaps they would see . . . It was best if Gaute won Jofrid with the consent of her kinsmen—now that she was already his.

"But what if they don't see things that way? And demand revenge for abducting a woman?"

Sir Sigurd squirmed and scratched even more.

"I suppose it's an unredeemable offense,"[2] he said quietly. "I'm not quite certain . . ."

Kristin did not reply.

Then Sir Sigurd continued, his voice imploring, "Gaute said . . . He expected that you would welcome them kindly. He said that surely you are not so old that you've forgotten . . . Well, he said that you won the husband you insisted on having—do you understand?"

Kristin nodded.

"She's the fairest child I have ever seen in my life, Kristin," said Sigurd fervently. Tears welled up in his eyes. "It's terrible that the

Devil has lured Gaute into this misdeed, but surely you will receive these two poor children with kindness, won't you?"

Kristin nodded again.

The countryside was sodden the next day, pallid and black under torrents of rain when Gaute rode into the courtyard around mid-afternoon prayers.

Kristin felt a cold sweat on her brow as she leaned against the doorway. There stood Gaute, lifting down from her horse a woman dressed in a hooded black cloak. She was small in build, barely reaching up to his shoulders. Gaute tried to take her hand to lead her forward, but she pushed him away and came to meet Kristin alone. Gaute busied himself talking to the servants and giving orders to the men who had accompanied him. Then he cast another glance at the two women standing in front of the door; Kristin was holding both hands of the newly arrived girl. Gaute rushed over to them with a joyful greeting on his lips. In the entryway Sir Sigurd put his arm around his shoulder and gave him a fatherly pat, huffing and puffing after the strain.

Kristin was taken by surprise when the girl lifted her face, so white and so lovely inside the drenched hood of her cloak. And she was so young and as small as a child.

Then the girl said, "I do not expect to be welcomed by you, Gaute's mother, but now all doors have been closed to me except this one. If you will tolerate my presence here on the manor, mistress, then I will never forget that I arrived here without property or honor, but with good intentions to serve you and Gaute, my lord."

Before she knew it, Kristin had taken the girl's hands and said, "May God forgive my son for what he has brought upon you, my fair child. Come in, Jofrid. May God help both of you, just as I will help you as best I can!"

A moment later she realized that she had offered much too warm a welcome to this woman, whom she did not know. But by then Jofrid had taken off her outer garments. Her heavy winter gown, which was a pale blue woven homespun, was dripping wet at the hem, and the rain had soaked right through her cloak to her shoulders. There was a gentle, sorrowful dignity about this childlike girl. She kept her small head with its dark tresses gracefully bowed; two thick pitch-black braids fell past her waist. Kristin kindly took Jofrid's hand and led her to the warmest place on the bench next to the hearth. "You must be freezing," she said.

Gaute came over and gave his mother a hearty embrace. "Mother, things will happen as they must. Have you ever seen as beautiful a maiden as my Jofrid? I had to have her, whatever it may cost me. And you must treat her with kindness, my dearest mother. . . ."

Jofrid Helgesdatter was indeed beautiful; Kristin could not stop looking at her. She was rather short, with wide shoulders and hips, but a soft and charming figure. And her skin was so delicate and pure that she was lovely even though her face was quite pale. The features of her face were short and broad, but the expansive, strong arc of her cheeks and chin gave it beauty, and her wide mouth had thin, rosy lips with small, even teeth that looked like a child's first teeth. When she raised her heavy eyelids, her clear gray-green eyes were like shining stars beneath the long black eyelashes. Black hair, light-colored eyes—Kristin had always thought that was the most beautiful combination, ever since she had seen Erlend for the first time. Most of her own handsome sons had that coloring.

Kristin showed Jofrid to a place on the women's bench next to her own. She sat there, graceful and shy, among all the servants she didn't know, eating little and blushing every time Gaute drank a toast to her during the meal.

He was bursting with pride and restless elation as he sat in the high seat. To honor her son's return home, Kristin had spread a cloth over the table that evening and set two wax tapers in the candlesticks made of gilded copper. Gaute and Sir Sigurd were constantly toasting each other, and the old gentleman grew more and more maudlin, putting his arm around Gaute's shoulder and promising to speak on his behalf to his wealthy kinsmen, yes, even to King Magnus himself. Surely he would be able to obtain for him reconciliation with the maiden's offended kin. Sigurd Eldjarn himself had not a single foe; it was his father's rancorous temperament and his own misfortune with his wife that had made him so alone.

In the end Gaute sprang to his feet with the drinking horn in his hand. How handsome he is, thought Kristin, and how like Father!

Her father had been the same way when he was beginning to feel drunk—so radiant with joy, straight-backed and lively.

"Things are now such between this woman, Jofrid Helgesdatter, and myself that today we celebrate our homecoming, and later we will celebrate our wedding, if God grants us such happiness. You, Sigurd, we thank for your steadfast kinship, and you, Mother, for welcoming us as I expected you would, with your loyal, motherly warmth. As we brothers have often discussed, you seem to us the most magnanimous of women and the most loving mother. Therefore I ask you to honor us by preparing our bridal bed in such a fine and beautiful manner that without shame I can invite Jofrid to sleep there beside me. And I ask you to accompany Jofrid up to the loft yourself, so that she might retire with as much seemliness as possible since she has neither a mother still alive nor any kinswomen here."

Sir Sigurd was now quite drunk, and he burst out laughing. "You slept together in my loft; if I didn't know better . . . I thought the two of you had already shared a bed before."

Gaute shook his golden hair impatiently. "Yes, kinsman, but this is the first night Jofrid will sleep in my arms on her own manor, God willing.

"But I beg you good people to drink and be merry tonight. Now you have seen the woman who will be my wife here at Jørundgaard. This woman and no other—I swear this before God, our Lord, and on my Christian faith. I expect all of you to respect her, both servants and maids, and I expect you, my men, to help me keep and protect her in a seemly manner, my boys."

During all the shouting and commotion that accompanied Gaute's speech, Kristin quietly left the table and whispered to Ingrid to follow her up to the loft.

Lavrans Bjørgulfsøn's magnificent loft room had fallen into disrepair over the years, after the sons of Erlend had moved in. Kristin hadn't wanted to give the reckless boys any but the coarsest and most essential of bedclothes and pieces of furniture, and she seldom had the room cleaned, for it wasn't worth the effort. Gaute and his friends tracked in filth and manure as quickly as she swept it out. There was an ingrained smell from men coming in and flinging themselves onto the beds, soaked and sweaty and muddy from the woods and the farmyard—a smell of the stables and leather garments and wet dogs.

Now Kristin and her maid quickly swept and cleaned as best they could. The mistress brought in fine bed coverlets, blankets, and cushions and burned some juniper. On a little table which she moved close to the bed she placed a silver goblet filled with the last of the wine in the house, a loaf of wheat bread, and a candle in an iron holder. This was as elegant as she could make things on such short notice.

Weapons hung on the timbered wall next to the alcove: Erlend's heavy two-handed sword and the smaller sword he used to carry, along with felling axes and broadaxes; Bjørgulf's and Naakkve's axes still hung there too. And the two small axes that the boys seldom used because they considered them too lightweight. But these were the tools that her father had used to carve and shape all manner of objects with such skill and care that afterward he only had to do the fine polishing with his gouge and knife. Kristin carried the axes into the alcove and put them inside Erlend's chest, where his bloody shirt lay, along with the axe he was holding in his hand when he received the mortal wound.

Laughing, Gaute invited Lavrans to light the way up to the loft for his bride. The boy was both embarrassed and proud. Kristin saw that Lavrans understood his brother's unlawful wedding was a dangerous game, but he was high-spirited and giddy from these strange events; with sparkling eyes he gazed at Gaute and his beautiful betrothed.

On the stairs up to the loft the candle went out. Jofrid said to Kristin, "Gaute should not have asked you to do this, even though he was drunk. Don't come any farther with me, mistress. Have no fear that I might forget I'm a fallen woman, cut off from the counsel of my kin."

"I'm not too good to serve you," said Kristin, "not until my son has atoned for his sin against you and you can rightly call me mother-in-law. Sit down and I'll comb your hair. Your hair is beautiful beyond compare, child."

But after the servants were asleep and Kristin was lying in bed, she once again felt a certain uneasiness. Without thinking, she had told this Jofrid more than she meant to . . . yet. But she was so young, and she showed so clearly that she didn't expect to be regarded as any better than what she was: a child who had fled from honor and obedience.

So that's the way it looked . . . when people let the bridal procession and homeward journey come before the wedding. Kristin sighed. Once she too had been willing to risk the same for Erlend, but she didn't know whether she would have dared if his mother had been living at Husaby. No, no, she wouldn't make things any worse for the child upstairs.

Sir Sigurd was still staggering around the room; he was to sleep with Lavrans. In a mawkish way, but with sincere intentions, he talked about the two young people; he would spare nothing to help them find a good outcome to this reckless venture.

The next day Jofrid showed Gaute's mother what she had brought along to the manor: two leather sacks with clothes and a little chest made of walrus tusk in which she kept her jewelry. As if she had read Kristin's thoughts, Jofrid said that these possessions belonged to her; they had been given to her for her own use, as gifts and inherited items, mostly from her mother. She had taken nothing from her father.

Full of sorrow, Kristin sat leaning her cheek on her hand. On that night, an eternity ago, when she had collected her gold in a chest to steal away from home . . . Most of what *she* had put inside were gifts from the parents she had secretly shamed and whom she was openly going to offend and distress.

But if these were Jofrid's own possessions and if her mother's inheritance was only jewelry, then she must come from an exceedingly wealthy home. Kristin estimated that the goods she saw before her were worth more than thirty marks in silver. The scarlet gown alone, with its white fur and silver clasps and the silk-lined hood that went with it, must have cost ten or twelve marks. It was all well and good if the maiden's father would agree to reconcile with Gaute, but her son could never be considered an equal match for this woman. And if Helge brought such harsh charges against Gaute, as he had the right and ability to do, things looked quite bleak indeed.

"My mother always wore this ring," said Jofrid. "If you will accept it, mistress, then I'll know that you don't judge me as sternly as a good and highborn woman might be expected to do."

"Oh, but then I might be tempted to take the place of your mother," said Kristin with a smile, putting the ring on her finger. It was a little silver ring set with a lovely white agate, and Kristin thought the child must consider it especially precious because it reminded her of her mother. "I expect I must give you a gift in return." She brought over her chest and took out the gold ring with sapphires. "Gaute's father put this ring in my bed after I brought his son into the world."

Jofrid accepted the ring by kissing Kristin's hand. "Otherwise I had thought of asking you for another gift . . . Mother. . . ." She smiled so charmingly. "Don't be afraid that Gaute has brought home a lazy or incapable woman. But I own no proper work dress. Give me an old gown of yours and allow me to lend you a hand; perhaps then you will soon grow to like me better than it is reasonable for me to expect right now."

And then Kristin had to show the young maiden everything she had in her chests, and Jofrid praised all of Kristin's lovely handiwork with such rapt attention that the older woman ended up giving her one thing after another: two linen sheets with silk-knotted embroidery, a blue-trimmed towel, a coverlet woven in four panels, and finally the long tapestry with the falcon hunt woven into it. "I don't want these things to leave this manor, but with the help of God and the Virgin Mary, this house will someday be yours." Then they both went over to the storehouses and stayed there for many hours, enjoying each other's company.

Kristin wanted to give Jofrid her green homespun gown with the black tufts woven into the fabric, but Jofrid thought it much too fine for a work dress. Poor thing, she was just trying to flatter her husband's mother, thought Kristin, hiding a smile. At last they found an old brown dress Jofrid thought would be suitable if she cut it shorter and sewed patches under the arms and on the elbows. She asked to borrow a scissors and sewing things at once, and then she sat down to sew. Kristin took up some mending as well, and the two women were still sitting there together when Gaute and Sir Sigurd came in for the evening meal.

## CHAPTER 3

KRISTIN HAD TO admit with all her heart that Jofrid was a woman who knew how to use her hands. *If* things went well, then Gaute was certainly fortunate; he would have a wife who was as hardworking and diligent as she was rich and beautiful. Kristin herself could not have found a more capable woman to succeed her at Jørundgaard, not if she had searched through all of Norway. One day she said—and afterward she wasn't sure what had happened to make the words spill from her lips—that on the day Jofrid Helgesdatter became Gaute's lawful wife, she would give her keys to the young woman and move out to the old house with Lavrans.

Afterward she thought she should have considered these words more carefully before she uttered them. There were already many instances when she had spoken of something too soon when she was talking with Jofrid.

But there was the fact that Jofrid was not well. Kristin had noticed it almost at once after the young girl arrived. And Kristin remembered the first winter she had spent at Husaby; *she* at least had been married, and her husband and father were bound by kinship, no matter what might happen to their friendship after the sin came to light. All the same, she had suffered so terribly from remorse and shame, and her heart had felt bitter toward Erlend. But she was already nineteen winters old back then, while Jofrid was barely seventeen. And here she was now, abducted and without rights, far from her home and among strangers, carrying Gaute's child under her heart. Kristin could not deny that Jofrid seemed to be stronger and braver than she herself had been.

But Jofrid hadn't breached the sanctity of the convent; she hadn't broken promises and betrothal vows; she hadn't betrayed her parents or lied to them or stolen their honor behind their backs. Even though these two young people had dared sin against the laws, constraints, and moral customs of the land, they needn't have *such* an anguished conscience. Kristin prayed fervently for a good outcome to Gaute's foolhardy deed, and she consoled herself that God, in His fairness, couldn't possibly deal Gaute and Jofrid any harsher circumstances than she and Erlend had been given. And *they* had been married; their child of sin had been born to share in a lawful inheritance from all his kinsmen.

Since neither Gaute nor Jofrid spoke of the matter, Kristin didn't want to mention it either, although she longed to have a talk with the inexperienced young woman. Jofrid should spare herself and enjoy her morning rest instead of getting up before everyone else on the manor. Kristin saw that it was Jofrid's desire to rise before her mother-in-law and to accomplish more than she did. But Jofrid was not the kind of person Kristin could offer either help or solicitude. The only thing she could do was silently take the heaviest work away from her and treat her as if she were the rightful young mistress on the estate, both when they were alone and in front of the servants.

Frida was furious at having to relinquish her place next to her mistress and give it to Gaute's . . . She used an odious word to describe Jofrid one day when she and Kristin were together in the cookhouse. For once Kristin struck her maid.

"How splendid to hear such words from you, an old nag lusting after men as you do!"

Frida wiped the blood from her nose and mouth.

"Aren't you supposed to be better than a poor man's offspring, daughters of great chieftains such as yourself and this Jofrid? You know with certainty that a bridal bed with silken sheets awaits you. You're the ones who must be shameless and lusting after men if you can't wait but have to run off into the woods with young lads and end up with wayside bastards—for shame, I say to you!"

"Hold your tongue now. Go out and wash yourself. You're standing there bleeding into the dough," said her mistress quite calmly.

Frida met Jofrid in the doorway. Kristin saw from the young woman's face that she must have heard the conversation with the maid.

"The poor thing's chatter is as foolish as she is. I can't send her away; she has no place to go." Jofrid smiled scornfully. Then Kristin said, "She was the foster mother for two of my sons."

"But she wasn't Gaute's foster mother," replied Jofrid. "She reminds us both of that fact as often as she can. Can't you marry her off?" she asked sharply.

Kristin had to laugh. "Don't you think I've tried? But all it took was for the man to have a few words with his future bride. . . ."

Kristin thought she should seize the opportunity to talk with Jofrid, to let her know that here she would meet with only maternal goodwill. But Jofrid looked angry and defiant.

In the meantime it was now clearly evident that Jofrid was not walking alone. One day she was going to clean some feathers for new mattresses. Kristin advised her to tie back her hair so it wouldn't be covered with down. Jofrid bound a linen cloth around her head.

"No doubt this is now more fitting than going bareheaded," she said with a little laugh.

"That may well be," said Kristin curtly.

And yet she wasn't pleased that Jofrid should jest about such a thing.

A few days later Kristin came out of the cookhouse and saw Jofrid cutting open several black grouse; there was blood spattered all over her arms. Horror-stricken, Kristin pushed her aside.

"Child, you mustn't do this bloody work *now.* Don't you know better than that?"

"Oh, surely you don't believe everything women say is true," said Jofrid skeptically.

Then Kristin told her about the marks of fire that Naakkve had received on his chest. She purposely spoke of it in such a way that Jofrid would understand she was not yet married when she looked at the burning church.

"I suppose you hadn't thought such a thing of me," she said quietly.

"Oh yes, Gaute has already told me: Your father had promised you to Simon Andressøn, but you ran off with Erlend Nikulaussøn to his aunt, and then Lavrans had to give his consent."

"It wasn't exactly like that; we didn't run off. Simon released me as soon as he realized that I was more fond of Erlend than of him, and then my father gave his consent—unwillingly, but he placed my hand in Erlend's. I was betrothed for a year. Does that seem worse to you?" asked Kristin, for Jofrid had turned bright red and gave her a look of horror.

The girl used her knife to scrape off the blood from her white arms.

"Yes," she said in a low but firm voice. "I would not have squandered my good reputation and honor needlessly. But I won't say anything of this to Gaute," she said quickly. "He thinks his father carried you off by force because he could not win you with entreaty."

No doubt what she said was true, thought Kristin.

As time passed and Kristin continued to ponder the matter, it seemed to her that the most honorable thing to do was for Gaute to send word to Helge of Hovland, to place his case in his hands and ask to be given Jofrid as his wife on such terms as her father decided to grant them. But whenever she spoke of this to Gaute, he would look dismayed and refuse to answer. Finally he asked his mother crossly whether she could get a letter over the mountains in the wintertime. No, she told him, but Sira Dag could surely send a letter to Nes and then onward along the coast; the priests always managed to get their letters through, even during the winter. Gaute said it would be too costly.

"Then it will not be with your wife that you have a child this spring," said his mother indignantly.

"Even so, the matter cannot be arranged so quickly," said Gaute. Kristin could see that he was quite angry.

A terrible, dark fear seized hold of her as time went on. She couldn't help noticing that Gaute's first ardent joy over Jofrid had vanished completely; he went about looking sullen and ill tempered. From the very start this matter of Gaute abducting his bride had seemed as bad as it could be, but his mother thought it would be much worse if afterward the man turned cowardly. If the two young people regretted their sin, that was all well and good, but she had an ugly suspicion that there was more of an unmanly fear in Gaute toward the man he had offended than any god-fearing remorse. Gaute—all her days she had thought the most highly of this son of hers; it couldn't be true what people said: that he was unreliable and dealt carelessly with women, that he was already tired of Jofrid, now that his bride had faded and grown heavy and the day was approaching when he would have to answer for his actions to her kinsmen.

She sought excuses for her son. If Jofrid had allowed herself to be seduced so easily . . . she who had never witnessed anything during her upbringing other than the seemly behavior of pious people . . . Kristin's sons had known from childhood that their own mother had sinned, that their father had conceived children with another man's wife during his youth, and that he had sinned with a married woman when they were nearly grown boys. Ulf Haldorssøn, their foster father, and Frida's frivolous chatter . . . Oh, it wasn't so strange that these young men should be weak in that way. Gaute would have to marry Jofrid, if he could win the consent of her kinsmen, and be grateful for it. But it would be a shame for Jofrid if she should now see that Gaute married her reluctantly and without desire.

One day during Lent Kristin and Jofrid were preparing sacks of provisions for the woodcutters. They pounded dried fish thin and flat, pressed butter into containers, and filled wooden casks with ale and milk. Kristin saw that Jofrid now found it terribly difficult to stand or walk for very long, but she merely grew annoyed if Kristin told her to sit down and rest. To appease her a little, Kristin happened to mention the story about the stallion that Gaute had supposedly tamed with a maiden's hair ribbon. "Surely it must have been yours?"

"No," said Jofrid crossly, turning crimson. But then she added, "The ribbon belonged to Aasa, my sister." She laughed and said, "Gaute courted her first, but when I came home, he couldn't decide which of us he liked best. But Aasa was the one he had expected to find visiting Dagrun last summer when he went to Sogn. And he was angry when I teased him about her; he swore by God and man that he was not the sort to come too close to the daughters of worthy men. He said there had been nothing between him and Aasa that would prevent him from sleeping without sin in my arms that night. I took him at his word." She laughed again. When she saw Kristin's expression, she nodded stubbornly.

"Yes, I want Gaute to be my husband, and he will be, you can count on that, Mother. I most often get what I want."

Kristin woke up to pitch-darkness. The cold bit at her cheeks and chin; when she pulled the blanket more snugly around her, she noticed there was frost on it from her breath. It had to be nearly morning, but she dreaded getting up and seeing the stars. She curled up under the covers to warm herself a little more. At that moment she remembered her dream.

She seemed to be lying in bed in the little house at Husaby, and she had just given birth to a child. She was holding him in her arms, wrapped in a lambskin, which had rolled up and fallen away from the infant's little dark red body. He was holding his tiny clenched hands over his face, with his knees tucked up to his belly and his feet crossed; now and then he would stir a bit. It didn't occur to her to wonder why the boy wasn't swaddled properly and why there were no other women with them in the room. Her heat was still enveloping the child as he lay close to her; through her arm she could feel a tug at the roots of her heart every time he stirred. Weariness and pain were still shrouding her like a darkness that was starting to fade as she lay there and gazed at her son, feeling her joy and love for him ceaselessly growing the way the rim of daylight grows brighter along the mountain crest.

But at the same time as she lay there in bed, she was also standing outside the house. Below her stretched the countryside, lit by the morning sun. It was an early spring day. She drank in the sharp, fresh air; the wind was icy cold, but it tasted of the faraway sea and of thawing snow. The ridges were bathed with morning sunlight on the opposite side of the valley, with snowless patches around the farms. Pale crusted snow shone like silver in all the clearings amid the dark green forests. The sky was swept clean, a bright yellow and pale blue with only a few dark, windblown clusters of clouds hovering high above. But it was cold. Where she was standing the snowdrift was still frozen hard after the night frost, and between the buildings lay cold shadows, for the sun was directly above the eastern ridge, behind the manor. And right in front of her, where the shadows ended, the morning wind was rippling through the pale year-old grass; it moved and shimmered, with clumps of ice shiny as steel still among the roots.

Oh . . . Oh . . . Against her will, a sigh of lament rose up from her breast. She still had Lavrans; she could hear the boy's even breathing from the other bed. And Gaute. He was asleep up in the loft with his paramour. Kristin sighed again, moved restlessly, and Erlend's old dog settled against her legs, which were tucked up underneath the bedclothes.

Now she could hear that Jofrid was up and walking across the floor. Kristin quickly got out of bed and stuck her feet into her fur-lined boots, putting on her homespun dress and fur jacket. In the dark she fumbled her way over to the hearth, crouched down to stir the ashes and blow on them, but there was not the slightest spark; the fire had died out in the night.

She pulled her flint out of the pouch on her belt, but the tinder must have gotten wet and then froze. Finally she gave up trying, picked up the ember pan, and went upstairs to borrow some coals from Jofrid.

A good fire was burning in the little fireplace, lighting up the room. In the glow of the flames Jofrid sat stitching the copper clasp more securely to Gaute's reindeer coat. Over in the dim light of the bed, Kristin caught a glimpse of the man's naked torso. Gaute slept without covers even in the most biting cold. He was sitting up and having something to eat in bed.

Jofrid got to her feet heavily, with a proprietary air. Wouldn't Mother like a drop of ale? She had heated up the morning drink for Gaute. And Mother should take along this pitcher for Lavrans; he was going out with Gaute to cut wood that day. It would be cold for the men.

Kristin involuntarily grimaced when she was back downstairs and lit the fire. Seeing Jofrid busy with domestic chores and Gaute sitting there, openly allowing his wife to serve him . . . and his paramour's concern for her unlawful husband—all this seemed to Kristin so loathsome and immodest.

Lavrans stayed out in the forest, but Gaute came home that night, worn out and hungry. The women sat at the table after the servants had left, keeping the master company while he drank.

Kristin saw that Jofrid was not feeling well that evening. She kept letting her sewing sink to her lap as spasms of pain flickered across her face.

"Are you in pain, Jofrid?" asked Kristin softly.

"Yes, a little. In my feet and legs," replied the girl. She had toiled all day long, as usual, refusing to spare herself. Now pain had overtaken her, and her legs had swollen up.

Suddenly little tears spilled out from her lowered eyes. Kristin had never seen a woman cry in such a strange fashion; without a sound, her teeth clenched tight, she sat there weeping clear, round tears. Kristin thought they looked as hard as pearls, trickling down the haggard brown-flecked face. Jofrid looked angry that she was forced to surrender; reluctantly she allowed Kristin to help her over to the bed.

Gaute followed. "Are you in pain, my Jofrid?" he asked awkwardly. His face was fiery red from the cold, and he looked genuinely unhappy as he watched his mother helping Jofrid get settled, taking off her shoes and socks and tending to her swollen feet and legs. "Are you in pain, my Jofrid?" he kept asking.

"Yes," said Jofrid, in a low voice, biting back her rage. "Do you think I'd behave this way if I wasn't?"

"Are you in pain, my Jofrid?" he repeated.

"Surely you can see for yourself. Don't stand there moping like a foolish boy!" Kristin turned to face her son, her eyes blazing. The dull knot of fear about how things would turn out, of impatience because she had to tolerate the disorderly life of these two on her estate, of gnawing doubt about her son's manliness—all these things erupted in a ferocious rage: "Are you such a simpleton that you think she might be feeling *good*? She can see that you're not man enough to venture over the mountains because it's windy and snowing. You know full well that soon she'll have to crawl on her knees, this poor woman, and writhe in the greatest of torments—and her child will be called a bastard, because you don't dare go to her father. You sit here in the house warming the bench, not daring to lift a finger to protect the wife you have or your child soon to be born. *Your* father was not so afraid of my father that he didn't dare seek him out, or so fainthearted that he refused to ski through the mountains in the wintertime. Shame on you, Gaute, and pity me who must live to see the day when I call my son a timid man, one of the sons that Erlend gave me!"

Gaute picked up the heavy carved chair with both hands and slammed it against the floor; he ran over to the table and swept everything off. Then he rushed to the door, giving one last kick to the chair. They heard him cursing as he climbed the stairs to the loft.

"Oh no, Mother. You were much too hard on Gaute." Jofrid propped herself up on her elbow. "You can't reasonably expect him to risk his life going into the mountains in the winter in order to seek out my father and find out whether he'll be allowed to marry his seduced bride, with no dowry other than the shift I wore when he took me away, or else be driven from the land as an outlaw."

Waves of anger were still washing through Kristin's heart. She replied proudly, "And yet I don't believe *my* son would think that way!"

"No," said Jofrid. "If he didn't have me to think for him . . ." When she saw Kristin's expression, laughter crept into her voice. "Dear Mother, I've had trouble enough trying to restrain Gaute. I refuse to let him commit any more follies for my sake and cause our children to lose the riches that I can expect to inherit from my kinsmen if Gaute can come to an agreement that will be the best and most honorable one for all of us."

"What do you mean by that?" asked Kristin.

"I mean that when my kinsmen seek out Gaute, Sir Sigurd will meet them, so they will see that Gaute is not without kin. He will have to bear paying full restitution, but then Father will allow him to marry me, and I will regain my right to an inheritance along with my sisters."

"So you are partially to blame," said Kristin, "for the child coming into the world before you are married?"

"If I could run away with Gaute, then . . . Surely no one would believe that he has placed a sword blade in bed between us all these nights."

"Didn't he ever seek out your kinsmen to ask for your hand in marriage?" asked Kristin.

"No, we knew it would have been futile, even if Gaute had been a much richer man than he is." Jofrid burst out laughing again. "Don't you see, Mother? Father thinks he knows better than any man how to trade horses. But a person would have to be more alert than my father is if he wanted to fool Gaute Erlendssøn in an exchange of horses."

Kristin couldn't help smiling, in spite of her ill temper.

"I don't know the law very well in such cases," she said somberly. "But I'm not certain, Jofrid, that it will be easy for Gaute to obtain what you would consider a good reconciliation. If Gaute is sentenced as an outlaw, and your father takes you back home and lets you suffer his wrath, or if he demands that you enter a convent to atone for your sins . . ."

"He can't send me to a convent without sending splendid gifts along with me, and it will be less costly and more honorable if he reconciles with Gaute and demands restitution. You see, then he won't have to give up any cattle when he marries me off. And because of his dislike for Olav, my sister's husband, I think I will share in the inheritance with my sisters. If not, then my kinsmen will have to see to this child's welfare too. And I know Father would think twice before he tried to take me back home to Hovland with a bastard child, to let me suffer his wrath—knowing *me* as he does.

"I don't know much about the law either, but I know Father, and I know Gaute. And now enough time has already passed that this proposal cannot be presented until I myself am delivered and healthy again. Then, Mother, you will not see me weeping! Oh no, I have no doubt that Gaute will have his reconciliation on such terms as—

"No, Mother . . . Gaute, who is a descendant of highborn men and kings . . . And you, who come from the best of lineages in Norway . . . If you have had to endure seeing your sons sink below the rank that was their birthright, then you will see prosperity regained for your descendants in the children that Gaute and I shall have."

Kristin sat in silence. It was indeed conceivable that things might happen as Jofrid wished; she realized that she hadn't needed to worry so much on her behalf. The girl's face was now quite gaunt; the rounded softness of her cheeks had wasted away, and it was easier to see what a large, strong jaw she had.

Jofrid yawned, pushed herself up into a sitting position, and looked around for her shoes. Kristin helped her to put them on. Jofrid thanked her and said, "Don't trouble Gaute anymore,

Mother. He finds it hard to bear that we won't be married beforehand, but I refuse to make my child poor even before he's born."

Two weeks later Jofrid gave birth to a big, fair son, and Gaute sent word to Sundbu the very same day. Sir Sigurd came at once to Jørundgaard, and he held Erlend Gautessøn when the boy was baptized. But as happy as Kristin Lavransdatter was with her grandson, it still angered her that Erlend's name should be given for the first time to a paramour's child.

"Your father risked more to give his son his birthright," she told Gaute one evening as he sat in the weaving room and watched her get the boy ready for the night. Jofrid was already sleeping sweetly in her bed. "His love for old Sir Nikulaus was somewhat strained, but even so, he would never have shown his father such disrespect as to name his son after him if he were not lawfully born."

"And Orm . . . he was named for his maternal grandfather, wasn't he?" said Gaute. "Yes, I know, Mother, those may not be the words most becoming a good son. But you should realize that my brothers and I all noticed that while our father was alive, you didn't think he was the proper example for us in many matters. And yet now you talk about him constantly, as if he had been a holy man, or close to it. You should know that we realize he wasn't. All of us would be proud if we ever attained Father's stature—or even reached to his shoulders. We remember that he was noble and courageous, foremost among men in terms of those qualities that suit a man best. But you can't make us believe he was the most submissive or seemly of men in a woman's chamber or the most capable of farmers.

"And yet no one need wish anything better for you, my Erlend, than that you should take after him!" He picked up his child, now properly swaddled, and touched his chin to the tiny red face framed by the light-colored wool cloth. "This gifted and promising boy, Erlend Gautessøn of Jørundgaard—you should tell your grandmother that *you* aren't afraid your father will fail you." He made the sign of the cross over the child and put him back in Kristin's arms, then went over to the bed and looked down at the slumbering young mother.

"My Jofrid is as well as she can be, you say? She looks pale, but

I suppose you must know best. Sleep well in here, and may God's peace be with you."

One month after the birth of the boy, Gaute held a splendid christening feast, and his kinsmen came from far away to attend the celebration. Kristin assumed that Gaute had asked them to come in order to counsel him on his position; it was now spring, and he could soon expect to hear news from Jofrid's kin.

Kristin had the joy of seeing Ivar and Skule come home together. And her cousins came to Jørundgaard too: Sigurd Kyrning, who was married to her uncle's daughter from Skog, Ivar Gjesling of Ringheim, and Haavard Trondssøn. She hadn't seen the Trondssøns since Erlend had brought misfortune down upon the men of Sundbu. Now they were older; they had always been carefree and reckless, but intrepid and magnanimous, and they hadn't changed much at all. They greeted the sons of Erlend and Sir Sigurd, who was their cousin and successor at Sundbu, with a free and open manner befitting kinsmen. The ale and mead flowed in rivers in honor of little Erlend. Gaute and Jofrid welcomed their guests as unrestrainedly as if they had been wed and the king himself had married them. Everyone was joyous, and no one seemed to consider that the honor of these two young people was still at stake. But Kristin learned that Jofrid had not forgotten.

"The more bold and swaggering they are when they meet my father, the more easily he will comply," she said. "And Olav Piper could never hide the fact that he would be pleased to sit on the same bench as men from the ancient lineages."

The only one who did not seem to feel quite comfortable in this gathering of kin was Sir Jammælt Halvardssøn. King Magnus had made him a knight at Christmas; Ramborg Lavransdatter was now the wife of a knight.

This time Sir Jammælt had brought his eldest son, Andres Simonssøn, along with him. Kristin had asked him to do so the last time Jammælt came north, for she had heard a rumor that there was supposedly something strange about the boy. Then she grew terribly frightened; she wondered whether some harm might have been done to his soul or body because of what she had done in his behalf when he was a child. But his stepfather said no, the boy was healthy and strong, as good as gold, and perhaps cleverer than most people. But it was true that he had second sight. Sometimes he seemed to drift away, and when he came back, he would often do peculiar things. Such as the year before. One day he took his silver spoon, the one Kristin had given to him at his birth, and a torn shirt that had belonged to his father, and he left the manor and went down to a bridge that stretches across the river along the main road near Ælin. There he sat for many hours, waiting. Eventually three poor people came walking across the bridge: an old beggar and a young woman holding an infant. Andres went over and gave the things to them, and then asked if he might carry the child for the woman. Back home everyone was desperate with anguish when Andres didn't appear for meals or by nightfall. They went out looking for him, and at last Jammælt heard that Andres had been seen far north in the next parish, in the company of a couple known as Krepp and Kraaka; he was carrying their infant. When Jammælt finally found the boy on the following day, Andres explained that he had heard a voice during mass on the previous Sunday while he was looking at the images painted on the front of the altar. It showed the Mother of God and Saint Joseph leaving the land of Egypt and carrying a child, and he wished that he had lived back then, for he would have asked to accompany them and carry the child for the Virgin Mary. Then he heard a voice, the gentlest and sweetest voice in the world, and it promised to show him a sign if he would go out to Bjerkheim Bridge on a certain day.

Otherwise Andres was reluctant to speak of his visions, because their parish priest had said they were partly imagined and partly due to a confused and muddled state of mind, and he frightened his mother out of her wits with his strange ways. But he talked to an old servant woman, an exceedingly pious woman, and to a friar who used to wander through the countryside during Lent and Advent. The boy would doubtless choose the spiritual life, so Simon Simonssøn was sure to be the one who would settle at Formo when the time came. He was a healthy and lively child who looked a great deal like his father, and he was Ramborg's favorite.

Ramborg and Jammælt had not yet had a child of their own. Kristin had heard from those who had seen Ramborg at Raumarike that she had grown quite fat and lazy. She kept company with the wealthiest and mightiest people in the south, but she never wanted to make the trip to her home valley, and Kristin hadn't seen her only sister since they parted on that day at Formo. But Kristin was convinced that Ramborg's resentment toward her remained unchanged. She got on well with Jammælt, and he tended to the well-being of his stepchildren with loving care. If he should die with no children of his own, he had arranged for the eldest son of the man who would inherit most of his property to marry Ulvhild Simonsdatter; in that way at least the daughter of Simon Darre would have some benefit from his inheritance. Arngjerd had married Grunde of Eiken the year after her father's death; Gyrd Darre and Jammælt had provided her with a rich dowry, as they knew Simon would have wanted. And Jammælt said she was well. Grunde appeared to let his wife guide him in all manner of things, and they already had three handsome children.

Kristin was strangely moved when she saw Simon and Ramborg's oldest son again. He was the living image of Lavrans Bjørgulfsøn, even more than Gaute. And over the past few years Kristin had given up her belief that Gaute might be anything like her father in temperament.

Andres Darre was now twelve years old, tall and slender, fair and lovely and rather quiet, although he seemed robust and cheerful enough, with good physical abilities and a hearty appetite, except that he refused to eat meat. There was something that set him apart from other boys, but Kristin couldn't say what it was, although she watched him closely. Andres became good friends with his aunt, but he never mentioned his visions, and he didn't have any of his spells while in Sil.

The four sons of Erlend seemed to enjoy being together on their mother's estate, but Kristin didn't manage to talk much with her sons. When they were discussing things among themselves, she felt as if their lives and well-being had now slipped beyond her view. The two who came from far away had left their childhood home behind, and the two who lived on the manor were on the verge of taking its management out of her hands. The gathering took place in the midst of the springtime shortages, and she saw that Gaute must have been making preparations for it by rationing the fodder more strictly than usual that winter; he had also borrowed fodder from Sir Sigurd. But he had done all these things without consulting her. And all the advice regarding Gaute's case was also presented without including her, even though she sat in the same room with the men.

For this reason she was not surprised when Ivar came to her one day and said that Lavrans would be leaving with him when he went back to Rognheim.

Ivar Erlendssøn also told his mother on another day that he thought she should move to Rognheim with him after Gaute was married. "Signe is a more amenable daughter-in-law to live with, I think. And it can't possibly be easy for you to give up your charge of the household when you are used to running everything." But otherwise he seemed to be fond of Jofrid—he and all the other men. Only Sir Jammælt seemed to regard her with some coolness.

Kristin sat with her little grandson on her lap, thinking that it wouldn't be easy no matter where she was. It was difficult getting old. It seemed such a short time ago that she herself was the young woman, when it was her fate that prompted the clamor of the men's counsel and strife. Now she had been pushed into the background. Not long ago her own sons had been just like this little boy. She recalled her dream about the newborn child. During this time the thought of her own mother often came to her; she couldn't remember her mother except as an aging and melancholy woman. But she too had once been young, when she lay and warmed herself with the heat of her own body; her mother's body and soul had also been marked in her youth by carrying and giving birth to her children. And doubtless she hadn't given it any more thought than Kristin had when she sat with the sweet young life at her breast—that as long as they both should live, each day would take the child farther and farther away from her arms.

"After you had a child yourself, Kristin, I thought you would understand," her mother had once said. Now she realized that her mother's heart had been deeply etched with memories of her daughter, memories of her thoughts about the child from before she was born and from all the years the child could not remember, memories of fears and hopes and dreams that children would never know had been dreamed on their behalf, before it was their own turn to fear and hope and dream in secret.

Finally the gathering of kinsmen split up, and some went to stay with Jammælt at Formo while others accompanied Sigurd over to Vaagaa. Then one day two of Gaute's leaseholders from the south of the valley came racing into the courtyard. The sheriff was on his way north to seek out Gaute at home, and the maiden's father and kinsmen were with him. Young Lavrans ran straight to the stable. The next evening it looked as if an army had gathered at Jørundgaard; all of Gaute's kinsmen were there along with their armed men, and his friends from the countryside had come as well.

Then Helge of Hovland arrived in a great procession to demand his rights from the man who had abducted his daughter. Kristin caught a glimpse of Helge Duk as he rode into the courtyard alongside Sir Paal Sørkvessøn, the sheriff himself. Jofrid's father was an older, tall, and stoop-backed man who looked quite ill; it was evident that he limped when he got off his horse. Her sister's husband, Olav Piper, was short, wide, and thickset; both his face and hair were red.

Gaute stepped forward to meet them, his posture erect and dignified, and behind him he had an entire phalanx of kinsmen and friends. They stood in a semicircle in front of the stairs to the high loft; in the middle were the two older gentlemen holding the rank of knight: Sir Sigurd and Sir Jammælt. Kristin and Jofrid watched the meeting from the entryway to the weaving room, but they couldn't hear what was said.

The men went up to the loft, and the two women retreated inside the weaving room. Neither of them felt like talking. Kristin sat down near the hearth; Jofrid paced the floor, holding her child in her arms. They continued in this way for a while; then Jofrid wrapped a blanket around the boy and left the room with him. An hour later Jammælt Halvardssøn came in to find his wife's sister sitting alone, and he told her what had happened.

Gaute had offered Helge Duk sixteen marks in gold for Jofrid's honor and for taking her by force. This was the same amount that Helge's brother had been given in restitution for the life of his son. Gaute would then wed Jofrid with her father's consent and provide all the proper betrothal and wedding gifts, but in return Helge would have to accept Gaute and Jofrid with full reconciliation so that she would be given the same dowry as her sisters and share with them in the inheritance. Sir Sigurd, on behalf of Gaute's kinsmen, offered a guarantee that he would keep to this agreement. Helge Duk seemed willing to accept this offer at once, but his sons-in-law—Olav Piper and Nerid Kaaressøn, who was betrothed to Aasa—voiced objections. They said Gaute must be the most arrogant of men if he dared to think he could set his own terms for his marriage to a maiden he had shamed while she was at her brother-in-law's manor and had then been taken by force. Or to demand that she be allowed to share the inheritance with her sisters.

It was easy to see, said Jammælt, that Gaute was not pleased he would have to haggle over the price for marrying a highborn maiden whom he had seduced and who had now given birth to his son. But it was also easy to see that he had learned his lessons and prayers by heart, so he didn't have to read them out of a book.

In the midst of the discussion, as friends on both sides attempted to mediate, Jofrid came into the room with the child in her arms. Then her father broke down and could no longer hold back his tears. And so the matter was decided as she wished.

It was clear that Gaute could never have paid such a fine, but Jofrid's dowry was set at the same amount, so things came out even. The result of the meeting was that Gaute won Jofrid but received little more than what she had brought in her sacks when she arrived at Jørundgaard. But he gave her documents for almost all that he owned as betrothal and wedding gifts, and his brothers gave their assent. One day he would acquire great riches from her—provided their marriage was not childless, said Ivar Gjesling with a laugh, and the other men laughed too. But Kristin blushed crimson because Jammælt sat there listening to all the coarse jests that were uttered.

The next day Gaute Erlendssøn was betrothed to Jofrid Helgesdatter, and afterward she went to church for the first time after the birth, honored as if she had been a married woman. Sira Dag said she was entitled to this. Then she went to Sundbu with the child and remained under Sir Sigurd's protection until the wedding.

It took place a month later, just after Saint Jon's Day, and it was both beautiful and grand. The following morning Kristin Lavransdatter, with great ceremony, gave her keys to her son, and Gaute then fastened the ring to his wife's belt.

Afterward Sir Sigurd Eldjarn held a great banquet at Sundbu, and there he and his cousins, the former Sundbu men, solemnly swore and sealed a vow of friendship. Sir Sigurd generously presented costly gifts from his estate, both to the Gjeslings and to all his guests, according to how close they were as kin or friends—drinking horns, eating vessels, jewelry, weapons, furs, and horses. People then judged that Gaute Erlendssøn had brought this matter of abducting his bride to the most honorable of ends.

## CHAPTER 4

ONE SUMMER MORNING a year later Kristin was out on the gallery of the old hearth house, cleaning out several chests of tools that stood there. When she heard horses being led into the courtyard, she went to have a look, peering between the narrow pillars of the gallery. One of the servants was leading two horses, and Gaute had appeared in the stable doorway; the boy Erlend was sitting astride his father's shoulders. The bright little face looked over the top of the man's yellow hair, and Gaute was holding the boy's tiny hands clasped in his own big tan hands under his chin. He handed the child to a maid who came across the courtyard and then mounted his horse. But when Erlend screamed and reached for his father, Gaute took him back and set him in front of him on the saddle. At that moment Jofrid came out of the main house.

"Are you taking Erlend with you? Where are you headed?"

Gaute replied that he was going up to the mill; the river was threatening to carry it away. "And Erlend says he wants to go with his father."

"Have you lost your wits?" She quickly pulled the boy down, and Gaute roared with laughter.

"I think you actually believed I was going to take him along!"

"Yes." His wife laughed too. "You're always taking the poor boy everywhere. I think you'd do the same as the lynx: eat your own young before you'd let anyone else take him."

She lifted the child's hand to wave to Gaute as he rode off from the estate. Then she put the boy down on the grass and squatted down next to him for a moment to talk to him a bit before she continued on her way over to the new storeroom and up to the loft.

Kristin stood where she was, gazing at her grandson. The morning sun shone so brightly on the little child dressed in red. Young

Erlend twirled around in circles, staring down at the grass. Then he caught sight of a big pile of wood chips, and at once he busily began strewing them all around. Kristin laughed.

He was fifteen months old, but his parents thought he was ahead of his age, because he could walk and run and even say two or three words. Now he was heading straight for the little stream that ran through the lower part of the courtyard and became a gurgling creek whenever it rained in the mountains. Kristin ran over and picked him up in her arms.

"You mustn't. Your mother will be cross if you get wet."

The boy drew his lips into a pout; he was probably wondering whether to cry because he wasn't allowed to splash in the stream or to give in. Getting wet was quite a big sin for him. Jofrid was much too strict with him about such matters. But he looked so clever. Laughing, Kristin kissed the boy, put him down, and went back to the gallery. But she made little headway with her work; mostly she stood and looked out at the courtyard.

The morning sun glowed so gentle and lovely above the three storerooms across from her. Kristin felt as if she hadn't taken a good look at them for a long time. How splendid the buildings were with the pillars adorning their loft galleries and the elaborate carvings. The gilded weather vane on the crossed timbers of the gable of the new storeroom glittered against the blue haze covering the mountains in the distance. This year, after the wet spring, the grass was so fresh on the rooftops.

Kristin gave a little sigh, cast another glance at little Erlend, and then turned back to the chests.

Suddenly the wailing cry of a child pierced the air behind her. She threw down everything she was holding and rushed outside. Erlend was shrieking as he looked back and forth from his finger to a half-dead wasp lying in the grass. When his grandmother lifted him up to soothe him, he screamed even louder. And when she, amid much crying and complaining, put some damp earth and a cold green leaf on the sting, his wailing became quite dreadful.

Hushing and caressing him, Kristin carried the boy into her house, but he screamed as if he were in deadly pain—and then stopped short in the middle of a howl. He recognized the box and horn spoon that his grandmother was taking down from above the door. Kristin dipped pieces of *lefse* in honey and fed them to the child as she continued to soothe him, placing her cheek against his fair neck where the hair was still short and curly from the days when he lay in his cradle and rubbed his head against the pillow. And then Erlend forgot all about his sorrow and turned his face up toward Kristin, offering to pat and kiss her with sticky hands and lips.

As they sat there, Jofrid came into the room.

"Have you brought him indoors? You didn't need to do that, Mother. I was just upstairs in the loft."

Kristin mentioned what had happened to Erlend outside. "Didn't you hear him scream?"

Jofrid thanked her mother-in-law. "But now we won't trouble you anymore." And she picked up the child, who was now reaching out for his mother and wanted to go to her, and they left the room.

Kristin put away the honey box. Then she continued to sit there, with nothing to occupy her hands. The chests on the gallery could wait until Ingrid came in.

It had been intended that she would have Frida Styrkaarsdatter as her maid when she moved out to the old house. But then Frida married one of the servants who had come with Helge Duk, a lad young enough to be her son.

"It's the custom in our part of the country for our servants to listen to their masters when they're offered advice for their own good," said Jofrid when Kristin wondered how this marriage had come about.

"But here in this parish," said Kristin, "the commoners aren't accustomed to obeying us if we're unreasonable, nor do they follow our advice unless it's of equal benefit to them and to us. I'm giving you good advice, Jofrid; you should keep it in mind."

"What Mother says is true," added Gaute, but his voice was quite meek.

Even before he was married, Kristin had noticed that Gaute was very reluctant to speak against Jofrid. And he had become the most amenable of husbands.

Kristin didn't deny that Gaute could stand to listen to what his wife had to say about many things; she was more sensible, capable, and hardworking than most women. And she was no more loose in her ways than Kristin herself had been. She too had trampled on her duties as a daughter and sold her honor since she could not win the man she had set her heart on in any better way. After she had gotten what she wanted, she became the most honorable and faithful wife. Kristin could see that Jofrid had great love for her husband; she was proud of his handsome appearance and his esteemed lineage. Her sisters had married wealthy men, but it was best to look at their husbands at night, when the moon wasn't shining, and their ancestors weren't even worth mentioning, Jofrid said scornfully. She zealously tended to her husband's welfare and honor as she perceived it, and at home she indulged him as best she could. But if Gaute suggested that he might have a different opinion from his wife regarding even the smallest matter, Jofrid would first agree with such an expression that Gaute would begin to waver, and then she would bring him around to her point of view.

But Gaute was flourishing. No one could doubt that these two young people lived well together. Gaute loved his wife, and both of them were so proud of their son and loved him beyond all measure.

So everything should have been fine and good. If only Jofrid Helgesdatter hadn't been . . . well, she was stingy; Kristin couldn't find any other word for it. If she hadn't been stingy, Kristin wouldn't have felt annoyed that her daughter-in-law had such a desire to take charge.

During the grain harvest that very first autumn, right after Jofrid had returned to the estate as a married woman, Kristin could see that the servants were already discontented, although they seldom said anything. But the old mistress noticed it just the same.

Sometimes it had also happened in Kristin's day that the servants were forced to eat herring that was sour, or bacon as yellow and rancid as a resinous pine torch, or spoiled meat. But then everyone knew that their mistress was bound to make up for it with something particularly good at another meal: milk porridge or fresh cheese or good ale out of season. And if there was food that was about to go bad and had to be eaten, everyone simply felt as if Kristin's full storerooms were overflowing. If people were in need, the abundance at Jørundgaard offered security for everyone.

But now people were already uncertain whether Jofrid would prove to be generous with the food if there should be a shortage among the peasants.

This was what angered her mother-in-law, for she felt it diminished the honor of the manor and its owner.

It didn't trouble her as much that she had discovered firsthand, over the course of the year, that her daughter-in-law always saved the best for her own. On Saint Bartholomew's Day she received two goat carcasses instead of the four she should have been given. It was true that wolverines had ravaged the smaller livestock in the mountains the previous summer, and yet Kristin thought it petty to hold back from slaughtering two more goats on such a large estate. But she held her tongue. It was the same way with everything she was supposed to be given from the farm: the autumn slaughtering, grain and flour, fodder for her four cows and two horses. She received either smaller amounts or poor-quality goods. She saw that Gaute was both embarrassed and ashamed by this, but he didn't dare do anything for fear of his wife, and so he pretended not to notice.

Gaute was just as magnanimous as all of Erlend's sons. In his brothers Kristin had called it extravagance. But Gaute was a toiler, and frugal in his own way. As long as he had the best horses and dogs and a few good falcons, he would have been content to live like the smallholders of the valley. But whenever visitors came to the estate, he was a gracious host to all his guests and a generous man toward beggars—and thus a landowner after his mother's own heart. She felt this was the proper way of living for the gentry—those nobles who resided on the ancestral estates in their home districts. They should produce goods and squander nothing needlessly, but neither should they spare anything whenever love of God and His poor, or concern for furthering the honor of their lineage, demanded that goods should be handed out.

Now she saw that Jofrid liked Gaute's rich friends and highborn kinsmen best. And yet in this regard Gaute seemed less willing to comply with his wife's wishes; he tried to hold on to his old companions from his youth. His drinking cohorts, Jofrid called them, and Kristin now learned that Gaute had been much wilder than she knew. These friends never came to the manor uninvited after he was a married man. But as yet no poor supplicant had gone unaided by Gaute, although he gave fewer gifts if Jofrid was watching. Behind her back he dared to give more. But not much was allowed to take place behind her back.

And Kristin realized that Jofrid was jealous of her. She had possessed Gaute's friendship and trust so completely during all the years since he was a poor little child who was neither fully alive nor dead. Now she noticed that Jofrid wasn't pleased if Gaute sat down beside his mother to ask her advice or got her to talk about the way things were in the past. If the man stayed for long in the old house with his mother, Jofrid was certain to find an excuse to come over.

And she grew jealous if her mother-in-law paid too much attention to little Erlend.

Amid the short, trampled-down grass out in the courtyard grew several herbs with coarse, leathery dark leaves. Now, during the sunny days of midsummer, a little stalk had sprung up with tiny, delicate pale blue flowers in the center of each flattened rosette of leaves. Kristin thought the old outer leaves, scarred as they were by each time a servant's foot or a cow's hoof had crushed them, must love the sweet, bright blossoming shoot which sprang from its heart, just as she loved her son's son.

He seemed to her to be life from her life and flesh from her flesh, just as dear as her own children but even sweeter. Whenever she held him in her arms, she noticed that the boy's mother would keep a jealous eye on the two of them and would come to take him away as soon as she deemed it proper and then possessively put him to her breast, hugging him greedily. Then it occurred to Kristin Lavransdatter in a new way that the interpreters of God's words were right. Life on this earth was irredeemably tainted by strife; in this world, wherever people mingled, producing new descendants, allowing themselves to be drawn together by physical love and loving their own flesh, sorrows of the heart and broken expectations were bound to occur as surely as the frost appears in the autumn. Both life and death would separate friends in the end, as surely as the winter separates the tree from its leaves.

One evening, two weeks before Saint Olav's Day, a group of beggars happened to come to Jørundgaard and asked for lodgings for the night. Kristin was standing on the gallery of the old storeroom—it was now under her charge—and she heard Jofrid come out and tell the poor people that they would be given food, but she could not give them shelter. "There are many of us on this manor, and my mother-in-law lives here too; she owns half the buildings."

Anger flared up in the former mistress. Never before had any wayfarers been refused a night's lodging at Jørundgaard, and the sun was already touching the crest of the mountains. She ran downstairs and went over to Jofrid and the beggars.

"They may take shelter in my house, Jofrid, and I might as well be the one to give them food too. Here on this manor we have never refused lodging to a fellow Christian if he asked for it in the name of God."

"You must do as you please, Mother," replied Jofrid, her face blazing red.

When Kristin had a look at the beggars, she almost regretted her offer. It was not entirely without cause that the young wife had been unwilling to have these people on her estate overnight. Gaute and the servants had gone up to the hay meadows near Sil Lake and would not be home that evening. Jofrid was home alone with the parish's charity cases, two old people and two children, whose turn it was to stay at Jørundgaard, and Kristin had only her maid in the old house. Although Kristin was used to seeing all kinds of people among the wandering groups of beggars, she didn't like the looks of this lot. Four of them were big, strong young men; three of them had red hair and small, wild eyes. They seemed to be brothers. But the fourth one, whose nose had once been split open on both sides and who was missing his ears, sounded as if he might be a foreigner. There were also two old people. A short, bent old man with a greenish-yellow face, his hair and beard ravaged by dirt and age and his belly swollen as if with some illness. He walked on crutches, alongside an old woman wearing a wimple that was completely soaked with blood and pus, her neck and face covered with sores. Kristin shuddered at the thought of this woman getting near Erlend. All the same, for the sake of these two wretched old people, it was good that the group wouldn't have to wander through Hammer Ridge in the night.

The beggars behaved peaceably enough. Once the earless man tried to seize hold of Ingrid as she went back and forth to the table, but Bjørn got to his feet at once, barking and growling. Otherwise the group seemed despondent and weary; they had struggled much and gleaned little, they said in reply to the mistress's questions. Surely things would be better in Nidaros. The old woman was pleased when Kristin gave her a goat horn containing a soothing salve made from the purest lamb oil and the water of an infant. But she declined when Kristin offered to soak her wimple with warm water and give her a clean linen cloth; well, she would agree to accept the cloth.

Nevertheless, Kristin had her young maid, Ingrid, sleep on the side of the bed next to the wall. Several times during the night Bjørn growled, but otherwise everything was quiet. Shortly past midnight the dog ran over to the door and uttered a couple of short barks. Kristin heard horses in the courtyard and realized that Gaute had come home. She guessed that Jofrid must have sent word to him.

The next morning Kristin filled the sacks of the beggars generously, and they hadn't even passed the manor gate before she saw Jofrid and Gaute heading swiftly toward her house.

Kristin sat down and picked up her spindle. She greeted her children gently as they came in and asked Gaute about the hay. Jofrid sniffed; the guests had left a rank stench behind in the room. But her mother-in-law pretended not to notice. Gaute shifted his feet uneasily and seemed to have trouble telling her what the purpose of their visit might be.

Then Jofrid spoke. "There's something I think it would be best for us to talk about, Mother. I know that you feel I'm more tightfisted than you deem proper for the mistress of Jørundgaard. I know that's what you think and that you also think I'm diminishing Gaute's honor by acting this way. Now I don't have to tell you I was fearful last night about taking in that lot because I was alone on the estate with my infant and a few charity cases; I saw that you realized this as soon as you had a look at your guests. But I've noticed before that you think I'm miserly with food and inhospitable toward the poor.

"That is not so, Mother, but Jørundgaard is no longer a grand estate belonging to a royal retainer and wealthy man as it was in the time of your father and mother. You were the child of a rich man and kept company with rich and powerful kinsmen; you made a wealthy marriage, and your husband took you away to even greater power and splendor than you had grown up with. No one can expect that you in your old age should fully understand how different Gaute's position is now, having lost his father's inheritance and sharing half of your father's wealth with many brothers. But *I* dare not forget that I brought little more to his estate than the child I carried under my bosom and a heavy debt for my friend to bear because I consented to his act of force against my kinsmen. Things may get better with time, but I'm obliged to pray to God that my father might have a long life. We are young, Gaute and I, and don't know how many children we are destined to have. You *must* believe, mother-in-law, that I have no other thought behind my actions than what is best for my husband and our children."

"I believe you, Jofrid." Kristin gazed somberly at the flushed face of her son's wife. "And I have never meddled in your charge of the household or denied that you're a capable woman and a good and loyal wife for my son. But you must let me manage my own affairs as I am used to doing. As you say, I'm an old woman and no longer able to learn new ways."

The young people saw that Kristin had no more to say to them, and a few minutes later they took their leave.

As usual, Kristin had to agree that Jofrid was right—at first. But after she thought it over, it seemed to her . . . No, all the same, there was no use in comparing Gaute's alms with her father's. Gifts for the souls of the poor and strangers who had died in the parish, marriage contributions to fatherless maidens, banquets on the feast days of her father's favorite saints, stipends for sinners and those who were ill who wanted to seek out Saint Olav. Even if Gaute had been much richer than he was, no one would have expected him to pay for such expenses. Gaute gave no more thought to his Creator than was necessary. He was generous and kindhearted, but Kristin had seen that her father had a reverence for the poor people he helped because Jesus had chosen the lot of a poor man when he assumed human form. And her father had loved hard toil and thought all handwork should be honored because Mary, the Mother of God, chose to do spinning to earn food for her family and herself, even though she was the daughter of rich parents and belonged to the lineage of kings and the foremost priests of the Holy Land.

Two days later, early in the morning, when Jofrid was only half dressed and Gaute was still in bed, Kristin came into their room. She was wearing a robe and cape of gray homespun, with a wide-brimmed black felt hat over her wimple and sturdy shoes on her feet. Gaute turned blood-red when he saw his mother dressed in such attire. Kristin said she wanted to go to Nidaros for the Feast of Saint Olav, and she asked her son to look after her chores while she was gone.

Gaute protested vigorously; she should at least borrow horses and men to escort her and take her maid along. But his words had little authority, as might be expected from a man lying naked in bed before his mother's eyes. Kristin felt such pity for his bewilderment that she came up with the idea that she had had a dream.

"And I long to see your brothers again—" But then she had to turn away. She had not yet dared express in her heart how much she yearned for and dreaded this reunion with her two oldest sons.

Gaute insisted on accompanying his mother part of the way. While he dressed and had something to eat, Kristin sat laughing and playing with little Erlend; he chattered on, alert and lively with the morning. She kissed Jofrid farewell, and she had never done that before. Out in the courtyard all the servants had gathered; Ingrid had told them that Mistress Kristin was going on a pilgrimage to Nidaros.

Kristin picked up the heavy iron-shod staff, and since she didn't want to ride, Gaute put her travel bag on his horse's back and let the animal walk on ahead.

Up on the church hill Kristin turned around and looked down at her estate. How lovely it looked in the dewy, sun-drenched morning. The river shone white. The servants were still standing there; she could make out Jofrid's light-colored gown and wimple, and the child like a red speck in her arms. Gaute saw that his mother's face turned pale with emotion.

The road led up through the woods beneath the shadow of Hammer Ridge. Kristin walked as easily as a young maiden. She and her son said very little to each other. After they had walked for two hours, they reached the place where the road turns north under Rost Peak and the whole Dovre countryside stretches below, to the north. Then Kristin said that Gaute should go no farther with her, but first she wanted to sit down and rest for a while.

Beneath them lay the valley with the pale green ribbon of the river cutting through it and the farms like small green patches on the forested slopes. But higher up, the moss-covered heights, brown and lichen-yellow, arched against the gray scree and bare peaks, flecked with snowdrifts. The shadows of the clouds drifted over the valley and plains, but in the north the mountains were so brightly lit; one mountainous shape after another had freed itself from the misty cloak and loomed blue, one beyond the other. And Kristin's yearning glided north with the cloud clusters to the long road she had before her and raced across the valley, in among the great barricading slopes and the steep, narrow paths through the wilds across the plateaus. A few more days and she would be on her way down through the beautiful green valleys of Trøndelag, following the current of the river toward the great fjord. She shuddered at the memory of the familiar villages along the sea, where she had spent her youth. Erlend's handsome figure appeared before her eyes, shifting in stance and demeanor, swift and indistinct, as if she were seeing him mirrored in a rippling stream. At last she would reach Feginsbrekka, at the marble cross, and Nidaros would be lying there at the mouth of the river, between the blue fjord and the green Strind: on the shore the magnificent light-colored church with its dizzying towers and golden weather vanes, with the blaze of the evening sun on the rose in the middle of its breast. And deep inside the fjord, beneath the blue peaks of Frosta, lay Tautra, low and dark like the back of a whale, with its church tower like a dorsal fin. Oh, Bjørgulf . . . oh, Naakkve.

But when she looked back over her shoulder, she could still catch a glimpse of her home mountain beneath Høvringen. It lay in shadow, but with an accustomed eye she could see where the pasture path wound through the woods. She knew the gray domes that rose up over the carpet of forest; they surrounded the old meadows belonging to the people of Sil.

The sound of a *lur* echoed from the hills: several shrill tones that died away and then reappeared. It sounded as if children were practicing blowing the horn. A distant clanging of bells, the rush of the river fading lazily away, and the deep sighs of the forest in the quiet, warm day. Kristin's heart trembled anxiously in the silence.

Homesickness urged her forward; homesickness drew her back toward the village and the manor. Pictures of everyday things teemed before her eyes: She saw herself leaping with the goats along the path through the sparse woods south of their mountain pasture. A cow had strayed into the marsh; the sun was shining brightly. When she paused for a moment to listen, she felt her own sweat stinging her skin. She saw the courtyard back home in swirling snow—a dingy white, stormy day seething toward a wild winter night. She was almost blown back into the entryway when she opened the door; the blizzard took her breath away, but there they came, those two snow-covered bundles, men wearing long fur coats: Ivar and Skule had come home. The tips of their skis sank deep into the great snowdrift that always formed across the courtyard when the wind blew from the northwest. Then there were always huge drifts in two parts of the courtyard. All of a sudden she felt herself longing with love for those two drifts that she and all the manor servants had cursed each winter; she felt as if she were condemned never to see them again.

Feelings of longing seemed to burst from her heart; they ran in all directions, like streams of blood, seeking out paths to all the places in the wide landscape where she had lived, to all her sons roaming through the world, to all her dead lying under the earth. She wondered: Had she turned cowardly? She had never felt this way before.

Then she noticed that Gaute was staring at her. She gave him a fleeting, rueful smile. It was time now for them to say goodbye and for her to continue on.

Gaute called to his horse, which had been grazing across the green hillside. He ran to get him and then came back, and they said farewell. Kristin already had her travel bag over her shoulder and her son was putting his foot into the stirrup when he turned around and took a few steps toward her.

"Mother!" For a moment she looked into the depths of his helpless, shame-filled eyes. "You haven't been . . . no doubt you haven't been very pleased the last few years. Mother, Jofrid means well; she has great respect for you. Even so, I should have told her more about the kind of woman you are and have been all your days."

"Why do you happen to think about this now, my Gaute?" His mother's voice was gentle and surprised. "I'm quite aware that I'm no longer young, and old people are supposed to be difficult to please; all the same, I haven't aged so much that I don't have the wits to understand you or your wife. It would trouble me greatly if Jofrid should think that it has been a thankless struggle, after all she has done to spare me work and worry. Do not think, my son, that I fail to see your wife's virtues or your own loyal love for your mother. If I haven't shown it as much as you might have expected, you must have forbearance and remember that's the way old people are."

Gaute stared at his mother, open-mouthed. "Mother . . ." Then he burst into tears and leaned against his horse, shaking with sobs.

But Kristin stood her ground; her voice revealed nothing except amazement and maternal kindness.

"My Gaute, you are young, and you've been my little lamb all your days, as your father used to say. But you must not carry on like this, son. Now you're the master back home, and a grown man. If I were setting off for Romaborg or Jorsal, well . . . But it's unlikely that I will encounter any great dangers on this journey. I will find others to keep me company, you know; if not before, then when I reach Toftar. From there groups of pilgrims leave every morning during this time."

"Mother, Mother, don't leave us! Now that we've taken all power and authority out of your hands, pushed you aside into a corner . . ."

Kristin shook her head with a little smile. "I'm afraid my children seem to think I have an overbearing desire to take charge."

Gaute turned to face her. She took one of his hands in hers and placed her other hand on his shoulder as she implored him to believe that she was not ungrateful toward him or Jofrid; she asked God to be with him. Then she turned him toward his horse, and with a laugh she gave him a thump between his shoulders for good luck.

She stood gazing after him until he disappeared beneath the cliff. How handsome he looked riding the big blue-black horse.

She felt so strange. She sensed everything around her with such unusual clarity: the sun-sated air, the hot fragrance of the pine forest, the chittering of tiny sparrows in the grass. At the same time she was looking inside herself, seeing pictures the way someone with a high fever may believe she is peering at inner images. Inside her there was an empty house, completely silent, dimly lit, and with a smell of desolation. The scene shifted: a tidal shore from which the sea had retreated far away; rounded, light-colored stones, heaps of dark, lifeless seaweed, all sorts of flotsam.

Then she shifted her travel bag to a more comfortable position, picked up her staff, and set off down toward the valley. If she was not meant to come back, then it was God's will and useless to be frightened. But more likely it was because she was old. . . . She made the sign of the cross and strode faster, longing just the same to reach the hillside where the road passed among farms.

Only for one short section of the public road was it possible to see the buildings of Haugen high on the mountain crest. Her heart began hammering at the mere thought.

As she had predicted, she met more pilgrims when she reached Toftar late in the day. The next morning she was joined by several others as they all set off into the mountains.

A priest and his servant, along with two women, his mother and sister, were on horseback, and they soon pulled far ahead of those on foot. Kristin felt a pang in her heart as she gazed after another woman riding between her two children.

In her group there were two older peasants from a little farm in Dovre. There were also two younger men from Oslo, laborers from the town, and a farmer with his daughter and son-in-law, both of them quite young. They were traveling with the young couple's child, a tiny maiden about eighteen months old, and they had a horse, which they took turns riding. These three were from a parish far to the south called Andabu; Kristin didn't know exactly where it lay. On the first evening Kristin offered to take a look at the child because she was incessantly crying and moaning; she looked so pitiful with her big, bald head and tiny, limp body. She couldn't yet talk or sit up on her own. The mother seemed ashamed of her daughter. The next morning when Kristin offered to carry the child for a while, she was left in her care, and the other woman strode on ahead; she seemed a most neglectful mother. But they were so young, both she and her husband, hardly more than eighteen years old, and she must be weary of carrying the heavy child, who was always whining and weeping. The grandfather was an ugly, sullen, and cross middle-aged man, but he was the one who had urged this journey to Nidaros with his granddaughter, so he seemed to have some affection for her. Kristin walked at the back of the group with him and the two Franciscan monks, and it vexed her that the man from Andabu never offered to let the monks borrow his horse. Anyone could see that the younger monk was terribly ill.

The older one, Brother Arngrim, was a rotund little man with a round, red, freckled face, alert brown eyes, and a fox-red fringe of hair around his skull. He talked incessantly, mostly about the poverty of their daily life—the friars of Skidan. The order had recently acquired an estate in that town, but they were so impoverished that they were barely able to keep up the services, and the church they intended to erect would probably never be built. He placed the blame on the wealthy nuns in Gimsøy, who persecuted the poor friars with rancor and malice, and they had now brought a lawsuit against them. He spoke effusively about all their worst traits. Kristin wasn't pleased to hear the monk talk in this manner, and she didn't believe his claims that the abbess had not been chosen in accordance with Church law or that the nuns slept through their daily prayers, gossiped, and carried on unseemly conversations at the table in the refectory. Yes, he even said bluntly that people thought one of the sisters had not remained pure. But Kristin saw that Brother Arngrim was otherwise a good-hearted and kindly man. He carried the ill child for long stretches of the way whenever he saw that Kristin's arms were growing weary. If the girl began to howl too fiercely, he would set off running across the plain, with his robes lifted high so the juniper bushes scratched his dark, hairy legs and the mud splashed up from the marshy hollows, shouting and hollering for the mother to stop because the child was thirsty. Then he would hurry back to the ill man, Brother Torgils; toward him he was the most tender and loving father.

The sick monk made it impossible to reach Hjerdkinn that

night, but the two men from Dovre knew of a stone hut in a field a little to the south, near a lake, and so the pilgrims headed that way. The evening had turned cold. The shores of the lake were miry, and white mist swirled up from the marshes so the birch forest was dripping with dew. A slender crescent moon hung in the west above the mountain domes, almost as pale yellow and dull as the sky. More and more often Brother Torgils had to stop; he coughed so badly that it was terrible to hear. Brother Arngrim would support him and then wipe his face and mouth afterward, showing Kristin his hand with a shake of his head; it was bloody from the other man's spit.

They found the hut, but it had fallen in. Then they looked for a sheltered spot and made a fire. But the poor folks from the south hadn't expected that a night in the mountains would be so icy cold. Kristin pulled from her travel bag the cape Gaute had urged her to take because it was especially lightweight and warm, made from bought fabric and lined with beaver fur. When she wrapped it around Brother Torgils, he whispered—he was so hoarse that he could barely manage to speak—that the child should be allowed to lie next to him. And so she was placed beside him. She fretted, and the monk coughed, but now and then they both slept for a while.

Part of the night Kristin kept watch and tended the fire along with one of the Dovre men and Brother Arngrim. The pale yellow glimmer moved northward—the mountain lake lay white and still; fish rose up, rippling the surface—but beneath the towering dome on the opposite side, the water mirrored a deep blackness. Once they heard a hideous snarling shriek from the far shore; the monk cringed and grabbed the other two by the arm. Kristin and the farmer thought it must be some beast; then they heard stones falling, as if someone were walking across the scree over there, and another cry, like the coarse voice of a man. The monk began praying loudly: *"Jesus Kristus, Soter,"* Kristin heard. And *"vicit leo de tribu Juda."*[1] Then they heard a door slam somewhere on the slope.

The gray light of dawn began rising. The scree on the other side and the clusters of birch trees emerged. Then the other Dovre farmer and the man from Oslo relieved them. The last thing Kristin thought about before she fell asleep next to the fire was that if they made such little progress during the day—and she would have to give the friars a gift of money when they parted—then she would soon have to beg food from the farms when they reached Gauldal.

The sun was already high and the morning wind was darkening the lake with small swells when the frozen pilgrims gathered around Brother Arngrim as he said the morning prayers. Brother Torgils sat huddled on the ground, his teeth chattering, and tried to keep from coughing while he murmured along. When Kristin looked at the two ash-gray monk's cowls lit by the morning sun, she remembered she had been dreaming of Brother Edvin. She couldn't recall what it was about, but she kissed the hands of the kneeling monks and asked them to bless her companions.

Because of the beaver fur cape, the other pilgrims realized that Kristin was not a commoner. And when she happened to mention that she had traveled the king's road over the Dovre Range twice before, she became a sort of guide for the group. The men from Dovre had never been farther north than Hjerdkinn, and those from Vikvær did not know this region at all.

They reached Hjerdkinn just before vespers, and after the service in the chapel Kristin went out into the hills alone. She wanted to find the path she had taken with her father and the place beside the creek where she had sat with him. She didn't find the spot, but she thought she did find the slope she had climbed up in order to watch as he rode away. And yet the small, rocky hills along that stretch of path all looked much the same.

She knelt down among the bearberries at the top of the ridge. The light of the summer evening was fading. The birch-covered slopes of the low-lying hills, the gray scree, and the brown, marshy patches all melded together, but above the expanse of mountain plateaus arched the fathomless, clear bowl of the evening sky. It was mirrored white in all the puddles of water; scattered and paler was the mirrored shimmer of the sky in a little mountain stream, which raced briskly and restlessly over rocks and then trickled out onto the sandy bank of a small lake in the marsh.

Again it came upon her, that peculiar feverlike inner vision. The river seemed to be showing her a picture of her own life: She too had restlessly rushed through the wilderness of her earthly days, rising up with an agitated roar at every rock she had to pass over. Faint and scattered and pale was the only way the eternal light had been mirrored in her life. But it dimly occurred to the mother that in her anguish and sorrow and love, each time the fruit of sin had ripened to sorrow, that was when her earthbound and willful soul managed to capture a trace of the heavenly light.

Hail Mary, full of grace. Blessed are you among women and blessed is the fruit of your womb, Jesus, who gave his sweat and blood for our sake . . .

As she said five *Ave Marias* in memory of the painful mysteries of the Redemption, she felt that it was with her sorrows that she dared to seek shelter under the cloak of the Mother of God. With her grief over the children she had lost, with the heavier sorrows over all the fateful blows that had struck her sons without her being able to ward them off. Mary, the perfection of purity, of humility, of obedience to the will of her Father—she had grieved more than any other mother, and her mercy would see the weak and pale glimmer in a sinful woman's heart, which had burned with a fiery and ravaging passion, and all the sins that belong to the nature of love: spite and defiance, hardened relentlessness, obstinacy, and pride. And yet it was still a mother's heart.

Kristin hid her face in her hands. For a moment it seemed more than she could bear: that now she had parted with all of them, all her sons.

Then she said her last *Pater noster*. She remembered the leave-taking with her father in this place so many years in the past, and her leave-taking with Gaute only two days ago. Out of childish thoughtlessness her sons had offended her, and yet she knew that even if they had offended her as she had offended her father, with her sinful will, it would never have altered her heart toward them. It was easy to forgive her children.

*Gloria Patri et Filio et Spiritui Sancto,* she prayed, and kissed the cross she had once been given by her father, humbly grateful to feel that in spite of everything, in spite of her willfulness, her restless heart had managed to capture a pale glimpse of the love that she had seen mirrored in her father's soul, clear and still, just as the bright sky now shimmered in the great mountain lake in the distance.

The next day the weather was so overcast, with such a cold wind and fog and showers, that Kristin was reluctant to continue on with the ill child and Brother Torgils. But the monk was the most eager of them all; she saw that he was afraid he would die before he reached Nidaros. So they set off over the heights, but now and then the rain was so heavy that Kristin didn't dare head down the steep paths with the sheer cliffs both above and below, which she recalled lay all the way to the hostel at Drivdal. They made a fire when they had climbed to the top of the pass and settled in for the night. After evening prayers Brother Arngrim told a splendid saga about a ship in distress that was saved through the intercession of an abbess who prayed to the Virgin Mary, who made the morning star appear over the sea.

The monk seemed to have developed a fondness for Kristin. As she sat near the fire and rocked the child so the others could sleep, he moved closer to her and in a whisper began talking about himself. He was the son of a poor fisherman, and when he was fourteen years old, he lost his father and brother at sea one winter night, but he was rescued by another boat. This seemed to him a miracle, and besides, he had acquired a fear of the sea; that was how he happened to decide that he would become a monk. But for three more years he had to stay at home with his mother, and they toiled arduously and went hungry, and he was always afraid in the boat. Then his sister was wed, and her husband took over the house and share of the fishing boat, and he could go to the Minorites in Tunsberg. At first he was subjected to scorn for his low birth, but the guardian was kind and took him under his protection. And ever since Brother Torgils Olavssøn had entered the brotherhood, all the monks had become more pious and peaceful, for he was so pious and humble, even though he came from the best lineage of any of them, from a wealthy farming family over in Slagn. And his mother and sisters were very generous toward the monastery. But after they had come to Skidan, and after Brother Torgils had fallen ill, everything had once again become difficult. Brother Arngrim let Kristin understand that he wondered how

Christ and the Virgin Mary could allow the road to be so full of stones for his poor brothers.

"They too chose poverty while they lived on this earth," said Kristin.

"That's easy for you to say, being the wealthy woman that you surely must be," replied the monk indignantly. "You've never had to go without food. . . ." And Kristin had to agree that this was true.

When they made their way down to the countryside and wandered through Updal and Soknadal, Brother Torgils was allowed to ride part of the way, but he grew weaker and weaker, and Kristin's companions changed steadily, as people left them and new pilgrims took their place. When she reached Staurin, no one remained from the group she had traveled across the mountain with except the two monks. And in the morning Brother Arngrim came to her, weeping, and said that Brother Torgils had coughed up a great deal of blood in the night; he could not go on. Now they would doubtless arrive in Nidaros too late to see the celebration.

Kristin thanked the brothers for their companionship, their spiritual guidance, and their help on her journey. Brother Arngrim seemed surprised by the richness of her farewell gift, for his face lit up. He wanted to give her something in return. He pulled from his bag a box containing several documents. Each of them was a lovely prayer followed by all the names of God; a space had been left on the parchment in which the supplicant's name could be printed.

Kristin realized that it was unreasonable to expect the monk to know anything about her: the name of her husband or his fate, even if she mentioned her family name. And so she simply asked him to write "the widow Kristin."

Walking down through Gauldal, she took the paths on the outskirts of the villages, for she thought if she met people from the large estates, it might turn out that they recognized the former mistress of Husaby. She didn't fully know why, but she was reluctant for this to happen. The following day she set off along the paths through the woods on the mountain ridge to the little church at Vatsfjeld, which had been consecrated to John the Baptist, although the people called it Saint Edvin's Church.

The chapel stood in a clearing in dense forest; both the building and the mountain behind were mirrored in a pond from which a curative spring flowed. A wooden cross stood near the creek, and all around lay crutches and walking sticks, and on the bushes hung shreds of old bandages.

There was a small fence around the church, but the gate was locked. Kristin knelt down outside and thought about the time she had sat inside with Gaute on her lap. Back then she was dressed in silk, one of the group of magnificently attired noblemen and women from the surrounding parishes. Sira Eiliv stood nearby, holding Naakkve and Bjørgulf firmly by the hand; among the crowd outside were her maids and servants. Then she had prayed so fervently that if this suffering child would be given his wits and health, she would ask for nothing more, not even to be freed from the terrible pain in her back which had plagued her ever since the birth of the twins.

She thought about Gaute, so stalwart and handsome he looked on his huge blue-black horse. And about herself. Not many women her age, now close to half a century, enjoyed such good health; that was something she had noticed on her way through the mountains. Lord, if only you would give me this and this and this, then I will thank you and ask for nothing more except for this and this and this. . . .

Surely she had never asked God for anything except that He should let her have her will. And every time she had been granted what she asked for—for the most part. Now here she sat with a contrite heart—not because she had sinned against God but because she was unhappy that she had been allowed to follow her will to the road's end.

She had not come to God with her wreath or with her sins and sorrows, not as long as the world still possessed a drop of sweetness to add to her goblet. But now she had come, after she had learned that the world is like an alehouse: The person who has no more to spend is thrown outside the door.

She felt no joy at her decision, but it seemed to Kristin that she herself had not made the choice. The poor beggars who had entered her house had come to invite her away. A will that was not her own had put her among that group of impoverished and ill people and invited her to go with them, away from the home she had managed as the mistress and ruled as the mother of men. And when she had consented without much protest, she knew that she did so because she saw that Gaute would thrive better if she left the estate. She had bent fate to her will; she had obtained the circumstances she wanted. Her sons she could not shape according to her will; they were the way God had created them, and their obstinacy drove them. With them she could never win. Gaute was a good farmer, a good husband, and a faithful father, a capable man and as honorable as most people. But he did not have the makings of a chieftain, nor did he have the inclination to long for what she had desired on his behalf. Yet he loved her enough to feel tormented because he knew she expected something else of him. That was why she now intended to beg for food and shelter, even though it hurt her pride to arrive so impoverished; she had nothing to give.

But she realized that she *had* to come. The spruce forest covering the slopes stood drinking in the seeping sunlight and swayed softly; the little church sat silent and closed, sweating an odor of tar. With longing Kristin thought about the dead monk who had taken her hand and led her into the light emanating from the cloak of God's love when she was an innocent child, who had reached out his hand to lead her home, time after time, from the paths on which she had strayed. Suddenly she remembered so clearly her dream about him the night before, up in the mountains:

She dreamed that she was standing in the sunshine in a courtyard of some grand estate, and Brother Edvin was walking toward her from the doorway to the main house. His hands were full of bread, and when he reached her, she saw that she had been forced to do as she envisioned, to ask for alms when she came to the villages. But somehow she had arrived in the company of Brother Edvin, and the two of them were traveling together and begging. But at the same time she knew that her dream had a double meaning; the estate was not merely a noble manor, but it seemed to her to signify a holy place, and Brother Edvin belonged to the servants there, and the bread which he offered her was not simply flatbread the way it looked; it signified the Host, *panis angelorum*, and she accepted the food of angels from his hand. And now she gave her promise into Brother Edvin's hands.

## CHAPTER 5

FINALLY SHE HAD arrived. Kristin Lavransdatter sat and rested in a haystack on the road beneath Sion Castle. The sun was shining, and the wind was blowing; the part of the field that had not yet been cut undulated with blossoming straw, red and shiny like silk. Only the fields of Trøndelag were ever that color red. At the bottom of the slope she could see a glimpse of the fjord, dark blue and dotted with foam; fresh white sea swells crashed against the cliffs of the shore for as far as she could see below the green-forested promontory of the town.

Kristin let out a long breath. All the same, it was good to be back here, good even though it was also strange to know that she would never leave here again. The gray-clad sisters out at Rein followed the same rules, Saint Bernard's rules, as the brothers of Tautra. When she rose before dawn and went to church, she knew that Naakkve and Bjørgulf would also be taking their places in the monks' choir. So she would end up living out her old age with some of her sons after all, although not in the way she might have imagined.

She took off her hose and shoes to wash her feet in the creek. She would walk to Nidaros barefoot.

Behind her on the path leading up over the castle's summit several boys now appeared, gathering around the portal to see if they could find a way into the fortress ruins. When they caught sight of Kristin, they began shouting crude words at her while they laughed and hooted. She pretended not to hear until a small boy—he couldn't have been more than eight—happened to roll down the steep incline and nearly rammed into her, uttering several loathsome words he had boldly learned from the older ones.

Kristin turned around and said with a little laugh, "You don't need to scream for me to know you're a troll child; I can see that by the tumbling pants that you're wearing."

When the boys noticed the woman was speaking, they came bounding down, the whole pack of them. But they fell silent and grew shamefaced when they saw she was an older woman wearing pilgrim's garb. She didn't scold them for their coarse words but sat there looking at them with big, clear, calm eyes and a secretive smile on her lips. She had a round, thin face with a broad forehead and a small, curving chin. She was sunburned and had many wrinkles under her eyes, yet she didn't look particularly old.

Then the most fearless of the boys started talking and asking questions in order to conceal the confusion of the others. Kristin felt so merry. These boys seemed to her much like her own daredevils, the twins, when they were small, although she hoped to God that *her* sons had never had such filthy mouths. These boys seemed to be the children of smallholders from town.

When the moment came that she had longed for during the whole journey, when she stood beneath the cross on Feginsbrekka and looked down at Nidaros, she wasn't able to muster her soul for prayers and devotion. All the bells of the town began pealing at once, summoning everyone to vespers, and the boys all started talking at once, eager to point out to her everything in sight.

She couldn't see Tautra because a squall was blowing across the fjord toward Frosta, bringing fog and torrents of rain.

Surrounded by the group of boys, she made her way down the steep paths through the Steinberg cliffs, as cowbells began ringing and herders shouted from all sides. The cows were heading home from the town pastures. At the gate in the town ramparts near Nidareid, Kristin and her young companions had to wait while the livestock was driven through. The herders hooted and yelled and scolded, the oxen butted, the cows jostled each other, and the boys told her who owned each and every bull. When they finally went through the gate and walked toward the fenced lanes, Kristin had more than enough to do watching where she set her bare feet between the cow dung in the churned-up track.

Without asking, a few of the boys followed her all the way to Christ Church. And when she stood amid the dim forest of pillars and looked toward the candles and gold of the choir, the boys kept tugging at Kristin to show her things: from the colored patches of light that the sun on the rose window cast through the arches, to the gravestones on the floor, to the canopies of costly cloth above the altars—all things that were most likely to catch a child's eye. Kristin had no peace to collect her thoughts, but every word the boys uttered aroused a dull, deep longing in her heart: for her sons, above all else, but also for the manor, the houses, the outbuildings, the livestock. A mother's toil and a mother's domain.

She was still feeling reluctant to be recognized by people who might have been friends with Erlend or her in the past. They always used to spend the feast days at their town estate and have guests staying with them. She dreaded running into a whole entourage. She would have to seek out Ulf Haldorssøn, for he had been acting as her envoy with regard to the property shares she still owned up here in the north and that she now wanted to give to the Rein Convent in exchange for a corrody.[1] But she knew that a man who had served as one of Erlend's guardsmen while he was sheriff was supposed to be living on a small farm out near Bratør; he fished for white-sided dolphins and porpoises in the fjord and kept a hostel for seafarers.

All the lodgings were full, she was told, but then Aamunde, the owner himself, appeared and recognized her at once. It was strange to hear him call out her old name.

"If I'm not mistaken . . . aren't you Erlend Nikulaussøn's wife from Husaby? Greetings, Kristin. How is it that you've come to my house?"

He was more than happy if she would accept such lodgings for the night as he could offer, and he promised that he himself would sail to Tautra with her on the day after the feast.

Late into the night she sat outside in the courtyard, talking with her host, and she was greatly moved when she saw that Erlend's former subordinate still loved and esteemed the memory of his young chieftain. Aamunde used that word about him several times: young. They had heard from Ulf Haldorssøn about his unfortunate death, and Aamunde said that he never met any of his old companions from the Husaby days without drinking a toast to the memory of their intrepid master. Twice some of them had collected money and paid for a mass to be said for his soul on the anniversary of his death. Aamunde asked many questions about Erlend's sons, and Kristin in turn asked about old acquaintances. It was midnight before she went to bed, lying down beside Aamunde's wife. He had wanted both of them to give up their bed for her, and in the end she had to agree to take at least his half.

The next day was the Vigil of Saint Olav. Early in the morning Kristin went down to the skerries to watch the bustle along the wharves. Her heart began pounding when she saw the lord abbot of Tautra come ashore, but the monks who accompanied him were all older men.

Just before midafternoon prayers the crowds began heading toward Christ Church, carrying and supporting the ill and the lame, to find room for them in the nave so they would be close to the shrine when it was carried past in procession the following day after high mass.

When Kristin made her way up to the stalls that had been put up near the cemetery wall—they were mostly selling food and drink, wax candles, and cushions woven from reeds or birch twigs to kneel on inside the church—she happened to meet the people from Andabu again. Kristin held the child while the young mother went to get a drink of local ale. At that moment a procession of English pilgrims appeared, singing and carrying banners and lighted tapers. In the confusion that ensued as they passed through the great crowds around the stalls, Kristin lost sight of the people from Andabu, and afterward she couldn't find them.

For a long time she wandered back and forth on the outskirts of the throngs, hushing the screaming child. When she pressed the girl's face against her throat, caressing and consoling her, the child would put her lips to Kristin's skin and try to suckle. She could tell the child was thirsty, but she didn't know what to do. It would be futile to search for the mother; she would have to go into the streets and see if she could find some milk. But when she reached Upper Langstræte and tried to turn north, there was again a great crush of people. An entourage of horsemen was coming from the south, and at the same time a procession of guardsmen from the king's palace had entered the square between the church and the residence of the Brothers of the Cross. Kristin was pressed back into the nearest alleyway, but there too people on horseback and on foot were streaming toward the church, and the crowds grew so fierce that she finally had to save herself by climbing up onto a stone wall.

The air above her was filled with the clanging of bells; from the cathedral the *nona hora*[2] was rung. At the sound the child stopped screaming; she looked up at the sky, and a glimmer of understanding appeared in her dull eyes; she smiled a bit. Touched, the old mother bent down and kissed the poor little thing. Then she noticed that she was sitting on the stone wall surrounding the hops garden of Nikulaus Manor, their old town estate.

She should have recognized the brick chimney rising up from the sod roof, which was at the back of their house. Closest to her stood the buildings of the hospital, which had vexed Erlend so much because it had shared the rights to their garden.

She hugged the stranger's child to her breast, kissing her over and over. Then someone touched her knee.

A monk wearing the white robes and black cowl of a friar. She looked down into the sallow, lined visage of an old man, with a thin, sunken mouth and two big amber eyes set deep in his face.

"Could it be . . . is that you, Kristin Lavransdatter?" The monk placed his crossed arms atop the stone wall and buried his face in them. "Are you here?"

"Gunnulf!"

Then he moved his head so that he touched her knee as she sat there. "Do you think it so strange that I should be here?"

She remembered that she was sitting on the wall of the manor that had been his first home and later her own house, and she had to agree that it was rather odd after all.

"But what child is this you're holding on your knee? Surely this couldn't be Gaute's son?"

"No . . ." At the thought of little Erlend's healthy, sweet face and strong, well-formed body, she pressed the tiny child close, overcome with pity. "This is the daughter of a woman who traveled with me over the mountains."

But then she suddenly recalled what Andres Simonssøn had said in his childish wisdom. Filled with reverence, she looked down at the pitiful creature who lay in her arms.

Now the child was crying again, and the first thing Kristin had to do was ask the monk if he could tell her where she might find some milk. Gunnulf led her east, around the church to the friars' residence and brought her some milk in a bowl. While Kristin fed her foster child, they talked, but the conversation seemed to halt along rather strangely.

"So much time has passed and so much has happened since we last met," she said sadly. "And no doubt the news was hard to bear when you heard about your brother."

"May God have mercy on his poor soul," whispered Brother Gunnulf, sounding shaken.

Not until she asked about her sons at Tautra did Gunnulf become more talkative. With heartfelt joy the monastery had welcomed the two novices who belonged to one of the land's best lineages. Nikulaus seemed to have such splendid spiritual talents and made such progress in his learning and devotions that the abbot was reminded of his glorious ancestor, the gifted defender of the Church, Nikulaus Arnessøn. That was in the beginning. But after the brothers had donned cloister attire, Nikulaus had started behaving quite badly, and he had caused great unrest in the monastery. Gunnulf wasn't sure of all the reasons, but one was that Abbot Johannes would not allow young brothers to become ordained as priests until they were thirty, and he refused to make an exception to this rule for Nikulaus. And because the venerable father thought that Nikulaus prayed and brooded more than he was spiritually prepared for and was thereby ruining his health with his pious exercises, he wanted to send the young man to one of the cloister's farms on the island of Inder; there, under the supervision of several older monks, he was to plant an apple orchard. Then Nikulaus had apparently openly disobeyed the abbot's orders, accusing his brothers of depleting the cloister's property through extravagant living, of indolence in their service to God, and of unseemly talk. Most of this incident was never reported beyond the monastery walls, Gunnulf said, but Nikulaus had evidently also rebelled against the brother appointed by the abbot to reprimand him. Gunnulf knew that for a period of time he had been locked in a cell, but at last he had been chastened when the abbot threatened to separate him from his brother Bjørgulf and send one of them to Munkabu; it was no doubt the blind brother who had urged him to do this. Then Nikulaus had grown contrite and meek.

"It's their father's temperament in them," said Gunnulf bitterly. "Nothing else could have been expected but that my brother's sons would have a difficult time learning obedience and would show inconstancy in a godly endeavor."

"It could just as well be their mother's inheritance," replied Kristin sorrowfully. "Disobedience is my gravest sin, Gunnulf, and I was inconstant too. All my days I have longed equally to travel the right road and to take my own errant path."

"Erlend's errant paths, you mean," said the monk gloomily. "It was not just once that my brother led you astray, Kristin; I think he led you astray every day you lived with him. He made you forgetful, so you wouldn't notice when you had thoughts that should have made you blush, because from God the Almighty you could not hide what you were thinking."

Kristin stared straight ahead.

"I don't know whether you're right, Gunnulf. I don't know whether I've ever forgotten that God could see into my heart, and so my sin may be even greater. And yet it was not, as you might think, that I needed to blush the most over my shameful boldness or my weakness, but rather over my thoughts that my husband was many times more poisonous than the venom of snakes. But surely the latter has to follow the former. You were the one who once told me that those who have loved each other with the most ardent desire are the ones who will end up like two snakes, biting each other's tails.

"But it has been my consolation over these past few years, Gunnulf, that as often as I thought about Erlend meeting God's judgment, unconfessed and without receiving the sacraments, struck down with anger in his heart and blood on his hands, *he* never became what you said or what I myself became. He never held on to anger or injustice any more than he held on to anything else. Gunnulf, he was so handsome, and he looked at peace when I laid out his body. I'm certain that God the Almighty knows that Erlend never harbored rancor toward any man, for any reason."

Erlend's brother looked at her, his eyes wide. Then he nodded.

After a moment the monk asked, "Did you know that Eiliv Serkssøn is the priest and adviser for the nuns at Rein?"

"No!" exclaimed Kristin jubilantly.

"I thought that was why you had chosen to go there yourself," said Gunnulf. Soon afterward he said that he would have to go back to his cloister.

The first nocturn had begun as Kristin entered the church. In the nave and around all the altars there were great throngs of people. But a verger noticed that she was carrying a pitiful child in her arms, and he began pushing a path for her through the crowds so that she could make her way up to the front among the groups of those most crippled and ill, who occupied the middle of the church beneath the vault of the main tower, with a good view of the choir.

Many hundreds of candles were burning inside the church. Vergers accepted the tapers of pilgrims and placed them on the small mound-shaped towers bedecked with spikes that had been set up throughout the church. As the daylight faded behind the colored panes of glass, the church grew warm with the smell of burning wax, but gradually it also filled with a sour stench from the rags worn by the sick and the poor.

When the choral voices surged beneath the vaults, the organ swelled, and the flutes, drums, and stringed instruments resounded, Kristin understood why the church might be called a ship. In the mighty stone building all these people seemed to be on board a vessel, and the song was the roar of the sea on which it sailed. Now and then calm would settle over the ship, as if the waves had subsided, and the voice of a solitary man would carry the lessons out over the masses.

Face after face, and they all grew paler and more weary as the vigil night wore on. Almost no one left between the services, at least none of those who had found places in the center of the church. In the pauses between nocturns they would doze or pray. The child slept nearly all night long; a couple of times Kristin had to rock her or give her milk from the wooden flask Gunnulf had brought her from the cloister.

The encounter with Erlend's brother had oddly distressed her, coming as it did after each step on the road north had led her closer and closer to the memory of her dead husband. She had given little *thought* to him over the past few years, as the toil for her growing sons had left her scant time to dwell on her own fate, and yet the thought of him had always seemed to be right behind her, but she simply never had a moment to turn around. Now she seemed to be looking back at her soul during those years: It had lived the way people live on farms during the busy summer half of the year, when everyone moves out of the main house and into the lofts over the storerooms. But they walk and run past the winter house all day long, never thinking of going inside, even though all it would take was a lift of the latch and a push on the door. Then one day, when someone finally has a reason to go inside, the house has turned strange and almost solemn because it has acquired the smell of solitude and silence.

But as she talked to the man who was the last remaining witness to the interplay of sowing and harvesting in her life together with her dead husband, then it seemed to her that she had come to view her life in a new way: like a person who clambers up to a ridge overlooking his home parish, to a place where he has never been before, and gazes down on his own valley. Each farm and fence, each thicket and creek bed are familiar to him, but he seems to see for the first time how everything is laid out on the surface of the earth that bears the lands. And with this new view she suddenly found words to release both her bitterness toward Erlend and her anguish for his soul, which had departed life so abruptly. He had never known rancor; she saw that now, and God had seen it always.

She had finally come so far that she seemed to be seeing her own life from the uppermost summit of a mountain pass. Now her path led down into the darkening valley, but first she had been allowed to see that in the solitude of the cloister and in the doorway of death someone was waiting for her who had always seen the lives of people the way villages look from a mountain crest. He had seen sin and sorrow, love and hatred in their hearts, the way the wealthy estates and poor hovels, the bountiful acres and the abandoned wastelands are all borne by the same earth. And he had come down among them, his feet had wandered among the lands, stood in castles and in huts, gathering the sorrows and sins of the rich and the poor, and lifting them high up with him on the cross. Not my happiness or my pride, but my sin and my sorrow, oh sweet Lord of mine. She looked up at the crucifix, where it hung high overhead, above the triumphal arch.

The morning sun lit the tall, colored panes of glass deep within the forest of pillars in the choir and a glow, as if from red and brown, green and blue gemstones, dimmed the candlelight from the altar and the gold shrine behind it. Kristin listened to the last vigil mass, matins. She knew that the lessons of this service were about God's miraculous healing powers as invested in His faithful knight, King Olav Haraldssøn. She lifted the ill child toward the choir and prayed for her.

But she was so cold that her teeth were chattering after the long hours spent in the chill of the church, and she felt weak from fasting. The stench of the crowds and the sickening breath of the ill and the poor blended with the reek of candle wax and settled, thick and damp and heavy, upon those kneeling on the floor, cold in the cold morning. A stout, kind, and cheerful peasant woman had been sitting and dozing at the foot of a pillar right behind them, with a bearskin under her and another one over her lame legs. Now she woke up and drew Kristin's weary head onto her spacious lap. "Rest for a little while, sister. I think you must need to rest."

Kristin fell asleep in the woman's lap and dreamed:

She was stepping over the threshold into the old hearth room back home. She was young and unmarried, because she could see her own thick brown braids, which hung down in front of her shoulders. She was with Erlend, for he had just straightened up after ducking through the doorway ahead of her.

Near the hearth sat her father, whittling arrows; his lap was covered with bundles of sinews, and on the bench on either side of him lay heaps of arrowpoints and pointed shafts. At the very moment they stepped inside, he was bending forward over the embers, about to pick up the little three-legged metal cup in which he always used to melt resin. Suddenly he pulled his hand back, shook it in the air, and then stuck his burned fingertips in his mouth, sucking on them as he turned his head toward her and Erlend and looked at them with a furrowed brow and a smile on his lips.

Then she woke up, her face wet with tears.

She knelt during the high mass, when the archbishop himself performed the service before the main altar. Clouds of frankincense billowed through the intoning church, where the radiance of colored sunlight mingled with the glow of candles; the fresh, pungent scent of incense seeped over everyone, blunting the smell of poverty and illness. Her heart burst with a feeling of oneness with these destitute and suffering people, among whom God had placed her; she prayed in a surge of sisterly tenderness for all those who were poor as she was and who suffered as she herself had suffered.

"I will rise up and go home to my Father."

## CHAPTER 6

THE CONVENT STOOD on a low ridge near the fjord, so that when the wind blew, the crash of the waves on the shore would usually drown out the rustling of the pine forest that covered the slopes to the north and west and hid any view of the sea.

Kristin had seen the church tower above the trees when she sailed past with Erlend, and he had said several times they ought to pay a visit to this convent, which his ancestor had founded, but nothing had ever come of it. She had never set foot in Rein Convent until she came there to stay.

She had imagined that life here would be similar to what she knew of life in the convents in Oslo or at Bakke, but things were quite different and much more quiet. Here the sisters were truly dead to the world. Fru Ragnhild, the abbess, was proud of the fact that it had been five years since she had been to Nidaros and just as long since any of her nuns had set foot outside the cloister walls.

No children were being raised there, and at the time Kristin came to Rein, there were no novices at the convent either. It had been so many years since any young maiden had sought admittance to the order that it was already six winters ago that the newest member, Sister Borghild Marcellina, had taken her vows. The youngest in years was Sister Turid, but she had been sent to Rein at the age of six by her grandfather, who was a priest at Saint Clement's Church and a very stern and somber man. The child's hands had been crippled from birth, and she was misshapen in other ways too, so she had taken the veil as soon as she reached the proper age. Now she was thirty years old and quite sickly, but she had a lovely face. From the first day Kristin arrived at the convent, she made a special attempt to serve Sister Turid, for the nun reminded her of her own little sister Ulvhild, who had died so young.

Sira Eiliv said that low birth should not be a hindrance for any maiden who came to serve God. And yet ever since the convent at Rein had been founded, it was usually only the daughters or widows of powerful and highborn men from Trøndelag who had sought refuge there. But during the wicked and turbulent times that had descended upon the realm after the death of blessed King Haakon Haalegg, piety seemed to have diminished greatly among the nobility. Now it was mostly the daughters of merchants and prosperous farmers who considered the life of a nun. And they were more likely to go to Bakke, where many of them had spent time learning their devotions and womanly skills and where more of the sisters came from families of lower standing. There the rule prohibiting venturing outside the convent was less strict, and the cloister was not as isolated.

Otherwise Kristin seldom had the chance to speak with Sira Eiliv, but she soon realized that the priest's position at the convent was both a wearisome and troubled one. Although Rein was a wealthy cloister and the order included only half as many members as it could have supported, the nuns' money matters were in great disarray, and they had difficulty managing their expenses. The last three abbesses had been more pious than worldly women. Even so, they and their convent had vowed tooth and nail not to submit to the authority of the archbishop; their conviction was so strong that they also refused to accept any advice offered out of fatherly goodwill. And the brothers of their order from Tautra and Munkabu, who had been priests at their church, had all been old men so that no slanderous gossip might arise, but they had been only moderately successful at managing the convent's material welfare. When King Skule built the beautiful stone church and gave his ancestral estate to the cloister, the houses were first built of wood; they all had burned down thirty years ago. Fru Audhild, who was abbess at the time, began rebuilding with stone; in her day many improvements had been made to the church and the lovely convent hall. She had also made a journey to the general chapter at the mother cloister of the order, Tart in Burgundy. From that journey she had brought back the magnificent tower of ivory that stood in the choir near the high altar, a fitting receptacle for the body of the Lord, the most splendid adornment of the church, and the pride and cherished treasure of the nuns. Fru Audhild had died with the fairest of reputations for piety and virtue, but her ignorance in dealing with the builders and her imprudent property ventures had damaged the convent's well-being. And the abbesses who succeeded her had not been able to repair that damage.

How Sira Eiliv happened to come to Rein as priest and adviser, Kristin never knew, but this much she did know: From the very beginning the abbess and the sisters had received a secular priest with reluctance and suspicion. Sira Eiliv's position at Rein was such that he was the nuns' priest and spiritual adviser; he was also supposed to see about putting the estate back on its feet and restoring order to the convent's finances. All the while he was to acknowledge the supremacy of the abbess, the independence of the sisters, and the supervisory right of Tautra. He was also supposed to maintain a friendship with the other priest at the church, a monk from Tautra. Sira Eiliv's age and renown for unblemished moral conduct, humble devotion to God, and insight into both canonical laws and the laws of the land had certainly served him well, but he had to be constantly vigilant about everything he did. Along with the other priest and the vergers, he lived on a small manor that lay northeast of the convent. This also served as the lodgings for the monks who came from Tautra from time to time on various errands. When Nikulaus was eventually ordained as a priest, Kristin knew that if she lived long enough, she would also one day hear her eldest son say mass in the cloister church.

Kristin Lavransdatter was first accepted as a corrodian. Later she had promised Fru Ragnhild and the sisters, in the presence of Sira Eiliv and two monks from Tautra, to live a chaste life and obey the abbess and nuns. As a sign that she had renounced all command over earthly goods she had placed in Sira Eiliv's hands her seal, which he had broken in half. Then she was allowed to wear the same attire as the sisters: a grayish white woolen robe—but without the scapular—a white wimple, and a black veil. After some time had passed, the intention was for her to seek admittance into the order and to take the vows of a nun.

But it still was difficult for her to think too much about things of the past. For reading aloud during meals in the refectory, Sira Eiliv had translated into the Norwegian language a book about the life of Christ, which the learned and pious Doctor Bonaventura had written. While Kristin listened, her eyes would fill with tears whenever she thought about how blessed a person must be who could love Christ and his Mother, the cross and its torment, poverty and humility, in the way the book described. And then she couldn't help thinking about that day at Husaby when Gunnulf and Sira Eiliv had shown her the book in Latin from which this one had been copied. It was a thick little book written on such thin and dazzling white parchment that she never would have believed calfskin could be prepared so finely, and it had the most beautiful pictures and capital letters; the colors glowed like gemstones against gold. All the while Gunnulf had talked merrily—and Sira Eiliv had nodded in agreement with his quiet smile—about how the purchase of this book had made them penniless, so they had been forced to sell their clothes and take their meals with those receiving alms at a cloister until they received word of some Norwegian clerics who had come to Paris; from them they could borrow funds.

After matins, when the sisters went back to the dormitory, Kristin always stayed behind in the church. On summer mornings it seemed to her sweet and lovely inside, but during the winter it was terribly cold, and she was afraid of the darkness among all the gravestones, even though she steadily fixed her eyes on the little lamp which always burned in front of the ivory tower containing the Host. But winter or summer, as she lingered in her corner of the nuns' choir, she always thought that now Naakkve and Bjørgulf must also be praying for their father's soul; it was Nikulaus who had asked her to say these prayers and psalms of penance as they did every morning after matins.

Always, always she would then picture the two of them as she had seen them on that gray, rainy day when she went out to the monastery. Nikulaus had suddenly appeared before her in the parlatory, looking oddly tall and unfamiliar in the grayish white monk's robes, with his hands hidden under his scapular—her son—and yet he had changed so little. It was mostly his resemblance to his father that seized her so strongly; it was like seeing Erlend in a monk's cowl.

As they sat and talked and she told him everything that had happened on the estate since he left home, she kept waiting and waiting. Finally she asked anxiously if Bjørgulf would be coming soon.

"I don't know, Mother," replied her son. A moment later he added, "It has been a hard struggle for Bjørgulf to submit to his cross and serve God. And it seemed to worry him when he heard you were here, that too many thoughts might be torn open."

Afterward she felt only deadly despair as she sat and looked at Nikulaus while he talked. His face was very sunburned, and his hands were worn with toil; he mentioned with a little smile that he had been forced to learn after all to guide a plow and use a sickle and scythe. She didn't sleep that night in the hostel, and she hurried to church when the bells rang for matins. But the monks were standing so that she could see only a few faces, and her sons were not among them.

The following day she walked in the garden with a lay brother who worked there, and he showed her all the rare plants and trees for which it was renowned. As they wandered, the clouds scattered, the sun emerged, and a fragrance of celery, onion, and thyme rose up; the large shrubs of yellow lilies and blue columbine that adorned the corners of the beds glittered, weighted down with raindrops. Then her sons appeared; both of them came out of the little arched doorway in the stone building. Kristin felt as if she had been given a foretaste of the joys of paradise when she saw the two tall brothers, dressed in light-colored attire, coming toward her along the path beneath the apple trees.

But they didn't talk much with each other; Bjørgulf said almost nothing the entire time. He had become an enormous man, now that he was full-grown. And it was as if the long separation had sharpened Kristin's sight. For the first time she understood what this son of hers had had to struggle with and was doubtless still struggling with as he grew so big and strong in body, and his inner astuteness grew, but he felt his eyesight failing.

Once he asked about his foster mother, Frida Styrkaarsdatter. Kristin told him that she was now married.

"May God bless her," said the monk. "She was a good woman; toward me she was a good and faithful foster mother."

"Yes, I think she was more of a mother to you than I was," said

Kristin sadly. "You felt little trace of my mother's heart when such harsh trials were placed upon you in your youth."

Bjørgulf answered in a low voice, "And yet I thank God that the Devil never managed to bend me to such unmanliness that I should test your mother's heart in such a manner, even though I was close to it. . . . But I saw that you were carrying much too heavy a burden, and aside from God it was Nikulaus here who saved me those times when I was about to fall to temptation."

No more was said about that, or about how they were faring at the monastery or that they had acted badly and brought disfavor upon themselves. But they seemed quite pleased when they heard of their mother's intention to join the convent at Rein.

After her morning prayers, when Kristin walked back through the dormitory and looked at the sisters, sleeping on the beds, two to each straw mattress, and wearing their robes, which they never took off, she would think how unlike these women she must be, since from their youth they had devoted themselves solely to serving their Creator. The world was a master from whom it was difficult to flee once a person had submitted to its power. Surely she would not have fled either, but she had been cast out, the way a harsh master chases a used-up vassal out the door. Now she had been taken in here, the way a merciful master takes in an old servant and out of compassion gives her a little work while he houses and feeds the worn-out and friendless old soul.

From the nuns' dormitory a covered gallery led to the weaving room. Kristin sat there alone, spinning. The sisters of Rein were famous for their flax. Those days during the summer and fall when all the sisters and lay sisters went out to work in the flax fields were like feast days at the convent, especially when they pulled up the ripe plants. Preparing, spinning, and weaving the flax and then sewing the cloth into clerical garments were the main activities of the nuns during their work hours. None of them copied or illustrated books as the sisters in Oslo had done with such great skill under the guidance of Fru Groa Guttormsdatter, nor did they practice much the artful work of embroidering with silk and gold threads.

After some time Kristin was pleased to hear the sounds of the estate waking up. The lay sisters would go over to the cookhouse to prepare food for the servants; the nuns never touched food or drink until after the morning mass unless they were ill. When the bells rang for prime, Kristin would go over to the infirmary if anyone was sick, to relieve Sister Agata or one of the other nuns. Sister Turid, poor thing, often lay there.

Then she would begin looking forward to breakfast, which was served after the third hour of prayer and the mass for the convent's servants. Each day, with equal joy, Kristin would look forward to this noble and solemn meal. The refectory was built of wood, but it was a handsome hall, and all the women of the convent ate there together. The nuns sat at the highest table, where the abbess occupied the high seat, along with the three old women besides Kristin who were corrodians. The lay sisters were seated farther down. When the prayer was over, food and drink were brought in and everyone ate and drank in silence, with quiet and proper manners. While one of the sisters read aloud from a book, Kristin would think that if people out in the world could enjoy their meals with such propriety, it would be much clearer to them that food and drink are gifts from God, and they would be more generous toward their fellow Christians and think less about hoarding things for themselves and their own. But she herself had felt quite different back when she set out food for her flock of spirited and boisterous men who laughed and roared, while the dogs sniffed around under the table, sticking up their snouts to receive bones or blows, depending on what humor the boys were in.

Visitors seldom came to Rein. An occasional ship with people from the noble estates might put in when they were sailing into or out of the fjord, and then men and their wives, with children and youths, would walk up to the cloister to bring greetings to a kinswoman among the sisters. There were also the envoys from the convent's farms and fishing villages, and now and then messengers from Tautra. On the feast days that were celebrated with the most splendor—the feast days of the Virgin Mary, Corpus Christi Day, and the Feast of the Apostle Saint Andreas—people from the nearest villages on both sides of the fjord would come to the nuns' church. Otherwise only the convent's tenants and workers who lived close by would attend mass. They took up very little space in the vast church.

And then there were the poor—the regular charity cases who received ale and drink on specific days when masses were said for the souls of the dead, as provided for in the testaments of wealthy people—and others who came up to Rein almost every day. They would sit against the cookhouse wall to eat and seek out the nuns when they came into the courtyard, telling the sisters about their sorrows and troubles. The ill, the crippled, and the leprous were always coming and going. There were many who suffered from leprosy, but Fru Ragnhild said that was always true of villages near the sea. Leaseholders came to ask for reductions or deferments in their payments, and then they always had much to report about setbacks and difficulties. The more wretched and unhappy the people were, the more openly and freely they talked to the sisters about their circumstances, although they usually gave others the blame for their misfortunes, and they spoke in the most pious of terms. It was no wonder that when the nuns rested or while they worked in the weaving room, their conversation should turn to the lives of these people. Yes, Sister Turid even told Kristin that when the nuns in the convent were supposed to deliberate about trade and the like, the discussion would often slip into talk about the people who were involved in the cases. Kristin could tell from the sisters' words that they knew little more about what they were discussing than what they had heard from the people themselves or from the lay servants who had been out in the parish. They were very trusting, whether their subordinates spoke well of themselves or ill of their neighbors. And then Kristin would think with indignation about all the times she had heard ungodly lay people, yes, even a mendicant monk such as Brother Arngrim, accuse the convents of being nests of gossip and the sisters of swallowing greedily all rumors and unseemly talk. Even the very people who came moaning to Fru Ragnhild or any of the sisters who would speak to them, filling their ears with gossip, would berate the nuns because they discussed the cries that reached them from the outside world, which they themselves had renounced. She thought it was the same thing with gossip about the comfortable life of convent women; it stemmed from people who had often received an early breakfast from the sisters' hands, while God's servants fasted, kept vigil, prayed, and worked before they all gathered for the first solemn meal in the refectory.

Kristin served the nuns with loving reverence during the time before her admittance to the order. She didn't think she would ever be a good nun—she had squandered her abilities for edification and piety too much for that—but she would be as humble and faithful as God would allow her to be. It was late in the summer of A.D. 1349, she had been at Rein Convent for two years, and she was to take the vows of a nun before Christmas. She received the joyous message that both her sons would come to her ordination as part of Abbot Johannes's entourage.

Brother Bjørgulf had said, when he heard of his mother's intention, "Now my dream will be realized. I've dreamed twice this year that before Christmas we both would see her, although it won't be *exactly* as it was revealed to me, since in my dream I actually *saw* her."

Brother Nikulaus was also overjoyed. But at the same time Kristin heard other news about him that was not as good. He had laid hands on several farmers over by Steinker; they were in the midst of a dispute with the monastery about some fishing rights. When the monks came upon them one night as they were proceeding to destroy the monastery's salmon pens, Brother Nikulaus had given one man a beating and thrown another into the river, at the same time sinning gravely with his cursing.

## CHAPTER 7

A FEW DAYS later Kristin went to the spruce forest with several of the nuns and lay sisters to gather moss for green dye. This moss was rather rare, growing mostly on toppled trees and dry branches. The women soon scattered through the forest and lost sight of each other in the fog.

This strange weather had already lasted for several days: no wind, a thick haze with a peculiar leaden blue color that could be seen out over the sea and toward the mountains whenever it lifted enough so that a little of the countryside became visible. Now and then it would grow denser, becoming a downpour; now and then it would disperse so much that a whitish patch would appear where the sun hovered amid the shrouded peaks. But an odd heavy bathhouse heat hung on, quite unusual for that region down by the fjord and particularly at that time of year. It was two days before the Feast of the Birth of Mary. Everyone was talking about the weather and wondering what it could mean.

Kristin was sweating in the dead, damp heat, and the thought of the news she had heard about Naakkve was making her chest ache. She had reached the outskirts of the woods and come to the rough fence along the road to the sea; as she stood there, scraping moss off the rails, Sira Eiliv came riding toward home in the fog. He reined in his horse, said a few words about the weather, and they fell to talking. Then she asked the priest whether he knew anything about the incident with Naakkve, even though she knew it was futile. Sira Eiliv always pretended to know nothing about the private matters of the monastery at Tautra.

"I don't think you need to worry that he won't come to Rein this winter because of that, Kristin," said the priest. "For surely that's what you fear?"

"It's more than that, Sira Eiliv. I fear that Naakkve was never meant to be a monk."

"Do you mean you would presume to judge about such things?" asked the priest with a frown. Then he got down from his horse, tied the reins to the fence, and bent down to slip under the railing as he gave the woman a steady, searching glance.

Kristin said, "I fear that Naakkve finds it most difficult to submit to the discipline of the order. And he was so young when he entered the monastery; he didn't realize what he was giving up or know his own mind. But everything that happened during his youth—losing his father's inheritance and the discord that he saw between his father and mother, which ended with Erlend's death—all this caused him to lose his desire to live in this world. But I never noticed that it made him pious."

"You didn't? It may well be that Nikulaus has found it as difficult to submit to the discipline of the order as many a good monk has. He's hot-tempered and a young man, perhaps too young for him to have realized, before he turned away from this world, that the world is just as harsh a taskmaster as any other lord, and in the end it's a lord without mercy. Of that I think you yourself can judge, sister.

"And if it's true that Naakkve entered the monastery more for his brother's sake than out of love for his Creator . . . Even so, I don't think God will let it go unrewarded that he took up the cross on his brother's behalf. Mary, the Mother of God, whom I know Naakkve has honored and loved from the time he was a little boy, will doubtless show him clearly one day that her son came down to this earth to be his brother and to carry the cross for him.

"No . . ." The horse snuffled against the priest's chest. He stroked the animal as he murmured, as if to himself, "Ever since he was a child, my Nikulaus has had remarkable capacities for love and suffering; I think he has the makings of a fine priest.

"But you, Kristin," he said, turning toward her. "It seems to me that you should have seen so much by now that you would put more trust in God the Almighty. Haven't you realized yet that He will hold up each soul as long as that soul clings to Him? Do you think—child that you still are in your old age—that God would punish the sin when you must reap sorrow and humiliation because you followed your desire and your pride along pathways God has forbidden His children to tread? Will you say that *you* punished your children if they scalded their hands when they picked up the boiling kettle you had forbidden them to touch? Or the slippery ice broke beneath them when you had warned them not to go out there? Haven't you noticed when the brittle ice broke beneath you? You were drawn under each time you let go of God's hand, and you were rescued from the depths each time you called out to Him. Even when you defied your father and set your willfulness against his will, wasn't the love that was the bond of flesh between you and your father consolation and balm for the heart when you had to reap the fruit of your disobedience to him?

"Haven't you realized yet, sister, that God has helped you each time you prayed, even when you prayed with half a heart or with little faith, and He gave you much more than you asked for. You loved God the way you loved your father: not as much as you loved your own will, but still enough that you always grieved when you had to part from him. And then you were blessed with having good grow from the bad which you had to reap from the seed of your stubborn will.

"Your sons . . . Two of them He took when they were innocent children; for them you need never fear. And the others have turned out well—even if they haven't turned out the way *you* would have liked. No doubt Lavrans thought the same about you.

"And your husband, Kristin . . . May God protect his soul. I know you have chastised him in your heart both night and day because of his reckless folly. It seems to me that it must have been much harder for a proud woman to remember that Erlend Nikulaussøn had taken you with him through shame and betrayal and blood guilt if you had seen even once that the man could act with cold intent. And yet I believe it was because you were as faithful in anger and harshness as in love that you were able to hold on to Erlend as long as you both lived. For him it was out of sight, out of mind with everything except you. May God help Erlend. I fear he never had the wits to feel true remorse for his sins, but the sins that your husband committed against you—those he did regret and grieve over. That was a lesson we dare to believe has served Erlend well after death."

Kristin stood motionless, without speaking, and Sira Eiliv said no more. He untied his reins and said, "May peace be with you." Then he mounted his horse and rode away.

Later, when Kristin arrived back at the convent, Sister Ingrid met her at the gate with the message that one of her sons had come to see her; he called himself Skule, and he was waiting at the speaking gate.

He was conversing with his fellow seamen but leaped to his feet when his mother came to the door. Oh, she recognized her son by his agile movements: his small head, held high on his broad shoulders, and his long-limbed, slender figure. Beaming, she stepped forward to greet him, but she stopped abruptly and caught her breath when she saw his face. Oh, who had done such a thing to her handsome son?

His upper lip was completely flattened; a blow must have crushed it, and then it had grown back flat and long and ruined, striped with shiny white scar tissue. It had pulled his mouth askew, so he looked as if he were always sneering scornfully. And his nose had been broken and then healed crooked. He lisped slightly when he spoke; he was missing a front tooth, and another one was blue-black and dead.

Skule blushed under his mother's gaze. "Could it be that you don't know me, Mother?" He chuckled and touched a finger to his lip, not necessarily to point out his injury; it might simply have been an involuntary gesture.

"We haven't been parted so many years, my son, that your mother wouldn't recognize you," replied Kristin calmly, smiling without restraint.

Skule Erlendssøn had arrived on a swift sailing ship from Bjørgvin two days before with letters from Bjarne Erlingssøn for the archbishop and the royal treasurer in Nidaros. Later that day mother and son walked down to the garden beneath the apple trees, and when they could finally talk to each other alone, Skule told his mother news of his brothers.

Lavrans was still in Iceland; Kristin hadn't even known that he'd gone there. Oh yes, said Skule, he had met his youngest brother in Oslo the previous winter at a meeting of the nobles; he was there with Jammælt Halvardssøn. But the boy had always had a desire to go out and see the world, and so he had entered the service of the bishop of Skaalholt and left Norway.

Skule himself had accompanied Sir Bjarne to Sweden and then on a war campaign to Russia. His mother silently shook her head; she hadn't known about that either! The life suited him, he said with a laugh. He had finally had a chance to meet all the old friends his father had talked so much about: Karelians, Ingrians, Russians. No, his splendid scar of honor had not been won in a war. He gave a chuckle. Yes, it was in a brawl; the fellow who gave it to him would never have need to beg for his bread again. Otherwise Skule seemed to have little interest in telling her any more about the incident or about the campaign. He was now the head of Sir Bjarne's guardsmen, and the knight had promised to regain for him several properties his father had once owned in Orkedal that were now in the possession of the Crown. But Kristin noticed that Skule's big steel-gray eyes had a strange look in them as he spoke of this.

"But you think that such a promise cannot be counted on?" asked his mother.

"No, no." Skule shook his head. "The documents are being drawn up at this very time. Sir Bjarne has always kept his promises, in all the days I've been in his service; he calls me kinsman and friend. My position on his estate is much like that of Ulf back home with us." He laughed. It didn't suit his damaged face.

But he was the handsomest of men in terms of bearing, now that he was full-grown. The clothing he wore was cut according to the new fashion, with close-fitting hose and a snug, short *cotehardi,* which reached only to mid-thigh and was fastened with tiny brass buttons all the way down the front, revealing with almost unseemly boldness the supple power of his body. It looked as if he were wearing only undergarments, thought his mother. But his forehead and handsome eyes were unchanged.

"You look as if something were weighing on your heart, Skule," ventured his mother.

"No, no, no." It was just the weather, he said, giving himself a shake. There was a strange reddish brown sheen to the fog as the veiled sun set. The church towered above the treetops in the garden, eerie and dark and indistinct in a liver-red haze. They had been forced to row all the way into the fjord in the becalmed sea, said Skule. Then he shifted his clothes a bit and told her more about his brothers.

He had been sent on a mission by Sir Bjarne to southern Norway in the spring, so he could bring her recent news from Ivar and Gaute because he had traveled back north through the countryside and over the mountains from Vaagaa, home to Vestland. Ivar was well; he and his wife had two small sons at Rognheim, Erlend and Gamal, both handsome children. "At Jørundgaard I arrived for a christening feast. And Jofrid and Gaute said that since you were now dead to the world, they would name their little maiden after you; Jofrid is so proud of the fact that you're her mother-in-law. Yes, you may laugh, but now that the two of you don't have to live on the same manor, you can be sure that Jofrid thinks it splendid to speak of her mother-in-law, Kristin Lavransdatter. And I gave Kristin Gautesdatter my best gold ring, for she has such lovely eyes that I think she will come to look much like you."

Kristin smiled sadly.

"Soon you'll have me believing, my Skule, that my sons thought I was as fine and grand as old people always become as soon as they're in their graves."

"Don't talk like that, Mother," said the man, his voice strangely vehement. Then he laughed a little. "You know quite well that my brothers and I have always thought, ever since we wore our first pair of breeches, that you were the most splendid and magnanimous woman, even though you clutched us tightly under your wings so many times that we had to flap hard before we could escape the nest.

"But you were right that Gaute was the one with the makings of a chieftain among us brothers," he added, and he roared with laughter.

"You don't need to mock me about that, Skule," said Kristin, and Skule saw that his mother blushed, looking young and lovely.

Then he laughed even harder. "It's true, my mother. Gaute Erlendssøn of Jørundgaard has become a powerful man in the northern valleys. He won quite a reputation for himself by abducting his bride." Skule bellowed with laughter; it didn't suit his ruined mouth. "People are singing a ballad about it; yes, they're even singing that he took the maiden with iron and steel and that he fought with her kinsmen for three long days up on the moors. And the banquet that Sir Sigurd held at Sundbu, making peace among kin with gold and silver: Gaute is given credit for that too in the ballad. But it doesn't seem to have caused any harm by being a lie. Gaute rules the entire parish and some distance beyond, and Jofrid rules Gaute."

Kristin shook her head with a sad little smile. But her face looked young as she gazed at Skule. Now she thought that *he* looked most like his father; this young soldier with the ravaged face had so much of Erlend's lively courage. And the fact that he had been forced to take his own fate into his hands early on had given him a cool and steadfast spirit, which brought an odd sense of comfort to his mother's heart. With the words Sira Eiliv had spoken the day before still in her mind, she suddenly realized that as fearful as she had been for her reckless sons and as sternly as she had often admonished them because she was tormented with anguish for their sakes, she would have been less content with her children if they had been meek and timid.

Then she asked again and again about her grandson, little Erlend, but Skule had not seen much of him; yes, he was healthy and handsome and used to having his own way at all times.

The uncanny fog, tinged like clotted blood, had faded, and darkness began to fall. The church bells started ringing; Kristin and her son rose to their feet. Then Skule took her hand.

"Mother," he said in a low voice, "do you remember that I once laid hands on you? I threw a wooden bat at you, and it struck you on the forehead. Do you remember? Mother, while we're alone, tell me that you've fully forgiven me for that!"

Kristin let out a deep breath. Yes, she remembered. She had asked the twins to go up to the mountain pastures for her, but when she came out to the courtyard, she found their horse still there, grazing and wearing the pack saddle, and her sons were running about, batting a ball. When she reprimanded them sternly, Skule threw the bat at her in fierce anger. What she remembered most was walking around with her eyelid so swollen that it seemed to have grown shut; her other sons would look at her and then at Skule and shun the boy as if he were a leper. First Naakkve had beat him mercilessly. And Skule had wandered around, boiling with defiance and shame behind his stony, scornful expression. But that evening, as she was undressing in the dark, he came creeping into the room. Without saying a word, he took her hand and kissed it. When she touched his shoulder, he threw his arms around her neck and pressed his cheek to hers. His skin felt cool and soft and slightly rounded—still a child's cheek, she realized. He was just a child, after all, this headstrong, quick-tempered boy.

"Yes, I have, Skule—so completely, that God alone can understand, for I can't tell you how completely I've forgiven you, my son!"

For a moment she stood with her hand on his shoulder. Then he seized her wrists and squeezed them so tight that she cried out; the next instant he put his arms around her, as tender and frightened and ashamed as he had been back then.

"My son . . . what is it?" whispered his mother in alarm.

In the dark she could feel the man shaking his head. Then he let her go, and they walked back up to the church.

During the mass Kristin happened to remember that she had once again forgotten about the cloak for the blind Fru Aasa when they were sitting on the bench outside the priest's door that morning. After the service she went around the church to get it.

In the archway stood Skule and Sira Eiliv, holding a lantern in his hand. "He died when we put in at the wharf," she heard Skule say, his voice full of a peculiar, wild despair.

"Who?"

Both men started violently when they saw her.

"One of my seamen," said Skule softly.

Kristin looked from one man to the other. In the glow of the lantern she caught sight of their faces, incomprehensibly strained, and she uttered a little involuntary cry of fear. The priest bit his lip; she saw that his chin was trembling faintly.

"It's just as well that you tell your mother, my son. It's better if we all prepare ourselves to bear it if it should be God's will for our people to be stricken with such a harsh—" But Skule merely moaned and refused to speak. Then the priest said, "A sickness has come to Bjørgvin, Kristin. The terrible pestilence we've heard rumors about, which is ravaging countries abroad."

"The black plague?" whispered Kristin.

"It would do no good if I tried to tell you how things were in Bjørgvin when I left there," said Skule. "No one could imagine it who hasn't seen it for himself. Sir Bjarne took stern measures at first to put out the fire where it broke out in the buildings around Saint Jon's Monastery. He wanted to cut off all of Nordnes with guardsmen from the castle, even though the monks at Saint Michael's Monastery threatened him with excommunication. An English ship had arrived with sick men on board, and he refused to allow them to unload their cargo or leave the ship. Every single man on that vessel perished, and then he had it scuttled. But some of the goods had already been brought ashore, and some of the townsmen smuggled more off the ship one night, and the brothers of Saint Jon's Church demanded that the dying be given the last rites. When people started dying all over town, we realized it was hopeless. Now there's no one left in Bjørgvin except for the men carrying the corpses. Everyone has fled the town who could, but the sickness follows them."

"Oh, Jesus Christus!"

"Mother . . . Do you remember the last time there was a lemming year back home in Sil? The hordes that tumbled along all the roads and pathways . . . Do you remember how they lay dying in every bush, rotting and tainting every waterway with their stench and poison?" He clenched his fists. His mother shuddered.

"Lord, have mercy on us all. Praise be to God and the Virgin Mary that you were sent up here, my Skule."

The man gnashed his teeth in the dark.

"That's what we said too, my men and I, the morning we hoisted sail and set off for Vaag. When we came north to Moldøsund, the first one fell ill. We tied stones to his feet and put a cross on his breast when he died, promising him a mass for his soul when we reached Nidaros; then we threw his body into the sea. May God forgive us. With the next two, we put into shore and gave them the last rites and burial in a proper grave. It's not possible to flee from fate after all. The fourth one died as we rowed into the river, and the fifth one died last night."

"Do you have to go back to town?" asked his mother a moment later. "Can't you stay here?"

Skule shook his head and laughed without mirth. "Oh, I think soon it won't matter where I am. It's useless to be frightened; fearful men are half dead already. But if only I was as old as you are, Mother!"

"No one knows what he has been spared by dying in his youth," said his mother quietly.

"Silence, Mother! Think about the time when you yourself were twenty-three years old. Would you have wanted to lose all the years you've lived since then?"

Fourteen days later Kristin saw for the first time someone who was ill with the plague. Rumors had reached Rissa that the scourge was laying waste to Nidaros and had spread to the countryside; how this had happened was difficult to say, for everyone was staying inside, and anyone who saw an unknown wayfarer on the road would flee into the woods or thickets. No one opened the door to strangers.

But one morning two fishermen came up to the convent, carrying between them a man in a sail. When they had gone down to their boats at dawn, they found an unfamiliar fishing vessel at the dock, and in the bottom lay this man, unconscious. He had managed to tie up his boat but could not climb out of it. The man had been born in a house belonging to the convent, but his family had since moved away from the region.

The dying man lay in the wet sail in the middle of the courtyard green; the fishermen stood at a distance, talking to Sira Eiliv. The lay sisters and servingwomen all had fled into the buildings, but the nuns—a flock of trembling, terrified, and bewildered old women—were clustered near the door to the convent hall.

Then Fru Ragnhild stepped forward. She was a short, thin old woman with a wide, flat face and a little, round red nose that looked like a button. Her big light brown eyes were red-rimmed and always slightly teary.

"*In nomine Patris et Filii et Spiritus Sancti,*" she said clearly, and then swallowed hard. "Bring him to the guesthouse."

Sister Agata, the oldest of the nuns, elbowed her way through the others and, unbidden, followed the abbess and the fishermen who carried the sick man.

Kristin went over there that night with a potion she had prepared in the pantry, and Sister Agata asked if she would stay and tend the fire.

She thought she would have been hardened, familiar as she was with birth and death; she had seen worse sights than this. She tried to recall the very worst she had ever witnessed. The plague patient sat bolt upright, for he was about to choke on the bloody vomit he coughed up with every spasm. Sister Agata had strapped him up with a harness across his gaunt, sallow red-haired chest; his head hung limply, and his face was a leaden grayish blue. All of a sudden he would start shaking with cold. But Sister Agata sat calmly, saying her prayers. When the fits of coughing seized hold of him, she would stand up, put one arm around his head, and hold a cup under his mouth. The ill man bellowed with pain, rolling his eyes terribly, and finally thrust a blackened tongue all the way out of his mouth as his terrible cries ended in a pitiful groan. The nun emptied the cup into the fire. As Kristin added more juniper and the wet branches first filled the room with a sharp yellow smoke and then made the flames crackle, she watched Sister Agata straighten the pillows and comforters behind the sick man's back and shoulders, swab his face and crusted brown lips with vinegar water, and pull the soiled coverlet up around his body. It would soon be over, she told Kristin. He was already cold; in the beginning he had been as hot as an ember. But Sira Eiliv had prepared him for his leave-taking. Then she sat down beside his bed, pushed the calamus root back into her cheek with her tongue, and continued praying.

Kristin tried to conquer the ghastly horror she felt. She had seen people die a more difficult death. But it was all in vain. This was the plague—God's punishment for the secret hardheartedness of every human being, which only God the Almighty could see. She felt dizzy, as if she were rocking on a sea where all the bitter and angry thoughts she had ever had in this world rose up like a single wave among thousands and broke into desperate anguish and lamenting. Lord, help us, we are perishing. . . .

Sira Eiliv came in later that night. He reprimanded Sister Agata sharply for not following his advice to tie a linen cloth, dipped in vinegar, around her mouth and nose. She murmured crossly that it would do no good, but now both she and Kristin had to do as he ordered.

The calm and steadfast manner of the priest gave Kristin courage, or perhaps it aroused a sense of shame; she ventured out of the juniper smoke to lend Sister Agata a helping hand. There was a suffocating stench surrounding the sick man which the smoke could not mask: excrement, blood, sour sweat, and a rotten odor coming from his throat. She thought of Skule's words about the swarms of lemmings; she still had a dreadful urge to flee, even though she knew there was nowhere to flee from this. But after she had finally persuaded herself to touch the dying man, the worst was over, and she helped as much as she could until he breathed his last. By then his face had turned completely black.

The nuns walked in procession carrying reliquaries, crosses, and burning tapers around the church and convent hill, and everyone in the parish who could crawl or walk went with them. But a few days later a woman died over by Strømmen, and then the pestilence broke out in earnest in every hamlet throughout the countryside.

Death and horror and suffering seemed to push people into a world without time. No more than a few weeks had passed, if the days were to be counted, and yet it already seemed as if the world that had existed before the plague and death began wandering naked through the land had disappeared from everyone's memory—the way the coastline sinks away when a ship heads out to sea on a rushing wind. It was as if no living soul dared hold on to the memory that life and the progression of workdays had once seemed close, while death was far away; nor was anyone capable of imagining that things might be that way again, if all human beings did not perish. But "we are all going to die," said the men who brought their motherless children to the convent. Some of them spoke with dull or harsh voices; some of them wept and moaned. They said the same thing when they came to get the priest for the dying; they said it again when they carried the bodies to the parish church at the foot of the hill and to the cemetery at the convent church. Often they had to dig the graves themselves. Sira Eiliv had sent the men who were left among the lay servants out to the convent fields to bring in the grain, and wherever he went in the parish, he urged everyone to harvest the crops and help each other tend to the livestock so that those who remained wouldn't suffer from hunger after the scourge had spent its fury.

The nuns at the convent met the first trials with a sense of desperate composure. They moved into the convent hall for good, kept a fire going day and night in the big brick fireplace, and ate and slept in there. Sira Eiliv advised everyone to keep great fires burning in the courtyards and in all the houses, but the sisters were afraid of fire. The oldest sisters had told them so often about the blaze thirty years before. Mealtimes and work regimens were no longer adhered to, and the duties of the various sisters were no longer kept separate as children began to arrive, asking for food and help. The sick were brought inside; they were mostly wealthy people who could pay for gravesites and masses for their souls in the convent, as well as those who were destitute and alone, who had no help at home. Those whose circumstances were somewhere in between stayed in their own beds and died at home. On some farms every single person perished. But in spite of everything, the nuns had still managed to keep to the schedule of prayers.

The first of the nuns to fall ill was Sister Inga, a woman Kristin's age, almost fifty, and yet she was so terrified of death that it was a horror to see and hear. The chills came over her in church during mass; shaking, her teeth chattering, she crawled on her hands and knees as she begged and implored God and the Virgin Mary to spare her life. A moment later she lay prostrate with a burning fever, in agony, with blood seeping out of her skin. Kristin's heart was filled with dread; no doubt she would be just as pitifully frightened when her turn came. It was not just the fact that death was certain, but it was the horrifying fear that accompanied death from the plague.

Then Fru Ragnhild herself fell ill. Kristin had sometimes wondered how this woman had come to be chosen for the high position of abbess. She was a quiet, slightly morose old woman, uneducated and apparently without great spiritual gifts. And yet when death placed its hand on her, she showed that she was a true bride of Christ. In her the illness erupted in boils. She refused to allow her spiritual daughters to unclothe her old body, but the swelling finally grew as big as an apple under one arm, and she had boils under her chin; they turned hard and blood-red, becoming black in the end. She endured unbearable agony from them and burned with fever, but each time her mind would clear, she lay in bed like an example of holy patience—sighing to God, asking forgiveness for her sins, and uttering beautiful, fervent prayers for her convent and her daughters, for all those who were sick and sorrowful, and for the peace of everyone's soul, who would now have to leave this life. Even Sira Eiliv wept after he had given her the viaticum; his steadfast and tireless zeal in the midst of all the misery had otherwise been a thing of wonder. Fru Ragnhild had already surrendered her soul into God's hands many times and prayed that He would take the nuns under His protection when the boils on her body began to split open. But this turned out to be a turn toward life, and later others experienced the same thing: Those who were stricken with boils gradually recovered, while those stricken with bloody vomiting all died.

Because of the example of the abbess and because they had witnessed a plague victim who did not die, the nuns seemed to find new courage. They now had to do the milking and chores in the cowshed themselves; they cooked their own food, and they brought back juniper and fresh evergreen branches for the cleansing smoke. Everyone did whatever task needed doing. They nursed the sick as best they could and handed out healing remedies: their supplies of theriac and calamus root were gone, but they doled out ginger, pepper, saffron, and vinegar against the sickness, along with milk and food. When the bread ran out, they baked at night; when the spices were gone, people had to chew on juniper berries and pine needles against the sickness. One by one the sisters succumbed and died. Night and day the bells for the dead rang from the convent church and from the parish church in the heavy air, for the unnatural fog hung on; there seemed to be a secret bond between the haze and the pestilence. Sometimes it became a frosty mist, drizzling down needles of ice and half-frozen sleet, covering the fields with rime. Then mild weather would set in, and the fog returned. People took it as an evil omen that all the seabirds had suddenly disappeared. They usually flocked by the thousands along the stream that flows through the countryside from the fjord and resembles a river in the low stretches of meadow but widens into a lake with salt water north of Rein Convent. In their place came ravens in unheard-of numbers. On every stone along the water sat the black birds in the fog, uttering their hideous shrill cries, while flocks of crows more numerous than anyone had ever seen before settled in all the forests and groves and flew with loathsome shrieks over the wretched land.

Once in a while Kristin would think of her own family—her sons, who were spread so far and wide, the grandchildren she would never see; little Erlend's golden neck would hover before her eyes. But they seemed to grow distant and faded. Now it almost seemed as if all people were equally close and distant to each other in this time of great need. And she had her hands full all day long; it now served her well that she was used to all sorts of work. While she sat and did the milking, starving little children whom she had never seen before would suddenly appear beside her, and she seldom even thought to ask where they were from or how things were back home. She gave them food and took them into the chapter hall or some other room where a fire was lit or tucked them into bed in the dormitory.

With a feeling of wonder she noticed that in this time of great misfortune, when it was more necessary than ever for everyone to attend to their prayers with vigilance, she never had time to collect her thoughts to pray. She would sink to her knees in front of the tabernacle in the church whenever she had a free moment, but she could manage nothing more than wordless sighs and dully murmured *Pater nosters* and *Ave Marias*. She wasn't aware of it herself, but the nunlike demeanor and manners she had assumed over the past two years swiftly began to fall away; she again became like the mistress she had been in the past, as the flock of nuns diminished, the routines of the convent were abandoned, and the abbess still lay in bed, weak and with her tongue partially paralyzed. And the work mounted for the few who were left to tend to everything.

One day she happened to hear that Skule was still in Nidaros. The members of his crew had either died or fled, and he hadn't been able to find new men. He was well, but he had cast himself into a wild life, just as many young people, out of despair, had done. They said that whoever was afraid would be sure to die, and so they blunted their fear with carousing and drinking, playing cards, dancing, and carrying on with women. Even the wives of honorable townsmen and young daughters from the best of families ran off from their homes during these evil times. In the company of wanton women they would revel in the alehouses and taverns among the dissolute men. God forgive them, thought Kristin, but she felt as if her heart was too weary to grieve over these things properly.

And apparently even in the villages there was plenty of sin and depravity. They heard little about it at the convent because there they had no time to waste on such talk. But Sira Eiliv, who went everywhere, ceaselessly and tirelessly tending to the sick and dying, told Kristin one day that the agony of people's souls was worse than that of their bodies.

Then one evening they were sitting around the fireplace in the convent hall, the little group of people left alive at Rein Convent. Huddled around the fire were four nuns and two lay sisters, an old beggar and a half-grown boy, two women who received alms from the convent, and several children. On the high seat bench, above which a large crucifix could be glimpsed in the dusk hanging on the light-colored wall, lay the abbess with Sister Kristin and Sister Turid sitting at her head and feet.

It was nine days since the last death had occurred among the sisters and five days since anyone had died in the convent or the nearest houses. The plague seemed to be waning throughout the countryside as well, said Sira Eiliv. For the first time in three months a glimmer of peace and security and comfort fell over the silent, weary people sitting there. Old Sister Torunn Marta let her rosary sink into her lap and took the hand of the little girl standing at her knee.

"What do you think she could mean? Well, child, now we seem to be seeing that Mary, the Mother of God, never withdraws her mercy from her children for long."

"No, it's not the Virgin Mary, Sister Torunn. It's Hel. She'll leave the parish, taking her rakes and brooms, when they sacrifice an innocent man at the gate of the cemetery. By tomorrow she'll be far away."

"What can she mean?" asked the nun, again uneasy. "Shame on you, Magnhild, for spreading such loathsome, heathen gossip. You deserve to taste the rod for that. . . ."

"Tell us what you mean, Magnhild. Don't be afraid." Sister Kristin was standing behind them; her voice sounded strained. She had suddenly remembered that in her youth she had heard Fru Aashild talk about dreadful, unmentionably sinful measures which the Devil tempted desperate men to try.

The children had been down in the grove near the parish church at twilight, and some of the boys had wandered over to a sod hut that stood there; they had spied on several men who were making plans. It seemed that these men had captured a small boy named Tore, the son of Steinunn from down by the shore. That night they were going to sacrifice him to Hel, the plague giantess. The children began talking eagerly, proud to have sparked the attention of the grown-ups. It didn't seem to occur to them to feel pity for this poor Tore; he was a sort of outcast who roamed the countryside, begging, but never came near the convent. When Sira Eiliv or any of the abbess's envoys went looking for his mother, she would flee or refuse to talk to them, no matter whether they spoke to her kindly or sternly. She had spent ten years living in the alleyways of Nidaros, but then she acquired a sickness that disfigured her so badly that finally she could no longer earn a living in the manner she had before. And so she had come to the parish and lived in a hovel out on the shore. Occasionally a beggar or the like would move in and share her hut for a time. Who the father of her boy might be, she herself didn't know.

"We must go out there," said Kristin. "We can't just sit here while Christian souls sell themselves to the Devil right on our doorstep."

The nuns whimpered. They were the worst men of the parish, coarse, ungodly fellows, and surely the latest calamity and despair must have turned them into regular demons. If only Sira Eiliv was home, they lamented. Ever since the onset of the plague, the priest's position had changed, and the sisters expected him to do everything.

Kristin wrung her hands. "If I have to go alone . . . Mother, may I have your permission to go out there myself?"

The abbess gripped her arm so tightly that she gave a little cry. The old woman, who was unable to speak, struggled to her feet; by gesturing she made them understand that she wanted to be dressed to go out. She demanded to be given the gold cross, the symbol of her office, and her staff. Then she held on to Kristin's arm since she was the youngest and strongest of the women. All the nuns stood up and followed.

Passing through the door of the little room between the chapter hall and the church choir, they stepped out into the raw, cold winter night. Fru Ragnhild began shivering, and her teeth chattered. She still sweated incessantly from the illness, and the sores left by the plague boils were not fully healed; walking caused her great pain. But she snarled angrily and shook her head when the sisters implored her to turn around. She gripped Kristin's arm harder, and shaking with cold, she trudged ahead of them through the garden. As their eyes grew used to the dark, the women glimpsed light patches of withered leaves scattered beneath their feet and a pale scrap of cloudy sky above the bare crowns of the trees. Drops of cold water trickled down, and gusts of wind murmured faintly. Sluggish and heavy, the drone of the fjord sighed against the shore beyond the cliffs.

At the bottom of the garden was a small gate; the sisters shuddered at the shriek of the rusted iron bolt as Kristin struggled to shove it open. Then they crept onward through the grove, down toward the parish church. They caught a glimpse of the tarred timber shape, darker against the night, and they saw the roof and ridge turret with its animal-head carvings and cross on the top against the pale gleam of the clouds above the slopes on the other side of the fjord.

Yes, there were people in the cemetery; they sensed their presence rather than saw or heard anything. Now a low, faint gleam of light appeared, as if from a lantern standing on the ground. Something moved in the darkness nearby.

The nuns huddled together, whimpering faintly under their whispered prayers; they took several steps forward, stopped to listen, and moved forward again. They had almost reached the cemetery gate.

Then out of the darkness they heard the shrill cry of a child's voice: "Hey, stop, you're getting dirt on my bread!"

Kristin let go of the abbess's arm and ran forward, through the churchyard gate. She pushed aside several shadowy men's backs, stumbled on piles of shoveled dirt, and came to the edge of the open grave. She fell to her knees, bent down, and pulled out the little boy who was standing in the bottom, still complaining because there was earth on the good piece of *lefse* he had been given for sitting still in the pit.

The men were frightened out of their wits and ready to flee. Several were stomping in place; Kristin could see their feet in the light from the lantern on the ground. Then she thought that one of them seemed about to leap at her. At that moment the grayish-white habits of the nuns came into view, and the group of men stood there, in confusion.

Kristin still held the boy in her arms; he was crying for his *lefse*. She set him down, picked up the bread, and brushed it off.

"Here, eat it. Now your bread is as good as ever. And you men should go on home." The quaver in her voice forced her to pause for a moment. "Go home and thank God that you were saved before you committed an act you might never be able to atone for." Now she spoke the way a mistress speaks to her servants: kindly, but as if it would never occur to her that they might disobey. Without thinking, several of the men turned toward the gate.

Then one of them shouted, "Wait a minute, don't you see it's a matter of life itself, maybe even all we own? Now that these overstuffed monks' whores have stuck their noses in it, we can't let them leave here to talk about what went on!"

None of the men moved, but Sister Agata began shrieking and yelling, with sobs in her voice, "Oh, sweet Jesus, my bridegroom. I thank you for allowing us, your servant maidens, to die for the glory of your name!"

Fru Ragnhild shoved her sternly aside, staggered forward, and picked up the lantern from the ground. No one raised a hand to stop her. When she lifted it up, the gold cross on her breast glittered. She stood leaning on her staff and slowly shone the light down the line, giving a slight nod to each man as she looked at him. Then she gestured to Kristin that she wished her to speak.

Kristin said, "Go home in peace, dear brothers. Have faith that the worthy Mother and these good sisters will be as merciful as God and the honor of His Church will allow them to be. But move aside now so that we might take away this child, and then each of you should return to your own home."

The men stood there, irresolute. Then one of them shouted in the greatest agitation, "Isn't it better to sacrifice *one* than for all of us to perish? This boy here, who belongs to no one—"

"He belongs to Christ. Better for all of us to perish than for us to harm one of his children."

But the man who had spoken first began yelling again. "Stop saying words like that or I'll stuff them back into your mouth with this." He waved his knife in the air. "Go home, go to bed, and ask your priest to comfort you, and keep silent about this—or I swear by the name of Satan that you'll find out it was the worst thing you've ever done, trying to meddle in our affairs."

"You don't have to shout so loudly for the one you mentioned to hear you, Arntor. Be assured that he isn't far away," said Kristin calmly. Several of the men seemed to grow fearful and involuntarily crept closer to the abbess holding the lantern. "The worst thing, for both us and for you, would have been if we had stayed home while you went about building your home in the hottest Hell."

But the man, Arntor, cursed and raged. Kristin knew that he hated the nuns because his father had mortgaged his farm to them in order to pay penalties for murder and blood guilt with his wife's niece. Now he continued slinging out the Fiend's most hateful lies about the sisters, accusing them of sins so black and unnatural that only the Devil himself could have put such thoughts into a man's mind.

The poor nuns, terrified and weeping, bowed under the vicious words, but they stood stalwartly around the old abbess, and she held the lantern in the air, shining it at the man and gazing calmly at his face as he raged.

But anger flared up inside Kristin like the flames of a newly lit fire.

"Silence! Have you lost your senses? Or has God struck you blind? Should we dare breathe a word under His admonishment? We who have seen His wedded brides stand up to the sword that was drawn for the sake of the world's sins? They kept vigil and prayed while we sinned and forgot our Creator every single day; they shut themselves inside the fortress of prayer while we roamed through the world, urged on by avarice for treasures, both great and small, for our own pleasure and our own anger. But they came out to us when the angel of death was sent among us; they gathered up the ill, the defenseless, and the poor. Twelve of our sisters have died from this sickness; all of you know this. Not one of them turned away, not one of them refused to pray for us all with sisterly love, until their tongues dried up in their mouths and their life blood ebbed out."

"How beautifully you speak about yourself and those like you—"

"*I* am like *you,*" she screamed, beside herself. "I'm not one of the holy sisters. I am one of you."

"How submissive you've become, woman," said Arntor derisively. "I see that you're afraid. When the end comes, you'll be saying you're like *her*, the mother of that boy."

"God must be the judge of that; he died for her as well as for me, and he knows us both. Where is she? Where is Steinunn?"

"Go out to her hovel, and I'm sure you'll find her there," replied Arntor.

"Yes, someone should send word to the poor woman that we have her boy here," said Kristin to the nuns. "We can go out to see her tomorrow."

Arntor snickered, but another man shouted reluctantly, "No, no . . . She's dead." He told Kristin, "Fourteen days ago Bjarne went out to her place and bolted the door shut. She was lying there, close to death."

"She was lying there?" Kristin gave the men a look of horror. "Didn't anyone bring a priest to her? Is . . . the body . . . still lying there? And no one has had enough mercy to put her into consecrated ground? And her child you were going to . . ."

Seeing her horror seemed to make the men lose their wits from fear and shame; they began shouting all at once.

Above all the other voices, one man cried out, "Go and get her yourself, sister!"

"Yes! Which of you will go with me?"

No one answered.

Arntor shouted, "You'll have to go alone."

"Tomorrow, as soon as it's light, we will go to get her, Arntor. I myself will pay for her resting place and a mass for her soul."

"Go out there now. Go there tonight. Then I'll believe that you're all full of holiness and virtue."

Arntor had thrust his face close to hers. Kristin raised her clenched fist up before his eyes; she uttered a loud sob of fury and terror.

Fru Ragnhild came over and stood at Kristin's side; she struggled to speak. The nuns cried that the next day the dead woman would be brought to her grave.

But the Devil seemed to have robbed Arntor of all reason; he kept on screaming, "Go now. Then we'll believe in the mercy of God."

Kristin straightened up; pale and rigid, she said, "I will go."

She lifted up the child and put him into Sister Torunn's arms; she shoved the men aside and began running swiftly toward the gate, stumbling over hillocks and heaps of earth, as the wailing nuns raced after her and Sister Agata yelled that she would go with her. The abbess shook her fists to say that Kristin should stop, but she seemed completely beside herself.

At that moment there was a great commotion in the darkness over by the cemetery gate. In the next instant Sira Eiliv's voice asked: "Who is holding a *ting* here?" He stepped into the glow of the lantern; they saw that he was carrying an axe in his hand. The nuns crowded around him; the men made haste to disappear into the darkness, but at the gate they were met by a man holding a drawn sword in his hand. A tumult ensued, with the clang of weapons, and Sira Eiliv called out: "Woe to any man who breaks the peace of the cemetery." Kristin heard someone say it was the mighty smith from Credoveit. A moment later a tall, broad-shouldered man with white hair appeared at her side. It was Ulf Haldorssøn.

The priest handed him the axe—he had borrowed it from Ulf—and then took the boy, Tore, from the nun as he said, "It's already past midnight. All the same, it would be best if you all came back to the church. I want to tend to these matters tonight."

No one had any other thought but to comply. But when they reached the road, one of the pale gray figures slipped away from the flock of women and headed for the path leading into the woods. The priest shouted, ordering her to come with the others.

Kristin's voice replied from the dark; she was already a good way down the path: "I can't come, Sira Eiliv, until I've kept my promise."

The priest and several others set off running. She was leaning against the fence when Sira Eiliv reached her. He raised the lantern. Her face was dreadfully white, but when he looked into her eyes, he realized that she had not gone mad, as he first had feared.

"Come home, Kristin," he said. "Tomorrow we'll go with you, several men. I will go with you myself."

"I've given my word. I can't go home, Sira Eiliv, until I have done as I promised."

The priest stood in silence for a moment. Then he said softly, "Perhaps you are right. Go then, sister, in God's name."

Strangely shadowlike, Kristin slipped into the darkness, which swallowed up her gray-clad figure.

When Ulf Haldorssøn appeared at her side, she said in a halting and vehement voice, "Go back. I didn't ask you to come with me."

Ulf laughed quietly. "Kristin, my mistress, haven't you learned yet that things can happen without your request or orders? And I see you still don't realize, no matter how many times you've witnessed it, that you can't always manage alone everything that you've taken on. But I will help you to undertake this burden."

There was a rushing sound in the pine forest all around them, and the roar of the waves out on the shore grew louder and then fainter, carried on the gusts of wind. They were walking in pitch-darkness.

After a while Ulf said, "I've accompanied you before, Kristin, when you went out at night. I thought I could be of some help if I came with you this time as well."

She was breathing hard in the dark. Once she stumbled over something, and Ulf grabbed hold of her. Then he took her hand and led the way. After a moment he noticed that she was weeping as she walked along, and he asked her what she was crying about.

"I'm crying because I was thinking that you've always been so kind and loyal toward us, Ulf. What can I say? I know that it was mostly for Erlend's sake, but I almost think, kinsman . . . you've always judged me less harshly than you had the right to, after what you first saw of my actions."

"I have always been fond of you, Kristin—no less than I was of him." He fell silent. Kristin saw that he was overcome by great emotion. Then he continued, "That's why it was so hard for me as I sailed over here today. I came to bring you news that I find difficult to tell you. May God give you strength, Kristin."

"Is it Skule?" asked Kristin in a low voice after a moment. "Is Skule dead?"

"No, Skule was fine when I spoke to him yesterday, and now few people are dying in town. But I received news from Tautra this morning—" He heard her give a deep sigh, but she did not speak.

After a moment he said, "It's already been ten days since they died. But there are only four brothers left alive at the monastery, and the island is almost swept clean of people."

They had now reached the edge of the woods. Over the flat expanse of land before them came the roaring din of the wind and sea. Up ahead in the darkness shone a patch of white—sea swells in a small inlet, with a steep pale sand dune above.

"That's where she lives," said Kristin. Ulf noticed that slow, fitful tremors passed over her. He gripped her hand hard.

"You've chosen to take this burden upon yourself. Keep that in mind, and don't lose your wits now."

Kristin said in an oddly thin, pure voice, which the wind seized and carried off, "Now Bjørgulf's dream will come true. I trust in the mercy of God and the Virgin Mary."

Ulf tried to see her face, but it was too dark. They walked across the tide flats; several places were so narrow beneath the cliff that a wave or two surged all the way up to their feet. They made their way over tangled seaweed and large rocks. After a while they glimpsed a bulky dark shape against the sand dune.

"Stay here," said Ulf curtly. He went over and threw himself against the door. She heard him hack away at the osier latches and then throw himself at the door again. She saw it fall inward, and he stepped inside the black cave.

It was not a particularly stormy night. But it was so dark that Kristin could see nothing but the sea, alive with tiny glints of foam rolling forward and then sliding back at once, and the gleam of the waves lapping along the shore of the inlet. She could also make out the dark shape against the hillside. She felt as if she were standing in a cavern of night, and it was the hiding place of death. The crash of the breaking waves and the trickle of water ebbing between the tidal rocks merged with the flush of blood inside her, although her body seemed to shatter, the way a keg splinters into slats. She had a throbbing in her breast, as if it would burst from within. Her head felt hollow and empty, as if it were leaking, and the gusts of wind swirled around her, blowing right through her. In a strangely listless way she realized that now she must be suffering from the plague herself—but she seemed to be waiting for the darkness to be split by a light that would roar and drown out the crash of the sea, and then she would succumb to terror. She pulled up her hood, which had been blown back, drew the black nun's cloak closer, and then stood there with her arms crossed underneath, but it didn't occur to her to pray. Her soul had more than enough to do, working its way out of its collapsing house, and that was what made her breast ache as she breathed.

She saw a flame flare up inside the hovel. A moment later Ulf Haldorssøn called to her. "You must come here and light the way for me, Kristin." He stood in the doorway and handed her a torch of charred wood.

The stench of the corpse nearly suffocated her, even though the hut was so drafty and the door was gone. Wide-eyed, with her lips parted—and her jaw and lips felt as rigid as wood—she looked for the dead woman. But she saw only a long bundle lying in the corner on the earthen floor. Wrapped around it was Ulf's cape.

He had pulled loose several long boards from somewhere and placed the door on top. As he cursed the clumsy tools, he made notches and holes with his axe and dagger and struggled to bind the door to the boards. Several times he cast a quick glance up at her, and each time his dark gray-bearded face grew stonier.

"I wonder how you thought you would manage to do this all alone," he said, bending over his work. He looked up, but the rigid, lifeless face in the red glow of the tarred torch remained unchanged—the face of a dead woman or a mad creature. "Can you tell me that, Kristin?" He laughed harshly, but it did no good. "I think it's about time for you to say a few prayers."

In the same stiff and listless tone she began to pray: "*Pater noster qui es in celis. Adveniat regnum tuum. Fiat voluntas tua sicut in celo et in terra.*" Then she came to a halt.

Ulf looked at her. Then he took up the prayer, "*Panum nostrum quotidianum da nobis hodie . . .*" Swiftly and firmly he said the words of the *Pater noster* to the end, then went over and made the sign of the cross over the bundle; swiftly and firmly he picked it up and carried it over to the litter that he had made.

"You take the front," he said. "It may be a little heavier, but you won't notice the stench as much. Throw the torch away; we'll see better without it. And don't stumble, Kristin; I would rather not have to touch this poor corpse again."

The raging pain in her breast seemed to rise up in protest when she lifted the poles of the litter over her shoulders; her chest *refused* to bear the weight. But she clenched her teeth. As long as they walked along the shore, where the wind blew, she hardly noticed the smell of the body.

"I'd better climb up first and pull the litter up after me," said Ulf when they reached the slope where they had come down.

"We can go a little farther," said Kristin. "Over to the place where they bring down the seaweed sledges; it's not as steep."

The man could hear that her voice sounded calm and composed. And now that it was over, he started sweating and shivering; he had thought she was going to lose her wits that night.

They struggled onward over the sandy path that led across the clearing to the pine forest. The wind blew freely but not as strongly as it had on the shore, and as they walked farther and farther away from the roar of the tide flats, she felt as if it was a journey home from the uttermost terrors of darkness. The land was pale on both sides of the path—a field of grain, but there had been no one to harvest it. The smell of the grain and the sight of the withering straw welcomed her back home, and her eyes filled with the tears of sisterly compassion. Out of her own desperate terror and need she had come home to the community of the living and the dead.

From time to time the dreadful stink of decay would wash over her if the wind blew at her back, but it wasn't as foul as when she was standing inside the hut. Here the air was full of the fresh, wet, and cold purity of the breeze.

And stronger than the feeling that she was carrying something gruesome on the litter behind her was the sense that Ulf Haldorssøn was walking along, protecting her back against the living and black horror they had left behind; its crashing sound became fainter and fainter.

When they reached the outskirts of the pine forest, they noticed lights. "They're coming to meet us," said Ulf.

A moment later they were met by an entire throng of men carrying torches, a couple of lanterns, and a bier covered with a shroud. Sira Eiliv was with them, and Kristin was surprised to see that the group included several men who had been in the cemetery earlier that night; many of them were weeping. When they lifted the burden from her shoulders, she nearly collapsed. Sira Eiliv was about to catch her when she said quickly, "Don't touch me. Don't come near me. I can feel that I have the plague myself."

But Sira Eiliv put his hand under her arm all the same.

"Then it should be of comfort for you to remember, woman, what Our Lord has said: That which you have done unto one of my poorest brothers or sisters, you have also done unto me."

Kristin stared at the priest. Then she shifted her glance to the men, who were moving the body to the bier from the litter Ulf had made. Ulf's cape fell aside; the tip of a worn shoe gleamed, dark with rain in the light of the torches.

Kristin went over, knelt down between the poles of the litter, and kissed the shoe.

"May God bless you, sister. May God bathe your soul in His light. May God have mercy on all of us here in the darkness."

Then she thought it was life itself working its way out of her—an unthinkable, piercing pain as if something inside, firmly rooted to the utmost ends of her limbs, had been torn loose. All that was contained within her breast was ripped out; she felt it fill her throat. Her mouth filled with blood that tasted of salt and filthy copper; a moment later her entire robe was covered with glistening, dark wetness. Jesus, can there be so much blood in an old woman? she thought.

Ulf Haldorssøn lifted her up in his arms and carried her.

In the convent portal the nuns met the procession, carrying lighted tapers in their hands. Kristin no longer had her full wits about her, but she sensed that she was half carried, half supported through the doorway. The white-plastered vaulted room was filled with flickering light from yellow candle flames and red pinewood torches, and the stomping of feet roared like the sea—but for the dying woman it was like a mirror of her own sinking life flame, and the footsteps on the flagstones seemed to be the crash of death's current, rising up toward her.

Then the glow of light spread outward to a larger space; she was once again under a dark, open sky—out in the courtyard. The light played over a gray stone wall with heavy pillars and tall windows: the church. Someone was carrying her—it was Ulf again—but now he became one with all those who had ever carried her.

When she put her arms around his neck and pressed her cheek against his prickly bearded neck, she felt like a child again, with her father, but she also felt as if she were taking a child in her own arms. Behind his dark head there were red lights, and they seemed to be shining from the fire that nourishes all love.

Some time later she opened her eyes and her mind was clear. She was sitting propped up in a bed in the dormitory; a nun stood leaning over her, wearing a linen cloth on the lower half of her face, and she noticed the smell of vinegar. It was Sister Agnes; she could tell by the eyes and the tiny red wart on her forehead. And it was daytime. A clear gray light entered the room through the little windowpane.

She was not suffering now, but she was soaked with sweat, terribly weak and tired, and she had a sharp, stabbing pain in her breast when she breathed. Greedily she drank a soothing potion that Sister Agnes held to her lips. But she was freezing.

Kristin leaned back against the pillows, and now she remembered everything that had happened the night before. The wild shimmer of a dream had vanished completely; she realized that she must have been slightly out of her wits. But it was good that she had done what she had: rescued the little boy and prevented those poor people from being burdened with such a misdeed. She knew she should be overjoyed that *she* had been fortunate enough to do this before she died, but she didn't have the strength to rejoice as she ought to. She had more a sense of contentment, the way she felt lying in bed back home at Jørundgaard, weary from a day's work well done. And she had to thank Ulf. . . .

She had spoken his name, and he must have been sitting in the shadows near the door and heard her, for he crossed the room and stood before her bed. She stretched out her hand to him, and he took it, clasping it firmly and warmly in his.

Suddenly the dying woman grew uneasy; her hands fumbled under the folds of bedclothes around her neck.

"What is it, Kristin?" asked Ulf.

"The cross," she whispered, and pulled out her father's gilded cross. She recalled that she had promised the day before to offer a gift for the soul of poor Steinunn. But she had forgotten that she owned no more earthly possessions. She owned nothing more than this cross, which her father had given her, and her wedding ring. She still wore that on her finger.

She took it off and looked at it. It lay heavy in her hand, pure gold and set with large red stones. Erlend, she thought. And she realized that now she should give it away; she didn't know why, but she felt that she should. She closed her eyes in pain and handed the ring to Ulf.

"Who do you want to leave it to?" he asked softly. When she didn't reply, he said, "Should I give it to Skule?"

Kristin shook her head, keeping her eyes closed tight.

"Steinunn . . . I promised . . . masses for her. . . ."

She opened her eyes and looked at the ring lying in the dark palm of the smith. And her tears burst forth in torrents, for she felt as if she had never before fully understood what it signified. The life to which this ring had married her, over which she had complained and grumbled, raged and rebelled. And yet she had loved it so, rejoicing over it, with both the bad and the good, so that there was not a single day she would have given back to God without lament or a single sorrow she would have relinquished without regret.

Ulf and the nun exchanged a few words that she couldn't hear, and he left the room. Kristin tried to lift her hand to wipe her eyes but didn't have the strength; her hand remained lying on her breast. It hurt so terribly inside, her hand seemed so heavy, and she felt as if the ring were still on her finger. Her mind was becoming confused again; she *must* see if it was true that the ring was gone, that she hadn't merely dreamed she'd given it away. She was also becoming uncertain. Everything that had happened in the night, the child in the grave, the black sea with the small, swift glimpses of the waves, the body she had carried . . . she didn't know whether she had dreamed it all or been awake. And she didn't have the strength to open her eyes.

"Sister," said the nun, "you mustn't sleep yet. Ulf has gone to bring the priest to you."

Kristin woke up with a start and fixed her eyes on her hand. The gold ring was gone; that was certain enough. There was a shiny, worn mark where it had sat on her middle finger. On the brown, rough flesh it was quite clear—like a scar of thin white skin. She thought she could even make out two round circles from the rubies on either side and a tiny scratch, an *M* from the center of the ring where the holy symbol of the Virgin Mary had been etched into the gold.

The last clear thought that took shape in her mind was that she was going to die before the mark had time to fade, and it made her happy. It seemed to her a mystery that she could not comprehend, but she was certain that God had held her firmly in a pact which had been made for her, without her knowing it, from a love that had been poured over her—and in spite of her willfulness, in spite of her melancholy, earthbound heart, some of that love had *stayed* inside her, had worked on her like sun on the earth, had driven forth a crop that neither the fiercest fire of passion nor its stormiest anger could completely destroy. She had been a servant of God—a stubborn, defiant maid, most often an eye-servant in her prayers and unfaithful in her heart, indolent and neglectful, impatient toward admonishments, inconstant in her deeds. And yet He had held her firmly in His service, and under the glittering gold ring a mark had been secretly impressed upon her, showing that she was His servant, owned by the Lord and King who would now come, borne on the consecrated hands of the priest, to give her release and salvation.

As soon as Sira Eiliv had anointed her with the last oil and viaticum, Kristin Lavransdatter again lost consciousness. She lay there, violently vomiting blood, with a blazing fever, and the priest who was sitting with her told the nuns that the end would come quickly.

Several times the dying woman's mind cleared enough that she could recognize one face or another: Sira Eiliv or the sisters. Fru Ragnhild herself was there once, and she saw Ulf. She struggled to show that she knew them and that it was good they were with her and wished her well. But for those who stood at her bedside, it merely looked as if she were flailing her hands in the throes of death.

Once she saw Munan's face; her little son was peeking at her through a crack in the door. Then he pulled back his head, and his mother lay there, staring at the door to see if the boy would look through it again. Instead Fru Ragnhild appeared and wiped her face with a damp cloth, and that too felt good. Then everything disappeared in a dark red haze and a roar, which at first grew fearfully loud, but then the din gradually died away, and the red fog became thinner and lighter, and at last it was like a fine morning mist before the sun breaks through, and there was not a sound, and she knew that now she was dying.

Sira Eiliv and Ulf Haldorssøn left the deathbed together. In the doorway leading out to the convent courtyard, they stopped.

Snow had fallen. None of them had noticed this as they sat with her and she struggled with death. The white sheen was strangely dazzling on the steep slant of the church roof opposite them; the tower was pale against the murky gray sky. The snow lay so fine and white on all the window frames and all the jutting gray stones of the church walls. And the two men seemed to hesitate, not wanting to mar the new snow in the courtyard with their footprints.

They breathed in the air. After the suffocating smell that always surrounded someone stricken with the plague, it tasted sweet and cool, a little empty and thin, but as if this snowfall had washed sickness and contagion out of the air; it was as good as fresh water.

The bell in the tower began ringing again; the two men looked up to the movement behind the sound holes. Tiny snowflakes were shaken loose, rolling down to become little balls; some of the black shingles could be seen underneath.

"This snow won't last," said Ulf.

"No, it will melt away before evening," replied the priest. There were pale golden rifts in the clouds, and a faint, tentative ray of sunshine fell across the snow.

The men stayed where they were. Then Ulf Haldorssøn said quietly, "I've been thinking, Sira Eiliv . . . I want to give some land to this church . . . and a goblet she gave me that once belonged to Lavrans Bjørgulfsøn . . . to establish a mass for her . . . and my foster sons . . . and for him, Erlend, my kinsman."

The priest's voice was equally quiet, and he did not look at the man. "I think you might also mean that you want to show Him your gratitude for leading you here last night. You must be grateful that you were allowed to help her through this night."

"Yes, that was what I meant," said Ulf Haldorssøn. Then he

laughed a little. "And now I almost regret, priest, that I have been such a pious man—toward her."

"It's useless to waste your time over such futile regrets," replied the priest.

"What do you mean?"

"I mean that it's only a man's sins that it does any good for him to regret."

"Why is that?"

"Because no one is good without God. And we can do nothing good without Him. So it's futile to regret a good deed, Ulf, for the good you have done cannot be taken back; even if all the mountains should fall, it would still stand."

"Well, well. That's not how I see things, my Sira. I'm tired . . ."

"Yes . . . and you must be hungry too. Come with me over to the cookhouse, Ulf," said the priest.

"Thank you, but I have no wish to eat anything," said Ulf Haldorssøn.

"All the same, you must come with me and have some food," said Sira Eiliv, placing his hand on Ulf's sleeve and pulling him along. They headed across the courtyard and over toward the cookhouse. Without thinking, they both walked as lightly and carefully as they could in the new snow.

# EXPLANATORY NOTES

*References Used*

Blangstrup, Chr., ed. *Salmonsens Konversations Leksikon.* 2nd ed. Copenhagen: J.H. Schultz Forlagsboghandel, 1928.

Knudsen, Trygve, and Alf Sommerfelt, eds. *Norsk Riksmåls Ordbok.* Oslo: Det Norske Academi for Sprog og Litteratur og Kunnskapsforlaget, 1983.

Mørkhagen, Sverre. *Kristins Verden: Om norsk middelalder på Kristin Lavransdatters tid.* Oslo: J. W. Cappelens Forlag, 1995.

Pulsiano, Phillip. ed. *Medieval Scandinavia: An Encyclopedia.* New York: Garland Publishing Co., 1993.

Sawyer, Birgit, and Peter Sawyer. *Medieval Scandinavia: From Conversion to Reformation, circa 800–1500.* Minneapolis: University of Minnesota Press, 1993.

## I: THE WREATH

## PART I

### CHAPTER 1

1. *Nidaros*: One of five episcopal seats in Norway during the Middle Ages; now the city of Trondheim. The cathedral in Nidaros housed the famous shrine of Saint Olav and was the destination of thousands of pilgrims every year, particularly during the Feast of Saint Olav in late July. The main road between Oslo and Nidaros passed through Gudbrandsdal, the valley where most of Undset's novel takes place.
2. *vigil nights*: Festive celebrations, called "vigils," were held on the night before many religious holidays.

3. *courtyard*: The multiple buildings of Norwegian farms were laid out around two courtyards: an "inner" courtyard surrounded by the various living quarters, storehouses, and cookhouse; and next to it an "outer" courtyard (or farmyard) surrounded by the stables, cowshed, barn, and other outbuildings. All of the buildings were constructed of wood, and most consisted of a single room that served a specific function on the farm. None of the buildings was more than two stories high. Many had an external gallery (a type of balcony) and stairway along one side. Lofts built above the storerooms were used as bedchambers for both family members and guests. At Jørundgaard, the high loft in the main house was the finest room on the manor and the one used for feasts and celebrations. Hearth fires in the center of the room (or corner fireplaces on the finer estates) provided the only heat in the living quarters.
4. *his daughter*: Christianity was introduced in Norway in the 11th century, but it wasn't until 1270 that celibacy for priests became part of Norwegian Church law. Even then, it was not strictly enforced, particularly in the countryside.
5. *village*: Unlike villages in the rest of Europe, rural villages in medieval Norway consisted of little more than hamletlike clusters of several large farm-estates, each surrounded by smaller leaseholdings. A settlement of at least three farms constituted a village. Many of them also included a small parish church. Norwegian villages were situated in remote valleys, separated from other settlements by rugged mountains.
6. *river sprite*: In medieval Norway a clear demarcation was made between inside and outside, between the protective circle of human habitation and the dark forces of the wilderness beyond. People believed that the forests and mountains were populated by many types of supernatural beings, which were both unpredictable and menacing.
7. *tar-burners*: Men who produced wood tar, a distilled liquid used for caulking and for preserving wood and rope.
8. *hawk hunters*: Hawks rather than falcons were generally used for hunting in Norway, due to the mountainous, forested terrain. Hawks follow the prey from behind and have an astonishing ability to steer around trees and bushes.
9. *lefse*: A thin pancake of rolled-out dough, folded and served with butter.

## CHAPTER 2

1. *allodial property*: Land held in absolute ownership, without obligation or service to any feudal overlord. In Norway this was an ancient institution in which a man's inherited allodial rights depended on proof that the land had been possessed continuously by his family or kin group for at least four generations. If there was no male heir, the land could be passed down to a female family member.
2. *canons' house*: Canon was an ecclesiastical title for a member of a group of priests who served in a cathedral and who were usually expected to live a communal life.
3. *Minorite*: A widespread order of friars founded by Saint Francis of Assisi in 1223. The monastic movement in Norway began at Selje, outside Bergen, where a Benedictine monastery was dedicated to Saint Alban in the early 12th century. Cistercians later settled on Hovedø, an island in the Oslo fjord. During the 13th century mendicant orders of Dominican and Franciscan monks established cloisters in the Norwegian bishoprics and trading centers.
4. *windowpane*: The introduction of Christianity brought the art of making stained-glass windows to Scandinavia. Most 14th-century Norwegian manors and farmhouses, however, did not have windows of any kind. Light came into the room from the smoke vent in the roof and from the doorway. In some cases small openings might be cut in the wall and then covered either with horn or with a translucent membrane, usually made from a cow's stomach.
5. *Selje men*: According to legend, Sunniva (a Christian princess of Irish blood) found it necessary to flee England in the 10th century along with her entourage. They sought refuge on the Norwegian island of Selje and took up residence in the caves, where a rock slide eventually buried them. Rumors of a strange light over the island brought the authorities to investigate, and the body of Sunniva was discovered, completely unmarked.

## CHAPTER 3

1. *Saint Olav*: During his reign from 1015 to 1030, King Olav Haraldssøn firmly established Christianity in Norway. Churches were built, priests were appointed, and Nidaros regained its stature as a spiritual center after years of neglect. The king also unified the

country under a single monarchy by driving out the noblemen pretenders who had risen up against him. When King Olav died a hero's death in battle, rumors began to circulate that he was a holy man and that miracles had occurred at his grave in Nidaros. Pilgrims began streaming to the cathedral, and the cult of Saint Olav grew rapidly. Olav churches and altars were built throughout Norway, and cloisters were dedicated to the holy man. Although never officially canonized, Olav became the most popular of Norwegian saints and was recognized as the patron saint of the country.

2. *medical things*: The parish priest was often the only one in an isolated settlement who could offer some type of medical skill, based on what he had been taught of the principles of monastic medicine from southern Europe. Otherwise the community had to rely on local people with special knowledge of traditional remedies and curative herbs.

## CHAPTER 4

1. *King Sverre*: Sverre Sigurdssøn asserted his right to the Norwegian throne in 1177 by ousting King Magnus Erlingssøn with the help of the "Birch-Leg" party (see chapter 7, note 2). King Sverre's reign, which lasted until 1202, was marked by a continuous struggle to maintain his right to succession. This period of strife was just the beginning of years of civil war in Norway.
2. *high seat*: The place of honor at the dining table, reserved for the male head of the family or an honored guest. The high seat was in the middle of the table, on the side against the wall.

## CHAPTER 5

1. *ting*: A meeting of free, adult men (women rarely attended) which took place at regular intervals to discuss matters of concern to a particular community. On the local level, the *ting* might consider such issues as pasture rights, fencing, bridge and road construction, taxes, and the maintenance of the local warship. A regional *ting*, attended by chieftains or appointed deputies, would address such issues as defense and legal jurisdiction. The regional *ting* also functioned as a court, although its authority diminished as the power of the king grew. In addition to its regular meetings, a *ting*

could be called for a specific purpose, such as the acclamation of a new king.

### CHAPTER 7

1. *prebendary*: A clergyman who received a stipend provided by a special endowment or derived from the revenues of his cathedral or church.
2. *"Birch-Leg" followers*: A political group formed in 1174 in southeastern Norway during the conflict over the rightful successor to the throne. They gained their name from the birchbark they tied to their feet because many were too poor to own shoes. The Birch-Legs supported Sverre in his successful bid to become king in 1177, and many of them were later rewarded by being allowed to marry into distinguished families and enter the higher circles of society.

## PART II

### CHAPTER 1

1. *corrodians*: People who donated land or property to a cloister in exchange for a pension or allowance (called a corrody), which permitted the holder to retire into the cloister as a boarder. Some corrodians took their meals at the cloister but lived outside unless they were ill. They were often clothed by the cloister as well.

### CHAPTER 2

1. *townyard*: A plot of land in an urban area where several wooden buildings, each serving a specific function, were clustered around a central courtyard. A townyard might have one or more owners, or it could be subdivided into tenements or other types of property.
2. *ørtug*: A coin equal in value to one-third of an *øre* or 10 *penninger*. One *øre* was equal to one-eighth of a *mark*.
3. *silver spurs*: Golden spurs, not silver, were a sign of knighthood.

### CHAPTER 4

1. *campaign*: The support of war campaigns initiated by the king was based on a defense system which divided Norway first into counties and then into parishes. Each county was required to supply and equip a warship, and each parish had to provide a member of the ship's crew. In addition, taxes were levied to finance the campaigns. Wealthy landowners, who had both horses and weapons needed for the war, were required to do military service and were thus exempted from these taxes.
2. *Duke Eirik's devastating incursion*: Duke Eirik Magnussön of Sweden attempted to extend his power by attacking Oslo in 1308 and again in 1310. Both incursions were repelled, but after the second one the Norwegian king launched a retaliatory campaign, which was a great drain on the country's resources.

### CHAPTER 5

1. *against the orders of the bishop*: Duke Haakon Magnussøn provided land for a Franciscan monastery to be built in Oslo, but bitter opposition from the bishop led to a prohibition against the building project. The monks, however, were not subject to the bishop's authority and proceeded with their plans. The bishop then refused them permission to preach in his dioceses, which rankled the Franciscans but did not stop them. Infuriated, the local ecclesiastical officials finally ordered armed men to attack and destroy the building site. The friars complained to the Pope, who interceded on their behalf in 1291, and the monastery in Oslo was finally built.

## PART III

### CHAPTER 5

1. *Bretland*: Old Norwegian name for Wales.

### CHAPTER 8

1. *escorted to bed*: A pre-Christian wedding ritual, still prevalent in medieval times, which required that six people witness the couple openly going to bed; only then would the marriage be considered legally binding.
2. *lur* horn: A trumpetlike wind instrument without a mouthpiece, made from a hollow piece of wood wrapped with bark.

## II: THE WIFE

## PART I

### CHAPTER 1

1. *courtyard:* The multiple buildings of Norwegian farms were laid out around two courtyards: an "inner" courtyard surrounded by the various living quarters, storehouses, and cookhouse; and next to it an "outer" courtyard (or farmyard) surrounded by the stables, cowshed, barn, and other outbuildings. All of the buildings were constructed of wood, and most consisted of a single room that served a specific function on the farm. The buildings were usually no more than two stories high, although Husaby, once a particularly magnificent estate, had an armory with a third story. Many buildings had an external gallery and stairway along one side. Lofts built above the storerooms were used as bedchambers for both family members and guests.
2. *high seat:* The place of honor, reserved for the male head of the family or an honored guest. The high seat was usually in the middle of the table, on the side against the wall. Servants often sat on the opposite bench.
3. *Trøndelag:* In medieval times this was the name given to the vast area of Norway stretching from Romsdal, the valley south of Nidaros (today the city of Trondheim), all the way up to the northernmost Norwegian settlements in Haalogaland.
4. *turnover day:* The day on which tenants and servants were allowed to give up their positions and move to new ones. The exact day varied by area, but was often Summer Day (April 14) and Winter Day (October 14) of each year.

5. *she had been to church after giving birth:* After giving birth, a woman's first attendance of a church service marked the religious celebration of her recovery. Among women of the nobility, this event ideally occurred after a six- to eight-week rest period following the birth. Many women, however, probably could not afford such a long convalescence before resuming their household responsibilities.

## CHAPTER 2

1. *inherit my ancestral property after me:* As Erlend's illegitimate son, Orm could not inherit his father's ancestral estates, which were the allodial property of his lineage. This was land held in absolute ownership, without obligation or service to any feudal overlord. In Norway it was an ancient institution in which a man's inherited allodial rights depended on proof that the land had been possessed continuously by his family or kin group for at least four generations. Children born of an adulterous relationship held a precarious position in medieval society, since they were usually not entitled to property or other privileges of kinship.
2. *inadvertently looked at a fire:* According to pre-Christian belief, it was dangerous for a pregnant woman to look at a fire that had been started by some accident or misfortune (such as lightning). Disfigurement of the unborn child could result.
3. *Saint Olav:* During his reign from 1016 to 1030, King Olav Haraldssøn firmly established Christianity in Norway. Churches were built, priests were appointed, and Nidaros regained its stature as a spiritual center after years of neglect. The king also unified the country under one monarchy by driving out those noblemen who had risen up against him. When King Olav died a hero's death in battle, rumors began to circulate that he was a holy man and that miracles had occurred at his grave in Nidaros. Pilgrims began streaming to the cathedral, and the cult of Saint Olav grew rapidly. Olav churches and altars were built throughout Norway, and cloisters were dedicated to the holy man. Although never officially canonized, Olav became the most popular of Norwegian saints and was recognized as the patron saint of the country.
4. *Nidaros:* One of five episcopal seats in Norway during the Middle Ages; now the city of Trondheim. Nidaros Cathedral housed the famous shrine of Saint Olav and was the destination of thousands of

pilgrims every year, particularly during the Feast of Saint Olav in late July.

5. *Verbum caro . . . :* And the Word was made flesh, and dwelt among us. John 1:14.
6. *Blessed Mary, you who are the clear star of the sea:* The North Star (*maris stella*) was identified with the Virgin Mary, and both served as the guide and protector of seamen.
7. *the spirits of the dead:* In pagan times it was believed that those people who had not received a proper, ritual burial would restlessly roam the earth in midwinter, when sacrifices were made to the gods to ask for a bountiful coming year. With the advent of Christianity, the Church adopted and modified this belief. It was thought that during Christmas, the souls of those people who had not yet passed through purgatory would wander around disconsolately, not having found peace in the grave. These spirits were both pitied and feared. It was considered unwise to go outdoors at all, except to Christmas mass, and never alone. Food was set out for the dead souls during the entire holiday.
8. *Saint Joseph of Arimathea:* A disciple of Christ mentioned in all four Gospels who obtained permission from Pontius Pilate to give the Savior's body an honorable burial. In later literature Joseph was described as the first witness of the Resurrection and as the recipient of the Holy Grail. Other accounts placed him in Glastonbury (in Somerset), leading a group of missionaries sent by the apostle Saint Philip. Bretland was the medieval name for Wales.
9. *the spirit of the first owner lives underneath:* Another commonly held pagan belief that the spirit of the original owner of an estate continued to offer protection from his grave.

## CHAPTER 3

1. *ting:* A meeting of free, adult men (women rarely attended) which met at regular intervals to discuss matters of concern to a particular community. On the local level, the *ting* might consider such issues as pasture rights, fencing, bridge and road construction, taxes, and the maintenance of the local warship. A regional *ting,* attended by chieftains or appointed deputies, would address such issues as defense and legal jurisdiction. The regional *ting* also functioned as a court, although its authority diminished as the power of the king grew. In addition to its regular meetings, a *ting*

could be called for a specific purpose, such as the acclamation of a new king.

2. *when her time came to kneel on the floor:* Women gave birth by kneeling on the floor, supported by women family members and skilled helpers or midwives called in from the surrounding village or parish. The birth took place in a building separate from the normal living quarters in order to prevent infection. A birth chair, common elsewhere in medieval Europe, was not used in Norway.

## CHAPTER 4

1. *Tristan and Isolde:* Tristan was the legendary Celtic warrior and hunter most famous for his love affair with the Irish princess Isolde, whom he had courted on behalf of his uncle. When Tristan and the princess accidentally shared a love potion intended for Isolde's betrothed, the two fell passionately in love. In the end, the two lovers were parted, and Tristan married another Isolde, but he never forgot his first love. Both of them came to a tragic end. The story was made famous in two French poems from the twelfth century.
2. *Saint Martin's story:* Saint Martin is the patron saint of France and father of monasticism, famous for the miracles he performed during his lifetime (A.D. 316–397).
3. *Averte faciem . . . :* Hide thy face from my sins, and blot out all mine iniquities.

> Create in me a clean heart, O God; and renew a right spirit within me. Cast me not away from thy presence; and take not thy holy spirit from me. Psalm 51:9–11.

4. *leprosy:* A much-feared disease that was common throughout Europe during the Middle Ages. Many Scandinavian monasteries took care of patients, and numerous hospitals were founded to offer treatment.
5. *corrody:* A pension or allowance granted by a cloister in exchange for donated land or property; it permitted the holder to retire into the cloister as a boarder.

## CHAPTER 5

1. *Halland:* Region on the west coast of Sweden between 56°19′ and 57°38′, roughly between the present-day cities of Halmstad and Göteborg, north of the region of Skaane (cf. Part III, Chapter 1, note 4). Originally the northern portion was under Danish control, but Earl Jacob (a descendant of the Danish king Valdemar Sejr) brought it under Norwegian rule. In 1305 it was passed on to the Swedish Duke Eirik upon his marriage to Lady Ingebjørg.
2. *The new manor priest:* Privately owned churches, called "convenience churches," were often built by noblemen on their own manors and by the king on his royal estates in the country and in towns. Priests were appointed by the bishops, but the owner retained certain patronage rights. Many of these private churches eventually became parish churches.

## CHAPTER 6

1. *Winter Night:* October 14, considered the beginning of the winter halfyear.
2. *Magnificat anima . . . :* My soul praises the Lord. And my spirit rejoices in the Lord, my Savior.
3. *Cor mundum . . . :* Create in me a clean heart, O God; and renew a right spirit within me.
   Cast me not away from thy presence.
   Deliver me from bloodguiltiness, O God, thou God of my salvation. Psalms 51:10–11, 14.
4. *Minorites:* A widespread order of friars founded by Saint Francis of Assisi in 1223.

# PART II

## CHAPTER 1

1. *underaged boy:* In 1319 Magnus Eirikssøn became king of both Norway and Sweden at the age of three. He was the son of the Norwegian Princess Ingebjørg (daughter of King Haakon V) and the Swedish Duke Eirik. For the first few years of Magnus's minority, his mother served as regent and exerted much power in both

countries. Discontent with her rule grew rapidly, however, and in 1322 the Swedish lords joined forces to deprive Lady Ingebjørg of authority; the following year the Norwegians followed suit. Each country was then ruled by a separate regent and council of noblemen until King Magnus came of age in 1331.

2. *Skara:* The ecclesiastical and royal seat of southern Sweden during the Middle Ages.

3. *a full campaign:* The support of war campaigns initiated by the king was based on a defense system which divided Norway first into counties and then into parishes. Because of the mountainous and heavily forested topography of Norway, war expeditions were largely launched by sea. Each county was thus required to supply and equip a warship, and each parish had to provide a member of the ship's crew. In addition, taxes were levied to finance the campaigns. Wealthy landowners, who had both horses and weapons needed for the war, were usually required to do military service but were exempted from these taxes.

4. *Eufemia's betrothal:* Eufemia was the sister of King Magnus. In 1321, at the age of four, she was betrothed to the German Prince Albrecht of Mecklenburg, who was himself only three. This marriage was arranged by her mother, Lady Ingebjørg, in return for the services of 200 fully armed men. These soldiers stood ready to support her plans for bringing the rich area of Skaane, then part o Denmark, under her control.

5. *Sir Knut:* Knut Porse was an ambitious nobleman from Hallan who played a key role in proclaiming the underaged Magnus as king of Sweden in 1319. He then joined forces with the king's mother, Lady Ingebjørg, in various intrigues against the Danish Crown that were not supported by either the Swedish or Norwegian nobles. In 1326 Porse supported the Danish uprising against King Christoffer II and was rewarded by the new Danish king with the duchy of Halland, other vast properties, and numerous castles in Denmark. As a duke, Porse was finally in a position to marry Lady Ingebjørg, and the wedding took place in 1327.

6. *Bjørgvin:* Medieval name for Bergen, which was the royal and ecclesiastical center of West Norway. In the twelth century it became the first port in Scandinavia to have international commercial importance, and it was the main market for the export of dried cod, or stockfish. By the fourteenth century Bjørgvin was the largest Norwegian town, with approximately 7,000 inhabitants. The pop-

ulation of the other foremost Norwegian towns was as follows: Nidaros: 3,000; Oslo: 2,000; and Tunsberg: 1,500.

7. *chapter:* An assembly of the canons of a cathedral. Canon was an ecclesiastical title for a member of a group of priests who served in a cathedral and who were usually expected to live a communal life.
8. *Haalogaland:* The medieval name for the northernmost inhabited territory of Norway, extending from present-day Nordland County to the middle of Troms County. The name derives from Old Norse, meaning "high blaze" land or "midnight sun" land.
9. *Lavrans Lagmanssøn:* As explained in Volume I of *Kristin Lavransdatter,* Lavrans was descended from the noble Swedish lineage known as the "sons of Lagmand."

## CHAPTER 2

1. *cantor:* The priest who was in charge of b[illegible]h the cathedral choir and school.
2. *benefice:* An ecclesiastical position to whic[illegible]ecific revenues or properties were attached.
3. *The Finns and the other half-wild peoples:* Sin[illegible]ga times the inhabitants of Finnmark, both Finns and Sam[illegible]ay no longer called by the derogatory name of Lapps), were [illegible]ered skilled in witchcraft and sorcery. The Norwegians also [illegible]d them as heathens.
4. *Gandvik Sea:* Medieval name for the White Sea, n[illegible]nt-day Arkhangel'sk, Russia. During the Middle Ages the are[illegible]urrounding the White Sea was called Bjarmeland. It was separated from Finnmark, which was under the Norwegian Crown, by a great river and promontory. The Norwegians discovered the passage to Bjarmeland around the North Cape in the ninth century, and frequent raids were made in subsequent centuries. The Russians were also interested in the area because it was an important fur-trading center, and by the thirteenth century it had come under the rule of Novgorod.

## CHAPTER 3

1. *Karelians:* Inhabitants of eastern Finland and the Russian territory around the White Sea. Karelia was the stage for a centuries-long border dispute between Sweden and Russia that was not settled until a treaty was signed in 1323.

2. *Santiago de Compostela:* Town in Galicia in northwestern Spain which became the third most important Christian pilgrimage site (after Jerusalem and Rome) during the Middle Ages. According to legend, the bones of Saint James the Apostle were taken there, and his tomb was purportedly discovered in A.D. 813.

## CHAPTER 4

1. *Sami woman from Kola:* The nomadic people called the Samis (formerly known as Lapps) today still inhabit the vast region of northern Europe which extends above the Arctic Circle. The Kola peninsula stretches northeast from Finland, between the Arctic Ocean and the White Sea.
2. *Saint Sunniva:* According to legend, Sunniva (a Christian princess of Irish blood) was driven from England in the tenth century along with a large entourage. They set sail in three ships that had neither oars nor sails, but they miraculously made it safely to the Norwegian island of Selje, where they sought refuge in the caves. Eventually a rock slide buried them all. Rumors of a strange light over the island brought both the king and bishop to investigate, and the bodies of the Selje men and Sunniva were discovered, hers completely unscathed by injury or decay. In the twelfth century her body was taken to Bjørgvin (Bergen) and buried in the cathedra there.
3. *prebends:* Stipends received by clergymen which were provided b a special endowment or derived from the revenues of their cathedral or church.

## CHAPTER 5

1. *the inheritance had been settled:* Simon Andressøn was not entitled to inherit Mandvik, the estate of his deceased wife, because their child died before she did. If the infant had survived the mother by even a brief time, the property would have passed on to the father.
2. *dispensation:* In 1215 the laws of the Church were changed to allow marriage between third cousins (considered kinship to the fourth degree), although only with special dispensation. Before that time marriage was not allowed up to the seventh degree, which covered such a wide group of kinsmen that it proved impractical in medieval society.

## CHAPTER 7

1. *Venite ad me . . . :* Come unto me, all ye that labour and are heavy laden, and I will give you rest. Matthew 11:28.

## CHAPTER 8

1. *Soten:* The Norwegian word for "soot."
2. *weapons*-ting: Assembly called to ensure that each man had in his possession the weapons prescribed by law.
3. *Summer Day:* April 14, considered the beginning of the summer half-year.
4. *campaign against Duke Eirik:* Duke Eirik Magnussön of Sweden attempted to extend his power by attacking Oslo in 1308 and again in 1310. Both incursions were fought back, but after the second one the Norwegian king launched a retaliatory campaign, in which Lavrans apparently participated during Kristin's childhood.
5. *Exsurrexi, et adhuc . . . :* When I awake, I am still with thee. Psalms 139:18.

# PART III

## CHAPTER 1

1. *allowed to remain in the country:* The king could grant permission for a man to remain in Norway even though he had either been sentenced to banishment, or had committed acts punishable by banishment.
2. *Frosta* ting: One of the four independent law assemblies in Norway during the Middle Ages. Founded by King Haakon the Good in the tenth century, the Frosta *ting* was usually held in the summer on the Frosta peninsula in Trondheim Fjord, although Sigrid Undset has moved the setting to Nidaros in her novel.
3. *cote-hardi:* A lined outer garment with sleeves and hood, worn by both men and women; it fit snugly to the body and was buttoned down the front.
4. *Skaane:* A rich agricultural region in the southernmost section of present-day Sweden that belonged to Denmark during the Middle Ages. The great demand for salt herring made the Öresund coast a

key trading area, and the Skaane Fair was one of the foremost fairs in medieval Europe. Every year merchants would arrive overland and by sea to trade their wares when the market opened on August 15. In 1289 the Norwegians unsuccessfully attempted to seize Skaane. King Magnus Eirikssøn tried again in 1332 and subsequently held the area for nearly thirty years.

### CHAPTER 2

1. *letter-breaching:* The punishable offense of breaking the seal on letters addressed to someone else. In medieval Norway letters were often safeguarded and conveyed in carved wooden boxes that could be securely closed.

# III: THE CROSS

## PART I

### CHAPTER 1

1. *high seat:* The place of honor, reserved for the male head of the family or an honored guest. The high seat was usually in the middle of the table, on the side against the wall. Servants often sat on the opposite bench.

### CHAPTER 2

1. *try to lure her inside:* In medieval Norway people believed that the forests and mountains were populated by many types of supernatural beings, which were both unpredicatable and menacing.
2. *the transparent hide:* Both window openings and smoke vents were often covered with a transparent membrane, usually made from a cow's stomach.

### CHAPTER 3

1. *His two motherless daughters had been taken in:* An arrangement by which a number of neighboring estates agreed to provide a certain amount of food for the poor. Each manor fulfilled its obliga-

tions either by distributing food to needy individuals or by taking in charity cases for a specified length of time.

2. *Convertere, Domine . . . :* Return, O Lord, how long? and let it repent thee concerning thy servants. Psalms 30:13. Be not wroth very sore, O Lord, neither remember iniquity for ever: behold, see, we beseech thee, we are all thy people. Isaiah 64:9.

## CHAPTER 4

1. *ting:* A meeting of free, adult men (women rarely attended) which met at regular intervals to discuss matters of concern to a particular community. On the local level, the *ting* might consider such issues as pasture rights, fencing, bridge and road construction, taxes, and the maintenance of the local warship. A regional *ting,* attended by chieftains or appointed deputies, would address such issues as defense and legal jurisdiction. The regional *ting* also functioned as a court, although its authority diminished as the power of the king grew. In addition to its regular meetings, a *ting* could be called for a specific purpose, such as the acclamation of a new king.

## CHAPTER 5

1. *Duke Skule when he rallied the forces:* In 1238 the Norwegian Duke Skule Baardssøn challenged King Haakon Haakonssøn's right to the throne by having himself proclaimed king at the Øre *ting.* He and his army of followers waged war in several parts of Norway, but after losing a battle in Oslo, he fled to Nidaros. Skule was eventually slain at Elgeseter Cloister. His death brought to an end the century-long strife over succession to the throne.
2. *offering the land to the heirs:* In accordance with the laws of the time, ancestral land had to be offered for sale to the descendants of the original owners before it could be sold to anyone else.
3. *his father had acknowledged him as his own:* Not until 1270 did celibacy for priests become part of Norwegian Church law. Even then, it was not strictly enforced, particularly in the countryside.
4. *the murder of the dukes:* In 1318 the Swedish dukes Eirik and Valdemar were murdered by their older brother, King Birger Magnussön, after a long-standing power struggle.

5. *a letter of reprieve:* Permission, granted by the king, for a man to remain in Norway even though he either had been sentenced to banishment or had committed acts punishable by banishment.

### CHAPTER 6

1. *merchants of Bjørgvin:* Medieval name for Bergen, which was the royal and ecclesiastical center of West Norway. In the twelfth century it became the first port in Scandinavia to have international commercial importance, and it was the main market for the export of dried cod, or stockfish. By the fourteenth century Bjørgvin was the largest Norwegian town.
2. *woodpile dance:* Dance often performed around a large woodpile on the day after a wedding. First the bride and groom and then other couples, by turn, would share a piece of bread and drink from the same cup and then dance around the woodpile.
3. *Abishag the Shunammite:* A beautiful young woman who came under David's care when he was an old man. Adonijah sought in vain to make her his wife.

## PART II

### CHAPTER 1

1. *the Gandvik coast:* The Gandvik Sea was the medieval name for the White Sea, near present-day Arkhangel'sk, Russia.
2. *mare:* A supernatural female creature which, according to folk belief, torments people in their sleep by perching heavily on their chests.

### CHAPTER 2

1. *prime:* The second of the seven canonical hours, usually about 6 A.M. According to Church law, specific prayers were to be recited at seven prescribed times of the day.
2. *chapter:* An assembly of the canons of a cathedral. Canon was an ecclesiastical title for a member of a group of priests who served in a cathedral and who were usually expected to live a communal life.

### CHAPTER 3

1. *Venite: revertamur . . . :* Come, and let us return unto the Lord: for he hath torn, and he will heal us; he hath smitten, and he will bind us up. . . . Then shall we know, if we follow on to know the Lord: his going forth is prepared as the morning; and he shall come unto us as the rain, as the latter and former rain unto the earth. Hosea 6:1 and 3.
2. *Salvator mundi . . . :* Savior of the world, save us all.
3. *turnover day:* The day on which tenants and servants were allowed to give up their positions and move to new ones. The exact day varied by area, but was often Summer Day (April 14) and Winter Day (October 14) of each year.

### CHAPTER 7

1. *with either five or eleven others:* Two types of oath could exonerate a person from a charge brought against him. One required five people to swear to the person's veracity; the other required eleven people. In the case of an accused woman all the others had to be women.
2. *King David and Bathsheba:* Old Testament story about the beautiful Bathsheba, wife of Uriah the Hittite. She was seduced by King David and conceived a child who later died. After the death of Uriah, Bathsheba married David and gave birth to Solomon.

## PART III

### CHAPTER 1

1. *the farmer in the mound:* A commonly held pagan belief that the spirit of the original owner of an estate continued to offer protection from the grave.
2. *Quid mihi . . . :* Woman, what have I to do with thee? mine hour is not yet come. John 2:4.

## CHAPTER 2

1. *Winter Day:* October 14, considered the beginning of the winter half year.
2. *an unredeemable offense:* A crime that could not be absolved through the payment of fines; a crime punishable by unconditional banishment.

## CHAPTER 4

1. *Jesus Kristus Soter . . . :* Jesus Christ the Savior. The lion of the tribe of Judah is victorious.

## CHAPTER 5

1. *corrody:* A pension or allowance granted by a cloister in exchange for donated land or property; it permitted the holder to retire into the cloister as a boarder.
2. *nona hora:* The fifth of the seven canonical hours set aside for prayer, usually the ninth hour after sunrise.

## LIST OF HOLY DAYS

| | |
|---|---|
| Saint Paal's Day | January 15 |
| Candlemas | February 2 |
| Saint Gregor's Day | March 12 |
| Saint Gertrud's Day | March 17 |
| Feast of the Annunciation | March 25 |
| Summer Day | April 14 |
| Feast Day of the Apostles | May 1 |
| Holy Cross Day | May 3 |
| Saint Halvard's Day | May 15 |
| Saint Botolv's Day | June 17 |
| Saint Jon's Day (Midsummer) | June 24 |
| Selje Men's Feast Day | July 8 |
| Saint Margareta's Day | July 20 |
| Feast of Mary Magdalena | July 22 |
| Saint Jacob's Day | July 25 |
| Saint Olav's Day (Feast of Saint Olav) | July 29 |
| Saint Lavrans's Day | August 10 |
| Assumption Day | August 15 |
| Saint Bartholomew's Day | August 24 |
| Feast of the Birth of Mary | September 8 |
| Holy Cross Day | September 14 |
| Saint Matthew's Day | September 21 |
| Saint Michael's Day (Michaelmas) | September 29 |
| Winter Day | October 14 |
| Saint Simon's Day | October 28 |
| The Feast of Saint Jude | October 28 |
| All Saints' Day | November 1 |
| Corpus Christi Day | November 9 |
| Saint Martin's Day | November 11 |
| Saint Clement's Day | November 23 |

| | |
|---|---|
| Saint Catherine's Day | November 25 |
| Saint Andreas's Day (Feast of the Apostle Saint Andreas) | November 30 |
| Saint Lucia's Day | December 13 |
| Saint Stefan's Day | December 25 |
| Children's Day | December 28 |
| Ascension Day | Fortieth day after Easter |
| Lent | Winter (*varies annually*) |
| Whitsunday | Seventh Sunday after Easter |
| Whitsuntide | The week beginning with Pentecost, the fiftieth day after Easter |
| Advent | December (*varies annually*) |